By Gary Jennings

RAPTOR

SPANGLE

THE JOURNEYER

AZTEC

Raptor

RAPTOR

GARY JENNINGS

DOUBLEDAY

NEW YORK LONDON TORONTO
SYDNEY AUCKLAND

PUBLISHED BY DOUBLEDAY
A division of Bantam Doubleday Dell Publishing Group, Inc.
666 Fifth Avenue, New York, New York 10103

DOUBLEDAY and the portrayal of an anchor with a dolphin are
trademarks of Doubleday, a division of Bantam Doubleday Dell
Publishing Group, Inc.

Library of Congress Cataloging-in-Publication Data

Jennings, Gary.
Raptor / Gary Jennings. — 1st ed.
p.   cm.
1. Theodoric, King of the Ostrogoths, 454?-526—Fiction.
2. Europe—History—392-814—Fiction. 3. Goths—History—Fiction.
I. Title.
PS3560.E518R3   1992
813'.54—dc20   92-9433
                                                              CIP

ISBN 0-385-24632-3
Copyright © 1992 by Gary Jennings

Map Illustration by Jim Kemp & Anita Karl/Compass Projections

BOOK DESIGN AND ORNAMENTATION BY CAROL MALCOLM-RUSSO

FOR JOYCE

Nous revenons toujours
À nos premiers amours

RAPTOR: (fr. Latin *raptere*, to ravish)
A bird of prey, as the eagle or
hawk, characterized by carnivorous
appetite, great powers of flight
and extreme keenness of vision.
— WEBSTER'S

MORTAL, *it was you yourself who cast your lot*
not with Security but with Fortune.
Never rejoice overmuch when she leads
you to great victories; never repine
when she leads you into sad adversity.
Remember, mortal, if Fortune ever
should stand still, she is no longer
Fortune.
— BOETHIUS, A.D. 524

TRANSLATOR'S NOTE

lthough Thorn's narrative begins in the traditional style of the Goths—"Read these runes!"—it was in fact written almost entirely in a fluent and articulate Latin. Only here and there did Thorn put in a name, word or phrase in the "Old Language" of Gothic or in some other tongue. The Roman alphabet of that time being inadequate for transcribing such sounds as the Gothic "kh," Thorn wrote those words in the Gothic script, which *was* in part derived from the ancient runes. I have rendered those words in today's Roman alphabet, in a manner that I hope will convey to the reader of English some notion of their original pronunciation: for example, Balsan Hrinkhen, "Ring of Balsam," the name of the valley where Thorn's childhood was spent.

Thorn's page after page of continuous, unbroken, unspaced narrative I have divided into sections and chapters as I thought appropriate. To further ease the reading of it, I have provided occasional italics for emphasis, and paragraphing and punctuation, devices which were only seldom or haphazardly employed in manuscripts of that time. And I have taken one major liberty. In many places where Thorn uses the Latin word *barbarus* or the Gothic equivalent, *gasts*, I have translated it as "outlander." In Thorn's day, practically every nation, tribe and clan referred to every other as "barbarian," but the epithet—except when delivered as an outright insult—did not usually have the brute-savage connotation that it bears now. In most instances here, "outlander" says it better.

At the time of Thorn's birth, in the fifth century A.D., the map of Europe was a confusion of borders being continually shifted by migrations of nations, wars between nations, the emergence or subsidence of one nation and then another. But the reader needs only to remember that the Goths—most powerful of the several Germanic peoples—were at that period divided into the Visigoths of western Europe and the Ostrogoths living in the east. The Roman Empire was likewise geographically divided into west and east, each half ruled by a separate emperor, the eastern emperor having as his capital the "New Rome" of Constantinople.

There is no knowing how many years Thorn may have taken in writing this chronicle, but it concludes in A.D. 526. Many of the cities, towns and other sites mentioned in the narrative still exist, and have modern names. But many others, of course, have vanished from the earth. So, for the sake of consistency, I have chosen to leave all the place names as Thorn knew them. For the reader's convenience, this book's maps show their locations and the names that the still-surviving sites wear today.

Out of curiosity, I went myself in search of the very first place mentioned in the text—that Balsan Hrinkhen—which, according to Thorn, was in the Burgund Kingdom, between Vesontio and Lugdunum (the cities now called Besançon and Lyon, in what is now France). And there I did indeed find the Ring of Balsam, in the Jura countryside not far from the Switzerland border. Amazingly, after fifteen centuries, the steep-walled valley and, down inside it, the cascades, the labyrinthine cave, the tiny village and the two abbeys are little changed from Thorn's description of them. Even more amazingly, the place is still so named: in French, le Cirque de Baume.

It is also still the habitat of the raptorial bird that Thorn so much admired—the juika-bloth, the "I fight for blood" bird. This is the harrier eagle, known elsewhere in France as *l'aigle brunâtre*, but the inhabitants of the Cirque de Baume call it *l'aigle Jean-Blanc*—and that name I take to be only a folk-corruption of the Gothic *juika-bloth*. The bird is much valued because, as Thorn relates, it preys mainly on reptiles, including the venomous adder. Mindful of Thorn's own extraordinary and paradoxical nature, I was interested to learn that the Cirque de Baume folk are of divided opinion: as to whether the male eagle or the female is the more relentless raptor.

G.J.

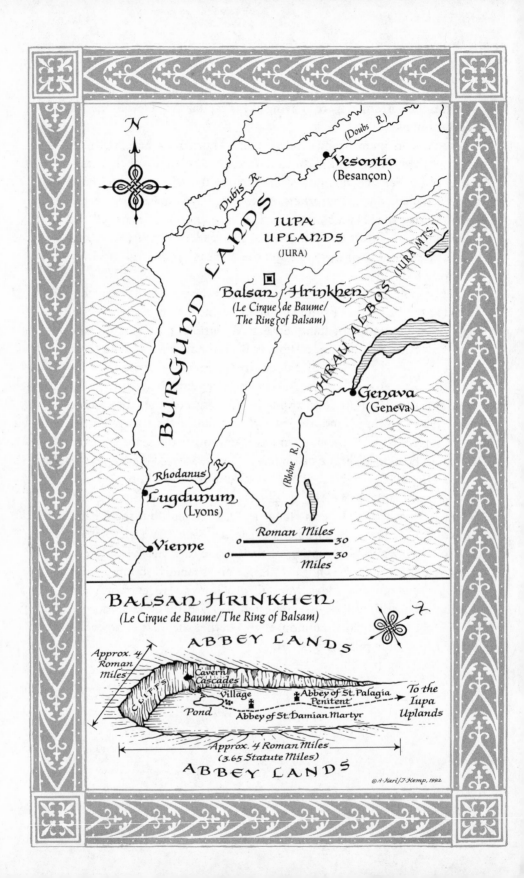

N

(Doubs R.)

Vesontio
(Besançon)

Dubis R.

IUPA
UPLANDS
(JURA)

BURGUND LANDS

Balsan Hrinkhen
(Le Cirque de Baume/
The Ring of Balsam)

HRAU ALBOS (JURA MTS.)

Genava
(Geneva)

Rhodanus R.

(Rhône R.)

Lugdunum
(Lyons)

Vienne

Roman Miles
0   30
0   30
Miles

BALSAN HRINKHEN
(Le Cirque de Baume/The Ring of Balsam)

N

ABBEY LANDS

Approx. 4
Roman
Miles

CLIFFS

Cavern
Cascades

Village
Pond

Abbey of St. Palagia
Penitent

Abbey of St. Damian Martyr

To the
Iupa
Uplands

Approx. 4 Roman Miles
(3.65 Statute Miles)

ABBEY LANDS

© A. Karl/J. Kemp, 1992.

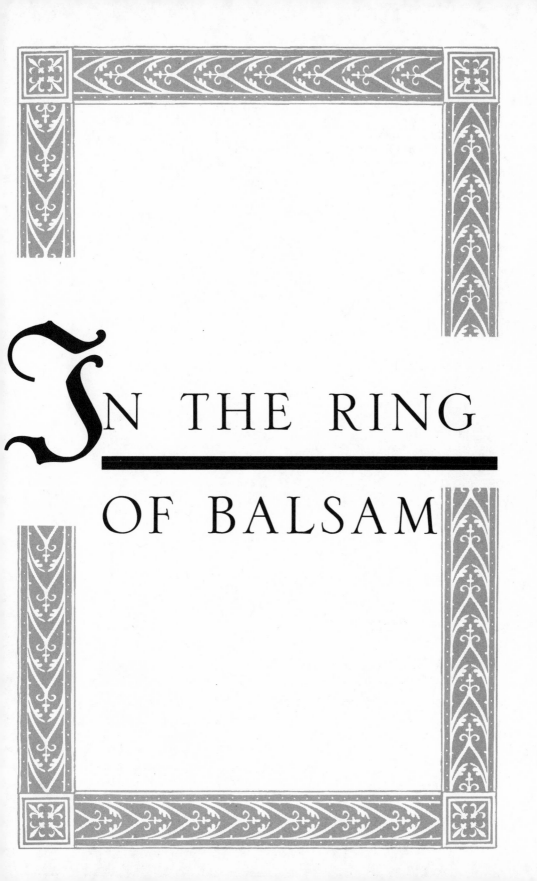

IN THE RING

OF BALSAM

1

Read these runes! They were inscribed by Thorn the Mannamavi, and at no master's dictation, but in Thorn's own words.

Hearken to me, you who live, you who have found these pages that I wrote when I, like you, was alive. This is the true history of a time that was. It may be that these pages have lain gathering dust for so long that, in your lifetime, the olden days are remembered only in your minstrels' songs. But *akh!* every minstrel meddles with the history of which he sings, trimming it or elaborating it, the better to beguile his listeners or to flatter his patron, his ruler, his god—or to malign the enemies of his patron, his ruler, his god—until the truth is obscured by veils of falsehood and sanctimonious laudation and invented myth. So that the truth of the events of my time might be known, I here set them down without poetics or partiality or fear of reprisal.

However, I had best commence by telling you one thing about myself, a truth that was known to very few even of my own time. You who read these pages, whether you be man, woman or eunuch, must understand that I was totally unlike you, or much of what I have later to tell would be incomprehensible. Now, I have sought long and hard for some way to explain my peculiar nature—some way that would not make you recoil in loathing or laugh in contempt—but there can be no tiptoeing around the truth. So, to make you comprehend my difference from all other human beings, I can think of no better way than to tell you how I came to realize it myself.

✠   ✠   ✠

That happened during my childhood in the great round valley called the Balsan Hrinkhen. I was perhaps twelve years old, and I was at my scullion labors in the abbey's cookhouse, and a certain Brother Peter was then the kitchener. He was a Burgund, who had been named Willaume Robei in the outside world. He was middle-aged, stout, wheezy of breath and so red of face that his dead-white tonsure could have been mistaken for a cloth cap set upon his graying red hair. Since this monk had but recently joined us, he was the lowest on the roster of the Abbey of St. Damian Martyr, and therefore was assigned to be kitchener, because that was the duty that the other monks liked least to have. He knew that his brothers would not even venture into the cookhouse while he was at his cooking, lest they be seized upon to do some odious kitchen chore. So Peter felt safe from being surprised or interrupted in the act when he lifted the back of my smock and caressed my bare buttocks and said, in his harsh Burgund way of speaking the Old Language:

"Akh, you have a fetching bottom, my lad. To be honest, you have also quite a comely face when it is clean."

I was somewhat bewildered at his so familiarly touching me, but I was more offended by his words. At my scullion tasks I was of course dirtied by the soot and smuts and ashes of the cookhouse. However, as a general thing—because I went frequently to disport myself in the nearby cascades, meaning that I was the only person in the valley ever to take all his clothes off at once—I was far cleaner than Peter or any other brother except perhaps the abbot.

"Anyway, this part of you is clean," Peter went on, still fondling my bare bottom. "Come. I will show you something. My last boy, Terentius, learned much from me. Here, lad, look at this."

I turned and saw that he had lifted the front of his heavy burlap robe. He was showing me nothing that I had not seen before. Because six-month-old human urine is the best manure for vines and fruit trees, the twice-yearly dredging of the rere-dorter's liquid contents into buckets was another of my duties, so I had seen the brothers make water in the rere-dorter while I worked. But truly I had never seen a man's urinary tube stand up, large and stiff and ruddy-knobbed, as Peter's was at this moment. It would be some while yet before I learned that the male member in this condition is called in Latin a fascinum, whence comes the word "fascinate."

Now Peter reached into the kitchen's crock of goose grease—muttering, "First, the holy chrism"—and slathered an amount of that on himself, making the rigid thing shiny red, as if it were fired within. Awed and wondering, I let Peter tug me over to the massive section of oak

4

trunk that the kitcheners used for a chopping block, and there he bent me so that I was lying across it on my stomach.

"What are you doing, Brother?" I asked, as he flipped the back of my smock up over my head, and began fumbling with his hands to part my buttocks.

"Hush, boy. I am showing you a new way to make your devotions. Pretend you are kneeling at a prayer-stool."

His hands were hurriedly fluttering, so one of them slipped farther between my legs, and Peter was plainly startled by what he encountered there.

"Well! I will be damned!"

And I trust that he has been. The man is long dead, and, if the God he pretended to serve is a just god, Peter has been all these years in hell.

"You cunning little fraud," he said, with a coarse laugh, bending his mouth close to my ear. "But what a fortunate surprise for me! I am saved from having to commit the sin of Sodom." Down below, with a trembling hand, he guided his fascinum into the place he had found. "Can it be that no other brother has ever suspected the presence in the cloister of a little *sister*? Am I the first to discover this? Ja, I am indeed! By God, it still has its membrane! No one else has yet taken the kernel from the fruit!"

Even though the goose grease lubricated his entry, I felt a piercing pain and gave a screech of protest.

"Hush . . . hush . . ." he panted. He was lying atop me now, while his lower body thumped repeatedly against the back of my thighs and that thing of his slid thickly back and forth inside me. "You are learning . . . a new manner of . . . of partaking of the Host . . ."

I thought to myself that I vastly preferred the old accustomed manner.

"Hoc est enim corpus meum . . ." Peter chanted, between his pantings. "Caro corpore Christi . . . aa-*aah!* Take! Eee-ee-*eat!*" He shuddered all along his length. I felt the warm gush upon my inner tissues, and thought he had nastily made water inside me. But no water drizzled out when he withdrew himself. Not until I was upright again did I feel the wetness begin to ooze down the inside of my thighs. Cleaning myself with a rag, I saw that the leakage—besides a small trace of blood, which was my own—was a viscous, pearly-white substance, as if Brother Peter really had deposited a bit of Eucharist bread inside me and it had dissolved there. So I had no reason to disbelieve his assertion that I had

5

been introduced to a new method of making Holy Communion, and I was a bit puzzled when he enjoined me to secrecy about it.

"Take heed," he said sternly, when he had recovered his breath and had wiped clean his again normally limp tube and decently rearranged his robe. "Boy—I shall continue to call you boy—you have by fraudulent means somehow contrived a cozy situation for yourself here among the brothers of St. Damian. I daresay you wish to keep that situation—not to be exposed and expelled."

He paused, and I nodded.

"Very well. Then I shall not say a word about your secret, your imposture. If!" He raised an admonishing finger. "If you do not say a word about our private devotions. We will continue practicing them hereafter, but they are not to be mentioned outside this cookhouse. Agreed, young Thorn? My silence for your silence."

I had no clear idea of what I was trading my silence and complaisance for, but Brother Peter seemed satisfied when I mumbled that I never did discuss with anyone my private devotions. And, true to my word, I never once spoke to any monk or the abbot regarding what occurred in the cookhouse, two or three noontimes in every week, when Peter had finished cooking the midday refection—the day's only hot meal—and before he and I carried the food to the monks at the tables in the frater.

After another time or two of being impaled, I ceased to find it painful. After several more times, I found it only a nuisance and a boredom, but bearable. And then there came a time when both Peter and I realized that he no longer needed the goose grease to ease his entrance. On that occasion, he exclaimed in delight, "Akh, the dear little grotto lubricates itself! It *invites* me in!"

That was all he noticed: that I now got moist down there in expectation of being gored. I supposed that it was something my body had learned to do to avert discomfort for itself. But I was aware that the devotions were having another effect on me besides that—and the fact gave me further wonderment and perplexity. Now the devotions also aroused the same part of myself as that which Brother Peter employed, making mine strive to stand and stiffen like his. In addition, I felt a new feeling: a sort of aching urgency, not painful, more like being hungry, though not for food.

But Peter never realized any of that. He always performed that particular act by having me bend forward over the chopping block, and he always hastened to enter me from the rear. He never glimpsed, never touched with his hand, never once realized that I had anything other than an oblong orifice between my legs. During a whole spring and most of a summer I shared—or endured—those devotions. Then in late summer, Peter and I were caught in the act, and by the abbot himself.

Dom Clement walked into the cookhouse just before the hour of refection one day, to find Peter straddling me and pumping away. The abbot cried, "Liufs Guth!" which is "Dear God!" in the Old Language, as Peter disengaged from me and leapt clear. Then the abbot wailed, "Invisan unsar heiva-gudei!" which meant "Within our godly house!" Then he absolutely roared, "Kalkinassus Sodomiza!" which at that time meant nothing to me, though I remembered once having heard Peter use one of those words. Wondering why the abbot should sound so distressed at our making devotions, I simply lay where I was, my smock bunched up at the back of my neck.

"Ne, ne!" bawled Brother Peter, in terror. "Nist, Nonnus Clement, nist Sodomiza! Ni allis!"

"Im ik blinda, niu?" demanded the abbot.

"Ne, Dom Clement," whined Peter. "And, since you are not blind, I beseech you to look here where I am pointing. There was nothing sodomitical about it, Nonnus. Akh, I was wrong, ja. I succumbed shamefully to temptation, ja. But only *look*, Nonnus Clement, at the perfidious, long-hidden thing that tempted me."

The abbot glared wrathfully at him, but moved around behind me, out of my sight, and I could guess what Peter was pointing at, for Dom Clement gasped yet again, "Liufs Guth!"

"Ja!" said Peter, adding piously, "And I can only thank the liufs Guth that it was none but myself, a lowly newcomer and a mere pedisequus, whom this spurious man-child, this sneaking, secret Eve seduced with her forbidden fruit. I thank the liufs Guth that she did not ensnare one of the worthier brothers or—"

"Sláváith!" the abbot snapped at him—"Be silent!"—and yanked my smock down to cover me, because a number of other monks, drawn by the shouting, had come to peer inquisitively in at the cookhouse door. "Go to your place in the dorter, Peter, and stay there by your pallet. I will deal with you later. Brother Babylas, Brother Stephanos, come in here and carry these platters and pitchers to the frater tables." He turned to me. "Thorn, my son—er, my child—come with me."

Dom Clement's quarters consisted of only one room. It was set apart from the monks' communal dorter, but was equally bleak and austere. The abbot seemed rather confused as to what he should say to me, so first he prayed at me for a long time, while presumably he waited for

7

inspiration. Then he got up from his bony old knees, and motioned for me to stand up also, and he questioned me for a time, and then he told me what he would have to do with me, now that my "secret" was out. This caused a good deal of melancholy on the part of us both, for the abbot and I had been very fond of one another.

✠ ✠ ✠

I was taken, next day—Dom Clement himself leading me and helping me to carry my few personal belongings—to the far other side of the valley, to St. Damian's sister establishment, the Abbey of St. Pelagia Penitent, the nunnery of virgins and widows who had dedicated themselves to the cenobitic life.

Dom Clement presented me to the old abbess, Domina Aetherea, who was quite taken aback, for she had often seen me at my daytime work in the fields of St. Damian's. The abbot had to ask her to take us to a private chamber, where he made me bend forward in the posture Brother Peter had so often commanded, and Dom Clement averted his eyes while he flipped up the back of my smock to expose my nether portions to the abbess. She uttered an appalled exclamation—the Gothic "Liufs Guth!" again—and herself snatched my smock back down to cover me. Then she and the abbot engaged in a rather agitated conversation, in Latin, but muttered too low for me to overhear. The interview ended with my being admitted to the convent in the same status I had enjoyed at the monastery: an oblate, a postulant and the jack-of-all-work—or rather, now, jenny-of-all-work.

Of my time at St. Pelagia's I will have more to tell later. Suffice it here to say that I had been working and worshipping and receiving instruction at the nunnery for many weeks when, on a warm day in early autumn, I was accosted by a convent counterpart of Brother Peter.

This time, however, the person who slid a hand under the back of my smock, and caressed my buttocks, and remarked on the shapeliness of my figure, was not a beefy Burgund monk. Sister Deidamia was also a Burgund, true, but she was a pretty and winsome novice nun—only a few years older than myself—whom I had for some while been admiring from afar. I did not mind at all when, as she fondled me, Deidamia pretended accidentally to let her hand move farther, where a dainty finger slipped into the oblong opening Peter had used. And, very like him, she said in delight, "Oo-ooh, were you anxious for affection, little sister? You are noticeably warm and moist and palpitant in that place."

We were in the abbey's byre, whither I had just brought the four cows in from their pasture for milking, and Sister Deidamia was carrying a milk pail. I did not inquire whether she had been sent this day to help me with the milking, because it seemed much more likely that she carried the pail simply to justify her visit and thus enable the accosting of me in private.

She now came leisurely around in front of me and began tentatively to lift the front of my smock, saying, as if asking permission, "I have never seen another female entirely unclad."

I said, and my voice was husky, "Neither have I."

She said coyly, lifting my smock a trifle higher, "You show me first."

I have related how the attentions of Peter had sometimes caused a disconcerting physical change in myself. I may say now that the intimate touch of Sister Deidamia's hand had already had the same engorging and erecting effect. I felt a little embarrassed, though I did not know why, to have her see that. However, before I could object, she had raised my smock all the way up.

"Gudisks Himins!" she breathed, her eyes widening. The Old Language words mean "Great Heavens!" and I told myself that I had rightly been reluctant—now I had shocked the girl. And so I had, but for a reason I could not have known. "Oh vái! I always suspected that I was deficient as a woman. And now I know it."

"Eh?" said I.

"I had hoped that we might . . . you and I . . . enjoy ourselves as I have seen Sister Agnes and Sister Thaïs do. At night, I mean. I have spied on them. They kiss their lips together, and run their hands all over one another, and rub their . . . well, that part of them . . . against one another, and they moan and laugh and sob as if it gives them great joy. I have long wondered how that pleasured them. But I never could see. They never undress entirely."

"Sister Thaïs is much comelier than I am," I managed to say, through my constricted throat. "Why did you not approach her instead of me?" I was trying mightily to seem in possession of my faculties, but that was difficult. Deidamia was still holding my smock high and staring at me. The ambient air was cool on my bare body, but I felt mostly the pulsing warmth at the focus of her gaze.

"Oh vái!" she exclaimed. "Be impudent to Sister Thaïs? Ne, I could not! She is older . . . and she has been granted the veil . . . and I am but a callow postulant. Anyway, seeing you, I can divine now what it must be that she and Sister Agnes do at night. If all other women have a thing like that . . ."

9

"You do not?" I asked hoarsely.

"Ni allis," she said, with much sadness. "Small wonder that I have always felt inferior."

"Let me see," I said.

Now it was she who was reluctant, but I reminded her, "You said me first, big sister, and I showed you. Now you must, too."

So she let go of my smock and, with tremulous fingers, untied her belt rope to let her burlap robe fall open in front. If the physical enlargement of myself could have got any more pronounced, surely it did so then.

"You perceive," she said shyly, "I am at least normal enough *here*. Feel." And she took my hand and guided it. "Warm and moist and widely opened, as yours is, Sister Thorn. I can even, when I insert a small gourd or a sausage, feel some small pleasure in there. But *here* I have only this little nub. It stands, much as yours does—you feel it?— and playing with that also gives me pleasure. But it is so insignificant, no bigger than the wart on Nonna Aetherea's chin. Not at all like yours. It can barely be seen." And she sniffled.

"Well," I said, to console her, "*I* do not have hair around mine. And I do not have those things." I indicated her breasts, where there were also nubs standing pert and pink.

"Akh," she said dismissively. "That is only because you are still a child, Sister Thorn. I would wager that you have not even had your first menstruum yet. You will commence to sororiare before you are my age."

"What does that mean?"

"Sororiare? The breasts, to do their first swelling. The menstruum you will recognize, when it comes. But already you have *that*"—she touched it and I gave a violent start—"which clearly I never will. As I suspected, I am not a complete woman."

"I would be glad," I said, "to rub mine against you, if you think that would make you feel joy, as it does those other sisters."

"Would you, dear girl?" she said eagerly. "Perhaps I can *take* pleasure even if I cannot give it. Here. Here is some clean straw. Let us lie down. That is how Thaïs and Agnes do it."

So we lay down and stretched out and, after some awkward essaying of different positions, we at last brought our naked lower bodies into contact, and I began the rubbing of that part of myself against that part of her.

"Oo-ooh," she said, panting like Peter. "It—it *is* most pleasant."

"Ja," I said faintly.

10

"Let it . . . let it go in."

"Ja."

I did not have to do any manipulation. It found its own way. Deidamia made many incoherent noises, and her body bucked against mine, and her hands groped wildly all over the rest of me. Then there seemed to occur inside her, inside me, inside both of us, a sort of gathering and rushing and then a soft bursting. Deidamia and I gleefully cried aloud when it happened, and the enjoyable sensations subsided into a radiant and happy peacefulness that was almost equally enjoyable. Though my enlargement seemed to have had its urgent yearning satisfied, and it dwindled back to normal size, it did not slip out of Deidamia. The membranes of her grotto went on doing a kind of soft, repeated *swallowing* movement that held me gripped tight. The same soft convulsions were going on inside me, too, though my grotto had nothing to hold on to.

Not until everything inside both of us had subsided to tranquillity did Deidamia speak, in a quavering voice. "Ooh . . . thags. Thags izvis, leitils svistar. It was wonderful beyond belief."

"Ne, ne . . . thags *izvis*, Svistar Deidamia," I said. "It was wonderful for me, as well. I am so pleased that you thought of doing it with me."

"Liufs Guth!" she suddenly exclaimed, with a small laugh. "I am much wetter here than I was before." She felt of herself, then of the same place on me. "You are not near so wet as I. What *is* this, leaking out of me?"

I said, with some diffidence, "I believe, big sister, you are supposed to think of that fluid as the Eucharist bread, only liquefied. And I have been told that what we did, just now, is merely a more private way of making Holy Communion."

"Say you so? But how marvelous! Much nicer than stale bread and sour wine. No wonder the Sisters Thaïs and Agnes do it so often. They are exceedingly devout. And this lovely substance came out of *you*, little sister?" Her happy face abruptly got less bright. "There, you see? I cannot do that. I am deficient. Why, the pleasure must have been *twice* as much for you . . ."

To prevent her starting again to pity herself for her deficiencies, I changed the subject. "If this way of making Communion gratifies you so, Sister Deidamia, why do you not simply take a man, niu? Men have even more of a—"

"Akh, ne!" she interrupted. "I may have been ignorant of the female body until now. That was because there were no other girls in our

11

family and my mother died when I was born and I had no female playmates. But brothers I did have, and them I have seen unclad. Ugh! Let
me tell you, Sister Thorn, men are ugly. All hairy and bulgy and leathery, like the great wild ox úrus. You are right in saying that they are —
in that part — of substantial size. But it is a gross and gruesome thing.
And under it they have dangling a hideous, puckered, heavy leather
bag. Ugh!"

"That is so," I said. "I too have seen it on men, and wondered if I
would grow one."

"That, never, thags Guth," she assured me. "Some modest hair down
there, ja, and some delectable breasts up here, ja, but not that horrible
sack of stones." She went on, "A eunuch, you know, does not have that
sack either, any more than we girls do."

"I did not know," I said. "What is a eunuch?"

"That is a man who has had his stones cut off, usually in childhood."

"Liufs Guth!" I exclaimed. "Cut off? Whatever for?"

"So that he can no longer function — in that respect — as a man.
Some have it deliberately done to themselves, even after they are fully
grown men. The great church teacher Origen, it is said, had himself
emasculated so that when he taught women or nuns he would not be
distracted by their femininity. Many slave men are made eunuchs by
their masters, so that they can attend upon the women of the household with no danger to the chastity of those women."

"A woman would never lie down with a eunuch?"

"Of course not. To what purpose? But I — even if I were surrounded
with servants who were all real and stalwart men — I would never, never
lie with one. Even if I could quell my nausea at the mere thought, I
could not do so. Lying with you, little sister, I make Holy Communion.
But to lie with a man would pollute my chastity, and that I have dedicated to God alone, so that I may be granted the veil when I reach the
age of forty. Ne, I will never lie down with a man."

"Then I rejoice that I am a female," I said. "Otherwise, I would never
even have met you."

"Not to mention lain with me," she said, smiling blissfully. "And this
we must do often, Sister Thorn."

And we did, often and often, and we taught one another many and
various ways to do our devotions, and of those occasions there is much
more to tell — but that, also, I will save for later. Meanwhile, Deidamia
and I were so besotted with one another that we got lamentably careless. One day shortly before the onset of winter, we were in such trans-

12

ports of ecstasy that we failed to notice the near approach of a certain meddlesome Sister Elissa. We did not notice until, presumably after having watched slack-jawed for a while, she departed and returned with the abbess, in time to find us still intertwined.

"You see, Nonna?" said Sister Elissa's gloating voice.

"Liufs Guth!" shrieked Domina Aetherea. "Kalkinassus!" I had learned by now that that word means fornication, which is a mortal sin. I hastily redonned my smock, and I cowered in anguish. But Deidamia calmly wrapped her robe about her and said:

"Kalkinassus it was not, Nonna Aetherea. Perhaps we were wrong to making Holy Communion during work hours, but—"

"Holy Communion?!"

"—but we committed no sin. There is not any hazard to chastity when one female lies with another. I am as virginal as I always was, and so is little Sister Thorn."

"Slaváith!" bellowed Domina Aetherea. "How dare you speak so? Virginal, is he?"

"He?" echoed Deidamia, nonplussed.

"This is the first time I have seen the impostor's front," the abbess said icily. "But you seem well acquainted with it, daughter. Can you deny that this is a he-thing?" And she indicated it—not by touching me with her hand; she picked up a stick and used that to raise the hem of my smock. All three women regarded my privities, with varying expressions on their faces, and only the liufs Guth knows what expression I must have been wearing.

"A he he is," said Sister Elissa, with a simper.

Deidamia stammered, "But . . . but Thorn has no . . . er . . ."

"He has enough to make him indubitably a he!" barked the abbess. "And to make of you, deluded daughter, a sordid fornicatrix."

"Oh vái, worse than that, Nonna Aetherea!" wailed poor Deidamia, in genuine despair. "I am become an anthropophagus! Beguiled by this impostor, I have devoured the flesh of human infants!"

The other two women stared at her with shocked amazement. However, before Deidamia could elaborate, she swooned dead away on the ground. I knew what those words had meant, but, quaking though I was, I had sense enough not to volunteer any explanation. After a moment, Sister Elissa said:

"If this—this person—is a he, Nonna Aetherea, how did he come to be here at St. Pelagia's, niu?"

"How indeed?" the abbess said grimly.

13

So once again I and my bundled few belongings were dragged across the wide valley, back to the Abbey of St. Damian. There the abbess had a monk shut me in an outbuilding, that I should not hear what she said when she confronted the abbot. But the monk had other duties to attend to, and left me alone, so I slipped out, and crouched beneath the window aperture of the abbot's quarters, and listened. They were conversing very loudly, and not in guarded Latin this time, but in the Old Language.

". . . *dare* you bring that to me," the abbess was roaring, "and represent it as a *girl*-child?"

"You *took* it to be a girl-child," retorted the abbot, not quite so stridently. "You saw all of it that I had seen, and you are a *woman*. Can I be blamed because I take seriously my vow of celibacy, niu? Because I am one priest who never has fathered any *nephews*? Because I have seen females unclad only on their sickbed or deathbed?"

"Well, now we both know what it is, Clement, and what must be done with it. Send a monk to fetch it here."

I scurried back to the outbuilding, to be fetched, and in my confusion and consternation only one thought was clear in my head. Over the past year or so, I had been variously described, but this was the first time I had been called "it."

Thus it was that I was banished from both abbeys, and commanded to depart from the valley of the Balsan Hrinkhen, and not to show my face in it ever again. I was being banished for my sins, said Dom Clement, when he engaged me in a private colloquy before I left, though he admitted that even he could not put an exact ecclesiastical label to those sins. I was allowed to keep my personal belongings, but the abbot cautioned me against taking with me anything of either abbey's property — except that he then kindly slipped into my hand a coin, a whole silver solidus.

He also told me, finally, what I was, and he said he was desolated to have to tell me. I was, he said, the kind of creature called in the Old Language a mannamavi, a "man-maiden" — what is called in Latin an androgynus and in Greek an arsenothélus. I was not a boy-child or a girl-child, but both, and therefore neither. I think, right then and there, I ceased to be any kind of child whatever, and grew up considerably.

Contrary to the abbot's admonition, I did take with me when I went away two things that were not strictly my own, and I will tell later what they were. However, I took with me nothing that was to prove of so much enduring value to me as the knowledge — of which I did not at that time realize the value—that in my entire life to come I would never be the victim of love for any other human being. Since I was not a male, I neither could nor would truly love any woman. Since I was not a female, I neither could nor would truly love any man. I would be forever free of the entangling ties, the enfeebling tendernesses, the degrading tyrannies of love.

I was Thorn the Mannamavi, and no man or woman in all Creation would ever be anything more to me than prey.

2

have said that I was "perhaps" twelve years old when Brother Peter first lifted my smock. I cannot be any more precise about my age, because I do not know when I was born, or even where. For one who would eventually journey so far, among so many different lands and peoples . . . for one who would take part in so many events that now are reckoned to have changed the course of civilization . . . for one who would someday stand at the right hand of the greatest man in our world . . . mine was a lowly and ignominious beginning.

Of my beginning, all I know for certain is that, about the 1,208th Year of the Founding of Rome, during the brief reign of the Emperor Avitus, sometime in the Year of Our Lord 455 or 456—which is to say, a year or two after the birth of that man who would be the greatest in our world—my infant self was found one morning on the muddy doorsill of the Abbey of St. Damian Martyr. I may have been days old, weeks old, months old, I do not know. There was no message left there with me, and no identification except that the peasant hemp cloth in which I was swaddled bore the chalked character þ.

The runic alphabet of the Old Language is called the "futhark," because those letters—F and U and so on—are the letters commencing it, as A, B and C are in the Roman alphabet. The futhark's third letter is the þ, and it is called "thorn" because it represents the "th" sound. If the mark on my swaddling clothes meant anything at all, it might have been the initial letter of a name like Thrasamund or Theudebert, indicating that I could have been a Burgund child, a Frank, a Gepid, a Thuringian, a Suevian, a Vandal or any other of the nationalities of Germanic origin. However, of all the peoples speaking the Old Language, only the Ostrogoths and Visigoths are still employing the ancient runes in some of their writings. So the then abbot of St. Damian's took the chalked initial as proof that I was of Gothic parentage. Only, instead of endowing me with any pure-Gothic baptismal name beginning with "th"—which would have required him to choose a masculine or a feminine name—he simply gave me the name of that runic character: Thorn.

Now, it might be supposed that I should have harbored a lifelong resentment against my mother, whoever she was, for her having abandoned me to the mercy of strangers. But no, I do not disprize or condemn that woman. On the contrary, I have always been grateful to her, for otherwise I should not have lived at all.

Had she, at my birth, made known my freakishness to her people, whoever they might have been, they would naturally have assumed that such an abnormal infant must have been conceived on a Sunday or some other holy day (sexual intercourse on such days being well known to have dire consequences); or that I was the product of my mother's having mated with a skohl, one of the forest demons left over from the Old Religion; or that my mother had for some reason been the victim of an insandjis, a Sending. That is a malevolent curse cast by what is called in Gothic a haliuruns, meaning someone—usually an ancient hag—still faithful to the Old Religion, still capable of writing and Sending the dread runes of Halja, old-time goddess of the underworld. (It must have been from the name Halja that we northern Christians derived the world "hell," for we preferred that word to the Latin word "Gehenna," *that* having come from the language of the Jews, whom we despised even more than we despised pagans.)

Only when a community has been severely diminished by war or pestilence or famine or some other calamity will it sometimes let its illbegotten infants live—cripples, weaklings, the feebleminded and other undesirables—or at least let them live for a while, to see if they can be nurtured up to some measure of usefulness. Should such a child's own mother and father be too ashamed of it to rear it, the community elders might even pay for the maimed child to be "knee-seated" on some pair of childless and needy foster parents. However, at the time I was born, there was peace in the Burgund lands—that war-making hellion the Khan Attila having recently died and the rest of his predacious Huns having fled back eastward toward Sarmatia, whence they had come. And in any land enjoying comparative peace and prosperity, when an infant is born deformed or defective in any way—or often if it merely happens to be born a lowly female—that child is declared "the unborn born," and is summarily slain or starved or left to die of exposure, for the obvious good of the race.

My mother would have realized very soon, if not at first sight of me, that she had given birth to something inferior even to a normal female, and something more monstrous even than a skohl-child. That she dared to defy every civilized people's custom of destroying the unborn born is to the woman's credit—or it is in my opinion, anyway, I having been the beneficiary of her defiance—that she did not immediately toss me onto the midden heap or leave me in the woods for the wolves to devour. She was maternally softhearted enough to let the brothers of St. Damian determine my destiny.

17

The abbot of that time—and the abbey's infirmarian—of course unwrapped and examined the foundling, so they too soon knew what an anomalous creature I was; hence the meaningless and ambiguous name with which I was baptized. It may have been only out of curiosity that the abbot, like my mother, decided to let me live. Still, he decided also to have me brought up as a boy-child, and it must have been out of real compassion that he so decided, for he thereby accorded me (if I should survive to adulthood) the male status, privileges and rights-at-law that, in every Christian country, are unattainable by even the highest-born woman.

And so it was that I was accepted into the abbey, just as if I had been an ordinary boy oblate given by his parents to be raised in holy orders, and a village woman was recruited to be my wet nurse until I was of an age for weaning. It is difficult to believe, but apparently none of those three persons who knew the truth about me ever whispered it to anyone else, either inside or outside the abbey. And, when I was perhaps four years old, a plague of disease descended upon the Burgund Kingdom. Among the inhabitants of the Balsan Hrinkhen who perished of the plague were that abbot, that infirmarian and that woman who had nursed me, so I afterward had only the vaguest recollection of them.

Bishop Patiens of Lugdunum soon appointed a new abbot for St.

Damian's—Dom Clement, come from teaching at the seminary at Condatus—and Dom Clement naturally took me for the boy-child I seemed to be and believed myself to be. So did the other monks continue to regard me, and so did all the village people whom the pestilence had spared. Thus my equivocal nature went unnoticed or unsuspected by everybody in my small world, including myself, during another eight years or so, until the lecherous Brother Peter accidentally and gleefully discovered it.

Life in the monastery was not easy, but neither was it unbearably onerous, for St. Damian's did not adhere to such strict rules of asceticism and abstinence as did the much older cenobitic communities in lands like Africa, Egypt and Palestine. Our more rigorous northern climate, and the amount of physical work we did, required us of St. Damian's to be better nourished, and even to have our inwards warmed by wine in winter or cooled by ale and beer in summer. Since our abbey lands produced quite prodigious quantities of every sort of food and drink, neither our abbot nor our bishop saw any reason to inhibit our consumption of them. Also, we worked so hard that most of us cleansed ourselves of sweat and dirt oftener than once a week. Unfortunately, not all of us did. Those brothers who bathed but seldom—and the rest of the time went about smelling like goats—said sanctimoniously that they were heeding St. Jerome's dictum: "A clean skin means a dirty soul."

Every brother did obey the first two precepts of monasticism, the foremost being Obedience, which is founded on the second, Humility—but the third precept, which is Love of Silence, was not very rigidly observed at our abbey. Since the monks' various labors required considerable communication among them, they were not bidden to be mute, although any talking not absolutely necessary was discouraged after Vespers.

There are some monastic orders that take also a vow of poverty, but at St. Damian's that condition was simply taken for granted, and was considered not so much a virtue as the absence of a vice. Every brother, on admission, disposed of all his worldly belongings, right down to his garments, and thereafter possessed little that he could call his own, except his two hooded burlap robes—one for daytime wear, one for after working hours—plus a light summer surcoat and a heavy woolen one for winter, his indoor sandals, his work shoes or boots, two pairs of waist-high hose and the rope girdle that he doffed only on going to his pallet at night.

There are also communities of monks that take a vow of celibacy, in the manner of convent sisters. But at St. Damian's that condition, like poverty, was rather taken for granted. It was only comparatively recently, just some seventy years before the time of which I write, that the Church had demanded celibacy, and then only of its bishops, priests and deacons. Thus a man in holy orders might marry while he was still a young minor clerk—a lector, an exorcist or a doorkeeper—and then could father children while he rose through the ranks of acolyte and subdeacon, and not have to part from his wife and family until he became a full deacon. Needless to remark, many clerics of all degrees have flouted both the tradition of celibacy and St. Augustine's pronouncement that "God hates copulation." They have had wives or concubines, or swarms of them, all their lives long, and have sired innumerable "nephews" and "nieces."

Most of the monks of St. Damian's were natives of the surrounding Burgund lands, but we also had numerous Franks and Vandals, several Suevians and a few representatives of other Germanic nations and tribes. All of them, on entering the abbey, dropped their Old Language names and took the Latin or Greek names of saints, prophets, martyrs or venerable bishops of the past—a man named Kniva-the-Squint-Eyed becoming Brother Commodian, and Avilf-the-Arm-Strong becoming brother Addian, and so on.

As I have said, every monk had a job to fill or a daily labor to perform, and Dom Clement did his best to assign each brother to a duty that was as near as possible to what the man had worked at in the outside world. Our infirmarian, Brother Hormisdas, had formerly been the medicus to a noble household in Vesontio. Brother Stephanos, who had been steward to some great estate, was now our cellarius, in charge of all our stores and provisions.

Monks who were literate in Latin became preceptores, copying scrolls and codices in the abbey's scriptorium, while any who had some artistic ability illuminated those works. Brothers who could read and write the Old Language were made responsible for the chartularium, where were filed all the records of St. Damian's, plus the marriage, birth and death rosters, the land deeds and contracts transacted among the lay residents of the valley. Brother Paulus, who was amazingly adept and swift at writing in both languages, was Dom Clement's personal exceptor, scratching onto wax tablets the abbot's dictated correspondence, as fast as it was spoken, and then writing the missives on vellum in a fine hand. Within our abbey grounds were herb and truck gardens, barns and yards

19

containing poultry, pigs and milk cows, and those were tended by monks who had formerly been farmers. But the abbey also owned, both inside and outside the valley, extensive tracts of farmland, vineyards, orchards and pastures of sheep and cattle. Unlike many monasteries, St. Damian's did not possess slaves, but employed the local rustics to till those lands and manage those herds.

Even the dullest-witted of all our brothers at St. Damian's—he was a poor lout whose tonsure topped a head that was very nearly conical— was given some simple tasks to do, and he did them with great pride and self-satisfaction. That fellow had previously been called Nethla Io-hannes—presumably on account of the shape of his head, for that name meant Needle, John's Son—but he had assumed the even more ridiculous name of Brother Joseph. I say "ridiculous" because no monk, cleric, monastery or church has ever been known to name itself after St. Joseph—that personage being considered, if anything, the patron saint of cuckolds. On Sundays and other holy days, our Brother Joseph had the job of shaking the sacra ligna, the loud wooden rattles that summoned the valley and village folk to services in our abbey's chapel. On other days, Brother Joseph stood as a scarecrow in this or that field of crops and rattled the sacra ligna to drive the scavenger birds away.

My own duties, when I was very young, were almost as menial as those of Brother Joseph, but at least they were numerous and various enough so that no job ever got too tedious. One day I might assist in the scriptorium, giving sheets of new-made vellum their final polish— this was always done with a mole pelt, because mole fur has the peculiar property of lying smooth in whatever direction it is rubbed—and then abrading the sheets with pumice dust to make their surface suitably gripping for the preceptores' swan-quill pens. Oftener than not, it was I who had earlier noose-trapped the moles to get those pelts, and I who had collected the oak galls from which the pens' ink was made, and I who had suffered painful nips and buffetings while plucking the quills from the swans.

Another day I might be in the fields collecting sweet gale, from which our infirmarian brother brewed a medicinal tea, or collecting thistle cotton, with which our sempster brother would stuff pillows (our geese and swans provided ample down, but such a soft luxury in a monastery dorter was unthinkable). Another day I might spend in dropping a frantically shrieking and flapping hen down one after another of the abbey's flues to clean them out, and then taking the dislodged soot to our dyer brother, who would boil it with beer to make a good brown tincture for coloring the monks' robes.

As I grew older, the brothers entrusted me with slightly more responsible tasks. The dairy-house brother, Sebastian, pouring cream into two pannier tubs slung across the back of our old draft mare, solemnly informed me, "Cream is the daughter of milk and the mother of butter." Then he set me atop the mare and had me jog her at a shambling fast walk around and around the barnyard, until the cream did indeed magically turn into butter.

On the day Brother Lucas, a carpenter, fell off a roof and broke his arm, the infirmarian, Brother Hormisdas, told me, "The comfrey plant is named for the comfort and curing it provides," and he sent me out to the fields to find and uproot enough of those plants to fill several bustellus baskets. By the time I brought them back, the infirmarian had laid Lucas's arm in a sort of wooden trough. Hormisdas let me help him mash the comfrey roots to a mucilaginous pulp, then he packed that around the broken arm. By the end of the day, the pulp had dried hard, like gypsum. The trough was removed and Brother Lucas was able to get up and get about, wearing the comfrey cast until his arm knitted, and he was as good a carpenter as before.

I always hoped mightily that I might be asked by our vintner brother, Commodian, to tramp around in the grape-pressing vat with his assistant monks, all of them barefooted but heavily clothed so their sweat would not drip into the juice. To me, that work looked more merry than wearisome. But I never got to try it; I was not heavy enough to have been worth the room I would have taken up in the vat. But I *was* able to work the leather bellows for Brother Adrian, while he forged sickle and scythe blades, billhooks, bits for the local people's horses and rimshoes for any of those horses that had to work on stony ground. I was especially happy whenever I was sent afield to take the place of some peasant shepherd who was ill or drunk or otherwise incapacitated, for I enjoyed being by myself in the green pastures, and the herding of sheep is no backbreaking job. Each time, I carried with me a wallet containing (for myself) a cantlet of bread, a wedge of cheese, an onion and (for the sheep) a box of broom-jelly with which to daub cuts, scratches and fly-bites. I also carried a crook for grabbing any sheep that needed treatment.

Except when I was afield, my work—like that of every monk—had to be planned and arranged to accommodate all our religious obliga-

21

tions, for our every day, week and year was most rigidly regulated. We rose in the dark each morning for the cockcrow office of Vigil. Then we (or most of us) took a wash before the sunrise service of Matins. After breaking our fast with a bit of bread and water came the first-hour office of Prime. In midmorning came the third-hour office of Terce. In late morning, at the fifth hour, we had the prandium, our one hot and hearty meal of the day, then performed the sixth-hour office of Sext. After that, unless work called, we were allowed the sexta nap or rest. In midafternoon came the ninth-hour office of Nones, and at sundown came Vespers, after which almost all the workers, except the brothers who had to tend animals, were free to take care of private business: reading, mending, bathing or whatever. At almost any hour of the day, though, if a monk had an unoccupied moment, he could be found kneeling and doing private, silent, lip-moving devotions, tossing pebbles from one pile to another—small pebbles for the Aves, larger ones for the Paternosters and Glorias—to count his imposed allotment of prayers, and at the end of each prayer making the sign of the cross upon his forehead.

22

Besides the offices of each day, we were required each week to chant all the hundred and fifty of the psalms, plus the canticles appointed for each week. Those monks who were literate were required to read for two hours each day, and three hours a day during Lent. During each year, of course, we all attended Sunday and holy-day and feast-day masses, the Easter baptismal services and frequently wedding or funeral masses. On sixty days of each year, we fasted. In addition to making those numerous observances, I, as an oblate and postulant, had to include time for religious instruction and secular education as well.

Very well. From my earliest years, I was made to work hard and to study hard, and only seldom was I let to go briefly beyond the cliff walls that enclose the Ring of Balsam. But, not ever having known any other kind of life, I might have remained satisfied with that one, and never have known any other. Sometimes, in after years, in moments of mellow mood—when I have been flushed with wine, say, or languorous after lovemaking—I have reflected that perhaps I should not have dealt so harshly with that Brother Peter as I eventually did. Had it not been for that wretch, I might this minute be still immured in the Abbey of St. Damian's or some other cloister or a church, and the secret of my nature would be a secret still, even to me, concealed beneath the robe of a monk—or of an acolyte, a deacon, a priest, an abbot, perchance even the robe of a bishop.

For I had a thorough grounding in the Catholic Christian Scriptures and doctrines and canonics and liturgy—a much more thorough grounding than most postulants ever receive. That was because Dom Clement, from his first arrival as abbot of St. Damian's, took a personal interest in my instruction, and often personally applied himself to it. Like everyone else, he assumed me to be of Gothic parentage, and evidently he also assumed that I had been born with inbred Gothic beliefs—or disbeliefs, or nonbeliefs—and so devoted some of his own time to expunging those and replacing them with firm Catholic orthodoxy.

On the Catholic Church: "It is our mother, prolific of offspring. Of her we are born, by her milk we are nourished, by her spirit we are made alive. It would not be decent of us to speak of any other woman."

On other women: "Should a monk have to carry even his own mother or sister across a brook, he will first carefully swathe her in a cloak, for the very touch of any female's flesh is fire."

On me: "Like a wounded man, young Thorn, you have had your life saved by the sacrament of baptism. But for the rest of your life you must endure a protracted and precarious convalescence. Not until you die in the arms of Mother Church can you ever be fully recovered."

And every time the abbot sat with me, he made sure to say, with repugnance in his voice, something like this: "The Goths, my son, are outlanders—men with wolfish names and wolfish souls—to be shunned and execrated by all decent folk."

"But, Nonnus Clement," I said, on one of those occasions, "it was to outlanders that our Lord Jesus first revealed himself after his glorious Nativity. For he was of the land of Galilee, and the Wise Men came from the outland of Persia."

"Ah, well," said the abbot, "there are outlanders and there are outlanders. The Goths are *barbaric* outlanders. Savages. Beasts. As is clearly evident from their tribal name, the Goths are the terrible Gog and Magog, the hostile powers whose coming was ominously foretold in the Books of Ezekiel and Revelation."

"Then," I mused, "the Goths are beings as detestable as pagans. Or even Jews."

"Ne, ne, Thorn. The Goths are far more reprehensible, for they are heretics—*Arians*. An Arian is one who has been *shown* the light of truth, and has chosen a foul heresy instead of the Catholic faith. The sainted Ambrose has declared that heretics are more blasphemous than the Antichrist, more than even the devil himself. Akh, son Thorn, if the

23

Ostrogoths and Visigoths were only outlanders, and only savages, they might be tolerated. As Arians, they must be *loathed.*"

Not Dom Clement or anyone else could then have foretold that, within my own lifetime, all the world about us would be ruled by those Arian Goths—and that one man among them would be the first ruler since Constantine to be universally acclaimed "the Great"—and that he would be the first man since Alexander to *deserve* to be called "the Great"—and that I, Thorn, would be beside him when he was.

3

What worldly education I received at St. Damian's began when I was very young, taking instruction from a Gepid monk, Brother Methodius, who spoke in the Old Language. As children will do, I kept asking foolish questions, and the monk had to exert all his patience to answer those queries as best he could.

"To God all things are possible," he was reciting in Gothic—"Allata áuk mahteigs ist fram Gutha"—when I interrupted:

"If everything is possible to God, Brother Methodius, and if God made everything for the good of mankind, then why did God make bedbugs, niu?"

"Um, well, one philosopher once suggested that God created bedbugs to prevent us from sleeping overmuch." He shrugged. "Or perhaps God originally intended for the bugs to torment only the pagans and—"

Again I interrupted. "Why are unbelievers called pagans, Brother Methodius? Brother Hilarion, who is teaching me to talk Latin correctly, says the word 'paganus' means only 'a simple countryman.'"

"So it does," said the monk, sighing and then taking a deep breath. "The countryside is harder for Mother Church to purge of misbeliefs than are the cities, so the Old Religion has persisted longest among the countryfolk. Hence the word 'pagan,' meaning a rustic, came also to mean anyone who is still mired in ignorance and superstition. The country clods are also oftenest guilty of heresy and—"

Again I interrupted. "Brother Hilarion says the Latin word 'haeresis' means only 'a choice.' "

"Akh!" grunted the monk, grinding his teeth a little. "Well, *now* it means an *evil* choice, believe me, and it has become a *filthy* word."

Again I interrupted. "If Jesus were still alive today, Brother Methodius, would he be a bishop?"

"The Lord Jesus?" Methodius sketched the sign of the cross on his forehead. "Ne, ne, ni allis! Jesus would be—or rather, he is—something infinitely grander than any bishop. The cornerstone of our faith, the sainted Paul calls him." Brother Methodius consulted the Gothic Bible he held on his lap. "Ja, right here, St. Paul says to the Ephesians, regarding the divine purpose, 'Af apaústuleis jah praúfeteis—' "

"How do you know, Brother, what St. Paul says? I did not hear the book say any words at all."

"Akh, liufs Guth!" groaned the monk, almost writhing. "The book says nothing aloud, child. It says its words in strokes of ink. I am reading what it says. What St. Paul has said."

"Then," said I, "you must teach me how to read, Brother Methodius, so that I too can hear the words of Paul and all the other saints and prophets."

So there began my secular education. Brother Methodius, perhaps in simple self-defense, commenced teaching me to read the Old Language, and I persuaded Brother Hilarion to teach me to read Latin. To this day, those are the only two languages of which I can boast any considerable command. Of Greek I have learned only enough to hold my own in conversation, and of other tongues only a smattering. But then, consider: in all the world, no one has ever been fluent in *every* language, except the pagan nymph Echo.

My Latin reading Brother Hilarion taught me by using the Vulgate Bible that St. Jerome had translated from the Greek of the Septuagint Bible, and St. Jerome's Latin was quite comprehensible, even for a beginner. But learning to read Gothic was a matter of more difficulty because, for his teaching, Brother Methodius employed the Bible rendered into the Old Language by the Bishop Wulfilas. Before that bishop's time, the Goths had had no mode of writing except the age-old runes, and Wulfilas found those inadequate for a proper rendition of the Holy Scriptures. So he *invented* an entire new alphabet for the

25

Gothic language—making some of its letters from the runic futhark, some from Greek, some from Roman—and that alphabet has been widely in use among most of the Germanic nations ever since.

Once I had some grasp of the art of reading, I found in the abbey's scriptorium books less difficult and more interesting—the *Biuhtjos jah Anabusteis af Gutam*, which was a compilation of the "Laws and Customs of the Goths," and the *Saggwasteis af Gut-Thiudam*, which was a collection of many of the "Epic Songs of the Gothic Peoples"—and numerous other works, both in Gothic and in Latin, relating to my ancestors and kinfolk, such as Ablabius's *De Origine Actibusque Getarum*, which was a history of the Goths from their earliest encounters with the Roman Empire.

In mentioning such works, I use the word "was" because I have reason to suspect that I and others of my generation will have been the last persons ever to read any of those books I have cited. Even when I was first perusing them, the Church had for long been frowning darkly on every work written by a Goth, or written about the Goths, or written in the Old Language, whether in the futhark runes or in the more modern alphabet concocted by Wulfilas.

The Church's disapproval was founded, of course, on the fact that both the Ostrogoths and the Visigoths were of the detested Arian faith. Over the years, all those books have been ever more fervently preached against by Catholic Christian clerics, and more relentlessly banned, burned, obliterated from existence. After my time, I fear, there will remain not so much as one written fragment of Gothic history or heritage, and the very name of "Goth" will have become only one more among the long roster of peoples extinct and unworthy of remembrance.

Dom Clement was as steadfastly opposed to Arianism as was every proper Catholic Christian cleric, but he had what most churchmen do not: a loving regard for the sanctity of books in themselves. That was why he allowed those various works dealing with the Visigoths and Ostrogoths to remain in St. Damian's scriptorium. During his years as a seminary teacher, Dom Clement had acquired a considerable library of his own, and had brought with him to our abbey a whole cartload of his codices and scrolls. He had continued ever since to procure for us more and more works, until we had a library that would have been admired by any book-collecting rich man.

Of course the religious instruction and secular education of any postulant like myself was supposed to be restricted to the study of only pious works to which Mother Church could not take exception. Dom Clement never forbade me to open any book I might discover in the scriptorium. So, while I dutifully read the Latin writings of the Church fathers and those works sanctioned by the Church fathers: Sallust's histories, Cicero on oratory, Lucan on rhetoric, I also read many that were discountenanced by the Church. In addition to the comedies of Terence, approved because they were "uplifting," I read the comedies of Plautus and the satires of Persius, disapproved because they were "misanthropic."

As a result of my voracious curiosity, my young mind eventually teemed with a mishmash of contradictory beliefs and philosophies. I even came upon books that refuted not only the Church-approved chorographies of Seneca and Strabo but also the evidence of my own eyes. Those books denied that the earth is what it looks to be—what all the far-travelers who have wandered over this world have found it to be—an expanse of land and waters stretching limitlessly east and west between the forever-frozen north and the forever-sizzling south. Those books averred that the earth is a round ball, meaning that a traveler who left home and went far enough eastward—farther than any man has yet gone—would eventually find himself again approaching his home, but from the west.

What amazed me more, some of those books maintained that our earth is *not* the centerpiece of all Creation, with the sun vaulting over it and ducking under it to provide us with day and night. The philosopher Philolaus, for instance, who wrote some four hundred years before the time of Christ, solemnly stated that the sun *stands still* while the sphere called earth simultaneously turns on its own axis and revolves once a year *around* the sun. And Manilius, who lived about the same time as Christ, said that the earth is as round as a turtle's egg, a fact which is evident from the circular shadow it casts on the moon during an eclipse, and also from the way a ship sailing off from harbor gradually dips and disappears beneath the far horizon.

Never, at that time in my life, having seen an eclipse, a harbor, a sea or a ship, I asked one of my tutors, Brother Hilarion, if those phenomena really did occur and really did prove the earth to be a sphere.

"Gerrae!" he growled in Latin, and then repeated it in the Old Language, "Balgs-daddja!" both of which words mean "nonsense!"

"Then you have seen an eclipse, Brother?" I asked. "And a ship going to sea?"

"I do not *need* to see any such things," he said. "The mere idea of a

27

ball-shaped earth contravenes Holy Scripture, and that is sufficient for me. It is nothing but a pagan notion, that the earth is other than what we see and know it to be. Remember, Thorn, those ideas were put forth by the ancients, who were not nearly so educated and wise as we Christians are today. I might also remark that if any philosophers *were* uttering such things in this enlightened modern age, they would be liable to a charge of heresy." He concluded, somewhat ominously, "And so would any persons who paid heed to them."

Before my time was up at St. Damian's, I fancied myself quite as brimming with erudition as any *twenty*-year-old of noble family. I probably was, too; twenty-year-olds of whatever social status are not overfraught with knowledge and wisdom, however good and expensive their education. Like them, I was crammed full of juiceless facts and rote arguments and categorical absolutes. And foolish pomposity. On any of the topics I had been made to memorize, I could discourse at length, either in the Old Language or in quite good Latin, but in my preposterously piping twelve-year-old voice:

"Brothers, we can find in the Scriptures every trope and schema of rhetoric. For example, notice how Psalm Forty-three illustrates the use of anaphora, or deliberate repetition: *You have made us turn . . . you have given us up . . . you have sold your people . . . you have made us a reproach . . .* Psalm Seventy is a perfect instance of ethopoeia, or the delineation of character . . ." All of that precocious posturing greatly pleased my instructors, but my talent for rhetoric proved, in my later life, to be of no use whatever to me or to anyone else.

Also, most of the facts I had been made to learn I would in time find to be untrue, most of the absolutes to be baseless, most of the arguments to be specious. And a lot of what a child might learn to its advantage, no monk could or would teach. For example, it was continually drummed into me that sexual activity was sinful, sordid, evil, never to be thought of, let alone indulged in. But no one ever taught me what it *was* that I was supposed to beware of—hence my imbecilic ignorance when I encountered first Brother Peter and later Sister Deidamia.

However, if much of my education was sheer dross, and much else of it totally neglected, I did learn to read and write and use numbers. Those abilities—and Dom Clement's tolerance in allowing me free run of the scriptorium—enabled me, while still at St. Damian's, to ingest a good deal of information and opinion not included in the approved curriculum. And what I thus learned, on my own, in turn enabled me

28

at least to question and challenge—mentally, I mean; I seldom dared to do so aloud—many of the postulates so piously fed me by my teachers. I was able in time to learn much more for myself, and to unlearn the deadweight misinformation and pathetic falsehoods those tutors were impelled to teach.

And, a year or so before I left St. Damian's, my education-beyond-my-age made it possible for me to get my first vicarious glimpses of the world outside the abbey and the valley and the surrounding highlands and even outside the Burgund nation. Our Brother Paulus, the swift-writer who was Dom Clement's exceptor, was afflicted with an apo-steme, and before long was bedridden. Despite all our prayers and the best ministrations of our infirmarian, Brother Paulus suffered and dwin-dled, and at length he died.

Dom Clement then did me the unexpected honor of appointing me to the post of exceptor (or, rather, to have me take it on in addition to my numerous other duties). I was by then adept at reading and writ-ing—and in both the Old Language and Latin, which none of the pre-ceptores in the scriptorium or chartularium could claim to be, so those monks muttered and grumbled only a little at my having won prefer-ment instead of one of them. I hardly need remark that I was nowhere near as quick and accurate as Brother Paulus had been at catching the abbot's utterances on wax and then transcribing them onto vellum. But Dom Clement made allowances for my inexperience. He dictated more slowly and precisely than heretofore, and he had me first write drafts of his dictation, on which he could correct any mistakes, before I did the finished writings.

Much of Dom Clement's correspondence dealt with minuscule points of Church doctrine and interpretations of scriptural arcana. And not all of the views I thus got of the Church's ways and workings were inspiring of boyish admiration. There seemed to me to be something wrong about a letter from Bishop Patiens in which he unnecessarily reminded Dom Clement of Christ's words in the Book of John: "The poor you have always with you."

"And happy it is for us Christians that we do," wrote the bishop. "By giving alms to the poor we do our souls much good, and lay up for ourselves a reward in the hereafter. Meanwhile, looking after the poor makes a worthy avocation for our women who might otherwise be idle. As we ourself tell the rich families who hospitably open their doors to us when we travel, 'Whatever you give to another, you are sending on before you into heaven.' And so, where once a wealthy man might have built an aqueduct for his town, now, heeding our preachments, he builds for us a fine church. As is well known, the rich always have the most sins to atone for, and we ourself are ever ready to give our best prayers toward the palliation of the sins of a rich and liberal patron. Needless to add, it is far more profitable than our tithing of the common folk."

I was even inclined once to view askance my own abbot, whom I otherwise loved and respected, when he dictated to me a letter to be sent to a recent graduate of the Condatus seminary, where he had once taught. That young man having just been ordained a priest, Dom Clement was moved to give him some advice on how best to address his congregation:

"One must preach without overpassing the simple folk; to them give milk—but without boring the more intelligent; to them give meat. However, nothing should be made too clear; therefore, stir the milk and meat into a gravy. If the laity ever were able to comprehend the Word of God unaided, if they ever were able to pray without an intermediary, what need then of the priest's benediction? Of his authority? Of the priesthood itself?"

Yes, I gained at least a few glimmerings of the world out there, before I was thrust into it.

4

 do not want to give the impression that the thirteen years I spent in the Balsan Hrinkhen consisted of nothing but hard labor and hard study. Our valley was a spacious and a pleasant place, and I managed to steal some free time from my duties and my studies, to enjoy the natural beauties of the Ring of Balsam. I may very well have learned as much of value from the wide outdoors as I did from the teachers and scrolls and codices indoors at the abbey.

I ought to describe the Balsan Hrinkhen for the benefit of those who have never been there. The valley is about four Roman miles long and wide, encircled by a vertical rock cliff, shaped like a giant horse's rimshoe and fluted like a hanging drapery, that rises from and encloses the valley. The wall is highest—at least thirty times a man's height—at the front-end arc of the rimshoe. Along the curved sides of the shoe, the cliff wall gradually diminishes in height—or it appears to; actually, the enclosed ground within gradually rises—until, at the open end of the rimshoe, the valley land merges into the land above and surrounding it: the immense, undulating plateau called in the Old Language the Iupa, the highlands. The only road out of the Balsan Hrinkhen goes up through that open end of the rimshoe. On reaching the uplands, the road forks, going northeast to Vesontio and southwest to Lugdunum on the great river Rhodanus. There are many lesser rivers traversing that plateau, and many villages, even the occasional small town, between Vesontio and Lugdunum.

There was also a village down inside the Ring of Balsam, but it covered no more area than did the buildings of either of the two abbeys. It consisted only of the wattle-and-daub, straw-thatched cottages of the local folk who farmed St. Damian's lands or their own—plus the workshops of artisans: one potter, one currier, one cartwright, a few others. The village had none of the amenities of civilization, not even a market square, because there was no buying or selling of provender or anything else. Whatever necessities were not produced by the local folk themselves had to be carted in from one of the bigger communities up on the Iupa.

Our valley's water supply was not an ordinary river, like those on the plateau, but a stream that issued rather mysteriously from our cliff wall, and no man could divine the whereabouts of its source. High up in the cliff, at what I have called "the front-end arc of the rimshoe," there was a vast, deep, dark cavern, and the water poured out of there. From the cavern's mossy and lichened lip, the stream ran down a series of terraces, making a pool at each one before running on to the next lower. Finally, after rambling hither and yon for a considerable distance from the foot of the cliff through the declivity of the valley there, the stream became a broad, deep, placid pond, and on the far side of that was where the village had grown up.

The best part of the stream, though, was that where it leapt from the cavern's rock ledge and came sparkling and laughing down the random, staggered rock terraces. Around the crystalline pools on all the terraces were banks of soil, brought as silt from wherever in the earth's

31

bowels the stream originated. Since those plots of ground were too small and hard of access for any farmer to bother tilling, they had been let to grow wildflowers, sweet grasses, fragrant herbs and blossoming shrubs. Thus that whole area, during the clement months of the year, was an enchanting place to bathe, to play or just to loll and dream.

Many a time I ventured inside the cavern whence the water came, and I may have gone farther in there than any of the timorous and incurious local folk ever have done. I always chose a time when the sunlight penetrated as far in as it ever did—which was never very far; we of the Balsan Hrinkhen were accustomed to the sun's always "setting early" behind our western clifftops. Even when I made my entry at exactly the right time, when the green mosses on the cavern's lip and the green vines dangling from its upper arch were all set glowing golden by the sun, that glow did not light my way for more than twenty paces inside. But I would grope my way through the thickening gloom for as far as I could, to delay lighting and expending my torch. I always brought at least one along: a hollow stem of hemlock, packed with wax-soaked flax, and in my waist wallet the flint, steel and puffball tinder with which to set it alight. Such a torch burns as long as a candle, and much more brightly.

If the stream of water ever had been broad enough to cover the cavern floor from wall to wall, it was not so in my time. There was ample walking room on either side. Of course, the rock underfoot was exceedingly slippery, from splashings of the stream and drizzlings from the domed roof. But fortunately my boots, the one pair I owned, were made of the untanned skin of a cow's legs, with the hairy side out. The hoofs had been removed, but the cow's dewclaws had been left on either side of each boot's heel, so they gripped excellently even on the cavern's treacherous flooring.

I never did get all the way to the stream's source, even on the time or two when I brought a whole bundle of hemlock torches. But I did go far in other directions. I early discovered that the tunnel through which the water ran, and which emerged as the cavern opening in the cliffside, was only one of many interconnected tunnels. At first I was hesitant to delve into any of the side tunnels, fearing that some skohl might have been hiding in them ever since the days of the Old Religion—or even some monster that a Christian could rightly be wary of, such as an evil demon or a lustful succuba. Even if none of those lurked hereabout, I feared that the tunnels might go on branching and I should get lost in

them. But after a while, when I had become less uncomfortable underground, I did begin exploring those side tunnels, and eventually explored all that I could find, even when they were such small holes that
I had to proceed on hands and knees, or sometimes wriggling on my
belly. I never encountered any inhabitants more fearsome than pale,
eyeless lizards and a lot of bats hanging upside down from the tunnels'
roofs, which woke only to rustle and squeak and spatter me with droppings. The tunnels did often branch, and the branchings branched
again, but I was always able to retrace my route by the soot trail my
torch left on the roof rocks.

If I cannot claim that I discovered the stream's source, I can say that
I found more marvelous things, and I wonder if anyone else has ever
set eyes on them. The tunnels not only divided and intermeshed like
the Labyrinth of olden time, they often opened out into underground
rooms far bigger than the cliffside cavern, so vast that my torchlight
was too feeble to reach their roofs. And those immense rooms were
wondrously furnished: footstools and benches and pinnacles and spires
of rock had *grown* from the rock floor, and the rock of which they were
made seemed at some time to have been *melted*. From the ceilings depended great hangings that variously resembled icicles and draperies,
but were also made of that melted-looking rock. On one particularly
exquisite tracery of melted-then-congealed rock, I wrote with the
smoke of my torch the initial of my name: þ, just to show that I,
Thorn, had been there, but then I realized that it marred the pristine
beauty of the place, and I used my smock hem to scrub it off.

For all the mysterious and extraordinary things I found underground,
however, the one *most* mysterious and extraordinary I found outside,
on one of the familiar ledges of the cascades. It was only an ordinary
rock, beside one of the cascade pools, a sharp-edged rock that resembled a giant-sized ax blade stood on end. Like the other rocks roundabout, it was mossy all over—or almost all over. What I noticed about it
was that it had a V-shaped notch in its thin edge, as if it really had
been used by an axman and he had carelessly struck it against something hard that had nicked its edge. But the rock was not an ax, and
never had been. The groove appeared to have been gouged as if by an
ironsmith's file, a good file that had not quickly dulled, for the notch
was about as broad and deep as my little finger. It was also bare of moss,
and the inner surfaces of it were sleekly polished, as vellum is polished
by a moleskin. I could not imagine how the notch had been cut or by

33

whom or for what reason. It was some while before I found out, and realized how truly wonderful that simple thing was, and how much more wonderful the reason for it.

But of that I will tell in due course. For now, I will continue describing the Balsan Hrinkhen.

As I have mentioned, there were sheep and cow pastures inside the valley—not so extensive, of course, as those up on the Iupa. Around the village there were neat kitchen gardens and, farther out, small fields of various crops, orchards of various fruits, vineyards, hop fields, even olive groves, for the Ring of Balsam's cliff-protected situation allowed those trees to flourish this far north of their native Mediterranean lands. And among all the cultivated fields were others left fallow for a season and let to grow wild.

In the gardens and orchards and pastures and fields, there were always men, women and children hard at work. A newcomer watching the work going on in the Ring of Balsam would have been hard put to tell which of the adult humans were peasants and which were the brothers of St. Damian, for all wore the same drab robes of burlap, with cowls to pull over their heads for protection from sun or rain. The dress of every man and woman in holy orders—from monk or nun on up to exalted bishop—was deliberately intended to be no more rich than the lowliest peasant's garb.

When working afield, the monks and the peasants not only looked alike, they all worked equally silently, except for a few shepherds and goatherds who might be tweedling on reed pipes. (I am convinced that the pagan god Pan invented his pipes for the same reason that all herders play them: out of sheer boredom.) The monks would speak or at least nod to me when I strolled among them. The peasant men and women seemed never to see me, or anything else except the task immediately under their noses; their gaze was as vacant as that of their cows. They were not being either aloof or unfriendly; it was merely their normal torpor.

One day I came upon an elderly man and woman forking sheep dung into the ground under their olive trees, and I asked why their neat and tidy rows of trees were interrupted by a tremendous circular gap in the middle of the grove. The old man merely grunted and went on with his labor, but the old woman paused to say, "Look you, boy, at what is growing in that gap."

"Only two other trees," I said. "Shade trees."

"Ja, and one of them an oak. Olives dislike oak trees. They will not bear if they are planted close to an oak."

"I wonder why that should be," I said. "The other tree, right beside the oak, is a linden. It does not seem to mind."

"Akh, *always* you will see an oak and a linden growing together, boy. Ever since a loving man and wife of the olden time—of the Old Religion—once asked the old gods please to let them die at the same moment. The compassionate old gods made that happen, and more than that. When the aged couple died, they were reborn as an oak and a linden, lovingly growing side by side. And so those two trees have ever afterward lovingly continued to do."

"Slaváith, old gossip!" growled her husband. "Get on with your work!"

The woman murmured—to herself, not to me—"Oh vái, the olden days were the good days," and resumed her manure-forking.

But even the peasants did not labor during every minute of every day. In the evenings, the menfolk would often forgather to play at dice, and to get quite drunk on wine or ale at the same time. As they tossed the three little dotted cubes of bone, they raucously invoked the help of Jupiter, Halja, Nerthus, Dus, Venus and other demons. Of course, they could not call on any Christian saints to intercede in an activity that involved wagers. But the game of dice was evidently older than Christianity, for the highest possible cast—three sixes—was known as "the Venus throw."

Like the peasants' penchant for gambling, some of their other doings appeared to me to be rather contrary to the Church's "you shall not" admonitions. Every summer they indulged in a riotously jolly celebration of the pagan Feast of Isis and Osiris, with much eating, drinking, dancing and apparently other enjoyments, for a spate of children always got born nine months afterward. Also, while it was usual for a newborn peasant baby to be christened or a peasant couple to be married or a dead peasant to be buried according to the Christian sacraments, the peasants performed for all of those persons an additional kind of blessing. Over the infant or the bride or the grave, a village elder would swing in circles a hammer crudely made of a stone bound by thongs to a stout stick. I recognized that object, from my readings in the Old Language, to be a replica of the hammer of the Old Religion's god Thor. Sometimes, on a wall of the house where the child had been born, or of that where the new bride would live, or in the loose earth covering the new grave, would be scrawled a sign—the gammadion cross of four equal, angular, crooked arms; what some call the "cramped" cross— intended to represent Thor's hammer being swung in a circle.

✠   ✠   ✠

In my wanderings and adventurings, I think I acquainted myself with every tree, plant, insect, bird and animal in the Balsan Hrinkhen. Of the wild creatures that lived or visited there, only the venomous adder was to be always avoided, or quickly killed if possible. Even the mischievous redheaded woodpecker was not dangerous in the daytime. I often followed one's flutterings from tree to tree, because it was said that that bird could lead a person to a hidden treasure, though none ever revealed any such thing to me. But I took care never to stretch out for a nap when a woodpecker was about, for it also had the reputation of boring a hole in a sleeping person's head and inserting maggots therein, so the person would wake up insane. Of the other birds, the white storks that arrived every spring were sometimes almost unbearably noisy, talking among themselves by clattering their bills, so they sounded like mobs of people dancing in wooden shoes. But their presence was welcome, because they were known to bring good luck to any house on the roof of which they chose to nest.

Once, while ambling about, I encountered a full-grown wolf, and another time a fox. But I did not have to flee from either, for on each occasion the beast was feebly staggering, and a farmer came hastening with a mattock to bludgeon the animal to death and skin it for its pelt. Ordinarily, those predators entered the Ring of Balsam only by night, and prowled only the end of it farthest from any human habitation. But the local folk put out bits of raw meat into which they had put a quantity of powdered bugloss herb, and that was what made the wolves and foxes blind and addled, to totter helplessly about in broad daylight.

The peasant who slew the wolf told me, while he was skinning it, "If ever you come upon a *lynx* fuddled by bugloss, boy, do not kill it. The lynx *looks* like a large cat, but it is really the offspring of a mating between a wolf and a fox, and therefore it is magical. Nurse it to health, give it sweet wine to drink, then catch its urine in tiny bottles. Bury those bottles for fifteen days and you will find that they contain bright red lynx-stones. Gems as beautiful and as valuable as carbuncles."

I never got to try that, for I never came upon a lynx. But I did have another encounter with a predator—and this one not fuddled—when I climbed a tree one afternoon. Like any boy, I liked to climb trees, and some of them, such as beeches and maples, having many limbs set near the ground, are easy to get into. Others, such as the stone pine, are like pillars, with their branches only high up, but I had devised a way of scaling those, too. I would undo the waist rope from my smock, knot a loop into either end, stick my feet in the loops and put them astraddle the tree trunk while I embraced it with my arms. The taut rope's friction against the bark enabled me to kick my way upward almost as easily as if I had been climbing ladder rungs.

Well, that was what I was doing that afternoon: climbing a stone pine tree, because I knew there was a bird nest up there, a nest of the bird called the wryneck. I had often marveled at the queer snakelike way in which the wrynecks waggle their heads, but I had never seen a chick of that bird, and I was curious to know what *it* looked like. However, a large glutton had also decided to investigate that nest, and had incautiously come out of its burrow before nightfall, and had got up the tree before me. We came face to face, away above the ground, and the animal snarled and bared its teeth at me. I had never heard of a glutton's attacking a human, but in our situation this one might forget its scruples. So I immediately abandoned my project and slid back down the tree trunk.

I stood on the ground, and the glutton and I glowered at one another. I wanted to kill the thing—for one reason, it had a fine brown fur side-banded with yellow-white; for another, it was probably the thief that had so often stolen moles from my noose-traps before I could get to them. But I had no kind of weapon with me, and the animal would make its escape the minute I went to fetch one. Then I had an idea. I took off my smock and high hose and stuffed them with the dead brush lying under the tree. I propped that limp simulacrum of myself against the trunk, sneaked out of the glutton's sight and then ran as fast as I could, stark naked, to the abbey. Numerous monks and peasants working afield goggled as I flashed past them, and Brother Vitalis was sweeping the dorter when I lunged in there. He gave a cry of scandalized astonishment, dropped his broom and went running himself—probably to tell the abbot that little Thorn had eaten of bugloss and gone demented.

I got from under my pallet the leather sling I had made myself, and yanked on my other smock, and raced back the way I had come. Sure enough, the glutton was still up the tree and still glaring down at the mock me. I had to try four or five times—I was no David with my sling—but a stone finally hit the animal, and hard enough to topple it

37

from its branch. It came flailing down, and thumped on the ground, and I already had a thick piece of tree limb handy to brain it with. The glutton weighed almost as much as I did, but I managed to drag it to the abbey, where Brother Polycarp helped me skin it, and Brother Ignatius, our sempster, helped me sew the fur into a cowl for my winter blanket-surcoat.

There was one wild creature that no one disliked or feared or wanted for its skin or tried to kill. It was a small brown eagle that nested not in trees but on high ledges of our cliffsides. The Ring of Balsam had other raptorial birds—hawks and vultures—but those were despised, the hawks because they habitually raided the poultry flocks, the vultures merely because they were so ugly and such foul feeders. The little eagle was treasured, because its chief prey was reptiles, including the one snake in all this continent that has a poisonous bite: the slender, greeny-black adder.

Either the eagle was adroit enough to avoid the adder's fangs or it was impervious to the venom, for I frequently saw the bird and the serpent in a thrashing, flapping struggle, and it was always the eagle that emerged victorious. The largest adder is not very big or heavy, but I have also seen one of those eagles fight and vanquish a ladder snake that was as long as I was tall and must have weighed six times as much as the bird. Since the slain serpent was far too heavy to be carried entire, the eagle then proceeded with its beak and talons to tear the cadaver into manageable pieces and fly those one by one to its high nest. From then on, out of admiration, I called the eagle the juika-bloth, meaning in the Old Language "I fight for blood." And the valley folk, who had never called it anything but aquila, the Latin word for "eagle," liked my new name and adopted it and used it ever after.

That was not to be my only association with the bird. During my very last year at St. Damian's, the juika-bloth solved for me the mystery of that deep and polished groove in that rock beside one of the cascade pools. At twilight one day, I chanced to bathe in that particular pool, and then lay floating lazily on the surface. The water being no longer agitated, and I making no noise, a juika-bloth came fluttering down from the cliff above the cavern, and made straight for that rock. It put its hooked beak into the rock's groove and busily worked the beak back and forth, sideways, up and down—*sharpening* it, as a warrior might whet his sword. I was surprised and thrilled to see that, and somewhat awed, too. How many, many generations of those eagles must have done the same, and over how many, many centuries, to have worn that notch so deep in solid rock! I stayed quiet and watched the juika-bloth until it was satisfied that its weapon was formidably ready for its next opponent, and then it flew up and away again.

What I did, on the following day, I would now regard as unforgivable. But I was then still only a child, and unthinking that a bird might value its freedom from mastery as much as a child does. I went again to the cascades, a little earlier in the afternoon, carrying my winter surcoat and a stout, lidded basket. At the rock, I smeared into the groove some birdlime made from the inner bark of a holly, which must be the stickiest substance there is. But that would hold a strong juika-bloth no longer than a moment. So next I carefully laid out at the foot of the rock a loop of rawhide—I had made a larger version of the noose-trap I used in mole burrows—and disguised that with scattered leaves. Then, taking with me the far end of the long rawhide, I crept deep under a nearby shrub, lay quiet and waited.

At twilight again, an eagle came. Whether it was the same one I could not tell, but it did the same thing: put its beak into that groove. Then it made an angry noise and began back-flapping its wings—much as I moved my arms when swimming on my back—while it pushed with its widespread talons against the imprisoning rock. But I suddenly stood erect, and in the same instant pulled the rawhide loop up and around the bird's hinder body, just above its tail, and yanked the noose tight. Then I leapt, flinging my sheepskin over the eagle. The next few minutes are only a blur in my memory, and they must have been a blur in reality, for the juika-bloth was only tethered, not bound. It had its wings, beak and talons free to fight with—which it did—much tattering my coat and tearing some bloody bits out of my desperately grappling arms. Tufts of wool and down wafted all about us. But at last I had the bird fast inside the coat and, holding the bundle tight with both arms, I scrambled to where I had left the basket, dumped the eagle into it and latched down the lid.

I kept that bird—and kept it secret, because, in that time and place, a person would have been considered lunatic to maintain a creature that did not in some way earn its keep. I housed my eagle in a large unused coop in the pigeon loft, where no one ever went but me, and I fed it on frogs and lizards and mice and such things that I could catch or trap.

Back then, I had never even heard of "falconry," so I certainly knew nothing about that sport and art, unless I had inherited from my Goth forebears some instinct for it. And well I may have done, because, all

39

by myself, I succeeded in taming and training my eagle. I began by clipping enough of the bird's wing feathers to prevent its flying any better than a chicken does, and whenever I first took it afield, I had it on a tether. With trial and error—and maybe instinct—I learned that the eagle could be kept quietly sitting on my shoulder if its eyes were covered, so I made a little leather hood for it. I caught and killed a harmless garden snake, and used that for a lure. By doling out rewards of morsels of meat, I taught my eagle to pounce upon that lure when I shouted, "Sláit!" meaning "Kill!"—I had to keep on catching snakes to use for that, as one after another got mangled—and also taught the bird to return to me when I called, "Juika-bloth!"

The bird and I had got that far by the time its wing feathers grew again. So one day, in an empty field, I threw my snake lure as far from me as I could. Then, with a small prayer, I slipped the eagle's tether and let it fly free, and immediately cried, "Sláit!" The bird could have flown straight back to its life in the wild, but it did not. It evidently had decided to look on me as its companion and protector and provider. The eagle obediently swooped down upon the dead snake and gleefully tore at it and tossed it about, until I called, "Juika-bloth!" at which it flew back to perch on my shoulder.

That admirable eagle continued to stay with me, and to serve me in ways of which I will tell later. I will only mention here that it and I had something in common. During all the time we were companions, the eagle of course had no opportunity to mate with another, so I never knew whether my juika-bloth was male or female.

40

5

uring the time at St. Damian's when I was smugly congratulating myself on having got educated far beyond my years, there were of course many, many things that I had yet to learn—even about the Christian religion, though I had been all my life immersed in it.

Of two things in particular I was then as ignorant as any unquestioning peasant. One was that Christianity was not so catholically universal as the Catholic Church would have liked its believers to believe. The other was that Christianity was not the solid, indivisible, unyielding edifice that all its priests pronounced it to be. None of my instructors ever divulged those truths to me, if they ever acknowledged such unpalatable facts in their own minds. However, since I never did conquer the curiosity that my tutors so much deplored, I continued to wonder about things and to scrutinize them, instead of merely accepting them, as I was expected to do.

41

Of all the things and occurrences pertaining to our religion that gave me cause for wondering or doubt, I remember most vividly one wintertime Sunday's mass.

Dom Clement, besides being abbot of our monastery, was parish priest to our whole valley, and our abbey's chapel served as the sole church of the valley's inhabitants. It was merely a large room, plank-floored, with no furnishings except the ambo reading-table at the front, and with no decorations whatever. Naturally, the congregation was separated by sex and status to stand in appointed places. Our resident monks, and I, stood to one side of the ambo, together with any visiting clerics and any distinguished lay Christian guests. The local peasant men stood in a body on the right of the room, the peasant women on the left. And off in one corner were segregated any sinners under sentence of penance.

Not until everyone else was in place did Dom Clement enter, wearing over his brown burlap robe the pure-white, priestly linen stola. The congregation saluted him with the "Alleluia!" He returned the salute by chanting the "Holy, holy, holy," and the people—signing the cross on their foreheads—responded with the "Kyrie eleison." Then Dom Clement took his place behind the ambo, laid his Bible on its top and announced that his Prophetica lection that Sunday would be the Eighty-third Psalm—"O God, who shall be like to you?"—the psalm that inveighs against the wicked Edomites, Ammonites and Amalekites.

He read it loudly and slowly, in the Old Language, but not from the Bible. He read it from a parchment scroll that had been written out in the Gothic script, and written large, so that the scroll was considerable in length. Also, it had been illuminated by our scriptorium limners with pictures illustrating various things mentioned in the lection. Those pictures were set upside down in the text. That was done so that, as Dom Clement read, and let the free end of the scroll unroll down the front of the ambo, the pictures were right side up in the view of the congregation. Almost all of the local people except the penitents came close to the ambo—politely taking turns, not crowding—to examine the illustrations. Since no peasant owned a Bible, or could read one, and since many of them were too ox-witted even to comprehend a priest's reading of it aloud, those pictures enabled the peasants to get at least a dim idea of what was being told to them. When Dom Clement had finished reading the psalm, and then began to preach his homily on it, I was more surprised than impressed by his solemnly telling us:

"The tribal name of the Edomites comes from the Latin word 'edere,' 'to devour,' hence we perceive that they were guilty of the sin of gluttony. The name of the Ammonites comes from the pagan ram-demon Jupiter Ammon, hence they were a tribe of idolaters. The name of the Amalekites comes from the Latin word 'amare,' 'to love passionately,' hence they were guity of the sin of lust . . ."

After the homily, Dom Clement prayed, still in the Old Language, for the Holy Catholic Church, for our Bishop Patiens, for our Burgund Kingdom's two co-ruling brothers, for their queens and their families, for the commonfolk of the kingdom, for the harvest here in the Balsan Hrinkhen, for widows, orphans, captives and penitents everywhere. He concluded in Latin: "Exaudi nos, Deus, in omni oratione atque deprecatione nostra . . ."

The congregation responded, "Domine exaudi et miserere," then went silent, while the monks acting as exorcist clerks herded all the sin-stained penitents out of the room and the doorkeeper clerks barred the portals against them. Next there came the Procession of the Oblation. The monks acting as deacon and acolytes brought into the chapel the three bronze vessels—each covered with a fine white veil of the cobweb cloth called goose-summer—the chalice of the wine-and-water; the paten bearing the Fraction, those being bits of the Host arranged on the tray in the shape of a human body; and the tower-shaped pyx in which was reserved the rest of the consecrated bread.

After the Eucharistic Prayer, the body-shaped Fraction was dismembered and the fragments distributed to Dom Clement, his assistant celebrants, the other monks, myself and any properly baptized guests that the monastery may have been entertaining that Sunday. Then Dom Clement did the Commixtio, dipping his bit of bread into the chalice, and pronounced the Benediction. The rest of the Host, from the pyx, was distributed to the congregation, each man receiving it in a bare hand, each woman in a hand covered with the dominical linen cloth she had brought with her. As each communicant swallowed the Host and was given a sip from the chalice, the others of the congregation chanted the Trecanum: "Gustate et videte . . . !"

When all had partaken, Dom Clement recited the Thanksgiving, but then, before pronouncing the Dismissal, he interposed a message that was not in the liturgy. You see, it was the custom of many among the congregation to swallow only a particle of the Host given them, then to take the remainder home and receive bits of it privately after their family prayers during the week. And Dom Clement warned those communicants, every Sunday, against leaving that consecrated bread carelessly about their houses, where a rat or a mouse—"or worse, some person not baptized in the Holy Catholic Church"—might accidentally or atrociously eat of it. Then he dismissed the worshippers: "Benedicat et exaudiat nos, Deus. Missa acta est. In pace."

Although I had heard him utter that caution about the Host innumerable times, never before had I thought to wonder why there should be any *but* Catholic Christians among the local folk. As I have told, I had for long been seeing the peasants do various things that seemed to me not quite—or not at all—in accord with Christian custom and practice. I had also long ago noticed that there were a good many folk of the Balsan Hrinkhen who did not attend our church services even on high holy days. Of course, in any community there are a few energumens, those "possessed by demons," which is to say insane, who are *forbidden* entry to a church. I had assumed that most of those who ig-

43

nored our services were merely impious and lazy louts. But the very
next day I learned that some were guilty of a waywardness far more to
be reprehended.

At the appointed hour, I took my wax tablets to Dom Clement's
quarters, to sit down and do the exceptor work of transcribing his correspondence. As he usually did on Mondays, the abbot asked if I had
any questions about what he had preached at the previous day's mass.
I replied that yes, I did, but I tried not to sound audacious or disrespectful as I said:

"Those Hebrew tribes mentioned in the psalm, Nonnus Clement—
you told the congregation how their names derived from the Latin
tongue or from an old Roman demon-god. Surely, Nonnus, those Old
Testament peoples named themselves long before Romans occupied the
Holy Land and brought to it their language and their pagan gods . . ."

"Good for you, Thorn," said the abbot, smiling. "You are maturing
into a very alert young man."

"But . . . then . . . how could you utter what you knew to be an
untruth?"

"The better to convince the congregation of the sinfulness of those
enemies of the Lord," said Dom Clement. He had ceased to smile, but
he spoke without anger. "I trust God will overlook that small deception,
lad, even if you do not. Most of my congregation are simple folk. To
persuade such rustics to keep the faith, Mother Church allows her ministers occasionally to assist the cause of truth with the aid of pious
artifice."

I pondered this, then asked, "Is that also why Mother Church set
Christ's birthday on the same date as that of the demon Mithras?"

Now the abbot frowned. "I fear I may have been allowing you too
much liberty, my boy, in your choice of studies. That question might
have been posed by a pervicacious pagan, not a good Christian who
believes the Church's teachings. Of those teachings, one is this: *If it
ought to be, it will be. If it is, it ought to be.*"

I mumbled humbly, "I stand chastised, Nonnus Clement."

"Whatever you have read or heard about Mithras," he said, more
kindly, "wipe it from your mind. The superstitious belief in Mithras was
doomed even before Christianity overwhelmed it. Mithraism could
never have survived, because it excluded females from its worship. To
grow and thrive, a religion must appeal, above all, to those most easily
led, those most amenable to paying tithes, those most susceptible and
even gullible—meaning women, of course."

Still humbly, I nodded, then waited for a moment before I said, "Another thing, Nonnus Clement. That warning you speak every Sunday—about the people taking care not to let the consecrated bread be eaten by a person not a Catholic Christian. Are you speaking of woefully errant Christians? Or merely tepid Christians?"

He gave me a long, appraising look, and at last said, "They are not Catholic Christians at all. They are Arians."

He said it quietly, but I was inexpressibly shocked. Remember, during all my life I had been taught to hate and condemn the Arianism of the Goths. And I had let myself learn well that hatred and contempt, not so much for the Goths themselves (since I probably *was* one) as for their odious religion. Now, suddenly, I was being informed that real, living, breathing Arians could be found within a few stadia of where Dom Clement and I were conversing. He clearly realized my astonishment, for he continued:

"I believe you are old enough now, Thorn, to know. The Burgund people, like the Goths, are *mostly* of the Arian persuasion. From the brother kings, Gundiok in Lugdunum and Khilperic in Genava, down through their princelings and nobles and courtiers, to the majority of their subjects. I would estimate that about a quarter of the villagers and peasants here in our Ring of Balsam are Arians, and another quarter are still unregenerate pagans. Those include even many of the people who raise crops or livestock on land belonging to St. Damian's, and who pay our abbey a share of their harvests."

"And you *allow* them to be Arians? You let *Arians* work side by side with our Christian brothers?"

Dom Clement sighed. "The fact is that our monastic community and our congregation of Catholic faithful constitute something like an outpost in an alien land. We exist only through the toleration of the surrounding Arians and pagans. Look at this sensibly, Thorn. The rulers of this kingdom are both Arians. Their administrators and soldiers and tax collectors are Arians. At Lugdunum, in addition to our bishop's Basilica of St. Justus, there is another, even loftier church, on the cathedra of which sits an Arian bishop."

"They too have bishops?" I muttered, dazed.

"Fortunately for us, the Arians are not forever vigilant against the least divergence from what they consider their true faith, as we are in respect to what we *know* is the true faith. Nor are they forever ready, as we are, either to convert or relentlessly to extirpate the unbelievers. It is only because the Arians are so lackadaisically lenient about others'

45

beliefs that we Catholics can live and work and worship and proselytize here."

"I can scarcely comprehend it all so suddenly," I said. "Arians everywhere around us."

"It was not always so. As recently as forty years ago, the Burgunds were merely pagans, the ignorant victims of superstition, revering all the teeming pantheon of pagan gods. They were converted by Arian missionaries from the Ostrogoth lands to the eastward."

I may still have been thunderstruck, but my usual curiosity had not been diminished. "Excuse me, Nonnus Clement," I ventured to say. "If the Arians hereabout are so many, and we Christians so few, is it remotely possible that the Arian god *is* of some worth and—?"

"Akh, ne!" the abbot interrupted, raising his hands in horror. "Not a word more, lad! Never even *speculate* on the legitimacy of the Arians or their beliefs or anything else about them. The councils of our Church have declared them evil, and that is sufficient."

"Can it be wrong of me, Nonnus, to wish to know the adversary better, so that I may the better contend against him?"

"Perhaps not wrong, son. But one must not even do *right* if it is the devil who provokes one to do it. Let us now leave that ugly subject. Come, take up your tablet."

I obediently bent to my exceptor work, but I was not yet ready to abandon the "ugly subject" Dom Clement had so abruptly thrust into my consciousness. When the abbot dismissed me, I went on to my next appointed activity of the day, my instruction in ethics by Brother Cosmas. Before he could commence one of his juiceless lectures, I asked him if it did not bother him that we were but a few Christians among a population mostly Arian.

"Oh vái," he said, and mockingly. And he dealt me the second shock I endured that day. "With all your furtive reading and prying, you have not descried for yourself that the Arians also are Christians?"

"*Christians?!* They? The *Arians?*"

"Or so they claim to be. And in truth they were, originally, when the Arian Bishop Wulfilas converted the Goths from—"

"The Wulfilas who wrote the Gothic *Bible?* He was *Arian?*"

"Ja, but that was no disgrace at that time, when Wulfilas turned the Goths from their age-old worship of the Germanic pagan gods. It was only later that Arian Christianity was damned as a heresy, and Catholicism decreed the only true Christianity."

I must have been reeling where I stood, for Cosmas gave me a look and said, "Here, sit down, young Thorn. You appear to have been much affected by these disclosures."

Brother Cosmas was rightfully vain of his knowledge of ecclesiastic history, so now he was pleased to tell me:

"In the early years of the last century, Christianity was woefully fragmented by schisms into a dozen or more disparate sects. The disputes between bishops were numerous and complex, but I will simplify them, for the purpose of this discussion, by saying that the two bishops who were eventually to be most influential and controversial were Arius and Athanasius."

"I know that Christians—or *we* Christians—follow the Athanasian teaching."

"We do, ja—Bishop Athanasius's true teaching that Christ the Son is of *one substance* with God the Father. But Bishop Arius contended that the Son is only *like* the Father. Since Jesus was tempted as a man can be tempted, suffered as a man suffers, and died as a man must die—he could not be equal to the immutable Father who is beyond temptation and pain and death. He had to have been *created* by the Father, as a man is."

"Well . . ." I said uncertainly, for I had never before meditated on any such distinction.

"Well, Constantine was then the emperor of both the Western and the Eastern Empire," Brother Cosmas went on. "He saw the adoption of Christianity as a means of cementing his empire against disintegration. But he was no theologian to understand the vast gulf between the Arian and Athanasian creeds, so he convened a Church council at Nicaea to determine which was the true belief."

"Frankly, Brother Cosmas," I said, "I do not entirely understand the difference either."

"Come, come!" he said impatiently. "Arius, clearly inspired by the devil, asserted that Christ was only a creation of God the Father. Inferior to the Father. In effect, no more than a messenger of the Father. But if that were so, you see, then God might at any time send to earth another such redeemer. If another messiah were even remotely possible, then Christ's priests would have no unique, unrepeatable, uncontestable truth to preach. And so Arius's scandalous notion naturally horrified most of the Christian priesthood, because it would have abolished their very reason for being."

"I see," I said, though I myself would have rejoiced in the hope that God might send another Son to earth in my own lifetime.

47

"The Nicene council rejected the Arian thesis, but did not then condemn it thoroughly enough. So Constantine tended to lean toward Arianism throughout his reign. As a matter of fact, the Eastern Church—the so-called Orthodox Church—*still* inclines toward some of the Arian teachings. While we Western Christians rightly regard sin as vice, and its cure as discipline, the insipid Eastern Christians regard sin as ignorance, and its cure as education."

"So when was Arianism finally condemned?"

"About fifty years after Arius died, when a synod was convened at Aquileia. Happily, the sainted Bishop Ambrose had the foresight to weight that synod with other Athanasian bishops. Only two Arian bishops attended, and they were literally shouted down, vilified, anathematized and expelled from the Christian episcopate. Arianism was overthrown, and the Catholic Church has had to suffer no stain of that heresy ever since."

"Then how did the Goths become Arians?"

"Sometime before Arianism was made anathema, the Arian Bishop Wulfilas went as a missionary into the wilds where the Visigoths had their wolfish dens. He converted them, they converted their neighboring brother Ostrogoths, *they* converted the Burgunds and other outlanders."

"But surely, Brother Cosmas, there must also have been Catholic missionaries going among the outlanders."

"Akh, ja. But you must remember that most of the Germanic people are of only brute intellect. They simply cannot realize how two divine entities, the Christ and the Father, can be of one substance. It requires an exertion of faith, not reason. Of the heart, not the head. Ignorance is the mother of devotion. But the Arian creed, that the Son is merely *like* the Father—*that* the outlanders can understand in their brute heads, and not have to employ their brute hearts."

"Yet you have called them Christians."

Cosmas spread his hands. "Only because they undeniably do follow Christ's admonitions—love your neighbor, and so on. But they do not properly worship Christ; they worship only God; I could as well call them Jews. No matter. Among their absurd beliefs is the belief that two or more forms of worship can be equally valid. So they stupidly allow the incursion of other religions—including ours, Thorn—and ours will inevitably triumph over theirs."

✠　　✠　　✠

It may seem odd—it seemed odd even to me at the time—that I alone of our entire Catholic Christian community should have dared to question, to challenge, even to begin to doubt the precepts, rules, strictures and beliefs by which we all lived. Looking back, though, I believe I can explain my dare-the-devil inquisitiveness and my incipient tendency to rebel against my upbringing. I believe, now, that it was the first emergence of the female aspect of my character. In my lifetime I was eventually and often to observe that most women, particularly those with a modicum of intelligence and a touch of education, are very much like what I was in my youth—vulnerable to uncertainty, liable to doubt, ready to suspect.

I might have gone on indefinitely poring over books and scrolls, and intensely questioning my instructors, and keeping a watchful eye on other persons, trying to resolve my doubts about what was supposed to be a God-given religion—what was supposed to be *my* religion—trying to reconcile, by perception and not merely assumption, the many inconsistencies I found in it. But it was at this time that the ruttish Brother Peter began using me in the manner of a female slave.

Though I had long prided myself on my acquisition of much knowledge, and even some measure of worldliness, I was totally unprepared for Peter's molestation, and knew not what it really was. I did know—Peter himself made it clear—that what we did together was something to be kept quiet and hidden. So I surely must have realized, though I just as surely refused to allow the realization room in my conscious mind, that ours was grossly impermissible behavior. Still, for all my independence and even contrariness in other matters, I had for so long been imbued with respect for authority—meaning subservience to everyone older in years or superior in rank—that I never tried to repel Peter's advances.

I think also, after the first assault, I was secretly so ashamed of what had been done to me that I could not disclose it to Dom Clement or anyone else, and have others feel the same revulsion and disgust at my pollution that I felt myself. Besides, Peter had accused me of being an impostor among the brothers—and what he had found between my legs evidently confirmed that accusation—so I had to heed his warning that, if anyone else learned of it, I should be expelled in disgrace from St. Damian's.

When that sordid business *was* discovered, and I *was* expelled, I had first to undergo Dom Clement's sad and compassionate but searching inquisition:

49

"This is extremely difficult for me, Thorn, my—daughter. Any imputation of sin to a female, or any female's voluntary confession of sin, is customarily made to Domina Aetherea of St. Pelagia's, or to one of her deaconesses. But I must ask, and you must tell me truthfully. Were you a virgin, Thorn, when this nastiness commenced?"

I must have been as red in the face as he was, but I tried to make a coherent reply. "Why . . . I . . . I hardly know. It is only just now, Nonnus Clement, that you have begun to call me a female. I am so . . . so astonished and bewildered to know that I *am* one . . . Well, Brother Peter also told me so, but I could not believe it . . . Since I never have thought of myself as a female, Nonnus Clement, how could I ever have wondered whether I was a virgin or not?"

Dom Clement looked away from me, and said to the empty air, "Let us make this easier on us both, Thorn. Do me the favor of telling me that you were *not* a virgin."

"If that is what you wish, Nonnus. But I truly do not know if—"

"Please. Just say it."

"Very well, Nonnus. I was not a virgin."

50

He breathed a sigh of relief. "And I shall accept your word. You see, if you *had* been a virgin, and had allowed Brother Peter to take advantage of you, and this had come to my knowledge, I should have had to sentence you to a hundred lashes of punishment."

I swallowed loudly, and nodded silently.

"Now, another question. Did you take pleasure in the sin you have been committing?"

"Again, Nonnus Clement, I . . . I hardly know what to reply. What pleasure *is* to be found in that sin? I cannot be sure whether I found any or not."

The abbot coughed and went red once more. "I am not intimately acquainted with any of the venereal sins, but I have it on good report that you would recognize the pleasure if you did experience it. And the intensity of the pleasure taken in any sin is a reliable measure of that sin's gravity. Also, the more irresistible one's impulse to repeat and to reexperience that pleasure, the more certain one can be that it is at the devil's instigation."

For the first time in this colloquy, I spoke firmly. "Both the sin and the repetition were at the demand of Brother Peter." I added, "All that I know of pleasure, Nonnus . . . well, pleasure is what I feel when . . . akh, when I bathe in the cascades . . . or when I see a juika-bloth take wing . . ."

The abbot looked even more troubled, and bent forward to peer narrowly at me, and asked, "Have you ever, perchance, seen *omens* in the flowing of those waters? Or in the flight of those birds?"

"Omens? No, I have never seen omens in anything, Nonnus Clement. It never occurred to me to seek for any."

"It is well," he said, obviously again relieved. "This affair is already complicated enough. Have the goodness now, Thorn, to take yourself out of sight of the brothers for the remainder of the day, and sleep tonight in the stable's hayloft. After Vigil tomorrow, I will escort you to the chapel for absolution."

"Ja, Nonnus. But may I ask . . . ? You said I risked being punished with the lash. What of Brother Peter, niu?"

"Akh, ja, he will be punished, never fear. Not so severely as in the case of your having been a virgin. But he will be confined and made to do lengthy penance with the Computus."

I went meekly off to the stable, as bidden, but I was harboring an unchristian resentment that Peter should be so lightly dealt with. The Computus is the treatise dealing with the calculations of the sun's and moon's movements that determine the variable date of Easter, hence every other Church date during nearly a third of the year. Granted, it is fiendishly difficult to study. But I did think that Peter's merely being confined to his pallet space in the dorter, while he deliberated on the mystic complexities of the Computus, was not at all the punishment he deserved.

My gloom was hardly lightened by the realization that I could not take my juika-bloth with me to the nunnery. But I was at least able to tell my stable-hand friend, kindly Brother Polycarp, of the eagle's existence in a coop of the pigeon loft. He promised to feed and water it until—Guth wiljis—I could somehow return and retrieve it.

✠　✠　✠

The next morning, after my absolution, I went—again meekly—with Dom Clement, to be delivered to Domina Aetherea at St. Pelagia's. I may seem to have been *exceedingly* meek about my disgrace and dismissal. But now, in thinking back on that time, I believe I can perceive the reason. I believe that I was evincing more of my female nature. I felt that somehow I *was* to blame for all that had happened—that perhaps I had unwittingly *invited* Peter's loathsome attentions—and so had no ground for complaint about the consequences. That was a feeling possible only to a female. No male would so readily indict himself in his own mind.

Yet, at the same time, I *was* a male. And, like any normal male, I was disinclined to let the matter stand, without the urge to put the blame elsewhere, and to see the culprit properly punished. This contrast and conflict of masculine and feminine attitudes was hard for even myself to understand, so I hardly could expect anyone else to. That is why I did not protest my humiliating expulsion from St. Damian's, and Peter's being allowed to stay. That is why I determined to keep quiet, but to effect my own requital. That is what I did eventually do, and I will tell of that in its place. Let me now recount more than the little I have so far told of my stay in the nunnery of St. Pelagia Penitent.

6

 cannot deny that it had been the worst shock of my life, to learn that I was not a boy, but, as I then believed, a lowly girl-child. It was hardly less of a shock to be thrown out of my accustomed and more or less comfortable monastery surroundings, to be ejected from the hearty masculine companionship of monks, into what I expected would be the soft, silly and twittery company of unintelligent, uneducated, ingenuous widows and virgins. Still, I was not entirely dreading that prospect.

For one reason, I had been much confused or upset or repelled by various things I had been regaled with during the past year or so at St. Damian's—the revelation that there were Arians all around me; the discovery that Arians were not necessarily subhuman savages, but only believers in a variant sort of Christianity; my realization that paganism overlapped disturbingly with *all* Christianity; and, not least, my suffering the abuse inflicted by Brother Peter. So I may even have felt some relief at being removed from that arena of unsettling disclosures and events.

But also I was young. I had the resilience and optimism of youth. Just as I had dared to explore the caves beyond the cascades, had caught and tamed a juika-bloth, had welcomed and dealt with the responsibility of being an abbot's exceptor—just so, I now regarded my banishment to St. Pelagia's as giving promise of being one more new adventure. For that matter, I thought the novelty of being a female might provide new experiences, too.

I could not, of course, expect those to be more than *small* adventures and experiences. I had long known that the women and girls of St. Pelagia's were kept closely cloistered. Except for their Sunday and other holy-day crossings of the valley to attend mass and Communion in St. Damian's chapel, they were not allowed ever to leave the nunnery grounds. The local peasants who supplied certain comestibles and necessities to St. Pelagia's, even the monks who brought from St. Damian's things like tools and beer and leather articles that the nuns did not make for themselves—none of those, male or female, could approach any closer than the gate of the convent's main yard.

The discipline inside the nunnery was equally strict, and any infraction of its rules incurred drastic punishment. I soon learned that the mind of a convent inhabitant was no more free to roam than her body was. I forget what was the first question I raised during one of Domina Aetherea's catechism classes—I know I asked something quite innocuous—but I do remember her slapping me nearly halfway across the room. At any given time, about one in three of us younger girls wore a puffed and fiery red cheek from the fearsome slap of the abbess's meaty hand—and the older women unsympathetically told us that we should not mind those chastisements, because those brisk facial massages would do wonders for our complexion. Well, we did *not* mind too much, because when Domina Aetherea wielded her hand, it meant that she had nothing more hurtful within her reach. When she had opportunity, she could use any weapon from the ferula birch switch to the flagrum whip of stiff, rough oxhide.

The other aspects of convent life did not much compensate for the miseries of it. Well, we did each have an individual cell, even the novices, instead of having to sleep in a communal dorter. And I will also admit that the food was decent, and usually plentiful, as it should have been in our bountifully producing Balsan Hrinkhen, so we did not starve, except intellectually, and I was probably the only female who realized that. St. Pelagia's had no scriptorium, and any codices or scrolls that the abbess owned she would not have shared with anyone. Not a

53

single other nun knew how to read, even among the older women who had lived long in the outside world before immuring themselves here.

The only learning available to us was that imparted in lectures, sermons and admonitions, sometimes delivered by the abbess, but oftener by one or another of the elderly nuns who were our chief instructors.

On the importance of virginity: "The human race fell into bondage through the misdeed of the once virginal Eve, but it was redeemed through the virtue of the ever virginal Mary. Thus virginal disobedience was balanced in the opposite scale by virginal obedience. You see, my daughters, so meritorious is virginity that it is even capable of atoning for the sins of others."

On the practical advantages of virginity: "Even a good marriage, said St. Ambrose, is abject slavery. And he asked *what*, then, must a bad one be, niu?"

On the solemnity of virginity: "Silence is the most ornamental robe a virgin can wear, and it is her stoutest armor as well. Even to speak what is good is a breach of virginal good conduct. And laughter is even more unseemly."

54   Although it had been impressed on me that my education, from now on, would consist only of what was preached by our instructor nuns, I had some other and urgent learning to acquire that I could not get from that source. I had to learn how to be a girl.

I found no trouble in getting used to some of the basic exigencies of being female: the accepted way to relieve my bladder, for instance. Since our rere-dorter was not partitioned for privacy, like our dorter cells, learning that was necessary. So I did it as does every other female, lifting up my smock and sitting down. But to master some of the other female peculiarities required concentration, practice and the example or advice of my sometimes puzzled sister novices, none of whom knew—and I did not want to invite ridicule by confessing—that I had spent all my life until now as a boy.

"You walk with too long a stride," commented Sister Tilde, a young Alaman novice who worked in the abbey dairy. "Where were you brought up, Sister Thorn? In a swamp that you had to cross on stepping-stones?" And once, when she saw me chasing a pig that had escaped from the pen: "You run like a boy, Sister Thorn. You absolutely *lope* along."

I stopped running and said, with some exasperation, "Then *you* go and catch the wretched beast." And I peevishly threw a stone at it.

"You also throw just like a boy, with a wide sweep of your arm," said

Tilde. "You must have grown up among brothers, you imitate boys so well."

She threw a stone herself, and then went chasing the pig, and I took note of how she did both those things. A girl throws with a constricted and ungainly movement of her arm, and she runs as if her legs were tied loosely together at the knees. And so did I, from then on.

On the rare occasions when we novices had some free time from the day's many religious observances and the instruction classes and the jobs of work assigned to us—I should say, on the even rarer occasions when we were simultaneously free *and* unobserved by any of our elders—the girls sometimes played at "being city ladies." They would variously arrange their hair, with strings and bone pins, into elaborate tortuosities that they believed, or pretended, were in perfect simulation of city-lady stylishness. With mixed soot and tallow they would darken and exaggerate their eyebrows and lashes. With crushed bilberries they would empurple their eyelids, or tinge them green with buckthorn berry juice. With raspberry juice they would paint their lips red and put a flush to their cheeks (unless Domina Aetherea had already done that with her hand).

They would stuff the upper part of their smocks or shifts with the tow from their spinning-wheel distaffs, to give themselves prominent bosoms. They would drape and swathe themselves in any handy length of cloth, pretending that they were wearing fashionable tunicae and dalmaticae of gold-threaded samite. They would put embroidery hoops around their necks, and hang nuts or berry clusters by thread loops from their ears, and twine candle wicks about their wrists and ankles, playing that they were wearing necklaces, earrings, bracelets and anklets of pearls and gems.

I closely watched those romps, and entered into them, and copied all those little artifices. Often the other girls insisted on doing the decorating of me, because, they said, I was the most beautiful of them and deserved to be made even more so. Sister Tilde, who was very plain, said wistfully, "You have those curly tresses of pale gold, Sister Thorn, and those immense and luminous gray eyes, and a mouth most tender-looking . . ." What I thus learned about painting and adorning myself and doing up my hair would in after years be most useful to me, though of course I later learned to do those things with more artistry and subtlety.

The other girls probably did not realize it, but I also was determinedly learning to copy their movements and mannerisms and the

55

postures they assumed while they were making "city ladies" of themselves. For example, a woman's deliberately slow way of bending her arm, so the biceps muscle does not bulge as it does when a man makes that movement more abruptly and tensely. The likewise deliberately slow way in which an arm is raised, and the shoulder put back at the same time, so the combined movement raises the breast (whether of flesh or padding) in a most sensuous manner. The way, when gesturing with one's hand, of always keeping its middle and ring finger together, to give the hand its most fluid and willowy appearance. The way, when raising one's head, of slightly tilting it at the same time, to give one's neck and throat the most flowing line. The way of never looking at another person *quite* directly, but always just a trifle obliquely or, depending on the circumstances, looking haughtily down the nose or coyly from under the lashes . . .

I decided that, since I was henceforth to be female, I might as well aspire to being someday the finest of fine ladies. Even fine ladies, though, have no advantage over the lowliest slovens in some regards. As I was to learn, there are physical afflictions unknown to males but suffered by all females. Sister Tilde and I had one day been given the job of scrubbing the dorter floors, when we suddenly noticed strange noises coming from one of the cells. We crept close and peeked in. It was the cell of Sister Leoda, a novice of about our own age, and she was writhing on her pallet, whimpering and moaning, and the lower half of her shift was nearly sodden with blood.

"Gudisks Himins," I muttered in horror. "Leoda has somehow injured herself."

"Ne," said Tilde, unperturbed. "It is only the menoths. The menstruum. Nonna Aetherea must have excused Leoda from her duties today."

"But the girl is in pain! She is bleeding! We must do something to help!"

"There is nothing *to* do, Sister Thorn. It is a normal occurrence. All of us must endure that for a few days every month."

I said, "But you do not. Or not that I know of. And certainly I do not."

"You and I will, though, in time. We are of the northern peoples. Sister Leoda is from Massilia in the south. Girls of the warmer lands mature at a younger age."

"That is *maturity?!*" I exclaimed, appalled, looking in again at Leoda, who was paying no attention to us or to anything else but her private and lonely torment.

"Maturity, ja," said Tilde. "It is the curse we inherited from Eve. When a girl becomes a woman—of an age to conceive and bear children—she suffers her first menstruum. Then it recurs every month, unless she does get pregnant. The misery lasts for some days each time, and it goes on happening, every month of a woman's life, until she can no longer conceive, until all her juices dry up, and she is an old woman of forty years or so."

"Liufs Guth," I muttered. "Then I should think every woman would wish and strive to *get* pregnant, if that brings surcease."

"Akh, ne, say not so! Be happy that we of St. Pelagia's have renounced men and marriage and childbirth. The menstruum may be a curse, but it is as nothing compared to the agonies of giving birth. Remember what the Lord said to Eve, 'In sorrow shall you bring forth children.' Ne, ne, Sister Thorn, be glad that we are to be forever virgins."

"If you say so," I sighed. "I will not eagerly look forward to my maturity, but I shall resign myself to it."

57

Although I had to exert constant and painstaking effort in learning how to *behave* like a female, I was pleased to find that I had little trouble in coming to *feel* like one. I have already told how, before I ever knew of my physical peculiarity, I seemed to be manifesting various feminine traits—uncertainty, doubt, suspicion, even the extremely unmasculine sense of guilt.

Once I had accepted my femaleness, it appeared that all my emotions came closer to the surface of me, so to speak, and were more easily indulged, expressed and influenced. Where once, boylike, I might only have admired Christ's manly fortitude on the cross, I could now reflect almost maternally on the pain he had suffered, and could unashamedly let tears come to my eyes. And I could be femininely mercurial in my moods. Like my sister novices, I could take joy in such frivolous things as dressing up and feeling pretty. Like them, I could just as readily get sullen at some real or fancied slight, and sulk about it.

I came to realize that, like them, I was acutely sensitive to odors, whether appealing or repellent—and later in life, when I encountered perfumes and incenses, I would find that they could profoundly affect my mood or emotion or disposition. Like my sisters, I could discern when another female was having her monthly indisposition, from the

look of her face, as well as from the subtle blood-scent she gave off—
and in the outside world, I would still be able to do so, even when a
woman tried to conceal her condition with a veil or a cloud of perfume.
Like my sisters, I somehow knew—what no male ever has learned to do
very well—how to dissemble my most tempestuous or deepest feelings,
when I wanted to, behind a mask of impassivity. That is to say, the
mask would have been inscrutable to a male, but was transparent to
any other female. Like every one of my sisters, I could tell when another
was being happy or sad, forthright or guileful.

Furthermore, my attitudes had changed. I could now appreciate my
feminine deftness of touch and aptitude for sympathy as much as I had
formerly gloried in my masculine strength and coolheadedness. I could
take as much pride in sewing a fine seam, or comforting a homesick
younger sister, as I formerly had done when I single-handedly slew that
wild glutton. Where before I had seen things in terms of their substance
and function, I now looked at things more keenly, noticing in them
gradations of palpability, pattern, color, texture, even sounds. Where
before a tree had been to me a solid object to be climbed, I now could
discern its intricacies—rough bark below, supple and tender extremities,
no two leaves of exactly the same shape or the same green, and the
whole tree forever making *some* sound, from the merest whisper to the
fiercest thrashing complaint. When the nuns of St. Pelagia's chanted a
canticle, any dullard male could have remarked that their voices were
infinitely more dulcet than those of St. Damian's monks—but my own
hearing was now acute enough to detect the gentleness in Sister Ursu-
la's voice even when she was scolding, and to detect the rancor in
Domina Aetherea's even when she spoke most unctuously.

Perhaps it is because women, through all the generations since Eve,
have mainly done close and delicate work that their girl-children by
now are born with such refined senses and abilities. Or maybe it is the
other way about: their inborn subtle talents make them excel at work
of minute precision. I do not know. But I was then—and still am—very
happy that I, like other females, had been endowed with those attributes of sensitiveness and discernment.

However, not then—and not since—did I ever lose or outgrow or
slough off any of the less refined but still valuable faculties and profi-
ciencies inherent in the male half of my nature. Because the independent boy-child part of me found the atmosphere inside St. Pelagia's to
be so oppressive and inhibiting, I contrived to spend as much time as

possible outdoors, volunteering to take on those chores that the nuns and novices most disliked: the care of the cattle and swine, for instance.

I had another reason, a more personal and even more boyish reason, for spending time in the outbuildings and barnyard. For that same secret reason, I managed fairly frequently, after dark, to steal away from the nunnery grounds entirely. I was able to do that simply because it was inconceivable to our elders that a girl *would* play truant, especially in the dark, for all the girls and women considered the night the time when demons were oftenest abroad. Nevertheless, I always took the precaution of waiting until after Domina Aetherea had made her head count of all the nuns and novices retiring to their cells at nightfall, before I slipped out of my own cell and out of the building and out of the grounds.

What took me outdoors whenever I could go there—besides my getting away from the convent's dour discipline, and besides my desire for an occasional all-over bath in the sparkling water of the cascades—was the need to care for and continue the training of my juika-bloth.

Here at St. Pelagia's, as soon as I could, I had established myself as "that girl who does most of the dirty work outdoors." Then, at my earliest opportunity, I sneaked out one night, ran all the way across the Balsan Hrinkhen to St. Damian's, climbed unobserved into the pigeon loft, retrieved my bird and ran back to the convent. Part of the way, the juika-bloth seemed to enjoy being carried on my shoulder, jouncing lightly to my stride. The rest of the way, it took wing and flew just ahead of me, as if encouraging me in my hard-breathing haste. Back at the convent barnyard, I installed the bird in the cows' hayloft, in a wicker cage I had woven myself, and made it feel at home by giving it a hearty meal of live mice I had trapped and saved for the occasion.

Thereafter, I managed to keep the presence of the juika-bloth secret from everyone else at St. Pelagia's, and also managed to keep it adequately fed and watered, and—usually at night—I let it exercise by flying free. Now and then a milk snake would come stealthily slithering about the cows' byre in hope of drinking a meal from an unguarded milk pail. I would catch it and keep it until I had a chance to rehearse my eagle in swooping down on that lure at my command of "Sláit!" As soon as I was sure that the juika-bloth was still obedient, and had forgotten nothing of what I had taught it, I commenced to teach it a new accomplishment that I had devised.

But it was at about this time that, on a balmy autumn day, I was startled to be suddenly and intimately caressed by a small hand, and to hear a sweet voice saying, "Oo-ooh . . ." That was when Sister Deidamia came into my life.

7

 have told of my first encounter with Deidamia at St. Pelagia's, and of my last. There were many in between, during which, as I have said, we taught one another numerous things. Since Deidamia never ceased to fret about her not being "a complete and developed woman"—because the "little nub" between her legs spurted no juice, as mine did—I was continually trying to console her, and even tried to help her remedy that lack that bothered her so.

I said guardedly, "I once overheard a *man* . . . talking of his own, er, thing . . . and he said *its* growth could be much enhanced, although his was already quite sizable."

"Say you so?" Deidamia exclaimed hopefully. "Do you suppose my thing could similarly benefit? How did this man say it could be done?"

"Well . . . in his case . . . by a female's taking it in her mouth from time to time . . . and, uh, massaging it vigorously with her lips and tongue."

"That would make it grow?"

"So he said."

"Did he say whether it actually *did?*"

"I am sorry, big sister, but I overheard no more." I was being most circumspect in the telling, so as not to risk Deidamia's suspecting that I had not *heard* of that but had *done* that. I was sure it would disgust her, as the recollection of it has ever since disgusted me.

She said in a shy voice, but with eagerness in her eyes, "Do you think . . . ?"

"It might. It cannot hurt to try."

"And you would not mind . . . doing such a thing?"

"Not at all," I said, and truthfully. What had been repulsive when Brother Peter forced me to it seemed not at all so, now, with the beautiful Deidamia. As I bent my head down there, I said, "This may even give you a new kind of pleasure."

Well, I knew it would, and it did, on the instant. As soon as I put my mouth there, Deidamia's whole body jolted as if I had touched that sensitive little nub with a piece of briskly rubbed amber.

"Akh, my *dear!*" she gasped. "Akh, meins *Guth!*" It was a pleasure to me, too, to give her so much joy. She threshed and twisted so wildly that, after a while, I had to clasp my arms about her hips to keep my mouth where it belonged. At last, after a long, long time, she gasped weakly, breathlessly, "Ganohs . . . enough. Ganohs, leitils svistar . . ." I raised up, to lie supine beside her again, and she went on panting for a while. Then, when she had got her breath, she said, "But how selfish I have been! All that for me and nothing for you."

"Ne, ne, I quite enjoyed—"

"Hush. You must be totally fatigued."

"Well, not totally," I said, and grinned.

"Akh, ja, I see," she said, smiling. "Now, do you not move, Sister Thorn. Lie there just as you are, and let me roll atop you . . . so. Now let this warm and grateful inside place of mine envelope *your* precious, patient thing . . . so . . . and softly give it Holy Communion . . . so . . ."

On perhaps the third or fourth occasion of my paying my particular attention to Deidamia's undeveloped little nub, she stopped me before she had become too excited. She tugged gently at my hair to lift my head away from there, and said, "Sister Thorn, would you . . . turn your body . . . so . . . while you do that?"

I asked, "It would make it better for you? If I am, so to speak, upside down?"

"Akh, it *could* not be better for me, dear girl!" Then she blushed as she said, "I think you deserve to experience the same pleasure you have been giving to me."

And when we *both* bent our mouths to that mutual enterprise, we *both* instantly convulsed in a paroxysm that made Deidamia's previous spasms seem like mere palsy by comparison. When at last we wafted slowly down from the heights, I could do no more than pant and perspire, but Deidamia was swallowing, then licking her lips, then swallowing again, over and over. I must have made some sort of noise of inquiry, for she smiled at me, a little shakily, and her voice was a trifle hoarse when she said, "Now . . . I truly have . . . taken and eaten . . ."

61

I said humbly, "I am sorry . . . if it was unpleasant . . ."

"Ne, ne. It tasted rather like . . . let me think . . . like the thick milk of crushed hazelnuts. Warm, and with salt in it. *Ever* so much nicer than stale Eucharist bread."

"I am glad."

"And I am glad that it was yours. Do you know—if a woman ever did that with a *man*—do you know that she would be guilty of anthropophagy? According to the venerable theologian Tertullian, the juice of a man—what he ejaculates inside a woman to make a baby—is *already* in fact a baby at the moment the juice spurts from him. Therefore, should a woman ever do with a man what I have just done with you, Sister Thorn, she would be guilty of the hideous sin of eating a human child."

On another occasion, Deidamia said to me, "If licking and sucking can work to the benefit of other organs, little sister, let me apply that same encouragement to your nipples."

"Whatever for?" I asked.

"To sororiare your breasts, of course. The earlier one begins to play with them, the earlier they will begin to blossom, and the handsomer they will be when you are full-grown."

"But why should I want them to be so?"

"Sister Thorn," she said patiently, "the breasts, along with a pretty face and a luxuriance of hair, constitute a woman's most attractive features. Regard my own breasts. Are they not beautiful, niu?"

"They are indeed, big sister. But, aside from their being enjoyable playthings, what purpose do they serve?"

"Well, none really—for a nun. But in other women they have the same function as a cow's udder. The breasts are where a woman makes milk for her suckling infants."

"I have tasted your nipples often, Sister Deidamia, and I have never tasted any milk."

"Oh vái! Do not be sacrilegious! I am a virgin. And, of all the virgins who ever have lived, only the blessed Mary was able to exude real milk from her breasts."

"Ah, so that is why they say that Mary spilled the milk that put the via lactea across the night sky. I did not realize they meant milk from her *breasts*."

"More than that," said Deidamia, lowering her voice in a confiding way. "Mary's milk is also the reason for Nonna Aetherea's having been appointed abbess of St. Pelagia's."

"Eh?"

"Thanks to the abbess, our convent is the proud possessor of a genuine, recognized *relic.*"

"Well? What abbey is not? At St. Damian's there is a toe bone of that martyr Damian. And also a splinter of the true cross, found in the Holy Land by the sainted Helena."

"Akh, there are splinters and nails of the true cross all over Christendom. But Nonna Aetherea brought to St. Pelagia's something much more rare. She owns a crystal phial in which there reposes one drop—just one drop—of the Virgin Mary's breast milk."

"Indeed? Where is it? I have never seen it. And how did she come by it?"

"I know not how she got it. Perhaps from some pilgrim, or during a pilgrimage of her own. But she keeps it on a thong about her neck, nestled safely within her own bosom. And she shows it only to us older novices—we who have breasts—and only at the Christmas season, when she catechizes us on the story of the Nativity."

✠ ✠ ✠ 63

In exchange for Deidamia's sharing so many confidences with me, I shared one of mine with her. I introduced her to my juika-bloth and showed her how I was secretly training the bird.

"The name you gave it means 'I fight for blood,' " said Deidamia. "But you are teaching it to attack an *egg?*"

"Well, the juika-bloth's natural prey is snakes, and those it *does* swoop down upon most fiercely. But it also likes to eat the eggs of reptiles. And those, of course, it does not have to attack with force, because they just lie on the ground and cannot flee or fight back."

"But that is not a reptile's egg," she said, of the one I was holding. "That is an ordinary chicken's egg. Much larger and quite different in appearance."

"Dear Deidamia, I do not have leisure and opportunity to go seeking real snake eggs. I must make do with what is at hand. But I will now smear this one with cooking grease, so it looks as shiny and gelatinous as the genuine thing. And I will set it in this seeming nest that I made of red moss."

"The egg is still far too large."

"So much the better target for my juika-bloth. As I say, I am training it to *attack* the egg, plunging down upon it from high aloft, and tearing at it with beak and talons. Ordinarily, the bird would merely hop to where an egg lies on the ground, and only casually peck it open."

"Interesting," said Deidamia, though she did not sound greatly interested. "So you trick a bird into behavior contrary to its nature."

"Or I am hoping to. Let us see how well it is learning."

I slipped the hood from its head and tossed the juika-bloth into the air, where it began spiraling to climb high above us. Then I laid my wad of red moss on the ground and set upon it the slimily glistening egg. I pointed to it and called to the bird, "Sláit!" It stayed hovering only long enough to fix its gaze and aim on the target, then folded its wings and came down like a thrown spear. With beak and talons all close together it struck so hard that the egg quite disintegrated, spattering bits of shell and drops of yolk and glair all about. I let the bird go on tearing at the mess on the ground, and gobbling it up, then I called, "Juika-bloth!" and it promptly returned to my shoulder.

"Impressive," said Deidamia, though she did not sound greatly impressed. "But this is a most *boyish* pastime. Do you think it fitting for a maiden novice to play at such games?"

"I do not see why boys and men should have the exciting games all to themselves, and we only the dainty ones."

"Because we *are* dainty. I prefer to leave to the males anything that requires strenuous exertion." She affected an exaggerated yawn, then smiled elfishly. "But you play as you please, little sister. I have had no fault to find with any of your games."

But of course the grim Domina Aetherea (and the skulking, tattling Sister Elissa) did have fault to find, and I have already told how they one day caught me and Deidamia in flagrante delicto.

The infuriated abbess did not, as Dom Clement had done, put me to any compassionate questioning, or grant me any least absolution, or even wait until the next morning to haul me from St. Pelagia's back to St. Damian's. I was rather grateful for my being expelled that very same day, for I was sure that, if Domina Aetherea had taken time to consider my crime, it would have occurred to her that this was one occasion on which she would well uncoil her dreaded flagrum, and a beating with that might well have killed me. However, I was also sad at being rushed away. Sister Deidamia had been carried to her cell still in a swoon, so I had no chance to see her one last time, to plead for her forgiveness and to say a farewell.

✠   ✠   ✠

I have already told, also, how Dom Clement—before he evicted me that day from the Balsan Hrinkhen altogether—informed me as to what kind of perverse and paradoxical creature I really was. But I have told of that disconcerting disclosure only in brief summary. The fact is that, before Dom Clement called me to his quarters for our final conversation, he had spent a good deal of time in the chartularium, delving deep into the abbey's archives.

"Thorn, my child," he said, looking as glum as I must have looked, too. "As you know, the abbot and the infirmarian who first examined you, when you were left on this abbey's doorsill, both were deceased by the time I arrived here. And neither I nor that infirmarian's successor, our Brother Hormisdas, ever had reason to examine you again. But I have succeeded in finding a report of what that earlier brother—he was called Chrysogonus—discovered when he unswaddled your infant self. I only wish I had thought to search for this before now, but any report on a new oblate is seldom worth writing down, and even more rarely is preserved in an abbey's archive. Of course, this one was made and kept only because you yourself proved to be such a rarity. And Brother Chrysogonus's report not only describes you as you were, but also records what that good brother did to you in his capacity of medicus."

"Did to me?!" I demanded, almost angrily. "Are you saying this Chrysogonus *made* me what I am, niu?"

"Ne, ne, Thorn. A mannamavi—an androgynus—you were from birth. But, as well as I can gather from these pages, that brother kindly performed some minor syrurgery upon you. That is to say, he made a few small adjustments of, er, your private parts. And those, I judge, saved you from enduring a lifetime of discomfort or pain or even a crippling deformity."

"I do not understand, Nonnus."

"Nor do I, not entirely. That long-ago Brother Chrysogonus was either a Grecian by birth or he chose to be discreet in this matter, for he wrote his report in Greek. I can read the words—'chord,' for example— but their exact meaning in a medical sense eludes me."

"Could you not ask Brother Hormisdas to explain them?"

The abbot looked a little uncomfortable. "I had rather not. Hormisdas is, after all, a dedicated medicus. He might well wish to keep you here. For study . . . for experimentation . . . even for exhibit. Other monasteries have been known to increase their fame and fortune by attracting pilgrims with the promise of a . . . a seemingly miraculous sight."

65

"You mean a freakish specimen," I said bluntly.

"In any case, I prefer to spare you such an indignity, my child. We shall not ask Brother Hormisdas to interpret this report. Let my own attempt at explanation suffice. Brother Chrysogonus wrote that he made 'a slight incision' which enabled him to remove 'the tethering bands' that had forced your, er, your principal organ into an abnormal curvature. As I say, Thorn, you should be thankful to that good man."

"Is that all he wrote about me?"

"Not quite. He went on to remark that, although you have the . . . external equipment of both male and female, he was certain that you would be forever incapable of having children. Either of siring them or of bearing them."

I muttered, "I rejoice to hear it. I would not risk bringing another like myself into this world."

"But that will impose on you another constraint, Thorn, and a heavy one. Just as persons eat so that they may go on living, so do they mate solely for the purpose of perpetuating the human race. And that is the only excuse for sexual intercourse that our Mother Church condones. Since you cannot ever have children, it would be a mortal sin for you ever to have carnal knowledge of another person. Of . . . ahem . . . either sex. Your former innocent ignorance absolves you of those delinquencies you have committed to date. But from now on, now that you are aware of the true state of affairs, you must be steadfastly celibate."

I said, very nearly pleading like a woman, "But God must have had some reason for making me a mannamavi, Nonnus Clement. What could the Lord have intended for me? What am I to do with my life?"

"Well . . . I am told that the Mishnah of the Jews lays down rules for the social and religious behavior of a mannamavi. Unfortunately, our own Scriptures neglect to treat of that subject. However . . . let me suggest something. Your work as my exceptor showed great promise, Thorn, back when all of us believed you to be a male. Needless to say, such a thing as a female exceptor or scribe would be unnatural and unthinkable. But I daresay, if you were to introduce yourself *as a male* to some other abbot or a bishop, in some place well distant from here— and if you were forever celibate, forever careful not to reveal any of your, um, aspects of feminity, forever careful not to expose yourself even in the rere-dorter—you might find satisfying employment as that high churchman's exceptor."

"So, when I come to die," I said bitterly, "I shall leave no trace that I ever have lived, except my copies of other people's words. And all during that bleak life, I must suppress every normal human appetite, even an entire half of my own God-given nature."

The abbot frowned and said in a stern voice, "Anything that is possible to a Christian is obligatory to a Christian. It is possible for a Christian to be perfect; hence it is obligatory that he or she strain to *be* perfect. Morally, spiritually, intellectually, even physically. If he or she persists in imperfection—ja, *even in being a freak*, as you described yourself—then it must be a willful imperfection, therefore execrable, therefore punishable."

I stared at him, aghast, and finally said, "You can believe in a virgin birth, Nonnus Clement. You can believe in a resurrection from the dead. You can believe that angels are neither male nor female. Yet you find *me* incredible and intolerable."

"Slaváith, Thorn! You verge on blasphemy. How *dare* you compare yourself to one of God's angels?" He struggled to put down his surge of wrath, and after a moment said more calmly, but tremulously, "Let us not part on that sour note, my child. We have been friends too long. I have given you the friendliest advice I know how to give, and now in friendship I give you this silver solidus. It will buy you food and shelter for a month or more of days. Be friendly to yourself, and go as far as possible from here—where you have been known—before you settle down to start your new life, whether that be the life I have suggested or any other you may choose. I pray that God will go with you and be with you always. Vade in pace. Huarbodáu mith gawaírthja. May you fare in peace."

67

✠   ✠   ✠

So I parted from Dom Clement, and both our hearts were heavy, and I never saw him again. But I did not immediately depart from the Ring of Balsam, as commanded, for I had some things to attend to before I went—first of all, to retrieve my juika-bloth from the cow byre at St. Pelagia's. That same night, I stole back to the nunnery, as I had frequently done before. Well knowing my way, I did not need to strike a light even to climb the ladder to the loft. I was feeling my way across the hay toward the wicker cage when a feminine voice suddenly said, "Who is that?" and I think my hair stood on end.

But I recognized the voice, and my hair subsided to its proper place. "It is I—Thorn. Is that Sister Tilde?"

"Ja. Is it really you, Sister Thorn? I mean . . . Brother Thorn, is it now? Oh vái, good brother, please *do not rape me!*"

"Hush, little sister. Keep your voice down. I have never raped any-body and I never will—least of all a dear friend. But what are you doing up here? And at this hour?"

"I came to make sure that your bird had food and water. Is it true then, Thorn, what we all have been told? That you have been a . . . a male person all this time? Why did you pass yourself off on us as a—?"

"Hush," I said again. "It is a long story, and I do not yet fully com-prehend it myself. But how did you know about my bird hidden here?"

"Sister Deidamia told me. While she still could talk. And bade me care for it. Have you come to take it away?"

"Ja. But it was kind of you and Deidamia to give thought to its welfare. Wait. What do you mean, Tilde? While she still could talk?"

Tilde gave a small whimper and said, "I think something is broken inside her now. Nonna Aetherea has been beating Deidamia most fe-rociously—and with the horrible flagrum—at intervals, all this day long, whenever Deidamia came to consciousness after the previous beating."

"Atrocissimus sus!" I said through gritted teeth. "The old sow neg-lected her opportunity to beat me. So now she makes poor Deidamia suffer for us both."

Tilde sniffled and said, "I doubt that any male person would concern himself with Deidamia any longer. She is not pretty now, or shapely, as she used to be. Nonna Aetherea flailed the flagrum most wildly and indiscriminately."

I swore a dreadful curse: "May the devil take her napping!" Then I paused and considered. "Napping, that is it. The abbess sleeps very soundly, ne?"

"Akh, exceedingly so, when she has well tired herself with the violent exercise of wielding a whip."

"Very well. I shall arrange that she has something to think about tomorrow besides Deidamia. Come, Tilde. I will leave my bird here, while I make my way to the abbess's quarters. You will keep watch there for me.

"Gudisks Himins! You do talk now like a boy, and a foolhardy one. No well-disciplined sister would dream of intruding on—"

"As you have said, I am no longer a well-disciplined sister. But you need have no fear. If anyone approaches while I am visiting Nonna Aetherea, simply give a hiss of warning and scurry away to safety. Come, do it for Deidamia's sake."

"I could hardly do anything for *your* sake, you being male. But even for the sake of a sister, it is a heinous crime. What is that you intend to do? To harm the abbess somehow?"

"Ne, ne, only to teach the fiendish Halja-woman that she would do better to emulate another woman, one of long ago, one of tenderness and loving kindness."

So Tilde came with me to the window aperture of Domina Aetherea's quarters, whence we could hear her snoring as loudly as any peasant wife. I climbed in through the opening and, by now having been so long in deep darkness, could see well enough to sneak silently to her pallet-side. Except for the horrendous noise she was making, the abbess was sleeping the sound, serene sleep of a woman well satisfied and clean of conscience. Gingerly, I felt about her throat until I found the small but heavy crystal phial. It was capped with a stout brass ring threaded on a rawhide thong that hung loosely from her neck but was tied in a tight, hard knot.

Hearing no warning from Tilde and no sound of anyone else at large inside the building, I trusted that I had plenty of time. So I copiously wet the knot with my spittle and worked the wetness into it until the rawhide swelled of itself. When it did, my fingers were small and nimble enough to untie it. As I did that, I took note that the knot was quite an intricate one, evidently of the abbess's own devising. I slid the phial off the thong and dropped it into the top half of my belted surcoat. Then I painstakingly re-created the knot as it had been before.

I slipped out the window and rejoined Tilde, but I waited until we were back at the byre before I told her what I had done. She almost shrieked, "You stole the holy relic?! The Virgin's breast milk?!"

"Hush. No one else will ever know that. By morning the rawhide will have dried and shrunk tight again. When Domina Aetherea wakes and finds her most precious possession gone, but the knot apparently un-tampered with, she will have to conclude that the phial was removed by no human agency. I hope she will believe that Mary herself took back her own drop of milk. The abbess may infer that she has been chastised and bidden to mend her ways. If so, our Sister Deidamia may be spared further torment."

"I hope so," said Tilde. "What will you do with the relic?"

"I do not know. But I have few other possessions. It may serve me in some way."

"I hope so," Tilde said again, and she sounded sincere. So I quickly

69

leaned forward and pecked a kiss on her snub little nose. She recoiled as violently as if she thought that a prelude to rape, but then she giggled delightedly, and we parted friends still.

✠ ✠ ✠

I have earlier told that I left the Balsan Hrinkhen with two things that did not belong to me. Well, I had them now—the captured juika-bloth and the pilfered reliquary phial—but I did not yet depart from the valley. I had one more self-appointed task to accomplish. While it was still night, I stole into the cookhouse garden of St. Damian's and plucked up a few winter turnips that would keep me from hungering and thirsting overmuch, and took them with me as I climbed a tree overlooking one edge of that garden. I climbed awkwardly, for I still had my bird in its cage; I could not take the chance of letting it go hunting before I wanted it to.

When Domina Aetherea had brought me back to St. Damian's and told one of the monks to keep me in an outbuilding, I had inquired of him what job Brother Peter, the former kitchener, had now been assigned. He had told me. Peter was now (and probably permanently) the lowly spreader of dung—human, fowl and animal ordure—on whatever abbey fields and plots needed top-dressing. So I knew that soon or later Peter would be bestowing that nourishment on this garden. I was prepared to wait, through many cold days and nights if necessary, until he did so.

As it turned out, I had to perch and shiver in my tree for only the remainder of that night, the next day and all the next night. During that one, I descended again to replenish my supply of turnips, and even found a few earthworms for the juika-bloth; it clearly did not relish them, but it ate them. Then, on the following day, after I had heard the brothers indoors chanting the Matins service to greet the sunrise, and after a short interval for the monks' breaking of their fast, the several outside doors of the abbey—two of them visible to me, the others not—began to disgorge the field-working brothers.

From one of the doors within my view came Peter. He went into a shed, emerged with a pitchfork and a hod heaped with ordure and carried them straight to the garden between the cookhouse and my tree. He set down the heavy hod, steaming in the sun, and with the pitchfork began laggardly to scatter the dung along the rows of vegetables.

Still I bided my time, until he was almost directly beneath me. Moving slowly and quietly, I reached my arm into the juika-bloth's cage and nudged my wrist against the back of its legs. In reflex, the bird stepped backward onto my arm. I withdrew it, slipped off the juika-bloth's hood and waited some more. By now, Brother Peter had got warm with exertion and had tossed back the cowl of his robe. But he necessarily worked bent over, so the bird and I could see only the back of his head. I waited until he stood up straight and stretched to unkink his spine. Now, with his head up, his grease-smeared, dead-white tonsure, fringed by gray-red hair, was a passable simulacrum of the slimy and glistening egg in a red-moss nest with which I had in recent weeks been training the eagle. I pointed and whispered to the juika-bloth, "Sláit."

My arm jerked upward as the bird eagerly vaulted off it, and the limb on which I sat bounced. Peter must have heard the swish of branches and leaves, or the drumming of the juika-bloth's wings as it reached for altitude, because he looked puzzledly around him. But he did not look up, so, though his head turned about, it still resembled an egg in a nest, and down toward that the eagle hurled itself from on high.

It plummeted, on rigid pinions, almost vertically downward and with incredible speed. But the raptor's shadow, cast by the low morning sun, came racing even faster, because it had farther to travel. The small dark shadow dropped abruptly down a western cliff, rippled urgently over the intervening fields, at the last dashed furiously across the garden below me. The juika-bloth and its shadow and their target met and merged all in one fraction of an instant.

The eagle hit Peter's head with a loud *thump* and clenched its talons in his fringe of hair—probably into his scalp as well, for Peter uttered an unearthly scream. But the scream did not last for long. The juika-bloth immediately drove its fearsome hooked beak into the monk's skull, at the very center of his tonsure, and at that the white egg turned redder than the moss around it. Peter fell silent and fell prone between two rows of high-growing kale. The bird continued to raise and ram down its beak, again and again, seeming infuriated that this egg had such an osseous shell.

Two other monks, drawn by the brief scream, came around a corner of the monastery and peered out over the garden, but they could not have seen Peter stretched out among the leafy kale. I called quietly, "Juika-bloth," and the eagle obediently flapped upward—its beak clamped on a strand of gray matter that stretched out of Peter's broken head, then came loose and trailed behind as the bird, its head feathers all bloody, returned to settle on the limb beside me. "Akh," said one of the monks, "that noise was only a rabbit or a vole struck by yonder eagle," and they both disappeared again to their own labors.

I took the juika-bloth on my shoulder—it still avidly champing on its long, limp string of gray substance—and tucked the wicker cage under one arm, and clambered down the tree. I no longer needed the cage, but I wanted to leave no evidence, so I carried it a good way before I hid it in a copse dense with underbrush. I had earlier left in that same place my bundled other few belongings, and now retrieved them.

It was time for me to go. I was both Adam and Eve, banished from the Garden. As a presumed Goth by birth, I had long been an object of some suspicion on the part of the Catholic Christian Church, and now, as a mannamavi, I was an abomination to that Church. Now, also, besides all the other dubieties, criminalities and sinfulnesses inherent in my nature—a nature not of my own making—I had two nights ago deliberately become the thief of a sacred relic, and this day had deliberately become as much a raptor as the juika-bloth. Of those two sins, thievery and murder, I wondered: to which was I impelled by the Adam in me and to which by the Eve?

No matter. It was time for me to go, and go I would, to *be* a Goth—*and* an Arian, if the Arian Christians would accept a mannamavi more charitably than the Catholic Christians had done. So, when I trudged upward from the Ring of Balsam and gained the Iupa highlands, I turned left on the road there, toward the northeast, toward the land that civilized folk called the "barbaricum," where the Ostrogoth tribes were said to live—or lurk like savages—deep in the fastnesses of their forbidding forests.

72

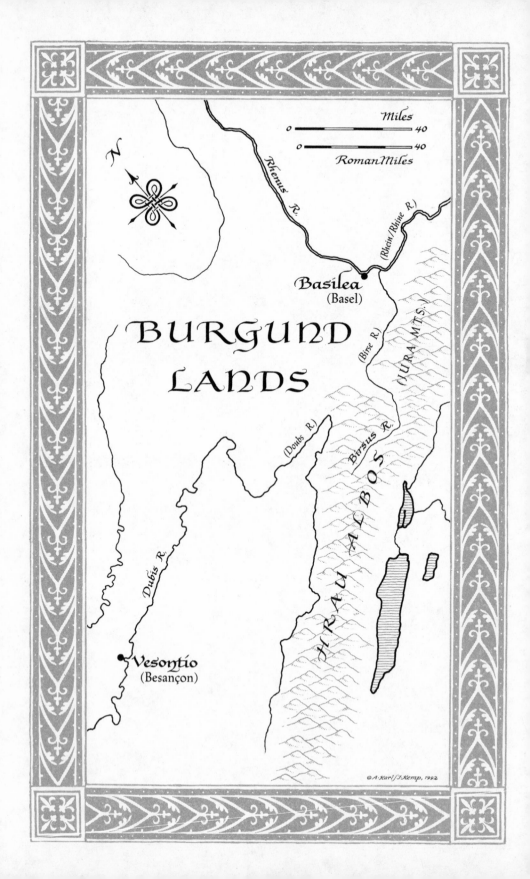

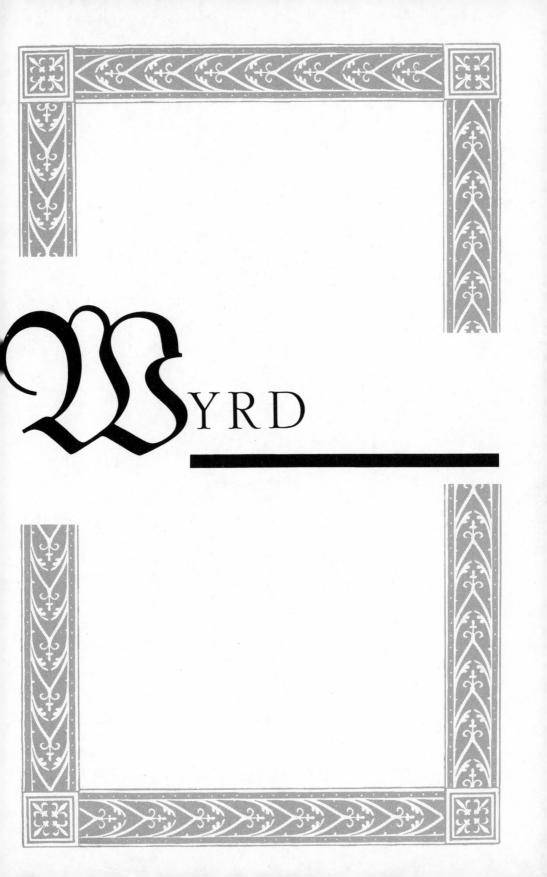

WYRD

1

I emerged from the Ring of Balsam into a world that was very nearly as uncertain about its identity and destiny as I was about my own. Of course, for a long time, the chroniclers had been writing and the minstrels singing dolefully of the disarray into which had fallen the once orderly, steadfast and mighty Roman Empire. Not that anyone had to read books or hear songs to be aware of that fact. Even a person as young and lowly as myself, cloistered in an abbey that was sequestered in a valley nook remote from most of the outside world's doings, had been able to discern that the empire was getting ever more fragmented and feeble.

The man who occupied the imperial throne at Rome when I arrived as an infant on the doorsill of St. Damian's, the Emperor Avitus, had ruled only briefly before being deposed and exiled. Since then, in just my own short lifetime, three other men had been emperors at Rome.

I ought to explain that we citizens of the Western Empire dutifully *spoke* of the emperor and the imperial court as being "at Rome," rather in the conventional way that Christians speak of dead loved ones as being "in heaven." Nobody knows anything for certain about the situation of his dead loved ones, but everybody knew where his emperor was, and that place was not in Rome. Though the Roman Senate still met there, and the Bishop of Rome still commanded much of Christendom from there, no Emperor of Rome now ruled the Western Empire from there. For fifty years past, the emperors had resided and maintained their courts—for the sake of safety, not to say cowardice—in the north Italia city of Ravenna, because it is surrounded by swamps and therefore easily defensible.

Anyway, the imperial throne "at Rome" was no shakier than all the rest of the Western Empire had been for some ages now. As I have mentioned, it was only the death of Attila, which occurred shortly before my own time, that made the Huns withdraw from Europe into the wilds of Sarmatia, whence they had erupted a full century before. But the Huns had left their traces on the empire because, in their advance, they had pushed various Germanic peoples off their longtime home grounds and onto new ones, where now they remained.

The Goths had been uprooted from their lands around the Black Sea, and now the Ostrogothic half of that nation was settled in the province of Moesia, the Visigoths in the provinces of Aquitania and Hispania. The next most eminent Germanic people, the Vandals, had migrated clear out of Europe and now ruled the entire northern coast of Libya. Others of Germanic origin, the Burgunds, held the land in which I was born, and the Franks most of Gallia north of there. While all those lands were still nominally Roman provinces, and ostensibly owed fealty to the empire, Rome regarded them with suspicion that their occupying "barbarians" might at any time turn belligerent.

The one force that should have held the *whole* empire intact, the Christian Church, was too often busy with its own internal rivalries and jealousies. The Christianity professed in the Western Empire was doctrinally at odds with that in the Eastern. Meanwhile, the patriarch bishops of the five principal Christian sees — Rome, Constantinople, Alexandria, Antioch and Jerusalem — were forever vying to be the *one* bishop acknowledged as sovereign in Christendom, to be the *one* fondly called Papa, and to have *his* see recognized as primate over every other. Also, despite Christianity's having been the state religion of the empire for two centuries now, heretical sects and pagan cults abounded. The empire's Germanic population either was still faithful to the Old Religion — of Wotan and his family of gods — or had embraced the "heretical" Arian Christianity. Many Romans still adhered to their old worship of Jupiter and *his* god family, while Rome's military men swore by the "manly" Persian cult of Mithras.

So this was the confused and forlorn outside world into which I, myself confused and forlorn, was now setting foot. I was not aware that I was taking the first steps of my journey toward meeting the one person destined to restore peace and unity, law and order to the Roman Empire in Europe. How could I have known? The empire itself was not aware that such a person existed, for Theodoric — one day to be known worldwide as Theodoric the Great — was then, like Thorn the Mannamavi, still a child.

For that matter, he was probably much more childlike than I was at that age—in virtue and innocence, I mean—because I had already, during the past many months, learned the numerous pleasures and the occasional pangs and the sometimes grievous consequences of functioning as a very nearly mature sexual being, and not of just one sex, either.

I should remark here that, when I *did* come to maturity, I was—as that long-ago infirmarian Chrysogonus had predicted—spared at least some of the infelicities of both my sexes. I never did bear a child; I never even once suffered the menstruum that afflicts other females. And, as far as I know, I never sired any children. So I was happily exempted from the frets and impediments and responsibilities of home and family that shackle most men and women.

Akh, I will confess that once in a while, when my life was being unusually hectic, hazardous or just uncomfortable, the feminine part of me might wish for nestlike safety and security. But that happened only infrequently and briefly, and I never did settle down to what most people would regard as normality. Looking back, from both my masculine and feminine points of view, I am glad of that. Had I ever been content with commonplace standards and values and morality—or even been content to choose one sex, and forever comport myself as either a man or a woman—my life would have been far easier and more free of blemish, but it would also have been far less full of excitement and adventure. I often wonder about the normal, virtuous, domesticated folk: what have they ever *done* to look back on, to remember with either a reminiscent smile or a rueful frown, to boast of or lament or even be ashamed of having done?

My physical appearance stayed as ambiguous as my sexual nature, even when I was full-grown, and I have been called a handsome boy or man as often as I have been complimented on being a beautiful girl or woman. I have met many women taller than I was, and many men shorter. I kept my wavy hair at a medium length, suitable to either a man or a woman. My voice never broke and changed, as does that of most adolescent males, so I could pass for either a soft-spoken man or a provocatively husky-voiced woman. Whenever I traveled alone, I usually went as a man, but even then my appearance was conveniently ambiguous. Because I was gray-eyed and fair-haired, the darker people of southern Europe took me for a northerner. Because I was slim-figured and beardless, the northmen took me for a Roman.

No, I never sprouted a beard or chest hair—and only tufts under my arms—but neither did I grow much in the way of breasts. As female mammaries, they were almost indistinguishable from male pectorals.

79

What soft fleshiness they did have, I could either flatten altogether beneath a binding cloth or enhance into the appearance of a real bosom by tying the cloth in the manner of a strophion so that it squeezed them upward. Their pale pink areolae and nipples were somewhat larger than those of a man—and certainly more erectile when excited—but no woman who thought me a man ever seemed to find them disagreeably unmanly. At any rate, when I was undressed to the skin, no other female after Deidamia ever mistook me for a sister female.

I did grow an escutcheon of pubic hair, a shade or two darker than that on my head. It was neither diffuse in outline like a man's nor distinctly delta-shaped like a woman's, but almost nobody except the occasional medicus is aware of that difference between the sexes. My navel was not precisely at my waistline, as a man's is, and not much below it, as a woman's is, but that is another difference that few people know about. My male organ was of sufficiently normal size that, with the hair around it—and if I took care about the postures I assumed when I was naked—no one noticed my lack of scrotum and testicles. But the organ could be made next to invisible, held tight up against my belly by a girdling band, when I was being a woman.

80

It may sound as if I early accepted my peculiar nature and easily adapted to it, but that is not so. As I shall tell, my adapting to it and to other people took a very long time and involved sundry encounters, both social and sexual, with both males and females. Some of those encounters were experimental, some became quite emotional and some turned out to be frankly embarrassing or downright painful. It also took several years for me to come to terms of acceptance with my own self. Often and often I wondered: should I rightly be wearing the soccus of comedy or the cothurnus of tragedy? During those years I was not only inclined to be uneasy in the presence of normal men and women, I could even feel so in the presence of normal lesser animals like horses and mares—and mules, of course. Akh, I could be made uncomfortable and unhappy with myself even when I happened to glimpse one particular *flower.*

All flower blossoms, however beautiful to look at and aromatic to smell, are really nothing but the sexual organs of those plants. The one flower, though, that I personally disliked in those days was the lily. That was because the lily, with its fleshy spadix standing erect from among its vulvate spathe of petals, always seemed to me a mockery of what my own sexual organs look like.

I was not really able to begin to accept my dual nature until I had done a great deal more of reading pagan histories and listening to old pagan songs that I would not have found in a Christian abbey. I learned that I was not by any means the first of my kind—that not the Gothic word mannamavi or the Latin word androgynus or the Greek word arsenothélus had been coined *just in case* someone like myself should be born. As Pliny wrote, "Nature in sportive mood can produce almost anything," and, if the pagan tales were true, nature had produced other freaks before me.

For example, those legends tell of an ancient, Tiresias by name, who during his life wavered back and forth from being a man to being a woman to being a man again. And Ovid wrote about the minor god Hermaphroditus, son of Hermes and Aphrodite (which is to say, Mercury and Venus). That boy was loved by a wood nymph, but he spurned her advances, at which she appealed to the other gods, asking that he never be parted from her, nor she from him. The gods mischievously complied, on a day when Hermaphroditus and the nymph chanced to be bathing in the same pond, by merging him and her into one being of both sexes. The gods then let their enchantment remain on that pond, which is somewhere in Lycia, so that, to this day, any man who bathes in it comes out of the water half female, any woman comes out half male. I used to wonder what *I* might become, if I could find that pond, but I never got into that Lycian region of the Eastern Empire.

There was also the godling Agdistis, who, like me, was *born* a mannamavi. But the other gods cut off the male organ and left only the female, after which Agdistis was the goddess known as Cybele. Among the ancient mortals, as well as the gods, there were others besides Tiresias who changed sex during their lifetimes. And Rome's own early Emperor Nero, though no androgynus either, took as much pleasure in lying with males as with females. When he publicly "took in marriage" one of his love-boys, a bystander at the wedding made the caustic remark that "the world would have been happy if Nero's father had had such a wife."

Not only did I learn of all those persons of equivocal or inconstant sex who has lived before me, I also came to believe that others of my mannamavi nature were still being born into humankind. There seemed, for instance, to be some of them extant among the degenerate remnants of the Scythian people. In the ancient world, the Scythians had been notorious for being fat, indolent, and their men and women alike so indifferent to sexual pleasure that that was the reason for the diminishment and decline of their race. Nevertheless, their scattered

81

few descendants still had a word, enarios, meaning a "man-woman," and surely that must refer to a mannamavi of my sort.

What I learned from my reading made me feel less alone and lonely in the world, or at least not unbearably unique. If there were others like myself, then I might someday meet one of them. I even thought once of betaking myself to those torrid Libyan lands south of Africa and Egypt, whence come the curious double animals—the tiger-horse and the camel-bird and such—because in those lands there might exist some patchwork humans, too, of my sort. But I never went, so I can recount nothing about those lands.

And, anyway, I am getting far ahead of my chronicle.

2

That second and final time that I was expelled from St. Damian's, I again departed, as I had when I was banished to St. Pelagia's, with a mixture of anticipation and trepidation, now wondering what adventures or misadventures I might encounter *outside* the Balsan Hrinkhen. I had previously been no farther beyond the valley than the nearest upland villages and farms, and then not often and never alone. I had gone only when one of the brothers took me in an abbey wagon to help him load some kind of provender or supplies that had to be fetched from there. Now, as I ascended from the Ring of Balsam onto the great undulating Iupa plateau, though I was warmly bundled in my fur-trimmed sheepskin and had my eagle riding on my shoulder for company, I felt almost naked against the fast-deepening winter and defenseless against whatever might befall me in the times to come. At the abbey, everything had been predictable. But I was on the road: the unwalled, wide-open, unprotected and endlessly reaching-out road, where there almost never is any predicting of what might occur from one day and one place to the next.

The first two or three villages I came to along that road, I had earlier visited, so I was recognized as "the monastery boy" and—though the villagers eyed my juika-bloth with much surprise and curiosity—they doubtless assumed that I had been sent afoot on some errand for St. Damian's. But once I was past those places and in territory unfamiliar to me, I had good reason to be wary of one particular hazard. That was the very real possibility that anyone I met would assume or falsely claim that I was a runaway slave and would seize possession of me.

I carried no certificate of manumission because, not having been a slave, I had been given none. And there is truly no other way for a person to *prove* that he or she is of genuinely free status. Of course, grown-up men and women seldom have to prove any such thing, unless they bear the scars and calluses of the slave's iron collar or shackles, or unless they are unfortunate enough to fit the circulated description of a real fugitive. But a young person, wandering alone in the countryside, can easily be accosted and accused and apprehended by anyone wishing a slave of his own. The youngster's most vociferous protestations or plausible explanations of his vagrant wayfaring would do him no good whatever, for the adult's word would outweigh his even in a court of law.

83

Boys are especially prized catches because, even if they be of only toddling age, they are worth the cost of upbringing until they are big enough to work. However, I was already old enough to be useful and desirable as a slave, whether I was boy or girl. The garb I wore was common to both sexes in those rural lands. Still, even if I had worn a placard proclaiming me male or female, I should have been in danger of abduction. If I were taken for a boy, I should have been put to heavy drudgery; if for a girl, I might have been given lighter labors, but I should most certainly have been required also to share my "new" master's bed.

So, whenever I spied another tramp or a horseman or teamster on the road, I dodged aside and crouched in a copse or hedgerow until he was safely past. Whenever I approached a village new to me, I skirted it at a discreet distance. I never appealed for shelter or sustenance at any wayside house. Even in the bitterest, snowy weather, I slept comfortably enough in farm hayricks or byres, and was up and away in the early morning before the farmer came out to do his chores, and for nourishment I foraged. Out of necessity, I was getting better at using my sling for a weapon, but, even so, I could only seldom bring down a rabbit or an edible bird. My raptor did much better at hunting, but I never got hungry enough to share any of its kills of snakes and mice and such.

There was little to pluck from the winter-fallow farm fields except an occasional overlooked and frozen turnip. So, I confess, when I had no other recourse, I raided henhouses for their eggs and, now and again, a whole chicken. And one of those forays very nearly brought my journeying to an abrupt end.

At one farm, in the early morning, my juika-bloth went off to seek some fare with which to break its own night's fast, and I slunk into the henhouse. I was filching from under the hens some of their warm, new-laid eggs—and I was doing it so deftly that the hens only mildly and sleepily clucked complaint—when a heavy hand gripped hard on my shoulder, yanked me out into the dawn light of the barnyard and threw me down on the iron-hard ground. The farmer, a huge man, as red of face and eyes as he was of beard, glared down at me, waved a heavy club and growled fiercely:

"Sai! Gafaífah thanna aiweino faihugairns thiufs!"

That explained his being awake and about even earlier than most farmers—"Behold! I have caught the everlastingly greedy thief!" Obviously his henhouse had been regularly plundered by another before me, and he had lain in wait. The earlier thief had probably been a fox or weasel, but I got no opportunity to suggest that, for now he had caught a human pilferer—and he went on to tell me how he would beat me bloody before he chained me up for a slave. He hit me in the ribs with his club before I could yell, "Juika-bloth!" I started to scramble to my feet, and caught another blow, this one right across my face, before the eagle could get back from wherever it had gone.

When it flapped between me and my assailant, and settled on my shoulder, and gazed curiously at the farmer, that man's eyes widened and he froze with his club held aloft. The juika-bloth of course had no animosity toward the stranger, but a raptor does not have to gaze very hard at a person to look fearsomely raptorial indeed. The farmer backed away from us, and muttered wonderingly, "Unhultha skohl . . ." I gave him no chance to collect his wits, but ran away as fast as I could go. I even ran out from under my eagle, so it had to fly to keep up with me. That must have awed the farmer still more, for he did not give chase. And I would wager that for the rest of his life he awed other people by telling how he had once given battle, in his own barnyard, to an "unclean demon" and its winged evil spirit.

Not until I was well away from that farm and hiding in a clump of shrubbery did I stop to wipe off the blood that was streaming down my face. And not until then did my ribs begin to hurt. The pain was excruciating, and I could feel a wetness there, too, and I supposed it was blood. But it was not. I had tucked the eggs, as I stole them, inside my upper smock above my belt rope, and the farmer's club had broken them. That made quite a mess inside my clothes, but I was able to scrape up enough of the mangled egg meat to allay my hunger a little. My ribs went on hurting for some days afterward, but, if any were broken, they knit of themselves.

For even longer, my face was also painful, swollen, black and blue. But the bleeding, though copious, had come from just one small cut, and that soon healed, leaving only a trivial scar, paler than my skin, that bisected my left eyebrow. Later, whenever I was a man, the scar was assumed by others to be an honorable memento of some manly combat. And whenever I was a woman, people remarked that the interestingly disjunct eyebrow made a striking addition to the beauty of my visage.

Shortly after that incident, the road brought me close beside the river Dubis, and for the first time in many days I was able to give myself a good washing. The water was bitingly cold—I had to break the bankside ice to get at it—but it helped to numb the pain of my ribs and to reduce the puffiness of my face. The river also enabled me to supplement my diet with fish, so that I had to make no more raids on henhouses from there on. There were many vineyards along the Dubis, and of course they bore no grapes in wintertime, but they were useful to me nonetheless. I stole several of the bits of twine with which the vines were tied to their stakes, and tied those together to make a fishing line, and improvised fishhooks from the spiny twigs of hawthorn shrubs.

Hawthorn is a very hard wood, and I owned no knife, but I induced my juika-bloth to bite off the twigs for me with its formidable beak. That took a great deal of imploring and encouraging, and patient trying and failing, before I could make the bird understand what I wanted. But once it had grasped the idea, it enthusiastically went on snipping off thorned twigs until I had many more than I could use. It was even the bird that provided bait for me; I took a fragment of mouse meat from one of its kills. In gratitude, I gave the eagle the first fish I caught, a small grayling. For several more days, every time the juika-bloth returned from one of its own foraging expeditions, it brought me a beakful more of hawthorn twigs. I think it must have thought I wanted to build myself a thorny nest.

Thereafter, and as long as I trudged upstream alongside the Dubis, I caught other grayling, trout and loach to cook for myself. (My primitive

85

hooks and line were not stout enough to land any of the larger fish, like pike-perch.) Because almost every day a river barge or two floated past me, bearing loads of salt or timber downstream toward the great cross-roads city of Lugdunum, I had to hide from them as I had hidden from passersby on the road. Bargemen would have been equally eager to snatch me from the shore and put me to slave labor on board. So I did most of my fishing by night, and it was actually easier then. I would make a torch of dead brush and set it afire, and that light would attract the fish closer to the bank.

My northeastward course led me always uphill, but so imperceptibly that I would not have realized it except that the Dubis gradually got constricted between higher and higher banks. Eventually I came to the river's abrupt bend where it flows around the hill on which is set the city of Vesontio. The Dubis very nearly encircles that hill, making it a peninsula, and on the narrow neck of that peninsula, the highest part, stands the city's cathedral. So the impressive brown-brick bulk of the Basilica of St. John was the first bit of Vesontio that I saw from afar.

For two or three miles before it passed through the city gate, the road was partially paved with four parallel rows of cobblestones, so that wheeled vehicles coming and going should not get mired in the muddy season, and the road was left uncobbled between those rows, to spare the hoofs of the vehicles' draft horses, mules and oxen. Since there was so much traffic entering and leaving Vesontio—people afoot or on horseback, carts and wagons full of various sorts of goods—I could now leave the river and get back on that road and be inconspicuous among the multitude. Even the juika-bloth on my shoulder drew few glances, because many of the other travelers were peddlers, and some of them carried wicker cages of nightingales and other songbirds, and I suppose I was taken to be also a peddler of exotic birds.

Some folk cannot abide cities and city life, but I am not one of those, and that is probably because the first city I ever visited, Vesontio, is such a pleasant place. From the eminence of its peninsula, its citizens enjoy a scenic view of the Dubis's great bend and the lesser hills all about. The riverside is fringed with innumerable quays, to and from which are constantly going freight barges, and the city's entire circle of river frontage is lined with a broad, paved promenade for summertime strollers. Vesontio is a clean and quiet city, too. There are few smokes and no stinks in the air, no repellent colors or taints in the water, no overwhelming clangor of smithies and workshops, as are to be found in cities where cloth is made and dyed, or leather is tanned, or stone cut, or metals worked. Vesontio imports all such things as those, and pays for them by exporting the clean salt from the mines in the vicinity and the fragrant woods from the forests roundabout. The city's other chief trade is the housing and feeding and entertaining of hordes of summer visitors from all over the Western Empire. They come to seek health and rejuvenation in the several elegant baths, fed by mineral and hot springs, in the city's suburb of Paluster on the other side of the river, and that makes for Vesontio a cleanly business indeed.

The stone bridge crossing the Dubis from Vesontio to Paluster was the first bridge that ever I saw in my life, and, on first seeing it, I marveled that stone could be made to float upon water. But then I discerned that the bridge's thick stone piers in fact went down through and under the water, and were planted firmly on the riverbed. Many other things, too, I saw for the first time in Vesontio. There is a grand triumphal arch spanning the entire width of the road at the entrance to the city. It was built by the Emperor Marcus Aurelius, so it is much aged and weathered by now, but I could still make out the reliefs carved on it, commemorating that emperor's victories. And there is an amphitheater, so immense that it looked to me—at first sight, anyway—as big as the whole Ring of Balsam. It is not, of course, but its high-soaring tiers of stone seats would certainly accommodate twenty times as many people as live in that valley.

The fine marble buildings housing the baths I admired only from the outside, for one must pay to luxuriate within, and I had no money to spare for that. But I did go into the cathedral, and this was the first time I had ever seen any church other than the chapel at St. Damian's. The Basilica of St. John could have enclosed a score or more of such chapels, and its walls were splendidly decorated with mosaic murals of biblical scenes and personages.

However, what I found the most striking novelty in Vesontio was that city people dressed differently—not just differently from country-folk, but differently according to whether they were men or women, boys or girls, even those as young as myself. There was considerable variance of costume among those of the same sex, but in general the females were all robed to the ankles in gowns adorned with much embroidery, and those who did not go bareheaded—proud of their long, freely streaming tresses—had gaily colored kerchiefs tied about their heads. The men wore short, belted leather tunics, and under them cloth coats that hung to their knees, and either ankle-length trousers or trousers that were wrapped from the knees down in leggings crisscrossed with leather thongs. Most men went bareheaded, but some wore leather caps of various fanciful shapes.

The wealth or social standing of both men and women could be discerned by the fabrics of their costumes—some flaunting sumptuous woolens from Baetica or Mutina and fine linens from Camaracum— and by the number and costliness of the ornaments they wore. Rich men wore a fibula on their right shoulder, rich women wore them on both shoulders. Men wore elaborate belt buckles, women wore bracelets or anklets or both. And much of that jewelry was fashioned of gold and set with gems—garnets, carbuncles or cut glass. Of course, this being wintertime, on the streets both men and women wore coats or cloaks of fur.

Well, I could hardly afford to buy clothing for the sake of sheer display, and there were enough other country people forever going in and out of Vesontio so that I was not conspicuous in my sheepskin and smock and hose. But I decided that it could eventually be to my advantage to acquire some additional apparel so that I could choose between dressing as a male or as a female. There was one other thing, though, that I needed to buy before clothing, as I had learned from experience while on the road and the river—a knife to cut with.

On my first day in Vesontio, I found a cutler's shop, but did not immediately go in. I waited until, at midday, the man tending it was joined by a woman, and then he left the place and she remained. Clearly, the cutler's wife had arrived to inform him that his prandium meal was ready. So then I entered and examined the knives laid out for sale. The world's best blades are those forged and wrought by the swordsmiths of the Goths, but such a thing is understandably expensive. I thumbed the wares of lesser quality, selected a case knife that I deemed the best of a poor lot, and haggled with the smithwife over the price of it. When we had agreed on that, I handed her my silver solidus—at which she gasped and gave me a very sharp look. But I had the eagle on my shoulder, and it returned her look much more coldly than I could have done. The woman quailed, let me have the knife and the change from my solidus, and let me depart in peace.

That was why I had waited for her husband to absent himself. He might not have been so easily daunted by the juika-bloth, and might have summoned some patrolling vigiles to interrogate me or confiscate my one piece of money or even arrest me. Of course, a silver solidus is worth only one-sixteenth of the value of a gold solidus, but, nevertheless, it was an extraordinary amount of money to be carried by a scruffy peasant youth. My possession of it could have proclaimed me not just a runaway slave but a thieving one as well.

Since there *were* cohortes vigilum patrolling Vesontio during all the watches of both day and night, I did not risk stealing anything to eat or seeking some hideaway in which to sleep. My knife had cost me half of my solidus, but the purchase had left in my waist wallet a comfortably jingling number of denarius and sesterce coins. And now, in wintertime, the city's many gasts-razna and hospitium inns that catered to summer visitors were quite empty, so they had accordingly reduced the prices they demanded for bed and board. I managed to find one of the very cheapest boardinghouses—a small hut with a single guest room let by an old widow woman so nearly blind that she did not comment on my uncouth appearance or even my companion eagle. I stayed there for two or three days, sleeping on a pallet not much more soft or warm than the bare riverside ground I had lately been used to, and living on the simple gruels that were all the old woman could cook in her nearly sightless condition. Meanwhile, I roamed the city's humbler quarters, in search of clothing I could afford.

There were numerous mean little shops, all of them kept by elderly Jews, that traded in the apparel cast off by folk of higher classes. In one of them, after I and the cringing and hand-wringing old proprietor had haggled long over the price, I bought a woman's gown, much worn and faded, but still serviceable. And while the Jew tied it into a bundle, muttering that I had denied him the least nummus of profit on the transaction, I filched and stuck inside my smock a woman's kerchief, and got away without paying for that. In another shop, I bought a man's leather tunic, much scuffed and wrinkled, and trousers of coarse Ligurian wool, not yet quite threadbare, that terminated in heavier-woven "foot-mittens." And there, too, while the Jew was rolling and tying them, I purloined another item, a man's leather cap. It shames me now to remember how I pilfered from those shopkeepers who were almost as poor as myself. But I was young then, and inexperienced in the world, and I shared the attitude of the rest of that world—which is to say that not even the law-enforcing cohortes vigilum would have frowned at anyone's stealing from a *Jew.*

What little money remained to me after those purchases I spent for a substantial string of smoked sausage that would keep for a long time. Then, on my last evening in Vesontio, I tested my two disparate identities and their effect on other people. First, in my rented room, I donned the leather tunic over my smock, and drew on the trousers,

89

tucking the skirt of my smock down inside them, and put on my boots over the foot-mittens, and set the leather cap on my head. Leaving the juika-bloth in the room, and wearing my sheepskin only casually slung across my shoulders, I went down to the waterfront street of prostitutes, and strolled along it with manly stride. The painted women sitting in doorways and on windowsills flipped open their heavy furs to give me glimpses of their bodies, while they variously cooed at me, whistled at me, called, "Hiri, aggilus, du badi!" and several of them all but leapt into the street to drag me into their lairs. I gave them a cool, manly, distant smile and continued walking, quite pleased that they had considered me worth soliciting.

I returned to my room and changed clothes, now shedding everything but my waist-high hose, putting on the gown, tying the kerchief over my head, and wearing my sandals instead of my boots. Again draping the sheepskin loosely over my costume, I went back to that waterfront street, and sauntered along it with a feminine gait. Where before the prostitutes had called, "Come here, angel, to bed!" they now eyed me coldly, kept their furs bundled about them, and some sneered or hissed at me, and some snarled, "Huarboza, horina, uh big daúr iz-war!"—"Keep going, whore, and find your own perch!" Since I was wearing neither jewelry nor paint, they took me for a female of low class, and a newcomer who might be competition for them. I gave them a warm, womanly, compassionate smile and continued walking, quite pleased that they had considered me femininely pretty enough to be a fledgling prostitute.

So I was satisfied that I could dress as befitted either of my two natures, and do it sufficiently well to convince other people. Alone in the world I might be, and friendless and poor and defenseless and fearful of my fate, but I could at least—like the creatures of the wild—assume the patterns and colors and configurations of my surroundings, and blend into them, and be taken for a normal human being. I was even encouraged to vow to myself that, if I lived long enough, someday I would dress and adorn myself as the very *highest* class of man *and* woman.

Right now, though, since I was about to go again across country, there was no need for me to be either male or female. I did put on the masculine trousers over my hose, but only for their welcome warmth. With my head uncovered by either kerchief or cap, with my smock and sheepskin and boots my only visible apparel, I was once more a rustic peasant of indeterminate sex. I threaded my new knife's sheath onto my waist rope, rolled my sausage and my other acquisitions into the bundle I carried, lifted the juika-bloth to my shoulder and left Vesontio behind.

3

 his time I went due east, away from the busy road and the busy Dubis River and every other evidence of civilization. After passing Vesontio's outlying salt works and timbering camps, I was in the deep woods, the track-less wilderness.

Except for the comparatively few places on this continent where men have long been settled—as farmers, herders, vine growers, orchardists, miners, timber cutters—almost all of Europe, from Britannia to the Black Sea, has been densely forested since the beginning of time, and still was when I wandered over it, and still is, for all I know. However extensive may be the cleared and cultivated patches, and however numerous may be their human inhabitants, and however imposing may be their towns and cities, those clearings are but islands in the great primeval sea of trees.

As I tramped eastward into the forest, I was leaving the lands of the Burgund people for those of the Alamanni. Here I could expect to find no henhouses to plunder or hayricks to take shelter in. The Alamanni are nomads, who have never planted farms or vineyards or even home-steads. As the saying goes, "they live all their lives on the backs of their horses." The Alamanni do not have one king, as most nations do—or even two kings, as the Burgunds then did—but have a multitude, be-cause they call "king" the petty chief of every paltry tribe of them. Those Alaman bands constantly roam the forests, and live off the land, and live by their wits and woodcraft, and so should I now have to do.

Up to this point in my journeying, the winter weather had been tolerably mild. But here I was in the high forelands of the immensely higher peaks named in Latin the Alpes. And these lower mountains that

91

I was traversing are called in the Old Language the Hrau Albos—the *Raw Alpes*—because of their savage winters. Savage indeed was this year's winter, and ever more savage it became as I pressed on eastward. Even at midday, the woods were dark and bleak and cold, and snow fell on snow, and I was forever breasting an ice-flecked wind that might have flayed an ox.

Of woodcraft, all I knew was what little I had learned from experience while roving about the Balsan Hrinkhen. I did know enough to take care not to lose my flint and puffball tinder from my waist wallet. I guarded them as conscientiously as I did the precious phial of the Virgin's milk. And I was capable enough at finding deadwood with which to build a fire, and I knew never to make a fire under a tree or rock shelf burdened with snow that would loosen in the heat and fall and kill the fire.

I had become proficient enough with my sling to drop an occasional tree squirrel or snow hare, but even the squirrels were few, while the white hares were difficult to see against the snow. The mountain brooks were too small to contain any fish larger than minnows. So I was often weak and faint with hunger, but I only infrequently ate of my coil of sausage. For one reason, I wanted to make it last as long as possible and, for another, eating it made me insatiably thirsty. I would have thought that eating snow would allay that thirst but, curiously, it did not. Therefore I resorted to the sausage only when I camped beside a brook that was of a size to have some water flowing beneath its coating of ice.

It was my juika-bloth that taught me how to find food more easily. The eagle remained always plump and healthy and strong, and never seemed to have to fly far or for long to find some prey. I watched, and saw that it simply investigated rock clefts and found therein all manner of serpents and lizards deep asleep in hibernation—sometimes great bundles of snakes intertwined for mutual warmth.

So I emulated the bird, and carried a long stick that I poked repeatedly through the deep snow as I slogged along, and by that means sometimes found a small cave in the rocks or a cranny in the ground that turned out to be the den of a hibernating hedgehog or dormouse or tortoise. I was most pleased, though, when I came upon the dens of sleeping marmots. Marmot meat is both tasty and loaded with fat, which helped maintain my body heat for a long time after I had eaten it. Also, a marmot's den is always full of nuts, roots, seeds and dried berries that it has stored for a light repast in case it awakens betimes, and those make a delicious side dish for the marmot meat.

I was prudent enough not to investigate any large caves that I came across, in case they might be the winter quarters of hibernating bears. I was not at all certain that I could kill a bear, even in its deepest sleep, with one thrust of my knife—and I knew that the one thrust would be all that I would be allowed. I also took care to avoid some other animals, bigger than myself, that were still awake and active in winter. Several times I climbed trees to get out of the way of a massively antlered elk or a high-humped bison. And once I had to stay high in a tree all night, while a gigantic úrus—it was at least a foot taller than myself at its shoulders—enraged at not being able to get at me, rampaged and bellowed and tore up the ground with its hoofs and chopped at the tree trunk with its fearsome horns.

There were many days when I thought I would die of hunger or thirst, and many nights when I thought I would freeze to death. I kept wishing that I would come across one of those wandering bands of Alamanni, who might let me join them and share in their hunts and learn how to live and thrive as a nomad.

Almost as often, I wished that I *might* die, if only I could go to the pagan afterland called in the Old Language "the abode of the chosen"—Walis-Halla—which some pagans believe is situated on the far side of the moon. (The pagan Romans contorted the name Walis-Halla into Avalonnis, and believe it to be some sort of Fortunate Isles, situated far west of Europe in the Ocean Sea.) Anyway, both the pagan Germanic peoples and the pagan Romans say that the afterland has six seasons a year, *and none of them winter.* The seasons consist of two bright springs, two sweet summers and two golden autumns of bounteous harvest. In my frequent moods of despair, that notion held much appeal for me. However, considering the sinful life I had led so far, it was more probable that I would "die twice," as the Germanic Christians believed the wicked do—dying first into a fiery hell, then into a frozen "Foggy Hell." Or perhaps, I mused, especially when I was dizzy with hunger, I already *had* died twice and was *in* that unbearably cold Foggy Hell.

Occasionally on my way I came upon evidence that the Alamanni had passed that way before me, but not recently. Sometimes I would find nothing more than some split stones, but on looking closely I could tell that they had been split by fire, meaning that some person or some body of persons had laid a campfire there. Sometimes I would emerge from the forest into a broad clearing, where a goodly number of people obviously had camped for quite some time, but the growth of underbrush indicated that that had been a long while ago. In some of those

93

places I found other tokens of Alaman occupation. There might be a flat rock or a rough wooden plank in which was chiseled the cross of four right-angled arms that represents Thor's hammer being swung, and under it would be runes inscribed in a circle or triangle or in serpentine loops.

Only one of those artifacts could I decipher in its entirety, and this is all it said: *"I, Wiw, made these runes"* — as if Wiw, whoever he was, had laboriously carved the message just to proclaim to posterity that he had carved the message. But others I could at least make out to be what were called in Gothic "the favorable runes, the victorious runes, the medicinal runes, the bitter runes." Each kind carved slightly differently, those were employed, respectively, to thank some pagan god for some blessing or favor, to thank some god for having helped win some battle, to invoke some god to heal some wound or illness and to call upon some god for vengeance against some hated person or enemy tribe.

And in one of those old clearings I found a very large piece of wood, lying flat on the ground, bearing a long message that was carved entirely in the more modern Gothic script. The wood was weatherworn and mossy, but the words had not been obliterated, and I could read them all:

> Passerby, short is my say.
> Stop and read these runes.
> This somber slab covers a beautiful woman.
> Her name was Juhiza.
> She was my light and my only love.
> What I wished she wished also.
> What I shunned she shunned also.
> Good she was, and chaste, loyal, discreet.
> She walked nobly and spoke kindly.
> Passerby, I have finished.
> Go.

I went on, as commanded. But I pondered on that epitaph as I went. It contained no reference to God or Jesus or the angels, no unctuous sentiment like "rest in peace," not even any supplication that the pagan Manes protect the grave from desecration. Whoever was the bereaved husband who carved that crude marker, he had not been a Christian, either Catholic or Arian, and apparently had worshipped no gods of any other faith. A barbarus and a nomad he certainly would have been,

94

and he doubtless would have been regarded by civilized folk as a *savage outlander*. But in doing that labor of love—and just in plain, unaffected words, nothing fancy or flowery—he had displayed a sensitive and deep feeling, a tenderness that was anything but barbaric. I am sure that any woman, even a Christian woman, even the most patrician *Roman* Christian woman—and I speak as a woman myself—instead of being honored after death with a grandiose marble monument and fulsomely pious platitudes, would rest more contentedly under those simple words: "She walked nobly and spoke kindly."

I had been journeying for weeks before I came upon the first live human being I found in the Hrau Albos. It happened toward twilight one snowy day, when I was bone-weary, famished, thirsty and numb with cold. Because the forest was fast darkening, I was rather desperately seeking some source of water where I could get my first drink of the day, and near which I might find some hibernating creature's den, and beside which I could roll myself in my sheepskin for the night. It was then that the juika-bloth on my shoulder gave a slight flutter of its wings to catch my attention. I raised my head, squinted through the falling snow and saw, some distance ahead of me, a ruddy light.

I approached it cautiously, and saw that it was a modest campfire with a hunched figure seated to one side of it. Still cautiously and quietly, I circled around to the back of that creature and crept closer. All I could make out was that it was a person with a great deal of unkempt gray hair, for the rest of it was bundled in a heavy fur. It was probably a man, I decided, but there was no horse tethered anywhere about, and no other people or campfires in sight. Would any Alaman, I wondered, be roaming the Hrau Albos all by himself and without a mount? I stood shivering, debating whether I should announce my presence or back off and go safely far away—when suddenly the hunched person said, without turning its head or raising its voice:

"Galithans faúr nehu. Jau anagimis hirjith and fon uh thraftsjan thusis."

It was a man's voice, and gruff, and he spoke the Old Language with an accent unfamiliar to me, but I could easily comprehend what he had said:

"You have come this close. You might as well approach the fire and warm yourself."

But I had taken such pains to steal upon him slowly and in silence. Was this some kind of forest skohl with eyes in the back of his head? I might yet have crept away and taken to my heels, but the cheerfully

95

flickering fire was too strong a temptation. I sidled around to the far side of it, and hunkered down close to it, and asked somewhat sheepishly:

"How did you know I was here?"

"Iésus!" the man grunted disgustedly. It was the first time I had ever heard the Lord's name used as an expletive. "You stupid urchin, I have known for at least a week that you were stumbling and blundering along behind me."

If he *was* a skohl with supernatural senses, he at least looked like an ordinary mortal, shaggy of hair and long of beard. He was an old man— not feeble-old but sturdy-old, in the way good leather is when it has been long suppled and limbered. In fact, what I could see of his skin behind all the hair resembled well-tanned leather. His eyes were not dim or rheumy but a sharp and piercing blue. He seemed to have all his teeth, and they were not yellow but brightly white, as if he nourished himself by *chewing* leather.

He went on grumbling, "All kinds of forest animals have come galloping past me, fleeing from the noise and commotion you made. Iésus! As a woodsman, you are a damnable bumbler, and obviously new to the woods. I have occasionally halted just to get a look at you, and to marvel at how clumsily you trudge along, and how unskillfully you wield your sling, and how you so often fail to see good meaty animals that stand still while you pass. You are not fit to kiss the backside of the hunting goddess Diana. Finally, when it became painfully obvious that you would soon entirely spoil my own hunting—that you might even awaken sleeping bears untimely early—I decided to wait and let you catch up to me. Who are you, imbecile?"

Even more sheepishly than before, I said, "I am called Thorn."

He laughed, but without amusement. "Well named, you are. A thorn in my side, you are. Interfering with my work and my livelihood, you are. What brings you here, urchin Thorn? You do not hunt game, except to eat, and you hunt ineptly. By the cuckold horns of St. Joseph, but I am amazed that you have not starved to death before now. Since you possess so pitifully little of woodcraft, how did you ever catch and man that eagle you carry, niu? Are you alive only because it lets you share its kills of serpents? Are you hungry now, urchin?"

"And thirsty," I mumbled.

"There is a brook trickling just behind those bushes yonder, if you are still robust enough to crack the ice on it."

He kept on talking while I went and gratefully took a long drink. I was rather awed by the old man's loquacity—and by the unabashed impiety and blasphemy of many of the expressions he used. But I had to admit that at least he was impartial in the gods and venerable personages he chose to profane with his figures of speech.

"There are other raptors in these woods besides that bird of yours, urchin. And hellishly worse ones. They would strip you of bag and baggage, scrip and scrippage, and then what they would do to your stripped body is beyond imagining. I am astounded that you have not yet fallen prey to some one of those skulking sons of haliuruns bitches. If you are hungry . . . here, take this."

As I hunkered down again, he tossed across the fire a raw, brown and flabby something that splashed blood when I caught it.

"Elk's liver. I was saving it as a delicacy for myself, but I have had many a one before. And, by the seven sorrows of the Virgin, you behave as if you lack a stout liver of your own. Get a stick and roast it in the flames."

"Thags izvis, fráuja," I murmured, respectfully calling him by the Gothic word meaning "master."

"Vái, you do not talk much, do you, urchin? Another mark of a newcomer to the woods. When you have lived in them as long as I have, and talked and damned and blasphemed at nobody but yourself, *you* will talk, too, whenever you have an audience, even if it be only a vulture."

And talk he did, incessantly, while I ate. I was so avid for the meat that I gave it only the merest crisping of fire, and then—using not my knife but my teeth—voraciously began tearing and gnawing at it. The shreds that fell from my lips I held up to the juika-bloth on my shoulder.

"The snow is thickening," said the old man. "That is good. It will make a warmer blanket when it covers us. You have not yet said, urchin, what brought you to these Hrau Albos. If you are, as I suppose, a runagate slave, why did you run to these inhospitable forests, niu? In this solitude you are as conspicuously out of place as a crocodilus of the torrid lands. Why did you not run to a city, where you could mingle and be invisible in the multitudes?"

"I am not a slave, fráuja," I said thickly, my mouth full and blood running down my chin. "I never have been a slave. Until recently, I was a postulant in a monastery. But I was—I decided I had no true calling to take the tonsure and the cowl."

"Did you now?" he said, eyeing me shrewdly. "A boy about to be-come a monk, were you? Then why have I seen you sometimes relieving yourself retromingently?"

I gaped at him, now with my mouth open and speechless, for I had no idea of what he was talking about. So he loudly repeated the query, putting it in more vulgar but more comprehensible words:

"Why have I seen you sometimes squatting to piss like a girl?"

The blunt question caught me unprepared. Anyway, how could I explain that I did it either upright or squatting depending on whether—at the moment I found urination necessary—I was thinking of myself as male or female?

I stammered, "Well, because . . . because I was less vulnerable that way . . . than if I stood with my . . . my urinary organ hanging out . . . in case I were to be suddenly attacked . . ."

"Akh, balgs-daddja! Cease your witless lying," he said, but not un-kindly. "I must declare, when you do talk, you use some mincing words to skirt indecency." He snorted a laugh. "Urinary organ, by the kunte of the lewd goddess Cotytto! What you mean is your svans. Listen, urchin, I do not care if you be girl or boy, nymph or faun, or both. I am an old man and, these many years, there has been no marrow in my bone. Were you as beautiful as the fabled Lady Poppaea or the legendary lad Hyacinthus, you would need fear no molesting from me."

I stared at him. After my years among monks and nuns constantly inquiring and interrogating and catechizing—especially on the subject of sex—it was a refreshing surprise to come upon a person totally un-interested in another's most private concerns.

He added, "Nor do I care, one tord's worth, from what or from whom you are running away, or why."

The meal of good meat had considerably invigorated me. I said with some spirit, "I am not running away, fráuja, I am running to. I am trav-eling eastward in search of my own people among the Goths."

"Are you now? To the eastern lands of the Ostrogoths? What makes you think you have been going eastward, niu?"

"Do you mean I have not?" I asked, dismayed. "When I left Vesontio, I know I headed due east. But all the time I have been in these accursed mountains, the heavy clouds have hidden both the sun and the north star Phoenice. Still, I thought, as long as I followed these forelands of the high Alpes in the south . . ."

The old man shook his shaggy gray head. "There has been a wind in your face all the way, has there not? That is Aquilo, the northeast wind.

Akh, *eventually* these forelands will veer and lead you eastward. But right now you are headed toward the Roman garrison town of Basilea, where I am going."

"Iésus," I muttered, the first time I myself ever had used the Lord's name profanely. And for the first time, I did not sign the cross upon my forehead at mention of the Holy Name. "How *does* one find direction, then, when both the sun and the north star are not to be seen?"

"Ignorant urchin, one uses a sun-stone." He took something from inside his voluminous swaddling of furs and held it out to me. It was only a piece of that common stone called glitmuns in Gothic, mica in Latin—the opaline and blurrily transparent stone composed of many overlaid flaky leaves.

"It will not show you the star Phoenice," he said, "for it works only in daylight. But, no matter how dark and cloudy the day, hold that to your eye and scan the heavens. Seen through the stone, most of the sky will look pink. But in the place where the sun stands unseen, the stone makes the sky look pale blue. Thus you easily determine your direction."

"I have much to learn," I said with a sigh.

"If you would be a woodsman and a hunter, ja."

"But, fráuja, you yourself are an experienced woodsman and hunter. You said you have lived long in these forests. Why are you now going to a town?"

"Woods-addled I may be," he said crossly, "but I am not yet totally insane or senile. I do not hunt from force of habit or for frivolity or to satisfy a mad blood-lust or even just to feed my gut. I hunt to acquire pelts, skins, furs. Those are all bearskins."

He pointed to a great thong-tied bale of them, which I had not earlier noticed, safely lodged in the crotch of a tree.

"I sell them to the Roman colonists at Basilea and other places who are too timid and effete to venture out of their fortified towns and collect their own. Iésus, small wonder the empire is in such sad state. Did you know, urchin, that many of the insipid Romans nowadays—even the colonials—are so preciously refined that they will dine only on fish and fowl? They deem good red flesh-meat fit only for laborers, peasants and us uncultivated outlanders."

"I did not know that. But it makes me glad to be an outlander Goth if that entitles me to eat those meats spurned by the overcivilized. And you, fráuja, are you of the Alaman outlanders?"

He did not answer directly, but said, "The Alamanni have not been

99

up in these Hrau Albos for some years past. They have lately confined their peregrinations to the lower lands, between the rivers Rhenus and Danuvius. I told you, these upper forests are haunted by evil outlaws."

"If not the Alamanni, then who?"

"Akh, the Alamanni are nomads and fierce of temper and fond of combat, but they do have laws and they do abide by them. Urchin, I speak of *Huns*. Stragglers, deserters, outcasts and dregs who stayed behind when the rest went back to whatever hell they came from."

"From Sarmatia, I have heard."

"Perhaps," he grunted. "It is said that, long ago, among the Goths were haliuruns women of such despicably wicked ways that their own tribes expelled them. And those outcast witches, wandering in exile, met and mated with wilderness demons, and consequently gave birth to the Huns. By the seventeen teats of the Ephesian Diana, I believe that tale! Only the black blood of witches and demons commingled could account for the fiendish ferocity of the Huns. Most of them are gone now, but those remaining have gathered into bands, complete with mates and offspring—of their own foul race or abducted from other nations—and those women and children, let me tell you, are as unspeakably vicious as their menfolk. The bands lurk here in the Hrau Albos, and dash out on forays against the lowland villages and farmsteads, then withdraw again into these woods. No Roman garrison's legatus would be foolish enough to send a legion in pursuit of them. Legionaries are accustomed to fighting in open terrain; they would be slaughtered in here. And the native Alamanni, though fond of combat, are disinclined to suicide. So, rather than contend with the terrible Huns, they have abandoned these highlands that were once their own."

"But you have not, fráuja," I said. "Do you not share the universal fear of the Huns?"

He sniffed contemptuously. "I was fifty years old when the Khan Etzel-called-Attila died. Before that, I had been hunting in one forest or another, man and boy, during some thirty-five years. Since Etzel's time, I have been hunting in *these* woods. I know them as no Hun ever can. Compared to me, the scavenger Huns now infesting the Hrau Albos are almost as much newcomers and fledglings as you are."

"You will return here, then, after you have been to Basilea?"

"Not to this precise spot, but ja, I will stay at the garrison only long enough to peddle my bearskins and purchase fresh supplies for myself. Towns are not for me, nor I for them. I will make my way eastward then, toward the great lake Brigantinus, for the springtime breakup of the ice on the streams thereabout, when the beavers emerge from their burrows and their pelts are at their prime."

I pondered. The old man seemed to detest or despise every other person in the world. He was ill-mannered and foulmouthed and blasphemously irreligious (toward *every* existing religion, I gathered). Why, I might be tainted and irredeemably damned through mere closeness to him. And I could hardly expect to be tenderly treated by the old scoundrel. Still, he did know the lore of the woods. And if he had spoken true about the dangers lurking in wait . . .

I said hesitantly, "Fráuja, since we both are going in the same direction . . . do you suppose we might travel together . . . so that I might learn some woodcraft from you?"

Now it was his turn to ponder. He eyed me for a long time before he said, "Akh, you might be useful, at that. Can you carry that big bale of furs yonder?"

Poor old brute, I thought; he is not so stalwart as he would wish to appear. He will probably dodder and totter and, crabby as he is, complain every step of the way. I could probably get along better without him, and take care of myself, and travel much more quickly alone. But I said, "Ja, I believe I can do that."

"Agreed, then. Now, enough of talking for tonight. And here, urchin, you might as well sleep more warmly than you have been doing." He doffed one of his furs and tossed it to me.

When he lay down close to the now very small fire, he took out from somewhere a brass basin that was evidently the dish from which he ate and drank. Then he picked up a pebble, held it in his fist and adjusted his sleeping position so that that hand was extended above the basin. I started to ask myself why he did that, but then I discerned the reason myself. If he were startled in the nighttime by any slightest sound, that hand would drop the pebble into the basin and the clang would wake him. Well, he had me now to help him repel any assailant.

As I thankfully rolled myself into the fur he had lent me, I said, "Fráuja, if we are to be companions for a time, what do I call you?"

He never had said whether or not he was an Alaman, or of some other nation, and I had not yet been able to identify the accent with which he spoke. Nor did his name—though it might have been a variant of the name of the old god Wotan—tell me anything of his origins. He said, "I am called Wyrd the Forest-Stalker," and in a moment more was sleeping, breathing deep, but uttering no snore that might be heard by any predator, raptor or night-prowling Hun.

101

4

e woke at first light—what light there was from the still overcast but no longer snowing sky. My juika-bloth flew off to seek its morning meal, and Wyrd and I made water behind separate trees. I deliberately did it boy-fashion this time, but he gave no sign of noticing or caring. Then we went to the brook to bathe our faces in the painfully cold water.

I said, "I surely do thank you, fráuja Wyrd, for the loan of that fur. It made a most comfortable—"

"Shut up," he growled, as grumpy as ever. "Until I have broken my fast, I do not attain to my accustomed good humor, and until then I have no patience with prattle. Come, I have some dried rashers you may share."

"And I have some smoked sausage," I volunteered. "It makes one dreadfully thirsty, so let us eat that up, since we have ample water here."

While we chewed on the tough, dry sausage, I remarked, "I have several times tried to quench a raging thirst with snow, and I cannot understand why it does not serve as well as water. After all, snow is nothing *but* water that has—"

"Iésus," grunted Wyrd. "I regret that I ever encouraged you to talk. An ignorant dotterel indeed, you are. A man can die of thirst in a snowfield as big as an Alb."

I said, a little testily myself, "So I have discovered. But I do not know why that should be so."

He gave a sigh of exasperation. "Attend closely, urchin. I do not explain things twice. When a man—or a woman, whichever you be—eats snow, it chills his mouth and throat and gullet so that they constrict, and cannot swallow enough of the snow to allay his thirst. Even to melt snow over a fire would keep a man so frantically collecting wood that he would get thirstier and thirstier, faster than he could melt water enough to quench that thirst. Let us make ready to move on. I will carry both our packs. You heft those bearskins down, and I will strap them on your back."

"Since we are leaving," I said, "why are you stoking the fire?"

"I am not," he said, though he had laid a fresh branch on the few remaining embers and was blowing on them to set the branch's tip aflame. "When I travel on a day as cold as this, I always carry a firebrand and hold its flame near my mouth and inhale the warm air. Very comforting, it is. I told you to fetch those skins."

I went, and discovered that their perch was so high that I had to find a windfall limb to reach up and poke them loose and make them fall into the snow beside me. I wondered how Wyrd had got them up to that crotch, since he was only a hand's span taller than myself, and I certainly could not imagine him climbing a tree. When I picked up the bale, I staggered and again said, "Iésus!" I had no idea how many bears' skins were in the bundle, or how much even a single one might weigh, but they were tightly compacted and, all together, weighed perhaps half as much as I did. How *had* the old man lifted the bale to the tree crotch? And how was I to carry this monstrous burden any distance? When I wobbled with it in my arms, back to the now snow-smothered fire, Wyrd said, as though he had anticipated my misgivings:

103

"If an old ferta like myself could carry that, so can you. It will seem to weigh less when I get it onto your back."

He had his burning brand stuck upright in the snow, and already had rolled my bundle of extra clothing and other belongings inside the fur I had slept in. I said nothing, but ruefully took note that I was not to be wearing the fur today, and also that he had not provided a firebrand for me. Again as if he were reading my mind, Wyrd said:

"Playing pack mule for me will keep you warm enough. You will see."

And he began rolling his own belongings into the fur that had been his bed and blanket. This disclosed to my view two objects on which he had protectively lain all night: a bow and a quiver of numerous arrows.

I said, "I have heard you twice invoke the pagan goddess Diana. I should have known that you must hunt with a bow."

"Did you suppose that I slay bear and elk with my bare hands?" he asked scornfully. But his voice softened as he picked up and fondled the bow. "Ja, this is my beauty, my treasure, my ever-reliable."

"Some of the men where I came from had bows," I said. "But theirs were much longer, and shaped in a simple arc, like the Roman letter C.

I have never seen one like yours before. It looks more like the crooked rune called sauil."

"Ja, each arm curves one way, then the other." He went on, very proudly, "Notice, urchin. Where an ordinary bow is made of wood, and has only the recoil strength of wood bent and tensed, this war bow *starts* with wood and adds to it." He gently stroked the outer curves. "See, the back of it here—"

"I should call that the front of it," I commented.

"Shut up. Here, the bow's wood is backed with dried animal sinews, because they resist being stretched. And it is bellied with horn, because that substance resists being compressed. So, to the recoil of the bent wood's trying to straighten is added the horn's strong urge to stretch and the sinews' strong urge to shrink. With all that power together, this bow will—at sixty paces—make an arrow pierce clear through a good-sized sapling, and at that range is so deadly accurate that it would bring down yonder bird *on the wing.*"

He pointed to my returning juika-bloth as it gracefully swooped and glided toward us through the trees, then added:

104

"Even at nearly two hundred paces, the arrow—should it hit a man—will usually hit hard enough to kill him. That is, if he is wearing only quilted or leather armor, not the sturdier scale armor. Let me tell you, urchin, it may take a bowyer fully five years to fashion a single bow like this one. First, the finding of the various materials—the wood, the bone, the horn—and selecting only the best of each. Then the ageing of them, and then the cutting to shape of them, and then the intervals of drying and seasoning them between the several operations, and then the putting together of them, and then the reshaping of them for the best proportions, and then the making of minute adjustments to the bow many times during its first months of use. Truly, all that can take as long as five years before the bowyer pronounces the work finished. Akh, ja, urchin, the Goths make the world's best swords and knives. But the Huns—oh vái, it must be conceded—the Huns make the world's best war bows."

"A Hun gave you that bow? I thought you were no friend to any Hun."

Wyrd uttered one of his laugh-snorts. "Ne, ni allis. I took it from him."

"You *took* a bow from a *Hun?!*"

He said drily, "Well, not until I was sure that he had no further use for it."

"I see," I murmured, with unfeigned awe. And then cautiously, not to rouse his choleric temper, I said, "I suppose, fráuja Wyrd, you were, uh, quite a bit younger in those days?"

"Ja," he said, sounding not at all insulted. "That was three years ago. Before then, I had had to rely on an ordinary hunting bow, such as you say you have seen. Now, we are wasting time. Let me load you, pack mule. This deep and fresh snow will make for difficult walking. And I wish to reach our destination well before dark."

As he easily lifted the bundle of bearskins and hung it on me, using broad canvas straps that went over my shoulders, crossed at my chest and were drawn securely about my waist, I managed to say, "Destination? *Oof!* What is our—*oof!*—destination?"

"A certain cave that I know of." He held up his sun-stone and scanned the sky. "That way. Atgadjats!"

The command meant "Let us be off!" and off he went. The business of using the sun-stone must have been only for show, because he headed directly into the teeth of the northeast wind, the same direction we both had been traveling for many days now. Wyrd strode through the knee-deep snow as briskly as a young man, and the trench he left in the snow afforded slightly easier going for me as I lurched along behind.

I was thinking that I might have been brashly mistaken in my assumption that this "old ferta"—as Wyrd had vulgarly described himself—was in any degree enfeebled or decrepit. He said he had been fifty years old when Attila died. So, unless he was lying with every word he spoke, he was now sixty-five, an extreme of longevity that few men attained, except idle, pampered townsfolk and ecclesiastics. Yet, at the age of sixty-two, he had somehow slain a savage Hun to acquire his war bow. Wyrd might no longer have any "marrow in his bone," as he had vulgarly said of himself. But if he was too old to indulge in sexual activity—or even to evince any interest in whether his new companion was male or female or eunuch—that seemed the *only* thing he was too old for. I now had no doubt that Wyrd could carry my bearskin burden more easily than I was doing, that he could hoist or even *throw* it high into a tree every night. This night, though, we were evidently going to camp inside a sheltered and cozy cave. That was something to look forward to.

But we were a long and weary time getting there. Even with Wyrd breaking a trail for me, I reeled and stumbled along, and was soon breathing in labored gasps. The old man had been right: I needed no

extra fur wrapping or even a firebrand to warm the air I inhaled. Cold
and blustery though the day was, I actually perspired, and copiously.
The bale on my back reached from my waist to somewhere above my
head—I could not raise my head to see how high—and my juika-bloth
rode on top of it. Or the bird did until I got so tired that I urged it to
fly along with us, and thereby relieve me of even that inconsiderable
weight.

Without once breaking stride or ever failing of breath, Wyrd talked
ceaselessly—or shouted, rather, to be heard above the Aquilo wind. He
provided a continuous commentary on the weather, the terrain, the
local fauna and flora, other weathers and terrains and fauna and flora
he had known, and liberally larded his speech with his usual profanities,
blasphemies and obscenities.

"Look yonder, in that patch of ground blown clear of snow. Do you
see the shriveled remains of that plant, urchin? That is the laser plant,
and glad you will be to find it if ever you are constipated and in need
of a good skeit. Wring out some of the laser's gum and take a dose of
it. You will skeit yourself empty, you will."

"Useful . . . to know . . . fráuja . . ." I gasped.

"You think these Hrau Albos forests are monotonous, urchin? Just
wait until you get to the swampy plains around Singidunum in the lands
of the Goths. So flat and barren of vegetation are those plains, the
tallest thing to be seen in the landscape may be a solitary standing
peasant. Or his goat. Or even his goose."

"Very . . . interesting . . . fráuja Wyrd . . ." I gasped.

"And now we are coming to some pine woods, urchin. Did you know
that pinecones, if you roast them first and then burn them, make a
sweet-smelling incense? More than that, the resin aroma of their burning is a sure stimulant of women's venereal desires. Certain pagans use
them in their temple orgies, to arouse the lust of their female votaries.
Ja, by the forty-nine fornicating daughters of Thespios, but roast pinecone incense makes a kunte as hot as the incense itself!"

Without a sound, I fell flat on my face in the snow, and lay there,
too winded and weak to try to raise even my own weight, let alone the
weight on top of me. Wyrd went hiking on, unaware, and talking:
"Iésus, but I smell more snow in the offing. We had best make haste . . ."
until his voice was lost in the gale. Then I suppose he noticed that I
was no longer wheezing behind him, for after a minute or two I heard
the whispery fluff-fluffing of his strides through the snow. The sound

stopped, and I had to assume—for my head was covered by the bale—
that he was standing right over me when he said disgustedly:

"By Murtia, the goddess of laziness, are you pretending to be already
tired? It is only barely past midday."

I had regained enough breath to say, my voice muffled, "Pretending
. . . I am not . . . fráuja . . ."

With one foot, and with no apparent strain, he turned the bale over,
and of course me with it, so that I was lying face up. Wyrd regarded me
as if he had overturned a rock and found a slimy slug stuck to its underside. My juika-bloth circled the scene, cocking its head to peer curiously at us.

"I am weary," I said, "and thirsty, and the pack straps have rubbed
my shoulders raw. Could we rest for just a little while?"

Wyrd grunted contemptuously, but he sat down beside me. "Only a
little," he said, "or your muscles will stiffen."

Well, well, I thought, it was *he* who had been pretending—forcing
himself to press on, to keep shouting his incessant soliloquy, feigning
freedom from fatigue or breathlessness—until *I* should be the one to
call a halt that was as welcome to him as to me.

107

He plunged an arm under the snow and felt about on the ground
until he brought up a smooth pebble. "Here, urchin. When we move
on, mouth this pebble while you walk. It will make you feel less thirsty.
And before we move on I shall arrange two paw ends of the furs so that
they pad your shoulder straps. In time, of course, you will get nicely
callused there."

"Perhaps, when we move on," I suggested, "we might trade packs for
a while?"

"Ne," he said firmly. "You *said* you could carry that bale. You must
learn, urchin, always to keep your word. And it was you who asked to
accompany me. I was rightly apprehensive that you might slow my progress, but out of my great good nature I agreed to let you do so. You
must learn, urchin, always to be careful of what you ask for, because
you might get it. But, once having got it, you must learn, urchin, always
to make the best of it."

"Ja, fráuja," I mumbled, though grudgingly.

"In my company, you may not be unremittingly happy or comfortable, but you will be hugely benefiting. Learning woodcraft, for example, and making strong both your body and your senses. Ja, urchin
Thorn, get strong"—he thumped his chest—"as *I* am strong!"

Rubbing my lacerated shoulders, I made bold to say, "It takes no great strength to disparage another's miseries."

He threw up his hands. "By Momus, the god of grumbling, but you are an ungrateful whelp!"

I muttered, "I never heard of any such thing as a god of grumbling."

"Ja, a Greek god, as you might expect of the Greeks. The grumbling god Momus once even chided Zeus for putting the bull's horns on its head, and not on its shoulders, where the bull is the strongest."

Simply to keep him sitting and talking, I said, "You are acquainted with so many gods, fráuja Wyrd, that I assume you are not a Christian."

He replied rather cryptically, "I was at one time. I got cured."

"You must not have had a very good priest. Or chaplain. Or pastor. Whatever."

Wyrd grunted. "The word 'pastor' means 'shepherd,' and sheep are for fleecing. I chose not to be a sheep."

"And the word 'cynic' comes from the Greek for 'dog,'" I said disapprovingly. "Cynics are so called because they are forever snarling at men of rectitude."

108

He did snarl then. "Much you know, puppy! The cynics gave *themselves* that name, because a dog—if it is offered any kind of tidbit—will sniff and scrutinize it carefully before swallowing it. Now, on your feet, urchin. We can still reach the cave before dark, if you do not do any more falling down. Atgadjats!"

We went on, he freely striding and I stiffly lumbering along. I was determined that I would finish our day's march, to wherever we were going, without again faltering for any reason short of my sudden death. As I lurched along, I deliberately set myself enigmas to solve, such as: assuming that a bear weighs as much as a hefty draft horse, how much of the bear's weight is bearskin? (And, for that matter, how much does an entire horsehide weigh? I had no idea.) Which kept my mind off my misery and fatigue, and I actually succeeded in completing that terrible march without again collapsing. I would have sworn it had lasted four years—Wyrd said it had been four hours of Church time—before he finally announced, "We are here."

In my relief and gratitude, I almost fell down, but managed not to. I panted, "Where . . . is the cave? I shall not . . . unstrap this bale . . . until I get it there."

"The cave is yonder," said Wyrd, pointing to a heavily shrubbed hillside not far ahead of us. "But you may as well drop your burden right here. We shall not be going in until he comes out."

"He?" I croaked.

"Or she," Wyrd said indifferently as he laid down his own bundles.

Stung by the seemingly sly reference to interchangeable sex, I found breath enough to cry, "Are you making jape of me, old man?"

"Hush!" he said sternly. "Lest you wake him—or her, as the case may be. I speak of the bear, not *you*, you tetchy urchin. How do I know which sex it is? I know only that the cave is a favorable hibernating den for bears, and I have reason to believe that one of them is sleeping in there now."

Sagging under my already agonizing load, I gasped, "You are . . . going to kill . . . another bear?"

"Well, not necessarily," said Wyrd, with withering sarcasm. "He *might* willingly peel off his own skin and hand it out to me. By the Styx, urchin, I told you to let fall that load. Do it before you fall yourself."

Feebly, I wriggled free of the straps and let the bale topple onto the snow behind me. I did not immediately sit or lie down, because I found myself still bent in a posture that I feared might be permanent. I staggered and stamped about, trying to unkink my spine, while Wyrd strung his war bow and tested its pull, then slung his quiver on his back so that the arrows' feathered ends extended just above his right shoulder.

109

I asked, "Are you going in alone?" for I was more than a little uneasy at the possibility of his commanding me to go with him.

"Going in?" He glared at me. "I have told you, urchin, that I am neither insane nor feebleminded. Are *you*? A bear has the strength of twelve men and the wit of eleven. By Jalk the Giant-Killer, have you in your wanderings never *seen* a bear?"

I was pleased to be able to say complacently, "I have, ja. On a street in Vesontio, there was a gleeman leading a bear with a ring in its nose. The beast danced to the man's flute music. It did not dance very elegantly, but—"

Wyrd uttered another of his laugh-snorts. "You might as well compare a farm ox to a savage úrus as compare a ringed bear to a wild one. Stay here and watch, and learn something."

With narrowed eyes, he studied the hillside shrubbery, and muttered in his beard, "Let me recollect. There are so many caves. As I recall, this one has a bend about ten paces inside. Ja, a slight bend to the left. That affords only a narrow embrasure, so to speak, through which to shoot. I must edge around to the right of the entrance . . ."

He left me and, with an arrow already nocked to his bow, went cautiously up and across the hillside, walking bent over—rather in the position I was still in—so his head did not top the snow-laden shrubbery. I had not yet espied the cave opening, so I could not estimate how close he got to it, but I could see him clearly as he crouched behind one bush, fixed his gaze, slowly raised his bow and took careful aim.

I heard the distant thrum of the bowstring and the whir of the flying arrow as it disappeared into the cave, wherever that was. But then I was astounded to hear a rapidly repeated thrum-thrum-thrum and whir-whir-whir. The old man, with the speed and agility of a young athlete, was whipping other arrows from his quiver and nocking them to his bow and shooting them after the first, so fast that his right arm was almost a blur, while his left, holding the bow grip, stayed as steady as a statue's. I could not count how many arrows he let fly before the very hill itself seemed to convulse and emit a mighty roar of outrage. Safely far away though I was, I quailed at the terrific noise, but Wyrd merely ceased his blur of movement and calmly, deliberately nocked one more arrow and stayed where he was, waiting.

He had to wait for only a moment. The hill that had bellowed like a volcano now erupted like one. From the invisible cave burst forth an immense brown object, momentarily as blurred as Wyrd's arm had been, in a cloud of snow and a spray of twigs and branches violently torn from the surrounding shrubs. Roaring as it emerged, the great bear skidded to a halt and, when the upthrown snow cleared, I could see that it had an arrow through one of its forelegs. It stood still, except for shaking that wounded leg and swiveling its massive head back and forth, its red eyes looking for its tormentor, while it bawled its death challenge over and over again. Now, slavering white froth from its fearsome jaws, it reared erect on its hind legs, to see better over the undergrowth.

At that, Wyrd again took careful aim and shot. Although that final arrow, as well as I could see, only pierced the underside of the bear's lower jaw, the giant beast concluded its roaring with a sort of strangled and hopeless bleat. Then, slowly, like a vast column crumpling, it fell over backward, rolled onto its side and lay inert, only its sickle-clawed paws still twitching.

I ran up the hill, along the trough Wyrd had broken in the snow—as well as I could run, with my spine and muscles not yet limbered—but when I got to where he stood, still behind the same bush, he motioned for me to stop.

"I have known a bear to have one final spasm," he said. "And those claws, even in death, can rip both your feet off."

110

So we waited until there was no least twitching still evident, and then warily approached and circled the gigantic brown mound of fur. My juika-bloth also came to swoop about us and peer down at the fallen beast.

"A male, this one," Wyrd murmured. "We will find no cubs inside the cave."

I could see, now, that Wyrd had not at all exaggerated when he spoke of the power of a Hunnish war bow. That last arrow had, as I thought, pierced the bear's underjaw, but it had gone farther, through all the bones and muscles inside the bear's head, to penetrate its brain and then smash through the incalculably thick and solid skull, so that the arrow's point protruded nearly my hand's span from the occiput of the beast's head.

"Never will you pry *that* arrow loose," I commented, as Wyrd knelt and worked to extract the other from the bear's foreleg.

"I know of no better way to forfeit an arrow," he said. "But you can retrieve those others from the cave. It will be dark in there, so first let us choose our camping place, and lay a fire, and you can take a brand into the den to give you light to search. I shot eight others; see that you fetch them all."

"Ja, fráuja," I said, with genuine respect. "And will you be cooking us a meal of good bear meat?"

"Ne, ne," he said. "Look here." He took out from somewhere in his clothes a small knife, parted the animal's belly fur and made a slit in the leathery skin. From it bulged out a considerable blob of yellow fat. "Too lardy to be worth the trouble of brittling."

"A pity," I said. "You must be as hungry as I am. Perhaps a haunch . . . ?"

"Ne," he said again. "We cannot disjoint the beast until I have skinned it entire. That is no quick and easy task, and night will soon be on us." He stood up and looked around. "Do as I told you and get a fire going. That looks the best place, down yonder."

"Do you mean, fráuja, with all this fresh red meat lying here, we will dine on dry brown rashers?"

"Ne," he said yet again, but absently still looking about. "I wager that the commotion we have made will bring some creature of curiosity—and akh, there *is* one."

He had glanced past my own shoulder, but before I could turn, he had swiftly brought up his bow, snatched an arrow from the quiver behind him, nocked it, bent the bow and let fly. The arrow went by my

111

ear so close that its sound was no mere whir, but a hair-ruffling flutter as loud as that of my eagle alighting. By the time I did turn, Wyrd's new prey had already fallen, some thirty paces distant. It was something like a goat, except that it had horns much more impressive than any goat's: thick, long, backward-curving, handsomely ridged on their fronts. I had never before seen such an animal, and said so.

"Ibex," said Wyrd. "They usually stay high on the peaks of the upper Albos. Only come this far down in deep winter. Inquisitive as cats, they are, to our good fortune. Lean of meat, too, since they do not fatten up to hibernate. Better eating than the best mutton. *Now* will you light a fire, niu?"

I did that, and in the place he had indicated, and I was not greatly surprised to find, under the snow and a coating of ice, a rill of sweet water. When Wyrd commenced to skin the ibex, I noticed that his saying knife was Goth-made, one with the distinctive "coiling snake" pattern ingrained in the metal. The knife had been so often used and well worn that its blade was little more than a sliver, but he was employing it skillfully in the skinning—and most meticulously, too.

I asked, "Are you saving the ibex's skin to sell also?"

He shook his shaggy head. "In summer I would. The coarse winter coat has not enough value to make it worth your carrying. The horns, though, I will get a good price for those. I am removing the skin only to cook the meat in."

"Cook it in the skin? How?"

"*Iésus!* You will see, when you have come back with those arrows of mine. If you ever do."

I took a brand from the fire and went back to where the dead bear lay, and soon found the cave opening, which was quite high enough for me to walk in upright. There was indeed a bend to the left, as Wyrd had remembered, and I found three of his arrows in the leaf mold and litter outside that bend, where they had hit the rock wall; one of them had bent its steel tip double in doing that. Beyond the bend, the cave ended, and back there it was cozily piled with dry leaves and a great deal of dry moss, all collected by this bear or others that had slept here before it. I scrabbled among the leaves and moss, being careful not to set them afire with my torch, and eventually found all the other five arrows that had failed to hit their mark.

When I returned to our camping place, I realized why Wyrd had taken so much care in flaying the ibex. He had left the hoofs and a pocket of skin at the four corners of the hide. Then he had stuck four

112

sticks into the ground around the fire, and used the hide's corner pockets to hang it over the blaze, its fur side down. Once the fur was singed away, he had filled the sagging hide with water. While that came to a boil, he had brittled the carcass into wieldy chunks—brisket, ribs, flank and so on—and put those into the water. The remaining meat scraps and the numbles he had tossed aside for my juika-bloth, and it was obviously enjoying its feast.

Wyrd and I had to wait a while for ours to cook, and our mouths watered as the delectable aroma wafted from the skin pot and the bubbling water darkened and the bobbing chunks of meat turned from red to brown. At last, when I was about to swoon from either famishment or the delight of anticipation, Wyrd produced his Goth knife and prodded a piece of the meat and pronounced it "done." It was done to perfection—so tender that we did not have to gnaw at all, and hardly had to chew; we had only to lip it off the bones—and so delicious that we gorged on it. We could not, of course, eat all there was. Wyrd set some by for the morning, and hung other bits over the fire to smoke and cure for carrying with us. Then, well and fully fed, we rolled into our furs for the night.

113

✠ ✠ ✠

That same night, but far away to the east, in the "New Rome" of Constantinople, a boy of about my own age had presumably also been amply fed before he retired to bed. However, he was the boy Theodoric, son and prince and heir of Thiudamer the Amaling, King of the Ostrogoths, so he slept as an honored guest in the magnificent Purple Palace of Leo, Emperor of the Eastern Roman Empire. And young Theodoric doubtless slept on silken sheets in a warm and downy bed, and before he slept he doubtless had dined on the most exotic and costly of dishes.

Well, so have I, in the years since that night. I have savored many a choice viand at many a festal board in many an elegant hall. In fact, I would dine often and often with Theodoric himself, in the several palaces he eventually won for his own, where we ate of the finest delicacies, in the company of patrician lords and ladies, and were attended by many stewards and servants. But I swear, I cannot remember relishing any meal in all my life so much as I enjoyed that simple repast that Wyrd so primitively prepared, that night in the cold and bleak and inhospitable Hrau Albos.

5

The next morning, though I again woke at first light, Wyrd was already absent from our camping place. I found him up where the bear had fallen, and well along in the labor of skinning the carcass. I gave him a murmured "gods dags" and then, unbidden, brought up from the campfire some warmed-over ibex meat, and from the rill some water, with which he could break his fast. He grunted acknowledgment, and snatched bites of the meat and gulps of the water while carrying on with his bloody and greasy work.

Then I busied myself with rolling up our bedding furs, and tucking inside them our other separate belongings, including the smoked meat. I also, as always, made sure that my phial of the Virgin's milk had not been lost or broken during the previous day's journey. Those chores did not take me long, so I picked up the discarded head of the ibex. My juika-bloth had made its own morning meal by pecking out the eyes and most of the tongue of it, but what I wanted was to remove the splendid horns. I found a suitable rock and used that as a hammer to crush the skull. When I was done, I laid one horn on each of our bundles and lashed them there.

Wyrd and I both finished our tasks at about the same time, and it was nearly midday. I regarded with dismay the great skin he brought wadded in his arms, and waited with resignation for him to add it to the bale I had borne the day before. But he nodded approval of my having separated the ibex's horns, and said:

"You already have enough to carry, urchin. Anyway, you could scarcely tolerate the smell this skin will soon develop, for I have not fleshed it as well as might be, and of course I will not take the time and trouble to stretch and dry it. I am accustomed to rank odors, so I will add this to my own load."

"Thags izvis," I said feelingly. "And will you be killing still others, fráuja Wyrd?"

"Ne, we *both* have enough to carry. And I know of no other favored hibernating dens between here and Basilea, so we might as well bend our best steps toward that garrison. Ja, we will get out of this raw weather and into a luxuriously hot Roman bath."

"Ought I go and carve some meat off the bear, in case we should need it on the way?"

"Ne. Once a cadaver has stiffened in death, the flesh is forever tough, however long one cooks it. Let it lie."

"It seems a shame to waste it."

"Nothing in nature ever goes to waste, urchin. That carcass will nourish a myriad of other animals, birds, insects. And if a pack of wolves should come upon it first, it will divert them from trailing us by the scent of this fresh skin. Better yet, if the bear is found by a scavenging band of Huns, it will keep them here for a good long while."

"I once saw a wolf," I said, "and it looked capable of killing a man with ease. I have never seen a Hun. But I take it, fráuja, that you had rather be the prey of wolves than of Huns?"

"By the infernal Styx, anyone would! Wolves might ravage our belongings, or our horses, if we had any. They would not attack us. I will never understand how the intelligent and respectable and resourceful wolves got their reputation of man-eating savagery. But I know how the Huns got *theirs*. Now, urchin—atgadjats!"

✠   ✠   ✠

I forget how many, many days we were on the march after leaving that place. But almost every day, now, we were tending downhill, and with almost every day the weather got slightly more clement, and with almost every day—impossible though I would have thought it—my burden of baled bearskins seemed to lighten. As Wyrd had predicted, the skin and muscles of my shoulders and back gradually got accustomed to the hard usage, and all my other muscles and sinews were likewise getting stronger. I no longer lurched and lumbered along, but kept pace with the tireless old Forest-Stalker.

He also instructed me in the ways of walking quietly—and he often did that with a snarl, when I erred—so I learned always to place each foot before putting weight on it, lest I snap a dead stick or crunch dry leaves concealed beneath the snow, and I learned never to let branches whip free after I had parted them for my passage, and I learned various

115

other tricks of woodcraft. Sometimes, when Wyrd and I had traversed a wind-bared stretch of rock and then found snow again on the other side, he would have us both walk *backward* until we came to bare rock again. That, he said, would confuse no forest beast, but might confuse any Huns who came upon our tracks.

Wyrd sometimes cut short our day's march in midafternoon, or extended it until after dark, so that we unfailingly made camp near an iced-over pool or streamlet. Often, too, as we went along, he would abruptly halt—and stop me with a gesture—silently set down his bundles, unsling his bow and shoot a snow hare or stoat that, standing immobile against the equally white landscape, had completely escaped my notice. It seemed to me that Wyrd must have two or three more senses than other people do, and I admiringly told him so.

"Skeit," he grunted, picking up his latest kill. "It was your eagle that spotted this one, and I was watching the *bird*. It may prefer to dine on reptiles, but it sees everything. And, watching it, so do I. A very useful companion, that eagle. Your own eyesight is merely lazy, urchin. You must sharpen it as you would any other skill. As for your sense of smell, you have simply lived too long between walls and under a roof. Spend enough time in the outdoors and you will learn to discern the different smells of snow, ice and water."

Well, I never did develop Wyrd's facility for sniffing out water. But I did try to use my eyes better, and, rather to my surprise, found that one *can*, with practice, see things previously unseeable. For instance, I learned that movement is best perceived by looking directly *at* a place where movement might be expected (or feared). But small or still or dim objects, and difference in color, are best perceived at the edges of one's vision. Eventually I could, like Wyrd, "see from the sides of my eyes," so to speak, and distinguish a winter-white small animal from the only slightly different white of the snow in which it stood stone-still, waiting for us to pass it by.

When I had become able to espy those little beasts, and when we were not desperate for some game to cook that night, Wyrd would let me take first try at bringing one down, using my sling. But he usually had an arrow already nocked to let fly in case I missed—which, early on, I did oftener than not.

"That is because you wield the sling in David's biblical style," Wyrd said sourly. "A result, no doubt, of your having been reared in a monastery. Twirling it over your head like that, before loosing the stone, indeed throws far and hard, but not with much precision. Your intent should not be to heave a stone clear across the Albos, and indiscriminately. It should be to *hit* something, and something that is fairly nearby, such as a small animal—or a Goliath, for that matter. You will get better accuracy, urchin, if you twirl the sling perpendicular to your side."

Obediently, I tried. And naturally, unused to that mode of throwing, I did it with atrocious awkwardness.

"Ne, ne!" Wyrd said disgustedly. "You need not spin it like a teetotum. Two or three spins are ample. Anyway, you are twirling it the wrong way, so you fling the stone underhand. Take note of this, urchin. The arm muscles work in such a way that you can *raise* your arm much more rapidly and forcefully than you can *lower* it. So twirl the sling the other way, and let fly with a strong overhand throw."

I tried again and, though I was still awkward at it, Wyrd's method did give me a feeling of more assurance with the sling. So I practiced at it, every chance I got, and before that journey was over I was bringing down most of our small venison.

At last we emerged from under the perpetual gray overcast sky of the Albos, and the days were intermittently, then frequently bright with sunlight. Fortunately, in those lower lands, we were in forests so dense that, even leafless, they afforded some shade from that sunshine; otherwise, the glare off the snow would have been blinding. Here, in the Roman province known as Rhaetia Prima, we came to the river Birsus, a stream so narrow that it was frozen all the way across, just like any of the mountain brooks and rills.

We followed the Birsus downstream and, where it joins the great river Rhenus, came in sight of Basilea—first seeing from afar the wall garrison built on a terrace that towers high above the rivers' junction. Wyrd explained to me that here the westward-flowing, narrow and rapid Rhenus makes an abrupt bend to flow northward, and also widens into a broad and easy-running water. So here is the upstream limit of navigation on that much traveled river that stretches all the way north across Europe to the Germanic Ocean.

Now, Basilea is only a small and minor Roman garrison town, compared to others I have visited since. But all are alike in the way they have grown and developed over time. The walled camp or fort occupies the most prominent and easily defensible place, and is usually immense in extent. It is encircled by ramparts, revetments, sentry towers, ditches, moats, thorny hedges and other such barriers against invasion. Immediately outside those barricades, and all around the fort, are clustered

117

the cabanae. Although that word means only "the booths," they are actually quite substantial buildings, divided by streets into blocks, market squares and every other aspect of a real town. No doubt they *were* at first only the shanty booths of camp followers peddling commodities that the Roman army does not always supply to its troops—rich foods, good wines, cheap women and lusty entertainments—but in every long-settled garrison town, the cabanae now constitute the civic community, busy with commerce, activity and conviviality.

Beyond the cabanae, the outskirts of the town contain those industries necessary to supply both the troops and the citizens—timber yards, tileries, stockyards, potteries, smithies and such—most of those belonging to the descendants of discharged Roman veterans who long ago married into the local population. In addition to all those appurtenances of any garrison town, Basilea also had a fringe of docks, repair shops, chandleries and warehouses along the Rhenus riverfront.

Because the Rhenus is the water highway for so much traffic of travelers and traders, there are only two narrow and ill-kept roads leading into Basilea, and on one of those Wyrd and I entered the town. It was to be expected that the roads would be little used, but we had this one *entirely* to ourselves. There were no carts, wagons, riders or pedestrians to be seen at all, and Wyrd muttered wonderingly about that. In the town's outskirts, we still saw no people, no one working or moving about or even sitting idle. All the gates we passed were shut and barred, no forge or kiln fires were burning, there was none of the usual hive noise of a populated community. We could not even hear a dog barking anywhere.

"By the oven-baked body of St. Polycarp," growled Wyrd, "but this is most peculiar."

"But look up ahead, fráuja," I said. "There are at least smokes rising from the cabanae."

"Ja. Come, urchin, and I will introduce you to my favorite taberna. It belongs to an old friend of mine, and he does not water his wine. We shall ask him if a plague has afflicted Basilea."

But when we arrived at the taberna, although its smoke indicated a hearth fire within, its door was shut fast, like every other in town. Wyrd hammered angrily on the panel and shouted some hideous obscenities and demanded, "Open this door, Dylas! May all the gods damn you, I know you are in there!"

Not until after Wyrd had done much more hammering and invoking of curses did a window shutter open, just a crack, and a bleary red eye peered out and a gruff voice said, speaking the Old Language as did Wyrd, with an unidentifiable accent, "Wyrd, old kinsman, is that you?"

"Ne, I am the lissome lad Hyacinthus, come to seduce and debauch you!" Wyrd bellowed, so loudly that various other shutters in houses roundabout also opened a crack. "Unbar this door or, by Iésus, I will kick it in!"

"I cannot open it, friend Wyrd," said the eye. "I am forbidden to open to any stranger."

"What? Forbidden? By the boils of Job, both you and I have contracted and survived every kind of pox and plague there is! We hazard no contamination of one another, or of anybody else. And I am no *stranger!* I say again, if you do not open—"

"If ever once in your life, old ferta, you would shut your yammering mouth, your ears might open. This door is barred by order of the legatus Calidius. So is every other door in Basilea. We have not been visited by any plague, but by the Huns."

"Iésus! Does Calidius barricade the barn after the horses are stolen, niu?"

"You speak truer than you may think. This time it was a unique mare and foal that got stolen.'"

"Perdition, Pluto and Pandemonium!" Wyrd raged. "Let me in and tell me about it!"

"I am forbidden even to speak of what has occurred here. So is every other citizen. All strangers and visitors are to report to the garrison, Wyrd. That is the only door that may be opened to you."

"Dylas, you wretch, what *is* going on? There are not enough Huns in this part of the world to mount an attack on a Roman garrison."

"I can tell you no more, old friend. Go to the garrison."

So we went on, through the streets that led uphill between the cabanae, Wyrd muttering foul words in his beard the whole way, and I staying prudently silent. Approaching the fort atop the terrace, we walked the zigzag path leading through the thorn thickets, bridging the ditches and trapfalls—a path easy enough for a pedestrian to negotiate, but capable of stopping any headlong charge of either foot or horse soldiers. Finally Wyrd and I stood at the base of the high wall. As I have said, Basilea's was one of the lesser garrisons, but it looked grand enough to me then. Just this one side of it was some four hundred paces from corner to corner. The wall, though doubtless of stone or brick, was entirely faced on the outside with a heavy layer of peat turfs, to soften the battering of any ram. Above the great timber gate hung a board with words incised and the letters picked out with paint: in gold the name of the long-ago emperor who had established the fort, VALEN-TINIAN, and in red the name of the legion to which the garrison troops belonged, LEGIO XI CLAUDIA.

That massive gate was tight shut, like every other door in town, and from one of the towers on either side of it a voice shouted down, challenging us first in Latin, then in the Old Language:

"Quis accedit? Huarjis anaquimith?"

Rather to my surprise, Wyrd replied in both of those tongues:

"Est caecus, quisquis? Ist jus blinda, niu? Who do you *think* approaches, Paccius? You presumptuous puppy, I am clearly your mother the bitch! You know my voice, Signifer, as well as I know yours."

I heard the sentry chuckle, but then he called again, "I know you, yes, old man. But some of the threescore archers on these battlements may not, and their arrows are already aimed at you. Announce yourself."

Wyrd furiously stamped his foot and roared, "By the twenty-four testicles of the twelve apostles! I am called Wyrd the Forest-Stalker!"

"And your companion?"

"Only another puppy, you impudent puppy. My apprentice forester, called Thorn the Worthless."

"And *his* companion?"

"What?" said Wyrd, nonplussed. He looked around at me. "Akh, the bird. Surely, Paccius, a Roman legionary recognizes an *eagle*. Shall I now announce my separate toes, which are itching to kick your skeit-smeared rump?"

"Wait there."

Although Wyrd kept on shouting, getting ever more obscene and blasphemous, there ensued only silence from above. I heartily wished that he would be quiet, too, considering that we were the potential target of more arrows than had ever been aimed at St. Sebastian.

But we did not have long to wait. There came from within the gate the thuds, grindings and creaks of timber balks being withdrawn. Then the heavy gate opened, with ponderous slowness, and only far enough to admit us. We were met by the sentry Paccius, who was, like the other legionaries flanking the entrance, in full battle dress. It was the first time I had ever seen soldiers, not to mention armor.

Each man wore a round iron helmet that flared out behind into a neck guard, and had hinged cheek guards on either side, and the whole of which was ornately wrought and chased. His body armor was of innumerable metal scales, densely overlapped and fastened to a leather undercorselet, and around his neck each man wore a scarf to prevent the stiff garment from chafing his skin. Around his waist, each wore a wide belt, studded with decorative metal bosses. From the left side of the belt depended a sheathed, leaf-bladed dagger, and from the right a much ornamented scabbard; the men all had their short-swords ready in their hands. From the front of the belt hung a sort of apron of iron plates on leather thongs, so they would swing between a man's legs as easily as the skirt of his woolen tunic but in a fight would protect his belly and private parts. All the men—especially the one named Paccius, who seemed to be of some rank higher than the others—looked so strong, tanned, capable, brave and warlike that I momentarily wished that I were a male, and a man grown, so that I could enlist as a legionary, too.

"Salve, Uiridus, ambulator silvae," Paccius said pleasantly, raising his clenched right fist in the Roman salute.

"Salve, Signifer," Wyrd grunted, his arms too laden to return the salute. "It took you long enough."

"I had to make known your arrival to the legatus praesidio. He not only grants you entrance, old Wyrd, he expresses great gladness that you are here, and bids you attend upon him on the instant."

"Vái! The perfumed Calidius would not want to receive me in my present condition. You must have been able to smell me, Paccius, even before you condescended to open the gate. I am going to the baths. Come, urchin."

"Siste!" snapped Paccius, before Wyrd and I had gone three paces. "When the legatus says come, he means come now."

Wyrd glared at him. "You are a soldier under the command of every other soldier above the rank of signifer. I am a free citizen."

"The jus belli has been imposed. And under martial law, as you well know, citizens also must take orders. But if necessary, you stubborn old man, Calidius would *beg* that you attend. When you speak with him, you will see that I do not exaggerate."

"Akh, very well," Wyrd sighed impatiently. "First, at least, show us to a barrack where we can dispose of our burdens."

"Venite," said Paccius, and led the way. "Almost all of our spare facilities are crowded with civilians. Calidius ordered in here everyone from the outlying countryside, and also every newcomer to Basilea. Everyone who could not be billeted in the cabanae nearest the garrison's protection. We are even playing host to a traveling Syrian slave dealer and his whole shackled train of charismatics. But I will find quarters for you two — or throw out the Syrian, if I have to."

"What is all this?" asked Wyrd. "Down in the town, the caupo Dylas — you know him, Paccius — spoke of Huns, but I thought the man deranged. You cannot be expecting an assault by the *Huns.*"

"Not an assault, a visit from time to time," the signifer said uncomfortably. "And by only one Hun each time. The legatus has sequestered everybody so that none but himself has communication with that visitor, and so that no one does him harm as he comes and goes, or tries to trail him to his lair."

Wyrd stared unbelievingly. "Has *every* last man in Basilea gone demented? You have been allowing a filthy Hun simply to stroll in here unscathed? And letting him walk *out* again? Without his louse-ridden head under his arm?"

"Please," said Paccius, in a voice almost of shame. "Let the legatus explain it to you. Here is your billet."

The long wooden barrack had a roofed portico running its full length, and several soldiers, presumably off duty, were lounging there to take the air. The building's long wall had a dozen doors in it, and beside each door, sunken into a hole in the portico floor, was a lidded bin for trash. Paccius led us through one of the doors, and I found myself in the choicest sleeping quarters I had yet been offered in my life. The room was only of raw wood, and had not a trace of ornament. But it contained eight pallets and they were *not on the floor.* They were raised above it — above the reach of all but extremely energetic vermin — on frames that stood on little legs. At the foot of each bed was a chest for the occupant's belongings, and it could be *locked* against pilfering. Opposite the beds was an alcove with a stand on which was soap and a ewer of water, and in its floor was an opening to be used for a rere-dorter, and those facilities were *not* for everyone in the building but *only* for this room's occupants.

When we three entered, all the beds were already taken. On one sat a black-bearded, brown-skinned, hook-nosed man in heavy woolen traveling robes. On the others sat smaller persons — young boys, in fact, aged about five to twelve years — each of them wearing iron rings on both ankles, with a chain between, and all of them raggedly dressed and morose of aspect.

"Foedissimus Syrus, apage te!" Paccius snarled at the man. "Abi, you Syrian swine! Take these brats and cram them in the next room with your others. And you go with them. We have guests who deserve a room to themselves, not to be shared with a greasy slaver and his capon charismatics."

The Syrian, whose name I later learned was Bar Nar Natquin, somehow managed to smile ingratiatingly and to sneer at the same time, and he wrung his hands, and said, in heavily Greek-tinged Latin, "I hasten to obey, Centurio. May I have the centurio's permission to take my young wards to the baths before I put them to bed, please, Centurio?"

"You know I am not a centurio, you lickspittle toad. You may drop your toad spawn down the latrina for all I care. Apage te!"

The boys all hid smiles of glee at hearing their master reviled, even though the revilement included them as well. And when they smiled, I could see that they were all exceptionally pretty boys. As the Syrian herded them out the door, Paccius said:

"That unctuous panderer Natquin keeps his wares as clean and sweet and appetizing as they can be. He even tried to peddle one of them to me. But I swear the barbarus himself has never washed in his life. Uiridus, just drop your things here and let *your* brat stow them properly while you come with me to the—"

"By all the thunders of Thor!" Wyrd erupted. "You cannot order us about like Syrians and slaves. Thorn is my apprentice, learning his craft from the fráuja Wyrd—the magister Uiridus, if you prefer. And whatever I am about to learn from the legatus, I intend that Thorn shall learn also. We go together to see Calidius."

"Heu me miserum! As you will," said the signifer, flinging up his hands in exasperation. "But let us go forthwith."

So I tethered my juika-bloth to the bedstead, and Wyrd and I again followed Paccius. This time he led us along the via praetoria, the other main street that ran crosswise to the via principalis, and at the far end of it was the praetorium, the residence of the legatus and his family and retinue. As Paccius strode along ahead of us, I said to Wyrd in an undertone:

"Tell me, fráuja, what are charismatics?"

"Why, those boys we just saw." He jerked his thumb backward.

"Ja, but why are they called by that name?"

He turned to look at me, with a strange sort of look. "You do not know?"

"How should I know? I never heard the word before."

"It is from the Greek—khárismata," he said, still eyeing me askance as we walked. "You *do* know what a eunuch is?"

"I have heard tell. I have not yet encountered one."

His look at me was frankly perplexed. "The Greek khárisma used to mean a special gift or talent possessed by a person. In modern language, a charismatic is a special sort of eunuch. The most exquisite and expensive sort."

"But I thought a eunuch was a . . . well, a nothing, a neuter. How can there be varying degrees of nothingness."

"A eunuch is a man unmanned by being shorn of his testicles. A charismatic is one shorn of *everything* down there. Svans and all."

"Iésus!" I exclaimed. "Why?"

Now averting his gaze, Wyrd said, "There are masters who want them that way. An ordinary eunuch is only a servant who can be trusted not to molest his master's women. A charismatic is a plaything for the master himself. And those masters prefer them young and winsome. The ones we just saw I would wager are Franks. Making charismatics—of beautiful boys orphaned, bought from their parents, abducted, whatever—is the special trade of the Frankish city of Verodunum, and a thriving trade it is. Of course, because so many of the boys perish during the drastic syrurgery involved, the few who survive fetch an extravagant price indeed. That villainous Syrian is shepherding a fortune on the hoof, so to speak."

"Iésus," I said again, and we walked on in silence until Paccius, well ahead of us, beckoned from the entryway of the praetorium for us to make haste. Then Wyrd turned to me once more and said, with what sounded like contrition:

"Forgive me, urchin. When you inquired about the charismatics, I showed surprise because . . . akh, well, because I took you to be one of them."

"I am nothing of the sort!" I said hotly. "I am not mutilated in any of my parts!"

He shrugged. "I have asked your forgiveness, and I will ask nothing else—not even to inquire whether you are offspring of the godling Hermaphroditus. I earlier said that I do not care one ferta *what* you may be, and I still do not, and I never will. Let us speak of the subject no more. Now come with me into the praitoriaún and we will find out why the august Calidius seems so overjoyed to have us here."

6

accius led us through a hall and several
rooms, all splendidly furnished and deco-
rated with wall and floor mosaics, couches,
tables, draperies, lamps and other objects
of which I could not even ascertain the use. I thought
the maintenance of such an establishment must require innumerable servants or slaves or military orderlies, but we encountered no other persons at all. Then Paccius ushered us outdoors again, into a colonnaded garden courtyard set in the
center of the building. There was of course snow on the ground there,
and nothing in bloom, but a man was striding up and down a flagstone
terrace—distractedly, it seemed, for he was wringing his hands much as
the Syrian slaver had done.

He was white of hair, and had wrinkles in his weather-tanned, clean-
shaven face, but he walked erect and looked hardy for his age. He wore
no sort of uniform, but a long coat of fine Mutina wool, elegantly
trimmed with miniver. To such a noble, Wyrd and I must certainly have
looked like savages that his signifer had grubbed from out of some
squalid underground den. Nevertheless, at sight of us, his somber face
brightened and he briskly approached, crying, "Caius Uiridus! Salve,
salve!"

"Salve, Clarissimus Calidius," said Wyrd, as each clasped his right
hand about the other's right wrist.

"I must light a flame to Mithras," said Calidius, "for his having sent
you in our time of dire distress, old warrior."

Wyrd said sardonically, "I wonder why I should be so favored by
Mithras. What *is* this trouble, Legatus?"

Calidius gestured to Paccius to depart, but took no notice of the
insignificant me, saying, "The Huns have abducted a Roman woman
and child, and are holding them for ransom, and are making impossible
demands of me for their return."

Wyrd made a face. "Whatever ransom you might pay, surely you do not expect the hostages' return."

"Verily, I had no faintest hope of it . . . until I heard that *you* were at the gate, old comrade."

"Akh, this comrade is old indeed. I am here only to peddle some bearskins and—"

"Eheu! You need not go about bargaining and haggling with every merchant in Basilea. I myself will buy everything you are carrying, and at whatever exorbitant price you ask. I want you to hunt down those Huns and rescue that woman and child."

"Calidius, nowadays I do not kill Huns, only bears. A dead bear's surviving relatives are less likely to hunt *me* across the world and across the years."

The legatus said sharply, "You did not always speak so. And you did not always answer to the proletarian address of caius." His next words made me turn and regard Wyrd with surprise and wonder and a new awe. "Uiridus, when we defeated Attila on the plains of Catalauni, you were then respectfully addressed as a decurio of the auxiliaries, and you were with the antesignani, fighting *out ahead of the standards.* Those fifteen years ago, you were not fastidious about killing Huns."

"Not then or now, you upjumped centurio!" Wyrd snapped back at him. "I simply do not any longer go out of my way to seek enemies to slay. Were I you, Calidius, I should be less concerned with the victims of this abduction than with the weakling men of your own command here. If any scavenger Huns could snatch so much as a horse-tord from a Roman garrison town, then they also deserve all the wheat and wine in your stores. And from now on your every legionary, stationary and auxiliary ought to be shamefacedly feeding on only the barley and vinegar of disgrace."

The legatus dolefully shook his head. "There was really no disgrace involved, only a headstrong woman." He grimaced. "A woman named, not very fittingly, Placidia. Her six-year-old son—named Calidius, in honor of myself—has a pony. That pony, not having been ridden over the winter, had got stilted in the hoofs and needed trimming. The stable of Basilea's best ferrarius is on the farthermost outskirts of the town, but young Calidius wished to go along with his pony to see the work done. So, although Placidia is pregnant with another child, and very near her term, and in no decent condition to be seen in public, the willful woman insisted on accompanying her son. So, without a by-your-pleave, she and the boy went recklessly off, with only four house slaves

126

to carry the lectica in which they rode, and one yard slave to lead the pony, and with no military escort at all. Then—"

"Excuse me, Calidius," Wyrd interrupted, yawning. "I and my apprentice are weary, and in grievous need of a good hot bath. Is all this trivial detail really necessary?"

"Quin taces! You can be long-winded enough, as I know very well. And the details are relevant, because the Huns must have been lurking outside the town, awaiting just such an opportunity. A band of them fell upon the little train, slew the four carriers and dashed off, carrying the lectica themselves. The surviving slave returned here with the pony. And the horrid news."

"You killed him, of course."

"That would have been too merciful. He is confined for life in the pistrinum pit—what the slaves call 'the living hell'—turning a millstone to grind grain. A life sentence there is not a long one, considering the bone-cracking labor in the stifling heat and the strangling dust. Anyway, two days later there came, under a white flag, a Hun who spoke some Latin. Enough to tell me that Placidia and little Calidius had been taken alive, and were still alive. They would remain alive, he said, if I let him return safely to his band, and if I warranted him safe passage to come here again with the instructions his fellows were preparing for me. Well, I gave my warrant, and the same scurvy Hun came back another two days later, with a list of ransom demands. I will not recite them all— stores of food, horses and saddles, weapons—but suffice it to say, the demands are insufferable and impossible of my compliance. I temporized, telling him that I needed time to decide whether the hostages were worth the price, and that I would give him an answer three days hence. That means the damnable yellow dwarf will be back again tomorrow. So you can see why I was in blackest despair, and why I rejoiced when I heard of your arrival, and why—"

"No, I do not quite see," said Wyrd. "Forgive me, Calidius, for reopening old wounds. But I remember, when your son Junius fell at Catalauni, you told us others of your men not to mourn. The death of one soldier, you said, was not an intolerable loss to an army. And that was your own son. Why, now, for a mere foolhardy woman and her hapless boy, even if he is named—?"

"Uiridus, I had and still have one other son, the younger brother of Junius. He serves under me here."

"I know. The optio Fabius. A fine lad."

"Well, the headstrong woman Placidia is his wife, my affinal daugh-

127

ter. Her small son and the child still in her womb are my only grand-children. If they live . . . no, they *must* live, for they are the last of my line."

"Now I see," muttered Wyrd, looking as grave as did the legatus. "Fabius must immediately have gone in pursuit of them, and gone to his own death."

"He would have done. But, by a ruse, I had him locked in the guard-house before he heard of the abduction. He is still in there, raging at me as frenziedly as at the Huns."

"Then, again, I do not see why you despair," said Wyrd. "I dislike to sound heartless. But I know well that a man can withstand the loss of a wife—perhaps in time even forget her—at least such a one as this Pla-cidia seems to have been. Fabius is young, and there are many other women, including more placid ones. And children are the easiest com-modity in the world to produce. Your familial line need not die out, Calidius."

The legatus sighed. "I have said exactly that to him. And I am heart-ily glad that there were iron bars between us when I did. No, Uiridus, for whatever reason, Fabius is besotted with that woman, and he dotes on young Calidius, and he is keenly anticipating the birth of their next child. He swears that, if they are lost, he will take the first opportunity to fall on his sword. He will do it, too; he is his father's son. I *must* get those hostages back."

"You mean I must," Wyrd said surlily. "But why do you think the Hun tells the truth? That they are still alive?"

"He has each time brought proof." The legatus sighed again, delved in a pocket of his coat and took out two small, white, limp things, and handed them to Wyrd. "Each time, one of Placidia's fingers."

I turned away, to keep from retching. While Wyrd examined those things, the legatus went on, almost absentmindedly, "Each time one has arrived, I have personally amputated *two* fingers from that miserable slave confined in the pistrinum. If the ransom negotiations should somehow be protracted, he will be pushing the millstone with his el-bows."

"Both of these are forefingers," Wyrd murmured. "But this one he brought first, yes? Its rigor has relaxed. And this one he brought on his latest visit. This finger was recently alive. Very well, I agree. The woman was at least not dead two days ago. Calidius, have that slave fetched here—this instant—before you whittle him any further."

The legatus bellowed, "Paccius!" and the signifer promptly emerged from a distant doorway of the building, and as promptly vanished again when he was given the order.

"One thing I have learned about Huns," said Wyrd while we waited. "They are dismally short on patience. A band of them might have lurked outside the town, hoping to seize *somebody*. But they would not have waited there for long, on the very slim chance that the somebody would prove to be the most precious persons they could hold hostage against the tenderhearted Clarissimus Calidius. They knew for whom they were waiting, and when those persons would appear, and how vulnerable they would be. It strikes me as suspicious that one of the five accompanying slaves so miraculously escaped unharmed."

"Mithras be thanked," gasped the legatus, "that *I* did not yet kill him."

When Paccius returned, there were two guards with him, dragging the slave between them so that he half ran, half stumbled. He was husky and fair-skinned, but trembly and frightened-looking, and he was naked except for a loincloth and dirty, bloody rags for bandages on both hands. When the man was propped up before us, the legatus's own hands twitched, as if eager to get at the man's throat. But Wyrd only calmly addressed the slave in the Old Language:

129

"Tetzte, ik kann alls," which means "Wretch, I know all." He went on, "You have but to verify it, and I promise you freedom from the pistrinum."

When Wyrd translated that remark into Latin, the legatus made a choked noise of protest, but Wyrd hushed him with a gesture and continued, "On the other hand, tetzte, refuse to admit the truth and I promise you will *yearn* to go back to the pit."

"Kunnáith, niu?" croaked the slave. "You *know*?"

"I do," Wyrd said complacently, as if he really did. He continued to translate his and the slave's words into Latin for the benefit of the legatus. "I know how you first met a skulking Hun on the outskirts of Basilea when making an earlier visit to the ferrarius. How you arranged for the Hunnish conspirators to be waiting when the Lady Placidia and her son went to call on that ferrarius. How you assured her that there would be no danger, and so lulled her that she summoned no guards for an escort. How you stood cowardly by while your fellow slaves tried bare-handed to fight off the Huns, and died doing it."

"Ja, fráuja," mumbled the tetzte. Cold though it was in the garden, he was suddenly perspiring. "You do know all."

"All but two things," said Wyrd. "For one, why did you do it?"

"Those yellow reptiles promised to take me with them, to let me roam free with them in the forest, to be a slave no more. But then, when they had what they wanted, they laughed and told me to be off— and to be thankful that they had left me my life. I had no recourse but to return here and pretend I had been a victim myself." He gave a fearful sidelong glance at the legatus, who was silently seething. "And I *had* been a victim, had I not?"

Wyrd only sniffed and said, "The other thing I wish to know. Where did they take the lady and the boy?"

"Meins fráuja, I have no idea."

"Then where is their camp, their den, their hiding place? It cannot be too far from here, if they have spent so much time sneaking about these precincts. And if they had to transport a heavy lectica there."

"Meins fráuja, I truly do not know. If, as they promised, they had taken me with them, then I would know. But I do not."

"I assure you, simpleminded tetzte, you would not have gone far with them. But you *have* talked with those Huns. Did they never mention a place, a landmark, a direction?"

The slave frowned and sweated in an effort to remember, but at last could say only, "They pointed, now and then, but in the general direction of the Hrau Albos, nothing more. I swear it, fráuja."

"I believe you," said Wyrd resignedly. "The Huns are much more cunning and prudent than you are, wretch."

"Then you will keep your promise?" the slave asked piteously.

"I will," said Wyrd, at which the legatus roared and reached with hooked hands for the slave's neck. But Wyrd had anticipated him. In one smooth motion, Wyrd drew his snake knife and plunged it into the slave's abdomen, just above his loincloth, and ripped him up the front until the blade struck against his breastbone. The slave's eyes bulged at the same time his intestines did, but he made no sound, and sagged dead upon the supporting arms of the two guards. Paccius led them and their burden of carrion out of the garden.

The legatus said through his teeth, "By the Styx, Uiridus, why did you do that?"

"I keep my promises. I promised to free him from the pistrinum."

"So would I have done, but infinitely more slowly. Anyway, the brute told us nothing useful."

"Nihil," Wyrd glumly agreed. "Now I shall have to wait for the Hun to get here, and follow him when he leaves. Tell him, Calidius, that you agree to all his demands, so that he will go speedily back to tell his band."

"Very well. Then what will you do?"

"By the ponderous brass feet of the Furies, how do I know? I must give this some thought."

"And preparation. Warriors, horses, weapons—I will give you whatever you need."

"You cannot. The emperor could not. What I need is the invisibility of Alberikh and the unfailing good luck of Arion. Like the Huns, I must effect a secret abduction. But I cannot afterward flee through the forest with a weakling woman—one who is both heavily pregnant and injured besides. On foot or on horseback, we would surely be caught."

The legatus pondered, then said, "This will sound as heartless as your own earlier words, Uiridus. But could you bring back at least the boy Calidius?"

"Akh, that would certainly be a more feasible venture, yes, and one with more chance of success. You said he is six years old? He should be able to keep pace with me. Still, it will be no easy matter to steal even a small boy out of an encampment well guarded and on the alert."

There was a long, thoughtful silence.

Then I spoke. For the first time, and unbidden, and most reluctantly, and in a very small voice, I spoke one word: "Substitutus."

Both men turned to stare at me in astonishment, as if I had abruptly sprouted up from between the flagstones at their feet. They continued to stare silently at me, and not because, like them, I spoke in Latin, or because of my presumption in speaking at all, but because they were agog at what I said next:

"Substitute one of the charismatics."

After another long interval, the men ceased staring at me and turned to look at one another.

"By Mithras, an ingenious idea," the legatus said to Wyrd, and then, with as much humor as he could muster, asked him, "Which of you two did you say is the apprentice?"

"By Mithras, Jupiter *and* Guth, the urchin learns quickly," Wyrd said with pride. "Already the apprentice has absorbed much of the misanthropy of the master. Substitution is an ingenious idea, indeed, and of a charismatic. You could hardly appropriate one of your garrison or town children, Calidius."

The legatus said, and this time to me, "I have not seen that slave-monger's flock of capons. Is there one that might serve?"

I said, "Two or three seem to be of a suitable age, clarissimus. You yourself would have to decide whether there is one of sufficient resemblance to your grandson. The Syrian took them all to the baths, but, if you wish to inspect them, they are probably back at the barrack by now."

The legatus said, "No, I will wager that they are still doing their bathing." He added, though not unkindly, "You are evidently unfamiliar with Roman baths, lad, if in fact you have ever been acquainted with any baths at all."

Wyrd snorted loudly. "Ill manners, Calidius, to repay a favor with an insult. This is an uncommonly cleanly youngster. Like myself, Thorn has been *trying* to get a bath ever since we arrived here."

"My apologies, Torn," said the legatus. "I, too, would like an extra bath today, after being near that unspeakably foul slave. Let us all three go to the bath this instant. Signifer Paccius will know which of them the Syrian went to."

As we walked there, I was thinking that Calidius had misheard and misspoken my name. But I would eventually learn that Rome-born Romans are constitutionally unable to pronounce the "th" sound, even though a great many of their words, derived from the Greek or the Gothic, are spelled that way. By every native Roman, I would be always addressed as Torn, and mine was not the only name thus elided. The Romans habitually referred to both of their onetime emperors Theodosius as Teodosius. And when, in time, the entire Western Empire came to be ruled by Theodoric, he would be known to every one of his Roman-born subjects as Teodoric.

At the bathhouse, I realized why Calidius had been so certain that the Syrian and his young eunuchs would still be occupied with their bathing, for I found that a Roman bath is a long and leisurely and luxurious ritual. A garrison bathhouse is, of course, nowhere near as opulent as any of the thermae in any real Roman city, but even this one was furnished with pools and basins and fountains of water of varying temperatures, from icy cold to tepid to comfortably warm to near-scalding hot. It was also equipped with other conveniences: an indoor court for athletic exercising or games-playing, couches for lounging, reading or holding converse, and ornaments of sculpture and mosaic for contemplation. Numerous off-duty soldiers were enjoying the accommodations: two of them were wrestling nude while their fellows cheered or jeered, others were rolling dice, a group lay listening as one of their number read a poem aloud. And everywhere about were the loinclothed slaves who did the actual bathing of the bathers and attended to their other wants or demands.

Calidius, Wyrd and I undressed in the room called the apodyterium, with a slave assisting each of us. Before we commenced to bathe, however, we hurried first to the farthest room, the balineum. There the charismatics, as naked and supple and glossy as newts—and as sexually featureless—were frolicking in the after-bath swimming pool. On the other side of the pool from us, the Syrian, still fully clothed, sat on a marble bench, possessively watching his wares. Some soldiers on other benches were also ogling them, and making comments variously comical, scornful or lecherous.

After surveying the scene only briefly, the legatus murmured to Wyrd, "That child yonder, trying to splash water up on the Syrian. That one is of an age and size like enough to my grandson. Only he is dark, and young Calidius is fair of hair. Also, his features are not very close of resemblance."

"The features do not matter," said Wyrd. "All westerners look alike to the oriental Huns, as all of them do to us. Right now, while the boy is here, have one of the slaves bleach his hair with struthium ashes. That is all that will be necessary."

When the legatus raised an arm to beckon a slave, the gesture caught the Syrian's eye. He came scurrying around the pool, to bow and scrape before us, and say:

"Ah, clarissimus magister, you waited to view my young charmers until you could see them as they *should* be seen. Naked and alluring and irresistible. Do I perceive that one of them has already taken your magisterial fancy?"

"Yes," the legatus said curtly, and then, to the slave who knelt before him, "That one," and he pointed. The slave went to fetch the child from the pool.

"Ashtaret!" exclaimed Natquin, ecstatically clasping his hands together. "The legatus has a magisterial eye, to be sure! Little Becga, the very one I might have decided to keep for myself. Almost pass for a genuine female, that one, eh? Well, clarissimus, it will nigh break my heart to part with pretty Becga. However, your humble servant would not dare to protest your selection. Instead, in admiration of your good taste, I will set a specially low price and—"

"Silence, you vile panderer!" snarled the legatus. "I am not buying, I am taking."

The trader gasped and stammered, "Quid? . . . Quidnam? . . ."

133

"Under the jus belli, I am empowered to seize private property by the rule of eminent dominion. I am seizing this one."

The small charismatic now stood before us, dripping wet, and it was clear that the operation of mutilation had been most expertly performed on him. There was nothing but a dimple to mark where his private parts had been. I wondered what sort of "plaything" such a totally sexless creature could possibly be for any sort of master. The young eunuch must have been wondering the same thing, because his eyes were fearful as they flicked from one to another of us. In his fright, the child involuntarily added to the water that was dripping off him, for a sudden slight trickle of amber liquid issued from that dimple between his thighs.

"Take him away," Wyrd said to the slave who had brought him. "Bleach his hair with struthium. The legatus will tell you when it is pale enough."

"Ger-qatleh!" bleated the trader, whatever that meant in his Syrian language. "Please, magisters, struthium is for bleaching linen. After such treatment, dear Becga's hair will eventually all fall out."

"I am aware of that," said Wyrd. "But it will not until after we have made the use of him that we intend."

"Magisters!" Natquin pleaded. "If you desire to have sport with a fair-haired charismatic, why not Blara yonder? Or Buffa? They are even prettier and more tender than Becga."

"Swine!" The legatus slapped the Syrian so hard that the man's head swiveled on his neck. "No Roman or decent outlander would ever wallow in the obscene vices of you easterners. This one of your suckling swinelets will have the honor of doing something heroic, not perverted and disgusting. Now you and the rest of them, get out of my sight!" He turned to the waiting slave. "Start treating the boy's hair while we three bathe. I will then see how the work is progressing."

So the legatus, Wyrd and I went back to the first of the bathing rooms, the unctuarium, where our attending slaves rubbed us all over with olive oil—Wyrd's slave and mine wrinkling their noses in disapproval of our exceedingly grubby condition. We went next to the athletic court, and the slaves produced for each of us a sort of paddle, its handle supporting a round and open wooden frame, the open part of it crisscrossed by strings of gut. With those paddles, we batted a round ball of felt back and forth among us until we had mixed considerable perspiration with the oil on our bodies.

Then we went to the sudatorium, a room full of steam, more dense than any Hrau Albos fog, and we sat on marble benches until the commingled oil and sweat streamed down off us. Then we lay at full length on slatted wooden tables in a room called the laconicum, while our slaves scraped the ooze off every part of us, using an assortment of different-sized, curved, spoonlike things called strigiles. Only when my slave brought his strigiles near my private parts did I push his hand away, indicating that I would do my own cleansing there. Neither Calidius nor Wyrd took any notice of that, and the slave merely shrugged, evidently supposing me to be a typically prudish country lout.

Next we immersed ourselves in the very hot pool of the calidarium, and bobbed and ducked and splashed about in that for as long as we could endure it. When we emerged, the slaves washed our hair, and Wyrd's beard, with fragrant soaps. Then we went to the tepidarium and splashed about in pools of gradually decreasing warmth, until we were able, without too great a shock, to plunge into the chilly pool of the frigidarium. When we came out of that, I felt frozen stiff, but the slaves briskly rubbed us down with thick towels, and very soon I felt wonderfully tingly, alert and alive all over—and also extremely hungry. Finally the slaves dusted us with delicately scented talcus, and we returned to the apodyterium to get dressed again.

135

We had not been overlong in our bathing—having omitted the after-bath swim and any lounging about—but somehow the therma slaves had, in that time, beautifully laundered and dried all our clothes. Even my sheepskin and Wyrd's massive bearskin cloak had been cleansed of their clotted mud and blood and their accumulation of dead leaves and twigs. My sheepskin was again white and springy, Wyrd's bearskin was shiny and fluffy—and, above it, his formerly matted gray hair and beard were as feathered-out as dandelion down, so he looked bristly all over, as quite befitted his prickly personality.

The signifer Paccius was waiting for us outside the apodyterium, and so was the slave attendant on the charismatic Becga. The little eunuch was still naked, but no longer looked frightened. In fact, he was holding a speculum and smiling at his new reflection, for his hair that had been a dark brown was now a pale gold in color, much the same hue as my own.

The legatus would not touch the creature, but had the slave tilt Becga's head this way and that. After studying the child, he said, "Yes, that is about the color I remember. Well done, slave. Paccius, take the boy to Fabius's chambers. Dress him in young Calidius's garments—they should fit nearly perfectly—and bring him again to me."

The signifer saluted, but before he could turn away, Wyrd demanded, "Paccius, what has the garrison coquus prepared for the convivium? I could eat an entire úrus, horns and hoofs and all."

"Come, come, Uiridus," said the legatus. "You will not eat of the soldiers' common convivium. You and your apprentice—now that you both look and smell human—will dine with me."

And so it was that, in the sumptuous triclinium of Calidius's mansion, I dined for the first time in the Roman fashion. That is to say, it was also the first time I had ever eaten a meal while lying down and supporting myself on one elbow. We all reclined that way, on a trio of soft couches set rather in the shape of a letter C laid flat, with the table in the middle, and the servitor slaves coming and going through the open side of the C. It was clearly not the first time that Wyrd had dined so, for he sprawled out most comfortably and ate without giving any hint of being ill at ease. I still knew nothing of Wyrd's origins, but I did know, now, that he had not always been just an outlander woodsman, and I was beginning to suspect that the rough and gruff old Forest-Stalker had also, at some time, enjoyed a social status somewhat higher than that of a decurio commanding ten auxiliaries in some Roman legion.

I myself felt extremely out of place in these surroundings, but, as young people will, I of course tried to pretend utter equanimity, and Calidius and Wyrd—and even the servants—had the good grace not to snicker at my many awkwardnesses. I was well accustomed to eating with a knife, and frequently in both of the abbeys had employed a spoon, but even those were difficult for me to use in my reclining position. Worse, there was at this table a third implement for each of us—a metal thing of two pointed tines, to be used for spearing one's cutoff bits of food and conveying them to one's mouth—and that thing really caused me some fumbling.

I took so much care to appear *not* uncomfortable in this setting that I ate slowly, but I ate voraciously. I was hungry enough, after that invigorating bath, to have eaten my own sheepskin. But this food, needless to remark, was much more elegant than would have been served in the soldiers' cenaculum, and also much more elegant than had ever been served to me anywhere else.

"I apologize for the wine," said the legatus, pouring a goblet of it for each of us. "A merely decent Formian. I wish I had a Campanian or a Lesbian with which to drink to the success of your venture, Uiridus."

Wyrd made a face, because the wine was not only watered, it was also flavored with resin. But I personally thought it more than decent.

The meal began with a soup of mashed chestnuts and lentils. The main dish was ham cooked inside an envelope of pastry crust and served in slices, with stewed figs roundabout. There was a side dish of beets and leeks cooked in raisin wine and dressed with oil and vinegar, and another side dish of something like pastry, drawn out and cut into very long, very narrow strips, dressed with garlic-flavored oil. That dish caused me the most difficulty in eating, for it was supposed to be conveyed to the mouth (I watched the others do it) by coiling the strings with the two-tined implement into knots of bite size. Even by the close of the meal, I was not managing that very well. Happily for my pretense of composure and competence, the dinner concluded with sweets easy to eat—an airy and delicate cheesecake topped with preserved Damascene plums, accompanied by tiny cups of violet wine.

At one point during the meal, a servant brought word that the signifer Paccius stood without, and the legatus ordered him shown in. He brought with him the little charismatic, now fully dressed, and more finely dressed than any child I had ever seen even in the city of Vesontio. His costume was a miniature of that worn indoors by the legatus, but more brightly colored: a tight, pale blue linen tunic, of the fashion called an alicula, embroidered with flowers all around the hem, cotton stockings and soft leather buskins of a color more yellow than the child's own new hair. Over the alicula was almost casually flung a cloak of rich red wool, pinned at one shoulder with a silver clasp.

The legatus lay where he was, and chewed while he silently inspected the child, rather like a ruminating bull. Then he only nodded approval and motioned for Paccius to take him away again. Not until they had gone did the legatus swallow loudly, heave a sigh and say with great emotion, "It could almost have *been* my lost grandson."

"Then why not just keep this one?" Wyrd asked unfeelingly. "Instead of putting *me* at mortal hazard along with the genuine grandson."

"What?!" cried the legatus, appalled. "Keep a eunuch for a—?" Then he perceived the jest. "Your mockery is not very funny, Uiridus. However, since the subject has obtruded itself upon our repast, tell me. How do you intend to substitute the one child for the other?"

"I already *have* told you," growled Wyrd. "I do not know. I must give it thought. And I refuse to think while I eat. It interferes with both the immediate enjoyment and the subsequent digestion."

"But we must prepare. Make plans. The Hun will be here within a matter of hours. Have you at least decided how many men you will take with you?"

"I know I shall need one helping pair of hands. But I would ask no one to volunteer for what may be suicide."

Once more I presumed to speak. "You need not even ask, fráuja. I mean magister. I am your apprentice in this as in everything else."

Wyrd inclined his head toward me in acknowledgment, and said to the legatus, "I will require no one else."

"Perhaps not. But there is one other I should like you to take also. My son Fabius."

"Look, man," said Wyrd. "I am attempting, and with only the faintest hope, to rescue one small remaining seed of your family tree. If I fail, everyone involved will die. That would include Fabius. And there will end all prospect of *ever* reseeding your line. This task demands cunning, patience, stealth. A rightfully outraged and distraught and desperate husband—"

"Fabius was a Roman soldier before he was a husband. He still is a Roman soldier above all else. If I put him under your command, he will obey. Think how you would feel, Uiridus, if you were he—or if you were I. As for risking his life and our family line, I have already told you that Fabius will not let himself live for long if this venture fails. He deserves the right to participate, and the opportunity of dying by some other sword than his own."

Wyrd rolled his eyes. "I remember Fabius as a robust fellow. May I at least see if he still is that?"

The legatus turned to a servant and gave the order that his son be brought, but well manacled and guarded. We were finishing our sweet when we heard a noise of jingling and of many footsteps, and in a moment there appeared in the doorway a young man who unmistakably resembled the legatus. He was in full battle dress, carrying his helmet under one arm and its parade crest under the other, but both his wrists were iron-cuffed to chains held securely by two other soldiers walking warily on either side of him. I should have expected Fabius, if it took four men to hold him, to come raging and trying to get his hands on his captor father. But he only glared at Calidius with red eyes that seemed even redder for the cold pallor of his grim visage. I think I also heard him grind his teeth, but then he saw that his father was not alone in the triclinium, and shifted his glare to me, then to Wyrd.

"Salve, Optio Fabius," Wyrd said, genially enough.

138

"Uiridus?" said the young man, peering in puzzlement, possibly because he had never seen Wyrd clean before. "Salve, Caius Uiridus. What do you here?"

"I and my apprentice Thorn are preparing to make a foray against those Huns who hold your wife and child. It is more than likely that we and they will all die of this foolhardiness. But your father suggests that you may wish to die with us."

"Wish?" gasped Fabius, some color coming into his face. "I *forbid* you to go without me!"

"I shall be in command. You must obey my every—"

"Say no more, Decurio Uiridus!" barked Fabius. "I am an optio of the Eleventh Legion!" With a sudden movement that yanked his chains and nearly jerked his warders off their feet, he snatched out from under his arm the rakishly curved metal-and-horsehair crest, and clicked it into the slot atop his helmet, and clapped the helmet on his head. "I am ready to go this instant."

"Iésus," muttered Wyrd to himself. "A Roman soldier indeed." With heavy sarcasm, he said to the young man, "What, you are bringing no trumpet to herald our parade? Go, you ninny, and discard those trappings. Tomorrow get dressed in rough woods garb. I will summon you when the time comes."

139

The four other soldiers led Fabius away, though this time he struggled against them, and shouted back, "But what do you intend, Uiridus? . . . How do we attack? . . . How many men?" and so on, to which questions neither Wyrd nor the legatus replied, and the shouting faded off in the distance.

"Iésus," Wyrd muttered again. "The Jews have a wise saying: that not even Adam would ever have taken a wife if Jehovah had not knocked him unconscious."

Calidius said nothing to that, so I made bold to speak up again. I asked permission to take some of our table scraps to feed my eagle that had been unattended all this time. The legatus only distractedly murmured, "An eagle?" but kindly gave me leave to go. So I heard no more of what he and Wyrd discussed, until somewhat later that night.

7

At the barrack, when I fed to my juika-bloth the scraps of ham left over from the dinner, all the remaining charismatic boys gathered to watch, themselves twittering like birds. They were dressed again in their rags and tatters, and again wearing their shackles, and they twittered in the Frankish version of the Old Language that I found very hard to comprehend—not that I supposed such creatures would have anything to say worth the hearing.

The swarthy Bar Nar Natquin, never far from his slave merchandise, also stood by and scowled at me and my bird. When the eagle had eaten all it wanted, and there was nothing more to watch, the boys scattered to play in the slush of the barrack yard—or to play as well as they could in leg chains. The Syrian remained, leaning against the doorpost of the room, regarding me blackly, and grumbling about the injustice of Calidius's having confiscated his little Becga without payment.

"Why, that lovely boy would have fetched ten gold nomisma in Constantinople," he said with a sniffle. "But what do I get for him? Ashtaret! Not a nummus. Meaning that I am the poorer by the five gold solidi he *cost* me. And then that prig Calidius has the audacity to inform me that my purloined charismatic will not even be put to the use for which he was created."

I said, "I cannot imagine any of your pitiful whelps being of any use at all. Certainly none that would make them as valuable as you claim."

"Ah, you must be a *Christian*," said Natquin with a sneer, as if that was a despicable thing to be. "And you are still a young one, so you doubtless still believe in all the prudish Christian inhibitions. But you will mature, you will get wiser, you will learn what every man and woman and eunuch must eventually come to know."

"And what is that?"

"You will endure the many, many aches and pains and annoyances and travails and embarrassments that the human body can inflict on its possessor. So you will come to realize that anyone would have to be an imbecile to stifle or repel the comparatively few *good* feelings that his or her or its body can provide." And he walked away.

I busied myself with unrolling the packs of Wyrd and myself, and hanging up various articles to air or unwrinkle themselves on the wall pegs the room provided. I had put there one of my own possessions, and was eyeing it speculatively, when Wyrd returned from the praesidium, carrying a number of things in his arms. He also looked at the garment I had hung up, and raised his tufty eyebrows and asked:

"What are you doing with a townswoman's gown?"

"I was thinking," I said. "You have often implied that I could pass for a female. I wondered if, when we get to the Huns' encampment, I might perhaps pass for that Lady Placidia. At least long enough for us to get her safely away."

Wyrd said drily, "I doubt that you could convincingly make yourself appear nine months pregnant. And I doubt that you would wish to lop off some of your fingers for the lady's sake."

"I had forgotten that detail," I muttered.

141

"Look you, urchin. We can thank half of all the gods there are if we get *ourselves* safely away from the Huns. Bear that in mind, and do not dream of trying any other heroics. If we also manage to rescue the boy Calidius, at the cost of only a lowly charismatic, we can thank all the rest of the gods. Now look here, what I have brought."

He dropped onto one of the bed pallets a wash-leather bag that clinked musically.

"The quickest sale I have ever made of my fur harvest, and the best price I have ever been paid, and Calidius bought them sight unseen. He also paid a handsome premium for the ibex horns. I would rejoice at all this bounty were I not unsure whether we will survive to enjoy it."

He dropped the other things he was holding.

"The legatus also made us some gifts that we may keep, if we live. A gladius short-sword for you and a securis battle-ax for me, each of them in a nicely wool-lined scabbard, so the fleece oils will prevent the blades' ever rusting. And for each of us, because we may have to lie in wait for a thirsty long time, a tin flask for carrying water, leather-bound to keep the water cold, and resined on the inside to make even stale water taste sweet."

I said, "I have never owned any things so fine."

"You will also have, courtesy of the legatus, a horse of your own."

"A horse? My own? To *keep*?"

"Ja. The Hun comes on horseback, so we will trail him the same way. We could actually do that better on foot, but we may need speed on the return trip, if there is a return trip. Have you ever ridden before, urchin?"

"Our old draft mare at the abbey."

"Sufficient. This ride will require no perfect seat or artful handling. A slow pace out, and a frantic gallop back. The charismatic Becga will ride pillion with you—and later, let us hope, the boy Calidius will."

"What exactly is your plan, fráuja?"

Wyrd scratched in his beard. "In ancient times, there was an architect named Dinocrates, who set about building a temple to Diana in which, by means of Magnes stones, a statue of that goddess would be suspended in midair. But Dinocrates died before he could finish it—or impart his plans to anyone else."

"Does that mean you will not tell me?"

"Or that my plan is equally impossible of achievement. Or that I have none at all. Take your choice. Suffice it that we will hide in the stableyard of that ferrarius on the fringe of town until the Hun makes his departure. I have bidden the legatus to detain that messenger in conversation—if he can keep from strangling the creature—until well into twilight. Then we will follow him to wherever he goes in the Hrau Albos. Until we are all gone, Basilea will remain tight-shuttered and everyone indoors. Which means I cannot go this minute, as I should dearly like, to old Dylas's taberna for some good, strong, unfancy wine. Just as well, no doubt. We shall want clear heads tomorrow."

We spent almost all of the next day in that stableyard, for we and the horses had to be there before the Hun arrived, so that he would notice no suspicious activity while he was in town. As when Wyrd and I had first come, the whole of Basilea was as silent as if every one of its citizens was holding his breath, and its streets and alleys and approach roads were empty of people, horses, dogs, even the pigs and chickens that usually wander about, rooting and pecking, in a town of whatever size. Wyrd and Fabius and I talked only desultorily, and in low tones. The boy Becga said nothing; I had never yet heard him say anything.

Fabius spoke mainly to complain, mainly about the fact that we were so few and inadequate a force—and *why* had not Wyrd enlisted more and sturdier men?

"By Mithras," grumbled the optio. "Not even letting me bring my shield-bearer. We are but two men, one boy, one eunuch and a tame *eagle.*"

"I repeat," said Wyrd. "We are not attacking, we are infiltrating. The fewer of us, the better. And if you merely feel that your rank is being insufficiently respected, I give you leave to regard Thorn here as your shield-bearer."

Then Fabius complained about the long wait:

"I want this business to be over with, and my Placidia and Calidius and the unborn young one to be back where they belong. Eheu, I am already resigned to realizing that every Hun in that camp must have raped my dear wife by now. But I shall take her back, and cherish her, nevertheless."

Wyrd shook his head. "That is one thing, Fabius, that need not trouble your mind. Your wife will still be chaste and undefiled. Not because the Huns are gallant, but because they are superstitious. They will readily rape anything from a sheep to a senator, but they will not molest a woman who is either pregnant or tainted with her monthly bleeding. They believe that would taint *them.*"

"Well," sighed the optio. "That is the best news I have heard since this ordeal began."

But I took note that Wyrd said nothing about the wife's amputated fingers, and from that I assumed that no one else had mentioned her mutilation to Fabius either. Nor did Wyrd tell Fabius that he planned not even to *attempt* to rescue his wife.

Meanwhile, I was mainly preoccupied with admiring the splendid horse that was now mine. It was a well-muscled young black stallion, with a white blaze, an alert eye and a comely stance. He even had a name—Velox—that promised speed of movement. As far as I could see, the horse had only a single physical flaw: an indentation like a large dimple on the lower left side of his neck. When I remarked on that, the optio Fabius forgot his grievances enough to say condescendingly:

"Ignorant Torn. That is a mark much to be valued on a horse. It is called 'the prophet's thumbprint.' Of what prophet, I know not, but it promises a good steed, and one of good omen. Anyway, all our horses here are of the unsurpassable Kehailan breed, from the land of Arabia Deserta. It is said that the Kehailans date from the time of Baz, the great-great-grandson of Noah."

I was properly awed to have been given a mount of such ancient lineage, and I was about to say so, but Wyrd made a sudden gesture for

143

us to be quiet. We joined him where he stood, crouched and peering through a chink in the wattles of the stableyard wall. There, we could hear the distant but approaching thwock-thwock of a horse plodding along the slushy road. It came into view, a very shaggy horse considerably smaller than our three. "One of the scruffy Zhmud breed," muttered Fabius, and Wyrd again motioned for him to hush.

I was more interested to see the rider, for this was my first glimpse of a Hun. He rather resembled his horse, in being smaller than the average, for he was shorter even than myself, and exceedingly ugly. He was of a dirty yellowish-brown complexion, with long, stringy, greasy black hair, eyes that were only slitted pouches, and no beard, but some straggly wisps of mustache. Unprepossessing though he was, he sat his horse superbly, and he might have been born to do that, for his legs were so bowed as to clasp tightly his horse's barrel body. The Hun was dressed about as raggedly as the boy Becga had earlier been, and his horse was winter-worn and ribby. The man carried the same sort of bow as did Wyrd, but his was unstrung, and he held it high to display a scrap of dirty white cloth tied to its tip.

Fabius was beside me, and I could feel him twitching during the long minutes it took the Hun to pass beyond our vision. The charismatic Becga, though—because no one had yet suggested to him that this or some other Hun would probably be his new master—peered only incuriously through the wattles. As soon as the rider was well out of earshot, Wyrd stood erect and said:

"I shall creep along after him, and make sure that he does enter the garrison, and that the legatus welcomes him—with no trickery on either part. Now, it is midday, and the ferrarius here has been ordered to provide a meal for us. So you go, Thorn, and tell him his wife can commence cooking. When I return, we will all eat—and eat to bursting, for not even Mithras knows when we may get another chance."

I duly went and told the ferrarius to see that his wife supplied ample provender. She was setting it out for us—a hearty fish stew ladled onto large round trenchers of bread, which served both as our plates and as part of the meal—when Wyrd came back. He reported that the messenger and the legatus were not killing or even assailing one another, and that Calidius was, as requested, obviously going to draw out the negotiations and keep the Hun there as late in the day as possible.

"But eat quickly," he told us. "At any instant, the little fiend may suspect something amiss and make a dash for the forest. If he does not, then let us go *on* eating for as long as we can stuff ourselves."

Wyrd also said, and to me only, out of Fabius's hearing, "I presume the hostages are still alive. At any rate, the villain brought another of the Lady Placidia's fingers, and, as best I could see from concealment, it appeared freshly cut."

Evidently nothing untoward occurred up at the garrison to alarm the visiting Hun, or to arouse his suspicion. And the legatus must have kept him pleasantly plied with wine and viands, while arguing over the details of delivering Roman army property—how much and when and where—in exchange for the Huns' captives, because that day dragged uneventfully but suspensefully on and on.

The agitated Fabius cursed and paced about the stableyard, and the placid Becga simply sat impassively waiting. I passed the time in befriending my new horse, Velox, as the ferrarius suggested I do. The man gave me some calamint, and I rubbed and crumbled that fragrant herb between my hands, then carressed Velox's muzzle and neck and chest and withers, an attention the horse obviously enjoyed. Meanwhile, Wyrd, to the vexation of the smithwife, kept demanding additional food from her, and kept making the rest of us gorge on it, to repletion and beyond.

145

But finally Wyrd cocked an ear in the direction of the town's center, then put an abrupt halt to all our noise and activity by waving his arms violently. Again we all stole close to the yard wall to watch through the cracks. The Hun was now in more of a hurry, or his nag had been refreshed by its long rest, or both, for it was coming at a brisk trot through the early dusk. Horse and rider crossed our vision again, going the other way, and were no sooner past the yard than Fabius hissed, "Let us hasten! Before he is out of sight!"

"I want him out of sight!" snapped Wyrd, but not loudly. "The Huns have eyes in their anuses. Anyway, his tracks will be fresh and distinct enough. There has been little traffic on these roads in recent days."

So we had to wait some more, until Wyrd at last gave the word to mount. I set my juika-bloth on my shoulder, then led Velox by his reins to a mounting block. From that eminence, I clambered awkwardly into the saddle, then reached down to hoist Becga to the pillow fastened behind me. My saddle and bridle and reins were not, of course, bedizened with medallions and pendants and inlays, as were those of Optio Fabius, but they were genuine military gear. The saddle was of leather stiffened inside with bronze plates, and had projections molded into it to help a rider keep his seat. I was not surprised to see Fabius mount his horse more dashingly than I had done—vaulting clear from the ground to the saddle—and not *too* surprised to see old Wyrd just as lithely make the same leap.

The ferrarius opened a gate for us, and we filed out into the road. We proceeded at only a slow walk, Wyrd in the lead, bent over in his saddle to scan the road's churned mud and slush, and Fabius crowded close behind him, doing the same. I was at first excited to be on the trail of a hellion Hun, but after a while the plodding nature of the chase got tiresome, and I thrilled more to the simple fact of being astride a fine horse. Even at a walk, and even with a saddle between us, Velox communicated to me a feeling of coiled tension, of muscles charged with unleashed energy, of the fire and might of a horse-sized volcano just waiting for permission to erupt. I do not know whether little Becga, behind me, could feel that, too, but he kept his arms clasped tight about my waist, as if fearful that I might urge Velox into a gallop that would take the horse right out from under him.

Then, suddenly, Wyrd halted his own horse and said, in some puzzlement, "The Hun turned off the road here. Why so soon?"

Fabius, from sitting on his saddle, gave another athletic bound and was *standing* on it. He peered through the trees bordering the road on the left, the direction Wyrd had indicated, and after a moment said, "He is out of sight. But the tracks are not."

So, Wyrd still leading, we too turned off the road there and continued on, through stands of trees and open pastures and farmlands. We went even more slowly than before, lest we should get too close and come within our quarry's sight. Then Wyrd again halted suddenly, and growled:

"By the self-castrated priests of Cybele, but the Hun has turned again! Turned *back* toward Basilea."

Fabius asked, "Could he be seeking to discover if he *is* being followed?"

"Perhaps. Still, we have no choice but to stay on his trail."

And we did, though now very, very slowly, and after a long, long while—by which time the twilight had deepened almost to darkness—Wyrd halted yet again, and loudly bellowed a string of curses that must have jarred every god and saint in every heaven of every religion. I should have thought the noise would have alerted the Hun ahead of us, but apparently that was no matter, because Wyrd concluded his profanity thus:

"By the bloat and bursting of Judas Iscariot, the creature did not head for Basilea at all! He has circled around it to the riverside well above the town. He would have had some kind of scow waiting for him and his horse, and he is probably across the Rhenus by now. Optio Fabius! Ride like the wind—to the Basilea docks. Get barges and barge-men, enough to ferry all of us. Bring them, rush them—whip them if necessary—upstream to where you find us waiting. Go!"

The optio was off like an arrow, and my Velox seemed to await only a nudge to lunge away just as fast, but Wyrd said:

"No need for us to hurry, urchin. Oh vái, if that traitor slave told the truth—and I believe he did—that the Huns had gestured south toward the Hrau Albos as their lurking place, then they were deliber-ately deceiving even him. And now me. They are somewhere to the north of the river Rhenus, and perhaps not very far from it, for who would think to look for mountain bandits there in the lowlands?"

So we kept on following the tracks, neither hurrying nor dawdling, and the darkness came down so that I could not even see the trail in the snow, but Wyrd seemed to have no difficulty. Eventually that led us to a shelving gravel bank of the river and, as Wyrd had predicted, there were discernible scrapes and gouges in the shingle to indicate that a flat-bottomed vessel of some sort had first landed, then been shoved off from there. Wyrd cursed some more, but there was little else we could do, so we dismounted and topped up our flasks with river water, and waited.

147

We did not have to wait for too long. A chronic complainer Fabius might have been, but he was a decisive man of action when action was called for. The night was not far along when Wyrd and Becga and I saw the darkness begin to lighten a little in the west, and then the light became separate lanterns, three of them, casting long, contorted, zig-zagging reflections on the turbulent river waters. As I have said, the Rhenus upstream of Basilea is of very rapid current, so the three barges, although they were poled by many men in each, had indeed made good time in reaching us. I should have not been surprised to see Fabius actually flailing and lashing the bargemen as they approached. But the boats were out in the water, and he of course came riding along the bank. When he found us, Fabius did not shout to the bargemen, but hooted like an owl—evidently a prearranged signal—to summon them to turn toward shore.

"Good work, Optio," Wyrd said as Fabius dismounted. "If the Huns left a watchman on the opposite bank, he will have seen nothing but three lanterns. So do not extinguish those lights. Detach three of the bargemen to carry one lantern apiece, and to continue afoot along this bank. They are to stay beside the water, and keep on until morning, or until they drop, whichever happens first. The remaining men will have to ferry us across in the dark—and in silence."

Accordingly, three of the newcomers, at slightly staggered intervals, trudged upriver carrying the lanterns. Any Hun spying from the other side would have supposed the barges to have gone past him without stopping. Meanwhile, as quietly as possible, we trackers boarded for the crossing. I might have expected our horses to balk at what must have seemed to them an unnatural mode of transport, but they were evidently veterans at the practice and made no demur. Neither did Becga, who must have crossed other waters on his way from the Frankish lands. The only hesitant and awkward boarder was myself—"Vái, you step like a mincing woman!" sneered one of the bargemen, who had to grab my elbow to steady me—because this was the first time in my life I had ever got into a boat of any sort.

Wyrd said there was no way of guessing how far the river's swift current might have carried the Hun's barge downstream during its crossing, so he commanded our bargemen to pole as strongly as they could, to take us as straight across the Rhenus as possible. Once we were on the other side, he said, we could make our own way down along the bank and find where the Hun had landed. So the men at the poles did their strenuous best, but, in the darkness, I doubt that any of our party could tell—certainly I could not—whether we made the passage in a direct line or on a long diagonal. All I knew for sure was that the river raged and foamed against the upstream side of our barge, and repeatedly lapped and splashed over its edge. Not to get totally soaked by the frigid water, we passengers in the three boats, like the polers, all stood during the crossing. And, for fear that the river might get even rowdier and come pouring in to sink us, I clung protectively to Becga with my one arm and hooked my other securely about the neck of the imperturbable and solid-standing Velox. The juika-bloth, as if it was being protective of *me*, clung tight to my shoulder, though it could have winged its way across with ease.

We were a long time upon the cold, black river—or so it seemed to me—and the black air was much colder than it had been on land, chilling us first to discomfort, then to misery, then to near numbness. But suddenly there were branches clawing at my coat's cowl and my horse's mane. Either the river was high enough to have overflowed the roots of the bankside trees or we had come to shore in a grove of some kind of water-growing trees. Anyway, the water gurgled and swashed so loudly among those trees as to cover all the noises of our disembarking. And we did make noise, because even the horses were stiff with cold, and clumsy as they clambered overboard and scrabbled from the shallows up to dry ground.

Wyrd bade Becga hold the horses' reins, and drew me and Fabius aside and told us, "From here, to find the spot where the Hun landed, we must go quietly. That means we go afoot."

"Why?" demanded Fabius. "That could take until morning, or even all of tomorrow. The Hun and his boatmen may have been swept many miles downstream, perhaps far beyond Basilea itself."

"And they may not, so keep your voice down. They may have come ashore just a few stadia from this spot. That is why we go on foot and in silence—my apprentice, the eunuch and myself. Optio, you will stay here with the horses, the barges and their men."

"What?! Gerrae! For how long?"

"I said keep your voice down. And *you* said you would obey my commands. You will remain here until Thorn and I return—bringing that which we came for, I devoutly hope."

"What?!" Fabius fairly roared it this time, and Wyrd slapped him across the face with the back of his hand. That did not silence the irate soldier, but it made him argue less loudly. "You and two children will make the chase and the assault without me? And I am to play nursemaid to horses and dockside drudges? I will be damned by Mithras if I do!"

"Damned or not, Optio, that is precisely what you are to do. When we three find the Hun's landing place, we cannot take time to come back and collect you. We must pursue him as closely as we can. Then, afterward—whatever happens—if we return at all, we will be in a headlong hurry. We must know exactly where the horses are, and they must *be* right here, and so must the barges and their polers. Do you imagine those dockside drudges—knowing that there are savage Huns somewhere in this vicinity—would obligingly wait here for us without someone to *make* them wait? You are the only one who can do that, and do it you will."

Fabius continued to argue and demand and cajole—reasonably, bitterly, angrily, piteously by turns—while Wyrd and I prepared to leave, but Wyrd did not trouble to refute or even reply to any of his plaints. I took my belted short-sword from where it hung on Velox's saddle

149

horn, and buckled that about my waist, and tucked my sling also into the belt where it would be handy, and, with my juika-bloth on my shoulder, I was ready to go. Wyrd belted on his short-handled ax, and arranged his war bow and quiver of arrows behind his shoulder. Little Becga had nothing to do but hand over the horses' reins to Fabius, who finally, reluctantly, resignedly ceased his pleading and said only, "Ave, Uiridus, atque vale."

"Te morituri salutamus," Wyrd said, not entirely ironically, and beckoned for me and Becga to follow him.

I was amazed by Wyrd's ability to lead us through the enveloping darkness and the dense riverside brush, keeping us always close beside the water without any of us ever falling into it. Despite the heavy going and the fast pace that Wyrd set, he made his way almost silently, and somehow traced a path that enabled me and Becga to follow him not much more noisily, though after a while I was nearly having to drag the poor feeble little charismatic like a sack behind me. And after our having been quite frozen during the river crossing, we were now so arduously exercised that we sweated beneath our woods clothing.

150

I have no idea how long or how far we traveled, but it was not a matter of hours or miles. The Hun messenger must have had almost as many men poling his vessel as ours had had, for his also had crossed without much deflection by the current, and had landed well upstream of Basilea. Only when, in the dark, I bumped into Wyrd's back did I realize that he had espied the beached boat and stopped still. Peering over his shoulder, I could make out a rough-hewn scow that had been pulled up from the water, well into the concealing brush, and I could see that it was empty. We three stood motionless, trying not to pant or even to breathe, while Wyrd listened and looked all about. At last, he put a hand on my chest, indicating that Becga and I should stay where we were, and he disappeared into the darkness as silently and completely as a shadow. After another while, he just as magically reappeared in front of me, and whispered:

"They seem to have left no guards. Help me shove the scow back into the stream—and quietly, quietly."

Of course, that could not be done entirely without sound; the vessel was much too heavy for us to lift, and our shoving it over the bankside ground made much scraping noise. But I realized why we were doing that. When—or if—we crossed the river again in our barges, the Huns would be hampered in their pursuit of us. Anyway, when we had got the scow launched, and seen it drift away, slowly revolving on the current, no Hun had yet materialized to challenge us. So Wyrd said without whispering, but still in a guarded voice:

"I followed their trail a little way. They were in too much of a hurry to take great precaution against leaving tracks. And from their hurry, I judge that they knew they had not too far to go. We cannot move as fast—we *must* be cautious and quiet—but we should come upon their lair well before morning light. You and the eunuch stay as far behind me as you can without losing me entirely. There may yet be sentries posted along the way, and there certainly will be some picketed around the perimeter of their camp. When you see or hear me halt, you two freeze stone-still."

The Huns must have supposed themselves entirely free of pursuers, because, as Wyrd had commented, they would have expected no one to seek them in the lowlands. At any rate, we came upon no guards along the trail. The first and only time that Wyrd paused that night was when he—and Becga and I, too—saw beyond the trees a dim red glow that might have been the first pale flush of dawn, except that it was in the north. Wyrd, however, well out ahead of us, saw something that Becga and I did not. He slid silently sideways into some trees, so we two hunkered down where we were. I heard a distant and momentary small noise, as of a brief scuffle among the dry bushes, and then Wyrd reappeared where we had last seen him, waving an arm to summon us to join him.

When we did, we found him bending over a Hun who lay dead on the ground, and Wyrd was loosing his own war bow from around the neck of the corpse, for he had throttled the man with his bowstring. Wyrd said nothing, and neither did we, and all together we crept toward the red glow. It gradually brightened as we got nearer to it, and finally outlined for us a hilltop crested with trees, among which we could discern no other lurking sentries. So, on hands and knees, we climbed the low hill and, toward its top, we lay flat on our bellies and crawled like beetles.

When we breasted the crown of the hill, we were looking down into a dale nearly barren of trees and lighted by a number of campfires. The trees had been felled, as we could see by the firelight, for the makeshift construction of a few crude huts, and those were encircled by a number of mean, patchwork hide tents. At the farther side of the dale was a picket line of tethered horses, all of them gaunt and shaggy scrubs. And

151

moving about in the clearing, even at this hour, were some twoscore persons. Since Wyrd, Becga and I were more than a hundred paces above and distant from the camp, I could not tell, by the people's ragged and shabby dress, which were men and which women. But, from their stunted stature and bandy legs, they all were unmistakably Huns.

8

152

"The woman and boy will be together, and in one of those huts. Easier for their captors to guard them that way." Wyrd had edged over beside me so he could speak quietly into my ear. "You keep watch, and see if there is any indication of which hut they occupy. I have more killing to do."

I said, "I have seen you shoot arrows with incredible rapidity and accuracy, but surely there are too many Huns down there for you to—"

"Ja. Still, the very number of them may later prove to be to our advantage. I shall only be killing the other sentries roundabout, and I must do that while it is full night. Meantime, you plaster your face and hands with mud, so they do not shine so. Yours and the eunuch's. At least you two will pass as Huns in the dark, if necessary, which I cannot, with this beard."

"What do you mean—if necessary?"

"I mean in case I do not return. Should one of the sentries catch me before I catch him, there will be some uproar attendant on my dying. In that commotion, you two may be able to make your escape unnoticed. Or even proceed with the rescue attempt, if you can devise some way to do it."

"Iésus!" I gasped. "I hope I do not have to try."

"So do I," Wyrd said drily, and wriggled away.

With my sword, I dug up and crumbled some clods of earth, then poured a dollop of water from my flask and made mud. I coated Becga's face with it, and he mine, and that sufficiently dirtied our hands as well. We were not exactly Hun-colored when we got done, but we were much less visible. Then I told Becga to keep a lookout behind and about, lest some vagrant Hun stumble upon us, and I concentrated on watching the encampment.

Time passed—what seemed to me a great deal of time—but nothing in the nature of an uproar erupted anywhere beyond the dale, and the activity down there continued to appear placid enough. Then I and the juika-bloth on my shoulder started in unison as Becga tapped my back to warn me of someone's approach. I could almost have sobbed with grateful relief when it turned out to be Wyrd.

"There were five more," he said into my ear as he stretched out beside me. "That would be about the usual guard roster for an encampment of this size, so I can hope that I have got them all."

I only gazed at him in wide-eyed admiration—this old man had silently and efficiently slain six armed, alert, murderous savages, and he was not even panting from the exertion—until he said with some impatience, "Well? What occurs here?"

I pointed and said, "At most of the huts, there have been at least one or two persons going in and out through their door flaps. But that one yonder, farthest from us—the hut backed up against the hill opposite—the hide flap has been lifted just once, and from inside. A Hun leaned out but did not emerge—a female, I think it was—and handed some kind of bowl to another Hun who was passing by. That one filled it with coals from one of the fires and returned it to the female, and she took it inside and has not opened the flap again."

"A brazier to keep the prisoners comfortable," said Wyrd. "And the hut farthest from the approach route. That has to be the one. Good work, urchin. Let us make our way around to that hill behind it."

Wyrd having already once made the circuit of the dale, and with no guards to impede us—we passed two of them, lying inert—we were able to proceed fairly rapidly along the heights surrounding the clearing. Nevertheless, the night was well along by now, and I thought I could detect a faint lightening of the sky in the east. Atop the low hill behind the selected hut, we three again lay down and regarded the scene below.

None of the ramshackle huts had a back door flap or any window openings. Of this one, all we could see was the rear wall of slovenly cut limbs and branches, standing more or less upright but leaning untidily this way and that, and above the wall a roof of nothing but piled brush. Both in front and back of the hut, an occasional Hun went by on some

153

errand or another—carrying wood for the fires or armloads of torn-up dry grass for the horses.

Wyrd said, as if thinking aloud, "I doubt that there is more than one woman in there, guarding the captives. The chief of the band and his best warriors and the newly returned messenger will all be elsewhere, in one or more of the other huts, discussing and celebrating the garrison's surrender of ransom. But let us make sure. Urchin, give me your eagle to hold. You go down there and sneak a look through the gaps in that hut wall."

"What? But there are Huns going back and forth."

"As I said, there is sometimes safety in numbers. These Huns cannot all know every other of them at a glance, at least not in the dark. Simply walk bowlegged and, if you meet one, grumble, 'Aruv zerko kara.' In the Hunnish tongue that means, more or less, 'What a skeity foul night.'"

"But this has been quite a clement night."

"To the Huns, all things are foul. Move."

Not with great enthusiasm, I slithered on my belly down the low hillside, then waited until no one was about before I stood up and sauntered toward the hut. One Hun did come along, burdened with a tangle of leather harness, and to him I said, in the hoarsest voice I could manage, "Aruv zerko kara." He grunted back only, "Vakh!"—which sounded as if he agreed with me—and kept on going. I sidled close along the hut wall and peered in through one of the many chinks. The brazier glowing within gave enough light for me to see at least the number of occupants. When I had, without incident, returned to lie down again between Wyrd and Becga, I reported:

"Ja, fráuja, only the one woman Hun—if it is a woman—awake and tending the coals. There are two other figures, one woman-sized, one smaller, seated and swaddled in furs and evidently asleep, but they do not seem to be bound or shackled. There is very little else to be seen in there—a water jar, some mats, no more. And the hut is no impregnable prison. The wall's sticks are held upright and together only by magpie bits and pieces of thong. I could easily cut my way inside, except that the guardian woman would instantly screech an alarm."

"Perhaps she would not, if her attention was bent on something else. I notice that these people are extremely careless of the sparks from their fires, and this hollow seems to catch some wind and swirl it about. The Huns will suppose it to be only an accident when one of those other huts' roof brush catches fire, but it ought to cause some turmoil. You and the eunuch get back down there. Walk about, but never far from the prison hut, and wait for me to arrange the turmoil."

"We dare not wait too long," I cautioned. "The day is coming perceptibly upon us."

"Vái! Since I do not look as Hun-like as you two, I cannot so easily stroll about, but I will be as quick as I can. Anyway, as soon as the camp is in confusion, here is what you are to do." He gave us our instructions in very few words, set my eagle again on my shoulder, and then he was gone, circling toward a different side of the clearing.

As bidden, Becga and I slid down the hill, then quite brazenly stood up and ambled about—now both of us walking bowlegged—back and forth behind the hut. Twice a Hun passed us, and each time I growled, "Aruv zerko kara," and got the same grunted "Vakh!" in reply, but neither man gave even my juika-bloth a second look. Becga as usual said nothing, but each time screwed up his muddy face in disgust at the repellent body smell wafted by the passing man. Because the little charismatic never *had* said a word in my hearing, and because his apathy had for so long continued undisturbed, and because he did now at least demonstrate a distaste for the Huns, I feared he might take this last chance to bolt for freedom, so I kept tight hold of his upper arm.

The light in the clearing beyond the hut suddenly became a much brighter red, and I briefly heard the crackling noise of brush on fire. Then that noise was drowned by a loud cacophony of shouts—"Vakh!" audible among them, in several voices—and the pounding of running feet. I swiftly drew my short-sword and hauled Becga to the hut's back wall and peered again through a crack. The Hun woman inside moved from the brazier to the door flap, lifted it and looked out. Over her shoulder I could see a confusion of running figures and, above them, the roof of a hut across the dale burning merrily. As quietly but quickly as possible, I began slashing the thongs that held the hut wall together, and yanking away the pieces of wood as they came loose.

It was just a moment's work for me to breach the wall and shoulder my way inside, dragging Becga behind me. But he, or some part of his garments, caught on some projection of the wood there. We were momentarily halted and, despite the noise out front, the Hun woman heard us behind her. She turned, dropping the hide flap and opening her mouth. Too far from her to use my sword, I gasped, "Sláit!" and my juika-bloth leapt from me toward the woman.

The bird was doubtless as surprised and confounded as she was, for

155

I had never before commanded it to "kill!" another human being—
except Brother Peter, and that time I had made certain that Peter
seemed to the eagle to be something other than a human being. So
now, though the juika-bloth obediently flew straight at the Hun female,
it made no attempt to drive beak or talons into her. Still, its fluttering
full in her face made the woman dodge violently and neglect to scream
for help, at least long enough for me to get entirely inside the hut, and
for me to lunge and swing my sword and cut the woman's throat. A
scream did come out of her, but an almost soundless scream, a gush and
spray of blood from the severed vessels and windpipe of her neck.

Meanwhile, the captive woman and boy had awakened, and were
whimpering as they struggled out of the stinking furs in which they
were wrapped. No doubt they, now finding new and mud-faced persons
looming over them, were more terrified than they already had been. I
quickly knelt beside the woman and clapped a hand over her mouth.
Becga, imitating me, did the same with the boy.

"Clarissima Placidia, we are friends, come to help," I whispered to
her, as she clawed futilely at my muffling hand with what remained of
both of her own. "Do not make a sound. If there is to be any rescue,
you must do just as I say. Tell that to your son as well."

My speaking in Latin must have given her confidence in us. She
nodded and I removed my hand, and she told young Calidius to follow
our instructions. Shed of the furs, the lady Placidia was clad only in a
sheer, almost transparent undershirt, bulged out by her grossly swollen
abdomen and its protruding knob of navel. Her long hair was a mare's
nest of tangles and snarls, and her face was haggard, but her eyes still
showed some spirit. I turned to her son, and in the dim light from the
brazier he *could* have passed for Becga, or vice versa. He was of exactly
the same height and slightness, and he was fair of hair and complexion,
and he was dressed in much the same sort of fine garments that the
charismatic wore under his heavy woods clothing.

"Becga, take off your cloak and boots," I said to him, and to the
woman: "Lady Placidia, help your son get quickly into them."

That occasioned quite a flurry of activity among us, because, while
the exchange was being made, I was also—with water from the jar in
the hut—washing off Becga's face mud and smearing what I could of it
onto the face of young Calidius.

"Now, my lady—" I began, but was interrupted. The tumult of noise
outside had been still going on, but it suddenly got louder and different.

Now, to the crackle of brush fire and the hubbub of shouts and curses was added the muted rumble of hoofs. I went to the door, stepping over the dead Hun—where my juika-bloth was calmly making a meal at the gaping neck wound—moved the hide flap just a little aside and peeked out. All of the Huns' scruffy horses were loose in the clearing. Obviously Wyrd had cut their picket line and driven them in among the huts and tents and campfires. Now, confused by their freedom, frightened by the still-blazing brush roof, the glary-eyed animals were milling about, running hither and yon, dodging the frantic grabs of their likewise milling masters.

"More distraction. Good," I murmured, then bent and picked up one of the blanket furs. Using it to protect my hands, I lifted the hot clay dish of coals and held it against the underside of the hut's roof, where the dry brush immediately began to burn. "Lady Placidia, as soon as this roof is well aflame, I want you to clasp your son to your side—not your son, but this substitute child—and together run out into the clearing, as if you are fleeing the blaze."

"But—" she said, then stopped, for she had fully comprehended our plan on the instant. She shut her eyes and swallowed once or twice, and I could see a tremor go all down her nearly nude body. But then she opened her eyes, looked at me squarely and bravely and said, "Take good care of Calidius."

"I will, my lady. Go now," I said, for the roof was already burning so fiercely that we were all crouching away from the heat.

She paused only long enough to hug her son and kiss him, then put an arm around the charismatic—then paused again, and bent to kiss *him*—before she and he leapt over the dead Hun woman guardian and burst out through the door flap. Because the hide went on flapping several times afterward, I could see that one of the Hun men out there had presence of mind enough to leave off chasing the horses, and to seize both Placidia and Becga, and to hold them tight.

I called softly, "Juika-bloth," and the bird came not too reluctantly away from its feeding, for now sparks and embers were falling from the roof. I took Calidius's hand and led him out through the gap I had torn in the rear wall. As might have been expected, there were no Huns going back and forth behind that hut on routine errands. But the dawn was now far enough along—and the whole dale so brightly lighted, besides, by the two flaming roofs—that I feared we would be sighted if we tried to climb the hillside. So, holding the boy close, I slipped behind

157

a thick tree's trunk, where I could peek around it and watch what happened in the clearing, while we waited for Wyrd to come and tell us what to do next.

Some of the Huns had caught some of the horses, some were still chasing other horses that continued to elude them, some were busily carrying out various contents of the first hut that had caught fire, and the one Hun was still holding Placidia and Becga in grim embrace. I was afraid that soon the Huns would think to come and look inside the newly burning hut, to see why the captives' guardian had not also fled the fire. But that did not happen. Something else did, and something that was not in Wyrd's plan.

The turmoil in the clearing suddenly became chaos. Those Huns holding horses let go of them, and men and horses were all again running wildly about, for yet another horse had galloped into the encampment. There was a man astride it and he was violently, efficiently swinging a battle-ax. He had already cut down two Huns before I realized that the attacker was not Wyrd.

It was Optio Fabius, of course, but he was not riding the bay horse on which he had left Basilea. He was riding my black Velox, no doubt because Velox's saddle was backed with a pillow seat, and on that Fabius no doubt hoped that his wife and son would soon be riding. It was a vain hope, and he had been foolish to follow us. Had Wyrd not already disposed of the guards beyond the camp perimeter, the optio would have been dead before he got anywhere near here. And now, despite Wyrd's prepared distractions, despite Fabius's own advantage of surprise assault, the odds were simply too much against him.

Impatient, impetuous and foolish he certainly was, but valiant he most certainly was, too. His galloping about the clearing took him several times out of my sight, but he hacked down at least two more Huns that I could see, before something occurred to check his furiously swinging ax arm. The Hun who was holding the two captives threw Becga to the ground, and planted a foot on him, to free an arm to draw his sword, and that blade he laid across Placidia's throat, while he yanked back on her hair to raise her head. Where they stood, they were well illuminated by the blaze of the hut I had set afire, so Fabius saw them. When he did, he reined Velox so abruptly to a halt that the horse reared. What the optio might have done next will never be known. For, in that moment when he was off balance, unable to swing his ax or otherwise defend himself, the surrounding Huns leapt upon him. They did not use their own weapons, but merely by weight of numbers dragged Fabius off his saddle and down to the ground, and let Velox trot away unscathed.

When Fabius was down, and struggling under a heap of the savages, the Hun holding Placidia removed his sword from across the woman's throat, but only to allow for a good swing backward. Then, still clutching her hair, he shoved her body away from him, and slashed with the sword as hard as he might have hewn at a tree, and cut her head cleanly off her neck. It must have been the female half of my nature that made me instantly and instinctively cover little Calidius's eyes. And I kept my hand over them during the subsequent occurrences.

The head dangling by its hair from the Hun's fist drizzled only a little blood and other substances from its stump, and its eyes blinked only a few times before ceasing, half-lidded. But the body lying supine on the ground spouted a good deal of blood from its neck stalk, and its arms and legs convulsed so that the light shift it wore got rucked up to expose all its nether parts. They were exposed not just to the degenerate Huns, but also to Fabius. He was by now pinned prone on the ground, two or three Huns holding each of his extremities, but another holding his head so that he had to regard what had been his wife. Then another Hun did something even more outrageous. He tore at the optio's lower garments, and ripped them away, so that *his* bottom also was exposed. Next, that Hun hiked up his own ragged tunic to reveal that his male organ was erect, and he flung himself down upon the helpless Fabius to rape him intra rectum.

However, Fabius was not yet entirely helpless. He was unable to break free of his captors, but he could writhe and twist enough to prevent the rapist's penetration. At last, frustrated, the Hun stood up again, snarled "Vakh!" and spoke some words of apparent instruction to his fellows. They, holding tight and tugging at Fabius's hands and feet, turned him over onto his back, and one of their number in charge of his head turned it again so he had to regard his wife's dead body. This time, when he did, such an expression of horror came over the optio's face that I looked away from his predicament to see what he saw.

The Hun who had slain Placidia was now striding away, with Becga like a sack of meal under one arm. He had dropped Placidia's head so that it lay also seeming to regard her body with its half-opened eyes. The body had ceased convulsing, and now its limbs only twitched, as do those of a horse flicking off flies. But its legs twitched themselves apart, and farther apart, and farther apart. And the swollen abdomen

159

above slowly collapsed, with little heavings and ripplings, like a blown-up bladder that had been pricked with a splinter. And out from between the twitching legs there gushed a quantity of fluids of various viscosities, and then there slowly, very slowly extruded a slimy, shapeless mass of something pulpy, colored dark red and bluish purple. When it was entirely out on the ground, the mass briefly throbbed and gave a wail—only a short, thin sound, but audible where I was—and then lay still and shiny and silent.

Its wail was echoed by Fabius with an agonized scream. I do not know whether he screamed at what he had just seen or at what was being done to him. The lecherous Hun so eager to violate him now took out a blade—no sword, just a belt knife—and carefully, almost delicately made a short incision in the optio's belly skin, just above the crotch hair. Then the Hun tucked his knife away, lowered himself onto Fabius's pinned-down body, thrust his fascinum into that slit and began pumping away as he would have done with a woman. Fabius did not scream again, and he did not even struggle any more, but only hopelessly stared, with eyes that had gone quite mad, at the remnants of his wife and second child.

Then I nearly gave a squeal myself, when again a hand fell upon my shoulder from behind. But it was Wyrd, looking very tired and rather melancholy, as he gazed upon the scene before us.

"Pluto would come up from hell to see such things," he murmured, then beckoned for me and Calidius to follow him.

He led us, all of us loping along in a crouch, around the outer edge of the clearing to where he had two horses tethered to a tree. One was my Velox, the other was one of the Huns' shaggy Zhmud horses, wearing a saddle and bridle even more decrepit than itself.

"We must steal quietly away," Wyrd whispered to me. "But once out of their hearing, we can break into a gallop and, I think, get clean away. The Huns will be so happily entertaining themselves with Fabius that it ought to be a good while before they even begin to wonder how their guards let him through."

He hoisted the little boy up onto Velox's saddle, telling him, "You have been a very good and brave Roman, so far, Calidius. Just continue to do so, and to remain silent, and we will soon have you home."

"And my mother and father?" asked the boy, frowning in puzzled recollection of what he had seen before I covered his eyes. "Will they be coming, too?"

"Soon or later, boy, everyone gets home. Now hush, and enjoy the ride."

Wyrd and I leading the horses at a quick but quiet pace, we headed due west. At first I thought we were taking a circuitous route to confuse the eventual pursuers, but we kept on going west, and finally I asked Wyrd why we were not returning to the barges. "Because they will not still be there," he growled. "Or at least we cannot trust that they are, without Fabius holding the bargemen at sword's point. So we are going to the broad, slow and shallower north-flowing stretch of the Rhenus, where we and the horses can swim across. If we can make it to the western bank before the Huns catch up to us, they will not dare follow us into garrison territory."

After a moment, I said, "Fabius was foolish. But he was gallant."

"Ja," Wyrd sighed. "I was not too much surprised at his arrival. And I could only hope that you had effected the substitution of sons before Fabius came to disarrange our plans. By Wotan the Goer, but you did well, urchin."

"The lady Placidia was also gallant, or I could not have done it. And Fabius, what will become of him?"

"The Huns will go on doing what you saw — taking turns — until they tire of him, or until he is about to bleed to death. Then, while he is yet alive and conscious, they will give Fabius to their women."

"What? The female Huns will likewise use him so?"

"Ne, ne. They will take their pleasure in putting him to death, and they have a unique way of doing that. The Hun men do not allow their women to wield knives — probably for good reasons of self-protection. So the women will use sharp shards of broken pottery to nick and chip and mince the prisoner to death. That takes quite a while. Fabius will be glad when it is over."

"And Becga, what of him?"

Wyrd shrugged. "Akh, the charismatics are bred and broken to be basely used, and are corrupted in their minds to accept such usage passively. But that one — I think Becga is safe even from molestation, for a time at least."

I could not see why, if the Huns would so eagerly take turns at raping a ruggedly masculine Roman man, they would restrain themselves with a compliant little eunuch in their grasp. But before I could inquire about that, Wyrd said, "I believe we have sneaked far enough. Let us mount now and gallop. Atgadjats!"

I stood upon a stump to get into my saddle, and Calidius moved to the pillow behind, and held me tightly about the waist, as Becga had done. Wyrd again vaulted from the ground to his horse's back, and, scraggy though this one was in appearance, it answered the kick of his heels with an instant burst of speed, and tirelessly kept up that pace.

So, while all about us the dawn brightened to full daylight, I did two more things for the first time in my life. For one, I rode a fine horse at full gallop, which is among the most breathtakingly exhilarating experiences a person can ever have. My juika-bloth also seemed to find it so; the bird remained on my shoulder and did not take to the air, but frequently spread its wings just to rejoice in the wind of our speed. During that ride, though, I repeatedly gave silent thanks to old Wyrd for his having earlier made me travel afoot as rigorously as he had made me do. If those forest journeys had not so strengthened my thighs, I could never have kept my seat on Velox throughout that morning's long gallop. As it was, the inside of my thighs got so painfully chafed that I might well have been moaning if I had not been so deliriously enjoying the ride.

162   We saw no more Huns. And eventually we came to the river Rhenus at a place where the bank shelved very gradually down to and under the water, and that water was very little roiled by the gentle current there. So we rested and watered the horses and ourselves, and let the animals browse on some of the dry foliage roundabout. None of us humans ate anything, because there was nothing to eat—and also because, in my case at least, the long ride had made my belly muscles so stiff and tight that I could not feel any emptiness in the stomach behind them. That must have been true for Calidius as well, because he made no complaint of hunger, and of course Wyrd was never much troubled by missing any number of meals.

When we moved on, I did that day's other first-time thing, which was to cross a river *not* in a boat. Though I had paddled often in the cascade pools of the Balsan Hrinkhen, and was not afraid of water, I would never have been capable of swimming across the Rhenus, which here I judged to be at least two stadia in breadth. Wyrd showed me how to do it. He set Calidius on my saddle, and bade him hold fast to it, and put my juika-bloth on the boy's shoulder. Then, following Wyrd's example, I led my horse by his bridle into the water. Neither Velox nor the Zhmud nag balked at that; it was evidently not a first time for either of them.

As we and the horses gradually submerged, Wyrd and I shifted our hold from the bridles to their tails. My juika-bloth, once it perceived our intent—and not to get water splashed on itself—soared off Calidius's shoulder and circled companionably above us as we more clumsily made the crossing. Holding tight to the horses' tails, Wyrd and I let the animals tow us, and they did the swimming more strongly and steadfastly than any man could have done. Just the biting cold of that water, let alone the daunting expanse of it, would have been enough to discourage and drown a man before he got halfway across. Being towed as we were, though, I personally found the passage almost pleasurable. Where the river shallowed on the other side, the horses even picked a convenient place to find their footing, and Wyrd and I likewise easily followed them out of the water. There, we and the animals shook ourselves as dogs do, and, while the horses rested, Wyrd and Calidius and I jogged up and down the bank to restore our body warmth. When at last we remounted and turned upstream again toward Basilea, we went in no hurry, for we were safe now from the hideous Huns.

163

9

After the legatus Calidius had embraced and fondled his namesake grandson, and then had sent him away with his nurse slaves to be cleaned and fed and cared for, Wyrd told the legatus a kindly lie:

"Your son Fabius died standing, clarissimus, a Roman soldier to the last." And then he told the truth. "His wife, Placidia, died bravely, as a Roman matron should." And then he mentioned something of which, at the time, I had not realized the significance: "I saw the Huns take care to spare the life of that unhappy charismatic, which means they believe they still hold your grandson captive. Therefore they think they still have a hold upon you."

The legatus said thoughtfully, "So they will not yet have dispersed and fled away."

"No. They will suppose that a few of us made a desperate foray—

perhaps even without your sanction—and that we failed. Tell me, Calidius, in your negotiations with the Hun messenger, when and whither did you agree to send ransom?"

"This very afternoon. To a certain bend of the river Birsus, south of here."

"Toward the Hrau Albos," said Wyrd, nodding. "And on this side of the river Rhenus. Very well. I suggest that, without delay, without waiting for any renewed demand, you *send* that ransom there—as if you have no knowledge of the failed rescue mission, as if you have no knowledge that the Huns are really camped north of the Rhenus, as if you truly expect to receive the hostages in exchange for the ransom."

"You mean, of course, send a *seeming* ransom."

"Of course. The specified number of horses, bearing the specified packs of weapons, provender, whatever, all herded by—I presume—the specified few slaves. But, of course, on arrival, the Trojan packs turn out to contain well-armed and angry soldiers. And then, I trust, a well-deserved slaughter ensues."

I presumed to interpose a question: "Perhaps, if the innocent victim Becga is encountered there, he might be exempted from the slaughter?"

Both men ignored me, and Wyrd went on, "Meanwhile, Calidius, you will send another and bigger troop to the Huns' encampment and—"

"You will lead them, Decurio Uiridus?"

"Begging your indulgence, clarissimus," Wyrd said, with some vexation, "I am rather weary of riding and very empty of belly and extremely sick of the sight and smell of Huns. So is my impudent apprentice here. I can give your men adequate directions, and I recommend that my old acquaintance Paccius lead them. It is time he earned a promotion from signifer."

"Yes, yes. I am sorry, Uiridus. You have earned your rest, and more," said the legatus, with evident sincerity. "I was so overjoyed at having my grandson safely back—my family line restored—and equally joyful in the prospect of annihilating those Hun vermin, that I spoke without thinking. I shall give the orders instanter, and also order food for—"

"Thank you, no. I am not hungry for dainty viands and resinous urine. I want gut-filling food and drunk-making wine. We are going down the hill to the cabanae, to the taberna of old Dylas. Send Paccius to me there when he is ready for my instructions."

"Very well. I will have a herald accompany you, to make official announcement to the people that they may again unbar their doors and freely move about the streets. Uiridus, you have lifted a heavy weight from Basilea. I thank you most heartily—and you, too, Thorn."

So this time we did not have to hammer at Dylas's taberna door. The caupo flung it hospitably wide, and I got my first look at more than his bleary red eye. Dylas was at least as old as Wyrd, and equally gray of hair and beard, but considerably taller and barrel-stout, with a face like a slab of raw beef. He and Wyrd rushed into one another's arms, and ferociously pounded their fists on one another's back, and called one another affectionately filthy names in both Latin and Gothic. Dylas bawled to someone in a back room to "fetch meat and cheese and bread!" and then himself lifted down a wineskin and some horns hanging from a low rafter, and motioned us to sit at one of the four tables in the room.

Wyrd introduced me to Dylas, who grunted and nodded amiably, and handed me one of the horns. I held it with my thumb over the hole in the small end while Dylas filled it. When we each had a brimming horn, he laid down the wineskin, raised his own horn to Wyrd and me and said, "Iwch fy nghar, Caer Wyrd, Caer Thorn." It was clearly a salutation, but I did not recognize the language. We held up the horns, tilted back our heads, unstopped the small ends and let the wine pour into our mouths. As Wyrd had said, this was not watered or flavored, but strong, ripe, red Oglasa. Since one cannot put down a horn until it is empty, we all soon emptied ours, and I was made quite giddy, so I politely declined when Dylas refilled the other two.

"The word preceded you, old Wyrd," said Dylas, "that the easing of Basilea's plight was somehow your doing. How did you manage it?"

Wyrd told him—or so I assumed, for he spoke in the alien tongue that Dylas had previously used.

"Akh, remindful of the good old days," Dylas said admiringly, and the conversation resumed in a mixture of Gothic and Latin. "But you are no longer a legionary in line for promotion. What did that risky adventure profit you?"

"A very good price for my furs, and the gift of a fine horse and gear. I had to abandon the first steed Calidius gave me, but I will choose another. Those are better wages for a single day's work than I ever was paid as a decurio."

"By all the heifers of Hertha, that is the truth! Do you know, when once I had learned to count, I calculated that my thirty years of service earned me my discharge pay at less than half a denarius a day. But are you not getting somewhat antiquated, Wyrd, for such caperings and posturings?"

"Speak for yourself, lard-belly."

"Good times or bad, a caupo eats well," Dylas said complacently, patting that belly of his, "and without having to prowl the woods to catch his food before it can be cooked. I always said that you and Juhiza should have set up in a taberna, as we did. My old woman, Magdalan, was never beautiful, like Juhiza, and she may have the brains of a hitching post and the graces of an úrus, but she knows how to cook."

As if she had been summoned by those words, an old, fat and slatternly woman emerged from the back room, in a cloud of steam of delicious aroma. She brought each of us a trencher of bread on which was mounded boiled sour cabbage and, on top of that, racks of boiled pork ribs. After those were set before us, she also brought a platter of the region's cheeses: wedges of Greyerz and Emmen and loaves of creamy white Novum Castellum. For drink, besides the wine, we had tall tankards of a dark beer that Dylas proudly told us he brewed himself.

166

Dylas and Wyrd repeatedly interrupted their two-fisted eating to draw with a finger, in the puddles of spilled wine on the table, diagrams of long-ago battles in which they had seen action. They spoke of comrades who had fallen in this or that fray, and Wyrd would correct Dylas, or vice versa, when he misremembered some detail of those engagements—and in general the two old warriors appeared to be having a good time reliving their young days. But all the battles had been fought years before my birth, and in places of which I had never heard. And since the two men frequently used words of that alien language, I could not really make out what the battles had been about, or who had won or lost them, or even who had fought whom.

We were finishing our trenchers—the bread now delectably soaked with the good juices—when we heard a clashing of metal and creaking of leather, and Paccius entered the taberna, dressed in full battle armor. Wyrd, with a hiccup, excused himself from our company and, staggering slightly, went to sit with the signifer at a clean table, to give him directions to the Hun encampment and instructions on the assault of it.

Just to have a topic on which to converse with Dylas, I asked, "Who is or was Juhiza?"

He drained another horn of wine and shook his big head. "I should not have mentioned her. You saw how old Wyrd's face went stiff. Do not you mention her either."

So I changed the subject: "It is obvious that you and Wyrd have known one another for a very long time."

He wiped grease from his beard—or, rather, he absentmindedly rubbed the grease well into it. "Ever since he and I were rank recruits in the Twentieth Legion, at Deva. I remember when he first acquired the name Wyrd the Friend of Wolves."

"Now he calls himself Wyrd the Forest-Stalker," I said. "But I know he has a fondness for wolves."

Dylas again shook his head. "The name did not refer to any sentimentality. It meant that he slew a great many of the enemy and left their cadavers for the scavenger animals. He was also sometimes called Wyrd the Carrion-Maker. He was very popular with the wolves—and the worms—around Deva."

"I do not know where Deva is."

"In the Cornovian region of the province of Britannia. In the Tin Islands, as you of this continent call them. Wyrd and I are Roman citizens by dint of our military service, but we were Brythons by birth, so we sometimes still speak the Brythonic for old times' sake."

"I never knew *what* he was, until now. Why did you and he leave those islands?"

"A soldier goes where he is bidden. We were only two men of the many thousands that Rome gradually withdrew from Britannia when the outlanders here in Europe began to threaten the colonies closer to Rome's heart. Wyrd and I finished our service in the auxiliaries of the Eleventh Legion, fighting the Huns."

He gestured toward one wall of the taberna, and I saw a metal tablet hanging there, so I went over to examine it. There displayed was Dylas's diplomata, two linked bronze plates, each about the size of a man's hand. On them was engraved his name (or a Latin rendition of it: Diligens Britannus), his retirement rank and unit (Optio Aquilifer, Cohors IV Auxiliarum, Legio XI, Claudia Pia Fidelis), the name of his last commanding officer, the date of his discharge (sixteen years before), the names of witnesses and the province where he had been discharged: Gallia Lugdunensis.

He said, "By the dun cow that sustained St. Piran, we should much have preferred—if a soldier were allowed any preference—to have gone on defending our own home region of Cornovia, against the Picti and Scoti and Saxones."

"Well, now that you are retired, you could return there, surely."

"Akh, who would want to? Now that Rome has totally abandoned Britannia, that land has degenerated again to the barbarism that prevailed before the Romans ever came. The fine cities and forts and farms and villas are now but the squalid camps of people as savage and filthy as those Huns from whom you and Wyrd escaped this morning."

"I see." I said. "That is a pity."

"Gwyn bendigeid Annwn, faghaim," he sighed, and then translated that for me: "Fair blessed Avalonnis, farewell."

A faraway look came into his bleared old eyes, and he said, more to himself than to me, "It must suffice us now just to take pride in the memory . . . that we *were* once of the Twentieth, the Valeria Victrix, one of the four mighty legions that first subdued and civilized that land. Why, in the great days of the Twentieth—in the great days of the empire—a man might travel from the Tin Islands in the west to the Pepper Ports in the east, and travel safely, and speak and hear the Latin tongue the whole way."

He poured another horn of wine, and raised it to me again: "Iwch fy nghar, Caer Thorn. You, like us, were born too late," and drained the horn.

"You are not drinking, urchin," said Wyrd, with a hiccup, as he rejoined us and Paccius went out the door, raising his clenched right fist in salute to us all. "And you will certainly fall asleep if you stay on here, being bored by the reminiscences of two old campaigners. Go and sleep in comfort at the barrack. But first—take this."

He unfastened his wallet from his belt, upended it over my hand and let jingle into my palm a considerable number of coins—copper and brass and silver and even one of gold.

I asked, "What would you have me do with this, fráuja?"

"Whatever you like. It is your share of the money our furs brought us."

I gasped, "I never did anything to earn this much!"

"Sláváith. I am the master. Hic. You are the apprentice. I am the judge of the worth of your services. Go and buy anything you think you may need during the continuance of our journey. Or anything that strikes your fancy."

I thanked him most sincerely for his munificence, and thanked Dylas for the good meal, and wished both of the old friends an enjoyable and satisfyingly drunken confabulation, and took my leave. I waited until I was outside to count the money. There was one gold solidus, numerous

168

silver solidi and siliquae, and many brass sestertii and copper nummi—in all, to the dazzling value of about *two* gold solidi,

I looked about me, and took note that Basilea had come again to life. Men, women and children moved freely about the streets. Nearby houses had their shutters open, and from them I could hear the thin, shrill sound of housewives' loom shuttles going back and forth. On the downslope of the hill behind the garrison, where the ground was shaded and snow still clung, several off-duty soldiers were playing like boys, sitting down on their shields and merrily shouting as they slid and spun downhill. The cabanae shops all had their fronts open, and many people were going in and out of them, replenishing the household supplies they had used up while they were barricaded indoors.

I myself could think of no supplies that I might need for my further journeying. I had already and fortuitously acquired more treasures than most persons amass in a lifetime—a splendid horse, its saddle and bridle, a sword and scabbard, a military flask, plus all the other goods I had bought in Vesontio. But it hardly made sense for me to carry money into the wilderness, where it would be of no use whatever, and I now had enough money to purchase just about anything that was for sale in Basilea—or anything except one of the Syrian's ten-solidi charismatics. I had no least wish to buy one, but the thought of those pathetically sexless creatures made me think of something else, since I was the very antithesis of sexlessness.

169

I owned the rudiments of female costume—a gown and a kerchief—in the likelihood that I should find it advantageous, somewhere, sometime, to be publicly a girl. But I lacked the refining touches of coloring and adornment. So, as I ambled among the cabanae, I sought first a myropola, and found one. I went into the shop and—partly to conceal the fact that I wanted the commodities for myself, partly to account for my having so much money to spend—told the woman tending the place that I was the servant of a femina clarissima. Since this shopwoman would doubtless have known of all the fine ladies already resident in Basilea, I told her that *my* fine lady was shortly to arrive here, and that, on the road, she had lost her entire casket of cosmetics.

"Naturally," I said, "my lady will desire to appear at her best when she arrives, so she sent me on ahead to purchase replacements for her—dyes and lotions and so forth. However, I knowing nothing of such things, caia myropola, I will trust you to provide everything a fine lady would require."

The woman smiled—rather greedily, at this opportunity to make such an extravagant sale—and said, "I shall need to know your lady's complexion and hair color."

"Which is why she sent me," I said, "instead of one of her female servants, because her coloring and mine are almost identical."

"Hm," murmured the myropola, her head on one side, eyeing me professionally. "I think . . . a fucus of blushing peach . . . a creta of ashy brown . . ." And then she bustled about the shop, collecting jars and phials and pencils.

It was a costly purchase, but I could well afford it, and I left there bearing a neatly wrapped parcel of potted unguents and powders, bottled liquids and sticks of chalk, a real woman's counterparts of all those berry juices and soots and tallows that we primping girls had slathered on ourselves at St. Pelagia's.

My next purchase was even costlier, at the workshop of an aurifex, where I bought jewelry for my "soon-to-arrive fine lady." Though I passed over the smith's excellent goldwork, and selected only silver pieces without any inset gems, the prodigality much depleted my newly come fortune. I bought a fibula that looked like a knotted rope of silver for either shoulder of my gown, and a necklace, a bracelet and earrings that were all of a match, each of them having been made to resemble chain links of silver. Afterward, going on uphill toward the garrison, I worried a little about my choices and my taste. Did jewelry that simulated ropes and chains look exactly *feminine*? But finally I decided that, if it was perhaps the male half of me that had selected them, then any man seeing me as a girl thus adorned ought to admire the jewels—and therefore admire me. And wasn't that what women wore jewelry *for*?

The garrison was not so crowded as it had been, most of the countryfolk and travelers who had been sequestered there having now gone on about their business. But the Syrian and his charismatics were still in residence, still in the same barrack as Wyrd and myself, the slaver evidently waiting in the hope that Paccius might bring Becga safely back with him.

In the barrack room, I resisted my very feminine eagerness to unwrap and gloat over and play with my latest acquisitions, because I had a very masculine job to do first, and I wanted to get that done before Wyrd should return and berate me for my having to do it. What it was—the night before, when I slashed the throat of that Hun hag, I had neglected to wipe the blood off my short-sword before I sheathed it again in my scabbard. Overnight, of course, the blood had dried, and now the sword was inextricably glued to the scabbard's wool lining. So I borrowed a washtub from one of the barrack soldiers, and filled it with water, and swashed the scabbard around in it until I could work the sword loose. Then I carefully wiped the blade clean and dry and left the scabbard in the tub to soak until the wool could get white again.

I was getting extremely sleepy by now, but I *was* girlishly yearning to try on my new jewelry and cosmetics. Since I had no speculum—and was hesitant to ask any soldier if he owned such a foppish piece of equipment—I had no way of seeing how those things looked on me. So, the Syrian being nowhere about at that moment, I summoned to my barrack room one of the charismatics, a boy near my own age and coloring, and he compliantly—even delightedly—sat still while I put my ornaments on him, and daubed fucus on his cheeks, and chalked darker his lashes and brows, and reddened his lips with one of the unguents. Then I stood back and eyed him, while he beamed pridefully at me. His ragged garb notwithstanding, the silver jewelry looked very fine, and accorded well with his pale hair. But what I had done to his face I had lamentably overdone, and garishly, so that he looked like what I imagined one of the more fiendish skohls might look like.

171

I was about to wipe it off, but he protested so pitiably—saying it made him "happy to be pretty"—that I let him go on wearing the skohl face, and called over another boy of about the same age and fairness. This time I employed a lighter touch, and applied the cosmetics more deftly, and, when I stepped back, was pleased with the result I had achieved. It gave me considerable assurance that, when I had access to a speculum and could make up my own face, and had the added advantage of being able to *feel* that application, I ought to be able to do a more than passable job of it. I took the jewelry off the skohl-boy and hung it on this other one. The skohl-boy and I enthusiastically agreed that he made a very lovely girl indeed, and he himself said that he truly felt like one, and then all three of us jumped, when the Syrian Natquin snarled behind us:

"Ashtaret! You meddling whelp, first you steal my Becga. *Now* what are you doing to my Buffa and Blara?"

"Making them as attractive as young girls," I said blandly. "What objection could you have to that?"

"Bah! Anybody who wants a lowly female can get one of those for a hundredth the price of a charismatic. You brats go and wash that scum off your faces."

They gave me back my jewelry and meekly trotted away. I went into the barrack room to put my things in my pack, and to swash my scabbard around in its water some more. The Syrian followed me inside, saying in a whine:

"Ashtaret! I am sick and tired of being treated like a vile whoremonger, when I am a respectable dealer in exceedingly valuable commodities."

I stretched out on my pallet bed and asked, though I did not really care, "Who or what is that Ashtaret you so frequently invoke?"

"Ashtaret is a mighty goddess, whom I highly revere. She was previously the Astarte of the Babylonians, and before that the Ishtar of the Phoenicians."

"I do not believe," I said drowsily, but with malice, "that I should wish to worship a goddess of the second or third handing down."

He snorted. "There is no god or goddess or demigod of any religion that would welcome close investigation into his or her antecedents. The pagan Romans' foremost goddess, Juno, was born as Uni of the Etruscan religion. The Greeks' Apóllon was originally the Etruscan Aplu." The Syrian laughed mockingly. "Now, as for what I could tell you about the true origins of *your* Lord God and Satan and Jesus . . ."

172

I have no doubt that he did tell me, and maybe even truthfully, but by then I had fallen fast asleep.

I woke in the dark, in the middle of the night, when two half-drunk soldiers half carried and half dragged an unconscious Wyrd into our room. After lurching about and cursing for a bit, they found the empty bed and toppled him onto it. When I asked, in some alarm, what was wrong with Wyrd, they only laughed and suggested that I lean over and smell his breath.

When the soldiers were gone, I did that—just to make sure he *was* breathing—and then reeled away from him, almost dizzied by the fumes of wine. I was glad I had been awakened, though, because my sword's scabbard was still in the washtub. I took it out, wiped it as dry as I could, then slipped it between my pallet's pad and the bed's board, and lay down on it, so that my weight would keep the leather from warping as it dried, and immediately fell asleep again.

When I next woke it was daylight, and quite late in the morning. Wyrd was already up, and bending over the borrowed washtub, repeatedly dunking his head under the water. I wondered why he had not noticed that the water was tinged very pink—that he was soaking his head in the diluted blood of a Hun—until he stood erect and turned around and I could see that his eyes were a considerably more vivid pink than the water was.

"Oh vái," he muttered, wringing out his beard. "I have the father and mother of a headache. That Oglasa wine exacts a fearsome penalty from its votaries. But worth it . . . worth it . . ."

I grinned and said, "Perhaps breaking your fast would make you feel better. Let us go to the convivium and see if they will feed us at this hour."

"Dead men do not eat. Let us go first to the therma and see if a thorough bathing will restore me to life."

But Wyrd was at least somewhat revivified before he ever got into the bath, because in the apodyterium we found Paccius. He was just then removing his armor, the metal and leather of which were dirty, scuffed in places and stained with dried blood. Paccius himself was dirty and weary-looking, but nonetheless bright of eye and smile.

"Ah, Signifer—salve, salve," said Wyrd. "It went well, then?"

"It went well, it is over, it is done," Paccius said jovially. "And I will thank you to address me properly, as the centurio I now am become."

Both Wyrd and I said, "Gratulatio, Centurio."

173

"Yes, we exterminated every last one of the savages at the encampment," said Paccius. "And Calidius tells me that the Trojan column did likewise at the river Birsus. Those scurvy scavengers will trouble us no more. Not that band of them, anyway."

"And . . . ?" prompted Wyrd, as he too began to undress.

"And, as you instructed," said Paccius, rather more soberly, "we did not attempt to bring back the remains of Fabius and Placidia. We burned those with all the other corpses, and I told the legatus that the bodies of his son and his son's wife had already been destroyed before we arrived there. He will not be able to give them decent Roman burial, but neither will he be further grieved by knowing how Fabius died."

"Thank you for the good news, Centurio," said Wyrd. "I was delaying the departure of Thorn and myself only until I heard how the reprisal raid had gone. Not that I expected anything less than total success from you and your men, Paccius. In fact, I had already celebrated in anticipation of it." Again he gingerly felt of his forehead. "Now I shall delay our departure only until I have fully recovered from that."

I asked Paccius, "But what of the charismatic Becga?"

He said indifferently, "That one is dead, too."

"By a Hun's hand—or a Roman's?"

"By my own hand," he said to me, and then said to Wyrd, "As you instructed, Uiridus. It was done quickly, and the eunuch did not suffer."

"*You* instructed?" I demanded of Wyrd. "But you agreed that Becga was only an innocent victim of circumstances."

"Not so loud, urchin," said Wyrd, wincing. "And you forget that it was *you* who volunteered a victim. Calidius would never have forgiven us the insult to his pride if we had let his grandson's impersonator live—perhaps even someday to *boast* of having done that impersonation—and the impersonator being a contemptible charismatic whore."

"Slaying him to soothe the legatus's feelings," I said heatedly, "seems unnecessarily cruel to the contemptible Becga."

"It was not *cruel!*" snapped Wyrd, his own loud voice also making him wince. "You know what that creature's life would have been like if it had lived. Now slaváith, and let us proceed to the unctuarium."

Wyrd was right, I had to admit, and I obediently followed him into the bath's interior. It was I who had said "substitutus," and thereby started Becga on his way to death. Even if it had been only the male half of myself that did the deed, then it was unbecoming of me now to feel any twinge of feminine guilt on that account—or to indulge in any feminine grieving over it.

I remembered having taken comfort in the realization that my being a mannamavi conferred one enormous benefit: that I need never have to love any other person, of whatever sex, and never have to endure all the miseries that loving entails. But now I realized another thing: if I *was* immune to the torments that accompany every such weakling emotion, I should have to learn to quell or at least ignore the discords and contentions that might arise between the male and female halves of my nature.

Very well, I said to myself, I *would* be glad that I had not known Becga well enough or long enough to have risked any sentimental attachment to the child. I *would* abjure any responsibility for his death or any regret about it. I *would*, now and always, take full advantage of my being Thorn the Mannamavi—a being uninhibited by conscience, compassion, remorse—a being as implacably amoral as the juika-bloth and every other raptor on this earth. I *would*.

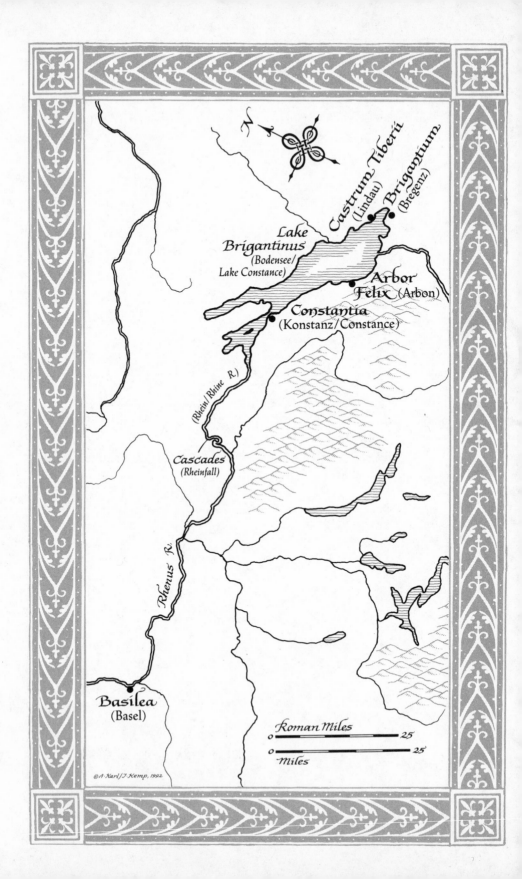

N

Castrum Tiberii
(Lindau)

Brigantium
(Bregenz)

Lake
Brigantinus
(Bodensee/
Lake Constance)

Arbor
Felix (Arbon)

Constantia
(Konstanz/Constance)

(Rhein/Rhine R.)

Cascades
(Rheinfall)

Rhenus R.

Basilea
(Basel)

Roman Miles
0   25

0   25
Miles

© A. Karl/J. Kemp, 1992

AT THE LAKE

BRIGANTINUS

1

We continued on from Basilea still together, myself and Wyrd the Forest-Stalker, the Friend of Wolves, the Carrion-Maker. His own peregrinations during that time tended eastward, the direction I was going, toward the lands occupied by the Goths. And since I had no reason to *hurry* to get there, and since I was forever learning something new and useful from the wise old woodsman, I was more than content to continue in his company and travel at his pace.

During the weeks after we left Basilea, most of Wyrd's teaching dealt with the care and management of horses and the finer points of horsemanship. As I soon learned, I had *not* yet learned much about riding a horse. My one outing on Velox had all been done either at a walk or at a stretch-out gallop, and any novice can easily ride at those gaits. When now Velox introduced me to the trot, I was extremely glad that I had no testicles between me and the saddle. Wyrd showed me how to post—rising and sinking in the saddle in time to the motion of the horse—and that made the trotting gait considerably less jolting, but still I wondered how a normal man equipped with testicles could endure it. And, as I continued to learn from Wyrd, the owning and keeping and riding of a horse required of me much more than just strong and callused thighs and the knack of posting to the trot.

He said, "Remember, urchin, that the gods of nature never intended a horse to be anything but a horse, untamed and free and masterless. The animal's size and shape make it appear to have been *designed* by nature to carry a rider, but it was not. When you are astride it, you are really only a parasite burden on the creature. Therefore, you must not let the horse ever suspect that you are just a parasite. You must cajole the horse into accepting you as a partner—and the dominant partner."

So, because Velox was sometimes coyly and friskily averse to being put to work in the early mornings, Wyrd showed me how to humor him into submission. I was to stand close to the horse, gently scratching his withers—while softly, tunelessly whistling to him—then gradually scratching up along the root of his mane to his poll, by which time he was quite amenable to being bridled and saddled and mounted. I learned also to correct Velox every time he showed a trace of disobedient impudence, rather than put up with his skittishness ten times and then lose my patience at the eleventh. "Because," Wyrd told me, "your single display of ill temper will spoil the *good* temper of any horse."

On another day Wyrd said, "Remember, urchin, have your horse shod with rimshoes if you are going to do much traveling over rocky ground. But traveling on earthen ground as we are doing, leave him always unshod, and he will be your best sentry and watchman. If someone steals upon you, the horse will feel the vibration in the ground long before you can hear the footsteps or see the person approaching."

On another day, Wyrd and I were both riding at an easy walk, myself in the lead, through a dense but very ordinary forest, and the sun was near to setting, when suddenly my Velox gave a vaulting bound that left me sitting in midair. My juika-bloth, though it had been dozing on my shoulder, also leapt so that it stayed in the air—which of course I did not. I landed heavily on my rump on the ground. The horse stopped a little farther on, as abruptly calm as it had been abruptly energetic, and turned its head to regard me inquiringly. The juika-bloth looked down at me accusingly, as it circled overhead, and Wyrd, drawing rein, hoarsely laughed at me.

"What did I do wrong *now?*" I said plaintively, rubbing my bruised backside as I got stiffly to my feet.

"Nothing," said Wyrd, still laughing. "But, by the flayed skin of St. Bartholomew, I will wager you will be more alert in the future. Look you, urchin, at that one lone stray beam of the sun shining low across the path. Remember that a horse will always try to hurdle such a sunbeam, because it looks like a barrier in his way. Also, I think it is time we started you in practice at jumping."

So, in the days thereafter, whenever we came upon a fallen tree lying in a suitable position, Wyrd would put his horse over it, then have me do the same with Velox—first over slender fallen saplings low to the earth, then over thicker boles higher off the ground. But almost every time I tried, Wyrd would scold me:

"Ne, ne, ne! At the moment the horse launches into the jump, you must lean well back in the saddle. That takes your weight off his fore-quarters as they lift."

"I will try to do better," I promised.

And I did try, leaning back at every jump, until Wyrd finally approved of my form. But the jumping still felt awkward to me—and I sensed that it felt so to the horse as well. So we went off at times to a distance from Wyrd, and practiced in private, and I tried different modes of sitting while we leapt hurdles both low and high, and finally I hit on a way of jumping that felt to me more comfortable and graceful, and it seemed preferable to Velox, too. When we had rehearsed that to smoothness, I demonstrated it for Wyrd.

"What is this?" he said, with mixed puzzlement and annoyance. "You are leaning *forward* to jump. Very bad form, that."

"Ja, fráuja, if you say so. But it seems to free Velox to launch himself with a much more powerful thrust of his hind legs, with my weight off them. And also my bending forward at that precise moment seems to give him greater momentum."

"Vái!" cried Wyrd, reeling in mock astonishment. "For some two hundred years, the Roman cavalry has been teaching recruits and horses how to jump properly, but you know better, eh?"

"Ne, fráuja, I do not pretend to *know* anything. But I can *feel* somehow that it works better, both for myself and for Velox."

"Vái! You speak for the horse, too, eh? Perhaps that abdicating parent who left you an orphan was a centaur, eh?"

"All I can tell you is that I seem to have a kinship of feeling with the horse, just as I have always had with my juika-bloth. In some way, we know . . . without the need of words . . ."

Wyrd regarded me levelly, then shifted his gaze to the eagle on my shoulder, then to the horse I sat on. Then he shrugged.

"Well, if it suits you better. And your Velox. But only you two. May I be damned to Gehenna if I should change a lifetime's habits at my advanced age."

One other time I challenged Wyrd's rules and his reverence for the long-standing traditions of equitation. Under his tutelage, I was playing at combat on horseback, whacking with my short-sword at various enemy bushes and trees while Velox capered and plunged and danced at my direction.

"That is the way!" Wyrd shouted. "Now the backhand stroke! Remember, you can make your horse do a complete right-about within its own length and at a full canter! Sit him hard, urchin! Now the flank cut! Now the disengage! Well done, urchin!"

"It would be . . . a lot easier," I said, panting from my exertions, "if one had some bracing . . . for the feet . . . to help one stay astride . . ."

"That is what thighs are for," Wyrd said. "Your own have lengthened and strengthened just in the time I have known you."

"Still . . ." I said, thinking. "If there were some way to hold the feet from flapping about . . ."

"Since the beginning of time, men have been riding without any such thing, and riding well. You must master the art and cease your quibbling."

But again I went off in private and made some tries at invention. I remembered how I had ridden the old draft mare around St. Damian's barnyard, churning milk into butter. I had then had thighs that were neither long nor strong, but I had kept my seat on the animal's broad back by tucking my feet under the milk panniers slung on either side. It would be impractical to make a war-horse wear panniers, and it would look ridiculous, but if I had *something* under which to tuck my feet . . . Then I remembered how, in the Balsan Hrinkhen, I had employed my belt rope to give me the friction that enabled me to climb limbless tree trunks . . .

"Now what?" Wyrd said grumpily when I came proudly to demonstrate to him what I had finally devised. "You have *tied* yourself onto your horse?"

"Not quite," I said, preening. "See? I took three of our stout pack ropes and braided them into a very thick rope, and then tied that around Velox just forward of his ribs, so it will not slide back, and tied it not too tight, but loosely enough to allow me to slip my feet within it on each side—and behold, fráuja! The friction holds me as firmly here as if I sat in a chair with my feet on the floor."

"And what," Wyrd asked, with sarcasm, "does your horse tell you—without words, of course—regarding his own opinion of this clumsy contrivance? How does he like having the rope's huge knot down there behind his forelegs?"

"Well, I grant that the knot is bothersome. I try to keep it up here at his withers, but it keeps shifting around and down. Except for that, I do believe that my being lodged securely here pleases Velox more than my slipping even a little in the saddle whenever he changes pace or direction."

182

"Lodged securely, are you? I have seen the Alani horsemen try some such rope trick to coddle their feet, and I have seen them regret it. Just wait, urchin, until you are once unseated by an opponent's blow, and that harness drags you head-down all over the landscape."

"Then I must endeavor," I said smugly, "not ever to let myself get unseated."

Wyrd shook his head as if in deprecation, but partly too, I think, in admiration, for he said, "You may get many opportunities for such endeavor. You look so quaint that every passing Goliath may wish to test your mettle. But ride as you will, urchin. And I will show you how to splice that rope instead of tying it, to eliminate that cumbersome great knot."

"Velox will thank you, fráuja," I said warmly. "And so do I."

Of course, I learned about things other than riding and horses during my travels with Wyrd. During our first summer together, when we were riding through some terrain only patchily wooded, under a gray sky as heavy and hot as a woolen blanket:

"Do you hear that call, urchin?"

"I hear only a crow. In that farther treetop."

"Only a crow, eh? Listen to him."

I did, and heard "Caw! Caw! Scraw-aw-awwk!" It sounded rather more deliberate than a crow's usually indiscriminate cawing, but it told me nothing, and I said so.

"He is uttering the crows' special call," said Wyrd. "Warning of a storm approaching. Learn to recognize that call. But right now, keep an eye out for shelter. I am not eager to stay on this open ground in a thunderstorm."

We found a shallow cave just before the storm broke, bringing blinding black gloom and blinding white flashes and an uproar of noise and a downpour of rain. It was fearsome enough, but not unnatural. However, after a time, our cave was suddenly—and steadily, not flickeringly—lighted by an eerie blue glow. We looked out, to find that every tree in sight was outlined by a blue fire that burned along every one of its limbs and streamed skyward from the tip of every branch.

"Iésus!" I cried, scrambling to my feet. "Let us save the horses! They are tied to one of those trees."

"Be easy, urchin," said Wyrd, staying placidly seated. "Those are the fires of the Gemini, a good omen."

"A forest fire is a *good omen?!*"

"Look closely. The fires are not consuming a single leaf of any tree.

183

They are all light and no heat. The twin divinities Castor and Pollux are beloved by mariners because, when their fires are seen during a storm at sea, it means the tempest and the high waves will soon abate. Behold—our own storm is dying away even as the cold blue Gemini fires diminish."

And that autumn, while I was chasing a doe, to herd it within the range of Wyrd, waiting with bow and arrow, I took a heavy bump against a tree. Had I not been riding with my feet securely tucked inside Velox's rope girth, I would probably have been toppled from my saddle. As it was, I suffered no injury beyond a large bruise on my hip. What did get hurt was my handsome leather-and-tin water flask—a deep dent that bent it nearly double—and I was inconsolable at having clumsily damaged that gift of great value and utility. But Wyrd told me:

"Do not grieve so, urchin. While I am skinning and brittling this fine doe for our meal, you go and thresh the bushes and grasses roundabout for every kind of seed you can collect."

When I returned, holding my smock hem up for a hamper, and with it full of assorted seeds, he said:

184   "Pour them into your dented flask, as full as it will hold. Now take this"—he handed me his own flask—"and pour water in, to the brim. Now cork the flask as tightly as you can and put it aside and forget it. Here, feed these entrails to your eagle. Then come and stir these good meats and juices, and keep up the fire under them, while I take a well-deserved rest. Wake me when the meal is ready."

The fresh venison, boiled in the doe's own well-fatted skin and lent a slight tanginess from Wyrd's having made the fire of aromatic laurel, was so delicious as to distract me from any thought of my flask. But while Wyrd and I were still gobbling and slurping, I heard a distinct popping noise from the direction of my unrolled blankets. I went to look, and found that my flask was unbent and undented and, except for a slight scuff on the leather binding, as good as new.

"Seeds, grain, beans, anything of that sort," said Wyrd. "Simply wet them, and their urge to grow will immediately start to exert an incredible amount of pressure. Now empty them out, urchin, before they blow your cork over the trees—or burst the metal flask itself."

Of course, not all the colloquies between Wyrd and myself consisted of his teaching and my learning—or my quibbling, as he so frequently complained. More often than not, we conversed of less consequential things. I remember how, once, he asked me idly how I had come to have only an initial and not a proper name. I told him that it was because, when I was found by the monks of St. Damian's, they discovered that single rune, þ, marked on my swaddling garments.

"I suppose," I said, "it might have stood for Theodahad or Theudis or something of the sort."

"More likely Theodoric," said Wyrd. "That was a name often bestowed on the boys newborn in the west around that time, because Theodoric the Balthing, King of the Visigoths, had but recently died heroically on the plains of Catalauni, in combat against the Huns. And he was shortly succeeded by a son, also named Theodoric, who reigned wisely and kindly and was widely admired."

I said nothing. I had heard of those Theodorics, but I doubted very much that my mother had named her mannamavi infant after a king.

"Nowadays, in the east somewhere," Wyrd went on, "there is another Theodoric—Theodoric Strabo—a minor kinglet of some portion of the Ostrogoths. But since his name means Theodoric the Wall-Eyed, I wager that not many parents will name their sons in his honor. And there is yet another Theodoric, a lad about your own age, urchin—Theodoric the Amaling—whose father, uncle, grandfather and probably *all* his distant forebears have been kings among the Ostrogoths."

185

That was the first time I had heard spoken the name of the Theodoric with whose life my own would eventually be so intertwined. However, since I was not a wise-sayer or a haliuruns of prophetic powers, I listened with only mild interest as Wyrd continued:

"Right now, that young Theodoric is a hostage at the imperial palace in Constantinople, as surety that his father-king and uncle-king will not disrupt the peace in the Eastern Empire. Happily for the boy, to be a hostage of the Emperor Leo is rather more pleasant than to be, say, a hostage of the Huns. I have heard that Theodoric is being brought up with all the privileges that would be accorded the son of a Roman gloriosissimus patricius. He is said to be a great favorite at court, and excels at learning, at languages and at athletic feats as well. So, no doubt, when he is of age, he will succeed to the kingship of the Ostrogoths. And probably be a nuisance to the Roman Empire. And his name—who knows?—may get bestowed on whole generations of infants."

2

hen Wyrd and I came to the city of Constantia, we were afoot and leading our horses, for their saddles were overslung and piled high with pelts. We had come upstream along the river Rhenus from Basilea, on the way taking whatever fur-bearing creatures presented themselves. Those were mostly small animals—stoat, marten, fitchet—and most of them slain by my sling stones, because an arrow would have torn them up so badly as to make their fur unmarketable. But Wyrd did use his Hunnish bow to bring down three or four gluttons and a single lynx. When, one twilight, we espied that large and handsome spotted gray lynx incautiously perched in a tree—it was eyeing *us*, perhaps hoping to pounce at the juika-bloth on my shoulder—I made a gesture for Wyrd to stay his arrow, but he was too quick for me, and shot it dead.

"You should have taken it alive," I said, and told him what a peasant had told me long ago.

"An ignorant superstition," said Wyrd, with one of his contemptuous snorts. "The lynx is no magical mongrel fox-wolf. Look for yourself. You can see it is a greater cousin to the wildcat. As for making lynx-stones or any other kind of precious gems, you would do as well to bottle the piss of that peasant who told you the story. Do not put your faith in fables, urchin, whether they are related by a booby or a bishop. Or even by wise old me. Use your own eyes, your own experience, your own reason to determine the truth of things."

At intervals, when we had a good stock of freshly flayed skins, we would pause in our journey and make camp for a while. Wyrd showed me how to scrape the pelts clean of flesh, and how to stretch them on willow hoops, and then we would laze about while they dried and cured.

One of our stops was beside the falls of the Rhenus, a grandly high and tumultuous, three-tiered cataract across the whole breadth of the river. They made my remembered cascades of the Balsan Hrinkhen seem tame by comparison, and they were most gorgeously beautiful—rainbowed in daylight, moonbowed at night—but they were a nuisance much cursed by the watermen whose shallow skiffs plied up and down the stream. Coming from either direction, the boatmen had to unload their goods and manhandle them up or down the riverside around the falls, and then wait for another skiff to arrive from the other direction, when the two crews would exchange vessels to keep going. So there were permanent skiff houses built above and below the falls, to shelter men and freight if they had to wait for long. In a temporarily empty skiff house Wyrd and I resided in comfort for some days, taking our time with the fleshing and stretching of our pelts, meanwhile enjoying the spectacle and tumult of the cataract.

"A splendid sight, ja," said Wyrd. "But yonder, on the other side of the river, that is the Black Forest. Akh, I know, I know, it is no blacker than any other dense forest, but that has been its name since time immemorial. And in there, some minor streams unite to become the beginning of a far mightier river than this Rhenus. That is the Danuvius, which flows all the way from the Black Forest to the Black Sea. If you continue on your quest to find your Gothic kinfolk, urchin, you will one day see the Danuvius."

187

Farther upstream on the Rhenus, we stopped at a Roman army station called Gunodorum. It was no considerable garrison like that at Basilea, but we were hospitably received and housed, for Wyrd had some acquaintances there. We traded a few of our skins for a few traveling necessities—salt and rope and fishhooks—and the station's coquus regaled us with the viands of the region. I ate my fill of broiled steaks of a giant fish called the wels, and of the delectable hard Sbrinz cheese that Romans consider the best of all cheeses, and drank my fill of white Staineins and red Rhenanus wine—and Wyrd had *more* than his fill of those.

During that journey, Wyrd and I did not exert ourselves to chase any game, except to get meat for the pot, until we came near the great lake from which the Rhenus flows. The lake Brigantinus is fed by innumerable small streams and, as Wyrd had told me at our first meeting, those lesser waters are the habitat of beavers. They were just then emerging from their burrows and working heroically to repair their winter-worn dams, to keep the stream waters at the level they prefer to live in. Wyrd wanted to gather as many of them as possible before they began to molt their rich, thick winter pelts, so now we hunted in earnest. Or, rather, Wyrd did, because beavers are too big to be felled by slung stones. Beavers are also very wary and alert, so he seldom had an opportunity to shoot more than one arrow at one target in any one day, but he seldom missed when he did. And when he skinned a beaver, he took more than its fur; he also cut away and kept the little sacs situated near the animal's anus.

"Castoreum," he explained. "I can sell it to the makers of medicinals."

"Iésus," I said, holding my nose. "Will they pay enough to make it worth the carrying? It smells worse than my fitchet skins."

For a long time, we skirted the lake Brigantinus at a considerable distance, and I got not a glimpse of it. The lake is completely encircled by a broad, well-paved, heavily traveled Roman highway, and is set about with forts, garrisons, settlements and thriving towns. There is even one city, Constantia, and it is a busy center of commerce, because several other Roman roads merge there, including the roads leading directly to and from Rome itself, those that climb over the Alpis Poenina, the Alpis Graia and other passes through the high mountains. With all the traffic and bustle around the margins of the Brigantinus, Wyrd and I had to stay well away from it to find our prey, so we ranged the upper reaches of the streams running down to the lake from the west. Twice—one time with an arrow, one time with his battle-ax wielded from horseback and at a gallop—Wyrd slew a wild boar that had come to wallow in the streamside mud. A boar's bristly and patchy pelt is worthless as a fur, but its meat is superbly good eating.

I did feel somewhat guilty about helping in the slaughter of the hardworking beavers, just to get their coats and castoreum, since the only edible part of a beaver is its tail meat—though that does make a most succulent dish. One night, as we dined on beaver tail, I said:

"I wonder why it is that I should feel more of a pang at the death of a wild creature than at that of a human being."

"Perhaps it is because the animals make no cringing appeal or hand-wringing when they are threatened by an executioner or a disease or a god. They die nobly and unafraid and uncomplaining." Wyrd sucked his teeth for a thoughtful moment, then said, "People used to be that way, too, long ago. The pagans and the Jews still are. They may not welcome death, but they know it to be natural and inevitable. Then along came Christianity. And, to make people obey its every you-shall-not in this life, Christianity had to invent something more terrible than death. It invented hell."

I know there was one creature at whose death I actually shed tears, and I do not remember ever having wept in my whole life before that. For many weeks, my juika-bloth had gone off hunting reptiles only for sport, or to keep in practice, because it fed so well on the offal of our animal prey. When, after a while, the eagle seemed *never* to go hunting any more, and seldom even to go flying, but preferred to remain logily perched on my shoulder or on my saddle cantle or on a campsite tree limb, I thought it was only being fatly lazy. But then one day it did an unmannerly thing that it had never previously done to me. While riding on my shoulder, it dropped skeit on my tunic, and I noticed that its mute was not the usual white with a black dot, but a greenish-yellow.

I commented worriedly on that to Wyrd, and he took hold of the bird—it listlessly let him—and he examined it closely, and then shook his head.

"Its eyes are dull, and the winking membrane is reluctant to unwink. The flesh around the beak is dry and pale. I fear it may have contracted one of the swine fevers."

"Swine fever?! This is an eagle."

"An eagle that has been feeding on uncooked boar entrails. Some swine are infested with a parasite that can be transmitted to another host."

"Like a louse? I can comb the bird's feathers and—"

"Ne, urchin," Wyrd said sadly. "This parasite is a kind of worm. It eats from the inside outward. It can kill a man. It will almost surely kill the bird. I can think of nothing to do but try feeding it a bit of castoreum now and then, as a stimulant."

So he tried that, and the juika-bloth listlessly swallowed it, though formerly it would fastidiously have refused anything so malodorous. I continued to give the bird bits of the castoreum from time to time, but it had no apparent effect. I even, in secret, pried the heavy brass cap from the crystal phial I had never yet shown or mentioned to Wyrd, and shamelessly invited the eagle to take a taste of the precious milk of the Virgin. But it only gave me a look, half scornful, half pitying, from its membrane-filmed eyes, and disdained the offering.

As the juika-bloth got even weaker, and its once bright and burnished but now untended plumage got faded and frazzled, I reproached myself again and again, and sometimes aloud:

189

"This stalwart bird has never done a single thing but good for me, and I have repaid that now by doing it harm. My friend is dying."

"Stop your sniveling," said Wyrd. "The eagle is doing none of that, and would despise you for it. Urchin, every one of us must die of *something*. And a raptor, of all creatures, knows that even raptors do not live forever."

"But this was my fault," I insisted. "Had I not interfered with its natural habits and way of life, it would have eaten only of cleanly things." I added, with bitterness, "I should have known—from knowing how *I* would feel—never to meddle with another's nature."

Wyrd looked uncomprehending and said nothing to that. He probably thought that I was babbling, demented by my sorrow.

"If the juika-bloth had to die," I went on, "it should have died while fighting for blood. *That* was its nature. Or at least it should have died in the air, in its element, where it was most at home and happy."

"That," said Wyrd, "it still can do. Take this"—he held out his war bow, an arrow already nocked—"and toss the eagle aloft."

"I would," I said wretchedly, "but, fráuja, I have practiced only seldom with that bow. I could never hit a bird on the wing."

"Try. Do it now. While your friend still can fly."

I leaned my head over toward my shoulder, so I could rub my cheek against the eagle's side, and it moved to nestle closer to my face. I reached up my hand and, for the first time in days, the bird stepped of its own accord onto my finger. I looked one last time into the eyes that had been so keen and were now so bleared, and the eagle looked back at me, as fiercely and proudly as it was able. I was saying a silent farewell to my only living tie to the Ring of Balsam, and to my childhood, and I believe the bird was saying goodbye, too, in its own way.

I flicked my hand and the juika-bloth flew. It did not vault eagerly upward, in the gladsome way that had been its wont. It went anxiously thrashing its wings now, as if they could no longer instinctively feel and seize and master the air. Still, it went valiantly, and not fleeing away from me, but up and to the front of me, so that it could easily hear and obey, and come quickly back, if I should call. But I did not call, and I lost sight of it, for my eyes had filled with tears.

Blind, I drew the bow and loosed the arrow, and I heard the feather-burst sound of the impact, and then the sad, soft sound of the broken body hitting the ground. I had not aimed; I could not have done. I know full well that the juika-bloth flew to meet the arrow. And from that day of that brave example, I have promised myself: when my own time comes, I will strive to welcome it as gallantly.

After a while, when I could speak, I murmured to the bird, "Huarbodáu mith gawaírthja," and then said to Wyrd, "The eagle deserves a hero's burial."

"Burial is for *tame* animals," he growled, "such as soldiers and women and Christians. Ne, leave the corpse for the ants and beetles. Eagle meat is tough and not tasty, so no higher creature is likely to eat it and get infected. But the insects will reduce it to compost, and thereby your friend will attain to the afterlife."

"What? How?"

"Perhaps as a flower. In time, that may nourish a butterfly, and the butterfly may nourish a lark, and the lark may nourish a future eagle."

I scoffed, "That is hardly any way to attain to heaven."

"That *is* heaven. At each dying, to give new life and beauty to this earth. Not many of us get to do that. Leave your friend here. Atgadjats!"

✠ ✠ ✠

When Wyrd finally decreed that we had furs enough, and that in any case our most recently collected pelts were past their prime, it was very nearly summer. From the headwaters of whatever stream we were then on, we came down it and out of the woods to the lake Brigantinus, and I at last got to see the vastest body of water I had yet seen in my life. Wyrd told me how many Roman miles long and broad it was, and also that, at its deepest point, a hundred and fifty men standing on each other's shoulders would not reach from its bottom to its surface. But I needed no numbers to grasp its immensity. The fact that I could not *see* across it, at its narrowest point, was enough to awe a native of a land-locked valley.

That lake, however, is not my favorite of lakes. Since it has no nearby mountains to shelter it, the least wind makes it turbulent and, on a really stormy day, it seethes and boils and surges most fearsomely. Even on a calm and sunny day, when its waters are dotted with a multitude of the local fishermen's little smacks—the tomi, or "chips," as the fishers call them—the Brigantinus is shrouded in a gray haze and seems to be sullenly brooding. Its surroundings, though, I found more cheerful; all about the lake, trim orchards and vineyards and flower gardens were in bounteous, colorful, fragrant bloom.

Constantia is not so big a city as Vesontio, and does not stand on a hill, and has no grand cathedral, and its only vista is of the melancholic Brigantinus. But otherwise it is fairly similar to Vesontio: a waterfront city and a crossroads of trade and travel. Most of its permanent denizens are descended from the Helvetii. Those were a people once wandering and warlike, but they long ago settled down, became Roman citizens, and their descendants now peaceably prosper by catering to the needs of *today's* nomads—merchants, teamsters, traders, missionaries and even other nations' armies marching hither and yonder to make war. It is said that the Helvetii, making of neutrality a vocation, profit more from war than any victors do.

Because Constantia stands at the confluence of so many Roman highways, the Helvetic residents are much outnumbered by the transient visitors, who hail from every province and corner of the empire. But the citizens seem to have learned to speak the language of every one of those. And every building in the city that is not a place of buying, selling, trading or warehousing of goods seems to be a hospitium or a deversorium for lodging those visitors, or a therma for bathing and refreshing them, or a taberna or caupona for feeding them, or a lupanar for their sexual diversion. Where the Helvetii themselves— when they were not occupied with business—did their own sleeping and eating and bathing and copulating, I could not make out, so I asked Wyrd if they ever *did*.

"Ja, in private," he said. "Always in private. So much of their time they spend in pandering to the public that some few things they do in private. But even in copulation they are as businesslike as in every other dealing. It is done only after dark, *in* the dark, under the covers, in one unvarying position. And besides being good Roman citizens, they are good Catholic Christians. So their coupling is done only for procreation, never recreation. Also, a decent woman is expected always to keep wearing at least one of her undergarments while doing it."

"She is? Why?"

Wyrd snorted. "Not being Helvetic or Christian or a decent woman, I do not know why. Now come, urchin. We have earned the right to luxuriate for a while. I know a comfortable deversorium here, and I will even engage separate rooms for each of us. Then, as soon as the horses are unloaded and stabled, we will be off to the best bathhouse in Constantia. And thence to a taberna that has never disappointed me yet."

The deversorium was well appointed and well kept. Besides providing us with a room apiece, it allowed us a separate room entirely for the safe storage of our furs. Once again I had a bed that stood on legs off the floor, and my room had both a closet and a trunk for storing my personal possessions, and another closet that enclosed a rere-dorter for my use alone. The establishment's stable was as clean as the lodgings for humans, and each horse's stall even contained a small goat for company to keep the horse from getting bored.

"In the woods, urchin, we were hunters," said Wyrd, when we left the therma after a welcome and long and leisurely bath there. "Now we are merchants. The taberna to which I am taking you is much favored by us traveling merchants."

There we also took our time, as we savored our platters of broiled Brigantinus whitefish and our horns of heady Staineins. Many other patrons came and went while we loitered, and Wyrd identified for me those merchants whose places of origin I could not divine for myself. Since I had previously known men of most of the Germanic nationalities, I could recognize a Burgund, a Frank, a Vandal, a Gepid, a Suevian, even though they dressed and spoke and even looked much alike. I could also recognize as Jews three men who sat together, and several of the shifty-eyed Syrians, who sat as far from one another as possible. But others were new to me.

"That rough-dressed man in the corner," said Wyrd. "From hearing him order his meal, I take him to be of the Germanic tribe called the Rugii, who live on the Amber Coast around the far northern Wendic Gulf. If so, the fellow is far wealthier than he looks, for he is doubtless a merchant of the gemstone amber. At the table just behind us, the big man with all the yellow hair is one of your Gothic cousins. An Ostrogoth from Moesia, I judge, and—"

"What?" I said, surprised. "A *merchant* Goth?"

"Why not? Even a warrior people must have a livelihood in times when there is no war in progress. And peddling usually pays better than pillaging."

"But peddling what? Their plunder from other nations?"

"Not necessarily. By the torn-off breasts of St. Agatha, urchin, do you suppose every Goth to be a ravening savage? Do you expect to see him clad in skins stained with gore and hung with plucked-out maidenheads?"

"Well . . . I know the Goths only by reputation. I have read the Roman historians. They all tell how the Goths love idleness, but hate peace. And Tacitus said that they scorn to earn by honest labor anything that they might acquire by shedding someone else's blood."

"Humph. Typical Roman slander of anyone not a Roman born. And meanwhile, no Roman will ever admit that he learned from the Goths how to bathe himself cleaner with soap than with oil alone. Or that he learned from the Goths the cultivation of hops." Wyrd shrugged. "Minor contributions to civilization, perhaps. But contributions, nonetheless."

I eyed that burly, yellow-haired merchant with new interest.

"As for merchandise," Wyrd went on, "the Gothic armorers forge the so-called snake blades, the best swords and knives ever made. They do not often deign to part with many of those, but they get princely payment when they do. And the Gothic aurifices are renowned for their artistry in jewelry of filigree, of enamel fillet, of gold and silver inlay. Those things, too, are in great demand and fetch handsome prices."

"The armorers I already knew about," I said. "But Gothic *artists?*"

Wyrd laughed. "Hard to believe, is it, when the rest of the world insists that the Goths are brutes less than human? Well, I doubt that you would find even the most refined Gothic artist to be a kittenish effeminate. But sensitive perception? Ja, the Goths are as capable of that as of belligerence and ferocity."

194

✣   ✣   ✣

Over the next several days, Wyrd went about Constantia, haggling with one buyer after another to get the best possible price for our various furs and our castoreum. I, being still only a novice at grading the quality and value of such things, and even less than a novice at trading and bartering with experienced buyers, could be of no help to Wyrd in those transactions. So, on my own, I simply wandered about Constantia, getting to know the city.

I soon discovered, from what I overheard in public places, that the citizens were in a state of some commotion. Wyrd and I had heard nothing of it in any bathhouse or taberna or in our deversorium, because it was nothing that would have concerned merely temporary lodgers like ourselves and other travelers passing through. But the Helvetic permanent residents of the city were excited—or at least as excited as the stolid Helvetii can ever get—over the matter of choosing a new priest for the city's Basilica of St. Beatus, its old priest having but recently died (of a surfeit of beer, it was rumored). The matter of deciding on a new priest was of consuming interest to the cityfolk, and I, as always, was inquisitive. So, whenever I heard any persons discussing the subject in a language that I could comprehend, I would loiter in the vicinity and listen.

"I shall nominate Tigurinex," said one of a group of middle-aged men, all of whom looked exceedingly prosperous and well fed, and all of whom were speaking Latin. "Caius Tigurinex has long itched to be something even more noble than a successful and tightfisted merchant."

"A good choice," said another man. "Tigurinex owns more business establishments and warehouses—he employs more commoners and purchases more slaves—than any other proprietor in Constantia."

"There are rumors from the other end of the lake," said a third man, "that Brigantium too will soon be needing a new priest. Suppose *those* people should think of Tigurinex."

"Negligible town though that is," said a fourth, "Tigurinex would almost certainly remove all his holdings to Brigantium—per Christo! he would remove them to the pits of Gehenna!—if he were offered a priesthood there."

"Eheu! We must keep him here!"

"Offer the stola to Tigurinex!"

So my curiosity took me to the Basilica of St. Beatus to see the merchant Tigurinex become a priest. He was, like the men I had heard talking about him, of middle age, of amply well-fed girth, nearly bald; he would not need to shave a tonsure. He was also beardless and, I think, even powdered about the face to dull what would have been a skin as oily as a Syrian's.

Without any stammering of his voice or modest bobbing of his head or awkward shuffling of his feet, he announced his acceptance of the priesthood in a strong voice, as if the honor had been always his due and impatiently awaited. Nevertheless, Tigurinex had not condescended this day to dress humbly in robe and cowl. He was dressed as what he was and would always be, priest or not: a peddler of the products of other people's labor—a very successful, rich, vain and preening peddler. It should have been offensive even to his merchant friends and colleagues and sycophants to see the pure and simple white stola draped across both his shoulders, over the expensive and gaudy garments he wore.

"As my priestly name," he concluded his announcement, "I am taking Tiburnius, in reverence to that long-ago saint. I shall henceforth be your stern but adoring father, Tata Tiburnius. However, as tradition requires, I ask if there is any single person among this congregation who challenges my fitness for this priestly service."

The church was crowded to the very doors, but no one of the congregation raised his voice. It was understandable, for they were all eminently practical Helvetii, all engaged in commerce, and the man standing before and above them could, with one word or even a glance of rebuke, have withered any parishioner's business prospects forever.

To my surprise, though, one voice *was* raised. To my further surprise, it did not speak in a Helvetic accent, for it was Wyrd's voice. I knew he could not have cared whether the Basilica of St. Beatus had for its priest Tigurinex or Satan himself. Perhaps he was drunk and merely making mischief. Anyway, he called loudly up to the altar:

"Dear father, dear *Tata* Tiburnius, how do you reconcile your Christian principles with the fact that this city owes much of its prosperity to the perpetual waging of war between various factions of the empire? Will you preach against that?"

"I will not!" Tiburnius snapped without hesitation, sending a blazing glare in Wyrd's direction. "Christianity does not forbid the making of war, so long as it is a just war. Since every war has its end in peace, and since peace is a divine blessing, then *every* war can be called just."

Tiburnius solicited no further challenges—and Wyrd did not volunteer any more—and went on to say:

"Before I pronounce the Dismissal of this service, my sons and daughters, I beg leave to read to you a lection from the Epistles of Paul."

Tiburnius had cunningly culled from the saint's letters to please his fellow tradesmen among the congregation . . . to intimidate the commoners, workers, laborers and any slaves attending this day . . . and, in case some resident or visiting noble was present, to flatter him fulsomely.

"St. Paul says it thus. Let every man abide in the same calling in which he was called. Whosoever are servants under the yoke, let them count their masters worthy of all honor, lest the name of the Lord and his doctrine be blasphemed. Let every soul be subject to higher powers, for those that are, are ordained by God. Render therefore to all men their dues. Tribute, to whom tribute is due; custom, to whom custom; fear, to whom fear; honor, to whom honor. So says the sainted Paul."

By now, I was edging my way through the enraptured crowd, to be early out the door, and I was thinking that Constantia had acquired not only the priest it wanted but one that it fully deserved. He was coming to the end of his address:

"Let St. Augustine speak the only homily on that text. The saint wrote, 'It is you, Mother Church, who makes wives subject to their husbands and sets husbands over their wives. You teach slaves to be loyal to their masters. You teach kings to rule for the benefit of their people, and you it is who warn the peoples to be subservient to their kings . . .'"

In my haste, I collided at the doorway with a young man also evidently eager to escape. We backed apart, murmured apologies, motioned to one another to go first, stepped forward together, collided again, laughed, then carefully departed side by side.

And that was how I came to meet Gudinand.

3

Although Gudinand was three or four years older than myself, we became friends, and remained so during all the rest of that summer. His only family, I discovered, was an invalid mother, and he worked to support her and himself. But whenever he had free time after work, and all day on Sundays, we were almost constantly together. We frequently entertained ourselves with boyishly mischievous recreations (though I would have thought, at his age, Gudinand would have considered such playfulness beneath his dignity)—snatching fruit from a peddler's cart and running off without paying; tying a line of twine to a street post and hiding behind something on the other side of the street, then, when some pompous-looking man came along, raising and tightening the string to trip him and make him fall in a most comical fashion; things like that. We engaged in less roguish activities, too. We ran races against one another, and held tree-climbing contests and wrestling matches, and Gudinand now and again borrowed a tomus in which we went fishing on the lake.

While Wyrd was still in Constantia, selling our pelts—and getting a very good price for them, and giving me a sufficiency of money for my day-to-day spending (the rest of my share of our earnings he tucked away for safekeeping)—he met Gudinand once or twice and appeared to approve of my having found a new friend.

After I had first introduced Gudinand to Wyrd, the young man said to me, "He looks too old to be your father. Is he your grandfather?"

"No relation at all," I said. And then, not wanting to diminish myself in Gudinand's esteem by admitting that I was but an apprentice to a master, I lied and said, as if I were the coddled offspring of some noble family, "I am his ward. Wyrd is my guardian."

Gudinand might well have wondered what I was being guarded *against,* and why any noble scion would have been made the ward of a rough-hewn old woodsman, but he did not inquire further.

When Wyrd had concluded all our business transactions in Constantia, since there would be no more fur-hunting for us to do until autumn, he spent the summer rambling on horseback around the margins of the lake, calling on other old-soldier comrades of his—at the fort of Arbor Felix, and in the hill city of Brigantium, and at the island garrison of Castrum Tiberii. I was not overeager to idle away the summer in drinking with him and his elderly fellows, and listening to their interminable reminiscences. I was satisfied to remain in Constantia and consort with Gudinand as often as I could.

I was free to gambol and sport and make mischief with Gudinand, and I enjoyed that immensely, never having had such a congenial friend before. But there were things about Gudinand that puzzled me. Here was a young man, eighteen or nineteen years old, tall, well built, handsome, intelligent and of almost unfailingly cheerful demeanor—yet *he* seemed never to have had *any* friend, male or female, until I came along. I knew he was an only child, and maybe I was a surrogate younger brother for him. But I could not make out whether he shunned every other person of his own age or whether they shunned him. All I knew was that I never once saw him in the company of anyone else, and that he and I were never joined in our games and frolics by any other boy or girl.

Furthermore, while I had cowardly misrepresented to him my status as a mere apprentice, Gudinand made no secret of what *he* was—even more lowly by any social measurement than I was myself, for he held the meanest and dirtiest employment in one of the local fur-dressing establishments. For five years, he had been an apprentice in that furrier's yard where newly acquired pelts were "leathered"—that is, immersed in a pit full of human urine, to which are added various mineral salts and other substances, and then continuously agitated, pressed, squeezed, wrung out and agitated some more.

That was Gudinand's job: standing day-long and neck-deep in a pit full of rancid urine and other smelly ingredients and even smellier raw pelts, trudging and trampling them with his feet, wringing one after another after another with his hands. Gudinand always, after his day's work was done, either spent a long time in one of the city's cheaper thermae or took several successive soap baths in the lake, before meeting me for our playing times together. And he strictly forbade me ever to visit him while he worked, but I had seen that revolting work done at other furriers' establishments in Constantia. So I knew what the work entailed—Iésus, I thought, Gudinand was probably leathering some of the pelts I myself had procured!—and I also knew it to be such a vile employment that usually only the most worthless slaves were compelled to do it.

I could not understand why Gudinand should ever have accepted that dismal occupation, or why his superiors had never promoted him from the pit to some more estimable position, or why he had uncomplainingly done that filthy work for so many years, or why he seemed reconciled to doing it for perhaps the rest of his life. I say again: here was a fine-looking, personable, affable young man, never very talkative but not at all slow-witted—he had not had my advantages of schooling, but he *had* been taught by his late father to read and write the Gothic script.

Every merchant in Constantia should have been vying to hire him as a welcomer of customers, to do the first dealings with them, and to put them in an expansive mood, before the merchant himself would slither out to handle the hard haggling of whatever business was to be transacted. Gudinand would have made a superb welcomer. Why he had never applied for such a position, or why no merchant had ever sought him out for it, was beyond my comprehension. However, since Gudinand asked me few questions about myself, I forbore from pestering him for answers to my puzzlements about him and his reclusive way of life. He was my friend and I was his. What more do two good friends really need to know about one another?

There was, however, one additional aspect of him that not only bewildered me but actually troubled me. Now and again—and we might be engaged in some merrily active game—Gudinand would suddenly stop still, look solemn or even worried, and ask me something like:

"Thorn, did you see that green bird that just flew past?"

"Ne, Gudinand. I saw no bird at all. And I never saw a *green* bird in all my life."

Or he might remark on the hot wind, or the cold wind, that had sprung up—when I felt no wind whatever, and no nearby bush or tree had so much as rustled its leaves. It was not until after Gudinand had several times seen or felt something imperceptible to me that I noticed something else about him. On each of those occasions, he would draw his thumbs so tightly against his palms that he appeared to have hands with only four fingers apiece. And if he chanced to be barefooted, his toes would curl so tightly under his soles that he seemed almost to have hoofs like an animal. Even more disturbing to me, at that moment and without another word, Gudinand would go running off, as fast as he could run on those hoof-feet, and I would not see him again for the rest of the day. Then, when we did next meet, he never proffered any explanation or apology for his odd behavior and abrupt abandonment of me. Each time, he acted as if he had totally forgotten having behaved so, and that was more mystifying yet.

Still, those occasions were seldom enough that they did not seriously interfere with our companionship, so—on this subject, too—I forbore from prying. Anyway, I must confess that, by this time, I had recognized that *I* was having strange emotions and thoughts and daydreams of a sort I had never had before, and that realization gave me more cause for perplexity than any of Gudinand's eccentricities.

During the early days of our friendship, I had admired Gudinand as any younger boy would do—for his being older, more athletic, more self-assured, and for his befriending me without any hint of elder-brother haughtiness. After a while, though, especially when we would both strip down to mere loincloths for a footrace or a wrestling bout, and I could see Gudinand all but naked, I found myself admiring him more as a moonling adolescent girl would do—for his handsomeness, muscularity, manly grace and attractiveness.

I would be putting it mildly to say that this surprised me. I had supposed that the female half of my nature was soft and passive and shyly retiring. Now I was discovering that it could manifest appetites and urges just as assertively as did my male half. Here again, as had happened when the child Becga was slain, I was troubled by the disharmony between the disparate components of myself. Back then, I had with only *some* difficulty made the masculine part of me subdue the sentimentality of the feminine. But now it seemed that the feminine

200

was being the dominant part, while the masculine was able only to look on, so to speak, and view with some alarm what was happening to me.

Before long, it was costing me an effort to stay my hand from reaching out to caress Gudinand's bare bronzed skin or to tousle his tawny hair. Eventually, it required all my determination, but somehow I managed to conceal those impulses and feelings. I knew that Gudinand would be astonished, disconcerted or even repulsed if ever he should glimpse that aspect of myself. And I valued our masculine friendship too much to risk impairing it, just for some brief and trivial gratification of my transitory whims. Except that they were not whims and they were not transitory. They were yearnings, and, after a time, instead of occurring only now and then, they more and more often possessed me, even when Gudinand and I were strenuously engaged in some definitely boyish activity, until they were a constant hunger in me aching to be allayed.

When we wrestled together, I more often than not was the one who was finally pinned helpless on his back. Though I was strong for my age and slender size, Gudinand was the heavier and more adroit in the holds and twists of that athletic contest. So, every time he prevailed, I pretended petulance and anger at my having lost the struggle. But in fact I enjoyed having him masterfully atop me, pinioning my wrists with his hands, my legs with his, both of us panting while he easily restrained my heaving to get free, and while he grinned down at me and dripped warm sweat from his face onto mine. On the few occasions that I pinned *him* to the ground and victoriously straddled his supine body, I had an almost irresistible urge to lower myself full length upon him, to clasp him gently instead of forcefully, and to roll both of us over to set him on top.

201

I realized—with perhaps as much dismay and near-horror as Gudinand would have felt if he had realized—that I wanted him to hold me, to fondle me, to kiss me, even to possess me sexually. But while my rational mind was recoiling from the thought of any such absurd doings, some less rational recess of my mind was thrilled and titillated whenever I imagined those things happening. And so was my body, in ways quite new to me.

In times past, when I knew that Deidamia and I would soon be lying entwined—and more recently, when I might espy a beautiful and desirable girl or young woman on the streets of some place like Vesontio, even here in Constantia—that caused me to feel a curious but pleasant sensation in my throat. I felt it below the hinges of my jaw—why there, I do not know—and from beneath my tongue came an increase of salivation that made me have to swallow repeatedly. Whether that particular response to sexual arousal was peculiar to me alone, I have no idea, and never asked another man whether it happened likewise to him. But I am sure it was a distinctly *male* response.

Because now, when I was in Gudinand's company, I felt a different, though still curious, still pleasant sensation. This one I felt in and about my *eyes*—and why there, again I do not know. They felt heavy-lidded but not sleepy, and if at such a moment I looked at my reflection in a speculum, I could see that my pupils were widely dilated, even in brightest daylight. So I am certain that this response must have been the female counterpart of the male's sensation in the throat.

I felt physical changes in more expectable places, too. My nipples stood up and became so tender that just the cloth of my tunic brushing against them made me fairly ripple with excitement. My nether female parts I could feel getting engorged and warm and moist. But, oddly, although my male organ at those times became even more sensitive to touch than did my nipples, it did not get rigid and rear up into a fascinum, as it had done when I was sexually engaged with Brother Peter and Sister Deidamia.

This new and anomalous condition—an access of sexual agitation but no upraising of a fascinum—I could only attribute to the fact that, all the while Peter was molesting me, I had believed myself to be a boy, and when Deidamia and I frolicked, she had been indubitably an alluring girl. So, in both cases, my virile organ had evidently responded as a boy's would be expected to. But now I knew—and all my organs seemed to know—that Gudinand was indubitably a male, that I wanted him as a female would, and that my female self was in control of every part of me.

At last, I was so much obsessed by my wishful daydreams, and so frustrated by the impossibility of their ever coming true, that I seriously considered saying farewell to Gudinand and wandering southward down the lake after old Wyrd. But then, one Sunday—it was a day too hot and sticky for any arduous play—Gudinand and I were lolling in a field of wildflowers outside the city. We were eating bread and cheese that we had brought, while we idly discussed impish ways of spending the day, such as our going into the back alleys of Constantia to taunt and harass the Jew shopkeepers there—when suddenly Gudinand said:

"Listen, Thorn. I hear an owl hooting."

202

I laughed. "An owl awake at midday in midsummer? I do not think—"

And then Gudinand got an anguished look on his face, and his thumbs curled tight against his palms. There was one thing different this time: just before he ran away from me, he uttered a dolorous cry, as of real pain. I had never before followed him when those episodes occurred. Now I did. Perhaps I chased after him just because of that unusual noise he had made, perhaps because I had lately been entertaining so many feminine feelings that they may even have afflicted me with a trace of maternal solicitude.

Gudinand might have been able to outrun me, even on his hoof-feet, but I caught up to him in a copse near the lake, because he had fallen to the ground there. Clearly, he had run only far enough to find a place of concealment before succumbing to the convulsion that now had him in its grip. He was not thrashing about; he lay on his back and his body was rock-rigid, but his head, arms and legs were in spasm, all quivering as does a bowstring after the arrow is loosed. His face was so contorted that I would not have recognized it. His eyes were rolled back in his head so that only the whites showed. His tongue was thrust far out of his mouth, and an excessive salivation spilled out around it. He also stank most revoltingly, for he had voided both urine and feces.

I had never seen such a convulsion before, but I knew what it was: the falling sickness. An elderly monk at St. Damian's, a Brother Philotheus, had suffered from that infirmity—which was why he had taken the cowl, his seizures having been so frequent that he was unfit for any other vocation. Philotheus never endured an attack in my presence, and he died while I was still quite young. Nevertheless, our infirmarian, Brother Hormisdas, told all of us at the abbey what those fits were like, and gave us some rudimentary instruction in what to do to help our brother if we *should* be nearby when he fell into one.

So now I followed those instructions. I broke a twig from one of the saplings in the copse and, braving the awful smell and appearance of Gudinand, went to him and thrust the twig between his upper teeth and his tongue, to prevent his biting it off. Having with me the waist wallet in which I had carried my meal, I took from it my screw of salt, and sprinkled that on Gudinand's thrust-out tongue, hoping some of it would trickle down his throat. I had also on my belt my case knife, so I took it from its sheath and wedged the blade under one of Gudinand's clenched thumbs so he held it against that palm. Brother Hormisdas had said, "Put a piece of cold metal in the victim's hand," and the knife

203

was barely cool, but it was the only metal I had about me. Last of all—
and breathing through my mouth as best I could, to keep Gudinand's
smell out of my nostrils—I leaned over and pressed my hands on his
abdomen and maintained the pressure there. Those several assistances,
the infirmarian had said, would ameliorate and shorten the seizure.

Whether they did or not, I do not know, for it seemed to me that I
remained leaning on Gudinand's belly for an excruciating long time.
But finally, and as abruptly as he had spoken of the owl's hoot, Gudinand's tense abdominal muscles relaxed under my hands. His extremities ceased quivering, his eyes rolled into their proper position and
wearily closed, his tongue retracted into his mouth and my twig fell
away. His countenance was again that of the Gudinand I knew. Then
he merely lay there, breathing so that his breast shuddered, as if he had
just then collapsed after running a long footrace. I plucked a wisp of
grass and wiped from his chin and neck and cheeks the spittle that
slimed them. There was nothing I could do about his other excretions,
for they were inside his clothes. So I, rather thankfully, withdrew to a
distance and sat down against a tree and waited.

Gradually, Gudinand's ragged breathing subsided. After another
while, he opened his eyes and, without moving his head, he looked up,
down, to either side, obviously trying to calculate where he was and
how he had got there. Then, cautiously, he raised himself to a sitting
position and turned his head this way and that for a better look around.
He caught sight of me, sitting well away, and what he did then
astounded me. I might have expected him to grimace in embarrassment
or distress at my having witnessed his seizure. Instead, he smiled
brightly and called buoyantly to me, as if our mealtime conversation
had never been interrupted:

"Well, *are* we off to make mischief among the Jews? Or are we simply
going to laze about all day?"

As I have said, I had often wondered, when at other times we had
met again after one of his disappearances, whether he had forgotten
having done so, or merely preferred to appear that he had forgotten.
Now I knew that he truly never had any remembrance of anything that
happened on those occasions. Because it certainly was evident, this
time, that Gudinand had no least recollection of his mention of that
nonexistent owl, of his having cried out and dashed away, of the agonies he had gone through in this copse, of how much time had elapsed
since either of us last spoke of making mischief. I could only sit where I
was and gawk at him.

So he got to his feet, rather stiffly, for his muscles must have been painfully cramped by their recent rigor, and started to saunter over to me. But when he stood up, the movement gave him a whiff of his stench, and he stopped as if lightning-struck. Now his face did crumple, almost to weeping, with dismay and self-disgust, and he shut his eyes tightly and shook his head in abject sadness. He said, so quietly that I barely heard him, "You saw. Goodbye, Thorn. I go to wash," and he stalked stiffly off toward the lake, taking care to walk well wide of me.

When he returned, he was wearing only his athletic loincloth, dripping wet, and carrying in his arms the rest of his equally wet clothing. At sight of me, still sitting against my tree, he looked genuinely surprised.

"Thorn! You did not leave?"

"Ne. Why should I?"

"Except for my old mother, everyone else who has ever learned of my—learned about *me*—has gone away from me, and stayed away. Surely you must have wondered why I have no friends. I used to have, from time to time, but I lost them all."

"Then they were not worthy to be called friends," I said. "Is that also why you continue in that squalid occupation at the furrier's?"

He nodded. "No one else will hire a worker who is liable to fall into a fit in public view. Where I work now, I am out of sight, and"—he laughed bleakly—"if I suffer a convulsion in the pit, it does not much interrupt my labors. It actually *helps* in the agitation of the pelts. My only worry is that sometime I may not have sufficient warning of the attack, and will not have time to seize the pit's edge to hold myself upright. If that happens, I shall drown in that ghastly liquid."

I said, "I once knew an aged monk who suffered from the same affliction. His medicus made him regularly drink a decoction of darnel grass seeds. It was supposed to make his attacks less frequent or less severe. Have you tried that?"

Gudinand nodded again. "My mother used to spoon it into me religiously. But a too heavy dose of darnel extract—and the dosage is difficult to judge—can be a lethal poison. So she stopped doing that. She would rather have a live monstrosity than a dead one."

"You are no monstrosity!" I snapped. "Why, some of the great men of history have been afflicted with the falling sickness all their lives long. Alexander, the Caesar Julius, even the sainted Paul. It did not hinder their being great men."

205

"Well," he said with a sigh, "there is a remote chance that I may *not* have it all my life long."

"How so? I thought it an incurable ailment."

"It is, for someone who first gets infected with it when he or she is full-grown—as I assume was the case with your aged monk. But for one who has it from birth, as I have . . . well, they say that it will disappear when a girl has her first menstruum or a boy his, er, sexual initiation." Gudinand blushed deeply. "Which I have not."

"That really will cure it?" I said excitedly. "But how marvelous! Then why in the world have you remained a virgin for so long? You could have lain with a female when you were my age. Or even younger."

"Do not make mock of me, Thorn," he said miserably. "Lain with *what* female? Every woman in Constantia and for miles around knows about me. Every girl-child is early warned against me by her parents. No female would risk getting pregnant by me and bearing an equally afflicted child. Even men and boys avoid me, for fear I will infect them. I should have to go very far away from here to befriend or seduce an unwary female, and I cannot leave my ailing mother."

206   "Akh, come now, Gudinand! There are the local lupanares. They do not cost much for a—"

"Ne. Every prostitute has refused me, either from fear of catching my disease or for fear that I might go into convulsion in the middle of the copulative act and somehow injure her. My only hope is to encounter some girl or woman newly come to the city, and win her love—or at least her acquiescence—before the gossips warn her against me. But female travelers are few. And anyway, I hardly know how I would accost her. I have been a solitary for so long that I am awkward and tongue-tied with other people. I thought it a blessed circumstance that I met *you* as I did, sheerly by accident."

I pondered for a bit, and an outrageous idea came into my head (and my eyes got heavy-lidded), and now it was I who blushed. But I reminded myself: I had long ago sworn that I would never be inhibited by conscience or what the world calls morality. Besides, even if my idea was inspired in part by my own selfish desires, the most fanatical moralist ought to condone it as a good deed, since it might be the one thing that could liberate dear Gudinand from his hideous affliction.

I said, "As it happens, Gudinand, there *is* a newcome young female in Constantia, and I can arrange for you to meet her."

He said eagerly, "There is? You can?" Then his face got glum again. "But she is sure to hear all about me before I could possibly—"

"I will *tell* her all about you. And you need waste no time in prolonged courtship or elaborate seduction. She would not, in any case, fall in love with you. She has vowed never to fall in love with anybody. But she will gladly lie with you, and will do it as often as it takes to cure your falling sickness."

"What?!" Gudinand exclaimed unbelievingly. "Why in the name of heaven *would* she?"

"For one reason, she fears no pregnancy. Her medicus long ago told her that she will be forever barren. For another reason, she will do it to oblige me."

"What?!" Gudinand exclaimed again, now utterly awestruck. *"Why?"*

"Because I am your friend, and she is my sister. My twin sister."

"Liufs Guth!" cried Gudinand. "You would play panderer of your own *sister?!"*

"Ne. I really have no need to. I have been praising you to her all this summer, so she knows of your many good qualities. And she has seen you, when you accompanied me sometimes to the door of our lodgings, so she knows that you are comely. Most important, she is a very kind, warmhearted person, and she would unhesitatingly do anything to ease your suffering."

"How could she have seen me without my seeing her? I did not even know you *had* a sister. What is she called?"

"Ah . . . er . . . Juhiza," I said, snatching at the first feminine name that came to my mind, recalling it from my conversation with the caupo Dylas in Basilea. "Like myself, Juhiza is a ward of the old man Wyrd you have met. And he is most strict with her. She is forbidden to set foot outside our lodgings until we all three are ready to move on from here. It was from her window at the deversorium that she saw you. However, now that Wyrd is out of the city, I shall disobey his orders and arrange for you to meet her. Juhiza will not confess the misdeed to our guardian, and neither will I, and surely you would not tell on us."

"Of course not," said Gudinand dazedly. "But . . . but if she is your twin . . . a girl so young . . ."

"Alas," I said, assuming an air of melancholy. "Not young enough to have her virginity still. There was a tragic love affair. With one of her tutors—but he proved faithless, and married someone else. That is why our guardian keeps Juhiza under such strict restraint. That is also why she has determined never to love again."

"Well . . ." said Gudinand, looking radiant at the happy prospect.

207

"Probably it is better that she is not virgin, because she will know . . . er . . . what to do."

"I daresay. And she ought to be a most enlightening teacher at your initiation, as you call it. You will be a better lover of other women afterward, when your affliction is removed and you can *have* other women."

"Liufs Guth," Gudinand whispered to himself. Then he said, "Not that it matters, but . . . is she pretty?"

I shrugged. "What brother ever can admire or even assess his own sister? Still, Juhiza *is* my twin, and people do say that we resemble one another."

"And you are fair of countenance, indeed. Well . . . what can I say, Thorn? If Juhiza really is amenable to doing this extreme kindness for an absolute stranger, I can only thank and bless her. And you, too. How might we arrange the meeting?"

"Why not right here in this copse?" I suggested. "There are no prying eyes hereabout. And it might be of some significance—perhaps even make the cure more quick and sure—if you and she lie together in this place where I first witnessed your suffering. Who knows? That seizure may prove to have been your *last*. Ja, I think it should be here. And you two will certainly not want me around. So I shall not even come along to introduce her. I will simply direct her to this place, and send her here tomorrow night, at the hour you and I have been accustomed to meet."

"Audagei af Guth faúr jah iggar!" Gudinand said feelingly: "God's blessing on both of you!"

And that was how "Juhiza" came to meet Gudinand.

4

The next day, when I went to the lakeside copse at the appointed twilight hour, I of course wore my feminine garb—gown, kerchief, some beautifying but not excessive touches of cosmetics on my face and a modest but becoming number of the baubles I had bought in Basilea. Under my clothes, I wore the binding strophion around my chest to upraise and enhance my breasts, and a girdling band to clasp my virile member tight against my lower belly and render it imperceptible. I also wore my feminine sandals, because, every other time I had been with Gudinand, except when we were barefooted, I had worn my cowhide boots—so the sandals made "Juhiza," at first sight, seem a trifle shorter than Thorn.

Some still-conscious trace of my male self kept trying to insinuate into my mind the accusation that I was doing nothing but disguising myself, as I had done in Vesontio to test the response of the riverfront prostitutes—and that I was being nothing better than a prostitute myself, soliciting the favors of an innocent young man for my own base purposes. But my female self put that troublesome idea firmly out of my head. Yes, I was taking advantage of this opportunity to consummate a union with the Gudinand for whom my admiration, affection and yearning had been building during these months I had known him. But I could not believe that to be an utterly *base* motive. After all, I was the only female anywhere who would willingly do this for him, to liberate him from his crippling affliction and let him henceforward lead a normal life—*not* with me, Juhiza, for I would be moving on eastward at summer's end—but with some lover or wife of his own choosing, and in some higher employment than the miserable occupation he had for so long been enduring.

As for my male self's nagging insistence that Juhiza was merely Thorn in disguise . . . well, it is true that both gods and mortals have been known to adopt the garb of the opposite sex, either for frolic or for mischief. The pagans say that Wotan wooed Rhind the Winter Queen by dressing himself in female attire, because Rhind scorned all male suitors. But I was not dissembling; I *was* female; I was entitled by nature to *appear* the female that I was and am.

Long ages before my time, the poet Terence wrote, "I am a man. Nothing human is alien to me." I do not think I was presumptuous in believing, because I was both a man *and* a woman, that I was even better qualified than Terence to aver that "nothing human is alien to me." So when I went as Juhiza to meet Gudinand, I left behind every doubt and uncertainty. I was a female and I would *be* a female. I was firmly convinced that, if I were a man, I could unhesitatingly have fallen in love with the young woman I was then. But I would let circumstances decide that. I would simply wait for the outcome of this encounter: to prove or disprove how authentic and successful a female I was.

Gudinand had admitted to being tongue-tied with strangers, and today he was most noticeably fidgety and flushed of face. However, the moment I introduced myself, he blurted in amazed admiration, "Why, you *are* almost identical to my friend Thorn. I mean your brother Thorn. Except"—and he blushed even redder—"Thorn is only a handsome boy and you are a most beautiful girl." I smiled and inclined my head in maidenly thanks for the compliment, and he babbled on, "You are also just a little smaller and more slender than he. And . . . you have protuberances and curves where a boy does not."

Well, *he* also had a protuberance, quite evident at the crotch of his trousers. And, I confess, I had been heavy-lidded with desire since the day before. Now my various female organs were all but palpitating. So I said brazenly:

"Gudinand, we both know why we are met here. Would you not like a clearer look at my curves?" His blush deepened almost to maroon. I went on, "I know what *I* look like underneath my clothes, but I have never seen you otherwise than full-clad. Why do not we both undress at the same time? That way, we will spare ourselves all the time-wasting feints and coynesses of new-met lovers getting acquainted with one another."

I am sure that, if Gudinand had ever in his life had any normal social relations with any girl or woman, he would have been scandalized by my blatant shamelessness. But he appeared to take it for granted that I was a woman of the world and knew the proper ways of boy-meeting-girl, and he obediently if awkwardly began to doff his garments. So did I, not awkwardly but with provocative grace and slowness. As I revealed more and more of myself, Gudinand's eyes bulged and his mouth opened and his breathing became a panting. I tried to seem in cool possession of myself, and to restrain my own responses at seeing him totally naked for the first time. But that was difficult. The moment I saw his fascinum—as ruddy, large and rigid as Brother Peter's ever had been—I felt a warm, thick wetness issue from my female parts and ooze down the inside of one thigh. A little surprised at that, I let one of my hands brush myself there, and found that those parts had opened most invitingly. Also, they were so sensitive to that merest touch that I shuddered at the thrill.

Gudinand's wide and wondering gaze roamed up and down me, from my face to my breasts to my groin, and the blush that had suffused only his face now spread midway down his chest. He moved his lips several times, and had to moisten them with a lick of his tongue before he could get out the next words. (I have to say that my whole body thrilled, then, as if he had licked *me*; though at the same time I worried that he might be getting so very agitated that it could bring on one of his seizures.) But all he said was:

"Why do you not remove that last bit of apparel—that band you wear around your hips?"

I said primly, repeating what Wyrd had told me, "A decent Christian woman is expected always to keep wearing at least one of her undergarments while doing—what we are about to do. It will not impede our pleasure, Gudinand." I spread wide my arms. "Come, let us give pleasure to one another."

Now with his eyes downcast, he muttered, "I . . . I do not really know . . . well . . . how that is done . . ."

"Be not embarrassed. Thorn already told me that. You will find that it comes easily and naturally. First . . ." I took him in my arms and eased us both gently down onto the soft grass, lying on our sides, our bodies pressed close together. And immediately, startlingly, with no more excitation than our closeness, Gudinand experienced what must have been his first-ever sexual release.

I could only assume that he had never once indulged in what the monks of St. Damian's condemned as "the solitary vice," or that he had ever even experienced a succuba-inspired dream resulting in self-pollution. Because his fascinum gave a mighty throb against my belly and

211

spurted nearly up to my breasts a most incredibly copious, warm, almost-hot jet of that fluid. When it did, Gudinand uttered a long, loud cry of surprise, relief and unfeigned joy.

What is more, I cried out, too. Without having had any other stimulation—merely from the realization that I, as a female, had so easily given this young man such pleasure—my own body emulated, in its fashion, what had happened to him. I felt that indescribable gathering and rushing and bursting inside myself, and my body convulsed almost as if *I* were in the throes of a falling-sickness fit, and I too gave a long, loud ululation in accompaniment. I had not been as long deprived of sexual enjoyment as had Gudinand, but this *was* the first time I had engaged in it since I last had lain with Deidamia.

There ensued a rather lengthy and quiet interval, while we lay as we had been, still tightly clasped together—indeed, almost glued together by our exudations—and gradually the thrillings of our bodies and the gasping of our breathing subsided. At last, Gudinand murmured shyly in my ear:

"So that is how it is done?"

"Well . . ." I said, with a small laugh, "that is one way. It gets even better, Gudinand. This having been your first time, you were, let us say, a bit too eager. Now your body will require a short rest before that can happen again, and I promise you the next will surpass the first one. In the meantime, let us simply play with each other's . . . well . . . let me demonstrate. And you do to me, more or less, what I do to you."

So I showed him every means of mutual sexual arousal that Deidamia and I had taught to one another—and the numerous variations and gradations she and I had devised—though this time the partners' functions were reversed: I being Sister Deidamia, so to speak, and Gudinand being Brother Thorn. For me, this encounter was exhilarating enough, simply because it was my first as a genuine female, but I believe that the seeming capability of Gudinand and myself to keep on changing our identities in such dizzying variegation—at least in my own imagination—gave an additional zest to my raptures.

After a considerable while of our doing everything *but* the conventional joining of man and woman, I held Gudinand away at arm's length and said, "Your fountain seems inexhaustible. But do save some of it until I can show you another way. These variant couplings are enjoyable, I know, but—"

"Enjoyable . . ." he gasped, "is a pale word . . . for what they are . . ."

"Still, they are but variations. According to what you told Thorn—

and he told me—your falling sickness can only be cured by your sexual initiation. And I would take that to mean your initiation into what Christian husbands and wives and priests regard as the sole and single normal, orthodox, decent and allowable manner of sexual intercourse. If the conventional manner *is* the one necessary to rid you of your affliction, we really ought to employ it at least once."

"Ja, Juhiza. And how do we do that?"

"Look here," I said, and pointed. "This place of mine where you just now had your finger. When next your organ has raised itself into a fascinum, you put *it* in there, but slowly, gently, to its very hilt. And then . . . well . . . akh, Gudinand, surely you have seen street dogs and farm animals do this thing!"

"Of course, of course. Then . . . let me see . . . you will have to raise yourself on elbows and knees, while I—"

"Ne, ni allis!" I snapped, rather angrily, for that was the posture in which I had been used by the vile Brother Peter. "We are not street dogs! Akh, in time, no doubt, if we lie together on other occasions, we will try that variation also. But, for now, I will show you how the devout Christian men and women do it, as soon as you are ready again."

"Very soon," said Gudinand, smiling beatifically. "Just the thought of it—see—is already arousing me and . . . akh, *Juhiza!*"

He gave that exclamation because I had embraced him with one of my arms and rolled him prone atop my supine body, while with my other hand I guided his only-limber but quickly hardening organ.

"Liufs Guth!" he cried, as it slid in, stiffening even more quickly as it did so.

I likewise made several fervent exclamations, then and thereafter, but, if they were coherent words at all, I do not remember what they were. I felt whole-souled gratification when Gudinand was inside me, and I cannot say whether I experienced such sublime joy because I felt so much affection and desire for Gudinand, or whether it was simply because now I knew what I was doing, and *wanted* to be doing it.

Also, in this particular position: the male partner atop the female— a position as novel to me as it was to Gudinand—I could enjoy two new stimulants to my arousal. Though Gudinand tried not to lie too heavily on me, his chest now and again brushed tantalizingly against my eagerly upthrust nipples. And I could feel, as I never had with Brother Peter in the street-dog position *he* always insisted on, Gudinand's heavy male scrotal sac thumping voluptuously against the delicate frenulum below my orifice. Furthermore, and best of all for me,

213

having Gudinand lying on top of me meant that his every thrust rubbed his lower body against the cloth band under which was my own sometimes-male organ. It was not now being male; it remained limp and passive; but it had become tender and sensitive to an almost intolerably exaggerated degree. Gudinand's rhythmic rubbing against it added such a stimulus to all the others I was feeling that I was soon quite delirious, nearly to the point of swooning.

But I did not swoon. I began to feel the familiar, but this time immeasurably enhanced, sensation of a gathering of indefinable forces within myself—not just in my sexual parts but throughout my entire body—and then the delicious rushing sensation, as of drunken giddiness. The inner sheath of my female cavity, through no volition of mine, began that same sort of engulfing, swallowing spasm with which Deidamia's inner muscles had used to clasp at my own fascinum. My thighs, widespread on either side of Gudinand's hips, also went into a spasm that was new to me. Their sinews and muscles quivered, twitched, convulsed uncontrollably. And all those things kept on happening while my ecstasy culminated in the most eruptive, tempestuous, surpassingly blissful release I had ever yet enjoyed in any sexual act.

It must have been much the same for Gudinand, though I was too happily preoccupied with my own gratification even to feel the geyser of his ejaculation inside me. At any rate, his burst of release was certainly simultaneous with my own, for together we uttered such long, loud cries and moans and exclamations that we might have been heard by fishers in their tomi far out on the lake.

When he was spent, Gudinand collapsed upon me as if *he* indeed had swooned, but I did not feel his weight. I felt feather-light, disembodied, euphoric, and I would not have been surprised to hear myself purring like a comfortable cat. But then, suddenly, something *did* surprise me. Without any help from Gudinand—his organ having gone flaccid inside me until I could no longer be sure it was still there—I experienced again an internal gathering and a rushing and a burst of pleasurable release. It was softer, milder, nowhere near so epic as the previous one had been, but it did happen, and apparently of its own accord, and it was assuredly not unwelcome.

I wondered at that. And I wondered even more when, some few minutes later, it happened *again*. And, after another short while, *again*. Each time it was lesser in intensity, but never less than enjoyable. Finally, those inexplicable happenings diminished and ceased entirely, but they had taught me another new thing about my female self. I was blessed with the capacity for the additional enjoyment, after a really grand episode of sexual release, of what I can only describe as after-claps—like the continuing, sporadic, gradually dwindling echoes one hears after a tumultuous crash of thunder. That wondrous capability of enjoying additional little blissfulnesses may have been peculiar to my-self alone, or all women may be so fortunate; I have never inquired of another female. I do know, though, that it has never happened to me when I was being the male partner in sexual intercourse.

Something else I learned—not just about my own female self but about women in general—is that there is one thing no woman can feign or pretend.

A woman, for whatever reason—to flatter a lover, or to beguile one, or to deceive one—can pretend that she is experiencing all kinds of loverlike sensations. She can make her face falsely express any degree of rapture. She can will her nipples to stand enticingly upright—or the nipples can innocently do that of themselves, from their being chilled, or from their merely being stared at by a man. A woman can make the petals of her sexual organs part invitingly and become alluringly moist, by secretly manipulating them herself—or they, too, can do that inno-cently, depending on the time of the month and the phase of the moon. A woman can feign any degree of sexual arousal, from first girlish blush to final, thrashing, wailing culmination—and she can do it so convinc-ingly as to delude her own long-married husband or the most widely experienced seducer.

215

But one thing she *cannot* simulate, strive though she might. That is the convulsive spasm of the thews of her inner thighs, the quivering, twitching, throbbing of them—as I have described having happened with my own. A woman has no least control over that particular mani-festation; she can neither quell it when it occurs nor counterfeit it when it does not. It happens only when she is entwined and coupled with a partner who can send her *genuinely* into the throes of that final joyous burst of sexual release.

✠   ✠   ✠

It was long after nightfall when Gudinand and I had finally exhausted all our physical capacities and our imaginative faculties, and drained ourselves of our various juices, and I had taught him just about all I had ever learned about sexual coupling. As we redonned our clothing in the dark—a task made more difficult by our both being rather weak and trembly—Gudinand told me, and fervently, and over and over again, what a splendid girl I was, and what an unbelievably enjoyable time it had been for him, and how slavishly grateful he was to me. I tried to convey, with equal gratitude but with maidenly demureness, that he had given as good as he had got. I added that I hoped we *had* effected the cure of his falling sickness.

We were taking different roads back to the city, so we parted with a kiss, and I—probably he, too—wobbled off toward Constantia on legs that seemed to have turned to jelly. I went directly to a therma that was reserved for women only, and was admitted without demur. In the apodyterium, when I undressed, I again did not strip entirely, but kept the binding band around my hips. This caused no comment, for many of the other female bathers likewise retained one or another small undergarment. One woman might keep her pudendum covered, another her breasts, and I assumed that that was simply for token modesty. But others kept concealed innocuous parts of their bodies—just one foot or one shoulder or one thigh. I could only suppose that they were hiding a minor deformity or a birthmark, or perhaps the imprint of a lover's nibble. Some of the attendant slaves were women themselves, and others were eunuchs, but all were evidently well trained in discretion. When I was anointed with oil in the unctuarium, and later scraped clean of it in the sudatorium, none of the attendants remarked on my having to be cleansed of several encrustations that the human body normally does not accumulate in the course of a day.

In the last room of the therma, as I splashed luxuriously about in the balineum's warm waters, I eyed the other females who were doing the same. They were of all ages and sizes and degrees of comeliness or plainness, from children to budding maids to obese or scrawny old ladies. I wondered idly how many of them had come to the baths to recover from just such a session of amorous dalliance as I had enjoyed.

There was at least one in the pool who was attractive enough to make me suspect that she might have done just that, and she was drifting about as lazily and languorously as if she *had*. She was a matron perhaps old enough to have been my mother—or even Gudinand's— but she was dark-haired, dark-eyed, beautiful and shapely, unmarked by time and clearly proud to show the fact. Even here in the company of none but other females, she was displaying her charms as if for the benefit of a whole legion of lovers, for she was one of the few among us swimming entirely nude.

No doubt I let my speculative gaze linger overlong on her. She returned my look, then swam sinuously over to me, and I expected her to scold me for having stared so rudely. But she did not; she merely spoke some trite pleasantries: how refreshing it was to see a new face hereabout . . . and was not the bath blissfully stimulating to all one's senses? . . . and her own name was Robeya and what was mine? Then, as she talked, she reached out, took my hand and cupped it over one of her bare breasts, while her other hand caressed my own (much less ample) bosom. I gasped at her unexpected audacity, and I gasped again when she leaned close, to whisper in my ear a decidedly explicit invitation.

She added, "We need not even leave the water. We can go to that far and darker corner yonder to do it."

Had I been Thorn, I might readily have accepted. But, being Juhiza, I merely smiled at her a sweetly satisfied smile and said, "Thank you, dear Robeya, but I have spent this entire evening being extremely well pleasured by an extremely *manly* lover."

She let go of me as if she had scalded herself, and snarled a word— no doubt some Helvetic expletive that I had not yet learned—and thrashed angrily away across the pool. I simply went on smiling, and was still smiling as I dressed and left the therma, and I smiled all the way to my room at the deversorium, and I think I went on smiling the night long, as I slept the good sleep of the sexually well-satisfied female.

217

✠   ✠   ✠

By the next day, I was revivified, no longer trembly of body, no longer awash in sentimental recollection of those emotional hours with Gudinand. Having now experienced *such* a transcendental release and assuaging of all my feminine desires, I believe the female half of me had— at least temporarily—subsided to a sort of slumbrous abdication, and my male half was again in control of me. I was able to dress as Thorn, and act as Thorn, and think as Thorn, and *be* Thorn, when I went again to the lakeside copse to meet Gudinand after his stint that day in the furrier's pit. I was able to greet him and regard him, not with any feminine yearnings or stirrings, but with the same simple boy-to-boy comradeship I had earlier felt when we were first friends and playmates.

In truth, I was again so much Thorn, so much the male, that it rather annoyed me to hear Gudinand exult about the marvelous girl and the marvelous doings he had enjoyed the night before. (I mention this only to make plain how many and disparate were the feelings that I, as a mannamavi not yet grown, had to learn to deal with.) I really ought to have been flattered by Gudinand's compliments and plaudits to my other self, Juhiza. But I suppose any normal boy—and at the moment I was *being* a normal boy—hearing another boy crow about an amorous adventure, and he being unable to counter with any braggart stories of his own, is bound to harbor some envy of the other boy's superiority in that regard. Anyway, Gudinand went on declaiming at length:

"Liufs Guth, friend Thorn, but your sister is extraordinary! Extraordinary in her beauty, her kindness, her courage, her talents, her . . . er . . ."

Well, he was decently reticent about the details, but *I* knew every one of them. So, among all my numerous conflicting feelings was another, and this one *not* normal but irrational. I actually felt resentful of my friend Gudinand's having had such pleasure with me, but *without* me, if that makes any sense at all. I said to myself: Stop this! You are verging on dementia!—and managed to interrupt Gudinand's effusions by remarking:

"I know Juhiza to be a loving girl-child, and I am sure her company was pleasant to you. But the most important thing is this. Do you think her—her attentions have allayed that affliction of yours?"

He shrugged helplessly. "How can I know? Unless I never again suffer a seizure. That can be the only test." He gave me a weak half-smile. "I could almost be grateful for having *had* the falling sickness, since it led me to such a gloriously memorable remedy. Indeed . . . and the liufs Guth knows I should not say such a thing . . . I could almost wish that the one cure might prove to have been less than totally efficacious . . ."

For an instant, the slumbering Juhiza woke inside me, and made me say, "Well, you know, for some ailments a medicus does prescribe a *course* of treatment . . ." But I sternly suppressed that lascivious impulse, and said, "My sister and I have already once disobeyed our guardian's command. If we do it more often, Wyrd is likely to hear of it from some gossip. Or even return here unexpectedly and find Juhiza absent from our lodgings."

"Ja," Gudinand said despondently. "I have no right to put you two in peril of his anger."

"However," I said, "your peril is greater than ours. If you do suffer another attack, do not conceal it from me. Tell me . . . and I will tell Juhiza . . . and . . ."

His face brightened and he gave me a full smile. "Let us hope that the one cure did serve. Right now, I feel healthier and happier than I have ever felt in my life. That should be a good augury, should it not? Let us put it out of mind. Let us be the Thorn and Gudinand that we were before any of this happened. What say you? Shall we enjoy what is left of today? Shall we race or wrestle or go out fishing on the lake or go back to town and make life livelier for the Jew shopkeepers?"

✠   ✠   ✠

Let me tell only briefly of ensuing events. It was not more than a week later that Gudinand came to our meeting place looking haggard and wretched. That afternoon, he said, while laboring in the leathering pit, he had gone into another convulsion, so suddenly that he had barely had time to seize the brink of the pit and support himself from sinking and drowning. He was sorry to have to tell me, he said, but it appeared that the "sexual initiation" cure had been ineffective . . . or at least insufficient . . .

Thus, the next evening, it was Juhiza who met him in the lakeside copse. What then occurred was much the same as on the previous occasion, so I need not repeat myself; I will say only that it was an even longer and more rapturous coupling than the first had been.

Nor was that time the last. At intervals of perhaps a week thereafter, Gudinand would shamefacedly report to me that he had endured another seizure. I never actually witnessed any of those, but I never doubted him. I refused to believe that he would lie to take advantage of either his friend Thorn or his lover Juhiza. So, every time, I took him at his word, and every time arranged for another meeting between him and Juhiza.

During one of those encounters, besides expressing his earnest thanks and gratitude, as he always did, Gudinand abruptly added, "I love you, Juhiza. As you know, I am—clumsy at expressing my feelings to other people. But you must have suspected that I regard you as far more than a gracious benefactor. I love you. I adore you. If ever I *am* relieved of this cursed affliction, I should like us to—"

I laid a finger across his lips, and I smiled, but I shook my head. "You know that I would not be doing this, my dear, if I did not feel real affection for you. And I confess that I enjoy it as much as you do. But I have sworn never to be in thrall to real love. Even if I were to break my vow, it would be unfair to both of us, for I shall be leaving Constantia at summer's end and—"

"I could leave with you!"

"And drag along your invalid mother as well?" I chided him. "Ne, let us speak of this no more. Let us relish what we have while we have it. Any thought of tomorrow—or of permanence—would only cast a pall

219

over our today and now. Not another word, Gudinand. The darkness is coming fast upon us, and we have better things to do than talk."

✠　✠　✠

I have told of these episodes in as few words as possible, because the next part I cannot tell so briefly. That summer of those many strange and wondrous events ended at last, and there came the autumn, and with it came catastrophe: for Gudinand, for Juhiza and—how could it be otherwise?—for me.

5

220

I should remark that I did not live in a vacuum during those summer months in Constantia. With Wyrd away, and with Gudinand at his labors during most of every day except Sundays, and with no work of my own to occupy me, I had a great deal of time to fill. I did not waste it by simply sitting in my room at the deversorium, waiting for my next meeting with Gudinand, either as Thorn or as Juhiza. True, some of my time I did pass at the deversorium, helping the stable hands feed and groom my horse Velox, or helping them keep soaped and shiny and supple my saddle and bridle leathers.

But much of my free time I spent, either on foot or on horseback, indulging my natural curiosity by exploring Constantia and its environs. I sometimes rode out to meet merchant trains of wagons and pack animals heaped high with trade goods coming into the city, or I might ride for some miles with an outgoing train. I conversed with the teamsters and riders, and learned much about the lands from which they had come and to which they were going.

In the city, I loitered in the markets and warehouses, and made the acquaintance of both sellers and buyers of every sort of goods, and learned much about the art of bargaining to one's best advantage. I even spent some time in Constantia's slave mart, and eventually so ingratiated myself with one Egyptian slave dealer that he, furtively but proudly, gave me a private showing of a particular item of his stock, which, he said, would never be displayed on the public auction block.

"Oukh," he said, which in the Greek tongue means "no." "She is for private, secret sale . . . to some buyer of *very* special requirements . . . because this sort of slave is so *very* rare and expensive."

I looked at her and saw only a naked girl of about my own age— quite a pretty and fetching girl, except that she was an Ethiope. I politely greeted her in every language and dialect that I knew, but she only shyly smiled and shook her head.

"She speaks nothing but her native tongue," the dealer said indifferently. "I do not even know her name. I call her Monkey."

"Well," I said, "she is black, but that is only an uncommon color, no great rarity. And I suppose, at her age, she is still a virgin, but virgins are not rare, either. And she cannot even make love-talk in bed. How much money do you ask for her?"

The Egyptian mentioned a price that took my breath away. It amounted approximately to the entire and considerable sum that Wyrd and I together had earned from our whole winter of hunting.

"Why, one could buy a whole *string* of beautiful virgin slaves for that!" I gasped. "What in the world would make this one worth so much? And why do you reserve her for only private showing?"

"Ah, young master. Monkey's true virtues and talents are not readily apparent, because they reside in the way she was reared from birth. She is not only black, not only comely, not only a virgin, she is also a venefica."

"And what is that?"

He told me, and what he told me was fantastic. I stared anew at the shy little black girl, and I was awed and aghast and almost unbelieving of what she was.

"Liufs Guth!" I choked out. "Who would purchase such a monster?"

"Oh, someone will," said the Egyptian with a shrug. "I may have to feed and house Monkey for quite a while, but—soon or later—there will come someone who can make use of her, and will cheerfully pay the price I demand. Begging your indulgence, young master, but at some time in your life, you may be glad to know that—if you search hard enough and pay dearly enough—you can find a venefica for your own use."

221

"Pray God . . ." I muttered sickly. "Pray *all* the gods that I never have to. Nevertheless, I thank you, Egyptian, for furthering my education in the wicked ways of the world." And I went away from there.

✠   ✠   ✠

At mealtimes, I frequented the tabernae favored by merchants and travelers, and ate and drank with them, and heard their tales of hardship and hazard on the road, their boasts of dizzying profits or their bemoanings of dismal losses at their various journeys' ends.

I attended athletic games and horse or chariot races and bouts of pugiles at Constantia's amphitheater—it was smaller than the one I had seen in Vesontio—and learned how to place wagers, and I sometimes even won on one of my gambles. I spent numerous other hours in the various thermae reserved for men, and made acquaintances with whom I exercised or wrestled, or we played at dice or at the twelve-line game or at the ludus game of batting a felt ball with the gut-stringed open paddles—or we simply lounged about and listened to someone of orotund voice reading poetry or singing the Latin carmina priscae or the Germanic saggwasteis fram aldrs.

Constantia also had a public library, but I went there only infrequently, for it was inferior even to the scriptorium at St. Damian's, and I could find few codices or scrolls that I had not already read. Nor did I often attend the city's Basilica of St. John, unless I was absolutely chafing with boredom, because I had conceived a dislike for the priest Tiburnius from the day I had witnessed his "involuntary" ordination and heard his self-serving first lection.

The streets and marts and squares of Constantia were forever thronged with people, but eventually I could recognize many of the permanent residents and distinguish them from the passers-through and summer visitors like myself. Two persons in particular I had reason to take note of. The street crowds were generally unruly and unmannerly, pushing and shoving and elbowing each other, but they *did* meekly step aside and make way and even cringe in doorways when a certain one of their fellows desired passage. Not for a long time did I even catch sight of that person, because he always came through the streets in an immense, lavishly decorated, curtained Liburnian car, its poles borne on the shoulders of eight trotting and sweating slaves, who bellowed, "Way! Way for the legatus!" and who would run right over anybody who did not dodge. When I inquired, I was told that that was the vehicle of Latobrigex—the dux, as he was known in Latin—or the herizogo, as he would be called in the Old Language. Latobrigex, said my informant, was Constantia's only native-born citizen of really noble lineage, and on that account he was at least nominally Rome's legatus of this prosperous outpost of her empire.

The other person whom I came to recognize, because I saw him so frequently, was a heavyset, hulking young man of slack and dull visage, with a hairline that began not far above his beetling eyebrows. He was about as old as Gudinand, meaning of an age to be gainfully employed, but he seemed to do as much leisurely ambling about the city as I did. At least *I* was going about noticing and inspecting and learning things; that young man's vacant gaze seemed to reflect nothing but contempt or disgust for whatever part of the city I saw him in. And I never saw him *do* anything, except to be even more unmannerly than others in the crowds, shouldering them out of his way, always with a curse and a growl.

So I inquired about him, too, and I inquired of an elderly man who had just then been shoved so hard that he had fallen. I helped the old man to his feet, and asked, "Who *is* that lout, anyway?"

"The damnable whelp is named Claudius Jaeirus. He has not the free enjoyment of his senses—except for his overbearing sense of superiority to all lesser citizens. He has no occupation, no obligations, no interests beyond vapid idleness and mindless brutality."

As the old fellow tried to brush off the mud he had accumulated from his fall into the street, I asked, "Then why do not the lesser citizens put some restraint upon him? *I* would, and gladly, even though he is twice my size."

"Do not try, young fellow. None of us dares cross wills with him, because he is the only child of the dux Latobrigex. Mind you, our dux is a mild and inoffensive man, no tyrant. He is lenient with us, his inferiors, and even more so with that misbegotten spawn of his. Would that Jaeirus partook of his father's weakling temperament. But he is also the son of his mother, and she is a bitch-dragon of the first degree. I thank you, young sir, for your assistance and sympathy. In return, I warn you to stay well away from that intolerable but inviolate Jaeirus."

And so I did, or at least for as long as I was able.

I hardly need say that it was always as Thorn that I did my wanderings about the city and the countryside, and my attending of public functions, and my mingling with the citizenry. When I went out in my guise and garb of Juhiza, it was on those twilight occasions of my meeting Gudinand for another episode in our course of his treatment. I took

223

pains, even in the dusk, that no one saw me slip out of the deversorium, and I would sneak through back alleys to the lakeside outskirts of the city, and thence to our familiar copse. Usually, also, after those episodes—and under cover of full darkness—I would repair to one of the women's thermae for my cleansing and resuscitation. A few times, in one or another of those baths, I saw again the lewd woman Robeya. But she never again accosted me, and if our glances did chance to meet, I would give her a sweetly malicious smile and she would give me a venomously malicious glare before we mutually averted our eyes.

Only twice or thrice did I deliberately, in broad daylight, venture out into public view as Juhiza. The one feminine gown I owned had already been faded and shabby when I bought it in Vesontio. Now, after my several sessions with Gudinand, it really showed signs of wear and tear from its being so often doffed and donned again. I now had ample money with which to purchase new garments—and I had no further need to pretend to be buying for an absent mistress. So, to ensure that I obtained raiment that both fit me properly and looked well on me, I went as Juhiza to the shops of clothiers catering to fine ladies. Dowdily dressed as I was, I was received with some coolness. But since I treated the shopkeepers as condescendingly as if I *were* a fine lady, and insisted on only the very best-quality goods, those clothiers were soon bowing and scraping obsequiously before me. Over the course of those few daylight ventures into the city, I acquired three new gowns, exquisitely embroidered, plus various accessories: new kerchiefs and sandals, some pins and ribbons and bars with which to dress my hair in different arrangements. I repeat: my outings as Juhiza were few, but they turned out to have been one too many.

That one time, I chanced to be emerging from the shop of a myropola, where I had been replenishing my supply of cosmetic unguents and powders and such, when I heard the pounding of many feet and the cries of "Way! Make way for the legatus!" So I drew back into the doorway of the shop, and everyone else on the street scurried to clear a passage, and along came the Liburnian car. On this occasion, however, and not far from me, the slaves halted and gently lowered the great enclosed chair. If the legatus was inside it, he did not get out. The passengers who alighted were an exceptionally handsome woman and an exceedingly ill-favored young man. He was, not too surprisingly, that loutish Jaeirus, son of the dux Latobrigex. But the woman, to my vast amazement, was that Robeya whom I knew from the women's baths. I instantly realized that she must be the "bitch-dragon" mother of the lout.

I ought to have covered my face, or turned and scuttled unobtrusively away. But I stood eyeing them and thinking: well, even a woman of Robeya's peculiar proclivities probably *could* marry—and would, if given the chance to marry into the local nobility. And then, having acquired a husband, she must have lain still and compliant at least *once* and for long enough to get impregnated by him. But it was small wonder that the fruit of such a dry and loveless womb should have been a male child as paltry and unlovable as Jaeirus.

But I stood there musing too long, and Robeya saw me. She and I had never seen one another in any state other than nudity, but she recognized me as easily as I had known her. Robeya's dark eyes widened, then narrowed, and she leaned to nudge her son and direct his attention to me, and she put her face close to his and spoke rapidly. I could not hear what she said, but it made Jaeirus's eyes narrow, too, and he swept them up and down me, as if his mother had bidden him to memorize every detail of me. At that, I did depart—in the opposite direction and at a modest gait. But as soon as I came to a cross street, I turned down it and made off as swiftly as I could without actually breaking into an unseemly run. Only once did I look back, and saw neither Jaeirus nor Robeya pelting after me.

225

I was grateful to reach my lodgings unmolested, and relieved at having escaped what might have been a nasty confrontation. I put away my newly purchased parcels and quickly stripped off every vestige of Juhiza, and made a silent vow never again to be Juhiza in public in daylight. And I never did. For many days thereafter, it was as Thorn that I did my perambulations about the city and made my meetings with Gudinand for boy-type sport and games. After those days, my anxiety abated somewhat, and so, when Gudinand glumly told me that he had suffered yet another convulsion, it was with only a minimum of trepidation that I arranged to have Juhiza meet and treat him once again.

"But I fear, good friend," I said, "this *has* to be the last time. Autumn is upon us, and our guardian Wyrd will be back here any day. Besides . . . if the treatment has not worked a cure by now . . ."

"I know, I know," said Gudinand with weary resignation. "Still, if nothing else, I shall have had this one last time . . ."

The next evening, when I dressed as Juhiza, I was nervous and my fingers fumbled, and I twice had to redo the creta with which I accentuated my eyes' lashes and brows. But, since this *was* one of the first days of autumn, the dusk came early, so it was very nearly dark when I slipped out of the deversorium. It was my first time outdoors as Juhiza since my street encounter with Robeya and Jaeirus, but I saw neither of them lurking about, nor anyone who might have been a spy of theirs. And as well as I could tell, I was not followed by anybody when I made my accustomed way through Constantia's back alleys toward the lake.

But of course I *was* followed — or, rather, Juhiza was — and obviously had been ever since I had seen Jaeirus and Robeya together. The moment I fled from them, they must have sent one of their car-bearer slaves chasing after me, and I would not have noticed such an anonymous pursuer among the street crowds. Apparently that slave or some other person, or series of persons, had kept an unremitting watch on my lodgings from that day to this. He, or they, must have had a tedious and frustrating wait, not seeing Juhiza ever emerge again, and having no reason to remark on my comings and goings as Thorn. But *someone* had at last been rewarded for the long wait, when tonight Juhiza did leave the deversorium.

Gudinand and I had often before become goose-prickled of skin when in our transports of passion, but this night the air was so crisp that we got goose-fleshed as soon as we had undressed. And at the instant we both were naked, our goose bumps and even our hair must have lifted higher, because there was a sudden rustling in the brush nearby and a hoarse voice — the voice of Jaeirus — said loudly:

"You have had many a turn with that wench, Gudinand, you stinkard cripple. Now it is a *real* man's turn. Tonight is *my* turn!"

Gudinand and I were defenseless. We were both nude, unprotected, unarmed, and Jaeirus came out of his hiding place swinging a heavy wooden cudgel. I was lying flat on my back, Gudinand bending over me, when I heard the simultaneous sounds of the cudgel's thud and Gudinand's grunt, and my friend fairly flew off into the darkness to one side of me.

Next moment I was pinned under the heavy, sweaty weight of Jaeirus. He was fully clothed, but had disarranged his garments sufficiently to free his fascinum, and he began jabbing with that at my nether parts. I struggled and flailed and cried for Gudinand's help — but Gudinand was either stunned or dead — and Jaeirus only laughed at me.

"You know you like this sport, little girl. And from me you do not risk catching the falling sickness, as you would from your freak friend yonder."

"Get off me!" I raged. "I *choose* my friends!"

"And you will choose me, once you have enjoyed me. Now cease your foolish fighting and listen to me."

I did not cease struggling as fiercely as I was able, but I could not help listening.

"You know my mother, Robeya. And she says you know her *well*."

I gasped, "I know that she is an unnatural—"

"Hush your blithering and pay heed. For her latest lover, my mother took the tonstrix who dyes her hair, a little slut of a commoner named Maralena. When my mother finally tired of Maralena's bedtime inadequacies, she bequeathed the slut to me. Mother told me and showed me how to pleasure Maralena, and Mother watched and instructed as we two frolicked. And—would you believe?—Maralena enjoyed my attentions even more than those she had had from my mother. I promise that you will, too, child. Here, give me your hand. Just *feel* the size of my fascinum. So now let us proceed to—"

There was another sound of *thud!* and, just as suddenly, Jaeirus whisked away sidewise into the darkness as Gudinand had done, and I was lying alone. Well, it was all I *could* do: lie there, dazed, and try to get my breath back, and try to sort out the bewildering series of events that had so rapidly occurred. Then a callused hard hand was laid on my forehead, but gently, and a voice that I knew said:

"Be easy, urchin. You are safe now. Take your time and collect your wits."

I croaked, "Fráuja, is it really you?"

"If you do not recognize whiskered old Wyrd, your wits must really be disordered."

"Ne . . . ne . . . I think I am all right. But what of Gudinand?"

"He is slowly coming awake. He will have a headache, nothing worse. So will this other friend of yours. I did not bludgeon him hard enough to kill."

"*Friend?!*" I croaked indignantly. "That is the son of a bitch-dragon—"

"I know who it is," said Wyrd. "By the nose and ears that Zopyrus cut off his own head, but you do have a talent, urchin, for making acquaintances. First Gudinand, the city's laughingstock. Now Jaeirus, the city's best-hated bastard."

"I did not invite the acquaintance of—"

"Shut up," Wyrd said, as gruffly as of old. "Put some clothes on. I do not care a ferta if you comport yourself indecorously, but you do not have to *look* it."

I fumblingly began to get dressed. So did Gudinand, removing himself to some distance, obviously fearful of Wyrd's anger at finding him and me in such a situation. As my confusion cleared, I said contritely and in a low voice:

"Fráuja, I never meant for you to see me thus."

"Shut up," Wyrd growled again. "I am an old man, and I have seen much else. So much that it would take more than anything you might do to scandalize me. I told you long ago that I have not the slightest interest in . . . well, whether you piss standing up or sitting down. Or whatever else you choose to do with your private parts."

"But . . ." I said, as I fumblingly began to get dressed again. "Come to think of it . . . how do you happen to be here, fráuja? Just when Gudinand and I needed help."

"Skeit, urchin, I returned to Constantia a week ago. However, when I saw a watcher posted outside our deversorium, I decided to take lodging elsewhere, and to keep watch myself. I have seen you going in and out, sometimes in that womanly garb you once showed me in Basilea. Then, tonight, when you emerged and were followed, I simply followed the follower. Now the question is: what do we do with this son of a bitch-dragon?"

Jaeirus had heard none of this, but was now sitting up, groggily fingering the lump on his skull. As well as I could see in the darkness, he looked thoroughly apprehensive.

"Tie a large rock to him," I said viciously, "and sink him in the lake yonder."

"It would be a pleasure," said Wyrd, and Jaeirus's face turned white enough to be quite visible in the darkness. "Under Gothic law the creature would be accounted a nauthing—a person so worthless that the law would not punish, fine or even scold the killer of him." But Wyrd went on:

"I would slay him without hesitation if he were any ordinary brute rapist. However, he is the son of the dux Latobrigex. While every inhabitant of Constantia—and even his father, the dux himself—might rejoice at the disappearance of Jaeirus, there would inevitably be questions asked. Also, his spying minions—and no doubt his mother—must have some notion of where he is at this moment. So those questions would be asked of *you*, urchin, and of your friend Gudinand, and the questions would probably be asked with the persuasive aid of a professional torturer. I recommend that we spare Jaeirus his life, and thereby avoid putting you two at such hazard."

As usual, Wyrd's advice made good sense, so I only inquired sullenly, "What do you suggest, then, fráuja? That we ask the cohortes vigilum or the judicium to decide his punishment?"

"Ne," Wyrd said, with scorn. "Only a weakling or a coward resorts to the law to resolve a dispute involving personal honor. In any event, Jaeirus being who he is, he would be instantly acquitted." Wyrd turned to Gudinand and said, "You and this eminent personage are of about the same age and size. Would you agree to face him in fair and equal and public trial by combat?"

Gudinand, looking relieved that he was not already being belabored by Juhiza's fearsome guardian, said that a fight with a mere Jaeirus would be a pleasure.

"So be it," said Wyrd. "Let us escort him to the city and invoke the ancient law of ordeal by battle."

"What?!" squealed Jaeirus. "I, the son of the dux Latobrigex, fight hand to hand with a *commoner*? With the city's most contemptible cripple and simpleton? I absolutely reject such an outrageous—"

"Shut up," said Wyrd, as indifferently as if he were addressing me. "Urchin, bind his wrists with that kerchief of yours. His own belt will serve me for a leash to lead him along. Gudinand, bring that stout cudgel that has already twice tonight been wielded. If the prisoner tries to flee, use the cudgel again, and with a will."

✠   ✠   ✠

So once more, and that very night, I appeared in public as Juhiza, this time in the Basilica of St. John. Like most provincial churches, it served also—between churchly functions—as the site of civic tribunals. There I stood before the hastily convened judicium of Constantia, and accused Jaeirus of assault and attempted rape, and asked that his guilt or innocence be adjudicated by the rite of ordeal, and begged the three judges' permission to let Gudinand serve as my champion in that combat.

"I suggest, my lords," said Wyrd, who was acting as my jurisconsultus, "that the matter be settled in the city amphitheater—so that all of Constantia may see that justice is done—and that the weapons be cudgels, since the cudgel appears to be the favorite implement of the accused."

There was considerable frowning and muttering among the judges, and that was hardly surprising because—in addition to myself, Gudinand, Wyrd and the still kerchief-bound Jaeirus—there was also present the dux Latobrigex, his wife, Robeya, and of course the church's priest, Tiburnius. This was the first time I had seen Latobrigex, and, as he had been described to me, he was a nondescript man of very modest demeanor. His only objection to the proceedings was delivered in a voice almost meek:

"My lords," he said, "the petitor making this accusation is but a stranger to this city, a wandering waif. I will not impugn her probity, but I do submit that her morals might be questionable. This incident allegedly occurred when she went unattended, well after dark, to a remote and deserted patch of shrubbery, which no decent female—"

He was interrupted by his wife. Her dark eyes glaring hatred at me, Robeya barked ferociously:

"*And* this wanton wench of a stranger dares to accuse a native citizen of our own Constantia. The son of our dux. The son of Rome's legatus. A scion of the ancient house of Colonna. I *demand*, my lords, that this slanderous accusation be dismissed, that Jaeirus be absolved of all taint upon his reputation—*and* that this wayfaring little whore be publicly stripped naked and *whipped* beyond the city precincts!"

The judges put their heads together again, to mutter some more, and I said aside to Wyrd, "It is as we might have expected. But what was that about the house of Colonna?"

"At one time," Wyrd whispered back, "one of the first families of Rome, but now dismally degenerate. Well, just look at the spunkless Latobrigex Colonna yonder. Would a man of any family less enfeebled have married such a virago as Robeya? And sired such a wretch as Jaeirus? Of course, each of them still pretentiously affects the status of clarissimus, but—"

There was another interruption, and this time from the priest Tiburnius, who said unctuously:

"My lords, the Church does not interfere in purely civil matters, and neither will I, as a servant of the Church. But I was a Constantia merchant long before I became Constantia's priest, and I beg leave to say a few words that may possibly be worth consideration in these proceedings."

Naturally the judicium deferred to him, and naturally I expected Tiburnius to say something that would truckle to the dux Latobrigex. But the newly made priest had clearly been inflated by his newly be-

230

stowed ecclesiastical authority—and must have welcomed this opportunity to exert it—because he astounded me by saying:

"True, it is a mere and meager passing stranger who has made this grave accusation against a respected citizen of Constantia. But I remind you, my lords, that our Constantia derives its prosperity from none *but* the strangers who pass through its gates. Every citizen, from highest to lowest, earns his every least nummus coin of profit from those strangers: the traveling merchants and traders and purveyors. Now, were the word to go abroad that only Constantia's citizens are protected by Constantia's laws—that a stranger might here be the victim of injustice, even such a nonentity as this apparent young vagrant whore—what then, my lords, might happen to the prosperity of Constantia? And that of yourselves? And of this, God's church? I recommend that you grant the petitor's appeal for a trial by combat between Jaeirus and Gudinand. It will relieve you of the onus of finding for or against either of the contending parties. In the rite of ordeal, it is the *Lord* who will judge."

"How dare you?" flared Robeya, while her husband simply stood silent and her son began perceptibly to perspire. "You frocked shopkeeper, who are *you* to consign a member of the nobility to a vulgar public fight against that outcast and brainsick vermin—just for the sake of this worthless piece of female trash?"

"Clarissima Robeya." The priest addressed her respectfully enough, but also leveled at her a stern forefinger. "The duties and dignities of the nobility are in truth weighty matters. But far weightier is the office of the priest, because, come the day of the divine judgment, he must give account even for *kings*. Clarissima Robeya, should you excel all the rest of the human race in dignity, still your pride must bow before the stewards of the Christian mysteries. When your priest speaks, it is for you to pay respect, not to dissent. I most solemnly warn you of this. I warn you as your priest, and it is Christ who warns you through me."

"That," murmured Wyrd, "scared even the bitch-dragon."

Indeed, the lady had gone quite ashen-faced during the rebuke, and she said nothing further, and Jaeirus sweated more copiously than before. After a moment of silence, it was Latobrigex who spoke. He laid a hand on Robeya's arm and said in his mild voice:

"Tata Tiburnius is right, my dear. Justice must be served, and in the ordeal it is God who will decide the right. Let us trust in God—and in our son's strong arm." He turned to the three men of the judicium. "My lords, I concur in the appeal. Let the combat take place tomorrow morning."

231

6

The news must have gone overnight to every corner of the city, and beyond. Next morning, when Wyrd and I arrived at the amphitheater—and I was being Thorn again, incidentally—the entire population of Constantia and its surroundings seemed to be at the gates, clamoring to buy the clay tesserae tokens of admission.

The Church had long frowned on gladiatorial contests, and most of the Christian emperors had forbidden them. Some such bouts may have been privily arranged and fought in distant provinces, but there had not been one publicly held in Rome itself for fifty years before my own birth. Today's combat was not, of course, being waged with the gladius sword or any other of the traditional weapons—the trident, the mace, the cast net—only with the fustis staff. Nevertheless, it promised to be a real blood contest, and that was an event unprecedented enough to throng the amphitheater.

The crowd comprised not just fishers and artisans and countryfolk and the other sorts of commoners who generally frequented the arena's games and sports. Even the city's merchants and traders and shop-keepers—who otherwise would hardly have closed their markets and warehouses to mourn the death of a popular emperor—seemed today to have shuttered their establishments, or left them in the charge of minor clerks and slaves, so they could attend this spectacle. Also present were all the transient visitors in the city who had heard of this unique offering of entertainment.

Long before the time for the combat to begin, I think every seat in every cuneus and every maenianum of the amphitheater was filled. As usual, the commonfolk sat on the ledges of the upper tiers, but Wyrd paid a stiff price for tesserae that admitted him and myself to the numbered seats on the second tier, ordinarily accessible only to the noble or wealthy. In the arena-level tier, reserved for high officials and other dignitaries, the central podium was occupied by the dux Latobrigex, his lady Robeya and the priest Tiburnius, all of them sumptuously and almost festively dressed. The dux was as expressionless as he had been the night before, but his wife practically radiated white-hot fury, and the priest looked as bland as if he were about to watch a troupe of ritum players devoutly reenact the Passion.

I turned to Wyrd and said, "Of all the money you and I have earned and tucked safely away, fráuja, I will wager my whole share against yours that Gudinand is the victor here this morning."

He uttered one of his snort-laughs. "By Laverna, the goddess of thieves, traitors and fugitives, you ask *me* to back that swine Jaeirus? Preposterous! But akh, at any arena I have never been able to resist making some kind of wager. I *will* put up my half of all our earnings against your half, and put *mine* on Gudinand."

"What? That would be even more preposterous. I would be disloyally—"

But I was interrupted before I could remonstrate further, by a single trumpet's blast from the arena below and the concerted eager murmur and stirring of the whole crowd. Jaeirus and Gudinand had emerged from gates on opposite sides of the perimeter wall.

233

Each of the young men carried a stout ash fustis, longer than he was tall and as thick as his wrist. Each wore only an athlete's loincloth and over the rest of his body a coating of oil to help slip the cudgels' blows. They approached one another in the center of the arena and then walked abreast to stand beneath the podium and raise their staffs in salute to the dux. To each of them impartially, Latobrigex raised his right fist, in which he held a white cloth. Then the trumpet blared again and the dux let drop the cloth. Jaeirus and Gudinand instantly wheeled to face one another and took the fighting stance, each gripping his fustis with one hand at its middle and the other hand halfway between middle and end. The two young men were well matched for the combat. Gudinand was the taller and had a longer arm's reach, but Jaeirus was broader and more beefy of muscle. Their skills with the staffs seemed also to be about equal. I knew that Gudinand had never had a friend with whom to engage in mock cudgel-fighting, but he must have amused himself sometimes with solitary pretend-battles. Jaeirus probably *had* had many opportunities to compete against other young men in the sport, but, Jaeirus being who he was, those others had doubtless restrained their blows and let him win easily. Though neither of these combatants could long have stood against a real, professional, experienced fustis wielder, they were right now giving a far better than fair show of swinging, parrying, thrusting, dodging—and the spectators had no reason to grumble that they had wasted their money to watch a bumbling novice performance.

To Wyrd, I said with exasperation, "See here, you cannot appropriate my wager. It was I who *sent* Jaeirus into that arena to be beaten to a pulp. It would be insane for me even unwillingly to wager *against* the man I chose for my defensor and champion. I insist—"

"Balgs-daddja," Wyrd said calmly. "I was right to back Gudinand, and I refuse to retract the wager. Just look yonder—how Jaeirus is beginning to cringe and flinch and retreat."

The opponents had begun the fight by trying every stroke and move that is possible in fustis combat, both offensive and defensive, to judge one another's courage and dexterity and strong or weak aspects. The various defensive moves include, of course, quick and firm parrying with the staff itself, but there are also many adroit means of dodging or ducking or even—if one's opponent makes a violent swing with the entire length of his fustis—of vaulting right over it as deftly as an acrobat. Basically, the cudgel-fighter's only offensive moves are the swing and the thrust, but they too can be delivered in various ways: for example, a feint of swing that suddenly becomes a thrust.

After Jaeirus and Gudinand had for some time battered at one another with all those different sorts of strokes—the body blows heavy and loud enough to make several of the onlookers grunt in sympathy—and both had, successfully or not, tried the several means of defense, they evidently decided they knew one another's weakest points and thereafter concentrated on those.

Jaeirus, lacking length of arm, less often thrust with the end of his staff, but relied on swinging it, and he swung most often at Gudinand's head. I think Jaeirus must have remembered his mother's reference to Gudinand as "brainsick," and was hoping that even a glancing blow to the head would severely stun the young man.

Gudinand, for his part, soon realized that Jaeirus's squat, square body could hardly be toppled or even much budged by sidewise swings of his cudgel. So Gudinand began to rely on his longer reach, on lunging thrusts. He aimed alternately at the pit of Jaeirus's stomach, trying to ram the wind from his body, and at Jaeirus's hands, trying to break or weaken his grip on his own fustis.

Gudinand, leaner and lithe, was able to dodge or parry Jaeirus's swings toward his head, or most of them, anyway. But the heavyset

234

Jaeirus was not agile enough to avoid Gudinand's thrusts with the end of his staff. Several of those jabs to the stomach made Jaeirus utter an audible *whoosh!* and stagger backward long enough to snatch a new gulp of air. Several of Gudinand's thrusts we heard crunch against his opponent's fingers, and once Jaeirus's right hand nearly dropped its hold on the fustis. From then on, Jaeirus did not so much wield his cudgel offensively; he fought to prevent its being wrested from his grasp. He appeared to have abandoned hope of victory and to be merely defying defeat. Gudinand pressed the advantage, forcing Jaeirus ever backward until the two of them were almost directly before the central podium.

"Look yonder," Wyrd said again. "The tetzte wretch is sweating the oil right off his body."

So he was. Where Jaeirus now stood, but shakily, shuffling his feet to keep his balance against Gudinand's relentless pummeling, there was a stain spreading on the sand, and I do not think it consisted entirely of sweat and oil. Jaeirus was flicking his eyes frantically from side to side, as if seeking a refuge—or a rescue, for he flicked his gaze most often toward the podium where sat his father and mother. The dux's face had not changed expression in the least, but Robeya's . . . well, if she *had* been a dragon, I am certain she would have swooped down into the arena beside her boy, belching flames at Gudinand.

Wyrd remarked with satisfaction, "A brute swaggerer is always a coward, and this one is publicly proving it. Urchin, you ought not complain at paying me even such a heavy wager, since it has brought you the pleasure of seeing your friend victorious."

But, all at once, Gudinand stopped his battering of Jaeirus and stepped away from him. The spectators may have thought he was simply according his defeated opponent the clementia: not killing him outright, not breaking his bones so that he would be forever a cripple, not even beating Jaeirus until he lay prostrate on the sand and had to make the humiliating gesture of the lifted finger, pleading that his life be spared. However, I knew it was not thought of clementia that so abruptly paralyzed Gudinand. He had ceased even to look at Jaeirus; his eyes slowly lifted above the arena, above the tiers of the amphitheater, on up to the morning sky above, as if perhaps he had seen a strange green bird fly over, or heard an owl unnaturally hoot in daylight.

All through the bruising battle, Gudinand had shown no least evidence of his affliction. But I had long ago noticed that it oftenest came upon him not in moments of stress or duress, but when he was feeling

235

happiest and most healthy. And so it did now, when he was on the verge of what would have been the grandest moment of his life, the moment that would have changed him from Constantia's lowliest outcast to its triumphant hero.

The fustis simply dropped from his hands, and I could see why: his thumbs had curled tightly into his palms and his hands were useless as hands. Jaeirus stood, staggering slightly, but in his astonishment almost as benumbed as his opponent. Every other person in the amphitheater was similarly stupefied, absolutely silent. Then Gudinand uttered the cry I had heard him cry once before, as if he had already been dealt his deathblow, and the ululation echoed eerily through the breathless hush that prevailed. One other voice spoke, but so quietly that no one except Jaeirus heard it. His mother leaned far over the balustrade of the podium and hissed something down to him.

Jaeirus had continued to stand bewildered, bleeding from his nose and from his almost crushed right hand, clearly unsure of what to do next—until Robeya told him. Now, suddenly, while Gudinand yet had his head far back and was still giving that unearthly howl, Jaeirus struck with all his strength. The cudgel caught Gudinand in the throat, and cut short his piteous wail, and he fell backward as stiffly as a downed tree.

The blow may not have critically injured him; he might have risen to fight again; but the fit was upon him. He lay supine and rigid, only his extremities quivering, and Jaeirus rained vicious blows all up and down his body. Gudinand could still have made the plea for clementia—the raising of one forefinger—and the dux Latobrigex would have been obliged to halt the combat while he solicited the verdict of the crowd: life or death? But poor Gudinand could not open one of his convulsion-clenched hands even to lift that single finger.

His quivering slowed and ceased; he lay flaccid while Jaeirus beat and beat upon his body until it was almost unrecognizable as human; the only thing about Gudinand that still moved was the saliva pouring from his mouth. He was surely dead by then, but Jaeirus went on flailing at the shapeless corpse, as if he were exultantly disposing of a sackful of kittens. The sight was so gruesome that, unsolicited, the crowd of spectators sprang to their feet, as one man, and roared, "Clementia! Clementia!"

Jaeirus paused just long enough to glance toward the podium. But the dux did not have time to make the traditional gesture: thumb downward as a signal for the victor to drop his weapon—because Robeya too quickly made the other traditional gesture: jabbing her thumb toward her breast, which in gladiator days had meant "Stab him!" And of course Jaeirus obeyed his mother. While the crowd still bellowed, "*Clementia!*" he raised his cudgel vertically and brought it down in the manner of a tamping rod, three or four times, directly on his victim's head. Gudinand's skull shattered like an eggshell, and the tragically disordered brain that had made his blameless life so miserable would never now be repaired by Juhiza's attentions or any other means, for it spilled in a gray-pink sludge onto the sand.

At that, the crowd, which had formerly seemed so bloodthirsty, began to bawl its sickened outrage, and in a cacophony of tongues: "Skanda! Atrocitas! Unhrains slauts! Saevitia!" — "Shame! Atrocity! Filthy slaughter! Savagery!" The people were now milling about and, I think, in a moment more they would have been pouring down from the seats and ledges and into the arena, to rend Jaeirus in pieces.

But the priest Tiburnius was also on his feet and holding his arms high for attention. As one spectator after another noticed him, the crowd gradually quietened so he could be heard. He shouted alternately in Latin and in the Old Language, to make sure everyone understood him:

"*Cives mei! Thiuda! My people!* Cease your impious protest and accept God's verdict. The Lord is just and wise and of righteous judgment; in him there is no iniquity. To put a stop to any doubt in this controversy, and to disclose the truth to all, God decreed that Gudinand should be overcome, and Jaeirus gain the victory. Do not dare dispute the Lord's wisdom as he chose to reveal it to all of you this day. Nolumus! Interdicimus! Prohibemus! Gutha waírthai wilja theins, swe in himina jah ana aírthai! God's will be done, on earth as it is in heaven!"

No one in the crowd was prepared to defy that priestly command. Though still muttering, the mob began to disperse and leave the amphitheater. Tiburnius, Latobrigex, Robeya and Jaeirus must have had a special door for leaving the podium, because they were suddenly gone as well. Not a single person except Wyrd and myself even lingered to watch the arena slaves — ironically known as the Charons, the ferrymen of the dead — remove from the sand the meat that had been Gudinand.

"Hua ist so sunja?" growled Wyrd. "What is truth? I do not know which is the slimier serpent: Jaeirus or his dragon mother or that reptilian priest."

I too could quote from the Bible. "Mis fraweit letaidáu; ik fragilda. Vengeance is mine; I will repay."

"It is I who am paying," Wyrd grumbled as we got up to leave. "It cannot console you for the loss of your friend, but you have won a tidy little fortune. I might make one remark, however. You never told me that Gudinand was an uslitha, liable to the falling sickness."

"I *did* tell you to recant the wager!" I snapped. "I give you free leave to do so now."

"By the pale, emaciated goddess Paupertas, I never in my life reneged on a debt. I will not start now, by defrauding a friend."

"Good," I said as we emerged onto the street. "I need the money. And I promise to work harder than ever during this coming winter, to help us earn another fortune."

"You *need* the money?" Wyrd asked, surprised. "May I inquire what for?"

"Ne, fráuja, not until after I have spent it. You might try to dissuade me from the uses I wish to make of it."

He shrugged, and we proceeded in silence toward our deversorium. Actually I walked weeping, though not Wyrd or anyone else could have perceived it, for no tears flowed from my eyes. The grief that I felt, as Thorn, on being bereaved of Gudinand-who-had-been-my-friend, I was bearing manfully dry-eyed. It was the female half of me that was unashamedly *weeping* for Gudinand-who-had-loved-me. And, my femaleness being at present suppressed deep within my outwardly male self, the tears flowed, so to speak, from my heart. I wondered: if I were at this moment Juhiza instead of Thorn, would those tears be visibly issuing from my eyes and streaming down my face?

I was led to reflect yet again on the peculiar nature of myself, and the frequently dire effects it seemed to wreak in the world around me. Was it my mannamavi incapacity to love, I wondered, or was it just my ordained fate, to make others suffer so? All Romans used to believe, and those who remained pagan still believed, that every human being is guarded and guided through life by a personal godling, invisible but ever-present. Those of male persons are called the genii, those of females the junones. According to that pagan belief, the individual has little volition of his own, but generally must follow the whims and dictates of his tutelary spirit. Then was I, as an androgynus, attended by both a genius and a junone? Were they perhaps in perpetual conflict for control of me? Or was I perhaps attended by neither? I *thought* that many of the things I had done in my life so far had been done of my own free will, but of others I could not be sure. I had willfully, deliberately and with malice slain the reprehensible Brother Peter. But, for all

I knew—and with no intent on my part—the innocent Sister Deidamia might also now be dead, from the flagrum beating she endured because of her involvement with me. I had had good reason and right to slay the savage woman in the Hun encampment, but no reason, right or wish to have impelled also the death of the little charismatic Becga. By Iésus, even my companion juika-bloth had died because of me—because I had ignorantly meddled with its true nature. And now . . . now I had, without wanting to, been the direct cause of Gudinand's self-sacrifice.

Liufs Guth! Whether it was my own doing or that of a tutelary genius or junone—or both—had I *really*, already, so early, become a raptor, as I once had vowed, marauding my way through life? And through others' lives?

Well, if I had, I said to myself, at least I knew what my next prey would be.

✠   ✠   ✠

"Khaîre!" The Egyptian slave trader uttered the Greek exclamation of salute when I told him what I had come for. "Did I not say, young master, that someday even *you* might find use for a venefica of your own? I confess, I did not expect that to be so soon, when you are still so young and—"

"Spare me the homily," I said. "Let us discuss price."

"You know the price."

Nevertheless, I managed to bargain at least a little to my advantage. As I have told, the Egyptian had earlier demanded for the slave called Monkey an amount approximately equal to the entire contents of my purse. But, after much wrangling, I bought the Ethiope girl for a trifle less than that amount, leaving enough money for me and Wyrd to pay what we would owe at the deversorium by the time we left there, and to supply ourselves for the coming winter, and even a few siliquae to spare, for another purpose I had in mind.

"Very well," I said, when the transaction was concluded, and the trader had signed, sealed and given to me the certificate of Monkey's servitium. "Have the girl clothed and ready to go with me—because I may call for her most suddenly—when I require her services."

"She will be waiting at your command." And the Egyptian smiled evilly. "When the time comes, I wish you—let us say—complete and utter satisfaction. Khaîre, young master."

✠   ✠   ✠

During the next several days, *I* was a secret watcher, lurking outside the domicile of the dux Latobrigex. I spied only during the daylight hours, because that was when the concatenation of events for which I waited was likeliest to occur. The nights I again spent in company with Wyrd, dining at a taberna or bathing at a therma, and we talked of only inconsequential things. Wyrd was obviously itching with curiosity, but he patiently forbore from asking questions or complaining that I was delaying our start upon the hunting season.

Numerous times I watched the Liburnian car leave the ducal residence, its bearer slaves shouting, "Way for the legatus!" On occasion Latobrigex rode out alone, on other occasions with his wife, on others with his son. But not until the day the slaves brought out the car bearing *just* Jaeirus and Robeya did I follow it, trotting at a discreet distance behind. As I had hoped, the car stopped to let Jaeirus descend at one of the men's baths. Then it went on again, and I continued to follow, silently praying. My prayer was answered: the car stopped next at one of the women's thermae, and Robeya descended there.

I ran as fast as I could to the Egyptian's establishment, fairly snatched Monkey out of the place and, dragging her, ran back to the therma where Jaeirus was bathing. It was not at all uncommon for a man to arrive anywhere with either a male or a female slave in attendance, but of course I could not take a female inside a men's bath. However, like all the better-class thermae, this one was equipped with small but comfortably furnished exedria waiting rooms, and I installed Monkey in one that contained a couch.

It was impossible for me to tell the little black girl anything in words, but I contrived to convey my instructions to her by gestures, and she nodded compliantly as she comprehended each point. She was to undress to the skin; she was to recline upon the couch and wait a while; then she was to perform the function for which she had been bred and trained. Immediately afterward, she was to dress herself again, leave the exedrium, leave the building and meet me in the street outside the therma.

Hoping mightily that Monkey *had* understood everything, I left her there and went on into the apodyterium to take off my own clothes. Then, wearing a robe of toweling, I hurried through the series of other rooms, searching for Jaeirus. After all the running I had done, I really needed a bath, so I was quite grateful to find my prey in the steam-filled sudatorium. There were several other men in there, sitting and sweating and talking among themselves, but they were grouped at an aloof distance from Jaeirus. I had rather expected that. Over these past days I had noticed that all the people of Constantia—even the louts like himself whom I had sometimes seen in Jaeirus's company—were now shunning any contact with him. Since the day of that trial by ordeal, probably no one but his mother and father, and perhaps the self-serving priest, had given him a friendly word or glance.

So, here in the sudatorium, Jaeirus sat in a corner all alone and looking morose, nude except for a bandage on his right hand. He stared at me in genuine surprise when I sat down beside him and introduced myself as "Thorn, an admirer of yours, Clarissimus Jaeirus." It might be supposed that he was surprised to be accosted by someone so close in age and resemblance to the girl Juhiza. But he had seen Juhiza—close up, anyway—only in the darkness of the copse and the dimness of the church where the judicium had convened. Also, I was patently a male, for I was here in a men's therma, was I not? I am sure he was surprised merely to have *somebody* speak to him, persona non grata that he had become.

"Clarissimus," I said, "you do not know me, for I am but an apprentice to a traveling merchant, and we have only recently arrived in your fair city. However, I must tell you that I owe you a great debt."

"What debt?" he asked huskily, and sidled a little away from me on the bench. I think he was instantly frightened that I was some friend or relation of the late Gudinand, and that the debt I mentioned was of a sort he would not wish paid.

I hastened to say, "Thanks to you, I won a wager of considerable money. Considerable for one of my humble station, at least. You see, I attended the arena combat the other day, and on you I staked every last nummus of my wages and savings."

"Indeed?" he said, less warily. "I should hardly have believed that *anyone* wagered on me."

"But I did. And I was given extravagant odds."

"*That* I can believe," he said glumly.

"So, for the fortune you earned this lowly apprentice, I desire to reward you. I know, of course, clarissimus, that you would never accept a pars honorarium. So I have brought you a gift."

"Eh?"

"I spent part of my winnings to buy you a slave."

"I own ample slaves, thank you, apprentice."

"None like this one, clarissimus. A young virgin, just ripe for the taking of the kernel from the fruit."

241

"Thank you again, but I have enjoyed many such kernels."

"None like this one," I repeated. "The girl-child is not only virgin, not only beautiful, she is *black*. A young Ethiope."

"Say you so?" he murmured, and his gloomy face brightened. "I have never bedded a black girl."

"You can bed this one this very instant. I took the liberty of fetching her here to the therma. She awaits you, stark naked, in the exedrium numbered three beside the entry hall."

He narrowed his eyes. "You are not making some elaborate jest of me?"

"I am *thanking* you, clarissimus. You have but to go and look. If you do not like what you see . . . well, here I sit. Simply come back and tell me you decline the gift."

Jaeirus still looked suspicious, but he looked eagerly lustful as well. He stood up, wrapped a towel around himself and said, "Wait, then, apprentice. If I do not return immediately and throttle you as a prankster, I shall return—afterward—and make most gracious acceptance of your gift." And he went off toward the front of the building.

I did not wait; I was close behind him. I had too closely calculated my timing to waste any of it. When Jaeirus went through the exedrium door, and it did not open again after a very brief interval, I scurried into the apodyterium and—happy to have steamed off some of my sweat—hastily redonned my clothes. Then, again running like mad, I dashed to the deversorium and to my room, ripped off my masculine garments and donned those of Juhiza. I did not take time to adorn myself with cosmetics and ornaments, but immediately ran back to the therma I had just left.

Monkey was, as instructed, already waiting for me on the street corner, placidly eyeing the passersby. Many of those slowed or paused to give her a look, too, because the merchant trains that visited Constantia did sometimes bring blacks with them, but not that often, and very seldom a pretty black girl. When I took her arm, little Monkey flinched away; I was a female and a stranger. But then she recognized me as her new owner, and she smiled, though looking understandably puzzled at what she must have taken to be extremely odd behavior. I gestured inquiringly toward the therma, and her smile broadened and she nodded vigorously.

So next I trotted her to the women's therma, and there, of course, it was commonplace for a gentlewoman to bring along her own female slave, even a black one. Monkey and I both disrobed in the apodyter-

242

ium and then together went searching the rooms. Enough time had passed by now so that Robeya was already in the farthest room, the balineum, floating about in the warm after-bath pool, as lazily and languorously as when I had first seen her. However, it was obvious that she, too, was being shunned by her peers, for the several other women and girls in the pool were letting her have one whole end of it to herself—that far and darker corner where Robeya had once suggested that she and I go to frolic.

Taking care that Robeya did not see me, I pointed her out to Monkey and again, with gestures, conveyed my instructions. She was to swim over to Robeya, in the most enticing manner possible, and accede to whatever the lady suggested. Then, after performing her function, Monkey was to *hurry* to the apodyterium, hurry into her clothes, hurry out of the therma, and this time I would be waiting for *her* outside. Monkey nodded and nodded and then slipped gracefully into the water, while I returned to the apodyterium and got dressed as Juhiza for the very last time.

I stood fidgeting in the street, while time seemed to pass with excruciating slowness. But actually it took no longer than it had with Jaeirus. In fact, I could hear a distinct commotion inside the therma—the sounds of women screaming, feet running, children bawling, attendants shouting—for a minute or two before Monkey came scuttling out the door, still doing up some of her outer garments. Before I even inquired, the little black girl beamed a broad white smile and nodded.

So now, much more leisurely, I walked Monkey to our final destination, in the poorest residential district on the far outskirts of the city. Gudinand had once shown me which was his house, but had never invited me inside—he being ashamed of such a shabby and squalid shack. I indicated that Monkey was to enter there, and gave her my purse to take with her. Then, somewhat gingerly, I gave her a thank-you kiss on her ebony forehead, waved goodbye to her and watched until she had gone inside.

The purse she took with her contained the few silver siliquae I had saved for this purpose, and Monkey's certificate of servitium, now countersigned by myself, and a note I had written in the Old Language and the Gothic script: "Máizein thizai friathwai manna ni habáith, ei huas sáiwala seina lagjith faúr frijonds seinans."

I had never met Gudinand's invalid mother, and did not even know whether she could read. But the widow would welcome the money, and surely some kind neighbor could translate for her the two documents.

The certificate would inform the twice-bereaved old woman that she now owned a slave, who would take Gudinand's place in providing and caring for her. And the other document would remind her of what, if she was a devout Christian, she must already know: "Greater love than this no man can have, that he lay down his life for a friend."

✠ ✠ ✠

I was back at the deversorium, and dressed as Thorn, and taking a well-earned rest in my room, when Wyrd came in, more than a little drunk, his hair and beard all bristly. He glared red-eyed at me and said, "No doubt you will already have heard that the bitch-dragon Robeya and her dragon-worm Jaeirus both are dead."

"Ne, fráuja, I had not heard, but I had hoped to."

"They died while bathing, but not by drowning. And they seemed to have died almost simultaneously, though in separate thermae."

"I had expected to hear that."

"They died under most curious circumstances. Most curiously *similar* circumstances."

244

"I am gratified to hear that."

"It is said that Jaeirus's face wore a grimace almost unbearable to behold, that his body was hideously contorted and lying in a puddle of his own skeit. It is said that Robeya's face wore an equally ghastly rictus, that her body was also convulsed into a knot, that she was floating in a balineum pool stained brown with her own skeit."

"I could not be more happy to hear that."

"Oddly, in view of everything else that has occurred today, the priest Tiburnius is still alive."

"I am sorry about that. But I thought it might be imprudent of me to rid Constantia of *all* its evildoers at one stroke. I shall leave the priest's judgment to the God he professes to serve."

"He may do little serving from now on. At least, not in public. I daresay he will cower for the rest of his life behind bolted and guarded doors."

When I did not remark on that, but only grinned, Wyrd scratched meditatively in his beard and said:

"So this is why you needed all our money. But, by the vengeful stone statue of Mitys, urchin, what did you *buy* with that money?"

"A slave."

"*What?* What kind of slave? A gladiator? A killer sicarius? But there was not a single mark of violence, they say, on either of those corpses."

"I bought a venefica."

"*What?!*" He was shocked almost to sobriety. "What would *you* know of a venefica? *How* would you know?"

"I have an inquisitive nature, fráuja. I inquired. I learned that certain girl slaves are, from their infancy, fed certain poisons. First in minute amounts, then in increasing doses throughout their upbringing. By the time they are grown to maidenhood, their own bodies are accustomed to those substances and unharmed by them. However, so virulent is the accumulated poison that a man who beds with a venefica—or anyone who partakes of any of her juices—dies on the instant."

In a hushed voice, Wyrd said, "And you bought one. And you presented her—"

"Quite a *special* one. This girl, like most such girls, had been fed on aconite, because that poison has a not unpleasant flavor. But she had also, all her life long, been fed on elaterium. If you do not know, fráuja, that is a poison extracted from the weed-fruit called the squirting cucumber."

"Iésus," said Wyrd, regarding me with a sort of horrified awe. "No wonder they died so disgustingly—squirting like the cucumber." Wyrd was not only sober now; he looked slightly ill at ease. "Tell me, urchin, are you going to *keep* this venefica creature?"

"Be not concerned, fráuja. Her work here is done, and so is mine. I suggest that now you and I get on with ours, and elsewhere. As soon as we can pack and prepare, I am ready to leave Constantia. Forever."

245

N

Miles
0   40
0   40
Roman Miles

Lentia
(Linz)

Castra
Batava
(Passau)

Haustaths
Saiws
(Hallstatt
See)

(Danube R.)

Haustaths
(Hallstatt)

Juvavum
(Salzburg)

SALTHUZDLAND
(REGIO
SALINARUM)

(SALZKAMMERGUT)

(Isere R.)

(Isar R.)

Danuvius R.

BAJO-
VARIA

(Inn R.)

Veldidena
(Innsbruck)

Aenus R.

Lake
Brigantinus
(Bodensee/Lake
Constance)

Brigantium
(Bregenz)

© 1992 A·Karl / J·Kemp

THE PLACE OF
ECHOES

1

uring what was left of that autumn, and during the whole of the winter and well into the next spring, I worked harder than ever before—as I had promised Wyrd I would—to procure the pelts and hides and ibex horns and beavers' castoreum sacs that would replenish our common fortune. Of course, it would have been difficult for anybody to hunt more skillfully and bring down more game than Wyrd himself could. He still far excelled me at woodcraft and keen observation. However, as I began to notice, and as Wyrd half peevishly, half dolefully admitted, his advancing age was adversely affecting his eyesight in any light dimmer than broadest day.

"By Allfather Wotan," he growled, "I wonder how many people would wish and hope and pray to live long, if they fully realized it would mean getting *old*."

So, as each day deepened to dusk, I would put away my sling and Wyrd would lend me his Hunnish bow, and I could go on hunting longer than he could have done alone. With practice, wielding that weapon for a while every day, I became quite proficient with it—though never as expert as Wyrd at his best—and, for an hour or two after he would have had to abandon the hunt, I brought down additional game both for skinning and for our evening meal.

With either my sling or Wyrd's bow—and once even with my shortsword, when I had stopped to relieve myself in a thicket, and an ibex, exceptionally curious or exceptionally stupid, came to investigate me—during those months I slew at least one specimen of every breed of fur-bearing animal . . . except two. Because I never attained Wyrd's astonishing ability to nock and draw and let fly arrows, one almost directly behind another, it was always he who did that feat of waking and flushing a hibernating bear from its den and then, with one final arrow, felling it when it emerged. Also, though a wolf's rich and heavy winter coat would fetch a price equal to that of a glutton, Wyrd the Friend of Wolves would not let me kill one.

I have to say that I, too, while not quite a *friend* to wolves, did begin to admire them, especially for their hardihood. There is an old country expression: "come winter and the wolf . . ." and it is an apt coupling. Wolves seem to love the winter best of all the seasons. Whenever I was wading through drifts of snow and was cold to the bone, and then would espy a wolf lying under a tree, I could only marvel at the fact that the wolf was every time—intentionally and apparently happily—lying on the *shady* side of that tree.

Long before springtime, Wyrd and I were walking alongside our horses, because their saddles were piled so high with pelts, and still we continued to collect more. So Wyrd and I built sledges of sturdy but pliant boughs, lashed together with strips of rawhide and with their runners' front ends upcurved so they could be dragged fairly easily over obstacles in our path.

When we left Constantia and circled around the southern end of Lake Brigantinus and continued eastward, we had entered the Roman province called Rhaetia Secunda in Latin and Bajo-Varia in the Old Language. As we had done during the previous winter, we mostly made our way along the foothills of the Alpes. But, this winter being considerably more clement, we frequently went higher up the mountainsides in search of ibex or to investigate some cave that Wyrd knew of, and in several of those found bears.

Bajo-Varia is the least populated of the Western Empire's remaining provinces. In our traverse of it, Wyrd and I came upon not a single Roman road, not a city or a village or a fortress, not even an outpost station of legionaries. The only inhabitants were nomad Alamanni, and several times we encountered one of those "nations," so called—none really more than a very large tribe—either moving from one place to another or encamped for the winter. We accompanied one of the traveling tribes for as long as it was going in our direction. At the winter camp of another, we enjoyed its hospitality for a few days and nights.

Considering the bellicose reputation of the Alamanni, it might be supposed that they would have resented the presence of aliens on their lands. And true, if Wyrd and I had been a lengthy merchant train or a foreign army on the march, the Alamanni would have regarded us as intruders, and attacked and looted us, and either killed or enslaved us. But we were so obviously nomads like themselves that they warmly welcomed us into their company. The encampment where we stayed for a while was that of the most populous nation in the province. They called themselves the Baiuvarja, and said that the whole province had derived its Gothic name from theirs, because of their preeminence in it. The tribe's chief, one Ediulf, of course called himself King of the Baiuvarja, but he was as hospitable as his "subjects," and did not accuse us of trespassing on his domain. Well, no Germanic king ever would do such a thing, for none claimed to *have* a domain. Like this backwoods King Ediulf, even the most august Germanic rulers—such as Khilderic, King of the Franks, or Gaiseric, King of the Vandals—were, as they styled themselves, the kings of *peoples*, not of territories.

On the continents of Europe and Libya, only the emperors of Rome have regarded themselves as the rulers of *lands*, and have set boundaries about the portions of the earth they claim as their own, and have fortified those borders—or tried to—against the encroachment of other rulers and peoples. Ever since the time of Constantine, when the empire divided into western and eastern, even the two halves of itself have been squabbling over the location of the border line between them in Europe. And the eastern half has often had to fight to maintain its farthest eastern boundary—on the continent of Asia, where the Roman Empire abuts on Persia—because Persia's "King of Kings," so called, also regards himself as reigning over lands as well as the people on them.

The Baiuvarja were all unregenerate pagans, and almost every one of them wore the amulet representing Thor's primitive hammer—made of carefully chipped stone or of iron or bronze, according to the person's affluence or status in the tribe—hanging hammerhead down from a rawhide string around his or her neck.

"However," King Ediulf told Wyrd and me, with a sly wink, "in our wanderings we are occasionally approached by a likewise wandering Christian missionary. And some of us do occasionally have to visit a Christian town, to buy tools or salt or some such thing that we cannot supply for ourselves. So, to keep from being preached at or prayed over or viciously reviled on those occasions, we simply hang Thor's hammer upside down on our neck strings. See? It is easily mistaken for a Christian cross. That makes us look even more pious and devout than any genuine Christian, who only makes the *gesture* of the cross, but has never bethought himself to wear one. Believe me, it saves us a good deal of annoyance."

With a small smile hidden behind his beard, Wyrd said, "It would seem rather less trouble for all of you to convert and *be* Christians."

"Ne! Ni allis!" exclaimed Ediulf, taking him to be serious. "Our Old Religion is like a table well laden with every kind of viand, from strong beer to delicate sweets. One can choose whichever god or belief one likes best. Ne, we will be content with our Old Religion, and will have no priests dictating to us, and if we require counsel or guidance from our gods, our frodei-qithans will divine it for us."

A frodei-qithans is a wise-sayer, but this one of the Baiuvarja nation would be called in Latin a sternutospex, for he did his divinations by the not very common method of interpreting *sneezes*. Whenever King Ediulf convened a council of the nation's elders, he and they sitting in a circle, the aged wise-sayer, Winguric by name, would be among them. If the council deemed that it needed the gods' advice about some decision it had to make—or worried that the gods might be displeased by some plan proposed—the elders would defer to Winguric. He would go around the circle, blowing from his hand some kind of flower pollen into each man's face, including the king's. Then he would sit back and listen to the number and frequency and rhythm of the resulting sneezes. When all present had had their sneeze-say, and were dashing

the tears from their eyes and blowing their noses on the ground or on the hems of their tunics, Winguric would make his pronouncement as to the gods' opinions or admonitions or objections regarding the matter under discussion. That might or might not alter the council's decision, but it would always be weighed and considered before a final decision was made.

As Wyrd and I were preparing to leave the Baiuvarja and go on our way eastward, that ancient wise-sayer volunteered to divine our fortune along the way. Wyrd only grudgingly accepted the offer, but I did so rather eagerly, for I had never before had my sneezes interpreted. So we sat down before old Winguric, and he blew that pollen at us, and we sneezed indeed. It would have been impossible not to. But it was evident to me—and to the wise-sayer, for he frowned most disapprovingly—that Wyrd exaggerated and prolonged his sneezing spasm, out of sheer mischievous contrariety.

When Wyrd finally finished, and pinched one nostril, then the other, to blow his nose onto the ground, and then wiped quite another lot of snot out of his beard, old Winguric gave each of us a black look and said venomously, "Unbelievers cannot deceive the gods with pretense."

"Akh, who?" said Wyrd, mock-innocently. "Would *I* dare to try flouting all the powers of—?"

"You," spat Winguric, stabbing a bony finger at him, "will be slain by a friend. So say the gods and so say I."

That may have stunned even the cynical Wyrd. It certainly stunned me. Then, before either of us could utter a word, the wise-sayer swung his finger to point at me.

"You," he spat, "will slay a friend. So say the gods and so say I."

Then he creakily stood up and, without so much as another look at us, strode away.

I still could not speak, but Wyrd serenely hummed to himself as he completed the packing and tying of our sledges. And as we led our horses from the encampment, he waved and called "huarbodáu mith gawaírthja" to King Ediulf and the other Baiuvarja who watched us depart. Not until we were some distance from the camp could I speak, and then my voice came out with a bit of a quaver to it.

"If—if the frodei-qithans is right, fráuja, it almost sounds as though—as though I am sometime going to kill you."

"Just try," he said drily.

"You put no credence in the predictions?"

"By the sin-sniffing St. Jerome, of course I do not! Every time I encounter a wise-sayer or an astrologus or an augur of whatever sort, I recall the warning that Nero got from the oracle at Delphi. 'Beware of seventy-three years.' Nero was overjoyed to believe that he would live to such an age. But it was the seventy-three-year-old Galba who dethroned him. Nero took his own life at the age of thirty-two. Predictions are always couched in such a way that they can mean anything or nothing at all. Most often, urchin, they mean nothing at all. Like Cato, I marvel that one augur can look another in the face."

253

Considerably relieved by Wyrd's calm indifference, I said, "I know you share King Ediulf's low opinion of Christianity. But I should have thought you might be a *little* inclined toward the Old Religion. It has at least the virtue of antiquity."

"Vái! Those who revere the antique seem never to realize that a *pebble* is older than anything man ever made. Including all the religions invented by the so-called ancients. Everyone speaks with veneration of those 'ancients' and how wise they were. But they were neither. Consider, urchin. The ancient peoples, the ancient kingdoms, the ancient sages and prophets—why, they all existed in the ignorant youthtime of the world. So many ages have passed since then that even the stars have moved. In those times, it was Thuban that marked true north;

now the star Phoenice shines there instead. Ne, ne, it is *we* who are the ancients—and the wiser, or at least we ought to be—we who live today, when mankind and the world have grown old."

I thought it over, then said, "That would never have occurred to me."

"Of course, there were intelligent and clever men, however ignorant, at the very beginning of the world, and then as now they took advantage of others' ignorance. That is why I hold all religions to be equally valid—or equally absurd—because all religions are myths, and no myth can be superior to any other, and men made those myths."

He stopped, both talking and walking, so suddenly that his horse bumped into him and the sledge bumped into the horse.

"Look here! Elk tracks! Come, urchin. We shall dine tonight on elk's liver. A delicacy far superior to every juiceless, tasteless, indigestible myth ever made!"

✠　✠　✠

Well, neither of us killed the other, and eventually, somewhere, we crossed an invisible boundary line in the forest, passing eastward from Bajo-Varia into the province called Noricum. Although Alamanni tribes wander about Noricum, too, there are also small settlements of Roman colonists whose ancestors emigrated from Italia, mainly because there is much iron in the ground here, and the Noricans prosper by making the fine Noric steel that Rome buys for making weapons. So every settlement that Wyrd and I came upon was centered on a mine or a forge or a foundry.

In early spring, we came downstream along the river Aenus, taking many beaver, and at last saw a real road, wider than a footpath. It was the Roman road that descends the Alpes by way of the Alpis Ambusta, probably the most traveled pass through those mountains, so the road bore a heavy traffic of persons and animals and wagons and carts going to or from or beyond the cities of Tridentum in Italia to the south and Castra Regina on the great river Danuvius to the north. The road crosses the Aenus on a well-constructed bridge, and so did Wyrd and I, finding the eastern end of the bridge guarded by the Roman station of Veldidena, garrisoned by troops of the Legio II Italica Pia. As elsewhere, the station's surrounding cabanae—shops, tabernae, forges, tanneries and the like—had mostly been built and were tended by legion veterans, and here, as elsewhere, Wyrd had several old acquaintances. And here, as elsewhere, he got drunk with them, though not until after he

254

had sold a quantity of furs and horns and, to the garrison's medicus, even some of our castoreum. Then, while he swilled and guzzled and wallowed for many days in happy drunkenness, I did the buying of what supplies we needed for the next stage of our journey.

That stage, when Wyrd had recovered and we went on, took us farther down the ever-widening Aenus, and then—when the river bent northward—away from it, over lands that were watered by only small streams. We traveled faster now, because most of the fur-bearing animals were past their winter prime and we hunted chiefly for the cooking fire. So, in late spring, we came to the trading city and provincial capital, Juvavum. As soon as we had sold all our goods—and sold them for a fortune far surpassing what we had earned in Constantia the year before—Wyrd said to me:

"I have no acquaintances here with whom to dawdle and drink and reminisce, and cities do not greatly appeal to me otherwise. Besides, I believe we have earned ourselves a real holiday. Let us stay here only a few more days, urchin, long enough to soak the wilderness out of us in several good leisurely baths, and eat our fill of voluptuous city viands, and replenish our wardrobes and other necessities. Then let us depart, and I will take you to one of the most enchanting places in which one *can* make holiday. What say you?"

255

I still had painful memories of the last city in which I had tarried for long, so I concurred without any hesitation and, about a week later, Wyrd and I rode out of Juvavum, leaving our empty sledges behind. We did not take any of the many Roman roads that converge on Juvavum, but went southeast through the gradually heightening forelands of the range known to the local folk as the Roofstone Alpes.

After just a few days of easy riding, we were in the part of Noricum called in Latin the Regio Salinarum, in the Old Language the Salthuzd-land, both names meaning "the place of much salt." That did not signify a barren desert of salt (which sort of wastelands do exist, I am told, but only in Asia and Libya). Far from it. The region *is* amply supplied with salt mines, but they are all deep underground and the entrances to those caverns only infrequently pock the countryside. The rest of the landscape is truly grand, the loveliest country I had yet traveled through. Lush alpine meadows of wildflowers and sweet grasses alternated with forests that were—I do not know why—different from all those we had earlier traversed. These forests were much like the parklands I would eventually see on rich men's great estates: not clogged with underbrush, the trees standing fastidiously apart, so that every one had room to spread its crown most bountifully, and between the trees were flowering shrubs and grass as lawnlike as the prata of those carefully tailored and groomed estates.

"This is the prettiest country I have ever laid eyes on," I said to Wyrd, in genuine awe and rapture. "Do you suppose there might be centaurs and satyrs and nymphs in these woods?"

"As many here as anywhere," he said wryly, but he looked pleased to have me commend his choice of a place for our holiday.

The journey was marred by only one unfortunate incident. We had stopped for the night beside a crystalline brook that flowed through a flowery and fragrant arbor. I had gone off to collect windfall branches and twigs to build a fire, and was returning with an armload when I heard Wyrd shout a wordless exclamation of surprise, and then heard a strange animal noise, something between a whine and a growl, and then heard a scuffling noise that ceased abruptly. I ran then and, at the campsite, found Wyrd standing with his short-sword in hand, its blade all bloody. He was gazing morosely down at what he had slain, a very handsome bitch-wolf.

"What is this?" I asked. "I thought you were a friend to wolves."

"I am," he said, without lifting his gaze from the animal. "This one tried to attack me."

I could believe that it must have been a sudden and fierce attack, for I saw a spatter of blood on one of Wyrd's laced leggings, and he was ordinarily very neat in his kills, even when it was a charging boar.

I said, "I also thought a wolf would never accost a man. You told me so."

"This one was ill," he said glumly. "She was afflicted with a sickness I have seen before. She would have died in terrible torments. I killed her out of mercy."

Wyrd looked so mournful that I forbore from inquiry about that sickness, and said only, "Well, at least you got her before she savaged you or the horses."

"Ja," said Wyrd, but still gloomily. Then he almost angrily rumpled his hair and beard, and said, "While I go to wash my sword and myself, urchin, please take the firewood farther along the brook to make camp. I would rather not spend the night so close to this poor dead creature."

I had earlier brought down a hare with my sling. As we dined on it— broiled on a spit over the fire and well seasoned with salt, because salt was so cheap in these parts—it occurred to me to remark:

"You know something, fráuja? He *did* prophesy rightly—that aged

Winguric we met back in the winter—only he got our fortunes reversed. It is you who have slain a friend, not me."

Wyrd did not even grunt at that. I fancied that he was peeved to have been wrong about oracles and divination, so I twitted him:

"Probably you confused the old frodei-qithans with all that extravagant sneezing you did."

Again he made no reply whatsoever, and I realized that I was being boorish and insensitive. It appeared that Wyrd was grieving over the dead wolf, much as I had done over my dead juika-bloth. So I shut my foolish mouth and we passed the evening in silence. By the next morning, though, Wyrd was his old self again—gruff and sarcastic and snappish—and the rest of our journey through those wondrous woods was carefree and gladsome.

I thought I had already seen beauty enough on our way, but all of that paled in my memory when I saw our destination. At about noon one day we rode around the shoulder of a high Alpe, and Wyrd reined his horse to a halt, and made a sweeping gesture of his arm to show me what lay below, and the sight made me catch my breath.

"Haustaths," Wyrd said proudly. "The Place of Echoes."

257

2

n my lifetime I have seen Roma Flora and Konstantinopólis Anthusa—the Latin agnomen and the Greek both mean "the flourishing," and both cities are sumptuous indeed. I have seen Vindobona, the second-oldest city, after Rome itself, in the entire empire; and I have seen Ravenna; and I have seen many other historic cities. I have seen the lands that border the river Danuvius, from the Black Sea to the Black Forest, and I have taken ship on both the Mediterranean Sea and the Sarmatic Ocean. In sum, I have seen more of the world than most people ever will. But still I remember Haustaths as the most ravishingly beautiful and beguiling piece of this earth that I have ever beheld.

From the mountain whence Wyrd and I gazed down, the Place of Echoes was very like an oblong bowl made all of Alpes, the bowl holding some water in its bottom. But that water was a lake, and it had to be a tremendously deep one, for the mountains' flanks went almost straight down into it, to meet conjoined somewhere far, far below. Only at intervals between the flanks, at lakeside, were there small patches of land sloping down to the water, and there were a few shelflike meadows visible on some of the mountainsides. Several of the Alpes on the farther side of the bowl were so tall that their peaks—even now, in early summer—were still white with snow. Here and there, the mountains also showed crags and cliffs of bare brown rock. But the bulk of them was clad in forest—from our distance, looking like billows and pleats of rich green fleece, dappled a dark blue-green wherever a cloud shadow undulated across it.

The lake, the Haustaths-Saiws, was a miniature compared to the Brigantinus, but it was incomparably more radiant and inviting. The blue—akh! the blue of it!—made it seem, from where I first saw it, a precious blue gem nestled among the mountains' folds of green fleece. Not until long afterward did I have opportunity to see a dark-yet-glowing blue sapphire, but when I did, I was instantly reminded of the color of that Haustaths lake.

✠ ✠ ✠

Floating about on the water were some objects unidentifiably tiny from this distance, and directly below us—so far below us that it appeared to be one of those toy villages that wood-carvers make for children—was the town of Haustaths, occupying the whole of one of the few meager patches of lakeside land. I could see only the roofs of the town, every one steep-pitched to shed the snow in winter, and an open market square among the roofs, and some piers jutting out onto the water. But there were *many* roofs, so many that I could not imagine how the houses under them all huddled together in a space so constricted.

Then we rode down from our Alpe, along a trail that ran close beside a wide stream bounding merrily down a series of cataracts toward the lake. And as we got nearer to Haustaths, I could see how the town was built. There was very little flat land alongside the lake here, so only a comparative few of the houses—and a sizable church and the town square, with shops and tabernae and gasts-razna all around it—stood on level ground. The other houses and establishments of the town were stacked almost one atop another, halfway up the steep mountainside. They were separated not by crosswise streets but by tiny alleyways, and up and downhill ran not streets but stone *staircases*. The houses were so cramped and crowded that some were very narrow, but those compensated for the squeeze by being two or even three stories high.

At first sight, Haustaths looked precariously perched, but there was no doubting that it had been there for a long, long time. All the buildings were solidly constructed of stone or stout timbers, with roofs of slate or tiles or thick shingles. Almost every one had its front plastered white and then brightly decorated, some with scrollwork designs painted in many colors, some with a flowering vine, or even a flowering *tree*, artfully trained to grow up flat against the housefront and around its door and window openings. The market square had in the middle a fountain with four spouts continuously gushing water, piped from the stream we had followed. And all the shops around that square were gaily adorned with tubs or boxes of flowers set about their sills.

I had never seen a community, from smallest hamlet to biggest city, that went to so much effort to put such a cheerful face on itself. I believe it must have been the heart-lifting loveliness of its surroundings that inspired the people to make their town worthy of its setting. Also, they could well afford those nonessential but comely embellishments of their buildings. On one of the Alpes high above Haustaths is a vast salt mine that, I was told, is the oldest in the world. The modern-day miners have found in there crude primitive tools and the salt-preserved corpses of men evidently killed by cave-ins aeons ago—creatures so ugly and dwarfish but massively muscled that they might have been skohls of the sort that live always underground, except that they wore the same kind of leather garments that salt miners still wear. So, say the folk of Haustaths, that mine must have been worked since the time Noah's children dispersed about the earth.

Anyway, the mine is still inexhaustibly rich in the purest grade of salt, and it keeps the townspeople rich in purse. All of them have lived here for generations, and they are of such mingled blood—descendants of settlers from just about every Germanic tribe, who long ago intermarried with Roman colonists come from Italia—that it would be difficult to say today what their nationality is, beyond their being, of course, citizens of the Roman province of Noricum.

Wyrd and I came down to lake level at the outskirts of the town, where its only stables are situated. In one of them we left our horses,

259

and paid for their keep and care. Then we hefted our packs of personal belongings and strolled along Haustaths's one wide street, the lakeside promenade, whence I could now make out what the objects on the water were. Those closest inshore were gray herons and purple herons wading in the shallows or standing meditatively on one leg. A little farther out were gorgeous white swans drifting serenely about. And farthest out were fishing boats, of a sort that I have never seen elsewhere. The local fishers call them the faúrda, which would mean roughly "the goers," though the boats have no need to go anywhere at speed. Each is shaped exactly like a slice of melon chopped in half at the middle. Its prow curves high out of the water and its stern, where the boatman stands to row it, is flat and abrupt. The reason for the shape—or the name—no one could tell me, but I do not think such a boat could be a speedy goer.

Wyrd and I dined that first evening on delicious grilled slabs of pikeperch, caught only an hour or so earlier. The taberna in which we took our meal was one of those facing on the town square, its caupo, a burly man named Andraías, being yet another of Wyrd's longtime acquaintances. The building's front was all painted with curlicues and its door was flanked by flower boxes, but its rear wall, right at lakeside, was made of panels which the caupo laid away during fine weather. So, as we ate and drank, we had a fine full view of the Haustaths-Saiws at twilight, and the still sun-tipped mountains beyond; and we tossed bits of bread to the swans that glided by below our terrace; and we several times shouted loudly over the water to hear the nymph Echo shout faintly and ever more faintly back to us from one far black peak after another; and when we were done with our meal we retired to our quilted bed upstairs; and I lay long awake with my head turned to the window, watching the moon come over a mountain to frost that blue, blue lake with glints of silver; and when my eyes closed at last they closed on what I still remember as one of the most peacefully happy days of all my life.

✠   ✠   ✠

I awoke the next morning to find Wyrd already up, washed and getting dressed. He paused before wrapping on his leggings to examine a small red lesion on one of his bare shanks.

"Have you hurt yourself?" I inquired sleepily.

"That wolf," he muttered. "She gave me a nip before I slew her. I was worried about that, but it is healing nicely."

"Why should such a tiny wound worry you? I have seen you agonize more after slaying the contents of a wine jug."

"Be not impudent to your elders, urchin. That she-wolf was suffering from the hundswoths, and that awful affliction can be communicated by a bite. But I hoped that her fang, having to pierce my thick legging, would have been wiped clean of its venomous saliva . . . and so it seems to have been. Believe me, that is a great relief, to see the puncture healthily scabbed over. Now I think I shall stagger downstairs and seek the tail of that other wolf that bit me just last evening."

I had heard of the hundswoths—it means "dog-madness"—and had heard that it meant certain death, but I had never seen any animal afflicted with it. I would have worried as much as Wyrd had I known of his injury, but now that he so airily dismissed it, I was glad he had not told me of it before.

I joined Wyrd in the taberna, where he was breaking his fast with nothing but black bread and some more wine, and appeared likely to go on drinking with his friend the caupo for the rest of the day. I hastily gobbled a sausage, a boiled duck egg and a tumbler of milk, for I was eager to be out in the pearly early sunshine, exploring Haustaths.

261

It might seem that so small and isolated a town would hold few attractions for a young man, but I found much to charm me, on that and succeeding days, and I looked forward to spending the whole summer here. That first morning, I decided to explore the region from the top down, so to speak, and set off up the streamside trail that Wyrd and I had descended the day before. It was a rigorous climb on foot, but that gave me excuse to pause at intervals. While I regained my wind and relaxed my muscles, I could leisurely examine and admire the view from increasingly higher altitudes. I went on past the place where Wyrd and I had come around the shoulder of the mountain, and took a fork in the trail that kept me going upward, and I came at last to the saltwaúrstwa—the mine that was the reason for Haustaths's existence.

The miners hobbled out of the arched entrance bearing on their backs long cone-shaped baskets filled with lumps of gray rock salt, while their fellows, having emptied their baskets, slouched back in. The mine itself was the center of a whole community and a considerable manufactory. There was quite a grand house for the mine's director, less grand ones for his supervisors and foremen, and an entire village of rude huts and small gardens for the workers. On the mountain slopes roundabout, wherever there was one of those shelflike meadows, its borders were diked and the meadow filled with water. The rock salt was dissolved in those pools, leached of any impurities and discoloration, then dried and re-created as granular pure-white salt ready for use. There was a shed for bagging the salt, and an immense shed for storing the bags, and stockades for the mules used to haul the bags over the Alpes to their various destinations.

The miners who worked underground and the teamsters were all men, of course, but the aboveground work was mostly done by their wives and children. There must have been as many people up here as there were in Haustaths below. Some of them, I would learn later, were slaves recently conscripted to this drudgery, but most were descendants of slaves who had ages ago saved their meager wages to buy their liberty—and these, their great-grandsons and -daughters, though freemen, continued in the same drudgery because it was the only work they knew how to do.

I was standing apart, scanning the scene, when an authoritative but youthful voice spoke from behind me: "Are you seeking work, stranger? Are you a free laborer or someone's slave?"

I turned and beheld the girl who would be my friend and companion for as long as I stayed in Haustaths. I hasten to say that this never became an amorous attachment, for she was only a child, about half my age, Romanly brown-haired, doe-eyed, fawn-skinned and very pretty.

"I am neither," I said. "And I do not seek work. I merely came up from the town to see what the saltwaurtswa looks like."

"Then you must be a traveler from beyond these mountains. Everyone hereabouts is wearily familiar with this place." She sighed dramatically. "The liufs Guth knows I am."

"And what would you be?" I asked, smiling, because she was finely dressed in alicula and cloak, like a little lady. "Laborer or slave?"

"I," she said loftily, "am the only daughter of the mine's director, Georgius Honoratus. My name is Livia. Who are you?"

I told her my name, and we chatted for some time—she seemed pleased to have someone new to talk to—and she pointed out to me various features of the workings, told me the names of the various alpine peaks around the lake, advised me as to which merchants in town were the least likely to cheat strangers making purchases. Finally she asked:

"Have you ever seen the inside of a salt mine?" When I confessed that I had not, she went on, "The inside of this one is much more worth seeing than everything outside. Come and meet my father, and I will ask his permission to let me escort you."

262

She introduced me to him thus: "Father, this is Thorn, a newcomer to our neighborhood and a new friend of mine. Thorn, give respectful greeting to the director of this eminent and ancient enterprise, Georgius Honoratus."

He was a slight man, gray-white of hair, and obviously he took his responsibilities seriously, spending much of his own time underground, for his skin was as colorless as his hair. I would later be told, by Livia and others, that Georgius was one of the few citizens of Haustaths whose family had descended from Roman colonists *without*, as yet, any admixture of other blood, and he never let anybody forget that. When he signed any least document, he always added the Roman numeral designating his generation of the family. As I remember, he was the XIIIth or XIVth of his line. He had even imported from Rome a woman to be his wife; she had died giving birth to Livia, and he showed no lingering signs of bereavement; he was married to the mine.

Georgius affected the agnomen of Honoratus, usually reserved for public officials of at least the rank of magistrate, because he, like his XII or XIII forefathers, had been appointed to this directorship by the Haustaths council of elders. Like those forebears—and, in my opinion, exactly like the wretched menials who drudged for him—Georgius had never traveled beyond the nearest horizon, never raised his eyes or his aspirations above it, and knew nothing whatever of the outside world except its voracious appetite for salt. He was rearing his two sons to be just as provincial and limited of outlook as he was himself. In fact, they were so reclusive that it was some while before I discovered that Georgius *had* sons, respectively two and four years older than Livia. If I ever saw those boys, I did not recognize them, for their father was teaching them his trade literally from the underground up, and they were currently among the leather-clad, sweaty, dusty miners lugging baskets of rock salt.

I wondered sometimes if perhaps Georgius's late wife *had* contrived to introduce some alien blood into the family line. I could think of no other explanation for Livia's being so unlike her lackluster father and docile brothers, because I found her to be a bright, perceptive, vivacious child, and rightly discontented with her prospects.

Whether Livia was really Georgius's daughter or not, he clearly treasured her more than he did his sons, and maybe almost as much as he did his mine. He could not have been too pleased to have her befriending a Germanic-looking stranger, but at least, given the difference in our ages, he did not have to worry about the hazard of my becoming a

263

son-in-law. So he merely asked me a few questions about my lineage, occupation and reason for being in Haustaths. I avoided being too specific about my origins, but answered truthfully enough that I was the partner of a fur merchant, that in summer we had little business to occupy us and that he and I were simply here on holiday. That seemed to satisfy Georgius, for he indulgently gave Livia leave to take me underground, and said he hoped I would enjoy touring the establishment of which he was so proud.

Inside the great dark entrance, the ingoing and outcoming miners deferentially made way for Livia and me, as she picked from a stack of leather aprons one for each of us. I started to tie mine about my waist, but she laughed and said:

"Not that way. Put it on hindside to. Here, turn around."

Puzzled, I turned my back to her, so I was facing the blackness of the mine's interior, and she arranged the apron to drape its long flap over my backside.

"Now tie the thongs in front," she said. "Now pull the flap up between your legs and hold on to it with both hands."

264 I did so, and Livia dealt me a surprise. With a giggle, she gave me a violent shove that propelled me into the darkness, where my feet instantly slid out from under me. I found myself breathlessly hurtling on my apron down a steep chute worn in the solid salt, polished by maybe millions of such slidings so that it was as slippery as ice. For what seemed a long time, but was probably only a few heartbeats, I plunged through utter blackness into the bowels of the earth. But then the chute's incline became less and less acute, until it was almost level, and I saw light ahead of me. I was still moving at a great rate, however, when the chute abruptly ended, so I was briefly airborne before I landed on a cushioning pile of springy pine sprigs. I sat stunned for a moment, then I was *really* knocked breathless, as Livia's feet slammed into my back and we both tumbled off the pile of pine.

"Dotterel," she called me, giggling again, as we disentangled from one another. "Such a dawdler would not long survive underground. Come. *Move!* Or you will have a whole heap of miners on top of you."

I rolled well away from the chute, and just in time. A spate of those men, each holding an empty basket, came shooting from out of the darkness into the torchlit, salt-walled corridor in which we had landed. Each man spryly sprang to his feet from the pile of pine boughs, to make way for the next, and then less eagerly plodded on along the hall. Beyond the procession of men, I could see another file of them coming from inside the mine, bent under their baskets, being waved on or briefly halted by a foreman who stood at the bottom of a ladder—an exceptionally tall ladder, built of very thick beams and rungs—up which the miners toiled into the darkness above.

When I could breathe again, little Livia led me along the corridor, around various corners, along other halls that branched off one another. Each was brightly and quite enchantingly lighted, and it required torches only at distant intervals to accomplish that because, from each torch, the translucent salt walls gathered the illumination and diffracted and diffused it for a long way in either direction. So, between the brilliant red-yellow splotches of torchlight, we walked in a mellower glow of orange radiance, emanating equally from walls, floor and ceiling, as if we were inside the world's largest jacinth gem. In some manner that I could not discern, every part of the mine was vented and the vents were interconnecting, reaching clear to the outside of the mountain. Everywhere inside, there was a faint but perceptible breeze that not only supplied fresh air at even the deepest levels but also whisked away the torches' smoke and prevented its discoloring the salt at all. In almost every hallway there was a constant traffic of heavy-laden men passing opposite to Livia and myself, and empty-basketed men trudging along with us, but some of the side corridors were totally empty, and I asked why.

"They lead to places where the salt has been worked down to bare rock, and is exhausted," said the child. "But I am not going to take you to any of the mine's faces currently being worked, for there is always danger of a cave-in, and I would not expose a guest to such peril."

"Thank you," I said sincerely.

"However, there is one particular place I wish to show you. And that is quite a long way. Both in and down."

She gestured, and I saw that we stood at the head of another dark chute, the miners again standing aside for us. Here Livia played no fooleries, and I bowed politely for her to go first. This time, as I followed, I found the swooping ride on my apron rather exhilarating. But we again wound our way through many corridors, then down another long chute—and more corridors, and more chutes—and I began to feel uncomfortable. In my youth, as I have told, I spent much time inside the tunnels and caves behind my beloved cascades in the Balsan Hrinkhen, but those had only taken me deep within a cliffside, not down and down and down *under* it.

It seemed to me that Livia and I must by now be back on a level with the town I had left in early morning. That would mean that I had a whole, huge, high Alpe bulking over my head, held from collapsing onto me only by walls and ceilings of salt. And salt, I reflected, is a notably fragile substance. But the passing miners showed no signs of fearfulness, and the girl went blithely along, so I gulped down my discomfiture and followed where she led. Now she turned off from the traveled corridors into an empty but nevertheless torchlit one. That got wider and higher as we progressed, and suddenly opened out, and we were standing on the edge of a vast cavern, empty of any other people but more brightly lighted than any of the busy walkways had been.

It was very like those Balsan Hrinkhen caves that I have described, but this surpassed them, both in size and in splendor—for what had there been formed by apparently melted-then-congealed rock was here fashioned of salt: fluted columns between floor and ceiling, lacework and draperies and motionless waterfalls around the walls, spires and steeples and pinnacles upthrust from the floor, long icicle-like pendants dangling from the vaulted ceiling. Everything was of good and market-able salt, but so marvelous were the salt sculptures that, in all the centuries or millennia that the mine had been worked, these things had been preserved undefiled.

The miners had gone to a great deal of trouble to illuminate this place. It must have been harder work than mining, to affix torches all around and up the arching walls to the very roof of the vault, as they had done. The resultant firelight, diffused throughout the translucent salt shapes, reflected back and forth inside the soaring dome of salt, almost like echoes made visible, gave me the feeling that I stood no longer within a jacinth gem but at the heart of a flame.

With proprietary pride, Livia said, "All this was made by nature, but the miners added some things man-made. No one knows how long ago."

She beckoned me to one side of the cavern and showed me. Into a wall that nature had neglected to adorn, the miners had carved a small but entire Christian chapel—hollowed out, then furnished with an ambo table built of salt blocks and slab, and on the ambo stood a tall pyx and a taller chalice, both sculptured from rock salt.

"Like the better people in Haustaths, some of the miners have long been good Christians," said Livia. "But most are still pagan, and they too, long ago, added a work of their own."

Into the side of the cavern directly across from the chapel, they had carved a temple. This hollowed-out space contained only a man-sized salt statue, crudely done but more or less man-shaped, and evidently meant to be some god. Then I saw that the figure's lumpy right hand leaned on the wooden haft of a hammer with a stone head tied on by thongs, and I realized that the statue represented Thor. One other thing about the temple: its interior was caked with soot and smelled of smoke—the only place in the mine that I had found thus blemished—and I asked Livia how that came to be.

"Why, the pagan miners make sacrifices here," she said. "They bring the animal here—a lamb, a kid, a piglet. A fire is laid, the animal is slain in the name of some god, then it is cooked. The celebrants eat the meat." She shrugged her slender shoulders. "The gods get only the smoke."

"And your Christian father *lets* the pagans do that?"

"The Christian elders of Haustaths make *sure* he lets them. It keeps the workers contented and it costs the mine nothing. Now, Thorn, are you well rested? It is a long way back, and we cannot slide *up*." I grinned and said, "I believe I can negotiate the ladders. Would you like me to carry you, little girl?"

"Carry me?" she said scornfully. "Vái! Try to *catch* me!" And she scampered off along the corridor that had brought us here.

With my longer legs I did not have to strain to keep up with her, and I made sure that I kept up, or I should assuredly have got lost along the way. I do admit that, when we climbed the last ladder and emerged from the mine's entrance, I was panting and perspiring and she was not. But then, I had climbed that mountain *twice* that day, once on the outside of it and again on the inside.

267

3

hen I got back to the taberna, the caupo Andraías told me, with hiccups, that Wyrd had already gone to sleep and then gone to bed. I must have given him an inquiring look, for he said:

"Ja, in that order. He fell asleep at the table— hic—so my old woman and I conveyed him upstairs."

So I dined alone, and I ate voraciously. When I likewise went up to bed, Wyrd's snoring was like a mortal combat between a boar and an úrus, and the room was well-nigh foggy with wine fumes, but I was too tired for that to keep me from sleeping soundly.

Next morning, when we broke our fast together, and Wyrd again took wine, I waited for that wine to clear his head before I recounted my doings of the previous day. I told him of my having visited the mine, and what I saw there, and of my having met Livia and Georgius, and what they were like.

He grunted and said, "I take it that the daughter is a tolerable creature, but the father is one of those self-important mediocrities found in any rustic town."

"That is my opinion, too," I said. "But I feel I ought at least to feign respect. He *is* an Honoratus."

"Balgs-daddja! He is only a plump oyster in a small oyster bed."

"You sound even more fractious than your usual self, fráuja. Is the wine so sour?"

He scratched in his beard, and said soberly, "Forgive me, urchin. I am lately despondent and uneasy of mind. The mood will pass. The wine will help it to pass."

"Why the mood? On our arrival here, you had no such mood. Consider, fráuja. We have plenty of money, we need not work, we need only enjoy ourselves and we are in the pleasantest of places for doing that. What have you to be despondent about? Or uneasy?"

He continued to fidget with his beard, and muttered, "By his own head that St. Denis carried under his arm, I do not know. Perhaps only because I am an old man. No doubt fretfulness is another sign of growing old, like the dimming of my eyesight. Go, urchin, and disport yourself with your new friend. Leave this old one to drink away his melancholy." He quaffed a long draft from his mug, and belched. "When I recover . . . in a few days . . . I will take you hunting. Hic. Just for sport . . . a kind of game you have not hunted before."

He disappeared behind the mug again, so I made no remark except a noise of exasperation, and strode angrily from the taberna into the market square. As on every morning, it was full of people, mostly women buying their comestibles for the day, and the vendors from whom they bought. I was surprised to see Livia loitering among that crowd. I had told her where I was lodging, but I wondered what had brought her all the way down from the mountain at this early hour.

"I came to visit you, of course," she said. "And to show you our town."

That day she showed me the interior of the Church of Mount Calvary, which also served as the chamber for the town council's meetings and as a repository of oddments from Haustaths's past: things discovered by local miners, house-builders and gravediggers over the years. Those included numerous articles of bronze jewelry, corroded and green with verdigris; and the much better-preserved corpse—as wrinkled, brown and leathery as its garments—of one of those dwarfish ancient miners found by his ages-after fellow miners.

269

Then we visited the workshop of an aizasmitha. He did not make jewelry in the modern fashion, such as I had seen (and occasionally purchased) elsewhere. He deliberately copied those antique articles in the Calvary church repository, only restoring them to what they would have looked like when new: arm and ankle bracelets, shoulder fibulae, dainty daggers that were not so much weapons as ornaments for the waist, necklaces and breast pins, all of bright shining bronze.

When it was time for Livia to return home and sit down with her tutor, I walked with her as far as the upper heights of the town. Then I went back to that aizasmitha's shop, for I had seen there something I wished to buy for myself, but had not wanted Livia to *see* me buy. That would have perplexed or shocked her, because it was an article definitely made to be worn by a woman. It was a breast guard of a style so old-fashioned that I never afterward saw another for sale anywhere, or worn by any other woman but myself.

It was a simple contrivance, as would be expected from the early artisans who made all those primitive ornaments, but it was at the same time most ingeniously designed and extremely handsome. It consisted basically of a very long, slender rod of bronze, about the thickness of an eagle quill, but artfully curled into twin spirals that wound in opposite directions. The left side spiraled to encase a woman's left breast from the nipple outward, then, from the upper bulge of that breast, the rod curled down into and across the cleft of the bosom to coil again, from the outside of the right breast inward to end at its nipple. To either side was attached a thong, for the wearer to tie behind her back. On the smith's bench the whole apparatus simply lay flat, but when clasped across the bosom, those spirals opened and expanded to become a sheath for the separate breasts, both a protection and a decoration. So I bought one, not for armor, but to enhance the visible protuberance of my breasts whenever I should next dress as my female self. It was a rather costly purchase, but I judged it worth the price to make me, when I chose to be a woman, look that much more feminine, shapely and attractive.

270 The better part of many days thereafter I spent in company with Livia, because Wyrd remained sunk in his inexplicable despondency, sodden with drink. I returned to the taberna only to take an occasional evening meal and to sleep and to break my fast before going out again. Other meals Livia and I would occasionally buy at some other taberna in the town, and once we dined with her father in his grand house. But most often she and I would be far out in the countryside when hunger overtook us, so we would seek the cottage of some woodcutter or charcoal-burner or herb-gatherer, where the housewife could be induced, for a modest sum, to lay out some simple fare for us.

One morning, when Livia and I had planned to spend the day exploring an area that she knew to be totally uninhabited, I went into the taberna kitchen and asked the caupo's old woman to pack for us a hamper of bread and cheese and sausage and to fill my flask with milk. While I waited, Andraías also came into the kitchen and drew me aside to say:

"Akh, Thorn, I am worried about our friend Wyrd. He has visited here many times before, but I have never seen him like this. Now he is refusing even to *eat*. He subsists entirely on wine and beer. He says his mind is too troubled for him to be able to swallow food. Does that make any sense? Cannot you persuade him to get out into the invigorating forests or onto the lake or *somewhere?*"

"I have tried persuasion," I said. "And I can hardly order him out. He would so resent a minor's giving orders to an elder that he would likely get drunker than ever. But you are more nearly his age, Andraías. Suppose you simply tell him that, for his own good, you will serve him nothing more."

"Vái! Then he would have not even the small nourishment of the wine and beer."

"I am sorry I can be of no help," I said. "But I have seen Wyrd drink before, and for more days than he has so far done this time. It will end with him sick abed and remorseful and intolerably ill-humored, but it will end."

On most days, I would get my Velox from his stable and ride up to the mine. Either I would leave Velox in the company of the mine mules, and Livia and I would go off on foot, or, if we were going far, we would go on horseback, she riding pillion behind me. I always took along my sling, which I tried to teach Livia how to wield. But she never got very adept at that, so it was I who brought down the small game—hares, squirrels, rabbits, partridges—that we always fetched back with us and divided. She would present her share to her family's cook, and I would carry mine down to the taberna, where both Andraías and his wife, as well as myself, found game meat a welcome change from their more usual fish dishes. But even those viands did not tempt Wyrd to eat, even when he was comparatively sober and lucid.

"I simply cannot swallow," he insisted. "Age has not only dampened my intellect and my sense of sight and my enthusiasm, but also has constricted my gullet."

"Iésus," I said. "There is nothing wrong with your throat if you can keep on guzzling strong drink."

"Even that gets more and more difficult," he muttered, "and less and less curative." But he swigged some more of it, so again I stalked out of his presence.

Livia and I, in our peregrinations, went everywhere she could think to take me. Once, we went more than halfway up the highest peak in the vicinity—the Roofstone, which gave its name to that whole range of the Alpes—so Livia could show me what she called an eisflodus. The term "ice-flow" meant nothing to me, until we rode Velox up to its edge, and then I was enthralled.

Broad as a river, the eisflodus lay in a wide, winding cleft in the mountain, and had in it ripples and waves and eddies and cascades exactly like those in the stream of water that bounded down past Haus-

271

taths and into the lake. But all of these were motionless, for they were made of solid ice—or they were motionless to the eye, at any rate. Livia said that the ice did move, but only at a creeping pace, so slowly that if I were to make an ineradicable mark on the ice, it would not have moved downhill the length of my own body before my body's life ended.

Except for wisps and whorls of old snow blowing across it like white spindrift, the eisflodus was almost as blue as the Haustaths-Saiws, and it was such an inviting novelty that I wanted to ride Velox out onto its surface. But Livia tightened her grip around my waist and warned me not to.

"This is summer, Thorn. There will be many runaruneis out there."

Another word that meant nothing to me, so I ventured a guess: "Ice demons?"

"Ne, you goose," she said, laughing at me. "Hidden crevices. During the warm daytime, the ice melts into rivulets that run here and there, and cut deep fissures, but the blowing snow at night can freeze gradually and bridge them over. You step onto what looks like solid ice, and find to your dismay that it is only a crust, and you fall and get wedged in a bottomless crevice and never get out again. I would not want that to happen to someone I—" She stopped so abruptly that I turned in the saddle to look at her, and she was blushing, and she said very quickly, "I would not want that to happen to me or you or Velox."

"Then I will not hazard it," I said, getting down from the horse. "Instead, I will chip both our names here in this flat slab of the ice, right by this black blade of rock, which is easily recognizable. One of us must come back here before dying—and you will outlive me, Livia—to see if the names have moved a body's length."

"Or moved closer together," she murmured, as I began chipping with the point of my sword. "Or farther apart."

"Or if our names have endured at all," I said, and to that she made no remark.

I knew that little Livia was fond of me, and I did not believe she thought of me as an elder brother, because she already had two of those, and understandably disprized them. I supposed that she regarded me as an exceptionally congenial and indulgent uncle or—I have remarked that she was a perceptive child—even perhaps as an *aunt*. She often spoke to me as one female does to another, talking of raiment and ornament and the like, things that a girl does not ordinarily discuss with a man. And I frequently caught her giving me speculative sidelong looks. She was obviously obsessed with curiosity about me, and determined to satisfy it, because one day, at a secluded spot on the lakeside, Livia stripped to the skin to take a swim, and urged me to do likewise.

"I never learned to swim," I said untruthfully.

"Then come in and wade, or just splash around," she called, while she frolicked like a furless young otter. "It is delightful!"

"It is not," I said, dabbling my fingers in the lake's wavelets and pretending to shiver all over. "Br-r-r! You are accustomed to ice water. I come from a warmer clime."

"Liar! You are either a prude or a coward or you have some hideous deformity to conceal."

Well, she was near enough right about that, so I continued to resist her taunts and blandishments. I sat down on the shingle and just enjoyed watching her cavort until she tired of the sport. She left the water and sat beside me to dry in the sun before she put her clothes on again, and now *she* shivered, and snuggled close against me, and I held her in a warming embrace, and she cooed with pleasure.

And meanwhile I was thinking. I had long ago made a mental note that I must never—by changing from male to female, or vice versa—attempt the deception of anyone in the presence of a dog, because I knew that a dog's keen sense of smell would disclose the imposture. Now Livia's behavior caused me to add another cautionary note. Evidently a child's instincts are as detective as a dog's. I must ever be careful around children.

273

As it happened, I did not need for long to be careful in Livia's company. The very next morning, when I rode Velox up to the mine, she was nowhere in evidence, but her father was. He told me that Livia had caught a catarrh, that the mine's resident medicus had ordered her confined to her room—and it all shuttered and curtained and filled with medicated steam—until she was well. Georgius imparted that information as accusingly as if I were to blame, though I was sure that brave little Livia had told him of her swim, and that she had gone swimming of her own volition.

Anyway, I could see a chink between the shutters at the window of Livia's upstairs room. I rode close to the house, and she cracked the shutters farther, and I could see how glum she looked, and that she was bundled in quilting. So I waved cheeringly and made gestures that I hoped indicated that I would be at her beck whenever she was free of confinement. Her face brightened and she replied with gestures of frustration, and then held up four fingers to tell me how many days she expected to be immured. Then she blew me a kiss and I rode away from her.

We never know when the last time comes.

☩   ☩   ☩

I went down the hill, wondering how I was going to pass the day—the next four days—because I had become quite used to having Livia with me during at least half of the daylight hours. But then, when I went to the stables to return Velox to his stall, I was thunderstruck to see Wyrd there. For the first time since we had arrived in Haustaths, he was brushing his horse and grumbling tenderly at it. Now that Wyrd was not slumped behind a table or stretched out on his bed, I could see that he had got lamentably gaunt, and his voice was hoarse—whether because his throat was constricted, as he claimed, or because it had been abraded to rawness by so much wine—but he seemed sober and in full command of his senses.

"What is this?" I asked skeptically. "After Andraías and his woman and I have been trying for so long to wean you from your inebriating teat, now you have done it all by yourself?"

He hawked and spat in the stable straw, and said, "When I discovered this morning that I can no longer swallow even Romanly watered wine or thin beer, I decided my inwards must *really* be rebelling. Now I do not wish even to speak or hear about drink. I promised you a hunt, urchin. What say you? Are you too disgusted with this old wretch to accompany him one more time?"

"Ne, fráuja, ni allis," I said humbly, feeling sorry that I had so repeatedly carped at him like a nagging wife. "I have been hoping for your recovery, so we *could* adventure again."

"We will be out for some days. Will your Livia let you go? Can you suspend your cradle-robbing proclivities for that while?"

"Of course. It may be that I have had childish company too often of late. It will be good to sally forth once more without feeling like a dry nurse."

"And I see you have your sword and sling. I brought my bow and arrows. Let us load the horses and be off, then."

We did not have to return to the taberna for anything, because we had left all our outdoor equipment at the stables. We selected a sleeping fur apiece, and rolled into the furs what other supplies we would need, and tied the rolls behind our saddles, and mounted and rode out of Haustaths. Wyrd did not take the trail that had brought us into town—

the one that I had just descended from the mine—but the one that had led Livia and me up to the Roofstone's eisflodus.

While the trail was yet wide enough for us to ride side by side, I said, "You earlier remarked, fráuja, that we would be hunting some unique kind of game. What is it?"

"The bird called the auths-hana. Not really unique, but it is shy and seldom seen, and it does require a unique style of hunting. We have never yet encountered an auths-hana in our travels together, and I thought it time I showed you one, and how to track it, and what good eating you will find it provides."

Its name, "wilderness cock," told me nothing, but Wyrd went on:

"The bird has the fierce look and awesome beak and hooked talons of a raptor, and it is of a bulky size, and it has a cry like the bawling of a maddened úrus, but it is a harmless plant feeder. I should say that it is *only* at this season, when the bird has been feeding on bilberries and such, that it makes good eating. In the winter it feeds on pine needles, so a taste of it would pucker the mouth of even an Illyrian jackal. Some woodsmen call the bird the *daufs*-hana, because, when it is bellowing its horrifically loud cry, it is totally deaf to everything else. So that is how one hunts it, urchin. When you hear an auths-hana utter that ear-shattering noise, you make for the tree it is perched in. You keep always in concealment, and you pause whenever it is silent, then hurry toward it when it yells. It will not hear you during those moments, however heavy-footed you may be. Eventually, taking advantage of the auths-hana's intermittent deafening of itself, you will get close enough to bring it down with an arrow."

275

Wyrd went on talking, but the trail had narrowed by now, and I had moved my horse behind his, so I missed hearing any more of his lore of the auths-hana. I did not mind; I would probably hear it all again. Wyrd had always been talkative, as he said every woodsman came to be, purely from lack of someone to talk to. Of late, however, during his siege of despondency and drunkenness, he had seemed—when he was capable of speaking at all—to overflow with words, as if he had some urgent need to spill out every word there was in him, and not much time to do it.

Well, I did not mind his garrulity, either. I was just glad to have back again the Wyrd I had known, in his right mind and in his proper function of fráuja to me the apprentice. Of course, he was not *quite* the old Wyrd. He was pitifully lank and haggard, and his voice had coarsened, and his hair and beard were slovenly matted, and he slouched in his saddle, where formerly he had ridden arrow-upright. I cursed myself now for my recently having been such an ungrateful and unreasonable scold, deriding and denouncing him when he was drunk, in the foolish assumption that he was *enjoying* himself, because now I realized that he had been suffering. He probably was suffering still, but putting a brave face on it. I prayed that his being on the trail again would invigorate him to his once-formidable strength and health, and I promised myself that I would do everything I could to help him. However gruff and irascible and insufferably tyrannical he might be, I would not resent that; I would happily welcome it as evidence of his recovery. And perhaps our faring forth together this time would prove to be the resumption of all the many good times we had used to have.

But we never know when the last time comes.

4

276

 kh, do you see that?" Wyrd exclaimed in his newly hoarse voice, and pointed.

It was the morning of the next day, and we were riding around a flank of the Roofstone mountain, about halfway up it, where the old snow still clung in hollows and pockets shaded from the sun. What Wyrd was showing me was a track in the snow. It was not hoof or paw prints, but a sort of triple furrow down a snow slope, as if perhaps three animals had slid, side by side, from top to bottom of the slope.

"Can you tell what made the track?" I asked. "Surely there are not three otters frisking about at this altitude."

"Ne. Not otters. And it was made by only one creature, not three. As you see, the track is totally different from that left by any other denizen of these heights. A woodsman recognizes it, but ignorant peasants are stricken with dread when they come upon it, because they believe it to be made by some kind of fearsome mountain skohl. However, that is merely the track of a single auths-hana."

"The bird we seek, fráuja? How does a bird do *that*?"

"It slides on its belly down a slope with its wings outspread and trailing. Purely giving vent to high spirits, as best I can judge. Anyway, there is obviously an auths-hana somewhere in the vicinity, for that track was made this morning. Here, urchin, take my bow and arrows, and go and hunt the bird. I fear I am too feeble, myself, to draw a steady bow. I shall descend below the snow line and bask my old bones in the warm sun and wait for you."

So I took the weapons, and Velox and I went on without him. We had not gone very far before I heard—with amazement, as Wyrd had said I would—the cry of the auths-hana. At least, that is what I assumed it must be. Just as the bird, in its playful sliding, behaved like no other bird in my experience, neither did it sound like any other I had ever heard. As well as I can describe the noise, it was a startingly loud hoot, clatter and screech all combined—and prolonged. I could well understand how the local peasants would have come to believe in the presence of mountain demons.

I got down from Velox and tethered him to a shrub, and nocked an arrow to the bow. I was just starting off in the direction of the bird's call, trying not too loudly to crunch the old snow's crust as I walked, when I was even more startled by another noise. This time it was unmistakably the long-drawn howl of a wolf, coming from behind me and down the hill, approximately where Wyrd would have been by now. I stopped where I was, puzzling, because it was most uncommon for a wolf to be baying at midday. Then the auths-hana gave its shattering cry once more and, as if in reply, the wolf howled again. I glanced indecisively from one direction to the other, but the wolf had sounded as if it was either in dire pain or in a ravening rage. Perhaps it was another sick one, I thought—and Wyrd was down there with no defense but his short-handled battle-ax. So I left Velox tethered and left the auths-hana unpursued and, bow in hand, I went running and bounding down the mountain to make sure that Wyrd was safe.

Some way below the snow line, I found his horse wandering about, idly browsing on what few edible greens grew at these heights. I wondered why he had not fled or did not even manifest any nervousness at knowing that a wolf was somewhere near. I looped the horse's reins over my free arm and looked all about me, but saw nothing beyond the underbrush. Not until I heard another howl, much closer now, was I able to plunge through the shrubbery toward the sound, my bow and arrow at the ready.

277

Thus it was that I came upon Wyrd—and I felt my back hair prickle when I realized that it was *he* doing the howling, exactly as a wolf does, his mouth impossibly wide agape and baying skyward, his extended tongue waggling and making the sound pulsate. Worse yet, Wyrd was lying on his back on the ground, but not *entirely* on it. His whole body was bent in a rigid arc, like the C shape of a bent bow, so that only his heels and the back of his head rested on the earth, while his clenched fists furiously drummed on it.

However, as I pushed through the last bushes to reach him, the rigor seemed suddenly to leave him, for his body collapsed flat onto the ground. He ceased that awful howling and the pounding of his fists, and simply lay flaccid, except that his chest heaved as he panted for breath. I quickly tangled his horse's reins in a sturdy shrub, laid down my weapon and went to kneel beside him. Wyrd was blinking rapidly, and his mouth was still open, but no longer so gruesomely wide. He was not sweating from his exertions, as I would have expected, but his face was as gray as his hair and beard, and, when I touched it, cold and clammy.

At my touch, he flicked his bloodshot eyes to look at me and asked, hoarsely but quite rationally, "What are you doing here, urchin?"

"What am I *doing* here? I came at a breakneck run. It sounded as if you were being attacked by an entire wolf pack."

"Akh, was I so loud?" he said apologetically. "I am sorry if I interrupted your hunt. I was . . . I was merely clearing my throat."

"You were *what*? You must have cleared this whole range of the Alpes. Every goatherd, every woodcutter, every—"

"I mean to say . . . I was striving mightily to eruct the phlegm or whatever it is that has for so long congested my throat and my windpipe."

"Iésus, fráuja," I said, though a trifle relieved to hear that he had intentionally been behaving so. "You were practically standing on your head. There must be an easier way to flush your throat. Where is your flask? Here, have a drink from mine."

He instantly twisted away from me, and made a gargling sound like the start of another howl—"*Argh-rgh-rgh!*"—and seemed about to contort again into that bent-bow rigidity. But, with an obvious effort, he regained control of himself, and panted:

"Please . . . ne, urchin . . . do not torment me . . ."

"I am only trying to help you, fráuja," I said, holding my flask close to his lips. "A sip of water may—"

"*Argh-rgh-rgh!*" he roared again, and again strained to keep his body from stiffening, but managed with one hand to slap mine aside. When he could speak, he growled fiercely, "Whatever you do . . . keep away . . . from my mouth . . . my teeth . . ."

I sat back on my heels and regarded him with concern, and said, "What is this? Andraías told me you have not eaten for some days, and all yesterday and today you have taken neither food nor drink. Now you refuse even good fresh wa—"

"Do not speak the word!" he pleaded, flinching as if I had struck at him. "In mercy, urchin . . . hand me my fur and lay a fire. It is so early getting dark . . . and I am cold . . ."

Wonderingly, I looked about at the brightly sunlit mountain. Then, worried but obedient, I got his sleeping fur from behind his saddle, helped him roll himself into it, and gathered dry moss, twigs and windfall branches, and set them alight near where he lay. By the time the fire was burning well, Wyrd was asleep and snoring. I hoped that was a good sign, so I took care to steal away silently and not wake him.

I climbed the mountain to where I had left Velox, and, just as I was about to undo his tether, I heard again that raucous, shrill, rattling cry of the auths-hana. It seemed that every animal in the neighborhood, except myself, had recognized that Wyrd's howling had come from no real wolf, and had not fled in fright. So I again nocked an arrow to the war bow and set off in the direction of the bird's call. Following Wyrd's instructions, I waited until the auths-hana was bellowing, and dodged from one concealment to another—a tree, a boulder—and hid behind it for as long as the bird was silent. Eventually I came in sight of it, perched on a low bough of a distant pine tree.

Once more I waited until the bird—stretching its head high and unfolding a great crescent of tail feathers—gave its self-deafening cry, and I scuttled quickly to a nearer point of vantage. I wanted to make sure not to miss felling it, because, if Wyrd was right about the bird's being very good eating, a meal of it might tempt him to eat. My arrow did strike it, so clean and true that the auths-hana died in the middle of its next yell, and dropped with a thud at the foot of the tree.

It was such a distinctive creature, even in death, that I stood and admired it for a moment. It was as big of body as a goose, but had a fantail like that of a blackcock, only much larger. Its taloned feet could have been those of a juika-bloth, and its head resembled that of the Scythian monster called the gryps, for it had a cruel, raptorial, yellow

279

beak and fierce red eyebrows. Its plumage was mostly black, though with bronze and white dapplings, and all of it was of such a metallic sheen that it flashed other colors in the sunlight: purple, blue, green.

I did not waste too much time admiring it, though. I plucked it clean of that remarkable plumage before the rigor of death should clamp the feathers tight. I chopped off the head and feet, and gutted the bird and scrubbed it in a snowbank, then carried it back to where Velox waited. When I got to the campfire, Wyrd was still asleep, so I merely singed the pinfeathers off the bird's skin, then waited until sundown to spit it and start it cooking over the fire.

I sat and occasionally laid new fuel on the flames, and gave the spit an occasional quarter turn, and listened to Wyrd's snoring, while the dark gradually, really did come down. I must have dozed, myself, out of worry and boredom and helplessness, because I suddenly came alert at the cessation of the snoring. The spitted fowl was sizzling and crackling merrily and, beyond it, on the other side of the fire—an alarming sight—two wolfish yellow eyes shone at me from the darkness. Before I could shout or scramble to my feet, though, Wyrd spoke, and I realized that he was sitting upright, that the eyes were his.

"The auths-hana even *smells* delicious, does it not? Eat it, urchin, before it chars."

I had never seen Wyrd's eyes glow in the darkness like that. But I said nothing except "There is enough here to feed four people. Let me help you to some, fráuja."

"Ne, ne, I could not swallow it. Perhaps I *could*, however, now try a gulp of water. At this moment, for some reason, I am not repelled by the very thought of it."

I handed my flask across the fire to him, then tore a leg and thigh off the bird and began hungrily to eat. In fact, I ate less mannerly than I usually did, deliberately making loud, juicy smacks and gobblings, hoping that my evident enjoyment would arouse Wyrd's appetite. But all he did was tilt my flask to his mouth, and he did that gingerly, almost warily.

"You were right about the auths-hana, fráuja," I said with enthusiasm. "The most savory bird I have ever eaten. And its own diet of bilberries has given just the right tartness to the sweet flesh. Do have some. Here. A slice of the tender breast."

"Ne, ne," he said again. "But I did manage to get a trickle of water down my gullet. It did not make me gag or recoil. And hark! I can even

speak the word 'water' without strangling on it. I must be on the mend."
He regarded the flask as appreciatively as if it had contained rare wine,
and said the word several times. "Water. Water. See? *Water.* No ill effects.
Have you ever read the *Georgics* of Vergil, urchin?"

Taken aback, and indeed surprised to learn that *he* had, I said, "Ja.
His poems were approved reading at St. Damian's."

"Well, unless your monastery owned the two disparate renditions,
you probably do not know this. In his original poem, somewhere in the
second book, Vergil put in the name of the town of Nola. But a while
later he happened to pass through that town, and he asked someone
for a drink of water. See? I can say it with ease. *Water.* Anyway, that
townsman churlishly refused him the drink. So Vergil rewrote his poem
and expunged the name of Nola. He put in 'ora' instead—'region,'
simply to preserve the poem's scansion. And I would wager that the
mean and grudging little town of Nola has never again seen itself mentioned in literature by *any* writer."

I said, "No doubt the town now regrets its treatment of him."

Without another word, not even wishing me a good night, Wyrd lay
down on his side, tugged his fur closer about him and fell asleep. He
snored, so I knew he was not dead, and again I hoped that sleeping was
the best treatment for his illness. I wrapped the remainder of the auths-
hana for eating on the morrow, and banked the coals of the fire with
turfs, and rolled myself into my own fur and likewise fell asleep.

For how long I slept I do not know, but it was still dark night when I
was yanked bolt upright and wide awake by another blood-chilling wolf
howl. I wished it *had* been that of a wolf, because it was Wyrd again,
and his body was again arched into that bent-bow contortion, so
strained beyond human endurance that I could hear his bones and
sinews creaking, and his repeated howls were of unmistakable agony.
For some while I could only watch and listen in helpless horror, and
wait for the paroxysm to abate. But when it did not—when Wyrd continued to lie propped on his head and heels, beating his fists on the
ground, roaring with pain—I bethought myself of something. I sprang
up to rummage in my pack of belongings for the crystal phial I had
carried for so long.

I had tried to make my dying juika-bloth taste just the merest smear
of the precious drop of milk. Now I bent over Wyrd and, when he had
to draw breath between howls, I let fall the remainder of that drop into
his mouth. Whether the milk did it, or just Wyrd's realization of my

281

being near, the rigor once more relaxed its cruel grip and let him collapse supine on the ground. But, in the same instant, he gave a savage sweep of his arm that sent me sprawling.

"Perdition!" he rasped. "Told you . . . keep *away!*"

So I remained where I was, and when Wyrd had got some air back into his lungs, he said hoarsely but calmly:

"Forgive my violence, urchin. I repel you for your own good. What was that you fed me?"

"My best hope of helping you. A drop of milk from the breast of the Virgin Mary."

He turned his haggard face to give me a look of disbelief, and said, "I thought it was I who had the madness. Did that auths-hana peck out your brains?"

"Verily, fráuja, the milk of the Virgin. I stole it from an abbess who did not deserve to possess it." I held out the phial for him to see. "But there was only a single drop. I have no more to give you."

Wyrd tried to laugh, but could not breathe deep enough to do that. Instead, he growled the most blasphemous oath I had ever heard him utter:

"By the discarded and never resurrected little foreskin of the circumcised little svans of the little infant Iésus! You tried *magic* on me?"

"Magic? Ni allis. The milk was a genuine *relic.* And such a sacred treasure has the power to—"

"A relic," he said sourly, "has exactly as much power as a Sending done by a haliuruns or an incantation recited by a magus. Any cheap and trifling magic may work prodigies among those fools who believe in it. But none will work against the hundswoths, urchin. I fear you have wasted your treasure."

"The hundswoths? I feared as much. But you said—"

"That I had escaped the infection. I thought I had, when the bite wound healed, but I was mistaken. I should have remembered—I once knew a case in which it took a full twelvemonth for the dog-madness to manifest itself in a human victim."

"But . . . but . . . what are we to do? If even the Virgin's milk is powerless . . ."

"There is nothing *to* do but let the affliction run its course. What *you* are to do is stay well away from me. Go and sleep at a safe distance. Should I start raving and slavering, the merest flying fleck of my spittle could put you at hazard. And I *will* rave, and talk nonsense, and at intervals endure bone-bending convulsions, and at other intervals fall comatose. Unless one of those convulsions cracks my neck or spine, we can only hope that they will become less frequent and longer apart and eventually cease altogether. Until then . . ." He shrugged.

"You are not raving now," I said. "You are talking most lucidly."

"There will be intervals of that, too."

"Well . . ." I said hesitantly. "I know that you do not value religion any more than magic. But . . . while you can . . . might you, just this once, consider praying?"

He snorted, "Skeit! What is that but incantation? Prayer is as meaningless as the augur's sonivium tripudium. Ne, urchin. It would be an ignoble resort, to seek compassion from some god because I am now in need, when I sought none all the while I had my health and strength. I shall not turn craven in my extremity. Go now. Get your rest."

I did as he told me, and moved my fur well apart from his, but not too far to hear if he should need me and call. But I got little rest, sleeping only fitfully, for I knew he had gallantly lied when he spoke of hope. The dog-madness is invariably fatal, and its wrenching attacks would not diminish but increase, both in frequency and in agonizing intensity.

283

And so they did. I was awakened from my uneasy sleep shortly after dawn by the now familiar but no less horrifying howling. Wyrd's body was again arched, even more tautly than before, it seemed to me, if that were possible. Every visible blood vessel and tendon in his face and neck was distended and purple and throbbing, and his red eyes appeared almost to be starting out of his head, and his mouth gushed enough saliva to beslobber his whole beard. That convulsion lasted longer than the two I had earlier witnessed, and I could not comprehend how he survived it without his backbone snapping or some vein or organ bursting. But after that spasm and after each of those that followed, all during that dreadful day, Wyrd collapsed for at least a brief while of relief, and his complexion faded from bruise color to a cadaverous gray.

When, at those times, he did not succumb to sleep and snoring, he would struggle to get his breath back and use it to talk—but only to himself. During those spells of deliverance, he seemed to have forgotten me, and instead remembered days long before my time. His speech was disjointed, and often so hoarse that it was inaudible, but the few coherent snatches that I heard sounded wistful, and consisted of words much more gentle than those the rough-hewn old woodsman customarily employed.

He said, "If I was never again to set foot in Cornovia . . . then Cornovia it would be wherever I was . . ."

And he said, "Once upon a time . . . in a valley where four ways met . . . she and I met also . . ."

And he said, "She walked nobly and spoke kindly . . ."

And he said, "We were young then . . . and we frolicked in the dancing-places of the dawn . . ."

✠ ✠ ✠

At one point, when he was in the throes of another attack, it occurred to me that I might ease his suffering by lending some support to his high-arched back. I bundled various things into my sleeping fur to make a sort of pillow, then crept close and was wedging that under his spine, when, without any warning, Wyrd snapped at me exactly as a wolf might do.

There had been no easing of his contortion, no cessation of his pounding his fists on the earth. He merely stopped his howling long enough to turn his head, lunge it at me and make a bite that missed my upper arm by only a hairbreadth. His teeth clashed together so loudly that I would have thought they must shatter—and I knew for certain that they would have gone clear through my tunic and taken a great gobbet of my flesh if they had reached it. As it was, Wyrd's spittle sprayed my sleeve. While he continued in his terrible convulsion, making no attempt to snap again, I used some leaves and some water from my flask to wipe away that lethal saliva. And from then on, I did stay well away from him.

When, at last, that seizure released him and Wyrd slumped, the unaccustomed pressure of my pillow beneath him seemed to bring him back to himself, and to the present. After he had regained his breath, he did not speak of olden days. He squinted up at the sky, then shifted his gaze in my general direction, and cleared his throat and spat out a blob of that pus-like saliva, and asked huskily, "What time of night is it?"

"Daytime, fráuja," I said unhappily. "It is late afternoon."

"Akh, then I have been at it for long. Did it much frighten you, urchin?"

"Only when you bit at me."

"*What?*" He snapped his head around at me as if he were about to try that again. "Are you hurt?"

"Ne, ne." I made light of it. "For once in your life, you missed your target."

"By Bonus Eventus, the god of happy endings, but I am glad of that." He peered about, then, with immense effort, dragged himself over to a nearby tree and propped himself against it. When he had again got his breath after that exertion, he said, "Urchin, I wish you to do two things for me. First, use the ropes from our packs and tie me securely to this tree trunk."

"What are you saying? You are ill! I will do no such—"

"Do as your master tells you, apprentice, and do it while he still can give sensible commands. Hurry!" I wondered if he really was in his right senses, but I complied. As I began to bind him to the tree, he added, "Leave my arms free. Only my mouth is dangerous. And I must not be able to snap at anyone else who might come along while I am in delirium."

"No one else will come," I said. "Livia told me that this part of the Roofstone is unpopulated."

"I must not be a menace to any woodland creatures either. The animals, even more than most of the people I have met in my life, deserve immunity from a suffering such as this. Iésus, urchin, tie me *tighter.* And make sure the knots are fast. Now, next, I want you to take both our horses away, because there is here no . . . there is no . . ."

Meaning to be helpful, I finished the sentence for him. "No decent grazing or browsing. And no water whatso—"

"*Argh-rgh-rgh!*" he bellowed, and writhed so frenziedly that I was glad I already had him bound. With another heroic effort, he fought for control of himself, until finally he could gasp, "In the names of all the gods . . . spare me that word. I must not lose my mind again . . . before I have finished . . . what I have to say . . ."

I obediently, wretchedly stood silent until he could go on.

"Take the horses and our packs and weapons. All our possessions. Return the horses to the stable, and—"

"But fráuja," I protested, with a sob in my voice. "I cannot in conscience—"

"*Hush your quibbling!* There is no necessity for you to stay here and watch me play the tetzte weakling, to watch me make a spectacle and a filthy mess of myself. There is nothing that you or your superstitions or your magical nostrums can do for me—nothing but wait for the affliction to pass. So begone. Wait for me at the taberna, and I will join you there as soon as . . . as soon as I am able."

285

"How join me?" I wailed imploringly, for I was beginning openly to weep. "You are *tied!*"

"Vái, you conceited cockerel," he said, as roughly as he would have chided me in former days. "Once I have my mind clear and my strength back, I can easily undo any binding put on me by such a puny urchin as you are. I command you—go now."

With tears running down my face, I bundled together almost everything we had brought from Haustaths, and put the packs on the horses. I kept out only Wyrd's war bow and quiver, which I slung on my back, and the remains of last night's cooked fowl. That, and Wyrd's flask, I laid within his reach, in case he should have another remission, as he had earlier done, that might enable him to drink and even to eat.

"Thags izvis," he grunted. "Though I doubt that I shall require them. By tomorrow morning, I hope to be breaking fast with you and Andraías. But I do not wish to see you before then. Now—huarbodáu mith gawaírthja, Thorn."

And he did not see me, ever again. I rode Velox and led Wyrd's horse down the mountain, but only far enough that he could not hear them if they whinnied. Then I dismounted, tethered them once more, and climbed uphill again, slowly, taking every precaution of silence and invisibility that Wyrd had taught me. I succeeded in creeping to where I could see him through a screen of underbrush, without his having espied or heard me, and there I crouched and watched—having frequently to blink away the tears that obscured my vision.

For a long while, he simply lay there propped against his tree, staring vacantly at nothing, and looking pitifully scrawny, feeble, limp, matted of beard and hair. But it became evident that he was only waiting until he could assume that I was far down the mountain—because now he reached out a shaky hand, picked up the flask I had left him, unstoppered it and poured the water over his head.

It immediately made him utter that long-drawn wolf howl, and his arms flailed and the flask went flying. His body arched as it had so many times done—or it tried to; it could only buck and strain and jolt against its bonds, and that must have hurt him more than the earlier contortions—and the mucous sputum oozed from his open mouth, and he drummed desperately with his fists on the ground at his sides. I knew that Wyrd had deliberately employed the water to bring on this convulsion, clearly hoping that it would be so unbearably excruciating that it would prove to be his last.

So I made sure that it was. Unslinging the war bow and nocking an arrow and drawing the bowstring and blinking to clear my eyes and taking aim most carefully and then loosing the arrow—all that took only a moment, but it was not done impulsively.

In the infinitesimal interval between Wyrd's going into his seizure and my shooting the arrow—in just that brief flicker of time—I had remembered many things. How Wyrd had given me the strength to accord a mercifully quick death to my stricken juika-bloth. How he himself had killed the bitch-wolf—and done that from kindness, to end her misery, even while suspecting that she had cursed him with the same dog-madness. How he had, this very afternoon, remarked that not even the merest animals should be made to suffer as he was suffering. How, a little time before that, he had been dreaming of his native land, and of other places of fond memory, and of his youth, and of a woman who walked nobly and spoke kindly.

No, I did not slay him on impulse. I did it so he could have peace and rest comfortably and go on dreaming those good dreams.

Wyrd sagged still and silent as instantaneously as the auths-hana had done. When I could stanch my weeping, I went and stood close to him and looked sadly down at him. The arrow had precisely pierced his heart, and struck so deep that it now pinned him to the tree, so I wrenched it loose. I could easily have buried my friend—the ground was summer-soft even at this altitude—but I recalled another remark of his: that burial is only for *tame* creatures. I hoped that his body would soon be consumed by the scavengers that are the cleaners and tidiers and purifiers of the forest, so that Wyrd would, by nourishing them, live the afterlife he had spoken of: "That *is* heaven." I made only one final gesture. With my belt knife, I pried and scraped away a patch of the tree's bark above Wyrd's head, and there, in the smooth and softer sapwood, I carved in the Gothic script, "He walked nobly and he spoke truly."

287

✠ ✠ ✠

By the time I finished that, the twilight was well upon me. So I picked up Wyrd's flask and hurried downhill again, without once looking back, to get to where the horses were. They whuffled at me small complaints of hunger and thirst, but I could not lead them in search of forage in the dark. So I rolled myself in my fur and fell into an exhausted sleep, and rose at earliest light to take the horses down to the Haustaths stable.

At the taberna, before Andraías could even frame a question, I told him, "Our friend Wyrd is dead."

"What? How? He lurched out of here three days ago and—"

"He knew then that he was dying," I said. "Indeed, it had been foretold to him. And to me. Now, if you will respect my grief, good Andraías, I prefer not to discuss his death. I wish only to settle our account here and dispose of my fráuja's belongings and be on my way."

"I understand. Perhaps you would allow me to purchase some of his effects? What I cannot use myself, I can find other buyers for."

So, in just that one day's time, I disencumbered myself of everything I did not care to take with me. Of Wyrd's possessions, I kept his war bow and quiver of arrows, his fishing hooks and lines, his glitmuns sun-stone, his brass eating basin and his Goth-forged saying knife. The latter I slid into my belt sheath, and threw away my own much inferior old knife. Andraías bought Wyrd's securis battle-ax and his sleeping fur and his leather-bound flask and all of his extra clothing. The stable proprietor most eagerly, and for a handsome price, bought Wyrd's horse, its saddle and bridle—for he owned nothing so fine as a Kehailan steed and its genuine Roman army trappings.

The sale of all those things left me a surplus of money even after paying the taberna and stable bills. Since I also now carried the contents of both my own and Wyrd's wallet, I was quite wealthy, at least for a commoner, at least for a commoner of my age. I did not take much pleasure in that, however, considering the circumstances that had made me so. I stayed one more night at the taberna, then said goodbye to Andraías and his old woman, and went to finish packing my belongings on my Velox. In doing that, I discovered that I still had Domina Aetherea's crystal phial. Empty of the Virgin's milk, it was of no use to me—for that matter, it had been of no use when it *did* contain Mary's milk—but I deemed it too pretty to discard, and packed that with my other goods.

When I rode out of the stable and out of Haustaths, I paused at the foot of the trail that led up to the saltwaúrtswa, and considered going to say farewell also to little Livia. But no, I thought, I would only be riding away from her again, and I had done that once already. She had now had four days to get accustomed to not seeing me—possibly she had even forgotten me; most children do not long remember a brief friendship, however close it has been—so I decided it would be kinder not to renew our acquaintance only to end it immediately.

I merely sat where I was for some little while, turning in my saddle to regard for the last time the beauty all about me — the blue, blue lake, the swans and herons and faúrda upon the water, the high-stacked and handsome houses of Haustaths, the jagged horizon of snow-crowned Alpes. I was leaving the Place of Echoes with much regret, partly because it *was* so beautiful, but mainly because I was leaving there the man who had been most dear to me in my life so far — leaving behind, indeed, a most significant *part* of my life. I tried to take some comfort from the thought that Wyrd at least had a serenely exquisite place in which to rest. And I gave rein to Velox and continued eastward on my journey, as I had begun it, alone.

289

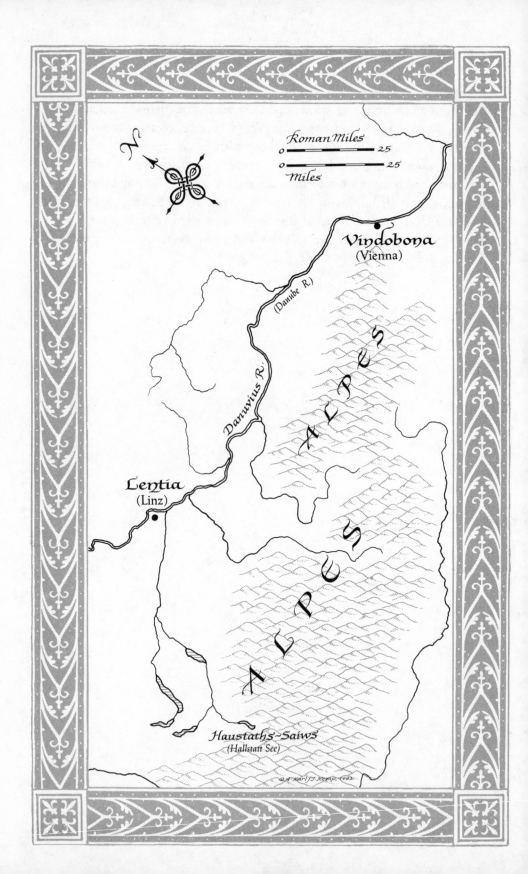

Roman Miles

0 _____ 25

0 _____ 25

Miles

N

Vindobona
(Vienna)

(Danube R.)

Danuvius R.

ALPES

Lentia
(Linz)

ALPES

Haustaths-Saiws
(Hallstatt See)

© A. Karl / J. Kemp, 1992

VINDOBONA

1

 had not really left Wyrd behind. Every day for months thereafter, from cat-gray morning to matron-gray evening, the old Forest-Stalker seemed still to be stalking at my side. Whenever I woke, I could almost see him waking nearby, scratching in his tousled hair and beard, being his usual surly old self until he had broken his fast. In the heat of noonday, when even the lizards slept in their rock crannies and even the larks were silent, I could almost hear Wyrd's gruff voice, telling some long and many-skeined story. Whenever I made camp, I dutifully heeded his imagined criticisms of the way I laid the fire or brittled the day's game into pieces of cooking size.

There were many times, too, that I would absentmindedly speak to *him*. If in my journeying I espied a peculiarly shaped mountain, I might inquire, "Which of the Oreades is the nymph of that particular peak, fráuja?" Or, of an especially refreshing spring, I would ask, "What is the name of the Naiad who is nymph of this sweet water, fráuja?" Or, of a lush forest, "Which of the Dryades . . . ?" Of a still and dreaming pond, "Which of the Limniades . . . ?" I never heard an answer, or expected to, any more than I ever glimpsed one of those elusive nymphs, or expected to.

However, during the nights, I often did see and hear old Wyrd. Perhaps the pagans are right in their saying that Night is the mother of both Sleep and the thousand Dreams—and that her cleverest Dream-child is Morpheus, the one who can impersonate any human, alive or dead. If that pagan belief is true, then Morpheus came to me many nights in the guise of Wyrd, to give me advice and instruction and helpful bits of woods lore. But I do not know if he communicated any of those from the afterworld, because the only dream-counsels that I could recall when I awoke were those that Wyrd had already imparted to me while he was still of this world.

Anyway, I was glad to retain that sense of Wyrd's continued and constant company. It made me feel less alone as I ventured on, and it helped gradually to diminish my grief at having lost the man who had verily been my foster father. That I have for so long remembered all of Wyrd's teachings, even the most cynical of them—and have so frequently employed them for the guidance of my later life—is evidence that I never totally dismissed him as dead and gone, and probably never will, to the end of my own days.

✣   ✣   ✣

Since I still had no compelling reason to hurry to find my presumed Gothic kindred, I proceeded only leisurely across the rest of the province of Noricum. Since I had no need or greed for additional wealth, I did not hunt to secure pelts or horns or anything else to sell, but slew only small game with which to feed myself. And since I had by this time attained my full adult stature—and was well mounted and well armed, besides—I no longer had to fear being apprehended as a slave. Nevertheless, I was in a territory and among peoples unknown to me, and I had no Wyrd to warn me where hazards might lurk. So, as I rode, I stayed ever alert and wary, and at night I slept as Wyrd had done, with a pebble clenched in my fist and the brass basin for it to fall into in case I should, however deep in sleep, sense anything untoward.

I was again traversing a region where there were no Roman roads, and only an occasional cart track or cattle trail or trodden footpath. I would follow one of those whenever it tended in the eastward direction I was going. But if I became aware of another traveler anywhere near, or discerned that the track was leading me toward a settlement, I would ride well to one side of the trail or halt invisible in the woods, at least until I could ascertain that the wayfaring person or the settled body of people posed no danger to me.

Velox knew, as well as I did, how to travel quietly, so either of us could hear from afar the noise made by a teamster's wagon or a herder and his animals or just an incautious walker on the trail. And even a bumbling newcomer to the forest—such as I had used to be—can tell when a settlement is nearby, simply by watching the birds. As long as there were black storks about, and the blue-and-buff magpies, I knew that I was in the wild. Whenever I began to see the white storks that

294

nest on rooftops, and the black-and-white magpies that live by theft, I of course knew that I was approaching some place of human habitation.

I gradually learned that the population hereabout comprised only scattered groups of people of the lesser Germanic nations—Heruli, Warni, Langobardi—most of whom lived by herding cattle. So the terrain consisted of great stretches of dense forest, interrupted at distant intervals by cleared pastures and the huts in which the herders and their families lived, clustered together for mutual protection as much as for sociability. Those settlements were sometimes mere hamlets, sometimes large enough to be called villages, but none was big enough to rank as a town. A hamlet would be inhabited only by a sibja, a group of people all related to each other, the oldest or wisest or strongest among them being the sibja's headman. A village would be inhabited by a gau, an agglomeration of several sibja groups, combined into a subtribe and headed by a hereditary petty chieftain.

Besides watching the birds, I soon recognized another sign that told me when I was nearing the habitation of a sibja or a gau, and whether I wished to visit it or more prudently ride wide around it. I discovered that each settlement in this region judged its self-importance and its inviolability according to the extent of the solitude it could make and maintain around itself. Therefore, if I came upon cleared land in the forest—and if it was a considerably vast clearing, with its settlement too distant to be visible from the forest's edge—I could assume that the people there were probably inhospitable to strangers and possibly would even repel one by force.

In any event, I was not much tempted to stop at even the least forbidding of those places, except when I was in need of something like salt, or had a yearning for a good drink of milk, provisions I could not acquire on my own. The villages and hamlets offered little other attraction to a wayfarer, for they were all squalid and impoverished and their residents were uniformly peasant-ignorant, peasant-slovenly and peasant-ugly.

Now and again, when I was riding on one of the trodden trails and encountered an obviously inoffensive teamster or herdsman, I would go a way with him, just for the sake of conversing with someone other than the gáis of Wyrd. The peasant and I would converse, I should say, if I could comprehend his backcountry dialect of the Old Language—Herulian or Langobard or whatever—sufficiently to make conversation possible at all.

295

Most of the peasants I encountered did not know much about the world beyond their immediate homeplaces, and did not care to know. When I begged one man for news of happenings more momentous than the marriage of local nonentities, he spoke vaguely of having heard rumors of wars and battles "somewhere yonder"—whereabouts he could not say, except that nothing of the sort had lately happened hereabouts. When I inquired of another man whither the trail we were traveling led to—besides his home village—he could say only:

"I have heard," as if it were a rumor he did not wholly believe, "that eventually it takes one from this province into another, and that there is a great river somewhere there, and on that river a city of substantial size."

"So—what is the next province? What is the river? What is the city?"

"Their names? Akh, stranger, if they have names, I could not tell them to you."

One day, when I was riding unaccompanied along a broad and well-beaten cart track, Velox suddenly pricked his ears up and forward. Almost as soon as he, I heard from far ahead of us the sound of many hoofs pounding the ground at the trot. I halted Velox and listened harder. After some moments, I could also hear the jingle and creak—and of more than just saddles and harness—the noises made by jouncing armor and weapons. So I reined Velox off the track, and a healthy distance away from it, because a mounted military troop would certainly have speculatores—outriding scouts—ranging ahead and well to either flank.

Deep in the forest, I found a small eminence of ground where, by climbing some way up a tree, I could see a fragment of that trail without being seen myself, unless a speculator should chance to ride right under me and find Velox tethered there. None did, and, after a long while, I watched the mounted men pass by, below and far away from me. There must have been more than two hundred of them, and they were a curious assortment. The leaders were recognizably uniformed, armored and helmeted Roman cavalrymen, perhaps one turma of them altogether. But the remainder of the column, the majority, wore an incongruous variety of headgear and costumes, none familiar to me, and they all wore beards, which the Romans did not. They could hardly be prisoners of war, I thought, or the turma would have been divided in half—fifteen cavalrymen riding before the captives and fifteen behind. So the bearded foreigners had to be allies or hired warriors under the Romans' command.

I toyed briefly with the notion of intercepting the band and introducing myself. They appeared to be riding on some combative errand, and I had never witnessed a war. The Romans would probably welcome my joining them, seeing me caparisoned like themselves, especially when I told them how I had earned my steed and weapons as a gift from the legatus Calidius and the Legio XI Claudia. But then I dismissed the idea. For one reason, the troop was headed in a direction opposite to my eventual destination. For all I knew, my kinfolk Ostrogoths might at present be engaged in a war against the Roman Empire. It would not do for me to take sides until I knew which side I belonged on. So I waited until a good while after the long column had passed and its hoofbeats had become inaudible—because a troop on the move often has singulares trailing along as a rear guard—and then remounted Velox and continued on my journey.

It was not until some time later, after I had crossed the imperceptible boundary line in the forest that meant I was now in the province of Pannonia, that I learned the identity of that oddly mixed troop of cavalry. I learned it from the first man I had met in months who had *anything* interesting to tell—indeed, it was he who told me that I was in Pannonia—and who introduced me to the first settlement in those forests that was in any way out of the ordinary.

I espied the man from far off, and, as usual, I watched him until I made sure he was alone and looked harmless. He was merely gathering windfall branches for firewood, and piling them on a rack set on a swaybacked old horse, and even that simple chore he seemed to be doing extremely slowly and awkwardly. When I rode up to him, I could see why. He had no hands, and was having to do the job with arms that ended in blunt stumps at the wrists.

"Háils, frijonds," I greeted him. "Might I be of assistance?"

"Health to you, stranger," he responded, speaking with the Langobard accent. "Only collecting wood for the village against the coming of winter and the wolf." He squinted up at the bright blue September sky. "No hurry about it. Not yet, anyway."

"Still," I said, "your village might have sent a man better equipped for picking up sticks. Let me help."

"Thags izvis," he said as I got down from Velox. Then he muttered, "Our village is sadly lacking in capable hands."

In minutes, I had collected more wood than he had done the whole while I had been watching him. I stacked his old horse high, then collected more, and tied it into bundles and slung those over Velox's saddle. Then I took the reins of both horses and, the man leading the way, went on with him through the forest to the clearing in which stood his hamlet. As we crossed the clearing, I noticed that it had not been kept very well cleared; grass and weeds stood high in it, and many sizable saplings were growing up.

The residents came out to stare, curious at seeing a stranger approach, and I realized the real import of the wood-gatherer's muttered last remark. *Nobody* in the hamlet had hands. Men, women, boys and girls, all had only wrist stumps. No, that was not quite true, I saw, as I looked around in horrified amazement. There were some infants crawling or toddling about, playing in the dirt, and they had hands to play with. For a moment I had thought—knowing these people to be a sibja, all interrelated—that I had stumbled upon a freak family that bred only handless progeny. But if the very youngest among them were normal, evidently all the children of two years or so and younger, surely they did not shed those hands when they grew older. So the hands of every person in this hamlet had been *chopped* off, about two years before.

"In the name of the liufs Guth," I gasped, too shocked to be tactful. "What happened here?"

"Edika," said the wood-gatherer, and those people near enough to hear him appeared to tremble. "Edika happened here."

"What or who was Edika?" I asked, as someone handlessly took the horses' reins from me and some others handlessly began to unload the wood.

"Edika is a periodic calamity," the man said with a sigh. "He is King of the Scyrri. They are a very terrible people."

Possibly the man's handlessness, hence his inability to do manual labor like peasants elsewhere, had made him more meditative and articulate than all those louts I had lately met. At any rate, he went on, with commendable fluency and much angry fervor, to tell me some things that I already knew and some that I did not.

The province of Pannonia, he said, was more or less the point in Europe where the separate influences and interests of the Eastern and Western Empires collided. So the Emperor Anthemius at Rome—or, rather, the "King-Maker" Rikimer, who was the real power there—and the Emperor Leo at Constantinople were forever contending and conspiring against one another to push Pannonia's imaginary dividing line this way or the other, to extend their respective domains of influence. Rome had long held and still maintained a firm grip on the garrison city of Vindobona at the Danuvius River frontier of the *entire* Roman Empire. But the southern reaches of Pannonia—including such sizable towns as Siscia and Sirmium, and such lesser settlements as this one—were continually being overrun by troops of one or the other half of the empire, and made to pledge allegiance, now to Rome, now to Constantinople.

Clearly, neither Rikimer nor Leo could be so brazen as to order any imperial legions in his half of the empire to go into combat against brother legions in the other's half. So each contender employed foreign allies, or hired mercenaries, and put them under the command of supposedly "renegade" Roman officers. The hireling forces of Rome included the Scyrri of King Edika and troops imported from Asia, such as the Sarmatae of a king named Babai. That explained the mixed composition of that column I had seen on the move. The Emperor Leo, said my informant, relied mainly on his longtime confederates, the Ostrogoths, under their King Theudemir. Hearing that, of course, made me glad that I had not chosen to join the troop I saw that day.

"But what," I asked, "accounts for the atrocity that happened here?"

"About thirty months ago," said the wood-gatherer, "that conflict's battle line was shifting back and forth in this very vicinity. But we assumed that we were, at the time, safely on the eastern side of the line. And, in our innocence, we gave provender to the men and horses of a troop of Theudemir's Ostrogoths. That was a mistake. Very soon, Edika's Scyrri made an assault that pushed the Ostrogoths well east of here. We were accused of having collaborated with the enemy, and it was Edika himself who decreed that we all suffer the same punishment of dismemberment. Those children whom you see with hands have been born since then. We are most anxious to see them grow up, and we earnestly hope that Edika will not return before they do. Now, stranger, can we offer you anything for your kind help with the wood? A meal? A pallet for the night?"

I declined the offer, and I believe it must have been the sentimental feminine part of my nature that inclined me to do so. I could imagine what toil and trouble it must have been for any of the hamlet's women to prepare the meals she *had* to prepare. And I felt such pity and helplessness at the sight of all those maimed wretches that I had no wish to spend any more time among them. So I merely asked in which direction lay the city of Vindobona, and how far away.

"I have never gone there," said the man. "But I know that there is a fine Roman road due east of here. It will take you north to the Danuvius and the city. The road is perhaps twenty-five Roman miles distant. From there to Vindobona, perhaps another twenty-five."

Only one day's steady riding, dawn to dusk, to reach the road, I calculated. Or two days riding leisurely. And to the city, another two days.

"But keep your eyes and ears wide open," the man added. "The imperial ambitions and conflicts may be only simmering right now, but they can come to a boil in a moment, and you could find yourself in the cauldron. Remember, too, that anyone you meet may be a partisan of Rome or Constantinople, of Edika or Babai or Theudemir. If perhaps you favor one of those, and should foolishly confide it to the serpent spy of a different one, well . . ." And he showed me both his stumps.

I said I would be careful and closemouthed, and I wished him and his people a future happier than their past had been, and then I rode on.

However, even before I came to the Roman road, I fell victim to misadventure, and it involved no human serpent, but a real one. In late afternoon of the next day, I paused at a sparkling streamlet, dismounted to let Velox drink and knelt a little way upstream of him to take a drink of my own. I steadied myself with my right hand against a rock, a blackish rock mottled with green. Then those colors suddenly and violently squirmed, and I felt a sharp pain in my forearm. Of all the places where I might have leaned for support, I had picked the one where a snake was soaking up some last warm sunlight. And, of all the snakes that might have been sunning itself, this was the greenish-black and lethally venomous adder.

I snarled a curse and instantly smashed the reptile's head with another rock. But then what to do? I had had no experience of dealing with snakebite, but I knew that my life could be at stake. All I could think of was that my juika-bloth, if it had been alive, would never have given the adder a chance to bite me. And Wyrd, if he had been still alive, would have told me now what to do.

"Whatever you do, do not move," said a voice of authority, but it was not Wyrd's.

I looked up to see a young man standing on the other side of the stream. He was of about my own age, but considerably taller and broader. He had long fair hair and a pale fuzz of first-growth beard, and he wore woods dress, but he was too handsome to be one of the local peasantry. Now I saw him reach for the knife in his belt and, remembering what Handless had told me about spies and speculatores, I made a grab for the short-sword at my own side.

"I said do not move!" the young man barked, and leapt easily across the streamlet. "You should not even have exerted yourself to kill the adder. Any movement makes the venom course more quickly through the veins."

Well, I thought, if he was concerned about my welfare, then he was no enemy. I left my sword in its sheath and obeyed his order to stay still. Kneeling beside me, he slashed the right sleeve of my tunic and bared my arm, where, near the elbow, the twin punctures were bright red.

"Grit your teeth," he said, as he pinched my skin there between his thumb and forefinger, then carefully positioned his blade to cut me.

"Hold, stranger," I protested. "I had as soon die of poison as bleed to death."

"Slaváith!" he said sternly. "Bleeding is what you need. But you will not bleed overmuch. You can rejoice that the serpent bit you where it did. Any part of the body's flesh that can be pinched up between two fingers can be safely cut without risk of severing any vital blood vessel. Do as I say. Grit your teeth and look elsewhere."

301

So I did, and gave only a stifled whimper at the fierce pain of his slashing away that collop of my skin and flesh.

I swallowed and asked, "Am I saved, then?"

"Ne, but that will help. So will this." He whipped off his belt, wound it around my upper arm and cinched it tight. "Now put your forearm under the cold water. Hold it there and let it bleed. I must go and tether both our horses before they wander off. We will be here for some time."

I was puzzled as to what sort of person this young man might be, and was more so when I saw him lead his horse out of the woods beyond the stream. It was as fine a Kehailan steed as my Velox, and the saddle and bridle were similar to my own, but richly garnished with silver bangles and studs. The young man was definitely of Germanic origin, though I could not identify the accent with which he spoke the Old Language. And, since he was neither a Roman nor any of those Asiatics whom Handless had mentioned, why was he equipped like a Roman cavalryman? For the time being, however, I was grateful enough to have his help that I asked only one question when he returned:

"Might we introduce ourselves before I die? My name is Thorn."

"Then we have the same initial. I am called Thiuda."

He did not inquire why my name was *only* an initial, perhaps because his own name was quite as odd as mine. Thiuda is a *plural* noun, and means "people."

"Anyway," he went on, "you are not likely to die, though you may wish you could when the snake's poison takes effect. Here, drink this."

He had plucked and brought back with him some stalks of the common spurge plant, and now he squeezed their milky, sticky sap into his flask—one exactly like my own—added water from the stream, briskly shook the mixture and handed the flask to me.

While I struggled to drink the bitter potion without gagging on it, Thiuda murmured, "That adder truly was most obliging. It was lying coiled upon its own best antidote." He scraped a quantity of the green moss off the black rock, lifted my gashed arm from the water—the bleeding had diminished to an ooze—plastered the moss upon the wound and tied it there with a strip of cloth torn from the hem of his own tunic. He also loosened, then tightened again the belt around my upper arm.

I asked, in a thin voice, for the infusion of spurge had rather puckered my mouth, "Do you wander these forests just to minister to unfortunate vagrants?"

302

"I daresay I would aid anyone who had been struck by an adder. But I take you to be no ordinary vagrant peasant, since you are Romanly caparisoned. Would you perhaps be a deserter from some cavalry turma?"

"Ne, ni allis!" I said indignantly, but then had to laugh. "I wondered the same about you."

He laughed too, and shook his head. "You tell first, Thorn. While you can talk coherently."

He might yet, I thought, turn out to be a spy or speculator for one of the contenders here in Pannonia, but he would hardly be patching me together just to lop off my hands. So I told him truthfully how I had, some time back, been temporarily in service against the Huns with the Claudian Legion, and how I had been rewarded with my Velox and weapons and other items. I also told him, rather too condescendingly, that I had lately earned a respectable fortune in the fur trade, that I was nowadays traveling only for pleasure, and I concluded, "I shall of course be happy to pay you for your ministrations, Thiuda, as I would pay a professional medicus."

"Akh, one of the *benevolent* rich, are you?" He gave me a hard look and said, even more loftily than I had spoken, "Hear me, you malapert.

I am an Ostrogoth. I would not ask pay or thanks for my good deeds any more than I would ask shrift of my wicked ones."

Contrite, I said, "It is for me to ask forgiveness. That remark of mine was exceedingly stupid. I should have known better, for I am myself of Gothic lineage and pride." But I had to add, "I have heard other Goths speak, and you do not sound like one."

He laughed again. "Naí—I mean ja. You are right. I must endeavor to shed my Greek accent. I have lived too long in the east, and only recently returned to my own nation. Only recently, but too late."

"I do not understand."

"I hastened here to join my people in combat against the loathly Scyrri. But the battle was over before I could lend assistance. It was fought on the river Bolia, one of the Danuvius tributaries, and I did not hear of the engagement until too late."

He sounded downcast, so I said sincerely, "I am sorry your people were defeated."

"Oukh—I mean ne! They were not! How dare you even think so?" he said severely, but laughed yet again. He was obviously a merry-natured young man, at least when I was not foolishly provoking him to haughtiness. "My people simply did not need me, and only for that am I sorry. Ja, they soundly trounced the Scyrri. They slaughtered many and sent the remnants fleeing westward."

"I believe I saw some of those retreating."

"There could not have been many of them," Thiuda said with satisfaction, and added proudly, "I hear that it was my own father who slew their contemptible King Edika."

"I am pleased to learn that someone did," I said, remembering Handless and his fellow villagers.

"Akh, well, there still remain the Sarmatae of King Babai to be fought, so I shall yet have an opportunity to bloody my blade. But at present, after what happened to their Scyrri allies, the Sarmatae are prudently in hiding. So I decided, during this lull, to visit the city of Vindobona. I was born near there, and have not seen my birthplace in many years."

"Indeed? I am also going—" I began, but was interrupted by a sudden sensation of giddiness. "I mean . . . I will . . . when I feel better . . ." Then I could say no more, for there was a rush of bile into my throat.

"Go ahead, lean over the water and vomit," Thiuda said cheerfully. "You may as well start getting used to it. Let me just loosen and tighten that belt again. Then I will lay a fire and spread our sleeping furs."

303

He continued to chatter good-humoredly while he went about those chores, but I have no recollection of what he said. Nor do I remember much about my ensuing period of illness, though Thiuda later told me that it endured for three nights and nearly three days, during which, he said, I frequently complained of seeing two of everything about me, including himself, and at other times talked so confusedly that I could not be comprehended.

I do recall that Thiuda now and then cooked a meal, but not because I ate any of it; quite the contrary, because the smell of its cooking so violently nauseated me. I recall also that I was most of the time in excruciating pain, my stomach cramping, my head and every muscle aching; and that Thiuda at regular intervals, day and night, loosened or tightened the belt about my right arm, until he finally dispensed with it altogether; and that Thiuda also had often to restrain me—sometimes waking from his sleep to do it—to prevent my clawing the moss poultice off my forearm, because the scab forming on the gash itched so maddeningly.

The only thing, as I recall, that I was capable of doing for myself— and the only thing that Thiuda would let me do, either to spare me embarrassment or to spare himself disgust—was to go lurching off into the woods on the many, many occasions that I had to spew my bowels empty. I am thankful that I had at least the will and the strength to do that, and to undress my nether parts myself, thereby to keep from soiling my clothes and, not incidentally, to keep secret from Thiuda the nature of those parts of myself.

Anyway, on what Thiuda said was the third day after our meeting, my head finally ceased aching and my mind cleared and I was speaking rationally and my various other pains and cramps diminished—everything but the itching of the wound—and Thiuda declared that I had survived my envenoming.

I mumbled, "I feel as weak as a baby."

"I wondered if perhaps you *always* did," Thiuda said mockingly.

"Eh?"

"Why else would you ride *tied* to your horse?"

I blinked at the unexpected question, then realized what he meant. "Akh, my foot-rope?" I explained how I had come to invent that contrivance, and how it served to brace me more securely in my saddle.

"Say you so?" murmured Thiuda, as if he, like Wyrd, mistrusted new notions. "I prefer to rely on the grip of my own two thighs. However, if you have found the rope of help, then you will find it even more so while you are regaining your strength. And you should be fully fit again by the time you get to Vindobona. Shall we ride there together?"

"Ja, I should like that. And, no offense to your dignity as an Ostrogoth, but will you permit me to buy you a sumptuous banquet at the best gasts-razn in the city?"

He grinned broadly and said, "Only if it includes a Dionysian indulgence in wine-guzzling." Then, even more mischievously: "Since you persist in playing the profligate young rich man, I shall play your abjectly fawning servant, and ride before you into the city, crying to all, 'Way for my fráuja Thornareikhs!' "

That Gothic dignification of my name would mean something like "Thorn the Ruler" or, in Latin, "Thorn Rex."

I scoffed, "Oh vái, I am nothing of the sort. I began life as a doorstep foundling, and was raised in an abbey."

"No matter. Be not humble," Thiuda said earnestly. "If you go into a city, or a gathering, or *any* encounter, thinking of yourself as a nobody, that is how you will be received. In Vindobona, for example, the landlord of the meanest gasts-razn would demand to see your money before he served you a meal or allotted you a room. But go in there trumpeting yourself as a personage—*believing* yourself truly to be one—and you will be warmly greeted, expansively welcomed, treated with reverence and deference and subservience. The choicest of everything—viands, wines, women, attendants—will be pressed upon you, and you can fastidiously pick and choose, and you can disdain paying so much as a nummus for as long as you like."

"Akh, come now, Thiuda!"

"I do not exaggerate. A rich personage is allowed always to owe and is never importuned to settle. Only little people owe little debts, and few of them, and must pay them promptly. The more and the bigger the debts of a personage, and the longer outstanding, the greater distinction he confers on all his creditors. They would be dismayed if he were to pay, for they could no longer boast of Lord So-and-So's being obligated to them."

"I think you have become woods-addled, Thiuda. Do I *look* like a personage?"

He waved his hand dismissively. "Rich youths are known to be often eccentric in their dress and comportment. The fact that I, your slave, will be sitting a saddle more ornate than your own will even add to that impression. I told you, cease *thinking* of yourself as anything less than noble. If I precede you into the city, exuberantly heralding the approach

305

of my illustrious young lord and master, that is what you will be taken to be. Thereafter, you have only to behave arrogantly, imperiously, overbearingly, and thus live up to people's expectations of a personage. Khaîre! You will genuinely *be* one!"

His enthusiastic prankishness was irresistibly infectious. And so, some days later, that is how we entered through the main gate of Vindobona. I slouched indolently in my saddle, not even deigning to look about me at the fine city and its finely appareled inhabitants, and trying hard not to break into laughter. Thiuda rode a little way before me, flinging his arms about, turning in his saddle this way and that, to shout in all directions, variously in Latin and in the Old Language and even in Greek:

"Way! Make way for my lordly fráuja Thornareikhs, who comes from his distant palace to spend some time and much gold in Vindobona! Way for the illustrissimus Thornareikhs, who comes unpretentiously, without his retinue of courtiers, to honor Vindobona with his august presence! Make way for Thornareikhs, all you lesser folk, and bid him *háils!*"

The people on that crowded thoroughfare, afoot or mounted or riding in slave-carried cars, stopped and craned their necks and turned their heads to gawk at my approach. And, as I passed them, contemptuously indifferent to their interest, all the heads respectfully bowed.

2

indobona is, like Basilea, a community that has grown up around a garrison that guards the Roman Empire's frontier. But it is many times larger and busier and more populous and more grand than Basilea, because it stands where several Roman roads converge and also alongside the swift, broad, brown Danuvius River, the most heavily traveled of all Europe's waterways.

On this mighty river, there are more than just barges and scows and fishing boats; there are freighting craft nearly as big as seagoing ships. The heavy Danuvius trading vessels are propelled by many oarsmen, sometimes two or three banks of them, aided, when the wind is right, by square sails held aloft on masts. Those freighting craft travel safely, without fear of being intercepted and plundered by pirates or war parties, because well-armed, beak-prowed dromo vessels of the Roman navy's Pannonian Fleet constantly patrol between their bases upriver at Lentia and downstream at Mursa.

307

Vindobona's fortress, manned by the Legio X Gemina, could contain at least six garrisons of the size of that at Basilea, and its surrounding defenses of ramparts, trapfalls, ditches, stakes and spikes are proportionately more numerous and more stoutly constructed. The fortress sprawls atop a slight eminence of ground that overlooks a narrow arm of the Danuvius, but the city around the fortress long ago spread clear to the banks of the river's main channel and far over the level land in every other direction.

It is not, like Basilea, a community of merely modest houses, cabanae and workshops. Most of its buildings are of stone or brick, many of them immense in area and three or four stories high. They include luxurious residences and thermae and lupanares, travelers' deversoria and gasts-razna, riverside warehouses and extensive market arcades housing shops and smiths and tradesmen of every kind of wares. However, tucked among the more imposing edifices are also snug neighborhood tabernae and exquisite small shops vending jewels, silks, perfumes and other precious sorts of merchandise. Vindobona even has a number of temples dedicated to the worship of various pagan gods, because the population includes people of so many different races and nations and religions. It would appear that not many of those are Christians, or at least not very devout Christians. In the whole city I saw only one Catholic and one Arian church, and both were small, of humble aspect and in some disrepair, while the temples were elegant, well attended and well maintained.

Otherwise, Vindobona is as modern and civilized and refined in its culture as is Rome, though on a lesser scale, of course. And it claims to be of an age second only to Rome itself in all the empire. Its historians say that, about the time Remus and Romulus were founding *their* city (and quarreling over the street plans of it), a primitive and now long-departed tribe of Celtic people made permanent camp where Vindobona now stands. That settlement endured until, some three centuries ago, Marcus Aurelius fortified the empire's entire northern boundary — meaning the whole length of the south and west banks of the Rhenus and the Danuvius — with watchtowers and castella and burgi and outpost stations, and set one of those here.

308

✠   ✠   ✠

Thiuda did not commence his shouted extolling of me and my splendiferousness until we had made our way through Vindobona's suburbs and outskirts and had entered the city proper. Then, while he ranted and I feigned utter boredom and the passersby made bewildered but solicitous salute, we proceeded along a wide avenue, at the distant end of which was visible the high palisade of the fortress. After a while, Thiuda halted his bellowed panegyric, and our two-man procession, to shout a demand at every person within our hearing:

"Tell me, people! Tell me the most excellent, most palatial *and most costly* lodging place in this city, for my princely fráuja will tolerate none but the finest of accommodations!"

Various of the folk about us obligingly suggested various places, but most of them seemed to agree that "the deversorium of Amalric the Dumpling-Plump" would best meet our requirements. So Thiuda pointed at one of the men who had said that, and commanded:

"Lead us there, then!" He stabbed his finger at another man who had recommended the same place. "And you, good fellow, run ahead to announce our coming to Amalric the Dumpling-Plump! That will give ample time for him and all his family and servitors to assemble before his door and make appropriate greeting to Thornareikhs, the most distinguished guest ever to honor Amalric's establishment with a visit."

Thiuda's outrageous high-handedness made me blush and mutter "Iésus" to myself. But, astonishingly, he was obeyed. The one man instantly set off at a run, and the other not only walked ahead of our horses but joined Thiuda in bawling, "Way! Make way for Thornareikhs!" So I subdued that one flush of embarrassment at our imposture, and only shook my head in wonderment. Evidently Thiuda was right. Proclaim that you are Somebody, and believe that you are, and you *are*.

The deversorium was indeed a fine one, of brick, three stories high, its front and doorway decorated almost as colorfully as those in Haustaths. And its proprietor was indeed plump, and so was the woman I took to be his wife, and the two adolescents I took to be his sons. They all had obviously put on their best clothes, and obviously had done so hastily, for some of their garments were fastened awry. The deversorium's broad and hospitable forecourt was quite filled with all those servitors who, like the family, had come forth to greet me, some of them wearing aprons, some with cooking ladles or goose-wing brooms in hand. From several windows in the upper stories, the establishment's already resident guests peered curiously down.

Plump though he was, the proprietor managed a deep bow and said in Latin, in Gothic, in Greek, "Salve! Háils! Khaîre! I bid welcome to Your Worship." That is not the address prescribed for anyone of royal, noble, governmental, clerical or any other rank, but inasmuch as Thiuda, in all his shouting, had cannily avoided saying exactly *what* I was supposed to be, the man had to do the best he could.

I looked aloofly down at him from my mount and asked, "Ist jus Amalric, niu?" but as if it mattered little to me whether he was or not.

"I am, Your Worship. Your inadequate servant Amalric, if it please Your Worship to command me in the Old Language. The Greek-speakers make of my name Eméra, and the Celtic-speakers Amerigo, and the Latin-speakers Americus."

"I believe," I said languidly, "I shall call you . . . Dumpling." Someone in the courtyard tittered, and Thiuda threw me an amused nod of approving my rudeness, but Amalric only bowed the deeper. "Then what are you waiting for, Dumpling? Summon a groom to take our horses."

309

As Dumpling and his wife escorted me indoors, he said, "I regret that I was not apprised of your visit before now, Your Worship." And he wrung his hands. "I would have offered you the very best quarters in our house. As it is . . ."

"As it is," I said, "you may offer them to me now that I am here." I was finding incivility an attitude very easy to assume.

"Oh vái!" the man moaned. "But I am expecting, this very afternoon, the exceptionally rich merchant who *always* occupies those rooms and who—"

"Say you so? How much is this rich man worth?" I asked, and saw Thiuda laughing gleefully but silently behind the Dumplings. "When he arrives, I will buy him. I can always use an extra slave."

"Ne, ne, Your Worship," Dumpling pleaded, beginning to sweat slightly. "I will put him off with some excuse that might not offend him quite so much as . . . I mean to say, *of course* the rooms are yours. You boys, bring in His Worship's belongings. And may I inquire, Your Worship, will you be wishing a room also for your, er, your herald? Your servant? Your slave? Or does he customarily sleep with your horses?"

I might have said something else obnoxious, befitting my new station, but Thiuda spoke first.

"Ne, good landlord Dumpling. If you will but direct me to the nearest, cheapest, most vermin-ridden house of lodging, I shall be satisfied with a pallet there. I am staying but this one night in Vindobona, you see, for I must be off at dawn on important and far-flung errands for my fráuja Thornareikhs." He leaned close to the man and, behind a raised hand, whispered confidingly, "Urgent and secret messages, you understand."

"Of course, of course," said Dumpling, impressed. "Well . . . the nearest . . . um, let me see." He scratched his sweat-shiny bald head. "That would be the lowly hovel of the widuwo Dengla. She sometimes inveigles unwary strangers into taking board and lodging there, but no one ever stays for long, because she steals from their belongings."

"I will sleep *on* my belongings," said Thiuda. "Now . . . I shall linger here only long enough, landlord, to take a sample taste of each of the many excellent hot dishes and cold wines of the elaborate meal that I am sure you will momentarily be setting before my master. Thornareikhs naturally will not condescend to eat the least morsel of a meal until I have declared every dish wholesome, pure, nourishing and prepared *precisely* to his liking."

"Naturally, naturally," said the poor man, now sweating so much that he looked as boiled as a real dumpling. "By the time His Worship has washed and refreshed himself, the board will be laid with all the most delectable treats from our larder and our cellar." To me he said, with something like desperation, "If Your Worship would be pleased to follow me, I will personally show you to your chambers."

Thiuda trailed us upstairs, along with the two Dumpling sons bearing my modest pack and saddlebags. The quarters were most comfortable, well furnished, clean and light and airy. But of course I peered about me and sniffed as if I had been led into a sty, and dismissed the Dumplings with a contemptuous flick of my hand. As soon as they were out of hearing, Thiuda and I collapsed against one another, roaring with hilarity and pounding on one another's back.

"You are the most shameless sinner I have ever met!" I exclaimed, when I could. "And here am I, falling in with your schemes. Deluding all of Vindobona . . . and that pitiable fat man . . ."

"May the devil take them napping," said Thiuda, still laughing. "The fat man, whether he knows it or not, is no less of a fraud than you are. He may bear the name Amalric, but I can guarantee that he is not remotely related to the Ostrogoths' royal Amal line. Delude him as long as you like."

"Akh, it is enjoyable to do so," I said, but then I sobered somewhat. "However, it may prove expensive. Did you see the other guests gaping from the windows and then sneaking to get a look at us in the entry hall? From their dress, they *are* all rich and prominent personages."

Thiuda shrugged. "In my experience, the pompous and pretentious are even easier to deceive than suspicious landlords and tradesmen."

"I mean, if I am to keep up appearances, I must invest in equally estimable apparel."

Thiuda shrugged again. "If you wish. But I should say that you have done very well just as you are. You might try the effect of dressing even more grubbily and behaving even more vilely. But now, speaking of grubbiness, let us wash off some of our road dust. Then we will descend to the dining hall and scowl because the table is not set, and thereby force Amalric the Dumpling-Plump to placate us with quantities of his best wine."

That is what we did. Since we had demanded to be fed at such an inconvenient hour, between midday prandium and evening cena, we were the only persons in the hall. And I must say that the hall was quite as inviting as that one Roman-style dining room I had seen at Basilea; its tables were covered with clean linen cloths and provided with

311

couches instead of chairs, stools or benches. Thiuda and I reclined at one of the tables, and impatiently drummed our fingers on it, and Dumpling came running. He apologized profusely because the meal was not waiting for us, and yelled for his sons to bring wine.

They came in carrying an obviously heavy amphora. Both Thiuda and I regarded it with some surprise and happy anticipation, because, in these days of modern barrels and casks, it is so rare to see a genuine, old-fashioned, baked-clay amphora. Besides, this was one of the sort that is not flat on the bottom but tapers to a point, the kind that cannot be stood upright. So we knew that it had been sunk in the earth of the deversorium's cellar, for its contents to mature and ripen, and that gave promise that it held no common taberna wine.

Nevertheless, when Dumpling broke the seal and let a small ladle down into the amphora and then tipped the ruby liquid into a goblet, Thiuda peremptorily grabbed the drink, suspiciously smelled of it, sipped of it, rolled it around in his mouth and rolled his eyes as well. I think he might have dared to declare the wine unfit and called for a different amphora to be broached had he and I not been very thirsty from traveling. So he grudgingly grunted, "A decent Falernian. It will do," and let the grateful Dumpling fill goblets for us both.

Then, when the food began to arrive—and it came in courses, the first being a hot soup of calves' brains and peas—I ignored it until Thiuda had ceremoniously taken a taste. Only after a suspenseful pause would Thiuda pronounce the dish "tolerable" or "adequate" and once even "satisfactory," which made Dumpling almost dance for joy. But, after each of those little games, Thiuda would dive into the provender and eat of everything as ravenously as I did.

Between the two main dishes—Danuvius eel broiled with herbs, then braised hare in wine gravy—I paused to belch and to take breath and to ask Thiuda, "Are you really departing so soon? To go and revisit your birthplace?"

"For that, ja, but not just for that. It has been a long time, too, since I have seen my father. So next I will wend my way on down the Danuvius into Moesia, to the city of Novae. That is the capital city of all us Ostrogoths, so I should find him there."

"I shall be sorry to see you go."

"Vái. You are fully recovered from your snakebite, and now you are well established here as a personage. You will be treated as such. Take advantage of it. Vindobona is a pleasant place in which to pass the winter. As for me, I will spend tonight at that widow's house, so I can get early away without having to wait for stable grooms to wake and fetch me my horse."

"Then let me say now, Thiuda, how much I have enjoyed your company. And I am indebted to you for having saved my life. I know you will not accept thanks, you stubborn Ostrogoth, but I hope someday to have the chance to do you a good turn."

"Very well," he said genially. "Whenever you hear that King Babai and his Sarmatae have again started to rampage somewhere, go there. You will find me in combat against them, and I heartily invite you to fight beside me."

"I will. On my word, I will. Huarbodáu mith gawaírthja."

"Thags izvis, Thorn, but I care not to fare always in peace. To a warrior, peace is only a corroding rust. Say to me as I say to you: huarbodáu mith *blotha*."

"Mith blotha," I echoed, and raised my goblet to salute him with the wine the color of blood.

✠ ✠ ✠

I did remain in Vindobona throughout the winter, and longer, because there is much in that city to divert and entertain a person—or I should say a *personage*, one who can afford the diversions offered, and thereby merit an invitation to partake of them.

While I possessed nothing like the fortune I pretended to have, the pretense was enough. I maintained my haughty attitude toward inferiors, and acted as if most people *were* my inferiors, and that made them bow and scrape and defer to me as if they concurred in their being inferior. But I allowed myself to unbend toward persons of approximately the same lofty station I had assumed. So I let myself become sociable with a select few of my fellow guests in the deversorium, which seemed to flatter and honor them. They introduced me to their better-class acquaintances residing in the city, and those introduced me to others. Eventually I was being invited to the homes of Vindobona's most prominent citizens, attending intimate family gatherings as well as the grand feasts and elaborate festivals that enliven the winter season there, and I made many friends of my own among the city's notables.

It may be hard to believe, but, during all the time I spent in Vindobona, not a single person—not even any of those who became my friends—ever inquired of me what exactly *was* my status or distinction or lineage or rightful title, or how I had acquired my ostensible wealth. Those close to me called me familiarly "Thorn"; others of my equals more formally said "clarissimus" or the Gothic equivalent, "liudaheins."

I might add that I was not the only person in those circles affecting a pose. Many others, even those of Germanic lineage, had adopted Roman manners to the extent that they were unable—or pretended to be unable—to pronounce the Gothic rune "thorn," and the "kaun-plus-hagl" runes as well. So they took great care to avoid those "th" and "kh" sounds, and invariably spoke my name in the Roman fashion, as Torn or Tornaricus.

I hasten to say that, while I continued my imposture and continued to be accepted at the high value I had set upon myself, I never used my position to defraud anyone materially. I even, contrary to Thiuda's suggestion, at intervals paid the deversorium's proprietor what I owed him to date—and also ceased to call him contemptuously Dumpling, but began to address him as Amalric. Those concessions made him, too, a friend of mine, and he gave me many useful hints as to how best to enjoy and profit from my being accepted as an equal among Vindobona's best families.

314

Early on, I decided to dress the part that I was playing. I informed Amalric that, although I was content to travel without ostentation, only woodsily garbed, I now desired to embellish my wardrobe, and I asked him to tell me where to find the city's most exclusive clothiers, cobblers, jewelers and such.

"Akh, Your Worship!" he exclaimed. "A man of your station does not go to *them*; they come to you. Allow me to summon them hither. Be assured that I will choose for you only those who purvey to the legatus and the praefectus and the herizogo and all the other liudaheins gentry."

So, the next day, there came to my chambers a sartor and his assistants, to take my measurements and to give me my choice of diverse patterns of garments and numerous bolts of cloth. There were cottons from Kos, linens from Camaracum, woolens from Mutina, even goose-summer from Gaza—and an incredibly fine, soft, lovely, almost fluid fabric that I had never seen before.

"Silk," said the sartor. "It is spun and woven by a people called the Seres. I am told that they make it from a kind of fleece, or perhaps a down, that they comb from the leaves of a certain tree that grows only in their land. I do not even know where their land lies, except that it is far away to the east. So rare and precious is this textile that only rich men like yourself, illustrissimus, can afford to wear it."

Then he told me the price—not by the standard cloth measure of tres pedes, not even by the pes, but by the *uncia*. I tried not to look stunned, but I thought *Iésus*, spun gold would cost less, and I knew very well that the illustrious Thornareikhs was not rich enough to afford such an extravagance. I did not tell the sartor that, of course; I mumbled something about the silk's appearing too frail for the wear I would give it.

"Frail?! Why, illustrissimus, a silk tunic will outlast *armor!*"

I gave him a hard look and he quailed and was silent, and I chose cheaper fabrics, but only after much deliberation and much grumbling about their poor quality. And I picked out patterns for tunics, undercoats, trousers, a woolen winter cloak and even a Roman-style toga that the sartor insisted I would need "for state occasions."

On another day there came to me a sutor, also with patterns and with swatches of felt and leather—every kind of hide from soft roebuck to garish crocodilus—and I commissioned him to make for me various pairs of indoor sandals, street shoes latcheted in the Scythian manner and a petasus hat for winter wear. On another day there came an unguentarius with a casket full of phials, which he opened one after another to let me sample the scents of the perfumes they contained.

"This one, illustrissimus, is the essence of the flowers from the plain of Enna in Trinacria, where even the hounds are confounded in their hunting by the ambient aromas of so many fragrant blossoms. And this one is the pure attar imported from the Valley of Roses in Midland Dacia, that valley where the inhabitants allow not a single other plant of any kind to grow, lest it pollute the impeccability of the roses. Then I have this other attar of roses which is less expensive, because it comes from Paestum, where the roses bloom twice each year."

Partly from thriftiness, partly because I could smell no difference between the two rose perfumes, I chose the cheaper. On another day— or, rather, at night—there came an aurifex, to show me rings and pins and armlets and fibulae all ready to wear, plus many unset gems with which he could fashion any sort of jewelry to my own design. He showed me diamonds, rubies, sapphires, emeralds, colored glass, beryls, jacinths and others, some loose, some set in gold, some in silver.

"If you prefer not so flagrantly to flaunt your wealth, illustrissimus, here are various gems set in the metal called Corinthium aes, a copper

315

alloyed with small amounts of gold and silver to make it blaze far more brilliantly than other copper. It got its name, as perhaps you know, illustrissimus, because it was invented—or rather, discovered—when in ancient times the Romans burned Corinth and all the precious metals there puddled together."

So, thriftily again, I selected from the aurifex's wares only two matching fibulae made of the Corinthium aes and set with deep-purple almandines. All in all, I think I was not grossly prodigal in my spending, and the things I chose to buy and wear were nowise flamboyant. For example, when the sartor returned with the clothes I had ordered— each garment only temporarily basted together—for his final fitting of them on me, he said:

"I have of course not presumed to add any colors yet, neither to the hems of your tunics or toga nor to the panels of your cloak. Having consistently addressed you as illustrissimus, and not yet having been corrected, I could not be sure whether that is indeed your rank—in which case you would naturally wish your clothes adorned with green— or if perhaps you are in fact of patricius status and therefore merit the purple. Nor have you indicated whether you wish the hems and panels merely dyed or done in figures."

"Nothing," I said, grateful that his babbling had enlightened me. "No colors, no figures. I prefer the materials unadorned and in their natural colors—white, buff, dun, whatever."

The sartor clapped his hands delightedly. "Euax! Now there speaks a man of good taste! I perceive your reasoning, illustrissimus. Nature did not make those fabrics gaudy, so why should their wearer? Why, the very simplicity of your garb will make you stand out in any company, more distinctively than if you wore all the gauds of a peacock."

I half suspected that he might be merely flattering me, but evidently he was not. When later I wore those clothes to the gatherings to which I was invited, several eminent and intelligent personages, far more worldly than I was, paid me sincere compliments on the tastefulness of my dress.

That little episode with the sartor taught me a valuable lesson: to keep my mouth shut when I was confronted with some subject that I ought to know about but did not. With my mouth closed, I could not utter any embarrassing disclosure of my callowness. And if I stayed silent long enough, someone or something would let drop a hint that would give me some grasp of the matter.

On occasion, when I prudently kept silent, masking my ignorance

with a seeming disdain for speech, I not only might avoid acting foolishly, but might be deemed by others to be wiser than they. One night,
after a dinner in the triclinium of Vindobona's elderly and massively
fat praefectus, Maecius, the women had retired from the room and we
men were embarking on a serious drinking session, when a messenger
slipped in and unobtrusively handed something to our host. The praefectus looked at it, then coughed for attention. Everyone stopped conversing and turned to him.

Maecius said solemnly, "Friends and fellow Roman citizens, I must
announce some startling news. This message was urgently relayed
hither from my agents in Ravenna, so you are hearing it well before any
official word can get here. The news is that Olybrius is dead."

There was a chorus of astonished exclamation:

"What? Now Olybrius *too?*"

"How did he die?"

"*Another* assassination?"

I did not blurt, as I might once have done, "Who on earth is or was
Olybrius?" I merely sniffed indifferently and took a draft of my wine.

"Not assassination this time," said Maecius. "The emperor died of
the dropsy."

There was a chorus of murmuring:

"Well, that at least is a relief to hear."

"But what a *peasant* sort of death for an emperor."

"It makes one wonder. What next?"

I did not blurt, as I might once have done, "But I thought *Anthemius*
was the emperor at Rome!" I simply indulged in another long drink of
wine.

The praefectus echoed that other guest's question: "What next? I
suggest you ask the illustrious young Tornaricus yonder, though I
strongly suspect that he would not tell. Behold him, friends. Only he
among all of us seems both unsurprised and unmoved by this news."

Everyone in the triclinium turned to stare at me. I could do nothing
but look blandly back at them. I did not think a laugh or even a smile
was called for, but I was disinclined, too, to burst into tears.

"Did you ever see such an innocent aspect?" Maecius demanded of
the room at large. "Now *there* sits a young man possessed of secret
knowledge!" But he sounded more admiring than accusing, and so were
all the faces regarding me.

The praefectus went on, "Here am I, appointed to this praefectura
by the empire itself, and what do *I* know? Only that in July the Emperor

317

Anthemius was most foully murdered, and at the instigation of his own affinal son, the very man who had set him on the throne, the King-Maker Rikimer. Exactly forty days later, Rikimer himself is dead, *allegedly* of natural causes, and another of his puppets, Olybrius, rules the Western Empire. Now, just two months after his accession, *Olybrius* is dead. Come, Tornaricus. Tell us. I know that you know. Who next will be our emperor, and for how long?"

"Tell us," urged others around the room. "Tell, Tornaricus."

"But I cannot," I said, smiling in spite of myself at their nonsense.

"There! Did I not say so?" Maecius roared, but jovially. "Some of you others who aspire to be men of affairs, take example from Tornaricus. A man who can be trusted with secret knowledge *will* be trusted with it. By the Styx, I wish I had your sources of information, young Tornaricus! Who are your agents? Can I bribe them away from you?"

"Come, Tornaricus," said another of the city's elders. "If you refuse to speak the name of Olybrius's successor, could you not at least give us a hint of what we may expect to hear from Ravenna in the future? Turmoil? Calamity? What?"

"I cannot," I said again. "I know nothing that I can tell you of affairs in Ravenna."

I heard whisperings around me:

"He *could* tell, but he will not."

"Still, take note that he did not *exclude* turmoil and calamity."

"Only not in *Ravenna*, he says."

And so, when Vindobona got the news, three weeks later, that the volcano Vesuvius in Campania had erupted in its mightiest convulsion in four hundred years, my acquaintances regarded me with immeasurably increased respect and awe. All agreed that I was omniscient not only in affairs of state but in those of the gods.

Thereafter, I was often accosted, in corners of rooms and in unfrequented streets, by this or that rich man seeking my counsel on the wisdom of investing in this or that commodity . . . by this or that matron asking what I thought of the latest advice she had been given by her astrologus . . . by this or that young man begging me to divine what his superiors *really* thought of his work and his prospects for advancement . . . by this or that young woman pleading to know her father's *real* opinion of this or that suitor of hers.

But I refused them all—my equals politely, my inferiors coolly—because it was by being silent on matters of which I knew nothing that I had gained some reputation.

3

 learned that the high and mighty of Vindobona were exceedingly selective as to the sorts of people they would admit into their circles of intimacy. For that matter, I would find the high and mighty everywhere in the empire to be so. An aspirant to the upper levels of society had to be more than sociable, personable and respectable. As I once heard the resident herizogo, Sunnja, declare:

"Respectability is only a virtue, and even a commoner can attain to that. But dignity, now, that is a glory. It belongs only to those persons who have distinguished themselves—in war, in letters, in service to the empire—and that dignity is not diminished by their sometimes disdaining to behave in the conventional, narrow-minded, self-righteous manner that is called respectability."

319

Neither was the possession of riches a sufficient qualification for admission to the company of the best people, because even men who once were slaves have sometimes amassed fortunes. Among the patricians, those families that derived their wealth from owning land were regarded as the highest-ranking. Although trade and commerce were generally looked down on, the next rank comprised those families that had earned their riches from commerce on a *large* scale, meaning that they or their forebears had been negotiatores, importing or exporting goods in vast quantities. The mere mercator families, whose trade consisted in keeping shops or warehouses or markets—no matter if they had been engaged in the business for generations, no matter if they built palaces to live in—were unfit to mingle with their betters. The most contemptible class of cityfolk contained all those who worked with their hands— smiths and artisans and laborers, of course, but aurifices, fine painters, mosaicists and sculptors were lumped in with them, and considered little better than toiling peasants.

I do not mean to say that wealth was at all scorned, or regarded as something to be kept hidden. Indeed, if one possessed the qualities of distinction, dignity and status necessary for being accepted in the best company, then it was essential to have also the money to maintain oneself in a style likewise acceptable. Of all newcomers to those lofty circles, the most warmly welcomed would be a genteel man or woman who was rich, unmarried *and* childless. That was because he or she, if young enough, might marry and thereby augment the wealth of some local spinster or bachelor. If the newcomer was too old for that, but was without heirs, there was still hope that some local patrician child might become that person's surrogate son or daughter and eventually inherit his or her fortune.

The Vindobona families who possessed great wealth were not shy about showing it. Many of them lived in lavish Roman-style villas, and even the grounds surrounding their residences were tailored to their owners' tastes. In addition to gardens and arbors and bowers, there were shrubs and hedges sculptured—in what I was told was "the Mattian manner"—into the shapes of gods, animals, urns and other forms, all in living green. Among them stood statues, some of gods but mostly of the family's more distinguished ancestors. Those were expensively made of bronze or marble, but they might as well have been carved of cheap wood, because their costly materials were covered all over with even costlier gold leaf. The insides of the houses were resplendent with mosaics and murals; many of the furnishings were crafted of warm ivory and sweet-smelling thuja wood; the floors were intricate geometries of patterned inlay.

Several of the villas contained, in a position of prominence, where its proud owners could frequently and ostentatiously consult it, an Egyptian-made clepsydra. That is a machine which marks off the hours of the day—the proper time for the prandium or the sexta rest or the cena or whatever—and even the hours of the night, for it does not depend on sunshine, but functions by means of water trickling through it and regulated by a modulus gate.

The upper-class Vindobonans were as fond of display in public, out among the commonfolk, as they were in private. Men and women alike went abroad in garments bordered with Girba purple or Janus green or whatever other color accorded with their rank. And they would find frequent necessity "accidentally" to slip open their cloak or coat to let passersby glimpse their undercoats or skirts or hose of shining silk. On the few occasions when a patrician woman walked anywhere, she always carried a gilded umbraculum over her head—or had a servant carry it—to protect her dainty skin from the sun or rain or wind or snow. More often, though, such a woman would be carried about in a chair, if she wished to be noticed, or in a Liburnian car, if she wished not to be. And if she had to undertake a long journey, it would be in the horse-drawn vehicle called a carruca dormitoria, a heavy, boxy, four-wheeled and closed carriage in which she could recline and *sleep* along the way.

Of the money those fine folk spent on their comfort and adornment, a good deal went for the buying or hiring of domestics. Besides the stewards and gardeners and stable hands and cooks and chambermaids that I would naturally have expected to find employed in those large households, there were others whose jobs—even whose *titles*—I had never before heard of. The master of the house would have his nomenclator, who went everywhere with him, to nudge him and remind him of the names of other personages he might meet on the street. A mistress would have her ornatrix, whose sole duty was to help her get dressed and do her hair and paint her face. The scion of a house would have his adversator, to see him home from his nighttime revels, warning the young master of obstacles in his path over which he might otherwise drunkenly stumble. The praefectus Maecius even employed one out-door servant whose title was phasianarius, because he had charge of feeding and caring for Maecius's penned flock of rare birds—all of them being the breed of wildfowl that Wyrd had told me was the pheasant, but which the praefectus said was properly called "the Phasian bird," because its original habitat was the river Phasis in far-off Colchis.

All those servants charged with such specific tasks were almost as haughty as their masters, in being vain of their particular employments and titles, and they would recoil if anyone asked them to do anything in the least removed from their defined duties. An ornatrix, for instance, would have resigned her post rather than obey a command to run an errand, because that was the job of the lowly pedisequa. I remember once, when I had been a dinner guest at some villa, I thought I was paying a compliment to one of the kitchen stewards who had helped prepare the meal, but I addressed the man as "my good coquus—" and he coldly interrupted me:

"Excuse me, illustrissimus, but I am no commonplace coquus, who shops for his cooking materials at the market stalls. I am my master's obsonator. I buy only from the most exclusive purveyors, and I prepare only dainties and delicacies."

It appeared, also, that such servants took their titles and honors with them all the way to the afterworld. In the legionaries' graveyard at the fortress, I came upon the headstone of one Tryphon, who, according to the stone, had been tabularius to the legatus Balburius. And he was further described as "pariator," which I suppose is the most praiseful epitaph a bookkeeper could desire. It meant that, after Tryphon's death, his ledgers of income and expenditure had been added up and found to come out perfectly even.

✠　✠　✠

I need hardly point out that I could boast not a single one of the attributes and qualities that I have said were necessary for acceptance in Vindobona's upper circles. I was not of any family whatsoever, let alone a family of eminent lineage. I was not a landowner or even a mercantile negotiator. I had never distinguished myself in war or letters or imperial service or anything else. The one and only "servant" that anyone had ever seen attending me was now gone away. I had some money, but nothing approaching riches. Really the sole attribute that I had was audacity, but I kept being surprised by the way it kept on serving me.

322　　　Everyone knew me by the name that Thiuda had invented, Thorna-reikhs (or, oftener, Tornaricus), and all seemed to take that as evidence of my having come from *some* wellborn Gothic family. When a conversation afforded the opportunity, I would occasionally and casually drop in a passing mention of "my estates," and that seemed to persuade my listeners that I owned land *somewhere.* The praefectus Maecius had already asserted that I commanded some body of secret agents, hence that I possessed privileged knowledge of everything occurring in the empire. That fiction was widely repeated, and the coincidence of Vesuvius's subsequent eruption gave me my undeserved reputation for prescience, so I acquired the "distinction" I could not otherwise have claimed. Since I did have enough money to dress well and to lodge in the city's best deversorium, and to stand my rounds of drinks whenever other young men and I disported ourselves in the tabernae—and since I did *not*, like so many genuinely affluent men, ceaselessly complain about expenses, taxes and wages—I was assumed to have much more money than I did. Most important, I was a young man, unmarried, childless and, so I was told, comely of face and figure.

　　Of course, I had embarked upon this imposture with one intangible but demonstrable advantage. I was far better educated than even the sons of such personages as Maecius and Sunnja. And, during my travels, I had garnered enough of politeness and poise that I was no cloddish rustic. Now, in Vindobona, at dinners and other gatherings, I took care to mimic the manners of my elders, and thereby to put further polish on my deportment. I learned to dilute my wine with water and to spice it with cinnamon and cassia, and to drink that abomination without making a wry face or uttering one of Wyrd's oaths. I learned to refer contemptuously to commoners as the plebecula, "the rabble." I learned to knock at doors in the Romanly approved manner, with a genteel tap of my sandaled foot instead of my knuckles. And I must confess that I frequently had occasion to knock at closed doors, and to do it most discreetly.

The girls and women of high degree, like their menfolk, unquestioningly accepted my imposture. And the females—dowagers, matrons, maidens—even more than the males, seemed intrigued by my reputation for omniscience. At any rate, they took advantage of every opportunity to meet me, to be introduced to me, to engage me in conversation. Before long, this revealed to me something about myself that I had never had reason to realize before. Rather to my own surprise, I found that I could make friends with women more easily than other men could. I do not mean briefly reciprocated flirtations or even passionate love affairs; I mean close relationships, whether or not they included romantic or sexual involvement. And gradually I came to understand *why* I was more fortunate than other men in that respect. It was simply because of the fact that men and women see each other differently.

The way the world works, men in general are regarded as superior to and dominant over women in general. So it is only natural for the ordinary man to look on women as creatures bred just for his use and convenience. That ordinary man—though he may be ugly, aged, ignorant, stupid, crippled, poor and worthless—will yet regard every woman on earth as *available* to him, if he should want her. Even if she is a noblewoman and he the tetzte slave of a slave, he is convinced that, if he cared to, he could woo and win her, or abduct and rape her, simply because she is female and he is male. Well, I too had been inculcated with the attitudes that the world considers right and proper. I was by nature half male, and had lived most of my life as a male among males. Now, as a man grown, I was certainly not immune to the allure of a beautiful girl or woman, and not above yearning to possess her. On the other hand, I could not consider any female to be my inferior or subordinate, because in part I *was* one. Even in my male embodiment, when I was behaving and thinking like other men, feeling myself to be as

323

manly as they, involved in purely masculine pursuits, still the female half of my nature was never entirely submerged.

Of other females, most that I had known heretofore had been peasant drudges or cowering nuns, barring some notable exceptions—the errant Sister Deidamia, the gallant Lady Placidia, the sprightly little Livia—and those vicious viragines, the Domina Aetherea and the clarissima Robeya. But now I was consorting with females of good breeding, of some liberty and leisure, of intelligence and education—several of them could even read and write—so I was able now to observe the ways of women who had not been broken in spirit by lifelong toil or religiosity, not been made terrible by overweening ambition. And I realized that their thoughts and feelings were precisely the same as my own when my female nature was manifest.

Although men and tradition and laws and religious dogma have declared that a woman is only a receptacle to be filled, she knows she is more than that. So she does not perceive any man as being simply a fascinum capable of filling her. She looks at a man differently from the way he looks at her. He first assesses only attractiveness and desirability. She tries to see what underlies his surface. I know, because I had looked at Gudinand the same way.

The females of Vindobona may at first have felt drawn to the newcomer Thornareikhs simply by their curiosity about the stranger and his supposedly mysterious knowledge of many matters. But they warmed to me and clove to me for an even simpler reason: I did not regard them or treat them as an ordinary man would do. I behaved toward them as I, in my female embodiment, would wish a man to behave toward me. That was all it took. Many of the women and girls became intimate friends of mine, and many made it clear that they desired to become even more intimate than that, and a number of them did.

I daresay that an ordinary man, left to choose from such an abundant garden, would have picked only the flowers that were fairest and most perfectly formed. But I had seen beyond those surfaces, so I chose the ones that I had come to *like* best, regardless of their age and comeliness. Some were beautiful, but not all. Some were maidens barely nubile, and I was their first lover, and they had to be tenderly taught, and I believe I taught them well. Some were matrons past their prime, but no woman is ever too old to delight in carnal pleasures, and some of those had things to teach *me*.

✠   ✠   ✠

The first unequivocally amorous invitation I received, and accepted, came from a highborn lady whom I will here call Dona. I will say that this one *was* a beautiful woman, with eyes the veritable color of violets, but I will give no detailed description that might hint at her real identity.

I went to her chambers eagerly that night, but also a little apprehensively. Even undressing in her presence caused me some small anxiety—not about my masculine organ, which was already an ardent fascinum—nor about my maidenly breasts, because, by consciously tightening my pectoral muscles, I could keep them almost indiscernible. I was more concerned about the lack of hair on my body. I still had only the pubic escutcheon and the tufts under my arms, and I feared that Dona might find it odd that I had no manly hair on my chest, legs or forearms, not even a sandy roughness of beard beneath my facial skin.

I need not have worried about that. Dona cheerfully stripped off her own clothing, keeping on only one article, as feminine modesty dictated. But she was cheerfully unprudish about that, too; the one thing she retained was merely a fine gold chain linked around her tiny waist. So I could clearly see that Dona herself was entirely devoid of hair, except for the raven-black tresses of her head—and she expressed some mild surprise that I was not likewise sleek and smooth all over. Thus I learned another new thing: that it was the upper-class Romans' custom, men as well as women, to depilate themselves of every hair on the body, from the cheeks on down.

325

Dona explained, as if to a backward child, "We do our utmost not to resemble the savage barbarians who are as hairy as the furs they wear. Have you some reason, dear Torn, for not waxing away those three useless little traces?"

"It is the custom of *my* people," I said, "to regard them as ornament." After all, I needed the pubescence to conceal my lack of scrotum and testicles.

"Alius alia via," Dona said, airily dismissing the subject. "You are otherwise a very sightly young man." She ran her gaze appreciatively over me. "That little tick of a scar in your eyebrow is invitingly kissable. But that crescent scar on your right arm is the one thing marring the purity of your body. What caused that?"

"A certain lady," I lied, "who, in the transports of her ecstasy one night, could not restrain her ravening desire and took a *taste* of me."

"Euax!" Dona exclaimed, her eyes now glistening like those of a cat. "Already you excite me, Torn." And she stretched like a cat on her soft and capacious bed.

And here was the moment that mainly caused me concern, because I had coupled with only one woman before, and then under false pretenses. Although I was to do nothing with Dona this night that I had not done in the long-ago with Deidamia, I had at that time been Sister Thorn, and thought myself totally female. Now I was doing those same things as a male, and zealously, as Gudinand had done them to Juhiza.

So, when Dona and I passionately intertwined, I found that, at least in some corner of my consciousness—how do I make this understandable?—I was *reminding* myself of the ways in which I had instructed Gudinand to employ his fingers and lips and fascinum. And at the same time, for Dona's benefit, I was also reminding myself of those particular attentions that had best pleased both Juhiza and Deidamia. Happily, this reminding myself did not at all distract me from my performance as a male, and did not in the least diminish my virility. I was as unflagging as Gudinand had been, and Dona was as gratefully and insatiably responsive as Juhiza had been.

Furthermore, while she and I both unreservedly reveled in my maleness, I was again having that sensation of our both being several and various persons simultaneously—Thornareikhs and Dona, Juhiza and Gudinand, Sister Thorn and Sister Deidamia—active and passive, penetrator and engulfer, giving and receiving, spurting and swallowing. As had happened before, my feeling that we two were of many mingled personalities, of composite sexes and of fluctuating, alternating functions, gave an indescribable extra intensity to my enjoyment. I believe that it somehow added to Dona's, too, even though she could not possibly have shared that sensation of more-than-human multiplicity.

At any rate, when at last she could speak intelligibly, Dona gasped with joy, "Macte virtute!" and humorously added, "I shall recommend you to my friends."

"Benigne," I thanked her, mock solemnly. "But I scarcely think it will be necessary. A number of your lady friends have already signified their eagerness to—"

"Eheu! Hush, you braggart! You are likely to be drawn into more contests than you can cope with. Let me tell you a story of a man who once had two extremely possessive lovers. One was a handsome but elderly lady and the other a very young and winsome girl. Can you conjecture what happened to the man?"

"Is this an enigma, Dona? I should *imagine* that he lived happily ever after."

"Not at all. He very soon went completely bald."

"I do not understand. Even excessive—ahem—excessive exertion would not make a man go *bald*."

"I told you his two lovers were jealously possessive. The elderly lady plucked out all of his dark hairs, and the young girl plucked out all his gray ones."

She laughed at her own story, and Dona was the blithesome sort of person who laughs all over, and that made her lovely body jiggle so invitingly that I was again inspired to find other things for us to do than talk.

I will recount no further details of that occasion, or of other occasions with Dona, or of other occasions with other Vindobona women and girls—except to say that I never went bald. So I went on, for some months more, thoroughly enjoying my being Thornareikhs, continually seeing and learning and experiencing new things.

In December, I participated—along with every other person in Vindobona, from the herizogo down to the meanest slave—in celebrating the seven days of Saturnalia. In the grander residences, the better families spread sumptuous feasts, and each of those lasted from dusk to near dawn. Though they commenced with stiff formality, they eased, as the hours went on, into drunkenness and bawdry.

The most riotous of the festivities I attended was the one the legatus Balburius furnished for his Gemina Legion. Since the ostensible excuse for the Saturnalia is the ascent of the sun from its midwinter low point in the sky, and since the god Mithras is regarded by his devotees as the Deus Solis, and since almost all Roman soldiers still worship Mithras, those troops naturally celebrate the festival with real debauchery.

I was loitering in one of the fortress barracks, watching the soldiers carouse with the harlots who had come up from the city's low quarter, when I was accosted by a decurio far gone in wine. He flung a comradely arm around my shoulders and launched into a harangue intended to persuade me to abandon my current religion, whatever that might be, and convert to the loftier creed of Mithraism.

"You would have to begin, of course, in one of the probationary grades, hic, as a Raven or a Secret One or a Soldier. But then, with study and application and due piety, hic, you would be initiated into the Lion grade, and be accounted a confirmed Mithraist. With further study, and by doing good works, you could then rise to the grade of

327

Persian. Now, at some legion posts, that would be as hic as you could go. But here in the Gemina Legion, we have *several* Sun-Runners, of which I have the honor to be one. And—believe this or not, hic—we even have a Mithraist of the very highest, most coveted title, the Father. He is, I hardly need hic, our esteemed legatus. Now, young Tornaricus, I am willing to sponsor your acceptance on probation. What say you, hic?"

"What I say is *hic*," I replied, making jape of him. "In my lifetime, Decurio Sun-Runner, I have known many persons who wished to convert others. Every single one of them insists, 'You must embrace *my* god and *my* religion and *my* priesthood and *my* beliefs.' I say to all of them— and to you, Decurio—thags izvis, benigne, eúkharistô, but I respectfully decline the offer."

Then, in February, the whole city celebrated the Lupercalia. Long ages ago, it is said, this festival included the ritual sacrifice of he-goats, and the flaying of them, and the slicing of their hides into thongs for the making of whips. For aeons, though, the Lupercalia had been but a tame holiday. The whips were made of cloth ribbons, and the only remainder of the earlier ceremony was that small naked boys ran through the streets wielding those soft whips, and numerous women would step in the boys' path to get "lashed" by them. The superstition was that, because the original whips had been fashioned from lustful he-goats, the "whipping" would cure a woman's barrenness or increase her fecundity. Otherwise, the Lupercalia existed only as one more excuse for feasts and convivia and revels.

Then, in March, Vindobona and every other community in the empire was given another reason for celebration, on a day that was not ordinarily marked with the red creta chalk on the calendar. In the first week of that month, messengers went all about the provinces with the announcement that a certain Glycerius was to assume the imperial purple on the sixteenth day before the calends of April. No one knew much about this Glycerius, except that he had been a soldier who had been yanked from obscurity to be interim keeper of the empire after the almost simultaneous deaths of the Emperor Anthemius and the King-Maker Rikimer. Now Glycerius was to be invested with the title, and all Roman citizens were bidden to celebrate his ascension on that March day, and to wish the new emperor "salve atque flore!" A nonentity he might be, but Vindobona always gladly welcomed any excuse to hold a convivium. This being a state occasion, at least by proxy, every woman attending the festivities wore a stola, and every man a toga, and I was pleased that my sartor had insisted on making one of those for me.

However, truth to tell, I was beginning to weary of a life that was an almost continuous round of social gatherings and entertainments, of seeing the same people everywhere I went, of having almost nothing to occupy my days except what those people themselves called "weaving Penelope's web," meaning endlessly purposeless pursuits.

I decided that I had by now learned everything that those people had to teach me about the manners and proprieties and preoccupations of the upper classes. Both their conduct and their conversation now seemed to me mostly artificial, affected and trivial.

I wanted to seek some new acquaintances among people less refined, but people perhaps more real. Of the male friends I had so far had in my life, the very best, the old woodsman Wyrd, had begun life as a lowly colonial soldier. And Gudinand, my best male friend nearer my own age, had come from the absolute dregs of society. I hoped that, if I descended again to those levels, I might encounter other persons of equally admirable character and companionability.

Akh, I did not intend to disengage myself entirely from the higher ranks of Vindobona; I was not at all weary of the private company of the many *female* friends I had made there. Also, I could not simply saunter down to the low quarter of the city and ingratiate myself among the commoners. The plebecula might admire, envy or detest their betters, but they certainly recognized every one of them, including the illustrissimus Thornareikhs. What I required was a new identity that I could assume and discard whenever I chose. That necessitated no elaborate disguise. I had only to change from male to female: a different name, a few touches of cosmetics, the donning of feminine clothes and feminine graces. That was easier for me to do convincingly than it probably would have been for any other.

I would also need a separate domicile for this alternate self of mine. I remembered that when Thiuda had inquired about cheap lodging, Amalric had directed him to the house of some widow. So I asked Amalric how to find the place.

"The hovel of the widuwo Dengla?" he said, making a face of repugnance. "Vái, Your Worship, why would you wish to go there?"

"Only to collect some secret messages," I lied, "and to dispatch my replies to them. I arranged with Thiuda, my servant and agent, that the widow's house would be our address of convenience for relaying such things."

329

"Gudisks Himins," muttered Amalric. "Then I fear your communications are no longer secret. The woman will certainly have opened and read every one, and either noised its contents abroad or somehow used them to her own advantage."

I laughed. "You have a low opinion of this Dengla."

"Not I alone, Your Worship. Everyone in Vindobona, high and low. Besides stealing anything she can get away with, the widuwo also by stealth ferrets out the delicta and peccata of eminent persons, and bleeds them of much gold under threat of disclosing those embarrassing secrets. Some say she learns such things through the basest arts of haliuruns sorcery. However she does it, she knows so many privities of our magistrates and legislators that they dare not banish her from the city, as they ought to do. Anyway, I hope I have convinced you to stay well away from her."

I laughed again. "Ni allis. You have kindled my curiosity. I seek always to learn new things. And just to glimpse a creature of such venal enterprise might prove instructive."

330

4

y stay with the widuwo Dengla did indeed prove instructive, but I would be loath to instruct anyone else in the things I learned during that time.

When I presented myself at her door one forenoon, I wore my oldest and shabbiest feminine garb, and carried only a few belongings tied in a cloth, to assure that my appearance was in keeping with my new identity as a lowly plebeia. The warped and splintery door was opened by a short, scrawny woman of about Amalric's age. She was a bit better dressed than I was, though by no means in patrician garb. She was dish-faced and her complexion would have been sallow except that it was so heavily laminated with fucus and Chian earth and mastic; her hair would

probably have been starting to gray, except that it was artificially reddened with anchusa.

"Caia Dengla," I said respectfully. "I am newcome to Vindobona, and
I seek domicile for some weeks. I am told that you sometimes accommodate boarders."

She looked me up and down, much more searchingly than I had
inspected her. Then, even before asking my name, she demanded, "Can
you pay, girl?"

I held out my hand, several silver siliquae in my palm. Though her
little eyes glittered greedily, she sniffed with disdain.

"A week's worth of board and lodging only."

I did not remark that her rates were outrageous, but said humbly, "I
expect to earn more."

"By harlotry?" she snapped. However, she evidently had no moral
objections to that trade, for she added, "If you intend to entertain your
stupratores here, it will cost you more."

"I am not an ipsitilla, Caia Dengla," I said, but without manifesting
either resentment or amusement, still speaking meekly. "Like yourself, I
was widowed young, and these few siliquae are all that my husband left
me. But I have some competence in the craft of fur-stretching. I hope
to obtain employment in some local establishment."

"Come inside. What is your name, girl?"

"I am called Veleda," I said. The Old Language name that I now
assumed—it means "unveiler of secrets"—had been that of an ancient
Germanic poet-priestess. I was determined never again to appropriate
the name of the Juhiza who had been Wyrd's beloved, and the other
Juhiza who had been Gudinand's.

Dengla's house was nothing like Amalric's opulent deversorium, but
it was considerably more luxurious inside than it appeared from outside. Of course, I could not expect to share the well-appointed family
rooms, and the upstairs chamber to which she showed me was pinched
and skimpily furnished with the cheapest of wares, but it was adequate
for my requirements.

Without the least embarrassment, she said, "If you made inquiry of
me before coming here, you will have been told that I steal. Pay it no
mind. You need not be concerned for your own possessions. I steal only
from men. But then, speaking frankly, as between sister females, do not
we all?"

I murmured, "I have never yet had any opportunity."

"I shall teach you," she said matter-of-factly, "if you stay long

331

enough. I have no other boarders at present on whom we could practice. But I shall teach you that—and other things to your advantage
and profit and even pleasure. You will not regret having taken lodging
here, Caia Veleda. Give me those siliquae, then. But remember, I will
not refund so much as a nummus if you change your mind before the
week is up."

"Why should I change my mind?"

She made a wry grimace that almost cracked the lamination of her
face. "Once upon a time, and just once in my life, I made one mistake,
and I was doubly punished for it. I regret to say that I have twin sons,
of which I have not yet been able to rid myself. They live here."

I said, "I have no complaint about there being children in the
house."

"Well, I do," she said through her teeth. "If only I had dropped
daughters, they would be now of an age to be . . . to be of some use
and enjoyment. But *boys!* What are boys but small men? *Beasts!*"

She told me that a prandium would soon be served, and departed. I
unpacked my few belongings and distributed them tidily about my
room, then went downstairs for my first meal at Dengla's board. I was
not overly surprised to find that, for all her professed poverty, the
widow employed a servant to do the cooking and waiting on table. That
was a swarthy woman named Melbai, about the same age as her mistress, and equally plain of face, but she used no plasters and powders to
prettify herself. Well, a servant would not, of course.

On being introduced to the woman, I said, just to be genial, "Melbai?
That is an Etruscan name, is it not?"

She gave me a curt nod, then fairly barked at me, "And the word
'Etruscan' is Latin, and we do not like to be called that. We of that
race—far older than the Roman—call ourselves the Rasenar. I am a
Rasna. Try to remember that, young Veleda!"

I was rather taken aback to have a servant speak so to a paying guest.
But then she sat down with us to the prandium, and I later heard her
bark orders at the two boys, too, and I frequently afterward heard her
speaking as an equal to her presumed mistress. So I began to perceive
that Melbai was not exactly a servant in the house, and Dengla not at
all her mistress, but it would also be some while before I realized their
actual relation to one another.

The two boys might have been the real servants in the house, or
even slaves. Robein and Filippus were not quite twelve years old and,
as might have been expected, were not at all handsome children, nor

were they very bright. They were, however, well behaved at table that day and at subsequent mealtimes and on the few other occasions that I was in their company. In fact, they were cowed almost to muteness and invisibility, because either their mother or Melbai was forever commanding them to do some chore or loudly ordering them to take themselves out of her sight.

On my second day at Dengla's, I went out early in the morning, on the pretext of looking for employment with a furrier. I probably could have got it, if I really had wanted it, but I wanted only to look at the city through my new eyes, so to speak. And it was surprising how many things I saw as Veleda that I had not when I had walked the same streets as Thornareikhs. Now being *of* the people, not looking down on them from an illustrissimus height, I could observe their activities without their having to stop whatever they were doing to salute me, or step clear of my path, or self-consciously try to lessen the noise of their work, or desist from their quarrels, or put out a hand to beg alms of me. They merely went on with their day's doings and paid me no heed.

I watched a potter throw an elegant urn and then, when he got up from his kick wheel to carry it to his kiln, I saw how he walked atilt, because every potter's pedaling leg is so much stouter and more muscular than the other. I watched a housewife wash a tubful of clothes, then wrap a piece at a time around a wooden roller and roll that up and down a flat board to wring it clean. I watched a stonecutter polishing a new-cut block of marble with a pumice stone, and he frequently had to pause while he coughed and hawked and spat phlegm, it being well known that stonecutters, like quarriers and miners, usually die young of the lung impairment that the Greeks call phthisis, or "the wasting away."

333

Another thing that I noticed now, as Veleda, was one particular sound of Vindobona. Of course, neither Thornareikhs nor the highest patricius could ever disregard the sheer *noise* of such a busy and populous city. There was the cacophony of hoofs and wheels, the neighing and braying and bawling of draft animals, the barking of dogs, squealing of pigs, cackling of chickens. Also there was the hammering of carpenters, the clanging of metalworkers, the jingle of money-changers' coins, the rumble of wine casks being rolled, the tweedling or twanging of street musicians, the bellows of hucksters and itinerant barbers, the yells of drunken soldiers and the intermittent screechings of contentions between women or roarings of fistfights between men. But now I heard the singing. That washerwoman sang over her tub, the potter hummed along with his wheel. From the Catholic church came the sound of children singing their cathechism questions and answers, the better to memorize them. It seemed that everybody sang while he worked.

When I returned to the house that evening, I told Dengla that I *had* found employment as a fur-stretcher and that I was to be paid by the piece and therefore, since I was so adept at that craft, I would be earning rather more than the usual starvation wage. So, I said, I would be able to afford to stay on in her lodgings for some while to come. Dengla congratulated me—and sincerely, I am sure, because my news must have been gratifying to her avaricious nature. She even gave me a knowing smirk of approval when, after cena, I said I was going out again "to seek diversion" after my hard day's work.

Going out alone at night was something I could not have done if I had been a woman of the upper classes. As one of the plebecula, I enjoyed considerably more liberty to wander where and when I chose to go. Of course, I could not sit down in a taberna and drink and make the acquaintance of good fellows like Wyrd and *his* drinking companions. Also, sometimes at night—when I was strolling along the torchlit streets, or eating at a street stall, or watching a band of mummers at their comic capers—I might be accosted by a drunken man or solicited by a sober one. But a good-humored bit of banter was usually enough to discourage any molester and, if it did not, I was capable of leaving him lying flat on the ground with a broken nose or missing teeth and a new respect for womanhood. However, the lower-class folk in general were a good deal less criminal and a good deal more mannerly than their betters gave them credit for being. Both by day and by night, I encountered decent men and women who became my friends, though I never met anyone to whom I was attracted as I had been to Gudinand. So, whenever I felt the urge for carnal relations, I would resume my identity as Thornareikhs and go calling on one of my nobler lady friends.

When I completed my first week's "employment," I paid Dengla her exorbitant price for my next week's lodging. As it happened, I had not slept in her house the previous night, having spent it with a very young clarissima whose parents were away from home. So, as she accepted my money, Dengla favored me with a gangrene smile and the sly remark that she saw nothing wrong with my "augmenting" my income as I pleased.

"The virtuous and censorious folk like to believe that an ipsitilla sells her body, but I do not agree. An ipsitilla or even the cheapest noctiluca does not give herself for pay, any more than a lady does. She is *rewarded* with money after having given herself of her own free will, exactly as is the case with the most respectably married wife. If ever you are inclined to feel ashamed of yourself, young Veleda, look at it that way. I do, because I once similarly disported myself. I mean *precisely* once, with a hairy Suevian named Denglys, and that once was enough to disgust me with men forever. Of course, I did take everything in his purse when I stole away, and later decided to take even his name, it being rather more distinguished than"—she tittered coyly—"than other names I have worn. However, as you know, my only *tangible* reward for having so disported myself was *those*."

She gestured toward her twins, at which the boys quailed timorously.

"But if *you* are not afflicted with fecundity, Veleda, and are not repulsed by men, then I say cavort with them as much as you like. Only be sure they pay every last nummus you can wrest from them. The priests and preachers and philosophers, who are all men, would like everybody—especially women—to believe that the seven moral virtues are precious heirlooms, to be handed down from mother to daughter. But we women know better. Every kind of virtue exists only to be bartered, either to the earliest or to the highest bidder. As for myself, I refuse to see any immorality in any act by which I benefit. And you, Veleda, I will advise you as if you *were* my own dear daughter. I can give you some hints that will make you even prettier than you are, therefore a more valuable commodity. For instance, when you go out at night, carry a handcloth doused with oil of thyme. On meeting a prospective stuprator, waft the cloth before your face. It will make your eyes gleam and sparkle alluringly. Also—"

"I am not a commodity, Caia Dengla," I said, to stop her spate. "I earn my every nummus by honest labor. And I imagine, if I ever *were* to become a mother, I would be proud to have two such loving sons."

"Loving!" she snorted. "If I had had daughters, they would by now be loving me most voluptuously indeed. But *these*? From their infancy, when I had to abase myself by serving as their nutrix, they have been repellent to me. A small *man* sucking on each of my paps—*eheu!* I could not even sell them to be charismatics, for they were not beautiful enough, or to be brought up as slaves, for they were not intelligent enough. However, thanks be to Bacchus, they will soon turn twelve and I will be rid of them."

Clearly, she did not and never would believe that I was anything but the cheapest street-corner night-moth, especially since I continued to

335

spend at least one night a week away from her house. For my part, I would have supposed, from the lip-licking way in which Dengla had spoken of her nonexistent daughters, that she and the Rasen woman Melbai must be sorores stuprae—except that they never exchanged affectionate caresses or words or even glances and, so far as I could tell, never spent any substantial length of time, day or night, in the same room. They did, however, go out together every Friday evening after cena and stayed out all night. I had no least interest in making inquiry about that, and Dengla proffered no further comment or advice on my own nighttime pursuits, and for some weeks I simply went on living my double life without significant incident.

During Holy Week, I several times went to mass at the city's Arian church, to see wherein the Arian Christian services differed from the Catholic. The priest, one Tata Avilf, was an Ostrogoth and all his deacons, subdeacons and acolytes were of one or another Germanic nation or tribe. But they were hardly ravening savages; they were as benign and bland and routinely, even lethargically, devout in their observances of ritual as any similar group of Catholic clerics.

336

On Easter Eve, there were five or six catechumen Competents to be received into the Christian mysteries, and the priest did their baptism very nearly the same way I had so frequently seen it done in St. Damian's chapel, except that each Competent was three times immersed in the baptismal water, not just once, as is required of Catholics. On the Saturday after Easter, I sought audience with Tata Avilf, pretending to be a Catholic contemplating conversion to Arianism, and respectfully asked him to explain the difference in baptismal immersion. He obligingly told me:

"In the early days of Christianity, my daughter, all catechumens were thrice immersed at their baptism. It was only with the emergence of Arianism that the Catholics changed their liturgy to specify a single immersion. It was done simply to set their creed apart from ours, you see, much as the Church had long ago made Sunday its Sabbath day, to dissociate itself from the Jews' Saturday Sabbath, and also had made Easter a movable feast, simply to set it as far as possible from the fixed Passover of the Jews. But we Arians do not dwell on the differences between the Catholics and ourselves. We believe that Jesus desired his followers to practice generosity and tolerance, not exclusivity. If you were to decide this minute, Caia Veleda, that you want to convert to, say, Judaismus—or even revert to the paganism of our ancestors—why, I should simply wish you happiness in your choice."

I was astounded. "But St. Paul said, 'Preach the word; reprove, entreat, rebuke; do the work of an evangelist.' Tata Avilf, you would not even *counsel* against my making such a drastic departure from the Christian Church?"

"Ne, ni allis. So long as you live a virtuous life, daughter, doing harm to no other, we Arians would aver that you *are* obeying what St. Paul called 'the word.' "

✠ ✠ ✠

Quite by coincidence, on my way through the streets after leaving the Arian church, I glimpsed the widuwo Dengla and the Rasen woman Melbai coming out of another—or out of a pagan temple, rather: the temple dedicated to Bacchus. They and numerous other women—and a few men—were emerging furtively, by twos and threes, all deeply muffled in their cloaks, but Dengla was distinguishable by her vivid red hair. Those people looked in all directions, evidently to see whether there was anyone about who might recognize them, then scuttled hastily away from the place. That was a reasonable precaution. Even among the most unregenerate pagans, the worship of Bacchus had for ages been considered dissolute and reprehensible. The temple's exterior walls were much bedaubed with lewd verses and imprecations written by disapproving passersby.

I remembered Dengla's having invoked the name of Bacchus. And it is well known that the Romans who displaced the Etruscans, or Rasenar, from the Italia peninsula had regarded them—and still regarded the scattered remnants of them—as a people steeped in sordid superstition and sorcery. So Dengla and Melbai were Bacchantes. And this was a Saturday morning, so the Bacchic temple was where those women spent their Friday nights. But what kind of worshipping, I wondered, could they and those other people find to *do* in there all night long?

"Would you like to find out?" Melbai bluntly asked me, when all three of us had got back to the house. "I saw that you saw us, girl, as we left the shrine. Many prurient folk are itching to know what occurs inside that temple, and I would wager that you are, too. As it happens, I am a Venerable—a priestess—of the Bacchic society, and I can introduce you there. You might even relish the rites enough that you would wish to become an initiate."

I said indifferently, "A minor god. Of wine merely. I know that all his votaries are women, but I cannot imagine what he has to offer that would interest me."

"Not merely the god of wine, Veleda," Dengla put in. "Also of youth and feasting and joy. We Bacchantes do drink much wine, but the music and singing and dancing intoxicate us far more ardently. We are exalted to the state that the Greeks call hysterikà zêlos, passion of the womb—but of more than the womb, actually—of the whole body and all its senses. A woman is excited to wild ecstatic ferocity and to strength enough that she can, bare-handed, tear apart a live kid for the ritual sacrifice."

"It sounds enchanting," I said drily.

"Nor are all his votaries female," Dengla went on, as if I had not spoken. "Originally they were, but some centuries ago a Campanian woman had a vision in which the god instructed her to induct her own two adolescent sons, and the Bacchic societies have been conjuncti ever since. You must have seen some men leaving the temple with us, Veleda. Or perhaps you would not call them *entirely* men. The Venerables among them are all eunuchs. Some of those willingly castrated *themselves*, just so they would qualify for our priesthood. And the male lay worshippers are all fratres stupri."

338   I said, "It sounds ever more enchanting."

"Well, they are amusing to watch," Dengla said, snickering.

"And Bacchus is not any *minor* god," said Melbai. "Only nowadays in the Roman Empire is he so shamefully neglected. As you may be aware, girl, the Greeks have long and highly regarded him as Diónysos. But you probably are not aware that we Rasenar were even earlier devoted to that same god, calling him Fufluns. The ceremonies of his worship are older yet, for they derive from ancient Egypt, where, long before he became Fufluns and Diónysos and Bacchus, he was revered as the goddess Isis."

Yet another divinity of mutable sex, I thought. Perhaps I, as a brother-sister mannamavi, *should* at least pay my respects to him-her.

"And next Friday," Dengla said eagerly, "is our highest holy night of the year. That is the date of the annual Dionýsia Arkhióteza. The Bacchanalia. There could be no more thrilling time for you to visit."

I was surprised. "I thought the Bacchanalia had been banned by the Senate aeons ago."

Dengla said contemptuously, "An edict was pronounced, yes. But that was simply to placate the hypocrites of the time. The Bacchantes had only to become less visible and more anonymous. The revels never really ceased, nor would the authorities wish them to."

"After all," said Melbai, "they provide a vent for the emotions and lusts and urges of all the persons prone to the hysterikà zêlos. Emotions that might otherwise erupt in ways harmful to the public order."

"*Furthermore,*" said Dengla, pointing to her twins, who cringed from the gesture, "Filippus and Robein will celebrate their twelfth birthday on Tuesday. So they will fortuitously enjoy the eminence of being initiated into the rites next Friday, which is not just *any* Friday, but the night of the Great Dionysia. You might like to honor the event with your presence, Veleda. You seem tolerably fond of the brats, and you will not be seeing them again thereafter, unless you continue to attend services at the shrine."

"You would impel your own sons into a den of fratres stupri? And abandon them there?"

"What higher calling could the louts aspire to? Their lives will be dedicated to serving Bacchus."

"Serving him how?"

"You will see, if you come to the Bacchanalia. Do come."

So I went.

339

5

 ver the weeks, I had brought to my room in the widow's house some of my other feminine clothes and trinkets, of rather better quality than I had worn on first arrival there—each time, of course, pretending they were new purchases enabled by my "wages." So, on the Bacchanal Friday, when I was being as self-conscious as any other young woman about to make her entrance into an unfamiliar circle, I said to Dengla:

"I suppose I ought to wear my very best raiment on an occasion like this."

"If you like," she said carelessly. "But it does not matter. You will be taking it all off before the night is over."

"I will?" I said, in some slight alarm.

"Eheu, do not look so scandalized. Why is it that girls of your station are always the most prudishly modest of females when they go anywhere except streetwalking?"

"I have told you, Caia Dengla, I am not a whore."

"And I have told *you* that you need not put on any poses for my sake. I know that no furrier pays you enough to have afforded that 'very best raiment' of yours. But even if you stole the things, I do not care, so long as they were not stolen from me. Why, I have acquired much of my *own* best raiment, and many other valuable possessions, by the very same means. Anyway, it is not *demanded* that you disrobe during the rites, though you would look most conspicuous and rude if you do not, when everyone else does. However, if you subscribe to the Roman custom, you may keep on one of your undergarments. Also, you need not—um—participate in the rites if you do not care to. Many of our most devout votaries attend the shrine only to observe, and they seem to attain a marvelously high degree of hysterikà zêlos by doing nothing but watching. Now, if you are going to change clothes, Veleda, go and do so. It will soon be time for us to be on our way. Melbai has already gone ahead, to don her vestments as a Venerable. I will collect the twins, and let us each hold one firmly by the arm, so he does not try to flee. The little imbeciles are as fearful as if they were kittens going to visit a kennel of wolves."

Well, I thought, the Latin word "lupa" strictly means "bitch-wolf" but it is informally employed—though it grossly slanders the wolves—to mean an "unchaste woman." So, more than likely, the kittens had *reason* to fear. But I got dressed in my best undergarments and amiculum overdress—and put on, last of all, my most fetching feminine adornment, that coiled bronze breast guard I had bought at Haustaths—and then obediently took fast hold of one of the boys, and the four of us proceeded to the temple of Bacchus.

The interior of that temple was, as Dengla had said, dimly illuminated; only a single torch was bracketed on either side of the capacious, high-ceilinged room. But there was light enough for me to see that the furnishings consisted mainly of soft couches, perhaps twoscore of them, set at random about an open space in the middle of the mosaic floor. Among the couches were set tall vases of irises, daisies, primroses—all white flowers, to be visible in the dimness. There were also scattered about the floor little pots in which roasted pinecones smoldered, and I remembered what old Wyrd had long ago told me about that resinous incense: that it "makes a kunte as hot as the incense itself." At the

340

front of the room, where I would have expected an altar or ambo, there was only a tremendous marble table that might have stood in an extraordinarily elegant taberna, because it bore a pyramid of ten wine casks—stacked on their sides and fitted with taps in their vents, ready to pour—an array of goblets and cups and numerous trays piled high with grapes of various colors.

"Where in the world do the grapes come from?" I asked, as Dengla and the boys and I sat down on one of the couches. "It is not even summertime yet."

"Did you not know? If ripe grapes are buried among a bin of radish roots, they will stay fresh and sweet for months. And of course we *must* have grapes, all year round, to eat in honor of the god of wine."

Soft music was being played by a group of women seated on one of the couches nearest the table. As my eyes got accustomed to the dim light, I could see that one was plucking a lyre, another shaking a sistrum, another gently tapping on a lap drum, another tootling on the panpipes and the fifth singing quietly into an onion flute. All five of the women were naked.

There seemed to be not much formality about the Bacchic ceremonies. Quite a number of people were already there when we four arrived, and others slipped in after us, by ones and twos. Almost all were women; there were perhaps ten or twelve men at most. And every one of the celebrants, even before claiming a seat, went straight to the marble table and filled a cup or goblet with wine. All made repeated returns to the casks, probably drinking hard to rid themselves as quickly as possible of any timidity or demureness. Dengla drank as deeply and frequently as any, and pressed many cups of wine on both the twins, and urged me to drink as well. I did go and get a goblet for myself, and refilled it several times, so as not to appear unmannerly, but each time I surreptitiously spilled most of my wine into a nearby flower vase.

Also, not to appear overly inquisitive, I refrained from craning about and peering at other people. But I could easily discern that the gathered Bacchantes were not all from the ranks of the plebecula. Without turning my head, I could see several women attired in fine gowns, and I recognized three whom I had met at the banquets and convivia that I had attended as Thornareikhs. They were women of the sort I have already mentioned with disdain: the sort of witless woman who is forever consulting an astrologus. One elderly, inordinately fat man I likewise recognized, and with astonishment, as the praefectus Maecius.

So, I thought, the widow Dengla did not pry out secrets about her betters by haliuruns sorcery. She did not have to. For her extortionate purposes, she had only to threaten to make public the fact that Maecius and those highborn women—and probably other persons whom I had not yet seen here—were practicing Bacchantes. Melbai had already warned me of the one most sacrosanct rule of the Bacchic societies: that no participant ever disclose to the uninvited what occurred inside the temple doors. Perhaps Melbai and the others never did, but I judged Dengla to be capable of violating any trust, if it profited her to do so.

After some while, the five naked women paused in their playing of music, and the murmur of conversation and gulping of wine ceased. Then the musicians began again to play, and more loudly, what I took to be the anthem of Bacchus, and it was not at all melodious, but jarringly discordant. A door opened in the wall behind the marble table and the priests and priestesses made their entrance. There were three men and eleven women, one of them Melbai, and each was dragging on leash a reluctant and dolorously bleating kid. The Bacchantes shouted to greet them: "Io!" and "Salve!" and "Euoi!" and here and there a "Háils!"—and kept on shouting as the fourteen paraded around the circumference of the room. They did not do that solemnly, but lurched and staggered in real or pretended drunkenness, sometimes tripping over their little goats and nearly falling.

"Always fourteen Venerables," Dengla said in a slurred voice, leaning close to my ear to be heard above the noise. "Because, when Bacchus was an infant, he was reared by the fourteen nymphs of Nysa. And of course we sacrifice kids to him because goats are detested by the god. They eat his grapevines."

The fourteen wore crowns of ivy and grape leaves, and about their shoulders panther-skin cloaks. They wore nothing else, and a panther skin is not very large or very concealing. The nearly nude priestesses were nothing to ogle at, all of them being of about Melbai's age and plainness. Two of the priests were clearly eunuchs, pale and fat and flabby. The other must have been one of the men who had castrated himself late in life, for he was very skinny, but he was so old that I wondered why he had bothered with the castration. Each of the Venerables, in the hand not holding a leash, carried and waved and waggled what Dengla called a "thyrsos," a tall staff topped with a pinecone.

I said loudly, over the shouting and bleating and dissonant music, "I know that the panther is sacred to Bacchus, hence the skins. But what does the pinecone stand for?"

She hiccuped and said only, "It represents the *reaming*," and giggled drunkenly.

When the procession of Venerables arrived again at the front of the room, thirteen of them stood back against the wall and the old man took a commanding but unsteady stance before the marble table. The musicians muted their playing and the congregation gradually ceased to shout, while the priest drew himself a brimming cup of wine from one of the casks and took a long, refreshing drink. Then he began to speak—what I assumed were the Bacchic versions of invocation, homily, benediction and so on.

"*Euoi Bacche! Io Bacche!*" he commenced, almost in a shriek. Much of his preaching was in Greek, and I was not too well versed in that language. Anyway, his tongue was so wine-twisted that I doubt that even a native Greek could have understood him. Other parts of his harangue were in a language that I could not even identify—the speech of the Rasenar or the Egyptians, for all I know. The one brief utterance that he made in Latin quite startled me, for it was from the Christian Bible, from the Book of Luke. The priest absolutely bellowed it:

"*Blessed are the barren, and the wombs that have not borne, and the paps that have not given suck!*"

343

Apparently that was the only part of the sermon requiring or inviting a response from the congregation. All the women in the room, Dengla included, cried in their several languages: "True!" and "Blessed are they!"

After some more incomprehensible babble, the priest concluded, "Now for the singing and the dancing and the feasting and more drinking. Euoi! Io!" He tossed away his panther-skin cloak, the music soared into a rollicking Lydian cantus, and the old man was the first to leap into the clear space on the floor, dancing rowdily and bonily, all knobby knees and elbows. The two fat eunuch priests, and five or six of the female Venerables, including Melbai, also dropped their cloaks and began to dance, leaving the other priestesses to hold the leashes of the frightened, fidgeting, bleating kids. There was a rush of lay worshippers—the more drunken ones—to join the frolic. All danced, just as furiously as the first and oldest priest, and few of them any more gracefully, and they began to fling off one garment after another. While they did so, they cried the name of the god: "Bacchus!" or "Diónysos!" or "Fufluns!" interspersed with screeches of "Io!" and "Euoi!"

Dengla doffed her outdoor cloak, dropped it on our couch and, without urging me or the boys to accompany her, vaulted onto the dance floor, where she loped and bounded and shrieked and began to peel like the rest of them. That revealed Dengla's legs to be short and stumpy, but with long, narrow feet that flapped against the mosaic floor with smacks and slaps audible even above the general pandemonium. Nor did the other naked dancers make a captivating sight. The few men and many women were all Dengla's age or older, and no more alluring than she was. Except for Filippus and Robein, I was the youngest person in the temple, and I must aver, however immodestly, that I was by far the handsomest. Even though still fully clothed, I was being stared at, waved at and winked at by various of the women on the couches roundabout.

The light was too dim for me to see whether the dancing women were manifesting any signs of sexual arousal—tumescent nipples, for example—and their wild contortions and ululations could as easily have passed for insanity as for the stirrings of carnal passion. So could those of the men, for none of them had yet developed a fascinum; the torchlight *was* sufficient for me to see that. The praefectus Maecius, for one, had excited himself only to the point of discarding all his dignity along with his clothes. He bounced lumpishly about, jiggling his bulges and billows of suety old fat, but the thing that dangled below his wobbling sack of belly was visibly not yet any more amatory than an earlobe.

The dancers, whenever they danced past the marble table, would snatch a few grapes or a cluster of them from the heaped trays, and then would slovenly spray juice and seeds as they went on singing. Whenever a dancer got winded, he or she would drop out of the milling crowd for a replenishment of wine. Some simply lay down supine under a cask and let the wine pour directly from tap to mouth, with the result that the floor was soon sloshy and slippery. More than one dancer fell asprawl, evoking much merriment among the others.

By now, there were only a few women, and no men, still seated on the couches. Those seemed content to observe, like myself, but they had all disrobed, though three or four of them Romanly kept on a single undergarment: a strophion about the breasts, a belt around the waist, a skimpy loincloth. And they were casting reproachful glances at me and the twins, so I leaned down and said to the boys what St. Ambrose had once said:

"Si fueris Romae, Romano vivito more . . ."

They probably did not understand the Latin, but, when they saw me begin to undress, they did likewise. The boys stripped to the skin; I of course retained the band around my hips to conceal the evidence of my maleness. To disguise the fact that it *was* a disguise, I had worn a decorative band of fine linen sewn all over with colored beads. And now I made sure to relax my chest muscles, and sat somewhat bent forward, to make my small breasts as prominent as possible.

However, when I and the twins were conformingly nude and re-seated—each boy sitting with his hands primly cupped over his private parts—I discovered that no one was casting glances at us any longer. The gaze of every onlooker was fixed on the front of the room, where now occurred the only ritual sacrifice I had ever witnessed. Dengla and numerous others of the naked female dancers ceased their deranged dancing and, just as maniacally, flung themselves upon the leashed kids.

Every woman—all the while screaming, "Io Bacche! Euoi Bacche!"—snatched and grabbed and clutched to get one of the kids for herself alone. If she did, and Dengla did, she went for the little goat's vitals, crooking her hands into claws and using her fingernails like talons, tearing the belly skin open, then plunging her face inside to gnash and gnaw. Where two or more women had to settle for sharing a kid among them, they yanked or bit at its extremities to take it apart. The wretched animals screamed more shrilly even than the women were doing, as their legs were torn off, and their ears and tails were chewed off, and their lower jaws were ripped off, and they stopped screaming only when their heads were twisted off their necks.

When eventually all the fourteen kids had been completely dismantled into bits and pieces, what pieces the butcher women had not already devoured were picked up by the Venerables and flung broadcast about the room. Some of the dancers had gone on deliriously dancing during all that bloody activity, even when they were struck by a flying goat rib or eyeball or tangle of intestines. But most of the Bacchantes had stopped dancing in expectation of the bestowal, and all the non-dancing spectators had run from their couches to stand with the crowd.

Now everybody in that mass of people elbowed and fought and scrambled to get a fragment of the meat—even something unidentifiable because it had been stepped on, even something as recognizably revolting as a goat's pizzle—and blissfully to eat it raw. Most then rushed to the casks for wine with which to wash it down. The twins were making small gurgling sounds, so I looked down again at them. They were heaving, gagging and adding vomit to the puddle of spilled wine that by now had flowed as far as our couch.

345

If the abundant nudity, the music, singing and dancing had not excited much sexual fervor among the Bacchantes, their bestial eating of raw meat certainly had done so. The male votaries now *were* displaying erect fascina, and began to employ those organs, though not on any of their female co-worshippers. Maecius seized onto one of the eunuch Venerables, a man as obese as himself, and impelled him to a couch. There, without caresses, kisses or any other preliminaries, Maecius bent the priest face down across the edge of the couch, humped himself atop the man's vast buttocks and proceeded to penetrate him per anum. The other males were doing the same, and all of them, the ones on the bottom as well as the ones on top, writhed and moaned and whimpered happily, just as if they had been in the thrilling throes of normal man-woman intercourse.

Everything that I had so far witnessed of these ceremonies could have come straight from the *Satyricon* of Petronius, except that none of this was meant to be humorous, lighthearted or sardonic; it was all being done in sanctimonious earnest. Small wonder that persons such as Maecius paid money to the extortionist Dengla. He and others of his status had reason enough to prevent her revealing them to be even attendants at the Bacchic rites. He would have far more reason to fear her making it known that he was what Roman law calls concacatus, "besmeared with excrement," which is to say a male who copulates with a male. The law decrees a heavy fine and punishment for that crime against nature, and assuredly Maecius would have lost his eminent station as praefectus of Vindobona.

And the female Bacchantes were doing very much the same unnatural thing. I had, of course, assumed them all to be sorores stuprae, and they were indeed. But I would have expected them to pleasure each other in the warm, close, loving, intimate ways that Deidamia and I had done when we *thought* we were sorores. These women did not. Melbai and several others had produced olisboí from somewhere, and strapped those implements at their crotches. An olisbós is an artificial fascinum made of smooth leather or polished wood, and some of these olisboí were of a normal man's size and coloring, but others were grotesquely immense or studded with warts or shaped all crooked, and some were dyed Ethiope black or were gilded or were painted in other garishly inhuman colors.

Now I realized what Dengla must have meant by "reaming," because the women equipped with olisboí behaved as Maecius was doing with his passive partner. Without any show of flirtation or affection or seduction, they simply pushed other women down on the couches, flung themselves on top and *raped* those women. Or perhaps "rape" is not exactly the correct term, for the victims were clearly *willing* to be raped. Melbai was pumping away at one of the highborn women I had earlier recognized, Dengla was being pumped upon by a hideously ancient hag, and neither the clarissima nor Dengla was struggling or crying to get loose from her assailant.

In fact, just like the men and their Ganymedes, both of the women participants in every such coupling were wriggling and gasping and squealing with joy. I could, albeit with some difficulty, suppose that the woman underneath might experience *some* pleasant feeling even from an artificial fascinum. But it was beyond my comprehension that the woman wielding the olisbós could feel anything whatever, unless it was purely in her head: some kind of perverse relish in playing a man and a stuprator and a conqueror and a violator.

Anyway, after a while I saw the women exchanging places, exchanging partners, even handing the now glistening-wet olisboí from one to another. So they were all getting their turn at playing violator and victim, or pleasure-giver and pleasure-taker, or whatever they conceived themselves to be. For that matter, some of the females got to play both kinds of partner simultaneously, because one of them produced a very long and double-ended olisbós that required no strapping on. With that, any two women could crouch on hands and knees, rump to rump, and insert the thing into both of themselves, then simply rock back and forth to attain their enjoyment.

347

True, some women were not participating at all, merely looking on. But they—I suppose as their manifestation of the hysterikà zêlos—were meanwhile making slobbery noises as they tickled, rubbed, manipulated what was between their thighs. And some other women lounging on couches near me, being temporarily without partners, smiled and beckoned to me. But I was nowise inclined to join in the counterfeit copulation. I had frolicked with many a female by now—once upon a time as a female myself and often since as a male—but in every case I had used my own flesh to excite and enjoy *her* own flesh. These women's mode of satisfying each other was not only cold, distant and brutal, it was also ridiculous; they resembled so many cows, utilizing the elongated, pendent dugs of their udders to penetrate each other.

Neither had I any wish to join the male Bacchantes in their Neronian method of mock copulation, though they at least were employing each other's own bodies, not paltry substitutes. I had already learned, from experience, the glorious gratification of lying with a male *as a female*, and I refused to believe that the concacatus practice of these men could be in any way comparable.

All this while, the five musicians had been playing a slow, sweet, almost cloying Phrygian music—to induce in the Bacchantes amorous emotions, no doubt. Now they again ceased playing, so that the oldest priest—not at the moment being reamed by any of the male votaries—could make a proclamation. In much the bombastic manner of a praeco announcing an amphitheater's games, he shouted, first in Greek, then in Latin and in Gothic:

"Pray, holy silence, all! For now we are about to witness and partake in a truly significant event that will embellish even further this holiest and most festive of Bacchic nights!"

Most of the crowd went silent, but a number were still copulating, in one way or another, and grunting or squealing or giggling while they did it. The old Venerable shouted louder:

"I am proud to announce that two new, young, male novitiates are this night to be dedicated to the god and initiated in his worship! The Bacchante Dengla honors us tonight by presenting to Bacchus her own two sons!"

348

The twins, now sitting on either side of me, gave piteous whimpers and each clutched one of my arms. The musicians were setting aside their lighter instruments and taking up heavier ones: drums and cymbals.

"The mother herself will conduct the ceremony of initiation," the old man went on, *"and* in the traditional fashion first introduced by that ancient Campanian Bacchante whose long-ago dedication of *her* sons we still remember and revere! Give heed now, on this momentous occasion!"

All the Bacchantes not otherwise occupied instantly began to applaud and stamp their bare feet and shriek their "Euoi Bacche! Io Bacche!" I wondered if I ought to seize the twins and run away with them. I honestly feared that the Bacchantes were preparing to rend and eat Filippus and Robein as they had done with those other young animals. However, before I could decide whether or not to interfere in the proceedings, Dengla and Melbai were looming over us.

Their hair was matted and snarled, and there was a crazed look in their eyes. Their thighs and shaven groins and the nether lips that flaccidly protruded there were all mucously slimy. Their breath was foul with wine, but my femininely acute sense of smell found even more revolting their bodies' rancid fish odor of overripe sexual surfeit. Their mouths were crusted with dried blood, and there were flecks of blood on their pendulous breasts. Melbai seized each boy by a wrist, while Dengla fumbled in the cloak she had left on the couch. She took from its folds an olisbós, but of a kind that I had not yet seen. This one was a *cluster* of olisboí, like a mushroom of several stems and caps: imitation male organs of graduated sizes, from young-boy small to grown man's fully erect.

"Come now, my sons," said Dengla. "And come without protest or complaint. It is this—or the thyrsos."

Melbai hauled the boys to a couch near where the musicians sat, and Dengla followed, not taking the horrid new olisbós for any Venerable to use, but strapping it onto herself. From where I was, and in the dim light, I could no longer discern which twin was which, but Melbai and a sister priestess bent one of them forward over the couch's edge. All the other Bacchantes stood about the room at respectful distances, so that all should have a good view, and all continued chanting, "Io Bacche! Euoi Bacche!"

Dengla stood behind the bent-over boy and looked all around as if to make sure that she was indeed the center of attention. She caught the eye of the skinny old-man Venerable, and he solemnly nodded. Immediately, the crowd's chant rose to a roar, and all the musicians started pounding drums and clashing cymbals, to drown the sound of the boy's scream when he was impaled with the first, the smallest of the multiple olisboí. No one heard him scream, but I know he did, because his body contorted, his head jerked back and his mouth flew incredibly wide open. Almost as wide were the eyes of his watching twin.

The thunderous uproar continued, as Dengla wiggled her hips for some moments, then withdrew and stood back. The boy sagged onto the couch, twitching, but he had only a brief respite. He convulsed again, and soundlessly screamed again, when the next olisbós was rammed into him, and the next, and the next. The final one, the largest, was worked back and forth in him for some time, and Melbai and all the watching other Bacchantes smiled, as the boy seemed to have accommodated to the violation, to be now relaxed and enduring it, perhaps even enjoying it.

Dengla at last stepped away from him, unstrapped and dropped her multiple olisbós, and turned the boy around to face the room. We could all see that his little organ, as if it had been somehow stimulated from the inside, had magically grown into a respectable little fascinum. To

349

make sure it stayed that way, Dengla made a fist and worked it up and down, while she leant close to talk to her son. Her wheedling and caressing made the expression on his face gradually change from woeful to wondering and then to a beatific smile.

Melbai had been watching for that. Now she snatched the other twin onto the couch and forced him face down. The Bacchantes resumed their bellowing and the musicians again began drumming and crashing, as Dengla pushed the first boy up against his brother's buttocks, and with the one hand guided his fascinum to the proper place, and with the other hand gave him a sharp push in the small of his back. The prone twin convulsed as the first had done, and silently screamed, and writhed. His brother might have withdrawn, but Dengla held him there, and herself moved his hips in a rocking motion. In a few moments he was doing it himself. Without any further urging, he took tight hold of his twin, and bucked most energetically, until finally, suddenly, he shuddered all over and threw his head back, his face wreathed with a joyous grin.

"Euoi! Io! Euoi Bacche!" the crowd screeched triumphantly.

350 "The initiation is successfully concluded!" shouted the old-man Venerable, prancing to the fore again. "*And* in the time-honored manner of the Campanian mother and her sons! *Io* Mater Dengla! *Euoi* Méter Dengla! Now . . . let us sing welcome to the new Bacchantes Filippus and Robein!"

At which, the musicians, playing their more melodious instruments, launched into a recognizable carmen, and all the male and eunuch Bacchantes sang the extremely obscene verses, a poem in praise of the practice of men loving men.

"Now," the old eunuch bawled again, "who would wish to be *second* to enjoy the favors of either of the boys?"

There was a chorus of "I!" and "I claim!" from the non-eunuch men present. But Dengla raised her hands for silence.

"No! The honor of first choice should go to our eldest and most notable and most highly respected Bacchante." She turned her gangrene smile on Maecius, who simpered back at her. Then he waddled forward, in all his flesh, and embraced one of the boys and led him to a couch.

Dengla was not only a lupa, I decided; she was also a lena, which is the Latin word for the lowest, filthiest sort of procuress — and she was a lena dealing in her own children. I could hardly be surprised at her having so magnanimously handed them over first to the praefectus, since she was already in his pay, so to speak. And no doubt this—what he was now doing to that boy on that couch—would enable her to extort even more money from him.

Among the other fratres stupri, there was some quarreling going on, as to which should get the other boy, and the old priest was trying to quell them:

"Patience, brothers, patience. There is still time for all of you to partake before dawn and disbandment. And remember, these new Bacchantes belong now to Bacchus and the temple. They will be participating in the rites every Friday night from now on. Remember also, they may be privately visited, by appointment and on payment of a trifling donation to the society's coffers, on any other occasion you find convenient or"—he cackled salaciously—"of urgent necessity."

Well, I said to myself, Filippus and Robein would probably be happier dwelling here in the temple than they had been with their mother. They might even, given their dullard intellects, learn eventually to *like* living out their lives as mere meat for hire. To be honest, I felt sorrier for the slain little goats, which might have grown up to be handsome and intelligent, as well as more useful in the world.

351

Anyway, I wished to see nothing further of the Bacchanalia, and I was not going to stay here until "dawn and disbandment." I wanted to get away from this nest of vipers, and I would claw my way past any that tried to stop me. But no one did. Practically everybody else in the temple was occupied in one nasty way or another—or was helplessly raddled with wine—so the few who noticed my getting dressed again gave me only mildly disapproving looks. And, though the temple door had been prudently barred, the bar was on the inside, so I easily and ever so gladly let myself out.

6

I hurried through the dark, empty, predawn streets, back to the widow's house, to get in and out of it again before Dengla or Melbai should return. There I cleaned my face and changed into the few necessary Thornareikhs garments that I had kept secreted among my Veleda wardrobe. Then I baled together everything else belonging to me, and made my last departure from the place.

I half thought of setting fire to the house as I went. I half thought also of somehow sending word to the twins, to suggest that they wreak vengeance on their odious lupa-lena mother. However, I did nothing to further it. Although that loathsome woman indubitably deserved a return of evil for evil, it was not my place to provide it. She would surely sometime be judged by a tribunal even more merciless than myself. Abyssus abyssum invocat, as the saying goes—hell calls to hell.

✠   ✠   ✠

Dawn was just breaking when I arrived at the deversorium of Amalric the Dumpling-Plump, but some of the domestics were already up and about. So, in my old Thornareikhs-imperious manner, I called for food and drink with which to break my fast. I took my belongings to my chambers, and a table was set for me by the time I came downstairs again. While I sipped a Cephalene wine, and ate of Sassinan cheese and preserved Caunian figs and a manchet of fine white bread, I reflected on what new things I had lately been learning about the world and men and women and gods. For one thing, if anybody should ever inquire of me about the nature of an orgy, I could truthfully say that it was *not* deliciously wicked, but disgustingly so.

Of the several gods to whom I had been introduced, Bacchus was certainly the most repellent. The soldiers' favorite, Mithras, held no attraction for me either, because Mithraism excluded women, and I *was* one. The only human being I had yet met who seemed to get even the least usefulness out of any of the pagan gods had been that old wise-sayer Winguric of King Ediulf's tribe—but Winguric had communicated with his deity through the preposterous medium of *sneezes*. The single admirable deity I had so far encountered, in all my life, was the god of the Arian Christians, who did not seem to *care* whether a person worshipped him or some rival god, so long as that person lived his life not ignobly.

I was still meditating on such things, and, being now full of a good meal, was feeling drowsy after my night without sleep. But then Amalric entered the room, and I roused myself.

"Come, join me, Amalric," I said. "Help me quaff this good Cephalene wine of yours."

"Thags izvis, Your Worship, I will." He stretched out on a couch adjoining mine, and beckoned for a servant to bring him a goblet. "It has been some while since we conversed."

"I have been . . . occupied," I said, and thought it would do no harm to add another increment to my continuing imposture. "I have been exploring all parts of your fair city. Seeking ventures in which I might care to make investment."

He poured some wine for himself, and said, "Forgive my presumption, Your Worship, but, considering the newly and suddenly unsettled condition of the empire, you might be wise to keep your money hidden under your pallet for the time being."

"Indeed? I have not lately been following the affairs of state. Much too busy with my own. I have not even bothered to collect and decipher any messages from my agents abroad. And my converse with—with those persons to whom I have talked—well, we never touched on matters of great moment. What is so new and so sudden, Amalric?"

He said slyly, "You must have been exploring, ahem, fair parts of our city, indeed. The chief topic of other people's conversation is, of course, our new emperor in Ravenna."

"What? *Another?!* So soon?"

"Ja. Glycerius was toppled from the imperial throne and replaced by one Julius Nepos. Glycerius has been consoled for his loss by being made bishop of Salona in Illyricum."

"Iésus! Glycerius was a soldier, then an emperor. Now he is a *bishop?* And who in the world is Julius Nepos?"

"A favorite of the Emperor Leo of Constantinople. Nepos and Leo were somehow related by marriage."

353

"Were? They no longer are?"

"How can they be?" Amalric shook his head at me. "Have you not even heard the most resounding news of all: that Leo is dead?"

"Credat Judaeus Apella!" I exclaimed. That was a fashionably smart remark that I had picked up from my acquaintances in higher society. It meant "Let Apella the Jew believe it!" or, in other words, "I find it hard to!"

"Believe it, believe it," said Amalric. "I told you these are confusing times. Almost catastrophic in their rapid succession of events."

"Iésus," I said again. "Leo had been ruling the Eastern Empire all my life, I think. And I assumed he would go on ruling forever."

"Akh, there is still an Emperor Leo in Constantinople. But now it is his grandson, Leo the Second. That one is just a child, five or six years old, so there will certainly be some regent helping him rule. Meanwhile, if you have not heard this—both of the brother kings of the Burgunds have died in this same springtime, both Gundiok and Khilperic."

"Gudisks Himins," I muttered. "Those two certainly had ruled all during my life."

354   "Now their sons are co-regnant. Gundobad at Lugdunum and God-egisel at Genava. And will you yet have heard this? That the king of the Ostrogoths, Theudemir, also has died. Not of old age, like the others, but of a fever."

"I had not heard. And does his death, too, somehow contribute to the unsettled condition of the empire?"

"Oh vái, of course it does. Theudemir had for years been paid by the late Leo the First to keep the peace along the northern borders of the Eastern Empire. Actually, it was more of a bribe—to keep the Ostrogoths themselves from being troublesome. Theudemir did that, but he also efficiently fought off invasions and depredations by other outlander tribes and nations."

"Ja," I said. "I have seen and heard something of Theudemir's prowess in that respect."

"Well, then. With both the Western and Eastern Empires now in disarray, from kings and emperors on down, and with the Ostrogoths now leaderless, those outlanders who have long been held at bay could judge this to be their moment of opportunity. Indeed, one nation already has. The Sarmatae of King Babai."

"I have heard of that people, too," I said. "What have they done now?"

"They have seized and occupied the castrum city of Singidunum, on that northern border of the empire. But—let us hope—perhaps not for long. There comes word that Theudemir's son has succeeded to kingship of the Ostrogoths, and he may prove to be his father's son in more than name. He is reported to be leading the Ostrogoths on a march to besiege and retake that city."

I remembered Thiuda's words: "You will find me in combat . . . and I invite you to fight beside me." I asked Amalric, "Where is that city of Singidunum?"

"In Moesia Prima, Your Worship. Far downstream on this very river Danuvius"—he gestured toward it—"where the Danuvius becomes the boundary between Moesia Prima and that barbarian land now called Old Dacia. Perhaps three hundred and sixty Roman miles from here."

"Then the quickest way to get there would be by the river?"

"Akh, ja. No sane man would wish to ride horseback all that way, through forest wilderness and probably hostile peoples . . ." He paused and blinked. "But surely, Your Worship, you do not contemplate *going* there?"

"I do."

"Into the middle of a *war*? You will find there no prospects for investment. No comforts and diversions such as you have enjoyed here. Nothing fair—and, if I may make so bold, no *body* fair—to explore, as you phrased it."

I smiled. "There are things more important, and far more interesting, than crass commerce. More inviting than indolence and entertainment and even fair bodies."

"But . . . but . . ."

"Right now, I am in need of a refreshing long sleep. However, before I retire, I shall visit a fletcher and purchase a good stock of arrows. While I am doing that, Amalric, send someone to the riverside. Have him hire for me a boatman willing to transport me to Singidunum—or, if the man is timorous, somewhere reasonably close to that city. And he must have a scow or barge big enough to carry my horse as well. Then see to the stocking of the vessel. Provisions for myself and the crew. Ample fodder for my horse—and not just hay, but good grain to strengthen him for the rigors ahead. Has Velox been properly exercised every day while I have been here? He will have to stand idle during the voyage."

"*Really*, Your Worship," Amalric protested, looking hurt.

355

"Akh, I know, I know. I need not inquire, or instruct you, and I apologize. I trust you to take care of everything needful. Then have ready your reckoning of all I owe you, for I wish to depart at dawn."

✠   ✠   ✠

The departure had not been forced on me, nor had I only impetuously decided on it, but the reason for it had come at an opportune time. Neither Thornareikhs nor Veleda would regret leaving Vindobona. I could happily live the rest of my life without ever again so much as glimpsing on some street the despicable widuwo Dengla. As for those women and girls who had been my friends, or more than friends . . . well, I had every expectation that there would be more of those wherever I went.

I was ready and eager to be journeying again. I looked forward to renewing my friendship with Thiuda, and mingling for the first time with my other Gothic kinsmen, and paying my respects to their—to our—new king. I also was eager, as I long had been, to experience and partake of a real war. So it was with no reluctance whatever, no looking back, that I shed my identities of Thornareikhs and Thornaricus—and, at least for now, that of Veleda—and set forth into the river mists of the next day's dawn, once more as Thorn.

356

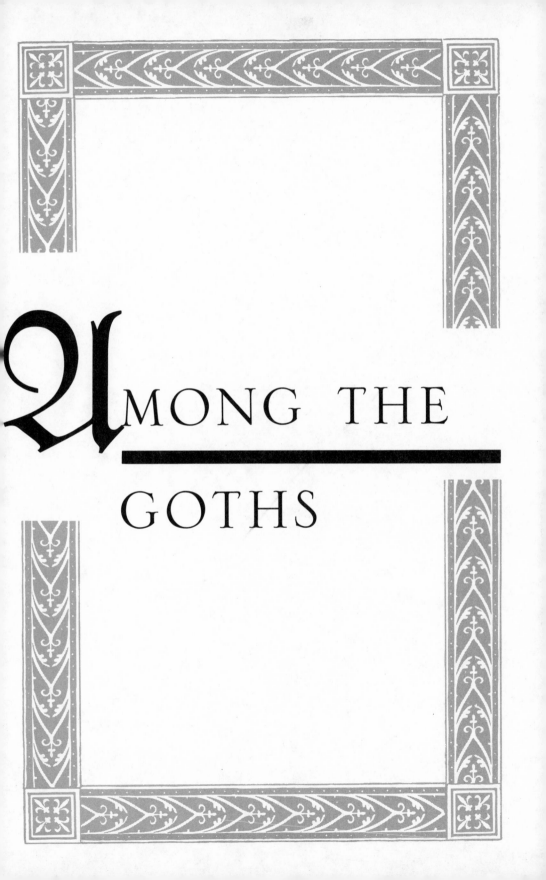

AMONG THE GOTHS

1

The voyage downriver was lazily pleasant, for the Danuvius wended first eastward from Vindobona, then, after some days, turned due south, so it took me and Velox and the bargemen quite quickly into the golden summer that was moving north. There was a great deal of traffic on the water, every sort of craft from barges like ours to the navy's patrolling dromo boats to immense merchant vessels, some of those wearing sails as well as banks of oars. But there was not much else to catch the eye along the way, because the river's banks were thickly and monotonously forested, except where those green walls were interrupted, here and there, by a logging camp or a small farmstead or a fisher village. At several of those we stopped to purchase fresh produce or fish to supplement the rations Amalric had loaded aboard for us.

We came upon only two settlements of any size, both of them on the river's right bank. The first, situated in the province of Valeria, where the Danuvius makes its great bend to the south, was the onetime frontier castrum city of Aquincum. But that place was all tumbledown ruins, and the barge's master, a man named Oppas, told me why. Over the past century, Aquincum had been so often devastated by marauding Huns and other outlanders that Rome had withdrawn its Legio II Adiutrix from the castrum there, after which the city was deserted by all its once numerous inhabitants.

The other settlement we came to was the naval base of Mursa, situated where the river Dravus pours into the Danuvius. That was a purely utilitarian place of wharfs, piers, dry docks, repair yards, warehouses, horrea storehouses and many drab barracks. There we were peremptorily flagged by a watchtower sentry. When the boatmen steered us close to the tower and poled us to a stop, the sentry leaned from his parapet to impart a piece of advice from his commanding navarchus: that we travel no farther downstream.

South of here, the sentry informed us, there was disorder and danger, what with the rampageous Sarmatae in control of Old Dacia on the far side of the Danuvius, and with the Ostrogoths controlling Moesia Prima on the near side, and with the strategic city of Singidunum being contested between the two foes, perhaps doomed to become another ruin like Aquincum. So the Roman navy had bidden its Pannonian Fleet no longer to patrol the Danuvius between here and the gorge called the Iron Gate, far downstream. Of course, said the sentry, beyond that point and all the way to the Black Sea, the river's shipping was under the protection of the Moesian Fleet. But here and now, along a stretch of nearly three hundred Roman miles, from Mursa to the Iron Gate, the Danuvius was undefended by dromo vessels, and any trading or freighting or passenger craft must proceed at their own risk.

In some consternation, Oppas asked, "But what of your fleet's other base, down at Taurunum?"

"Have you never been there, bargeman? Taurunum is directly across the Savus River from the afflicted Singidunum, and will likely share its fate. Our navarchus is not fool enough to keep any of our vessels based there, until and unless the Sarmatae are repulsed."

"By the Styx!" growled Oppas. "I had reckoned on finding some kind of freight there, to bring back upriver."

The sentry shrugged. "The navarchus has not *forbidden* anybody's voyaging to and fro along that length of the Danuvius. My orders are only to counsel against your doing so."

The barge's master and his four crewmen all turned to look at me, and not very kindly. That was understandable; my destination, Singidunum, was almost exactly midway down that unpatrolled stretch of the river. During the exchange with the sentry, I had been honing my short-sword with a whetstone, and idly went on doing so, as I said:

"If other vessels are heeding that counsel and going into hiding, Oppas, then there very well may be freight waiting—even spoiling while it waits—and you should get a very good price for its transport."

"Balgs-daddja!" he snorted. "Only to have it pirated from me before I can get it safely upriver. Or to have my barge sunk under me. Ne, ne. Under the circumstances, we would be foolhardy to travel on."

"The circumstances," I calmly reminded him, "include my having already paid you for my passage."

"Akh! Without a load that my men and I can bring back, and live to deliver, and get paid for doing it, then I charged you only *half* what I should have demanded."

"That was not specified when we made our contract," I said, still imperturbably, and still honing my sword. "Besides, when I paid what you earlier asked"—this was the truth—"it took very nearly the last nummus in my purse. Now you will honor your contract."

Although I had put Thornareikhs behind me, I would still—and, in fact, still do—employ that useful stratagem I had learned by being Thornareikhs. That is, if one assumes an air of authority and fully *expects* to be obeyed, then other people, more often than not, do obey. I went on:

"I will allow this concession. You may land me well short of Singidunum, and thereby not take yourselves too close into hazard. But to that I append a specification of my own. I must *see* the city, however far distant, before I disembark. I will not be landed in some remote forest."

Oppas could only grind his teeth and say uncertainly, "What if we choose to unship you right here? What if we help you hasten ashore by pitching you overboard?" His men all nodded and muttered menacingly.

I said, "I have told you that I go to Singidunum to fight the Sarmatae." I plucked a hair from my head and stroked it along the edge of my blade; the long hair became two short hairs. "It might profit me to practice some slaying beforehand. And I imagine this barge, even unmanned, would eventually drift me to my destination."

"Well said, stripling!" the sentry shouted from above us. To Oppas he said, "If I were you, bargeman, I would chance the pirates and barbarians."

So Oppas, though grudgingly and with many ugly profanities, bade his men lift their poles and let the barge go on. The remainder of the voyage was not very pleasurable, and Oppas and I had no further friendly converse, and his men grumbled mutinously and continuously. I took care, from this time on, never to turn my back on any of them, and at night I slept as Wyrd had done, with my sword unsheathed and near, with one hand clenching a pebble over a basin and my other hand wound with Velox's halter rope, so I could feel if he gave a start for any reason.

Although this run from Mursa to Singidunum was only a third as long as the distance we had come from Vindobona to Mursa—conditions being what they were, this stage of the voyage seemed to take many more days and nights. However, we traveled the whole way unmolested. Except for the occasional fishing skiff or peat scow, timorously hugging the shore, we had the whole Danuvius to ourselves. It seemed that even the river pirates must have decided to go to ground until the warring Sarmatae and Ostrogoths went away.

Early one morning, our barge rounded a point of land and the boatmen stabbed their poles into the river bottom to bring us to a halt, and Oppas wordlessly pointed. On our right was the naval base of Taurunum, almost identical to Mursa, except that its piers and docks were empty of boats and people. Beyond that, the Danuvius was broadened to nearly twice its former width by the river Savus, flowing into it from the right. And beyond that confluence of waters, dim in the distance and the morning mist, was the city of Singidunum.

A triangular foreland sloped upward from the riverside to a vast plateau that ended inland where it dropped off at a dizzyingly high cliff. The entire foreland was an ideally defensible fortress, protected by that cliff face on one side, by the river on the other two sides. From this distance, I could not make out many details—presumably the city's residential outskirts occupied the sloping ground—but I could see that a formidable wall enclosed the whole plateau top, where obviously was the city proper. I looked for smoke rising there, but could espy none, and listened for sounds of battle, but could hear none. Well, if the Sarmatae were occupying the city, as reported, they would hardly be burning it down around themselves. But if the Ostrogoths were besieging the city, as reported, they were certainly not being very energetic or noisy about it.

"You may take me to shore now," I said to Oppas. "But I do not care to have to swim across either the Danuvius or the Savus."

"Vái! You want me to set you on the very riverfront of Singidunum? I absolutely refuse to get that close!"

"Very well. Then have your men pole us some way up the Savus. Take me as far from the city as you consider prudent, and I will disembark there."

The boatmen grumbled and cursed even more angrily than ever, at having really to exert themselves for the first time on this voyage, but they did as Oppas sullenly commanded. Meanwhile, I saddled and bridled Velox, and loaded my packs of belongings on him, and belted on my sword and slung ready my bow and quiver of new arrows. When we came to a conveniently shelving bank of the Savus, some two or three Roman miles upstream of that cliff face behind Singidunum, the barge slid close inshore and Oppas let its side ramp flop into the shallow water. I led Velox down it, myself walking backward to keep the men at my front, and cheerfully called to them:

"Thags izei, my fellow travelers. There is still a quantity remaining of the provisions that I paid for, but I leave all those dainties for your delectation, in gratitude for your unstinting services."

They all snarled at me, Oppas yanked the ramp up into place, the men jerked their restraining poles from the mud, and the barge drifted back down the Savus, the way it had come, toward the Danuvius again. I waited until I could be sure that none of the men would attempt a parting gesture of flinging some kind of missile at me, then I led Velox up the bank and into the forest. When we came to a footpath that paralleled the river, I mounted to the saddle, tucked the toes of my boots under my foot-rope and—ready for war or whatever else offered—I let the eager Velox uncramp his muscles and legs in a joyous stretch-out canter toward Singidunum.

✠   ✠   ✠

Before I got there, however, I came upon an arresting sight. Velox carried me to the top of a wooded ridge, and there the wood abruptly ended, so I reined the horse to a halt, for I was looking down into a bowl of land in which something curious was going on. In the bowl there were only a few scattered clumps of trees, and otherwise the ground was covered only with grass and low brush, so I had a clear view of what was occurring about three stadia below me. In each of two copses, not three hundred paces apart, a group of men had taken cover, each briskly shooting arrows at the other group. I could not judge how many men were involved all together, but there were about a score of horses, all in quilted war armor, tethered on the protected side of each clump of trees.

I backed Velox a little away from the ridge's skyline, to stay out of sight while I watched. But I wanted to do more than watch. These had to be Ostrogoths fighting Sarmatae, and of course I belonged on the side of the Ostrogoths—only which was which? I could see no standards anywhere, the horses and their quiltings were indistinguishable, and the men themselves were invisible within the copses. It was likewise impossible for me to tell whether one or the other side was winning, whether anybody on either side was being struck by any of the showering arrows. Those simply continued to fly ceaselessly back and forth, passing each other in midair, with no diminution in their number or frequency—because none of the bowmen would soon run out of ar-

365

rows; he had only to pick up and use the spent ones from the other side. After some while, I began to feel that I was watching an evenly matched, interminable, childish and pointless game.

But at last the men on one side seemed to tire of the inconclusive exchange of arrows, and came charging out of their cover with drawn swords. Of the score or so of them, two were stopped by arrows already flying, and they fell on the ground and writhed. The men in the other clump of trees did not emerge to meet their assailants, sword to sword, nor did they continue shooting arrows. Instead, they erupted from the *back* of their copse, leapt onto their horses and fled in the opposite direction from the attack.

So now I could tell which were the Ostrogoths and which the Sarmatae. I might have guessed just from the fact that the one group declined to engage in a sword fight. Those charging with swords had to be wielding the formidable "coiling snake" *Gothic* swords, before which the bravest foes have been known to quail. But also I could see that the men fleeing on horseback were wearing corselets of the scale armor made of horse-hoof parings, once described to me by old Wyrd as the invention of the Sarmatae warriors. Those, then, were *my* enemies, too. Since the Ostrogoth attackers seemed content only to dash into the suddenly evacuated copse—presumably to dispatch any wounded Sarmatae still there—and made no attempt to pursue the runaways, I decided I would do that for them.

I kicked Velox into a gallop down the slope of the ridge at a tangent that would intercept the Sarmatae before they could cross the bowl of clear ground and disappear among the surrounding woods. As our courses converged, the men turned to look in surprise at me—a lone horseman, unarmored, of indiscernible identity. Their looks of surprise turned to looks of chagrin, bafflement and terror when I began to loose arrows at them while I was still riding at a gallop.

As I have said, I was not nearly so adept at that rapid shooting as Wyrd had been, or as unerringly accurate. Most of my arrows flew astray, but I dropped two of the Sarmatae from their saddles before the rest of them recovered from their astonishment, dispersed from their bunched grouping and scattered in different directions. Even then, I managed to bring down one more, with an arrow in his back. None of the Sarmatae so much as tried to loose an arrow at me, and I had known they would not. Except for the Huns, whose bandy legs must give them a more than humanly firm grip on their horses, no warrior ever could shoot an arrow from a moving horse and hope to hit a mark. I should say, no warrior but a Hun *or myself*, firmly anchored on my mount by my foot-rope contrivance. And, as Wyrd had remarked, none but a Hunnish bow, like the one I had inherited from him, could propel an arrow at long range with force enough to penetrate the Sarmatian scale armor.

The fleeing men could have stopped, dismounted and *then* have been able to discharge any number of arrows at me, with a good chance of hitting me—and killing me, unarmored as I was. But I saw why they did not when I turned in my saddle and looked back. Four of the Ostrogoths had gone to get their own horses and now were riding headlong toward me, each of them carrying a long contus lance. These men did not wear the scale armor, but stout leather corselets from which depended quilted leather skirts. Their legs were encased in padded white cloth leggings, strapped with thongs that crisscrossed upward from their low boots. Their helmets were not conical, like those of the Sarmatae, but much resembled the Romans', only with broader cheek lappets and with a flat piece of metal projecting downward from the forehead rim to protect the nose. All that one could see of an Ostrogoth warrior's face was his fierce blue eyes and wavy yellow beard. I halted Velox and waited for the men to ride up to me.

One of them gestured to the other three, and those went to plunge their lance points into the Sarmatae I had unhorsed, to make sure they were dead. The other halted near me and couched his lance in its saddle socket so he could salute me. He did that by raising his right arm, but holding the hand open and stiffly extended, not clenched into a fist in the Roman manner. I took him to be the officer commanding this troop, for his helmet was much wrought with decorative figures and he wore at each shoulder of his corselet a richly jeweled fibula in the form of a rampant lion. I returned the same salute and he studied me keenly for some moments.

He was a formidable figure, masked by his helmet and beard, bulking huge in his armor and sitting tall upon his quilted horse. I felt quite diminutive and vulnerable under his gaze, rather as I imagine small forest creatures must have felt when, far from the safety of their dens and with no covert nearby in which to shelter, they realized they were being eyed by my raptorial juika-bloth. But then the warrior shed his fearsome aspect, for he gave a laugh and said:

"At first we thought you were a wandering Hun, and a Hun gone mad, attacking alone and without armor. But then we saw the rope that enables you to employ the bow while riding, and do it as deftly as any

367

Hun. Once upon a time, I scoffed at that rope of yours. I will not do so again."

"Thiuda!" I exclaimed.

"Waíla-gamotjands! Welcome, Thorn, to war. I invited you to join us, and you did, and you have acquitted yourself most handsomely from the moment of arrival."

"So must you have done," I said, "since you seem already to have risen to a position of command. Also your beard has become admirably luxuriant since I last saw you."

"Akh, we must both have much to tell one another. Come. Ride with me to the city, and we will talk as we go."

His three men fell in behind us, at a respectful distance. And, because we proceeded only at a leisurely walk, the other Ostrogoths also soon caught up to us. Some of them led the captured horses of dead Sarmatae, but some of the Ostrogoths rode draped limply over their saddles, either dead or badly wounded, and others had to be held upright on their mounts by companions riding beside them.

Thiuda asked me, "Have you been all this while in Vindobona? If so, then Thornareikhs must have found beguiling hospitality there."

"Ja, he did, thags izvis," I said, smiling. "I mean that. Thags izvis. He could not have found so much without your having prepared the way for him. But I should prefer to hear of your own adventures. Did you find your father? Is he with you in this campaign?"

"I did find him, ja. But no, he is not. I am happy that I got to see him when I did, for he was ill of a fever, and shortly died."

"Vái, Thiuda. I am sorry."

"So am I. He would much rather have died in combat."

"Is that why you are out on patrol—seeking combat—and not among those besieging Singidunum?"

"Ne. The patrolling is part of the siege. You see, there are only six thousand of us, and King Babai has nine thousand Sarmatae within the city's walls. Also, we had to ride hither too rapidly to fetch anything but what we could carry. Since we brought no siege engines and towers and rams with which to storm Singidunum, the best we could do was encircle it and keep Babai and his men from getting out. Also, to keep them from enjoying their occupancy in tranquillity, at random intervals we rain in arrows and sling-stones and fireballs. Also we make these sweeps of the countryside to prevent any reinforcements from coming to join Babai—or coming to attack us from behind. At present, we can do no more."

368

"Bithus contra Bacchium," I said. That was another fashionable phrase that I had acquired from my upper-class acquaintances in Vindobona. It refers to two famous gladiators of olden days, who were of exactly equal age and strength and skill, so that neither of them ever bested the other. Thiuda might have been vexed by my smart remark, but he had to concur in the sentiment.

"Ja," he grunted. "And we could be at this frustrating standstill for a hellishly long time. Or worse, we might *not*. We are ill supplied even with food and other necessities, while the Sarmatae possess ample horrea and granaries. Unless we can survive until our supply trains from the south manage to get here, we may have to withdraw. Meanwhile, our turmae take turns at squatting under the city walls and ranging roundabout on horseback. And you know how I chafe at inaction. So I try to ride out with every turma that goes afield. As you saw, we do occasionally find some action."

"I got only a brief glimpse of Singidunum from the river," I said. "But it appears well-nigh impregnable. How did the Sarmatae ever take it?"

"By surprise," he said sourly. "It was manned by only a skeleton garrison of Roman troops. Still, even those few—with the help of the inhabitants—should have been able to hold a city so strongly situated and fortified. The garrison's legatus has to have been either an inept clod or an outright traitor. His name is Camundus, and that is no Roman name, so he is of *some* outlander lineage—possibly even Sarmatian. He may have been long and secretly in league with King Babai. Anyway, whether fool or turncoat, if Camundus is still alive in there, I intend to slay him along with Babai."

I privately thought that Thiuda was talking somewhat presumptuously, as if he alone were responsible for this whole Ostrogothic campaign against the Sarmatae. But I said nothing of that, and, prodded by questions from him, regaled Thiuda with some account of my doings in Vindobona—only Thornareikhs's doings, of course, not Veleda's. Finally our little troop came to the outskirts of Singidunum, at the base of the ground's upward slope from the riverside, and, with a nearer view of the city now, I could better appreciate the difficulties the Ostrogoths faced in the besieging of it.

As in Vindobona and most other cities, these outskirts constituted the lower quarter of the city, the site of all the poorer inhabitants' houses, of workshops and warehouses and markets and cheap popina eating houses and such. The garrison fortress, the finer public buildings, the better mercantile houses, the more luxurious tabernae and dever-

369

soria, the residences of the richer folk, all those were atop the plateau. As I have said, that entire height was surrounded by a wall, and now I could see how the wall was built of huge stone blocks, firmly cemented, and built unassailably high. As Thiuda and his men and I rode up the main street from the riverside, I could see not so much as a roof peak, dome or spire thrusting above the height of the wall. Furthermore, that wall had only one gateway, visible at the top end of the street we were climbing, and that entrance was of course closed by a great arched double gate. Though the gate was of wood, it was constructed of beams so immense, so firmly held together by massive iron staples, and so studded all over with reinforcing iron bosses that it looked as indestructible as the stone wall.

There were people in the streets—almost as many Ostrogoths as cityfolk—and the daily life of Singidunum seemed to be going along fairly routinely, but I noticed that none of the citizens favored us with smiles or salutes or greetings as we rode by. When I remarked to Thiuda that the people did not appear to regard us jubilantly as welcome deliverers, he said:

370

"Well, they have reason. At least they do not object too much to our quartering ourselves in their shanties. But that is about all they can offer us. Babai ransacked their larders and cellars and shops, and took all their provender inside the walled city with him, so the people are as hungry as we are. Whether the richer folk within the walls are delighted to have the Sarmatae dwelling among them, I do not know. But these out here are equally disgruntled with Babai for having seized the city, with Camundus for having let him do so, and with us for our not being able to do much to remedy the situation."

I said, with due humility, "I doubt that I can do anything that is not already being done. But I should like to lend what help I can. Perhaps if I were granted audience with your chief commander, he might find some post to assign—"

Thiuda grinned and said, "You have already been blooded in combat, Thorn. Be not too eager to get yourself *bloodied*. First let me introduce you to our armorer, Ansila, and have him arrange for you and your steed to be properly equipped. Meanwhile, I must accompany my wounded men to the lekeis, and see that they are well doctored."

So he and I stopped at the workshop of a local faber armorum, where the smith was doing his work under the supervision of a hefty, middle-aged, bushy-bearded Ostrogoth. To that man Thiuda said:

"Custos Ansila, this is Thorn, my friend and a new recruit. Take his measurements for a complete outfitting. Helmet, armor, shield, lance, everything he currently lacks. His horse as well. Have the smith get to work on that immediately. Then show Thorn the way to my lodgings. Habái ita swe!" Ansila silently saluted, and to me Thiuda said, "I shall see you there, and we will talk further." And he was gone.

While the faber, with a length of string, measured the circumference of my head and chest, the length of my leg and so on, the custos Ansila eyed me with some curiosity and finally said:

"He called you his friend."

"Akh," I said offhandedly, "when we met we were both mere woods-men."

"Both mere woodsmen, eh?"

"I must say that Thiuda seems to have come well up in the world since then," I went on. "He issues orders as if he were commanding every man involved in this siege, not just a single turma of them."

"You do not know, then, who is our commander?"

"Why . . . ne," I said, realizing that I had not even thought to wonder about that. "I was told that your King Theudemir recently died, but I have not heard who succeeded him."

"Theudemir—that is the Alaman and Burgund pronunciation of his name," said Ansila, in a pedantic manner reminiscent of my abbey tutors. "We spoke our king's name as Thiudamer, the *mer* of course meaning 'the known, the famed.' Thiudamer, the Known of the People. He could rightly have taken the honorific suffixion of *reikhs*, 'the ruler.' But, for many years, he and his brother Wala equally shared the kingship of us Ostrogoths, so they more modestly styled themselves Thiudamer and Walamer, the Known of the People and the Known of the Chosen. Even after Walamer was slain in battle, his brother modestly still refused to change and exalt his name and title. Now, however, Thiudamer having died, and his son being the one and only king—"

"Wait a moment," I said, beginning to comprehend at last. "Are you saying that my friend Thiuda—?"

"Is the son and namesake and successor of Thiudamer. He is King of the Ostrogoths, and of course our commander-in-chief. He is Thiuda-reikhs, the Ruler of the People. Or however you wish to pronounce that name, in whatever dialect or language you customarily speak. The Romans and Greeks, for instance, call him Theodoric."

2

The Singidunum house that Thiudareikhs had appropriated for his residence and praitoriaún was very close to the walls of the inner city. As I approached it—on foot, having left Velox picketed with the troop's other mounts—I saw that the Ostrogoths were engaged in one of their spasmodic harassments of the enemy. Warriors stationed at intervals were variously discharging arrows or fire-tipped arrows, using slings to throw fist-sized stones or blazing balls of oil-soaked flax up and over the wall. From the battlements and towers of the rampart there came back only a few arrows in contemptuous reply.

Thiudareikhs's house was no better and no worse than any that quartered the lowest-ranking of his men—except that (I could not help noticing) the family living in it included a comely young daughter, who blushed every time she glanced at the king or he at her. And the family members were the only servitors that Thiudareikhs had about him. He clearly did not require to surround himself with a slavish retinue of courtiers, aides, orderlies and other such hangers-on. A few of his warriors stood at the street door, to serve as runners if he had messages to send, and now and again one of his centuriones or decuriones would enter the house to make a report or receive orders. But no guards or officious lackeys impeded my going inside to see him, and there was no ceremony about his receiving me.

Nevertheless, when I entered the simple room in which he sat—divested now of helmet and armor, clad only in common tunic and hose like my own, wearing no regalia either of command or of kingship—I felt compelled to go down on one knee before him and to bow my head.

"Vái, what is this?" he protested, with a chuckle. "Friends do not kneel to friends."

372

Without raising my head, I said to the packed-earth floor, "I really do not know how to salute a king. I have never met one before."

"When you met me first, I was not a king. Let us continue to behave as informally and comradely as we did then. Stand up, Thorn."

I did, and looked him in the face, man to man. But I knew that he was someone different from the Thiuda who had first befriended me, and I think I would have known it even if I had not been apprised of his true identity. Though he wore no trappings of royalty, there was a new regality in his very visage and posture. His blue eyes still could be as merry and mischievous as they had been when he was shouting praise of his "master Thornareikhs," but they were equally likely to darken with pensiveness or to smolder hotly when he spoke of combat and conquering. He had formerly been just a handsome, likable young man. Now he was an *exceptionally* handsome and personable young monarch—tall, graceful, well muscled, with a virile mane and beard of gold, with skin bronzed by sun and wind. His manners were courtly, his nature gracious, his intelligence manifest. He needed no crown or scepter or purple to confirm his eminence among men.

373

The thought flashed unbidden through my mind: "Akh, could I but be a *woman!*" and for an instant I felt distinct envy of the blushful peasant girl who was flicking a goose-wing duster about the sill of the room's one window. But I sternly quenched both the thought and the emotion, and asked Thiudareikhs:

"How, then, do I properly address you? I would not presume on our friendship, and I would not wish to seem disrespectful in the company of your other men. How *does* a commoner address a king? Your Majesty? Sire? Meins fráuja?"

" 'Poor wretch' might be most appropriate," he said, not entirely humorously. "But in fact, during the many years that I lived at the court of Constantinople, everyone there called me Theodoric, and I became quite accustomed to that name. My tutor even gave me this golden seal, as a gift on my sixteenth birthday, with which to affix a monogram of that name upon my lessons and letters and such. I still treasure it and use it. See?"

He was seated on a bench behind a rude deal table that was littered with parchments on which there were many scribbles of chalk. Onto one of the parchments he dripped candle tallow and stamped his seal upon it and showed it to me:

I had already recognized that the word "Theodoric"—accented on the second syllable, spoken more or less as "the odder rick"—represented a fair attempt by the speakers of Greek and Latin to approximate the pronunciation of the outlander name Thiudareikhs. Besides that, it possessed an extra distinction, for it incorporated two Greek words: *theós*, meaning "god," and *doron*, meaning "gift." So the name, in addition to its original significance of "King of the People," could be taken to mean also "the God-Given." No doubt the name was patterned, as well, on that of Theodosius, once emperor of the Eastern Empire, still reverently remembered as a most able and extremely popular ruler. All in all, I thought, a monarch could hardly hope to wear a name more fraught with good associations than Theodoric.

"Theodoric I shall call you, then," I said to him. "It is a name of rich augury. Why would you refer to yourself as a poor wretch?"

He swept an arm about and said glumly, "Does this poor and wretched hovel look to you like a royal palace?"

The girl who was dusting put on a mournful and contrite look, I suppose because she could not provide more luxurious quarters for him.

"Here am I," Theodoric went on, "master of six thousand men who are hungry for both food and conquest, and I can give them but little of either. Meanwhile, the rest of my people, in our lands south and east of here, are not enjoying much better fortunes. I cannot feel myself truly a king until I have proven myself one."

"By retaking Singidunum for the Roman Empire?"

"Well, ja. I must not fail in my first kingly endeavor. But ne, not exactly for the empire, and not simply to prove myself, either."

"For what, then?"

He explained to me some things of which I had first heard mention from old Wyrd. For nearly a hundred years, said Theodoric, his branch of the Gothic nation—the Amaling line, the Ostrogoths—had been a rootless, landless, wandering people, living by forage and plunder. But then his father and uncle, the brother kings Thiudamer and Walamer, had made treaties of alliance with Emperor Leo of the Eastern Roman Empire.

"That," he said, "is why I was sent as a child to live in Constantinople. I was hardly Leo's prisoner—he had me reared right royally—but I *was* his hostage. Against my people's breaking those treaties."

In accord with their alliance, Leo had paid the two kings a substantial consueta dona, a yearly sum of gold, to have their warriors police and defend the empire's northern borders. Leo also had granted to the Ostrogoths new lands of their own in Moesia Secunda. There they had lived secure and settled lives as farmers and herders and artisans and traders, and had striven to cultivate all the refinements and enlightenments of modern civilization, and had endeavored to be worthy Roman citizens. But their security had evaporated with the recent death of the Emperor Leo, because his successor grandson, Leo II—or, rather, whoever was the regent governing in his name, was respecting no treaties with any outlanders.

Theodoric sighed and said, "The Goths of the Balting line, now— our cousins the Visigoths—have long been firmly and prosperously settled in the far-west province of Aquitania. But, as of the day old Leo died, we Ostrogoths have no place anywhere to call our own. I want to take Singidunum and hold *it* hostage, as I once was. I trust that I could thereby force the younger Leo to observe his grandfather's obligations to us. This city overlooks and commands all the river commerce traveling between the upper and lower Danuvius. Both Rome and Constantinople ought to deem it a bargain—in exchange for my giving Singidunum back to the empire—to reaffirm our right to our lands in Moesia Secunda, and to resume the gold payments for our protecting the Danuvius frontier."

"I should think so, too," I said.

"But only *if*," he reminded me. "*If* I can wrest the city from King Babai. It may take weeks for my supply train to make its way here with those ponderous siege engines, and only the liufs Guth knows whether we can endure until then. We are literally living on horsemeat and horse fodder. The Sarmatae, having no need of mounts once they were within the walls, did not bother to ransack this outer city of all its oats and hay and bran, so *we* are dining on those dainty viands. The only nourishing flesh we get to eat is what we carve from any horses slain on patrol."

Both Theodoric's stomach and mine, as if they had been prompted by his words, rumbled loudly. The girl heard, and blushed, and scurried from the room.

Theodoric went on, "I could order my men to dismantle the heavier

375

shanties out here and use the timbers to construct siege towers. But they would be too weak, after that exertion, to climb the things, let alone grapple and fight from them. I have considered other possibilities." He gestured at the chalk-scribbled parchments on the table. "I thought we might undermine the walls on the western side of the city, where they rise abruptly from that precipice edge. But it *is* a precipice — no overhang, no footholds, no practicable way to arrange protection for the digging men — and certainly the Sarmatae have readied vats of boiling water, oil, tar, whatever, to repel any attempt at that."

"Speaking of overhang," I said, "I noticed that the gate to the inner city is set within a very deep arch in the wall. And, for some reason, that entryway was built without a portcullis or any other sort of grating to prevent besiegers' getting right to the gate. Quite a few warriors could congregate in there under that arch, where the Sarmatae would be unable to hit them with either oil or missiles."

"And then what? They put their shoulders to the gate?" Theodoric grimaced. "You must also have noticed how solidly that barrier is built. No newly cut-down and unseasoned tree trunk would be strong enough to breach it, or I would already have tried. And it is too old and petrified to be burned through in less than half a lifetime. To break it down will require an iron-headed, iron-bound, chain-slung battering ram — and my train will be bringing such a thing. But when?"

The girl came back into the room and set two steaming bowls on the table. Theodoric gave her a grateful look — causing her again to blush — and motioned for me to take the bench opposite his. He immediately and ravenously began eating from one bowl, but I looked first into mine to see what we had been served. It was a gluey porridge of oats boiled in water — not even salted, as I discovered when I tasted it. I deeply regretted not having managed to bring hither the remainder of the good Vindobona foods that Amalric had stocked aboard Oppas's barge.

"Do not turn up your nose at it," said Theodoric between slurpings. "The lower-rankers get only bran husks."

So I spooned up the pap, and tried to feel grateful for having *anything* to eat under the present circumstances. And suddenly the gummy mush made me remember something — an incident of long ago — and that kindled an idea within my head. But I decided not to mention it to Theodoric, not yet, not until I had thought upon it further.

I did say to him, though, "I should like to render any help that I can. In the siege, the patrols, whatever you command."

"I believe you already have been of some help," he said, wiping his mouth and grinning. "Of the warriors in the turma who saw you shooting arrows at a gallop, at least half are now busily splicing foot-ropes to put on their own mounts. They seem to think your invention a brilliant one."

I said modestly, "Akh, a contrivance that I adapted from a plaything of my childhood days. It will take your men some while of using it, and practice with the bow at various gaits, before they can make good use of it. I could give them demonstrations and drill, if you wish me to."

"Vái, Thorn, I cannot command you to anything. Not unless and until you are one of us, one of my subjects, one of my troops."

I said wryly, "I should think that just my having shared your awful meal of silage slops would already have qualified me."

"Ne, you must take the aiths."

"The aiths?"

"Swear allegiance to your fellow Ostrogoths and fealty to me, in the presence of a responsible witness."

"Very well. Call in your adjutant, or whomever it requires."

"Ne, ne. The wench will do. Girl, stand here beside us. Try to look responsible, and not to blush." At which, of course, she did blush.

I asked, "What are the words?"

"There is no set form. Speak your own."

So I extended my right arm and hand in the rigid salute and said, as solemnly as I knew how, "I, Thorn, a freeman of no former nationality, do now declare myself to be an Ostrogoth from this day on, and a subject of my King Theodoric the Amaling, to whom I pledge my lifelong fidelity. Er . . . will that do?"

"Splendidly," he said, and returned my salute. "Girl, bear witness."

She whispered shyly, "I do bear witness," and blushed almost Falernian-wine red.

Theodoric reached out to clasp my right wrist, and I clasped his, and he said warmly, "Welcome, kinsman, friend, warrior, good man and true."

"Thags izvis, and most sincerely. I feel that I have a people at last. But is there no more to the ceremony?"

"Well, I could have our chaplain baptize you as an Arian, but that is not a requisite."

"Then, with your permission, I will take my leave. The faber armorum bade me to return to his workshop for my helmet fittings."

"Ja. Go, Thorn. I will resume my gloomy perusal of my chalked diagrams. Perhaps some new notion will occur to me. Or I may just lie down"—he glanced at the girl, who blushed redder yet—"and meditate for a while. That might invite my genius, or even the junone of a serving wench, to visit me with inspiration."

I was out of the room and out of the house before I realized that I had cheated to some degree when swearing my allegiance to king and kinfolk. I had taken the aiths as "Thorn, a freeman." I wondered if it ever would or could matter that I had neglected to pledge to Theodoric—even silently, even only in my mind—the lifelong fidelity of Veleda, a freewoman.

✠   ✠   ✠

Before I went back downhill to the faber's smithy, I went to take a closer look at the inner city's gate. It was dark night by now, and the Ostrogoths were no longer ringing the wall and flinging missiles over it, and the paved open area before the gate was empty of any other people. In the dark I was able to scuttle across that open space without attracting notice—or at least without having to dodge arrows—from the Sarmatian sentries up above, and once I was under the arch I was invisible to them.

The entryway was broad enough to admit into the city the widest wagon ever built, and high enough to accommodate the most towering wagonload. But the darkness was of course even deeper in there than outside, so I had to make my examination of the gate mostly by feel. I ran my hands all over it—over both of its panels and the wicket door inset in one of them—from side to side and as high as I could reach. I found that the beams and planks of which the gate was built were indeed as massive as they had looked from a distance. And no doubt the planks that I could feel on this surface, running crosswise, were backed by others running vertically, maybe even another backing or two of planks running diagonally. And behind, the panels would be secured by immense side-to-side crossbars socketed in slots in the stone walls. The gate had no hinges that could be pried loose; each portal was hung to swivel on pivots top and bottom.

However, despite all that impregnability of design, and despite the two panels' being so formidably strengthened by iron staples and bosses, the entire gate *was* basically of wood, and it was old, and wood shrinks over the years. So I could feel a gap where the two panels met in the middle, and a gap at their bottom, between them and the pavement of the entryway, and a gap between each panel and its wooden jamb on either side of the stone arch, and lesser cracks around the edges of the inset wicket door. The widest of those gaps, the one at the roadway level, was only about two fingers in breadth, and none of the others was much more than a single finger's breadth. In other words, they all were too narrow to admit a pry bar big enough to do any useful forcing, even with any number of men putting their combined strength to it. Still, there *were* gaps, and *something* in the nature of destructiveness could be inserted into them. I thought I knew what that something might be.

So I broached my idea—in part, anyway—to the faber armorum and his Ostrogoth supervisor, the custos Ansila. The faber already had shaped and put together the shell of my new helmet. Now he laid a wad of cloth on top of my head—"because," he said, "there will be leather padding inside when the helmet is complete"—settled the shell on that, and proceeded to make chalk marks on the metal to show him where my cheek lappets and nosepiece were to be fastened on. As he worked, I said:

"I notice, faber, that some parts of this helmet are bound together with rivets. But other plates seem to be somehow *forged* together."

"Brazed together," Ansila corrected me.

"Ja," said the faber. "To braze two pieces of metal I score them with many shallow notches and put a spelter of powdered brass between. I clamp the work together and heat it red-hot and hammer it until the parts are inseparable."

I asked, "Could you assemble by that method a new sort of weaponry of my own pattern?"

He said haughtily, "I have never yet failed to fabricate anything asked of me that could be made of metal."

"Then lend me your chalk," I said, "and something on which to draw."

He and the custos looked on curiously as I sketched on a wooden shingle the thing I had in mind.

"Vái! What kind of weapon is that?" demanded Ansila. "It looks like nothing but an overgrown pea pod. A pea pod as long as my forearm."

"It is not a weapon for killing people," I said. "It is for breaking things. Think of it as the trumpet that brought down the walls of Jaíriko."

"But you could make that yourself, young man," said the faber, peering at my drawing. "Bend it from a piece of scrap metal, with the simplest of tools."

379

"Ne," I said. "I must fill it with the trumpet's noise, so to speak. And then it must be sealed as tightly as a wine bottle is sealed against spoilage. Sealed so tightly that not even its trumpet noise can get out."

"Akh, so that is why you wish it brazed. Ja, I can do that."

"Good. I shall need at least a score of the things. And as soon as possible."

"I said I *can* do that. But why should I?"

"Ja, why should he?" Ansila said testily. "I am the custos of all armory and weaponry. I give the orders."

"Best give this one then, Custos Ansila. That way the faber—and you too—can work on these weapons through the night, before Theodoric has to give you the order tomorrow. I assure you that he will."

✠ ✠ ✠

"*Oats?!*" Theodoric exclaimed in disbelief, when I accosted him while he was still getting dressed next morning. "You would batter down the gate with *oats?* Have you been deranged by hunger, Thorn?"

"Well, I cannot guarantee that this will work," I said. "But I did once see it work most magically on a less ambitious undertaking."

"Work *how?*"

He was examining the object I had brought, one of the several that Ansila and the faber had made overnight. In finished form, made of thin sheet iron, it looked rather less like a pod than my drawing of it had, and of course nothing like a trumpet. It more resembled a thick, single-edged sword blade, squared off at each end. And it was not quite finished, for I had told the faber to leave one of its ends open.

"Through that opening," I explained, "we fill it with the oat grains, tamped as full as it will hold. Then we pour in water to the top. Then the faber puts a cap on that end and brazes it tight shut. Then I and some other men rush these things to the gate, for we must work in a hurry. We insert the narrow edges of them into the cracks and gaps around the gate, as many of the things as possible, end to end. And we hammer them, like wedges, as far and firmly into the cracks as we can."

I paused for breath. Theodoric was regarding me meditatively, but with the hint of a smile. "And then?" he asked.

"Then we fall back and wait. So tightly packed and confined, the swelling grains ought to burst their containers with tremendous force. Not enough, perhaps, to bring the whole gate crashing down. But enough, I hope, to buckle the panels so that they snap the crossbars behind. And enough, I pray, to make the gate vulnerable to our assault—with only a raw tree trunk for a ram, wielded by your brawniest men."

Still regarding me with that assessing look, Theodoric said, "I do not possess a plan of Singidunum's fortifications, but I know the wall to be awesomely thick. There is probably a second gate solidly closing the other end of that arch."

"Then we must simply do the forcing procedure all over again. There is no way the defenders can prevent us. Of course, if and when we do get into the city, there is another aspect to consider. We will be six thousand going in against nine thousand."

Theodoric dismissed that with a wave. "You yourself dispatched three battle-hardened Sarmatae warriors. If each of my more experienced men is able merely to match your prowess, we could go confidently in against *eighteen* thousand."

"If we get in at all," I said. "But we risk nothing by trying the means I propose. And I personally would rather employ the oats this way than have to go on eating the slimy mush made of them."

"So would I," Theodoric said with a laugh. "Of course I will try your plan. Did you doubt that I would? I will immediately send men to chop down a tree for a ram. Meanwhile, you run and tell Ansila to find himself some assistants to go on making these . . . whatever you call these things. Let the faber be freed of that toil so he can finish your armoring. If this clever expedient of yours does succeed, you will want to be one of the first through the gate. And for that you need helmet, corselet and buckler. Hábái ita swe!"

That was the first direct order Theodoric ever gave me as my king and commander, but I would often afterward hear him utter that imperious final phrase, and would see it written at the end of every order and edict he ever published: "Be it so!"

381

3

hen I went again to the armory, the custos Ansila dutifully complied with Theodoric's instructions, setting a number of the smith's apprentices to the cutting, bending and brazing of the oat-grain containers. Then, while the master faber resumed his more painstaking work of completing my helmet, Ansila said to me:

"Let us see what else you will need. Show me your sword." I un-sheathed it, and the armorer sniffed disdainfully on seeing that it was the standard Roman army gladius. "Have you ever fought with that?" he asked. "Slain with it?"

"Once, ja, and it slew well enough." I did not tell him that its only victim had been an old and unarmed Hun woman.

He grunted. "Best keep it, then, for this battle. You will, of course, eventually want a Gothic snake-pattern blade. But that must be made of a weight and length and grip especially fitted to your own weight and arm length and hand size and style of fighting. For now, use the sword you are accustomed to, inferior though it is. And here, take any one of these bucklers. They do not have to be suited to the individual. They are all alike."

I lifted one down from an overlapping row of them hung on a rafter. It was not the large, heavy, rectangular Roman scutum shield, designed to hide and protect a man's whole body. It was round, made only of tight-woven wicker, except for its central boss and rim of iron, and it was no bigger than a basket cover, because its intended use was only to parry an enemy's blows or fend off his missiles. I took hold of the hand-grip behind the hollowed-out iron boss, and thrashed the buckler about for a bit to get the feel of it.

"Now," the custos went on, "you must also wait a while to have your personal corselet made, because that will likewise have to be specially fitted to you, and the making of it is a long process. The heavy leather is first boiled, then carefully molded to your torso while it is soft, then pounded into final shape, then baked to nearly iron-hardness. However, for the coming battle, you will need *some* kind of corselet. Here in this corner are a number of spares. Find the one that fits you best."

I could see why they were spares. All were much scuffed, many were gashed or pierced with holes or scorched by fire, and several still bore the stains of their former wearers' blood. I also saw that every corselet, besides having been molded to fit a particular warrior's body, had also been artfully shaped to exaggerate his shoulder breadth and his chest and stomach and back muscles. To make a choice for myself from among the heap of castoffs was easy. Since I was considerably shorter and slighter than even the smallest adult male Goth I had yet seen, I picked out the littlest corselet—which was not very little—and Ansila helped me hold up the front and back segments of it while I tightened the thongs on either side that bound them together.

Then he stepped back and looked me over, rather skeptically, and muttered, "A hazelnut in a walnut's shell."

I did feel somewhat ridiculous, with my slender neck protruding from a leather torso that was muscled like that of Hercules, and with the quilted leather skirts hanging below my knees. Still, this was the only armor available to me, so I said:

"It is commodious, ja, but it does not impede my movements. It will serve."

The custos shrugged. "Then you lack only the heavy leggings, and those you can procure for yourself. Here, the faber has your helmet ready. Try it on and see if it requires any adjustments."

It did not. Heavy though it was in my hands, it did not feel so on my head. The soft leather padding inside fitted snugly, and the straps depending from it buckled neither too tightly nor too loosely under my chin. The nosepiece properly covered my nose, but did not touch it. The lappets hung from in front of my ears exactly to my cheek-bones and down to my jawlines. The neck guard was deep enough to ward off any blows there, but not so low as to scrape against the back of my corselet. I fancied that I must look as formidable as Theodoric had looked when he approached me on the field. I was beginning to feel quite the genuine Ostrogoth warrior, until the faber said gruffly:

"I advise you, young man, to start growing a good Gothic beard. It will protect that exposed and skinny throat of yours."

383

I made no reply to that, but said of the helmet, "It does not have a top slot for the attachment of a parade plume."

Ansila all but roared: "Vái! Goths do not parade like preening Romans! When a Goth moves his legs, it is to march forward against some foe! When a Goth dons a helmet, it is to go into combat, not for ceremonial review by some effeminate Roman consul!"

The faber said, "Neither did I give the helmet any other embellishment. No raised or etched decorative figures. For one reason, I did not have time. For another, I cannot know what ornamentation might be appropriate, because I do not know what rank Theodoric has accorded you."

"None at all, that I know of," I said cheerfully. "But I thank you, comrades both—and your apprentices—for all your good work. Thags izei. I will return when the time comes to put the finishing caps on our trumpets of Jaíriko."

✠ ✠ ✠

Those men that Theodoric sent to chop down a suitable tree, he sent well upriver of the city, so the Sarmatae would not hear the noise of their activity. The men picked a tall, straight, strong cypress to fell, because that tree has many but not immense branches growing horizontally from the trunk. When the tree was on the ground, the men lopped some of those branches entirely off, but others along the length of the trunk they only shortened, so the stumps would serve as carrying handles for the warriors who would wield the ram. Then they whittled one end of the trunk to a blunt point, and hardened that in a hot fire. Then they floated the great thing downstream along the Savus, snaked it ashore and, under cover of darkness, hauled it uphill and dropped it at a place that was concealed but convenient for the assault.

"Very well, Thorn," said Theodoric. "The next move is yours."

"I have never stormed a city before," I said. "What is the best time? Daylight or darkness?"

"In this case, daylight, because the cityfolk are in there among the Sarmatae. I should prefer that we be able to tell them apart, so that we do not slay too many noncombatants."

"Then I suggest," I said, but with some hesitancy, "that we prepare the oat containers and hasten to get them placed just before dawn. I have no way of predicting how long they will take to burst, but I should *suppose* it would be sometime during the daylight hours. Perhaps not, though."

"In that event," Theodoric said indifferently, "the citizens must take their chances. Noon or midnight, if and when the gate comes down, we go in. As you say, then, start the preparations shortly before dawn."

He assigned six men to go with me, because the armory had by now constructed twenty-eight of the "trumpets of Jaíriko"—as everyone was now calling the things—and I had calculated that a man could carry four of them, plus a mallet, and still run fast. It took us seven not long to fill all the trumpets with oats. Because it was necessary to get them sealed as nearly simultaneously as possible, the faber's assistants put their twenty-eight iron caps on the forge all together, and heated them to red-hotness. Then I and my six helpers poured water into the containers, the faber did whatever it was that he did with his brazing spelter, clamped the cap on one trumpet after another, and he, Ansila and their apprentices all frantically did the hammering to seal them.

As soon as the trumpets had cooled enough to touch, I and my men each tucked four of them under our arms and picked up a wooden mallet apiece. We hurried uphill to the last row of houses before the open space in front of the gate, and there Theodoric and a host of archers were waiting in concealment.

"Ready?" said Theodoric, evincing no excitement at all. He pointed eastward. "The dawn is just beginning to blush, rather like that serving girl of mine. I think, from now on, I shall call the wench Aurora."

I perceived that he was being deliberately casual, to put all his men at ease—or me, anyway, since that sunrise yonder was heralding the first day of my life as an Ostrogoth warrior.

"When I give the signal," he said, "my bowmen will rain arrows over the ramparts. Under that cover, Thorn, you and your trumpeters should be safe to make the run. Let us commence, then. Be it so! Warriors, to position!" He led the archers as they poured out into the open, into the street that led to the gate. "Take stance! Take aim! Let fly!"

There was a noise like the sudden gust of a mighty gale as those many shafts flew together. Instantly, Theodoric and his archers were nocking new ones to their bows, and thereafter discharged them quite as rapidly as old Wyrd had used to do.

I cried, "My men! Follow me!" and we pelted for the entryway. The Sarmatian sentries above must have been so taken by surprise by Theodoric's flocks of arrows that they did not even notice us in the predawn dusk, for none of their answering missiles came our way, and all seven of us got in under the arch without a scratch.

I had already demonstrated to the men what we were to do, so there

385

was no time wasted. I and one other began wedging our containers, end to end, in the gap between the bottom of the gate panels and the paving stones, and hammering them in and under there as far as we could. Other men attended to the cracks at the side jambs, and the crack where the panels met in the middle, and the cracks around the wicket door. One man stood on another's shoulders, so he could place the things even higher up the vertical gaps than I had earlier been able to reach.

The Sarmatae inside surely heard the noise of our labors, and I could imagine their bewilderment. For defenders who might have been dreading to hear the powerful thuds of a battering ram, we must have sounded as if we were only politely knocking for admittance. When I and my six men were done, one of them had a single container left over, and was looking anxiously for some unoccupied place in which to jam it, but I said:

"Keep it. Bring it back with us. If we watch it, we will know how these others are behaving. It ought to tell us when—or if—they swell and burst, and whether that bursting appears likely to accomplish what we hope it will. Now, all together, let us make the run back to shelter. Go!"

Again we arrived unscathed, and Theodoric ordered his own men to cease that storm of arrows and to fall back behind the protecting row of houses. He and I had debated as to what the Ostrogoths should do while waiting for the trumpets of Jaíriko to do their work, and we had decided that there was not much *to* be done. Keeping up the harassment by missiles would not prevent the Sarmatae from going to see what had been done to their gate, and would only waste our arrows and energy. Anyway, even if the defenders came right up to the inside of that gate, they could not discern what we had done to it, and they certainly would not open it to examine the outside.

So Theodoric merely mustered his centuriones and decuriones and told them what their various bodies of warriors were to do, when and if the gate was weakened. First, of course, the biggest, heaviest and strongest men were immediately to dash forward from concealment with our makeshift, hand-carried battering ram. If, when the first gate was smashed, we found another gate tight shut inside the arch, the men with the ram would back out, and all our other men would stand in place, just as they were standing now, for however long it took us to prepare and place another set of Jaíriko trumpets, and wait for *them* to do their work. Then the ram would go in again. Whenever it finally *did* break through into the city, a turma of mounted men bearing contus lances would gallop in—these to be led by Theodoric himself—to mow down any close-packed crowd of defenders waiting right inside the gate. Next four contubernia of archers would surge in, to pick off any defenders perched high atop the wall or on the rooftops. Finally, all the rest of us six thousand, myself included, were to go in on foot with only swords and bucklers.

"The men are to commit slaughter," Theodoric flatly told the officers. "To confront and slay every foeman who stands against us, to seek out and slay everyone who tries to hide or flee. Take no prisoners. Succor no wounded. Only have your men try to avoid, insofar as possible, killing the hapless cityfolk. A warrior should be able to recognize the women and children, at least, and spare those. Habái ita swe!"

The centuriones and decuriones silently snapped their arms up, iron-rigid, in the Ostrogoth salute. Theodoric went on:

"Also hear this, and impress it on every man of your command. If any among them should encounter a foeman who might conceivably be King Babai or the legatus Camundus, he is to refrain from striking a blow. Those two are mine. If for some reason I fail to find and slay them, they are to be let to live until the city is taken, and then I will arrange for their execution. But remember—if during the battle I do not kill Babai and Camundus, no one does. Be it so!"

The officers again snapped the salute, and this time Theodoric returned it. Then the officers went to march their separate bodies of troops into the sidehill streets, where they would remain invisible to the Sarmatian sentries, and there disposed the various columns in the order in which they would storm the city. As the men dispersed, I remarked to Theodoric:

"Are you not making two very brash assumptions? First, that my simple weapons will work? And, if they do, that we will so surely take the city?"

"Akh, friend Thorn," he said jovially, clapping an arm around my shoulders. "Of the many saggwasteis fram aldrs that are sung about the hero Jalk the Giant-Killer, one old saggws relates that he somehow bested a giant by means of a beanstalk. I forget how that was done, but I shall have faith that Thorn's oats will somehow serve as heroically. As for the rest, well . . . I try to emulate my royal father. He used to say that he never doubted of victory, and that was why he never failed to achieve it. But tell me, friend, when did you eat last? Come and break your fast with me. My wench newly named Aurora is cooking a brisket

387

of meat newly named venison. That is to say, part of the remains of a defunct war-horse."

"I must keep an eye on this thing," I said, and showed him the metal container, and told him why.

"Bring it along. We can watch it while we eat."

Well, it did nothing during the brief time that we were at table; we could hardly have expected it to. I thanked Theodoric for the meal—and thanked Aurora, too, making her blush—and took the container and myself off to the side street where waited the turma to which I had been assigned.

And I waited, and I waited, and so did the other six thousand Ostrogoths wait, the whole day long. During that day, I think almost a thousand of the six thousand made excuse to amble along the street where my turma was posted, to take a look at me and my silent trumpet of Jaíriko. Early on, those looks were merely curious or wondering. But as the hours dragged on, the looks became suspicious, derisory, even resentful. After all, every man was in helmet and armor, and the day got hot, and we sweated and itched inside our metal and leather integuments, and the only nourishment (dispensed only once, at high noon) was bran biscuits and tepid water, and we were bidden not to make any noise with our weapons, and to talk only in low tones, and not to laugh or sing—as if there was anything to laugh or sing about.

Sundown brought some alleviation of our long-drawn-out torment, for the dusk was cool. But still my trumpet made not a sound or a twitch, and there was nothing for us to do but go on waiting and hoping that it would. So that is what we did, though there was much grumbling in the ranks. When the night came down, the men resignedly prepared to sleep in place on the hard street stones, and each turma's optio appointed men to take turns staying awake and alert. Since I was not one of those selected in my turma, I gave my container to our optio, a grizzled warrior named Daila, and asked that each succeeding guard be ordered to watch it.

"And wake me instantly," I said, "if it swells or bursts or fizzes or does *anything.*"

The optio gave a baleful look at the object I had handed him, and another at me in my ludicrously oversized armor, and said drily:

"Little beetle, I think you can sleep soundly and all night long. My father was a farmer. I could have told you that oats take at least seven days to germinate. If we have to wait for these to put out roots enough to pry apart those gates, we will *all* be sleeping right here for most of the summer."

I could only murmur, and halfheartedly, "I do not think the oats actually have to *grow* . . ." But Daila had gone off, to post the guards of the first watch.

He was right about one thing. I slept all night undisturbed, until the blushing dawn woke me. I hurried over to the guard, who yawned and tossed my container at me, grunting, "Nothing to report." I caught the thing, regarding it with almost as much contempt as the guard had done, and made my way through the other waking and stretching warriors to the optio Daila, and asked his permission to go and seek out Theodoric.

At the turma of lancers I was told that Theodoric, after having spent the night waiting like everyone else, had now gone to his praitoriaún. So I trudged off to his house, and I was so bowed down with discouragement and dejection that I think my leather skirts must have dragged the ground.

"Well, so much for that," sighed Theodoric, when I gave him the doleful news. "It was worth the try. Let me at least reward you for the try, Thorn. There is some of that horsemeat left." He called to Aurora to bring food. When she did, he handed her the mute trumpet and said, "Here, take this out of our sight."

It was a despondently silent meal that he and I shared, sitting there in our unneeded armor. Theodoric apparently had no alternative siege ideas to propose. Neither did I and, if I had, I would not now have dared to mention them. So, except for the sound of our chewing of the tough meat and our sips at our water goblets, there was not another noise until a small and whimpery one came from the kitchen:

"Eek!"

Theodoric and I looked at one another across the table, then simultaneously sprang up and through the door. The girl was backed against one wall of the tiny kitchen, and for a change she was pale instead of blush-pink, and she was staring wide-eyed at the brick cooking hearth. On one of its flat ledges she had deposited the trumpet, and evidently later had laid a long-handled ladle there, without noticing that she had propped it across the metal container. She was gazing now at that ladle, because it was creeping, seemingly of its own volition, almost eerily, sideways along the ledge. Even as we three watched, it slid a little more rapidly, overbalanced at the brink of the ledge and toppled onto the earthen floor.

389

"The trumpet sounds!" Theodoric exulted. "It has bulged!"

"But ever so slightly," I muttered.

"Perhaps enough. Bless you, Aurora!" He pecked a kiss on her pale cheek, then beckoned urgently to me. "Thorn, come!"

He clapped on his helmet, seized up the contus lance he had laid aside while we ate and hurried from the house. I put on my own helmet and followed him. We had no sooner got outdoors than we heard another sound commence. It was a low thrumming that seemed to vibrate all the air roundabout. Theodoric ran for the street that led directly to the gate, and I followed. As we ran, the noise ranged upward in pitch, to a sort of wordless singing, then to a shrill keening. The Ostrogoths we passed were all standing, milling somewhat, looking befuddled, tightly clutching their weapons. Many of their officers were craning their heads curiously around the edges of the sheltering houses, looking in the direction of the gate. Theodoric did not peer from concealment; he incautiously ran right to the edge of the open area fronting the entryway. But no arrows came down from the battlements; the Sarmatae must have been as perplexed and confused as were our own men.

When I caught up to Theodoric he was pointing and laughing and doing a kind of gleeful dance. That unearthly, air-quivering noise was coming from the gate itself, for it was being strained and imperceptibly deformed at every point where I and my men had inserted a container, and it was loudly complaining of its agony. The keening now became mixed with other noises: the groans of stubborn old wood being bent, the splinterings of overstressed wood giving way, the screeches of spikes and bolts being twisted. I could see and hear iron staples and bosses wrench themselves from the surface beams here and there, each with a harsh rasp or twang of noise.

Suddenly the weakest part of the gate, the wicket door inset in the right-hand panel, buckled and partly shattered. The wicket had of course been made of a size to admit one person at a time. When it splintered, we could see that the upper part of its opening was blocked by a crossbar inside. But the wicket was now a tangle of broken wood that could be cleared to make an entrance as wide as a man and half as high.

Theodoric instantly wheeled and shouted to the nearest waiting turma of foot soldiers, "Ten men with swords! To the gate! Break open that wicket! Get inside and raise all crossbars!"

The first ten men in that column unhesitatingly dashed forward and across the open area. The Sarmatian sentries above had regained their wits enough to send down a hail of arrows, so only nine of the ten men reached the gate, while Theodoric and I dodged to safety behind the corner of a nearby house. The first warriors to arrive at the buckled wicket hacked at it with their swords and tore at the fragments with their hands, and one after another the nine men stooped and lunged through the jagged opening. For all they knew, they were committing suicide by doing so, if there were Sarmatae waiting just inside, but they went eagerly.

Theodoric shouted now, "Bring up the ram!"

The blunt point of the thing poked out from behind the row of houses where it had been lurking. The long trunk had to be slowly manhandled around that corner by its carriers. But when it was in the main street, pointed toward us, the leading man bawled, "Left! Right! Double pace! Left-right! Left-right-run!" and the great ram came up the street as fast as the many men propelling it could race.

Although the other nine men had only just got inside the gate, and there was no telling what they might be doing or what might have happened to them in there, Theodoric waved the ram-bearers on. He gave a commanding sweep of his lance, ending with it pointing at the gate. He meant that they were not to pause for further orders, but to continue in their present headlong rush, gaining impetus as they did so, and they were to hit the gate regardless of whether it opened or showed signs of weakening or even if it stood as firm as before.

391

But just then the gate did open inward, though only a crack of about three hands' span, enough for me to see a commotion of indistinct activity within. In fact, as we would all soon realize, several things were happening at once. Our nine men had lunged through the wicket to find that they were—as Theodoric had earlier conjectured—actually between two gates, and the farther one was solidly shut. Nevertheless, as commanded, they proceeded to wrestle the two immense crossbars of the outer gate from their sockets in the arch walls and their brackets on the gate panels. The men were just starting to tug those panels open when the *inner* gate miraculously also began to open. The Sarmatian gate guards had ill-advisedly chosen that moment to emerge and investigate the strange noises they had been hearing from beyond that inner gate.

All in the same moment, our battering ram struck the crack already opened in the outer gate. The panels slammed inward against the arch walls, and such was the impetus of the running ram-bearers that their weapon went on to burst wide the inner gate as well. What with that great ram hurtling through and the heavy gate panels flinging open, there ensued a turmoil of tossed and mashed and falling and flailing bodies in there, and a clamor of yells, curses and screams. But what most caught my eye was what looked like a sudden small snowstorm of glinting metal—my numerous trumpets of Jaíriko flung high and wide and all about.

Theodoric shouted, "Lancers! Rally on me!" Then, without waiting for them, he ran for the gate, heedless of the arrows still pouring down from the walls, leaping over the bodies of two of the ram-bearers who had been felled by those missiles.

I was almost impelled by his ardor for combat to run after him. But I restrained myself and waited while the mounted lancers, then the contubernia of archers, then two or three turmae of dismounted swordsmen pelted past me, the foot soldiers all holding their bucklers overhead for protection against the deluge of arrows. I waited until my own assigned turma came by, and, as I fell in with them, I flashed a broad, triumphant, gloating grin at our optio, Daila.

4

I can give no real account of the battle for Singidunum. No man who took part in it could. Of any battle, the individual combatant can recount only the minute fragment in which he participated. During that, he sees none but his nearest fellows and foes, knows only whether those few are advancing or retreating, killing or dying. The rest of the action is as remote from him as if it took place on another continent, and he never knows whether it is being won or lost until it is concluded.

Even during his own small part in the battle, he may be less aware of the fighting in which he is engaged than he is of a multitude of inconsequential other things. A trained and experienced warrior can almost unconsciously wield his weapon and dodge an enemy's, while he gives his closer attention to annoying distractions. I myself had had enough practice at swordsmanship so that I was less concerned with doing it properly than I was with worrisome trifles:

The sweat that streamed from my forehead and blurred my vision . . . the irritation of a chafing rash under my arms, from having lived so long in my armor . . . the street dust, kicked up by so many struggling men, that clogged my nose and stung my eyes . . . the hotness and heaviness of my feet, swollen from having been so long booted . . . the overwhelming tumult of shouts and grunts and oaths and screams . . . the deafening din of sword blows on helmets and shields and corselets, deafening not just because those sounds were loud, but because they were stunningly concussive, like having one's ears clapped hard by cupped hands . . . the sickly sweet smell of spilled blood, and the stench of excrement voided by the bowels of the dying, and the acrid odor of fear, fear everywhere . . .

✠   ✠   ✠

There were fewer arrows raining from above, as our turma ran toward the ruined gateway in a column of fours, holding our bucklers above our heads. But we had to thread our way among many bodies, some of them limp, some feebly moving, on the open pavement before the wall and in the tunnel-like arch leading through it. Once inside the wall, our turma dissolved, and it was every man for himself.

As we spilled into the city, we met no organized resistance. If there had earlier been a heavily armed phalanx planted there to repel our invasion, Theodoric and his lancers had effectively scattered it. And his bowmen had easily picked off most of the Sarmatae atop this section of the wall, because the defenders' perch up there was only a wooden shelf with no protection behind. More bodies lay everywhere about the entrance and at the base of the wall, but there were at least twice as many Sarmatae as Ostrogoths.

I, like every other man of our turma, went running into the city's warren of streets, seeking an enemy to close with. And I stayed close to our optio, Daila, deeming him the likeliest to find action—and the best man to have near me when I found some. He and I passed numerous couples and knots and crowds of men fighting, but the Ostrogoths among them were clearly holding their own, so we did not interfere. Of other people, we espied only the occasional fearful face of a townsman or a woman, peering apprehensively from behind a shutter or through the crack of a door or over the edge of a roof.

Then, in one of the city's squares, we came upon a fiercely fighting group that Daila *did* elbow his way into, and I followed his lead. Six or seven Ostrogoths were dueling with about the same number of Sarmatae, and those latter were ranged in a protective ring about one other man. He was elderly, unarmed, clearly terrified and—considering the circumstances—very oddly dressed, for he wore a rich green toga hemmed with gold. Even above the clash of arms, he could be heard loudly crying for mercy in a number of languages: "Clementia! Eleéo! Armahaírtei!"

When the optio and I joined the fray, the Sarmatae were soon overpowered. But I must confess that I did not do much toward accomplishing that small victory. Though I delivered several sword blows, I discovered that my Roman gladius merely glanced off the Sarmatian scale armor. The Ostrogoths' snake-pattern blades did not; they sheared right through it. Three of the Sarmatae fell, and the others scampered away. Then one of the Ostrogoths made a lunge with his sword at the toga-clad old man, but Daila moved faster. To my vast astonishment, though, he did not slash at the old man, but skewered the Ostrogoth, who fell like a log. None of that man's fellow warriors showed any dismay at that, or even any surprise; they simply dashed off after their fleeing foes. But I exclaimed to the optio:

"You slew one of our own!"

"Ja," he grunted. "The man was disobeying orders, and disobedience must be instantly punished. This creature he was about to kill can only be the legatus Camundus."

The creature was abjectly babbling thanks for his deliverance, again in various languages, and might have thrown himself upon both of us in grateful embrace. But Daila leaned down behind him and, with a sudden, shallow, slicing stroke of his sword, severed the hamstrings at the back of the old man's knees. Camundus shrieked and toppled as if his legs had been totally cut out from under him.

"That will keep him where we know where to find him," growled the optio. "Little beetle, you stay and guard him from further molestation until Theodoric is ready for—*Look out!*"

Daila had glimpsed the lurking rooftop archer, and leapt aside even as he shouted, but the shout came too late for me. An arrow struck me like a mallet blow in the right side of my back. The impact threw me forward and to one side, and I fell prone on the cobblestones, my helmet hitting with such a crash that I was knocked nearly unconscious.

Dimly I heard Daila say, "Too bad, little beetle. But I will get him for that." And I dimly heard his boots pounding off into the distance. Well, he was only obeying orders. Theodoric had commanded, "Succor no wounded."

I could also hear the hamstrung legatus whining and blubbering, lying somewhere near me, but I was too dazed and aching to open my eyes to see where he was. I felt absolutely drained and flaccid, just from the shock of having been struck down, but I found that my right hand still clutched my sword, so I tried with that to lever myself over onto my back. However, the arrow that had pierced my leather armor was still embedded there, and the protruding shaft prevented me from turning more than partway supine. I might have squirmed and twisted to break the shaft, but I lay still, to recover and conserve my strength, because I heard other bootsteps. The injured legatus again began loudly pleading, not for mercy this time, but for help, and only in Greek: "Boé! Boethéos!"

A hoarse voice answered him, in heavily accented Greek, "Be easy, Camundus. First let me make sure your assailant is indeed dead."

I opened my eyes just enough of a slit to see a cone-helmeted, scale-armored warrior approaching me, apparently one of those who had earlier been guarding the legatus and had been routed. He glared down at my motionless body in its arrow-pierced, oversized armor, and muttered, "By Ares, are the Goths sending their children to war now?" Then he lifted his sword high with both hands to deliver my deathblow.

Summoning all my strength, I drove my blade upward between his legs, under his corselet's skirts, deep into his body there. The man uttered the loudest and most hair-raising scream I had ever heard in my life. He fell over backward, away from me, gushing blood from his crotch, and he scuttled and scrabbled on the pavement like a frenzied crab, not trying to get up or to get at me, but only to get away from his pain, which must have been agonizing.

I slowly and groggily climbed to my own feet, and had to stand for a moment, choking back nausea and waiting for my head to cease whirling. Then I stepped over to the fallen man and knelt on his chest to stop his flapping about. Because I could not breach his armor, I forced his head back to bare his throat and, as mercifully quickly as I could, sawed through his neck until my sword was stopped by the bone at the back.

That was the only hand-to-hand action in which I personally engaged during the battle for Singidunum, and I came out of it without so much as a scar for a memento. I was well slathered with blood, but it was all Sarmatian blood. Both that warrior and Daila had thought me impaled by the arrow that had felled me. But I was giving thanks to Mars, Ares, Tiw and whatever other war gods might exist, for my having been on this occasion "a hazelnut in a walnut shell." The arrow had pierced only my ill-fitting corselet and slid past my rib cage without even scratching me.

By dint of some contortion, I reached around behind me and managed to snap off the protruding shaft. Then I strode over to the legatus, who flinched away from my gory sword and bleated, "Armaha írtei! Clementia!"

"Akh, slaváith!" I snarled at him, and he kept his mouth shut while I used the gold-bordered hem of his fine toga to wipe my sword. I grabbed Camundus under the arms and dragged him away from the scene of carnage—his own injured legs leaving blood smears on the cobbles—to a deep-set doorway on the farther edge of the square.

We sheltered in there all the rest of that day, during which occasional bands of warriors—Sarmatae being chased by Ostrogoths or vice versa—either pounded through the square or paused to turn and fight there. By midafternoon, the passersby in the square were no longer pursuing, being pursued or stopping to fight, because they were all Ostrogoths, occupied with the final details of the city's purgation. Most of them were scouting for any Sarmatae in hiding, and making sure that all the fallen ones were thoroughly lifeless. Others were searching out and carrying or helping our own salvageable wounded to wherever the lekeis was working. I learned later that our warriors had combed every last building in Singidunum, and every room in every building, even to the rere-dorters, but had come upon very few Sarmatae cowering in hiding; almost every one had stood bravely in the open and fought until he died.

Toward sundown, two men came walking leisurely into the square where Camundus and I still sat in the doorway. They were both in scuffed and bloodstained armor, but unhelmeted—though one of them seemed to be carrying his helmet, or something like it, in a leather bag. They were Theodoric and Daila. The optio was bringing the king to show him where the legatus had been left for safekeeping—and evidently also to show Theodoric the corpse of his friend Thorn, because both the men exclaimed in surprise at finding me alive and still attending to my assigned duty of guarding Camundus.

"I might have known that Daila was mistaken!" Theodoric said with relief, clapping me on the shoulder instead of returning my salute. "The Thorn who could so dashingly play a clarissimus could as convincingly play dead."

"By the hammer of Thor, little beetle," Daila said with heavy humor, "you ought always to wear outsized armor! Maybe we all ought."

"It would have been a pity," Theodoric went on, "if you had got yourself killed before seeing us complete the conquest of the city, since you helped so greatly to get us in here. I am happy to report that every man of the nine thousand Sarmatae has been exterminated."

"And their King Babai?" I inquired

"He did the proper thing. He waited for me, and then fought as bravely and fiercely as any of his warriors. He might even have bested me had he been younger. So, in due respect, I accorded him a clean, swift death." He gestured to Daila, who was carrying the leather bag. "Thorn, meet the late King Babai."

The optio, grinning, opened the bag and held up by the hair Babai's severed head. Though it dripped blood and other substances from its neck, its eyes were still open, glaring, and its mouth was fixed in a rictus of rage. It might have been the head of any Sarmatian warrior, except that it was banded by a gold circlet.

Camundus, who had been whinnying behind us and trying to interpose a word, now fell suddenly silent, horrified. At that, we all three turned to stare at him. He had to open and shut his mouth several times before he could speak.

"Babai," he said in a creaky voice. "Babai *tricked* me into letting him take the city."

"The creature speaks ill of the dead, who cannot defend themselves," said Daila. "Also he lies. When we found this creature, he had an accompanying bodyguard of Sarmatae, ready to kill on his behalf."

"Of course he lies," said Theodoric. "If he spoke the truth, he would by now be decently dead. After losing the city, he would, like any good Roman, have fallen on his own sword. Instead, he must employ mine."

Theodoric drew his blade and, without any ceremony, with one stroke, sliced open both Camundus's fine toga and his abdomen. The legatus did not cry out—the cut must have been too quick and keen to pain him immediately—but he gasped and clutched the gaping wound to keep his intestines inside.

"You did not behead him," Daila said casually.

"A traitor does not merit the same death as an honorable enemy,"

397

said Theodoric. "That belly wound will give him hours of intolerable agony before he dies. Post a man to watch here until he expires, *then* to bring me his head. Be it so!"

"Ja, Theodoric," said Daila, with a crisp salute.

"Thorn, you no doubt are starving and thirsting. Come along. We are having a celebratory feast in the central square."

As he and I walked there, I said to Theodoric, "You spoke of the nine thousand vanquished. What of our own men?"

He said cheerfully, "We did very well, but of course I was certain that we would. Perhaps two thousand dead and another thousand or so wounded. Most of those will recover, though some may never fight again."

I had to agree that the Ostrogoths had done very well, considering the odds against them. But I also had to say, "You sound rather offhand about it. After all . . . those thousands *are* dead or crippled."

He gave me a sidelong look. "If you mean that I should be weeping for them, ne, I do not weep. I should not weep if all my highest officers were among the fallen—if you and all my other friends were—and I should expect no one to weep if *I* were. It is a warrior's vocation and duty and pleasure to fight. And to die, if need be. This day I rejoice— and so do the dead men, I am sure, in heaven or in Walis-Halla or wherever they may be—that, in this case, what they fought and died for was *won*."

"Ja, I cannot gainsay that. Still, as the optio Daila must already have reported to you, at least one of those men was slain by a fellow Ostrogoth—by Daila himself."

"The optio did right. As I did when I finally gave Camundus his mortal wound back yonder. Disobedience of a superior officer's order is a crime, just as the indisputable treachery of the legatus was a crime, and a criminal must be punished on the spot."

"But I think a fair trial might have shown Daila's victim to have been more impulsive than disobedient. Acting rashly, ja, but in the heat of battle . . ."

"A fair trial?" Theodoric said blankly, as if I had proposed unconditional forgiveness for all evildoers. "Vái, Thorn, you speak of Roman law. We abide by the ancient *Gothic* laws, which are much more sensible. When a criminal is caught in the act or is otherwise unquestionably guilty, a trial would be superfluous. Only if the crime is done in secret or if, for some other reason, there is doubt as to the guilty party, only then is a trial held. There is seldom occasion for that." He paused and smiled sunnily. "That is because we Goths tend to be as open and forthright in our sins as in our good deeds. Now, here is the square and the banquet. Let us forthrightly indulge in the sin of gluttony."

Theodoric's decuriones and signiferi and optiones had mustered every inhabitant of the inner city, except the smallest children, and given all of them work to do, and none of those looked very happy about that. To the upper-class and better-fed cityfolk, the liberation of Singidunum clearly meant nothing more than an exchange of masters. The men and boys had all been put to the dirty work of picking up the dead bodies, stripping them of armor, weapons and any other valuables, and then getting rid of them. Given the number of corpses, that task would likely occupy them for many days. As I later discovered, they were bidden simply to drop the cadavers from the top of the city's landward wall, down the cliff to the plain below, where other workers added oil and pitch and made of the pile a tremendous cremation pyre.

The inner city's women and girls had all been commanded to break out the hoarded stores of food, and to cook and serve them—to both the famished Ostrogoth troops and the equally starved people from the outer city. So there were cooking fires blazing in that central square and hearth smoke rising from the flues of houses all about. The women bustled back and forth with their household trays and platters heaped high, and with loaves of cheese and bread, and with tankards and pitchers and jugs. The square and every side street leading to it teemed with our warriors and the folk from beyond the wall—I saw Aurora and her parents among them—either reaching and grabbing for a portion of food, or clutching close an elegant tableware dish or bowl and wolfing from it without benefit of utensils.

The crowd parted respectfully to let Theodoric through and I sidled along with him. But once he and I had meat, bread and wine, we found an unoccupied spot on the street cobblestones, and Theodoric sat down there to eat just as unroyally (and as ravenously) as myself and every least ranker and urchin sharing the feast.

When our pangs of hunger and thirst had been blunted a bit, I asked Theodoric, "What happens next?"

"Nothing, I hope. At least not here, not for a while. These people of Singidunum are no more glad to see us than they were to see the Sarmatae. However, in the main, they have not been too much inconvenienced. The Sarmatae had no opportunity to carry off any plunder, and I have forbidden my own men to do any looting. Or any raping. Let them find their own Auroras, if they can. I want the city left intact and

399

unviolated, or it will be of no use to me as a hostage in my bargaining with the empire."

"So you must occupy and hold it for some time."

"Ja, and with only about three thousand of my men still whole and hale. North of that river Danuvius, in Old Dacia, there are many more of Babai's Sarmatae—and their allies, the Scyrri. But, because King Babai decided personally to lead the occupation of Singidunum and to plant himself here, those others of his forces are leaderless and lacking direction. Unless and until they get word from some spy that this city has fallen and Babai has perished, they are not likely to mount a massive counterattack."

"But surely they are awaiting *some* word from here," I said. "It was hardly any secret that this city and their king were under siege."

"True. So I have already posted sentries to prevent any treacherous or disaffected citizens from sneaking across the Danuvius to report. I will station half our men here to garrison the city, to look after the wounded, to rebuild the gates. While they are doing that, I and the rest of our men will continue our patrols roundabout, as before, to intercept any Sarmatae roaming hither, so that none of *them* escapes to take back word of Singidunum's fall. I have also sent messengers galloping southeastward, to meet and urge on my supply trains and to summon still more reinforcements."

"And in what capacity can I best serve?" I asked. "Sentry? Garrison? Messenger? Patrol?"

He said with some amusement, "Eager for more combat, are you, niu? Still consider yourself just a warrior of the ranks, do you, niu?"

"*Just* a warrior!" I protested. "It is what I traveled across half of Europe to become. What I have long been preparing and training myself to be. What you invited me, back in Vindobona, to come and be. A warrior of the *Ostrogoths.* What are you yourself, if not a warrior?"

"Well, I am also commander of all the warriors. And king of a great many other people besides. I must determine how to employ those warriors in the best interests of all those people."

"That is what I asked. That you assign me to some employment."

"Iésus, Thorn! I told you long ago—*be not humble.* And if you are merely *playing* at being modest, I will treat you as such a tetzte pretender deserves. I will assign you to be permanent scullion to the coquus in some kitchen tent far, far away from any action or hope of action."

"Gudisks Himins, anything but that," I said, though I knew he was jesting. "That was the first employment I ever had. I should hope my lot in life had improved by now."

"Vái, any rustic straight from the farm can learn to use a sword or lance or bow. And any rustic with any intelligence and ability can eventually win promotion—to decurio, signifer, optio, whatever."

"Fine," I said. "I am neither humble nor modest. I should not at all mind rising through the ranks."

"Balgs-daddja!" he said impatiently. "You have more than intelligence and ability. You have imagination and initiative. I laughed at your tying a rope around your horse, but that seems to be a useful invention. I laughed at your oat-filled trumpets of Jaíriko, and they *certainly* proved useful. I allowed you to participate as a lowly ranker in the taking of the city, just to give you the taste of hand-to-hand combat you desired. You did well at that, too, and I am very glad you survived it. But now, do you expect me to *go on* risking a valuable man as I would risk the rawest recruit?"

I spread my hands. "I have no more inventions to offer. Command me to whatever you will."

He said, almost to himself, "Some ancient historian once observed that the Macedonian general Parmenio won many victories without Alexander the Great, but Alexander not one without Parmenio." Then he said, directly to me, "I have at present only one marshal, the Saio Soas, who held the same office during my father's reign. I should like you to serve as another marshal to me."

"Theodoric, I do not even know what a marshal *does*."

"In earlier times, he was a king's marah-skalks, and his name denoted his post: keeper of the royal horses. Nowadays, his duties are different and inestimably more important. He is a king's envoy, carrying the king's commands and messages to his distant armies or high officials, to the courts or monarchs of other nations. He is not a mere messenger, for the marshal speaks in the king's name and bears the king's authority. It is a post of great responsibility, because the marshal is, so to speak, the long arm of the king himself."

I stared at him, hardly able to believe what I was hearing. It was giddying and a little frightening. When this day had dawned, I had been a common soldier. Even if I had been this day my alternate self, Veleda, my soldiering would not have been *too* unusual, because Amazons and other viragines have been known to fight like men, and even earn promotions to high military office. But now, as this day was ending, I was being offered not just promotion—practically apotheosis—elevation to a courtier of a king. That was because Theodoric assumed me to be as much a male as himself. I was fairly certain that no mannamavi had ever served as king's marshal, and I doubted also that any female ever had.

Theodoric seemed to take my hesitation for disinclination. He added, "The post of marshal carries with it the noble rank of herizogo."

That flustered me even more. A Gothic herizogo was the equivalent of a Roman dux. And, in the standings of Rome, a dux was the fifth-highest order; only the imperator, a rex, a princeps and a comes stood higher than a dux. I *knew* no female had ever borne that rank. Even if a woman married a dux, that conferred no title upon *her*. Of course, I was not being offered a ductus of the Roman Empire, but it would be no small thing to become a herizogo of the Goths and the marshal of King Theodoric of the Ostrogoths.

I briefly wondered if, before Theodoric or I consented to this new association, I ought frankly to confess to him the true nature of myself. But no, I decided not to. I had so far acquitted myself believably, even commendably, as a woodsman, a clarissimus, a bowman and a swordsman. I would try to do the same as a marshal and herizogo. Unless I failed at that and lost the post, or unless somehow I was revealed as a mannamavi, I might well continue in that office for the remainder of my life, and then rest in my grave under a stone bearing an imposing epitaph. It would be a splendid jape on history—for one of this era's marshals, one of its herizoge, one of its duces to have been, all unknown to the historians, not truly a man at all.

Still waiting for me to speak, Theodoric prodded, "You would be addressed respectfully as the Saio Thorn."

"Akh, I need no persuasion," I said. "I am flattered and honored and overwhelmed. I was but pondering one thing. I have to assume that a marshal does no fighting."

"That depends on where your royal missions take you. There could be times when you will have to fight to *get* there. Anyway, though you may not yet believe this, there are some things just as exhilarating as combat. There are machinations, complots, stratagems, intricacies of diplomacy, conspiracy, connivance—and there is *power*. A royal marshal gets to taste of them all, to engage in them all, to delight in wielding them all."

"I only hope there *will* still be fighting. And adventure."

"Then you accept the marshalcy? Good! Be it so! Háils, Saio Thorn! Now, find yourself some soft cobblestones and get a good night's sleep.

Report to my praitoriaún tomorrow morning and I will tell you of your first mission as marshal. This one, I promise, you will find both adventurous and pleasurable."

5

"Impossible!" I gasped when Theodoric, next morning, told me what he wanted me to do. "I? Talk to an emperor? Why, I would be struck as mute as a fish!"

"I doubt it," Theodoric said lightly. "Granted, I am only a lowly king, but you are hardly inarticulate in my presence. Indeed, you frequently talk *back* to me. How many of my subjects dare do that?"

"It is entirely different. As you have said, you were not a king when we met. And we are very much of an age. Please, Theodoric, consider. I am but an abbey brat. An unmannered rustic. I have never been anywhere near a capital or a court of the empire . . ."

"Balgs-daddja," he said, which did not much inspirit me. Ever since my abbey days, I had been hearing people declare my utterances to be "nonsense."

He leaned forward across his table and went on, "This new Leo is only a brat himself. You long ago told me, Thorn, how you served as exceptor to the abbot of that abbey, and dealt with his correspondence to and from many distinguished persons. So you have some acquaintance with the words and ways and wiles of such high-placed notables. You have boasted of your successful imposture among the upper classes of Vindobona. Well, what you will encounter at an imperial court is not much different from what you found in the society of those provincial dignitaries. And this time you will not be pretending prestige of your own; you will *have* it. You will present unimpeachable credentials as the marshal of the King of the Ostrogoths. Since I know that you speak Greek well enough, you are capable of dealing with little Emperor Leo the Second, and whatever man or group of men is helping the boy to

403

govern. That is why I am sending the Saio Soas to confront the Emperor Julius Nepos in Ravenna—because Soas speaks only Gothic and Latin—and why I am sending Saio Thorn to confront the Emperor of the Eastern Empire. Be it so!"

I nodded obediently, and even half saluted, though we were all sitting down—Theodoric and Soas and myself—and one does not customarily salute while seated. We three were conferring in the same simple little house outside the Singidunum wall where I had twice before talked with Theodoric. He could have appropriated for his praitoriaún and residence the grandest mansion in the inner city, but he had chosen to go on using the humble abode of Aurora and her parents.

Soas was a gray-haired and gray-bearded man almost as old as Wyrd had been, and indeed looked very much like him. But the resemblance ended there, for Soas was a man of few words. He raised no objections to the mission *he* was being sent on, and he evinced no jealousy or displeasure at my having been so suddenly appointed to share the office of marshalcy with him. And he and I, when we conversed at all, addressed one another respectfully as "Saio," despite the great disparity in our ages.

I had been honest in protesting myself unworthy of the mission Theodoric proposed for me, because I *did* view that with some trepidation. But, to be equally honest, I was just as much excited by the prospect. I would never in my life have supposed that I might ever visit the New Rome of Constantinople, let alone be admitted to the imperial court there, let alone be granted audience by the eastern emperor himself. I felt rather as I had felt that time I was exiled from the monastery to the nunnery: half apprehensive, half welcoming the opportunity for new and unforeseeable adventures.

"I have no least desire to keep possession of this city," Theodoric continued. "Like every other free-born and free-living Goth, I have no fondness for any walled city. I much prefer our Amaling city of Novae, wide open to the Danuvius and the riverside plains. However, you marshals will of course not confide that to the emperors. Make them believe that I love and treasure Singidunum, and yearn to stay here forever, and to make it my capital city instead of Novae. Because I *will* stay here until I get what I want in exchange for Singidunum. Or, to be realistic, I will hold this city as long as I can. So you two must deliver my demands to Ravenna and Constantinople before I *am* perhaps dispossessed by a Sarmatian counterattack."

He reached across the table to give to me and to Soas each a sheet of vellum, bearing many lines written in his own hand and sealed with his monogram stamped into purple wax.

"I sat up most of the night composing these," he said. "Yours in Latin, Saio Soas. Yours in Greek, Saio Thorn."

I murmured apologetically, "I speak some Greek, Theodoric, but I do not read it."

"You need not. Every official in Constantinople does. Anyway, both you and Soas know what I am communicating. The emperors are to demonstrate their gratitude for my having rescued Singidunum from the Sarmatae, by sending me a vadimonium—a pactum—a renewal and ratification of the treaties made between the empire and my late royal father. To wit, that we Ostrogoths be assured permanent owner-ship of the lands in Moesia Secunda granted to us by Leo the First. Also, we want a resumption of the consueta dona for our services as guardians of the empire's frontier—the payment of three hundred librae of gold annually, as before. Once I have that pactum, I will relinquish this city to whatever force the empire sends to garrison it. But not *until* I have the pactum. Not until I am satisfied of its good faith and validity and its imperviousness to being abrogated or dis-avowed or rewritten by any emperors who succeed Julius Nepos and this latest Leo."

I asked, "And how do the Saio Soas and I prove to our respective emperors that you have indeed taken Singidunum?"

Both of the men gave me glances of exasperation at my persisting in quibbling, but Theodoric said, "A king's word ought to be sufficient. However, since *you* impudently raise the question, others might also. Therefore, you and the Saio Soas will each carry irrefutable proof." He raised his voice and called, "Aurora, bring the meat."

At that curious command, I expected the girl to fetch in platters or trenchers. But she came from the kitchen carrying two leather bags, of a sort that I had seen before, and handed them to Theodoric. He opened one bag, looked into it, gave it to Soas and gave me the other, saying casually as he did so:

"Aurora has likewise been up most of the night. Smoking those things so they will not be too putrescent and stinking when you deliver them. Camundus's head to Julius Nepos. Babai's head to Leo the Sec-ond. Proof enough, Saio Thorn?"

Chastened, I only nodded again.

"Saio Soas, you have the longer way to go, all overland to Ravenna. You had best leave at once."

"I am there, Theodoric!" barked Soas, leaping to his feet, snapping the salute and vanishing out the street door.

Before I could ask how I was to get to Constantinople, Theodoric told me. "A barge awaits you at the riverside, well provisioned and with a trustworthy crew. You will continue on down the Danuvius to my Moesian city of Novae. Since you are already acquainted with the optio Daila, I am sending him with you, and also two bowmen, in case you meet pirates or other impediments on the river. The barge is big enough for all of you and your horses. However, I would wish you to have a more impressive body of retainers when you arrive at Constantinople. So here is another letter, to my sister Amalamena at Novae. It instructs her to provide more warriors and mounts. She may even wish to accompany you, with servants of her own. Like yourself, Amalamena has never yet visited Constantinople. You will enjoy her company; she is comely and charming and beloved by all who know her, including myself. Also, she will see that your entire retinue is grandly dressed and equipped and provisioned for the overland ride southeastward from Novae. There! Does that sound intolerable, Thorn? Are you still timorous of being my marshal to that imperial court?"

"Ne, ne, ni allis." What else *could* I say if, as he suggested, a mere female might readily make the same journey to confront the august Emperor Leo. "Have you any further instructions?"

"Ne, only high expectations. That you will speedily return, bearing the pactum I charge you with obtaining. Be it so!"

✠ ✠ ✠

The grizzled optio Daila, although he had known me the day before as the newest and least and lowest (both in stature and rank) of the turma of warriors he commanded, this day formally saluted me as I led Velox aboard the barge. Daila did so without a sneer or smirk—and so did the two bowmen, beefy veterans as old as he—but I returned their salutes rather sheepishly, and thereafter refrained from giving any orders that would have required them to go on saluting me. Anyway, there was no need for me to utter any commands, because the voyage was uneventful; they and I had to do no fighting off of river pirates or ambushes from the riverbanks. Nor did I have to give any orders to the bargemen, because they knew their work and the caprices of the Danuvius far better than I did.

In all the time I had spent on the Danuvius so far, it had been a swift-flowing but broad, brown stream. Because of the influx of the river

Savus above Singidunum, it was now broader than ever, more than half a Roman mile in width, and the forests of its farther bank were only dimly visible. But, just a day's voyage downstream from Singidunum, the river completely changed its character. Now it had to force its eastward way between two great mountain chains, the Carpatae to the north, the Haemus to the south.

Since the Danuvius had to squeeze through a defile between them, with precipitous cliffs of gray rock towering impossibly high on either side, the formerly broad river was here pinched to less than a stade in width. It turned from brown to foaming white, and roared through that narrow channel like a horizontal cascade. The horses all braced their legs wide apart, and Daila and the bowmen and I clutched anxiously for a firm grip on everything solid about the barge, because it slapped and skipped and bounded along with jaw-jarring and neck-whipping lunges and checks and yawings and veerings. However, the barge crew remained unruffled during the wild ride, as they expertly plied their poles and steering oar to keep us in midstream and well away from the rock walls that could have ground us to splinters.

Having myself been in combat, I can attest that it heightens all of one's senses and emotions and responses. And I have to say now that being in the midst of a contest between the elements of earth and water can be just as tumultuously invigorating as any contention of man against man. I was riding a river that apparently once had fought its way through solid rock, and still was triumphantly doing so. As in combat, I felt my awareness and alertness much enhanced. There was one difference, though, and it was not particularly pleasurable. When caught in a battle between two mighty elements, I found, you cannot take sides, you cannot have either element as an ally, you cannot strike a blow for yourself or parry one, you can only wait and cringe and hope to survive the outcome.

I daresay that is why the old-time pagans paid more reverence to the gods of earth, water, air and fire than they did even to the gods of creation and love and war.

That furious, turbulent, fearsome part of the voyage lasted for most of a day that seemed as long as a week, but then ended as abruptly as it had begun. The river spouted out of the gap between the mountains, the cliffs spread away from us on either side, and then the whole ranges of the Carpatae and the Haemus likewise backed away, giving room for riverside forests and meadows and underbrush. The Danuvius, as if it were grateful for its release from constriction, muted its noise from a

407

roar to a sort of contented sighing, slowed its pace from a headlong gallop to a placid amble, turned brown again and flattened out to its former breadth. The barge crew steered us to a grassy bank, where the horses could graze and we humans could thankfully relax on unheaving solid ground to eat our evening meal.

The crewmen laughed as we four warriors—and the horses, too—reeled and staggered ashore, the two archers grumbling that they had not enlisted in Theodoric's ranks to be white-water sailors. I am quite sure that the bargemen were as muscle-sore and bone-weary as we, and that they only put a brave face on their misery so they could be disdainfully amused at ours. While we all ate and drank, they told us that we "land-lobbes" had better enjoy the next few easy days on the river. They said that we had but negotiated what they called the Kazan Defile, and the next rapids downstream, the Iron Gate, would make the Kazan seem to us in retrospect as serene as the tepidarium in a Roman bathhouse.

At least we had the chance, over the ensuing several days, to unkink our limbs and spines and to recover from our aches and bruises. The Danuvius gradually became almost as broad as a lake between the mountain ranges, and it had no banks to speak of, but on either side of us dwindled off into stagnant marshes and bogs, and the main stream flowed so turgidly that the bargemen poled with vigor to move us along faster than the river moved. They could not, however, propel us fast enough to suit me and Daila and the bowmen, because now, instead of hurting, we itched intolerably. Blood-prickers, gnats, midges and every other kind of predatory flying insect rose from the riverside swamps in clouds as visible as *real* clouds, and feasted on us insatiably and tormented us fiendishly.

The crewmen—I suppose through long familiarity—seemed to pay the swarms no mind, except occasionally to wave a hand before their faces to clear the insects enough for them to see through. But we other four itched and scratched and bled so continuously, and were for so long unable to sleep, that we came very near the verge of madness. Every exposed bit of our skin was raked with the marks of our nails—the three bearded warriors had even gouged out patches of their facial hair—and the insect bites so overlapped that our faces and hands were bumpily bloated, our eyelids swollen nearly shut, our lips puffed and raw. The horses, though they had thicker hides, had also the disadvantage of being unable to scratch, so they twitched and fidgeted and thrashed and kicked until we feared that they would stave a hole in the barge and maroon us all forever in this hellish place.

It was a genuine relief when, after a seeming eternity, the Danuvius again began to narrow and to surge faster, and the wind of our passage diminished the number of insects. Eventually we left the last of them behind, when the river and the barge plunged into another narrow, cliff-walled pass. The buffeting we endured in here was, as the crewmen had warned, indeed worse than at the Kazan Defile, and lasted longer. But Daila, the archers and I—and even the horses, I imagine—found the pounding we suffered to be far less of a torture than the insects had been.

I could see why this defile was called Iron. The bordering precipices were not gray here, but of a rock that was the somber red color of rust. And I could see why it was also called a Gate. The cliff walls were so close together that any body of men, perched atop them, could have poured down onto the river enough arrows, fire, boulders or tree trunks to have barred the Iron Gate to any passing craft, even to all the gathered dromo vessels of the entire Roman navy. But no inimical force was at present doing any such thing. So our barge raced unimpeded down the white-water chute, bucking and slewing and wallowing and walloping. We got safely through, though we emerged from that ordeal even more sore and fatigued and stomach-sick than the Kazan had made us. The bargemen this time took pity on their passengers. They poled the barge to the river's left bank and moored it there for the two whole days it took us to recuperate.

Situated here was the first inhabited community we had yet encountered during our voyage. It was only a hamlet, but it boasted the distinguished name of Turris Severi, after a local landmark, the stone tower erected by the Emperor Severus, more than two centuries before, to commemorate his victory over the outlander tribes called Quadi and Marcomanni. Evidently one of the terms Severus imposed on the vanquished was that they settle here and devote their lives to succoring any voyagers who met mishap in the Iron Gate—or who, like us, came out of it in wretched condition. Anyway, the villagers *were* all descendants of the survivors of those tribes, and they *did* treat us most kindly. They gave us an ointment made from the flowers of the blue vervain, with which to daub our insect bites, and that helped greatly to ease our swellings and itchings. They gave us to drink a tincture of valerian root, to relieve our agitated nerves and settle our stomachs. When that had

409

been accomplished, and we were able to eat, the villagers fed us fresh fish from the Danuvius and fresh vegetables from their gardens.

During the remainder of the voyage there were no more turbulent waters to be endured, and less likelihood than ever that we might be attacked by river pirates. From Turris Severi onward, we were drifting down the lower Danuvius, where there was much other river traffic, including the armed patrol boats of the Moesian Fleet. The stream was once more brown and broad and flowed calmly, and the landscape we passed was utterly empty and monotonous, until we came to our destination, Novae, on the river's southern bank.

I privately thought that Theodoric had rather exaggerated when he spoke of Novae as a "city." I had seen several cities by now, and Novae was no more than a small town in comparison. The buildings were mostly of only a single story, there was no amphitheater at all, the one church was considerably less than majestic, the two or three thermae were of nothing like Roman-style grandeur, and what Daila pointed out to me as "the royal palace and gardens" was an estate much more modest than that of, say, the herizogo Sunnja back in Vindobona. Nevertheless, Novae was a pleasant-looking place, spreading from the riverside up a gentle rise of hill, and there were many market squares shaded by trees and brightened by flowers. The town was indeed unwalled, as Theodoric had said, but Daila explained that it was by no means complacent in its openness.

"Notice, Saio Thorn," he said, as we stepped ashore, "how every residence, shop and gasts-razn has its street door situated so it is not opposite the door of the building across the way. That is done so that, if the city is threatened and an alarm sounded, the men inside every building can seize their arms and dash outdoors and not collide with those emerging from the house opposite."

"Ja," I said. "Planned with foresight. I have not seen that precaution taken even in cities." I hastened to add, tactfully, "In bigger cities, I mean. Now tell me, Optio, what is expected of us? Do you and I and the bowmen take lodging in one of the gasts-razna?"

"Akh, ne. The men and I will proceed over the hill to the army encampment beyond, and we will take the horses with us. But you are a marshal. You will be hospitably received by the princess Amalamena, and given lodging in the royal palace."

I nodded, then said uncertainly, "I am new at being a marshal, as you know. Do you think I ought to wear full armor and arms when I present myself to the princess?"

Daila was tactful, too. "Um . . . considering that you do not yet have your own armor, tailored to fit your—er—your stature, Saio Thorn, I should recommend that you make your entrance in your everyday garb."

I decided to change into clean clothes, at least. To do that in privacy, I took my packs inside a dock shed, only to discover that every garment I owned was moist and musty from our passage through the two white-water gorges. I could not take time to dry all those things in the sun, so, damp though they were, I donned the best of the raiment I had bought and worn as Thornareikhs in Vindobona—not the toga, of course, but a fine tunic, undercoat and trousers, my Scythian-latcheted street shoes, and I pinned onto my tunic's shoulders my matching fibulae of aes and almandines. When I was fully clad, I smelled rather of mildew—even though I got out my phial of rose essence and dabbed some of that on me—and my shoes squished when I walked, but I thought I *looked* well enough dressed to pass for a marshal of the king.

Bearing no arms but my sheathed short-sword, just to show that I was sometimes a warrior, I went uphill toward the palace grounds. I noticed that most of the passersby, and the people in the market squares—and even those working at forges and potters' wheels and the like in the open-fronted shops—were female or very old or very young males, so I assumed that the men of Novae who were not with Theodoric in Singidunum must be either in the trains of supplies and reinforcements on their way there or camped in reserve on the other side of this hill, where Daila had gone.

411

The palace grounds were encircled by no wall, either, but only by a dense hedge that had a fretwork iron gate in its one opening. That was guarded by two sentries, the brawniest and bushiest-bearded Goths I had yet seen, wearing complete armor and helmets and holding contus lances. I strode up to them, told them who I was and why I wished admittance and showed them the letter I carried from Theodoric to his sister. I doubted that the men could read, but I expected them to recognize the seal, and they did. One man growled to the other to "go and fetch the faúragagga," and gruffly bade me wait for that steward to come and escort me. While I waited, still outside the gate, the sentry looked me thoroughly up and down, not so much suspiciously as with an air of mild incredulity.

The steward came from the palace and down the pathway, walking with a staff, for he was a very old, bent man with a long white beard, and he wore a heavy, ground-length robe even in this summer weather.

He introduced himself to me as the faúragagga Costula, bowed as I handed my letter through the gate, then broke the wax seal, unfolded the vellum and read it entirely through, occasionally glancing from it to me, his white eyebrows raised high. Finally he bowed again and handed it back to me, and ordered the sentries:

"Open the gate, guardsmen, and raise your lances in salute to the Saio Thorn, marshal of our King Theodoric."

They did that, and I walked between them, walking as tall as I could, but they loomed over me like the cliffs of the Iron Gate. The old steward courteously took my arm as we went up together up the path. But then he looked surprised, withdrew his hand from my sleeve and wiped it on his robe.

"Excuse my dampness, Costula," I said, embarrassed. "The river was very wet." He gave me a sidelong look, and I realized that I was sounding exceptionally stupid for a marshal, so I dropped the subject and asked, "What is the proper manner of saluting and addressing the princess Amalamena?"

"A dignified bow will suffice, Saio Thorn. And you may address her simply as Princess, until she gives you leave to call her Amalamena, as she probably will. She demands none of those grandiose Augusta or Maxima titles, as the Romans do. I will, however, ask one indulgence of you, Saio Thorn. Would you mind waiting for a while in an anteroom? I must announce your arrival and the princess must arise from bed and get dressed to receive you."

"From bed? It is midafternoon."

"Oh vái, she is no sleepy sloven. She has been ill, and under the care of a lekeis. But do not say I told you so. Amalamena is her father's daughter and her brother's sister. Just as she refuses to admit the least frailness, so would she disdain any show of sympathy or condescension on your part."

I murmured vague condolences and an assurance that I would not rudely remark on the princess's health. The steward ushered me through the big, double front door of the palace and to a couch in the entry hall, and bade another servant bring me refreshment. So I sat and sipped from a tankard of good, bitter, dark beer while I studied my surroundings.

The palace was constructed of the same red stone I had seen at the Iron Gate, and stood two stories high, at the center of well-tended prata and gravel paths and flower beds, all surrounded by the thorny hedge.

412

And the palace was no more ostentatious inside than out, for it was not cluttered with ornamentation, as a Roman-style villa would have been. Of what furniture there was, most of it, not surprisingly, represented trophies of the hunt. The couch on which I sat was covered with úrus hide, there were bearskin rugs scattered about on the mosaic floors and there were superb horns and racks of antlers mounted on the walls. There were also works of a kind of artistry I had never seen before: immense, elegantly shaped vases and urns of a black and cinnabar-colored ceramic, decorated with figures of graceful gods and goddesses, lithe boys and girls doing athletic feats, muscular hunters and their prey. Costula later told me that those things were of Grecian artistry, and also that the manner of furnishing a room sparsely—so that every item of adornment in it can be separately appreciated—was in the Greek fashion.

Now, at the inner end of the hall, another double door opened and old Costula beckoned to me from there. I set down my tankard to go to him, and he motioned me on into the room beyond. It was a most spacious and lofty chamber, lighted by many windows unshuttered to the summer day outside. It was mosaic-floored like the hall I had just come from, and likewise arrayed with hunt trophies and the Grecian urns. But there was only one functional piece of furniture, a high, thronelike chair set against the farther wall, a considerable distance from the door, and on it sat a slight feminine figure clad in white. She was holding Theodoric's unfolded letter, as if she were reading it, and without assistance. That somewhat surprised me: an "outlander" female, even a royal one, being able to read. But I would in time find out that the princess not only could read, and write besides, she was very *well* read.

413

I went toward her at a deliberate and stately pace, but it was a long march I had to make, and all the dignity I tried to assume was dispelled by the comical squish-squishing of my moist shoes, a sound horrendously amplified in this vaulted chamber. I felt less like a marshal and a herizogo than like a trudging water bug.

The Princess Amalamena must have been thinking much the same thing, because she kept her head lowered and her gaze fixed on my feet all the time I was approaching her. When at last I squish-squished to a stop a little way in front of her chair, she finally, languidly raised her head. She was smiling pleasantly enough, but the dimples about her mouth were visibly struggling; she would have preferred to laugh out loud. I know that I must have been blushing redder than Theodoric's Aurora had ever done, so I bowed deeply to hide my own face, and did not straighten up until I heard Amalamena say:

"Welcome, Saio Thorn." She had her expression under control, but now the smile was pensive, as she delicately sniffed the air. "Did you come hither by way of the Valley of Roses?"

"Ne, Princess," I said—through my teeth, because I was biting back the urge to remark that, whatever was her ailment, it was not a catarrh dulling her sense of smell. "I am wearing a perfume of rose essence, Princess."

"Ah! Say you so? How original!" Her dimples were again having difficulty maintaining the smile. "Most of my brother's emissaries come smelling of sweat and blood."

I did not need her to tell me that I was cutting a wretched figure as a marshal of the king. And I should very much have liked to impress this Amalamena, for she was as comely as every princess ought to be. I could discern the resemblance to her older brother, but her features were naturally more delicate, so, while Theodoric was handsome, she was beautiful. And of course she did not have his strong body; she was so slender as to seem almost wraithlike, and had not much more of a bosom than I did when I was Veleda. While Theodoric was Gothic-fair of complexion and hair, Amalamena had tresses of silver-gilt, lips of primrose and skin so ivory-translucent that I could see the pale blue of veins at her temples. She was well named—"moon of the Amals"—for she could have been an incarnation of the slim, wan, fragile new moon. Her overall pearliness made her Gothic-blue eyes as brilliant as those Gemini fires I had once seen—and right now her eyes were mischievously mocking of me, as she went on:

"Why, you are no bigger than I am, Saio Thorn, and I think not any older, and you have no more beard than I do. Perhaps I, too, could aspire to a marshalcy. Or does Theodoric nowadays, like Alexander, prefer to have only young *men* about him? If so, he has certainly changed since I saw him last."

I was probably apoplectic-red by this time, and I said in a voice constricted by vexation, "Princess, I was awarded my title because I helped Theodoric take the city of Singidunum, not for any other—"

At that, she finally let loose her laugh, a long and lilting one. She helplessly waved a slim white hand at me, and even old Costula began to chuckle, and I could gladly have melted into the floor where I stood. When her hilarity subsided, she dabbed at her gem-bright eyes and said, with kindly amusement, "Forgive me. I was being indecorous. But you *did* look so . . . so . . . And the lekeis tells me that laughter is the best medicine for any affliction."

I said icily, "I hope it proves so, Princess."

"Come. You are not young enough to go on addressing me as your senior. Call me Amalamena and I shall call you Thorn. Surely you could not have believed me serious in my raillery, for you must have read my brother's letter."

"I have not," I said, still stiffly. "It was your faúragagga yonder who broke the seal. Ask him."

"No matter. You should be proud to have anyone read it—or everyone. My brother praises you unstintingly, and calls you friend, not just marshal. He has many friends, of course, but they are friends of the king. You are the friend of Theodoric."

"I try to be a trustworthy one," I said, not yet entirely thawed by her warmth. "And I am on a mission of some urgency, Princess. I mean Amalamena. If you would merely provide what is necessary for the expedition, as I think your brother requests in that letter, I will be on my way and—"

"And I, too," she interrupted. "I wish to join your expedition. Theodoric himself suggests that I might do so."

I said, "I believe, when he wrote that, your brother was unaware that you are . . . er . . ." I broke off because old Costula, behind the princess's chair, was shaking his head so emphatically that his long beard rippled. "I mean to say . . . I know nothing of the way from here to Constantinople. The journey thither could be rigorous. Even hazardous."

She favored me again with that dimple-wreathed smile, and said persuasively, "But I have Thorn to guide and protect me. According to this letter, I could not travel more securely even under the aegis of Jupiter and Minerva. Would you deny me the opportunity to find out for myself?"

Now she was asking a question, not giving me a command. And this was a royal princess, sister of my king and my friend, doubtless dear to all her people, and she was suffering some illness of which I did not yet know even the name, and I would be held responsible for anything that happened to her in my keeping. So I had ample reason for misgivings and forebodings, and I should have voiced them with vigor. But in fact, as I gazed on that fragile and beauteous girl, the only thought in my head was "Akh, could I but be a *man!*" And all I could say was "I would never deny you anything, Amalamena."

415

6

Amalamena gave various instructions to the faúragagga regarding preparations for the expedition, and told him to send to her chambers various other servants and military aides to whom she would also give instructions. Then she said to me:

"The excitement of anticipation has already tired me somewhat. Or perhaps, Thorn, it was the salubrious laughter that you provided for me." And she laughed again. "Anyway, I would rest now. Costula will show you to your lodgings, and will arrange for your belongings to be brought there. I shall see you again when we dine at nahtamats."

So old Costula and I took our leave together. As soon as we were outside that throne room, I asked him, "This lekeis who is attending the princess, would it be some haliuruns, some astrologus, some other such qvaksalbons?"

"Akh, nothing of the sort. The lekeis Frithila would poison you if he heard you speak so. He is a man most learned and skillful, genuinely deserving of the Roman title of medicus. Would any qvaksalbons practitioner be employed by the royal family?"

"I should hope not. Take me to this Frithila. I must have his permission before I can let the princess — and you — get too far with the preparations for her traveling to Constantinople."

"That is so. We will go to Frithila at once. Let me but summon a chair, Saio Thorn. It is a long way for my old legs."

We went through a number of streets and turnings, and came to a respectable dwelling house, and went into its presence-chamber, which was full of waiting patients, all women and small children. I waited, too, while Costula continued into an inner room. After only a few minutes, a woman emerged from that room, doing up her vestments, and Costula's head poked out the door to nod to me.

416

"Well?" barked the lekeis, the instant I entered. He was a man nearly as ancient as the faúragagga, but far more bright-eyed and brisk of manner. "What is the necessity of this urgent call, niu? You look healthy enough."

"It is the health of the Princess Amalamena that I came to inquire about."

"Then you can go away at once. My oath of Hippocrates forbids me to speak of a patient's condition to anyone but a consulting physician."

I said to the steward, "Have you not told the lekeis who I am?"

"He has told me," said Frithila. "And I would not care if you were the Patriarch Bishop of—"

I slammed my hand loudly on the table behind which he stood. "I will waste no words. The princess wishes to accompany me on a mission to Constantinople."

He looked a trifle disconcerted, but only shrugged and said, "Fortunate young man. I see no reason why she should not."

"Look here, Lekeis Frithila. I am the king's marshal and his friend besides. I will not risk taking his sister on a lengthy journey without your assurance that she will survive it."

The physician now stroked his beard and pondered, regarding me narrowly the while. Then he turned to Costula and said, "Leave us." When the steward had gone, Frithila eyed me some more, and finally asked, "Have you a grasp of Latin and Greek?" I said I did. "Very well. Then even a layman like yourself will already have noticed the princess's very evident marasmus and cacochymia and cachexia."

I blinked. I had never heard of such things, in any language, and would not have recognized them in any person, but it sounded as if Amalamena was much more ill than she had looked to me. I said, "All I could see, Lekeis, is that she is pale and thin and inclined to weary easily."

He snapped, "That is precisely what I *said*. An appearance of malnutrition, of vitiated body fluids and of general ill health. When I first saw her looking so, I insisted on giving her an examination, although she protested that she felt as well as ever she had. Now, in the case of a debilitated female patient, a physician naturally thinks first of chlorosis or the fluor albus or some other such adustion of the womb. Niu?"

"Er . . . naturally."

"However, she maintained that she was suffering no aches or pains, that she was eating well, that all her functions were normal and regular. And I could detect no fever, no rapidity of the pulse, no purulent or

417

offensive or otherwise significant discharge from the female parts. *Except*"—he held up a forefinger—"except a very slight secretion of a limpid and pellucid lymph. This, of course, led me to suspect an infarct or renitency elsewhere than the womb. Niu?"

"Of course."

"But, on palpation and percussion of her thorax and abdomen, I could discover no such induration. Therefore, I prescribed only calorific epithems for her to apply—or have her maids apply to her—and, of medicines, a chalybeate to incrassate her blood and a deobstruent to clear any clogged intestinal passages."

None of this told me anything whatever, but I could read his expression, so I said, "And your remedies did not restore her to health?"

"Ne," he said grimly. "But still she felt nothing to complain of, and so did not return for further consultation, and I had other patients occupying my attention. Unfortunately, it was not for some months that I chanced to meet Amalamena on the street. I was shocked to see that her pallor and languor had not visibly improved. I insisted on making a call at her chambers. This time, when I palpated—oh vái—I *could* feel an induration in her abdomen."

418

"Lekeis, why do you say 'unfortunately' and 'oh vái'?"

"Because . . . if I had found it sooner . . ." He wagged his head and sighed. "It is a cacoëthic scirrhus. An occult scirrhus, since it has not yet bulged or broken the skin. An indolent scirrhus, since it took so long in making itself known, and still is giving her no pain. As well as I can determine, it is not in her womb or in her intestines, but in the mesenteries. So it must be of that category that we lekjos call—in detestation—kreps. But I cannot be sure of that until I can see whether the veins around it have turgesced to the shape of crab claws. And that I cannot see until I cut open the princess's abdomen."

"Cut her open!?" I cried, aghast.

"Akh, not while she lives, certainly not."

"*While* she lives?"

He demanded angrily, "How can you keep on repeating me, young man, when you apparently have not heard a word I have said? The princess has kreps, a consumptive scirrhus growing in her mesenteries. The carrion worm, as some call it. In time, it will infiltrate her other organs. Amalamena is not just ill, she is dying."

"Dying!?"

"Is not even *that* plain enough language for you to understand, niu?

Akh, marshal, *you* are dying. *I* am dying. The princess is dying *young*. I cannot predict how much time she has, but let us pray that it be brief."

"Brief!?"

"Iésus," he grunted, and threw up his hands. But then, with strained patience, he explained, "If the liufs Guth is merciful, she will die soon and painlessly and with her body unblemished. If the dying takes too long, the scirrhus will eventually erupt through the skin as a gruesomely gaping and suppurating abscess. Also, as that kreps clutches with its claws at her other organs, it will make her body bloated in some parts, skeletal in others, hideous in all. Such a prolonged death would entail an interminable suffering that I would not wish inflicted on the devil himself."

I too said, "Iésus," then asked, "Is there no medicine . . . or perhaps syrurgery . . . ?"

Again he wagged his head and sighed. "This is not a combat wound that I could heal with a simple vulnerary. And she is not a dim-witted slattern, believing in demons, whom I could delude by prescribing amuletics. And syrurgery would simply irritate the scirrhus into spreading faster. Akh, sometimes I wish we all still lived in the good old simple days. Back then, if a lekeis was confronted by a baffling and incurable disease, he would set his patient at a public crossroads, in hope that some passerby—perhaps a foreigner—would recognize the ailment and tell how he had seen it cured elsewhere."

419

"Is there *nothing* to be done?"

"Only desperate resorts. Some of the ancients prescribed the drinking of ass's milk and the bathing in water in which wheat bran has been boiled. So now I have the princess doing those things, though there is no record of their ever having done anything in the least remedial for anyone in history. Also, assuming that the scirrhus *is* the kreps, I am giving her powders of the calcareous substance called crab's-eye, for whatever homoeomeric good that may do. Beyond that, I can give her only a discutient and a lenitive—bryony, in hope of dissolving the morbific matter, and oil of the anchusa berries to calm her nerves. If and when the pain begins, I shall give her bits of the bark of the mandragoras root. But I do not wish to commence that lenitive until it is necessary, because she will need increasingly heavier doses."

I said disbelievingly, "And yet you would give her leave to travel?"

"Why not? Between here and Constantinople, there are plenty of milkable jenny asses, and much wheat to be sieved for its bran. Of the medicines, I can give her a supply to take along. To you I can give the mandragoras bark, to administer should it become necessary. A journey might be more beneficial for Amalamena than any amount of medicaments. I have already recommended that she seek diversion and cheerful company. Are you cheerful company, niu?"

"She seems to find me so," I murmured, and asked, but could not complete the question, "Have you told her . . . ?"

"Ne. But Amalamena is not stupid, and she knows what discutients and lenitives are for. If nothing else, her eagerness to seize on an opportunity for travel would indicate that she is cognizant of her fate. She evidently wishes to see something of the world before she dies. I doubt that she has ever been far from this city since she was born here. And if she prefers to die elsewhere than her birthplace, well . . . at least I will not have to watch her do it."

I said bitingly, "You seem to take lightly the fate of what is probably your most distinguished patient."

"Lightly!?" He whirled on me and jabbed his bony forefinger right against my nose. "You contumelious whelp! I will have you know that I attended at the *birth* of the child Amalamena. And a sweeter, happier, merrier babe I never birthed. Every other newborn infant, when held aloft and spanked, has seized its first breath of life with a wailing cry. But Amalamena? She did that with a *laugh!*"

While he railed at me, the old man had begun to weep.

"That is why I tell her now: try to laugh again, child, try to find things that will make you laugh. And she is only one of the many reasons why I have long cursed my ever having adopted a profession that can foresee death, can foretell all its horrible details, yet can do so little to prevent it." He wiped his eyes on his sleeve and said, to himself, "Youth passes . . . beauty fades . . . perfection fails . . ." Then he snarled again at me, "And I curse all the complacent fools like yourself, who sneer at the physician because he is only a man and not a god!"

"Be easy, Lekeis Frithila," I said, chastened and ashamed and near weeping myself. "I will let the princess go with me, as she desires, and I promise to take good care of her. As you desire, I will exert myself— even continue making a fool of myself—to be her cheerful companion, to give her cause for laughter, to help her enjoy the journey. And let me have the mandragoras medicine. If I am with Amalamena when her end comes, I will do my best to make it easy for her."

✠   ✠   ✠

When I rejoined old Costula outside, it was still full day, so I asked him to accompany me to some other places. We first went down to the dockside shed where I had left my belongings. I abstracted three things from among them, to carry myself, and the steward had his porters load the rest onto the poles of his chair. Next, I had him lead me to the workshop of the city's best gulthsmitha, or aurifex, and introduce me there. I gave to the jeweler one of the things I was carrying and asked if he could devise some way to mount it, with a touch of goldwork about it, to make it handsomely impressive for presentation as a gift.

He said, "I have never had *quite* such a commission before, Saio Thorn. But I will give careful thought to its design. And ja, I will have it ready before you depart the city."

Finally, I had Costula show me which street would take me up and over the hill to the army encampment beyond. Then I let him and his porters and my packs go on to the palace, and I continued alone. The sentries at the camp had evidently been told to expect me, for they neither challenged my identification of myself nor showed any least surprise at such an unlikely and young person's being a marshal of the king. They quite readily obeyed my request that a runner be sent for the optio Daila. And he, when he came to meet me, had already anticipated my next request.

"I have had our fillsmitha lay aside all his other work, Saio Thorn, to take the measurements for your armor. And our hairusmitha has commenced the forging of what will be your new sword's blade, when you have also been measured for that."

So he led me to the workshop of the armorer, and I handed to that man another of the things I had been carrying, the helmet made for me at Singidunum, and asked him to embellish it according to my rank. He said he would do that, and would add the same ornamentation to my corselet, for the making of which he now proceeded to take all my body measurements.

"Please try also, custos," I instructed him, facetiously, "to make me, when I am armed, look like something better than a little beetle." The fillsmitha only looked puzzled at that, but Daila had the grace to shuffle his feet and chuckle at my making jape of him.

Then he led me to the sword-smithy, where I was given the privilege—not accorded to many, even of the Ostrogoth warriors themselves—of seeing how the far-famed and highly esteemed "snake pattern" blades are made. Of course, the hairusmitha was already well along in the making of mine, but he cordially explained the entire process. Or *almost* the entire process.

A smith, he said, began that work by heating eight slender rods of iron to red-hotness, packing them in charcoal and keeping them red-hot until the iron's surface absorbed enough carbon to turn to steel, while the core of each rod remained pure iron. Those rods were then, while hot and flexible, twisted together rather in the way that a woman plaits her hair. When that plait cooled, it was reheated, hacksawed into pieces, reforged into eight new rods, those again heated in a charcoal packing and again twisted together. That procedure was repeated several times, the new rods each time being plaited in a different order, until the smith was satisfied that he had the proper composition for the blade's central portion.

On his anvil, he hammered that into a rough sword shape, then forged onto either side of it a strip of the very finest tempered steel, to be the cutting edges. The whole was next put to the grindstone, and ground to more finished shape, then was filed, burnished and polished to near-completion. During these stages the distinctive, bluish, shimmering pattern emerged along the central section, according to the several ways the central rods had been woven and rewoven, and not even the smith could say what the pattern would look like until he saw it begin to appear. Most often, as in the case of the sword he made for me, it looked like intercoiled snakes, but it might resemble a sheaf of grain, curly tresses of hair or eddying waves of water.

"And besides the blade's beauty," he said proudly, "it has flexibility. In battle it is three times less likely to be broken or bent awry than a sword made of a single piece of metal. The snake blade is incomparably superior to the weapons of the Romans or of any other nation. However, the one real secret to its manufacture is the last step of all."

He was now holding the finished blade—or what I supposed was the finished blade—in a pincers over his forge, while his apprentices labored at the bellows, making the wood coals and the metal glow the same pulsating red.

"And for this step, Saio Thorn," he went on, "I must ask you please to leave my smithy while I accomplish it."

I and Daila obediently went outside, and from there we heard a loud hissing, seething, boiling noise. After a moment, the smith came out, too, bearing the bluish-silvery blade still steaming from its bath, and said:

422

"It is done. Now I must measure the length of your arm, Saio Thorn, and the arc of your swing, in order to saw this blade to the proper length for you. Then we must choose a grip, a cross guard, a pommel, and must weight that hilt for the correct balance, and then—"

"But what was so secret about the last step of making it?" I asked. "The optio and I both heard. Clearly you quenched the hot blade in cold water."

"Quenched it, ja," he said slyly, "but not in water. *Other* smiths may do that, but not we makers of the snake swords. We long ago learned that to plunge hot metal into cold water instantly creates steam. We learned also that the steam makes a barrier between the metal and the water. That prevents the metal's being quenched suddenly enough to acquire the temper we desire and demand."

"May I make a guess then, fráuja hairusmitha, as to what you do use for that purpose? Cold oil? Cold honey? Perhaps cold wet clay?"

He only shook his head and grinned. "I fear, Saio Thorn, that you must be of far higher rank than a marshal—or even a king—to be told that. You must be a master smith, like myself. Only *we* know that secret, and have jealously guarded it for centuries. That is why only *we* can make the snake blades."

✠ ✠ ✠

The third thing that I had been carrying I handed across the table to Amalamena when we ate nahtamats in the palace dining hall that night.

"I have decided," I said, "that I will take you with me to Constantinople only if you agree to wear this, somewhere on your person, the whole way there and back."

"Gladly," she said, admiring the object of crystal and brass. "It is pretty. But what is it?"

"That phial until recently contained a drop of the milk of the Virgin Mary."

"Gudisks Himins! Could that be true? It is nearly five hundred years since the Virgin suckled the infant Jesus." At the name, Amalamena sketched the sign of the cross on her forehead.

"Well, the phial once belonged to an abbess, and *she* declared it genuine. My hope is that it will help to keep you safe while you are my responsibility. It certainly cannot hurt to wear it."

"Ne. And to lend it added efficacy, I too shall believe it genuine." She took off a thin gold chain that she wore around her neck, and

423

showed me the two baubles that already dangled from it. "My brother gave me these on my last birthday." She smiled, in the mischievous way that I had often seen him do. "So I ought to be well protected against harm. Niu?"

I had to agree. One of the ornaments, hanging as it did, was a tiny gold cross, slightly truncated at the top. And that was the reason for her mischievous smile—because that trinket could as well be hung upside down from the chain, when it would be the rough-hewn hammer of Thor. And the other ornament was a gold filigree tracing in miniature of Theodoric's monogram. Now that she was threading my Virgin's-milk phial on the same chain, the princess could be said to be *quadruply* guarded against harm. Truth to tell, though, I was secretly wishing for the phial to fend off worse things than misadventure. The lekeis Frithila had scoffed at "amuletic" medicines, and perhaps I was being just another of the "dim-witted slatterns" he had also contemned, but I hoped the phial might prove a *real* amulet and dispel Amalamena's dire affliction.

424

"Now that I am well armed," she said, still smiling, "tell me, Thorn. Why do you not grow a good Gothic beard so that—?"

"So that my skinny neck is protected? I have heard that before. Well, for one reason, I am Theodoric's emissary to the Greek-speaking lands. And the Greeks have not worn beards since Alexander abolished them. As St. Ambrose said, 'Si fueris Romae . . . ' Or, in this case, 'Epeí en Konstantinopólei . . .' "

Amalamena ceased to smile, and meditatively poked with her knife at the broiled cutlet of steerfish we each had been served. After a moment she said, "I know that you wish to be warmly received at Emperor Leo's court. But I wonder if you will be."

"Why should I not?"

"There are factors . . . and undercurrents . . . that you could not yet be aware of. When you were at the army camp this afternoon, did you notice anything about it? Anything surprising?"

"It is rather smaller and less populated with warriors than I would have expected." She nodded when I said that. "Are the majority of Theodoric's forces already on their way to join him at Singidunum, or are they stationed elsewhere?"

"Some are off to join him, ja, and some are manning other posts throughout Moesia. But you may be under a misapprehension as to the total number my brother commands."

"Well, I know he took only six thousand of cavalry for the siege of Singidunum. How many others are there?"

"Perhaps another thousand of horse. And about ten thousand of foot."

"What? But I have been told that your people—our people—number some two hundred thousand. If only a fifth of the Ostrogoths are warriors, they would be a force of *forty* thousand."

"True, *if* they all recognized my brother as King of the Ostrogoths. Have you not heard, then, of the other Theodoric?"

I remembered old Wyrd once, long years ago, discoursing as we sat beside a campfire. I said, "I seem to recall that there have been several Theodorics among the Goths."

"There are only two now of any consequence. My brother and an older Theodoric, distant cousin to our father, Thiudamer, and near his age, too—the Theodoric who affects the Romanly boastful auknamo of Triarius, 'most experienced of warriors.'"

I strove to recollect what Wyrd had told me so long ago. "Is that the one who bears yet another Roman agnomen? An auknamo rather derisive and disparaging?"

425

"Strabo. Ja, that is he. Theodoric the Wall-Eyed."

"Well, what of him, niu?"

"Many of our people account *him* their king. He does, after all, come from the same Amal line of descent as did my father and uncle. So, even before the deaths of Walamer and Thiudamer, the Ostrogothic nation was divided in its loyalties—between those brothers and that cousin. And Strabo does have other staunch allies. The Scyrri of King Edika, whom my father defeated shortly before his death. And those Sarmatae of King Babai, whom you and my brother have just now defeated. The Scyrri and Sarmatae may not *now* be such powerful supporters for him. Nevertheless, after my uncle and then my father died, Theodoric Strabo proclaimed himself sole king. Not only of the Ostrogoths, but also of the Balting line—those Visigoths long settled far away to the westward, who may never even have heard of him."

"The man's brain must be as addled as his eyeballs. Proclaiming himself king of any or every nation does not make him so."

"Ne. And most of our people who were formerly faithful to my father have acknowledged my brother as his rightful successor."

"Only *most* of them? Why not all? Our Theodoric is fighting to secure the lands and the livelihood and the rights of every Ostrogoth. Is the wall-eyed one doing anything like that?"

"He may not have to, Thorn. One or the other emperor, Leo or Julius Nepos, may *give* him all those things."

"I do not understand."

"As I said, there are many and various undercurrents at work here. From time immemorial, the Roman Empire has feared and hated all the Germanic nations, and has done its best to make them quarrel among themselves, thus to divert them from seeking to overrun the empire. That has been especially true ever since the empire adopted Catholic Christianity and the Germanic nations the Arian." She shrugged her delicate shoulders and her feathery pale eyebrows. "Akh, both Rome and Constantinople were happy to call the Germanic peoples their allies when the Huns were rampaging across the world. But, upon Attila's death and the dispersal of those savages, the emperors of both west and east resumed their policy of keeping the Germanic nations at each other's throats, instead of the empire's."

"Then why," I asked, "would either west or east favor one Theodoric above the other?"

"Neither ever will, not for long. But right now, with Theodoric Strabo having proclaimed himself king of every Ostrogoth and Visigoth everywhere, it is to the Roman Empire's advantage—for the time being—to recognize him as such. Thereby, when the empire deals with Strabo, it can at least *pretend* that it deals with all the Goths of Europe, and with all their allies, Germanic or otherwise."

This was a thing most unusual, to hear a female speaking of matters political, and sounding as if she knew whereof she spoke. So I had to ask, though I tried hard not to make my question seem either skeptical or patronizing, "Is this your own personal view of the situation, Amalamena, or is it widely shared?"

She gave me a look of Gemini fire, sharp but amused, and said, "Judge for yourself. The latest news is that Theodoric Strabo has sent his only son and heir, Rekitakh, a young man about your own age, to live at Constantinople—just as my father sent my brother in his infancy, many years ago—to be hostage and surety of Strabo's alliance with the Eastern Empire."

"No doubt about it, then," I muttered. "Strabo is indeed the currently favored Theodoric. Does your brother know all these things?"

"If he does not, he very soon will. And be assured that he will not passively accept the situation. The moment he can leave Singidunum, he will be ravening for a confrontation with Strabo." She sighed.

426

"Which, of course, is exactly what the empire wants and expects. Goth against Goth."

"Unless," I said hopefully, "our embassy to Constantinople is successful, and we procure the pactum that your brother demands."

Amalamena smiled—a sort of melancholy smile, as if she admired but pitied my apparent artlessness and baseless optimism. "I have told you how things stand, Thorn. The odds are against our success."

"Then, as I have warned before, we may even be venturing into hazard. I am the king's marshal, so I am in duty bound to this mission. You are not. I strongly recommend that you stay here."

She seemed to ponder that, in serious consideration, but at last shook her pretty head and said:

"Ne. I used to believe that a corner is a safe and sheltered place to stay. But even there, the Fates can seek one out."

Since I was unsure whether she realized that I knew what she meant, I said nothing at all, and she went on:

"I am a princess of the Amaling Goths. Any adversary, any challenge, I prefer to meet in the open. I shall come with you, Thorn, and I hope you will find me no impediment to your mission. Remember, I am now wearing the Virgin's-milk phial. Let us pray that it assists us in our cause."

"In all our causes, Princess Amalamena," I said softly. "Come with me, then, and welcome."

427

7

When we set out from Novae, we were a formidable column, and a splendid-looking one. We men constituted a full turma, thirty mounted warriors, and most of those were leading pack horses or spare steeds, including two elegant white mules. Only I, the optio Daila and the two bowmen we had brought were unencumbered with lead ropes, because I was senior officer, Daila was in command of the turma and the two archers were accounted my personal guard. Princess Amalamena, insisting that one attendant was enough of a retinue for her, was accompanied by a cosmeta, a lady's maid, of about her own age and nearly as comely, Swanilda by name. For much of the way, those two young women rode inside a horse-drawn, curtained carruca dormitoria, and slept in that at night. But whenever Amalamena felt hale enough, she would ride alongside me on one of the white mules, with Swanilda on the other a little way behind us. On those occasions, both women wore a sort of split skirt, and rode astride as easily as men do.

We warriors and our mounts were all caparisoned either to fight off any assailants we might encounter or to awe any ordinary folk who beheld us on the road. The horses wore war quiltings and the men wore leather armor and metal helmets, and both men and horses were hung about with various weapons. The men had polished to a high luster all of their leathers, and mine and Velox's, with a glaze of gum acacia, barberry juice, ale and vinegar. Every man, myself included, carried behind his saddle a glossy brown bearskin cloak, fringed with bears' teeth and claws, to wear in case we met inclement weather.

My own helmet now was tooled with ornamentation—and so was the exaggeratedly muscular torso of my new leather corselet—the figures of grapevines in full fruit, interspersed with the figures of wild boars, the animal emblematic of my marshalcy. Over the corselet I wore a new woolen mantle of the sort called a chlamys, its hem elaborately embroidered in green, and it was pinned at my right shoulder with a new jeweled fibula, also in the design of a boar. My sword belt was now clasped with a tremendous buckle of Corinthian aes, shaped like a demonic face with protruding tongue. That, its maker had informed me, would avert the wearer's being troubled by any lurking skohl or other such nuisances.

Though everything I wore was unequivocally masculine attire, I am sure it was the feminine aspect of my nature that made me preen so proudly in my gorgeousness, and even feel sorry because Gothic custom forbade my wearing a legionary-style plume atop my helmet. It may also have been feminine vainglory that made me wish I could put on a show for the company, by demonstrating how my foot-rope invention gave me extraordinary prowess on horseback with the bow and arrow. I also wished mightily that I could find some excuse to wield my new snake-blade sword, and do it impressively. But I could justify my doing that only by going out to hunt game for our meals, and of course that would have been beneath my dignity as a marshal.

So, whenever we desired fresh meat, it was my two bowmen who did the hunting. They, like Daila, had copied my contrivance and put foot-ropes on their own mounts. That made their horseback hunting as successful as mine would have been, and they always brought in ample venison. However, in order to find any game, they naturally had to range out far ahead of our glittering and clattering column. Thus none of our new company got to see how useful was the foot-rope, and none—including the princess and her maid—decided to adopt it.

There was really no need for *anybody* to hunt. When we ate the venison of boar, deer, elk or lesser game, it was a luxury and not from necessity. Old Costula and the other palace servants had laden our pack horses with every kind of staple food and daintier viands as well. The animals also carried changes of clothing for everyone in the company, spare bits of tack for the mounts and the carruca, extra arrows and bowstrings—and a number of sumptuous gifts, selected by Amalamena, for us to present to Emperor Leo: jewels of enamel fillet, jewels of gold or silver inlay, cases of perfumed soap, casks of the good bitter brown beer, and other articles that the Goths make better than anyone else. (We took him none of the snake blades, though.) Since we were so well supplied, and since the lands we traversed were well watered, mostly farm country where we could procure fresh eggs, bread, butter and vegetables, with wide meadows for our animals' forage—and where we

429

could frequently bed down in soft haystacks or sheltered barns—we traveled without any of the rigors and hardships I had feared for the princess's sake.

Obviously, she and the other people of Novae were better acquainted than I was with the state of the roads roundabout. I had looked doubtfully on the introduction of Amalamena's big and heavy carruca into our column of march. But, although we would not find a real, broad, paved Roman road until we were near our destination, the others we trod proved wide and firm enough and mostly of gentle gradient. On reflection, I realized that I should have expected them to be so. Not only because Constantinople is the New Rome of the East, but also because it is the prime port of several great seas, it is—like Rome— the center of a widely flung web of roadways. Those that we followed took us southeastward through the province of Moesia Secunda, of which Novae is the capital, then through the province of Haemimontus, across a corner of the province of Rhodope and finally into the province called Europa.

Besides being not very rigorous, our route turned out to be free of hazard; we never had to contend with any marauders or to circle wide of any unfriendly territory. Daila told me that the Ostrogoths loyal to our own Theodoric occupied the lands to the west of our way, and those of Theodoric the Wall-Eyed all lived off to the east of our route. For most of our journey, then, we were crossing a country settled only comparatively recently, and by a people who had migrated thither from less comfortable lands somewhere to the north of the Carpatae Mountains. They are called by the Goths the Wends, by the Romans the Venedae and by Greek-speakers the Sklaves, but they call themselves Slovenes. I had previously in my wanderings encountered one of them here and there, but this was the first time I had ever found myself among an entire population of those dark-haired, ruddy-skinned people with broad, flat noses and high cheekbones. And while the Slovenes did not seem too much resentful of our passage through their settlements, and did not too grudgingly consent to sell us supplies, we thought them a not very prepossessing people.

The Slovenes are not savages, like the Huns, but they are indisputably a barbaric people, for they have no written language and they are still enmired in pagan superstition. Their pantheon of gods is headed by what must be the oddest in any religion, because his name, Triglav, means "three-headed." The people acknowledge both a sun god, Dazbog, and a god of the heavens, Svarog. There is no grand adversary, like

Satan, but the people do fear a hostile storm god, Stribog. Their demons are collectively the Besy, and those seem to be ruled by a man-eating witch called the Bába-Yagá. No civilized person could possibly discern, from their names, which are the good spirits and which the bad, because *all* their names are so ugly.

Indeed, I found almost all the *words* in the Slovene language ugly, because most of them combine a disagreeable harshness and a repellent juiciness. We Ostrogoths were unable easily to pronounce any of those people's personal names, so we avoided even inquiring what they were. We arbitrarily addressed every one of them, man or woman, as "kak, syedlónos!"—because that raspy-mushy series of sounds is their own way of hailing "you, saddle-nose!"

I think it may be the peculiar shape of their noses that accounts for one other unloveliness of the Slovenes: their air of woeful and eternal melancholy, apparent even among the youngest children. And I will tell shortly why I think that.

It was in the Slovenes' part of Midland Dacia that we came to the only difficult stretch of our road, the incline leading up to and over the Thorny Pass—the Shipka, as it is called (or slurp-coughed) in the Slovene language. We had to hitch a double team to Amalamena's carruca to draw it up, over and gently down that pass, but it was not intolerably hard work. The Shipka took us across the same Haemus Mountains that I had earlier seen, because those mountains, after making a great arc down from the Danuvius, here run from west to east. And when we descended from the Shipka, we were in a broad, long, unwooded, fertile valley between that range and another parallel mountain chain which, because it is much less lofty than the Haemus, is called the Shadow Range.

431

The valley, of which I had previously heard mention, the Valley of Roses, *is* the world's most extensive garden of rosebushes. The oil extracted from the rose petals is avidly sought after by every myropola in both the Western and the Eastern Empire for the making of rose-scented perfumes. Since it takes nearly five thousand Roman *pounds* of rose petals to fill a single tiny hemina flask with their liquid essence, that oil sells for a higher price than the purest gold or the rarest spice.

During our company's whole journey so far, I had been trying at every opportunity—as I had promised the lekeis Frithila—to make the princess laugh, and to keep her in good cheer. I regaled her with nonsensical jocularia that I had heard in Vindobona, and bits of humorous gossip about the denizens of that and other places I had been. My prating caused her frequently to smile, occasionally to chuckle, sometimes to laugh aloud. But it was not I, it was the Valley of Roses that made her laugh more uproariously than I had ever yet heard her do.

We arrived in the valley in very late summer, so the rose harvesting season was some months past. But the valley was still abundantly flowered with countless millions of the more mature blossoms, and their voluptuous aroma was all about us at every hour, so intense that it seemed to tinge the very air a rose hue. We broke our journey briefly in the town of Beroea, so Amalamena and Swanilda could put up for a night in the town's one taberna—what the Slovenes somehow manage to call a krchma—and there have their clothes laundered, and replenish and refresh their sundries.

So, while at the krchma, the princess bought, among other things, two cosmetics compounded nowhere else but in that valley: a face powder ground from rose pollen and a pomade compounded from the rose petals. I was present when the princess graciously remarked to the proprietor that she envied his being able to dwell in such a sweet-scented place. The man grunted, in genuine surprise, "Sweet scent? Sladak miris?" Then he made a sour face and growled viciously, "Okh, taj prljav miris! Nosovi li neprestano blejo mnogo!" Translated from his barbarous language, it meant "Akh, that filthy stench! It gives all of us here a perpetual nose-ache!"

And that sent Amalamena off into peals of laughter, the notion that any people could be so obtuse as to disprize their privilege of living always surrounded by blissful beauty and fragrance. The incongruity of it must have been especially poignant to one who knew that she herself had little time to go on seeing and inhaling and admiring and enjoying the bounties of this world. But, as Frithila had said, the princess was ever inclined to laugh where others might have wept. And that occurrence at the krchma is what makes me believe that it must be the Slovenes' squashed-in noses, hence a deficient sense of smell, hence an inability to appreciate aromas and probably many other good things as well, that makes those people so incurably morose and unhappy.

✠ ✠ ✠

We went on, crossing the Shadow Range of mountains—no arduous feat—then proceeded southeastward through the Hebrus River valleys of Rhodope and Europa, the provinces that had anciently been the land called Thracia. Most of its inhabitants are as dark-haired as the Slovenes, but swarthy of skin instead of ruddy, and all speak the mellifluous Greek tongue and have comprehensible, pronounceable names for themselves and for everything else. Also, they all have unremarkable noses and dispositions much sunnier than the Slovenes'.

Throughout the journey, and notwithstanding the gossip and jocularia I told to Amalamena, she never found anything so hilariously funny as that episode in Beroea. However, she did seem pleased when I asked her to tell *me* things of which I was ignorant. So, whenever we rode side by side, she talked most entertainingly and instructively about her royal family, the Goths in general and the countries through which we traveled. Of course, those lands were as foreign to her as they were to me, but she had rather more deeply studied their annals than I had done. For example, at one place along the way, she told me:

"Not far west of here, two hundred years ago, the Roman Emperor Decius won a battle with the Goths. But thirty thousand Roman soldiers and Decius himself died doing it. Victory or defeat, no matter, it has always cost the Romans dearly when they have fought the Goths. So you see why the empire has long feared and hated us, but had to accommodate us, and has tried every other means than war to divide and fragment and exterminate us."

433

I muttered, "I hope to persuade the eastern court that *that* can be risky, too."

But I was less interested in remote history than in hearing Amalamena's more immediate and personal accounts of herself and her family. She told me of her late father's many kingly virtues and martial exploits, and she even more enthusiastically recounted his many beneficent deeds that had led his people to call him Thiudamer the Affectionate. "And my uncle was much the same," she said. "So he was fondly known by all as Walamer the Faithful."

She told me of her royal mother, Hereleuva—and her voice choked a little when she related how that queen died "of the dread disease called kreps" while still a comparatively young woman. Furthermore, said Amalamena, her mother had much distressed the family because, on her deathbed, she had renounced her lifelong Arianism and converted to Catholic Christianity. "Of course," said the princess, "she was in terrible agony, grasping for any slightest hope of relief, but that desperate measure gave her none. So we, her children, have forgiven her, and we trust God will. Or all the gods."

Then, as was her wont, Amalamena brightened again. She fingered the three talismans on the chain about her slender throat, and said lightly, "No doubt it was because of my mother's inconstancy that I do not now give my full devotion to any one religion. I am quite willing to accept whatever good *any* of them can vouchsafe. Does that make me despicable, Thorn?"

"I think not," I said. "It seems a very prudent course. But then, I am no slave to any religion myself. I have not yet found one that seems to me right and true."

The princess also told me of her sister Amalafrida, older than both herself and Theodoric, who was already married "to a herizogo named Wulteric the Worthy, much older even than she is."

"And you, Amalamena?" I asked. "When and whom do you plan to wed?"

She gave me such a sad look that I was ashamed of my jesting remark. But, after a moment's silence, she too spoke jestingly. She waved a hand at the land around us and said, "For that, I should have been born hereabouts, and a long time ago."

"What has the time and terrain got to do with marriage?"

"I have read that once, somewhere in these parts, there was a king who decreed that, on a certain day each year, every maiden, widow and other marriageable woman of whatever age should be herded inside an unwindowed dark hall. Then all the marriageable men of the kingdom were likewise herded in. Each man had to choose a woman—in the dark, only by sense of touch—and marry her. It was the law."

"Liufs Guth! Are you suggesting that *you* are an ugly woman? Or an old or an undesirable—?"

"How like a man to say that!" she interrupted, laughing. "Why do you instantly assume that only the *women* in that dark hall were ugly?"

"Well . . . now that you put it that way . . ." I mumbled, and I think I was blushing—not because she had caught me up, but because she had said of me, "How like a man . . ." Probably also I was blushing because I had made her laugh, and that pleased me, for I was eager to give Amalamena cause to be fond of Thorn: as a man, as a cheerful companion, as a congenial fool, as anything at all.

"Anyway," she went on, "I am certain that my sister Amalafrida married Wulteric only because she thought him very like our father. I have found no man that resembles our brother."

"Eh?"

"I was but a child, and so was he, when Theodoric went away to live in Constantinople. I had only a dim memory of him as a boy. And then, just months ago, he came back, a man grown, a young king—a man to catch the eye and fire the desire and inspire the adulation of any woman. Even his own silly sister." She laughed again, but with scant humor this time. "Akh, I need not tell you, Thorn. You know him. Although, of course, you would not regard him as a woman does."

Oh vái, I thought ruefully, would I not? *Had* I not? In one breath, the princess called me a man. In the next, though inadvertently, she reminded me of what I really was. It made me wonder: did I find Amalamena so attractive, even adorable, simply because she was blood sister to Theodoric? In any case, she had also made it plain that, in her eyes, *Thorn* was not at all comparable to him.

And she continued, albeit unwittingly, to twist the knife in my heart, saying, "Even if, like the Queen Artemisia of olden time, I could wed my own brother, he would not have me. During the brief time he was in Novae, and captivating all the maidens there, I could tell that he prefers women more . . . robust than I am." I remembered the sturdy peasant girl Aurora and silently agreed. Amalamena sighed and added, "So, since I am not likely to meet such another as he, perhaps it is just as well that I am . . . I mean to say, I am getting rather tired, Thorn. Would you help me down, and beckon Swanilda to attend me? I shall ride in the carruca for a while."

435

The princess was less and less often now riding her mule beside me, and was spending more of each day reclining in the carruca, as if it had been a sickbed. When she was at my side, she less and less often laughed aloud at my sallies of humor and my valiant attempts at playing the droll. Amalamena smiled only tolerantly, for instance, at the story I had heard in Vindobona: about the man with the two lady lovers who gradually plucked him bald. Still, the princess made no complaint of any distress. She did not appear drawn or haggard, and I never once saw her wince with pain. I did not know if she had been managing, during the journey, to continue drinking ass's milk and bathing in bran-water. But when, one day, I noticed on her the faint scent of a woman's monthly indisposition, though on her face no look of it, I took Swanilda aside to make discreet inquiry about Amalamena's condition. The cosmeta affirmed that "the princess has some slight bleeding," and, when pressed, would only add modestly that "it is not of the debilitating sort to interfere with her traveling."

Whether as a result of the bleeding or of the mere progress of her disease, Amalamena became still more pale and frail than when I had first met her, and I would hardly have believed that possible. I could now literally watch her pulse beating at her temples and at the side of her neck and at her slim wrists. Indeed, I almost fancied that I could see *through* her, so very nearly transparent had she become. Nevertheless, in my view at least, the princess looked not sickly or wasted, but increasingly more beautiful.

Partly because she had made it clear that I was not the man for her—and partly, I suppose, because I had always secretly known that I was not—my feminine feelings now came to the fore. I regarded Amalamena no longer as someone to be desired or sought, but as a dear sister to be cosseted and cared for. I stayed close by her whenever possible, tried to do every least thing for her that I could, often rode far off the road to pick flowers for her. In truth, I appropriated so many of Swanilda's less intimate duties that the cosmeta could scarcely hide her amusement. And Daila did not even try to hide his scowls, so I realized that I was behaving most unlike a marshal, and moderated my attentions to the princess. Anyway, we were getting close to our destination, and I intended there to entrust her care to Constantinople's foremost physician.

✠ ✠ ✠

436 Near the southern coast of the province of Europa, we came to the Via Egnatia, the wide, well-paved and fairly thronged Roman road that carries commerce and travelers west to east, all the way from the port of Dyrrachium on the Hadriatic Sea to the port of Thessalonika on the Aegean to the port of Perinthus on the Propontís, and to various lesser ports along its route, the road finally terminating at the great metropolitan port of Constantinople on the Bósporos. Our column joined the traffic on that thoroughfare and followed it into Perinthus, where we paused again for a day and a night, just to allow Amalamena rest and refreshment in the well-appointed sort of hospitium that is called in Greek a pandokheíon.

The princess told me that this port of Perinthus had once, long ago, rivaled Byzantium (as Constantinople was known then) in its harbor traffic, its prosperity and grandeur. Perinthus had much declined from that eminence in recent centuries, but still I was thrilled to be visiting it, because its view out over the seemingly limitless blue-green Propontís was my first-ever look at any sea anywhere. The city occupies a small peninsula, so on three sides there were piers and moorings where vessels were being loaded or unloaded and, out in the harbor roads, many more ships were waiting their turn.

I also, in the brief time we were there, got my first taste of many of the superb foods of the sea: locustae, oysters, crayfish, scallops, cuttlefish cooked in their own sepia. I did my omnivorous eating at Amala-mena's pandokheíon, because it had a terrace overlooking the harbor. While I ate, I could watch the slow but graceful movements of the war galleys called Liburnians, with their two or three banks of oars, some of them with high castles fore and aft—and watch the low, slim, speedy "raven" and "dolphin" patrol boats gliding about.

I saw also merchant craft more immense than I had ever seen on a river: two-masted and square-sailed ships, called "apple-bowed" because of their blunt prows; and the smaller, faster coastal traders, propelled by oars only. There was a constant coming and going of those merchant vessels, because their masters were eager to complete all their year's voyages before the coming of winter, when all but the coast-hugging cruising has to cease.

I so enjoyed our short stay in Perinthus that I might have been re-luctant to leave there, except that we were only three or four days' travel from what I knew to be a considerably richer and livelier seaport, and what I had been told was the most magnificent city in the entire Roman Empire: the one that had for long been named Byzantium, then for a time Augusta Antonina, but was now and forevermore the Great City of Great Constantine.

Serdica (Sofia)

Pautalia (Kyustendil)

Strymon R.
(Struma R.)

N

Euxine
(Black
Sea)

Perinthus
(Eregli)

Propontis
(Sea of
Marmara)

Constantinople
(Istanbul)

Chrysopolis
(Üsküdar)

Aegean
Sea

Assos

Pergamon
(Bergama)

ASIA

Smyrna
(Izmir)

MINOR

Miletus

Meander R.
(Büyük Menderes R.)

Mylasa (Milâs)

Halicarnassus (Bodrum)

KOS

Roman Miles

0 ——————— 100

0 ——————— 100

Miles

RÓDHOS
(RHODES)

Myra

© A. Karl / J. Kemp, 1992

Constanti-
NOPLE

n a manner of speaking, we saw Constantinople long before we could see it. Our column was still some two days distant from the city, and we were making camp for the night in a goat pasture beside the road, when several of our company exclaimed aloud on espying a yellow light in the night sky to the east.

I said, "The vast herds of goats on these shores have not left enough trees or shrubbery to feed a forest fire. What can be making that light? The Gemini fires of a storm? The draco volans of a swamp?"

"Ne, Saio Thorn," said one of our soldiers. "It is the pháros of Constantinople. I have been here before, and seen it. The pháros is a wood fire atop a very high tower, mainly intended to guide ships to safe harbor there. A light by night and a smoke by day, as you will see tomorrow."

Amalamena said, "We must be still at least thirty Roman miles from that city. A column of smoke, ja, we could see. But how can a mere wood fire's light be visible at such a distance?"

"It is magnified, Princess," the soldier explained, "by an ingenious contrivance, rather like a curved speculum. The fire is laid in an immense metal bowl that is lined with plaster. And in that concavity of plaster are embedded innumerable shards of glass, each backed with a silver foil, as gems are set in jewelry to make them glow the brighter. So glows the pháros fire."

"Ingenious, indeed," Amalamena murmured.

The soldier went on, "In time of war or other emergency, the fire-tenders can flicker that light by covering and uncovering the reflective bowl with a leather blanket, and thereby spell out a message. It can be read by sentries on distant hills. They in turn light beacons and likewise flicker them, to repeat that message over and over, and farther and farther, thereby to summon an army or divert it or whatever is required. Similarly, the sentries can relay to the city a warning of an approaching enemy, or any other urgent news from abroad."

The next novelty we encountered was not visible at all, because it was a smell—but such an *awful*, almost smiting smell that it fairly made me reel in my saddle. I coughed and retched, and my eyes watered, but through my tears I could see that the other wayfarers on the road seemed to consider it no very terrible occurrence. Everybody whose two hands were not totally occupied or burdened was either simultaneously or alternately pinching his nose and sketching the sign of the cross on his forehead.

"Gudisks Himins," I gasped to Daila. "This miasma would make even a normal man as gloomy-natured as a Slovene. Summon that soldier who has been here before. Let us ask him if Constantinople always stinks so putridly."

"Ja, Saio Thorn," said the soldier, cheerfully enough, though he too was holding his nose. "What you smell is the odor of sanctity, and Constantinople is quite proud to have it greet all comers. Indeed, the aroma actually attracts many pilgrims hither."

"In the name of whatever god they worship, *why?*"

"They come here to adore Daniel the Stylite. Look yonder."

He pointed across the fields on the left of the road. In the distance, I could descry what looked like a tall pole with an extremely untidy stork's nest built on top. It was surrounded by a number of people on the ground at its base, some of them moving about, but most of them kneeling.

The soldier said, "This man Daniel does it in emulation of the famous Simeon of Syria, who became St. Simeon by living atop a lofty column for thirty years. Daniel has been a pillar-hermit now for only some fifteen years, but I am told that his example of self-inflicted misery has converted many pagans."

"Converted them to what?" growled Daila. "Not even Circe's men-turned-swine would loiter in such nauseous surroundings."

"Devout Christians," said the soldier with a shrug. "Those who find pleasure in abasement and mortification, I suppose. They seem to find bliss in the smell of fifteen years' accumulation of Daniel's droppings."

"Then we shall leave him to them," I said. "And them to him. They appear to deserve each other."

We did eventually leave the stench behind us, and in just a few hours more we saw the walls of Constantinople begin to loom above the horizon ahead. I turned and told one of my bowmen:

"The princess was most eager for her first look at the city. Ride back to her carruca and advise her that it is imminent. Ask if she would like her mule saddled and readied for her to mount."

He came back, smiling a little, to report, "The princess thanks the marshal for his thoughtfulness, but she has decided to admire the city from her carruca, of which she has opened the curtains. She believes it would be unseemly for the sister and daughter of a king to enter Constantinople riding astride, like a barbarian woman."

That sounded unlike the free-spirited Amalamena who had heretofore laughingly dismissed "womanly" inhibitions and "seemly" behavior. Clearly she was inventing that excuse, so as not to have to admit that she did not feel well enough to sit a saddle. I reminded myself to seek out a physician for her at the first opportunity.

The walls that we were nearing were, of course, the walls built by the Emperor Theodosius II. The earlier wall, laid out by the city's founder, encompassed only five hills of the Byzantium promontory. Even at that, Constantine was thought overweening for having far exceeded the measure of the most spacious city. But he was proved right, because in his own lifetime the New Rome had grown beyond the wall, and now, like the Old Rome, it occupied fully seven hills.

Theodosius's later wall, fencing Constantinople off from all the rest of the continent of Europe, must be the most formidable protection ever built for any city. Stretching nearly three Roman miles between the waters on either side of the promontory, it is actually two walls, twenty paces apart, with a broad moat before them, and that moat is fronted with masonry breastworks. The dual walls are five times as high as a man, and are studded with ninety-six towers, higher yet. Those towers are alternately round and square, and the walls between them are zigged and zagged to permit concerted action by the warriors manning the fortifications.

Now I saw all the other travelers ahead of us on the Via Egnatia—the pedestrians, riders, teamsters, carters, drovers with their flocks, even the chairs and carriages of apparently important persons—moving to one or the other side of the road to make way for some procession coming from the city. Daila looked to me inquiringly, and I shook my head.

"Ne, Optio. We are Ostrogoths and royal deputies, not the local

443

Greeks and mongrels. We march as we are, at least until we see what approaches."

I was right to hold our ground, but there was no danger threatening, because it turned out that what approached was an imperial delegation coming to greet us. They were a splendidly mounted and caparisoned body of men. The elderly leader of them, the best dressed of all, raised his hand in salute—and his first words, though cordial, were an astonishment to me.

"Khaîre, Presbeutés Akantha!" That meant only "Hail, Ambassador Thorn!" in Greek, and it was puzzling enough that he should have known my name. But then he said, "Basileús Zeno éthe par ámmi philéseai!" and that meant "The Emperor Zeno bids you welcome!"

Once again in my life I had sense enough not to exclaim something witless like "Who is *Zeno*? I came here to meet the Emperor *Leo*," but my face must have gone blank, nevertheless. While I sat speechless, the elderly man went on, "The Emperor Zeno sends these gifts in the name of friendship," and he waved forward two heavily laden servants who rode behind him. I motioned for my two bowmen to receive the things, and composed myself enough to say, "Theodoric, King of the Ostrogoths, salutes his cousin Zeno, and we also bring gifts of friendship."

"You bring the king's royal sister, too, I believe," the man said, nodding down the column toward the carruca. "I am Myros, the emperor's oikonómos, his palace chamberlain. If I may escort you, then? There is a house prepared for you and the princess Amalamena and your attendants, and adequate quarters for your warriors." I gestured for the chamberlain to ride beside me, and the rest of the delegation fell in among my men, and thus we proceeded toward the city.

As we rode, I remarked to my new companion—pretending to make idle conversation, but really probing for information—"I have not yet lived a very long life, Oikonómos Myros, but, if I wished to enumerate all the emperors of east and west that have come and gone in my time, I should have to count on my fingers."

"Naí," he agreed, then astonished me again. "And now two of them displaced in the span of mere months."

"*Two* of them?" I blurted involuntarily.

"Naí. The younger Leo dead here, Julius Nepos deposed at Rome. Had you not heard?"

I was thinking: not only was I not going to meet the emperor I had been sent to see; neither was the Saio Soas. I mumbled, "I have been away. At war. Out of communication with current events."

Myros gave me the look that I suppose Romanized Greeks frequently bestow on barbarians. "And on your way hither, Marshal, you could not read the pháros fires and smokes? They have told of little else these past months. Except, of course, to advise us of your imminent arrival."

With some vexation, I admitted that I was illiterate in sky-writing, and added, "I should have hoped that I would at the very least recognize my own name written in the heavens. How were you apprised of that?"

He smiled slyly, as if to imply that "we Greeks are omniscient," but then told me frankly, "Our katáskopoi are everywhere. Soldiers who wear no uniform while they do their patrolling and scouting. Doubtless one of them heard you identified as the Saio Thorn when you and the princess stopped at Beroea or some other place."

"Indeed," I said coldly, not at all pleased that my company had been spied upon without my having realized it.

The oikonómos and I were now leading the column through the grandest of Constantinople's ten gates, the triple-arched Golden Gate. Set in handsomely black-streaked white marble, the massive bronze doors were hospitably wide open and polished so that they really looked like gold. Two of the sequential arches that compose the gate are, of course, passages through the two thick walls of the city. The third and innermost arch is different; it actually takes the arriving wayfarer through the foundations of the Church of St. Diomed. That church is built just within the walls, above and astride the road. The Via Egnatia ends there under the church—or simply changes its name—and becomes the Mése, the equally broad and well-paved central avenue of Constantinople.

I deliberately did not turn in my saddle to admire the high-built Church of St. Diomed when we emerged from under it. Instead, to indicate to the oikonómos Myros that I was not the least bit awed by the grandeur of the imperial city, I conversationally went on:

"Well, chamberlain, tell me of all these shifting and varying emperors of whom you spoke. I swear, I have seen children playing the game of all-fall-down, and do it without prostrating so many players as the empire has lately been doing."

"Dépou, dépou, papaí," Myros dolefully agreed. "True, true, alas. Now, what to say of the late Leo? During all his six years, Leo was ever a sickly boy. His namesake grandfather should not have appointed the lad to succeed him. Poor little Leo, even with the aid of his own father as his regent, had scarce the strength or heart or will for such responsibility. Anyway, both of the Leos being now dead, the regent-father has himself assumed the purple."

"That regent and father being Zeno?"

"Of course. Did you not know that he was affinal son of the first Leo? He is wedded to that emperor's daughter, Ariadne. The late Leo the Second was the son of Ariadne and her husband, now called Zeno."

"What do you mean—*now* called Zeno?"

"On his accession, he took that name. From the famous Stoic philosopher of olden time."

"I thought only the most pompous and pretentious bishops wore assumed names."

"You would understand and sympathize with Zeno if you knew that he is of Isaurian lineage, and that the Isaurians speak a horribly cumbersome dialect of Greek. His name at birth was Tarásikodissa Rusumbladeótes."

"Papaí!" I said. "I do understand. Thank you for explaining."

We were still riding along the Mése, and many were the marvels and novelties that I saw. The broad avenue was lined with trees and with countless bronze or marble statues of gods, heroes, sages, poets, and behind them stood almost as many palatial mansions of stone or brick—though down the narrow side streets I caught glimpses of much more plebeian residences. The Mése took us up and down the city's hills, through the lesser Golden Gate of Constantine's earlier, less impressive wall. After that, the avenue at intervals broadened out around us to become a spacious marble-paved square. From the Forum of Boûs, a square like a giant marble platform somehow suspended between the slopes of two hills, we were actually looking *down* on a small river running *beneath* the square—the Lúkos, which serves to flush away the city's wastes. At the Forum of Theodosius, we were looking *up* at a man-made river—one of the city's aqueducts, here upheld by graceful, towering stone arches as it crosses between two of the hills. In the Forum of Constantine, I saw the most grandiose statue in the whole city, the effigy of its founder, standing upon an immeasurably high column of marble and porphyry. That bronze statue shows Constantine with a corona of rays radiating from his head, thus representing him as either Apóllon with his aura of sunbeams or Jesus Christ with his crown of thorns; no city dweller of these latter days could quite decide which.

But still I tried determinedly not to stare or gape, and continued to make conversation with the chamberlain, saying:

"Very well, then. This Eastern Empire is now ruled by the Basileús

Zeno and his Basílissa Ariadne. Meanwhile, what has been happening in the west?"

"As I said, Julius Nepos was deposed. By a man named Orestes, whom he himself had raised up to be a general of the armies. Nepos thereupon fled to Salona in Illyricum."

"Wait a moment. Is not Salona the place where—?"

"Naí," said Myros, nodding and smiling maliciously. "Where the former Emperor Glycerius had been exiled after Nepos deposed *him*. Do not ask me why Nepos should have chosen Salona as his refuge, because there the resentful Glycerius—not surprisingly—had him assassinated."

"Gudisks Himins."

"Ouá, the story gets even juicier." Now, from the chamberlain's womanish relish in confiding gossip, I only belatedly realized that he must be a eunuch. He went on, "Evidently in reward for that deed, Glycerius has been elevated from the minor bishopric of Salona to the much grander *arch*bishopric of Mediolanum in Italia."

"Liufs Guth! A bishop commits regicide and the Church *promotes* him?"

Myros made a face of fastidious distaste. "Well, that is Rome's corrupt Catholic Church for you. Constantinople's good patriarch Akakiós would never permit any such thing to happen in our Orthodox Church of the east."

"I should hope not. So, who *is* emperor at Rome now?"

"The son of that General Orestes. Romulus, disdainfully called Augustulus."

"Disdainfully?"

"Not *Augustus*. Augustulus. *Little* Augustus. Little, and not very august. He is only fourteen years old. So his father, too, like the late young Leo's, is the real ruler. But no one expects either Orestes or Romulus Augustulus to last very long."

I sighed and said, "I wonder, has it occurred to anyone besides myself that the Roman Empire is in more pitiable disorder than ever before? Emperors flitting to and fro, as ephemeral as mayflies. Bishops turned assassins turned archbishops. Saints squatting on high poles and dropping skeit on their followers . . ."

"Here is your house, Presbeutés Akantha," said the chamberlain. "The finest xenodokheíon in the city. I believe you and your party will find it well appointed and more than comfortable. Would you be pleased to dismount and enter?"

The marble building and its enclosed grounds looked sumptuous indeed, but I would not let Myros see that I thought so. I sat my saddle and said:

"I am only the king's marshal. I am responsible for the comfort of his royal sister." I turned to my bowmen and told them, "Escort the princess forward, that she may decide if these humble lodgings are adequate."

The oikonómos looked rather irked, but got down from his own horse to salute Amalamena. When she came unhurriedly up to us, I saw that she had somehow managed, inside the moving carruca, to adorn herself in fine vestments and cosmetics and jewelry. As if I had instructed her to do so, she bestowed only a cool nod on the deeply bowing Myros, swept regally on past him and, with Swanilda and my bowmen beside her, went on into the courtyard and then the house.

The eunuch, now looking hurt, continued to praise the xenodokheíon to me: "A luxurious private therma for the females in the left wing, the one for you and your male attendants to the right. A plentiful staff of servants to assist your own . . . including some Khazar slave maids specially selected for their beauty. They will be ever eager to, ahem, serve your needs as well as those of the princess."

I pointedly ignored that, and cast about me a soldier's look of survey. The building's enclosing wall was not very high or constrictive, the gates were more decorative than ponderous, suggesting that we were not likely to be locked inside and held captive. Still, we *were* deep within the city and its own fortress walls. So, when Myros started to say, "The quarters for your other men—" I firmly shook my head.

"Oukh, oukh. The men are Ostrogoths. They need no roof over them or cushions under them. I shall dispose them about the courtyard here. And, regarding servants, the first I want to have serving us is the city's best physician. I should like assurance from him that the princess has not been discomposed by her long journey."

"The emperor's own iatrós, the venerable Alektor, will attend upon you without delay." He added, with eunuch spitefulness, "I could not help noticing that the princess looks rather older and more feeble than her reputed age."

I ignored that, too. When the women and their armed escort rejoined us, Amalamena sent me a glance of mischievous complicity before she gave Myros another cool nod, no more, to indicate that the house was acceptable. I dismounted from Velox and instructed my bowmen to unload from our pack animals the gifts we had brought, and to give those to the chamberlain's assistants. While that was being done, Myros went on:

"As you see, Princess and Marshal, your lodgings here are convenient to all sorts of amenities. The Hippodrome is yonder, where you may enjoy the games and races and theatrical performances. Yonder is the Church of Hagía Sophía, where you may care to attend worship services. The Purple Palace, yonder, is where the emperor will be granting you audience. The—"

"I hope," I said, "we will not be here long enough to require many diversions or even the making of devotions. When will Zeno see me?"

"Ouá . . . well, now. You will, of course, be advised of that in plenty of time to prepare for the meeting."

"Prepare? Prepare what? I am prepared right now."

"Oukh, not at all. Not at all. There are formalities to be observed. You will be told at least one day before the audience, so that you may spend that day fasting."

"*Fasting?* I am not here to receive Holy Communion."

"Ahem. Then, on the day, you will be conducted to the purple presence-chamber, where your gifts to the emperor will be all on display. As you walk toward the throne, you will three times halt and pause respectfully. When you are before the emperor, you need not throw yourself prone in the proskynésis, you being of ambassadorial rank. You will merely kneel to him and—"

"Hold, eunuch!" I said, hotly and rudely. "I am no humble petitioner, come to whine and wheedle!"

"Are you not?" he said, unruffled. "In my long experience as the palace chamberlain, every emissary from abroad has come either to present a declaration of war or to entreat the emperor to grant something to somebody. Are you here to declare war, then?"

It was a moment before I could reply, partly because I was choked with anger, partly because I had caught Amalamena's look of amusement, reminding me that I *was* here to ask Zeno to grant something. Myros took advantage of my silence to go on reciting:

"The emperor will not make you kneel for long before he bids you rise. Then you will give him greeting from your King Theodoric—and take care that you do not speak of that king as the emperor's 'cousin' or 'brother.' All lesser rulers are *sons*. The emperor will thank you and Theodoric for the gifts you have brought. Then he will name the day on which you are to return to the Purple Palace to discuss the matter

449

that occasioned your coming here." The chamberlain yawned right in my face. "War, or whatever it may be."

I finally gritted out, "Since you seem to have had us spied upon from the start of our journey, you must know why I am here."

"I did not, therefore I do not," Myros said with elaborate indifference. "Our katáskopoi first encountered your train in the Valley of Roses. I do not even know *whence* you came."

"Then I will tell all to your Emperor Zeno, and no later than tomorrow. This is urgent. I shall kneel, if that pleases his vanity, but I will not wait. See to it, eunuch, that the formalities and delays are dispensed with."

"That would be unheard of!"

"You are now hearing of it. And you may give Zeno a hint of the message I bring. Theodoric has taken the city of Singidunum from the occupying Sarmatae. He holds it firm. He could keep it. He could make of it his own stronghold, from which to launch incursions into either the Western or the Eastern Empire."

"This cannot be true!" gasped Myros. "Singidunum in Theodoric's possession? Surely we would have heard of it!"

"Then your spies and your pháros fires are not all-knowing, are they? However, I am here to say that Theodoric can be persuaded to cede that crucial city back to the empire. To the august Zeno or the less than august Romulus—to whichever emperor offers the better price for Singidunum, *and offers it soonest*. Go now. Tell Zeno that. And tell him I expect an audience tomorrow. Go!" I shouldered past the eunuch into the courtyard, leading Velox so that Myros had to dodge to save his toes from being trodden on. I turned back only to add, "Do not forget—on your way, send me that Iatrós Alektor of whom you spoke."

I tossed my reins to Daila and told him to see to the men's camping arrangements in the courtyard. As I walked with Amalamena to the house, she regarded me somewhat admiringly and said:

"I warned you that you might not be received warmly here. But it appears that you will at least be *received*. I think you did very well, snapping orders at that person in the true manner of an Ostrogoth."

"Thags izvis," I said, but grumbled, "I should not have had to make demands. My being marshal to a king ought to have been credentials enough."

"Remember what Aristotle wrote," she said. "Personal beauty is a greater recommendation than any letter of introduction. Ne, ne, do not snort. You *are* a fine-looking man." She laughed, but she was not laughing at me. "Remember also the reputation of these Greeks—how much their men love beautiful men."

I was not greatly flattered by her once again saying she regarded me as a genuine man, then making jape of me as the kind of man who attracts other men. Nevertheless, her quotation from Aristotle gave me something to think about.

✠ ✠ ✠

The oikonómos had not exaggerated the luxuriousness of the guest-house—nor, for that matter, the beauty and the complaisance of its Khazar slave maids. The princess and Swanilda, I and my archer-attendants immediately repaired to the baths—and I do not know how the women were served, but we men were not only voluptuously undressed and oiled and strigilated and bathed and dried and powdered by the maids, we also were treated to such sighs and eyelash-flutterings and even surreptitious ticklings that there was no mistaking the Khazars' willingness to serve us in other ways. No doubt my bowmen later availed themselves of that; I did not. I suppose I had for too long been too close to the pale "moon of the Amals." The dark-haired, dark-skinned Khazar girls did not appeal to me. Besides, I strongly suspected that they were katáskopoi, and I wanted no reports made to Myros or Zeno regarding my sensuality or carnality or pudicity or anything else about me.

451

I emerged from the therma, wrapped in toweling, to find the physician Alektor waiting for me, a hawk-nosed, gray-bearded man who eyed me as if he could see right through my swathing, making me feel just slightly uncomfortable in his presence. However, his presence was evidence that Myros had obeyed at least one of my commands. And Alektor's being privileged to wear a beard indicated that he was accorded the status of a sage, so I took him to be an eminent physician indeed.

"You are the Presbeutés Akantha?" he demanded. "Are you the patient?"

"Oukh, Iatrós Alektor," I said. "It is my royal companion, the princess Amalamena. Can I trust you with a confidence?"

He drew himself up and glared at me down his nose. "I am a Greek of the island of Kos. So was Hippokrátes."

"Forgive me, then," I said. "But I myself am not supposed to know what I am about to tell you."

So I confided to him everything that the lekeis Frithila had told me about Amalamena's affliction—the iatrós nodding solemnly and fingering his beard the while—and gave him certain instructions, then directed him to the women's chambers. He went thither, and I returned to the therma's apodyterium, to don comfortable indoor garb. Afterward, I simply wandered about the house, admiring our accommodations.

The floors were all of delicate stone mosaic, and some of the walls were of even more exquisite glass mosaic. Other walls were adorned by hangings showing turbulent sea battles, lovers flirting in sylvan bowers, scenes from pagan myth or Christian history. There were many other works of art about, and statues large and small—statues everywhere—some of historical figures, but most of gods, heroes, satyrs, nymphs and the like.

Although it was Constantine who decreed that Christianity would be the Roman Empire's state religion, his own capital and namesake city does not acknowledge a patron saint, but a tutelary deity, and that one the pagan goddess Tykhe, as Fortune is called in Greek. So there are statues of her all about the city, and there were several in our xenodokheíon. They were "Christianized" to the extent of each Fortune's having a cross affixed to her forehead, but there was something else about the statues that pleased me more. The Greeks had formerly represented Tykhe as an ugly, fat and raddled old woman. But, by Constantine's order, ever since his time she has been personified as a beauteous and blooming young maid.

I was looking over the gifts Zeno had sent for Theodoric—mostly gems, bolts of fine silk and other easily portable goods—when I was joined by Amalamena, her face flushed with an unaccustomed pink. She was a trifle angry, and she let me know it.

"Why did you presume to send a lekeis to me?" she demanded. "I asked for no such attention."

"I hold myself responsible for your safety, Princess, and that includes your good health." I added, "I am happy that the attention would seem to have been unnecessary. The iatrós just now departed, and without a word to me." I was able to say that truthfully, because I had instructed him to do just that.

"I could have told you myself that I feel well." She looked relieved, and I was sure that she, too, had commanded the iatrós to say nothing. She went on lightly, "Right now, I feel healthily hungry."

"Good. You will be well fed," I said, just as lightly. "I went to tell the cooks to be sure to feed also our men in the courtyard. And I am pleased to report that every cook in the kitchen is exceedingly obese.

That is always an augury of tasty and ample victuals. The dining chamber is yonder, Princess. Let me go and see that our men are encamped, and I shall join you there for nahtamats."

The iatrós was, as instructed, waiting for me in concealment in the courtyard, and he said immediately—but not happily:

"If the princess desires to die at home, wherever her home is, you had best waste no time in taking her there."

I winced. "She will perish so soon?"

"The scirrhus has eaten outward from the mesenteries, through the flesh and the skin. It is now an open, ugly aposteme, and there is no longer any doubt of its being a killing karkínos."

"Is she in pain, then?"

"She says no. She is lying. If it is not already excruciating, it very soon will be. You said you brought mandragoras. If you like, I can tell the cooks here how to serve it in her food without her knowledge."

I nodded bleakly, and commanded a nearby soldier to go and fetch my packet of the drug. "Is there nothing else that can be done?"

Old Alektor looked off into the distance and scratched in his beard for a while before replying, and then he did not reply directly.

453

"There was a time," he mused, "when we recognized the existence of goddesses, the equal of any gods. And in those days even mortal women were accounted equal to mortal males. Then along came Christianity, preaching that women are inferior to men, commanding women to be subservient to men, making of women mere cattle, as lowly as slave-owned slaves."

"True enough," I said, puzzled by this turn of the conversation. "But what of it?"

"Even a beautiful and intelligent princess is nowadays only an adornment, a bauble, at best fated to be the meek and self-effacing wife of some prince. She never *does* anything. Your Princess Amalamena, now— if she had a long life to live, what would she do with it?"

I still did not know why we were discussing abstractions, but I decided I could philosophize as well as he.

"A *flame* does nothing whatever," I said, "except burn itself to extinction, perhaps all the time in agonizing pain. Yet, in the process, it gives a blessed light and warmth."

He grunted sourly. "Not much for that flame to remember, when it is snuffed out."

"Excuse me, venerable Alektor," I said at last. "Why are we talking in enigmas?"

"I do not know what mission brings you here, young Akantha, but the princess seems most eager to have you succeed in it. I suggest—it is the only prescription I *can* suggest—that you invite her to *help* you achieve your mission. Unlike most women, she will have done one thing in this world—one thing in her very brief life—to remember and cherish during all her eternal afterlife. I have no more to say. I shall take this mandragoras to the kitchen and give instructions there. May Tykhe smile on you and your princess."

I fixed on my face what I hoped was a cheerful expression, and went to join Amalamena in the triclinium. She was already gracefully stretched out on a couch and eating heartily—whether or not that was mere pretense for my benefit—and a well-dressed young male servant stood behind her, evidently identifying for her the various unfamiliar dishes on the table. When I reclined on the couch at right angles to hers, Amalamena said, as gleefully as a girl-child dining away from home for the first time:

"Here, Thorn. Do try this. It is called marsh mutton—the meat of a sheep that has grazed all its life on sea grass. Uniquely delicious. And the sauce on it is of boiled laver fronds. Akh, and look here. Every single manchet of bread bears the embossed zeta initial of Zeno."

"So that we do not forget whom to thank for the meal?"

"Considering that bread is usually the plainest food on a table, I thought it a most elegant embellishment. I asked Seuthes how it is done." She indicated the young man standing behind her couch. "He says the kitchen's baker simply stamps the bread dough with an engraved wooden block before it goes into the oven. Akh, and did you notice the wondrous pictures on the draperies all through this house? Seuthes says those are done the same way—stamped with wooden blocks that are ever so intricately incised, dipped in different-colored dyes and ever so carefully pressed onto the cloth, one after another . . ."

I smiled tolerantly as she went on effervescing, and, when she finally ran out of praise for the meal and the house, I said idly to Seuthes:

"Are you slave or servant? Has your office a title?"

"I am neither, Presbeutés," he said, a little stiffly. "But I do have a title. I am the diermeneutés, the palace interpreter. I speak all the languages of Europe, and several of Asia. I shall interpret for you, Presbeutés, when you have your audience with the Basileús Zeno."

I thanked him. "Eúkharistô, Seuthes, but that will not be necessary. I excuse you from the duty."

454

He looked shocked and affronted. "But you must have me present. You are a bárbaros."

"I am aware of that. But why would your attendance make my being so any less barbaric?"

"Why . . . why . . . a bárbaros, by definition, is one who does not speak Greek."

"I am aware of that as well. But tell me, interpreter, in what language are you and I conversing at this moment?"

He did not answer that, but said stubbornly, "It is a known fact. No bárbaros can speak Greek."

"All received wisdom is not necessarily wise, or even true. Facts to the contrary, you are somehow understanding my speech, and I yours. Do you expect that Zeno and I will not?"

Still stiffly, he said, "I have always been needed—and present— whenever the basileús has granted audience to a bárbaros."

I assured him, "Naí, you will be present. Because the princess will also be there, and she is of course a barbará. She will be pleased to have you translate the words she speaks to Zeno, and he to her."

Now the man literally staggered where he stood. "The words *she* speaks?!"

455

Amalamena was looking more and more interested as this exchange got louder and louder, so I said, "Interpreter, you can commence by translating for her what you and I have just been saying."

He did so, speaking the Old Language quite well. And Amalamena, when she heard what I had proposed, looked almost as dazed as he. However, Seuthes had repeated all of that to her very hurriedly, because he was in such haste to turn to me again and tell me in Greek:

"She cannot be present! In all its history, the Eastern Empire has never been visited by a presbeutés of other than the male sex! The basileús would be insulted, outraged, *furious* if a woman pretended to be such a thing, and presented herself before him in that guise. It is unheard of!"

"You are now hearing of it." In Gothic, I added, "And you are now excused, until we convene in Zeno's purple presence-chamber. Go away and smooth your ruffled sensibilities."

As he departed, shaking his head, Amalamena looked at me with a mixture of amusement and gratitude. Her eyes of late had been clouded, but now they shone again like the Gemini fires.

"I thank you," she said, "for the delightful surprise gift—including me in your ambassadorial retinue. And I shall be overjoyed to go with you to the Purple Palace. But why did you decide on that? And insist on it?"

In reply, I told her not the whole truth, but a truth:

"You suggested it yourself, Princess, when you quoted Aristotle. Your beauty ought to help us accomplish great things together."

2

It happened as I had demanded: the eunuch chamberlain came to the house early the next day to inform me that the Basileús Zeno would see me that very morning. Clearly, the oikonómos would have liked to see me express gratified pleasure at that announcement. However, he found me waiting for him already dressed in my finest—newly polished corselet, my green-embroidered chlamys and my bearskin cloak, with my freshly burnished helmet under my arm—and his face rather fell. Pretending that my patience had been about to wear thin, I said tartly:

"Very well, Myros. We are ready. Are there any formalities we ought to be observing on the way to the palace?"

"We? Who are *we*?"

"Myself and the princess Amalamena, of course."

He cried, "Ouá, papaí!" and began to fizz and sputter and reel about, much as the interpreter had done the night before. I put a quick stop to that, declaring firmly that Amalamena *would* be accompanying me. He waved his arms and wailed, "But I brought mounts only for you and me!"

I looked out into the courtyard. There was a considerable body of men waiting to escort us—splendidly robed attendants, armed and armored guardsmen, even a band of musicians. One of the men was holding the reins of two horses, and the saddles of them were so ornate, high-backed and canopied that they looked like thrones.

"Khristós," I growled. "The palace gates are not three hundred paces from here. The notion of parading thither is ridiculous. But if we must, we must. The princess and I will ride. You can walk, Oikonómos, with the other escorts."

He gasped in horror, but that is how we went—Amalamena and I astride and aloft, Myros in his heavy long robes waddling and stumbling along behind us, and nearly getting overtrodden by the guardsmen stamping vigorously to the band's brisk Lydian marching music.

The Great Palace of Constantinople is not a single edifice; it is a city within the city. Inside the impressive bronze gates and the walls of Prokonéssos marble are fully *five* different palaces, big and small, but none really small; and two entire, separate living residences, the Oktágonos for the emperor and the Pantheón for the empress; and numerous churches and chapels, besides the massive Hagía Sophía just outside the walls; and quarters for the palace guardsmen, a building much too grand to be called a barrack; and one building used for nothing but a banquet hall; and numerous other edifices for the meetings of this and that council or tribunal; and an armory, and a depository for the imperial archives; and servants' quarters, slaves' quarters, stables, kennels, massed aviary cages . . .

457

The immaculately gardened grounds sweep all the way down to the city's seawall at the edge of the Propontís, and anywhere on the grounds one is standing in Europe but can gaze northeastward across the Bósporos strait and see the continent of Asia on the farther side. Down at the water's edge—although Constantinople has seven other artificial harbors, the finest in the world—there is a private harbor, the Boukóleon, for the use of ships and boats belonging to the palace or coming to it. And alongside the Boukóleon looms the cross-beamed, laddered tower that holds high the immense metal bowl of the pháros fire.

Most of the palace's building exteriors are faced with the black-streaked white marble from the little island of Prokonéssos. But the interior walls and columns and braziers and even sarkophágoi are mostly of Egyptian porphyry—and the draperies and hangings and upholsteries are colored to match that stone. That is why the entire site is popularly referred to as the Purple Palace. And, because the children born to the imperial and noble families residing there are known as "porphúro-genetós," many other languages have adopted a translation of that term to describe persons of high pedigree: "born to the purple."

Considering all the splendor that surrounded us there, it may seem odd that I was so taken with one rather trifling detail of the decorations. But it was this. The emperor's throne room, closed against the day by heavy purple silk hangings, was lighted only by a scattering of lamps and small braziers, so the very high ceiling of it was invisible in darkness—or almost invisible. When I looked upward, I realized why the big room was kept dim. It was to make shine—up there, where a dome or roof or rafters should have been—what looked to be the night sky spangled with multitudes of twinkling stars.

All the constellations were in the exact places they would occupy in the real sky on a clear summer midnight, and every star was of just the proper color and degree of brilliancy. What was most marvelous was the ingenious simplicity with which this had been done. As I later found out by inquiry, all the countless stars up there on the black-painted dome were nothing but humble, commonplace fish scales of varying tints and sizes, precisely glued in place to reflect the flickering light of the lamps below.

I had earlier seen Amalamena's face tighten with pain when one of our attendants had helped her onto her horse's elaborate saddle, and she had grimaced again when she was helped to dismount. But she walked proudly and serenely as we entered the one of the palaces to which our escorts had led us, and as we and Myros paced through the many halls and corridors. In one of those, the gifts we had brought to Zeno were displayed on purple-covered tables—or most of our gifts; one of them I had not handed over to the chamberlain and was now carrying myself, in a fancily carved ebony box. Because that was bulky and heavy, Amalamena was carrying Theodoric's folded, wax-sealed vellum.

Doing as Myros did, beside us, the princess and I walked slowly, with pauses, across the throne-room floor, and then knelt before the Basileús Zeno. His throne, of course, was of purple-upholstered porphyry, and it was wide enough for two men, but Zeno sat well over on the right side of it. I knew the reason for the over-commodious couch. On holy days, the emperor would sit on the left, with a Bible occupying the right side, to indicate that the Lord God reigned on those occasions. But on working days, like this one, the emperor took the Bible's place, to indicate that he represented God's vicar on earth, or at least in the Eastern Roman Empire.

Zeno was a bald man of early middle age, but his stocky body was still as solidly muscular as that of any warrior, and he had a complexion the color and texture of a brick. He was not wearing an imperial toga,

458

but the chlamys and tunic and even marching boots of a soldier. He made a notable contrast to the attendants standing beside and behind his throne. Most of those were Greekishly dark and willowy and perfumed and so impeccably dressed that they scarcely moved, so as not to disarrange the careful, almost sculptural folds and drapings of their robes. Only one among them, the one who stood closest to Zeno's right hand, though clad as elegantly as the others, was obviously no Greek. He was of about my own age and fairness, and might have been passably handsome, except that his face wore the dull, petulant expression of a gudgeon, and he had no more neck than that fish does.

"That has to be Rekitakh," the princess whispered to me, while we knelt with our heads bowed. "The son of Strabo."

When Zeno grunted for us to rise, I respectfully saluted him as "Sebastós," the Greek equivalent of Augustus, and introduced myself and the princess as ambassadors of his "son," Theodoric, King of the Ostrogoths. At that, young Rekitakh—for it *was* manifestly he, and evidently he understood some Greek—ceased to resemble a gudgeon for long enough to curl his lip in an unfishlike sneer. Another young man, this one the interpreter Seuthes, leaned forward from the ranks of attendants to start repeating to the emperor what I had just said, word for word. Zeno cut him off with an impatient gesture, nodded curtly at me and addressed me only by the Greek equivalent of Caius, and addressed the princess not at all.

"Kúrios Akantha," he growled. "It ill becomes a presbeutés, and it ill serves his master's interests, when he comes to this court rudely and recklessly trampling on its sacrosanct traditions."

"I did not intend sacrilege, Sebastós," I said. "I merely wished no delaying formalities to—"

"So I have noticed," he interrupted. "I watched your approach across the palace grounds." His brick face did not quite crack into a smile, but I thought I could hear one in his voice when he added, "I believe it is the first time I have ever seen the oikonómos Myros walk any distance farther than from table to koprón."

That word means a latrina, a rere-dorter, and it made the chamberlain snuffle embarrassedly at my side. I was emboldened to hope that Zeno was regarding my demand for this immediate audience more humorously than censoriously. I said:

"In all sincerity, I thought the Basileús Zeno would find my king's letter of consummate importance, and therefore should see it as soon as possible. I hope my impetuosity has not offended."

459

"Your unseemly haste I can understand," said Zeno, no longer sounding amused. "But a single presbeutés should be sufficient to deliver a single letter. Why am I confronted by a sympresbeutés as well, and that a *female* one?"

Since I really had no reason for that, I said only, "She is the king's own sister. A royal princess. An arkhegétis."

"My own wife is an empress. A basílissa. But she does not accompany me even to the Hippodrome games. Such audacious presumption in a woman would be unheard of."

I could hardly say to *him*, as I had said to others, "You are now hearing of it." But I was spared saying anything at all, because Amalamena had caught the tenor of the conservation, and herself now addressed Zeno:

"Another mighty monarch, called Darius, once granted audience to a lowly female."

Of course she said that in the Old Language, but Seuthes was quick to translate it into Greek. The emperor turned his eyes on the princess for the first time since our entrance, and his look was baleful. But he unbent enough to say coldly, "I am not ignorant that Darayavaush was one of the greatest kings of Persia." The interpreter told that to Amalamena in Gothic, and she was encouraged to go on, with Seuthes translating:

"That King Darius was preparing to execute three war prisoners when a woman came to plead that he pardon them, for her sake, because they were the only men she had in the world—her husband, her only brother and her only son. She begged so piteously that Darius finally acceded—to a degree. He said he would let *one* of them go free, and asked her to choose which it would be."

Amalamena waited until Zeno barked, "Well?"

"The woman chose her brother."

"*What!?* Why?"

"Darius said the very same thing. He was astonished that she chose neither her husband nor her son, and demanded to know why. The woman told him. She said she could always marry another husband, even give birth to other children. But, because her parents were both dead, she could never have another brother."

The basileús blinked in surprise, then looked silently at her, and his gaze seemed to warm somewhat. The princess concluded:

"Just so, Emperor Zeno, I come before you in company with the Saio

Thorn. To present to you King Theodoric's request for your wise and gracious granting of a pactum." She held out the sealed letter. "And to voice my own entreaty of your generosity, on behalf of the only brother I possess."

Seuthes had no sooner repeated that speech to Zeno in Greek than young Rekitakh shouted at Amalamena, in the Old Language, "Your brother Theodoric is not the *King* Theodoric! That title belongs to my—!" He stopped in midsentence, because Zeno, without waiting for any translation, turned and skewered him with an angry glare.

Then Zeno gave me very much the same sour look, and growled, "The young lady at least has better than barbarian manners, and knows how to comport herself with dignity at court." He returned his attention to the princess, and now politely addressed her with the title of co-ambassador, "Sympresbeutés Amalamena, give me Theodoric's letter."

She did, smiling, and he smiled back at her—and so did I and Myros, while Rekitakh glowered at her. The emperor broke all the waxen seals, unfolded the vellum and read through its contents, first rapidly, then more slowly, his free hand stroking his bald head and a new frown gathering on his face.

461

At last he said, "As already has been reported to me, Theodoric claims to have bested the Sarmatae of King Babai, and claims now to hold the city of Singidunum." Zeno rather stressed the *claims*, so I said:

"I fought in the siege and the taking of that city, Sebastós. I can affirm that everything asserted in the letter is true."

"You say so, do you, kúrios? I wonder—would you dare to say the same if the fearsome Babai himself were here?"

"But he is here, Sebastós." I set my ebony box down on the floor and undid the latches that let its sides fall apart. The head of King Babai, dried and browned and wizened by smoke, would not have been a very impressive sight, had it not been for the broad-cupped goblet of gold filigree in which I had the Novae gulthsmitha set it. I gestured and said:

"If you should wish to drink a fitting toast to Theodoric's victory at Singidunum, Sebastós, simply have a kheirourgós saw off the top of Babai's skull, and fix that piece of bone, inverted, in this exquisite golden shell. Then pour into it your best wine and—"

"Eúkharistô, Kúrios Akantha," the emperor said drily. "I have been a military man myself, and not infrequently a victorious one. So I already own other such skull cups, and now and then I do drink libations to the memory of the old enemies of which they are made. But that head could be anybody's."

"If you have never met King Babai, Sebastós," I said, "perhaps your attendant there has—the young man Rekitakh—and perhaps he can verify the identity. I understand that Babai and the young man's father, Theodoric Strabo, have long been—"

Rekitakh interrupted me by snarling, "Vái! My royal father's name is Theodoric *Triarius!*" I do not know whether he was more irate at my linking his father to the late Sarmatian king, or at my calling his father Theodoric the Wall-Eyed, or simply at my knowing who *he* was. However, when Zeno shot another glare at him, Rekitakh grudgingly admitted, "I have met King Babai. That is—that was he."

"Very well. I accept that," the emperor said blandly, and Seuthes went on translating for the benefit of Rekitakh and the princess. "Now, whether I can accept this request for a pactum . . . that is a matter not so readily to be decided. Theodoric says here that he has made the identical request to the Emperor of Rome. We cannot both grant it, I think. Tell me. Does the little Emperor Augustulus yet have this under consideration, do you know?"

"Oukh, Sebastós," I said. "We would have no way of knowing if my fellow marshal has even reached Ravenna yet. But I daresay . . . whichever emperor first grants the pactum will have possession of the captured city."

"You daresay, do you? Well, let us consider your Theodoric's terms. He asks a resumption of the consueta dona annually paid for the keeping of peace on the empire's northern borders. However, for that same service, I am now committed to paying those three hundred librae of gold to the *other* Theodoric. Now, am I expected to deprive the one to pay the—? *Siopáo!*" he snapped, as both Rekitakh and I opened our mouths. We instantly shut them again, and Zeno went on:

"Another thing. He asks for assured and permanent tenure of the lands in Moesia Secunda currently occupied by his tribe. But he and you, Kúrios Akantha, Kuría Amalamena, ought to be aware that there are numerous other claimants of those same lands. For one, the tribe of the other Theodoric."

Rekitakh looked affronted at having his nation described as a tribe, and I probably looked so, too. But Amalamena only said sweetly:

"Excuse me, Sebastós. The Saio Thorn and I have just now traveled all the way from the Danuvius. Between the lands of our people and the lands of the Thracian Greeks, north of here, we saw no other occupiers or colonists or settlers except some immigrant Wends. Those are not Roman citizens, and therefore are not *allowed* to lay claim to any lands."

Zeno coughed and said, "Human claimants aside, there is the Christian Church."

"The Church?"

"Perhaps, kuría, since you enjoy the enviable privileges of non-involvement afforded by your being a heretic Arian, you would not know that the Christian Church is the largest landowner in the entire Roman Empire. Once upon a time, rivers marked the boundaries between nations, but now those rivers may merely be flowing through and watering the croplands or timber forests or just the flower gardens of vast Church estates. And wherever any lands are not securely in the title of others, well, for those the Church makes extremely persuasive petition. To any donor of land, whether peasant or emperor, the Church promises eternal bliss in heaven. More to the point . . . but ouá!" He threw up his hands. "There is too much to explain."

"Allow me, Sebastós," said Myros, and, with the aid of the interpreter, he told me and Amalamena: "Every one of the five patriarch bishops of Christendom tries to increase and consolidate his power and authority, in hopes of reigning supreme in the Church. Naturally, our Basileús Zeno favors our Bishop Akakiós of the Orthodox Church here in the east. But the emperor must be ever mindful, as well, of his many far-flung subjects who adhere to the Catholic Church of the west. At the same time, he must conciliate all the conflicting desires and demands of the innumerable and mutually inimical sects in both Churches. The Chalcedonians versus the Monophysites versus the Dyophysites versus the Nestorians, to mention only four. Those Christians even fight in the streets, and slaughter each other, over their hairsplitting doctrinal differences. Therefore, when it comes to granting—"

463

"Now allow *me*," I interrupted, being deliberately rude and abrupt. "One item is getting obscured in this thicket of split hairs." Myros, Seuthes and Rekitakh all looked aghast at my effrontery, but I went on, "I have heard nothing to suggest that any claimant or inhabitant of the lands in question—not Wall-Eyed Theodoric, not the Sklaves, not any of the rapacious Christian elders—is offering anything tangible in exchange for those lands. The princess and I are here to offer, so to speak, the keys to the formidable city of Singidunum."

Everyone in the room, Amalamena included, turned to look at the emperor, as if expecting him to hurl a Jovian lightning bolt. But he surprised even me by saying:

"The presbeutés Akantha speaks the truth. To military men like him and myself, deeds are more important than words, and substance more important than promises. A city that dominates the whole of the river Danuvius, here on earth, I deem preferable to any nebulous hope of heaven hereafter. However, kúrios, I *will* require incontestable title to that city."

I said, "I believe you have it already, Sebastós, if you wish it. From what I hear of the new and less than august Emperor of Rome, neither he nor his regent-father is secure enough on the throne to make any binding agreement. I might suggest, though, that you date the pactum as of the day Singidunum fell. I give you my word and Theodoric's— and his sister is here to bear witness and swear asseveration—that your claim takes precedence over all others, and will be honorably upheld."

"The word of two military men and a fair princess, that is surety enough for me. Myros, summon a grammateús, so that I may dictate the pactum without delay."

464

Rekitakh uttered an anguished bleat, but Zeno silenced him with yet another look, and went on addressing me and Amalamena:

"I will grant to Theodoric's people their possession of the Moesia lands in perpetuity. I will resume payment of the annual consueta dona. And further, I will appoint Theodoric to the title that his father held during the reign of the elder Leo—magister militum praesentalis—commander-in-chief of all the border forces of the Eastern Empire."

The princess glowed happily and I murmured, "Most gracious of you, Sebastós."

"I will send another grammateús over to your xenodokheíon, so that you may dictate the quitclaim of Singidunum. Then, as soon as we have affixed signatures and seals, and exchanged the documents, I would wish that you depart immediately, to bear the pactum directly to Theodoric at Singidunum with all haste. I dislike to dismiss any guests so summarily, but I trust you both will return here—in company with our esteemed Magister Militum Theodoric—when you have ample leisure to enjoy all the charms of our imperial city."

✠ ✠ ✠

Amalamena contained her girlish joy until we were again riding side by side, while the same attendants and guardsmen and musicians escorted us back to the guesthouse that afternoon. Then she laughed, more musically than the music playing around us, and exclaimed:

"You did it, Thorn! You got from the emperor everything that Theodoric wanted, and more!"

"Ne, ne, Princess, not I. Aristotle was right. It was your *beauty* that swayed that crusty and crabby old ex-soldier. Your beauty and your winning ways. You are another Cleopatra, another Helen."

Her blush of pleasure made her glow even more radiantly, though I was instantly sorry that I had compared her to those two queens. According to Plutarch and Pausanias, both of those women died untimely and ingloriously. But at least, I thought, in their lifetimes they had done deeds worth remembering in their graves—and now so had Amalamena.

"I thank you, Thorn, for so gallantly sharing the credit. But the important thing is that Zeno *did* agree."

"He agreed, ja. Let us see if he keeps the agreement."

"What? You do not trust the word of an emperor?"

"He is an Isaurian, and an Isaurian is a Greek. Have you read Vergil, Princess? 'Quidquid id est, timeo Danaos . . .'"

465

"But—but Zeno is putting it all in writing. Why would you distrust him?"

"Three things. For one, that last look he threw at Rekitakh. It was not a look of *keep-silent!* It was a look of only keep-silent-*for-now!* However, even in tacit collusion, Rekitakh should have gone on loudly protesting, for the sake of appearances—certainly when Zeno ceded to us his father's claims, his father's gold and his father's military command. But Rekitakh was too gudgeon-stupid to do that. Lastly, although Zeno referred to your brother by various names and titles, he never once called him King of the Ostrogoths. Presumably he still reserves that honorific for Theodoric Strabo."

"Now that I recollect, ja, you are right." Amalamena's glow had diminished. "Still . . . if he is entrusting to us the pactum . . . sending the gold . . ."

"If I myself had that gold right now, Princess, I would wager every nummus of it on one guess. That the pháros back yonder—and you will notice, I have not looked behind me since we left the palace—is already wafting signal smokes, telling someone of all that has just occurred."

She swung around in her saddle—and gasped loudly. I turned also and saw that the lighthouse smoke was still a steady column, only a little breeze-blown. But I had not been wrong in my guess, merely premature, for a man was scrambling hurriedly up the ladders from the ground, almost certainly bearing a message to be sent by that means.

I was not too much concerned about that. What was more immediately worrisome was that gasp Amalamena had uttered. She had closed and clenched tight her eyes and mouth, and her face had gone from the rosy glow to a whiteness that was tinged with greenness, and she weaved in her saddle and clung desperately to its horn. Her sudden turning to look at the pháros, I decided, must have torn something inside her. So I took the reins of her horse, drew it close beside mine, put out an arm to steady the swaying girl and shouted to our escorts to double their pace.

At the same moment, even there in the open air, being nearer to Amalamena than I ever had been before, I caught a whiff of an unfamiliar scent coming from her. As I have said, I had long ago become accustomed to discerning the various odors given off by females, and divining from them the women's various moods or emotions or feminine indispositions. But this odor I had never encountered before. Because of my acute olfactory sense, I may have been the first, even before the princess, to have noticed that scent about her. It was a smell not especially strong, not overwhelming—like the miasma of Daniel the Stylite—but as penetrating, insidious and clinging as smoke. It would eventually pervade Amalamena's entire person, her clothing and bedding and everything she touched.

The Iatrós Alektor later told me what it was, and that it is by no means peculiar to females. It is exuded by anyone of any sex, he said, afflicted with the kind of killing kreps that erupts into an open ulcer. It is called in Greek the brómos musarós, the abominable stench. That name doubly describes the odor, because the word 'musarós,' 'disgusting,' contains the word 'mus,' meaning 'mouse.' And the smell truly is rather like that of a musty nest of mice, but commingled with a sharper odor, like that of a person's urine after he or she has eaten of asparagus. I can add, from my experience on battlefields, that the odor also resembles, though not exactly, the gangrenous stink of a neglected and purulent combat wound.

However, I am getting ahead of events.

When we arrived back at the xenodokheíon, I tenderly lifted the princess down from her mount, and Swanilda and some other servants came to help her to her chambers. Since Amalamena could hardly deny now that she was ill and in pain, and since she was too weak to protest that I was being meddlesome, I sent one of the Khazar maids running to fetch the iatrós.

Alektor came in company with the grammateús that Zeno had promised to send, a wispy old man who introduced himself as Eleón. I showed him to an empty room and bade him sit still until I was ready for his services. Then, while the iatrós was off attending the princess, I anxiously paced the floor of that room and watched old Eleón sharpen a number of his quills and stick them here and there in the white hair above his ears, and unroll sheets of parchment and give them an unnecessary burnishing with a moleskin, and stir his little pot of ink and somehow manage to splash stains of it onto himself and several pieces of furniture roundabout.

When Alektor came to the room, morosely shaking his head, he and I went aside and he said:

"There will be no need to disguise the mandragoras. She takes it willingly. But now that the carrion worm has revealed itself, it is eating ravenously and rapidly on her. She will require more and more massive doses of the drug. That I leave to you to administer. To her female attendant I have given instructions as to the changing of dressings and so forth. But I recommend that the princess be attended night and day. There will be times, increasingly frequent, when she is physically unable to effect her own, ahem, necessary functions. So her one servant will not be enough. There should be several, and strong ones—strong of stomach as well as of musculature. I seriously doubt that any of these giddy Khazar wenches would suffice."

467

"I pledge that she will have suitable and constant attention," I said. "And again I implore: is there nothing else that can be done for her?"

"Oukh. Nothing that I, as an iatrós, can in conscience even hint at. But I must say—something worthwhile seems already to have been done. For a young woman in such dismal straits, the princess appears to be in an admirably tranquil mood."

"Ouá . . . well . . . I did my best to administer your earlier prescription, Iatrós Alektor. She has accomplished something of considerable consequence."

"Good, good. Try to keep reminding her of that. Exaggerate the importance of it, if necessary. She will need all the inspiriting support that can be given her in the days to come."

When Alektor departed, I told the grammateús to wait a while longer. Then I made a brief visit to my own chambers before going on to Amalamena's. Swanilda politely left the room where her mistress lay on her bed, and I said:

"Princess, the lekeis now tells me that you are *not* in the prime of health. I have no doubt that I am asking a futile question, but, as your responsible safekeeper, I must ask it. Will you stay here, where you can be properly cared for, while I hasten back to Theodoric with the pactum?"

She smiled, a wan smile, but a smile. "As you say, a futile question. You also said earlier that I was at least partly responsible for the securing of the pactum. Surely you would not deny me the prideful pleasure of being able to join my brother in rejoicing over it."

I sighed and spread my hands. "I said yet another thing, once. That I would never deny you anything."

"In return, Thorn, I promise that I will not delay our column's progress on the road. That new medicine, the substance like shredded bark, whatever it is, it really does relieve my . . . this temporary indisposition . . . much more effectively than anything the lekeis Frithila formerly gave me. With the aid of that medicine, I will not need to loll in the carruca dormitoria like a lady of leisure. We can leave that here, and I will travel the whole way on my mule."

"Ne, ne, do not be foolish. I shall send an advance rider galloping with the document. The rest of us can proceed at an easier pace. Carruca and all. I have sworn to the lekeis Alektor that you will be pampered and coddled, even more so than Swanilda could do for you."

"Better than Swanilda? Nonsense. Swanilda has attended me since we both were girls. We are not mistress and servant, we are friends."

"Then she can now do you a really friendly favor. With your permission, I have a different task in mind for Swanilda. In her absence, *I* will do the attending of you. I have had some prior experience at ministering to ailing patients."

Of course, I thought, considering the eventual fate of those patients—my juika-bloth, young Gudinand, old Wyrd—it was not high recommendation of my ministering abilities. In any case, she only smiled again, and with fond gratitude, but said firmly:

"A male nurse for a female patient? Unthinkable."

"Amalamena, it was your beauty and bravery that *did* procure the pactum, and I will not let your accomplishment go for naught. The document must get safely and quickly to Theodoric. If it does not, Zeno can pretend that he never wrote it, never agreed to it, never was *asked* for it. And you know that I have suspicions of Zeno's good faith.

I intend to make sure that the document does get to Theodoric, so I ask for your further assistance in this mission. Indeed, what I plan to do cannot be done without your help. And to have that, I am ready to take a rather desperate measure of my own. It may shock you, distress you, revolt you, I do not know, but I am going to trust you to keep it a secret between just the two of us."

"What *do* you plan, Thorn?" she asked, in mock alarm, as I closed and latched the door. "Seduction or ravishment?"

I ignored the levity. Although I had promised to make the princess laugh whenever possible, this was anything but humorous to me. "I am about to introduce you to the female who will be attending you during our journey. Her name is Veleda."

"Her? I thought you said that *you* would—" She broke off, in real alarm now, and weakly tried to edge across the bed, farther away from me, when I began to disrobe. I believe the princess totally forgot her own troubles and everything else, for at least a moment, as I stripped off all my clothes except the "modesty" band around my hips, and she gasped, *"Liufs Guth!"*

469

3

ressed again, I returned to the room where Eleón the grammateús waited, and there I paced the floor some more while I dictated the covenant of cession of Singidunum. From my own scribe days, I remembered all the formal salutes and flowery phrases with which to begin the communication. But when it came to the meat of the matter, I could think of nothing better than to say simply, "For consideration received, I, Theodoric, King of the Ostrogoths, do hereby cede possession of the city of Singidunum in Moesia Prima to the Sebastós Zeno, Emperor of the Eastern Roman Empire."

"Ouá, papaí," groaned the grammateús. He shook his head over my words as unhappily as Alektor had skaken his head over the imminent demise of the princess. "Excuse me, young presbeutés, but that will not do. Oukh, oukh."

"Why not, Eleón? It says all that I wish to say. All that the emperor could wish to be said."

"But it says it too *plainly*, too forthrightly. Theodoric gives, Zeno accepts. Why, any shrewd practitioner of law would find such simple honesty a challenge, and would taken keen delight in contesting its legality. You must lard it with obfuscatory terms. 'The cedent irrevocably agrees, warrants and assigns . . . waives all rights forevermore . . . swears that the city is not subject to any other lien, levy or counterclaim . . .' Things like that, Presbeutés. And also make frequent referrals to the legal code. 'Pursuant to chapter number so-and-so, title number so-and-so, book number so-and-so of the Forum Judicum . . .'"

"I know nothing of titles and chapters and such."

"Then allow *me* to sprinkle those citations and some nicely dense legalities here and there in the conveyance, Presbeutés. They actually need have no cogency to the issue. They are only included to make legal heads nod in pretense of jurisprudent appreciation, and the heads of others to nod in drowsy boredom."

I laughed and said, "By all means, let us comply with the legalities."

He immediately set to, with much scritch-scritching of his quill, and I looked over his shoulder while he wrote. I was being as much a solemn pretender as any practitioner of law, because, for all I could read of the manuscript, Eleón could have been setting down a warrant for my execution. Finally he scattered sand over the document, blew it off and handed me a fresh-cut, unused quill with which to append my name and title. I wrote not nearly so beautifully as he had done, but I extravagantly praised the quality of the parchment on which I was putting my signature. "Ouá, an imperial court would of course use none but the costliest materials," he said proudly.

"I wonder . . ." I said, affecting humble reticence. "Do you suppose I might beg a sheet of this, grammateús, to take home with me and show our scribes how much finer resources you enjoy here?"

"Why, surely, surely, Presbeutés. I brought two, in case I might mar the writing of the one, but I did not."

I thanked him profusely, took great care in rolling the parchment, then tucked it down the front of my tunic. I was showing Eleón to the door, when he greeted by name another wispy old man just arriving:

470

"Khaîre, Artá. Have you already completed the emperor's pactum? Then I shall wait and we will return to the palace together."

This second grammateús was accompanied by the interpreter Seuthes, who asked if I would like him to read aloud what Zeno had written—and if so, in what language? I said Greek would do. He unrolled the document and declaimed, complete with oratorical gestures:

"The Sebastós Zeno Isauriós, Basileús of the Roman Empire in the East—the pious, fortunate, victorious, ever august Zeno, renowned conqueror of the Antae, the Avars and the Kutriguri—from his New Rome of Constantinople says Hail! to Thiudareikhs Amaling, son of Thiudamer Amaling, and to his generals, senators, consuls, praetors, tribunes and marshals, Hail! If you and your loved ones are in good health, Thiudareikhs, it is well. I and my loved ones are in good health also."

Then the communication proceeded to the business at hand, and Zeno's was as cluttered with ponderous legalities as Eleón had made mine. (From behind Seuthes's back, the old grammateús winked at me.) However, as I listened, I managed to filter those out, and was satisfied that Zeno *had* granted everything he had promised—the lands in Moesia Secunda, the annual gold payment, the command-in-chief of the border forces. He closed with another fulsome spate of fare-you-wells, though still noticeably neglecting ever to address Theodoric as King or Rex or anything else grander than Magister Militum. At last, Seuthes turned the parchment to show me Zeno's imperiously swashed signature, and under it his zeta-with-curlicues seal stamped upon purple wax.

471

I nodded and said, "It is acceptable. I trust Zeno will find my conveyance as much so."

Seuthes gave the pactum back to the grammateús Artá, who did not roll it, but folded it in quite an intricate manner. Seuthes plucked a purple candle from a wall sconce and dripped melted wax onto three different places on the folded parchment. Artá produced from inside his robes the emperor's heavy gold seal and, on those three places, again embossed the zeta-with-curlicues, then handed the compact package over to me.

"I thank you, good men all," I said. "I and my company are prepared to leave as soon as your emperor sends word that he is satisfied with my own document. As early as daybreak tomorrow, if he so commands. And we will bear this speedily to King Theodoric. Be so kind as to tell him that."

When they were gone, I sat down at a small porphyry table and contemplated the packaged pactum. I took out of my tunic the blank parchment I had been given by Eleón; it was of a size, tint and quality identical to the other. I could quite easily have counterfeited Zeno's flourish of signature, but I would have needed weeks of finicking forgery to duplicate all the words Artá had set down. Still, I really required no more than a simulacrum of the *package.* So I went to the kitchen and borrowed from the baker the wooden block with which he embossed Zeno's zeta on all the bread he made and served. I brought that back to the table, folded my blank parchment in exact imitation of what Artá had done, dripped purple wax onto the three same places and stamped the wax with the wooden block. The zeta thus embossed lacked the curlicues imparted by the real golden seal, but that was not evident except on close inspection. So I returned the bread stamp to the baker, then carried both of my parchment packages to Amalamena's chambers.

In just the little time I had been away from her, the odor peculiar to her disease seemed to have intensified—to me, anyway—and I hoped she could not yet smell it. But all I said was "Have you decided, Princess? Everything is ready except Swanilda."

She looked at me with the same expression she had worn when I left her earlier: a look somewhat wary, somewhat wondering, perhaps even a little sad. With a sigh, she said, "I still have enormous difficulty in thinking of you as a—in thinking of you as Veleda."

I shrugged and said lightly, "Sometimes I do, too."

That was a lie. Even when I was most Thorn, I was ever aware of my Veleda self. But I had stopped short of disclosing to the princess everything about me. I had led her to believe that I was a young woman only *disguised* as a young man, the better to find adventure and advancement in life.

She said wistfully, "I had got so accustomed to Thorn. Even fond of him."

"And Thorn of you, Amalamena."

"I shall be sorry to take leave of him."

Of course, considering her affliction, she would eventually have had to do that in any case, and she doubtless knew it. But I tried to make our having to end our man-and-woman companionship sound more heroic than inevitable. I said:

"Remember, Princess. You and Thorn are participants in a great matter that takes precedence over mere individuals. If either of you were found wanting of will and courage in the completion of that mission, would you not be even sorrier?"

"Ja . . . ja . . ." She sighed again, and squared her slender shoulders. "Veleda, you bear the name of a long-ago priestess of the Old Religion—an unveiler of secrets. So before I give permission to let Swanilda go, can you tell me, will she be at hazard?"

"Probably less than you and I will. The girl is an accomplished rider, and she and I are of much the same size. Dressed in some men's clothing of mine, astride one of our common pack horses instead of a lady's mule, Swanilda will seem just another wayfarer on the road. Anyway, I believe she is the only one of us who *can* depart from Constantinople unnoticed. So those are the orders I wish you to give her—that she ride out of here at the darkest hour of this night, and make all haste to Singidunum with this."

I held out to Amalamena the packet that was the real pactum. She still looked undecided, so I explained further:

"We must assume that every soldier of our company has been marked by Zeno's minions. Any man's sudden disappearance would be as noticeable as would be yours or mine. But I doubt that your cosmeta has attracted much attention, she having been in and out of the carruca with you. When our column does depart, you—and ostensibly Swanilda—will be inside that carriage. I will be riding in full armor and marshalish pomp, triumphantly waving aloft this imitation pactum." I showed her the other package. "To any watchers here in the city, or daylight spies along the way, our company will look complete. Any katáskopoi watching us by night will see a female servant waiting upon you—and retiring to sleep with you."

That made the princess blush slightly, and I was glad to see that she still had at least enough blood and vis vitae to *enable* her blushing. But I hastened to add:

"You have seen Veleda unclothed. She is not one whit different from Swanilda or yourself." That of course was another lie, but my next words were not. "Veleda's only intent is to wait upon you as devotedly as a servant or loving sister."

"I have never had either servant or sister who could so convincingly pass as a *man*." But Amalamena said that with a laugh, and I was glad to see that she also still could laugh, even if it was a slightly rueful laugh. "Very well. Summon Swanilda and I will give the orders. I will also tell her that I am replacing her with one of these Khazar palace maids." The princess added, in a commanding tone, with some of her

473

old mischievous mockery, "Now, *Veleda*, you go and have a horse and traveling provisions made ready for her."

I grinned, and bowed my way servilely out of the room, and went to tell Optio Daila why the princess's cosmeta would be making her midnight departure, and garbed as a man. I also told him the same small lie that Amalamena was telling Swanilda: that we had engaged one of the Khazars to attend the princess during our return journey. And I cautioned him:

"Do not request any provisions from the kitchen. Pack Swanilda's saddlebags with some of those supplies we brought ourselves. Then I will leave it to you, Optio, to lead her and her horse unobtrusively through back streets to one of the less busy city gates, and there set her on the right road."

"I shall see to it, Saio Thorn. And the mount will be ready when the girl is."

Back at the women's chambers again, I found Amalamena laughing right merrily, as from her bed she watched Swanilda awkwardly getting dressed in the tunic and undercoat and hose and shoes and cap I had provided.

"Ne, ne, Swanilda," the princess was saying. "You have the belt backward to the way a man wears it. For some reason unknown to us women, men bring the buckle around from the *left* and the tongue from the *right* . . ."

Laughing myself, I lent my assistance to the flustered Swanilda. When she was properly attired, I gave her also my ancient sheepskin surcoat to take along, because the nights would be getting chilly. Then I gave her a wallet containing money more than adequate to take her to Singidunum. I recommended that she carry only a few of the coins in that wallet, and hide most of them—along with Zeno's pactum— elsewhere on her person. Then, because Amalamena seemed now fairly revivified, I told her that the Khazars were laying a table in the triclinium, and asked if she felt like taking some nourishment.

"Akh, ne," she said with a small grimace. "But do take Swanilda with you, and make sure that she gorges herself. It may be the last decent meal she will have in some while."

In order to do that, I had to bid the girl to put on a feminine robe over her masculine garments, so that the servants would not marvel at her transformation. Swanilda may have been a bit uncomfortable, so heavily clothed at table—and the slave maids did regard her somewhat

474

oddly, because a cosmeta who ranked in status only slightly above themselves did not customarily dine with a presbeutés. However, neither of those circumstances prevented Swanilda's putting away an estimable portion of the meal we were served. And while she may have been distressed at leaving her mistress, even a little apprehensive of what lay ahead of her, still she was noticeably excited at the prospect of making such a responsible journey all alone.

During the meal, Swanilda shyly asked if I, as a man, could give her any intimations as to how best she might comport herself in her disguise. With such a short time available for instruction, I could think of only a single useful suggestion:

"I cannot imagine that you will have much occasion to run, Swanilda, or to throw anything, while other people are watching. But try to remember not to do either. The act of running or throwing will always give away a woman who is pretending to be a man."

She thanked me for my sage advice, then went to say goodbye to her mistress before she reported to Optio Daila and prepared to depart. I stayed on at our table to ask our serving maid to bring me a jar of the wine we had just drunk, hoping that I could get the princess to take **475** some of it. Then I went to a window that faced the Propontís, and looked out at the pháros. Its fire was blinking and flickering, undoubtedly either repeating or elaborating on the message it would earlier have sent by puffs of smoke. So I went next to my own chambers and untidily disarranged the linens on my bed. In case any spy should sneak a look in on me during the night, it would not be evident that I had not occupied my own bed. It would appear that I had been unable to sleep—and so had probably gone off to relax myself by using one of the Khazar maids.

Then I carried the wine jar to Amalamena's room, and steeled myself not to flinch when I caught the whiff of the brómos musarós. I found the princess again alone, still in bed, but once more looking almost as wan and woeful as she had done on coming back from the palace.

"Are you in pain, Princess?" I asked anxiously. "Do you require some attention? Were you left too long alone?"

She wearily shook her head. "Swanilda changed my dressing one last time before she left. I have to confess that it is dispiriting to see my— my wound uncovered."

"Then here—have some of this good Byblis wine," I said, pouring a goblet for her. "I brought it because I thought it might have some beneficially homoeomeric effect on your health, it being the color of rich blood. But whether it does or not, it is potent enough to lift you out of melancholy."

She sipped at it, than drank quite thirstily. I poured a goblet for myself and took it over to the corner of the room where stood the maidservant's smaller and lower bed, and there I began preparing myself for sleep. Among the Goths, this simply means stripping to the skin, except on bitterly cold nights—and except in my present case, of course, for I continued to affect Romanish modesty, and did not remove my hip band. In truth, my modesty was not entirely a pretense. Even after having earlier undressed to the same near-nudity in Amalamena's presence, I could not now do it *casually*. But I assumed that she would feel less uncomfortable being alone in a bedchamber with another woman rather than with a seeming man.

She did keep her eyes averted from me while I disrobed, and forbore even from speaking to me again until I had slipped on Swanilda's discarded light lounging robe. Then, evidently just to have *something* to say, Amalamena murmured, "The wine is delicious, Veleda. And it truly is blood-red."

476

"Ja," I agreed and, also just to have something to say, unthinkingly added, "I daresay that is why it got its name. After the nymph Byblis, who committed suicide when she failed in all her attempts to seduce her brother."

I instantly realized what a mistake that remark had been, for the princess turned on me a look of Gemini fire.

"And you, *Veleda?*" she demanded, this time not stressing that name with good-humored mockery. "How have *you* fared with my brother, niu?" Her eyes raked blue flame up and down my scantily clad body. "Surely you, too, are in love with him."

For a moment, I floundered, trying to frame a response that would cause her the least distress. At last I said, choosing my words most carefully:

"If I had been Veleda when I first met your brother, ja, I might very well have fallen in love with him. And perhaps he with me. And perhaps by now you would have real reason to suppose . . . However, Theodoric has known me always as Thorn. If I were now to reveal my . . . my true self to him, he would banish me from his sight forever. I would lose not only any chance of loving him as a woman, I would also lose his friendship for Thorn. And with it the marshalcy, the rank of herizogo—heights impossible to a woman—that I have achieved by being Thorn.

So . . ." I spread my hands. "As a matter of cold practicality, I have refused, I still refuse, I *will* refuse to let myself love Theodoric, or to entertain any smallest wishful thoughts of him. If I may speak even more frankly, Amalamena, let me say this. Were I really a man, or were I the mannish woman you may suspect Veleda of being, then it would be *you* that I would—"

She said abruptly, "That will do. I regret that I asked the question. This is ridiculous. Here I am, quarreling over a man who is my own brother, and with a woman who prefers to be a man, and who now professes to—*vái!*" She gulped the last of her wine, and said sorrowfully, "My parents had prescience in naming me Moon. This is a situation fraught with lunacy, if ever there was one."

"Ne, my dear Amalamena," I said gently. "There is nothing lunatic about loving. And if you can love a brother, surely you can let a sister love you." I waited, then said, "You have but to tell me how."

She made herself small in the bed, and pulled the covers almost up to her eyes, and trembled visibly, and finally said, in the voice of a tiny child, "Hold me. Only hold me, Veleda. I am so very frightened by my dying."

I did that. I doffed my robe and slid under the covers and slipped my parchment package under the pallet, beneath my body, and clasped Amalamena to me. Except for her ever present gold chain bearing the gold miniature of Theodoric's seal, the gold hammer of Thor and my Virgin's-milk phial, the princess wore only a hip band like my own, to keep the bandage pressed upon her abdomen. And, as I had noticed at our first meeting, her breasts were maidenly, no bigger than my own. So I was able to hold her close, safe, warm. And all the night I held her so, and during all the nights left to us thereafter, and that is all the loving we ever did, or ever needed to do.

✠ ✠ ✠

Though I was early up and dressed the next morning, the oikonómos Myros came calling before I had a chance to have a word with Daila. With a sniff, he said that Zeno was well satisfied with my document ceding Singidunum to him. Myros added, with another sniff, that the Sebastós even sent his compliments on my having dictated the covenant with such "legalistic" perfection. The chamberlain was not being eunuchally sarcastic or supercilious; he continued to sniff and wrinkle his nose, and I knew why. Amalamena's brómos musarós had permeated my own clothing, or perhaps my hair or even my skin. But Myros did not inquire about the smell, and I did not volunteer anything, so he concluded his message by saying:

"Therefore, Presbeutés Akantha, you and your company may depart whenever you are ready, and the emperor trusts that you will be doing so without delay."

"We are ready to leave," I said, "as soon as we all have broken our fast. And as soon as you can organize your marchers and musicians, and get them here to escort our column to the Golden Gate."

He stopped sniffing and blinked. "What? Another formal escort? Well, now . . ."

"Please do not tell me it is unheard of. I believe this is a most significant pact that your master and mine have agreed on. It deserves some public fanfare, would you not say so?"

He sighed, said, "The escort will be provided," and went away.

I immediately sought out Daila, who told me, before I could even ask, "The little cosmeta departed at the midnight hour, Saio Thorn, unobserved by any of the cohortes vigilum or, I think, by any secret spies or anyone else at all. I took her out through the Rhegium Gate, which is not much frequented even in daytime. From there, she will have had no trouble in finding her way around the city walls to the Via Egnatia. And she is a bright little wench; she will have no trouble, either, in finding the roads that will take her west and north to Singidunum."

"Good," I said. "But if any misadventure does befall her on the way, we ought to hear of it, because the rest of us will be traveling those same roads behind her."

"To Singidunum?" asked Daila in some surprise. "I thought, since you entrusted the pactum to the cosmeta, you would have other plans for us."

"She is carrying the document secretly. I hope to convince all and sundry that *we* are carrying it." I showed him the imitation I had made, and told him why I suspected that Zeno had no intention of its ever reaching Theodoric. "I shall have this on my person the whole way, and I fully expect an attempt will be made to snatch it from me. I do not know what kind of attempt—a sneak thief, a skulking slayer, an open attack by seeming road bandits . . ."

"Or something unpredictable," growled the optio. "An apparently fortuitous landslide, a forest fire, anything."

"Ja. Meanwhile, we are transporting to Theodoric one thing more precious even than the pactum—his royal sister. So I am going to stay always as close to the princess as her new maidservant does. During every day's journey, I will ride beside her carruca. Every night, whether we make camp or find lodging indoors, I will sleep at the foot of her bed, with one eye open and with my sword unsheathed. Since I will be thus occupied and frequently out of your sight, Daila, I am laying a heavy responsibility on you. I will do my best to protect Amalamena, but I am relying on you and your command of our men to protect her *and* me *and* the false document I will be carrying."

He said, a little frostily, "You could have relied on that in any case, Saio Thorn. What need for the second parchment and the ruse and the secret messenger?"

"A precaution only, old warrior, no reflection on your fighting ability. Remember, I have seen you in action. Still, if we *should* be overwhelmed, we can die knowing that our death has not furthered the perfidious aims of Zeno and his myrmidons Strabo and Rekitakh, but actually has thwarted them. Theodoric *will* have his pactum and everything it promises to him and our people."

Not much thawed, Daila said, "Better yet for us not to die at all. My every effort—and that of every man—will be devoted to that end."

"As you say, better yet. Now see that you and they break fast, and do it most gluttonously. One last good feed at Zeno's expense."

I ate voraciously myself, and personally carried a heaped tray to Amalamena, and—after she had downed a dose of mandragoras—demanded that she eat some food, though I could not force her to eat a great deal. Then, for the first time, doing as Swanilda had instructed me, I changed the dressing of the princess's ulcerated scirrhus. I had to do that over her objections that she was still capable of doing it herself—and while I did it, she turned her head away and gnawed at a fist and squeezed her eyes tight shut and trembled all over, consumed by embarrassment and shame.

I tried to ignore the fact that I was intimately touching the quivering bare belly of a beautiful young princess, that I was seeing her naked from her navel to her pudendal crease, it being not much concealed by its silver-gilt fluff of pubescence. I sternly reminded myself that she was now my beloved sister, that her body was not greatly different from my own, except that it was ailing and needed my sisterly attentions.

Peeling off the old bandage released the lesion's stench and—I repeat—there are no words for that. The appearance of the open sore I will not try to describe, for I have no wish to recall what it looked like. I will only say that I was heartily glad that both the princess and I had

479

already eaten. So, whatever had been my feelings when I began the task, they were all replaced by a sick horror—and that was replaced as swiftly by a surge of pity. Thereafter, at every subsequent change of Amalamena's dressing, I had to suppress—not any lust or salacity, not prurient curiosity, not even nausea at the dreadfulness of the job—only my impulse, every time, to weep for the poor girl, decaying before she was yet dead.

That morning, after my attentions, Amalamena was so weak and woebegone that I had to assist her to put on her traveling clothes, and then I had to call one of my bowmen to carry the princess's belongings while I and a Khazar maid helped her to the courtyard and into her waiting carruca. Then and later, I noticed that Amalamena seemed to wilt a little more each time her bandages were changed. I do not know whether it was the natural progression of her disease, or whether some of her vital spirit drained out with each released effluvium of odor, or whether, with each new reminder of her condition, she simply lost another degree of her will to live—but she was perceptibly fading, day by day and hour by hour. And every day, too, she required bigger and more frequent doses of mandragoras to keep the pain at bay.

That morning, though, the princess did seem to enjoy our festive traverse of the city, from the xenodokheíon to the Golden Gate, with palace attendants marching fore and aft of our column and making cheerfully loud music. She kept the curtains open on her side of the carriage, so she could see the sights and could wave to the people who watched us pass, but she kept the curtains closed on the other side, where ostensibly her servant was riding. Daila led the procession and, as I had instructed him, made sure it wound its way up and down many streets and avenues, and through many marketplaces and monumental squares.

I rode beside the carruca, again wearing all my finest and most martial and most marshalish regalia, now beaming broadly and flaunting the folded, purple-splotched parchment like a captured flag. The noise of our parade made the people on the streets stop and stare, and others came running from their houses or their work. They surely had no earthly notion of who we were, or what we represented, or what was the package I waved, but they cordially returned our waving and they cheered *íde!* and *blépo!* and *níke!* as if we were going off to war on their behalf. Should I ever need them, I thought, I could call several thousand inhabitants of Constantinople to testify that I had left their city carrying an official, emperor-sealed document. But I mainly hoped that Zeno was again eyeing us—along with everyone else in the Purple Palace—and was being equally deluded by my mummery.

The marchers and musicians stopped at the Golden Gate, but the music continued to play as our column went on, and only gradually faded behind us, and the high city walls even more gradually sank below the horizon, and we were again among the traffic of walkers and riders and carts and livestock on the Via Egnatia. Two days out from Constantinople, we again hastened past the obscene Daniel the Stylite, and for two or three nights we still could see behind us the glow of the pháros, but it was not discernibly sending any signals. We kept to the Via Egnatia, camping by the wayside each night, until we reached the port of Perinthus. There the princess and I (and, I told Daila, the princess's Khazar maid) lodged in the same harborside pandokheíon that had been such a pleasant place on our earlier stop in that city.

When our company left Perinthus, though, we did not take the road that had originally brought us south to it. We went more west than north, now, up the valleys of the Rhodope Mountains, across a corner of the province of Macedonia Secunda, to the town of Pautalia in the province of Dardania. That town, we were informed, was noted for its curative mineral springs, to which many ill and crippled persons resorted from all over the empire. So, in hope that Amalamena might get some benefit from those waters, I broke our journey there for three days and three nights, and the princess and I took lodging in another well-appointed pandokheíon. During the third night we spent there, something totally unexpected did happen—something that would indeed relieve Amalamena of that wasting and agonizing and killing carrion worm. But, before it did, it would very nearly put an end to the existence of both Veleda and Thorn.

481

4

We had not yet seen or suspected anything against which to defend ourselves. But Daila, as he had done at every stopping place so far, both posted sentries and set a mounted patrol roving randomly about. Our lodgings at Pautalia were as easy to guard as any camp we had made in the open, because Pautalia is not so much a town as a loose collection of hamlets. The numerous hot springs are scattered at some distance apart, so there has grown up around each of them a separate cluster of buildings. Each spring has a pandokheíon that consists of a central inn and a group of small cottages combining sleeping quarters and a private bathhouse. And each has accreted the shops of blacksmiths, suppliers of travel goods, cartwrights and the like. At the pandokheíon we chose, I engaged a cottage for myself and another for Amalamena "and her maidservant," and our men bedded down in courtyards and stableyards and in the fields roundabout. So we made a compact community around which the sentries and patrols could guard all the approaches.

Since we were all more or less within sight of each other, I instructed the princess to make occasional appearances in daylight, outside her quarters, but dressed in Swanilda's clothes and with a kerchief hiding her fair hair, to maintain the pretense that a cosmeta shared the cottage with her. And, at each sundown, I strolled conspicuously from my quarters to hers, wearing sword and armor and helmet, so all could assume that I was sleeping across her doorsill or at the foot of her bed.

As I have said, I slept *in* her bed, and held her close each night until she was fast asleep. I also helped her with her bathing, because the warm and astringent mineral waters sapped her strength more than any exertion did. At first, she was reluctant to make use of the therma, insisting that a piecemeal sponge bath would be adequate.

"Come now," I said. "According to local report, every visitor to

Pautalia since the Emperor Trajan himself has praised the healing power of these springs. Bathing in this water can hardly *worsen* your health."

"I am not concerned about that, Veleda. What in the world *could* make it worse? I simply refuse to uncover my . . . my blemish, and have it visible to both of us for that long a time."

"Very well," I said, pleased to have a good excuse not to remove my own concealing girdle. "We will both be Romanly modest while we bathe. Then, when we are done, I will promptly change your dressing for a dry one."

As we left the therma on the third night, the princess said, with some wonderment, "I can only half believe this, Veleda, and perhaps I should not mention it, lest I invite rebuke by the Fates, but I do think these waters are helping me. I am still weak, but I *feel* healthier—of both body and mind. And the pain has so much abated . . . Do you know, I have not had to take any mandragoras at all today."

I smiled and congratulated her. "I had thought that it might just be the baths' heating of your body that made you look rosier and happier. But it seems to me that the ulcer itself is smaller and less angry-looking than it was."

483

Well, I also thought that the open sore might have been shrunken and closed to some degree by the waters' astringency. And Amalamena's brómos musarós was not perceptibly diminished. Nevertheless, I decided to tell Daila on the morrow that we would all stay at Pautalia for some days more, just to see if the princess continued to improve. Anyway, she went to bed with me in a considerably more blithe mood than she had enjoyed for a long while past. And it was in the middle of that night that the unforeseen thing occurred.

"*Saio Thorn!*" boomed a voice from outside our quarters. I was instantly awake, and aware that the day had dawned. Almost equally instantly, I was out of the bed and scrambling to get into my Thorn garments and armor.

"Coming, Daila!" I shouted back, having recognized the voice. While tugging one of my boots on with one hand, I reached the other under the pallet for the folded parchment, to tuck it inside my tunic. It was not there. Startled even more wide awake, I flipped back that side of the pallet for a look. The package was nowhere in sight.

"Amalamena!" I gasped. She was sitting up, looking as shaken as I, clutching the covers over her bare breasts. "The parchment! Did you take it? Move it?"

She said faintly, "Ne, not I."

"Then, please, you get dressed too—in Swanilda's clothing. As soon as none of our men is close enough to identify you, make a brief appearance as the maidservant."

I did not wait for a reply, but clapped my helmet on over my disheveled hair and hurried out the door, still fastening various closures of my apparel. The optio was waiting for me, blackly scowling but—gods be praised—holding in his hand the purple-sealed parchment. He was not alone. Several others of our warriors were with him, and two of them were supporting one who appeared to have fainted or been injured.

"Saio Thorn," Daila greeted me sourly. "If you have been sleeping with one eye open, I recommend that you give it a rest and employ the other eye for a while."

I could hardly upbraid him for disrespect to a superior. I could only inquire, and apologetically, "How did the thing get stolen?"

"A traitor in our very midst." Daila indicated the man who hung slumped between two others. His face was so battered, bruised and bloody that it took me a moment to recognize him as one of my two bowmen. The optio took me a little apart from the group to speak confidentially.

"Our other sentries are still loyal, and they watch with both eyes open. They saw him steal into and out of the princess's quarters. They laid hands on him before he could break the seals and discover that he had pilfered a worthless imitation."

That was some relief, but I was still appalled—and doubly so. Not only had this personal guardsman of mine tried to subvert the plan that I had taken so many pains to arrange. He also must be now aware that I, the Saio Thorn, was not what I had for so long claimed to be. He had tweaked that package right out from under my sleeping head. Even in the dark, he would have realized that the Saio Thorn and the "Khazar servant girl" were one and the same. Well, I was as much to blame as the thief. The relationship between sisters Amalamena and Veleda had become so intimate and cozy that I had allowed myself to get scandalously comfortable and complacent. Now both Thorn and Veleda were at hazard of being denounced and unmasked, and eventually punished or banished or even eradicated. Still, Daila had not yet said anything on that subject, nor had he given me any searching or equivocal looks—only his understandable glare of disapproval—so I, too, spoke only of the matter of closest concern.

484

"Why would an Ostrogoth stoop to betraying his own king and nation and fellow Ostrogoths?"

The optio said drily, "We asked him that, and, as you can see, we asked him most emphatically. He finally confessed that he had got enamored of one of the Khazar maids back at the guesthouse in Constantinople. She inveigled him into this treachery."

Another thing, I thought, for which I had to share the blame, because it was I who had bidden the two bowmen to lodge indoors there, instead of in the courtyard with their company.

I sighed, "I have been woefully remiss."

Daila could not forbear grunting, "Jawaíla!"

"I naturally assumed that the xenodokheíon servants all were spies. It never occurred to me that they might persuade one of my own men to turn his coat."

"And for such a sordid cause," growled the optio. "For *love*, of all paltry things! For love of a guesthouse appliance already much used by innumerable previous guests. He will certainly be granted no warrior's death." Daila walked over to the slumped man and slapped his wobbling head several times back and forth. "Wake up, you wretched nauthing! Wake up, so you can be hanged!"

485

"He deserves it, true," I said. "But let us not put on a show that will amaze the local folk, and make them curious about this dissension in our ranks. Ne, Optio. Let us dispatch him quickly, then make of him just another pack on our pack animals, and dispose of his cadaver in some uninhabited place along the road."

Daila grumbled, but finally said, "Ja, you are right." He put his hand to his sword hilt. "Will you do it, Saio Thorn, or do I?"

"Hold," I said, suddenly struck by a worrisome thought, and I beckoned him aside again. "Might the bowman have told his lover about our advance messenger?"

"He could not have done. Not he or any other man except you and myself, Saio Thorn, knew of that. I alone escorted the girl to the city gate. And now the tetzte traitor cannot tell anyone, either, that we carry only a counterfeit pactum."

Daila's calling me a "man" emboldened me to ask, "And, in his confessing, has he spoken of . . . anything else?"

The optio shrugged. "The rest was babble. I fear I may have hit him too often and too hard."

As if that remark had waked him, the flaccid prisoner stirred and raised his head. He looked at me and Daila from the one of his eyes still working, and that red eye fixed malevolently on me. When the bowman spoke, he sprayed a mist of blood, and his speech was slurred by broken teeth and torn lips.

"You. You are not . . . not marshal . . . not warrior . . . not Thorn." He choked and swallowed and tried again. "There *is* no man Thorn."

"You see?" said Daila. "Babble."

"No Thorn . . . and the princess has no female serv—" There he stopped abruptly, because I had, in one movement, unsheathed my sword, stepped forward and cut his throat.

"Now get him out of sight," I told the men who held his corpse still upright. "Roll him in a blanket and sling him on a pack saddle."

I had finally made use of my new snake-pattern Gothic blade. But I could not be very proud of that, its first victim having been an Ostrogoth kinsman of mine. And I had slain him, not really for his attempted betrayal of us, but to prevent his disclosure of my own personal secret—because that would be a relevation that his and my fellow Ostrogoths might well deem more horrific even than his treachery. But, I reminded myself, I had not killed the man *entirely* for that reason. Right now, my chief motive for maintaining my secret was to enable Veleda to go on attending the ailing princess, and Amalamena's well-being was worth the slaying of any number of wretches such as this one. Still, I did wish that my sword could have been baptized with the blood of a fighting enemy warrior.

As the dead man was dragged away, the optio said, "I doubt that he was going to desert us and carry the parchment all the way back to Constantinople. He would have known that we would chase after him and hunt him down. More likely, he was going to hand the thing on to someone else. And, since he waited until now to steal it, probably he meant to meet that someone hereabout."

"I agree," I said. "And if we *do* have an enemy or enemies lurking hereabout, let us get speedily away from this place. Yonder is Amalamena's Khazar cosmeta now, plucking some autumn flowers for her mistress." (And, I noted approvingly, making sure that the blossoms obscured her face.) "So the princess must be up and about, as well. I will not let her leave until she has adequately broken her fast. See that the men and animals also are well fed, and have the company ready to ride immediately afterward."

I explained everything to Amalamena while she and I ate from the tray I had brought to her quarters—and it gladdened my heart to see her eating now with robust appetite.

"I should have liked to stay longer here," she said. "The thermae seem to have done me most miraculous good. I was truly hungry to break my fast this morning. But, as you have said, we have a mission to accomplish. I am ready—and I feel strong enough—to get on with it."

"Then hasten to don your princess regalia for the day's journey," I said. "But tonight, as soon as we make camp, dress again in Swanilda's apparel." I took from my tunic the retrieved parchment and said, "Also, tonight, I believe I will sleep with this clenched in my *teeth.*"

When the column was all formed and readied, and the horses were whuffling eagerly to be off, the optio rode back from the head of the company to where I sat on Velox beside Amalamena's carruca, and he said:

"There are two roads we could take from here, Saio Thorn. The dead traitor expected us to stay on the one we came by, the road going directly northwestward from here to Naissus and then to Singidunum."

"I see what you mean. So his accomplice—or band or army of accomplices—will likewise expect us to leave by that road. Thank you for the observation, Daila. And the other road?"

"It runs alongside the river Strymon from here, more northerly, eventually to the city of Serdica."

"Well, Serdica is far out of our way," I said. "But we will take that road, and stay on it until we are well away from here. Then we will hope to strike another road branching off toward the west, and resume our former course. Very good. You may put the column to the march, Daila."

487

✠   ✠   ✠

We seemed to be almost the only journeyers using the riverside road this day; we neither caught up to nor passed any other trains coming or going along it, except for some flocks of sheep and herds of pigs and their drovers. That made me—and optio Daila, too—vaguely uneasy about the safety of this particular stretch of the road.

What more concerned me was that, in making this departure from the shortest way to Singidunum, we were no longer following the course that Swanilda would have taken before us. At each stopping place so far, I had made discreet inquiry. No one I asked had any vivid recollection of a small, slight, fair-haired horseman having passed through—

and that was all to the good, because neither had anyone witnessed or heard of any such lone rider's being waylaid or falling ill or getting injured by an accident. I could assume that Swanilda had at least reached Pautalia without misadventure. But until we were back on her track, I could only trust that she was still making her way toward Theodoric or—as I devoutly hoped—had already found him and delivered the pactum.

Very soon, though, I stopped fretting about Swanilda's progress. I and Daila had more reason to be uneasy about our own, because the land began to close in on us at either side. We found ourselves in hilly country through which the river Strymon had cut a deep and narrow defile. With the river and our road beside it being hemmed in by steep cliffs, we felt uncomfortably vulnerable to ambuscade.

However, by the time the optio and I were mulling those apprehensions, our company was too far along the defile to have turned back and got out of it before dark. We had to forge onward, hoping to emerge from the farther end of the ravine before the day ended. We did not, but neither were we assaulted by anyone or anything, in daylight or dusk. So, when the twilight darkened enough to make further travel impractical, we took advantage of the next wide place in the gorge to move off the road and break column and prepare to camp.

"I do not want anyone rolling boulders down on us," said Daila, so the first thing he did was to send two men climbing the cliff that overhung us. They would take turns keeping watch overnight. Next he sent two warriors to watch the road, one in either direction, up the road and down, a considerable distance from our encampment, and he posted other sentries at intervals along the riverbank beside us.

While the rest of our men were tending to the animals, lighting cooking fires and laying out our provisions, I made sure that Amalamena was seen, and seen twice, by anyone who cared to look. First, she descended from the curtained carruca wearing her princess apparel, and made a pretty show of stretching the travel kinks out of her limbs. She got back into the carriage and—after a little, when the twilight was deeper—emerged again in her "Khazar maidservant" garb and head covering, carried a ewer down to the river, filled it and took that inside the carruca.

Then, just in case our sentries atop the cliff might *not* prevent some enemy's tumbling a landslide down onto our encampment, I took the reins of the carriage horses and led them back the way we had come, nearly to where the down-road sentry stood leaning on his spear, and positioned the carruca there safely apart from the rest of the company. I summoned another soldier and, while he unhitched the horses and took them and my Velox to be picketed on pasturage with the others of our animals, I entered the carriage to ask the princess how she had fared during the day's journey.

"Splendidly," she said, as chipper and merry as ever I had seen her. "Another whole day without any need of taking the drug."

"Your recovery seems miraculous, indeed. And far be it from me to play the doubting Thomas. I must remember to recommend the Pautalia waters to any invalids I may ever meet hereafter."

"Also I am as hungry as a she-wolf," she said, laughing. "I have been munching on fruits the entire way. But now I should very much like some heartier provender."

"The men are cooking now. Let me but change your dressing and, by then, the meal should be ready."

When she opened for me the Swanilda clothes she wore, and the ulcer was uncovered, she did not get downcast, as formerly, but said buoyantly, "See? It is smaller yet than it was this morning!" I could not be sure of that, but I said it was. "So this bothersome chore," she went on, "will not much longer be necessary. Go now and fetch our nahtamats. Then let us be early to bed and, after another good night's sleep, good Veleda, I should be in even better health yet."

489

As I walked back to the company, I was thinking that the cheerful cooking fires, shining their warm light upward along the cliffsides, made our encampment look like a lofty, roofless but snug and reposeful room, islanded in the black night. The men not working or on watch were already in line at the fires where the camp coquus and his helpers were serving, but they of course made room for me. One server gave me a full wineskin, and I slung its strap over my shoulder. Another handed me two wooden bowls, and the coquus was ladling into them a rich-looking stew, when we all started at a sudden bellow from the darkness up the road:

"*Hiri! Anaslaúhts!*

It was the road sentry yonder, frantically warning us, "Here! Onslaught!" He managed to shout one more word before he must have been cut down: "*Thusundi!*"

Well, there were not a thousand of them. But from the approaching thunder of hoofs on the hard-packed road, it was evident that they far outnumbered us. Next instant, they were upon us, and everywhere, but only briefly visible in the firelight—armed and mounted men, in Gothic

armor and helmets like our own—before their horses' hoofs tore the
fires apart, into flying embers and drifting sparks. But the attackers did
not wield their weapons; that first assault seemed intended only to
shock us and put out our fires, for the horses wheeled away again. As it
turned out, those assailants were slashing the picket ropes of our
mounts and stampeding them to deprive us of them.

Everyone of our company, myself included, had dropped his food or
utensils and whipped out his sword. All the others now went running
to where they had left their heavier weapons, but I paused, indecisive
as to where best I should make a stand. Then, abruptly, Optio Daila
was beside me, dimly visible in what was left of the fires, shouting commands:

"Men! Prepare to defend on foot! Butt your spears and impale their
horses!" Then he turned to me and barked, "Go! Get the princess
and—"

"She is guarded, Daila."

"Ne, she is not. That sentry had orders. If we were attacked. Slay the
other traitor, then rally with us. Here he comes running now. You go
and—"

"Slay?" I echoed, perplexed. "What other traitor?"

"It is obvious. Knew we decided to take this road. Must have sent
word somehow. The Khazar maidservant."

I said, or probably wailed, "Akh, Daila, Daila . . . misguided man . . ."

"Do you hear me? Go! If the princess is captured, she is hostage. Get
her to the river. Try to make it downstream, away from—"

But the attackers were on us again, this time furiously flailing their
swords, battle-axes and spiked maces. Daila threw up his shield to parry
one horseman's ax blow that would certainly have brained me, because
I was standing stunned and paralyzed until that *crunch!* of heavy steel
biting into leather woke me from my daze. I made a swing at the foeman with my own sword, and then went scampering as Daila had commanded.

It was very hard to run, with my heart so heavy that I might have
been weighted by a millstone inside my breast, but I ran. And, as I ran,
I reflected that Daila could not rightly be reprehended for his mistaken
assumption. After all, one Khazar maid *had* tried to disrupt our plans;
why not another? Of course, it was just as likely that any enemy eager
to confiscate our pactum would, when our own treacherous man failed
to deliver it, deduce that we had found him out—and that we, now
being alerted to an enemy presence, would leave Pautalia by an alter-

nate road. Still, even if it had been practical, in the middle of a thunderclap attack, for me to explain that to Daila, what point in it? I had gone to great lengths to make Daila believe that there *was* another Khazar servant in our company. So the grievous error was not so much to be blamed on him as on me. Once more, on me.

Inside the carruca, I found Amalamena as I had dreaded but expected. She had lighted only a single wick lamp in there; its dim glow would not have been sufficient for the sentry to see who "the Khazar" really was. But it had given him light enough to kill her with one sure stab of his blade—into her pale maidenly breast, just below the place where hung the Virgin's-milk phial. There was not much blood from the single puncture; my beloved sister had not contained much blood to spill.

Well, I thought, it had been a quicker, cleaner, more merciful death than the two physicians had predicted for her. And she had died with pride, neither trying desperately to hold on to her last flicker of life nor pleading for surcease from the terrible slow dwindling of it. She had been happy this day, and carefree, and she had died while still being so. There was still a trace of that dimple-wreathed smile on her face, and her open eyes, though they had lost their brilliance, were yet of the winsome color of the Gemini fires.

I gently closed the ivory lids over those blue eyes, and just as gently kissed her pink-pearl lips; they were still warm. Then, with a sigh, I turned to go and join my fellows in what could only be *their* dying, too. Even from this distance, I could hear the clangor of the combat, but I knew that would not last for long. Our enemy—and I assumed it was Theodoric Strabo—having failed at taking the parchment by subterfuge, was clearly now going to seize it by brute force, and had come with forces enough to annhiliate all of us. I sighed again, because it had been only this morning that I had wielded my snake blade for the first time; now I would be wielding it for the last. And Strabo's men, though they might be detestable renegades, were yet Ostrogoths. So the only blood my sword would ever have tasted would all be that of my kinsmen.

But then I paused. I had no fear about dying, and no reluctance to do it; that was a warrior's expectable and most honorable end. Still, it would be wasteful to die if I might possibly be of more value to my king and my people alive. Daila had wanted me to get Amalamena away to safety because, if she were not killed in this fray, she would have been Strabo's hostage. By holding her to ransom, he could demand from her

491

brother any kind of concession, even the giving up of all that the Emperor Zeno's pactum granted to him. Well, Strabo could not now use the princess for that extortionate purpose. But . . . suppose he were made to *believe* that he had captured her. Might not a counterfeit princess—a captive, yes, but a captive held inside the enemy's highest ranks and innermost stronghold—might she not prove a more valuable warrior than whole armies outside?

Hastily, I doffed my armor and boots and other trappings, and flung them into the bushes in the darkness beyond the carriage. I started to throw away even my precious snake blade, then thought better of that. I discarded its belt and scabbard, but I gave the sword one more blooding, though only a pretended and pathetic one. I carefully put its point into the wound the sentry had made in Amalamena's breast, silently mouthed some words of farewell to her, rammed the sword as deep as the other had gone, and left it there, its hilt an upright cross.

I stripped down to the hip band that I still wore, then got out from their storage chest the princess's best garments and appurtenances. With a strophion of hers, I bound my breasts so they were high and rounded and with a shadowed cleft between them. I put on one of Amalamena's gowns, a wispy white amiculum, and found a gilded leather belt to go around my waist, and a genuine gold fibula to pin at each shoulder, and some gilded leather sandals. My hair had been pressed down by my helmet, so I fluffed that out as femininely as I could make it. I would have liked to prettify my face with some cosmetics, but the distant clamor of battle had now quietened, so I merely dabbed some of the princess's rose-essence scent at my throat, behind my ears, at my wrists and between my breasts, just to mask the brómos musarós that clung to Amalamena's garments. Then I knelt beside her body and, with a murmured apology, unclasped the gold chain with its three bangles, took it from her neck and fastened it around my own. Last of all, I tucked the imitation pactum down inside the blousing of my gown—and I had barely done that when my captor came for me.

With a noise like that of lightning cleaving the sky, the curtains of the carruca were suddenly, violently thrown asunder and, simultaneously, the man who did it gave a roar of triumphant discovery. He was standing outside on the ground between the carriage's front and rear wheels, his thick-muscled arms holding the curtains wide apart, but so massive was he that his helmet nearly brushed the roof. He continued to utter that bestial roar as I instinctively—not pretending—shied away from him as would a real and fearful maiden. Because he wore a Gothic

492

helmet, I could see nothing of his face except his beard, his mouth and his eyes. The beard was yellow-gray, chest length, disheveled, bristling like the spines of a hedgehog. The roaring mouth was open, strung from lip to lip with strands of saliva, and behind them were long, almost equine yellow teeth. The red-lidded and red-veined eyes might have been those of a freakishly giant frog; they seemed to scan the carruca's entire interior from wall to wall without even swiveling, because each eyeball was unalterably skewed outward.

Constantiana
(Constanţa)

Axiopolis (Medgidia)

Euxine
(Black Sea)

Kallatis
(Mangalia)

Durostorum
(Silistra)

Odessus
(Varna)

Danuvius R.
(Danube R.)

Prista (Ruse)

Romula
(Rosiorii
de Vede)

Anchialus
(Burgas)

Novae
(Svishtov)

Serdica
(Sofia)

Pautalia
(Kyustendil)

Strymon R.
(Struma R.)

Roman Miles

0   40
0   40

Miles

©A.Karl/J.Kemp, 1992

STRABO

1

heodoric Strabo—or, as his sycophants obediently called him, Theodoric Triarius—ceased roaring at his discovery of me, and, in a voice that grated like tombstones rubbing together, demanded, "Ist jus Amalamena, niu?"

I nodded, as if unnerved to speechlessness, and lifted the gold chain to show him its hanging adornments. He leaned forward to peer at them in the dim light, first with one eye, then the other, and grunted contemptuously.

"Ja. As described to me. An imbecile female who wears, right next to a holy symbol, the monogram of her tetzte brother. Ja, you are she." He jerked his spiky beard toward the sword-impaled body of the princess. "And who is that, then?"

I said, with pretended difficulty, "She . . . was Swanilda. My cosmeta. She begged me . . . to do that. She was terrified of being . . . raped . . . or worse."

He laughed coarsely. "And you are not, niu?"

"I am well protected," I said, trying to sound as if I believed that, and I again showed him the chain's bangles.

"Protected? By which protector, niu? The pagan Thor? The Christ? Your nauthing brother?"

"Ne, by this third amulet." I held it up apart from the hammer-cross and the monogram. "My phial of Virgin's milk."

"Akh! *Your* milk, wretched maiden?" He guffawed so loudly as to make the closed curtains on the opposite side of the carruca tremble. "Why, virginity is a quality even more tempting to a ravisher than is your inviolable royalness. I shall greatly enjoy plucking the kernel from your—"

"The milk of the Virgin Mary," I interrupted. "A genuine relic." I cast my eyes aloft, put on a simpering devout expression and, with my free hand, sketched a cross on my forehead.

He instantly stopped laughing and dropped his voice from its loud grating to a hoarse whisper. "Say you so?" He leaned forward again and brought one of his eyes so close that it almost touched the phial, and he too made the sign of the cross. "Well, now," he said in the same hushed rasping, sounding both awed and disappointed. "A man cannot insult the Virgin Mary by despoiling a maiden wearing her holy relic, now, can he?"

I silently gave thanks—not to any sanctified virgin or to her improbably brimming breasts, but to my own quick thinking—for having revealed Strabo to be so superstitious and so easily subdued. But then he reached out one big hand and seized my wrist not very respectfully, and spoke my title with even less respect.

"Come, *Princess*, and join us at the campfires. We have matters to discuss."

He yanked me from the carriage so hard that I might have landed face first on the ground, but he had two warriors accompanying him, and they caught me and set me upright and held me pinioned by both arms. They also took the opportunity to fondle me in various places, while Strabo leaned again into the carruca and plucked my sword out of Amalamena's body.

"A good blade," he muttered, stroking some of her blood off it so he could see its pattern and try its edge. "But far too small for any of *my* soldiers. Here, Optio Ocer, you have an infant son." He tossed the sword to one of the men holding me. "Give him a proper start on his life's career."

Then Strabo led the way—his men supporting me as I deliberately did some feminine tottering over the rough ground—back toward where the encampment had been. It was being remade there, for others of his men were rekindling the fires, righting the overturned cooking kettles and other equipment, eating and drinking from the dropped bowls and wineskins. As we went thither, we came upon the bodies of several of my late company. One was quite near the carruca, others lay at intervals farther on. Every man had been facing up the road, in the direction from which the onslaught had come, and every man's wounds were all in his front. They had obviously fought to the last step, as they backed toward where their princess was, gallantly striving to keep the assailants from her.

At each corpse we came to, Strabo made me stop and look closely at each dead face. I recognized them all, of course. The one closest to the carruca had been the one of my personal bowmen who had remained loyal; among the many bodies strewn about our former encampment, one was that of the optio Daila. Though I wondered why I was being bidden to look at every face, I had a more pressing concern. My two guardians, in their furtive fondling of me, had not encountered the parchment package inside my blouse. So I was again doing some quick thinking. Should I try to keep the false document hidden? Try to destroy it? Try some other ruse before it was found and opened?

As it happened, I was worrying needlessly. When we came into the firelight, Strabo—and all his soldiers nearby—looked me appraisingly up and down. Then he asked, in his stone-grating voice:

"Which of those dead men, niu, was the Saio Thorn of whom I have heard?"

"None of them," I said truthfully, and added, with some show of spirit, "Perhaps he got away alive. I hope he did."

"Indeed. It was he who carried Zeno's pactum?"

I could also say truthfully, "The last time I saw him, it was, ja."

The optio Ocer spoke up. "Triarius, *no one* escaped alive. We know that none slipped up the road past us, and I have had men in disguise following this train ever since it left Pautalia. They have reported to me, and they report that no one fled past them down the road. However, some of the foemen did die at the riverside, and their bodies washed on downstream."

"Very well," said Strabo. "As soon as all of us have scavenged a few bites to eat, and the others have returned from rounding up the scattered horses, lead them and find every last man that was slain. Go all the way to the Aegean mouth of the Strymon, if necessary. Strip and search every one. Find me the pactum. But before that"—he jutted his beard at me—"start with this one."

I wriggled loose of the two grinning guards and cried, "Would you dare to humiliate an Amaling princess so?"

"Vái! Do you suppose I am being merely sportive? I want that document. If you wish to preserve your modesty, all you have to do is point to the man Thorn."

In a sense I did. I said through my teeth, "I have the pactum," and withdrew it from my blouse and tried to tear it with both my hands, but parchment is not easy to tear.

The optio and the other man instantly pinioned me again. Strabo uttered his rasping laugh, stepped close and took the package from my grasp. Then he only glanced at the folded document, nodded on seeing the purple wax seals indented with the Z monogram . . . and, to my astonishment, tossed the thing almost casually into the nearest fire. It was not until later that I learned that Strabo was unable to read. Of course, if he had simply opened the parchment and found it blank, all my planning would have gone for naught. But he forebore to open it, because it would have shamed him to have to *pretend* to read it, or to have to ask someone else to do so, and have me laugh at him for an ignorant barbarian.

I laughed anyway, scornfully, and said, "You have destroyed only a piece of parchment, not its significance. My brother still holds the strategic city of Singidunum. That was what persuaded the emperor to grant *this* pactum and all its endowments. My brother has only to ask, and you may be sure Zeno will write and sign and seal another such parchment."

Strabo grunted uncaringly. "Your brother holds Singidunum. I hold his sister. We shall see which weighs more in the balances." He turned from me to the optio and said:

500

"Very well, Ocer. Now we need not linger here overlong. Send two men to hitch draft horses again to the carruca, and to drag that dead wench out of it. Have two others take this *princess* back there, put her in the carriage and see that she stays in it." To me he said, "I regret having disturbed your night's rest, *Princess*. But I want us all to be on the road by daybreak. We will be riding hard and we will not make camp again until tomorrow night. So if you can snatch any sleep before we depart, I suggest that you do so."

I only gave him a look of disdain, so he turned once more to the optio, saying, "Meanwhile, Ocer . . ."

I should have liked to hear what other instructions Strabo gave, but I was hustled away into the darkness and, after the horses were harnessed to the carriage, my two guards rather roughly tossed me up into it. Amalamena's body was already gone, and there was nothing remaining of her except one small dried bloodstain where she had lain. I demanded of my guards to know what disposition had been made of her remains. I feared that such a lovely young corpse, still soft and pliable and penetrable, might have tempted brute soldiers to use it for all manner of depraved entertainment.

"We are Ostrogoths, like yourself," one of the men haughtily reminded me. "We do not defile the dead. Your maidservant will be treated just as is every warrior fallen in this fray."

The two guards were not, however, so punctiliously considerate toward a still-living young woman. When I started to close the carruca's curtains, they made me leave them wide open on both sides. Then they tried, with loutish japes and vulgar gestures, to persuade me to prepare myself for sleep—meaning for me to strip naked—while they watched me in the lamplight. I ignored them, and simply lay down on Amalamena's traveling couch, fully garbed, and closed my eyes and tried to rest while I pondered the recent rapid succession of events.

I wish I could say that I thought only of my poor dead princess, and mourned her deeply, and still felt her dear presence near me in the carruca. Her perfume was there, because I was wearing it. But the only other trace of her was the lingering brómos musarós, still discernible even overlaid with the heady scent of roses, and I did not care to be reminded of Amalamena moribund. I wanted to remember her as I had last seen her, vivacious and merry and looking forward to life. I hoped that I would soon have an opportunity to put on fresh clothing and to change every furnishing in the carriage impregnated with that ugly odor.

Meanwhile, I fingered the bangles on the chain about my neck, and prayed silently—though not to any particular deity—"*Please* let Swanilda have got safely to Theodoric!" Since my leaving Constantinople, things had not all gone precisely according to plan, but I was still alive and in a very advantageous position, especially if Theodoric *had* received his pactum and Strabo went on believing that he had not.

Still, there were some worrisome aspects. Lying there in the carruca, I could hear the noises from the encampment, and could divine what was going on. Strabo was having his men strip all of my men's corpses. The victors would plunder any weapons or armor or money purses or anything else they might find useful, and then would pitch the residue and all the naked cadavers into the river. I supposed that they had already done the same with Amalamena's body. Hardly the most honorable and dignified exequies for the departed, but I doubt that the dead really care for pomp. And that way, as old Wyrd had once asserted, they would live on, as fish, as waterfowl, as otters, as fish hawks, as fisherfolk . . .

What mattered most to me was that all those dead would not soon be missed. Floating corpses are common enough in any river so that the local streamside dwellers and boatmen would not make much fuss over encountering a few more. Since all of these would be floating naked, probably nobody would even haul one ashore to see what might be

501

pilfered from him. Certainly nobody would take any trouble about identifying any of them. Meanwhile, Strabo's column would continue along this same road that mine had been following. Though the train would consist of many more men, horses, spare mounts and pack animals, it would have the same carruca traveling with it.

Far away in Singidunum, Theodoric would not waste a great deal of time in fretting about what had become of his marshal Thorn and his sister Amalamena and his optio Daila and all the other warriors. Before long, he would send scouts galloping to backtrack our trail. But what would they discover? No scene of battle and no rumor of any. They would hear in Pautalia that *ja*, our column had left that place and had taken this road in doing so. And then, from travelers or residents or innkeepers along this road, they would hear that *ja*, a train of Ostrogoth horsemen did pass this way, and *ja*, it was escorting a handsome carriage with a pretty woman riding in it . . .

To Theodoric's scouts, it would seem that the Saio Thorn had simply, suddenly, incomprehensibly—perhaps traitorously—diverted his entire column away from its intended destination, and had led it off into Strabo's lands, or to the other side of the earth, or into oblivion. I had no idea where Strabo might now be taking me, and since I had deliberately arranged for him to do this, I did not much care where. However, I would have preferred that anyone who *did* care could follow me there.

At some point I drifted off to sleep, not to wake until the carriage abruptly jerked into motion. The darkness about was now dark indeed, for the carruca's one lamp had burned dry. The curtains were still open, and I could dimly make out my guardians riding close on either side. So I merely lay where I was, and listened to the hoofbeats and clinks and creaks and jangles of the whole train, continuing on up the road through the gorge, which gradually began to lighten as the sun rose. Strabo had warned me that we would set a good pace, and we did. The carruca was rumbling along faster and more joltingly than I had ever known its draft horses to haul it.

The column rode well strung out—so no rank had to eat too much road dust from the rank ahead—and my carriage was at about the middle of the train's considerable length. But the road sometimes curved enough so that I could glimpse the front and the rear of the column. I was pleased to see, among the spare mounts being herded along, my own fine Kehailan steed Velox. No one was riding him, even when the men traded wearied horses for fresh ones, and I decided they must be avoiding him because they were puzzled by the foot-rope he wore spliced around his chest. Perhaps they thought it some sort of check-rein, indicating that he was vicious or skittish of temperament. I smiled at that. Assuming that Velox and I arrived to be held captive at the same place, I would eventually—I devoutly hoped—have the opportunity to show our captors what Velox and his accustomed rider could do in the way of admirable riding.

We kept on traveling all that day, pausing only occasionally for the men to change their horses and to water all of them. At two or three of those stopping places, my guardians brought me food and drink from the column's traveling rations: cold smoked meat or salted fish, a hard manchet of bread, a leather cup of wine or beer. At those times also, I was allowed to descend briefly from the carruca, to stretch my legs and empty my bladder. Of course I did that in the female manner, and of course there was always one or another warrior standing guard nearby—and leering at being able to watch a royal princess have to relieve herself not a whit more royally than would the lowest peasant wench.

We continued northeastward, evidently heading directly for Serdica. I knew it to be a sizable city, but I did not know if it was counted among Strabo's dominions or if he simply deemed it a convenient place to hold me while he negotiated with Theodoric. Well, I thought, I would find out in time. However, even riding hard, we did not reach Serdica that day, and when we made camp by the roadside that night, I found out that Strabo had other and baser plans for the princess Amalamena than merely holding her to ransom.

503

The carruca, though still guarded by two men, was positioned well apart from the mass of soldiers, and I supposed it was to accord me some small privacy for my eating, sleeping and other functions. True, my food and wine were again brought over to me—hot food, this time—so I was spared having to jostle among the others at the cooking fires. But after I had eaten and had made a necessary trip into the bushes and had done what sketchy washing of myself was possible under the circumstances and was composing myself for sleep, Strabo himself suddenly loomed at the side of the carriage. Without any greeting to me, without asking my leave—with only a cavernous belch, indicating that he too had eaten well—he climbed into the carruca and lay down beside me.

"What does this mean?" I demanded frostily.

"Akh, girl, you could have slept only poorly last night." He belched again. "I shall graciously see to it that this night you slumber well. You will sleep with me, and you will sleep the sleep of the sated. Now you may snuff the lamp and close the curtains. Unless you want the two guardsmen to watch."

Not fearfully, but in genuine surprise—because I had congratulated myself that I *was* protected against molestation—I said, "You told me that you would respect my holy relic. That you would not rape me."

"I do not intend to. You are going to yield to me willingly."

"I shall most certainly do no such thing."

He shrugged his beefy shoulders. "Take your choice. Theodoric Triarius or the whole camp. Either I or all of them will have you this very night, and I will not wait long for you to decide. I should imagine that a presumptive princess would rather yield to one cousin of her own Amaling line than to a hundred and fifteen men of dubious lineage and gentility."

"Do not be too sure," I said boldly, but not feeling very bold. "Louts and vulgarians they may be, but I have seen none of them so abhorrently ugly as you are."

504

He laughed his tombstone laugh. "I have been ugly all my life, and in that time I have heard more gibes and jeers and insults than you could possibly fling at me, so save your breath for screaming 'rape!' "

"A princess does not scream," I said, trying to sound as lofty as a real princess. "It is impossible to express disgust and contempt and disdain in a scream. But these calm words I will speak, Strabo. You expect from my brother some concession, submission, ransom, whatever. You must be aware that he will not pay for damaged goods."

"Vái, he will have paid before he knows the goods are damaged. It may even be that he will not care about the so-called damage, when he does know."

"What?"

"Remember, he is only a minor pretender to kingship. Many a real monarch has found it to his advantage to pander a sister or a daughter to a mightier monarch. Your tetzte brother may have been long contemplating doing just that—offering you to be my wife or concubine— in exchange for some recognition of his pretensions."

I seriously doubted that, but there was one thing I was truly curious to know, so I asked, "Why the world, old man, would you *want* a mate who finds you repellent and detestable?"

"Beause I do not find *you* so," he said, calmly enough. But then, abruptly, he ceased being calm. He darted out one huge hand, clutched the neck of my blouse, gave a violent tug and ripped Amalamena's filmy white gown completely off me. Under it, I wore only the amulet chain, the strophion about my bosom and the decorative band around my hips. He cocked his head from side to side, so that first one eye, then the other could regard me appreciatively from top to bottom. After a moment, he went on, calmly again:

"Ne, I do not find you at all repellent. Rather less than ample, for my taste, but no doubt I can fatten you up in due time. But now, enough of this paltering. Let me see the rest of you. Or must I do it all myself?"

I was almost angry and outraged enough to fling away both of the concealing scraps of cloth, just to astonish the brute with the sight of a person possessed of not only female breasts but also a male member, and to enjoy seeing what his response would be. However, since good sense suggested that his most likely response would have been to slay me on the spot, I restrained myself, and peeled off only the strophion.

"Less than ample," he repeated. "But maidenly enticing, and they will of course swell with pregnancy."

He began leisurely removing his own outer garments, and I merely 505 glared at him without remark, so he continued:

"Ne, I do not find you repellent, and I have no other wives or mates or concubines at the moment. Your predecessors all died without giving me any male issue, except the one fish-faced son, Rekitakh, whom you have met. The Emperor Zeno thinks he is holding that son hostage to my good behavior. Vái! He is welcome to the dolt. But you are young. No older than Rekitakh, I think. Perhaps you will give me a more commendable heir. And then, you see, we will be inextricably united."

"Heaven forfend," I said, making an effort to keep my voice steady and icy. "Suppose that child should turn out to be as deformed as you are. Rekitakh only looks like a fish, not like a frog with—"

Slap! His hand again shot out, and I fell supine on the couch, half stunned, one whole side of my face burning.

"I told you, wench, do not spend your breath on idle insults. Use your mouth instead to spit copiously into your hand. Then apply that to moisten your nether parts, or they will hurt far worse than your face does. I do not waste time on preliminary play to prepare a woman, and I do not require any such play from you. No pretended arousal or endearments or caresses. Or, for that matter, even your undressing to the skin. If it makes you feel less wanton, you may go on wearing your pitiful amulets—even your affected and ever so coy Roman modesty band. Do you hear me? All I need from you is that you lie there and *endure!*"

That is what I did. That is all I could do.

There was some initial pain, because, old and grizzled though he was, he was immense and leathery and energetic. After only a short while, though, I suffered no more pain. I felt only abominably *used*, and thereafter managed to resign myself to being used, as if he had merely been pumping his member inside my armpit or along the cleft between my breasts. His sweating and slobbering over me might have been only that of a pestiferous large dog, and his other emissions I managed to regard as no more than disgustingly messy.

I do not mean to suggest that there is anything remotely extenuating to be said about the brutal act of rape, even—I suppose—if it were to be committed by the fairest and gentlest of men. But, in my particular situation, I could at least be thankful for three palliative circumstances. One was that, even if Strabo might be as potently fertile as a bull úrus, I had no fear of getting pregnant with a fish-faced child, a frog-faced child or any other sort of child.

506

Another gladsome circumstance was that I never had to look into my defiler's eyes. Even when Strabo's reddened and bloated and straining face was directly above mine, his eyes' irises were off to either side, and all I could see was the whites of his eyeballs. It might have been a blind man lying atop me and pumping at me. So I never had to see whether his eyes were glazed with bestial glee or triumphant with gloating—or whether they were searching my own for signs of anguish or terror or debasement or any other such response that might have heightened his feeling of domination over me.

The third small palliation for me, while this was going on, was my being able to keep Amalamena in mind. Earlier, I had been only reconciled to her having died comparatively mercifully, from a single sword thrust instead of a ghastly decay. But now I had good reason to *rejoice* that she had perished when she did, because she had died unsullied and unshamed. I was quite certain that I could survive this night much better than she could have done—or any other woman, and I include Veleda.

It must be remembered that, at this time, I was not in any way *being* Veleda. I was Thorn—purely, totally Thorn—only in Amalamena's clothing and semblance. Of course, to support my disguise, I had instinctively been exhibiting feminine graces and movements and mannerisms, but I was not *feeling* female. The distinction may seem trivial, but it really amounts to a vast difference. That is because every human female, from childhood to old age, has one realization ever infixed in her innermost mind. She may take pride and pleasure in it, if she early decides that she was born to be no more than a wife and a mother. She may despise the realization, try to deny and dismiss it, if she has other aspirations—anything from nunnish lifelong chastity to more worldly ambitions of achievement. Nevertheless, whoever the woman—even a mannish-seeming soror stupra or an Amazon—the realization is always there, the realization that *she was created by nature primarily as a receptacle, a vessel with a cavity shaped and ringent and lipped to be filled.*

But for now, since I was not Veleda, that realization was not engrossing my consciousness, was not even dormant in the recesses of my mind. Therefore I did not have to feel my femaleness being violated and polluted and defiled. During this night, I could almost have been an observer standing off to one side and indifferently watching Strabo rut upon an inert nonentity—just as, long ago, an observer might have watched the vile Brother Peter repeatedly abusing the still-unformed, still-unsexed, still-uncomprehending child Thorn.

None of this, needless to say, made the night any less of a misery and an indignity and an outrage for me. But I know that my evincing nothing more than bored listlessness made the night considerably less of a joy for Strabo than he must have anticipated. There transpired something more palpable, too, that further diminished his pride in conquest and mastery. After he had consummated his first assault upon my person, he reared off me, roughly pawed my crotch, examined his hand and bellowed:

"Damaged goods, indeed! Tight you are, ja, but not virgin! You fraudulent slut! Not a trace of blood!"

I merely looked coolly back at him.

"You have been deceiving your trusting brother, as well, have you not? I can tell that there have not been many before me, but there has to have been one. I know you were closely cloistered at Novae, but you have been long on the road lately. Who was it who plucked the kernel from the fruit? Who was it, niu? Was it that Saio Thorn with whom you journeyed?"

At that, I could not help laughing aloud. And my unexpected response seemed to disconcert him more than his discovery of my already lost virginity.

"Vái, you fitchet bitch! Well, your dear traveling companion Thorn is dead now. And I shall see to it that you make no more fond attach-

507

ments. From now on, you had better learn to enjoy *me!* You can start learning *now!"*

He lifted me and flipped me over so that I was on elbows and knees, and entered from behind, ramming himself into me more violently than the first time. The chain around my neck and its pendent hammer-cross, monogram and phial swung hectically—as if they were horrified to be witness to sacrilege—while I was rocked back and forth. But I cared little about the amulets' trepidation. The Virgin's-milk phial in particular I had frankly come to contemn. It had done nothing to save my juika-bloth from harm, or old Wyrd, or Amalamena, and now it was doing absolutely nothing to relieve my own distress. What really concerned me was the security of the beaded band around my hips that clasped my own male organ up against my belly. If Strabo, in his frenzy, should rip away the band and let that member dangle—small and limp and uninterested though it was in these particular proceedings—he could hardly fail to notice its presence.

But Strabo did not tear away the band. He did not then or ever afterward—for this was not the only night on which I was to suffer his foul attentions. I do not believe he simply neglected ever to remove the band; I believe he deliberately let me continue to wear it. Since I never once shrieked or whimpered or pled for mercy—however awful were the acts he performed on me or made me perform on him—I believe that his leaving in place my "modesty band" was the only way he could continue to convince himself that he *was* violating my modesty. So he never did discover what sort of creature he was forever futilely trying to despoil. To his mind, he was forever wreaking his lust upon the young, beautiful, desirable Princess Amalamena. In my mind, I was never other than Thorn, and my only real response to being thus used was to swear to myself that I would eventually make Strabo most bitterly regret it.

Once, and once only, I told him so, and I told him truthfully, and it was that very same night. When at last he was totally spent, and rolled off me, he panted wonderingly:

"This is most curious. This is the first time of lying with any woman that I have not, soon or later, smelled the sweet fragrance of the sweet spilled juices. Perhaps *you* have spilled none, you dry wench, but I cannot even discern the familiar aroma of my own. Why is this, niu? All I seem to scent is a faint but most unfragrant . . . a sort of . . ."

I said, "It is the smell of death approaching."

508

2

hen Strabo left me, sometime before dawn, to go and sleep elsewhere, he slung open the carruca curtains and commanded me to leave them that way. The two guards stationed outside smirked in at my nudity, they of course having heard and realized all that had occurred. I was past caring about things like that, and ignored them, and simply rolled myself in the couch coverings and fell asleep myself. However, in the morning, I got out another of Amalamena's gowns from among her belongings, and put it on, so that I should not have every passerby on the road gawking at me.

509

In late afternoon, we arrived at Serdica. As I discovered, it was not a city subservient to Strabo or to any other claimant except the Roman Empire. There was even a garrison of the Legio V Alaudae stationed there. However, since that legion belonged to the *Eastern* Empire, and since Strabo was currently in favor with the Emperor Zeno, this sudden arrival of a considerable troop of armed and armored Ostrogoths did not bring the legionaries swarming out of the garrison to repel us. Anyway, Strabo was not there to besiege or pillage, only to pause in our journey toward his own lands. So he left most of his men to make their own camp outside the city, and engaged lodgings at a deversorium for himself and me and his chief officers.

The deversorium was hardly of the luxuriousness that I had chosen when *I* was escorting an Amaling princess. I was given a room very poorly furnished; it did not even have a door or a curtain flap for privacy. And again there was a guard stationed outside to keep watch on me and to trudge with me whenever I had to go outdoors to the rere-dorter. Strabo's room was as sparsely appointed as my own, and directly across the hall, so that he too could keep an eye on me. (Even in my currently unenviable situation, I could find some mordant humor in that: reflecting that Strabo literally could keep *only* one eye on me at a time.)

But at least he did not object when I asked him to send one of his soldiers to fetch something for me from the packs that his men had plundered from my own ill-fated train. What I wanted was one particular saddlebag that Velox had carried, and I described the bag so that the soldier could find it. Doubtless the saddlebag was searched before it got to me, to make sure it contained no knife or poison or anything of that nature. It did not; its contents could have caused no remark, for they were only feminine garments and fripperies, which is to say Veleda's. When a deversorium servant brought a basin of water to my room, I was able to wash off not just the road dust of the day's journey, but also the various smears and encrustations of Strabo's múxa and smegma and bdélugma from the night before—and the brómos musarós that had clung about me ever since I began playing the part of poor Amalamena's maid. Then I put on one of my own Veleda gowns, and felt really clean and odorless for the first time in recent memory.

510   When Strabo and his officers went to the dining chamber for nahtamats, I had to stay in my room, under guard, and have my meal brought to me. I found the establishment's provender about equal to its accommodations. Still, just my being clean was inspiriting enough that I could take some pleasure in viewing Serdica from my room's one window. The city, I learned from the servant who brought my food, had been such a favored residence of Constantine the Great that he had *almost* chosen it, instead of Byzantium, to be the New Rome. I could understand why. Serdica sits in an upland basin of the Haemus Mountains, at an elevation that gives it a most salubrious air and pleasant climate and a nearly perpetual breeze that keeps it swept and fresh. The city is watched over by the highest peak in all the Haemus range; I could admire it from my window. That peak is called by the local folk Culmen Nigrum, but no one could tell me why. Black Top is certainly a misnomer, because it is crowned with gleaming white snow all the year around.

I had my room to myself that first night. Strabo did not come in to molest me, probably because he needed a full night's sleep as much as I did. But the next morning, my guard marched me to the building's courtyard, where were waiting Strabo, a military scribe, the optio Ocer and a few other officers.

"I wanted you to hear this, *Princess*," said Strabo, with his usual mocking emphasis on the title. "I am about to dictate my terms to your brother."

He proceeded to do so, slowly, because his scribe was not of great proficiency and had to write much more laboriously than I would have done. In brief, Strabo demanded that Thiudareikhs Amaling, son of Thiudamer Amaling, vacate the city of Singidunum and surrender it to imperial forces soon to be sent there by the Emperor Zeno. Further: that Theodoric cease and desist from importuning the emperor for concessions of land grants, military titles, the consueta dona of gold and any other such presumptuous entitlements. Further: that Theodoric cease and desist from styling himself King of the Ostrogoths, renounce all claims to that sovereignty and swear fealty and subjection to the true king, Thiudareikhs Triarius. In return for Theodoric's acceptance of those several terms, Strabo would *consider* what disposition might be made of the woman Amalamena Amaling, daughter of Thiudamer Amaling, recently captured by Strabo in fair combat and currently being detained by him as a prisoner of war. Strabo added some hints to the effect that that "disposition" of Amalamena might consist of her contracting a marriage of convenience—prospective spouse unspecified— thereby to heal the long-standing dissensions between the divergent Amal lines of the Ostrogoths and cement a lasting peace and concord.

511

"You will note," Strabo said to me, with a froggish wink, "that I make no complaint about the, ahem, already damaged state of the goods in question. Since I am sure that you have kept secret from your brother your woefully depreciated condition, I will not apprise him of it. He might deem you not worth his acceding to my demands."

I did not dignify that with comment. I merely sniffed and maintained my princessly mien of complete disdain. Strabo reached out, yanked me close to him, twisted his fingers in the gold chain about my neck, broke it and held on to it while he undid its three pendants.

Then he said, "Here," and tossed two of them and the chain back at me. "Keep your holy baubles, much good may they do you." The third ornament, the gold tracery of Theodoric's monogram, he folded inside the parchment that the scribe had finally handed to him. "This will convince your brother, if he needs convincing, that I truly do hold you hostage."

The scribe dripped some blobs of candle wax onto the folded document, and Strabo stamped the blobs with a seal of his own. His consisted of only two runes, the thorn and the teiws—þ↑—to signify Thiudareikhs Triarius. He thrust the packet at the optio and said:

"Ocer, take as many men as you think adequate against bandits or mishap. Gallop with this document to Singidunum. Give it into the hand of that tetzte pretender Theodoric and tell him you are bidden to wait for a written reply. If he wishes to know where his sister is being held, you can tell him honestly that you do not know, that she and I are somewhere on the road. We will rest here in Serdica one more night and then"—he paused and glanced at me—"we will proceed you know whither. Bring the reply to me there. You will be riding much more rapidly than our long train, so you should arrive there at about the same time we do. Be off!"

"I am there, Triarius!" barked the optio. He clapped on his helmet, beckoned to the other officers and led them out.

"You," said Strabo to me, "return to your quarters." He again winked a frog eye and grinned salaciously. "Rest—for the night is coming. And on the morrow you start a long journey indeed."

Well, I thought, as I sat in my room and stared morosely out at the white-topped Black Top, Strabo's message to Theodoric was more or less what I had expected it to be. But what would be Theodoric's response to it? Even if Swanilda had *not* reached him and delivered Zeno's pactum, I very much doubted that Theodoric would entertain any of Strabo's demands. No, not even for the sake of his dear sister's safety. He was, after all, the king of too many people to hazard their hopes for one young woman. Still, he was bound to be distressed by the news that Amalamena was in durance and in peril.

He would not be any less distressed to hear that Amalamena was already dead, but at least that would relieve him of trying to think of ways to save her, and thereby probably putting himself or others in danger. How could I get that word to him? Do not give in, Theodoric. Do not even *pretend* to comply with Strabo's extortionate terms. Your position is unassailable, Theodoric, and *somewhere* Zeno's genuine document still exists, confirming your position. Also, do not grieve too much for Amalamena. You did not know it, but her death was foreordained, and she died better than she or you could have hoped.

I had to tell him those things, but how? Tomorrow this company would be on the road again. And once we arrived at Strabo's aerie, wherever that was, I would be more tightly confined and closely watched than I was now. Right here in Serdica was my one best and probably last chance to send a message to Theodoric. But how? Offer my broken chain to one of the deversorium servants as a bribe of gold? Impossible. There was always a guard present whenever a servant was near me. And during the rest of this day there was a constant coming and going of Strabo's underofficers, visiting his room across the hall for instructions or orders.

I looked at my chain's two remaining ornaments, and the look I gave the reliquary phial was malignant to the point of desecration. Any virgin's milk would have to be void of nourishment and blandly tasteless; just so had the phial repeatedly proved itself barren of utility. But the other? Whether regarded as a Christian cross or the pagan Thor's hammer, it did have one useful attribute. It was of gold, and soft, and it would make a mark if scraped hard enough on a rough surface. I could write with it. I could leave a message on one of the room's walls, but with only a dim hope that some servant would see it after I had departed, and would recognize it as writing—and the dimmer hope that that servant would bother to fetch someone who could read it—and the hope, so dim as to be laughable, that the message might somehow get passed along to Theodoric. Still, even a preposterous hope is better than none. I glanced warily at the guard lounging just outside my door, and went to the wall in which the door was, so that he could not see me without leaning his head in. Then I asked myself: in what language should I write, and in what alphabet? The Old Language, I decided: likelier than Latin to be recognized by a menial. And in runes because, having originally been intended for carving into wood, they consist mostly of straight lines: easier to write with my makeshift instrument. Next I gave some thought to the message itself. It should be of as few words as possible, but persuasive . . .

And then I was so startled that I nearly dropped the hammer-cross, because the guard outside, as if he had divined my intentions, commanded me: "Princess, do not make any sudden move or noise."

My one or two guards had been ever present, but ever changing, of course, taking roster turns at the task. However, when I was not actively ignoring their insults or oglings or lewd solicitations, I was not paying any attention to them. So they could have been the same man or men, as far as I was concerned. But this one, when he spoke, did not barge into the room to do it. He spoke from outside the doorway, and in an undertone, and he spoke respectfully.

"Princess, I must talk quickly, for no one else is about at the moment."

Stammering slightly, I said, "Who . . . who are you?" and made a move toward the door, but stopped when he said:

"Ne, come no closer. We must not risk being seen conversing. My

513

name is Odwulf, Princess. You would not know me by sight, I am sure, and I have seen you only from a distance before now. But I was one of your column—a lancer of Optio Daila's turma—all the way from Novae to Constantinople to the slaughter on the river Strymon."

"But . . . but . . . why are you not dead with all the rest?"

"My misfortune, Princess," he said, and he sounded dolefully sincere. "You may remember, the optio set guards here and there along the road and the river. Two others—myself and a man named Augis—he sent to climb to the top of the gorge above the encampment, to keep watch from there."

"Ja . . . ja. I do remember."

"Augis and I were only just gaining the top when Strabo and his men attacked. When we realized what was happening, we immediately began clambering down the cliff again. But it was all over too soon. I am sorry, my princess. We both are sorry."

"Do not be, Odwulf. It is better that you lived. This day I have been casting about for a miracle, and you are it. But how do you come to be *here?*"

514

"After the battle, there was much confusion—Strabo's men running to catch the horses of ours that they had scattered, others stripping and looting our dead comrades. We saw you being led into the firelight. We hoped to see that Strabo had spared also our king's marshal. But of the Saio Thorn, we found merely his helmet and corselet. Those were the only two valuables that the marauders did not carry off—because the marshal was a small man, you know, and his armor would fit no one else. Anyway, I must regretfully report that the Saio Thorn evidently died with the others."

"Do not be too sure," I said, smiling for the first time that day. "The marshal was also a resourceful man."

"But never a coward," Odwulf staunchly defended me. "I have heard how he fought at Singidunum. Nevertheless, Augis and I brought along his armor—just in case. Or in hopes."

I restrained a joyful impulse to give loud thanks. My custom-made armor was still safe; I knew where my war-horse and my snake blade were; and now, unexpectedly, almost unbelievably, I had two brave allies nearby.

"But *you* had survived, Princess," Odwulf went on. "So Augis and I thought—if we stayed close—we might somehow find an opportunity to rescue you."

"And you followed Strabo's column all the way hither?"

"Ne, ne. We have been *in* it. We merely mingled with the others and rode when they did. Akh, we have been at some hazard of discovery, ja. However, the troop numbers more than a century. Of that many men, not every one knows every other. Perhaps the optio, Ocer, would have been the likeliest to espy us as strangers, but we have taken pains to avoid his eye. Only now that Ocer has departed did I let myself be grabbed by a signifer for this guard duty and— slaváith, Princess. Someone comes."

It was another underofficer tramping along the hall and into Strabo's room. Not until those two were loudly conversing in there did Odwulf speak again, and in low tones:

"You said, Princess, you sought a miracle. Tell me what, and I will attempt it."

"First I must tell you, gallant warrior, that I am not your Princess Amalamena. However—"

"What?" He nearly blurted it.

"However, I am acting on the princess's instructions, impersonating her, and Strabo also believes me to be she."

"But . . . but . . . who are *you*, then?"

"Only from a distance have you seen me, too. I am the princess's cosmeta, Swanilda."

Odwulf's sidewise muttering now became almost strangled. "Liufs Guth! Augis and I have been risking our lives to trail after a *maidservant*?

"Acting on Amalamena's instructions, I said. And so must you do, out of allegiance to her."

We were interrupted again, as Strabo and his visitor came out of that room and, laughing raucously about something, went off down the hall. When they were gone, Odwulf at last stepped inside my room and stared at me.

"You see?" I said. "I have gray eyes. Amalamena had blue."

He frowned and asked, "What do you mean—she *had*? Did Strabo slay the princess, too?"

"Ne. Strabo thinks he has her captive, and all he has is me."

Odwulf shook his head as if to clear it, then sighed, then said, "Very well. If you are all that is left, Augis and I will rescue you. We must plan how best to—"

"Ne," I said. "I do not wish to be rescued."

Now he *really* stared. "Are you brainsick, woman?"

"No more questions, lancer Odwulf. While we have the time, you must listen, and then do as I tell you."

515

He bridled somewhat and said, "May all the gods damn me if I understand what is going on here. But I am not accustomed to taking orders from a female domestic."

"When you hear them, you will gladly obey them. Now slaváith, and listen. You saw the optio Ocer leave here. He is off to Singidunum, to present Strabo's ransom demands to Theodoric, claiming that Strabo holds Amalamena hostage. Theodoric must be told that that is not true."

Odwulf thought it over, then said, "Ja, that I can understand. As soon as I am relieved of this guard duty—"

"Ne, ne. Do not you go. Now that I know and can recognize you, Odwulf, you remain with this company, and keep on doing your best not to be detected. Send to Theodoric your comrade Augis. Have him gallop after Ocer—or get to Singidunum ahead of Ocer, if possible. Here, have him carry this." I handed over the gold hammer of Thor. "That will be proof of the truth of his message. Have Augis tell Theodoric this. There is unfortunately nothing he can do to save his princess sister. The sad fact is that Amalamena is dead."

516

"Iésus." Odwulf signed the cross upon his forehead. "But you said she was not slain."

"She died of a wasting illness. Theodoric can verify that by sending a messenger to inquire of his court lekeis Frithila at Novae. But, before she died, the princess and I arranged this substitution. Me for her, to delude Strabo. You see, as long as he thinks he holds Amalamena, and waits for Theodoric to yield to his demands, Strabo is no menace or impediment. Theodoric can proceed with his own plans, tighten his hold on Moesia, strengthen his ties with Zeno, do almost anything else he pleases. Do you see?"

"I . . . I suppose I do. And that is why you do not wish to be rescued?"

"Ja. And also, while I remain in Strabo's company, I may see or hear or learn something of his own plans and designs—things that I can later impart to Theodoric, to Theodoric's advantage."

Odwulf nodded and was silent for a space. Then he said, "Forgive me, Swanilda, for having spoken rudely to you a moment ago. You are a brave and clever young woman. I shall have Augis tell Theodoric that, as well. Anything else?"

"Ja. Ocer will press Theodoric for an immediate reply to Strabo's demands. Theodoric is to send none at all. Leave Strabo waiting and wondering as long as possible. I recommend that Theodoric kill the optio and all his companions. When Ocer arrives at Singidunum, he will be armed with two snake blades, one shorter than the other. The shorter sword belonged to the Saio Thorn. Ask Theodoric please to slay Ocer with that one."

Odwulf smiled and nodded again. Then, at a noise from down the hall, he stuck his head out the door.

"My relief approaches. I will instantly instruct Augis and send him on his way. But quickly now. Is there anything more?"

"Only keep safe my—keep Thorn's armor safely stowed, and bring it along, wherever we go from here. That will be our memento of him."

The newcome guard had nothing to say to me except—with indecent simpers and gestures—how fetching I looked in the different gown I was wearing today, and how much more fetching I would look without it. So I simply sat and congratulated myself on the latest turn of events. Of course, I had not told Odwulf of all the secret circumstances that had affected or afflicted our mission ever since Constantinople. And some of the things I *had* told him were likely to cause confusion at Singidunum. For example, if Swanilda was already there, Theodoric would be puzzled to know who was the "Swanilda" now being held captive—or, rather, voluntarily playing the spy for him—among the forces of his enemy Strabo. Well, I had tried to keep my message as succinct as if I had had to resort to scrawling it on a wall.

517

I was feeling so elated that, even when Strabo came again that night to paw and maul and abuse and debauch and defile me, he found that he still could not make me weep or scream or swoon or give him any other such satisfaction at all. Instead, I spent the whole time quite impassively turning over in my mind one scheme after another by which someday I would repay Strabo for doing these things to me.

✠   ✠   ✠

The journey was a long one, for a fact. From Serdica to our destination turned out to be much, much farther than the distance that my own column had traveled from Novae to Constantinople. We went directly east from Serdica, along the southern foothills of the Haemus range, across the provinces of Thracia and Haemimontus. There are practically no roads in those regions, and obviously that was why Strabo chose that route: not to chance meeting any traveling troops of Theodoric's rival Ostrogoths. So, with only rough cart tracks and horse trials to follow, we progressed but slowly.

We could have moved rather faster if I had volunteered to ride a horse and let the big carruca dormitoria be abandoned. Strabo and others of my captors several times growled hints to me that I ought to do just that, but I was stubbornly resolved not to. If I was being carried into faraway captivity, I would be *carried.* After all, I was impersonating a princess; I would be treated like one. Since we came to no settlement anywhere along the way that was big enough to boast even the most primitive pandokheíon or taberna or gasts-razn or krchma, we had to make camp in the open every night. But I at least had the carruca's shelter from the increasingly cold and worsening weather, and—whenever Strabo did not crawl in with me for a while, which he did every third or fourth night—I could sleep the whole night away, comfortable on my couch in there.

Here and there along our way, we did come upon a decent Roman road, but always running north to south, across our route. One of them was the very road over the Shipka or Thorny Pass that I and Amalamena and Daila and our company had traveled. But Strabo did not avail himself of any deviations from our direct route, even if the longer way would have made for easier and faster progress; we pressed on continuously to the east. I still did not know to what city or town or fortress we were headed, but I knew that if we went eastward long enough, we had to come at last to the Black Sea.

And so we did. And I confess to have been a trifle disappointed to discover that the Black Sea does not consist, as one would naturally suppose, of a stygian-black liquid. It is, in truth, a beautiful body of water—azure with lacy trimmings of white foam where it laps the sands of the coastline, darkening through blue to blue-green to deep green as it gradually deepens offshore, and then dimming and paling again to blue and blending into the blue of the sky at the far-distant horizon. It is also much more pleasant to bathe in than are any of the waters around the Mediterranean, because it is only half as salty as they are. I should correctly say that the Black Sea is a beautiful sea when it *wants* to be. It got its gloomy name because, at unpredictable intervals, even on the sunniest day, the sea can decide to shroud itself in a fog so dense that it blinds and confounds a boatman as totally as would the blackest night.

I first saw the Black Sea when we arrived at an uninhabited stretch of its Haemimontus coast. Then we turned north along that shore, across the invisible border into the province of Moesia Secunda, meaning that we were in what was properly Theodoric's domain—so Strabo led us as rapidly as possible across those lands, continuing on a northward course that took us out of sight of the Black Sea. Not until we had crossed another invisible border, into the province of Scythia, did we turn east again, and eventually we came to the seaside city of Constantiana.

This is another city that was founded by Constantine the Great, and it gets its name from that emperor's sister Constantia. Rightly or wrongly, simply by force of occupation, Strabo was nowadays using it as his stronghold and apparently regarding it as his "capital." Well, Constantiana was then and still is worthy of an honorific title, for it is a fair and pleasant and populous city, and its capacious harbor is as crowded with vessels—both coastal and seagoing—as is that of Perinthus on the Propontís.

Strabo's residence and praitoriaún were under the same roof, but a most extensive roof, covering many buildings, barracks, storehouses, slave quarters, stables and such, rather in the manner of the Purple Palace at Constantinople, though not on such a grand scale. The combined palace-administrative-military buildings presented a flat, blank, unwindowed stone face to the rest of the city, but within were many small gardens, interior courtyards and an extensive parade ground. I was led to one of the courtyards, and Strabo told me that it would be my own personal exercise yard. It was enclosed by walls too high for me to climb, in one of which was a door—where a guard would be permanently stationed, of course—that gave onto my private quarters.

519

The rooms had windows looking out onto one of the gardens, but the garden was sere and barren in this season and the windows were stoutly barred. A servant girl was already installed, to be my constant attendant, and she had a small room of her own. Camilla could hardly be dignified as a cosmeta, for she was only a frumpish Greek peasant. And, I soon discovered, she was a deaf-mute, no doubt selected for that reason to be my maid, so that I could neither persuade her to relay messages for me nor try to ferret from her information about anyone or anything else connected with my captivity.

The lodgings were hardly regal, but I had lived in far worse, and at least I was not to be chained in some dark dungeon. I made sure not to let Strabo see from me any signs of satisfaction or resignation, but he seemed not to care a whit about what my state of mind might be.

"I trust that you will enjoy your stay here, Princess," he said. "And I do believe you will. I believe you will become so fond of these accommodations that you—and frequently I—and eventually our son also—will delight in residing in these chambers for a long, long time."

3

ven before he told me so, I was well aware that Strabo had no intention of setting me free, even if Theodoric had abjectly surrendered to his every demand. I knew that for a certainty, because Strabo had already confided to me one secret of his that he would never give me the chance to repeat to anyone else. At our very first encounter, he had told me how he despised his own son and heir apparent, and how Rekitakh's being at the court of Constantinople gave the Emperor Zeno only the *delusion* of holding a hostage with which to manipulate the young man's king-father. Had I been let loose to reveal just that one bit of information, Zeno surely would have shifted his imperial favor from Strabo's Ostrogoths to Theodoric's—or even have raised up some nonentity kinglet of some lesser Germanic nation. So I would not be let loose.

Whether Strabo intended to keep me as his plaything forevermore, or whether he truly expected me to conceive and bear a worthier heir for him, or whether (since I never would get pregnant) he eventually would tire of me and have me summarily slain—one thing I knew. When he said that I would be confined in his Constantiana palace for "a long, long time," he meant for the rest of my life.

Had I really been Princess Amalamena, I would likely have been plunged into despair on hearing myself sentenced to such a fate. But of course I had secrets of my own to comfort me, and a fair prospect that, with Odwulf's assistance, I could effect my escape whenever I judged that the time was right. I knew that Odwulf was still with us, for I had occasionally glimpsed him during our journey hither. On the first occasion, he had given me just the merest nod, to assure me that his fellow lancer Augis was on the way to Theodoric. Thereafter, Odwulf had communicated nothing more, and, if we chanced to pass one another, he might lewdly chaff or leer at me, as did all the other soldiers,

520

but neither of us gave any other sign of recognition. Since there were many more of Strabo's troops here in Constantiana—though nothing like a vast army, as well as I could tell—Odwulf probably (and gratefully) found it easier yet to mingle with them undetected as an intruder. Anyway, at intervals, he contrived to get himself assigned as the guard at my courtyard door, just to find out if I needed anything from him. I did not—not yet—but we could talk freely, the servant Camilla being unable to eavesdrop, and that was pleasing to me, because I had no one else to talk to except Strabo himself.

Strabo did talk, and often—and, when he was not panting or grunting or slobbering in the act of copulation, he could talk articulately enough—and he talked of many things that I found of compelling interest. He was most loquacious when he was spent and languid after having made carnal use of me, but it was not because he was besotted with love of me that he was so freely confiding. He talked out of his love for braggartry, and because of his certitude that I would never be able to make any use of the secrets he divulged.

Not everything that he said was a dark, dire secret, of course. On our first arrival at Constantiana, he expressed some surprise and displeasure—not just to me, to everyone within earshot—because his optio Ocer was not already there, waiting for him with Theodoric's message of contrition, concession and submission. But there could have been many innocuous reasons for Ocer's delay, so Strabo did not then make too much fuss about it. As time went on, though, and the optio did not appear, Strabo got more concerned and disgruntled, and frequently snarled at me something like:

"If your nauthing brother expects to wheedle any compromise from me simply by dawdling in making his reply, he is very much mistaken!"

To which remarks I simply shrugged indifferently, as if to say that I had nothing to do with the matter, cared nothing about it and could do nothing even if I would. Another time, Strabo threatened:

"Perhaps it would stiffen your brother's weakling irresolution if I began to send him your fingers, one a week."

I yawned and said, "Send him Camilla's fingers instead. Theodoric would hardly know the difference, and she would hardly miss them. She does little enough work with them around here."

"Iésus Xristus," said Strabo, in genuine awe. "You may be only a pretender of a princess, but an Ostrogoth you surely are. A predator! As ruthless as a haliuruns! And when you do give me a son, what a sturdy and staunch and steely son he will be!"

521

Another time, he spoke of another thing that was obviously no secret, but was thunderclap news to me. He had been boasting of how much the Emperor Zeno esteemed and supported and relied on him, when I made bold to say:

"But suppose my brother has enlisted the support of the emperor at *Rome*. Would not you and Theodoric then be evenly matched, and thus at deadlock?"

Strabo belched juicily and growled, "Vái! There *is* no emperor at Rome."

"Well, I mean Ravenna, of course. And I know he is only a boy, and disdainfully called Little Augustus . . ."

"Ne, ne. Aúdawakrs dethroned that boy Romulus Augustulus, and exiled him, and had his regent-father beheaded. For the first time in more than five hundred years, no Roman bears the resounding title of emperor. Why, the entire Roman Empire of the West is no more. Its name is expunged from the maps of the world."

"*What?*"

"Where have you been, girl, that you did not know?" Strabo cocked his head to stare one of his eyes at me in incredulity. "Akh, ja, I was forgetting. You were a long time on the road. You must have left Constantinople just before the word of it reached there."

"The word of what? Who is Aúdawakrs?"

"An outlander, like you and me. He is the son of the late King Edika of the Scyrri."

"Of Edika I have heard," I said, again remembering the little village of handless people. "Theodoric's—my father slew King Edika in battle, shortly before he died himself. But what has Edika's son to do with—?"

"Aúdawakrs joined the Roman army in his youth, and rose rapidly through the ranks to a position of high eminence. In emulation of Rikimer, that other outlander before him, he recently has been the 'King-Maker' at Rome. It was Aúdawakrs who put young Augustulus on the throne, and he who chose to throw the boy off it."

"Why? The King-Maker Rikimer, in his time, was the real ruler of the Western Empire, and everyone knew it, but he was satisfied to remain always behind the throne."

Strabo shrugged his shoulders and rotated his eyeballs. "Aúdawakrs is not. He waited only for a pretext. The outlanders in the army petitioned to be granted homestead lands on their retirement from service, which have always been granted to the Italia-born. Augustulus peremptorily refused, or his father, Orestes, did. So Aúdawakrs ousted the boy and executed Orestes, and announced that *he* was granting the petition. The outlander troops cheered and exulted and raised him on their shields. So now Aúdawakrs rules in name as well as in fact."

Strabo chuckled, taking pleasure in telling of the plight of Rome, and added, "Of course, his Old Language name is too difficult for the Romans to pronounce. They render it Odoacer, as much as to say in Latin 'Hated Blade.' "

"An outlander!" I breathed, agog. "The Emperor of Rome! Truly, an overthrow unprecedented in all time."

"Ne, he does not claim the imperial title. That would be too brazen, and he is too cunning. Neither the Roman citizens nor the Emperor Zeno would let him do that. Nevertheless, Zeno seems perfectly content to let Odoacer go on ruling in the west, so long as he continues to manifest subservience to the Emperor of the East. That is to say, the *only* emperor of all that *remains* of the Roman Empire."

Strabo belched again, as if totally uncaring that he had literally been speaking of the end of an era, perhaps the end of modern civilization, maybe the end of the whole world as we had known it.

Still dazed, I said, "I have lost count of all the emperors who have ruled at Rome or Ravenna in my lifetime. But I never dreamed that I should live to see an outlander—ne, a savage *barbarian*, if he is of the Scyrri—regnant at the dissolution of the greatest empire in all the annals of history."

"At any rate," Strabo said pointedly, "I very much doubt that Odoacer will ever ally himself with the son of the man who slew his father."

"Ne," I had to concede, and I sighed. "Theodoric can expect no friendship from that quarter."

"On the other hand," said Strabo, "if one outlander could attain to such eminence, so could another."

He slitted his frog eyes, like a frog espying a tasty fly, and he smiled slyly, and he spoke slowly, as if he had been waiting for some time to snap up that fly.

"Odoacer might well succeed in merging all the disparate nations and factions of the west. He might make of them a league so powerful that Zeno finds him a most uncomfortable neighbor next door to the Eastern Empire. I believe that the time will come. Until it does, I will continue to let Zeno, holding my worthless son Rekitakh, think that he has me subdued and in thrall. Let him think that I remain his meek and servile underling. Then, when Zeno needs someone to invade and

523

conquer and take over Odoacer's domains . . . who better than Zeno's longtime loyal and trustworthy minion, Thiudareikhs Triarius? Niu? And then . . . shall we make a wager on how long *Zeno's* empire will stand? Niu?"

✠   ✠   ✠

Very well. I had allowed myself to be captured solely in order to learn what I could of Strabo's ambitions and designs, and now I had learned them. They were marvelously simple: he intended to rule the world. It sounded so possible and so credible and so likely that I was tempted to start immediately on my preparations for escape, so I could ride at a stretch-out gallop to take the word to Theodoric.

However, there were a few more things I wanted to investigate — one thing in particular that had intrigued me since our first arrival in Constantiana. So, on another night, after Strabo's sweating, heaving, panting exertions had left him lying limp and drowsy, I broached the subject.

"You have spoken of the invincibility of your army and of how Zeno fears it," I said. "But I have seen here no army, only a garrison, and that numbers fewer men than Theodoric keeps in our city of Novae."

"Skeit!" Strabo grunted indelicately. "My army *is* an army, not a hive of drones. Garrison duty turns men into sluggards and incompetents. I keep most of mine in the field, where soldiers belong. Fighting, as soldiers should be doing."

"Fighting whom?"

"Anybody." He went on, sleepily, as if it were a matter of no great moment, "Recently, two of my subject tribes up north in the swamps of the Danuvius delta — two minor offshoots of the Heruli — for some reason had an altercation. Then, without my permission, they commenced a petty war between them. I sent my army to quell that."

"How did your army know which side to take?"

"What? They were ordered to obliterate *all* the fighting men, of course, and take as slaves their women and children. How else *should* I punish disobedience?" He stretched languidly and broke wind. "As it happened, though, a good number of the rebellious warriors cowardly surrendered before they could be slain. So a portion of my army is on its way back here right now, bringing those prisoners of war — some three hundred from each side, I am told. I shall execute them in a manner to give entertainment to everybody in Constantiana. The tunica molesta, perhaps. Or wild beasts. Or the patibulum. I have not decided."

I persisted, "But if you keep your army always afield, and only a small garrison here, what is to prevent Theodoric—or some other enemy—from laying siege to Constantiana? I should think that you and your garrison troops and all the citizens of Constantiana might be starved into capitulation before your army could get here to relieve you."

He snorted in disgust. "Vái! The words of women are wind! This city could not be effectively besieged by all the armies of Europe combined. You saw the harbor yonder. The Black Sea ships could keep Constantiana fed and armed and supplied and defiant for decades, if necessary. Only by all the *navies* of Europe could a blockade harm Constantiana. And no navy could get here without having to squeeze through the narrows of the Bósporos to get into the Black Sea. I would be long forewarned of the approach of any such fleet, and could take measures to repel it."

"Ja, I should have realized that myself."

"Listen, dotterel wench. The only way this city *might* be subverted is from the inside. An uprising of either the inhabitants or the troops. That is another reason why I keep the mass of my soldiers well away from here. Armies have been known to mutiny against their leaders. But I also maintain enough of a garrison—and have those men keep the people brutally intimidated—to discourage any potential revolutionaries among the cityfolk."

I commented daringly, "I should hardly suppose that either your troops or your people adore you for those measures."

"I do not give a ferta for their adoration, any more than I do for yours." He hawked up phlegm and spat it on the floor at my feet. "While I am no slavish imitator of the effete Romans, I do follow two of their ancient maxims. 'Divide et impera.' In order to rule, divide. That is wise advice. The second I like even better. 'Oderint dum metuant.' Let them hate . . . so long as they fear."

✠ ✠ ✠

Odwulf, when next he was assigned to guard my door, alluded to the same subject.

"Those few warriors with whom I have made slight acquaintance think I am an imbecile," he said. "To explain my newness among them, I have put out the story that I was formerly a lancer in Theodoric's army, that I was caught cheating at the dice and was severely punished at the whipping post, that I then deserted my fellows to join Strabo's forces instead."

"It seems to me a clever pretext," I said. "What do they find imbecilic about it?"

"They say that only a man with skeit for brains would prefer Strabo's army to Theodoric's."

"Why? Apparently *they* do."

"With them it is a matter of their families' long-standing allegiance to Strabo's branch of the Amal line. They feel obliged to serve him, but they are much discontented. Akh, they are good fighting men, ja, and Strabo gives them ample fighting to do. But even when there is no one to fight, he keeps them riding and trudging and lurking in one hinterland or another."

"So I have heard."

"Except for occasional reliefs to serve here in the Constantiana garrison, they seldom get to enjoy the diversions of a town. A good frolic in a lupanar, a good meal and a good drunk and perhaps a good brawl at a taberna, not even a good leisurely bath at a therma."

"Are you saying, Odwulf, that Strabo's men might desert him and go over to Theodoric?"

"Akh, ne. Not any time soon. They and their fathers and grandfathers have been for too long committed to the Amal line from which Strabo descended. I suppose their discontent *could* be aggravated into open dissension and rebellion, but it would require agitators as subtle as priests, and many of them, and maybe many years."

"However," I said thoughtfully, "if Strabo were eliminated . . . if they had no leader to be loyal to . . ."

Odwulf looked at me much as Strabo had done when I suggested his amputating the servant's fingers. He said, "Swanilda, I have heard of Amazons, but I never expected to meet one. Are you proposing to murder the man? Yourself? A slender young woman against a tough old warrior? Here in his own palace, inside his own city, deep within his own territories?"

"If I did—or if someone did—if his troops had no Strabo at their head, do you think they might accept Theodoric as their king instead?"

"How can I say? I am only a simple soldier myself. No doubt they would be considerably confused and uneasy. But remember, Swanilda. Strabo's authority would pass to his son Rekitakh."

I murmured, "I believe even Strabo would not wish his good men afflicted with a fish for a king. But tell me, Odwulf, how have you managed so well to remain undiscovered this long? Can you manage for a while longer?"

"I think so, ja. It is an odd and unsoldierly feeling for a soldier—not to be attached to some turma, not to answer to the roll call, not to have any duties at all. But I learned. Everywhere I go, I carry something. Something large and visible. An untrimmed log, a sheaf of lances needing polishing, a saddle needing repair. Every officer who sees me takes me to be doing some chore or some errand for some other officer."

"Then keep on doing so. Stay invisible. I have an inkling of an idea, and if I attempt it, I will have need of you. Sometime soon, a detachment of Strabo's troops will be returning from a minor battle somewhere north of here. They will be bringing some hundreds of Herulian war prisoners with them. When they arrive, get yourself assigned again to guard my door. I will tell you then what I have in mind. And I assure you, Odwulf, you will feel once more a soldier."

✠　✠　✠

Strabo was by this time being almost continuously irate and fulminant, and frequently staggering drunk, and his frog eyes, nowadays permanently bloodshot, were more horrible than ever—all because his optio Ocer still failed to appear. And of course Strabo raged and railed at me, as the most convenient target for his vilification. I really became apprehensive that he might incontinently strike out and injure me so badly that I could not carry out the plan I had formulated. One night he roared drunkenly:

"Fingers be damned! I think I will carve out your kunte and send it to your nauthing brother! Is Theodoric likely to recognize *that* as his sister's?"

"I doubt it," I said, as coolly as I could, and parried with a lie that I invented on the instant. "You should know it well enough yourself, but you do not always."

"Eh?"

"The other night, you were foully drunk and this room was dark, so I put Camilla in my bed for your use."

"Liufs Guth!" The eye careened again, to look aghast at Camilla, who was shuffling through the room just then. "That unappealing trull?" But then he recovered, to counter with a lie of his own. "I *wondered* why, that night, though still not making a sound, you evinced so much more spirit and cooperation and reciprocation than usual." He reached out, seized Camilla's thick wrist and growled:

"Let us see if she still does. You stay too, wench, and watch this. You may learn how to behave like a real woman in bed."

Well, I felt a little remorseful for having put the maidservant to that humiliation and distress and contamination. Still, I could not feel *too* sorry for her. It may have been the only such experience she would ever have. And for once, thags Guth, it was not *me* enduring it.

When Strabo was finally done with her, he fell back flat on the bed to catch his breath, and the naked Camilla, besmeared with múxa and bdélugma, tottered out the door. When Strabo was able to talk again, I took care to bring up a very different topic, calculated not to provoke him to another fit of temper.

"You have frequently called my brother a nauthing, and I have heard the word once or twice before, from other speakers of the Old Language. But I never have known exactly what a nauthing is."

He reached for the wine jar he had brought with him, and took a long drink from it before he said, "I am not surprised. You are a woman. It is a man's word."

"I do not take it to be an endearment. If you are insulting my brother, as I suppose, you might at least tell me what you are calling him."

"Are you acquainted with the word 'tetzte,' niu?"

"Ja. It means worthless."

"Well, nauthing means much the same, only it is infinitely more offensive. It comes from the rune called the nauths. The one that looks like two twigs crossed at an angle. Do you know the runic alphabet, niu?"

"Of course. Nauths indicates the 'n' sound. And by itself, nauths stands for misery."

"Just so, and a nauthing is a man worse than worthless. He is wretched, paltry, cowardly, vile, beneath contempt. It is the basest insult that one Goth can speak to another. And if a man *is* called a nauthing by another, he must fight the insulter—fight him to the death. If he does not, he is banished from the society of all other human beings, shunned by everyone of his nation, his tribe, his gau, his sibja, even his nearest family. He is scarce regarded as human himself. He is such a— well, such a nauthing—that if anyone else for any reason chances to kill him, the Gothic law traditionally does not bother to bring the killer to account."

"And have you called my brother a nauthing to his face?"

"Not yet. Distant cousins though we are, we have never met. But we will. When we do, I promise I shall look him squarely in the eye— what are you snickering at, wench?—and loudly and publicly declare

528

Theodoric to be a nauthing. At the same time, I will plant a nauthing-stake."

"What is a nauthing-stake?"

"Simply two twigs crossed at an angle to resemble the nauths rune. On uttering the insult, you stick that in the ground at the place of the encounter. It will go on working its evil bane, whether the man fights you right then, or later, or not at all, or even if he bests you in the fight. It is very much the same as an insandjis, a Sending by a malevolent haliuruns."

"Indeed? Then . . . if I call you a nauthing at this moment . . . and go and find sticks with which to make a nauthing-stake . . ."

It was Strabo's turn to laugh. "Do not trouble yourself, wench. Do not even try to spoil my mellow mood by threatening me. I told you: the nauthing challenge is a matter for *men*. For the sake of your own continued good health, wench, I suggest that you cease such impudent remarks, unless you can grow a svans to match your unwomanly disrespect of masculine superiority."

I made my voice meek and said, "You are right, ja. I must do that."

"Good . . . good . . ." he murmured, drowsy again, not seeing my grin of wickedly gleeful anticipation.

✠   ✠   ✠

For two or three days afterward, I devoted myself to acting as serving maid to my own servant. The poor ill-favored creature had apparently been unnerved and devastated and totally crushed; she stayed supine on her pallet in her room and did nothing but weep. So I sat with her and spoke words of comfort and condolence, and fetched tidbits for her to eat whenever she had appetite for them.

However, she and I contrived a rudimentary sort of communication by gestures and grimaces, and eventually Camilla made me understand that she was *not* prostrated by pain or enfeeblement or even unhappiness. On the contrary, she was weeping with joy, because she had briefly been "wife" to King Thiudareikhs Triarius himself. And she was lying idle and immobile only so that she should not jostle Strabo's slimy bdélugma out of her koilía, because she hoped mightily that some of his virile spérmata would make their way into her hystéra, and that she, though only a menial drab, would thereby become the mother of a bastard prince.

When Strabo next visited my chambers, he was too nearly in a state of apoplexy to indulge in molesting me, let alone Camilla. He came only to froth at the mouth and to bobble his boiled-looking eyes at me and to rant:

"My patience is well-nigh at an end! The trustworthy optio Ocer would not have dared to keep me waiting in perplexity. It *has* to be your nauthing brother's equivocation that is delaying Ocer's return hither. By all the gods, and by your cross and your hammer and your Virgin Mary's excretions, I will wait but two more days! Tonight those Herulian prisoners arrive. I am in a mood to make them dearly wish tomorrow that they had perished tidily on the battlefield. But when I have dealt with them, if there is still no word from Singidunum by the day after, I swear that I am going to—"

"I have an idea about those prisoners," I interrupted, before he could threaten again to remove my private parts.

"Eh?"

"Or have you decided yet on their fate? The wild beasts? The tunica? The patibulum?"

"Ne, ne," he said impatiently. "All those measures are too tame to slake my present ravening thirst for blood."

"Then let me recommend something really gory," I said, feigning eagerness. "Did I not see an amphitheater here in Constantiana when we rode in?"

"Ja, a fine big one, of white Parian marble. But if you are going to suggest gladiatorial contests, do not. Hand-to-hand contests are even more tame and tedious and boring than—"

"One *tremendous* contest," I said exuberantly. "Those tribesmen angered you because they tried to slaughter each other, niu? Then let them do so. All at once. *Make* them do so. Arm every man of those six centuries with a sword but no shield. Turn them all into the arena. Three hundred of the one tribe against the three hundred of the other. For added incentive, you might promise to let the one last survivor of each tribe live and go free. Why, a contest of that magnitude ought to equal anything ever devised by Caligula or Nero. The arena will probably be ankle-deep in blood."

Strabo shook his head admiringly, which made his eyeballs almost capsize, and said in a hushed voice:

"I devoutly hope that Ocer *does* get here in time to avert my having to mutilate you, Amalamena. It would be a pity to destroy the one woman I have ever met who shares so many of my own tastes. A predator, a haliuruns, I called you, and so you are. Caligula and Nero—in

Walis-Halla or Avalonnis, or wherever they now reside—must be dying all over again from envy of my having found you."

"Then show your gratitude," I said. "Let me sit beside you and watch the spectacle."

He scowled and muttered, "Well, now . . ."

"I have not once been out of these quarters since you put me here. And no one has been allowed inside except the garrison chaplain one Sunday. He told me that, soiled and sullied as I am, I have no hope of the Christian heaven. So let me damn myself irretrievably to hell. Come, Triarius. Would you deny to a predator the opportunity to be in at the kill? Would you deny a haliuruns the chance to gloat at the consummation of her Sending?"

Strabo snorted a short laugh. "Fair enough. But you will be manacled to a guard. And I hope you enjoy the spectacle, woman. I do not speak idly when I swear that the next blood spilled will be yours."

When the watch changed that evening, the relief guard who brought me and Camilla our trays of nahtamats was, as I had expected, the lancer Odwulf. He told me that the captive Heruli had indeed arrived in the city, some three hundred men of each tribe, and that they had been immediately herded into the dens beneath the floor of the Constantiana amphitheater. There were also several hundreds of their wives and children, he said, most of whom had already been distributed among the city's Syrian slave dealers.

"That is, except for the handsomer women and the girl-children old enough to be used as women. As you can imagine, the garrison soldiers are holding high revel."

"Are they getting thoroughly drunk?"

"Akh, exceedingly. I am regarded somewhat askance because I am not reeling and puking."

"And the male captives, are they wrathful at the treatment being dealt their wives and children?"

Odwulf shrugged. "Probably no more than I would be if I had lost a battle and then been captured. It is the expected thing."

"Ja, I suppose so," I had to agree. "Still, I should like those Herulian men stirred up as much as possible. Can you get in among them?"

"This night I can likely do anything you require, Swanilda, with all the rest of the garrison so drunk and, er, otherwise occupied."

"Then do that. Spread the word among the prisoners that Strabo's men are using their women and girl-children in—say—in the so-called Frankish manner. And the Greek."

531

Odwulf looked shocked. "They would not believe that! No one would believe any Ostrogoth capable of such perversions."

"*Make* them believe it. After all, these are Ostrogoths deep in drink, lost to inhibition and decency."

"You talk worse than any soldier," he growled, then shrugged again. "I will do my best. But why?"

I began to tell him of the mass gladiatorial contest that would be waged on the morrow, thanks to my having conceived it and having got Strabo to agree to it. Odwulf several times erupted with wondering exclamations—and again suggested that I *was* Amazonially inclined to atrocity. But he subsided and nodded approvingly when I went on to tell him what else I wanted him to say to the Heruli in the dens under the arena.

"By the hammer of Thor," he murmured, "but you do have an ingenious turn of mind. Whether or not it avails you and me in any way, it ought to be something to see."

"After you have properly agitated and provoked and instructed the prisoners—and well after dark, but while all the others of the garrison are still raddled—I want you to fetch the marshal Thorn's armor and his horse. Strabo and I will be seated tomorrow in the central podium on the arena-level tier of the amphitheater. So tether the horse and hide the armor somewhere convenient to that podium's private entrance."

"I thought we were keeping the armor merely as a memento. *You* wish to wear it?"

I said offhandedly, "The Saio Thorn was not much bigger than I am. It ought to fit me well enough. And he showed me how to ride his horse with that foot-rope around it. Remember, Odwulf, in times not too long past, the Ostrogoth women were no mean warriors themselves."

"Still . . . a female servant to a princess . . ."

"I hope I have not been domesticated to abject softness. Simply do as I say. And one other thing. Strabo tomorrow will surely select some well-trusted guard to be manacled to me. But *you* contrive to be as near me as you can."

"No fear," he said. "Everyone else will have a heavy head tomorrow. I will have no trouble in posting myself nearby. And, Swanilda, let us both be praying that your plan succeeds. If we do not escape, we most certainly will not outlive the day."

4

ext morning, I got dressed and adorned in the very finest of my Veleda garments and cosmetics and jewelry that I had brought from Novae, including even the bosom-enhancing breast guard of coiled bronze that I had bought years ago and far away in the Place of Echoes. I wanted Strabo to see me—this last time that he would ever see me—as wholly, genuinely, undeniably feminine, in no way threatening, so that he should not change his mind about letting me join him at the amphitheater.

533

Camilla did not help me with my dressing. As she had been doing for some mornings past, she was wistfully attending to her own bosom—baring and squeezing and stripping down one, then the other of her pillowy breasts—obviously seeking for the first appearance of maternal milk. Of course, she succeeded in squeezing out only the thin, pale areolar lymph that almost any corpulent woman or even a fat eunuch can express from her or his breast. Nevertheless, I was inspired to a malicious notion. I took off my golden neck chain, took off the brass cap of my reliquary phial and—to Camilla's dumb astonishment—myself milked some of that trickle of hers into the crystal and capped it again.

Strabo arrived then, also resplendently dressed, wearing instead of heavy armor a chlamys and tunic of fine, light fabrics, and a sword belt and scabbard richly jeweled. He was well groomed, too, with even his usually quilly beard neatly trimmed and combed to smoothness. He cocked his head to look me up and down with each eye separately, clasped and rubbed his hands, grinned and said warmly:

"Amalamena, I am truly glad that I do not have to amputate any part of you until tomorrow. You look more beautiful and enticing than I have yet seen you. After the contest in the arena has heated our mutual blood-lust, we ought both to enjoy our frolic tonight. I know I will. Too bad, really, that it must be the last time."

"Unless," I said, "Freya or Tykhe or some other goddess of fortune should choose to smile upon me before then."

"Akh, ja, if the overdue Ocer does suddenly materialize. But I fear that your time of reprieve is dwindling rapidly. Come, shall we go now to watch the slaughter you craved to see?"

He gestured to the armored soldier he had brought with him, and that man clasped a slave's iron bracelet about my right wrist and bolted it shut, the chain of it already attached to the identical bracelet that he wore on his left wrist. It was, in fact, fairly embedded in the man's arm, because he was even bigger than Strabo, being grossly fat. I suppose the intent was that, even if my guard should suddenly drop dead, I could not possibly drag such a weight and effect an escape.

With only a few other soldiers in attendance, the three of us went afoot to the amphitheater, it being no great distance from the palace. There we went through the entrance reserved for the city's notables, our attendant soldiers remaining outside. We ascended a short flight of stairs to the podium, and I found that a comfortable chair had been set there for me, and a high couch on which Strabo would recline. Before he did so, though, he slipped off his sandals and put on a pair of elegant slippers, densely and intricately embroidered with beads, even on the soles. The high couch made him visible, full length, to all his subjects in the amphitheater, and those slippers were to indicate to them that their King Thiudareikhs Triarius was so exalted, illustrious and indolent that he need never even *walk* unless it pleased him to do so.

It seemed that every single one of his Constantiana subjects was present to admire him. They filled every cuneus and maenianum of the amphitheater, from the best seats up to the hard ledges of the highest tier. Only our podium was not elbow to elbow with people; it contained none but myself, my attached guard standing slouched beside my chair, Strabo recumbent on his couch and a single other guard—it was Odwulf, thags Guth—standing armed and armored and at rigid attention behind Strabo's back.

That my chain was manacled to my right arm and to my guard's left was the customary way of fettering prisoners, because in most people (myself included) the right arm is the stronger. However, I had already noticed that my fat guard wore his sword sheathed on the *right* side of his belt, and his arm gave mine a yank now and then, when he picked his nose or scratched his crotch. So he was left-handed. Fortune, I decided, was indeed smiling on me this day.

Strabo languidly waved a white cloth and the doors in the arena's perimeter walls opened. Herded out by their numerous armed warders, the Herulian captives emerged onto the sand. Every man was stark naked, except for a blotch of blue or green paint daubed on his chest — to indicate which of the two tribes he belonged to — and the separate tribes were bunched on opposite sides of the arena. Each of the men carried a Roman gladius short-sword, meaning that the fighting would have to be done at very close quarters, with no protection at all, for the captives had not been issued shields.

Strabo signaled again. The guards went back inside the arena doors and stoutly bolted those portals behind them, so that none of the contestants could flee or hide. The Heruli on either side of the arena were milling about, apparently discussing the situation among themselves, other were pointing at the men across the way, smeared with a different color. But after a few moments they all turned and looked toward the podium. So did the cityfolk in the seats, and those shouted, *"Let faírweitl gaggan!"* — urging Strabo to "let the entertainment commence!" I turned also, but to steal a glance at Odwulf. He nodded that he had done as I had instructed, and then made a wry face of "we can but wait and see."

Strabo smiled and dallied for a mischievous little while, teasing his eager subjects. Then he lazily got up from the couch and stepped forward to the parapet of the podium to address the gladiators. If those men had never seen Strabo in person before, they must have marveled at how he was able to stare simultaneously at both companies of them. His declamation consisted of pretty much what I had said to him earlier: that these rebellious tribesmen, having flouted their king's authority by trying to butcher each other, would now be given the opportunity to do just that, Blues versus Greens. In the event that one last man should be left alive on each side, those two would not only be granted the keeping of their lives, they also would be enlisted as honored warriors in the king's own palace guard.

"Háifsts sleideis háifstjandáu!" Strabo concluded: "Fight a fierce fight!" Then he lazily returned to his couch and disposed himself upon it so his beaded feet could be seen by all, before he waved and let drop the white cloth for the combat to begin.

It did begin, but not in the way that Strabo and the other spectators had expected. It began in the way that I had planned and Odwulf had

535

fomented, and we both had been hoping for. At the drop of the cloth the Blues and Greens did not rush forward upon one another. They turned the other way, toward the arena's side walls. Some of the men, holding their swords in their teeth, leapt and grasped the parapet above them, and hefted themselves up and over it. Others stepped into the cupped hands of their fellows and were boosted over the wall. Then those above leaned down and hauled still others up. The spectators, finding naked and armed men tumbling headfirst into their laps, scrambled to get out of their way. But everyone else in the amphitheater—Strabo included—was so thunderstruck as only to sit forward and stare at the unprecedented disorder, and murmur in a chorus of astonishment.

But those murmurs turned to shrieks and bellows when the naked Heruli began wielding their swords. They struck indiscriminately, and the men, women and children tightly packed in the seats were helpless against them. Some of the spectators flung up their arms as shields, and the arms were severed and sent flying. So were fingers and hands and ears and noses and more than a few entire heads—mostly those of children, being the more easily sheared off—and also unrecognizable gobbets of flesh, and sprays and gouts and gushes and jets and spates of bright red blood.

The noise became a deafening cacophony. The Heruli yelled and laughed insanely as they slashed and stabbed. The victims who could scream did so, others only burbled through the gashes in their necks or elsewhere, and those yet unassailed were bawling and bleating and trampling each other, trying to swarm higher along the tiers as the Blues hacked their way up one side of the amphitheater and the Greens up the other. There were of course many of Strabo's warriors posted as guards in the aisles and on the staircases, and they strove to close with the attackers, but they were impeded and shoved backward, some of them toppled by the surge of the people they were trying to defend. Meanwhile, there were many more guards who could have been helping—those who had herded the Heruli into the arena—but those were now idling uselessly *under* the amphitheater, inside the doors they had shut and bolted behind them. No doubt they could hear the commotion that was going on outside, but no doubt they supposed it to be merely the noise of the Blues and Greens slaughtering each other.

Even before Strabo himself had fully grasped what was happening, my own personal guard came unstuck from his paralysis of stupefaction and reached his left hand across his body to seize his sword. But I yanked my manacled right arm at the same time, and prevented that. Leaning sideways on the chain, I had strength enough to draw his arm outstretched between us, and Odwulf's snake blade flashed down from behind us, chopping through the guard's forearm, a little way beyond the manacle. As I have said, because of that man's fatness, the iron bracelet was well embedded in his wrist flesh. So I was left with not just the chain and two manacles hung from my own wrist, but his heavy, bleeding, twitching hand as well. And I must give the guard credit for valor. Though grievously wounded, he managed somehow with his right hand to draw his sword, and fought desperately to ward off Odwulf's succeeding blows.

By then, Strabo was on his feet, roaring at me, "You fitchet bitch, this was *your* doing."

He had a sword, too, and he swung at me and, by rights, I should have died there at that moment. However, since I was merely an unarmed female, he had not troubled to take proper stance and careful aim, or even to swing with all his might. His sword only struck and glanced off the coiled bronze breast guard I wore. The blow alone was terribly painful and knocked the breath from my body and sent me staggering. But before Strabo could position himself and swing again, this time more lethally, Odwulf had felled the guard—and now lashed out with his sword once more, and Strabo dropped at our feet. Oddly, as I could notice even in my stunned condition, Strabo did not bleed.

"I hit him . . . with the flat . . . of my blade," Odwulf explained, panting. "You had not instructed . . . I did not know . . . whether you wished him dead . . . just yet."

"I . . . think . . . not . . ." I wheezed, struggling to get my breath, while I looked about the amphitheater.

The guards who had locked themselves inside the arena dens had finally emerged, seen what was occurring, and were scaling the walls and pursuing the Heruli. Everywhere on both sides of the amphitheater were bodies—limp bodies, writhing bodies, segments and bits of bodies—some lying where they had fallen, some slowly toppling off ledges or rolling down staircases. And, probably for the first time in the history of gladiatorial contests, the sand of the arena was spotless, while the great bowl of Parian white marble was running with red.

However, the Heruli had confined their depredations to the two longer sides of the amphitheater. They and their pursuers had not yet swerved toward either of the curved ends of the edifice. The people who had been sitting on those ends—including everybody seated about

537

and above our central podium—had been able to flee unmolested to the exit-ways. But there they funneled into such a crush—shoving, elbowing, butting, biting, squirming, tearing at each other—that they were doing as much crying and screaming as anybody being actively slain. And obviously some of those people fighting to get through the doors were dying, too—women and children, certainly—being beaten on and trodden on by the bigger and more terrified and more ruthless among them. At any rate, not another person in the amphitheater was paying the least attention to us few in the podium.

I said to Odwulf, "I do not wish Strabo dead . . . yet. I only wish *him* to wish he were. Here, unscrew the bolt and free me of this manacle. I have no need of three hands. Now give me the dead guard's blade. And lend your own sword and strength to assist me." I told him what we would do, and where. "The knees and elbows. It is easier to separate joints than to hack through bones."

Strabo was still unconscious when we commenced the cutting of him, but he instantly came wide awake. Of course he struggled like a madman, and he was an immense and powerful brute. But he had been somewhat weakened by Odwulf's having knocked him senseless, and he was quickly weakened even further as his blood began to stream out of him. Also, he was clad only in cloth, and Odwulf was heavy with armor, and I was not any *puny* female. So, toward the last, Strabo was only screaming and pleading for mercy, as pitifully and as uselessly as every one of his unfortunate Constantiana subjects.

The amputations did not take us long. The rest of the amphitheater was still in tumult and chaos—the dead and dying now included many Heruli and numerous guards—when I finally stood up and stood over the supine remains of Thiudareikhs Triarius. But I did not address him by that name.

"Swine-man," I called him, panting again, this time from exertion. "Until you bleed to death . . . you can walk about . . . on all fours. On your four stumps. Verily, a swine-man. Niu?"

He was silent now, but his sidewise eyes were weeping runnels of tears sidewise down his head, down his temples, to mingle with the pool of blood that was gradually covering the floor of the podium. I picked up one of his severed limbs—a calf and foot, the foot still wearing its beaded slipper—and propped that against the couch so it stood upright. Then I picked up another piece of limb—a forearm and hand—and leaned that across the other so that together they had the semblance of the crooked rune called nauths.

"And here with you I leave my nauthing-stake," I said. "You can gaze upon it while you slowly die. Gaze upon it with whichever eye you choose. As you yourself told me, the nauthing-stake will go on uttering my revilement of you until your swine heart beats its last."

"Come, Swanilda," said Odwulf. "The crowd has pushed on through that doorway yonder. We can mingle with them on the stairs, and get to the street unnoticed."

"Ja," I said, glancing where he pointed. "Our horses, Thorn's armor, where are they?"

"Well hidden and well housed," he said with a laugh. "Actually inside a house, I mean. Directly across the street from this podium's private entrance. The family were all absent—over here, to see the spectacle—so I thought: why not?"

"Well done. Go, then. I will be right behind you." I leaned again over Strabo, saying, "Just two things more."

His truncated limbs jerked and lifted as if to fend off a blow. But all I did was unclasp my reliquary phial from my neck chain, unstopper it and jam the crystal between Strabo's lips, which were now a pale blue in color.

539

"Here," I said. "This is the only shriving you will have. You sneered often enough at the Virgin's milk. Now, perhaps, you may care to suckle on it while you say your last prayers."

I stood up and looked about, to make sure that Odwulf was out of sight and hearing.

"The other thing," I said. "I give you one small consolation in your dying. Be not ashamed that you were slain by a mere woman. I am not the Princess Amalamena." Now I deliberately told him a lie, though I hoped that only half of it was a lie. "Amalamena is safe with her brother Theodoric—and so is the genuine pactum written and signed by the Emperor Zeno. My being captured and staying this long in captivity was only to keep you from knowing those things until too late."

He uttered a dismal groan, then croaked, froglike, "But who . . . you bitch . . . are you?"

I said airily, "No bitch at all, not even a female predator. I am a raptor. And you hoped to breed a human son of me, niu?" I laughed. "It was not with a woman that you lay those many times, and it is not a woman who now has branded you a nauthing."

I raised my blood-sodden skirt and undid my hip band and whisked it off. Strabo's eyeballs bulged so very much that I thought the irises of them would slide away, like his tears, down his temples, to dissolve in the pool of blood. Then he clenched his eyes tight shut, as I spoke my last words to him:

"You were deceived and you were derided and you were outwitted and you were cut down to a swine-man and you were slain by a raptor named Thorn the Mannamavi."

✠   ✠   ✠

I wish I could say that everything I had planned to happen that day happened exactly as I had planned it, but that was not to be.

Concealing my confiscated, bloodied sword in a fold of my bloodied gown, I ran in the direction that Odwulf had gone, through the exit-way and down some stairs—having to leap over various trampled bodies as I went. But at a landing of the staircase my way was blocked, and I saw that Odwulf had gone no farther either. A crowd of the just escaped spectators, enraged to frenzy, had surrounded him and seized him there, and were yanking and shoving him this way and that, and were screeching imprecations at him.

"One of Strabo's cowardly guards! Running away!"

"Why is he not back there fighting those demons?"

"My beautiful daughter was killed! But he lives!"

"Not for long!"

Odwulf was trying to expostulate with them, but could not be heard above their uproar. Of course he, a professional soldier, would not draw his sword against innocent cityfolk. *I* might have done that, simply to save his life, but the mob was too dense and surging for me to force my way to his side in time. The man who had shouted "Not for long!" had, in the same instant, snatched Odwulf's sword from its scabbard. Odwulf again tried to say something, and the man plunged the blade into his open mouth, so fiercely that its point emerged at the back of Odwulf's neck.

When the blameless Odwulf fell, with his sword standing upright from his mouth, like a cross already placed as his grave marker, the crowd seemed to come to its collective senses. Realizing what a horrendous crime they had just been party to—and not knowing that Strabo was beyond inflicting any punishment for it—they scurried guiltily on down the stairs and dispersed in the street beyond. I followed more slowly, pausing to give Odwulf the Gothic salute before I left him.

The city's streets were full of people. Most of them were clearly fugitives from the turmoil, for their fine holiday raiment was bloodstained or torn to rags. Some of those were running homeward, and others simply stood about, dazed and silent or weeping and keening. There were also many armed soldiers running, not away from the amphitheater but toward it, to reinforce their comrades inside. In all the confusion, one additional disheveled and bloodied female was unremarkable. Not entirely having to *pretend* weariness, I stumbled and staggered around the outside walls of the amphitheater until I came to the doorway that Strabo and I and my guard had earlier entered.

Across the street was a fine mansion, obviously that of some family of status. I pushed open its unfastened street door and found, in the well-furnished hallway just inside, my dear and long-missing Velox, still wearing my foot-rope and even—I had no idea how Odwulf had found them—my own saddle and bridle. Velox whickered in surprise and pleasure at seeing me again. There was another horse, too, but since Odwulf would have no use for it, I decided simply to leave it where it was, as one more astonishment that day for the persons who lived in this house, when and if they ever got back to it. On a corner table was neatly piled my helmet, my corselet and a bearskin cloak. I was considering how best to combine those with the feminine garb I already wore when I espied a face peering fearfully at me from around the inner door of the hall.

541

I beckoned as imperiously as if I owned the place, and he came shuffling—an aged house servant, left behind as a watchman while the family went to be entertained. He must have been baffled when Odwulf came to quarter two horses in his house, but he had to be much more dumbstruck now when an Amazonian young woman commanded him to doff his tunic, hose and leather shoes. Since I was holding a bare sword still clotted with blood, he made no demur, but hastened to obey. Then he stood shivering with either fright or cold when I took the garments from him.

Not to shock the old fellow any further, I concealed myself between the horses while I stripped off my own outer wear. My jeweled fibulae, my gold neck chain and the blessed bronze breast guard I stowed in Velox's saddlebags. The old man's tunic and hose fit me well enough; the shoes were far too large for me, but I would not have to do much walking; they would serve for riding. When I was decently covered, I ordered the watchman to help me buckle on my corselet. Then I clapped on my helmet and slung the bearskin about my shoulders. Having no sword belt, I tied a thong about the hilt of my substitute blade and hung it from my saddle horn. My red-sodden gown I tossed to the old servant, in case he had nothing else with which to clothe his skinny, quivering legs. I led Velox to the outer door, opened it a crack and waited until there were no soldiers visible in the street. I turned and said, "The other horse, old man—tell your masters that it was a gift to you from Thiudareikhs Triarius." Then I led Velox outside, mounted and set off at a canter—westward, inland from the seaside.

With the city still in utter confusion, one hurrying rider in Ostrogothic military costume was no more remarkable than one weary woman had been. Whenever I passed another soldier, or an outpost of soldiers, I merely shouted, "Gaírns bokos! Urgent message!" and none of them dared to wave me down. When I had thus got safely past the last guardhouse on the city's outskirts, I let Velox slow to an easier pace.

I had escaped.

So here I was, journeying again, as much alone and almost as devoid of resources as I had been when I left the Balsan Hrinkhen as a child. My only weapon was a purloined sword not very suitable to my size. Wyrd's fine Hunnish bow and arrows were gone; so were practically all of my other goods and belongings, except what I had left in Novae. However, I did have Amalamena's gold chain to use for money. I could barter its separate links and its one remaining ornament, the gold hammer-cross, for any necessities that I could not provide for myself. I had a long winter journey ahead of me, but I had endured others before. I anticipated no insuperable problems in making my way back to Theodoric.

"And what a wondrous tale I will have the pleasure of telling him!"

I could not help exclaiming that aloud. There was no one to hear me except Velox, but the horse turned his ears back toward me as if he were paying rapt attention. So I went on:

"Why, I have killed a king, just as Theodoric killed Babai of the Sarmatae. Or at least I have killed a rival and pretender to the kingship of the Ostrogoths. More than that, perhaps. I may have saved more than the Gothic people from being overwhelmed by that tyrant."

There I fell silent, because I had to admit that that deed and my escape had been of considerable cost to others. Only the gods knew how many Constantiana citizens I had sacrificed in the furtherance of my aims—not to mention the six hundred wretched Heruli. I had lost a good and faithful comrade, too, when Odwulf fell. But I could even find reason not to feel *overwhelmingly* sorry about that. It meant that I no longer had to live in disguise—or in varying disguises to suit varying situations—now that Odwulf was not accompanying me. And when I

542

rejoined Theodoric, my arriving alone would certainly make for less complicated explanations of who I was.

Oh vái, and who *are* you?

That was not said aloud, and it was not said of my conscious volition. It was some inner part of my mind demanding to know.

Or *what* are you, it went on—so readily to justify all of today's bloodshed as simply necessary to your own ends? Have you truly become as uncaring of all other earthly creatures as is the juika-bloth? Remember, you boastfully told Strabo that a raptor is what you are. Nor was that the first time in your life that you have arrogantly described yourself as a raptor.

Impatiently, angrily, I shook those thoughts away. I would *not* have my sentimental and susceptible feminine nature intruding, to dim or diminish my pride in my masculine accomplishments. For now, I was still Thorn. Thorn! *Thorn!*

"And, by all the gods," I shouted to the world at large, "if a raptor I am, I am a *live* raptor, and a raptor uncaged!"

I said no more. I pressed on westward, to find the river Danuvius and follow it upstream.

543

5

All the way from Constantiana westward to the Danuvius, I was crossing a tediously flat, treeless grassland, where the only movement was that of myself and Velox, and that of the dry brown grass, rippled by a constant chill wind. But even had I lacked the aid of the daytime sun and the night's star Phoenice, I could have made the crossing without straying, because I was following the tumbled remains of an incredibly long and once high stone wall constructed on orders from the Emperor Trajan, after he had pushed the Dacians north of here, nearly four hundred years ago.

When at last I came to the banks of the Danuvius, the river was flowing at an angle across my westerly course. So, to go upstream, I now turned southwest. Since I did not journey along any roads, I did not meet or get passed by any messengers, though I was sure that they must be galloping in all directions, to spread the news of the holocaust in Constantiana and the death of Strabo. I should have liked to hear what messages they carried abroad, and what messages they brought in return—from Zeno, from Rekitakh, from anybody else concerned. However, I was satisfied *not* to be on any much traveled routes, because, for all I knew, there were also patrols out vengefullly seeking the vanished "Princess Amalamena."

Now that I was following the river, though I still encountered no other land travelers, I was no longer the *only* traveler in evidence. The Danuvius was seldom empty of some kind of vessel—a sailing merchant ship, a drifting barge, a fishing boat or one of the swift-moving dromo craft of the Moesian Fleet—and those various travelers were going placidly or busily upstream and down, as if oblivious of the civic and military convulsions occurring among the "land-lobbes" in the nations bordering their river.

The Danuvius gradually bent until it was taking me more and more directly westward, and in time I came to Durostorum, a Roman fortress town that is also a river port for the merchant craft and a supply base of the Moesian Fleet. I had crossed from the province of Scythia into Theodoric's at least titular domain of Moesia Secunda again. The riverside fortress was manned by the Legio I Italica, which, despite its name, was a legion of Zeno's Eastern Empire. Also it was composed mostly of outlanders—Ostrogoths, Alamanni, Franks, Burgunds, other Germanic tribesmen. All those men considered themselves "Roman legionaries" and nothing else, and the Ostrogoths among them professed no partisanship for either Strabo or Theodoric.

They took me to be a messenger from Scythia—obviously no other had preceded me here from the north—and escorted me at once to the praetorium of their very capable-looking commander, Celerinus, who was a real Roman, meaning Italia-born. He likewise assumed that I was a messenger-at-large, and received me most cordially, so I gave him the one message I could: that Thiudareikhs Triarius was dead and his Black Sea port of Constantiana was a shambles. Celerinus, as a longtime soldier, either was well inured to astounding news or had schooled himself to show little emotion on such occasions. He only raised his eyebrows and wagged his head. But then, in return, he graciously told me the latest news he had had from the west. It was gratifying news indeed.

Thiudareikhs Amaling, *my* Theodoric, had successfully concluded a treaty with the Emperor Zeno. (I gave silent but fervent thanks to the gods; Swanilda *had* got safely to Theodoric with the pactum and Zeno could not abrogate it.) Thereupon, Celerinus had sent a sizable detachment of his own Italica Legion upriver to Singidunum. Theodoric had formally relinquished that city to them—hence to the Emperor Zeno, who would quickly be sending many more troops, to fortify it against future assaults by any barbarians.

Right now, said Celerinus, Theodoric was at his home city of Novae, regrouping and disposing his various Ostrogoth forces to defend what were now unequivocally *their* lands in Moesia. It was expected that Theodoric would next assume the command that Zeno had accorded him: magister militum praesentalis of every military force, including this Legio I Italica, guarding the Danuvius frontier of the empire. Celerinus looked forward, he said—and he said it sincerely—to swearing the auths to his new commander-in-chief.

I stayed that night, two days and two more nights in Durostorum, to take refreshing advantage of its fine thermae, to rest myself and Velox in comfortable quarters and to feed us both on nutriments superior to what we had so far been foraging. There was only one other sizable community on my way up the Danuvius—Prista, all tanneries, dye works, brick kilns, tileries and potteries—and I did not linger there.

And eventually I arrived again at Theodoric's Novae. In the considerable span of time since I had left the city, so very, very much had happened—little of it pleasant to recall, except for the too brief, bittersweet and ill-fated intimacy of Amalamena and myself—that it seemed I had been away for years, decades, ages beyond counting.

✠   ✠   ✠

"Thorn lives! The rumor was true!"

Those were Theodoric's glad words as I entered the throne room where I had first met Amalamena. Evidently I had been recognized as I rode through the city, and the news had been relayed to the Novae palace. Besides the king, there were four other people waiting to welcome me.

When I snapped up my arm in the stiff Gothic salute, Theodoric

laughingly slapped it down. We clasped right wrists in the more comradely Roman manner, then embraced like long-parted brothers, and
both of us exclaimed, almost in unison, "It is good to see you again, old
friend!" Two of the men in the room did give me the raised-arm salute,
one other man nodded gravely and a young woman shyly smiled at me.
All of them echoed Theodoric in warmly greeting me, "Waíla-gamotjands!"

"Well," I said to the king, "you seem to have convened almost everyone connected with that mission."

The middle-aged man who had saluted was my fellow marshal, Saio
Soas. The much older man who had only nodded was Lekeis Frithila.
The pretty young woman was Swanilda. The young man who had sa-
luted was a stranger to me, but I assumed him to be my messenger
Augis, fellow lancer to the late Odwulf. He had to be, because he was
staring at me as if I were the risen gáis of Thorn or a skohl taking the
semblance of Thorn—and it was Augis whom I had sent here to report
Thorn's death.

"There is only one person you have not summoned, Theodoric," I
said. "Strabo's optio Ocer. I am most anxious to have my own sword
again."

"The sword is already hanging in your quarters. The optio is beyond
anyone's summons. Augis delivered your suggestion as to what disposition I ought to make of Ocer and his attendants. Did you think I
would fail to comply?"

I said approvingly, "Thags izvis."

"We will have you fully caparisoned again in no time. But first, let
me congratulate you—let me praise you—on the surpassing success of
your mission. You have proven yourself a true Ostrogoth, an exemplary
marshal, a worthy herizogo. However, the accounts of that mission have
come only in bits and pieces. You must tell the whole story, fill in the
gaps. You might start by telling us—particularly the bewildered Augis
yonder—how it is that you are not dead."

I spread my arms in a gesture of woeful resignation and said, "Ne,
let me express my grief for those who *are*. Optio Daila and all the rest
of my turma, except for gallant Augis there. I hope the mission's success
was worth its lamentable cost. And, of all the lost, I grieve most deeply
for your dear sister, Theodoric. I had become more fond of Amalamena
than even you could be."

"I should not have laid that responsibility on you," he said contritely.
"But I had no idea that she was suffering the least illness. Frithila has,

of course, told me all about it—and that there was no way any mortal could have helped her."

"As best I could," I said, "I did what the lekeis commanded. I tried to keep up her spirits."

"And . . . she died bravely," said Theodoric, not quite making either a statement or a question of it.

Skirting the truth only a little, I said, "Ja, she bravely awaited the coming of her death, knowing it to be inevitable. But at the end she really had no need of bravery. The very last time I saw her alive, Amalamena was in seeming good health, good cheer, even good appetite. Most merrily she bade me go and fetch her evening meal. When I returned with it, she was gone. That quickly, that easily, that peacefully."

Theodoric sighed and said, "I am glad of that. And I am glad that you survived to tell me. It helps to lessen the heartache of bereavement. But who, then, was the captive woman that Strabo pretended was my sister? The woman for whom Optio Ocer demanded ransom?"

"Strabo was not pretending. He believed she *was* your princess sister. In truth, she was one of the Khazar servants who had attended us at the Purple Palace. Amalamena engaged the woman as her cosmeta after we sent Swanilda riding hither with Zeno's pactum. I presumed that when Augis later arrived here with the word that Strabo held not Amalamena but a substitute, the *genuine* Swanilda"—I gestured at her— "would have divined who that woman must be."

547

"And Swanilda did hazard that conjecture," said Theodoric. "But I found it hard to credit. How could Strabo have mistaken a dark-haired, olive-skinned Khazar maidservant for an *Amaling princess?*"

"Well, the woman was wonderfully adept as a cosmeta," I said, piling lie upon lie. "She bleached her hair and skin most skillfully. She even deluded all of our own men—from a distance. Did she not, Augis?" The lancer nodded, his eyes wide. "Later, when she was being held captive by Strabo, I managed to stay in communication with her. Like Augis and Odwulf, another of our stalwarts, I had mingled unnoticed with Strabo's own warriors."

Augis's eyes got even wider, and he did not nod to confirm that remark. He was clearly wondering how *he* could have failed to notice my lurking about. So I rather desperately went on, "I wished to bring here with me that transformed Khazar maid, for your amazement, Theodoric. And for your commendation, because she played her part with valor. Unfortunately, she was among the innocents who died during the bloodbath at Constantiana, when—"

"Hold, hold!" Theodoric interrupted, shaking his head and laughing. "I think it best that you commence your account from the beginning. Here, men, let us all draw couches close together. And Swanilda, would you go and ask the kitcheners to supply some refreshment? This will surely be a long story, and Thorn's throat is bound to get parched."

So I told of everything, or almost everything, that had happened from the day our company left Novae until this day of my return. I had barely begun when Swanilda and another woman came from the kitchens, bearing between them an immense, fluted, silver-gilt bowl full of fresh golden mead, in which stood a gracefully bird-shaped golden ladle. They set the bowl in the center of our circle and then departed, not presuming to sit in on men's talk. I did not interrupt my account, but I had recognized the second woman. She was much more richly garbed than I had last seen her, and she was tremendously pregnant, and from her manner she seemed to be the new mistress of Swanilda the cosmeta.

I was bemused, but I postponed making any query about the woman. When they were gone, and as I continued speaking, one or another of us men would at intervals dip from the bowl a drink of sweet mead. As is customarily served when several men are conferring, this was a "fraternal bowl," requiring all of us amicably to take turns drinking from the single ladle.

I told my story very much as I have told it here, only more concisely, omitting details like the ugly manifestations of Amalamena's illness. To account for my being alive at this moment, I had to make myself out to have been something less than a heroic warrior-to-the-death. I declared that Amalamena's death took place in Pautalia, and that Optio Daila and I secretly buried her there—not letting even our own men know of it—and that thereafter the Khazar-Swanilda rode alone in the carruca. I told how our discovery of the one bowman's treachery made me and Daila decide to deviate from our course and follow the river Strymon—eventually into the deep defile where, one dark night, Strabo's force swooped down upon us. There I fought alongside my men, I said (knowing that Augis could not denounce that as a lie, he having been high atop the cliff at the time).

Then, I said, I simultaneously realized that ours was a losing battle and saw Strabo's men drag the Khazar-Swanilda from the carruca—and thereupon conceived my notion of substitution. I doffed my own armor, because it proclaimed my rank and identity, and donned that of another smallish man who had fallen in the fray. I made my way to the Khazar-Swanilda's side, where I had time to whisper urgent instructions to her and to give her the princess's necklace to wear. Thus, when Strabo himself confronted her, she haughtily announced herself to be Princess Amalamena—and Strabo believed her.

"He never doubted her, from that day to her last," I said. "But that did not prevent his using her most foully, and in violation of all the conventions of honorable warfare. Rejoice, Theodoric, that she was *not* our Amalamena. Only two nights after capturing her, long before he sent Ocer to demand ransom of you, Strabo took the maidenhead of the woman he believed to be a princess—the woman who, by the code of all warriors, should have been under his protection during her captivity."

Theodoric growled and, though he was wearing no sword, his hand reached involuntarily toward his belt.

I went on to tell how I maintained my own disguise, unrecognized as an interloper by any of Strabo's men and even by those two of my own turma who had likewise insinuated themselves into the enemy company.

"It was at Serdica that Odwulf and I at last recognized one another. We sent Augis galloping hither to tell you that Strabo's ransom demand could be ignored. From then on, Odwulf and I alternated, whenever we could, as the guard assigned to the substitute Amalamena. We told her what to say and how to behave in Strabo's presence, to keep him beguiled and lulled and unwary, while we tried to think of what to do next."

549

I briefly recounted the rest of our journey, from Serdica to Constantiana, with Strabo getting increasingly restive about the disappearance of Ocer, and increasingly abusive of the Khazar woman.

"He continued to ravish her—every two or three nights, she told me. He said he was but anticipating his taking her to wife, and that he intended to beget upon her an heir more to his liking than his worthless son Rekitakh. Further, he asserted that you, Theodoric, would cowardly overlook that gross insult—because you would *welcome* being bound to the mighty Strabo by ties of marriage."

Theodoric uttered a horrendous obscenity and snarled, "Thags Guth it was not my sister. No matter. I will make that overweening reptile rue those words."

"Perhaps he already has," I said, and went on to tell how, when Strabo became so choleric that he was ready to mutilate the substitute princess, I had her persuade him to arrange the contest of the captured Heruli, and how Odwulf and I coerced those prisoners into making it quite a different kind of entertainment. I told how the outraged Strabo stabbed the Khazar woman before Odwulf or I could intervene, and how we two then punished Strabo by performing our syrurgery on him, and how the intrepid Odwulf was so unexpectedly slain during our run for freedom.

"So," I concluded humbly, "like the messenger of Job, I alone have escaped to tell these things."

Theodoric, calm again, said, "Nevertheless, you did most admirably accomplish the mission I sent you. I and all my people are indebted to you. I will of course have a splendid cenotaph raised to my beloved sister. And another, only slightly less splendid, to Odwulf and Daila and all their fellows who also perished. As for Augis here, I had some while ago promoted him to signifer of lancers. In gratitude to that Khazar woman who so nobly served, I will have our palace priest say a mass for her soul. Have I overlooked anyone, Saio Thorn?"

"Ne," I said. "And I have little else to tell, except some overheard tidings and tattle pertaining to matters of state. They would probably interest no one but yourself, Theodoric."

550

He took my meaning; he stood up, stretched, yawned and declared the meeting adjourned. As we all ambled toward the throne room's outer doors, Frithila took my arm to make us lag behind the other three.

"A very interesting story," he said. "I never before heard of any victim of the kreps having died so quickly, so peacefully. Perhaps I should invite you to visit the bedsides of my other patients being gnawed by the carrion worm."

I protested, "The princess did not die by my hand."

"No matter. From the tales you have told, I gather that mere proximity to Thorn is sufficient to kill."

"Please, Lekeis. I am already enduring enough regret for all those—"

"Indeed? I too can quote from the Book of Job. 'Will the eagle mount up at your command? From her nest in high places she seeks her prey, and she sees afar off. Wheresoever the carcass shall be, she is immediately there.'"

Frithila gave me a bleak smile, and went out the door. Why, I wondered, had he chosen to recite those particular words? And why, for that matter, does the Bible itself refer to that raptor as "she"?

The lekeis and the lancer took their leave. Theodoric and I and my fellow marshal, Soas, remained. While we strolled back to our couches, I said to Theodoric under my breath:

"That fine-looking and finely dressed young lady who helped bring in the mead bowl—is not that the Singidunum girl you used to call Aurora?"

"Ja," said Theodoric, without lowering his voice at all. "And I still call her Aurora. I never can remember her real name. It transpired that she was carrying my child, so . . ." He grinned, a little proudly, a little foolishly, and shrugged his shoulders.

"My felicitations to you both," I said. "But . . . you married her and you do not even recollect her *name?*"

"Married her? Gudisks Himins, ne, I could not do that. So she can of course be accorded no official title. But she now occupies what were Amalamena's chambers, and she fulfills all the duties of a royal consort. She will continue to do so until someday I find a woman of status enough to be my wife."

"And if you do not?"

He shrugged again. "My father never had a legitimate queen. The mother of myself and Amalamena and my other sister, Amalafrida, was but his concubine. That imparted no blemish or impediment to us. So long as I recognize Aurora's child or children as my own, that is all that matters in regard to the royal succession."

As he and I and Soas reclined again on our couches, I was reflecting that Theodoric's victory at Singidunum really had resulted in two additional and quite unlooked-for victories. Both I and Aurora-or-Whoever had vaulted from obscurity and nonentity to high places indeed: I becoming a marshal and herizogo, she a de facto queen. Probably I was the only person on earth, now, who knew how hurt Amalamena would have been to find her adored brother joined by paternity to another woman—and a woman much inferior in status to herself. Ja, Amalamena would probably have been heartbroken. And I? Was it possible that I felt some twinge of jealousy?

As we dipped up fresh drinks of mead, I said, "I have been talking for a long time. My other fragments of rumor and gossip and eavesdropped indiscretions can wait for a while. I should like to learn what has been happening here in the west while I was away."

Theodoric gestured to Soas, and that man of few words told, in very few words, of his own mission to an imperial court. As I already knew, the Saio Soas had arrived in Ravenna to find not Julius Nepos the

551

emperor there, but the boy Little Augustus about to assume the purple. What with the delays attendant on the change—the coronation ceremonies, the appointment of new councillors and so on—Soas had had to stand about, waiting to deliver Theodoric's message and the smoked head of the legatus Camundus. Even after the commotion had subsided, and the new young emperor was beginning to grant audiences, there were many other emissaries waiting in line ahead of Soas. Then, when his appointed time was finally approaching, there came the other convulsive overthrow—not just of the reign of Romulus Augustulus, but of the entire Western Roman Empire, and the very concept of an empire ruled by two equal emperors. Aúdawakrs, known as Odoacer, took the rule as king and subordinate of Zeno, Emperor of the East.

Soas concluded, "I knew better than to petition Odoacer in the name of the Theodoric who had slain the man's father. So I came away hoping mightily"—he inclined his head toward me—"that my young colleague had enjoyed better luck." Then Soas made a mild jape, the only attempt at humor I ever heard from him. "I still possess a fine smoked head, if anyone wants it."

552

Theodoric laughed and said to me, "Even if Soas *had* negotiated a treaty with Odoacer, it would have no validity without Zeno's approval. Now that I possess Zeno's own pactum, I care not an iota what Odoacer may think of it. These Moesian lands are ours, the consueta dona is again being paid, the military magistracy is mine."

I said, "But, as I told you, Zeno never really intended for you to receive that parchment. When it *was* delivered, did he not try to disavow it?"

"No doubt he wished that he could, but how could he? On Swanilda's arrival with it, I immediately dispatched a messenger, riding at full tilt, conveying to Zeno my hearty thanks and my auths of loyalty, and asking him to send legionaries to relieve me of my stewardship of Singidunum. In his reply, Zeno could scarce conceal his surprise—even displeasure—but *akh!* his toe was caught fast and pinched hard in the crack of his own making. Also he was much occupied with the dizzy round of affairs at Rome, rather more pressing than the rivalry between Theodoric Amaling and Theodoric Strabo."

"Also," I suggested, "he may perhaps by then have had some hint that Strabo was not quite the loyal and pliable adherent he pretended to be."

I went on to relate some of the confidences Strabo had revealed to "Amalamena"—that his son Rekitakh's being held hostage at Constantinople gave Zeno no real hold over him, and that he expected eventually to be incited by Zeno to evict the Scyrrian Odoacer from his Roman kingship. I recited Strabo's own words pertaining to Odoacer:

"If one outlander could attain to such eminence, so could another."

With a mischievous glint in his eye, Theodoric asked, "Are you proposing that I appropriate Strabo's plan? That *I* evict Odoacer and usurp his rule of the Western Empire?"

"You are at least entitled to unite all the Ostrogoths under your rule," I said. "Strabo's Constantiana is in an uproar, all of Scythia is in disarray. Now that Strabo is dead, and all those lands and peoples are leaderless, and you have Zeno's appointment as magister militum praesentalis, you could become truly king of *all* the Ostrogoths, without even wielding your blade."

"Except for one small detail," said the marshal Soas. "Strabo is not dead."

I wondered if I had drunk too much of the mead; I could not believe I had heard those words. Theodoric cast a sympathetic look at whatever stunned expression I must have had on my face, and explained:

"During your long ramble hither, Thorn, messengers from Constantiana have been galloping more directly and rapidly to Constantinople, to Ravenna and Singidunum and every other major city, including this one. They report Strabo injured but still alive."

"That is impossible!" I gasped. "Odwulf and I left the man with only four stumps of limbs, and every stump was spouting blood. Even his *lips* were bloodlessly blue."

"Akh, I do not doubt you, Thorn. The messengers said that he is bedridden, and has been seen by no one except his two or three most skillful and most trusted lekjos. Well, he would be, if he is now the swine-man you described to us. But evidently his remains were discovered before he lost every last drop of his life's blood. Or perhaps there was divine intervention. That is what is being told."

"Eh?"

"The word is that Strabo has rededicated himself to the Lord God, and swears he will henceforth be a better Arian Christian than ever before."

"He should not find that difficult. But why?"

"To show his gratitude for his miraculous escape from death, and for his continuing recovery. He credits it all to a drink of the breast milk of the Virgin Mary."

553

6

I was destined to see Strabo just one more time in my life, and then only from a distance, and that was some years later, so I will tell of that in its place.

In the meantime, the formerly rampageous old tyrant seemed to be living up to his near-deathbed vow of Christian piety and meek Christian behavior. It was a matter of wonder and conjecture among all people—how he never again bestrode a horse or flaunted a weapon or deflowered a maiden or personally led his men to war or pillage. He was henceforth so reclusive that he might have been a cave-dwelling anachoreta doing nothing but solitary devotions. His only attendant, it was said, was his new wife, Camilla, mother of his new son, Baíran. And she would not—because she could not, being deaf and mute—reveal anything of Strabo's private life. The few of his chief officers who were admitted to his presence, to be given orders or instructions or advice or chastisement, came away from those meetings as silent as his queen.

Naturally I believed the stories of Strabo's hermitry, because I knew the reasons for that. And I was much amused to hear that the lowly and unattractive servant woman had somehow married so far above her station. No doubt she had done it by letting Strabo know that his one drunken ravishment of her had impregnated her—and I was aware of the old man's eagerness to sire more progeny. Of course, he need not have *married* her, any more than Theodoric had had to marry Aurora. But I assumed that, given Strabo's inability now to pursue or abduct anything better than the frumpish Camilla, he had settled for what queen he could get.

However, regarding Strabo's rumored renunciation of all villainy and ambitions of conquest, I credited that not to any surge in him of Christian regeneration, but to force of circumstance. His apparent piety was merely his attempt to make a virtue of necessity. Once the news had been heard by everyone of every degree that Theodoric Amaling was now the true and sole King of the Ostrogoths, the greater part of Strabo's armies gratefully pledged their auths to King Theodoric. So did almost all of the cityfolk and countryfolk—not just Ostrogoths but many other peoples, even Slovenes—from Singidunum in the west to Constantiana in the east to Pautalia in the south.

Strabo was left with only the remnant of an army, mostly those men related by blood to his branch of the Amal line, and for his subject population he had not many more people than those soldiers' families. He and they became nomads, drifting from one to another of the "stronghold" cities of which he had boasted to me, but finding the cities strongholds no longer, and themselves no longer very welcome in those places. From time to time during the ensuing years, Strabo would summon up enough pushfulness to start a petty war or make a random raid for plunder. But those escapades were seldom more than minor nuisances to either Zeno or Theodoric, and either the emperor's legions or the king's would repel the marauders, usually with ease.

(I will mention that the one thing Strabo might have done that could have hurt or annoyed or embarrassed me personally, he never did do, or at least I never heard of his having done it. He never spoke a word to anyone about that occasion on which the presumed Princess Amalamena had exposed her private parts in front of him—her *very* private parts—and announced herself to be really Thorn the Mannamavi. I can only suppose that he had dismissed that incident from his own mind as having been an incredible hallucination engendered by his agony.)

Strabo's son Rekitakh never rejoined his father, but went on residing in Constantinople. If he had earlier been of little value to Zeno as a hostage, he was now of no value whatever, so he no longer dwelt in the Purple Palace. But evidently his father had long before provided him with an ample purse, perhaps more ample than Strabo himself now possessed. According to report, Rekitakh was able to afford fair lodgings in that fair city, and to enjoy the otiose, pleasurable life of an illustrissimus.

On my return to Novae and my reunion with Theodoric, I had expected to rest and refresh myself until my king should conceive some other mission on which to send his marshal Thorn. But Theodoric was naturally much occupied with many responsibilities of his own. A king's first duty is to take care of the needs and wants of his subjects. And now, as *truly* King of All the Ostrogoths, Theodoric had a superabundance of administrative details requiring his attention. And, in having

555

assumed command of the Danuvius frontier, he had to see to a multitude of military matters. Also, when in due course Aurora gave birth to their child, Theodoric proved to be an admirably uxorious and paternal man. If ever he brushed aside any pressing duties at all, it was so he could spend time with his consort and their infant daughter, Arevagni.

I do not mean to say that I was slighted or forgotten; quite the contrary. I was given all the due of an esteemed herizogo, and then was left to enjoy my good fortune in undisturbed tranquillity. Theodoric conferred upon me the estate of another herizogo who had recently died without widow or progeny or other heirs: a thriving farm on the Danuvius riverside, managed by tenant freemen and worked by slaves. With tilled fields, orchards, vineyards and pasture grounds, the property was almost as extensive as the Balsan Hrinkhen lands of St. Damian's Abbey. The main building, my residence, was no palace, only a rustic farmhouse, but it was solidly built, comfortably furnished and capacious enough to contain separate quarters for my indoor servants. There were outdwellings for my freemen and the slave laborers and their families. There was a smithy and a mill and a brewery and an apiary and a dairy house, all in working order and all being worked most productively. There were barns and stables and sties and cotes and cellars, full of every kind of bounty of the land: cattle, swine, horses, poultry, grain, grapes, cheeses, fruits and vegetables. If I had been disposed to live out the rest of my life as a nobleman farmer, I could have lived busily and gainfully and fatly indeed.

However, my tenant managers were clearly competent at everything that made the farm prosperous, so I was content to let them go on being so, without my playing the officious overseer. Instead, and somewhat to my men's surprise and admiration, I occasionally lent a hand, as humbly and industriously as any of the slaves, to those menial chores I had done in my youth—bellows-pumping, poultry-plucking, coop-cleaning and the like.

In only one field of husbandry did I exert authority and control. When I first took over the estate, the only equine stock in the stables and pastures consisted of nondescript horses not much superior to the Zhmuds ridden by the Huns. So I purchased two Kehailan mares—for a price that would well-nigh have bought me another whole farm—and bred my Velox to them, and later to their fillies. Within a few years, I owned a respectable herd of more than just respectable animals, from which I profited handsomely. When one of my mares threw a black colt

556

almost identical to its sire—even to the "prophet's thumbprint" on his lower neck—I told my stable steward:

"This one we will not sell. He is to be mine, the successor to his noble father, never to be straddled by anyone but myself. And since I believe such a superb bloodline as this is entitled to the same honorific designations as any succession of kings or bishops, I shall name this one Velox the Second."

From his first saddling, Velox II was accustomed to wear my foot-rope around his chest, and he learned readily to jump without ever balking on account of my eccentrically non-Roman seat, and he became as agile as Velox I at staying firmly under me when I practiced mock fighting from the saddle, however much he had to dance and dodge and contort. Eventually, if I had been blindfolded before going to the mounting block, I could hardly have told which of my two Veloxes I was riding.

Except for my equine occupations and my trivial chores, most of my time on the farm was spent as idly and purposelessly as, according to report, Rekitakh was doing in Constantinople. However, I was not always on the farm. I had lived too much of my life on the road to be ready, now, to settle down forever in one place. So, once in a while, I would simply throw a saddle and a pack on one of my Veloxes and go roaming abroad, for a span of days or a fortnight or sometimes as long as a month. (I more and more often chose Velox II for the longer rides, judging that his sire had well earned his retirement to pasture and the enjoyment of his mares.) On each of those occasions, of course, I sought Theodoric's permission before I absented myself, and asked if I could perform any services for him on my way. He might say, "Well, if you chance to see any barbarian forces roving about, make note of their number and strength and route of march, and report to me when you return." And I would punctiliously comply. But he never had any more specific missions to assign, so I wandered where I would.

As always, I found travel rewarding, but it was pleasant, too, having a home to come back to. That was something I had never had before. Because I still, and for a long time, mourned the loss of Amalamena—or, to say it more honestly, because my yearning for that winsome nymph had been unrequited, and now forever would be—I had no desire to take a consort to keep me company in my country retreat. In fact, I repeatedly had to fend off the lady Aurora's kindly intentioned efforts to make a match for me with various unattached females of the

557

Novae court, from noble widows to the pretty cosmeta Swanilda. Therefore, partly to keep myself from being tempted to make any such long-term alliance, and partly because imperious arrogation is expected of a slave owner, I occasionally took a female slave to warm my bed.

There were many of those about my premises, and I tried several, but only two were handsome and appealing enough that I made use of them with some frequency. Naranj, a woman of the Alan people, the wife of my mill steward, had exceptionally long hair as black as moonshade. Renata, a Suevian girl, daughter of my cellarer, had exceptionally long hair as silver-gilt as Amalamena's had been. I remember the names of those two, and I remember their gorgeous hair, and I remember how the woman and the girl showed their appreciation of the honor, in their eagerness to give me plentiful pleasure. But that is all I can now remember to recount of them.

Meanwhile, there was the other side of my nature to be satisfied, too. As Veleda, I wanted to be purged of the memory of the abominable Strabo and those odious insults he had inflicted on my person. Also, since I had so steadfastly suppressed my femininity every time he had defiled me, I now felt the need of some reassurance as to the adequacy of my female sexuality. I could easily have tested that by availing myself of a male slave or two; I possessed quite a stud of stalwart and passably attractive men. But I was disinclined to go to the trouble, again, of maintaining the disguises and jugglery that such an expedient would have entailed.

So I took some of my estate income and, as Veleda, purchased and furnished a small house in Novae. I had to be discreet in my employment of that, and in the ways in which I accosted and made the acquaintance of the men I judged eligible to share that sanctum with me—for an hour or a night or longer—because Novae was a considerably smaller city than, say, Vindobona, where I had previously been Veleda, or Constantia, where I had been Juhiza. Here in Novae I could not risk making myself conspicuous and causing gossip and speculation: who was this newcome woman and whence came she and what was she up to? I took care not to approach any high-ranking military men, with whom I might someday have to associate as Thorn, or any of Theodoric's familiars, or men of the nobility, or any other notables whom I might later meet at court.

Of course, I was pleased to find that I was still attractive to men, and could easily entice and enthrall them, and that my female apparatus and sensitivities and juices and emotions were all unimpaired. But no bedfellow there in Novae ever inspired in me anything quite to equal the affection and appetite I had felt for my very first male lover, Gudinand of Constantia. I kept none of the men about me for very long—I most quickly dismissed those who became abjectly enamored of me and pleaded for lasting attachment. I do not regret either Thorn's or Veleda's libertine behavior of those days, nor do I think I owe any apologies for it. That was one of the few periods in my life when I had leisure and opportunity to indulge myself—both of my selves—and I thoroughly enjoyed the indulgence.

Raptorial I may have seemed, in my taking and discarding of lovers, but not one of those, freeborn man or female slave, ever complained of being hurt by loving me. If I distressed anybody at all, it may have been those lovers' *future* lovers, or their wives or husbands, who very possibly were deemed inferior bedmates by comparison to me.

Of the male lovers, I recall the name of only one—Widamer—and his name I have reason to remember vividly. Though I was to be only twice in his company, my meeting with Widamer there in Novae would eventually lead to another encounter—the most astounding of my life, perhaps the most fantastic ever to tincture the life of *any* human being. I met Widamer in a Novae market square, the same way I had met other men, and we contrived some excuse to introduce ourselves and proceed to get acquainted. Widamer was some four or five years younger than myself, and he was dressed like any Gothic young man of estimable status, but there was a slightly foreign cut to his clothing, so I presumed him to be a Visigoth, not an Ostrogoth. In our first tentative skirmish of light conversation, he confirmed that guess. He had come hither, he said, all the way from Aquitania, merely to deliver a message, and would be in Novae only long enough to get a written reply to that message, and then he would be off again for his homeland.

559

That suited me. I preferred a transient visitor to a permanent resident. He would less likely want to become my one and only and everabiding lover, and thereby become a pestiferous nuisance. However, I should have interrogated Widamer at length, to satisfy myself as to his identity and credentials. I would have done so, except that I had been much taken with him at first sight. That was because Widamer was almost the twin of the young and anonymous Theodoric I had first known and traveled with, back in Pannonia. Widamer had much the same features and coloring and manly build, and he was *nearly* as handsome, and he had the same devil-me-care rakishness about him. So, contrary to my usual practice on meeting a new man, I took him home with me that very day, and accorded him rather more varieties of delight than I usually bestowed at the first bedding of a new lover.

Well, come to that, I too enjoyed rather more delight than I usually did during a first coupling. For one reason, Widamer looked so much like a younger Theodoric that I was able to imagine, even with my eyes open, that he *was* Theodoric. And there was another, realer reason. I had always imagined that Theodoric's amatory appendage must be of an admirable robustness. And that is what Widamer's proved to be, and he employed it with commendable prowess.

I wallowed for so long in such blissful rapture that, when Widamer and I at last uncoupled, I decided to reward him for the experience, and I shifted position in the bed to lavish on him an even more intimate attention. However, when I bent close to his fascinum, and saw it to be of an unnatural flamboyant maroon color, I recoiled and exclaimed:

"Liufs Guth! Are you diseased?"

"Ne, ne," he said, laughing. "That is only a birthmark, nothing worse. Taste it and see." And I did, and he had spoken the truth.

560

In the evening, I bade Widamer take his leave, because I had to dress for another engagement later that night. So he and I parted, with fervent mutual thanks and fulsome mutual compliments and the expression of hopes that we two might meet again sometime. I doubt that Widamer expected that we ever would, and I know that I had no such expectations.

But meet again we did, that same night. My engagement was at Theodoric's palace, where he had invited his marshal Thorn to attend a convivium feast. I had not known that the gathering was being convened in honor of a messenger named Widamer. Since quite a few courtiers were being introduced to that young man, he surely did not realize that a particular one among them he had already met under other circumstances. Still, I was understandably a little uncomfortable when Theodoric stood us face to face and said affably:

"Saio Thorn, be so good as to bid welcome to my cousin Widamer, son of my late mother's late brother. Though by birth a noble Amaling, Widamer chose to cast his fortune some years ago with the court of the Balting Euric, King of the Visigoths, at Tolosa in Aquitania."

I gave the raised-arm salute and said in my deepest, most masculine voice, "Waíla-gamotjands," and Widamer returned the greeting without evincing any recognition of me.

Theodoric went on, "Widamer comes as an emissary, with the news that our fellow king Euric and the Roman king Odoacer have concluded an agreement—to make the Alpes Maritimae henceforth the firm boundary between their domains. That is little business of ours, of course, but I am pleased to have the report, simply because it brought Widamer here for a visit. He and I had not seen one another since we were small children."

I said politely, "I wish you a pleasant stay in Novae, young Widamer."

"Akh, it already has been extremely pleasant," he replied, without any smirk or insinuation of double meaning.

Thereafter, while the many guests milled about and drank and conversed, I managed to keep away from Widamer. Then, when we all went to the dining chamber and reclined at tables for a midnight nahtamats, I took a couch at a distance from that of Theodoric and Widamer. But I must have drunk copiously and unwisely of the table's wines and mead, because, before the night was over, I would utter a horrendously imprudent remark.

Theodoric was recounting to his cousin some of the events of his career during the years they had been apart—and, in keeping with the festivity of this occasion, he was relating mainly the more lightsome and entertaining events. The other guests listened with interest, except when they were laughing uproariously or when they interrupted Theodoric to shout some recollection of their own, usually an indelicate or downright bawdy anecdote. And, for some reason, I too felt impelled to contribute a sally. I can only suppose that, seeing Theodoric and Widamer side by side there, the two so nearly indistinguishable, I had got drunkenly confused as to which of *my* identities I was currently inhabiting. At any rate, I had got too addled to remember that it behooved me to stay inconspicuous.

561

". . . And then, Widamer," Theodoric was saying, with great good humor, "when we laid siege to Singidunum, I took a local wench, just to while away the time. But she is with me yet. Not only have I not got rid of her—behold!" He gestured to where his consort reclined among some other court ladies. "She *multiplies!*"

True, Aurora was again visibly pregnant, but she was not embarrassed by the waggery. She only put out her tongue at Theodoric and, when the company laughed at that, she joined in. Then my own voice loudly overrode the laughter:

"And behold, too—Aurora blushes no more! Theodoric, tell Widamer how Aurora used to blush! Vái, she used to blush as dark a color as the birthmark that stains Widamer's svans!"

The room's laughter instantly stilled, except for a bewildered feminine giggle here and there. As if my blurting out such a privity were not unseemly enough, the word "svans" is frowned on in mixed company. A number of women *did* blush bright red—and so did Widamer—and *everyone* in the chamber turned to stare at me, appalled. The silence would doubtless have been broken, next moment, by a volley of demands to know if I was making a jest, and, if so, what was the point of it. But, belatedly aware of my own indiscretion, I now regained sense enough to feign sudden drunken unconsciousness, and toppled off my couch to fall asprawl on the marble floor. That occasioned several more feminine giggles and some contemptuous masculine growls of "Dumbsmunths!" I merely lay where I had fallen, with my eyes shut, and was relieved to hear Theodoric take up his storytelling again, with no one making further reference to my oafish outburst.

But I could not lie there forever. Happily, the marshal Soas and the physician Frithila came to my aid, though with disapproving sniffs. They poured cold water over my head and down my throat and, rather than strangle, I pretended to come back to some semblance of muddled consciousness. I thanked them in a slurred voice, and let them lead me to a far corner of the chamber, where they propped me on a bench against the wall. When they left me there, the pretty cosmeta Swanilda came over to stroke my wet head and murmur comforting words, and to her I mumbled indistinct apologies for my witlessness.

At last the gathering began to break up, and Swanilda left me. I was trying to figure out how best I could stagger convincingly but *unobtrusively* from the palace, when abruptly Widamer was standing in front of me, legs apart, hands on hips, and he asked, in a voice low enough not to be overheard but cold enough not to be ignored:

"How did you know about the birthmark?"

I grinned as foolishly as I knew how, and said, making my tongue fumble, "Edivently—I mean evidently—we have been in and out of the same warm bed."

"Indeed," he said, making of the word no question. He put a hand under my chin and tilted up my drooping head so he could closely scan my face. Still without making of it a question, he said, "It *would* have been warm, would it not, if you got into that bed in the brief time between my leaving it and your arriving at this convivium."

I could think of no rejoinder to that, so I gave him only another sloppy grin. He kept hold of my chin and keenly studied my face, then finally said, "Be easy. I am no gossip. But this I will ponder on . . . and remember . . ."

Then he was gone from the room, and shortly so was I.

✠ ✠ ✠

I might have been inclined to stay well away from the palace for some time after that night, until perhaps my atrociously dumbs-munths performance might be forgotten. But I was anxious to know whether I was to be permanently in disgrace with Theodoric and Aurora and everyone else of the court. I was even more anxious to find out whether Widamer had made vociferous complaint about my inhospitality toward a foreign emissary. So, despite my apprehensions (and a fearsome headache), I presented myself at the palace early the next day.

My misgivings were much allayed when Theodoric did not berate me, but only grinned and chaffed me for having drunk myself "aisanasa"—copper-nosed, as the Old Language has it. He also told me that Widamer had already, even earlier that morning, departed for Aquitania, without having done more than chuckle indulgently about my sottish impropriety. And Aurora took one look at me, did some motherly clucking and waddled out to the kitchen to prepare a beaker of Camerinum wine mixed with wormwood and costmary. She brought that to me, saying with a smile, "Tagl af wulfa"—as the Old Language calls it: the tail of the wolf that had bitten me—and most thankfully I quaffed it down.

563

So I was not in irremediable disgrace, and my brief spell of derangement was not held against me. Also, not Theodoric or Aurora or any other person ever afterward pressed me to know "what birthmark?" or anything else about the innocuous secret of Widamer's that I had divulged. Still, if no one else felt like despising me, I did, because I knew that Widamer had behaved much more decently than I. Whatever suspicions or intuitions he may have had about *my* deep, dark secret, he had not confided to anyone. Or so I then believed. Not until a later time—and in another land—would I realize all the repercussions of that one fateful day's encounters among Veleda and Widamer and Thorn.

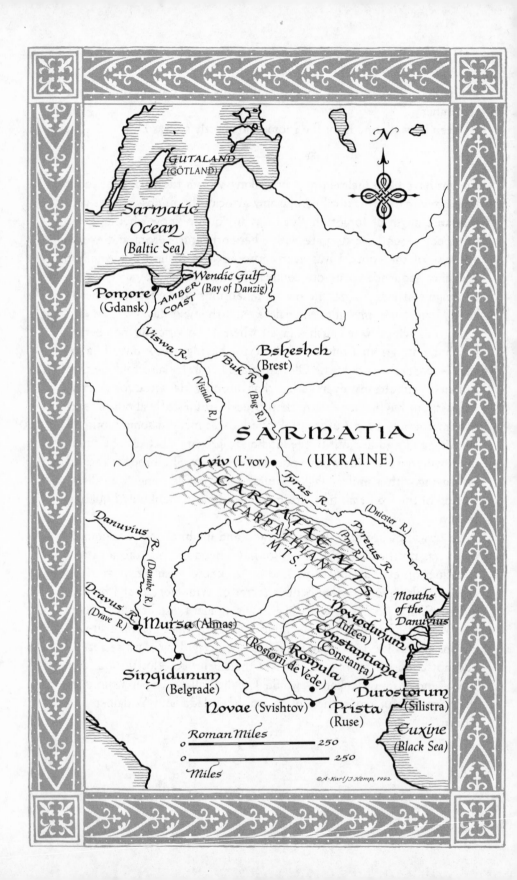

QUEST

1

So I went on passing my time in mere activity, which is not the same as action, until I was brought to an awareness of how very *much* time had gone by. That realization occurred when one day I rode from my farm into Novae and encountered the court physician Frithila on the street.

"Have you heard the news, Saio Thorn?" he asked. "Last night the lady Aurora gave birth to another daughter."

"Say you so? I must hurry to the palace and bestow felicitations and gifts. But . . . gudisks Himins . . ." I said, calculating. "This means that I have been stagnating in frivolous retirement since before the king's *first* child was born. And little Arevagni is no longer so little. Where has the time gone to?" Frithila only grunted, so I asked, "And why are you not overjoyed, Lekeis, to be spreading such glad news?"

"It is not entirely gladsome. The lady died in giving birth."

"Gudisks Himins!" I said again, for this was a real shock, and I had been brotherly fond of Aurora. "But she was such a sturdy woman, of good strong peasant stock. Were there untoward circumstances?"

"None," he sighed, and helplessly spread his hands. "She came to term and to labor as healthily as before. There seemed no more than the expectable amount of pain, and the midwife properly kept masturbating the lady to palliate that pain. The delivery was easily accomplished, the infant proved normal in every respect. But then the lady Aurora slipped into coma, and never awakened." He shrugged and concluded, "Gutheis wilja theins"—which means "God's will be done."

I spoke that same pietistic phrase to Theodoric when I went to condole with him: "Gutheis wilja theins."

"God's will, eh?" he said bitterly. "To take a blameless life? To deprive me of my loving consort? To deprive two children of their mother? That was God's will, was it?"

I said, "According to the Bible, God once deprived even himself. He gave his only begotten son—"

"Akh, balgs-daddja!" Theodoric snarled, and I was taken aback to hear him call the Holy Scriptures "nonsense." Even more blasphemously, he ranted on, "The mealymouthed mendacity of that particular Bible story is the reason why I refuse to revere Jesus Christ—or praise him—or even admire him."

"What are you saying?" I had never sounded Theodoric's views on the subject of religion in general, or of Christianity in particular, and I was profoundly astonished to hear the king speak such sacrilege.

"Consider, Thorn. We are told that, to atone for the sins of us mortals, Jesus gallantly suffered unspeakable agonies on the cross. But Jesus knew that on his death he would go straight to heaven, to share the celestial throne, to enjoy eternal life and the worship of all Christendom. Do you not see? Jesus risked nothing. The paltriest mother dares much more than he did. To give life to just one child, she endures the same agony. But if *she* should die in that torment, she has no knowledge of what fate awaits her, no assurance that her sacrifice will earn her heaven. Ne, ni allis. She is far braver than Jesus was, far more selfless, immeasurably more deserving of praise and exaltation and reverence."

"I think perhaps you are overwrought, old friend," I said. "Yet it may be that I agree with you. I never thought to ponder that comparison before. I wonder if any other Christian ever did. Nevertheless, Theodoric, I devoutly hope that you do not make a practice of proclaiming such things anywhere except among your closest—"

"Of course not," he said, with a rueful laugh. "I myself have no yearning for suicide. I am the king of a Christian nation, and I must publicly respect my people's beliefs, whatever may be my private opinion of them." He breathed a gusty sigh. "A king must ever be politic. I must even forbear from kicking old Saio Soas when he suggests—as he already has—that Aurora's death may have been for the best."

"*For the best?*" I exclaimed. "Why, that heartless, leather-hided, unfeeling old—"

"For the best, as regards my people's interests. The royal succession, that is. Soas suggests that a new consort—or better, a legitimate royal wife—might give me a male heir instead of only daughters."

I had to concede, "Ja, there is that to consider."

"In the meantime, just in case this latest daughter should turn out to be my last offspring, I have named her in honor of our nation. She will be christened Thiudagotha. She of the Gothic people."

"A really royal name," I said. "I am sure she will live up to it."

"But *akh*, I am going to miss dear Aurora. She was a comfortable woman. And a quiet one. There are not many like that. I doubt that Soas will find such another for me, but he is already making lists of eligible princesses. He hopes to find one whose marriage to me would mean for the Ostrogoths an advantageous alliance with some other strong monarch. However, to effect that, I myself really ought to be monarch of more than I am. Certainly, I and my people ought to be something more than Zeno's obedient watchdogs."

I cleared my throat and said guardedly, "On my way here, Theodoric, I was thinking. It has been quite a while since you—or I—have made any conquest of consequence. You used to say, 'Huarbodáu mith blotha!' but lately . . ."

"Ja, ja," he muttered. "I have not even bestirred myself to lead my men in the putting down of Strabo's three or four contumacious pesterings. I know, I know."

"Nor did either of us go with the men," I reminded him, "when they marched to subdue that unruly tribe of Suevi that I reported rampaging about the Isere plains. Is it possible, Theodoric, that both you and I have been—as you also used to say—corroded by the rust of peacetime?"

"Or of domesticity," he said, heaving another deep sigh. "But now that Aurora is no longer here . . . Well, some of my other speculatores report that Strabo threatens now to make a rather greater nuisance of himself. They say he is attempting to forge an alliance with an estimable force of dissident Rugii from the north. If that occurs, Thorn—ne, ne, *when* that occurs—there will be battle enough to satisfy us both."

"Before that happens, then, I would like my king's permission to go abroad, to whet my blade and limber my muscles and furbish my old fighting instincts. They have all been too long unused. Except for my random reportings from my idle wanderings, Theodoric, I have performed no mission on your behalf since my coming hither from Scythia."

"But those reports have always been accurate—and eminently useful. Your initiative has not gone unnoticed or unappreciated, Saio Thorn. Indeed, your dependable usefulness has already inspired me to conceive another mission for you. Something of a quest, actually. I bethought myself of it when I decided on that name for my new daughter—Thiudagotha. And when Saio Soas spoke of my seeking a bride."

569

"Eh?" I said, dumbfounded. "You wish me to go and appraise the prospective princesses?"

He laughed with real humor for the first time that day. "Ne, I wish you to go in quest of history. I believe that my new daughter, she of the Gothic people, ought to know all about her forebears. And if I am to secure a bride of the highest royalty, I must be able to prove to her that I too am of unimpeachable lineage. Not least, my people ought to know whence they came and how they came to be Ostrogoths."

Still puzzled, I said, "But you and your people already know those things. All the Goths everywhere are descended from a god-king named Gaut. Your daughter Thiudagotha, like yourself, is a descendant of a long-ago King Amal."

"But what was that Amal king *of*, and *how* long ago? And was there ever *really* any being named Gaut? You see, Thorn, all that we Goths have, by way of history—all we have ever had—is an assemblage of legends, myths, conjectures and old folks' reminiscences, none of that ever even written down. But here, let me call in one of those reminiscent old folks—your fellow marshal, Soas. He can better explain what you are being asked to do."

So old Soas joined us and, as usual, used no more words than absolutely necessary.

"Our certain knowledge of Gothic history goes back only a bit more than two centuries, to the time when all the Goths lived on the lands north of the Black Sea. From the times before that time, we have nothing more reliable than the saggwasteis fram aldrs, and those songs-from-old are notoriously untrustworthy. They all make mention, however, of an original Gothic homeland, called Skandza. They claim that the Goths emigrated from Skandza, crossed the Sarmatic Ocean into the Wendic Gulf and landed on the Amber Coast. From there, over some incalculable span of time, they made their way to the shores of the Black Sea."

"What I propose, Thorn," said Theodoric, "is that you retrace the Goths' migration, but backward. Start from the Black Sea and follow their trail northward, as far as you can find any evidence of there *being* a trail. You are an experienced and intrepid traveler. You have admirable facility with foreign languages, so you can question the people you find living now along the migration route. You are an accomplished scribe, so you can make notes of everything you learn, and later compile those into a coherent history. I should like you to track those long-ago Goths all the way to the Amber Coast where they ostensibly landed. And beyond—all the way to that Skandza homeland, if the Goths really came from there, and if you can find it."

Soas spoke up again. "Roman historians have made vague mention of an island called Scandia, somewhere far north in the Sarmatic Ocean. The similarity of name cannot be coincidental. But that island may be as fanciful as those other islands the Romans believe in, Avalonnis and Ultima Thule. Even if Scandia does exist, it is terra incognita to this day."

"Or at least, until you find it, Thorn, terra *nondum* cognita," said Theodoric. "Also I ought to warn you—should the faint old trail lead you only as far as the Amber Coast, you must be careful there. That is the native land of those Rugii that Strabo is reportedly inciting to join him in making war against us."

I said, "I understood that the Rugii are all wealthy from trading in the amber found thereabouts. Why would they suddenly be so unhappy that they are ready to abandon trading and go to war?"

"Akh, the amber *merchants* are wealthy, ja. But the drudges who *collect* the amber do not earn anything from it, and must subsist by farming and herding, and the land up there is wretchedly infertile. So, like any other plebecula, they are impoverished and resentful of their lot and ripe for revolt in any direction that offers."

571

Soas resumed, "Our Gothic forebears, from their first landing on the continent of Europe, seem already to have differentiated themselves— into the Baltings, who later called themselves Visigoths, the Amalings, who became Ostrogoths, and the Gepids, who are still known only as Gepids. That name would appear to derive from our word 'gepanta'— slow, torpid, sluggish—though I have never perceived any Gepid to be any more sluggish than anyone else."

Theodoric smiled and said, "Perhaps, Thorn, in your quest in search of history, you may also find for us an explanation of that curious name."

"And there was one group of persons," Soas continued, "that totally parted company from the other Goths along the way. According to the old songs, anyhow. It seems there was a body of women who got left alone while their men went off to some battle or another. Then the enemy outflanked the Gothic warriors and fell upon those unprotected women. But the women so ably defended themselves and so thoroughly annihilated all their attackers that, afterward, they decided that they would never again *need* any men. They elected a queen, went off on their own, settled somewhere in Sarmatia and—some say—gave rise to the legend of the Amazons."

"Not likely," said Theodoric. "If that were so, then our Gothic history would extend back into dim antiquity—to a time earlier than the Greeks who first wrote about Amazons, some nine hundred years ago."

"I might add," Soas said drily, "that no saggws fram aldrs explains how our Amazons managed to reproduce without any men among them."

I said, "I once heard another account involving Gothic women. That one told how the Goths' leaders expelled a number of hateful haliuruns women. And those hags *did* manage to reproduce. Wandering in the wilderness, they mated with skohl demons, and their progeny were the terrible Huns. Do you suppose that story and the Amazon story somehow overlap?"

"That is for you to ascertain and then tell us," said Theodoric, and he comradely clapped me on the back. "By the hammer of Thor, I wish I could go with you! Just think! To breast new horizons, to solve so many enigmas . . ."

"It does sound like a challenging quest," I said. "All the same, I would rather not be abroad when you confront Strabo and his allies."

He said lightly, "If the Rugii move south to join Strabo, you may know it before I do. You can come south *with* them. Or perhaps take some advantage of being in their rear. I should not at all mind having a Parmenio behind my enemy's lines. Anyway, before you depart, I will send messengers to all points of the compass. They will bid all the outlander monarchs and Roman legati of my acquaintance to open their lands to you and extend their hospitality and do what they can to facilitate your quest. And also to keep you informed, as you go, of what news they may have of occurrences hereabouts. Now, I will of course provide every kind of supplies and escorts and mounts you require. Would you wish an impressive retinue or just a few sturdy warriors?"

"None at all, I think, thags izvis. For such a very special quest, I prefer to be a man alone—especially if I am to do any slinking through hostile peoples. And I will go armed, but not armored. It may be best, in some places, if I am not readily identifiable as an Ostrogoth. I will need nothing but my own good horse, and what supplies I can carry behind my saddle. Ja, I shall go as just what I used to be, a wayfaring woodsman."

"Hábái ita swe!" said Theodoric, the first time in a long time that I had heard him utter to me that magisterial affirmative: "Be it so!"

✠　　✠　　✠

I went directly from the palace to my own house in the city. There I selected from closets and chests an assortment of my Veleda raiment, cosmetics and jewelry. I dressed myself in some of those things and rolled the rest, with the Thorn garb I had been wearing, into a bundle for carrying. When I left the house, I locked its street entrance behind me and then knocked at the door of the neighboring house. The old woman who lived there had been for some while a nodding acquaintance of Veleda, so she readily assented when I asked her to keep a watchful eye on my place while I was "absent for a time."

I rode a way outside the city, then off the road and into a copse, where I changed clothes again, so I could arrive back at my farm as its master Thorn. There, in my chambers, I laid all my Veleda garments and accessories ready for packing with whatever else I would be taking with me on my journey. I had in mind no particular use for those clothes; I simply wanted to be prepared for any future situation in which I might better perform as Veleda than as Thorn.

The next two days I spent mostly in consultation with one after another of my tenant freemen. I heard each man's report on the current state of the farm work that was his responsibility, and his plans for upcoming projects. Some of those I acquiesced in, some I ordered postponed or abandoned. I submitted ideas of my own for the men's consideration, in some cases gave definite instructions, and eventually was well satisfied that the farm would go on functioning smoothly and productively while I was gone. During those two days, also, I kept thinking of things that might be useful on my journey, and laying them aside to be packed—then usually discarding them as unnecessary. Finally, I rolled together only my Veleda things, extra Thorn garments, some emergency travel rations, fishing line and hooks, a flask and a bowl, a leather sling, flints and tinder—and the glitmuns sun-stone, my last surviving bequest from old Wyrd. And the nights of those two days I spent in bidding farewell, one night to the woman Naranj, the next to the girl Renata.

573

It was on a beautifully sunny, mild May morning that I rode away from my farm, hoping that I looked more like an aimless vagabond than like a king's marshal. There was no way I could disguise the quality of my Velox II, but I had deliberately bidden my stable grooms to refrain from currying or combing him during the past two days. Also, my outer garments were of the roughest, and though I had personally honed and polished my fine snake blade, I was wearing it in a scuffed old scabbard.

I went first into Novae and to the palace, to let Theodoric know that I was on my way. We made no great ceremony of our leave-taking, but he cordially wished me "raítos stáigos uh baírtos dagos"—straight ways and bright days—and, as he had done at another time, he gave me a mandatum identifying me and bearing his monogram seal. Then, when I emerged again into the palace yard, I found that the steward Costula, whom I had left holding the reins of my horse, was now holding the reins of two. On the second sat the cosmeta Swanilda, dressed for the road and with a pack behind her saddle.

"Gods dags, Swanilda," I greeted her. "Are you also traveling today?"

"Ja, if you will let me join you," she said, in a slightly wavery voice. As I approached, I saw that her face was puffy and her eyes red, and I judged that she must have been weeping ever since her mistress died.

I took the horses' reins, waved Costula away and said politely, "Of course, Swanilda, you are welcome to ride a way with me, until our ways diverge. Where are you going?"

"I wish to ride *all* the way with you," she said, her voice more firm. "I have heard of the long journey you are undertaking. I wish to be your shield-bearer, your servant, your companion, your . . . everything else you would like me to be."

"Come now. Hold a moment—" I began, but she talked on, eagerly, anxiously, even urgently.

"I have wept for two beloved mistresses, and now I have none, so now I beg to have a master. To have *you* for my master, Saio Thorn. Please do not refuse me. You know that I am a good rider and that I have traveled much. It was with you that I traveled from here to Constantinople. And later it was at your command that I traveled a greater distance—all alone—and dressed in your clothes. Do you remember? You taught me how to pass for a man. How I was never, in view of other persons, to run anywhere or throw anything . . ."

In the years that I had known Swanilda, I had never heard her speak so many words. But now she had run out of breath before she ran out of words, so I interposed a few of my own.

"Very true, good Swanilda. But on those journeys we were at least traversing the more or less civilized lands of the Roman Empire. This time I am venturing into terra incognita, among hostile peoples, possibly *savage* peoples, and—"

"Which is good reason to take me with you. A man alone is viewed with suspicion, seen as a menace. But a man with a woman close by his side appears tame and harmless."

"Tame, eh?" I said, and chuckled.

"Or, if you prefer, I can again wear some of your clothes. It might be equally advantageous if I am taken to be your apprentice. Or even"— she looked away in embarrassment—"your love-boy."

I said sternly, "See here, Swanilda, you must be aware that I have for all these years—partly in memory of your dear mistress Amalamena—forborne from taking wife or consort, although many choices were offered me. Vái, the lady Aurora even offered me *you*."

"Akh, I can understand your not having wanted to take me formally for wife or consort. I am no Amalamena in any respect, and I am not even a virgin, but neither have I had experience enough to be very competent in the ways of a woman with a man. However, if you will accept me informally, only for the span of our journey together, I will promise to do my best in that regard, and I will strive to learn whatever you care to teach. But I do not ask any promise in return, Saio Thorn. When the journey is over, or at any other time, you have only to say, 'Swanilda, enough.' I will uncomplainingly cease to be your loving companion and thenceforth will be only your humble servant." She held out a trembling hand, and her mouth trembled too when she said again, "Please do not refuse me, Saio Thorn. Without a mistress or a master, I am a forlorn and outcast orphan."

That touched me. I had myself once been an outcast orphan. So I said, "If you are to pretend to be my wife or my consort, you must try from now on not to address me as Saio or master, but simply as Thorn."

575

She brightened on the instant and, even with red eyes and puffy face, looked almost radiantly pretty again. "Then you *will* take me along?"

And I did. To my eventual and everlasting sorrow, I did.

2

gain I relied on the Danuvius as my guide, and Swanilda and I followed it downstream, retracing the route I had taken when I fled from Strabo's Scythia. Although, as I have said, I have ever been disinclined to do the same thing twice, I now took a rather proprietorial pride and pleasure in pointing out to Swanilda various landmarks and sights worth seeing, things I remembered from my earlier journey, and my doing that made this excursion seem quite new and different.

From having traveled with Swanilda before, I had not at all doubted that she would be a capable and congenial companion, and so she proved. She had not always been a dainty domestic, she told me; she had grown up in a forest clan of hunters and herders. She was as proficient as I at bringing down small game with the sling—and she was definitely better at the cooking of it. (She had even brought along a little iron cooking pot, which I would never have thought of doing.) In fact, she taught me some expedients of cookery and of eating that I think the old master woodsman Wyrd had not known. I learned that, when one cooked meat, a few birch twigs in the pot would prevent its burning or sticking. I learned that frogs are easy to spear at night, using just a reed torch and a sharp stick, and that their hind legs are meaty and delicious to eat—something else I would never have thought of— when boiled together with lion's-tooth greens.

I had always thought highly of Swanilda. Now I came to treasure her, not just for her practical comradely capacities, but also for her appealing feminine traits. I remember how, on our first night out from Novae, she almost magically transformed herself from the day's rough-dressed wayfarer to a soft, sleek and fetching young woman.

At twilight, we stopped at a wide, sun-warmed, grassy clearing beside the river, and cooked and dined on a hare I had taken along the way.

Then I went down to bathe in the shallows, dressed again and returned, and got under my sleeping fur before I undressed for sleep. Not until then, when the night was full dark, did Swanilda likewise go to bathe. She splashed about down there for a good while, and I wondered why she was dawdling. As it turned out, she had only been waiting for the moon to rise. She left her coarse traveling garments beside the river and came up the clearing—walking slowly, tantalizingly, visible to me the whole way—clothed in moonlight and nothing else.

As she melted into my arms, I said with a mixture of amusement and admiration, "My dear, you certainly know the right raiment to wear, whatever the occasion."

She laughed, then said shyly, "But . . . other things . . . I told you . . . you may have to teach me . . ."

Well, I have already indicated that there was little I could teach her about woods traveling. So, yes, I did teach her some other things, and she was an eager student and an apt learner—perhaps the more so because I accomplished that teaching more playfully than didactically. For example, I recall an occasion when I entertained her by recounting all the Greek words pertaining to the female breast, words I had learned while in Constantinople. Swanilda found them both instructive and humorously intriguing, because our own Old Language has but one single word to refer to everything in that area of the human anatomy.

"What we call the brusts, the entire bosom," I said, "is called in Greek the kolpós. But each of these"—tenderly I cupped one of hers—"is a mastós, and this cleft between them"—I stroked it—"is called the stenón. And this pink forepart of each mastós is the stetháne"—my finger drew a circle around one of them—"and this little nub in the middle of the stetháne is called the thelé. And akh, behold what the thelé does at my lightest touch. In that alert state, Swanilda, it is called the hrusós."

She shivered delightedly and asked, "Why do you suppose, Thorn, the Greeks saw fit to make up all those words?"

"They have always been a famously inventive people. And they are reputed to be far more sensual and abandoned than the northern races, such as ours. Perhaps the Greeks devised those words—and there are many others, descriptive of other human parts and functions—to aid them in the making of love most voluptuously. Or perhaps to instruct youths and virgins who are novices at the art of making love. As you have noticed—and at this moment are demonstrating—the mere telling of the words and the showing of where they apply have a marvelously exciting effect on those parts of a woman."

As might be surmised, we both were finding our journey so gratifying that we did not hurry it, but were rather more disposed to make it last as long as possible. Still, after a leisurely two weeks or so, we came to the riverside fortress town of Durostorum and there took lodging in a well-appointed hospitium. I left Swanilda luxuriating in the establishment's therma while I went to call at the praetorium of the Italica Legion. The commander whom I had met there before had, this long while later, been retired. But his replacement was, of course, also subordinate to Theodoric, so was most hospitable to a marshal of the king. We sat and drank of one of Durostorum's innumerable wines and he told me the latest news from Novae. He had had only routine reports, no word yet of any threatening movements by Strabo, with or without his presumptive Rugian allies. So there was no need or excuse for me to interrupt my quest and return to Theodoric's side.

"Neither is there any need," the commander said helpfully, "for you to go on plodding laboriously overland, Saio Thorn. Why do you not engage a barge here and float comfortably down the Danuvius? You will reach the Black Sea rather more quickly, and much less travel-worn."

I made inquiry along the riverside about the possibility of hiring a barge. And right there I came upon the first spoor of those early Goths whose trail I sought.

The second or third barge owner whom I approached was a man almost old enough himself to have been one of those ancients. He asked, somewhat incredulously, why I should want to pay the considerable price to ride a barge clear to the Black Sea when I would be freighting no trade goods. Since there was nothing secret about my mission, I told him forthrightly that I wished to look for the homeland that my Gothic ancestors had once occupied.

"Akh, then a river barge is the way to find it, right enough," he said. "You will not need to circumnavigate the whole long shore around that sea, searching for that land. I can tell you—the Goths long ago lived in just one particular area there. The delta called the Mouths of the Danuvius, where the great river debouches into that sea."

Somewhat incredulous in my turn, I asked, "How would you know that?"

"Vái, cannot you tell from my speech that I am of the Gepid Goths? Besides, it is the business of us bargemen to know who lives where on our river. So of course we know who *used* to live where. Not just last year, but centuries agone. And it is well known to us that in olden time the Goths dwelt among those Mouths of the Danuvius. Very well, then, if you have the money to squander, I and my crew will set you on that delta."

I engaged him on the spot, bade him make ready for departure on the morrow and gave him part of the money in advance, instructing him to stock the barge with ample provisions, including feed for two horses—and, I said as a happy afterthought, an assortment of good Durostorum wines sufficient for two passengers. Then I went back to the hospitium, to join Swanilda in bathing voluptuously and at length, for what would probably be the last time in such an elegant therma until we returned to civilization.

The next morning our barge shoved off as soon as the crewmen had led our horses aboard and tethered them securely amidships. I was helping Swanilda stow our belongings and lay out our sleeping furs in the canopy-covered stern of the barge, when the old owner called to me from his place at the steering oar:

"Would yonder horseman be looking for you?"

I raised up and saw, on the dock we had just left, another horse and rider. The man was sitting high in the saddle and shading his eyes to gaze after us, but he was not hailing or making any urgent gestures. I could see only that he was slight of figure—from our midstream distance I could not make out his features—but there was something vaguely familiar about him.

"A servant from the hospitium, perhaps," I said to Swanilda. "Did we go off and leave something of ours there?"

She cast a glance of inventory over our belongings and said, "Nothing of any consequence."

So I signaled to the old steersman to continue on, not to turn back. And as soon as we had rounded a curve of the river, that person on the dock was out of sight and forgotten.

✠　✠　✠

The whole of our voyage downriver might have been a continuation of the indolent life I had lived for so long in Novae. The Danuvius flowed at a much faster than horseback pace, but, here in its lower stretches, was not roiled by any rapids or interrupted by any cascades. I had no work to do, no exigencies of land travel to contend with, no need even to think about acquiring food. I did occasionally dangle a line in the water to add fresh fish to our provender, and a time or two, just for the experience, took a turn at the steering oar. Swanilda helpfully did some sewing repairs on the bargemen's clothing, and trimmed their hair and beards when they needed it. But she and I mainly lolled through day after day, basking in the warm summer weather and admiring the passing scenery and the other craft on the water. At night, we had other enjoyments. The only effort I made to pursue my quest was to inquire of the old barge owner whether he knew how his branch of the Gothic nation had come to be called the Gepids.

He did not; he could only say, "What do you mean? That is our *name*. You might as well ask why is this river called the Danuvius. It simply *is*."

Gradually the river widened and in time we floated on past the widest part of it that I had heretofore seen, and *still* the river broadened. Eventually we were drifting among wide-apart, low-lying, wooded but uninhabited islands and islets and knolls and hillocks. Then the forests on those bits of land and on the farther banks began to diminish, until there were no forests, but individual trees. Then there was only underbrush, eventually giving way to reed beds and swales of marsh grass and floating pallets of tangled weed. The circumjacence was not improved by the swarms of blood-prickers and other insects that arose from the mud flats, very nearly as numerous and predatory and maddening as I had known them upstream of the Iron Gate. But it was at about this point in our voyage that the barge owner swung his arm about and announced:

"Here you are, then. The Mouths of the Danuvius!"

"Iésus!" I exclaimed. "Our Gothic forefathers were satisfied to live *here*? In a *swamp*?"

"Akh, do not disdain it. This is a rich land and a vast one. We are yet more than forty Roman miles from where the many mouths of the river spill into the Black Sea. And these marshlands stretch for many more miles than that on either hand. In all, this delta is of more sprawling extent than many an entire Roman province. And far more bountiful than some."

"Not in beauty," murmured Swanilda.

The old man said drily, "I think, dear lady, our forefathers gave precedence to other things than beauty. They took heed first of livelihood, and these Mouths of the Danuvius gave abundantly of that. Look you at all the fishing boats still plying these channels, because the waters here teem with succulent fish. Perch, carp, catfish, a hundred other varieties. And have you not noticed the immense flocks of birds? Heron, egret, ibis, pelican. And the islets and hummocks are also home

580

to the animals that prey on the fish and the birds—boar and wildcat and glutton and marten . . ."

His enthusiasm was persuasive. I looked about me again, now seeing the place with the eyes of those long-ago Goths who had arrived here after crossing all of northern Europe, seeking a habitable place to settle, and who had more than likely arrived here hungry.

"Ja, the Goths waxed fat and happy in these parts," the barge owner went on. "They smoked and salted the surplus meat, and they collected the furs and feathers and down, and they traded most profitably in those commodities on all the shores of the Black Sea—even to Constantinople and beyond. Why, the Goths would never have left here had not the invading Huns uprooted them and swept them westward."

"Then who," I asked, "are the people manning all these fishing craft roundabout?"

"The inhabitants now are mostly Tauri and Khazars—who also know a good dwelling place when they see it. But some few of the old-time Goths managed to hide here from the marauding Huns—or they returned after the Huns were obliterated. Ja, here and there resides a family of Goths—perhaps a sibja or a gau, nothing so numerous as a tribe—still or again fishing and trapping and fowling and trading, and thereby living comfortably. You will find them if you stay here a while."

581

"But stay where?" asked Swanilda, because there was nothing in sight any larger than the fishing boats.

"Noviodunum," said the old man. "We will be there tomorrow. It once was a fair-sized city, until the Huns sacked and burned it. But what remains still thrives, because the river there is deep enough to give passage and anchorage to the Black Sea merchant vessels. So there are several gasts-razna offering decent enough lodging." He paused, then laughed. "And you will see quite a sight when you first espy one of those seagoing ships coming into Noviodunum."

He was right about that, because we saw one the next day, at the same time we sighted the town—both of them at a great distance. The waters and the riverbanks and the other bits of land thereabout are of almost equal flatness, and Noviodunum consists entirely of buildings only a single story in height. So the bulky, apple-bowed, two-masted Black Sea vessel looked like a misplaced mountain creeping across the level landscape and cautiously negotiating the twists of the channel, and its size was even more exaggerated by the smallness of the fishing boats and other minor craft that shared the river with it, and it fairly towered over the town it was approaching. It all made for a vision so incongruous as to seem dreamlike.

By the time our barge reached the town, the big merchantman had already tied up offshore, and small skiffs were busily ferrying goods to and from it. Our crewmen made us fast to a dock and I helped them coax and lead the two horses from barge to shore. Then I stepped onto the bustling dockside street for a look about. Of the throngs of people, most were dark-haired and dark-skinned: Khazars and the Tauri, whom I assume to be the Khazars' racial cousins. But there were a number of fair-haired and fair-skinned persons of clearly Germanic origin. Also, as would be expected in any port this close to a sea, there were other persons of just about every nationality on earth: Romans, Greeks, Syrians, Jews, Slovenes, Armenians, even here and there a black Nubian or Ethiope. And there were as many languages being spoken. Some were those of the individual peoples I have mentioned, but the most generally spoken (and loudest) was a sort of sermo pelagius, or port traders' speech, compounded of words of *all* those languages, the tongue evidently best spoken and understood by everybody.

582

Among the vessels moored near ours was a dromo of the Moesian Fleet, so I accosted its commanding navarchus, who of course spoke Latin, and asked him if he could recommend to me any particular hospitium or taberna in the town. While Swanilda and the bargemen put the saddles and packs on the horses, I paid the barge's owner, thanked him for a pleasant voyage and left him casting about the docks for a possible freight he could take back upriver. Then I led Swanilda and our mounts to the suggested lodging place. It called itself a pandokheíon, being kept by Greeks, but it was much less than luxurious and not overly clean. However, the navarchus had told me it was the best in Noviodunum, so I engaged a chamber for Swanilda and myself, and stable stalls for the horses.

The pandokheíon naturally boasted no therma, so Swanilda set the servants to drawing and heating water for the basins in our room, and prepared to bathe. Meanwhile, I asked the proprietor if the town had a praefectus—or a kúrios, or a city elder, or whatever his honorific might be—on whom I could pay a courtesy call as the king's marshal. The Greek had to ponder the question, then said:

"There is no one officially designated as master of the city. But you might call on Meíros the Mudman."

"Singular title," I muttered.

"He is probably the oldest resident, certainly one of the foremost merchants, hence he is acknowledged the senior personage here in Noviodunum. You will find him in his warehouse near the dock you just came from."

The warehouse would have been as undistinguished as any other I had ever visited, except that its dark, dank interior was pervaded by a rank, almost fetid odor. I stood in its street doorway, peering about, trying to see through the gloom the source of that smell. Then a man came out of the shadows, saying "Welcome, stranger" in six or eight different languages, a few of which I could comprehend. He was an old man, exceedingly stout, and I took him to be a Khazar from his olive complexion, hooked nose and voluminous curly beard, so black that it belied his evident age.

I returned his greeting—in just two languages: "Salve" and "Háils"— and held out to him my document of credentials. But as soon as he joined me in the light of the doorway, he seemed to recognize me, for he said amiably:

"Saio Thorn, of course. King Theodoric earlier sent an advice that you were to be expected, and just an hour ago I was apprised of your arrival. Allow me to introduce myself. Meirus Terranius in Latin. Meíros Terástios in Greek. Or, in my native tongue, Meir ben Teradion."

583

I blurted, in the Old Language, "Ist jus *Iudaíus*, niu?"

"Ik im, ja. You have an aversion to Jews?"

I hastened to say, "Ni allis. Nequaquam. But it is . . . well, unusual to find a Jew accounted the senior personage in any community of the Roman Empire."

"An anomaly, ja. Or perhaps an *inelegancy*, as the Khittim would say."

"The Khittim?"

"The Romans, as they are named in my native language. And I wager, Marshal, that you have already heard *me* called by another name."

"Er . . . ja, I have. But I would hesitate to address anyone as Mudman. I supposed the agnomen to be not exactly complimentary."

He chuckled. "Purely descriptive. I am the man who trades in that commodity."

"You trade in *mud*?"

"Surely you smell it. This building is full of it."

"But . . . to whom do you sell mud? And where? Is there any place in the world that does not already have its own mud?"

"Mine, as you have noticed, is especially odoriferous mud."

"I should think that would make it especially worthless."

"Akh, you do not allow for imagination, and the value that ingredient can add to anything."

"I suppose I do not, since I have no idea what you are talking about."

"Imagination, young man! Most merchants deal merely in *things*. They are but peddlers. I deal in *fancy*. You see, I was not always a merchant. In my young and wandering days I was variously a poet, a minstrel, a storyteller—in hard times, even a khazzen, which is an augur, a wise-sayer. But those were ill-paid occupations, and I was getting older, seeking to settle. So, on a day long, long ago, I found myself here at the Mouths of the Danuvius, and I looked around. I saw many a man getting wealthy, trading in furs or fish or feathers. The trouble was that all the profitable products of the delta were already spoken for. There was nothing left untaken in these marshlands except the marsh itself."

He paused and gave me an arch look, so I said, "The mud."

584

"Ja! The distinctively stinking mud of this delta. Mere peddlers would not have given it a second sniff. But I—I had imagination. Also I had the khutzpa of an augur, and my days as an augur had given me experience of human gullibility. So I bought little pots and filled them with that mud, and I offered it as a cataplasm for rheumatic joints or wrinkled flesh. And people bought it—vain, aging women and pain-racked old men—on the premise that the most efficacious medicine is always the most unappealing. I even had the audacity to give the awful mud an awful name—saprós pélethos, rotten ordure—and to set an exorbitant price on it. The repellent name and the outrageous price made it absolutely irresistible. For years and years now, I have been selling the ghastly muck to rich Khittim as far away as Rome and Ravenna, to rich Yevanim as far away as Athens and Constantinople and to rich men and women of every other nation in between. The saprós pélethos has made *me* as rich as any of them. Akh, I tell you, imagination is the magic ingredient!"

"I congratulate you. And your imagination."

"Thags izvis. Of course, once having exerted my imagination, there has since been little need for me to exert anything else. Selling mud takes no great attention or effort. I do not have to exist, as most tradesmen do, in a state of perpetual anxiety and desperation. That is why I have ample leisure to busy myself with civic and provincial affairs, and occasionally to perform as a wise-sayer for those requiring that service, and frequently to do favors for such notables as our military magister Theodoric. And his visiting marshal. Allow me, Saio Thorn, to present you with a potful of my miracle mud. You are too young to be rheumatic, but perhaps you have a wrinkled lady friend . . . ?"

"She is not yet aging, thags izvis. Anyway, I expect to be out in the marshlands myself. If need be, I can procure my own mud."

"Of course, of course. Now, how may I assist you, Marshal? Theodoric's message represented you as a traveling historian, and asked that you be accorded every convenience. Are you seeking history in these marshlands?"

"And wherever else it may be found," I said. "I know that this is where the ancestral Goths resided before they were pushed westward by the Huns. I know that, while they lived in these parts, in addition to their peaceable pursuits of fishing and trapping and trading, the Goths became also seafaring warriors, and raided many cities, from Trapezus to Athens."

"Not exactly," said the Mudman, raising a finger. "The Goths were ever foot soldiers and horse soldiers. Land-lobbes. The seafarers were the Cimmerii—so called in the old histories. Those were actually the people now called Alani, who also inhabited the Black Sea shores. The Goths persuaded the Alani to transport Gothic warriors on those raiding expeditions—just as you employed bargemen to bring you hither. The Alani provided the seamanship, the Goths did the fighting and plundering."

"I will make a note of the correction," I said.

Meirus went on, "Those sea-raiding Goths were famous—or infamous—for the brevity and cruelty of the message they always sent ahead of them to the next city their ships approached. In whatever language they employed, the message consisted of just three words. Tributum aut bellum. Gilstr aíththau baga. Tribute . . . or war."

"But that all ended, did it not, when the Goths eventually made alliance with Rome, and learned the ways of peace, and began to absorb Roman culture and customs . . . ?"

"Ja, the Goths then enjoyed a golden age of peace and plenty, for fifty years. Until the Huns came, under their chieftain Balamber." Meirus dolefully shook his head. "Earlier, the Romans had used to say of the Goths, 'God sent them forth as a punishment for our iniquities.' Then it was the Goths saying of the Huns, 'God sent them forth as a punishment for our iniquities.'"

"And all men know the history of the Goths since then," I said. "What I now hope to find out is what the Goths did, and where, before they settled here around the Black Sea."

585

The Mudman sighed a great, gusty sigh. "Truly I am old, old, oh vái, but not quite that old. And my powers of wise-saying extend only into the future, not the past. You have said you will prowl the marshlands. You will find there at least scattered remnants of the Goths. Perhaps among them you will find other old men, and perhaps they will remember things told by their fathers and fathers' fathers. Let me lend you a reliable guide, Saio Thorn." He turned and called to where some men were working deep in the shadows of the warehouse, "Here . . . *Maggot!*"

"Maggot?" I echoed, amused.

"His name is really Maghib. But he is the man I send afield for my raw material, and he has always been able to find for me the mud of the slimiest consistency and most nauseous stench. He grubs up mud"—Meirus shrugged—"hence: Maggot."

The man was an undersized, oily-skinned Armenian, rather mud-colored himself, and he groveled quite maggotlike as he said in heavily accented Gothic, "At your command, fráuja."

He stood in a cringing sort of crouch while the Mudman jabbered something at him in his own language. Then Maggot jabbered back at some length.

"Done," Meirus said to me. "Whenever you are ready to make an excursion into the outlying lands, come here and get Maggot to accompany you. He says he does indeed know of elderly Goths of all persuasions—Visigoth, Ostrogoth, Gepid—who may just know things of times past."

"Thags izei," I said to them both. As Maggot backed servilely away to become a part of the gloom again, I added, "Meanwhile, good Meirus, you yourself seem to know all there is to know about names—including the bestowing of them. Would you happen to know how the Gepid Goths came to be so called?"

He laughed and said, "Of course."

I waited a moment, then prodded him, "Would you be so kind, then, as to tell me?"

"Akh, I thought you were but trying me. You really do not know? The Gepids' name derives from the Gothic word 'gepanta'—slow, languid, apathetic."

"So I have heard conjectured. But why?"

The old Jew clasped his pudgy hands across his vast belly. "In my minstrel days, I used to have to sing all manner of the Goyim's songs-from-old—no doubt making my own forefathers twirl in their graves. There was one song that told how the Goths came from the far north to this continent of Europe. They came, it said, in three ships, one bearing each tribe—or sibja, or nation, or whatever they called their related divisions in those early times. And one of the ships lagged far behind the other two, and landed its passengers some while after the others, and those people continued ever afterward to tarry and dawdle behind the others, all during their subsequent travels. Hence"—he laughed again—"the slow ones, the Gepids."

I laughed with him. "A plausible story. I shall make a note of that as well. I am most grateful to you. Tomorrow I will come"—I smiled—"with my unwrinkled lady companion, and we will avail ourselves of the guide you have so generously offered. Shall I bring an extra horse for him?"

"Ne, ne, do not spoil the creature. Maggot is accustomed to trot alongside my carruca whenever I go myself afield. I promise to feed him some extra swill in the morning, to give him strength to trot. Until tomorrow, then."

✠ ✠ ✠

Next morning, after the old Jew had been introduced to Swanilda, and he gallantly had averred that she would *never* need his mud, he said to me:

"You and I, Saio Thorn, seem always to be talking of names. May I ask now—are you acquainted with the name Thor?"

"Who is not?" I said. "He is the Old Religion's god of thunder."

"And are you often followed about by a god? I must say, he did not look much like a god, but he had the arrogant temper and rudeness of one."

"*Who* did?"

"A newly come young man—or god, if Thor is really his name, as he claims it is. Also he is decked all over with the emblems of that god. He wears a Thor's-hammer pendant around his neck. His mantle fibula and his belt buckle are emblazoned with the ugly angular cross that symbolizes Thor's hammer being swung in a circle. He came ashore with his horse from another barge not long after you were here. A man of about your own age and size and coloring. And beardless, which I would not expect a god to be. He asked for you by name, and gave a recognizable description of you. I wondered if he might be your associate or assistant or apprentice, or something."

"He is not any such thing. He is no one I know."

"Strange. He knows you. He said he just missed catching up to you at Durostorum. And he seemed much put out about having had to chase you this far. He grumbled and growled and snarled, very like a god, indeed."

I remembered the horseman who had watched from the dock upriver

587

as our barge pulled away. But that gave me no hint of his identity or his reason for trailing me. I merely said, with some impatience, "Whoever it is, I dislike being followed."

"Then I am glad that I pretended to him that I had not seen or ever heard of you. But this Thor person did come to me, the Mudman, to inquire about you, so he must be quick and clever. He had so soon discovered that I am, so to speak, Noviodunum's fount of information. He *expected* that you would have visited me. He is sure to come here seeking you again."

Annoyed, but not sure why I was annoyed, I snapped, "I do not care what he does! I do not know him. I never heard of *anyone* assuming the name of a god."

But Swanilda spoke up, saying lightly, "If you think about it, the name Thor, in the Roman alphabet, is only one letter away from being *your* name, Thorn."

Her casual remark brought me up short. I murmured, "You are right. I have so seldom seen my name written down. Until this moment, I never took cognizance of that."

588   I might have wished to muse on that little revelation, but Meirus persisted in pestering me: "May I ask you in confidence, Marshal, might this person be some old enemy of yours?"

Again irked to an inexplicable degree, I said through my teeth, "To the best of my recollection, I have never had an enemy—not god or mortal—named Thor. But if this man is one, and he visits you again, you may tell him that I prefer my enemies to come at me from the front, not from behind."

"You would not care to wait and tell him yourself? I should think you would at least be curious to see him."

Yet again I could not have said why—unless I was feeling some premonition—but by now I was exceedingly vexed, and I burst out:

"Understand me, Mudman! I have no least interest in an unknown hanger-on. I have no more regard for this person who dogs my tracks than the vanguard Goths had for the laggard Gepids. Summon your man Maggot out here, and we will be off. If any godling or godlet or godkin is really determined to find me, he can slog through the marshlands after me."

"As you say, Saio Thorn. Then, if the person calls here again, shall I point him in the direction you have gone?"

"Iésus Xristus! I do not give a ferta if you drown him in a vat of your misbegotten mud!"

Meirus put up his hands defensively and said, "Oh vái! You sound as fierce and angry and commanding as he did. Very like a god yourself. By my fathers, I should like to be present when you two *do* meet. Thor and Thorn."

3

wanilda and I did not leave Noviodunum at a canter, because we had to hold our horses to a pace that Maggot could keep up with. At the outskirts of the town, Swanilda looked back and said, "We are not being followed by anybody, Thorn."

589

I grunted, "Maybe gods are late sleepers. Let the devil take that one napping."

"My fráuja the Mudman has explained to me your interests, fráuja Thorn," said Maggot, who evidently could talk without panting as he trotted. "I will introduce you to an aged Ostrogoth couple of my acquaintance who, like all old folk, are much given to reminiscence of the past."

"Very good, Maggot. But will we be able to do all our traveling in these swampy lands on horseback? Or will we have to take to the water now and again?"

"Ne, ne. You will find some of the ground unpleasantly soggy, but I am familiar with the paths that will take us around or across the marshier places. You can trust me, fráuja, to guide you without hazard or inconvenience."

The land was mostly flat and covered with silvery-green, feathery grass that would, if vertical, have stood higher than my head, even with me atop Velox. But such slender stems had bent to the ground while growing, so the grasses lay curved by the wind, and billowed like waves, about knee-high to Maggot and the horses. In the places where the grass did not choose to grow, the land was carpeted with blue-flowering salvia; it gave out a keen herbal scent when trodden on.

We frequently saw flocks of birds, many I had never seen elsewhere:

the graceful-beaked glossy ibis, the clumsy-beaked crispus pelican, the elegantly plumed egret. We did not glimpse any of the delta's native mammals, but we did come upon stray cattle and sheep, let run by their owners to forage for themselves, so they had become more wild than domesticated. As Maggot had warned, the ground often squished and heaved underfoot, but here and there the land rose up into a hillock dry and sturdy enough to support a house, and it was only on those higher places that the local inhabitants had built their houses.

At midmorning, the sky clouded over with dramatic suddenness, and we were enveloped in twilight. I had to take out my sun-stone to scan the sky and make sure we were still heading north. But very soon the cloud cover got too thick and black to let the glitmuns show me the pale blue patch where the sun stood. Then lightning began to flare and thunder to roll and the rain came down violently and drenchingly. The lightning sizzled and jagged all about, and I was more concerned about our being the tallest objects in that flat land. My concern was not eased by Swanilda's laughing remark:

"Do you suppose Thor sent his thunder to seek us out?"

I had put that person out of my mind, and was not much pleased to be reminded of him. Anyway, there was no shelter anywhere about, so Maggot could only lead us lumbering on, as best he could, through the curtain of rain. Then, abruptly, the three of us were cowering and covering our heads with our arms, and the horses were dancing in distress, because the rain changed to a fiercely lashing white hail. The cold pellets, as big as grapes, hit like hard-thrown gravel, and caromed and bounced and seethed, and beat down the feather grass around us, and turned the ground to an uneasily twitching and squirming white floor. The downpelt was sufficiently hurtful to make me almost believe that Thor *was* malignantly besetting us. Maggot raised his voice to shout to me over the ambient noise:

"Be not distraught, fráuja. These sudden squalls are common here in the delta. They never last for long."

Even as he spoke, the storm began to diminish, and we could see about us, and we went on, the horses' hoofs crunching and slithering on the ice-pebbled surface. But the hail ceased and the sun came out, as suddenly as it had disappeared, and the heavy glaze on the land melted, and the battered-down grasses began to shake themselves dry and unfold to their former feathery waves and whorls.

Toward sundown we approached a hillock on which stood a fairly well-built wooden house. As we went up the slope to it, Maggot gave a shout, and from the dwelling's leather-flapped doorway emerged two persons. He called to them, "Háils, Fillein uh Baúhts!" and they waved and responded, "Háils, Maghib!"

As is the case with so many aged couples, the husband and wife would have been indistinguishable—by their bent, frail figures or their garb or their wrinkled faces—except that the man wore a full white beard and the woman only a scanty mustache and some stray wild hairs sprouting from her chin and cheeks. Swanilda and I got down from our horses, and Maggot introduced us all around.

"This is the good man Fillein and his good woman Baúhts, Ostrogoths both." To them he said, "Old people, I am proud to present to you the fráuja Thorn, marshal of the King of the Ostrogoths, and his companion, the lady Swanilda."

Instead of greeting or saluting me, old Fillein surprised me by saying querulously, "Thorn? Thorn? This is no king's marshal. King Thiudamer's marshal is named Soas. I may be old and weak of mind, but I remember *that.*"

I smiled and said, "Excuse me, venerable Fillein. Soas still is marshal, true, but I am another. And King Thiudamer has been dead these many years. His son Thiuda the Younger reigns now in his stead, and is called Thiudareikhs—or more commonly Theodoric. It was he who appointed me fellow marshal to Saio Soas."

591

"You do not make jape of me, niu?" the old man said uncertainly. "This is true?"

"It could be so," his wife put in, her voice equally thin and quavery. "Do you not remember, husband, when that son was born? The child of victory, we all called him." To me she said, "Is that Thiuda now grown to manhood and kingship, niu? Vái, how the time does go."

"The time does go," Fillein echoed, with melancholy. "Then . . . waíla-gamotjands, Saio Thorn. Our humble house is yours. And you must be hungry. Come in, come in."

Maggot took the horses around to the rear of the house, to find some feed for them, and Swanilda and I followed the old folks inside. Fillein poked the hearth embers into flame while Baúhts used a long forked stick to reach a slab of venison bacon down from the rafters, and both of them talked the while, in their wispy old voices.

"Ja, I do remember when young Thiuda was born," said Fillein, meditatively champing his toothless mouth. "It was while our two kings, the brothers Thiudamer and Walamer, were in far-off Pannonia, fighting to overthrow the Hun oppressors, and—"

Baúhts interrupted him. "King Thiudamer we always called the Affectionate, and King Walamer the Faithful."

I nodded and said with fond recollection, "I once was told that by Thiudamer's daughter, the Princess Amalamena." Perhaps because of the tone of my voice, I got a thoughtful look from Swanilda, who was helping the old woman start a meal for us.

Fillein went on, "As I was saying, one day during that time, we got word here that the brother kings had finally bested the Huns, that no Ostrogoths anywhere were any longer in bondage. On that same day, we heard also that Thiudamer's consort had borne him a son."

"That is why," Baúhts put in, "we always spoke of the young Thiuda as the child of victory."

I said to Fillein, "Then, before the reign of Thiudamer and his brother, you knew no monarch or master except the Hun chieftains?"

"Akh, not so! Once upon a time, I was, like all Ostrogoths, a subject of the father of those brothers, King Wandalar."

"Known as the Vandal-Conqueror," said Baúhts, as she and Swanilda hefted a great iron pot to set on the fire.

"And Wandalar's father was before my time," said Fillein, "but I knew his name. King Widereikhs."

"Known as the Wend-Conqueror," said Baúhts, as she slid flat rounds of dough among the hearth ashes to bake into trenchers.

I had by now decided that Fillein must be this household's keeper of kings' names, and his wife the keeper of their auknamons. But I was puzzled by something, so I said:

"Venerable Fillein, how can you call those men kings? You said yourself that the entire Ostrogoth nation was in bondage to the Huns until the time of the brothers Thiudamer and Walamer."

"Ha!" he exclaimed, and his creaky old voice strengthened with pride as he explained. "That never stopped our kings from being kings, or our warriors from being warriors. And savages the Huns were, indeed, but clever savages. They knew our men would never take commands from *them*. So they let the royal succession continue uninterrupted, and our warriors took commands from our kings. The only difference was that we now fought not any of our ancestral enemies, but the enemies of the Huns. No matter. To a warrior, any fight is a worthwhile fight. When the Huns, driving westward, wished to vanquish the miserable Wends of the Carpatae valleys, it was our King Widereikhs who led our warriors in helping to accomplish that. And later, when the Huns wished to push the Vandals out of Germania, it was our King Wandalar who led our warriors in that exploit."

"As you say, the Huns pushed every other people westward, including almost all the Goths. How is it, then, that *you* are living here?"

"Young marshal, reflect. Romans or Huns or any other race of men may rampage back and forth across the earth. The various parcels of land may change masters many times. The ground may be drenched with blood or strewn with bones or pitted with graves or littered with rusting and rotting armor. But those things wear away and vanish within a single man's lifetime. I myself have seen them do so. *The earth itself does not change.*"

"Do you mean . . . a man owes loyalty only to the immutable earth? Not to any auths or king or kinship?"

He did not at once answer that, but went on:

"Balamer brought his ravaging Huns through here a hundred years ago. But our fathers had held and worked these lands for more than a hundred years before that. True, the Huns swarmed over our territory and called it theirs, but they did not lay it waste—and for good reason. They needed the produce of *all* the lands they conquered, to feed and clothe their armies, so they could go on marauding through Europe."

593

"Ja," I murmured. "I can see that."

"But what did those Huns know of harvesting from the earth? To make the earth keep on providing, there had to be people who could work the lands and marshes and waters. So, although the Huns forced our kings and warriors and young men either to go westward with them or to flee before them, they also allowed the old folks, women and children to keep possession of the homesteads—and to share their harvests with the Huns' supply trains."

There was a break in the conversation while Swanilda and old Baúhts fetched our meal from the hearth to the table—the wild-boar bacon boiled with goosefoot greens, heaped on the bread trenchers. Because the night was now full dark and the hearth fire was the only light in the room, old Fillein took two burning brands and stuck them into slitted blocks of wood, and set those on the table as torches for us to eat by. While his old wife took a trencher out to wherever Maggot was to eat, Fillein also drew mugs of beer from a cask in the room's corner and set them before us, saying, with a light cackle of laughter:

"Observe, Saio Thorn. We still do abide by some ancient Gothic traditions. Because this delta grows no decent beer-making grains, we must buy our beer from the traders in Noviodunum. We could as cheaply buy Roman or Greek wine. But in ages past, the strong-beer-drinking Goths scorned those watered-wine drinkers as effeminate weaklings. So . . ." He cackled again, raised his mug and wished us "Háils!" Then he reverted to the conversation:

"You asked earlier, Marshal, whether a man owes his loyalty to his native earth or to his ancestral auths. I suppose each man must make that choice for himself. When the Huns gave leave to the nonwarriors of the Ostrogoths to go on living and working here, the greater portion of them proudly disdained that concession. They refused to be parted from their warrior kinsmen, and went west with them, choosing homelessness and landlessness and often wretchedness for the rest of their lives."

I said, "For many thousands of those people, the rest of their lives was not long."

Fillein shrugged his meager shoulders and said, "Well, some few chose the assurance of survival. They stayed here. Among them were my great-grandparents, and other elders who were the great-grandparents of dear Baúhts here. Clearly, I cannot disprize those people for the choice they made, or Baúhts and I would probably never have existed. However, as subsequent generations were born, some of the young folks were not content to be perpetual drudges of the Huns. I was one of those. And believe me, Marshal, I was not always as you see me now."

He crammed the soggy last bit of his trencher into his mouth and, as he munched it with his gums, he regarded the hands with which he had been eating. They were old hands, gaunt and gnarled and veined and blotched with the spots of age.

"These hands were once young and strong, and I thought they deserved better work than marsh-grubbing."

"Akh, ja," his wife put in. "He was such a fine, strapping young man in those days that he was called Fillein the Firm. His parents and mine had arranged our marriage when we were little more than children. They wanted to make sure, you see, that we would stay on the land. But when Fillein decided to go for a soldier, I did not try to dissuade him. I was proud of him. I swore to our parents that I would stay and do the work of us both until he should return."

The old woman and the old man smiled toothlessly but warmly, lovingly at one another. Then he turned again to me.

"So I ran away and joined the forces of our King Wandalar, who was then marching against the Vandals. Like him and all his other warriors,

I was of course campaigning on behalf of our oppressor Huns. But at least it seemed a more manly work to be doing."

I said wonderingly, "You *fought* . . . with King Wandalar? But . . . but that would have to have been at least seventy years ago."

Fillein said simply, "I told you. I was young then."

Swanilda spoke up, just as wonderingly as I had done. "So you and your lady Baúhts have been married for even longer than *that* . . ."

He smiled and nodded. "And for most of that time living together, right here. I am glad that I have my warrior days to look back on. But I was glad, too, when I was wounded in battle, severely enough to be retired—and glad to come home to my dear Baúhts. And here we have dwelt ever since, under this very roof, on this land that was settled by our fathers' fathers' fathers."

The old woman said complacently, "When the hammer of Thor has been swung in its binding circle over a boy and a girl, they are bound for life."

I was again slightly nettled to hear mentioned the name of Thor, so I sought to change the subject. "Let us hark back even before the kings Wandalar and Wideric—"

"Ne, let us not," Fillein interrupted. "Not tonight. We old folk are accustomed to go to bed at dark, and it is long past that, and this room is where we sleep. Young Maghib has a hayrick behind the house. You two young people may take your sleeping furs to the loft above this room."

As Swanilda and I lay together in the dark loft, we refrained this night from doing anything that would make noise to disturb or scandalize the old folks in the room below. We only talked quietly for a time.

Swanilda said, "Do you not find it touching, Thorn? That a man and a woman could have been married for so long?"

"Well, out of the ordinary, certainly. A man of Fillein's great age could be expected to have outlived three or four wives, dead in childbirth."

Swanilda shook her head. "Baúhts told me, while we were preparing the meal, that God—or perhaps she meant the god Thor who bound them—never blessed them with children."

Because peevishness seemed to have become my usual response on hearing that name, I said sourly, "Perhaps that beneficent Thor sent them Maggot, not just for an acquaintance, but as a substitute son."

Swanilda was silent for a little. Then she said: "Thorn, did you notice the two trees growing behind this house?"

"Eh?"

"An oak and a linden."

That stirred something in my memory, but I was getting too drowsy to dredge for it. Anyway, Swanilda saved me the trouble.

"A story from the Old Religion," she said. "An aged man and woman once loved one another so long and so devotedly that the Old Gods, in admiration, offered to grant them any wish they might desire. The man and woman asked only that, when their time came to die—"

"They be allowed to die at the same moment," I said. "I remember now. I too once heard that story."

"The wish was granted," said Swanilda. "And the gods turned them into an oak and a linden, so that they might go on flourishing side by side."

"Swanilda," I chided her gently, "you are weaving a whole legend around two very ordinary old peasants."

"It was you who said just now that they are *out* of the ordinary. Tell me truthfully, Thorn. Do you think you could live happily with one woman for all the rest of your life?"

596

"Iésus, Swanilda! No person could possibly say that, except in retrospect. Fillein and Baúhts could never have *foretold* their long association. It is only now, in old age, that they can look back and *remember* it."

Swanilda said quickly and contritely, "Akh, Thorn, I was asking for no *vow* . . ."

"You were asking for a prediction. So I suggest that you put the question to old Meirus the Mudman. He claims to have some prowess as a wise-sayer. Ask him what you and I will be remembering when we are as ancient as Fillein and Baúhts. Now, please, dear girl, let us sleep."

✠ ✠ ✠

The next morning, Fillein wished to see what sort of catch he had made in some fowling nets he had lately spread in the marsh rushes, and invited me to go with him. Swanilda offered to stay at the hearthside and help Baúhts with some sewing, because, as the old woman admitted, her eyesight was "not what it used to be."

"And surely, venerable Fillein," I said, "your strength is hardly what it used to be. If your nets are far off, simply point the way, and Maggot and I will see to them."

"Vái, old I may be, but not yet as old as some. Why, King Ermanareikhs did not die until he was a hundred and ten years old. He would have got even older, had he not committed suicide."

"King Ermanareikhs?" I said. "Who was he?"

As I might have expected, old Baúhts readily supplied an auknamo for him. She said reminiscently, "Akh, Ermanareikhs, now. He was the king that many have called the 'Alexander the Great' of the Ostrogoth people."

But she had no more to add to that, so I waited to hear that king's history from Fillein on our way to inspect his nets. We descended the hillock and crossed several fields of the silvery-green feather grass, where the ground was firm enough. However, it soon became bogland, ever more fluid underfoot, and before long we were having to step high, lifting each foot with an audible *thwock* from the clinging muck. We were by now deep among the reeds that rose higher than our heads, and, as we sloshed and sidled through them, frogs jumped out of our way, water snakes undulated away, wading birds either took wing or stalked haughtily away. Meanwhile, for all his years and seeming fragility, Fillein slogged along as sturdily as I, and talked as he went.

"You inquired of Ermanareikhs, Marshal. When I was young, I heard from my elders what they, when young, had heard from *their* elders, and I was made to memorize it, and it was this. Ermanareikhs was the king who first brought the Ostrogoths from the far north to the Mouths of the Danuvius here. Then as now, this land was called Scythia, but today it is no longer inhabited by the degenerate Scythians. To make room here for his own nation, King Ermanareikhs drove those Scythians off into Sarmatia, where the remnants of them still live in their primitive squalid ways."

597

I murmured, "Ja, I have heard curious stories of those once-great Scythians."

Fillein nodded and went on, "However, before the Ostrogoths ever got *here*, they had passed through the lands of many other peoples. So, along the way, Ermanareikhs made all those sundry peoples acknowledge the Ostrogoths as their superiors and protectors. In effect, Ermanareikhs was king of many more peoples than just his Ostrogoths. Hence his being acclaimed an equal of that legendary Alexander the Great. Unfortunately, all his grand exploits went for naught when he suffered his first and only defeat. The Huns came swooping out of the remote east, and Ermanareikhs was by then a hundred and ten years old—too old to mount a proper defense. Seeing the Huns victorious, he took his own life as penance for his one failure. Now, be careful here, Saio Thorn. Walk only in my tracks. There are bottomless quaking-sands on either side of us."

As he bade me, I walked behind him. But I had been getting increasingly skeptical throughout his recital, and now I said:

"Gudisks Himins, man, that king would have had to live something like *two* hundred and ten years to have engaged in all those events, from the Goths' arrival here to their subjugation by the Huns."

Fillein said petulantly, "If you already know everything there is to know, why did you solicit what little I thought I knew?"

"Forgive me, venerable Fillein. Evidently there are many histories. I only wish to correlate them, to sift from them the *true* history."

He grumbled, "Well, there is one thing about King Ermanareikhs that cannot be disputed. After him, none *but* men of the Amal line have been kings of the Ostrogoths. Not necessarily the eldest son of each king, mind you, but the best-qualified Amal descendant. To illustrate, Ermanareikhs himself had an eldest son. That prince was called Hunimund the Handsome, but Ermanareikhs designated a less handsome, more capable nephew to be his successor."

"Very interesting, good Fillein," I said sincerely, "and information new to me."

That seemed to soothe Fillein's ruffled feelings. He said, "We are past the quaking-sands morass now, Saio Thorn. The path ahead is clear to see and easy to follow through the reeds." He even stepped aside to let me take the lead.

As I strode on ahead, I prompted him, "So Ermanareikhs bequeathed his crown to a nephew . . . ?"

"Ja, his nephew Walavarans. As Baúhts would tell you, that king is known to history as Walavarans the Cautious. Next came King Winithar the Just. And after him came the kings of whom I spoke last night. Tell me, Saio Thorn, has this latest king, Theodoric, yet earned an auknamo for my dear Baúhts to add to those she has memorized?"

"Ne, but I am sure he will. Doubtless a memorably complimentary auknamo." And then I bellowed suddenly and profanely, *"Akh! Skeit!"*

"Theodoric the Excrement?" Fillein said with a straight face. "Hardly complimentary. By the way, Marshal, I meant to warn you, there is open water ahead."

Since I was already standing neck-deep in it, I simply glared at him, high and dry on the bank above me, doing his best not to break into a triumphantly malicious cackle.

"As long as you are there, Saio Thorn, you might save an old man a wetting. Would you retrieve the catch for me, niu?"

He pointed off to my right and I saw the nets. They had been cunningly placed. The water in which I was immersed was either a tributary or some random small channel of the Danuvius, about as broad as a Roman road and evidently only man-deep, bordered on both sides by reedy banks, from one of which I had so foolishly toppled. In all this wilderness of reeds, the stream was an obvious place for water birds to alight when they came down to nest or feed or just to rest for the night. So Fillein had stretched three nets across the breadth of it, at intervals some distance apart, and each of those had snared five or six sizable birds that, like myself, had not paid sufficient attention to where they were going.

I breasted the water and, half walking, half bobbing, propelled myself to the closest net, finding it to be made not of any cord but of painstakingly braided and knotted reed fibers. I was starting to disentangle a large, dead egret—and noticing that the bird, in its death struggle, had severely torn the meshes—when Fillein called to me:

"Do not bother with that, Marshal. Drag the nets over here entire. They will all need mending, anyway."

While I was doing that, Fillein was going up and down the bank on his side of the stream, feeling about under the surface and bringing up small objects of some sort. When I had the last of the nets at the bankside, I hauled first myself, then them, up onto dry ground. Fillein joined me, carrying his tunic hem turned up before him like a basket. He let it fall and there spilled out a bustellus or so of glistening blue mussels.

I asked him, "How could you have carried this burden of nets and birds—and now shellfish—all the way back to your house? It is going to be a considerable challenge for both of us."

"Who wants the birds?" he said as he ripped an egret loose from the meshes, quickly plucked out its long dorsal plumes, then flung the cadaver far off into the reeds. "The martens and gluttons will thank us for them."

So he went on, taking only the shoulder plumes from egrets, the head plumes from herons, the curly crests from pelicans and—to my mystification—breaking off and keeping the slender curved beaks of the ibises.

I asked, "What possible market can there be for *beaks?*"

"The lekjos buy them. Medici. Physicians."

"What on earth for?"

"To be blunt, Marshal, for *skeit*—a word you used a little while ago. A physician binds the two parts of the beak tightly together, saws the tip off clean and ties a leather bag to the larger end. Then, to ease the misery of a costive patient, he rams the tip of the beak far up into the man's backside and gushes into him a curative, skeit-inducing clyster. Now, Saio Thorn, while I am working and you are just sitting there idle, you might usefully pluck one of those dead sheldrakes for us to take home. Ne, on second thought, let us take two of them. To celebrate this good catch, we might as well treat Maghib to a decent meal also."

So, when we were done with our separate labors, we went back the way we had come, I carrying the two ducks I had plucked and the bundle of nets enclosing the mussels, Fillein carrying the precious feathers and ibis beaks. And that night, though Maggot again was given his meal outdoors, all five of us feasted deliciously on wild duck stuffed with mussels and baked in the hearth ashes. Later, in the loft, as Swanilda and I lay replete and drowsy, I amused her by telling how the king's august marshal had spent the day being ordered about by an ancient peasant, and being given menial work to do, and even being unceremoniously dunked in a stream by that lowly old man—and how the king's marshal had meanwhile learned many things.

4

ext morning, when we were breaking our fast, the old man said, "I have decided, Saio Thorn, that today I am going to inflict you and your inquisitiveness and your disbelief on someone other than myself."

"Come now, venerable Fillein," I said. "There are other questions about the old times that I would like to put to you."

"Ne, ne. I and my old woman and your younger one will spend today in mending my nets. I wish to do that without distraction. You can go and put your questions to my neighbor Galindo."

"Your neighbor?" I echoed, for I had seen no other houses in the vicinity.

"Akh, there are no *near* neighbors anywhere in this delta, but you can get to Galindo's abode and back again by nightfall."

"Galindo. That is a Gepid name, is it not?"

"Ja. Since he is a Gepid, he may regale you with a totally different version of local history. He has traveled even farther than I ever did. In his youth, Galindo served with a Roman legion somewhere in Gallia."

"I am certain that I will find him less interesting to talk to than you, venerable Fillein. But I value your advice. How do I find him this Galindo?"

"I have already given directions to Maghib. He will guide you there. Galindo being a Gepid, therefore lethargic, he has burrowed himself away as reclusively as an oyster, in one of the remotest barrens of these marshes. He lives alone, without even a woman, and shuns any company. But at least the trails are on firm ground all the way from here to his hermitage, so you and Maghib can ride the horses."

"If he is so averse to company, how do you know he will see even a king's marshal?"

Fillein scratched in his beard. "True, your being a marshal will not impress Galindo. But mention my name and he should receive you not *too* grudgingly. Of course, being a Gepid layabout, he will not bestir himself to feed you. I will have Baúhts wrap some morsels from last night for you and Maghib to carry with you."

601

Outside, Maggot was saddling the two horses, and doing it with little hums and whistlings of childish good cheer. I remembered how Meirus the Mudman had said, "Do not spoil the creature," so I assumed that this must be one of the few occasions in Maggot's life when he had not had to lope alongside a mounted master. But when Baúhts and Swanilda brought our packets of provisions, Maggot watched me closely as I vaulted astride my Velox, then he tried to emulate me—but too energetically, for he went clear over his saddle and fell in a heap on the other side, to the great admiration of us all, including the horses. I realized that Maggot never *had* been "spoiled." He never had straddled a mount at all. So I bade him change horses with me, and that gave him the seating security of Velox's foot-rope. I was not just being the gracious master; I did not want to be repeatedly delayed on the trail while he fell off and got on again.

For part of the forenoon, Maggot was unwontedly quiet—concentrating either on trying to stay aboard Velox or on the trail directions Fillein had given him. After some time, though, he began tentatively to talk and before much longer was being the typically voluble Armenian. I was rather grateful for his prattle. In the endless grassland we were crossing, under its vast blue sky flecked with puffball clouds, there was nothing interesting to see or hear—or even to think about, except how *much* grassland and sky there was—so Maggot's garrulity was some relief from boredom.

His effusion consisted mainly of accounts of his fráuja Meirus's more marvelous feats of foreseeing and wise-saying, every instance of which, according to Maggot, had resulted in tremendously increased profits for the Meirus mud establishment, but none of which, according to Maggot, had put a single additional nummus in the purse of Maggot or any other of Meirus's workers. For which reason, said Maggot, he was exceedingly anxious to put his talents to more personally profitable exertion. If, he said, he had such a provably good nose for sniffing out the best grades of mud, he believed he could sniff out much more valuable substances in or on the ground. Having said that, he gave me a sidewise look and added:

"The fráuja Meirus said that you will retrace the old track of the Goths all the way from here to the distant shores of the Wendic Gulf."

"Ja."

"And that gulf shore, it is called the Amber Coast?"

"It is."

"And amber is found there in great quantities?"

"It is."

"Will you seek for amber yourself while you and the lady Swanilda are there?"

"Not seek it, ne. I have other business. But if I should stumble on some, I assuredly will not step over it."

There, Maggot dropped the subject of amber, and began to talk of inconsequentials, cleverly leaving it to me to argue with myself the possible utility of taking north with me a person who kept his nose to the ground, so to speak. Well, he did not *have* to say anything more; he being an Armenian, the nose in question was perpetually and obtrusively in plain sight. However, he did finally make another reference to his talents as we approached a miserable pimple of a hut.

"You see, fráuja, how good I am at finding things? This has to be the place to which old Fillein directed me, the residence of old Galindo."

If it was, then old Galindo was sitting outside it, visible for long before we got there, because either he was almost as big as his house or it was not much bigger than Galindo. Indeed, the "residence" was only a rough dome of sun-dried mud, looking no more habitable than the mud bubble that a swamp sometimes belches up. But its occupant had fenced it off from intruders as formidably as if it had been a fortress city. He could not have been often beset by horsemen on that trail—

602

Maggot and I had seen not one all morning—but, nearly two stadia distant from his door, he had dug a ditch across the path, wide and deep enough to halt a cavalry charge.

The ground was solid enough thereabout so that we could probably have circumvented the obstacle. But I decided to respect it, at least to the degree of dismounting and leaving Maggot to hold the horses while I went on foot, clambering across the ditch and then walking to where the man stolidly still sat. I waved amiably to him, and received no response, and not until I stood directly before him did he do or say anything at all. Then, without even looking at me, he said only:

"Go away."

He may not have been *quite* as old as Fillein, for he was somewhat less wrinkled, and possessed a few teeth, but he was at least as old as my onetime companion Wyrd would have been by this date. He was all gray hair and whiskers that merged into his gray wolfskin robe, so that he seemed only a heap of hair with some few facial features at its upper front. I could understand why he was outdoors, his windowless mud hut being obviously nothing but a sleeping shelter. His hearth was a few blackened stones on the ground, alongside which were ranged what appeared to be his only belongings—a cooking pot, an eating bowl, a water jug.

603

I said, "If you are Galindo, I have come a long distance to speak with you."

"Then you must know the way back to wherever you came from. Go there."

"I came here from the abode of Fillein, an acquaintance of yours. He told me that you once served with a Roman legion in Gallia."

"Fillein always has talked too much."

"Might that have been the Eleventh Legion, the Claudia Pia Fidelis, in Gallia Lugdunensis?"

He glanced at me for the first time. "If you are compiling a census, you have come a long way to assess the most insignificant property in the empire. Look around you."

"I am no censor. I am a historian, seeking only information, not taxes."

"I have no more of one than the other. But I too am curious. What would you know of the Claudia Pia, niu?"

"I had a very good friend once who was a veteran of service with that legion. A Brython from the Tin Islands, called Wyrd the Friend of Wolves. Or, in Latin, his name was Uiridus."

"Horse, was he, or foot?"

"Horse. In the battle of the Catalaunian Plains, Wyrd rode with the antesignani."

"Did he now? I was but a foot soldier, a pediculus."

Well, I thought, Galindo had a soldier's wry sense of humor. The Latin word for an infantryman is "pedes," but "pediculus" is not the diminutive of that. It means literally a louse.

"You did not know Wyrd, then?"

"If you are a historian, you must be aware that a legion comprises more than four thousand men. Would you expect us all to be close acquaintances, niu? *You* are close enough to me right now that you are making me sit in your shade, and I do not know *you*."

"Excuse me," I said, moving so he had the sunlight again. "My name is Thorn. I am a marshal of King Theodoric Amaling. He sent me to these parts to gather an accurate history of the Goths. Fillein thought you might tell me useful things about the Gepid part of that history."

"I would tell you to go straight to Gehenna, except for your mention of that legionary who once rode with the antesignani. I too fought the Huns on those plains near Cabillonum. If a man was courageous enough to have gone out ahead of the standards there, he was a man indeed. And if he later befriended you, then *you* must have some merits. Very well." He made a grand gesture, as if he were offering me a throne instead of the bare ground. "You may sit down—on the unsunny side of me. Now, what useful things would you like to know?"

"Well . . . I hope you will forgive my beginning this way, but . . . how do you Gepids feel about having the name Gepids?"

He stared stonily at me for a long moment, then said, "How do *you* feel about having no name at all, niu? Thorn is not a name, it is a character of the runic writing."

"I am aware of that. Nevertheless, it is my name. I can only say that I long ago became accustomed to it."

"And I to being a Gepid. Next question."

"I mean," I said, "considering the derogatory connotations of the name Gepid . . ."

"Vái!" he said, and spat on the ground. "That old fable? How Gepid derives from the word 'gepanta'? Sluggish, slow, slovenly, and all that? You profess to be a historian. But you believe that infantile balgs-daddja?"

"Why . . . I had it on good authority. On *several* good authorities."

He shrugged. "If you are satisfied, who am I to quibble with a historian? Next question."

"Ne, ne, ne. Please, good Galindo. If you know a different derivation of the name, I should very much like to hear it."

"I know *the* derivation of the name. In old Skandza, where all of us Goths originated, the Amalings and the Baltings were flatland dwellers. We Gepids were men of the baírgos, the mountains. When later the Amalings and Baltings came to call themselves the Eastern Goths and Western Goths, we proudly continued to call ourselves the Mountain Goths. Gepid is merely the modern, abbreviated pronunciation of 'ga-baírgs,' mountain-born. You may believe that or not, as you choose."

"Akh, I will, I will," I said, surprised but pleased by the new story. "It is much more believable than the accepted account."

"I advise you, young historian, do not put too much credence in any name. How many Placidias and Irenes and Virginias have you known who were in no way placid or peaceful or virginal? A name can be a flimsy thing, a fluctuating thing, even a delusive thing."

"That is so," I agreed, though I did not mention that I myself sometimes deliberately, even delusively, changed names.

"Regarding names, I remember one thing from my days with the Claudia Pia." Galindo gazed out across the limitless grass, his old face going pensive, as if he were seeing instead the Catalaunian Plains of nearly forty years before. "We sang many martial songs, and not all of them Roman, for we legionaries were of many different peoples—including men of the Tin Islands, as you know—but whatever the song, we sang it in the legion's common language of Latin. Now, those Brythons had songs of their own, but they also joined us Goths in singing our saggwasteis fram aldrs. And I remember us singing that old saggws that tells about the life and deeds of the great Visigoth hero Alareikhs. In Roman Latin his name would be properly Alaricus, but those Tin Islanders sang it in their corrupt Brythonic Latin as Arthurus." Old Galindo came abruptly back to the here and now, snapping, "Confound it, Marshal! You are interfering with my sunlight again!"

"Not I. It is another of your delta's accursedly instantaneous storms." Just that quickly, the puffball clouds had grown and spread and merged into a solid blanket that now was blackening.

"Akh, ja," said Galindo, almost approvingly. "Thor does love to fling his hammers hereabouts."

"You believe in Thor, do you?" I asked, with my now usual testiness on hearing that name. "Are you of the Old Religion, then?"

"If I am anything, I am a Mithraist, having once been a Roman legionary. But it does no harm, I think, to acknowledge the existence of other gods. And if Thor is not the god of thunder, who is, niu?"

As if Galindo had invoked it, a fork of lightning jabbed down at the eastern horizon and the air quivered to the following drumroll. The first drops of rain began to fall, and I growled a profanity.

The old man gave me a look. "Do you fear the anger of Thor?"

"Not his or any other's," I snapped. "I merely dislike storms when they inconvenience me."

"Myself, I find rainstorms no inconvenience whatever." To my amazement, he doffed his wolfskin and then the few rags of clothing he wore under it. "The rains save me from having to trudge a far distance to a stream to bathe. Will you not join me, Marshal?"

"Ne, thags izvis." I averted my eyes from his scrawny and hairy old body, bared to the rain that now came sluicing down. I could no longer see Maggot and the horses by the ditch where I had left them. I could only trust that the animals were safe—and Maggot, too, of course, since the horses might have run off without him to hold them. In the meantime, I sat uncomfortably and the naked Galindo sat contentedly and the rain poured on us both and I listened to his continued account of his people's history.

"As testimony that the Gepids have always been at least the equals of any other Goths, I will mention two battles that took place not far from here, but a long time ago, during the reign of Constantine the Great. That emperor was not yet called 'the Great' in those days, but he already showed symptoms of greatness—when he defeated a combined army of Ostrogoths and Visigoths. But then, eight or nine years later, when the *Gepid* Goths were fighting the Vandals, Constantine brought his army to fight on the side of the Vandals—and suffered the first defeat of his life. One of the *few* defeats of his life."

"Ja, that thoroughly vindicates the honor of the Gepids," I said, as enthusiastically as I could in the prevailing damp conditions.

"Notice, Marshal, now that I am spotlessly clean, Thor's storm conveniently diminishes. The beneficent sun of Mithras will be out in another minute to dry me."

"I rejoice that you are on such good terms with so many gods." I looked out through the thinning rain and was glad to see that Maggot and the horses were still where I had left them, and still upright. "But why do you live out here in the middle of nowhere, good Galindo, when you clearly have wit enough to make your own way in that outside world?"

He spat on the ground again. "I saw enough of the outside world while the Roman army marched me around in it for near thirty years."

"Still, you could be living in retirement without having to live in quite such isolation and deprivation."

"Isolation? Deprivation? When I have the company of such as Mithras and Thor, and the benisons of their sun and rain? I have birds' eggs and frogs and locusts and purslane for food. I have hanaf smoke for comfort. What more does a man need at my age?"

"Hanaf smoke?"

"One of the few bequests that the decadent Scythians left to us here. You have never tried it? There is some dry wood just inside the hut there, Marshal. Be so good as to light a fire in my hearth here and I will show you."

While I was laying the fire, I said, "I have now heard much of interest about the Goths' doings after they settled here among these Mouths of the Danuvius. But can you tell me anything of what their lives were like—how they fared during their long migration—before they arrived here?"

"Not a thing," he said cheerfully. "Here, set this pot on the fire, and put this hanaf into it." From the recesses of his wolfskin, in which he was now reclothing himself, he took out a handful of a desiccated and crumbly substance. I dropped it into the otherwise empty pot, recognizing it as the dried leaves and seeds of the wild plant called in Latin the cannabis.

607

"But I will tell you this," Galindo went on. "The best thing that ever happened to the Goths—to all of the Goths—was their being chased out of here by the Huns."

"Why do you say that?" I asked as we watched the heated weed begin to curl and char and smoke.

"They were too comfortable here. Once they settled down to be well-behaved Roman citizens of approved Roman ways and manners, they were fast becoming bland, smug and self-satisfied. They were forgetting their heritage of independence and willfulness and daring."

He leaned over the pot on the fire and inhaled deeply of the smoke that was now wafting profusely up from the scorching weeds, and he motioned for me to do likewise. I did, getting a lungful of sweet-acrid smell and taste, not repellent but not very pleasant either, nothing to explain why Galindo had called it a "comfort."

"Those settled and indolent Goths," he resumed, "even imitated the Romans in succumbing to the Christian religion, which was their most weakling submission of all."

"Why do you say that?" I asked again, rather stupidly. In truth, I spoke with some difficulty, for that whiff of smoke seemed to have made me slightly but suddenly thickheaded.

Galindo took another deep inhalation of smoke before he replied. "What need had the Goths to import an oriental religion? Christianity is a faith best suited to tradesmen—nothing but barter for profit. 'Do good,' it preaches, 'and you will be rewarded.' "

I could not have confuted him if I had wanted to, because I was feeling quite drunkenly addled. Though Galindo sat right before me, his words seemed to come from far away, and hollowly, with echoes jarring between them, as if the words were somehow *jostling* each other.

"Akh, Marshal, you are sitting at a tilt," he said to me, grinning. "You are feeling the effect of the hanaf smoke. However, it is better experienced in an enclosed space." He gestured for me to sniff again, but I woozily shook my head. When he bent over the fire this time, he flung a flap of the wolfskin over both his head and the pot, and the covering heaved as he took repeated drafts of the smoke. When at last he emerged from that enclosure, his eyes were glazed and his grin extremely loose and foolish. But he continued to talk and, to my hearing, his words still sounded clangorously distant.

608

"Happily for the Goths, the Huns uprooted them from here. Until just recent years, the Goths were hunted or shunted from place to place. They hungered, they thirsted, they suffered. Those that did not die in battle died of disease or exposure. But that was good, too."

"Why do you say that?"

I realized that I had stupidly asked the very same question a third time, as if I knew or could speak no other words. Well, I had a hard enough time speaking *those*—very slowly, with a pause after each one—because my own words, like Galindo's, seemed to reverberate inside my head.

"It was good because those who died were the weak and the spiritless. The ones that remain are the strong and the bold ones. Now, with the Roman Empire so pitifully fragmented, the time is ripe for a Gothic resurgence. They could be a greater force than they ever were before. They could be the *new Romans . . .*"

The old hermit was clearly drunk on his hanaf smoke, and babbling. But I hardly felt entitled to make mention of that, because my own organs of thinking and speaking were almost as badly impaired as his.

"And if the Goths should supplant the Romans as masters of the western world . . . well . . . the world would be grateful that the Goths adopted *Arian* Christianity and not the Athanasian, as the Romans did."

To my private horror, because I feared that I would never be able to utter anything else, I heard myself asking yet a fourth time, "Why do you say that?"

"Throughout history, Europeans of different faiths have fought and killed each other for this reason or that. But never until the coming of Christianity did men of our western world fight and kill each other *because* of their faiths—one seeking to impose his on the other." Galindo paused to take another draft of his awful smoke. "However, the Arian Christians are at least tolerant of every other religion, and of paganism, and of those persons who profess no religious beliefs at all. Therefore, if the Goths *should* prevail, they would not demand or even expect everyone else in the world to believe as they do. *Saggws was galiuthjon!*"

Those last words made me jump, for he sang them, or bawled them:

> *"Saggws was galiuthjon,*
> *Haífsts was gahaftjon!"*

It was a relic of his martial days, evidently—"Song was sung, battle was begun!" I was now convinced that Galindo, sane though he had sounded at first, must have been long addicted to his weed smoke and had been incurably demented by it.

609

We parted without much ceremony. I got to my feet, somewhat shakily, and bade goodbye to Galindo. He only gave me the Roman salute, for he was still lustily singing. Then I staggered dizzily off across the plain and floundered my way in and out of the ditch to join Maggot, faithfully holding the horses. I squeezed my eyes shut so I could concentrate before trying my voice, and was relieved to hear myself speak other words than "Why do you say that?" though these came out in a croak:

"Let us return to Fillein's abode."

Maggot gave me a searching look. "Are you all right, fráuja?"

"I hope so" was all I could reply, for I had no idea whether one exposure to hanaf smoke might be permanent in its effects.

However, the untainted, newly rain-washed air of the grassland and the exercise of riding at an easy canter gradually cleared the murk from my mind. I was feeling healthy and sober again when, sometime after dark, we got back to the house of Fillein and Baúhts. Maggot got down from Velox not nearly so precipitately as he had earlier tried to mount, and tottered and groaned when he was on the ground. It was my turn to ask, "Are you all right?"

"Ne, fráuja," he said weakly. "I do believe my legs are permanently bowed. And skinless. Does a horseman always feel this sore and stiff and raw after riding?"

"Only the first time or two," I said. "Or three."

"Akh, I hope not to have to do it twice. I shall be ever satisfied hereafter with running alongside, as I think Armenians must have been intended by nature to do."

"Balgs-daddja," I scoffed, but laughingly. "Go and dig up a horse-radish. Mash it and rub that on your sore places. You will feel better by morning."

Fillein and Baúhts had kindly waited nahtamats for our return, though this night it was only boar bacon and greens again. As usual, Maggot took his trencher to eat outdoors while he unsaddled and fed the horses. I sat down with Swanilda and the old couple and, while we ate, recounted some of what had passed at Galindo's place, including his adopted Scythian habit of indulging in lunacy-inducing weed smoke.

"I told you," said Fillein with malicious satisfaction, "that he is less intelligent than I. After all, Galindo is a Gepid."

610

5

hen we visitors took our leave next morning, Maggot jogged along between my horse and Swanilda's and again talked enough to relieve the tedium of our crossing of the grassland. For a while, his talk was merely gossip about various colorful inhabitants of Noviodunum. But finally, as I had expected, the Armenian broached the subject of future travel.

"Where will you and the lady Swanilda be going next, fráuja?"

"After I have put to Meirus a few questions I have in mind, we will repair to the pandokheíon for a night or two of rest and refreshment. Then we will pack the belongings we left there and simply ride far northward, toward the wilds of Sarmatia. According to all report, that is the direction the early Goths came from."

"And you will go ultimately to the Amber Coast?"

I laughed. "I have not forgotten your nose, Maggot."

"His nose?" said Swanilda in puzzlement.

She had not heard of the Armenian's ambitions, so I enlightened her.

"Seeking amber," she said to him, "certainly sounds a nobler occupation than seeking mud. But will not your fráuja Meirus be disconsolate when you announce that you are leaving his employ?"

"More likely irate, my lady," said Maggot. "And I doubt that I will even have to say a word. Meirus is what we call in my language a wardapet, or in his tongue a khazzen, or in yours a wise-sayer."

Truth to tell, when we got to the town, soon after dark, and went first to Meirus's warehouse, the stout old Jew was standing outside as if waiting for us. And, giving me and Swanilda the briefest of "háils," he thumped Maggot comradely on the shoulder and said, in a honeyed voice:

"Good to have you back, my boy. Your nose has been sorely missed. In these past days, the dredger men have brought in saprós not nearly pélethos enough. I was forced to realize that my expert mud-finder deserves to be better paid for his labors." The Armenian opened his mouth to speak, but was not given the chance. "Go now and rest at my house, Maggot—I mean Maghib. You have had a long run. We will discuss your new, increased wage as soon as I have made the marshal and his lady welcome."

Maggot, looking crestfallen, shuffled off along the street, leading our horses. The Mudman turned to us, expansively opening his arms.

"Now, waíla-gamotjands, Saio Thorn." He waved us inside the warehouse, where we sat down on some hay bales. "I am sure you are overwhelmingly anxious and curious to know—"

"To know first," I interrupted, "whether there has been any message from Theodoric."

"Ne, nothing but routine matters. Nothing about the expected uprising of Strabo and his Rugian allies, if that is what you mean."

"It is. No word, eh? I wonder what they could be waiting for."

"Akh, I wager I can tell you that. Very likely those forces will not march until they are well supplied. When the harvest is in. Ja, I predict that they will make their move in September or later, after the harvest. And before the winter clamps down."

611

"It sounds reasonable," I said, and nodded. "If so, I may be able to finish this quest and be back at Theodoric's side . . ."

"Come, come," Meirus prompted. "You have no *other* urgent questions to ask?"

I knew what he was hinting at, but I refused to give him the pleasure of hearing me ask for the latest news of the shadowy Thor. Instead I said:

"Ja, I have a question of . . . what would it be? History? Theology? Anyway, tell me—since it was you Jews who gave us Jesus—"

Meirus rocked back on his heels and exclaimed, "Al lo davár!" which I took to be an expression of surprise.

"And since it was Jesus who gave us Christianity," I continued, "perhaps you can verify something I recently was told. I believe, Meirus, from my reading of the Bible, that you Jews used often to go to war on behalf of Judaismus—trying forcibly to convert to your faith other peoples of the Orient."

"Akh, indeed, ja. I might cite for illustration the exploits of the Makhabai. That family name means 'hammer,' and it was an apt name. One of the Makhabai, when he defeated some other nation, did not even wait for them to submit to conversion. He had all the men circumcised on the instant."

"And you Jews also fought among yourselves, I understand, trying to make each other agree on matters of faith."

"Indeed, ja," he said again. "As the Book of Amos says, 'Shall two walk together except they be agreed?' There was, for example, the centuries-long rivalry, frequently violent, between the Perushim and the Tsedukim."

"But we western peoples, so I have been told, though we often warred on each other, never did so for religious reasons."

"To a Jew," Meirus said drily, "you never *had* a religion."

"I mean to say, we did not make war for that reason until Christianity became our prevailing religion."

"To a Jew, the Goyim *still* do not have a religion."

"Hear me out, please. We Europeans never had holy wars until the arrival of Christianity. It was born in the Orient, and came to us from there. And in the east, as you have just attested, holy wars are no novelty. And Jesus was a Jew, so . . ."

The Mudman clutched his head with both hands and bleated, "Bevakashá! I have heard many a mean Christian revile the Jews for slaying Jesus. You are the first I ever heard accuse us of *inflicting* him on you."

"Still . . . would that not be our heritage from the east?"

"Ayin haráh! Ask me a question I can answer!"

I shook my head. "I have nothing further to ask."

"I do," Swanilda said shyly. "I have a question, my lord Meirus."

With obvious relief, the Mudman turned from me to her. "Ja, child?"

"I was recently wondering about something, and Thorn and I talked it over, and he said that I might ask you about it."

Meirus leaned forward to see her better in the darkness. Then he turned the same searching gaze on me, and was silent for a moment before he said, "Ask. I will answer if I can."

"I would like to know . . . can you foretell . . . if Thorn and I will be . . . ?" Whatever she had started to say, she broke off and rephrased it. "If Thorn and I will long hold one another dear . . . ?"

Meirus gave each of us another piercing stare, then for some while indecisively stroked his black beard.

I said, "Can you not answer?"

"I have divined an answer, ja. But I do not know what it signifies. I can wise-say nothing about it. I would prefer not to give you an answer so dry and uninterpreted."

I said, "Come, come. You cannot simply tantalize us and then dismiss us."

"You are sure you wish to hear it?"

Swanilda and I said in unison, "I am."

Meirus squared his bulky shoulders. "As you command." He spoke first to me: "You will hold Swanilda dear for all the years of your life."

I could not imagine why he had hesitated to speak, for I saw nothing ominous or extraordinary or even very perceptive in that prediction. Swanilda seemed quite pleased with it. She was smiling happily when Meirus said to her:

"You will hold Thorn dear until midday tomorrow."

Swanilda's smile vanished and she looked totally dumbfounded. I was, too, but I recovered sufficiently to complain.

"What kind of prophecy is that? It does not make sense."

"I told you so. I can only say what I see."

"If you can divine that much, Mudman, you could at least venture a conjecture as to what it means."

"Confound it, Marshal! First you ask me to account for the atrocious behavior of all the world's Christians. Now you want to hold me responsible for what the future will bring. You might have some better idea of that yourself if you had asked me the question that must have

613

been longest on your mind. What news of the person who calls himself Thor?"

"All right! What news, then, of that lurking son of a fitchet bitch?"

"He came here again, of course. Just as arrogant and demanding and ill-humored as he was before. And as you are whenever you hear mention of him. I told him that you had gone traveling about the delta, but would eventually return. He growled that he was not going to muddy his feet tramping after you. He said he would await you here, that I was to tell you he has taken lodging in the same pandokheíon as you. And he hopes—he said this very mockingly—he hopes you will not go on cowardly dodging the hammer of Thor."

I snorted my contempt of that taunt. But then Meirus added, "He said also that he hopes you will not hide behind a woman's skirts. He must think that you keep the lady Swanilda by you merely as a shield against assault."

"I do not give two tords for what he thinks. Or says. I will go and find out what he is capable of *doing*."

"You will confront him?" the Mudman asked, almost eagerly.

"Right now?" Swanilda asked in alarm.

"Of course. I must not keep a god waiting. However, since he seems to scorn the company of ladies, I will go alone to meet him." I stood up and went outside, the other two following. "Meirus, is there another lodging place nearby where Swanilda can abide for a short while?"

"My own residence is just yonder," he said, pointing. "She will stay with me, and I will have my servants prepare nahtamats for her, and I will have Maggot see to the horses."

"But . . . Thorn . . ." Swanilda said beseechingly. "We have been companions for so long and so far. Must you separate us now?"

"Thor asked to see only me, and so he shall. I will go alone and on foot, and carry nothing but my sword. I should not be long, my dear. I wish to end his damnable bedevilment of us."

"Come, Lady Swanilda," Meirus said cheerfully, as he took her arm. "I am happy to have a visitor. I so seldom do. And I would welcome your advice about some commercial plans of mine." As they disappeared down the dark street, he was enthusiastically laying out those plans. "I have decided to expand my business to include trading in amber. Therefore, I should like to send Maggot north with you and the marshal, if you and he will allow it—to the Amber Coast—where Maggot will be my prospector and agent and . . ."

His voice trailed away, and I smiled—the old Jew evidently *did* have some skill at foreseeing—as I strode purposefully off in the opposite direction.

✠   ✠   ✠

I was longer at the pandokheíon than I had expected or intended to be. When I finally left there, I realized that Swanilda must be fretting and worrying about me—and Meirus no doubt slavering to know the outcome of my encounter—so, on my way back to them, I tried to hurry, but I could walk only numbly, woodenly. And my mind was in such a whirl that, when I did get back to the riverside warehouse district, I had to cast about for yet a while longer before I could recognize the house that Meirus had pointed out to me. All the way from the pandokheíon I had been composing a coherent story to tell. But I must not have composed my face very well, because, when I rapped my boot against the doorframe and Meirus himself let me in, he gave me one look and exclaimed:

"Akh, Saio Thorn, you are as pale as a gáis! Come in, come in quickly. And here, have a long pull at this wineskin."

I did, and drank gratefully, while he and Swanilda and Maggot, crowding into the entry hall behind him, watched me with mingled concern, expectation and apprehension.

"Was there a duel, Thorn?" Swanilda asked breathlessly when I at last lowered the wineskin.

"Did you prevail, fráuja Thorn?" Maggot asked timidly.

Meirus said, "Well, he is here, and upright, and not visibly bleeding."

"Did you defeat a god, fráuja Thorn?" Maggot persisted. "In hand-to-hand combat?"

"Thor is no god," I said, trying to laugh lightly. "And there was no duel. He is no enemy. His seeming angry pursuit of us was all pretense and prank."

"Akh, I had hoped it was!" cried Swanilda, laughing with me and throwing her arms about me. "I am so glad it was!"

Meirus said nothing, but narrowed his eyes as he regarded me.

"I am surprised, old wise-sayer," I chaffed him, doing my best to seem offhandedly devil-me-care, "that you did not divine something of the sort."

"So am I," he muttered, still eyeing my face.

It occurred to me to say, "If I am pale, it is doubtless because I went there anticipating a duel, and have not yet quite recovered from that gloomy mood." I laughed again. "But our supposedly fearsome stalker turns out to be . . . well, very much what you originally thought him to be, Meirus. An associate of mine, so to speak, sent to assist me in my historical quest."

Now the Mudman was frowning thoughtfully, so it occurred to me that I might be seeming *over*-ready to laugh away everyone's earlier anxieties.

But Meirus said only, "Come then, Marshal. Come and eat. There is food still on the table."

"And tell us all about it," Swanilda said merrily. "Who Thor really is, and why he is here."

I had a good many more things on my mind than the appeasement of simple hunger, but I tried to conceal my inward agitation and to make as good a show of appetite as I could. Swanilda and Meirus apparently had already eaten their fill, so they merely sipped wine as they listened to me. I daresay Maggot also had dined to repletion, but he companionably and voraciously continued to eat for as long as I did, perhaps because this may have been the first time he had ever been allowed to eat at a table indoors. When I told my story, I tried not to talk too glibly, as if I had been practicing it—which I had, in my head—so I spoke in snatches, between bites of food and gulps of wine.

"I do not know if it was coincidence," I said, "or it may be that all kings simply think alike. Anyway, at almost the same time Theodoric decided to seek an accurate history of the Goths, so did his cousin-king, Euric of the Visigoths, over in Aquitania. And Euric, like Theodoric, sent a man to retrace the old trail of those early migratory Goths. Of course, Euric bade his man Thor stop in Novae to pay his respects to Theodoric and explain his mission. And of course Theodoric told him that I was doing the same thing and was already on my way. So Thor made haste to catch up to me. As we all know now, he just missed us at Durostorum. But he stayed on our trail and, I suppose just to enliven his journey, took the notion of making a japery of that pursuit—pretending to be trailing us for some dark, mysterious purpose." I airily waved the bone I had been gnawing. "As I said, pure prankishness. And coincidence."

"Almighty coincidence," grunted Meirus. "Including the names of Thor and Thorn."

"Ja," Swanilda said gaily. "Was the name Thor only part of his japery?"

"Ne," I said. "Coincidence or not, Thor really *is* his name." And that was the first time in this telling that I told the truth—or part of the truth. "Well, our meeting was not at all friendly, at least not at first. I made the Greek at the pandokheíon show me which was Thor's chamber, and I burst in upon him with my sword drawn. If his own blade had been near to hand, we very well *might* have slain one another before any explanations could have been made. But he was undressed, ready for bed, and unarmed, so I refrained from striking the first blow. And then, of course, when his tale was told, we both had a hearty laugh over it." Swanilda and Maggot laughed as if they had been there, too, but the old Jew did not. "That is the whole story. Now Thor will be joining me on this mission, and—"

"Joining *us*," said Swanilda, laying a hand on mine.

I went on, "We will quest together, from here northward. And it may be—I have not yet had time to question him—that he already possesses knowledge that I do not. Ideas of where we might most profitably search . . . better evidence than old songs and dim recollections . . ."

"I think," said Swanilda, "that Maghib also will be wishing to join us, if that is agreeable to you."

"Ja," said the Mudman, starting suddenly from his brooding. "I am trying to persuade Maghib to go and prospect for amber on my behalf."

"But I wished to do it for *myself*," the Armenian said plaintively.

Meirus said, "Maghib, if you are willing to take your nose into those far places, that is risk enough for you. Let *me* shoulder the other risks of the venture. I will continue your wages unabated, and *then* pay you a handsome portion of the profits from all the amber you can deliver here in Noviodunum. You see? You take no risk in case amber proves undetectable to your nose."

That pendulous organ was drooping more and more, and Maggot sniffled sadly through it.

Meirus added expansively, "I will even present you with a horse of your own, young Maghib, so you do not have to trudge on foot all the way to the Amber Coast."

At that, Maggot flinched slightly. But then he sighed and helplessly spread his hands in a gesture of resigned surrender.

"There we are, then!" the Mudman crowed triumphantly. "Saio Thorn, as marshal of the king, will you see this worthy subject of the king safely to the shores of the Wendic Gulf?"

"Well, now . . ." I said, and drummed my fingers on the table. "Look here. What I undertook as a solitary mission has been accreting company all along the way." Swanilda gave me a startled look, so I addressed her directly. "I told you in the beginning, my dear, that there is terra incognita ahead,

617

possibly teeming with savages. It is certain that the fewer we are, the more likely we are to survive—to get the information we seek." I glanced around at the others. "I cannot refuse to take along my new associate, for Thor is the emissary of another king, and charged with the same mission. But I have to say that this quest is becoming a *clutter*."

Swanilda was now looking dreadfully hurt, and Maggot very downcast, and Meirus was regarding me steadily, but with no expression at all. I concluded my argument:

"I trust you all understand. I must talk this over with Thor. I cannot decide, on my own, who will compose this company from this point onward."

Swanilda nodded, but sadly, and so did Maggot.

"Now," I said, "I will return to the pandokheíon and sit down with Thor in my chambers, where I have certain notes and maps that I made earlier in this journey. I will share with him all that I have learned so far, and solicit what knowledge he has—and discuss what he and I will do next, and with what companions, if any. That will probably keep us up all night, and when we finally do sleep we will no doubt sleep late. Since that chamber is also Swanilda's, and Thor and I will be monopolizing it, I would ask you, Meirus, if you might be hospitable enough to let her stay here until I come tomorrow and call for her."

618

"I will do that," he said to me, very frostily, and then to Swanilda, most warmly, "Will you do an old man the honor of accepting his invitation to lodge here this night?"

She nodded again, looking stricken, and she said nothing, not even a "gods nahts" to me as I departed.

✠　　✠　　✠

Thor was already in my chambers when I arrived there, and asked, "What did you tell them?"

I said, "I lied."

6

"ou lied?" said Thor, but indifferently, uncaringly. "Why bother?"

"Because the Mudman was carping at all the coincidences attendant on our encounter. If he—or anyone—knew how many coincidences really conspired to bring us together . . ."

"Incredible, ja. But *you* are incredible. *I* am incredible. So let the ignorant be incredulous. Why should you and I care what anyone besides ourselves may think of us? And you have not yet told me . . . what *do* you think of me? Am I not personable? Desirable? Irresistible?"

Thor was lying naked on my bed, and now smiled provocatively and stretched voluptuously in the warm lamplight, to show off a face and body that I would indeed have praised, acclaimed, exalted—except that to do so would have been most shamelessly immodest of me, because the face and body were so very nearly my own.

Still smiling and slightly undulating, Thor murmured, "I once heard a priest say that the only irredeemably credulous people are those who do *not* believe in miracles."

I remembered how I had first seen Thor, at a distance, on the dock at Durostorum as my barge pulled away from there, and even then, from afar, I had discerned something curiously familiar in that figure. Thor was a Visigoth, two years younger than the age I estimated myself to be, and was a finger's breadth shorter than my height, and was of the same slight build and fine-textured fair skin. We were not twin-identical of face, Thor's being more triangular and sharper of features, but we both would have been called exceptionally handsome—or beautiful. We both were beardless, and Thor's hair was the same pale gold as mine, worn at the same medium length, suitable to either a man or a woman. Thor's voice was equally ambiguous, soft but husky. The most

619

immediately noticeable difference between us, when we both were clothed, was that Thor's eyes were blue and mine gray.

Unclothed . . .

"Look at me," said Thor, standing up and standing close to me.

"I have been looking."

"Look at me some more. It has taken us all our lives to find one another. Look at me and tell me how jubilant you are that I have found you and you have found me. Tell me how much you long to possess me . .. . while I undress you . . . like this. Then I will gaze at *you*, Thorn. And tell *you* tender things."

Except for having seen my own reflection in water or in a speculum, where of course I could not have seen even my own self reflected entire, I had never before had the opportunity of looking my fill at a naked mannamavi. During our brief earlier meeting, Thor had stunned me by proudly exposing to me only what I might call the essentials, and, though more reticently, I had reciprocated, and thus we two manna-mavjos had identified ourselves to one another, as it were.

Now, seeing Thor totally disrobed, I decided that the exuberantly tip-tilted breasts might be a trifle more full than mine, their nipples and areolae larger, darker, more feminine. Thor's navel was a dimple as unobtrusive as mine; the pubic escutcheon was of curlier hair and more distinctly delta-shaped. I could make no comparison of our buttocks, never having seen my own, but I hoped that mine were that firm and peach-tinted and nicely contoured. Thor's male organ, at this moment standing as if to invite inspection, was shorter, thicker than mine—I might say stubby, more like a woman's genital nub extraordinarily overgrown—and, in fascinum erection, it pointed forward rather than upward. Behind it, there was no testicular sac, but a cloven purse, like my own, and Thor's was at this moment pouting a little open, like a mouth about to kiss . . .

Now I was naked, too, and assuredly displaying similar signs of arousal, but Thor was raptly gazing at only my throat.

"I am so glad to see that you also wear the Venus collar."

"What?"

"You were not aware that you have one? You did not notice that I do?"

"I am wearing nothing whatsoever. Or nothing but the gooseflesh of excitement. I do not know what a Venus collar is."

"This little crease that encircles your throat, just here." Thor traced it with a fingertip, making my gooseflesh positively ripple. "Men do not have it, and only certain women. And at least we two happy mannamavjos. It is not a wrinkle, for it is evident in the smallest girl-child, long before she merits it."

"Merits it *how?*"

"The Venus collar is the certain indication of a prodigious appetite for sexual indulgence. Have you not seen some women wearing a ribbon about their neck, right there? They are chastely trying to conceal that evidence"—Thor laughed—"or trying to pretend that they *have* it."

Though I had not noticed our matching Venus collars, I could not have missed seeing the one glaring difference between our bodies. My own bore only trivial marks of misfortunes past—the tiny scar that bisected my left eyebrow, where I had long ago been clubbed by that Burgund farmer, and the crescent scar on my right forearm, where Theodoric had excised the snakebite. But Thor's upper back, between the shoulder blades, was blemished by a really gruesome scar. It was shiny white and puckered, so old a scar that Thor must have acquired it in childhood. It was as big as my palm, and it was the memento of no accident, for it was in the shape of the "cramped cross," those four right-angled arms that represent the god Thor's hammer being swung in a circle. It hurt me just to look at the scar, as if I could feel the searing pain of its being cut or burned into the child Thor's smooth skin.

621

I asked, "How did you get that?"

"My very first male lover," said Thor, as casually as if neither the lover nor the injury mattered at all. "I was very young and not very faithful. He was very jealous and not very forgiving. Hence the brand of shame."

"Why brand you with the gammadion?"

Thor shrugged carelessly. "Ironic humor, I suppose. Because Thor's hammer is swung over the newlywed, to assure constancy. But I try to make *some* use of everything that comes my way. The scar at least gave me the idea of adopting Thor as my masculine name."

"And you said your feminine name is Genovefa. How long have you had that?"

"As long as I can remember. The nuns gave me that one in my infancy. They named me after the queen-wife of the great Visigoth warrior Alareikhs."

"Interesting," I said. "I got my names just the other way about. The masculine Thorn in my infancy, and I later chose Veleda for the feminine."

Thor gave me an inviting smile and an intimate caress. "Are you nervous, Thorn-Veleda? Is that why you prolong the talking? Really, Thorn! This night was a long time coming. Here. Let us lie down and prove what our Venus collars promise."

As we reclined, I said, a trifle shakily, "I thought myself experienced and worldly. But this is a . . . first time . . ."

"Akh, for me as well. And *vái!* for all I know, it may be a first time in human history. So . . . this first time . . . who shall we be? Will you be Thorn or Veleda? Shall I be Thor or Genovefa?"

"I . . . frankly, I do not even know how to begin . . ."

"Let us hold one another in tight embrace, and begin with kissing, and simply see what happens . . ."

We had been doing that for only a short time before one of us, I forget which, quietly laughed and then murmured:

"I am finding it difficult to clasp you as close as I would wish."

"Ja. Something encroaches between us."

"Two things, actually."

"They want satisfaction."

"Most insistent, are they not?"

"We ought to oblige at least one of them."

"Ja. This one. Yours."

"Ja . . . ah-h-h . . ."

Right here, I have to confess that, when Thor and I coupled, my fond recollections of the delights accorded me by previous lovers began to dim and dwindle. The pleasures I had so recently been relishing with Swanilda seemed tepid in comparison to what I was now given to savor. So did every other consummation, every other partner, in all my life past—Widamer, Renata, Naranj, Dona, Deidamia, the others whose names I have forgotten—even the Gudinand of long-treasured memory.

It must be manifest to anyone of any other sex that the physical *means* of mutual stimulation and satisfaction possessed by two mannamavjos are not just numerous but capable of almost infinite variation and combination of application. It ought also to be self-evident that the multifarious pleasures thus produced are of nearly as infinite *duration*. Though our male parts would, like those of a normal male, require intervals of rest and regeneration, our female parts, like those of a normal female, could go on functioning almost indefinitely without depleting their energies, exudations, responses and sensations. And it may have been, as Thor claimed was indicated by our both wearing the Venus collars, that Thor and I had female resources even exceeding the normal.

What is probably not so manifest is the *intensity* of thrill, passion, ecstasy, delirium, paroxysm attainable by two mannamavjos in sexual embrace. I can only inadequately describe it by calculating that it must reach threefold the peak of sensation ever possible—or even imaginable—in the copulation of man and woman, or man and man, or woman and woman. In my dalliances with other partners, I had sometimes indulged the fantasy of picturing myself, or each of us, as being some other person, or several persons. But Thor and I really *were*. Each of us was literally, physically, authentically two persons. Therefore, at every blissful moment, each *one* of us was partaking of the rapture of all the other three.

"Let us do it in a different manner this time."

"Ja. Like this, shall we?"

"Ja . . . ah-h-h . . ."

If there was one thing that prevented my enjoying this night wholeheartedly, it was a small puzzlement lurking somewhere in my mind. Ever since Swanilda had remarked on the similarity of the names Thor and Thorn, I had been—what?—stirred? bothered? excited? disquieted?—every time I heard the name Thor spoken. But why? I might have had some premonition of who and what Thor really was. But the prospect of discovering that I was not unique among humankind should hardly have annoyed or affrighted me. After all, from my childhood days, when I had learned what *I* was, I had wistfully hoped to meet another like myself.

623

Then was it possible that I had had a premonition of something else? Of something *dire* in the coming together of Thor and Thorn? I could hardly believe that, either. If ever there had been two human beings designed by nature to give joy to one another, destined by nature to cleave to one another, it had to be Thor and Thorn. And certainly Thor had not been troubled by any misgivings. On first hearing a hint of my existence—that there might just be another mannamavi living in the same world at the same time—Thor had eagerly set out in search of me.

It was all the doing of Widamer, that emissary from the Visigoth court at Tolosa, because his visit to his cousin Theodoric at Novae had involved him first in some felicitous hours with a townswoman named Veleda, and then in an equivocal encounter with a herizogo named Thorn.

Widamer's parting words to me had been "This I will ponder on . . . and remember . . ." And so he obviously had done, though it seems he never did quite construe the real connection between Veleda and Thorn. Anyway, later, at a festive convivium in Tolosa, when he was perhaps inebriated, Widamer uttered some remark about the baffling two persons he had met in Novae. It may have been only a frivolous or even salacious speculation on the nature of those two persons. However, one among the guests at that convivium, hearing the remark, had instantly grasped what Widamer had not. The very next morning, Thor had saddled a horse and ridden eastward toward Novae. Learning there that I was off on a quest, Thor had followed, and kept on following, and finally had found me, and now here we were, intertwined.

"Vái," said Thor good-humoredly. "That last contortion has given me a cramp."

I laughed. "It must be what the apostle meant when he said that the spirit is willing, but the flesh is weak."

"Not so much the flesh as the muscles. I am less athletic and gymnastic than an outdoorsman like you. Let us rest a moment."

While we lay there, trembling slightly from our exertions, I asked, "Do you remember yet, Thor, exactly what it was that Widamer said?"

"Ne. But it gave me only a hint, not a certainty of what I would find. The woman Veleda that he mentioned, well, she *could* have been nothing but a real woman—deluding everyone in Novae with her impersonation of a man named Thorn. Nevertheless, I went . . . in hopes . . ."

I said admiringly, "You came all this way, sustained merely by those hopes."

"And a devilish chase you led me, I must say. I have always been a city dweller, and I was delicately reared, and I am not at all adventurous. I have no love of robust activities or of travel or of the wilderness."

"If you dislike travel, why do you own a horse?"

"I do not. I stole the one I am riding."

"You *stole* it?!" I exclaimed, aghast. "Why, that is a capital offense! You will be hanged . . . crucified . . ."

Thor said negligently, "Only if I am fool enough to go back to Tolosa, where I stole it."

I was stupefied. I had never heard of any criminal so recklessly confessing such a heinous crime. Granted, I personally had not always been the most law-abiding and sinless of mortals, but neither had I ever spoken blithely of my transgressions or, in my own mind, lightly regarded them. However, even the killings I had done, I could not count as vile as stealing the horse of another man of one's own people. That villainy is adjudged, in Gothic law and custom and general opprobrium, more reprehensible than murder. What bothered me most was that the evildoer in this case, unconscious or uncaring of having committed such a gross immorality, was the one person in the world nearest being my kindred spirit . . . or my twin . . . or my destined mate . . . nearest, in fact, being *me myself*.

Possibly sensing my dismay and disapproval, Thor got up and wandered about the room, then opened the closet in which I had stored my spare clothes before Swanilda and I rode out into the delta. Finding among them my Veleda garments, Thor got those out and began fingering and examining them. The coiled-bronze breast guard that I had bought in Haustaths seemed of particular fascination. Thor put it on and, otherwise still naked, went to lean over the water basin, bending this way and that to admire the reflection. I already had been shown the feminine attire that Thor also carried—including a hip-band undergarment, like my own, to bind and conceal the male organ—so I refrained from voicing annoyance at Thor's so impudently toying with my belongings. Also, eyeing that ugly gammadion scar on Thor's back, I felt inclined to leniency even in greater matters. Perhaps ill treatment in early life accounted for Thor's seemingly insensitive disregard of other people's property.

625

I said, "You do not intend ever to return to Tolosa? But I would have assumed, from your attending a convivium at the court there, that you must be a young noble of some degree."

"Would that I were," Thor said, then stunned me yet again. "I am—or I was—cosmeta and tonstrix to King Euric's wife, Queen Ragna."

"What? A *male* cosmeta? A cosmeta named *Thor?*"

"Named Genovefa. And not male. In my native Tolosa, and wherever else in the Visigoth lands that I have gone in company with the queen, I was known and respected as her skillful cosmeta Genovefa. I have striven not to sully that reputation. Genovefa's little indiscretions have always been conducted discreetly. Only when I had to satisfy my male urges have I become Thor, and on those occasions I would sneak off to a low lupanar where the women ask few questions of the men who rut upon them."

"Interesting," I said again. "I too go to great lengths to protect my identity, only the other way about. I live publicly as a male."

"I told you, I was delicately reared. I was a foundling, raised and trained by nuns, and taught the occupations suitable to a female. Sewing, cleaning, cooking, eventually the arts of applying cosmetics, dyeing and crimping hair. And then I left the convent to make my own way in the world."

"But, while you lived there, did not any of the nuns notice . . . well . . . that you were different?"

Thor smiled reminiscently. "What would nuns know of such things? When I was a child, they regarded me compassionately—a poor little girl afflicted with an unfortunate but not disabling abnormality. When I grew into puberty, they discovered that my abnormality had its uses. They may not have known what to call it, but they made use of it, in secret—everyone from the elderly prioress to the novices. Nevertheless, all the time I lived among them, they thought me just an oddly developed female. And so did I."

"How did you learn the truth?"

"When I was fourteen, the prioress found me employment as cosmeta to a Tolosa matron. And the lady's husband soon found other employment for such a pretty girl as I was. He was not at all disturbed, but overjoyed, when he encountered my . . . unique equipment. He called it my 'overblown rose,' and said it beguiled him, excited him. He seemed never to imagine that my equipment might someday compete with his. But the lady did, when one day we bathed together and *she* espied my overblown rose. It was she who taught me how to function as a male—in that regard, at least."

Thor paused and shrugged. "Akh, well, my namesake, King Alareikhs's Queen Genovefa, was an adulteress too. For more than a year, I alternated between serving master and mistress, sometimes both within the span of one sexta resting hour. The lady was well aware of my being her husband's nymph, and never objected to that. But when he caught me energetically playing satyr to his wife, he raged and then he wept. Then he burned the brand into my back and threw me out of the house."

"Well, let us hope that your hurts and your scandals and your sneakings-about are behind you now. Henceforth, perhaps you will be able to gratify *all* your urges without stealth, without having to seek. Or stray."

"You mean . . . with you?" Thor let drop my Veleda garments and smiled across the room at me. "Openly with you? And *only* with you?" Next moment, Thor was lying close against me again and making soft caresses. "Does that mean you love me already? Or is it merely lust? But akh! lust is love enough, surely!"

"Hold! Hold!" I said gently. "Let me tell you the lies that I told about you to my friends here."

"Why?"

"So that you will not contradict my account of our meeting when you talk to Meirus or Swanilda or Maggot."

"Why should I talk to them?"

"Because they are all involved, one way or another, in my mission of compiling a Gothic history."

Thor drew a little away. "I was hoping that, after tonight, you would abandon that silly mission."

"Abandon it? I am on the king's business!"

"Well? I rode away from a queen, without explanation or apology, just to find you. More than likely Queen Ragna has cursed me with a Sending." Apparently not worried by that prospect, Thor snickered and added, "I know very well that she must *look* like a haliuruns hag by now, bereft of my services."

"I am flattered that you were so eager to find me. But I must point out that you were a cosmeta. I am a king's marshal."

Thor drew farther away from me, and said petulantly, "Akh, ja. *Only* a cosmeta. This lowly domestic begs your pardon, clarissimus. You are ever so much better than I am. I must forever bow to your wishes."

"Now, now. I did not mean to sound belittling or—"

"You have the superiority of rank, Saio Thorn, but only when you are wearing your title and your insignia *and your clothes*. Right now, I see on this bed only two naked mannamavjos, both of them abnormities, outcasts from all normal folk. Neither of them one iota better or different or of higher status than the other."

"True enough," I said, but stiffly. "Still, you must concede that you had rather less to give up than a marshalcy."

Thor abruptly warmed again. "Vái, we are quarreling—like any commonplace man and wife. We must never do that. You and I are two against the world. Here . . . let me hold you again . . ."

In another moment we were doing something that would be anatomically impossible to any other two human beings of whatever sex. And the culmination of it was so sublimely paradisiacal as to be indescribable to anyone of any other sex except mannamavi—and then *only* to a mannamavi, like Thor or myself, who had had the transcendent good fortune, like Thor and myself, to have found and coupled with another mannamavi.

And here I must confess something else, or many of my subsequent actions will be unfathomable.

To be quite truthful, before this night was over, I was abjectly besotted. I had by no means fallen in love; I was not even moonily infatuated with Thor *as Thor*; I was simply overwhelmed and captivated by the superabundance of sexual gratification that Thor provided. I hardly need say that I

627

had never in my life suffered from the crippling Christian vice of pudicity, nor had I been abstemious of sexual appetite, nor had I been lacking for opportunities to slake that appetite. But suddenly I was like a gluttonous man who, long constrained to a frugal diet, at last comes upon an inexhaustibly bountiful table—and not just of staple fare but of ambrosial delicacies—wherewith to feed his insatiable gluttony over and over again. Finding myself now fettered by an addiction to sexual surfeit, I was able to understand how a drunkard gets enslaved by his wine, and why the old hermit Galindo repulsed every company and comfort except that afforded by his damnable weed smoke.

When, after that lyrical round of our debauch, we lay with our bodies glistening of sweat, I said:

"Since you followed me here, Thor, knowing of my quest, I would have expected you to join me in it, not speak of my abandoning it."

Thor said again, "I detest travel and hardship and the outdoor life. I much prefer a settled and sheltered existence. To attain that—*and with you*—I should be not at all reluctant to give up the dubious advantages of my dual identity. I should be not at all fearful to live as my true self, and cheerfully endure whatever infamy it might cost me. Why would you be averse to doing the same, Thorn? In Novae, I learned that you are passably wealthy, and I was shown your fine estate. Why should not you and I simply go back there, live comfortably and happily together in leisured retirement, and let the commonfolk think or say what they will?"

"Liufs Guth!" I exclaimed. "I worked, I fought, I killed to earn the rank and affluence of a herizogo. I have worked and fought and killed to deserve the keeping of my station. If King Theodoric were to learn that he had conferred nobility on a mannamavi, how long do you think I would be a herizogo? Or affluent? Or owner of that estate? Ne, I will not throw away everything I possess, merely to make a show of defiance to the normal world."

It occurred to me that I was sounding very like a Christian: staunchly insistent on being good and doing right only for the rewards attendant on such behavior. So I said also:

"Theodoric and I were friends long before he became king and I swore my auths and he made me his marshal. Our very first meeting occurred when he saved me from dying of an adder bite. I owe more than vassal fealty to the king, I owe comradely loyalty to the man. And with the privileges of herizogo rank, I took on responsibilities as well. More than that, I have my own self-respect to maintain. I accepted this mission; I will pursue it. You may come with me, Thor, or stay and wait for me, as you choose."

If those sound like firm and masterful words, they actually constituted a weakling evasion. I omitted to mention a third alternative: that Thor return to Tolosa or go elsewhere, and leave me forever. But remember, I was already besotted. Anyway, although Thor could not have helped noticing that I had laid down only two of the three choices open, I heard no exulting over that, only a sulky silence. So, while I waited somewhat anxiously for Thor to say, "I will go with you" or "I will wait for you," I remarked:

"By the way, my companion Swanilda was also formerly a cosmeta. First to Theodoric's princess-sister and then to his—"

That made Thor speak, and with vehemence: "Vái! You demand fidelity and constancy from me, but you have had that trull with you all the way from Novae!"

I tried to protest, "I have demanded nothing from—"

"You said I need seek no more. Or stray. Are you now telling me that, from here on, I will have to share you with that drab?"

"Ne, ne," I said irresolutely. "That would hardly be fair to either of you. And, expecting that you would travel with me, I have already spoken to Swanilda . . . intimating that I may soon be dispensing with her company . . ."

"I should hope so! And who is the Maggot of whom you spoke? Is that your male concubine?"

I had to laugh at that absurdity, which rather spoiled the severity of my cautioning Thor, "Now see here! I grant that you were right in what you said before—about our being equal when stripped of clothes and other superficialities. If we are to be a pair from now on, I promise not to be a dominating husband or a domineering wife. But so must you promise. And bear in mind: this is my quest. I will take with me whomever I choose and, however many or few we are, when it comes to matters of decision and command, I am the leader of our company."

"Vái, vái, vái!" Thor said, again abruptly in good humor. "Another quarrel? Why must you keep picking quarrels, Thorn, and wasting so much of our first night together? Come, let us kiss away the quarrel and then resume . . ."

"Really, Thor. It must be almost dawn."

"So? We will sleep when we have not vigor or imagination enough to do anything better. Then you will go a-questing—and ja, of course I will be going with you. But the Goths' trail is already centuries old; it can wait a while longer. My . . . urges . . . are more urgent. Are not yours, niu?"

Certain it is that I did not then love Thor, nor Thor me. But it is equally certain that we both were dazedly, nearly dementedly, obsessed with one another, from the very start of our association, as if we had been smitten by the Sending of a haliuruns or by the conjuration of Dus, the skohl of lechery. It is evidence of our mutual nympholepsy that, at some moment during our next intertwining that night, one of us gasped:

"Akh, I dearly wish I could give you a child . . ."

And the other: "Akh, I dearly wish I could bear your child . . ."

But I do not remember which of us voiced which words.

✠   ✠   ✠

"Iésus Xristus!"

She spoke not very loudly, but it woke me, and my first thought was that it was the only time I had ever heard Swanilda use the name of Jesus as an expletive. My second thought was of relief that Thor and I were fairly well tangled in our blankets, because full daylight was streaming in the chamber window, and Swanilda had obviously seen us lying in close embrace. Then the door banged as she backed out of the room. I scrambled from the bed, but Thor only laughed.

"She keeps close ward of you, niu?"

"Be quiet," I growled, fumblingly starting to get into my clothes.

"Well, if she did not share your secret before, she does now. And if I know women—and I do, I do—she will very soon be telling it to all creation."

"I think not," I muttered. "But I must make sure."

"There is only one sure way to stop a woman's mouth. And that is with the earth she gets buried in."

"*Will* you be quiet? Damnation, what has become of my other boot?"

Thor got up, rummaged under the bed and came grinning across the room to hand me the boot. Even in my state of mingled vexation, guilt and anxiety, I had to admire anew the beauty of Thor's naked body, bright in the morning sun. However ungallantly, I had to acknowledge that Thor moved with more lissome grace than Swanilda did. Then I winced, when the bright body turned and I saw the dead-white Thor's-hammer scar.

"I will escort Swanilda back to Meirus's house," I said. "You stay here,

Thor. Get dressed, break your fast, do whatever you will. Only stay well out of sight. Give me ample time to soothe Swanilda and find out how much she may have conjectured. I will meet you sometime later at Meirus's dockside warehouse."

I turned to go, but Thor detained me long enough to make the immemorial female gesture of possession: picking a bit of lint off my tunic before I went out in public. Then I hastened from the room and from the building. I thought Swanilda might have fled fast and far, but she was only shuffling miserably across the pandokheíon's stableyard. When I caught up to her, I said the first thing that came into my head:

"Have you broken your fast, Swanilda?"

She said sharply, "Of course. It is almost midday. Meirus fed me." But when she turned her face to me it was not angry; it was wet with tears.

I decided against delaying or dodging the issue. "My dear, you told me yourself, before we commenced this journey, that at any time I had only to say, 'Swanilda, enough.' "

She wiped at her eyes. "Akh, darling Thorn, I had nerved myself against the likelihood of someday losing you. Perhaps to another fair princess like Amalamena. I never dreamed I might lose you *to a man.*"

631

I sighed thankfully. Then Thor and I *had* been sufficiently covered by the blankets. Swanilda only thought she knew what she had seen.

I said, "But, as I told you earlier, Thor and I had much to discuss last night. Then, overcome by sleep, we simply collapsed."

"Into one another's arms. Do not dissemble, Thorn. I make no reproach. After all, I need not have walked in on you. I am troubled only because . . . because I believed I knew you well." She tried to laugh, and sobbed instead. "I did not, did I?"

I was less than pleased to have Thor and myself taken for a pair of despicable concacati, but that was preferable to our being recognized and perhaps loudly proclaimed for what we really were.

"I am sorry you found out, Swanilda. Or at least that you found out in such a jarring way. But there are still things of which you cannot possibly be aware. If you were, you might think more kindly of me."

"I do not think ill of you," she said, and sounded sincere. "I will leave you to your—your preferences. But I will not leave *you*. Let us get on with the mission."

"Ne, let us not."

She looked incredulous. "You would give up the quest?"

"Ne, I will give up only your company. I would like you to return to Novae."

Now she looked distressed. "Akh, Thorn, when I told you that you could say, 'Swanilda, enough,' I told you also that I would thenceforth be your humble servant. Please—let me be at least that to you."

I shook my head. "It would be intolerable for you, for me, for everybody. You are bound to realize that, and better now than later."

And now she looked desolated. *"Please, Thorn!"*

"Swanilda, I do not put much store in wise-sayers, but perhaps once in a great while they are worth heeding. Last night Meirus predicted that this very day you would cease to regard me fondly. I suggest that you do exactly that."

"I cannot!"

"Do. It will make our parting easier, and part we must. Now come, walk with me to the old Jew's house. I am quite befogged by lack of sleep. I will beg from him a waking drink of wine and a bit of food."

Meirus greeted me with only a grunt, and only grudgingly bade a servant fetch the meal I requested, and meanwhile flicked his beetling gaze back and forth from me to Swanilda. She had accompanied me in silence, but dragging her steps, and her countenance was woeful. Nevertheless, she said nothing to the Mudman of what she had found at the pandokheíon, saying only that she would get her horse and lead it back there, to retrieve and pack what belongings she had left in our chambers. It was left to me to tell Meirus that I was sending Swanilda home to Novae—to make our company less cumbersome, I said. That seemed to dye the old Jew's black mood even blacker, so I tried to lighten it by telling him:

"My associate Thor and I discussed the matter of your prospector. Between us, we have decided that we *will* let Maggot ride with us, and we shall strive to set him safe and sound on the Amber Coast."

"Thags izei to you both," Meirus grumbled sourly.

I went on leisurely eating and drinking until he unbent and said:

"Thags *izvis*, Saio Thorn. I hope to make great profit from that venture, and I am sure Maghib will benefit by seeing new horizons. I only hope that he and your new friend Thor together will prove half as worthy a companion to you as the girl Swanilda has been."

I did not deign to comment on that, and got up from the table. "Then let us go and tell Maggot to prepare to travel. I should also like to inspect the horse you promised him."

"Maghib is at the warehouse, waiting for you. I will tell my groom to bring a number of horses, from which you and he may choose."

632

"Good," I said. "Thor also will be joining us there. You two will get to meet again."

"Biy yom sameakh."

"What?"

"I said, 'O joyful day,'" he growled, and went out a back door as I went out the front.

Maggot was standing in the street door of the warehouse, as if he was awaiting me most impatiently, but he did not look *happy* to see me. He was holding the reins of Swanilda's horse, and it was saddled and wearing its pack, so I supposed that she also was here, waiting inside to say goodbye when we had all forgathered.

"Háils, Maggot! I have good news for you. If you are still of a mind to go adventuring, Thor and I invite you to ride with us."

He did not effusively thank me, or caper with glee, but said only, "The lady Swanilda . . ."

"She will not be coming with us."

"Ne," he said, in a sort of croak, and pointed to the building's dark interior. "The lady Swanilda . . ."

"I know," I said. "We will all say farewell to her."

"You *know?*" he said, in a sort of squeak, and goggled his eyes.

"What is the matter with you?" I demanded.

"With *me?!*" he said, in a sort of bleat, and pointed again inside the warehouse.

Wondering, I strode in there. It took some moments for my vision to adjust to the darkness. Then I saw what Maggot had meant. From a high corner beam hung a tangle of leather harness, stretched taut because its lower straps were knotted about the neck of the small dangling corpse.

633

7

I instantly drew my sword, slashed the leathers and caught her limp body in my arms, but I could as instantly tell that it was too late for resuscitation. Gently settling the still-warm corpse on a hay bale, I said, half to myself, half to the hovering Maggot:

"How could a living person go from such a beautiful sunny day as it is outside into such a dank and malodorous place as this and do to herself such a horrible thing?"

"She must have thought you would approve," said a rough voice, and I realized that Meirus had joined us. "Swanilda was ever ready to do anything that might please you."

There was too much truth in that for me to gainsay it, so I took refuge in equivocation. I wheeled on him and said angrily:

"Or did she simply do what you foretold, Mudman? Why try to blame this on me when you could have *prevented* it?"

He did not back away, but stood firm. "I foresaw only the cessation of her affection for you. I did not foresee the manner of its happening—in one last act of affection. Or of abnegation. She was giving you up, Saio Thorn. But to what?"

"To his duty and destiny, perhaps," said another voice, soft but smoky. "A man with a mission should not have to drag along the useless weight of a mere—"

"Be silent, Thor!" I barked, and Meirus gave the newcomer one of his black looks.

For a moment we were all quiet, gazing at the pitiable small cadaver. I said, again half to myself:

"I was sending her home to Novae, and alone. I had forgotten what she told me once. Without a mistress or a master, she was a forlorn orphan. I suppose that was what impelled her . . ." Then I looked up and saw Thor's eyes on me, mocking, almost challenging. So I tried hard to put on a semblance of manly induration.

"Well, whatever her reason," I said, as coolly as I could, "I wish . . . she had not done it . . ." There my voice threatened to break, so I turned to Meirus and said, "You see, as a Christian, she has sinned unforgivably against God's will and grace and judgment. She must be buried without priest or rites or absolution, only with execration, and in unhallowed ground, her grave unmarked."

Meirus scornfully spat, *"Tsephúwa!"* which sounded like an exceptionally filthy vituperation. "You may think little of Judaismus, Marshal, but it is not so cold and cruel a religion as Christianity. Leave the poor dead girl to me. I shall see that she is buried with unchristian compassion and decency and dignity."

"I am grateful to you, good Mudman," I said, and with heartfelt sincerity. "If I may return the favor in a small way, there will be no need for you to provide a horse for Maggot." I turned to the Armenian. "If you still wish to ride with us, yonder is Swanilda's mount, already saddled."

He looked rather indecisively from me to Meirus and Thor, until his master urged, "Take it, Maghib. It is a better steed than any in my stable." And Maggot made a gesture of resigned acceptance.

Then Meirus—oddly, I thought—asked Thor instead of me, "Would you examine this parchment I wrote, fráuja Thor, and see if it is in order? The document accredits Maghib to act in my interests in the amber trade."

Thor took a step back from the proffered parchment, a little flushed of face and seeming momentarily flustered. Then, recovering the demeanor that Meirus had repeatedly called "arrogant," Thor said loftily, "I know nothing of the amber trade *or* of the clerk's trade. Which is to say that I know nothing of the clerkish drudgery of reading."

"Say you so?" Meirus grunted, and handed the rolled parchment to me. "I should have supposed that the ability to read would be a necessity for an emissary sent by King Euric to compile a history."

Pretending indifference to that exchange of words, I opened the document, scanned it, nodded and tucked it inside my tunic. But in truth I was embarrassed far more than Thor appeared to be. Although I was no augur like the Mudman, I *might* have thought to assure myself of the qualifications of my "associate historian" before announcing Thor as such. I had simply taken it for granted that someone as well-spoken as Thor must logically be literate. But of course a cosmeta continually

635

exposed to the conversation of court ladies could easily accrete an over-
lay of *seeming* courtliness and cultivation. Anyway, I only said to Maggot:

"You may also find use for some of the things in Swanilda's packs.
Her sleeping furs, her winter traveling cloak. You are not much bigger
than she is—than she was. There are some cooking utensils in there,
too."

"Pardon, fráuja," Maggot said meekly. "I do not know how to cook."

"*That* much, Thor knows," I said, wickedly implying that Thor might
know little else, and it gave me some satisfaction to see Thor bridle
with indignation. I added my first command as leader of this company,
"Thor will do the cooking for us during this journey."

I bent to give Swanilda one last kiss, earning another indignant look
from Thor. But I kissed only the dead girl's hand, because the face of a
person who has strangled to death is too terrible to kiss. And I said a
silent farewell to her, and made a silent promise: that if I survived the
journey and completed the Gothic history, and wrote it down for others
to read, I would inscribe its dedication to Swanilda.

✠　　✠　　✠

After Maggot had packed his own belongings behind his saddle, we rode
three abreast out of Noviodunum. I did not again let the Armenian
ride my Velox, deciding that he might as well start learning some horsemanship unaided by the foot-rope. Also I figured that, since we were
getting a late start and so would be only half a day in the saddle, he
should not be *too* sore and stiff to recuperate overnight, and then be
able to ride again the next day.

Because I had already seen quite enough of the delta's monotonous
grasslands, I was glad that Maggot chose not to direct us straight northward. We went upstream along the Danuvius, back toward the west. In
two days or so, said Maggot, we would find a tributary river flowing
into the Danuvius from the north, the Pyretus, and we would turn
upstream along that. So we would be traveling northward through a
fairly well-wooded river valley, with a pleasantly verdant landscape to
look at and a variety of forest game to feed on.

One thing I noticed. Although Maggot rode his horse with all the
jouncing gracelessness of a sackful of assorted sticks, and had not the
least ability to keep his mount to a comfortably even gait, he did somehow manage always to be riding beside me, with me between him and
Thor. Maggot's obvious avoidance of our companion made me specu-

late on this Thor who rode with us—or, rather, on what little I knew of Thor.

And that little was hardly commendatory. Here was an impudently upjumped commoner, totally self-regarding, brazen enough to *boast* of ignorance and presumptuous enough to have assumed the name of a deity. Here was a self-confessed thief, devoid of simple decency, disrespectful of authority and law and custom, contemptuous of others' property and rights and feelings. Here was a person of a physical comeliness that should have made a friend of every stranger, but of a manner so ungracious as to ward off any friendliness. I was gradually having to admit that no one seemed to *like* this person Thor. Could even *I* say that I liked this person Thor?

As if having heard me utter the name aloud, Thor spoke up, saying conversationally:

"On this journey so far, I have found my god-name most useful. It seems to awe other men. Not once have I been beset by robbers during my travels, or plagued by thieves, or even cheated by a gasts-razn landlord. And I can only suppose that it was because my dread name went before me. As I have told you, I try to put every least thing to good use. Perhaps, Thorn, we ought now to send Maggot riding out ahead of us, to herald to all people the approach of Thor. It might prevent our having any untoward encounters."

I declined the suggestion. "I have journeyed many times, and across much of this continent, without the need of any such safeguard. I think we can do without it, Thor, and spare Maggot the humiliation of playing our slave."

Thor sniffed loudly and looked vexed, but did not press the issue, and I went on with my meditations.

Thor's personality was uninviting to others, including myself. I was not fond of this person Thor. But I had to admit to myself that, even had I found Thor thoroughly repellent of character, I would not have severed our association. And my reason for that reflects little credit on my own character. Like a drunkard or the old hermit Galindo—who would surely profess no fondness for cheap wine and foul weed, but only for the effects they produced—I could no more give up Thor than they could quit the wineskin or the smoke. However meretricious Thor's beauty, however questionable Thor's morals, I was enslaved by my lust for the gratifications that Thor, alone of all the persons in the world, could provide. Indeed, at this moment, I was rather regretting *not* having commanded Maggot to ride ahead of us. I was reluctant to waste a single night of embrace with Thor, but I did not want Maggot to see or overhear us. I soon learned, though, that Thor was nowise inhibited by such considerations.

"Vái," Thor said disdainfully when we stopped to camp and I mentioned my apprehensions. "Let the lout be scandalized. He is only an Armenian. And I would refuse to forgo my pleasures if he were a bishop."

"You, ja," I muttered, "but I still am concerned to remain anonymous. Surely you know how Armenians love to talk."

"Then let me be the one to cast away disguise, at least partially. While Maggot is tending the horses yonder, I shall dress in my Genovefa garments, and wear them henceforward as long as he is with us. We can tell him that it was only for secret state reasons that I passed as a man until now." It seemed a clever notion, and I thought it a most generous gesture, until Thor added sardonically, "You appointed me the cook of this company. I might as well dress the part, and behave as obsequiously as befits a great marshal's mere underling."

638

I tried to make a jest of that, saying, "Well, after dark we will take turns at being the *overling.*" But neither of us laughed at that poor sally, and I immediately felt ashamed of my stooping to vulgarity.

Still, the ruse worked well enough. When Maggot came, carrying an armload of wood with which to lay a fire, he evinced only mild surprise at finding me in converse with a young woman instead of Thor. He nodded courteously when I introduced "Genovefa," and if he had any doubts of the story we had confected, he did not voice them. He said only:

"Since none of us killed any game today, not even having seen any, you may be pleased to know—fráuja Thorn and fráujin Genovefa— that I took the precaution of bringing along some smoked meat and salt fish from the fráuja Meirus's kitchen."

We both expressed gladness and thanks for his thoughtfulness, and Genovefa even set to her cookery work with a will, taking a pot down to the river to get water for boiling the fare. Neither she nor Maggot chided or derided me, their leader, for having neglected to provide trail food myself. But I, realizing that this lapse was one more sign of my now fuddled intellect, resolved to be less preoccupied with my new companion, from now on, and to give more attention to my responsibilities.

When we had eaten our rude meal, and Genovefa had sand-scoured our few utensils, and I had banked the fire for the night, we each began to lay out sleeping furs—and Maggot took his a respectful distance off along the riverbank, well out of sight of us. I doubt, though, that he was out of hearing, for Genovefa-Thor and Thorn-Veleda made many loud and blithesome cries in the course of that night.

The next day, and all the days thereafter—during the daylight hours, at least—Thor remained in the guise of Genovefa, and Maggot addressed her always as fráujin, and I as Genovefa. I came to regard her as exclusively female—during the daylight hours, at least—and found that, in my thoughts as well as in my spoken words, I was referring to her *as* a "her." Until now, neither in speech nor in my mind had I employed "he" or "she" or "it" or *any* kind of referent pronoun, because there simply does not exist—in the Old Language or in Latin or Greek or, as far as I know, in any other language—a pronoun suitable to a mannamavi.

✠ ✠ ✠

As I well knew from having come down this stretch of the Danuvius, it did so much twisting and turning hereabout, and split so often into divergent channels, and was flanked by so many lakes and meres, that I might not have recognized the tributary river we were headed for, but Maggot did when we reached it. Though less imposing than the mighty Danuvius that it flowed into, the Pyretus was no inconsiderable stream itself. It bore a fair traffic of transport barges and, at open intervals in the woods that lined its banks, there were thriving farmsteads and now and again a village, sometimes of respectable size. The river was rich with fish, and Maggot proved adept at catching them. The woods were rich with game, and I could almost choose which meat I would bring down for us to eat each night.

This country north of the Danuvius was called Old Dacia and was considered, by all the Roman citizens south of the Danuvius, to be a primeval, trackless fastness populated only by savage barbarians. But I had early learned that "barbarians are everyone else," so I did not much fear meeting veritable wild men. And in fact I now discovered that most of the people of these lands, while they lacked many of the amenities and graces of civilization, had made domesticated islands in the wilderness, where they lived peaceably, productively and more or less contentedly. Akh, here and there we did encounter *real* barbarians, nomad families and tribes that merely wandered about and lived by hunting and gathering. They were remnants of the people called Avars and Kutriguri, clearly relatives of the Huns, for they were yellowish of skin, pouchy of eyes, hairy, filthy and verminous. None of those we met gave us any trouble beyond importunate begging—not for money, but just for salt or spare clothes or scraps from our kills of game.

The settled communities that we came upon were variously inhabited: by Slovenes, or by Goths of one of the three lineages, or by people of some other Germanic ancestry. But most were the villages of a people descended from the ancient Dacians, the original natives of these parts, who had long ago intermarried with Roman colonists and retired Roman soldiers. The descendants now spoke a corrupt but comprehensible Latin and called themselves Rumani. (By their Slovene and Germanic neighbors they were called a more derogatory name: the Walachi, meaning "babble-speakers.") Every community of any size, of course, also had its sprinkling of Greeks and Syrians and Jews. They were invariably the richest residents, for they were the traders dealing in the goods that accounted for the Pyretus River's barge traffic.

We three journeyers seldom paused for long in the Slovene villages, because, if any of them had a travelers' lodging place at all, it would be only an unlovely krchma. The Germanic communities always had a passable gasts-razn, and the Ruman ones usually had a tolerable hospitium (called "ospitun" in the Ruman dialect), sometimes even including a rudimentary bathing house. I myself would not have stopped overnight in so *many* such places, but Genovefa insisted on having a respite, as often as possible, from "the rigors of the outdoors." So I would engage a chamber for us—Maggot of course sleeping out in the stable with the horses. However, I did stoutly resist Genovefa's frequent attempts to *keep* us loitering and lolling in any one place, though she might prettily plead and implore or—like a genuine woman-wife of the Xantippe sort—berate me in angry tantrum.

Anyway, the time we spent in gasts-razna and ospitune was not all wasted, for in several of them I collected new items for my historical compilation. Any lodging place for travelers is of course situated on a well-traveled road, and generally has been there for as long as that road has *been* a road, and generally has been in the same family for all that time. Since the proprietor of such an establishment does not himself ever go anywhere, and has very little to occupy him besides routine chores, his sole entertainment is listening to the tales that his lodgers tell. Then he tells the stories to other people, including the sons who will succeed him as keepers of the family establishment. Consequently, any such person has an enormous stock of tales and gossip and anecdote, some of it recently acquired, but much of it old—even ancient—handed down from his father's father, perhaps through countless generations. And if the bored, moss-grown stay-at-home enjoys anything more than listening to other people, it is talking to them, so I was easily able to elicit from every Gothic and Ruman landlord whole spates of recital, recounting and recollection.

Not everything I heard could be considered strictly historical, and some of it was not entirely believable, and several of the stories I had heard before. Nevertheless, I would sometimes get so enthralled by some long-winded landlord that I would sit with him beside the ospitun hearth fire for hours after nightfall, until Genovefa would get restless and peevish, and would interrupt our host to say:

"That story has nothing to do with our quest, and it is long past midnight. Do come to bed, Thorn."

And I would have to tear myself away. But I did not necessarily miss much of value in so doing, because Genovefa frequently was right. Many of those Ruman narrators merely told variant versions of ancient pagan myths and fables. At one ospitun, the landlord solemnly assured me, "If you live always in virtue, young man, upon your death you will go to the Fortunate Isles of Avalonnis, and there you will dwell in bliss. But it is ordained that, after a time, you must be born again into this world in a new body. Naturally, no sensible man would willingly forsake the joys of the Fortunate Isles to do that. So you will be given a drink from the river Lethe, the water of forgetfulness. That will make you lose all memory of the happiness you enjoyed in Avalonnis, so you will be content to return to earth and suffer the innumerable tribulations of yet another mortal lifetime."

641

"Avalonnis, *bah!*" grunted the Gothic keeper of a gasts-razn. "That is only a Roman—and Ruman—perversion of the Gothic afterworld, Walis-Halla, Wotan's 'hall of the chosen.' And, as pagans still believe, the chosen Walr are those warriors who die bravely in battle. They are lifted up by the awesomely fierce but beautiful maidens called Walis-karja, 'the carers for the slain,' and are borne in honor to Walis-Halla."

Those things I already knew, but the Gothic landlords told me other things that I had *not* known, things more pertinent to my compilation of history. I was told that, when the Goths left their early inhabitation on the Amber Coast, it was a King Filimer who led them inland and southward, to find a new homeland around the Mouths of the Danuvius. And, I was told, it was a King Amal the Fortunate who had been the progenitor of the Amaling line.

I learned also of some of the ways and manners and customs of those earliest Goths.

"Before they ever owned horses and learned to ride," said one old man, "when they still hunted afoot, our ancestors improved the simple throwing-spear by inventing the twisting-spear. A hunter would wind a rope in a spiral coil about the shaft of his spear—not tying it fast, you understand—and then, holding tight to the rope end, would fling the spear with all his might. The rope, briskly unwinding, made the spear spin as it left his hand, so it would fly more straight and true and hard to strike its target prey."

"But then," said another elderly Goth, "during the long migration of our ancestors, they crossed the flatlands where in time they learned the many uses of horses and the skill of riding them. Thereafter, the Goths hunted and fought on horseback, using swords, spears, bows. But they also invented one weapon never known even by the world's *best* horsemen, the Huns. That was the sliuthr, a long rope with a loop at the end, made with a running knot. At full gallop, a Gothic warrior could throw that loop an immense distance, and yank it tight around his prey—whether it be a game animal or a man or the man's horse— and bind that prey instantly helpless. Best of all, it was a weapon even more silent than an arrow, ideal for ambushing an enemy rider or felling a posted guard."

And the Goths, during their ages-long migration, had acquired other things than weaponry.

"They learned, as well, the arts of the Alani and the ancient Dacians and the once cultured Scythians," an old woman told me. "Those peoples are all now dispersed or degenerate or totally extinct, but their arts live on in the minds and hands of Gothic artisans. Our jewelers know how to bend and twine gold wire into gorgeous filigree, how to back-hammer a design into a sheet of metal, how to rub enamel into graven designs, how to back a gem with gold or silver leaf so the stone gleams more brightly even than it would in nature."

But the Goths' gradual education and cultivation and refinement had not, it seemed, made them at all effete or neglectful of their some-times severe codes of conduct.

"No Gothic king has ever *imposed* a law on his subjects," said yet another old man. "The only Gothic laws are those that were conceived in antiquity and proved worthy by long observance. A man caught in a crime is held to be guilty of it. Say he slays a fellow tribesman without good reason. His punishment is to be slain by that man's kin, or else to mollify those kinfolk by paying a satisfactory wairgulth. That is why 'guilt' and 'debt' are the same word in our Old Language. Or if a crime is committed and a man is not caught, but only accused of it, he can best prove his innocence in the trial by ordeal. Alternatively, he may be tried before a judge, and have his innocence warranted by a sufficient number of oath-helpers, so called, those being witnesses as to the probity of his character."

The old man paused and smiled. "Of course, anyone having experience of *civilized* judges would hardly trust their adjudication, for they can be so easily swayed by bribery or self-interest. That was never so with any Gothic judge. His judgment seat was draped with a genuine human skin, flayed from some former judge who had proved corruptible. It may have been done so long ago that the skin was only a worn and tattered rag . . . because not many later judges would *ignore* such a reminder to be always fair and honest."

As I think I have made plain, the Gothic keepers of gasts-razna told me more useful things than did the Ruman keepers of ospitune. But both Goths and Rumani told me one thing that was the same, and it was a warning. A Ruman landlord was the first to voice it:

"Take care, young man, that you and your companions keep to the directly northern path you have been traveling so far. Or bear west of north, if your quest should take you that way, but do not, on any account, stray to the *eastward*. Some distance north of here, you will come to the river Tyras. Whatever you do, stay on the western bank of it. On the eastern bank begin the tablelands of Sarmatia, and in those pine forests lurk the terrible viramne."

"I do not comprehend your Ruman word 'viramne,'" I said.

"In Roman Latin it would be 'viragines.'"

"Akh, ja," I said. "Those females whom the ancient Greek historians called the Amazons. Are you telling me that they really do exist?"

"Whether they are veritably the Amazons, I could not say. I *can* say that they are a tribe of viciously warlike females."

Genovefa was present, and she asked, as a woman would, interested in measuring the possible competition, "Are those women as beautiful as they are reputed to be?"

The Ruman spread his hands. "That I cannot say either. I have never seen them, and I know no one who has."

"Then why do you fear them?" I asked. "How do you even know they are there?"

"The occasional vagrant traveler has wandered into their lands, and *very* occasionally one has escaped with his life, to tell hair-raising stories of what he suffered at their hands. I have never personally met such a survivor, but one does hear the stories. Also it is widely known that a band of Ruman colonists, yearning for farmland of their own, once got desperate enough to cross the Tyras, planning to clear a place for themselves in the Sarmatian forests. They have never been heard of since, not even by the relatives whom they left behind."

"Vái, mere rumors," Genovefa scoffed. "That is not evidence."

The landlord gave her a look. "For me, the rumors suffice. I am not eager to seek evidence. If you are wise, you will not risk *being* the evidence."

I said, "I have heard other tales of that virago tribe. But no tale has explained how, if they are all women, they propagate their kind."

"It is said that they detest both sexual congress and childbearing, but do those things as a duty, to keep their tribe from dwindling. Therefore they submit to infrequent connection with the males of other savage Sarmatian tribes—the wretched Kutriguri, perhaps. But when the infants are born, the viramne expose all the males and let them die, and keep and rear only the females. That is why no king has ever sent a force to try exterminating the viramne. What warrior would willingly go against them? If he did not get slain outright, he could have no hope of living as a captive until he might be ransomed. Could he expect mercy from women who murder even their infant sons?"

"What nonsense!" Genovefa said impatiently, and then to me, "Why do you listen to balgs-daddja that has nothing to do with our quest? It is long past bedtime, Thorn. Come, let us retire."

The Ruman gave her another look. "We have a saying in these parts. He is not an honest man who burns his tongue and fails to tell the others at table that the soup is scalding hot. I try my best to be an honest man."

"Still," I said, half humorously, "I *should* like to find out if the viragines are beautiful."

Genovefa gave me a smoldering look, and the Ruman gave her a pensive one. Then he said only, "The most inviting soup can be scalding hot."

And we heard the warning repeated by Gothic landlords, who called the Amazons baga-qinons, "war-women." I even paused one day in a Slovene village just to ask if those people also knew of such a female tribe. They did, and as best I could make out the Slovene word for them, it was something like pozorzheni, meaning something like "women to beware of." And everyone who spoke of those women told us they lived on the grasslands east of the river Tyras, and solemnly warned us, "Do not go there."

8

hen Genovefa, Maggot and I had traveled up the valley of the Pyretus for about a hundred and eighty Roman miles, the river's course abruptly swung off to the westward. So we left it, continuing directly north and traversing some miles of rolling hills until we came down into the valley of the Tyras, and we went upstream along that, northwestward. We kept to the river's western bank, not so much because we were heeding the warnings we had heard, but simply because we had no need or wish to cross over the water.

We were north of the Carpatae Mountains now, farther north than any of us had ever been before, and we saw numerous things new to us. Among the wild animals native to those parts, we came upon what must be the largest of all the world's deer: the great northern elk, immense creatures bearing palmate antler racks that rival the spread of some trees—and the smallest of all the world's horses: the dun-colored little ponies called tarpan by the local Slovenes. Since the lodging places for travelers were fewer hereabout, and longer distances apart, we spent many more nights camping in the open and having to rely on our own resources for food. I did not slay any of the elk for our meals, because we would have had to waste so much of its meat, and that would have been unthinkable for a woodsman. But we did dine twice or thrice on tarpan flesh, and Genovefa broiled it most tastily. From the Tyras waters Maggot could hook just about any kind of fish I had ever heard of, and, even more easily, could scoop up with an improvised net whole batches of the little white lavarets or silver bleaks or the still smaller gobies, all of which made delicious eating.

Though Genovefa was more than capable at cooking, she had no love for the chore, and sulked and muttered over it. So whenever we did come to a lodging place, even if it was only a Slovene krchma, she would insist on our taking advantage of it. I would have been willing in any case, just to give myself and Maggot a rest from hearing Genovefa's mealtime complaints. In those places, too, we encountered things new to us. The Slovenes of the north seemed to subsist mainly on thick soups, and to their lodgers the krchma keepers serve little else. So we ate soups made of unfamiliar ingredients—sorrel soup and beer soup and sour-rye soup and even a soup made of beef blood and cherries—and we found them all surprisingly good.

At one krchma, another traveler was staying the night, and I made his acquaintance right gladly, although he was a Rugian and therefore a possible future enemy of myself and my king. I was pleased to meet him simply because he was an amber trader, the first I had ever spoken to, and he was traveling south from the Amber Coast with a pack-horse load of that precious material to sell in whatever nearest market could best afford it. The man proudly showed me samples of his wares—translucent chunks of amber of every color from palest yellow through gold and red to bronze, some of the chunks holding in their depths perfectly preserved flower petals, bits of fern frond, whole dragonflies—and I admired them unreservedly. I called in Maggot from his stable quarters, and introduced him, and we three sat together by the fireside, sharing jugs of beer. Maggot and the trader were still deep in converse when Genovefa and I went off to our bedchamber.

There she grumbled, "I think it is time I resumed being Thor. I am tired of being slighted."

"Slighted? How?"

"Do I get introduced by name to a stranger? Ni allis! But that big-nosed Armenian creature? Ja waíla! The name Genovefa is perhaps negligible. The name Thor is not. It makes people take notice. And I prefer to be noticed, not treated as a mere appendage to the grand marshal Thorn. On the trail I am only your servile cook. In company I am regarded as your traveling whore, and am condescendingly ignored. I suggest that, from this place onward, we take turns. You ride for some days as Veleda, and I as Thor, and so on alternately. See how *you* like being the female and the mediocrity."

"I should not like it," I said with weary patience. "But not because I have ever felt inferior as a female. Only because I *am* the king's marshal, and I must maintain that identity while I am on the king's mission. You may do as you please. Be man or woman, whichever you please, when-ever you please."

"Very well. This night I wish to be Thor, and no one else. Here—put your hand here and you will realize that I am Thor."

So all that night I was Veleda, and no one else. And Thor rode me hard, punishingly, vindictively, using me as his receptacle in every way a female can be used, again and again. But if he was doing his utmost to make me feel inferior, he did not succeed. A woman can be soft and submissive without ever feeling subservient, all the while thoroughly—akh! *throbbingly!*—enjoying the experience.

During the intervals between our couplings that night, while Thor rested and recuperated, I reflected. Early in life, I had recognized in myself the various masculine and feminine traits of personality, and thereafter I had striven to cultivate the more admirable attributes of both sexes, and to subdue the baser. But, like a speculum image, in which everything is the same but reversed, this twin of mine seemed to have done just the opposite. Thor was everything reprehensible in a male: insensitive, overbearing, self-centered, demanding and greedy. Genovefa was everything unlovely in a female: fretful, suspicious, spite-ful, demanding and greedy. Both those entities were beautiful to look upon, and eminently satisfying in sexual embrace. But one cannot be always admiring or embracing one's mate. Had I been a woman, I could not long have endured the boorish Thor as a husband. Had I been a man, I could not have endured the shrewish Genovefa as a wife. Yet here was I, all but wedded to them *both*.

647

I was learning what my juika-bloth had learned when it fed on un-cooked boar entrails—that a raptor can be eaten by its prey, from the inside. Just so, as if my guts were invisibly bleeding, I was being sapped of my strength, my will, my *self*. For the regaining of my independence and individuality, perhaps for my very survival, I must disgorge this prey and wean myself from this disastrous diet. But how could I, when it was so irresistibly tasty as to be habit-forming?

Well, I should like to believe that I *could* eventually have done it of my own volition, but Genovefa did it for me. I have often since then wondered if her namesake, queen to the Visigoths' great King Alareikhs or Alaricus or Arthurus, had been anything like my Genovefa. If she was, and if the old songs are true—telling how that queen was caught in adultery with the king's best warrior, Landefrid—I have wondered whether Alareikhs felt, as I did, some relief mingled with his rage when he discovered the betrayal. To be truthful, my own rage may have been mixed also with some mordant amusement, because my latter-day Genovefa bestowed her favors on a person much less worthy than a warrior.

Thor's having performed entirely as Thor, that one night long, seemed for a time to have satisfied my consort's yearning for variety. There was no more talk of our alternating our male and female identities and costumes as we went on. Genovefa remained Genovefa and I remained Thorn, and every day we dressed that way, as we continued upstream along the Tyras. We came into another of the regions destitute of lodging places, so Genovefa had to work as our cook every night, but she did that with no more than nominal scowling and mutterings. To provide fish for the pot, Maggot had only to step aside from the trail to the riverbank and drop in a hook and line. But to procure flesh-meat I had to delve into the woods and go some way from the river. Though the road that ran beside it was hardly a crowded highway, there was always some human traffic on it, and that kept the wild animals at a distance.

One afternoon, I kneed Velox aside into the forest on one of those forays and, before I flushed and killed a good, plump auths-hana, I had to roam so far that it was well after sundown when I got back to where my companions had already laid camp. Maggot took Velox's reins without remarking on anything unusual having occurred during my absence, and Genovefa made no remark when I took the big bird to the fire she had lighted. But I instantly perceived something out of the ordinary.

Even there in the wide-open air, even over the pungent odor of the fire's wood smoke, I could *smell* that Genovefa had been engaging in sexual connection of some sort. Of course, that in itself was nothing exceptional; scarcely a night went by that we two did not; but I had become as intimately familiar with the aromas of her various emissions as I was with my own. This time there was an unaccustomed scent—corylaceous, not lactucaceous, so the source was male, not female, but that source was neither Thor nor Thorn.

I eyed Genovefa as she set to plucking the auths-hana, and for the moment I said nothing. I was going over in my mind the persons we had met or passed on the trail that day. There had been five: two men on horseback, with traveling packs behind; a man and woman on muleback; an aged charcoal-burner afoot, staggering under his high-heaped load. Each man had given at least a glance, if not a stare, at my comely riding companion. And some other or others might have come along while I was away hunting.

Genovefa was skewering the bird on a trimmed, straight branch when I asked grimly, "Who was it?"

"Who was what?" she said, without looking up, laying the spit over the fire on two forked upright sticks.

"You have very recently coupled with some man besides myself."

Now she glared at me, defiantly but warily at the same time. "Did you sneak to watch me? Did you see me do any such thing?"

"I need not. I can smell the ejecta of a male human being."

"Vái, I thought my own senses were acute. You must have the nose of a ferret." She shrugged indifferently. "Ja, I lay with a man."

"Why?"

"Why not? There was a man, there was an opportunity, you were not here. I pretended that my horse had picked up a stone in the frog of his hoof. I bade Maggot ride on ahead." She added coolly, "I had not ample time, but time enough."

I said, with feeling, "But why, why, Genovefa, would you do so sordid a thing? When, between us two, we have everything that either of us could possibly—"

"Spare me," she said, rolling her eyes as if she had been tried beyond endurance. "Are you going to preach fidelity and constancy? I told you, I am tired of being your appendage. I wish to be noticed for my own sake. This man noticed me."

I bellowed, "Who? Which man?" I seized her shoulders and shook her violently. "I have been reviewing every man who has passed. Which was it?"

The shaking chattered her teeth so that, when she spoke, she had to speak in spurts. "It was . . . it was the . . . the charcoal-burner . . ."

"What?!" I roared, so astounded that I let go of her. "Of the men on this trail today, why that derelict and filthy Slovene peasant?"

She smirked complacently. "Akh, I have had Slovenes before. But I had never before tried such an old man. Or such a dirty one. Except for the novelty of it, I must admit that I found it disappointing."

"You lie! You know I will go and kill the culprit. You are protecting the real one."

"Ni allis. I care not whom you kill, so long as it does not discommode me."

"Maggot!" I shouted. "Do not unsaddle Velox. Fetch him here."

Undoubtedly having heard all our uproar, Maggot came almost hiding behind the horse, creeping apprehensively. I told him, "Mind our meal. Turn the spit. We will be back before it is done."

649

Then I almost hurled Genovefa into the saddle and vaulted up behind her, and kicked Velox to a gallop. We had to retrace the trail only
a short way before we found the old man. He was sitting hunched
beside a small fire of his own charcoal, roasting mushrooms stuck on
twigs. He looked up in surprise as I dragged Genovefa from the horse
and pulled her over to him. Then I whipped out my sword and laid its
edge across his throat, and snarled at Genovefa:

"Tell him to confess. I wish to hear it from *him*."

The aged wretch was spluttering, "Prosím . . . prosím," the Slovene
for "please," and his eyes bulged in terror. Suddenly, instead of words,
he spluttered blood from his mouth, all over his beard and my sword
hand. Then, just as suddenly, he toppled away from me and I saw Genovefa's belt knife protruding from his back.

"There," she said, giving me a winsome smile. "Have I made amends,
Thorn?"

"I have no proof that he was the one."

"You do. Just look at him. That expression of serenity spreading over
his face. There is a man who died happy."

650

She bent to retrieve her knife, casually wiped it clean on the old
peasant's ragged cloak and returned it to her waist sheath.

"If I choose to believe you," I said icily, "then this makes twice you
have cheated me with the same man. I wanted to slay him myself." I
put the point of my sword under her chin. With my other hand, I
bunched her tunic and dragged her face close to mine. "I wanted you
to be convinced that I shall do the same to you if ever you stray again."

I saw genuine fright in her blue eyes, and she sounded sincere when
she said, "I believe you."

But on her breath I smelled that hazelnutty odor of male ejecta, so I
thrust her roughly away from me, saying:

"Believe, too, that I am talking to Thor as well as Genovefa. I will
not share you with other women any more than I will with other men."

"I believe you, I believe you. See? I continue to make amends." She
had found an empty sack belonging to the dead man, and was filling it
with chunks of his charcoal. "I am even making up for the wood I
squandered on our fire. Now let us pitch this corpse into the river and
go back to our camp and eat our nahtamats. All this excitement has
made me ravenous."

She did eat heartily, too, and chattered all through the meal, very
femininely, of inconsequential matters, as blithely as if the day had
been an ordinary day of uneventful travel. Maggot only picked at the

auths-hana carcass, as if he were trying to be inconspicuous to the point of invisibility. I ate no more than a bite or two, for I had lost my appetite.

Before we disposed ourselves for sleep, I took Maggot a distance out of Genovefa's hearing and gave him some instructions to follow from this time on.

"But, fráuja," he whimpered. "Who am I to spy on the fráujin? Or to disobey any of her commands? I am no more than baggage on this journey."

"You will do so because I tell you to, because I am the leader of this company. If ever again I have to be absent, you are to be my surrogate eyes and ears." I added, half to myself, with rueful humor, "I only wish your big nose were capable of—"

"My nose?" he cried, aghast, as if I had threatened to cut it off. "What of my nose, fráuja Thorn?"

"Nothing, nothing," I said. "Keep it safe for your amber-sniffing. Just be my eyes and ears. Do not again let the lady Genovefa out of your sight and hearing."

"But you have not told me what I am to watch and listen *for.*"

651

"Never mind," I grunted, loath to admit that I was now a cuckold, and gnawed by jealousy. "Simply report to me even the most commonplace occurrences, and let me be the judge of them. Now let us sleep."

At least for that night, I had lost my appetite for things other than food. It was one of the very few of our nights together that not Thorn or Thor or Veleda or Genovefa indulged in any sort of frolicking at all.

✠　　✠　　✠

During the subsequent week or so, there were no more than three days on which my hunting forays kept me long enough away from Genovefa for her to engage in any misconduct. And on each of those days, when I rejoined my companions, Genovefa looked luminously innocent, and I smelled on her no alien smells, and Maggot said nothing. He only raised his eyebrows and spread his hands to indicate that he had nothing *to* say. So there were no more wasted nights, either. As both Thorn and Veleda, I exerted myself to reward the chaste behavior of Genovefa and Thor, and they returned those attentions lustily enough to assure me that no outsider had been depleting their energies.

The river Tyras had been more and more flowing toward us from the west, and it was getting narrower and narrower, so we knew we were approaching its headwaters. At the last krchma we came to on that trail,

I asked directions of its keeper, and he recommended that we cross the Tyras, an easy fording at these narrows, and strike northward away from it. Some forty Roman miles overland, he said, we would find ourselves at the upper waters of another river, this one called in the Slovene tongue the Buk—it would be the first river I had ever encountered or heard of that flowed *from south to north*—and we would follow that downstream all the way to the Amber Coast.

So now we had traveled about half of those forty miles, on a surprisingly good road with considerable wheeled traffic, and the road brought us to the village called by its inhabitants Lviv. Notwithstanding its unpronounceable Slovene name, Lviv was a comfortable place to break our journey. Situated midway between the Tyras and the Buk, it was nearly big enough to be ranked as a town, because it was the market and trading center for all the area's farmers, herdsmen, artisans and others who brought to it their goods for shipping down one river or the other. We found a hospitium that was patronized by the wealthier visiting merchants and their families, so it was well enough appointed that it even contained separate thermae for men and for women.

Since Lviv was such an easeful place, and since it seemed a promising place for me to make historical inquiries, and since we likely would not come upon another such place for a long time, I decided that we would stay for more than just a night, perhaps for a few days. When Genovefa and I had carried our belongings to our chamber in the hospitium, she said to me:

"Now, Thorn, you cannot or will not abandon your august identity of masculine marshal and herizogo. But I can discard either of mine at will, and I intend to. I shall be alternately Thor and Genovefa, so I can amble about the various shops and smithies of this village and sample the wares offered to men and women, and perhaps purchase some items for one or both of my selves. Furthermore, as you know, I was delicately reared and I am of fastidious daintiness, and I have for too long been bathing only sketchily and in nothing better than river water. So I intend also to luxuriate alternately in the men's and women's thermae. There are enough people on the streets of this community, and enough of them lodging in this establishment, that none is apt to remark on the resemblance of my two selves. Even if someone does, what of it? Any gossip by these nobodies out here in the middle of nowhere can hardly harm or embarrass *you*."

I might rightly have been indignant at the ultimatum nature of that declaration, but I was more amused to hear such a person—horse thief, fornicatrix, murderer of a hapless old peasant—describing herself as delicate and dainty. So I only said indulgently, "As you please."

Nevertheless, I went to Maggot's stable quarters and told him that "again, for state reasons," the fráujin Genovefa would occasionally be posing here as the young man Thor. "In whichever guise she goes, I want you to be always secretly in close attendance. And give me full report whenever I ask for it."

"I will do my best," he said, but looking very unhappy about it. "There are some places a fráujin can enter that I cannot."

"Then wait and watch between her going in and her coming out," I said, exasperated—not so much by his aversion to spying as by my own ignoble instigation of it.

Thereafter, it was only when Genovefa dined with me in the hospitium's dining chamber that she accompanied me as my female consort, and once or twice strolled with me about the streets. Most of the time, Thor was being Thor. I always bathed alone as Thorn, of course, in the therma for men. If I encountered Thor in there, or elsewhere about the village, I and he took care not to recognize one another. But I trusted Maggot to be keeping watch when I was not, and, since he never reported anything suspicious, I was satisfied that both Thor and Genovefa were behaving virtuously. I spent most of my own time making the acquaintance of whatever elderly local men I found idling about the hospitium—or at wineshops or beer stalls around Lviv's market square—and inquiring of them what they could tell me of the history of their forebears in this region.

653

But I found very few in residence who were of any Germanic lineage. The majority of the men I met were the squashed-nose Slovenes, and they were ignorant even of their own people's origin and history. In their morose and melancholy way, they could tell me only that the Slovenes had come from somewhere far to the north and east of here, and over time had drifted southward and westward.

I asked one old man, as we sat in a marketside taberna, "Was it the Huns who drove your ancestors out of their original homeland?"

"Who knows?" he said uncaringly. "It may have been the pozor-zheni."

"What?" I said, for it had been some while since I had heard that word.

Laboriously he managed to render it in other words, and I comprehended. He meant those "women to beware of."

"Iésus," I muttered. "I have heard them mentioned in backwoods outposts, by superstitious rustics, but I would hardly have expected the civilized inhabitants of Lviv to be timorous of a tribe of *women*. Or even to believe in such a preposterous myth."

"We believe," he said simply. "We are careful not to provoke them to anger when they come here."

"What? They come here?"

"Every spring," he said. "Only a few of them. They ride in to Lviv to trade for necessities that their tribe cannot procure in the eastern wilderness. It is not difficult to tell them from the other women arriving at the market. They come heavily armed, and they come naked to the waist, as if they were leather-skinned barbarian men, and they brazenly strut and swagger, flaunting those bare breasts."

"What do they trade *with*?"

"They bring pack horses laden with their tribe's winter harvest of otter pelts. Also freshwater pearls that they have gathered. Of course, otter is not the most valuable kind of fur, nor are the mussel pearls worth very much. But, as I say, we are chary of provoking those terrible women, so we are extravagantly generous in our bartering with them. That is why they have not attacked this village, or even plundered any farmstead roundabout, within living memory."

I said skeptically, "Then, for all you really know, their swagger is no more than bluster. Whatever they may have been in times past, they may now be as feeble and docile as kittens."

"I doubt that," he said. "In my younger days, I was one of several men who stopped a runaway horse in the street yonder, as it came galloping headlong from the east. Its rider was clearly dying when we helped him down, and he died without telling of his adventures among the pozorzheni, or how he had escaped from them. He *could* not tell, because he was carrying his torn-out tongue in one hand. But his desperate ride from there to here must have been hideously painful, because he was raw flesh all over, with no skin anywhere on his body. Indeed, we only knew he was a *man* because in his other hand he was carrying his genitals."

I went back to the hospitium to eat, and I had chosen an inconvenient hour, for it was crowded. The dining chamber was no spacious hall of well-apart couches. It had only long, slatted tables, with benches alongside, and all close together. I wedged myself onto a bench between two other diners, and found that I was seated directly across from Thor. When our eyes met, his opened wide in surprise, and he gave a start as if to jump up abruptly from the table, but he too was tightly crammed in this place.

Instantly I knew why my unexpected arrival had startled him. Even above the other odors all about—of many human bodies, of lentil soup and hot bread and strong beer—I could scent from Thor the unmistakable lettucey aroma of a woman's most intimate exudation, still fresh. It had only recently been exuded—because when a woman's juice gets stale it smells of fish—and it had not come from either Veleda or Genovefa. Thor perhaps saw my nostrils dilate, for he again got that genuinely frightened look on his face, and his eyes darted about as if seeking a way of escape. But what he saw in the room seemed to fortify him. He put on an ingratiating smile and said across the table, just loud enough for me to hear over the room's hubbub:

"You caught me before I had the chance, this time, to bathe myself sweetly clean in the therma. But would you kill me here, dear Thorn, in such a crowded place? That *would* create a commotion loud enough to be heard by Thorn's king and all of Thorn's other friends."

He was right; I could do nothing to him at the moment. Again I had lost any appetite I had for food, so I shoved my way upright and out from between the men on either side of me—getting cursed for my rudeness—and elbowed my way out of the crowded room—getting more curses—and stormed off to the stable, my hands itching to get a stranglehold on Maggot.

"You tetzte tord!" I raged, seizing him and flapping him like a saddle blanket. "Are you merely lazy? Or totally incompetent? Or criminally disloyal to me?"

"Fr-fráuja," he pleaded, as best he could. "Wh-what have I done?"

"*Failed* to do!" I roared, slamming him against the stable wall. "Thor has been . . . I mean Genovefa, in the guise of Thor, has had illicit congress today with someone here in Lviv. How did she elude you? Anywhere a Thor could go, you could have followed. Were you too *lazy?*"

"Ne, fráuja," he whined, sliding limply down to the ground. "I did follow."

"Then where did Thor . . . where did she go in that disguise? Were you too incompetent to recognize a meeting with somebody? A tryst of some sort?"

"Ne, fráuja," he whimpered, doubling himself into a knot and wrapping his arms protectively over his head. "I knew the house to be a lupanar."

655

"What?" I said, taken aback. "A common whorehouse? You watched Thor go . . . you watched Genovefa go disguised into . . . you watched a *decent woman* walk boldly into a *lupanar*? And you did not come running to tell me of such an unheard-of happenstance?"

"I did not, fráuja," he moaned. But then Maggot proved to be more courageous than I would have thought. He raised his woebegone face from under his sheltering arms and said bravely, "You were right to accuse me, fráuja. I was being criminally disloyal to you."

I held back the fist I had poised to strike him, and said through gritted teeth, "Explain yourself."

"There is much I have not reported to you."

"Then do so this instant!"

In a sort of wail, sobbing occasionally, he said, "I do not know what manner of woman *is* the fráujin Genovefa. What sort *would* go into a lupanar? Back in Noviodunum, I supposed her to be a man named Thor. So, when our journey was first proposed, I worried that you and he might someday come to blows over the lovely lady Swanilda, and I feared for my own safety if that should occur. But then, no sooner was Swanilda dead than Thor was revealed to be also a female. I could not discern *where* the jealousies and rivalries might have lain, but *you* seemed happy enough, so—"

"This is not a report! This is gibberish!"

But he went right on, "So I determined to say nothing—to do nothing on the journey that might cause jealousy or trouble—to *see* nothing else that I was not supposed to see."

"Imbecile, I *told* you to see! I ordered you to keep your eyes on Genovefa!"

"But by then, fráuja, she had already once betrayed you. The very day you told me that."

I hated to admit it, but I said, "I knew she had. She bade you ride on ahead, and then she lay down with the charcoal-burner. That is *why* I told you not to let her out of your sight from then on."

Maggot was regarding me with a blank expression. "Charcoal-burner?"

I said impatiently, "The grimy old man who passed us on the trail earlier that day. Surely you saw him. An aged Slovene peasant. A nauthing." I laughed a bitter laugh. "*That* was the lowly lover she embraced."

"*Akh, ne,* a lover lowlier than a Slovene, fráuja Thorn!" Maggot cried, bowing his head and pounding his own fists on it. "You are mistaken

656

about the charcoal-burner, or you were misled. The only nauthing who embraced the fráujin Genovefa that day was an even lowlier Armenian!"

I stammered witlessly, "You? . . . *You!* . . . How *dared* you?"

"It was she who dared. I never would have." And he babbled rapidly, to get the story out before I cut him to pieces, but I was stricken too numb to draw my blade. "She said if I refused she would cry rape and I would be slain, so I might as well have the joy of her and merely *risk* being slain. She said she had long wondered whether it is true, what is said of men with big noses. That is why I was so affrighted, fráuja Thorn, when soon afterward you also made reference to my nose. Anyway, I told her there is no relation between a man's nose and his svans. I told her that *all* Armenians have big noses, but I have never known of one who had more of a svans than my own meager thing. Armenian *women* have big noses, too, and they do not have any svans at all." He paused and said thoughtfully, "But neither do those women have . . . a *something* down there . . . as big as what I encountered on the fráujin Genovefa . . ." I only stared at him, and he hurried on:

"But, for all I protested, she demanded demonstration. And then, when we were done, she said I was right, and she laughed and derided my puniness. And then you returned from the hunt, fráuja Thorn, and that was the second time I criminally neglected to speak. Then there were third and fourth and fifth times, because the fráujin Genovefa— sometimes in the dress of Thor—has been disporting herself, at least twice a day, with one man or woman after another, ever since the moment we arrived here in Lviv, and each time has rushed to the therma to cleanse herself before sharing your bed again. Indeed, I have been concerned that she might pick up some foul disease from these squalid Slovenes and inflict it on you. But, fráuja Thorn, how *could* I disclose all that without incriminating myself? Oh vái, of course I knew that I would have to, soon or later, that it would all be discovered. And I am ready to take my punishment. But, please, before you kill me, may I return to you one thing that belongs to you?"

657

I was too dazed to reply, so he scuttled off somewhere in the stable and immediately came back carrying something.

"I found it tucked away in the sleeping fur of the lady Swanilda when I first unrolled that," he said. "I thought you might have wondered what became of it. And since I am about to die . . ."

But I had never seen it before. And seeing it now, I was at least momentarily distracted from my rage and bafflement and distress. It was a circlet woven of leaves and tendrils, such as women idling in gardens often make of flowers as a pretty crown to wear around the head. At first I thought that Swanilda must have made it just as a pastime, for I had never seen her wear it. But then I realized what it was woven of—oak leaves, now dry and crumbly, and clusters of the tiny linden flowers, those still sweet-smelling though long withered. And I remembered the legend of the oak and the linden, and I knew why Swanilda had lovingly fashioned the circlet, and why she had kept it. I turned it over and over in my hands, and I said softly, sadly, tenderly:

"That prediction that the old wise-sayer Meirus made . . . I think he was wrong about the finality of it. I think Swanilda, wherever she is, has *not* ceased holding me dear."

"Wherever she is, ja," Maggot said, sniffling sympathetically. "Wherever she is, Thor put her there."

I raised my eyes from the rustic crown and fixed them hard on Maggot, and did not even have to ask. He flinched away from me, more guiltily and fearfully than before, saying:

"I thought you knew, fráuja. As I said, you seemed then happy enough. It was Thor who overpowered her and put the noose about her neck and hauled her, hand over hand, to the warehouse beam and let her hang there and twist and kick until she strangled. I think Thor knew that I was there in the shadows, and I think he did not care. That is why I assumed that you and he—or she, I mean—"

"Enough," I said hoarsely. "Be silent."

He shut his mouth with almost a click, and I stood pondering for some moments, still turning the oak-and-linden circlet in my hands. When at last I spoke again, I did not care what Maggot might make of my words.

"You were right. It is true. I have tacitly conspired in every evil deed that has been done by that fitchet bitch and son of a fitchet bitch. Thor and I are but the two sides of a single coin, and that coin is of base metal. It must be put to the smelter and refined and minted anew. To do that, I must first atone. I shall begin by letting you live, Maggot. I will even respectfully call you Maghib from now on. Get ready to ride. We are leaving this place. And there will be only the two of us. Saddle my horse and yours, and fasten our packs on the other."

I tossed the circlet away, so I would not be impeded, and drew my sword and went striding back across the stableyard to the hospitium and into its dining chamber, and swept my gaze about. Thor was no longer there. I pelted up the stairs to our chamber, and found the door

658

wide open. Thor had been there, and obviously had been in a great hurry to leave it again, for our belongings were all disarranged and scattered about. Hastily rummaging through the things he had left behind, I could tell that he had changed into Genovefa's garb and had carried away with him *only* his Genovefa clothes and appurtenances, none of Thor's except his sword. I discovered, also, that he had purloined one thing of mine—that coiled bronze breast guard that had taken his fancy when he first saw it.

I heard some loud outcry from downstairs, and went to the window. In the yard, the hospitium's keeper and a few of his servants and stable grooms were milling about, and the proprietor was shouting for someone to fetch a "lékar," meaning a medicus. I ran out again and to the stable, and found Maghib stretched supine on the straw between our two saddled horses. Protruding from his chest was the hilt of a knife I recognized. But this time Genovefa's thrust had been overhasty. Maghib was still alive, still conscious, and though the hovering attendants solicitously tried to hush him, he was still Armenianly able to talk, at least to choke out a few words through the blood bubbling from his mouth:

659

"Tried stop her . . . fráujin stuck me . . . took horse . . . rode east . . . *east* . . ."

I nodded, knowing why he stressed that word.

"Ja," I said. "She has heard the stories of those vicious viragines. She knows she has much in common with them. So that is where she is going."

I could not believe that such a *delicate* creature as Genovefa would commit herself permanently to the kind of rigorous life led by any nomad forest tribe. But it did seem likely that she would join those women just to hide among them for a while, and that she would expect to be safe there.

I said, "Your wound appears not to be mortal, Maghib, and here is the physician. Let him dress the injury and start your healing. When you are strong enough, continue on toward the Amber Coast. You have only to go to the river Buk and follow it downstream. I will join you after I have settled accounts with our betrayer."

I left Maghib to the ministrations of the lékar, and went to give the hospitium keeper ample money for his keep and care. Then I packed and mounted Velox, and I too rode away eastward, toward Sarmatia and the women to beware of.

9

The vast and only vaguely defined region called Sarmatia constitutes the westward extremity of Asia, and eastward beyond it lies *all* of Asia, a continent so immeasurably immense that its bounds are unknown even to chorographers. But I did not expect to have to explore the whole of it in pursuit of Genovefa. If she really had fled to hide among the Amazons—or the baga-qinons or viramne or pozorzheni or whatever was their own name for themselves—then I should find those women living not impossibly far from Lviv, since they annually sent emissaries there to trade. And I believed I might even locate them before Genovefa did, because I knew one thing that she likely did not. I had been informed that the Amazons traded in otter pelts and mussel pearls, meaning that they had to live somewhere near a clear running stream.

Two days' ride beyond the last outskirt habitations of Lviv and the farmsteads around it, when I was deep in the woods of pine and fir, I ceased to be Thorn. I stowed away the masculine garb and armor I had been wearing, and put on some of my Veleda clothing, so I could approach the Amazons as a woman and perhaps not be instantly repulsed. I even made myself look *flagrantly* female, because I had learned another thing about the Amazons that Genovefa probably had not. On my upper body I put no tunic or blouse, only a strophion band under my breasts to make them higher and fuller. I rode thus naked from the waist up, and I was thankful that the early autumn weather was still warm enough to make that not uncomfortable.

I was here traversing an almost unbroken evergreen forest, but I did come upon bodies of water here and there. At a brook, I might pause to drink or to fill my flask, but I did not look for the Amazons anywhere about there, because a brook is not big enough for otters to play in or for mussels to bed in. Nor did I look for the Amazons around the occasional marsh or stagnant pond or other sluggish water. But at last, five or six days out from Lviv, I came to a fairly broad, beautifully limpid, briskly flowing stream, ideal otter water. I decided to follow it downstream for a day or two, and then, if I found no trace of habitants, to cross it and try casting upstream. There was soft sod and moss lining the bank, so Velox walked almost as quietly as a wolf, and I kept a wary lookout as we moved along beneath the pines that overhung the water. As it turned out, though, I was not being wary enough.

Something silently flicked down past my face and front, and then something tightened hurtfully around me, just under my breasts, clamping my arms to my sides. Before I could grasp what was happening, I was yanked right off my saddle. I did not fall, but dangled in midair while Velox placidly walked out from under me. When he felt my weight leave him, he stopped and turned and gave a look of quite comic astonishment at the sight of his rider swinging in a rope noose horse-high from the ground. Only now did I remember having been told about the sliuthr, that silent weapon of the old-time Goths.

My pinioned arms could not draw sword or knife, so there was nothing for me to do but hang helpless there. I heard branches rustling as someone clambered down the tree, evidently having snubbed the rope's other end somewhere up there as soon as it took my weight. I was hardly surprised to see that it was a woman who dropped from a limb to stand on the ground and scowl up at me.

661

Now, I know that all the legends of the Amazons, from Homer and Herodotus to recent times, have described them as beautiful. I myself had been curious to learn if they really were. Well, I regret having to disillusion those who treasure such legends, but the Amazons are decidedly not. Even Homer should have known better, if he had given the matter any thought. Obviously, women living all their lives in the wild, living winter and summer in the open, surviving by their own might and main, without menfolk to do the harder labors for them, are far more likely to resemble brute beasts than lithe and lovely huntress Dianas. This first one I encountered was certainly beastly enough, and no more so than her sisters that I was soon to meet.

She had not slipped down from that tree limb with the grace of a nymph alighting; she had flumped heavily and squatly down like a dropped toad. It was scarcely to be wondered at; anyone dwelling outdoors the year around has to accrete a considerable layer of fat as insulation, but her coating was excessive. Although her arms were as brawnily muscular as a woodcutter's, and her legs as trunklike as a chariot-driver's, her torso, hips and buttocks were billows of bloat. Her skirt, the one garment she wore, was of some kind of hide, hence nearly indistinguishable from her own, which was as coarse, grainy and weather-tanned as that of an úrus. She was, like me, unclothed from the waist up, showing that, contrary to the stories and the statues, the Amazons do *not* hack off one breast for ease in drawing the bow. She had both of hers, and they were nothing to inspire a statue-sculptor: leathery dugs with barklike areolae and nipples. What the Amazons do hack off is their hair, and evidently do nothing else to it, even combing. This one's cap of dark hair was a nappy mat, like felt, and she had similar mats in her armpits. Her eyes, from a lifetime of peering into sun and wind and distance, were red and squinty. Her bare feet were long-toed, splayed and prehensile for tree climbing. Her hands were as broad and callused and horny-nailed as those of a blacksmith, and she now reached one of them up to snatch away the belt holding my sheathed sword and knife.

As she did that, she opened her bone-cruncher jaws to speak, disclosing a mouth full of snaggled yellow teeth. I could make out that she asked a question, partly in the Old Language but so mixed with alien words that I could not understand. Unable even to shrug, I tried to make a face of bafflement. So she asked again, choosing the words more carefully, all of them Gothic but more barbarously spoken than in any Old Language dialect I had ever previously heard. Anyway, I could comprehend that she was inquiring, and not warmly, who I was and what I was doing here. I did my best to indicate, with face and hands, that the rope had me squeezed too breathless to reply.

Besides having my weapons, she had a belt knife of her own and a bow and quiver slung on her back. But she studied me and pondered until evidently she decided that she was also superior in strength. She may well have been, because she now stepped close, clasped my legs and lifted me aloft until I could work the noose over my head, then lowered me to the ground. She twitched the dangling rope in a manner that somehow loosed it from its attachment above and let it all fall. Then she coiled the rope without looking at it, keeping her little red eyes fixed on me while I answered her query with the fiction I had concocted.

I said, and earnestly, that I was the wretched wife of an evil and violent husband, and after years of his curses and abuse — especially his vile lustfulness — I had determined to tolerate him no longer. So I had escaped his bondage and ridden hither to seek succor and shelter from my sisters of the forest.

Then I waited, apprehensive lest she remark that I was the second such fugitive to arrive here in the past few days. But she only flicked a glance at my Velox and said suspiciously, "Your cruel husband, svistar, affords you a fine horse."

"Akh, ne! *Him?* Ni allis. I stole it. That husband is no poor peasant, but a Lviv merchant, with a stable of steeds. I took his best Kehailan to be mine."

"Not yours," she grunted. "Ours now."

"Then you could acquire yet another," I said, smiling wickedly and indicating her sliuthr rope, "if he comes following me."

She pondered on that, and finally said, "Ja." She even brightened a bit. "And enjoy some diversion, besides."

I had a fair idea of what she meant, and I smiled more wickedly yet. "I should like to watch that. And participate."

She had seemed to accept my pretense of distaste for "lustfulness," and she seemed to approve my pretense of eagerness to join in other kinds of "diversion," but my captor now looked me critically up and down, then said, "You are not sturdy enough to become a Walis-kari."

So that was what they called themselves: the Walis-karja, after those pagan angels of the battlefield, the carers and bearers of the chosen slain. Could these women perhaps be descendants of *them?* If so, it was another grievous disillusionment, for the Walis-karja, too, were said to have been beautiful.

I lied some more. "Vái, svistar, I used to be as handsomely sturdy as you are. But that pitiless husband *starved* me. Still, I am stronger than I appear, and I know how to hunt and fish and trap for food. Let me but be allowed to feed myself and I promise to eat swinishly. I will soon get fat—obese—gross. I swear it. Do let me stay."

"It is not for me to decide."

"Then let me appeal to your queen. Or your headwoman. Or your chief Walis-kari. Or whatever is her title."

"Unsar modar. Our mother." She pondered again, and deeply. "Very well. Come."

Still carrying my weapons and her own coiled sliuthr, she also took Velox's reins, and stumped off downstream along the riverbank. I walked beside her, very glad to know that I *had* got here ahead of Genovefa.

I said, "Surely your headwoman is not the actual birth mother of every Walis-kari. Does she rule as the tribal mother by right of succession? By popular election? Acclamation? How? And how do I address her?"

My captor pondered once more, then said, "She rules because she is the oldest. She became the oldest by surviving longest. She survives by being the fiercest, most bloodthirsty, most merciless of us, capable of killing any or all of the rest of us. You will address her as we do, reverently, adoringly, as Modar Lubo. Mother Love."

I almost laughed aloud, because the name so belied the description—or the other way about—but I said only, "And what is your name, svistar?"

She had to ponder that one, too, but finally said that it was Ghashang. I remarked that I had never before heard such a name, so she told me it meant Pretty, and again I managed not to laugh.

Now we began to be joined by other women who came out from behind riverside trees or climbed down from them or came riding from the deeper woods, sitting bareback on small, shaggy, despondent-looking horses. They shouted raucously at sight of me and Velox, and screeched questions at Ghashang. But she, proudly possessive of her captives, refused to reply and only gestured for them to make way for us. Every one of those women, even the youngest of them, looked very much like Pretty, which is to say very much like the massive wild cow called the úrus.

Ghashang and I were leading a procession of eight or ten women when we got to their living place. I do not call it a village or even an encampment, because it was only a wide glade in the forest, scattered with cooking-fire rings of blackened stones carelessly tossed together, and with sleeping furs spread over pallets stuffed with fir sprigs, and with various cookery implements and skins stretched on drying hoops and bits of harness, and with saying knives and brittling knives, and with the gnawed bones and other remains of past meals. From two or three trees' lower limbs hung the blue-red carcasses of future meals, humming with flies. The women had obviously no need for shelter, or not enterprise enough to erect any, because there was nowhere a tent or lean-to, much less anything as elaborate as even a crude kryk house. I had never seen so squalid a community as this. Why, the *Huns* were of civilized refinement by comparison.

There were ten or twelve more women here, and several girls young enough to be still breastless, and half a dozen infants toddling or crawling about. The children being totally unclothed, except with dirt, I could see that every one of them was female. The girls and infants were not yet coarse of skin or bulging of musculature, but they were already sadly bulbous of body. Vái, the *Hun* females had been comely by comparison to these. And I, Veleda, most certainly shone here like a gold piece thrown among barnyard tords.

It could reasonably have been expected that such a herd of Gorgons would have stared agape—and with envy—at the sudden spectacle of my fair face and form. However, had I been the most vain and immodest of females, my reception by the Walis-karja would have humbled me. They did stare, yes, and admiringly, but at my Kehailan steed. At me, they threw only infrequent glances of disapproval, almost of revulsion, and otherwise kept their eyes averted from me, as if I had been a creature of such ghastly deformity as to cause nausea in normal folk. Well, by their standards of normality, I *was*. By their standards, the woman named Pretty had not been ludicrously misnamed.

Anyone hearing of the Amazons' unshakable abhorrence of men might suppose them to be a society of sorores stuprae, taking sexual pleasure only in each other. I soon learned that they were not. Although they possessed all the usual female organs, they were utterly sexless, not only uninterested in sexual intercourse but repulsed by the very notion of it. Small wonder that their concept of the ideal Walis-kari was a woman so ill-favored, shapeless and graceless as to be repugnant to men and socially acceptable only by women equally ugly. At this moment of my first arrival among the Walis-karja, I did not know the reasons for their being the way they were, but I did instantly comprehend that the one and only oddity in this crowd was Veleda. What would be the women's response if they discovered what I *really* was, I did not care to imagine.

Ghashang tethered my horse and then escorted me, many of her sisters following, through a screen of trees and into an adjacent smaller glade. This was their Modar Lubo's "palace" in the open air, and it was just as littered with food scraps and other trash, but it did boast two things that could have been called furniture. Over the sleeping pallet hung a roof of ragged deerskin slung between two tree branches. And in the middle of the clearing was a "throne" rudely hacked and adzed out of a tremendous tree stump that weather and decay had begun the hollowing of. Mother Love was imposingly seated on it now, rather overflowing it, in fact. At sight of her, I could readily believe that this oldest of the Walis-karja was indeed the most to be dreaded of them.

665

Each of her daughters was only as ugly as an úrus, but she was very like what one would conceive the fabled dragon of pagan superstition to have been. Mother Love's leathery hide had been wrinkled and mottled by age, as any old woman's might be. But hers had also been lapped into saurian scales and bunched into warts and wens; her flat old breasts looked as hard as two armor plates. Her fingernails and toenails were of talon length, and what teeth she still had were practically tusks. She far surpassed any of her daughters in bulk, and she was hairier, too; besides the scurfed gray mat on her head, she had hairs like fish barbels on either side of her mouth. While her breath was not visible as dragon fire, it was rancid enough to repel any adversary at eight paces.

The other women had regarded me only askance. This one glared balefully as I told her my name and began to repeat the tale I had spun for Ghashang. I had spoken but a few words when she growled at me what sounded like a question:

"Zaban ghadim, balad-id?" When I just looked blankly at her, she demanded in Gothic, "You do not speak the Old Language?"

That puzzled me even more, and I could only say, "I *am* speaking the Old Language. As *you* just did, Modar Lubo."

She curled her lip contemptuously from her tusks and sneered, "A townswoman," and imperiously waved a paw for me to get on with my story.

I did, and considerably elaborated on what I had told Pretty, ascribing all kinds of vilenesses to my invented husband. I laid particular emphasis on my having felt *violated* not just the first time but every time he exercised his conjugal privilege. And since I was feigning Amazonian loathing of the copulative act, I took care to keep my head down, so Mother Love should not glimpse the Venus crease about my throat, in case she might have known what that signifies about a woman's true sexuality. Having depicted my phantom spouse as a veritable monster of brutality and carnality, I concluded:

"I beg haven with you and your daughters, Modar Lubo—and I beg your protection, too, because that odious man will not lightly surrender the vessel into which he has enjoyed pouring his lustful juices. He is very apt to come ravening after me."

She shifted her bulk slightly on her throne and grunted testily, "No man in his right mind would come here."

"Akh, you do not know this one," I said. "He might come in disguise."

She snorted, very dragonlike, and said disbelievingly, "Disguise? Are you in *your* right mind?"

I hung my head and tried to force a blush. "I am mortally embarrassed to tell you this, Mother. But he . . . sometimes when he forced himself upon me, he liked to play that he was the wife and I the husband. He would lie passive and make me get atop him and—"

"This is sickening! Desist!" She and all the other women were squirming and making faces. "Anyway, what has this to do with disguise?"

"He became well practiced in travesty, if you know what that is, Mother—what is called in Latin transvestitus muliebris. He would dress in my garments. After some while, he could do that most convincingly. He even had our Lviv lékar cut pockets under his chest skin, in which he could insert wads of wax . . . here . . . and here . . ."

I inhaled deeply to protrude my breasts, and poked them with a finger, dimpling them to demonstrate that mine were genuine. The old dragon's little saurian eyes widened to almost human size, and so did those of the other Walis-karja gathered about us.

I sighed and added, "He would even go sometimes upon the street in his travesty, and strangers would take him for a woman."

"We would not! Would we, daughters?" They all determinedly shook their bovine heads. "However womanly he might look or behave, he could not pass the simple test of a campfire brand thrust at him. Wax melts. Wax *burns."*

Her daughters nodded briskly and cried, "Bakh! Bakh!" which I took to be their word of plaudit, so I joined in, "Macte virtute! What a brilliant thought, Mother!"

"But you," she said, fixing me with her lurid stare. "What have you to offer us? Besides your fine horse and your fine Latin phrases?"

"I have not always been a townswoman," I said. "I am adept at hunting, fishing, trapping . . ."

"But you lack the good substantial fat that would fit you for the cold work of diving for mussel pearls. You must put some flesh on those spindly bones. See to it. Now, how much do you know of us Walis-karja?"

"Well . . . I have heard many stories. I do not know which were true."

"You must learn." She indicated one of the women. "Morgh here is our ketab-zadan—as you would say, our singer of the old songs. She will sing to you tonight. That will also start your learning of our Old Language."

667

"Then I am accepted?"

"For now. Whether you will stay is another matter. Did you leave any children behind when you fled Lviv?"

That took me by surprise, but I said honestly, "Ne."

"Are you barren?"

I thought it best to lay the blame on that already well-heaped husband. "More probably *he* is, Mother. Considering his perversions and all . . ."

"We shall see." She spoke to my captor: "Ghashang, you will be responsible. Send word to the Kutriguri that we wish a Serving. When their man gets here, put this one to him." To me she said, "If you conceive, then you stay."

It seemed rather a stiff initiation requirement, to make a woman who had shunned her husband's attentions take on those of a stranger. And one of the yellow-skinned, verminous, hideously Hun-like Kutriguri, at that. But I said nothing, only bowed in acquiescence.

"Good. Then you are dismissed. Everyone, begone. Your mother would rest."

668

She gave a mighty heave and levered herself up from her throne to go stumping over to her pallet. Now that she was off the big chair, I could see that it was draped with a hide daubed with colors, evidently meant to be ornamental. Though the skin was much worn and rubbed thin and frayed at the edges, it was recognizably too delicate and pliant a hide to have come from any animal but a human one.

✠ ✠ ✠

Ghashang returned to me my belt and sword and knife, and showed me an unoccupied place in the glade in which to spread my sleeping fur and lay my pack. Then I spent what remained of the day being occupied with rope.

My new sisters still seemed uneasy about looking me in the face, and not all of them were fluent enough in Gothic to communicate with me, but they did express curiosity as to why my Velox wore that thick rope encircling his chest. So I vaulted onto him and demonstrated the purpose of it. Then, one after another, they tried it for themselves. Of course, such fat women did not vault to the saddle; they climbed Velox much as they would climb a tree. However, once astride, a Walis-kari could grip the foot-rope better with her prehensile toes than I could. The women were surprised and pleased to realize the utility of that contrivance, and several started to make foot-ropes for their own mounts. It quickly became obvious that none of the Walis-karja knew how to splice a rope, so I devoted some time to teaching them that craft.

I was equally curious about their silent weapon, the sliuthr. One of those was easy enough to make, and the women made the twirling and throwing of the noose end look easy, too. They could fling it and loop it over a tree stump or a crawling baby, and yank it tight about the target. But when I tried, I was so awkwardly inept as to make them all laugh. (That was more than mortifying, it was painful, their laugh being an ear-piercing squawk.) However, I was able to show them how to *improve* the sliuthr—putting an eye-splice in the rope's end, through which to bend the bight, instead of having a clumsy and impeding knot there. When I made one, and the women tried it, they found that it slid more smoothly, thus could be thrown even more deftly, and they ceased to laugh at me. They even lent me a sliuthr with which to go off and practice by myself, unlaughed-at.

While I played with it, and only *very* slowly got better at wielding it, I reflected on what I had thus far learned about the Walis-karja. They employed the sliuthr as a weapon. Their Modar Lubo draped her "judgment seat" with a hide flayed from a human being. In other words, these women maintained at least two usages of the very earliest Goths. That lent credence to the legend that, long ago, during the Goths' migration across these lands, certain of their women had proved so intolerable that they had been forcibly expelled from the company. It seemed reasonable to conclude that those women *had* managed to live on their own, had stayed hereabout, preserving the old ways and customs, never learning any of the arts and graces later acquired by the Goths—and these Walis-karja were their direct descendants. If so, I could well understand why the old-time Goths had cast out their great-great-great-grandmothers. According to the story, those original women had been vile haliuruns hags, but they need only have been as unsavory as I found their progeny to be.

My theory might validate the old songs as true history, but there was a question remaining. What could account for the women's commitment to total sexlessness? Those original outcasts might have been, as the legend said, so indignant at their expulsion that they swore to get along without men forever after. But the descendants of the present day had not just forsworn men and shed their own female sexuality; they had rid themselves of every other feminine instinct and attribute as well.

669

Bad enough that they were content to be fat and ugly, they also seemed deliberately to have cultivated disagreeable voices. I had heard many men speak with the hard clangor of iron, and most of the women I had known spoke in the sweet tones of silver, but these Walis-karja, young and old, spoke stridently in harsh voices of *brass*. Equally unfeminine was their sloth and slovenliness. They lived in a squalor that would horrify any normal woman. They let their children go dirty and stinking, even with the river water at hand. They dressed in skins because they had forgotten or never learned the feminine arts of spinning, weaving, sewing . . .

And now, when they summoned me to join them at nahtamats, I discovered that they did not even know how to cook. I was given a portion of some unidentifiable animal's viscera, so tepidly warmed as almost to be raw, and a mess of unrecognizable greens, the meal ladled onto a plane-tree leaf, because the women did not know how to make bread or bake a trencher. I muttered that even I could cook better than this, and Ghashang overheard me. She said I would get my turn, as every woman did, because none of them relished the job.

670   When we had all finished eating, the women next indulged in the one and only luxury they possessed. It was an indulgence I had seen before. Onto the embers of the cooking fires they sprinkled dried hanaf leaves, and then draped skins over the rude hearths, and took turns sticking their heads under those canopies to inhale the smoke. Even the young children did that, and some of the women lifted the tiniest infants so they could partake, too. The hanaf intoxication took the women in various ways, none of them dignified. Some women reeled giddily about in the dark, others danced bulkily about, others talked incoherently at the top of their brazen voices, others just fell over and snored. It did not elevate my opinion of the Walis-karja to see them behaving so. Only a few of us eschewed the indulgence: I because I did not care to get drunk, four or five others because they were to be that night's sentries perched in treetops roundabout, and the woman Morgh because Mother Love had bidden her sing to me.

The name Morgh means Bird, but she was no more birdlike in utterance than she was in size. If listening to a brass-voiced woman's speech was unpleasant, hearing one sing was excruciating. Nevertheless, the old song that she rendered was enlightening to me. Though it was of course sung in that welter of mixed Gothic and alien words, it was so interminably long that I could catch enough to comprehend its content. It was a saggws recounting the origin and early history of the Walis-kari tribe, and it most gratifyingly supported the conjectures I had been making only a while before.

It began by telling how, long ago, a number of women had left the main body of Goths—*left* it, mind you, not been thrown out of it. In this version of the story, there were no foul haliuruns witches being banished. The women were all chaste Gothic widows and maidens, and they were constantly having to fend off the Gothic men's lecherous attempts on their virtue. Finally wearying of that, the women sought refuge in flight, in voluntary exile. They departed into the wilderness, and wandered about in it. Even while suffering hunger, exposure, terror and all manner of other miseries, they somehow still found the leisure and composure to take an oath that their little band would remain in perpetuity all-female and staunchly misogamic.

Eventually, said the song, the women came to a splendid Scythian city, for in those days Sarmatia was not known as Sarmatia but as the nation of Scythia, and the Scythians were still a mighty people. The women of that city sisterly received the travel-worn Gothic women, and fed and clothed and pampered them, and wished them to stay. But the Gothic women resisted the temptation to settle down as city dwell-ers, for they were determined to survive and thrive on their own. They did learn certain Scythian customs, such as the intoxicating use of the hanaf smoke. And they did adopt from the Scythian religion two female deities, Tabiti and Argimpasa, to be their own matron goddesses. And they did accept from their Scythian sisters the gift of various things they would need in the wild. But then they departed, to go and live in the forest forever after. And when they left the city, they were accom-panied by numerous of the Scythian women whom they had converted to man-haters like themselves.

671

Morgh screeched on and on, telling how the combined Gothic and Scythian women were from that time free and independent and self-sufficient, and how they thereafter utilized an occasional man, at their own convenience, purely as an inseminator for the purpose of propa-gating their race. However, along about this point in the saggws, I ceased straining my ears and started conjecturing some more, because the song had already explained much to me.

For one thing, I realized why the women's native Old Language of Gothic had been mixed with and corrupted by what *they* called the Old Language. That was obviously the Scythian tongue and, for all I knew, it *was* older than the Gothic. At any rate, these Walis-karja were clearly hybrids, descendants of those earliest mingled Gothic and Scythian women, not to mention the men they had "utilized" for fertilization, who might have been of any number of other races. Frankly, I felt genuine relief at knowing that these awful women were at least not *full-blooded* sisters to me.

And Morgh's saggws told me something else, though it was not explicit in the words she sang. It told me the reason for the Walis-karja's physical unattractiveness *and* their total indifference to sexuality and femininity. From old history books I knew that the Scythians, once a handsome, intelligent and energetic people, had in time become fat, flabby and apathetic. Men and women alike became virtual eunuchs, losing all interest in sexual pleasures. And, according to the history books, that woeful combination of their loss of vigor and their failure to breed was what caused the Scythians' downfall.

It seemed clear to me, therefore, that these Walis-karja had not so much *decided* to become fat, ugly, stupid, languid and sexless; they had simply inherited those characteristics when they intermingled with the Scythians. I remembered how I had long ago taken special note of one word of the Scythian language—enarios, meaning a "man-woman"—because I then assumed that it signified a mannamavi like myself. But now I had to suppose that it referred only to a *mannish* woman. It must have been the Scythians' word for a Walis-kari.

In setting out from Lviv to pursue the perfidious Genovefa, I had thought that I was wantonly digressing from my historical mission. Instead, I had fortuitously found worthwhile information that I might never had found otherwise. Akh, I did not flatter myself that I had divined the sole source of the age-old Amazon legend, because I was aware that the Greeks had been discoursing on Amazons hundreds of years before the Walis-karja came into being. But I was satisfied that I *had* fathomed the Gothic contribution to the Amazon legend.

672

10

enovefa did not find her way to the Walis-karja until three days later. In the meantime, I pretended to be doing my utmost to become an acceptably awful Walis-kari.

As Mother Love had commanded, I made a great show of eating voraciously of every wretchedly cooked meal that the rotating cooks set before us, though I would usually slip away afterward and regurgitate most of it. Now and again, I would even emulate my sisters in sticking my head under a fire hood and inhaling just a little of the hanaf smoke, enough to make my eyes as glazed and my mouth as slack as theirs, but never enough to make me lose my wits. And I learned a smattering of their Scythian language.

673

In some respects, it was not too different from Gothic. The women might say "Madar Khobi" instead of "Modar Lubo," and "na" instead of "ne," and "dokhtar" instead of "daúhtar," and those words were easily comprehensible. Others were more like those of the Alan tongue—and the Alani, I believe, originally came from the Persian lands—so those words were foreign to my mouth. But I learned to address each woman as "khahar" instead of "svistar," and to call the looped throwing rope a "tanab" instead of a "sliuthr," and to refer to a woman's breasts as "kharbuzé" (the word means "melons," and it very well described the other women's breasts, though not mine). So I acquired enough Scythian to be able to converse more easily, but, in truth, the sisters had little more of interest to tell me.

They would bid me, "Khahar Veleda, mind that you make offering," whenever I brought down a rabbit or an auths-hana with my sling, or caught a pike-perch with my fishing line. So I would, as they instructed, cut off the thing's head and lay that on an otherwise undistinguished cypress stump that served as altar to both of the women's female deities. And that was the only recognition or service that I ever saw anyone pay to Tabiti and Argimpasa. As best I could discern, Tabiti was equivalent to the Roman pagans' Vesta, goddess of the hearth, and Argimpasa was the same as Venus, goddess of love and beauty. Inasmuch as the Walis-karja had only the crudest sort of hearth, and had nothing whatsoever of love and beauty, I thought it no wonder that their devotions were so scanty and offhand.

And the women showed me how they did their dokmé-shena, or pearl-diving. Their thick sheathing of fat made it possible for them to endure the coldest water, but it made them too buoyant to sink under that water unaided. So, stripped naked and carrying a withy-basket, a woman would slide into the river taking along also a rock heavy enough to sink her down to the bottom mud where the mussels were burrowed. Once she got below, she was able to stay there for much longer than I would have thought humanly possible. Behind those melon breasts must have been capacious lungs, because any one of the women could hold her breath down there long enough to fill her basket brimful of the blue shells. Then, on shore, she might have to open many hundreds of the things before she encountered a pearl. It would have taken me half a day to open that many with a knife, but she could do it speedily, prying them open with her horny thumbnail. She briskly flipped away those that contained only mussel meats, which might be every one in the basket—and in basket after basket—before she found a single pearl worth keeping.

The pearls were not so beautifully tinted as sea pearls, nor as lustrous, and only a very few were round. The majority were irregular blobs, some as small as a fly's eye, a few as large as my fingertip, most of them of varying sizes between those extremes. I doubt that the women could have traded them for much of value if the women had not been the Walis-karja, feared by the merchants of Lviv.

On the afternoon that I watched the pearl-diving, some other things caught my eye, plants growing along the riverbank. I borrowed one of the mussel baskets and collected enough of the plants to fill it. The women looked suspicious of that, so I said, and truthfully, "Flavorings for our meal, when it comes my turn to do the cooking."

During the time that I was with the Walis-karja, they made no assault on Lviv or any other inhabited place, so I did not get to see whether they really were such terrible marauders as legend and rumor painted them. However, on my third morning there, I did accompany them on a hunting foray. We were all just waking that morning when one of the night's sentries, a woman named Shirin, rode in to report having seen

674

a prime bull elk in the woods during her watch. Mother Love grinned like a hungry dragon and declared that we would add the good elk meat to our larder. She pointed and named a dozen other women to go with Shirin and kill it—then thought to add my name.

"But do not interfere with the hunt," she warned me. "Only observe and learn how we do it." Another thought struck her. "I too will go along. A good opportunity to try our new horse."

She meant my Velox, but I made no protest. I was interested to note that, for serious work like this, the women did not ride bareback. They put my good Roman army saddle on Velox, and put their old and dilapidated ones on the woebegone little horses that they and I were to ride. It took four of the women to hoist and heave their massive mother onto Velox—and he groaned lugubriously when they did—but she managed to stay firmly astride him, because we rode only at a cautious and quiet walking pace.

We came to a rise of ground where we overlooked a clearing in the forest, a long open swale of high grass, and there Shirin silently signaled that we were near the place where she had seen the elk. So we halted and Mother Love waved her tree-limb arms to direct the huntresses. They rode quietly off in different directions, and the old woman and I just sat our mounts and waited. The Walis-karja did not hunt as I would have done, dismounting and creeping up to within arrow-shot of the game. Evidently several of them rode wide around and well beyond the elk, then came galloping back at him, because after a while I heard the distant sound of many hoofbeats. And shortly the elk, fleeing those riders, broke from the woods at the far end of the clearing, frantically pounding this way.

675

Halfway down the swale of grass, though, the great animal abruptly interrupted his run. Though I saw no arrows loosed, the elk balked as if he had hit a wall, made a violent sidewise bound, and another, and then stayed where he was, still on his feet, but convulsively leaping left and right, twisting and flopping like a hooked fish. The rest of the women had, while their sisters rode on, stopped their horses at intervals among the trees on either side of the clearing, but I did not even see them until after the elk had halted, when their horses sidled skittishly out of the woods. Little though I esteemed the Walis-karja, I had to be impressed by their skill with the sliuthr. From their concealment, sitting their saddles, they had flung those rope loops—silently, almost invisibly, each throwing from a distance that must have been a good forty paces, and at a target moving at a headlong gallop. I would have deemed it impossible, but they had accurately snagged the elk's antlers—and on both sides, so he could do nothing *but* stop and struggle furiously.

Of course, even such hefty women as these could not long have held captive a maddened and thrashing bull elk. But they had snubbed their rope ends around their saddle pommels, and their mounts took the strain. Those horses were clearly accustomed to this work, because they leaned back against the ropes and adroitly shifted their weight or position as the elk flailed about. Small though they were, the horses kept the ropes from slacking and the nooses from slipping off the antlers, and thus held the elk where it was. The three or four women who had not thrown ropes rode closer to their quarry, dismounted and dashed in and out, dodging the elk's kicks and plunges, swinging their swords at his throat. By the time Mother Love and I rode down to join them, the beast was dead, its tremendous body prostrate on the grass but its head propped up by its big soft snout and one immense palmate antler.

The mother did not congratulate or thank her daughters for their success in the hunt, but only gave orders: "You and you, do the removal of the head for presentation to Tabiti and Argimpasa. You and you, start gutting the creature. You and you, commence the skinning."

Without waiting to be told, I got down from my horse and pitched in to help. The swordswomen had not killed cleanly; their hasty hacking had made of the elk's throat a gory purple hash, as if it had been ripped and worried and chewed by wolves. But they had at least confined their slashing to that place, so the rest of the handsome hide was unmarred. With saying knives, I and my sisters peeled it off intact, and finished that job even before some others of the women had managed to hew and saw and sever the massive head from its neck.

Of the tripes, we saved only the liver; that alone was a sufficient load for one woman to carry. And merely to have quartered the giant carcass would have made pieces that would have staggered our horses. So we brittled it right there into manageable chunks and slices, keeping only the best meat, leaving the remainder for the forest scavengers. When, some while after noon, we finally rode homeward, it required two women and two horses to transport the trophy for the goddesses, the women carrying it between them by the antler tips, the head dangling midway between their horses. And when those carriers were fatigued by the weight, they were spelled by others.

When we got to the river, not far from our destination, we met Ghashang, who came riding from the east. She kneed her horse along-

676

side Velox, at the head of our column, and spoke to Mother Love. Then the two of them dropped back to where I was riding.

"Ghashang has been to the Kutriguri," said our mother, "to tell them that we require a Serving. They will choose a man to do it. That sometimes takes a while, because of course those goatish savages all clamor for the honor. But the chosen man will be here in a day or two."

Not at all graciously, I muttered, "Mamnun," which is "thags izvis" in the Scythian tongue.

"And I command you, Dokhtar Veleda," she went on, "strive to conceive in the Serving. You are to repay our hospitality by proving fruitful."

Then she was gone, back to the head of the column, before I could ask sardonically whether one *can* conceive on command. Ghashang, still at my side, said in her ponderous way:

"Curious. Modar Lubo is mistaken. Those men usually quarrel over the choosing, ja, but clamoring *not* to be chosen. I have never known why."

I might have suggested that the Kutriguri, however savage, must have good sense, but I refrained.

677

"Still more curious," said Ghashang, "this time they are not being reluctant, although I told them frankly that you are a newcomer, a stranger, not at all fat, unwomanly soft and scrawny and pale."

Probably I should have commended the savages for having good taste, too. But still I made no reply, because I heard loud shouting up ahead. We were approaching the Walis-karja's place of habitation, and some of the women who had stayed behind were hailing us. They were not just crying a welcome-home to us hunters triumphant; they were calling urgently, and among the shouted words I could hear my name:

"Madar Khobi, come quickly! . . . Khahar Veleda, come and see!"

They were excited because Genovefa had arrived.

✠   ✠   ✠

"Is that the man?" Mother Love asked grimly, and I nodded.

"He rode directly under my sentry tree," said the woman who was proudly displaying her catch to us. "I had only to drop the tanab loop. And he was in disguise, right enough. He even wore *this* over his woman's clothes."

"It belongs to me," I muttered, for she held up the coiled bronze breast guard. She let me take it from her hand, and excitedly went on reporting.

"And he pretended—pedar sukhté! *how* he pretended—but I was not to be deceived by words any more than by disguise."

I gazed down at Genovefa, who lay supine in the middle of the glade, unconscious, wound all about with rope, tunic torn open to bare the chest. That part of Genovefa looked like the throat of the elk when it was first killed—a grisly purple hash of shredded flesh—except that it was not bleeding, but smoking. Genovefa would never be Genovefa again.

"And then he *pleaded*," the woman said gleefully, "when I put him to the test. But I refused to be dissuaded. The false kharbuté did not burn away so easily as I had expected. But I persisted and, as you can see, burn they finally did. Also, Madar Khobi, we now have another good horse, the one he was—"

Her mother angrily interrupted. "You did this all by yourself?"

The woman's happy face fell, and her sisters roundabout were quick to cry accusingly:

"She *did*, Modar Lubo!"

"Roshan did it all *alone*, the selfish sow!"

"She did not call us until the man was limp and senseless!"

"Roshan only wanted us to help carry him in!"

"She had the diversion all to *herself!*"

Mother Love glared at the miscreant and growled, "Such rare diversions are to be enjoyed only when I say so, and when I am present, and are to be shared by all."

The woman looked frightened. "You were not here . . . and he was. And you said . . . make a test . . ."

"You have been greedy. Disloyal. You have cheated not just your sisters but your loving mother."

Roshan whimpered, "But . . . but . . . there can be more diversion still. He is not dead." She flapped a trembling hand at the bound body. "See? He breathes. He will awaken to plead some more."

Mother Love scowled hatefully down at the captive, then grumbled to me, "It does not look like much of a man."

I pointed and said, "You can easily verify it."

Since Mother Love was too dignified and too fat to bend, she gestured to Shirin, who stood with us. Shirin knelt and fumbled at Genovefa's riding skirt, but the ropes held it wrapped. So she took out her short saying knife, still bloody from the elk. She cut the cloth and parted it, then recoiled slightly at the emergence of the virile organ—

not at this moment aggressively virile, but indisputably male. I was glad for the binding ropes; the legs were so tight together that the absence of testicles was not to be noticed.

Mother Love grunted, "Hand it to me."

Shirin smiled and licked her lips, then plied the knife. Even securely trussed and oblivious to everything else, the body writhed in a spasm of agony. Thor would never be Thor again. In at least some small measure, the murder of sweet Swanilda had been requited—and the needless slaying of the old charcoal-burner, and the dastardly attack on Maghib. Shirin handed the severed part up to her mother, who gave it only a glance of distaste and then tossed it into the nearest campfire.

I said, "Mamnun, Madar Khobi. I am quit of Thor."

She frowned. "Thor?"

"That is his name. He is so proud of it that he had the Lviv lékar engrave it upon him. Look at his back."

She gestured again. Ghashang helped Shirin roll the body over, and they cut away the remaining rags of the tunic. All the women's eyes widened at sight of the Thor's-hammer scar.

Mother Love rumbled in admiration, "Bakh! Bakh! I have been wanting a new pelt for my throne. This one will adorn it most elegantly."

679

I said, "Why not get some use out of the creature before you flay him? Now that he is no man, make him the tribe's slave. When you have worked him to death, *then* take his skin."

She snorted derisively, "We have little work for a merchant to do."

"Excuse me for saying so, but you could make good use of a good cook."

"Eh?"

"I told you he affected many womanly doings. He even made himself skilled at cookery. I promise, Mother, you will never have eaten so well as you will when Thor spends the rest of his life cooking for you. For us, I mean."

She looked disgustedly down at him. "A merchant, a husband, a player at travesty—and a *cook!*" She kicked at the body, and told Ghashang, "Put a brand to his newest wound and sear it shut, so he will heal. Then drag this—this *enarios*—out of my sight. Stand guard and call me when he awakens." She turned again to me and said crossly, "If you have been so dissatisfied with the provender here, Veleda, you can take your own turn at the cooking tonight."

"Gladly," I said, and I meant it, for I had planned to offer to do just that. "Will you wish me to cook a meal of the elk meat, Mother? It really ought to hang and age for a week or so before being—liufs Guth!"

The exclamation was of surprise, because she had turned from me, drawn her own belt knife and plunged it into the bulging bare belly of Roshan. The woman's eyes widened for the last time, then she toppled over backward and fairly jarred the ground when she hit it.

"Disloyalty must be punished," said Mother Love, without the least emotion, and her remaining daughters made no least outcry of protest or lament. "Now, Veleda, pay heed." She fixed her dragon glower on me again. "Your coming here—the relieving you of your Thor—has cost us one of our sisters. You had *better* conceive from the Serving, and it had *better* be a daughter born, to provide us with a replacement."

I only nodded. This was no time to make any insolent remark about whether such things could be done on command.

And Mother Love was not finished with giving imperious commands. To Shirin she said, indicating Roshan's still-twitching remains, "Take off her head and put it reverently with the elk's head, on the cypress altar."

Shirin unflinchingly set about doing that, and there was still no outcry from any of the other women. But Mother Love must have disliked the expression she saw on my face, for she snarled, "Have you some *other* complaint to make?"

"Ne, ne. It is just . . . I had thought that the offerings we made to the goddesses were only . . . like the elk's head . . . cut from the game for our table."

"So they are. Roshan will be our meal tonight. That is what you will cook for our nahtamats."

Whatever expression now came over my face, it at least induced the old dragon to take the trouble to explain.

"Ja, we consume our departed sisters. Someday I—and you—will be consumed in our turn. That is how we make sure that each departed Walis-kari is helped on her way to her happy afterlife in the company of Tabiti and Argimpasa. Obviously, the quicker the dissolution of her mortal remains, the more quickly she makes that journey into immortality. And being digested accomplishes the dissolution much sooner than simply being buried to await decay. Also it assures that no dead sister's body will ever be dug up from a grave to be violated by some man."

Well, I thought, I should by now be impervious to surprise at any new depravity the Walis-karja revealed to me. But, in truth, they had some precedent for the practice of anthropophagy. I remembered old Wyrd's having told me that certain of the Scythians did the same thing. Doubtless that was where these women's forebears had learned it. And everyone knows the story of Achilles and Penthesilea: how that hero of the Trojan War, after besting and slaying that Queen of the Amazons, further dishonored her by having sexual intercourse with her corpse. I was inclined to suspect, though, that Penthesilea had been more of a temptation to venery, even dead, than was this Roshan, even alive.

"I suggest you get started, Veleda," said Mother Love. "From past experience, I know that such a meal can take a good while to prepare. And look—the children are already eyeing it hungrily. Shirin, when you finish what you are doing, help Veleda with the butchering and brittling."

I will refrain from telling in detail what the preparation of that meal entailed. At least I was spared having to dissect the head. But when I would have thrown away the great gobs of yellow fat from the belly and buttocks, my assistant Shirin was appalled.

"Vái, Veleda, that is the tastiest substance of all. The red meat you will find very tough and stringy. Besides, the fat further pads our own bodies. Roshan would be pleased to know that her fat lives on in her sisters." And a moment later Shirin chided me, "Na, na! Do not throw away those bits either. When cooked, they are pleasantly chewy morsels."

681

I decline to say what those bits were. But all I *was* allowed to discard was the unquestionably inedible matter like toenails and armpit hair and the filthier entrails. Then Shirin showed me the pit in which were kept the tribe's few vegetable stores and their supply of dried hanaf. To the chopped and sliced meat I added wild onions and river cress, and some laurel leaves to give flavor. Of course, I had no intention of partaking of this ghastly refection—not just because of what it was, but because, when we had it stewing in cauldrons over the fires and Shirin had left me to stir it, I added some other ingredients.

I crumbled and sprinkled into the bubbling pots those plants I had collected from the riverbank and let dry. I had long known the stupefying effect of bugloss, and old Wyrd had once told me that ragwort will make a horse go mad, so I used them both, and lavishly. I might have hesitated to inflict those weeds on anybody of normal palate, because they are of bitter taste, but I had no apprehension that these omnivores would notice anything amiss. Indeed, they all lounged about the darkening glade in lip-licking anticipation; the young girls and infants visibly drooled. And some of the women, voluptuously sniffing the aroma rising from the cauldrons, exchanged witty remarks and stridently laughed over them—comments on how their sister Roshan, so recently reviled by one of them as a "sow," now smelled very much like good boar pork being cooked.

About the time the meal was ready to eat, Ghashang came to report to Mother Love that the new slave had awakened from his swoon, but was too delirious to be talking any sense.

"All he says is 'between my legs . . . look between my legs.' I do not care to look between his legs."

I realized what Thor was trying to tell her, but Mother Love did not. She only laughed her brass laugh and said, "Misses his svans, does he? Best keep him bound, Ghashang. However, let us assist his recuperation with some nourishment." So I ladled out some of Roshan onto a plane leaf to be taken and fed to him.

Then I heaped the leaves of all the others as they filed, toddled or were carried past the cauldrons. This being a ceremonial night, every tribeswoman was here, none having been sent out on sentry duty. Still, I should have thought that a carcass as big as Roshan's would have sufficed for at least two nights' nahtamats for twenty-some women and half that many children and infants. I was in error. They wolfed down their first portions and called for more. I emptied every pot, then gave them the boiled-clean bones to gnaw and crack, and finally I scraped out and served them the very last residue of congealed yellow grease. In all that gorging, no one paid any attention to whether I ate or not.

When every bit had been devoured, they all sat about and belched for a while, and one or two commended me on my cooking. Then Mother Love ordered me to bring out and scatter on the fires the night's ration of hanaf—and to bring more than usual, because the sentries were still with us. I had some ragwort and bugloss left over, so, just to make sure that I was giving the Walis-karja no parsimonious dose of those weeds, I mixed them in with the hanaf leaves. Then I sat back in the darkness to wait, and I did not have to wait long.

The women who were usually the more susceptible to the smoke— and those included the infants—fell over and began snoring after only a single inhalation. Those who on other nights had raucously sung or lumpishly danced did so again, but their songs got louder, the dancing more frenetic, until they were baying and bounding about, almost as furiously as I had once seen the Bacchantes do. The women who on other nights had only sat and talked nonsensically now raised their voices—to yammering, then to bellowing—and their exchanges became foam-lipped quarrels, and the quarrels became vicious contests of punching, wrestling, clawing and hair-pulling. Mother Love at first tried to quell the fights with indulgent scolding, but before long she was in the thick of a five-woman fray, screeching and kicking and gouging better than the best of them. Here and there a woman got knocked down and did not bother to get up again, but only lay where she fell and began to snore. Others simply lost interest in dancing or fighting, and reeled from the center of the glade to lie down and begin to snore . . .

I trusted that they all would be snoring before much longer, but I did not wait to see. They were already clearly incapable of noticing or caring what I did. If the bugloss and ragwort worked as warranted, the Walis-karja would probably still be demented and addled all day tomorrow, if not for many more days. Meanwhile, there were not even any sentries to try to stop me or cry the alarm of my escape. I went leisurely to change from my Veleda garb into my hidden Thorn clothing—and I did so gratefully; the nights were getting chilly for going about barebreasted. I stowed all my belongings and rolled my packs. I got Velox from among the tethered horses and saddled him, and took also the newly arrived horse to carry my packs. Then I mounted and slowly rode away.

683

No, I did not go to speak any words—either of gloating or of farewell—to that one who had been Thor and Genovefa, and was no longer. True, I had earlier intervened to save that one from being immediately slain or flayed alive. But *akh*, I had not done it out of mercy or remorse or forgiveness, or in memory of what that person—those persons—once had been to me. I had done it in the realization that there could be no more hideous punishment for any malefactor than having to spend a lifetime as a slave of the abominable Walis-karja.

What else might happen to that one, I could not predict. When the women recovered from their derangement, they would assuredly be irate at what I had done, and they might well vent their fury on their remaining captive. Or if the captive was not summarily butchered, the women would eventually discover what *was* between its legs, and there was no guessing what they would do then. Nor was there any guessing what would happen when that man from the Kutriguri tribe arrived to perform his Serving . . .

I did not even try to guess. I had no least interest in guessing.

Though I myself might be only half woman, I could make myself be as untouchably cold as any whole one. So I rode off into the night without looking back, without a qualm, without caring what happened to *any* of those I left behind in that place.

11

I did not go back to Lviv. Although I knew that Maghib could not yet have recovered from his wound, I did not care to loiter there until he did. I remembered the Mudman's prediction that the Rugii, if they *were* going south to ally themselves with Strabo against Theodoric, would make their move when the harvest was in and before the winter came down. In these northern climes, winter was fast approaching.

So I made straight for the Buk River, then followed it northward. Over the course of some hundred and fifty Roman miles, I found no more villages of even modest size, but only the occasional clustered huts and riverside stackyards of Slovene woodcutters. Eventually I emerged from the dense evergreen forests into one of the more dismal lands I have ever had to cross. It was a flat plain, clammy clay underfoot and coldly drizzling gray clouds above, where the trail wound among marshes and peat bogs. I could well understand why the migrating Goths had not paused hereabout, but had pressed on southward in search of more inviting lands.

So I was immensely grateful when I did at last come upon a village, though its populace was almost totally Slovene, and its only lodging for travelers a lowly krchma. The Slovene spoken here was even more atrociously juicy than I had heard elsewhere—the village's name I can only render in writing as Bsheshch—but the speakers were a rather higher grade of Slovenes. They were typically broad-faced, but they were taller, fair of skin and hair, quite clean, and they called themselves Polanie. My fellow lodgers in the krchma were all rivermen, stopping here while their boats unloaded and loaded again, for Bsheshch stands at the head of navigation on the Buk. Since I was mortally tired of traveling the boglands, I willingly traded my extra horse to the master of a freighting barge in payment for his carrying myself and Velox clear to the Wendic Gulf.

The big flatboat, laden with flax and furs and hides, riding the current and also being poled or paddled by its crewmen, moved much faster than I could have done on land. It was not until we were three or four days out from Bsheshch that I thought to inquire of the master what he could tell me of the Rugii who lived at the other end of his back-and-forth voyages. I was thunderstruck when he said:

"Right now, Pana Thorn, a goodly portion of them are *not* living there. All the able-bodied men are on the march, and by this time they are surely far south of where we are."

"What? On the march?"

"Tak," he said, which means "ja" in the Polanie dialect. "On our way toward Bsheshch this trip, we were passed by King Feva and his columns, also going southward. Even on horseback and on foot, they of course outpaced us because our barge was breasting the current. But also, of course, the king's troops were only lightly laden."

685

"They were on their way to join Strabo?"

"What or who is Strabo?"

"Theodoric Triarius," I said impatiently. "He who is preparing to make war against Theodoric Amaling."

The barge master spread his hands; he had never heard of either Theodoric. Well, I should have expected that. The man may have traveled thousands of miles in his lifetime, but never so much as a mile to either side of his river runs.

"All I can tell you, Pana Thorn, is that they went south. And tak, they certainly looked warlike."

"You said they were *of course* lightly laden. What did you mean by that?"

"On our several previous voyages upriver, we were not freighting trade goods. At the order of the Rugians' King Feva, we brought military provisions and supplies—and not just this barge, but many others—depositing those things at various points along the rivers Viswa and Buk. The king arranged that, so his men and horses would not have to carry everything they needed, but still could be sure of finding food and feed and such along their line of march."

A very well-planned campaign, I thought, and executed without my being aware of it until now. The Rugian army must have gone southward past me while I was off in the Amazon lands. Though I was somewhat chagrined at that, I did not feel impelled to leap overboard from the barge or demand to be set ashore. There was no point in my trailing after that army, or trying to get ahead of it to warn Theodoric. If even the common boatmen knew of the march, so would he.

When the war commenced, I ought rightly to be with my king, and I trusted that I would be. The hardiest warriors do not care to do battle in the wintertime, any more than they do in the nighttime, and for the same reason: the cold and ice and snow, like the darkness, can impede their movement. So, while Strabo would muster his forces before the onset of winter, and perhaps would make strategic disposition of them during the winter, he would not start the fighting until the spring. I had time to get there before then. But even when I did, I would be only one additional warrior in Theodoric's ranks. In the meantime, I might be of far more usefulness where I was. Theodoric had said that he would not at all mind having "a Parmenio" behind the enemy's lines.

So I stayed aboard the barge, and during the voyage I catechized the master and his crewmen to learn as much as I could about the Rugii. Since we had a long, long way to go—about a hundred and thirty Roman miles down the Buk to where it joined the much bigger river Viswa, and from there to the sea another two hundred and fifty miles— I had time to learn a fair amount, and to conjecture much more.

The Rugii, I was informed, were a Germanic people of some relation to the Vandals, who had always inhabited the lands along the coast of the Sarmatic Ocean. They were of the Old Religion, Christianity being still scorned by the far northern races. The Rugii shared those seaside lands with Slovene tribes called the Kashube and the Wilzi. Those Slovenes were the peasants who did the farming and fishing and other hard work, while the Rugii were their overlords, living on their labor, even taking the richer profit from the amber that the peasants found along the shore. For ages, the Rugii had been satisfied with their little kingdom and their semi-slaves. But now, belatedly becoming aware of the grander domains that the other Germanic peoples had carved out in the south—the Visigoths in Aquitania, the Suevians in Lusitania, their own Vandal cousins in Libya—the Rugii had been stirred by envy to ambition and emulation.

"So they march," said the barge master, "to see what *they* can win for themselves in the south."

686

I knew that their aims were not so vague as that. They were marching to help Strabo seize Moesia, because he had no doubt promised King Feva a piece of it. From what the bargemen told me of the supplies and foodstuffs they had deposited along the riversides, I calculated that the Rugian force was a substantial one, numbering perhaps eight thousand, horse and foot combined. And when the barge master happened to mention that Feva's wife, Giso, was a woman of an Amal Ostrogoth tribe, I was able to make further surmise.

I had thought it strange that Strabo, in seeking war allies, had not solicited any of the peoples near and convenient to him, but had enlisted the Rugii, even though they were so far away. I wagered that I now knew the reason. This Queen Giso must be a woman of his own branch of the Amaling line. His emissaries would have begged her, in kinship, to cajole her husband into participating in Strabo's uprising. I wagered, too, that Strabo had meanly and flagrantly lied to his kinswoman. She and her royal husband, being so far distant from Moesia, likely were not aware that Theodoric Amaling was the rightful and universally acknowledged ruler of that province—that the importuning Theodoric Strabo was only a desperate, outcast, impotent pretender. Therefore, to have won Queen Giso's sympathy to his cause and King Feva's army to help prosecute it, Strabo must grossly have misrepresented the true state of affairs.

I would have to see what I could do to rectify those matters.

✠   ✠   ✠

Like the Danuvius, the Viswa fanned out into a delta of lesser rivers and minor streams as it approached the sea. The land was mostly dunes and beaches that would have been pleasant places except that they were scoured and chilled by a continuous north wind. The barge master kept to the Viswa's main channel and that brought us to the Rugian capital, Pomore, right where the river debouched into the Wendic Gulf of the Sarmatic Ocean. Pomore means "by the sea" in the local language.

Actually the town was laid out so that it fronted as much on the river as on the sea, and was fringed with piers jutting out into both of those cold, gray, choppy bodies of water. Every building facing the waterfronts was solidly constructed of stone to withstand the perpetually wind-sprayed spume and sand. Handsome though that made the town, it also made Pomore look forbiddingly like a fortress. Our barge put in at one of the riverside docks, because, said the barge master, the docks around on the seafront were for the use of the Pomorenian fishing fleet and coastal freighters.

Before I led Velox off the boat, I paused to ask, "When will you be heading upriver again? Perhaps, when I conclude my business here, I could ride back south with you."

"Not unless your business keeps you here all winter. The Viswa will start to freeze any day now, and it will be solidly iced over for three months or more. Not I or any other master will be taking a barge out of here again until spring."

Even in my fur cloak, I shivered at the thought of being winterbound on this unappealing coast. I growled, "Guth wiljis, I shall be far from here by spring. Now, what are these two busybodies asking of me?"

None of the many people working about the docks had paid any attention to our barge's arrival, except for this pair of armed men—too old and overweight to be soldiers—who came on board officiously barking questions.

"Harbor officials," said the barge master, "here to assess my load of freight. But they also wish to know who you are and what brings you to Pomore."

I told the truth, or told it partway. "Inform them that I am the Saio Thorn, marshal to King Theodoric"—I did not say *which* Theodoric—"come to thank their Queen Giso for having sent their fellow Rugii to join in that king's war."

I showed the document I carried, confident that such lowly officials could not read it, but also that they would be impressed by the look of it. They were; when they next spoke, it was without barking. The barge master also sounded newly respectful as he interpreted:

"They say that a high personage should not have to lodge in a common boatmen's krchma. They will escort you to quarters at the palace, and have you announced to the queen."

I would have preferred being left to my own arrangements, but I could hardly refuse to be treated as a dignitary. So I let them lead me inland through the cold streets and to the palace grounds, where they summoned a steward to take charge of me. And I let the steward call a groom to stable Velox, and then lead me to a small house on the grounds, and there produce several pudding-faced Kashube servants to attend me, and then order a meal set for me.

The house was rather less palatial than my farm home back in Novae, and the servants of rather less quality than my own. Also, the meal turned out to consist almost entirely of herring dishes prepared in various ways, but none of the variations disguising the fact that it was herring. So I was glad I had not put up in a krchma offering accommodations of an *inferior* order. Anyway, the circumstances enabled me to make an appraisal of Queen Giso even before I met her. A hostess conscious of the shortcomings of her establishment ought rightly to make up for them by showing more than common courtesy. But Giso loftily refrained from granting me audience until late the next day.

My estimate of her as an affected posturer was confirmed when at last I was summoned to the main building. The "throne room" there was slightly pathetic in its pretense at splendor, and the queen spoke the Old Language in a deplorably rustic dialect, and her robes and jewels were less than rich, but she received me as if this had been the Purple Palace and she the Emperor Zeno. Giso had to be quite a young woman, for her son was also in attendance, and Prince Frido was only about nine years old. But, possibly because she was not a pretty woman—her teeth were so prominent that her lips had trouble closing—Giso affected the prickly condescension of an elderly dowager being bothered by an impubic youth.

689

"Exactly *what* is your business with us, Marshal?"

I proffered my parchment, but she waved it away as if to say that it was beneath her notice, and really indicating that she could not read. Nevertheless, she continued pretentiously to speak of herself in the royal plural.

"We accept that you come from our cousin Thiudareikhs Triarius. We hope he has not sent you to ask for further contribution from us."

I was momentarily tempted to deflate her pomposity by telling her which Theodoric I actually did represent, and making plain to her that the Rugii, at her instigation, had wasted their "contribution" on the wrong Theodoric. But before I could speak, she continued:

"Excepting the Slovenes, of course, since those wretches would be useless as warriors, we have already sent you every man older and abler than our dear son Frido here." The boy made a glum face; he did not seem happy for his exemption. "And we have much depleted our treasury to outfit that army for you. So, Marshal, if men or money or material is what you came to beg for, this audience is concluded and you have our leave to depart."

Though I had not yet spoken a single word, she stood up, erect on her throne's dais, and stared haughtily down at me, hugging her son close to her side, as if to prevent my snatching him away to war. So I resisted my temptation to tell her the truth. It was evident that plain facts and an appeal to common sense would not persuade Queen Giso to transfer her misplaced allegiance. Such a woman as this would never admit to having made a mistake—still less would she consent to correcting it—even if her stubborn vanity should cost the life of her king-husband and every soldier he was leading. So I said only, and unctuously:

"My lady queen, I petition for nothing of a material nature. My first purpose here is only to convey Theodoric's heartiest thanks for what you have already lent us. Theodoric is certain that your Rugian army will help establish him as the rightful ruler of all the Ostrogoths and all their domains. Once that is accomplished, you will be amply rewarded for your support—and for your kinship, since you and Theodoric's every other cousin will thereafter be acknowledged as belonging to the rightfully ruling branch of the Amal line."

That somewhat warmed her, as it was intended to do, and she showed the tentative beginning of a toothy smile. I went on:

"In expectation of that happy outcome of the war, Theodoric desires that the world be provided with a history of the Amals' august lineage, from remotest time to the present day. He wishes to assure that his and your family be deservedly admired, its origins honored, its virtues universally lauded. To that end, he has commissioned me to compile such a history."

"A worthy project," she said, widening her smile to display expanses of gums beyond the teeth. "It has our approbation."

"Therefore, my lady, my second purpose here is to ask your permission to acquaint myself with this coast and *its* history, because it is said that this is where the earliest Goths made landfall when they first came from the north across the sea to this continent of Europe."

"Ja, so it is said. And ja, of course you have our permission, Saio Thorn. Can we assist you in any way? Provide a knowledgeable guide, perhaps?"

"It would be most kind, my lady. And I was thinking . . . to make sure that my lady's branch of the Amal family is properly, copiously, *eminently* represented in the history, perhaps the young Prince Frido could be my guide and informant."

The boy's face went from glum to glad, then back to glum again when his mother said, with a sniff of disparagement, "Vái, the child knows more of his father's Rugian antecedents than of the Gothic."

"Then I would presume, my lady, that he also speaks the Rugian Germanic. And that dialect of the Old Language I do not speak with ease."

"Ja waíla, he even speaks the brutish Kashube Slovene"—Queen Giso laughed like a horse, toothily—"which not even the brute *Kashube* can speak with ease."

"Well, there we are! He would be invaluable to me as my interpreter hereabout." The prince was looking uncomfortable at being discussed in the third person, so I addressed him directly. "Would you do me that service and that honor, Prince Frido?"

He waited for his mother's grudging nod before he said, shyly but with pleasure, "I will, Saio Thorn."

So the next day, with proprietorial pride, young Frido showed me about the town of Pomore, though it had not a great deal to show, because it exists mainly as a center for the trade and shipping of products that come from elsewhere. Pomore's only really native product is amber, so Frido took me to various lapidary workshops to show me that material being fashioned into beads and buckles and fibulae.

Frido made a good guide, for he was a companionable lad, not at all vainglorious like his mother. Once he was away from her, he was just another boy, bright and cheerful, at least until he was reminded of her. When I asked if she was the reason he was not marching with his father the king, he got glum again and muttered:

"Mother says I am too young to go to war."

I said, under my breath, "Mother love," and that evoked recollections that made me laugh at myself for having said it. I went on, "I have known a variety of mothers, Frido, but I never had one of my own, so perhaps I am not qualified to judge them. However, I do believe that war is the province of fathers and sons, not of mothers."

"Then you think I am not too young to go?"

"Too young to fight, perhaps, but not to watch. You will be a man eventually, and every man should have some experience of war. It would be too bad if this were the only one to occur in your lifetime and you were to miss it. Still, you are only nine. You will probably have another chance. In the meantime, Frido, what *do* you do for manly excitement?"

"Well . . . I am let to play with the other palace children, so long as they respect my station and do not overstep theirs. I am let to ride my horse, and alone, without attendants, so long as I do not gallop. I am

691

let to roam the beach, and alone, and collect seashells, so long as I do not go into the water." He saw my look, and concluded lamely, "I have quite an estimable collection of seashells."

"Indeed," I said.

We walked on for a bit in silence, and then he asked, "What did you do for diversion, Saio Thorn, when you were my age?"

"At your age . . . let me see. I had no horse. Or beach. And most of the time I had to work very hard. But there was a waterfall, and a cave, and inside the cave I discovered caverns and tunnels going deep and dark into the earth, and over time I explored them all. I climbed trees, even unclimbable trees, and high up in one of them I once met a glutton face to face, and I slew it."

Frido's eyes were on my face, and they shone admiringly, enviously, wistfully. "How fortunate a boy you were," he murmured, "not to have had a mother."

Because I was concerned to merit Queen Giso's trust, I made sure to get Frido back to the palace grounds before dark. There the queen was waiting—outdoors, despite the cold, and with several of the palace guards about her—as nervous as a mother cat when someone is handling one of its kittens. And, like the cat, she was obviously relieved when I returned her son safely to his nest. So she acceded, not too grudgingly, when I asked if Frido and I might go out together again the next day. I was pleased at that, and pleased also to note that the queen had apparently not lied when she told me that every able Rugian male was gone abroad with her king-husband—for now I observed that all her palace guards were, like the harbor officials I had earlier met, men old and fat and not formidable.

The prince and queen went off to their nahtamats, and I went to my own in my guesthouse quarters. I found the meal to consist again of dishes variously prepared, and again all of them fish, and all the same fish, only this time the fish was cod.

In the succeeding days, Frido and I went farther afield, now on horseback, and now along the shores of the Amber Coast. Frido's horse was a sturdy bay gelding, though not so fine as my black, and the boy rode well, even at a stretch-out gallop, which I allowed him to do—vái, *encouraged* him to do—whenever there was no one about who might report to the palace. Frido rode even better after I helped him make a foot-rope like my own, and showed him the utility of it. One morning we would ride east along the beach, the next west, but each time going only half a day's journey out from Pomore. At noon I would turn us back for the town, to make sure that the prince arrived at the palace in time for nahtamats with his mother. And I hoped they were dining better than I was, for I was still being fed alternately on herring and cod. As a guest, I could hardly complain, but I did think it curious.

Nor could I rightly complain to anyone because I found the Amber Coast far less attractive than its name. The beach itself, as I have said, is all sand and, at least in summertime, might have been a pleasant place, except for the incessant north wind. But that beach has the insurmountable handicap of fronting on the Wendic Gulf of the Sarmatic Ocean. I had earlier looked out over other great salt waters—the Propontís and the Black Sea—and I had much enjoyed the view. But I think no one could enjoy looking at the Sarmatic Ocean. From land's edge to far horizon, it is an unrelieved gloomy gray, without so much as a lacing of white foam where it meets the beach.

During the days that Frido and I were riding the margins of the gulf, the weather got colder and colder, the winds more bitter, the Amber Coast decidedly ugly. Just upstream from the Pomore docks, the river Viswa was sheeted over with ice, and somewhere north of us even the *ocean* was freezing; the gray sea began to wash gray chunks of sea ice onto the beaches. Nevertheless, the prince and I found our outings a pleasure—he, no doubt, because he was temporarily free of his mother's strictures, I because I was learning new things. Not all of them were pertinent to my compilation of history, but some were interesting. For example, Frido took me to the stretch of sand that the Slovene peasants call nyebyesk povnó, "blue earth" (though it is more a dull green than blue), where are oftenest found the lumps and knobs and knots of amber in the raw. Frido did a competent job of interpreting whenever I questioned a coastal dweller or passerby, and he himself provided helpful information—not least when he enlightened me as to why I was being fed such monotonous meals at the palace.

693

"Of all the world's salt seas," he said, "the Sarmatic contains the least salt. And it has no tides to move and cleanse its water, so it is soupy with drifting particles of matter. Even in summer, its water is very cold, and in winter it often freezes solid enough that an army could march on the ice all the way from here to Gutaland in the north. It is for those several reasons, the fishermen say, that the Sarmatic cannot support oyster beds or deep-dwelling fish. Indeed, practically its *only* fish worth catching and eating are the cod and the herring."

So, I said to myself, the sea was as impoverished as the sandy land was infertile. Once more I was in a place where the early Goths had not cared to stay, and with good reason. I had to wonder why it had taken the later-come Rugii such a long time to tire of the Amber Coast and decide to seek better opportunities in the south. But something else in Frido's speech had interested me more.

I said, "You mentioned a place called Gutaland."

"Ja, a great island, far to the north of here. It was from there that the Goths sailed to this shore, back in the distant mists of time. My mother's forebears. Just as my father's Rugian forefathers sailed here from an island over to the west, called Rugiland."

"I believe I have heard of Gutaland," I said, "if we are speaking of the same island. I heard it called by the name of Skandza."

"Akh, *everything* yonder is called Skandza." Frido made a sweeping gesture that encompassed the whole seaward horizon, from west to east. "The lands of the Danisk, the Svear, the Fenni, the Litva, *all* the peoples who live beyond this ocean. But the different parts of Skandza have different names. Hence Rugiland, ancestral home of the Rugii. Gutaland, ancestral home of—"

I interrupted eagerly, "Is Gutaland still inhabited? Still by remnants of the Goths? Do your Pomorenian ships trade there?"

He said uncertainly, "Our ships call there. But I think there is little trade."

"Let us go and talk to a merchant ship's master."

So we did, and fortunately the master was a Rugian, meaning that he had taken some trouble to learn the history of his surroundings, which no Slovene would have done. With Frido translating, he told me:

"There is evidence that Gutaland was once, ages ago, a major center of trade and shipping. To this day, when money changes hands there, we often find ourselves receiving curious old coins—Roman, Greek, even Cretan. But that activity and prosperity must have come to an end when the Goths left, for the island has been of no consequence in all the centuries since. It is inhabited nowadays by a scant few families of Svear farmers. They manage a miserable living by raising barley and a breed of yellow cattle. We put in to buy the barley for beer-making and the distinctive hides of those cattle. I know of only one Goth still resident there, an aged woman, and she is quite mad."

"Nevertheless," I said, "I should like to be able to report to my king that I had seen the place. Would you take me there?"

"At this season? With the Sarmatic freezing over? Ni."

I urged, "My king will see that you are paid enough to compensate you and your crew for whatever danger is involved. And he does not pay in worthless antique coins."

"There is no *danger*," the master said impatiently. "Only dire discomfort and wasted effort. To cross the icy Sarmatic in the bitterness of winter to look at a worthless island, that is a fool's errand. Ni, ni. I cannot be bought."

"But you *can* be commanded," said Frido, surprising both me and the ship's master with his air of authority. "I, your crown prince, also wish to go there. You will take us."

The master argued and blustered and expostulated, but he could not flatly refuse a royal order. The prince sternly instructed him to be ready when we came again, and he and I took our leave. On our way back to the palace, I said:

"Thags izvis, Frido, for your princely intervention. But you know your mother will never let you do such a thing."

He gave me a sly look and said, "We shall see."

In every tongue at her command—Gothic and Rugian Germanic and Kashube Slovene—Queen Giso said no. "Ne! Ni! Nye! You must be mad, Frido, even to ask to go on a sea voyage."

695

I said, "The ship's master assures us there is no hazard, my lady, only the cold."

"The cold is hazard enough. The kingdom's sole heir cannot risk taking ill."

"If the boy is well bundled in furs—"

"Desist, Marshal!" she snapped. "I have already been unmotherly in letting you haul my son all about the countryside in the unhealthy open air. But that ceases here and now."

I entreated, "My lady, regard the lad. He looks ruddier and stronger now than when I came."

"I told you: be still."

I could not disobey her, but Frido could. He said, "Mother, I told the ship's master I would go. I ordered him to transport us. Can I renege on a royal decision and a royal command?"

That made her turn pale. And I realized why Frido had looked sly: he had hit on the one stratagem sure to win over a woman like Queen Giso. She had for so long insisted that he maintain his "station"—and that everyone else revere it—that she could not now let him disavow it. If she who was mother to the Crown Prince of the Rugii bade him go back on his given word, then she who was Queen of the Rugii would be sorely bruised in her overweening vanity. So, though it was no *easy* victory, Frido got his way. Giso did a great deal of agonizing and ranting and flinging her arms about, and even some weeping, but in the end her royal self-importance had to overrule her maternal solicitude.

"I hold *you* responsible for this!" she snarled at me, after she had finally capitulated. "Until you came along, Frido was a submissive and governable child. You have undermined his filial regard for his mother. Well, I promise you, this will be your last association with him."

She bellowed for servants, and barked orders at them, sending them scurrying to start the packing of everything the prince might conceivably need on the voyage. Then she again jutted at me her prognathous teeth and gums. I expected her to charge me with keeping the boy safe while we were gone. Instead she said:

"Four of my trustworthy palace guards will go along, and not solely to shield Frido from harm. They will be instructed to see that you are never alone with him, to infect him with any more of your seditious notions of rebellion. When the voyage is done, Marshal, you are to leave here. But if Frido shows any slightest sign of being still unruly, you will leave here with your back flogged to ribbons. Is that understood?"

I was not greatly frightened by that threat, for I did not intend to get flogged. But I had to concede in all honesty that I would eventually deserve to be. For I was planning to sin, not just against the laws of Gothic kinship, but worse, against the universal laws of hospitality given and received.

12

he ship's master, still averse to making the voyage, received us grumpily and with further remonstration. I think he might have contrived some last-minute excuse to keep from going—possibly even holing his ship's planking—except that Queen Giso had come with us to the docks and speedily made herself so disagreeable to everyone in sight that the Sarmatic Ocean seemed a better place to be than Pomore. So the master threw up his hands, ranged his men at their oars, and we cast off.

The ship was a broad, apple-bowed merchant vessel, much like those I had seen in the Propontís, only not so big. It had two masts, but of course any sails would have been impediments because we were heading directly into the north wind. So we had to depend for propulsion on the oarsmen. There being only a single bank of those at either side, the ship moved slowly enough to make me believe that the Sarmatic Ocean really was as "soupy" as Frido had described it. Except for the brutal cold, I found this sea travel not very different from being out in a tomus fishing smack on the almost as gloomy waters of Lake Brigantinus.

However, young Frido was thrilled and excited to be taking his first ride upon any water, and I was pleased for him, remembering my own first time, when old Wyrd and I had ridden a barge across the river Rhenus. Once we were out of sight of the Amber Coast, the ship's master too seemed inspirited by being on the open sea; he gradually shed his surliness and became friendly again. Of course, he and I and Frido, when we tired of loitering topside and gazing at the gray water—which we very soon did—could retire to shelter in the enclosed cabins at the stern of the ship. The four guards sent by Giso were already under cover there, and the ship's crewmen not on duty, and even the ship's two steersmen were sheltered by a canopy. But the men laboring at the oars had no protection and no reason to be glad at having put to sea. Though their benches were beneath the upper deck, hence roofed against the elements above, those men still had to endure the cruel cold wind and spiteful cold spindrift that lashed in at them through the rowports. I could not make out the Rugian words of the chant with which the rowing leader was setting the stroke, but I suspected that it was a long, protracted cursing of me and Frido.

As we went ever northward, the weather and the surrounding view changed, too, but only for the worse. The steel-cold air got ever colder, the glass-shard wind ever sharper, the sheet-lead sky ever heavier and lower. If the sea had been soup in the Wendic Gulf, it turned into slush as we proceeded across the Sarmatic Ocean proper. The water got genuinely thick with granular ice, and the rowing leader's chant got slower and slower because the oarsmen had to pull so hard against that pulpy muck. Though the steersmen in the stern had had little work to do in the first three or four days out from Pomore, having only to hold the straight northern course, they too began to find their task laborious. They soon were manipulating their sweeps almost continuously, to guide the ship between or around immense floating slabs of what those seamen call "toross"—ice piled on ice, layered, overlaid, heaped up into hummocky gray bulks as big around as our vessel and frequently as tall.

Even Frido, so enthusiastic at the start of the voyage, was finally going on deck only once a day, each morning, to see if the seascape had become any more worth looking at. Since it never did, he spent most of his time below, with myself and the ship's master, being our interpreter as we talked and drank beer. Queen Giso's four guardsmen never participated in that, and never tried to enforce the queen's order that Frido and I be kept apart. If the fat old men had tried, I would have pitched them overboard, and they probably knew that. The ship's master and I talked of many things of no consequence, but I did glean from our talks one more new scrap of information for my historical compilation, one more name to add to my roster of early Gothic kings.

"It was a King Berig," the master told me, "who commanded the ships that brought the Goths from Gutaland to the continent. The old songs say that there were three ships, but I dispute that. Unless they were each the size of Noah's Ark, I am sure there must have been many more ships—a whole fleet of them. I have sometimes wondered: what became of those ships after the crossing? Did Berig simply abandon them on the Wendic shore? Did their masters take them empty back to Gutaland? But akh, that was ages ago. The ships have long been rotted to nothing."

At last, after how many days I do not remember, when the cold and the dreariness and the confinement and the monotony had become well-nigh unendurable, the ship's master one afternoon broke off our three-way conversation. Without going to glance overside, without having received any notice or impulse that I could detect, he said suddenly and simply, "We ought to be raising the island right about now. Will you come and have a look?"

Frido went scrambling for the upper deck, and I followed almost as eagerly—and there was the first land we had seen since leaving Pomore behind. There was Gutaland, just emerging from the gray sea haze on the northwestern horizon, off to our left front. I wish I could report that what we saw was a land as enchantingly beautiful and alluring as the Fortunate Isles of Avalonnis are said to be. But it looked more like that other fabled island, Ultima Thule, the Farthest Place of All. Gutaland was but one more dismal feature of that dismal Sarmatic Ocean, only one more of the many abodes that I could see the Goths had had good reason to leave.

The prince and I gazed at it over the sea. Or rather—because for many days we had seen little actual water between the innumerable floating islands of toross—he and I gazed out over those drifting gray hillocks of pack ice. And if we had not been forewarned, we might have taken Gutaland to be just another and exceptionally gigantic toross. From our distance, I could not well judge dimensions, but the island was a long one, extending out of sight in the haze at either extremity. And it was a high one, consisting of cliffs that rose sheer from the gray sea. The cliffs were of gray rock columns like pillars bunched together, but here and there unbunched columns stood apart from the rest, individual spires and spikes sticking up from the water. Those could have been the fraying, raveling edges of the ragged last outskirts of the world.

The ship's master certainly saw our disappointment at having come this long and weary way to find so little, and he may have felt slightly gratified, because he had promised us exactly that. But he courteously refrained from saying, "I told you so," and said instead:

"I am sure you will wish to set foot on your ancestors' homeland. The only decent harbor is far around on the western coast of the island, and solidly icebound in this season, impossible to reach. So I have brought you along this high eastern shore because I know of a little half-moon cove here, where the water is deep enough for a mooring. Also it is the habitation of that aged and demented Gothic woman of

699

whom I earlier spoke. You may as well have a word with her. Who knows? She may prove to be your own many-times-great-grandmother."

I very much doubted that, and I also doubted that an old madwoman would have anything of interest to tell me. But the master was doing his best to be helpful, so I let him put the ship into the cove. It required closely concerted work by the steersmen, the rowing leader and the oarsmen — with the master confidently shouting instructions to them — to edge our vessel through the drifting, shifting, colliding, crunching toross ice. But before dark, the seamen had brought the ship in to a scooped-out cavity in the cliff wall, where the rock columns loomed above a tiny shelf of shingle, and there we anchored for the night.

Frido and I were awakened early the next morning by a thin but urgent outcry from somewhere. Thinking it must be the ship's sentry calling an alarm, we hastened on deck, and found that the shouting was coming from the shore. Over there a small and nondescript figure was doing a sort of dance on the shingle, gesticulating and shouting incoherently. So we went to where the ship's master was directing some men in lowering a small leather boat overside. But he was doing that with no hurry, and said offhandedly:

"No danger, no distress. It is only old Hildr. She gets wildly excited whenever any vessel puts in here, because every master brings her a gift of provisions. I think it is all she gets to live on, and I do not know how she manages to live between feedings."

The ship's cook dropped into the boat a large slab of smoked pork and a skin of beer, and the master himself rowed me and Frido over. There was only a short stretch of water between the ship and the cove shelf, and only a few chunks of drifting ice, no hindrance. As we closed the distance, I could see that the ash-colored cliffs were pocked with numerous hollows and caves. I could also espy the woman's pitiful abode, nothing but a heap of driftwood haphazardly piled against the cliff wall, thatched and chinked with dried seaweed.

When we stepped ashore, the woman danced up to us, dressed in gray rags and ribbons of some kind of very limp and flimsy leather. Without ceasing to dance — her lank white hair flopping, her sharp old knees and elbows madly jerking — she babbled and plucked at our sleeves as we hauled the boat up on the shingle. I could tell that she was speaking a dialect of the Old Language, but little more. She employed a great many words that I had seen in old Gothic manuscripts but never had heard uttered, and she spoke with bewildering rapidity.

700

Prince Frido's young ears were perhaps quicker than mine, for he translated, "She is thanking us for whatever we have brought her."

The master took from the boat the provisions the cook had loaded, and Hildr, still jigging and jogging in her old-bones dance, clasped them to her scrawny chest. She blithered some more, then turned and scuttled away toward her cliffside hut, but beckoning for us to follow.

Frido said, "To thank us, she offers to show us something of interest."

I glanced at the ship's master. He grinned and nodded. "Come along. She has shown it many times to me. I told you old Hildr is mad."

So we followed the aged woman, and had to get down on our hands and knees to squeeze into the hut behind her. There was nothing inside except a smoky fire of faggots laid in a ring of stones, and a pallet made of dried seaweed and filthy rags. The single room was scarcely big enough to contain all four of us, but there was unused space beyond; I could now see that the hut had been built by leaning the pieces of driftwood about the dark opening of a shoulder-high cave in the cliff wall.

However, if there was anything to show us, the crone had other things to do first. Without even heating her smoked pork slab over the fire, she was already tearing at it with her few snaggle teeth, and swigging from the spout of the beerskin. Hildr was incredibly old, so wrinkled and gnarled and leather-brown and ugly that she could have been one of the three Furies. She possessed only one eye, with a vacant hole where the other had been, and her nose and chin nearly touched when she munched. Her chewing did not stop her babbling, but it slowed the articulation to where I could comprehend it. I now heard her say, quite clearly, even quite sanely:

701

"The master will have told you I am mad. All say that I am mad. That is because I remember things from long ago, things other folk never knew, so they do not believe those things. Does that prove me mad?"

I asked gently, "What sort of things do you remember, good Hildr?"

Chewing hard, she waved a greasy old hand, as if to indicate that the things were too numerous to list. Then she swallowed and said, "Akh, among others . . . the great sea beasts that used to exist . . . the monster kraken, the creature grindl, the dragon fafnir . . ."

"Mythical monsters," the ship's master said aside to me. "Seamen's superstitions."

"Myths? Ni allis!" snapped old Hildr. "I can tell you, Sigurd hooked and netted and beached a many of them in his time." With the haughty pride of a grand lady, she fingered the sleazy rags she wore. "Sigurd slew those beasts so he could dress me in fine raiment." Seeing her leather rags up close, I could recognize them as dogfish-skin.

I said, "Good Hildr, you are a Gothic woman. Would you remember any of the other Goths once habitant in this Gutaland?"

Spraying chewed matter, she exclaimed, "Weaklings! Faint-hearts! Softlings! Nothing like Sigurd, they were! This Gutaland was too harsh for them, so they fled. Some went west with Beowa, most went south with Berig."

I had already calculated that King Berig must have lived about the time of Christ, so if old brown Hildr was claiming to remember him, she was either mad indeed or old indeed. Humoring her fancy, I asked, "Why did you not go with them?"

"Vái!" Her one bleary eye looked at me with astonishment. "I could not leave my Sigurd!"

"Are you saying that your Sigurd and King Berig lived at the same time?"

She bridled as if insulted, saying loudly, "Sigurd *still* lives!"

The master was grinning again and shaking his head in denial, so I did not pursue that. I asked, "Good Hildr, do you perhaps remember any other *names* of those times? Besides Sigurd and Berig?"

"Akh, ja." Her one eye now gave me a measuring look, and she chewed for a while before continuing. I had not yet said anything to her about history, but surprisingly she did. "If you would know the very beginning of things, you must cast back . . . beyond history . . . beyond Sigurd and Beowa and Berig . . . back to where you touch the night of time. There you would find no Goths, no people, no human beings at all, but only the Aesir—the family of the Old Gods—Wotan and Thor and Tiw and all the rest."

When she paused to tear off another bite of meat, I said encouragingly, "Those names I know, ja."

She nodded and swallowed. "Back there in the night of time, the Aesir appointed one of their minor kinfolk to become the father of the first human beings. His name was Gaut, and he dutifully sired the Gautar, the Many Peoples. Over the ages, they took various names. Here in the north, the Svear, the Rugii, the Seaxe, the Iutar, the Danisk . . ."

When she paused for a swig at the beerskin, I said, "I see. All the

Germanic peoples. In the south they took the names Alamanni, Franks, Burgunds, Vandals—"

"Notice!" she interrupted, pointing the skin's spout at me. "Of all those peoples, only we Goths have kept our first father's name through the centuries since. It changed some, ja—from Gautar to Gutans and finally to Goths—but we kept the name."

Well, that was the single most antique piece of historical information I had been given yet. I may be thought slightly mad myself to have taken that as worth recording, coming as it did from a madwoman. But Hildr sounded sane enough on this subject, and she certainly *looked* old enough to have been present in person at what she called "the beginning of things."

Now, rending the meat again, she said through a mouthful of it, "Good . . . tastes good . . ." And that obviously reminded her of something. She swallowed quickly so she could tell me, "It was also from our original father's name of Gaut that all the Many Peoples derived the word 'good.' "

Then she laid aside the meat and the beerskin, saying, "Come, my lords. I will take you to Sigurd." She picked up a brand from the fire, blew it to flame and, carrying it for a torch, shuffled into the cave mouth behind us.

Frido, looking just a little apprehensive, asked the ship's master, "You say you have seen her Sigurd?"

He grinned again. "I have. My father saw. My grandfather must have seen. Go see for yourselves. Old Hildr is only deranged, not dangerous."

I had to stoop to get inside the cave. It was not very deep, and at the farther end of it the aged woman was holding her torch with one hand, using the other to scrabble at a heap of damp seaweed until she uncovered a long, pale object lying on the rough stone floor.

"Sigurd," she said, pointing a withered finger.

Frido and I went closer, and saw that the object was a solid block of ice, as big as a sarcophagus. I motioned for old Hildr to hold the torch closer, but she croaked an objection.

"I must not risk melting the ice. That is why I keep it in here the year around, and keep it covered with weed, so it melts not even by a fraction."

As our eyes adjusted to the dim, flickering torchlight, we could see that the ice block truly *was* a sarcophagus, and the crone truly did possess a "Sigurd"—or at least a preserved male human being. Although

703

the ice block's irregular surface blurred our view of him, we could make out that he was clad in rude leather garments, and that in life he had been tall and muscular. Squinting more closely, I saw that he had clear young skin, an abundance of yellow hair, and that his still-open, surprised-looking eyes were a bright blue. His features were those of a peasant youth, somewhat slack and stupid. But, all in all, he had been a handsome young fellow, and still was. Meanwhile, old Hildr went on talking and, now that she was not chewing, her speech was again getting indistinct, so that I could catch only disconnected words and phrases:

"Many, many years ago . . . a bitter winter day. Sigurd went . . . with Beowa . . . Wiglaf . . . Heigila . . . in fishing boat. Sigurd overboard . . . among the toross. Companions dredged him out . . . encased in ice . . . brought him ashore thus . . . thus he has been ever since . . ."

"How tragic," murmured Frido. "Was he perhaps your son? Your grandson?"

Her reply was slurred, but it was unmistakably indignant. "Sigurd . . . my *husband!*"

I said, "Oh vái. Many years ago, indeed. We sincerely condole in your grief, Widuwo Hildr. And we admire your devoted caretaking of Sigurd. You must have loved him very much."

I would have expected the hag to sniffle or simper or give some other such widowly response. But old Hildr seemed much more emotionally moved. She flailed her torch about, and flaffed her fish-skin rags, and screeched so that the cave echoed, and Frido shrank back against the rock wall in fright. But I was able, just barely, to comprehend the wretched old crone's words of angry lament.

"Grief? . . . Love? . . . With all my heart, I *hate* the spiteful Sigurd! Just look, my lords! Look at my husband, then look at me. I ask you, is that fair? Is it *fair?*"

704

13

2ls we boarded the ship again, the master said affably, "Since we came so far, and are here now, we need be in no hurry to leave. You can go ashore as often as you like."

And Frido said hopefully, "Saio Thorn, we could ascend the cliffs and go roaming the island's interior."

"Ne," I said. "Thags izvis, master, but you may raise anchor as soon as you are ready. Take us back to Pomore." So he went off shouting orders, and I said to the prince, "Here ends my questing. Surely the history of the Goths *cannot* go further back than what we heard from old mad Hildr. I need see no more of this Gutaland and Skandza and the frozen far north. I appreciate your enterprise, young Frido, but winter travel on foot is hard enough even in less forbidding lands than these. I will not hazard your health, and have your queen-mother flog me to ribbons."

There was a short silence. This was the moment in which I would commit myself to sinning against the laws of both kinship and hospitality. However remote might be the Gothic kinship between Queen Giso and myself, I was about to be disloyal to it. However grudging had been her welcome of me, it *had* been hospitality, and I was about to repay it with treachery. But I waited, trusting that Prince Frido would broach the idea and save my suggesting it.

He finally said, "What *will* you do now, Saio Thorn?"

"Go south," I said airily, but still taking care to choose my words ambiguously. "Rejoin King Theodoric. Then go into battle with him— and with your own king-father—when the war commences."

"How will you go south? The river Viswa will not thaw for two months yet."

"Akh, I have a good mount. Winter travel is not impossibly difficult on horseback."

705

There was another short silence. Again I waited.

He said hopefully, "I too have a good mount."

I let his words hang there between us for a moment, then said, but not sternly, "You would flout the command of your queen-mother?"

"I believe . . . what you said . . . that war is not the province of mothers. I shall tell her that, to her face, and then—"

"Hold, Frido. I recommend that you forgo any confrontation." In counseling furtiveness, I was but being practical, for I had seen how the boy quailed in that woman's overbearing presence. "We have with us all our traveling needs. When we dock at Pomore, you have only to order one of your companion guards to go and fetch our saddled horses, as if you wished us to make triumphal entry at the palace. We fling our packs on the horses and . . . simply gallop out of town."

"Then I *am* going with you?" he cried, beaming brightly.

"You are. I look forward to presenting you to your king-father. That is, if we do not get waylaid. Your queen-mother is bound to send her guards galloping in pursuit of us."

"Akh!" He laughed disdainfully. "You and I can outgallop all those lumpish, grumbly, dice-playing, beer-bellied old men! Right, friend Thorn?"

"Right, friend Frido!" I said, and clapped him on the shoulder.

His smile got even broader, and he pointed upward. "See? An omen of good augury."

For the first time during the voyage, the leaden clouds were parting, showing patches of crystalline blue sky, and rays of sunlight came down to gild Gutaland's cliffs and the deck we stood on and the toross ice all around us. The crewmen were now hauling sails aloft on the two high masts, and the canvas billowed out as bright as cloth of gold in that new radiance, and the ship gave a jaunty forward bound as if it too was eager and happy to be returning southward.

But that night, when Gutaland was again below the horizon, there came another seeming omen, one that I might have regarded as foreboding, if I put any credence at all in omens. The sky was by then completely free of clouds, a clear blue-black instead of dirty gray, and full of brilliant stars. Under full sail, the ship was running briskly before the wind—actually putting a bow wave and wake of pearly white lace on the sullen Sarmatic waters—coursing due south and jinking only now and then to left or right to avoid the bigger toross packs. I was standing at the stern, admiring the deft work of the steersmen and being glad to see the north star Phoenice directly behind

706

us—when, in a matter of a moment, Phoenice was obscured from my sight.

Slowly, slowly but majestically, there came dropping from the zenith to the horizon in all directions great luminous swathes of drapery and curtains and veils, translucent and coldly colored pale green, pale blue, pale lavender. They waved and fluttered about the heavens, but only lazily, dreamily, in dead silence, like goose-summer cloth stirred by a gentle breeze—not by the north wind that was still blowing a gale down here on the world's surface. The sight was unutterably beautiful, but it stopped my breath because, had I been a superstitious person, a believer in gods, I could only have supposed that those gods had all died, and that these spectral draperies must be their *shrouds*. Fortunately, before I could do or say anything foolish, I looked to the steersmen, and saw them not transfixed as I was, but only cheerily regarding the show above and exchanging apparently untroubled comments on it.

I went to see if young Frido had been unsettled by this cosmic event, and found him just as cheerful as the steersmen. Indeed, when I mumbled to him something about heavenly omens, he perceived my concealment of my own concern. As if I had been the child and Frido the adult, he good-humoredly assured me, "If it is an omen, Thorn, it cannot portend much, for it is common in our skies, particularly in the wintertime. It is only what we Rugii call the murgtanzern, the merry dancers."

707

Well, that did not explain what the merry dancers *were*, or why they danced—and no one else has ever given me an explanation either—but I could hardly go on being concerned about a phenomenon so innocuous that it was called *merry*. So I ceased being so, and merely stayed awake to enjoy the spectacle during the remainder of that night. I am glad I did, because the morning brought back the low-hanging gray clouds, and I have never seen the murgtanzern again in all my life.

✠　✠　✠

The homecoming voyage was not so tedious and uncomfortable as the outgoing, because, with the wind behind us, we made it in about half the time. When we raised Pomore one forenoon, and the seamen slipped the sails and the ship slid toward the docks, slowing as it neared them, I saw someone excitedly waving from there. I had rather dreaded that Queen Giso would have arranged for advance notice of our approach and would be skulking in wait. But this was not the queen; it was my whilom companion Maghib. So I said to Prince Frido:

"It may be that we can elaborate our plan somewhat, and better assure our safe escape."

"What do you mean?"

"I am not sure yet. But hearken to me. The ship's master seems well disposed to obey your commands. Tell him not to make fast to the dock, but to tether the ship only loosely, and to have his oarsmen at the ready. Then, as we planned, order one of the guards to go and saddle and bring our mounts. But order him to do that *in secret*, to tell no one at the palace of our arrival, because you wish to surprise your mother. By the time he gets back here with our horses, I will know better what we might do next. Meanwhile, you wait here on board."

Frido proceeded unquestioningly to do as I suggested. As soon as the ship touched the dockside, I leapt ashore and ran to greet and embrace the joyously grinning Armenian. We thumped one another on the back and I said:

"It is good to see you, Maghib. I trust you are fully recovered."

"Ja, fráuja. I wish I could have recovered and come here sooner, to inform you that the Rugian army passed through Lviv only shortly after you left there. But I assume you must know that by now."

"I do. Have you any other news? Anything from Meirus? From Theodoric?"

"Ne, fráuja. Only travelers' reports—that both Theodoric and Strabo are preparing their forces for a clash in the spring."

"Hardly news, that." I was keeping an eye on the ship, and now saw one of the queen's guards step ashore and go off at a shuffling trot toward the palace. "Well, I have some small news for you, Maghib. Your injury has been avenged, and the dastardly Thor will never assail you or anyone again." He started an Armenianly wordy spate of thanks and undying gratitude, but I cut him short, asking, "What inspired you to meet this particular vessel this morning?"

"My lady Queen Giso told me that you and her son had gone a-voyaging on it, and that it was the only merchant ship at sea right now. So I have come down here to the docks each day."

"*Your* lady told you?" I said, wondering.

"As you know, I came to Pomore bearing the fráuja Meirus's letter accrediting me as his amber agent. I was advised to present that to the queen. It seems she oversees every mercantile matter here, however insignificant. So I gained audience with her, and told her of my acquaintance with you, and also mentioned having seen her royal husband pass through Lviv at the head of his troops. She most graciously gave me lodging in what had been your quarters at the palace. I am still installed there, and I am very much enjoying the luxurious accommodations, except that I begin to find the unvarying meals of fish rather—"

"Vái, Maghib!" I interrupted. "I led the queen to believe that I am here as a representative of Theodoric *Strabo*. Have you let slip that I am an impostor?"

"Ne, ne, fráuja. My lady Giso did make some remarks that puzzled me, early on. But I soon divined their import, so I have let her go on believing that we are both—you and I—firmly on the side of Strabo and his ally, her husband, King Feva. Your imposture is undisclosed."

"Thags izvis," I said, relieved. To repay Maghib's good offices, I went on to tell him what I had learned about amber-finding in the local "blue earth" and amber-working in the local lapidaries' shops, and told him where to find those places in order to learn more of his new trade. I concluded, "I have no doubt of your success as an amber trader, given your exemplary initiative. I must say that you and *your lady* Giso seem to have become very close very quickly."

He looked modestly proud. "She seems to favor me. I think she has never met an Armenian before, or ever even heard of such a thing, so she does not realize that a tetzte Armenian is unworthy of a respectable woman's notice." Now he looked sheepish, lowered his eyes and shuffled his feet. "She has even spoken admiringly of the length of my nose."

I blinked in surprise and murmured, "Well, well, well," for this opened possibilities. While I pondered them, I said absently, "I hope you complimented her in return, on the length of her teeth."

"Eh?"

"Nothing, nothing. So the queen favors you, does she?"

"Well . . . she even asked if, when I watched her husband ride through Lviv, I noticed *his* nose. How small it is."

"Gudisks Himins, man!" I said jovially, and pummeled his back again. "Why are you wasting time, then, standing here talking to me? Go and press your advantage."

"She is a queen!" he squeaked. "I am an Armenian."

"Many noble ladies have a secret taste for the squalid. Be not faint of heart, Maghib. Go. Make me proud of you."

"But . . . but . . . have you no need of my services?"

"You *will* be serving me. My work here is done, and now I must hasten back to Theodoric." I saw the guard returning, leading my Velox and Frido's gelding, so I spoke rapidly. "I am taking with me the queen's

709

son, for reasons you need not know. Giso is going to be irate when she finds out, but it will mollify her some to suppose that I am taking him to the encampment of Strabo and Feva. Still, the boy and I must get away with as much of a head start as possible. You will provide that—you and your long nose, so to speak—by keeping Queen Giso distracted."

He cried despairingly, "She will realize my complicity, fráuja! She will have me *hanged* by my—so to speak—nose."

"Ne. She will not even know that the prince and I have been here today. I will send the ship back to sea." Over Maghib's shoulder I now saw Frido come ashore from the vessel, the other guards carrying our packs, so I spoke even more rapidly. "Here is what you do. Exert yourself to win that queen's favor, this very day, and satisfy her curiosity about your nose. Keep her blissfully busy for as many days and nights as possible. When she has had enough, or you have, steal away to the place I told you of, the beach of the blue earth, and there make a good fire. The ship's master will be watching for it. The vessel will return to Pomore as if for the first time, and to stay. Then, ja, Queen Giso will learn that Frido and I are not aboard. But we will be long gone, and she will not even think to connect you with our escape. Now go. Do it."

He looked slightly dazed, but he nodded and clasped my hand in affirmation, then went hastily away. I rejoined Frido, who was directing the guards in fixing the packs behind our saddles, and I said in an undertone:

"Order all four guards back aboard the ship." He did that, and they muttered but obeyed, and I told him the rest. "Have the master take the vessel out of sight of Pomore. He is to stay away and stay unseen until there is lighted a watch fire on that beach where you showed me the blue earth. Then, but not until then, he can bring the ship and the guards home again."

Frido frowned a little. "As you said, Thorn, the master does seem to accede willingly to my commands. But can we expect that he will go on following my orders when I am not present?"

"Tell him you are playing a wicked and malicious jape on your mother. I have a feeling he will be pleased to help it succeed."

Frido went aboard one last time and, after only a brief colloquy with the man, came back humorously wagging his head. "You are right again. He said he would be happy to disoblige the queen. He seems to have taken a dislike to her at their one brief encounter."

"I cannot think why," I said drily. I waited only to make sure that the rowers really were backing oars and the ship moving astern, away from the dock. Then I said, "Very good. Mount up, Frido. But let us not depart, as we first planned, at a dare-the-devil gallop. Let us go quietly, unobtrusively, through back alleys."

I was satisfied that we were making a clean escape, and I thanked the goddess Fortune or whatever other agency had brought Maghib so fortuitously to our assistance. Queen Giso would, of course, erupt like Vesuvius, but her son and I would be beyond her reach, and there was no one on whom she could reasonably wreak reprisal. The ship's master would only have been following the prince's royal orders, and he had witnesses to vouch for that. The same with the four hapless guards. Maghib would have been innocently waiting for me to arrive, the whole time the queen was doing the same—and waiting *with* the queen, in her own bed and arms—so she could hardly suspect him of involvement in our ruse. Maghib might even help ameliorate the queen's fury (I smiled when I thought of it) by going on plying his nose, so to speak. Unless (and I stopped smiling and winced) Queen Giso, with those awful teeth, should incontinently *bite*.

Not until Frido and I had ridden as far as Pomore's scattered outskirt habitations did I turn again to him. "From here on and from now on, lad, you have leave to gallop as fast and far and freely as you please. *Come!*" And I put heels hard to my own steed.

711

✠   ✠   ✠

The long overland journey was uneventful, as far as I was concerned, but every mile and every day of it was an exciting adventure to the young prince, simply because everything outside the Pomore palace was so new to him. He had never before forded a river, and we forded many of them, or climbed a mountain, and we climbed many of them. He had never had to hunt or trap or fish to feed himself, but I showed him how and he learned quickly—even managing to rope small game with the sliuthr I had adopted from the Amazons. Except that there was not such a great difference in our ages, I felt very much like old Wyrd playing mentor and tutor to that inexperienced youth he had called "urchin"—because I taught Frido many of the same bits of woodcraft: how to recognize edible growth even in deep winter, how to cook venison in its own skin, how to use the sun-stone on a cloudy day to find direction . . .

The sun-stone was invaluable in helping us keep the course I judged the shortest way back to the Roman provinces—that is, going directly south. Of course, we had to deviate from that occasionally, where it was easier to go around obstacles than to struggle through or over them. I deliberately circled at a distance about every settled community we found in our way, to avoid having to answer all the questions that backwoods people always ask. But we encountered few such settlements and, after we left the Viswa River behind, there were almost none.

That straight-south course at last brought us to civilization, at the great bend in the river Danuvius. Or, I should say, it brought us within the borders of civilization, because there was nothing of that in evidence except the tumbledown remains of the old castrum city Aquincum, which I had seen before. Still, we *were* in the province of Valeria, and Prince Frido was as excited by that—his first setting foot in the Roman Empire—as he had been by every other novelty on the journey. I noted that the ice in the river was breaking up, meaning that springtime could not be far off, so I set us a brisker pace than we had yet traveled, hurrying downstream along the Danuvius, still directly southward.

That brought us to the naval base of the Pannonian Fleet at Mursa. While Frido ambled about, gazing wide-eyed at the first Romans he had ever seen, I introduced myself to the fleet's navarchus and produced my document of marshalcy signed by his chief commander. He was instantly ready to oblige any request I might make of him, so I asked first what news he had of war or other doings in Moesia Secunda. The war was still pending, he said, and probably imminent, but he had nothing yet to report except routine events. So I asked next for ink and parchment, and sat down to write a message. I bade the navarchus send it by his swiftest dromo vessel to the Iron Gate, and there have it handed on to the Moesian Fleet, and have *its* swiftest dromo rush it to Novae and to King Theodoric.

The navarchus had the document on its way downriver before Frido and I reclined at table (for our first civilized meal ever indoors together) in the triclinium of the navarchus's quarters. In my message to Theodoric I naturally had not wasted words to recount anything of my adventures and discoveries while on my mission to compile a history. I only explained, and succinctly, how I had been acting as his "Parmenio" in the land of the Rugii—and, in essence, my message was this:

Avoid engagement with Strabo and his allies until I get there. I bring a secret weapon.

14

y the time a barge brought me and Frido and our mounts downriver to Novae, there was no ice anywhere and the trees on either bank were in early bud. Because the Danuvius flowed past my farmlands before it reached the city, I had us put ashore there, and took the prince to lodge in my farmhouse, telling him, "You might as well be comfortable while I go and find out where your king-father is encamped."

The farm servants all gave welcoming cheers when I came home after so long away, and the women servants cooed and clucked with motherly delight at my putting in their charge a new young fráuja, and Frido himself made pleased exclamations at finding my house rather grander than the royal one in which he had grown up. I saw him installed in his quarters and then, without even taking time to bathe and change into fresh garments, I rode straightaway to Theodoric's palace.

713

I had thought that the king might be afield with his troops, but the aged steward Costula, greeting me most warmly, told me Theodoric was in residence, and ushered me immediately in to private audience. I found my friend looking more handsomely regal than ever. He had put on some weight—of muscle, not fat—and his beard had grown to heroic luxuriance, and he seemed to have a more deliberate air about him. That did not inhibit our embracing heartily and shouting salutations and assurance of our mutual good health. But then he held me at arm's length and said:

"I obeyed your admonition, Saio Thorn. No battle has yet been joined. But I confess this has made me chafe, having to hold off. I should have preferred to fall upon the enemy before giving him any chance to choose the place and time."

"Then you can do it now," I said, and told him what weapon I had brought, and what I advised be done with it. "The lad supposes that I will take him to join his father. And, in a sense, I will be doing exactly that. However, I realize that my plan could result in there being no battle at all, which would probably displease you. I well remember your telling me that you care not to fare in peace, but *mith blotha.*"

Theodoric smiled reminiscently, then surprised me by shaking his head. "I used to speak fondly of blood, ja, when I was a warrior among warriors. But the longer I am king, the more I see the good sense of being not needlessly wasteful of warriors. It may displease *them,* but I will not decline any stratagem that can win a quick and clean victory. I heartily congratulate you and sincerely thank you, Thorn, for having brought us the weapon that can accomplish that."

I asked, "Where is Strabo right now?"

"The other side of the Danuvius, a day's ride to the north of it, near a village called Romula. According to my speculatores, he has put Romula under tribute for victuals, and is watering from a small river there. All the time you have been away, he has been gathering forces by little and little. Those of his old adherents who have stayed with him or returned to him. Still-defiant remnants of the Sarmatae whom we defeated long ago. And, of other nationalities, this and that small tribe or gau or even sibja that he has persuaded to gamble for greatness. His most numerous troops, as you must know, are the Rugii of the ambitious King Feva." Theodoric paused to laugh. "However grudgingly, I must give credit to my cousin Triarius. Because of his swine-man mutilation, he remains a recluse, so he has somehow seduced all those ragtag constituents without any of them even laying eyes on him."

"And evidently," I said, "without any of them realizing what a foredoomed venture this is. Strabo is bound to lose. Why, your regular army aside, you could marshal all the Roman river-fortress legions against him."

"Of course. And the Emperor Zeno has offered me as many more legions as I might want from the Eastern Empire. But I prefer not to owe any obligation to Zeno. Ja, my cousin knows very well that this is his last gasp. That is why he has not yet made his assault. He hopes that merely by being a nuisance once more—and more of a threat this time—he can wring concessions. A small patch of homeland for his still-loyal Ostrogoths. A small measure of dominion for himself. Nothing for any of those hopeful allies of his. But he would not weep over their disappointment, once they had served their purpose."

Theodoric laughed again, and comradely thumped me on the back.

714

"Well! Now let us prepare to disappoint them *all!*" He strode to the throne-room door and gave orders to a page outside.

We were shortly joined by the chief military commanders, some but not all of whom I already knew, and Theodoric briskly issued instructions.

"Pitzias, commence the ferrying of our main forces across the Danuvius. Ibba, have your centuriones draw up those troops in battle array just out of bow-shot of Romula. The enemy will be hastening to dispose their own formations, so, Herduic, you go under a flag of truce and tell Strabo that I desire a parley before we engage. Recommend to him that he have King Feva in attendance as well. I and my marshals Soas and Thorn will be outside Romula by the time those arrangements are made. Go now, and see to it. Habái ita swe!"

They saluted smartly and departed, and Theodoric said to me:

"I will not detain you now, Thorn. I know you must be anxious to soak in a hot therma and get into clean clothes. But I am eager to hear the account of your other quest, the historical one. Come to nahtamats tonight and we will enjoy a long, leisurely colloquium. You can bring along Prince Frido if you like."

"Ne, let us not confuse the boy. He thinks I am reporting to Theodoric Strabo. You can hardly pretend to be that Theodoric without somehow similarly contorting your eyeballs. Frido is happy enough at my farm, well attended and well guarded. With your permission, I will keep him lodged there until we are ready to ride to Romula."

So I returned to my farmhouse, and luxuriated during the rest of the day in a steaming bath, and then dressed in my finest Thorn garb. On my way back to the palace, I stopped by my Novae house, just to make sure it was still intact, and to stow there the Veleda belongings I had carried all over the continent.

In the palace triclinium, over a sumptuous repast and much excellent wine, I told Theodoric of my adventures since he had sent me on the journey and the mission. In general, I told the truth, however much it might contradict the old songs and other treasured myths and legends and fables. However, not to invite too many searching questions, I considerably glossed over the reasons why a certain Thor had come unexpectedly from the Visigoth lands to join me in my quest. I also glossed over the circumstances by which both that person Thor and the one-time palace cosmeta Swanilda, while in my company, had "come to grief," as I phrased it. I told him of the folk I had met along my way, I

715

told him also the names of unfamiliar peoples of whom I had heard or actually walked among, I spoke also of the many curious customs and practices I had been told about or actually witnessed.

"Now, as to the history of us Goths," I said, "it appears to have begun far back in the mists of time, when that old, old god-family called the Aesir appointed one of their number to sire all the Germanic peoples. He was Gaut, evidently something less than a god but more than a king. And of his numerous descendant nations, only we Goths have kept his name, though it also lives on as the word meaning 'good' in every dialect of the Old Language."

"Why, so it does," murmured Theodoric, looking pleasantly surprised. "I never thought to make the connection."

"The first *mortal* name I encountered in Gothic history," I went on, "is that of King Berig, who commanded the ships that brought the Goths over the sea from Gutaland. Then, after they had dwelt on the shores of the Wendic Gulf for I do not know how long, it was a King Filimer who started them on their long migration southward across the continent. One thing I can tell you, Theodoric, from personal experience and observation. I have now seen the island called Gutaland, and I have seen the Amber Coast, and I have seen every other land that the Goths lived in or stopped in or traveled across. And I say this: I can well understand *why* they left or hastened past those places. I am heartily glad — and so should you be — that our ancestors did not remain in any of them, for it would have meant *our* being born in one of those bleak barrens. I am even glad that our forebears got evicted from the Mouths of the Danuvius, though they seem to have found those marshes and grasslands habitable enough. That place was so much to their taste, in fact, that they were becoming soft and complacent and phlegmatic. I was told, and I believe it, that the Huns did the Goths a great favor by driving them off those Black Sea lands before they could deteriorate into extinction, like the ancient Scythians, or worse, could generate into a race of pallid tradesmen."

"I quite agree," said Theodoric, raising his goblet in salute and then taking a deep swig from it.

"To get back to the sequence of kings," I said, "from Filimer onward, there is considerable confusion as to names and dates and order of succession." As I spoke, I was riffling through the notes I had taken during my journey, for I had brought with me to the palace the various scraps of parchment and wax tablets and even plane-tree leaves on which I had scribbled or scratched my memoranda. "For one thing, I was told the kings' names in a reverse listing, so to speak, because as I progressed northward I was, so to speak, progressing backward through time."

I read the many names to him, and at a few he nodded that he had heard them before, but at most he raised his eyebrows to indicate that he was hearing them for the first time.

"Here and there," I pointed out, "a name is recognizable as Visigoth or Gepid. Uffo the Once-Tetzte would have been a Gepid and Hunuil Immune-to-Magic would have been a Visigoth. Other names are clearly those of Ostrogoth kings—Amal the Fortunate and Ostrogotha the Patient, for example. But many others I cannot confidently identify. And I have not yet determined where in history the royal Amaling line diverged into the branches that became your family and Strabo's family—and, for that matter, the family of the overbearing and over-toothy Queen Giso."

Theodoric said, "I can appreciate the difficulties. There is really no way to substantiate any of those names and reigns until one gets down to fairly recent history."

"Ja," I said. "Until we arrive at that King Ermanareikhs who was called the Gothic equivalent of Alexander the Great. If he truly did commit suicide in despair at being overrun by the Huns, that would have been about the Christian year 375."

717

Theodoric mused, "He was likened to Alexander, eh?"

"He may have *been* great," I said, "and of great longevity, as I was told. But he could not have been the king who settled the Goths at the Mouths of the Danuvius. At least a century before the reign of Ermanareikhs, the Goths were already the terror of the Black Sea shores. They employed the seafaring Cimmerii—the people now called the Alani—to ferry them about on their raiding voyages. And, by the way, those pirate Goths used to send a wonderfully terse advice to every city they advanced upon. 'Tribute or war.'"

"Akh, I admire that!" Theodoric exclaimed. "In any language, easy to communicate and impossible to misinterpret. I shall hope to have opportunity to use it myself. Thank you, Thorn, for providing it."

"I am glad I heard of it," I said. "Anyway, to continue with the history . . . two kings *after* Ermanareikhs, we arrive at your great-grandfather Widereikhs the Wend-Conqueror. And from there on, the royal succession is well attested. After him, your grandfather Wandalar the Vandal-Conqueror. Then your co-ruling father and uncle." I began to shuffle my notes together again. "Well, as soon as I have leisure, I will puzzle and ponder over everything I have collected. I will do my best to make a coherent history of it, and accurately to trace your lineage right on down to your new daughter, Thiudagotha. She of the Gothic people."

"Hardly new any longer," said Theodoric, chuckling. "She of the Gothic people is old enough to be walking quite capably and talking most loquaciously."

"Then I must compile for her a lineage worth talking about. And you did say that you desired a genealogy that would enable marital alliances with the most distinguished of other royal houses. I can draw the stemma in such a way that you and your daughters are direct descendants of that Ermanareikhs who was the equal of Alexander the Great."

"That should improve the marriage prospects, ja," Theodoric said approvingly. Then, with a solemnity rare for him, he added, "Before I die, though, I shall hope to have earned some honorable auknamo of my own. I should hate to be one of those frayed-out remnants of a once estimable family who accomplish nothing themselves, who have nothing to boast of *but* their ancestry."

718   I said, just as solemnly, for I think I had foreseen it long before then, "You will be honoring Ermanareikhs to count him among your ancestors. In time, in the afterworld, he will surely be boasting of having the great Theodoric among his *posterity.*"

"Guth wiljis, habái ita swe," said my king, bestowing on me a fond smile. "God willing, be it so."

At that, I took my leave, and went back to my farm to wait until he should summon me and Frido for the parley with Strabo. I could have stayed at the palace, but I wished to sleep under my own roof—for the reason that I regarded my quest as not yet quite over and done with. Since the night I had slipped away from the Walis-karja, leaving in their hands the remains of my mannamavi lover, I had been wondering about something. Would I ever again, after Thor and Genovefa, find satisfaction in the embrace of any mere man or woman? On this, my first night back home, I would seek the answer to at least half of that question, with the collaboration of one of my slave women.

Well, I was told that the fair-haired Suevian girl Renata had, during my long absence, married one of my young slave men, so I graciously forbore from exercising my proprietorial rights to her. I availed myself of the dark-haired Alan woman Naranj, whose mill-steward husband had always been proud to lend her to his fráuja. To my delight, and thanks to Naranj's wholehearted collaboration, I rediscovered that one does not really need—all at one time and in one bed—*every* variety of probings and claspings and couplings. I rejoiced to rediscover that, while there are physical limits to the ways a female lover can give enjoyment and be enjoyed and take enjoyment, those ways are wonderfully numerous and assorted and enjoyable indeed. Then, the next night— when, as Veleda, I took to my Novae house a handsome young traveling trader whom I had met in the marketplace—I had the delight of rediscovering that the same can truthfully be said of coupling with a male lover, too.

✠ ✠ ✠

Five or six days later, not far from the village called Romula, I sat my saddle on Velox, wearing full armor and weaponry, looking out over a narrow, shallow river. Prince Frido, unarmed and unarmored, sat his bay gelding beside me, and some way behind us waited a formidable piece of Theodoric's army. At a distance beyond the farther bank of the river, Strabo's troops also waited. Their attention, like ours, was fixed on the bare little islet in midriver, where Strabo had stipulated that the leaders' parley take place. There were eight men occupying it, though only seven were really visible.

719

From our side, King Theodoric and Saio Soas had ridden over there through the shallow water. From the other side, King Feva had ridden, and four bearers had carried Strabo's litter, a curtained box on poles. It was clear why the swine-man had insisted that the meeting take place on the islet—so that he would be as far as possible from the sight of both his men and ours—because he could let nothing of himself be seen except his head, sticking out through the litter curtains, and that was hardly a dignified posture for an army's leader.

I leaned to ask Frido, "Do you recognize your father over there?"

"Ja, ja!" he said, and bounced happily in his saddle.

Quickly I bade him, "Ne, do not call or wave. You will be joining him shortly. For the time being, let us keep silent, like everyone else."

The boy obediently subsided, but he looked faintly bewildered, as he had looked ever since our arrival in Novae, and that was understandable. Not I nor any of my servants had yet told Frido that I was Theodoric's man, or that he himself was a hostage in Theodoric's keeping. On the way hither to Romula, I had kept him and myself in the rear of Theodoric's columns of centuries, so Frido did not even know that he had ridden here in company with the army marching to oppose his father. And right now, he did not know the circumstances of the parley being held on the islet yonder, or which of the participants in it were on which side.

All the men in both of the ranked armies were keeping silent, and were doing their best to keep horses from whinnying, and arms and armor and harness from clanking or creaking. We were listening to Theodoric and Strabo doing their conferring, because Strabo's part in it was being done at the full volume of that hoarse, coarse voice I well remembered. Evidently he hoped to inspirit his forces and dispirit ours by letting everyone hear the accusations and invective he bellowed at Theodoric.

"Renegade cousin! Reprobate Amaling! You have made toadies of the once proud Ostrogoths! Under your limp banner, they are only imitation Romans! They have become lickspittles of the Emperor Zeno, trading their independence for a few crumbs from the imperial table!"

Frido leaned to whisper a question to me: "The man in the box, doing the shouting, is that my father's ally Triarius?" I nodded that it was, and the boy subsided again, looking less bewildered but not very happy about King Feva's choice of a brother-in-arms.

720   "Kinsmen!" Strabo bawled. "I invite all of you, I urge you, I charge you! Join me and throw off the Roman yoke! Put an end to the false kingship of our traitor cousin!"

For a while longer, Theodoric only sat his horse patiently, and let that head poking out from the curtains rant on unchallenged, so Strabo could see what little effect his harangue was having on his kinsmen on our side of the river. Gradually, the swine-man's voice got strained with shouting and began to weaken, but he kept on:

"Brother Ostrogoths! Fellow Rugii! Friends and allies! Follow me into battle and—" And there Theodoric interrupted, in a voice that all could hear:

"Slaváith, nithjis! Be silent, cousin! It is my turn to speak!" But he spoke not to Strabo or the waiting armies; he turned to the horseman who had accompanied the litter and shouted, "Feva, is your eyesight keen?" That man rocked slightly in his saddle, as if surprised, and nodded his helmeted head. "Then look yonder!" commanded Theodoric, raising an arm and pointing.

"Sit tall in the saddle, Frido," I instructed the prince, as his father's head swiveled toward us. The boy did better than that. With the footrope I had helped him make, he could literally *stand* tall and visible—and he cheerily waved and called a "Háils, Fadar!" as loudly as his piping child's voice was able.

King Feva's horse took a step backward, seeming as startled as its rider had to have been. Then the islet became the scene of much agitation and hurried confabulation, though now we spectators could not hear the words. All three of the horsemen—Theodoric, Soas and Feva—did a good deal of pointing, toward me and Frido, toward Strabo, toward Strabo's troops. Feva rode back and forth in the little space of that islet—close to Theodoric and Soas, to speak to them with eloquent gestures, back to the litter to lean and speak with Strabo. The swineman would certainly also have been gesturing if he had been able, for his whole litter shook with the frantic bouncing of his body.

That commotion went on for some time, but was finally resolved when King Feva simply threw up his hands in seeming resignation, abandoned the parley, reined his horse about and splashed back through the water. He rode up the far riverbank and over to the left flank of the army still stolidly waiting there. He gesticulated some more, shouting orders that I could not hear. Then a great part of what I could see of that army's front—obviously Feva's Rugii—made the "down weapons" sign of truce. The horse warriors dismounted, the spearmen put their points to the ground, the swordsmen sheathed their weapons. That caused consternation in what I could see of the rest of the army. There was much milling about, and the signifers' flagstaffs wavered, and there came to my ears a murmur that must have been loud and angry quarreling among those troops.

721

Their consternation was nothing compared to Strabo's. He was now flailing and humping about inside the litter so that it was jouncing on the shoulders of its bearers, and those four men were having to dance to keep their footing. Theodoric and Soas merely sat their saddles and coolly regarded all the goings-on. I heard Strabo's voice one last time, hoarsely bellowing, "Take me back!" And his bearers, staggering tipsily, turned and carried the litter, rocking and yawing, across the waters to the far bank.

Frido asked me, in a wondering voice, "Am I not to see a war?"

"Not this day," I said, smiling at him. "You just *won* this one."

There now occurred the day's final event of significance, the one that historians in their books still mention with awe. Strabo was continuing to heave about inside his litter so furiously that his bearers had trouble lifting their burden up the riverbank. From the front rank of his nearer troops, several spearmen ran down to lend a hand. And then the litter gave such a violent bounce that Strabo pitched right out of it, visible to everybody, a thick torso wearing a cut-down tunic from which

protruded a bearded head and four stumps helplessly thrashing in distress. At that moment, the swine-man looked very much like a porker
indeed, splayed for display at a meatcutter's stall.

The history books nowadays give only meager mention to the lifetime doings, to the reign and the tyrannies and the atrocities of Thiudareikhs Triarius, called Strabo. But the books all tell how—after his
having outlived many enemies and surviving many battles and even
recovering from the gross mutilation that should have killed him—
Strabo finally came to die of an ignominious accident. He was tossed
from his litter onto the spearpoint of one of the soldiers hurrying to
assist him. The man tottered at the sudden shock, and his fellow soldiers confusedly leapt to help him hold his spear from falling. So the
last sight I had of Strabo was of his truncated body impaled and briefly
wobbling aloft before its deadweight bore the spear sideways and down,
and he disappeared among the shuffling feet of his remaining loyal men.

✠   ✠   ✠

Over wine in Theodoric's field tent that night, he and Soas and I discussed the happenings of the day.

Soas, somberly shaking his gray head, said, "It is certain that Strabo
did not deliberately seek the inglorious death he died. But he might as
well have done, after the dual humiliation of being denied battle and
of having his chief ally desert him in front of all his other men."

"Ja, he was finished and he knew it," said Theodoric. "Still, I am
happy that the world is now rid of him altogether. He was a blight on
the memory of my lamented sister Amalamena. I can hope that she,
and the woman who so gallantly took her place in Strabo's clutches,
and all Strabo's other victims of that time, are satisfied with his fate."

"I am sure they are," I murmured, for I knew that *one* of them was—
that one being me.

"And now that Strabo is gone," said Soas, "all this day, from the
moment of his misadventure, his last diehard, desperate Ostrogoth followers have been crossing the river, by twos and threes and whole
droves, to cast their lot with our forces. His other allies—that rabble of
Scyrri and Sarmatae tribesmen—are simply evaporating."

"And better news yet," said Theodoric. "Rather than march his
troops straight home again, King Feva has offered to put all of them at
my disposition."

I said sardonically, "Feva may be less than eager to return to his
queen, Giso. I would not blame him. And, by the way, I have as yet

seen King Feva only from a distance. Does he really have a nose smaller than the average?"

Both men blinked and said, "What?" and Theodoric said, "Well, he is a Rugian. He hardly has an imposingly *Roman* nose. Why on earth would you ask that?"

I laughed and told them of Queen Giso's eagerness for dalliance with my companion Maghib, because of his Armenian long nose and what she supposed that portended of his masculine equipment and prowess.

Both men joined in my laughter, and Theodoric said, "I wonder why that ancient myth persists, when it must so often have been proven a fallacy."

Old Soas scratched in his beard and said thoughtfully, "On the other hand, regarding the opposite sex, I have always found a woman's *mouth* a reliable indication of what her sexual parts are like. A large mouth means a capacious kunte. The wider and looser and wetter her mouth, the same with her nether aperture. And a woman with a small, pouty, rosebud mouth always has a similarly small mouth below, to match."

I stared at the marshal, finding it a little hard to think of him as having once been young enough to have experienced a variety of female mouths. But Theodoric only nodded and solemnly confirmed Soas's contention.

"Ja, the correspondence of a woman's two apertures is no fallacy. That is why, in many eastern countries, the women are made to keep their faces always covered in public, all but the eyes. Their men do not want other men lasciviously *measuring* their women, so to speak."

Soas also nodded and said sagely, "And a man might be expected always to *seek out* a woman with a small mouth—knowing how deliciously tight and clasping will be her kunte—except that all men also know that small-mouthed women are more than likely to be similarly small and tight and mean of temperament. A man must beware, above all, of the woman with a small mouth *and* thin lips. She will prove veritably vicious."

"True, true," said Theodoric. "Akh, well, in the matter of selecting a woman just for frolicking, it is best to follow the one simple rule. Seek a woman who wears the Venus collar. Whatever she may lack in beauty of face or form or temperament—and however anxious you may be to get rid of her next morning—she will be an irreproachably enjoyable bedfellow for the night."

It was apparent that Theodoric and Soas had seized on this lightsome subject just because they were glad to have, for a change, some-

723

thing more pleasant to discuss than weighty matters of statecraft and policy and strategy. However, I brought them back to the here and now by remarking:

"I am gratified but slightly surprised to hear that King Feva has so readily allied himself with us. I should have thought he would be wrathful at his son's having been abducted and held hostage."

"Ne," said Theodoric. "He seemed actually *pleased* to have so unexpectedly found his small prince in this far land, and to find that the boy had been well cared for. Also, Thorn, I believe it was as you conjectured. Not until Feva arrived here would he have realized that Strabo was only a pretender, a would-be usurper—and worse, that Strabo had woefully little chance of succeeding even at usurpation."

"Well, now," grumbled Soas, again being the sober and sententious old marshal. "For the loan of Feva's army, Strabo no doubt promised him half your kingdom, Theodoric. What are *you* promising for the use of that same army? Or what is Feva asking?"

"Nothing at all," Theodoric said lightly, "except his and his men's fair share of whatever they can win while under my command."

"But win where?" I asked. "Win what? From whom? Strabo was your only real rival, Theodoric, and the only real nuisance bothering the Emperor Zeno. Putting him down gained no one any land or plunder to be shared. True, there probably will in the future be other such petty upstarts to be conquered, but they will likely have even less of property worth winning. There is nowhere any rich king or nation affording an opportunity for a profitable war, so I do not see—"

"You forget," Theodoric interrupted. "Zeno has for some years now been annoyed by one chronic affliction. I expect he will eventually ask me to help cure it."

"What or who would that be?"

"Come, come, Thorn," he said mischievously. "You yourself once quoted the late Strabo on the subject of this person. And, Soas, you have actually been in the man's company."

We two marshals glanced questioningly at one another, and Theodoric grinned at us both as we instantly realized.

I breathed the name, "Aúdawakrs."

And Soas said, "Odoacer Rex."

And we both, in awe, spoke the resounding word: "Rome."

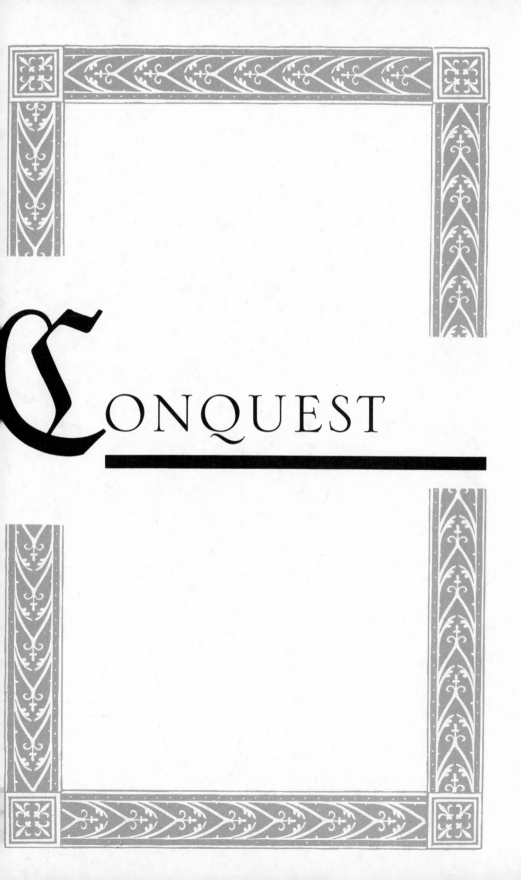

CONQUEST

ALPE

Alpis)(
Ambusta
(Brenner Pass)

Alpis Poenina
(Great St. Bernard Pass)

Tridentum
(Trento)

Bergomum
(Bergamo)

Alpis Graia)(
(Little St. Bernard Pass)

Augusta Praetoria
(Aosta)

Patavium
(Padua)

Augusta
Taurinorum
(Turin)

Mantua
(Mantova)

Verona

Athesis
R.

Alpis Cottia =
(Mont Genèvre Pass)

Novaria (Novara)

Mediolanum

Ticinum
(Pavia)

Padus R.

(Milan)

Mutina
(Modena)

Adda R.

Addua
R.

Adige R.

Altin

Con
Sagi
(Co
Altin

Bononia
(Bologna)

Ravenna

ITALI

Nicaea (Nice)

Genua
(Genoa)

Classi

Arin

LIGURIAN

SEA

Spoletu
(Spoleto)

R
Ostia

Roman Miles

Miles

© 1992 A·Karl/J·Kemp

Aemona
(Ljubljana)

Andautonia
(Zagreb)

ontius R.

quileia

Siscia
(Sisak)

Savus R.

Vadum
(Brod)

Danuvius R.

Singidunum
(Belgrade)

(Save R.)

Sirmium
(Sremska
Mitrovika)

(Danube R.)

DALMATIA

Salona
(Split)

HADRIATIC SEA

ium (Corfinio)

mo (Sulmona)

Aufidena
(Alfedena)

xur (Terracina)

Neapolis (Naples)

1

As the saying has it, all roads lead to Rome, but we would have to travel many of those roads and be a long time getting there.

Theodoric had first to go to Constantinople, and he took me and Soas and his generals Pitzias and Herduic and a sizable retinue of his finest troops with him, because he was summoned to that city to enjoy a signal honor, never before bestowed by a Roman emperor on any outlander. The Emperor Zeno, on being apprised of the bloodless victory over Strabo, insisted that Theodoric come to the capital and be threefold celebrated—with a triumph, with the name of Flavius and with the imperial consulship for the year.

Many a conquering Roman general has been accorded the grand public ceremony called a triumph. And numerous Roman citizens, even a few noncitizens, have had the nomen gentilicus Flavius formally prefixed to their names. And every year at least one notable Roman has been designated that year's consul of the empire (often having well-nigh bankrupted himself to *buy* that honor). But Theodoric was the first and only Goth ever to be given all three of those accolades, and all at the same time.

Some would later say that Zeno thereby bribed Theodoric, and to good effect; but I saw it more as a wooing. In the time since the emperor had recognized Theodoric as King of the Ostrogoths and appointed him the imperial commander-in-chief at the Danuvius frontier, Zeno had been loyally served and properly deferred to and faultlessly respected. But Theodoric had continued to be very much his own man, for example in declining the emperor's offer of reinforcements to help quell Strabo's uprising. So now, it seemed to me, Zeno wanted ties of more than mere concord between ruler and subordinate; he was seeking to weave bonds of equality and comradeship between two good men.

Thus it was that, at the side of Flavius Amalus Theodoricus, and followed by his splendidly caparisoned troop of horsemen, I was privileged to ride again along the Via Egnatia and through the Golden Gate of Constantinople. Under the gate's triple arches a crowd of the Eastern Empire's senators and magistrates and high churchmen awaited us. Theodoric dismounted from his horse so he could be crowned with laurel by the city's Patriarch Bishop Akakiós, who saluted him as "Christianorum Nobilissime et Nobilium Christianissime"—most noble of Christians and most Christian of nobles. The senators draped him in the gold-and-purple toga picta and presented him with a scepter to carry, addressing him as "Patricius" and welcoming him to his office as Consul Ordinarius of this Roman year 1237 ab urbe condita—or, in the Christian count, anno domini 484. Then Theodoric stepped into the distinctive circular-shaped chariot used only for triumphs, holding its four horses to a slow walk so the body of dignitaries could march ahead of him as an honor guard.

I and my fellow marshal Soas rode next after Theodoric, with our troop of warriors behind us. Since we totaled no impressive contingent, and since we had no captives or spoils of war to parade, our number was augmented by columns of marchers and horsemen from Zeno's Legio III Cyrenaica, and by several bands of musicians playing on military instruments. There were many drums and pipes, of course, but also other instruments of marvelous variety—the brass infantry trumpet, the lighter cavalry trumpet of wood and leather, the twisted horn called the bucina, the cornu that coils over its player's shoulder, the very long trumpet called the tuba and the *extremely* long lituus that requires two men to carry. Stepping out smartly to that brave music, we proceeded along the broad Mése, where the throngs lining both sides of the avenue cheered *níke!* and *blépo!* and *íde!* and children flung flower petals at us.

We Ostrogoths wore the war armor and embellishments that I was familiar with, but this was the first time I had seen Roman legionaries on parade. They were most gaudily outfitted in armor of colored leathers, and with towering plumes affixed atop their helmets, and those helmets were of odd construction. The everyday helmet protects skull and forehead and cheeks; this Roman parade helmet covered a man's whole face, with only eyeholes for him to see through. The legionaries also carried many bright flags and standards and guidons, some of which were not just cloth oblongs, but were ingeniously fashioned to imitate animals. There were dragon flags, for instance: multicolored ribbons braided into long tubes that, as they swept through the air, writhed and undulated and even *hissed* like serpents.

When we arrived at the Forum of Constantine, Zeno was waiting, and he escorted Theodoric from the chariot up onto a platform garlanded with flowers. The marchers and riders and musicians kept on moving, circling about the forum's great central column so the two monarchs could formally make review of the procession. Each body of men, as it passed the platform, in unison roared a mighty shout of "Io triumphe!" and gave the Roman salute of raised right fist or the Ostrogoth salute of stiffly extended right arm. And the cityfolk standing packed all around the circumference of the forum enthusiastically echoed each shout, "Io triumphe!" Zeno and Theodoric then repaired to the Church of Hagía Sophía to make devotions.

On his emergence from the church, Theodoric gave the order "Dismissed!" and when that was repeated by officers up and down the columns, the triumphal riders and marchers and musicians broke ranks. Then, from kitchens all over the city came obsonatores bearing high-heaped trays and platters and salvers, and brimful jugs and ewers and amphorae. Soldiers and citizen spectators alike fell to on the abundance of viands, while we higher-rankers proceeded to the Purple Palace for a more formal, less lusty feast.

We were escorted to the palace's most elegantly appointed triclinium, the room called the Dining Hall of the Nineteen Couches. Since there were *only* nineteen couches, no one of lesser title than myself and Soas and Bishop Akakiós could be accommodated, meaning that all the senators and magistrates and minor churchmen had to dine elsewhere. As we favored few lounged about—eating breast of pheasant cooked in raspberry wine, and roast kid doused with garon sauce, and drinking the finest Khíos wine—I heard Zeno's stout and middle-aged but still handsome empress, the Basílissa Ariadne, congratulating Theodoric on his consulship.

"Even the commonfolk seem to approve of your preferment," she said. "All the polloi were cheering you right heartily. You must be proud, Consul."

"I shall strive to maintain humility, my lady," Theodoric replied good-humoredly. "After all, the Emperor Caligula once proposed awarding the consulship to his favorite *horse.*"

The empress laughed, but Zeno looked half peeved, half rueful that his lavishing of honors evidently had not yet won Theodoric over to brotherly affection. However, Zeno was not going to give up on his courtship. During the subsequent days and weeks, he continued to ply Theodoric with blandishments—and of course we attendants of the king got to enjoy them as well. I, for one, was probably more impressed by all the entertainments and diversions than Theodoric was, because he had spent much of his childhood here among the wonders of Constantinople.

We were shown the city's religious treasures. A staff once belonging to

733

Moses is reverently kept within the Purple Palace itself. The Church of Hagía Sophía, besides housing what is said to be the well from which Jesus asked a drink of the Samaritan woman, also contains a robe and girdle once worn by the Virgin Mary. Still, as I have said, this city founded by the "Nobilium Christianissime" Emperor Constantine has yet to learn good Christian intolerance. The Church of Hagía Sophía is hedged all about with a multitude of statues—exactly 427 of them—most of which are of such non-Christian personages as the Pythian Apóllon, the Samian Hera, the Olympian Zeus and the like.

In an amphitheater overlooking the beautiful Propontís, we were treated to a whole afternoon of Pyrrhic dances done by a throng of graceful maidens impersonating not just goddesses—Venus, Juno, Minerva—but also godlings like Castor and Pollux, the Muses, the Graces, the Hours. The most amazing thing about this entertainment was the setting the theater's artificers had devised for it. On the stage sat an entire mountain covered with trees, a stream flowing down it, goats grazing on it while the dancers flitted merrily about to the music of massed pipes. The dancing depicted a series of well-known myths, and came to culmination with Paris presenting the golden apple to Venus. At that, the music and the dancing became even more than Pyrrhically lively and wild—and, believe me or not, the stage mountain *erupted*. From its peak jetted up a fountain of water, descending like rain on all the performers. That water was somehow tinted yellow, perhaps with powdered saffron, so that everything it sprayed—the dancers, the musicians, even the goats—turned to gold as we spectators stood and applauded and shouted in surprise and wonder.

There were games specially arranged for our amusement at the city's Hippodrome, the most magnificent such structure in the world. We went there, not through the common entrance gates, but straight from the palace, by way of the private staircase that led from Zeno's Oktágonos chambers to his imperial podium overlooking the vast oval arena. Towering above his podium was a column made of intertwined brass serpents, holding aloft a golden basin full of fire. The arena floor, exclusive of the high-soaring tiers of seats, measured at least a hundred paces in one direction and four hundred in the other. Around its perimeter stood massive obelisks brought from Egypt, statues from Messana and Panormus, tripods and incense-burners from Dodona and Delphi, the great bronze horses taken from Nero's arch in Rome. The contests of chariot-racing, riding, wrestling and pugilism between the city's Green and Blue factions were full of excitement, frenzied action and sometimes suspense. Theodoric and I and everyone else in our party laid heavy wagers, but even when I lost I deemed the

734

money had been well spent just for the opportunity of visiting the world's grandest Hippodrome.

When Theodoric and I and our companions were not being entertained or feasted or shown the sights of the city, we frequently sat in converse with the emperor—with interpreters present to make conversation easy for all, and with amphorae of Khíos wine to make the conversation fluent. I kept waiting for Zeno to broach the subject of dispossessing Odoacer from the throne of Rome—or, more likely, for him to take Theodoric into private, secret conference for that purpose—but he was evidently in no hurry to do so. He discoursed only elliptically on imperial affairs, and seemed content to have his interpreters pass along his words to all of our party, and he never yet mentioned Odoacer's name.

I remember him saying one night, reflectively, "You saw the helmets that my legionaries wore during the triumph. Those parade helmets are really masks, to maintain the fiction that the Roman legions still are composed entirely of *Romans*—all olive-skinned natives of the Italia peninsula. Without the masks, the legionaries would be seen to have pale Germanic complexions, and yellow Asiatic, and swarthy Greek, and even charcoal-black Libyan. Very few of them olive. But . . . papaí . . ." He shrugged. "That has been a fact for a long, long time now, and who am I to repine? I am called a Roman emperor, and I am an Isaurian Greek."

"Vái," grunted Soas. "The veriest Romans are likewise Greeks, if you trace back far enough, Sebastós. Every person native to Italia shares the blood of Albans, Samnites, Celts, Sabines, Etruscans *and* the Greeks who early set colonies on that peninsula."

"And in more recent times an infusion of Germanic blood as well," said Theodoric. "Not just in the peasant stock, mind you, but in the uppermost classes. Men like the Vandal Stilikho, and the Franks Bauto and Arbogast, and the Visigoth-Suevian Rikimer, after they came to renown at Rome, married their children into the best Roman families."

We all noticed that Theodoric stopped short of naming the Scyrrian Odoacer as the latest of those Germanic eminences.

Pitzias said, "Long before the peninsula was named Italia, it was called Oenotria—the Land of Wine—and it is said that an early Roman there got angry with his fellow Romans, and decided to do them an evil turn. So he spitefully sent samples of wine to the Germanic barbarians beyond the frontier, who had never before tasted wine. They were so enraptured by it that they swarmed into Oenotria. And that, says the story, was the first barbarian invasion of the empire."

We chuckled at that, and Zeno said, "A winsome fable, and not too far

735

from the truth. In olden time, the Romans did send gifts to the Vandals and Visigoths and others beyond their borders, and those novelties may well have included choice wines. Of course, the gifts were intended to persuade the outlanders to *stay* in the outlands, but they had the opposite effect. The outlanders so prized those exotic novelties that they wanted to acquire more. What better way than to descend on Rome and take them?"

Herduic spoke up. "But, as you say, Sebastós, that was in the olden time. Nowadays every Germanic inhabitant of the empire, west or east, thinks of himself, not as an Ostrogoth or a Suevian or a Gepid or whatever, but as a Roman citizen. He regards the empire as eternal, inviolate, sacred, an institution to be preserved, and he will do his utmost to keep it so. He may be a far better Roman than that olive-skinned native of Italia."

"The olive-skinned native would not agree," Zeno said coolly, "and I will tell you why. All those Germanic outlanders you have mentioned, those who rose high in the councils of Rome, every one of them—from Bauto to Rikimer—was a pagan or an Arian. That is why every one of them fell short of achieving any lasting eminence. The Western Empire being officially and predominantly Catholic Christian, and those men *not* being, the Catholic Roman populace might allow them to rise, but only so high, and for only so long. Now, friend guests, who is for more wine?"

Later, when the emperor had drunk his fill of Khíos, and he and his interpreters had departed, Theodoric said to the rest of us, "Zeno gave himself away in that speech. It explained why he wants Odoacer overthrown. Because Odoacer *is* a Catholic Christian."

"Ja," rumbled Herduic. "Odoacer even claims that it was a hermit Catholic priest whom he met in his youth, one Severinus, who foretold that he would one day take the throne of Rome."

Pitzias said, "Odoacer keeps old Severinus still by him, as his personal chaplain, only now he is *Saint* Severinus."

Soas explained, "The new Patriarch Bishop of Rome, Felix the Third, is said to have attained that high bishopric only after he agreed to sanctify old Severinus. Ja, ja, Odoacer is Catholic, right enough."

"So," said Theodoric, "Zeno fears that Odoacer *could* attain the renown impossible for his pagan and Arian predecessors. Perhaps even overshadowing Zeno himself in popular esteem and in the annals of the empire."

"Therefore the emperor wants him expelled," mused Soas, "and the replacement, besides being *able* to overthrow Odoacer, must *not* be another of the Catholic Christian faith."

I said, "Strabo fit those qualifications. Seasoned warrior. Leader of a warrior people. And an Arian Christian. So the emperor would have been willing to see even that loathsome tyrant on the throne of Rome. But now he has an equally qualified but far superior candidate in you, Consul."

Theodoric said firmly, "Not even for the winning of the whole Western Empire will I consent to be Zeno's creature. I shall not leap at the opportunity." Then he grinned and said, "I shall instead play the coy maiden. Make Zeno court me until he has to make his proposal most fervently, on bended knee. We will see then, my friends, what terms he offers, and decide among us whether we find them acceptable."

✠ ✠ ✠

Months passed, and still the emperor refrained from saying anything whatever about Odoacer, but only continued to regale us visitors with cornucopian hospitality and entertainment. Since Theodoric seemed happy enough to go on wearing the purple and living the irresponsible life of a hedonist, and since he needed no assistance in doing that, I asked his leave to go on a journey.

"As long as I am here in the Eastern Empire," I said, "I should like to see more of it, beyond Constantinople."

"By all means, Thorn," he said indulgently. "If I have need of you, I can send a messenger to find you."

So I had one of the palace boatmen ferry me and Velox from the Boukóleon harbor across the Propontís to Chrysopolis on the other shore—which is to say that I crossed from the continent of Europe to the continent of Asia. I kept mostly to the coastal plains and beaches, traveling at random, at leisure and generally at ease. With towns and villages not far apart, with good Roman roads connecting them and with a comfortable Greek pandokheíon in almost every community, there is no hazard or hardship in traveling. Also, the climate is Mediterranean-mild, and since I was wending more or less southward, I scarcely noticed when autumn became winter and winter became spring.

I passed first through the region, just south of the Propontís, where the Mysians live. In former times, those people were very warlike, but over the ages they were so often defeated and cast down and oppressed that they lost all their bellicosity. Indeed, so far have the Mysians degenerated that now they earn their living chiefly by hiring themselves out to be mourners at funerals. Because of their woeful history and melancholy heritage, they can spontaneously shed copious tears for any defunct stranger.

On the Aegean coast I came to many a community that clearly had been much more populous and prosperous in the long ago. Smyrna has been Smyrna since the remotest beginning of human history, and it still is a busy

737

seaport, but its great days are all behind it. Assos is only a rustic town now, but it must have been a mighty city in its time, for its terraces, carved from its high hilltop, hold the shells of once imposing edifices—theater, agora, baths—long empty, neglected, crumbling. At Pergamon and Ephesus and Miletus are ruins of temples and thermae and libraries that will never be used again but will doubtless endure forever, because they were most astonishingly cut in their entirety—columns, doorways, porticos, friezes—out of the living rock of cliffsides.

At Smyrna I saw camels for the first time; I even drank some camel milk, but I do not highly recommend it. In the wild, in the countryside between communities, I saw other creatures new to me—several jackals and hyenas and once (I think but cannot be sure) I fleetingly glimpsed a leopard. At Miletus I looked on the Meander, the vagrantly wandering river that is supposed to have inspired Daedalos with the idea for his impenetrable Labyrinth.

I went in a boat from the mainland over to the island of Kos, where the world's finest cotton goods are woven and the most precious purple dye is produced. The women of Kos are so proud of their island's produce that they wear it every day, and while doing the most mundane tasks, and when walking on the street. To do that, a woman has to be proud of her body, too, because a stola or tunic or chiton of Kos cotton is so sheer that it is scandalously transparent. I bought some of the purple dye and some cotton garments for my Veleda wardrobe, though I did not plan ever to wear them in public and shamelessly expose myself as the Kos women do.

From a promontory farther south on the mainland, I took a boat to the island of Ródhos, just to look at the long-fallen fragments of the famous colossus there. Until an earthquake threw it down, nearly seven centuries ago, that gigantic bronze statue of Apóllon stood to welcome ships into the Ródhos harbor, and it supposedly stood as tall as twenty men on end. I can believe that, because the *thumb* of it was too thick for me to wrap both arms around. And inside the crumpled torso one can see the winding staircase that once took visitors up to gaze out over the Aegean through Apóllon's eyes. The colossus would have looked, to people on the ground or on the sea, even taller than it was in fact. Before the time of this statue, sculptors had made their figures strictly to human proportions—a normal man or woman being seven and a half times as tall as the measure of his or her own head. But this Apóllon was sculptured by artists who had learned to make their figures eight or nine heads high, even ten, thereby giving them more heroic and graceful stature. And so statues—not just of gods but of men and women—have been proportioned that way ever since.

I had by now been long gone from the Purple Palace, but I had left a clear trail, identifying myself by name and title at every pandokheíon I had stayed in, and no messenger had yet come pounding after me. So I assumed that Theodoric still had no need of my presence. Therefore, when I at last turned Velox again toward Constantinople, I continued to travel only leisurely, stopping wherever I found anything of interest.

"What in the world," I brashly demanded of a priest in the town of Mylasa, "is that awful assemblage of trash supposed to represent?"

It appeared to be intended as a shrine, standing beside a church. The church itself was only a ramshackle affair of mud bricks and thatch, and it was not made any handsomer by the addition alongside. The shrine, if that was what it was, had begun life as an ordinary tree, but that had been lightning-blasted at some time, so it was now dead and leafless. The bolt had neatly split the trunk so that half of it lay on the ground, its upper side as flat and smooth as an ambo reading-table. To make it look *like* an ambo, there was a tattered old parchment scroll unrolled across it, and upon it was set some imitation Communion vessels—a tarnished old chalice, a common tray to represent a paten, a lump of wood rudely carved to resemble a pyx. And behind the simulated ambo was propped a straw figure garbed in priestly brown burlap robe and white stola. The other, upright half of the tree still had its branches, and those were hung with innumerable musical instruments. There were stringless harps, timbrels with torn drumheads, dented cymbals, badly bent trumpets—everything old, damaged, cast-off—mournfully tinkling, rustling or jangling in the wind. Try as I might, I could think of nothing in Scripture or in history that would explain such a curious accumulation.

739

"It is not apparent to you, pilgrim?" the priest asked, smiling proudly.

"Is it some kind of japery?"

"Oukh, not at all. Like you, every Christian pilgrim pauses to inquire. And most of them stay to admire—and adore."

"They adore that . . . mess?"

"And while they stay, they spend money on food and lodging in Mylasa, they make offerings in our humble church, they distribute alms, they even purchase trinket mementos blessed by our Bishop Spódos, such as this miniature reed flute. Allow me to sell you one."

I declined, on the ground that I was neither a pilgrim nor an Orthodox Christian, and said, "I can recognize the pretended priest and ambo yonder, but what is the meaning of all the musical instruments?"

The priest, seeing no profit in me, evidently saw no reason not to explain. He did that without the least embarrassment.

"Far to the east of here," he said, "stands Mount Ararat, where the Ark came to ground after the Great Flood. Near that mountain is a Christian church, much like ours here. Its enterprising and energetic congregation has built there an immense replica of Noah's Ark. They even hewed out great stone anchors for it. Christian pilgrims come from far and wide, in teeming droves, to admire and adore that artifact, and to make rich the church responsible for its construction. This land of Asia Minor abounds in copies of other biblical objects and sites."

"Excuse me, Tata, but what has all this to do with that overdressed tree yonder?"

With an expansive wave of his arm, he went on, "It was in these lands that St. Paul did much of his missionary journeying. So, reviewing Paul's life and works and words, we selected an inspiring passage and . . . behold!" He gestured triumphantly at the trumpery shrine. "Now pilgrims can come and pray where St. Paul preached!"

When I only blinked in bafflement, the priest said, somewhat testily, "Well? There is no proving he did *not* preach on this very spot."

"Forgive my thickheadedness, Tata, but I still do not understand. All the musical instruments . . . I cannot recall anything in the Bible about Paul's having been musically inclined . . ."

"Ouá!" he cried, in genuine glee. "We have been too clever for you! But there, there. You did confess that you are no Christian. If you were, you would know that in Paul's day the early Christians were much given to falling into trances or ecstasies, and babbling incoherent gibberish, and calling that divine inspiration. It was, of course, extremely *un*christian, imitating the behavior of the detestable pagan oracles, who always gave their nonsensical prophecies 'in tongues,' as they called it. So Paul, anxious to discourage that practice —"

"Wait, wait!" I interrupted, laughing, as realization dawned. "That passage where Paul tells the Corinthians, 'If I speak with the tongues —' "

"Exactly!" crowed the priest. " 'I am become as sounding brass, or a tinkling cymbal.' Well, look yonder on the tree. Brass horns, cymbals, tabors, all things that make meaningless noises. And there behind the ambo stands St. Paul, as best we can re-create him, preaching his admonition. 'I had rather speak five words with understanding than ten thousand words in a tongue.' "

I thanked the priest for his having so lucidly explained, and I made insincere noises of admiration, and I wished him and his church much profit from their endeavor, and I went on my way, shaking my head in marveling amusement.

✠ ✠ ✠

When I arrived again in Constantinople, I of course went immediately to report to Theodoric. In his chambers, I found him dandling one of the prettier Khazar palace maids on his knee, and looking mischievously pleased with himself. But the marshal Soas, the generals Pitzias and Herduic, also present, were looking unhappy and distracted. They gave me only curt nods of welcome, because they were sternly reproving their king.

"The victim was not just some back-street nonentity," said Herduic.

"An abuse of hospitality," said Pitzias, "a disgrace to your office and an insult to the emperor."

Soas growled, "Zeno must be appalled. Outraged. Furious."

But Theodoric greeted me jauntily, "Háils, Saio Thorn! You come just in time to see me tried and convicted and condemned."

"What? Whatever for?"

"Akh, nothing much. This morning I chanced to commit a minor murder."

741

2

"**M**urder? Nonsense!" snorted Zeno. "Perfectly justifiable. The man was nothing but an excrescence on the world."

We marshals and generals breathed sighs of relief. I think all of us except Theodoric had imagined ourselves being executed and hung from the city walls.

Theodoric said to the emperor, with no air of apology, "I merely wished to erase the last reminder of the insult to my royal sister."

He had already told me how, meeting the young man on the street, he had recognized the "gudgeon face" of Rekitakh, and there and then, in broad daylight, had drawn his belt knife and slain the son of Strabo.

"Nevertheless," said Zeno, his brick face unsmiling, "it was an unbecoming act for one who all last year wore the toga and cincture of a Roman consul. The purple does not confer impunity, Theodoric. I cannot have my people thinking that I am become lazily lenient in my old age. And that is what they would think if they were to see you still enjoying the freedom of my imperial city."

"I quite understand, Sebastós," said Theodoric. "You would have me go from Constantinople."

"I would. I would have you go all the way to Ravenna."

Theodoric raised his eyebrows.

"A man of your combative nature deserves a worthier antagonist than a discrowned princeling like Rekitakh."

"A king, perhaps?" Theodoric asked lightly. "You wish me to stick a blade in the King of Rome?"

"At least puncture the man's overinflated aspirations," said Zeno, and we of Theodoric's party exchanged glances. The emperor finally, after having been irresolute for so long, was speaking plainly. "Odoacer has at last tried my tolerance too far. He has recently appropriated to the crown a full one-third of the land of all the great estates in Italia. Or, I should say, he has appropriated from the lands belonging to private families. He has exempted Church holdings, so as not to imperil his hopes of the hereafter. This constitutes flagrant theft of land from its rightful owners, and not for the benefit of any landless commonfolk. No peasant will ever be given a single jugerum of it. Odoacer will merely apportion the land among his sycophant magistri and praefecti and vicarii. It is disgraceful behavior. Disgraceful!"

None of us smiled, though we knew very well that Zeno was only pretending to be righteously shocked. He did not care a nummus that Odoacer was filching from the Roman rich, or that Odoacer was being callously neglectful of the landless poor, or that Odoacer was squandering generosity on his court favorites. What vexed Zeno was the realization that this appropriation measure would enhance Odoacer's personal popularity. The estate owners whom he robbed were too few to cause him concern. The largest landowner of all, the Church, being exempt, would call him blessed. The legislators and administrators to whom he gave the land would be bound closer to him, making his regnancy more secure. Most important, Italia's entire population of commonfolk would praise his name, simply because the lower classes everywhere always rejoice to see someone despoil and discomfit their betters, even when it gains them nothing at all.

"I sent Odoacer a severe rebuke," Zeno went on, "for having so egregiously exceeded his authority. Of course he replied with fervent protestations of his undiminished fidelity and subservience. In token, he sent to me all the Roman imperial regalia—the purple diadem, the stellate crown, the jeweled scepter, the orb and victoria—the priceless ornamenta palatii that have adorned every emperor at Rome for the past five hundred years. This is presumably to assure me that Odoacer does not, at least, aspire to *that* supremacy. I am pleased to have the regalia, but I am not placated by it, because Odoacer still insolently thumbs his teeth at me. He has refused to rescind that order of land confiscation. I have too long endured his presumptuousness. Now I want the man removed. And I want you to do it, Theodoric."

"It will not be easy, Sebastós. Odoacer has the loyalty of all the western Roman legions, and he has cemented good relations with other western nations. The Burgunds, the Franks . . ."

"If it were going to be *easy*," Zeno said tartly, "I would send my wife, Ariadne, or the eunuch Myros to do it. Or the palace cat. Only *because* it will not be easy am I asking a strong warrior to undertake it."

"And I believe I could succeed at it, Sebastós. I only want you to be aware that it cannot be accomplished overnight. My own Ostrogoth army, even with King Feva's Rugii in support, will not suffice. I must rally other forces, and Odoacer will naturally know of that, so he will likewise be girding—"

The emperor interrupted. "I am going to make it even less easy for you. Those other forces you speak of—you must not expect to count among them the Danuvius legions currently under your command."

"Of course not," Theodoric said, rather stiffly. "We cannot have Roman legions marching against Roman legions. It would sunder what is left of the empire. It would do no good to excise a pimple from the body only to have the body die."

"And for that same reason," said Zeno, "I must impose another caveat. When your armies march from Novae toward Italia, for as long as they are treading the ground of the Eastern Empire, they are not to live off the land. During your crossing of the eastern provinces, you will not exact tribute or sustenance from any community. Not until you enter what used to be the Western Empire—in Pannonia—will you begin to victual your armies by foraging and looting."

743

Theodoric frowned. "That means our carrying food and supplies sufficient to march for some three hundred Roman miles. And to collect such a
mass of provisions means waiting for the next harvest to be reaped. Then,
by the time we reach Pannonia, the winter will be upon us. We shall have
to lay over until spring. Then there are another four hundred miles or so
between us and the Italia border. Depending on where we encounter the
first of Odoacer's forces—or where he sends them to find us—we may not
close with him until the following summer."

Zeno shrugged. "You warned me not to expect overnight success."

"Very well," said Theodoric, squaring his shoulders. "I understand my
mission and my objective, and I see the necessity for the strictures. Now,
may I be so bold as to ask, Sebastós, what do I win in the winning?"

"Everything. The entire peninsula of Italia. The venerable ground of
Latium, from which spread and flourished the greatest empire ever known.
The Eternal City of Rome, the city that once was the world. The imperial
capital of Ravenna. Every other rich city in Italia and all the rich lands
between them. Displace Odoacer Rex and you become Theodoricus Rex."

"Rex . . . Rex . . ." Theodoric reiterated, and pensively. "The title is
redundant. My own name, Thiudareikhs, already incorporates the rex."
Zeno's interpreter had a little trouble translating that speech, and the man
looked nervously apprehensive as he translated Theodoric's next bold
question: "And what will I be then, Sebastós—your ally, your subordinate
or your mere bondsman?"

For a long moment, the emperor gave Theodoric a hard glare. But then
his brick face relaxed and he said genially, "As you remark, titles are ambiguous things, easy and cheap to bestow. And we are both aware that you are
the only man who could perform this mission for me. So I shall not equiv-
ocate. If you can wrest from Odoacer the peninsula of Italia, you will govern
it as my deputy, my vicar, my trusted caretaker, and without meddling from
me. Make of it, if you like, the new Land of the Ostrogoths. It is far more
fertile, more sightly, more valuable than the lands your people now hold in
Moesia. And whatever more you can make of what you conquer—even if
you restore the Western Empire in all its onetime power and greatness—it
will be in your keeping. You will rule it in my name, but . . . *you will rule.*"

Theodoric took time to consider that. Then he nodded, smiled, bowed
his head to the emperor, motioned for the rest of us to do the same and
said, "Habái ita swe. Eíthe hoúto naí. Be it so."

✠　✠　✠

On our way back to Moesia, we traveled together only as far as Hadriano-polis. There Theodoric, Soas, Pitzias and Herduic, each taking with him a portion of our troops, fanned out in different directions from west to east, going off to canvass every least tribe and gau and sibja for new recruits to add to our army. I, with only two soldiers for attendants, kept straight on to Novae, because Theodoric had told me to resume my work on the Gothic history. If, he said, he was going to be monarch of more than he was already, he most certainly wished his people's archive and his own geneal-ogy to be in proper shape to be read and appreciated by all his contempo-rary monarchs.

So I retired to my farm and applied myself to putting that history into coherent, finished, written form. And of course I did what is expected of any notable man's biographer: adding some luster and illustriousness to the subject's background, however unnecessary that might be. A few historical facts I exaggerated and some others I bent and some others I omitted, and some events that actually had happened far apart in time I butted closer together. Thus I wove into the Gothic history an Amaling lineage that made Theodoric a direct descendant of King Ermanareikhs, the Goths' equivalent of Alexander the Great, and made Ermanareikhs a direct de-scendant of the shadowy god-king Gaut.

745

In so doing, I was struck by a realization that I found both instructive and amusing. To track back through the progenitors of a present-day person means doubling the number of contributory mothers and fathers in each bygone generation. If I could retrace the entire lineage of Theodoric or myself or anyone back, say, to the time of Christ—just fifteen generations ago—that person would have had 32,768 men and women contributing to his bloodline at that date. Even in the unlikely event that someone today could pride himself on being a direct descendant of Jesus Christ himself, who were those other 32,767 people? There might have been a notable warrior or sage or priestess here and there among them, but surely such a teeming throng must have included lowly goatherds, base publicans, prob-ably vicious criminals and drooling imbeciles. I decided that any man of this present day who wished to boast of his distinguished ancestry would have to be most carefully selective of which ancestors.

Akh, well, I said to myself, smiling, as I inscribed my finished composition on sheets of the finest vellum, in this case I had done my best. And even if future historians might cavil at certain details of my reconstructed annals of the Goths, none could object to what I wrote on the very first page: "Read these runes! They are written in memory of Swanilda, who helped."

What time I spent at the Novae palace before Theodoric got home, I frequently spent in company with his daughters Arevagni and Thiudagotha, latest offspring of the Amal line. Princess Arevagni had grown into adolescent young-ladyhood, and she had their mother's plumpness and ruddy coloring. The younger Princess Thiudagotha more resembled their late aunt Amalamena, having snowy skin, pale hair and a slender figure. Another palace resident often in our company was the Rugian Prince Frido, now a sturdy young fellow of about thirteen. Though King Feva had permanently encamped his army around the village of Romula, he had sent Frido to Novae for schooling under the same palace tutors responsible for the education of the two Ostrogoth princesses.

I was a close friend to all those young people, but each of them regarded me rather differently. Though Frido sometimes still addressed me deferentially as "Saio," he more often treated me as an admired older brother. Arevagni affectionately called me "awilas," uncle. However, she being at that uncertain and skittish age of budding into early womanhood, Arevagni was as modest and shy in my presence as she was with Frido and every other adult male. Thiudagotha, by contrast, was still a girl-child and, like another I had known in the long ago, she seemed instinctively to regard me more as an aunt than an uncle. I did not demur; after all, I had once, in a manner of speaking, *been* her aunt Amalamena. So Thiudagotha shared with me all her girlish notions and confidences—one of which was that, when she grew up, she hoped to marry "handsome Prince Frido."

It did not appear to bother any of those young people that each of them saw me differently. But it did sometimes make me feel, as I had felt at other times in my life, a trifle unsure of my *own* identity. On such occasions, I would repair to my farm again, to live for a while and reassure myself of my being the herizogo and marshal Thorn. Or I would go to my town abode, and live for a while equally secure in the identity of the independent lady Veleda.

Theodoric and his officers had to stay afield for quite a long time, because their mission of recruitment was not as simple as in the past, when the mere mention of a war in prospect would have made every able-bodied Ostrogoth rally instantly to the battle standards. Theodoric's people had now been habitant in these Moesia lands for long enough that many onetime warriors had turned farmers, herders, artisans, merchants—men with fixed domiciles and occupations and wives and families. They were, in the manner of the legendary Cincinnatus, understandably reluctant to be snatched from their plowed furrows and settled ways. So the men who came earliest flocking to Theodoric's colors came mainly from landless non-

Ostrogoth tribes, nomad tribes, even barbarian tribes. Then, of course, when the word got about that this was not just *any* war being planned, but the conquest of all Italia, even the most sedentary men could not resist the prospect of winning loot richer than had ever before been offered them. So the former warriors shed their commonplace obligations and their peacetime lethargy and their clinging womenfolk, to turn warriors again.

Many of the recruits—trained, experienced, practicing and *ready* soldiers—came from the Roman legions, and this was a thing unprecedented. Though Theodoric had agreed that no Roman legion should be employed to assail a brother legion, the fact was that *every* legion outside Italia consisted predominantly of men of Germanic heritage. Among the Danuvius forces under Theodoric's magistracy were the legions I Italica, VII Claudia and V Alaudae. Of their legionaries, numerous officers and many more rankers went to their superiors to resign their commissions or to take temporary leave or to request detached duty—or they downright deserted—and came over to our Ostrogoth army. Whether they came out of fondness for Theodoric or for the lure of plunder, those professional soldiers were most welcome. Still, it was a sad thing to see, for such a defection from the legions could never have been dreamed of in the great days of the empire.

By the time our army was ready to march, the new additions and the rejoining former warriors had swelled it to some 26,000 men. With King Feva's 8,000 Rugii, that gave Theodoric a force of foot and horse totaling about 34,000, or more in number than eight regular Roman legions. However, getting that many men ready to march took still more time, so Theodoric had to plunge into the formidable work of preparation as soon as he returned to Novae.

The entire force had to be apportioned and organized into manageable legions, cohorts, centuries, contubernia and turmae, with officers appointed for each level of organization. The newest recruits required training, and men joining after a while away from arms required reacquainting and practice with their weapons. For those men who brought no mounts, horses had to be rounded up and trained for war, some of them even requiring breaking to saddle. Supply wagons had to be procured, and new ones built. New torque-ropes had to be braided and new green-oak torque-posts cut for the siege catapults, and oxen procured to draw their massive carriages. Armor had to be made for men who had none; in some cases, even boots and basic clothing. Swords and spears and knives had to be forged for men who had none, and many more of those weapons made for spares. Countless new arrows had to be turned and tipped and fletched,

747

and extra bowstrings twisted and whipped. And *everybody* had to be fed, now here in encampment, later on the trail. So those men that did not need war training or practice were set to the work of bringing in the land's autumn harvest and doing the autumn butchering. When grain had been threshed and winnowed and bagged, when wine and oil and beer had been barreled, when meat had been dried or smoked or salted, Theodoric dispersed those stores as King Feva once had done. Barges took loads of the food and feed and other supplies upriver to deposit them at intervals along what would be our line of march.

None of that bustling activity could be done in secrecy, so of course Odoacer began making preparations of his own, and those could not be kept secret either. Travelers coming out of the west reported to us that troops from all parts of the Italia peninsula were moving north along it. Our military speculatores, sent to spy, reported in more detail—that the numbers of those troops were about equal to ours, and that they were being congregated in one defensive position. As I have told, the invisible dividing line between the Western and the Eastern Empire ran only vaguely through the province of Pannonia, and each empire had forever been trying to bend that border to take in more territory. Odoacer would have had every right to advance from the Italian provinces at least halfway into Pannonia and confront us there. But he was reportedly marshaling his forces much farther away, at the eastern border of Italia's easternmost province, Venetia, along the river Sontius, which runs from the Alpes Juliani down to the Hadriatic Sea.

748

On receiving those reports, Theodoric convened a council to discuss the situation. It consisted of himself, his marshals Soas and myself, his generals Ibba, Pitzias and Herduic, his ally King Feva and that king's son, Frido (who would at last be getting to see a war, as I had long ago promised him).

Theodoric said, "Odoacer could have chosen to engage us in the wilds of Pannonia, far from the doorstep of the Romans' home ground, and perhaps prevent us from laying waste any of that sacred ground. Instead, he is stoutly barring only the door itself. He might almost be telling me, 'Theodoric, you may keep and hold the disputed land of Pannonia, if you can. But here at the edge of Venetia, at the frontier of Italiae imperium, here I draw the line.' "

Herduic said, "It could be greatly to his advantage. An army fighting on its home ground always fights the more fiercely."

Pitzias said, "It means that we must march more than six hundred Roman miles just to get to him. A tiresome journey."

"At least," said Ibba, "we will not have to *fight* our way across all those intervening miles."

"And if we do not have to fight along the way, the journey should not be too debilitating," said Soas. "Eighty years ago, the Visigoth Alareikhs made the same march, with forces much less well equipped. He marched from here all the way to the gates of Rome, and broke them down."

"Ja," said Theodoric. "In planning our own march, I think we can do no better than to take the same course Alareikhs took. Follow the Danuvius Valley to Singidunum, then go up the river Savus to the city of Sirmium. That is just about exactly halfway to our destination, so we will winter at Sirmium. When we go on, following the Savus through the rest of Pannonia, through Savia and into Noricum Mediterraneum, there is nothing to forbid our sacking and foraging for our sustenance. Toward the headwaters of the Savus, we come to the city of Aemona, where we may get much useful plunder. And from there we have only an easy plain to cross to the river Sontius. We should be at Odoacer's door by late spring."

The rest of us nodded and murmured agreement to that plan. Then King Feva spoke for the first time in my hearing, saying in his heavy Rugian accent, "I wish to make an announcement of some importance."

We all looked at him.

"In the expectation and the conviction that I shall before long be ruling some piece of the once Roman Empire, I have determined to Romanize my outlander name." He turned up his nose—his notoriously short nose—and looked haughtily down it at us. "Henceforth, I desire to be styled Feletheus."

Prince Frido winced in embarrassment; the rest of us looked determinedly elsewhere and tried not to snicker. I decided that Feva-Feletheus was as pompously vainglorious as Queen Giso back in Pomore, and I wondered how the two of them had ever produced a son so unassuming but admirable.

"Feletheus it shall be," Theodoric said good-humoredly. "Now, friends, allies, staunch men all, let us go forth and earn the name of *warriors*."

So, on a deliciously crisp day of blue and gold, in the month that by the Goths used to be called Gáiru, the Spear Month, now called September, the first month of the Roman year 1241, the Christian year 488, Theodoric vaulted to the saddle of his Kehailan steed and gave the cry "Atgadjats!" Then the earth fairly trembled to the concerted tread of thousands of boots and hoofs, and the rolling of hundreds of wagon wheels, as our mighty host moved forward, westward, Romeward.

749

✠ ✠ ✠

The first two hundred and forty miles of our journey were, as we had expected, uncontested and unimpeded, not even very rigorous. September and October are months of good weather for traveling, neither too hot during the day's march nor too cold for comfortable sleeping at night. And the season well deserves its old-time name of Spear Month, because game animals are plentiful. We had outriders ranging at a distance ahead of and alongside our columns—frequently Frido and I took our turn among them—acting both as lookouts and as hunters. In addition to bringing down edible beasts and wild birds, the outriders plucked fruits from orchards, olives from groves, grapes from vineyards and fowl from farmyards. That of course defied the emperor's ban against pilfering from his local subjects, but even Zeno would have conceded that soldiers cannot be commanded to *too* good behavior.

Along the way, we were several times hailed and joined by additional contingents of warriors eager to march and fight with us. They were of various minor Germanic nationalities—Warni, Langobardi, Heruli—sometimes only a handful, sometimes all the able men of an entire tribe, and some of them had traveled far distances to meet us. It was a nuisance to integrate them into an already organized army, and that made the officers to whom they were assigned grit their teeth in exasperation, but Theodoric did not turn any of the newcomers away. In fact, he took some pains to make them feel welcome as close comrades. Every time a sizable group joined us, he would conduct a ritual of swearing auths, they to him and he to them. Although our army was accompanied by several Arian Christian priest-chaplains, Theodoric did not mind making the priests, too, grit their teeth in exasperation. As I well knew, our king wore his Christianity only lightly. So, since most of the new men were adherents of the Old Religion, Theodoric obligingly joined them in swearing the auths on the pagan Allfather Wotan.

Those first two hundred and forty miles of journeying brought us to where the Danuvius is joined by the river Savus, where stands the city of Singidunum. We made camp along the riverbank and stayed there for several days, partly to procure fresh supplies of one commodity and another, partly to give the troops brief leaves to avail themselves of the city's facilities. Singidunum was now garrisoned by the Legio IV Flavia and, while we were in the vicinity, many men decamped from that legion also, to join Theodoric.

This city having been the site of my initiation into battle, I felt quite proprietorial as I again walked its streets. My companion, Prince Frido, was even more thrilled to be visiting here, because, when he and I had come past the city on the barge taking us south to Novae, I had told him all about the siege of Singidunum and the defeat of King Babai's Sarmatae.

"So now, Saio Thorn," he said eagerly, "you must show me everything that earlier you only described."

"Very well," I said as we strolled. "Ahead of us yonder are the gates— though rebuilt now—that were breached by our trumpets of Jaíriko."

And anon I said, "In this square I skewered a scale-armored Sarmatian warrior. And on that farther side Theodoric disemboweled the traitor Camundus."

And anon I said, "From yonder wall the dead were dumped down the cliff to be burned. And here is the central square where we celebrated our victory with a banquet."

And finally I said, "I thank you, friend Frido, for letting me play the seasoned old campaigner revisiting his old stamping ground. But now please go and find some amusement of your own. I wish to seek out one of the diversions traditional to old campaigners."

He laughed understandingly and, with a cheery wave, went off by himself.

751

It is popularly supposed—at least by homefolk who have never been abroad on military service—that an army's officers go on leave just to soak themselves clean in a respectable therma, and that it is only the coarser-fibered enlisted men who go to tumble lupanar girls and get vilely drunk. But it has been my observation that about equal numbers of the lesser ranks go virtuously to wash and officers go wickedly to wench and tipple.

I myself went *first* to the city's best men's therma. While leisurely lolling there, I imbibed enough good wine to make me comfortably mellow. Then I went out to saunter the streets again, alert for other pleasures in prospect. I had no inclination to resort to a lupanar, nor had I any need to. I knew I was personable enough to attract women of better than ipsitilla grade, even if I had not been wearing the fine raiment and insignia of my own grade. I had gone only a little way from the therma when I caught the appreciative eye of a well-favored and well-dressed young woman, who, it soon developed, had also a well-appointed house. It was well furnished, that is to say, with every convenience a housewife could want—except a husband, hers being a merchant gone downriver on business. Not until very late in the evening did she and I even pause to introduce ourselves. Her name was Roscia.

When, two days later, I went again from camp into the city, I carried my

Veleda garments and adornments and cosmetics in a bag, and found a secluded alley where I could put them on unobserved. Then I went to the city's best *women's* therma and spent a long, luxurious time there. I left at nightfall, walking as languidly and assuredly—and as watchful-eyed—as Roscia had done. And, just as she had done, I soon caught the admiring eye of a personable male. But I had to make an effort to keep my face straight when he hesitantly approached. This was no townsman, but one of our warriors, and a very young one. Also, to judge from his breath, he had taken a good deal of wine to fortify himself for the accosting of female passersby.

He stammered awkwardly, "Please, gracious lady . . . may I walk a way with you?"

I looked coolly at him and said, with pretended severity and genuine amusement, "Your voice is only just now cracking and changing, boy. Have you your mother's permission to be out after dark, niu?"

Frido flinched guiltily and, as I had rather expected, wilted a bit at the mention of a mother. He could only mumble confusedly, "I need no permission . . ."

So I continued to tease him, demanding, "Or do you, boy, mistake *me* for your mother, niu?"

To his credit, he braced up at that and said firmly, "Stop calling me 'boy.' I am a prince and a warrior of the Rugii."

"And a raw beginner, obviously, at making conversation with strange women."

He shuffled his feet and muttered, "I did not know . . . I thought *you* would know what to say. I thought any woman out walking alone at night must be . . . well . . ."

"A noctiluca? A night moth? And what was I supposed to say? Come to bed with me and let me relieve your fruit of its kernel?"

Now Frido looked slightly alarmed. "What?"

"It means devirgination. The end of innocence. The onset of maturity. The first time ever. It *would* be your first time, would it not?"

"Well . . ."

"I thought so. Come along, then, prince and warrior. Here, you can carry my bag."

As I took his arm and guided him along the street, he said dazedly, "You mean . . . you will?"

"Not I, ne. I am old enough that you *might* mistake me for your mother."

752

"I assure you, gracious lady, I never would. No one ever would. If you but knew my—"

"Hush. I was only making jape of you. Now I am escorting you to meet a more complaisant lady. Very near here." Frido did not speak again, because he had to concentrate on walking without weaving. We came to a door and I pointed. "She lives there. You will enjoy Roscia. She wears the Venus collar."

"Are you not going to introduce me? I cannot simply come calling at a stranger's door and—"

"If you intend to dare maturity, young prince and warrior, you must get used to doing things on your own. Call her by name—Roscia—and tell her that you are a friend of her friend of the day before yesterday."

He stood undecided before the door, so I took my bag from him and departed, confident that he would not long remain undecided. I was also confident that Roscia would willingly and expertly induct young Frido into manhood. And I was glad; the lad could not too early begin learning how to function as Princess Thiudagotha's husband, even if he did not yet know that that was what he was to be.

I must confess that I *had* briefly toyed with the mischievous notion of playing noctiluca to Frido myself. He was a handsome and sturdy and likable boy, and I would have made sure that we both reveled in the experience of his first time ever. I could easily have managed it, as I had long ago done with Gudinand, without Frido's ever suspecting that I was *not* a female stranger casually encountered. Why, then, had I declined to take raptorial advantage of such a wickedly winsome opportunity? Perhaps because the prince was addled by drink, and it would have been unfair. Perhaps because I had for so long been "big brother"
to Frido and did not wish to be anything other. Perhaps because I felt it would be perverse of me, helping to prepare him for marriage to my "niece" Thiudagotha. Perhaps because, having spoken to Frido of maturity, I decided to demonstrate some myself, instead of my usual carefree impetuosity. Or was I perhaps secretly, slyly saying to myself that there would be plenty of time for "that" when the lad was older? Akh, it was all very complicated.

In any case, my having forgone that opportunity seemed to have dulled my appetite for adventure—for that night, anyway. As I continued walking through Singidunum, I caught admiring glances from other and more eligible males. But I primly parried the glances and kept on

753

walking, and found another secluded alley in which to change clothes, and went virtuously back to the camp.

✠ ✠ ✠

Not until our army had been on the march again for a day or two did Prince Frido ride up beside me and, after a few pleasantries, shyly remark, "I believe, Saio Thorn, we now have something in common. More than we used to, I mean."

"Indeed?"

"A common friend, a lady named Roscia, back in Singidunum."

I said lightly, "Akh, not *too* common, as I remember. Merely liberal."

He nodded knowingly. "I was told that she wore a Venus collar, and I did not know what that was, so I asked her. She laughed, but she showed it to me. And then she showed me . . . well . . . what the Venus collar signifies . . ."

He waited for me to say something, so I did. "Frido, we men of gallantry do not bruit the attributes or the talents or the enthusiasms of those women known to us by name. Only our anonymous wenches are fair game for discussion."

754

"Oh vái, I stand rebuked," he said contritely. "But . . . if nameless women can be talked about, there was one of those in Singidunum, too. The woman who introduced me to the lady Roscia. It was nighttime, and I was not very sober, so I remember only one of *her* attributes. She had a tiny scar bisecting her left eyebrow."

There were a number of things I might have said, but I said only, "So?"

"Well, it was a scar exactly like yours, rather distinctive. I wondered if you might have seen her and noticed it, too."

I decided simply to laugh it off. "A bisected eyebrow, eh? Frido, if you were *properly* drunk, I am surprised that you were not seeing five or six eyebrows on every face. Come, shall we join the outriders and see if we can flush something tasty for nahtamats?"

From Singidunum, the army had proceeded along the north bank of the river Savus, meaning that we were now well inside the province of Pannonia, and could forage at will without breaking any agreed-on rules. But we found few people to take anything from, and not much to take from them. The word of our march had gone before us, and it has long been proverbial that people in the path of an advancing army have only two choices: "flee or fast." The countryfolk having got their autumn harvests in, most of them had chosen to flee, taking produce, herds and flocks with them. However, we were not lacking in provender. The bargeloads of stores were still waiting for us at intervals along the Savus, and there was still plenty of wild game, and the riverbanks afforded dry but ample grazing for our horses.

Eighty miles upriver of Singidunum, when we approached the city of Sirmium, Theodoric sent ahead of us a herald bearing the message of warning that our marauder ancestors had employed: *"Tributum aut bellum. Gilstr aíththau baga. Tribute or war."* Though the main body of us had not yet sighted the city, we were downwind of it, and we all began gasping and gagging and commenting profanely on the foul smell of that place. When we arrived there, we found out why it stank so. It seems that the surrounding countryside is especially well suited to the breeding and raising of swine. So, in all of Pannonia—maybe in all of Europe—Sirmium is the leading slaughterhouse of swine and exporter of pig meat, pigskin, hog bristles and every other sort of pig product.

The city had prudently acceded to the first choice offered by Theodoric's message, but of course it did not receive us joyously when we entered into its smelly precincts. Cityfolk being not so readily able to pack up their possessions and take flight as country people are, the civic storehouses were well stocked with provisions—not only pork but also grain and wine and oil and cheeses and much else—a plenitude to support our army in comfort throughout the winter, and we appropriated all those goods. However, Sirmium's one defensive weapon—its awful odor—kept us sufficiently at bay that we did not occupy the city or devastate any of it or quarter troops in its houses or even molest any of its inhabitants, but set our winter camps at a sensible distance upwind.

We also had to do without some of the happier diversions and comforts we had enjoyed at Singidunum. That is to say, long after we had eaten every hog and sow and pig and piglet in the Sirmium stockyards, and then had eaten every vestige of preserved pork stored in the warehouses, the city still stank of sties and offal. Even its therma waters and its lupanar girls and its night moths reeked so terribly as to be unapproachable. None of us, including Prince Frido and myself, was at all tempted to go into the city either to wash or to wench. So our men stayed conscientiously at their posts and at their military duties in the cleaner air of the camps, the whole winter long.

755

3

When the early spring brought sufficiently clement weather, we resumed our march westward. But we were not to have easy going, as we had hoped, all the way to the Venetia border. About sixty Roman miles upriver of Sirmium, at a place called Vadum, we were ambushed by a hostile force. Vadum is not a city or town or settlement of any sort. The name means only a ford, because there the road crosses from the hilly north bank of the Savus to the southern, where the land is more level. And obviously our vast army of men, horses and wagons doing the slow, cumbersome crossing of a river ford—especially in water so frigid that our horses as well as men shied at stepping into it—was there most vulnerable to sudden assault.

The hidden warriors waited until a good half of our troops were over on the south bank, soaked, half frozen, tired and unready for fighting. Another quarter of us were in the process of crossing, and the remaining quarter were busy with preparations for doing so. Then the lurkers concealed in the woods on both banks launched volley after volley of high-arching arrows. When those seething showers first rained down on us, felling men and horses here and there, we naturally supposed that some of Odoacer's legionaries had somehow stolen a march on us. But when the attackers emerged from among the trees—archers and swordsmen running, mounted spearmen galloping, all of them bawling war cries—we saw that they wore armor and helmets and shields very similar to our own. Indeed, more surprising to us than the ambush was our realization that we were being assailed by fellow Goths—a Gepid tribe, as we learned later, commanded by a petty king named Thrausila.

Of course, the warriors of a single tribe were nowhere near numerous enough to entertain any hope of defeating an army the size of ours, even with their advantage of ambuscade. Our rear guard, still on the north bank of the river, therefore not yet wet, cold or weary, consisted of King Feletheus's Rugii. Ever since those men had marched from Pomore, so long ago, in expectation of a different war, they had been comparatively idle—and unhappy about it. Theodoric had had no employment for them except defensive garrison service, occasional escort duties and some minor skirmishes against road bandits and river pirates. So those warriors had long been bored, restive and itching for all-out combat. This was their first real opportunity, and every man of them, from Feletheus to young Frido to the least shield-bearer, went ravening into action. With commendable expedition, efficiency and gusto, they stopped those Gepids who attacked on the north bank, then beat them back.

I was among the men in the middle of the river at the time, so I took no part whatever in that day's combat. But Theodoric and Ibba were already on the farther bank, and they soon rallied our men there. Although our Ostrogoths were handicapped by waterlogged armor and numbed limbs, they so heavily outnumbered the Gepids that they likewise fought off their assailants, then threw them backward. The battle was very quickly over and, when casualties were counted, it was found that each side had lost only about a hundred men, slain or incapacitated, and about a score of horses. And when the surviving Gepids were rounded up, disarmed and taken prisoner, we learned why those kinsmen of ours had ambushed us.

Their king, Thrausila, said the prisoners, had been ambitious for more than petty kingship. He might, like King Feletheus, have chosen to ally his warriors with Theodoric's. But he had conjectured that no outlander army could ever prevail against Eternal Rome and Odoacer's legions. So Thrausila had cast his lot with what he concluded would have to be the winning side. He was well aware that he could not defeat our army, but he hoped perhaps to decimate it, at least to delay its advance, thereby winning himself approbation from Odoacer, and eventually being awarded some of the fruits of Odoacer's inevitable victory over us. However, even if time were to prove King Thrausila to have been right in his conjecture and decision, he would never benefit by it or even know about it, because Thrausila was one of two kings who lay among the slain that day at Vadum. The other was the posturing, preening (but undeniably valiant) King Feletheus of the Rugii.

Theodoric could have invited the surviving Gepid warriors to join his own forces. That was common enough practice after battles between outlanders, and eminently practical. But he declined to do so with these, because they had tried to deflect him from an objective intended to benefit their people as much as all other Goths. Theodoric simply set the prisoners

757

free and bade them go back to their tribe—in disgrace at having been both disarmed and dismissed—and he gave them a contemptuous parting suggestion:

"Take yourselves some extra wives from among the widows of your slain comrades. Then settle down to be soft, comfortable, insipid family men. It is all you are good for."

The rest of us lingered at Vadum long enough to dig graves for the dead of both sides. The corpses of Rugii and other fallen pagans, like those of Arian Ostrogoths and Gepids, were buried with their heads to the west. That is an age-old custom of all Germanic peoples—far older than Arian or Catholic or any other creed of Christianity—the notion being that the dead can thus go on "seeing the sun rise." The Church would dearly have liked to abolish such a pagan sun-worshipping practice, but, failing in that, had hypocritically decreed that Christians must be buried with their *feet to the east*, because "that is whither Christians must hasten on the Judgment Day."

While the burying was being done, and our accompanying physicians and chaplains were attending the wounded, Theodoric said to me and his other chief officers, "So now our Rugian allies have a stripling for their king. What think you? Should I appoint an older and seasoned man to help him command? The boy is only—what? Fifteen? Sixteen?"

Herduic said, "I saw young Frido wielding his blade in the thick of battle. The lad is not yet strong enough to deliver a cleaving downstroke. But he is capable enough at the thrust and the cuff cut."

"Ja," said Pitzias. "He staunchly pressed his opponents and ably defended himself."

I said, "I did not get to see Frido fight. But I can attest that in other respects he conducts himself as a man grown."

"And bear in mind, Theodoric," said Soas. "That Alexander whom you so much admire was commanding in Macedonia at the age of sixteen."

"Done, then," Theodoric said genially. "We shall let the boy prove himself. Hábái ita swe."

So, before we left Vadum, there was held another auths-swearing ceremony, the boy-king pledging on the name of Allfather Wotan that he would rule wisely and kindly over his people, the Rugian troops pledging that they would obediently and bravely follow wherever he led. At the start of the ritual, however, Frido made an announcement—"I give notice to all here. In assuming the regnancy of the Rugii, I am also assuming a new name"—which raised some eyebrows, because it sounded so much like his fustian father.

But Frido sent a reassuring glance at Theodoric and me, as he went on, "I wish no womanish Romanized name. In the venerable Germanic manner, I shall henceforth be styled Freidereikhs, King of Free Men."

At that, all the Rugii raised an approving cheer, and so did Theodoric and I and every other Ostrogoth and all our other allies

✠ ✠ ✠

Young Freidereikhs got his first taste of combat command—or, rather, his first lessons in that art—at Siscia, the next city we came to on the river Savus, in the province of Savia. The citizens of Siscia, like those of Sirmium, were not at all happy to see our army approaching, and they did their best to let us know we were unwelcome. The city had no garrison capable of fighting us off, no stout walls capable of shutting us out—it had not even a repellent smell like Sirmium's to make us voluntarily stay away—so it adopted the defensive tactic of a snail or tortoise. In effect, Siscia withdrew into a hard shell and defied us to pry that open.

Ever since the Huns had sacked and devastated this city, about half a century previous, it had never quite recovered its onetime stature and grandeur. But, in the days before the coming of Attila, Siscia had been one of the Roman Empire's mints and treasuries. Of its former grand edifices, that mint-and-treasury building was still standing intact, though nowadays unused for that purpose. A huge structure of solid stone walls, bossed and studded iron-and-oak doors, unburnable bronze roof, only arrow slits for windows, the treasury building had stood impregnable even under the siege of the Huns. Now, against our coming, the cityfolk had lugged inside there everything we might have wanted to confiscate, and set a guard to bolt and bar the doors behind them. So the building, on all four sides, presented to us a blank, closed face of stolid resistance—much like the face worn by the people still on the streets outside. Those were all the citizens too old or crippled or ugly not to have to fear conscription or rape. They had locked inside the treasury their males of warrior or laborer age, their chaste wives, nubile maidens and virgin boys, along with their civic and personal valuables, their weapons and tools and implements, the foodstuffs and other plunderable goods from their warehouses.

I walked with Theodoric and Freidereikhs and several other officers all the way around that impassive edifice, studying it for vulnerable spots, but seeing none. When we completed our circuit of it, we were confronted by four elderly men, the city fathers, who stood there wearing the bland, smug, self-satisfied smiles of so many priests.

Theodoric told them, "We are not Huns. We are not here to scour this

759

city down to its pavement stones. We merely wish to supply ourselves sufficiently to move on. Open your treasury, let us take only what we need, and I give you warrant that your gold and maidens and other such precious possessions will not be touched."

"Oh vái," murmured one of the old men, but still serenely smiling. "Had we known of your magnanimity, we would have made other arrangements. But now the guards inside have their strict orders. They are not to open the doors until they can see from their apertures that every last invader has departed from the city."

"I suggest you countermand those orders."

"I cannot. No one can."

"Akh, I imagine one of you will," Theodoric said easily, "and right gladly, when I set fire to your feet."

"It would be of no use. Command what we might, the guards are sworn to yield to no plea or pressure or persuasion, even should you bring here their own mothers to burn."

Theodoric nodded, as if admiring such obduracy. But he said, "I will not ask again. If we have to breach the building ourselves, my men will want reward for that drudgery. I will let them take every morsel and maidenhead they find inside."

"Oh vái," said the old man again, but still not looking the least concerned. "Then we must simply pray that you fail in the breaching."

"On your heads be it, then," said Theodoric, "when we smash the shell and devour the nutmeats. Go and do your praying elsewhere."

As the four men strolled complacently away, Saio Soas muttered to the rest of us, "Pride and honor, of course, forbid our allowing such intransigence. But, besides that, we *need* the contents of this treasury. Our traveling provisions are depleted and, from here westward, we will no longer find replenishments handily waiting for us along the way. The Savus is too shallow upstream of here. Our barges could not get up it to deposit any riverside stores farther on."

Freidereikhs said eagerly, "Let my men use your siege engines. Day and night, we will hurl great stones—"

"Ne," grunted Ibba. "Those walls are as thick as you are tall, young king. You could not batter them down if you took all summer."

"Very well, then," said Freidereikhs, his enthusiasm undiminished. "I have marksmen who can put fire arrows through the slits. A storm of them. The defenders cannot quench them all. We will torch the whole interior."

"And the contents, niu?" Pitzias said impatiently. "We do not wish just to deprive the city. We want those goods for ourselves."

Soas said to me, "Could we try your trumpets of Jaíriko, Saio Thorn?"

I shook my head. "We could, but I think it futile. Those doors are not big double panels like the gates of Singidunum. They are small, compact, not large enough to have any give to them. I doubt that the trumpets could rupture them."

"Even if we broke one down," said Herduic, "the opening is too narrow for a mass assault. The guards inside would easily mow down the few men who could go in at a time."

Theodoric had waited politely while we discarded possibilities. Now he said to Freidereikhs, "If you want to give your men employment, youngster, have them start digging. You see yonder? How the building's eastern corner stands atop that bluff? Put your Rugii to tunneling under the foundation there."

"Undermine it?" asked Freidereikhs uncertainly. "Are you ordering a suicide mission, Theodoric? If the foundation buckles, its falling stones will mash the diggers."

"Have them cut balks of timber, and prop up the foundation as they proceed. Not bendable green tree trunks, mind you. Find hard, dry timber."

"I do not understand," said the boy. "Why undermine the building only to leave it standing?"

761

Theodoric sighed. "Just go and order it done, there's a good lad. Tell your diggers that they will be earning first pick of the virgins inside. The faster they work, the sooner they will get those delicacies. Habái ita swe."

Freidereikhs looked still uncertain, but he repeated, "Habái ita swe," and went off to give the orders.

"Pitzias, Ibba, Herduic," said Theodoric. "Have your underofficers quarter all our men on the cityfolk. Make these inhospitable Siscians be hospitable. No reason for us to sleep in tents and the open air when we can be comfortable while we wait."

The digging was hard work, but at least not hazardous. Freidereikhs's men were under no rain of arrows or rocks or boiling liquids from above. And since they were gouging into a bluff, they simply dumped the excavated soil down the side, without having to cart it any distance. However, the stone walls were thick indeed, and Freidereikhs was not just drilling a tunnel, but making a good-sized cave, so all his workers not digging were kept busy cutting and fetching the timber supports.

When the work first began, those same four city fathers went to see what was going on. But I noticed that they did not look any more worried than they had done when they had conversed with Theodoric. I could only assume that they must know the treasury's floor to be as impenetrable as its walls and roof, so they felt no anxiety about our being able to dig *up* through it—if that was what Theodoric planned to do.

"How deep do you want the hole, Theodoric?" Freidereikhs asked on the fifth or sixth day of digging. "It is now about a quarter of a stade deep and broad, and we are beginning to have a hard time finding stout wood for the props."

"That size should do it," Theodoric said. "Now send men about the city to collect all the olive oil they can find."

"Olive oil?"

"Drench the timbers with it. Then set them afire. And withdraw your men to a safe distance from the bluff."

"Ah-h-h," breathed Freidereikhs, as comprehension dawned on his face—on mine too, probably—and he hurried away.

At least partial comprehension dawned also on the Siscians when smoke began to billow up and out of the diggings. The four city fathers came scuttling to Theodoric, no longer looking smug, but exceedingly distraught.

"Do you intend to roast all our young people inside a stone oven?" whimpered one of them. "The guards and the other men who might fight— that would be allowable by the rules of war. But wives, niu? Maidens? Children?"

Theodoric said, "We did not set the fires to roast anybody. Likely they will sweat a bit before the props burn through. But then the corner of the building will collapse of its own weight, and—"

"Oh vái, worse yet!" The old men wrung their hands. "The only decent building still standing in what was once our glorious Siscia! Even Attila left us that one. Please, mighty conqueror, damp the fires. We will open the treasury doors for you. Let us but go close enough. There is a secret signal we can make to the guards within."

"I rather supposed there would be," Theodoric said drily. "But I gave you your chance. And I do not so readily go back on *my* word. Our men have been put to hard labor by your stubbornness. I shall see that they get their reward. Those wives and maidens and children may wish they *had* been roasted."

The old men cried *akh!* and *vái!* and other expressions of dismay. But then they consulted together, and one of them said, "Spare us the building, and we willingly surrender everything and everybody inside it."

Theodoric gave them a long, sour look. "I assume you four are only the *city* fathers, not the fathers or other kin of any of the persons involved. You certainly do look after your city at the expense of its citizens. But what

762

have you to bargain with? What can you surrender that I am not already taking?"

"Then simply grant us mercy! The treasury building is all that makes Siscia merit being *called* a city."

"That is true. And I too have some regard for the city. When the Western Empire is mine, so will Siscia be. I ought not despoil my own property. Very well, I accept your offer. The shell survives, the nutmeats are ours. Go and give the signal."

As they went, under guard, Theodoric beckoned to a messenger. "Tell King Freidereikhs to have the treasury surrounded. When the doors open, he is to snuff his fires, and he is to let the grown men emerge unharmed from that building. Then, as promised, his warriors may do as they like with all the other persons."

Saio Soas grumbled, "I approve of your sparing the building, Theodoric. But those four old men, first crowing, then crawling—I hate to see you spare them."

"I do not intend to. Give the command, Soas, that all the people of Siscia are to turn out and witness what happens when the building is opened. Afterward, you make an announcement. Tell the citizens how the orgy was the doing of their own city fathers. I daresay the city's *other* fathers and husbands and brothers will give the old men the chastisement they deserve. Probably a far more dreadful requital than anything we could devise."

✠   ✠   ✠

When we moved on, resupplied by the provisions from Siscia's treasury building, we went only about fifty miles upriver before meeting another impediment in our way. This time it was an army of cone-helmeted, scale-armored Sarmatae and Scyrri, not skulking in ambush but drawn up in line of battle and forthrightly waiting to be discovered by our farthest vanguard outriders. I say it was an army only because it numbered perhaps four or five thousand horsemen. Actually it was an aggregation of the warriors from many different nomad Sarmatian and Scyrrian tribes, including the veterans and survivors of several previous defeats by the Ostrogoths—by Theodoric at Singidunum, by Theodoric's father and uncle before that. These people had two motives for moving against us. Having been so often defeated and fragmented, hence compelled to a wretched nomad existence, they now hoped—as the Gepids' ill-fated King Thrausila had hoped—to delay our advance on Venetia and thereby to win from a grateful Odoacer some grant of domain and recognition of them as something better than nomads. Also, since so many of the warriors were still smarting from past overthrows, they frankly yearned for revenge on all Ostrogoths.

However, they stood little chance of wreaking vengeance, and even smaller chance than King Thrausila had had of causing us serious damage or delay. Thrausila at least had been sole king and commander of a unified Gepid soldiery. These several petty tribal leaders, as we would soon realize, had jealously refused to cede overall military authority to any one of themselves. Their gathered troops had done no practicing of integrated battle tactics. What faced us was only an unorganized gang, brave enough and bellicose, but incapable of acting as a concerted force. That was made evident by our first skirmish with them.

When our foremost columns arrived at the nearer edge of the field where the enemy were ranked at the farther edge, about three stadia distant, our troops immediately began to spread out left and right, to form a similar line of preparedness for battle. The opponents sat their horses, waiting—as is the courteous battlefield custom—while more and more of our troops arrived and took their assigned preliminary places. Our two kings and highest officers, I among them, rode to a little rise of ground to study the situation. After a brief appraisal, Theodoric ordered that a single turma of our cavalry be dispatched to make a glancing feint at the enemy's front, just to judge the readiness and temper of those lines. Had the opposing horsemen been properly drilled and commanded, they would simply have stood stolid while raising their shields and lowering their spearpoints, like a hedgehog unconcernedly curling up and bristling its quills. But they did not; a score of them broke ranks to dash out toward our skirmishers, who of course instantly veered away and galloped back toward our side of the field.

"Look at that," Pitzias growled in disdain. "Overeager and undisciplined. They lunged before our men had ridden within even *cursing* range."

"What fools!" Freidereikhs exclaimed happily. "Theodoric, I know you will withhold further engagement until you have all your horse and foot arranged to your satisfaction. In the meantime, let me lead my Rugii all the way around to the enemy's rear, and—"

"Hush, boy, and learn something," Theodoric said gruffly, but not unkindly. Then he turned his back on the younger king, to give orders to Pitzias, Ibba and Herduic, directing them to position their centuries and cohorts and turmae here, there and yonder. Freidereikhs could barely contain his impatience, and his horse danced to be off, while the generals one after another saluted and departed. Finally Theodoric turned again to the lad.

"Let me explain to you what I am doing, and why, so that—"

"But I *already* understand, Theodoric!" the boy interrupted, and excitedly gushed a torrent of words. "As soon as the generals have massed and deployed and instructed their troops, and begun to advance, you will have the main assault made by Ibba's cavalry, riding in what is called the swine-array—the triangular formation originated by the great god Wotan when, in ancient times, he came down to earth to amuse himself for a while by being Jalk the Giant-Killer, and happened to notice how a herd of wild pigs, galloping through a forest in that form of a point-first triangle, swept every other animal helplessly before them." The boy had to pause to gulp for air, then went on in another rush of words, "You are also placing forces to protect the flanks of Ibba's cavalry, and other forces to deflect any counter-attack, and still other forces to abide in reserve, and of course diversionary forces to harry the enemy and distract them from the cavalry's swine-array assault." Again he ran out of breath, then grinned and concluded, "There! Have I not accurately described your disposition of forces?"

"You have not," Theodoric said bluntly, and the boy's face fell. "The cavalry in swine-array, ja, but *they* will be the diversionary force, not the main attack."

"What? Why?"

"Because the swine-array's traditional employment *is* attack, so the enemy will suppose our cavalry to be doing precisely that. You see, I try never to do the expected thing—except, of course, when I think my foes may be expecting me to do the *un*expected. In this case, I think they are not. Therefore, while they move to defend against and repel Ibba's cavalry, I shall attack instead with Herduic's infantry."

"With *foot* soldiers?"

"Observe, young king. The enemy forces consist entirely of mounted men, but they made an unwise choice of field on which to make their stand. The ground here is rough and rocky, much better suited to fighting on foot than on horseback. Observe also, young king, the sky and the weather and the time of day."

Theodoric waited, so Freidereikhs said, "Midafternoon. Bright sunshine. A westerly breeze."

"Observing which, I seize two other small advantages. I send Herduic and his men to attack from the west, so the afternoon sun will be shining into the enemy's eyes, and the dust scuffed up by the attackers' running feet will be blowing into the enemy's eyes."

765

Freidereikhs murmured admiringly, "Ja, I see. Very clever, very practical. Thags izvis, Theodoric, I *have* learned a few things here. But now—for my men's part, since yours will be facing and flanking the enemy—let me take my Rugii around to their rear to complete the surrounding."

"I do not want them surrounded."

Freidereikhs looked mystified. "What? Whyever not? We could crush them utterly."

"At an exorbitant and unnecessary price. Learn one more thing, young warrior. Except in a settled and lengthy siege, *never* entirely surround your enemy. If he is trapped, he will fight fiercely, to the last man, costing many of your own. If he is left an avenue of escape, he will flee the slaughter. I wish only to clear these nuisances out of our way, with as little of our blood spilled as possible."

In some frustration, Freidereikhs wailed, "Where *can* I fight, then?"

"Akh, I would not deny good warriors a good battle, and I do not at all mind shedding the *enemy's* blood. Take your Rugii to their rear, as you proposed, and line their avenue of escape. When they flee, let them flee, but scourge them as they go. Ravage them, terrify them, scatter them. Make sure they do not regroup to turn on us again. Go! Enjoy yourself!"

"Hábái ita swe!" cried Freidereikhs, and he was gone.

I need not recount the battle in detail, because it went just as Theodoric had planned and foreseen, and it was over before sundown. When the two armies came together, most of our mounted warriors, including Theodoric and myself, pressed the enemy's front and eastern flank, while Ibba's swine-array charged into them point-first. Then, in amongst the milling horsemen, Herduic's foot soldiers swarmed like a multitude of ants infiltrating a brawl of beetles. They arrived almost unnoticed, out of the sun and the dust. And the foemen on horseback, towering above them—hacking, slashing, bellowing war cries—were at first almost heedless of them as they nimbly scurried about, unobtrusively putting their swords into horses' bellies, cutting saddle girths, slicing the hamstrings of horses and unwary riders, quietly dispatching the unhorsed who fell among them. By the time the enemy realized that they were literally being undercut from beneath, there was little they could do about it. The sheer weight of our numbers was jamming them together, the vigor of our spear and sword work was forcing them to go on fighting at horse level, so they could not bend and lean to swipe at their ground-level tormentors. A good many of our infantrymen were getting trampled and crushed, but few were dying by the blade.

The enemy, finally noticing that they were being pressed from front, sides and underneath—but not from the rear—began to make for that avenue of escape Theodoric had provided. For a time they backed and sidled away from us, still wielding their blades as they went, but then a few of them, then more of them, then increasing numbers of them turned their horses and let the steeds gallop headlong. And as the enemy fled, they had to run the gantlet of Rugii planted along their way, so their retreat was not at all orderly, but became a disorganized and panicky rout.

When the fighting was all over, there were more than two thousand men lying on the ground, most of them Sarmatae and Scyrri, and most of them were lying still. Theodoric was not going to take prisoners or to waste the time and medical skill of his lekjos in treating the enemy wounded, so our foot soldiers continued their efficient dispatching of those fallen foemen still alive. And our army stayed in that place only long enough to dig proper graves for our own slain. Freidereikhs, in making his long ride around to the rear of the battlefield, had come upon a village on the way. It was smaller than its name—Andautonia—having a population of only about a hundred. But Freidereikhs conscripted all its able-bodied men and women, herded them onto the blood-soaked field and commanded them—however long it might take—to do the burying of the dead Sarmatae and Scyrri, or to do whatever other mode of corpse disposal they might contrive, so our army could go on without further delay.

767

✠   ✠   ✠

It was mid-July, and very hot, when we arrived at Aemona, the chief city of the province of Noricum Mediterraneum. That is a very old city—indeed, reputed to have been founded by the Argonaut Jason—and in spring and autumn it must be a surpassingly fair city. It occupies both banks of a clear-water Savus tributary, and its most notable feature is a single lofty hump of ground, from the top of which one gets a magnificent view of the distant Alpes Juliani and nearer mountains roundabout. However, all the rest of the city is on low land, and that is surrounded by a marshy plain that in summer exudes unwholesome miasmas and clouds of insects.

Aemona's one high piece of ground is crowned with a fortress quite as immense and formidable as that mint-and-treasury building in Siscia. The Aemona citizens might similarly have tried to secrete and barricade in there all their valuables and possessions, but evidently some traveler preceding our slow-moving army had told them of Siscia's failure to thwart our plundering. So Aemona let us march in unopposed and unhindered, and resignedly let us avail ourselves of what supplies and provisions and diversions it had to offer. There was a sufficiency of those—including thermae and lupanar women and wineshops and noctiluca streetwalkers—but we unearthed no great treasures of gold or jewelry or the like, because the city had been long ago sacked by our predecessor kinsman, the Visigoth Alareikhs, or Alaric, and later by Attila's Huns, and never had won back to its former wealth and opulence.

Theodoric and Freidereikhs and their higher-ranking officers took up residence in the fortress on the high ground, and we were comfortable enough there. Our men were not so, down in the pestilential airs of the lowlands, but Theodoric was having to weigh one discomfort against another. The remainder of our journey to the Venetia border would be across similarly low ground, and he thought it better to let his army abide in encampment around Aemona than to make it slog on through the summer heat. So we loitered there for nearly a month, waiting for the torrid weather to abate. But it did not, and the morbific swamp mists began to cause illnesses and grudges and quarrels among the men. Finally, nolens volens, Theodoric had to give the order to pick up and move on.

We left the marshlands behind, which was a blessing, but the weather continued oppressively hot and humid. And if that had not been enough to make traveling miserable, we soon found ourselves in a landscape most odd and ugly. The natives who have to live there call it "karst," and curse it, and so did we. Most of that land is bare limestone, punishing to men's feet and horses' hoofs. Worse, the naked rock both holds the sun's heat and reflects it, thus being twice as hot as any other terrain. What is most odd about the karst, though, is that it is everywhere tunneled by underground rivers. In ages past, many of the caves and caverns hollowed out by those rivers have collapsed, leaving the limestone surface pocked by sinkholes—ranging from the size of a sunken amphitheater to a circumference and depth capable of containing an entire town. And over the ages those hollows have accumulated silt in their bottoms, so that is where the natives live, on miniature round or oblong farms. At the occasional such hollow, a passerby can look down into it and see the river that made it, issuing from one side and disappearing into the other, going underground again.

Thags Guth, we came at last to a normal river again, the Sontius, flowing aboveground and through a more pleasant landscape, one of real soil and greenery and flowers. So we came to it with genuine relief and gladness, even though, on the farther side of it, where begins the Italian province of Venetia, we saw waiting the massed and mighty legions of Odoacer, poised to close with us and stop us and destroy us.

4

It was our speculatores riding farthest forward of our army's columns who got the first look at those forces defending the Venetia border. After discreetly scouting their front from south to north—from the Tergeste Gulf, where the river Sontius flows into the Hadriatic Sea, to the foothills of the Alpes Juliani, where the river has its source—the outriders returned to us to report. And when their optio spoke, there was some awe in his voice.

"King Theodoric, the enemy troops are of almost incalculable number. They are ranged for nearly four miles along the river's western bank. The heaviest concentration of those troops is, of course, at the farther end of the Pons Sontii, the only bridge across that river, directly to the front of your line of march."

"As I expected," Theodoric said, unawed. "After all, Odoacer has had plenty of time to mass his men. What other use has he made of the time, Optio? What manner of defenses have his legions prepared against us?"

"They appear to be relying on sheer force of numbers," said the outrider. "They have built nothing more substantial than the usual tidy Roman camps, all along the river. Orderly rows of their big butterfly sleeping tents, and among them supply sheds, horse pens, armory and smithy and cooking tents, sties and folds for the pigs and sheep they brought along to eat, all the ordinary appurtenances of military camps. But they have constructed no permanent buildings or walls or barricades."

Theodoric nodded. "They rightly expect that this will be a fierce hand-to-hand battle. They want ease and quickness of mobility. And what of the riverside terrain, Optio?"

"From the gulf to the foothills, all level land, the same as here, with one difference on their side of the river. They have cleared the trees as far as perhaps a quarter of a mile back from the water. Whether that was to allow the laying out of their campgrounds, or for freedom of movement when the fighting begins, or simply to procure campfire wood, I could not say."

"But on this side? The forest remains? All the way to the riverbank?"

"Ja, King Theodoric. As you say, they had plenty of time to clear that too, had they wished. Perhaps they hope the trees will hinder your disposition of your own troops."

Theodoric nodded again. "Anything else, Optio?"

"We noted only one other thing that might be worth reporting." He knelt to scratch with a twig in the dirt, drawing parallel lines to represent the river's course, and a mark to show where we were. "On the higher ground to the north, they have built two signal platforms. The fires or smokes will be visible all down the river."

"Platforms?" Theodoric asked. "Not towers?"

"Platforms, ja." The optio drew two little rectangles at the upriver end of his diagram. "Right about there. Not very high or sturdy platforms, and not very far apart."

"Well, well," said Theodoric. "The old Polybian system, eh? I must ride up there, one night soon, and see them signal. Thags izvis, good Optio. And thags izei to your fellow outriders. Now—Odoacer surely had his own speculatores in these woods to watch our advance. They will have counted our number, but I would prefer that they do not see our eventual deployment. Take as many other men as you need, Optio, and go out ahead of us again. Clear away those watchers before we get to the river. Habái ita swe."

The optio saluted, vaulted to his saddle and led his men off again. Theodoric remained kneeling by the twig-drawn sketch, and beckoned for his marshals, his generals and King Freidereikhs to join him.

"Let us start now to separate our columns and get some of them off this main trail." Pointing here and there on the diagram, he gave each man orders to move this or that body of horsemen or foot soldiers or supply wagons to this or that position. "And, Pitzias, the detachment I am sending here"—he indicated a spot upriver on the diagram—"have them equipped with tools for felling trees and hauling the trunks to the riverside, in case I decide we need them for floating men or supplies across." Theodoric turned last to young Freidereikhs. "You wanted once before to make use of our siege engines. You can do it here. I want them brought up and ranged—"

"Siege engines? But the outriders said there are no buildings or walls or barri—"

Theodoric interrupted, with some exasperation, "You must humor my eccentricities, young man! Perhaps I merely like to hear the twang and thump noises the engines make. What I do *not* like to hear is criticism of my battle plans."

Freidereikhs, abashed, said hastily, "Ja, ja, of course. My men will make them twang and thump most mightily."

✠   ✠   ✠

Three or four days later, our foremost columns, Theodoric in the lead, got to the Sontius, where he held them well back from the riverside, using the forest for concealment as various portions of them veered off upstream and down. He did not even go close to the river himself to take a look at the enemy on the farther bank. He seemed totally unconcerned about that vast army over there, and gave all his attention to the positioning of our own troops, as more and more of them arrived, and to the provisions made for keeping them fed and comfortable and in good cheer. During the several subsequent days and nights, Theodoric rode north and south, inspecting our lines and giving orders or making suggestions to his subordinate officers.

Meanwhile, all the forward ranks of both armies lay within easy bow-shot of each other. The range was too great for accuracy, with the river between, but a high-arching rain of arrows could have dealt considerable harm. Our troops were only concealed by the trees and shrubbery, not much protected, and Odoacer's troops did not have even that flimsy cover. But Theodoric sternly forbade any of our men to indulge the impulse to let fly even a single arrow, and apparently Odoacer was doing the same.

771

Theodoric explained his restraint when, one balmy night, he had me ride with him upriver to see where—or if—the Sontius got narrow and shallow enough to be fordable at some point.

On the way, he told me, "Because this is certain to be the most significant war I shall ever fight in my lifetime, I intend to observe the courtesy of formally declaring war before I commence it, and do so with scrupulous attention to the traditions recognized by both Romans and outlanders. When I judge the time to be right, I shall walk out upon the Pons Sontii and cry my challenge—demand that Odoacer surrender before he is defeated, that he stand out of my way to Rome, that he acknowledge me as his successor and overlord. Of course he will do no such thing. He or a lesser officer will also walk out upon the bridge and cry the refusal and defial. Thereupon we mutually declare that a state of war exists between us. Custom further requires only that he and I be allowed time to return safely to our separate sides. Then, on the instant, if we choose, we can wave our men forward to the attack."

"How much longer, then, before you do that, Theodoric? Are you merely letting our men get a good rest after their long march? Or are you tantalizing and taunting Odoacer, after his having waited so long for our arrival, making him wait some more?"

"Neither," said Theodoric. "And not all of our men have been resting. Some of them, you know, are former legionaries, and they wear Roman army dress. On each of the nights past, I have sent them quietly swimming across the river and, as soon as their clothes dry, mingling unobtrusively with the enemy, to see or hear what they might. I have also posted ample guards to make sure that no spies come over from that side."

"And have ours seen or heard anything useful?"

"One thing at least. Odoacer is of course an experienced and capable campaigner, but he is old—sixty or more. I was interested to learn that he has entrusted most of his command duties to a younger man, about our own age. A man named Tufa, who is of Rugian birth."

"Akh, then this Tufa would be familiar with all the Germanic strategies and tactics of battle. The swine-array and so on."

"Well, so would Odoacer. He has fought enough Germanic tribes in his time. Ne, I was not so much concerned about that. I was thinking . . . since this General Tufa is of the same origin as our young King Freidereikhs, he might just *possibly* be susceptible to seduction by a fellow Rugian . . ."

"To betray his King Odoacer? To subvert the Roman defenses? Even to change sides?"

"The possibility is interesting to speculate on, but I am not counting on it." Theodoric dropped the subject there, because we had come to the upriver body of troops prepared to do tree-cutting if necessary, and he told their commanding officer, "You might as well get them started at that, Decurio. If this river shallows anywhere at all, it would be too far north for the ford to be of much use to us. So have the men hew us a good supply of tree trunks, in case we should require them."

The decurio went off bawling orders into the night, and a few moments later we heard the first ax blows. Almost immediately after that, Theodoric said, "Behold, Thorn," and pointed across the river. The darkness over there was pierced by a point of light, and then a second, and then several more.

"Torches," I said.

"The Polybian signals," he said. "Torch-bearers up on those platforms we were told about." He dismounted from his horse. "Let us get out of these trees to where we can see better and read what they are saying."

"I never could read even the signals of the Constantinople pháros," I said as we sat down on the riverbank.

"The Polybian system is quite simple. With torches by night or smoke by day, it spells out words. The twenty standard letters of the Roman alphabet are divided into five groups of four. A, B, C, D and then E, F, G, H and so on. The five torches on the left-hand platform yonder tell which group. See there? One of the torches is raised for a moment above the others. And on the right-hand platform, one of the four torches is raised to tell which letter in the group."

"Ja, I see," I said. "On the left, the second torch is raised. On the right, the first torch. And now they are all being held level again. Now, over on the left, the first torch. On the right, the fourth."

"Keep calling them off," said Theodoric, who had bent down to the ground. "I am laying out twigs here, to make note of them."

"Very well. Now, on the left, the fourth torch. On the right, the third. On the left, now, the third—and on the right the third also. Now on the left the fourth, on the right the second."

Theodoric waited, then said, "Well?"

"That is all. Now they are signaling the same sequence over again. I assume they are spelling a single five-letter word."

773

"Let me see, then, if I can decipher my twigs here. Hm . . . second group, first letter . . . that is E. First group, fourth letter . . . D."

"Macte virtute," I murmured admiringly. "It does work."

"And P . . . and L . . . and O. Edplo. Edplo? Hm . . . it may *not* be working, after all. Edplo is not a word. Not in Latin or Gothic or Greek."

I was watching the torches again, and said, "Well, they are signaling the exact same thing, over and over. That makes four or five times now."

Theodoric growled in annoyance, "We got it right, then. But, confound it, what language are they—?"

"Wait," I said. "I think I have it. The language is Latin, right enough, but the alphabet is not the Roman. Very cunning of them. They are employing the *futhark*, the old runic alphabet. Not A, B, C, D, but faihu, úrus, thorn, ansus . . . Let me see: second group, first letter . . . that would be raida. First group, fourth letter . . . ansus. So we have R and A . . . then teiws . . . and eis . . . and sauil. The word is *ratis*. You see? Latin!"

Theodoric laughed like a boy. "Ja! Ratis, a raft!"

"They heard our woodcutters at work. They are signaling to Odoacer or Tufa that we are building rafts here upriver."

"Let them," Theodoric said gaily as we returned to our horses. "If

Odoacer and Tufa are fools enough to believe that *we* are fools enough to try building rafts for twenty-odd thousand men and half that many horses, let them believe it."

"And in the meantime, what *will* we be doing?"

"Attacking in full force," he said as we mounted and turned back the way we had come. "I have decided. Tomorrow, just before dawn, I shall cry my challenge. Then the war begins."

"Good. Where would you have me fight?"

"On horse or on foot this time?"

"Akh, my Velox would never forgive me if I left him behind." I fondly slapped his sleek neck.

"Velox?" Theodoric repeated, wonderingly, and leaned to peer through the darkness. "I thought only Wotan had an immortal steed, his Sleipnir. Surely, Thorn, that cannot be the same horse you were riding when we first met—fifteen years ago, was it?

It was my turn to laugh. "I ought to leave you in perplexity. But this is Velox the *Third.* I have been exceedingly fortunate that the bloodline has bred so true to the original."

"Indeed, ja. If ever you retire from the warrior's profession, you ought to devote yourself to horse-breeding. However, since you are still a warrior, and a well-mounted one, go in with Ibba tomorrow. His cavalry will be the vanguard."

"You would not rather I ride with young Freidereikhs?"

"He will not be riding. As I ordered, he and his Rugii will be working the catapults—the ballistae and onagri. His men have been collecting boulders and other missiles ever since we got here."

"Missiles for what, Theodoric? Are you going to knock down the Pons Sontii?"

"Why in the world would I do that? I need the bridge for our crossing."

"What else, then? As Freidereikhs said, there is not a single wall or barricade to be battered and broken."

"Akh, there is, Thorn. You fail to recognize it because it is not of stone and iron and timber. I only hope that Odoacer and Tufa think as you do— that I have no need or use for siege engines. But anything that impedes my way, I call a barricade, and I shall batter and break it."

✠   ✠   ✠

At dawn the next day, I realized what he meant: the barricade to be demolished was of flesh and bone and muscle.

It was not Odoacer but his Rugian-turned-Roman Tufa who faced Theodoric on the Pons Sontii. After the two men had gone through their ritual formalities—Theodoric crying his challenge, Tufa his counter-challenge, then both of them declaring, "This is war!"—Tufa returned to his end of the bridge. Theodoric stood where he was, drew his sword and swept it in the imperious overarm gesture calling for the "impetus!" But Ibba did not put us horsemen to the charge. Instead of our mounts' hoofs making a thunder, we heard an astonishingly loud thrumming noise from behind us, and next a staggered series of earthshaking thuds, and next a sort of swooshing noise overheard, like the beating of many immense wings. The pearly dawn light was suddenly and luridly brightened by what might have been a cascade of igneous meteors, blazing across the sky from somewhere behind us and crashing to earth with explosions of sparks on the farther side of the bridge.

Those fiery, smoke-and-spark-trailing objects were not, of course, bolides come from the heavens. They were projectiles hurled by the ballistae and onagri ranged in the woods behind us—boulders wrapped in dry, oil-soaked brush, set alight just before they were launched. And they continued to fly over us, as Freidereikhs's men briskly rewound and reloaded and reloosed the throwing arms of their siege engines. A ballista, discharging the power coiled into its tightly twisted torque-ropes, can catapult a rock weighing twice as much as a man a distance of two stadia. A massive onager, discharging the power squeezed into its tightly contorted torque-beams, can hurl the same weight twice that distance. So the ballistae were aimed at the farther end of the bridge and at the legions ranked along the riverside north and south. The onagri were flinging their missiles farther beyond, into the infantry and cavalry massed on the cleared ground between the riverside and the western tree line.

775

I do not know whether such machines, intended for the patient, deliberate hammering of heavy fortifications, had ever in any previous war been employed thus, against unprotected flesh and bone and muscle. But clearly Odoacer and his troops had not been expecting any such extraordinary assault. Many of those men and horses were straightway crushed by the plummeting boulders, but the most telling effect of the meteor shower was the consternation it caused. When a missile crashed down into the ranked and filed legionaries, that orderly formation exploded like the sparks, into a disorderly spray of dodging men. When a projectile landed among a troop of cavalry, that orderly array became a disorderly commotion of horses bolting, men thrown, horses plunging, men fighting for control of their terrified mounts. When a boulder flattened a stock pen or fold or sty and freed its contents, the horses and sheep and pigs scampered hither and yon, bleating, squealing, neighing, butting, kicking. When a missile fired one of the canvas supply and service tents, that contributed more sparks and smoke to the confusion. The eight-man butterfly tents, being of leather, did not burn, but their torn-loose panels blew about and tangled among the running feet and hoofs. Such was the chaos and catastrophe that, when our ranks of archers added a rain of arrows and fire arrows to the rain of rocks and flame, the rattled and disjointed Roman forces could return no concerted volley.

All of that was going on within range of my vision; no doubt much the same destruction was being worked to the north and south and farther west beyond my view. Now Theodoric's shield-bearer went running onto the bridge, leading the king's horse. He leapt to the saddle, again waved his sword in the command of "charge!" and this time Ibba and we of his cavalry clapped heels to our steeds. As evidently had been carefully arranged, Freidereikhs's lighter ballistae ceased their action as Theodoric and Ibba led us pounding across the bridge, so that we did not have to worry about getting battered by boulders when we reached the other bank. But there were more flares of red light and swooshing noises going over our heads, so the heavier onagri were still pounding the enemy forces out beyond.

In a frontal assault, the point men almost always suffer the most casualties and the worst damage. But we cavalrymen—charging in among those milling, disorganized, unnerved troops nearest the bridge end—were at first almost unopposed, and we slaughtered busily but easily, as if we had been reaping a grainfield. Our every leveled spear was wrested from us only because it lodged inextricably in a foeman's breast. Then we thrashed and slashed with our battle-axes and snake blades, and the enemy fell like mown wheat stalks, only not so quietly or juicelessly. And after us came more of our army, as we cleared the way for them and while the catapults and archers kept a canopy of missiles and arrows in the air over them—turmae and decades and centuries of horse and foot soldiers converging from north and south and east, and funneling onto and across the bridge.

Of course, our invasion did not go on for too long uncontested. This day we were not contemptuously brushing aside an undisciplined rabble of nomads or an unfriendly city's hastily contrived defenses. This was the Roman army. Despite its appalling initial losses and its having reeled before our onslaught, it was by no means defeated or routed. Above the uproar of combat—human and animal cries, clashing arms and shields and armor, missiles booming down, boots and hoofs clumping—the blare of Roman trumpets could be heard, blowing the "ordinem!" that began rallying *their* turmae and decades and centuries to regroup about their standards and commanders. And more distant trumpets could be heard, summoning re-inforcements from the long lines extending up and down the Sontius. Then, once the Romans recovered from their first unhappy fallback, they fought with courage and skill and more than ordinary ferocity (they being justifiably angry at having been seen to cringe from the projectiles). We were engaged in a major battle, and no mistake.

But it could have been worse for us. Had we made our dawn attack in any traditional, accepted, expectable manner, we would have had a hellish time trying to force our way across that bridge—or trying to cross the Sontius on rafts, or by swimming, or under cover of darkness, or on make-shift pontoon bridges, or by waiting for winter to freeze the river solid, or by any other means imaginable. But Theodoric's unconventional, maybe even unprecedented, employment of catapults and blazing missiles had given us two inestimable advantages. It did some of our killing and crippling for us before we even closed with the enemy. And it so surprised and discomposed and roiled those troops that they could put up no real resis-tance before we got a considerable force of our own in among them. And now, we having accomplished that, we *had* to keep fighting ever forward. If we had let the enemy repulse us, there could have been no retreating, because we were far too numerous to back onto that bridge without jam-ming ourselves solid and helpless. The only alternative would have been to back into the river, which would likewise have meant our extermination. We had to fight and we had to prevail.

777

The history books now judge that battle at the river Sontius to have been one of the mightier clashes between mighty armies in recent times, and a momentous episode in the annals of the later Roman Empire, and an epochal event that will influence the destiny of all the western world to the furthest future. But the books do not tell what that battle was like, and no more can I.

This I have said before: a participant in a battle can honestly recount nothing of it but his own individual, meager, narrow experience of it. At the start of this one, when I was thrusting with my cavalry spear . . . and later, when I was flailing with my sword, after I had left my spear in the corselet of a signifer whom I had impaled . . . and later still, when I was fighting afoot, after I had been unhorsed but not injured by the glancing blow of a centurio's battle-mace . . . all that while, I was conscious only of turmoil everywhere about me, except when I occasionally and briefly was conscious of a familiar face nearby. I glimpsed Theodoric hard at the fray, and Ibba, and other soldiers known to me, including young Freidereikhs, when his catapult work was done and he and his Rugii had come over the bridge to join us. I may at some point have crossed blades with such notable opponents as Odoacer and Tufa, but if I did I was too busy to recognize them. Like everyone else on that field, from the kings down to the camp cooks and clerks compelled to seize up arms, I was intent on doing just one thing—and that was *not* to make this battle worthy of inclusion in the history books, or to add anything to the annals of the Roman Empire, or to affect the future of western civilization. It was an aim rather less lofty, but much more immediate, and it was the one aim that every warrior had in common that day.

There are numerous ways to kill a man, without waiting for disease or old age to do it. He can be deprived of food or water or air, or all three, but that is a slow way of killing. He can be burned or crucified or poisoned, but those too take some time. He can be hit a crushing blow, as with a mace or a catapult's projectile, but that cannot be depended on to kill with certainty. No, the surest and swiftest way to kill a man is to put a hole in him and let his life-spirit spurt or ooze out with his blood. The hole can be made with something as common as a sharp stick or with something as unlikely as what I used upon my own earliest victim, the beak of a juika-bloth. What weapon the first recorded killer used, the Bible does not say, but blood is mentioned, so Cain obviously put a hole in Abel. Ever since then, through-out history, man has exercised his best ingenuity to invent means of putting holes in other men: spears, lances, swords, knives, arrows—and to invent ever sharper and surer versions of those things: the twisting spear, the barb-pointed arrow, the keen snake blade. Men of the future may have weapons that I and my fellow warriors could not even dream of, but this I know: chief among them, and most reliable, will be something recognizable as a hole-maker. The intent will be no whit different in the far future than it was in the dim past age of Cain or on that day beside the river Sontius: this man striving to put a hole in that man, before that man could put a hole in him. Akh, I realize that I am risking disbelief and reproach by making manly combat—and the fiercest battle, and the mightiest war—sound absurd instead of heroic. But ask any other man who has ever been to war.

Well, we did prevail at last. When the Roman trumpets blared one final time to call the legions to their standards, those trumpets were urgently but mournfully sounding the "receptus!" All those forces that had con-verged here now drew away, and those still engaged with ours fought their way clear of us, and the whole army shrank away westward, snatching up what it could of its camps' equipment and supplies, its dropped weapons and riderless mounts, and those of its wounded who could move or be moved. In its many centuries of waging war, the Roman army had not made

778

too many retreats, but it had learned to make them orderly and expeditiously. Our men naturally chased after the enemy, harrying their rear and their fringes and their stragglers, but Theodoric had his officers likewise call their troops to regroup, and sent after the retreating Roman army only a body of speculatores to keep track of where it went.

My first concern was to track down my own riderless mount, because Velox wore a Roman army saddle and might have been mistaken for one of their horses. But his also wearing the unusual foot-rope perhaps gave pause to the Romans' horse-collectors. At any rate, I found him safe and unscathed, down to the south of where he and I had fought, grazing on the cleared ground between the bridge and the trees. He was having to choose and pluck his grass-blades most fastidiously, because the grass and ground *everywhere* on this side of the river was soaked and reeking with blood. Velox too was spattered with it, and I was smeared with it, and so was almost every other horse and man on the field, alive or dead. When we survivors later went to wash ourselves and our gear, the Sontius ran red, bright red, for a long time. If there were any persons living between here and the Hadriatic who had been unaware of our armies' meeting, they soon knew of it, and knew that it had been a carnage.

When the Roman legions departed, they left behind none of their fighting men who were still fit. From those legions there were no defectors, no deserters. But there did remain on the field a number of their medici and capsarii—the physicians of officer grade and their assisting rankers— to tend the wounded also left there. And of course, the wounded enemies this time being men of worth, we victors did not summarily put them to death, but let them be doctored and cared for. Indeed, our own accompanying lekjos officers worked side by side with the Roman medici, and all those physicians impartially treated all the wounded of both sides. I do not know how many of the fallen were kept alive or nursed back to health, but there were at least four thousand of our men already dead, and half again that many more of Odoacer's. When our burial parties set about interring our slain, several officers suggested that it would save us much time and trouble if we simply dropped the enemies' corpses into the Sontius and let them go downstream, as their lifeblood was already doing.

"Ne, ni allis!" Theodoric said sternly. "These Roman dead are six thousand fewer impediments on our way to winning the whole land of Italia. And when we have won that land, these men's widows and children and other kinfolk will be my subjects, our fellow citizens and adopted kin. See to it that every one of the fallen Romans is buried as ceremoniously as we bury our own. Be it so!"

779

And so it was, though that task took our men many days to complete. At least our corpse-straighteners and gravediggers were spared any necessity of doing different offices for the various dead. That is to say, it would have been impossible to tell which of the corpses were Christians or pagans or Mithraists, except in the rare case where a dead man wore a cross or a Thor's hammer or a sun-disk somewhere on his person, but that made for no problem. Mithraists, like pagans, have always been buried with heads to the west. And Christians having decided to be buried "with feet to the east," our men had only to dig identical graves in parallel rows and inter the dead all the same. Anyway, no matter their religion in life, that is what dead men are: all the same.

Meanwhile, our armorers and smiths were also busy, repairing damaged corselets, reshaping dented helmets, straightening bent blades and sharpening blunted ones. Other soldiers were put to work collecting all the usable equipment and supplies and provisions the departing Romans had had to leave behind. Some of those things we made immediate use of—eating our fill of fresh-killed pork and mutton, for example, slathered with the Romans' good garon sauce—and the other salvaged goods were loaded on the Romans' discarded carts and wagons for taking along with us. Even our woodcutters who had chopped down all those trees upstream on the eastern bank finally got their chance to make them into rafts. We discovered that the Pons Sontii was too narrow to admit the immense carriages of our siege engines, so those got floated across the river.

Meanwhile, too, some of the speculatores who had gone following Odoacer came riding back to report to Theodoric. They said there was a very large and handsome city just a day's march to the west of us, Aquileia by name. Because that city sits on Venetia's flat coastal plain and faces on the open sea and is not at all walled about, its obvious vulnerability to assault had evidently decided Odoacer not to stop there. The speculatores said that his army had taken the fine Roman road that begins at Aquileia and, making good time, had continued along it, westward.

"The road is the Via Postumia," Theodoric said to us gathered officers. "It leads to Verona, a strong-walled city, two-thirds encircled by a river, therefore eminently defensible. I do not wonder that Odoacer is hastening there. But I am pleased that he abandoned Aquileia to our mercies. It is the capital of this province of Venetia, and is an exceedingly wealthy city—or was, before the Huns trampled through it fifty years ago. However, it still is one of the main bases of the Roman navy, with part of the Hadriatic Fleet stationed at its seaside Grado suburb. It ought to be a comfortable place to refresh ourselves after our year of endeavor, and reward ourselves for the grand victory we have had here. From what I have heard of travelers' tales, Aquileia has many elegant thermae, tasty Hadriatic seafoods and expert cooks to prepare them, beauteous Roman *and* Veneti women. So we will abide there for a time, but not for too long. As soon as we are all well rested, we will be off after Odoacer. Unless others of our speculatores return to report that he has veered off the Via Postumia, we will find him at Verona. And we must not allow him time to make that city more of a stronghold than it already is. That is where he will make his next stand. And I hope to make it his last."

5

e very much enjoyed the several days we spent in Aquileia. Not since my stay in Vindobona had I been in a city where Latin was the everyday language of even the commonfolk. However, since most of the citizens here were Veneti—small, wiry, gray-eyed people with more Celtic than Roman blood—they spoke their Latin rather curiously, using the sounds of *z*, *k* and *f* instead of the conventional *d*, *g* and *b*. They glumly saluted Theodoric as "Theozoric," and they amused him and the rest of us when, meaning to revile us as Gothi barbari, they cursed us as "Kothi farfari."

And they did curse us, because Aquileia was understandably weary of being invaded by outlanders every generation or so—Alaric's Visigoths, then Attila's Huns, now us. The people were not much conciliated when Theodoric demanded of them only tribute of such supplies and commodities as would be of military use to our army. Mindful of this being his own future property, he forbade our troops to do any wanton destruction in the city or any looting for their personal profit. However, the warriors did make free use of the Aquileian women and girls and possibly some few boys. The decent ones did not like that, nor did their kinfolk, and probably the local lupanar and noctiluca females even less liked being used, because they were accustomed to getting *paid* for that.

Not *every* leading citizen of Aquileia held us in total odium. The navarchus of the Hadriatic Fleet, a man named Lentinus, middle-aged but youthfully brisk of movement, came from the Grado docks to converse with Theodoric. He spoke disparagingly of Odoacer (and, being a native of Venetia, he pronounced that name in the local manner).

"I have no reason to love King Ozoacer," he said. "I watched his army's unseemly stampede through here, and I am disinclined to be bound in fealty to a king so quickly and thoroughly routed. However, that does not mean, Theozoric, that I will abjectly surrender to you my ships based here or down the coast at Altinum. If your men prepare to board or seize them, I shall have all the vessels put safely to sea. On the other hand, when you demonstrably have vanquished Ozoacer, and have the blessing of Emperor Zeno, from that moment I will acknowledge you as my superior officer, and the Hadriatic Fleet will be yours."

"Fair enough," said Theodoric. "I expect to be fighting only land battles to overthrow Odoacer. I should not need any sea forces. By such time as I have use for those, I expect to be your king, and universally recognized as such. I shall then welcome your allegiance, Navarchus Lentinus, but I promise first to earn it."

782

Also, while every other female in Aquileia seethed with loathing of us intruders, at least two of them—the exceptionally handsome women appropriated by Theodoric and young Freidereikhs—were absolutely enraptured at being the temporary bedmates of genuine *kings*, even conqueror kings. During their brief tenure as "queens," those two willingly imparted useful bits of information about the surrounding country, such as: "When you continue along the Via Postumia, twenty miles west of here you will come to Concorzia." (She meant Concordia.) "It once was a garrison and a manufactory of weapons for the Roman army. Ever since the Huns ravaged it, Concorzia has been in ruins, but it still is an important road juncture. There you will see another good Roman highway forking to the southwestward ..."

Thus, when our army finally moved on from Aquileia, and we came to the remains of Concordia, Theodoric summoned forward a cavalry centurio to be given orders, and was able to tell him:

"Centurio Brunjo, that fork to the left is a branch of the Via Aemilia. While the rest of us proceed toward Verona, you and your century of horsemen will take that road yonder. I am reliably informed that you will meet no opposing forces anywhere along it. The road will take you across both the rivers Athesis and Padus, all the way to the city of Bononia, where it joins the Aemilian Way's *main* road. You will post your men around that city, along that road in both directions and covering every possible round-about path. Should Odoacer try to communicate with Rome or Ravenna—to call for reinforcements or for any other purpose—his messengers from Verona must travel that Via Aemilia to get to either destination. I want any such messenger intercepted and his message brought to me by a fast-riding messenger of your own. Hábái ita swe."

A hundred Roman miles west of Concordia, our army came to Verona. A very old and a very sightly city, it had had the good fortune, before now, not to have been much mauled by war and warriors. Although Alaric the Visigoth had marched by here more than once, he had always been too much embattled in this vicinity to do any depredation of the city. And the later Huns of Attila, rampaging through Venetia, had stopped short of here. So, until our coming, Verona had not suffered a siege since the time of Constantine, nearly two centuries before. And now Verona was not very well prepared to withstand one.

True, the city was stoutly walled all about, and it was further protected by the Athesis River running swift and turbulent around two of its three sides, and in each of its high side walls there was only a single gate to afford entrance. However, past Roman emperors, out of affection and admiration for Verona's comeliness, had decided to make its outside as attractive as its inside. Whatever the city's gateways once had been like—probably forbidding portals flanked by massive towers and abutments—those emperors had replaced them with grandiose triumphal arches, much carved and ornamented. Although the arches were of stone, and sturdy enough, it is flatly impossible to hang and hinge and buttress a door of really impregnable solidity within a decorative monument. Fancy dress is flimsy armor.

All three gateways were vulnerable, but Theodoric ordered that we would besiege only the one in Verona's landward wall. Our onagri and ballistae were aimed at it and our archers commenced raining arrows on the defending troops ranged all along that wall's parapet. In the same way that Theodoric had left open an avenue of flight for the opponents who faced us at Andautonia, he left unassailed the other two of Verona's gates—which gave onto the two bridges spanning the Athesis—for Odoacer's men to escape through when inevitably they should realize that they were outfought. He dispatched only a few turmae of our cavalry to wait beside those bridges and harry the fugitives as they emerged and fled. Also, because Theodoric himself respected the venerable and handsome city, he commanded that our catapults hurl only unfired missiles—and only at the gate, not over the wall among the buildings—and that our archers shoot only unfired arrows.

Within two days, the pounding of the boulders flung by our siege splintered the gate's panels, and we brought up a heavy ram. Under a turtle cover of raised shields, our burliest men hefted and swung that ram until it butted through the remaining wood and iron—and our foremost ranks of spearmen and swordsmen were close behind. Odoacer and his General Tufa clearly had realized that the city's gates were inadequate barricades, and had done what little was possible to prepare against the certainty of their being breached. The defenders atop the wall had plentiful stores of arrows and spears and cobblestones, and they cast those down in such quantity and rapidity that the wall was almost obscured from our view, as by an endless hailstorm. The Roman soldiers also had many vats of melted pitch up there, and they lighted them, and poured down cascades of liquid fire. A man beneath had only to be touched by a single gobbet of that, and it would stick fast and go on burning him.

Scores of our troops advancing toward the broken gate did get pierced or struck or burned by those falling things—many got killed, many more were disabled. But any experienced warrior knows that such defensive weapons are really only weapons of desperate last resort, that far fewer attackers get repelled than succeed in getting past them. Thus it was that our men unhesitatingly swarmed in through the wall to meet the Romans' second line of defense, the spearmen and swordsmen solidly blocking the city street beyond.

With his fellow king Freidereikhs and several of his chief officers, Theodoric was still standing clear of the action, where he could best do the directing of it. I was there with them when one of our horsemen came galloping around the city wall from one of the other gates, to announce that both those farther gates had already been opened from within, disgorging a torrent of fleeing people.

"But no warriors," said the messenger. "Only the townsfolk. They are being let to run to safety."

Theodoric grunted and waved the man back to his station, then said to us, "It means that Odoacer intends to fight a holding action, street by street and house by house. That will cost both of us many dead and wounded. What an unkingly way of waging battle."

Ibba muttered, "Like a whore lying spraddled to be used, but scratching and biting at the same time."

"In wars past, Odoacer stood ever upright," said Herduic. "Age must have sapped the marrow from his bones."

"It surprises me," said Freidereikhs, "that his General Tufa would agree to fight so. He is, after all, a Rugian."

"Since the citizens are not being held hostage," said Pitzias, "why, we could simply station guard forces to block the gates, seal the Roman army inside Verona and go on our way, victorious without bloodshed. Eventually they would starve and rot in there."

Theodoric shook his head. "No good simply to bury Odoacer. I must make it plain to every Roman—and to Zeno—that I have utterly defeated him." Taking up shield and sword like any common foot soldier, he added, "So, comrades, if he and Tufa desire a battle fought inchmeal, let us oblige them."

And we did. Going in on foot, kings and officers and rankers alike, we fought with spears or contus lances as long as we had room to thrust—in Verona's many open squares and among the arcades of the city's immense amphitheater and up and down the seating tiers around its arena. Then we fought at closer quarters with swords—back and forth among the avenues and into ever narrower streets. And finally some of us were having to fight with our daggers, so cramped were the combats in alleys and in the atria of public buildings and even in the snug rooms of private houses. Odoacer's legionaries may have despised this hole-and-corner style of combat as much as we did, but they fought no less bravely or fiercely on that account. Had not our snake-blade steel been superior to that of the Roman gladius sword—keener to begin with, keeping its edge, less liable to bend or break—we invaders might not have prevailed at all. We did drive the enemy back and back, but as we cleared one street and one building after another, that place was left littered with as many of our fallen men as of theirs. In keeping with Theodoric's wishes, Verona was not dealt any structural damage, but it got sickeningly feculent with blood and the other fluids and substances that spill out of men in whom holes have been cut.

One thing I learned there in Verona. During the house-to-house fighting, I learned why every spiral staircase everywhere in the world has always been built the same way: so that it spirals upward to the right. It is done so that the central column of it will impede the right arm, the sword arm, of any intruder trying to fight his way up the stairs, while the defender, fighting from above, will have unconstricted space in which to swing his sword. That is how, in a house somewhere in the middle of the city, I got a sword cut on my left arm—not a totally incapacitating wound, but a gash that bled so profusely that I had to retire from the fray to be poulticed by a lekeis. I consoled myself that now I would be "balanced" with scars, one on

785

my left arm to match that on my right, incurred many years before, when Theodoric had treated me for snakebite.

I do not know how far into the city our men had made their way by the time the lekeis finished tending to me. I hurried back toward the clamor of battle, flexing my bandaged arm as I went, wondering if it could be trusted to hold a shield really firm again. I came to a small square in which many men were furiously engaged, hand to hand, while many others already lay still or writhing upon the pavement stones. Just as I prepared to plunge into the struggle, two other men entered the square from its far side, holding empty hands above their heads and shouting to be heard over the noise. The newcomer crying in the lighter voice was young Freidereikhs, the deeper-voiced a large man in Roman dress. Both of them were calling for "Truce! Indutiae! Gawaírthi!"

The Roman combatants, obeying the bigger man, lowered their weapons. So did our men, obeying Freidereikhs, and he then ordered several of them to run seeking Theodoric, and to fetch him hither. When the young king saw me approaching, he said cheerfully:

"Akh, Saio Thorn! You have been injured. Not badly, I hope. Allow me to introduce to you my Rugian cousin, the magister militum Tufa."

The general acknowledged me only with a grunt, so I did the same. While around us the city quieted, as word of the truce was spread, Freidereikhs pridefully told me how his "cousin" had sought him out to request a temporary halt in hostilities. Tufa wore the elegantly worked armor of his high rank, and he certainly filled it well. Though he was only about as old as Theodoric or myself, thirty-five or so, he wore a gingery beard more voluminous than any of our side's oldest officers boasted—and the wearing of a beard was in flagrant disregard or disdain of Roman army uniform regulations. Evidently disdain was the right word, because, when Theodoric joined us, Tufa sourly disavowed any further connection whatever with the entire Roman army.

"In the thick of battle, I espied the King of the Rugii," he said, nodding toward Freidereikhs, "and I begged of him a truce, so that I could seek audience with you, King Theodoric." Tufa had been speaking in Latin. Now, as if to emphasize the matter of kinship, he spoke in the Rugian dialect of the Old Language. "I come not to surrender—not *just* to surrender—but to take auths to you, and make your cause my own."

"Or, in less lofty words," Theodoric said drily, "to desert your high office and your own men."

"Any who are my own men will come with me. That will not be many more than my personal palace guard—Rugians like myself, who will be honored to serve under our King Freidereikhs. The rest of the army will remain loyal to Rome, little though they esteem Rome's King Odoacer."

"And why do you, magister militum of the Roman army, do this?"

"Vái! Look about you!" Tufa said disgustedly. "A battle in nooks and crannies! I am for Rome, ja, and I too would go on defending it, but is this any way to fight? This is Odoacer's doing, as was our ignominious retreat from the Sontius. You at least fight boldly, in the open, advancing. I say again, I am for Rome. That is why, since I expect that you will *manfully* defend it when you have it, I am with you."

"So much for your reasons. What of mine? Why should I accept your auths?"

"Because, first, I can reveal to you something of value. I can tell you that Odoacer has already eluded you, gone from here. When he let Verona's populace depart through the riverside gates, he went with them, unnoticed, just another old man. And now, this moment, while your warriors are embroiled in these streets, fighting only an expendable rear guard, the bulk of Odoacer's army is also streaming out through those gates."

Theodoric said, unruffled, "I have just been so advised by a messenger. You are telling me no news. And I deliberately left open those bolt-holes."

787

"Of course. But you would have wished them used only after you had inflicted a crushing, resounding, unequivocal defeat. And you will not have accomplished that. Odoacer is heartlessly abandoning all these dead and wounded, so his army can move at its best speed. He and it will join with another entire army not far from here. Verona was a trap set for you, Theodoric. What you declined to do to Odoacer, he intends to do to you. My orders were to keep you ensnarled in here while he returns with troops enough to *seal* you in, to finish you off at leisure."

My fellow marshal Soas and our General Herduic had now joined us— no doubt having come in some perplexity to ask Theodoric why the battle had so abruptly ceased—and they stood listening with interest.

"And now, Tufa?" Theodoric asked him, still coolly. "Now that you have divulged the plan, why should I not simply thank you with a sword thrust instead of a brotherly embrace?"

"My brotherly advice may be of use to you," Tufa went on. "I suggest that you need fight no longer for Verona. The city is yours, so bring no more of your men in here. Let those outside the walls remain there, where they are freely mobile. And I doubt that you will be as heartless as Odoacer. So, while you stay to tend your wounded and bury your dead, I suggest that you do not quarter your men within the city. Have them camp in the open roundabout. Odoacer's speculatores, seeing that, will report to him that you are *not* to be easily caged here. He will discard that plan and you will not be at hazard of his—"

"Enough!" Theodoric snapped. "My first consideration is not the avoiding of danger. It is putting the *enemy* into danger."

"Exactly so. And that is what I propose. Let me go and do that."

Theodoric snorted, "You?"

"I know where Odoacer is likeliest to go. I can catch him before—"

"Akh, Odoacer will not be hard to follow. My already pursuing cavalry are by now snapping and gnashing at his army's flanks. It can be traced by its trail of corpses."

"It will not move the slower for that. You have no hope of moving your entire army quickly enough to catch Odoacer before he does one of two things. He is racing for the river Addua, west of here, where that other army waits to be brought against you. However, when Odoacer realizes that his entrapment plan has gone awry, he may instead run south for Ravenna. And if he gets there, you probably never will get him out before Doomsday. That marshland city is impossible to surround, impervious to attack, unconquerable by siege. I say let me go this instant, Theodoric, and catch Odoacer before he can reach either of those destinations."

788

"You?" Theodoric said again. "You and your few palace guards?"

"And as many of your own men as you can entrust to me. Those that are already giving chase, and some more from here. I need a swift striking force—small enough to be fast and wieldy, but big enough to do damage when it engages. I would not hope to defeat that whole fleeing army, only to force it to halt and defend itself, thereby giving *your* army time to catch up to it. So, Theodoric, merely detach to me some of your cavalry. Or come along yourself, if you—"

"Ne, let *me!*" young Freidereikhs excitedly broke in. "Yonder outside the walls my Rugian horsemen are, like their horses, champing at the bit for action. Theodoric, let me and Tufa and *all* us Rugii together go after Odoacer."

When Theodoric did not immediately reply, but pondered the proposal, Herduic said helpfully, "If nothing else, that ought to dishearten Odoacer—the sight of his former commanding general and apparently the whole of the Rugian nation suddenly turned against him."

"He might totally despair," Freidereikhs added, with enthusiasm. "He might very well throw up his hands and surrender on the spot."

"I promise nothing like that," Tufa said. "But whatever happens, Theodoric, what have you to lose by sending us?"

"One thing is certain," rumbled solemn old Soas. "The longer we discuss the matter, the farther away Odoacer is getting."

"You are right," said Theodoric. "All of you are right. Go, then, Freidereikhs, and take ten turmae of your horsemen. Go with him and guide him, Tufa, but remember that you are only a probationary ally. On this foray, your Rugian king is your commander. Send messengers to keep me advised of what occurs—and where. Habái ita swe!"

Like Freidereikhs, Tufa responded with the Germanic salute, not the Roman, and both men went running for the gate by which we had entered the city.

I said to Theodoric, "Not long ago you were speculating on the chances of Tufa's defection. Why now were you seeming resistant to it?"

"I want more than his word that he *is* defecting. Let us see if he proves it with the deed he proposes. Even then, though—and Tufa must know it— a traitor never can be trusted, much less respected. Come now, my marshals, let us start restoring order to this city, so its inhabitants can return and restore life to it. Verona is too gracious a place to be left long in disarray."

✠   ✠   ✠

789

I have, in after years, heard many a traveler in Italia speak rapturously of the "rosy glow" of Verona, because so much of that city's architecture and statuary and ornamentation is made of warm red and pink and rust-colored stone and brick and tile. If Verona was so strikingly colorful during the time I fought there, I confess that I was too busy to be impressed by it. But I cannot help wondering if that much praised "rosy glow" might not be simply the lingering result of all the blood that stained Verona during our battle for it. The combat having been waged in so many separate corners and cubbies and coverts, the carnage was less immediately evident than it would have been in an open field. However, when we came to count and collect the fallen, we found that they amounted to more than four thousand lost from the Roman army, about the same number from ours. How woefully that may have weakened Odoacer's forces, we could not estimate. But, counting the other casualties we had suffered on the way hither, our army was only about two-thirds the size it had been when we marched out of Novae.

Well, this ruinous slaughter *had* won Verona for us. And we could congratulate ourselves that we had successfully forged our way deep into the Roman homeland, having now come a good third of the distance across the entire width of the Italian peninsula. Still, this battle—all of our fighting so far—had really been inconclusive, in that it had not yet overthrown Odoacer, or caused him to sue for peace, or won for us invaders the people's acceptance as their liberators. Taking Verona had not, apparently, made much difference to anybody at all.

Because of the suddenly called truce in the fighting, not all of the legionaries remaining in the city were dead or disabled. The survivors, some three thousand men, were taken prisoner. Though they were understandably resentful of Odoacer for his having left them to be only a suicidal rear guard—and perhaps were even more disgruntled that they had *not* died nobly in that task—none of them emulated Tufa in forswearing his Roman army auths and asking service with us. Theodoric naturally would not let them keep their arms or go free, even on condition of fides data. But he was of course mindful that these men, like all the legions of Rome, would presumably someday be his, so he ordered them treated with respect and courtesy and liberal rations while they were our captives. This put an extra onus on our depleted forces, who were already occupied with the multifarious chores involved in making camp, ministering to the wounded, burying the dead and evacuating the city so it could resume its normal life. With so much to be done, it is perhaps unsurprising that none of our generals made worried comment because the departed Freidereikhs and Tufa sent no immediate word back of where they had gone and what they were doing.

790

Theodoric did take note of that, though, and grumbled to me, "Four days without report. Is it possible that that young peacock plans to keep me stalled here in ignorance just so he can strut without the supervision of his elders?"

I said, "I do not believe the lad is capable of insubordination. But it might be that he hopes to present you with an already accomplished feat of some ostentatious sort."

"I prefer not to wait upon his whim," growled Theodoric. "Bid messengers ride west and south to seek and find him and report back here."

Before I could get them away, however, a messenger did come riding into camp from the south. He came on a lathered horse, riding hard, skidding to a halt at the tent bearing Theodoric's standard, nearly falling from fatigue when he dismounted. But he had not come from any of the ten turmae under Freidereikhs's command. This messenger came from the century that Theodoric had sent from Concordia to keep watch along the Via Aemilia.

"Centurio Brunjo's compliments, King Theodoric," he gasped. "You asked for word of any messenger dispatched by Odoacer toward Ravenna or Rome. I come to tell you he sent no messenger. Rather, he himself rides toward Ravenna—at the quick march—he and his General Tufa, at the head of what seems to be a full-sized army, and with our captive shackled men being dragged along behind the Romans' horses."

"Odoacer *and* Tufa?" Theodoric said, through clenched teeth. "And *what* men of ours?"

"Why, King Freidereikhs and two or three hundred of his Rugii, all much bloodied. The centurio assumed you must have suffered a significant defeat here, to have lost so many—"

"Hold!" snarled Theodoric, white with anger. "I have suffered a stinging slap in the face! But never mind the assumptions. Report what was seen and what was done about it."

"Ja waíla!" The messenger stood extremely erect and said smartly, "Odoacer's columns came from the west of Bononia and pelted straight on through that city, going southeastward. You had given no orders covering such a contingency, but Centurio Brunjo intended to attack with what men he had, and hoped to inflict some damage, though knowing the assault would mean death or capture. Only because he *commanded* it did I turn and run to bring the word. I would rather have stayed and—"

"Of course, of course. Anything else?"

"Since Odoacer is moving at quick-march pace, and did not turn south at Bononia along the shortest road to Rome, he is apparently not making for there. Our lookouts had earlier determined that the Via Aemilia can take one either to Ravenna or to Ariminum, but Centurio Brunjo conjectured that the former is the more probable destination. That is all I can tell you, King Theodoric, except that my centurio and all my comrades are most certainly—"

791

"Ja, ja. And you wish you were, too. What is your name, young man?"

"Witigis, optio of the second turma, Brunjo's century of cavalry, at your service, King Theod—"

"Well, Optio Witigis, go and tell General Ibba to prepare his entire cavalry force for immediate departure and an early combat. Tell him also to assign you to one of his vanguard turmae, where you may have your wish soon granted."

The young man saluted and strode away, and Theodoric muttered glumly, "It may soon be granted for all of us, nolens volens, with a fool like me conducting this campaign. How could I have been so easily duped by that perfidious Tufa?"

I said, "He spoke with seeming sincerity."

"Vái! So did Herduic, when he called Odoacer a boneless old man. What, then, should I be called? I must be getting as jelly-boned as a Gades dancing girl, to have let myself be thus deluded."

"Come now," I said. "I am seeing a Theodoric unfamiliar to me. Most other times, when I have known you to be wrathful, you seemed more dare-the-devil than desolated."

"I am less wrathful at Tufa than at myself. He told the truth about one thing, at least—about there being a trap set. Only it was not here in the city, it was waiting down the road." He barked a humorless laugh. "And the villain even had the brazen audacity to invite *me* to ride into it. What Odoacer wanted was to thumb his teeth at me *and* to assure his getting safely wherever he decided to go, by ambushing a sufficiency of hostages to be his traveling turtle armor. And what did I so obligingly send him? Not only ten turmae of my trusting allies but their crowned king besides!"

I reminded him, "You hold ten times that many of Odoacer's legionaries. The Roman army has always scrupulously observed the rules of civilized warfare, one of which allows for the ransom or exchange of prisoners. And the messenger reported Freidereikhs still alive."

"I hope he stays so. Odoacer was not too lovingly concerned for the lives of his own men here. He may be King of Rome, but neither he nor Tufa is Roman by birth, not necessarily respectful of Roman ideas of honor and civility and humanity. As soon as they know they have safely outpaced pursuit and interception, their hostages will only be burdensome to them."

"True," I said uneasily. "And we can hardly expect any more messengers reporting from there. Theodoric, I ask your leave to go myself and learn the fate of those captives."

"Can you ride, Thorn? You are wounded."

"A trifle. Already healing. And it does not hamper my using reins or sword."

"Go then. You may take along another ten turmae, if you like. The rest of the young king's Rugii will be ravening to retaliate."

"Not just yet. I will fare better alone. And so I will know where to find you again, may I ask what you plan to do next?"

"Ja," he said grimly. "I plan to enliven my spirits by doing some killing." He added, with a self-mocking smile, "I also plan to go on trusting the tales of Tufa."

"Eh?"

"He spoke of another Roman force camped on the river Addua, and that sounds like the truth. I believe Odoacer will expect me to come racing after him, addled by anger, blindly pounding south toward Ravenna. In which case, he would summon that Addua army—perhaps with his system of Polybian signals—to close in on me from behind."

I nodded. "Catching you in a pincers."

"Instead, the moment Ibba's cavalry is ready to ride, I will make a swift lunge westward at that Addua army. Catch it unawares, I devoutly hope, so I can *pulverize* it. I will leave Pitzias and Herduic and our infantry here to hold Verona, just in case there are other Roman armies somewhere about."

To cheer him, I grinned and said, "I had best be on my way, then, or you will have won the whole war before I get back."

When I saluted and took my leave, Theodoric was girding on his battle armor, but I left mine there in camp, and my snake-blade sword and belt knife, and everything else that would too readily identify me as an Ostrogoth and a warrior. I wore on my back and carried in my saddlebags only indifferent traveling garb, and slung on my pommel a captured, battered Roman short-sword. I let Velox walk gently across the Athesis River bridge, the stones being hard to his hoofs. On the other side, I put him on the turfed margin of the Via Postumia and gave him my heels, and we galloped southward.

✠   ✠   ✠

793

If you think about it, the human form is composed almost entirely of convex shapes. On the normal, typical, full-grown human body there are very few concave places. The palm of the hand, the arch under the foot, the chelidon, the axilla; are there any others? So it is repellent, even nauseating—simply because it is unusual, unexpected, unnatural—to view a human figure that *does* have spoon-concave dips and hollows defacing what should be the smooth roundness of its torso and limbs.

On a bright blue October day, some miles east of Bononia, in the stubble of a recently harvested grainfield beside the Via Aemilia, I stood looking at that ground's new sowing—a litter of more than two hundred corpses. Most of the men had been efficiently dispatched with one stab or a slash wound apiece; only a single well-placed hole is really necessary for letting out a man's lifeblood and spirit. But Odoacer's columns had been moving at the quick march; they could brook little delay; their slaughter of their prisoners had had to be done in a hurry. So a number of the victims, Centurio Brunjo and the young King Freidereikhs among them, had been so carelessly hacked to death—the skin and meat clumsily scalloped away in gobbets—that their corpses were gouged and pitted and cratered with concavities, rather like the ugly terrain of those karst lands across which they and I had once ridden together.

6

Perhaps it is unbecoming in a warrior writing of war, but I must belatedly confess that, on every battlefield after a battle, my feminine emotions always came unsoldierly to the fore: a deep pity and an unfeigned grief for *all* the fallen.

This day, though, in this grainfield, I felt a welter of other emotions as well. One of them was a sorrow that I can only describe as tenderly maternal. While I never have experienced maternity, I truly could shed motherly tears for Freidereikhs, if only because I knew that his real mother was unlikely ever to do anything of the sort. As I gazed on his poor desecrated corpse, I seemed to hear the words that once had been said to a genuinely loving mother: "Behold, this child is set for the fall . . . and your own soul a sword shall pierce." My soul, being the kind of soul it was, had at the same time to suffer the pangs of a *masculine* sadness, because I also mourned the loss of Freidereikhs as would a bereaved older brother. It was with the boy Frido that I had traveled in the lands and the lights of the "merry dancers." It was to the eager lad Frido that I had taught some lore of woodcraft. It was to the growing-up Frido that I had introduced his first-ever woman. And now, to my shame, as I remembered that occasion, I recognized in me another feminine emotion, and a base one. I felt a selfish, sulky regret that I had not *been* that first woman of his, or any of the later females who had given joy to the comely young king, and taken joy from him, because now there could never be another opportunity . . .

Still, for all my mixed and not entirely lofty emotions, my overriding feeling—I hope to my credit as man and woman both—was a cold, raptorial determination to redress the atrocity committed here.

Meanwhile, I was gradually becoming aware that there were live people in the grainfield too. The assembled local farm and village folk were lethargically digging large holes for mass graves, and they were growling, cursing and muttering about this offal that had been left for them to clean up. Not far beyond Freidereikhs's body, four old peasant men were digging in a group. The nearest of them, noticing my regard, shouldered his mattock, came over to me and said conversationally:

"You may wonder, friend, why we are all grumbling when we ought to be grateful. Except for the numerous bastards that our noble lord has fathered on our daughters, this generous gift of ground-enriching dung is the only gift he ever *has* given us."

"What lord?" I asked. "King Odoacer?"

He shook his head. "The clarissimus Tufa. Magister militum of Odoacer's armies. Also dux of this province of Flaminia and legatus of the city of Bononia."

I motioned at the field. "A Roman dux did such butchery?"

"A Roman? Nullo modo. No Roman he, but a sus barbaricus. And a barbarian swine in a tinted toga is still a barbarian swine. You are a stranger, then. I hope you are not traveling with wife or daughter. Second only to his fits of fury, Dux Tufa's *other* chief pleasure is the deflowering of maidens and dishonoring of matrons."

I indicated the field again. "Why did it pleasure Tufa to have this fit of fury?"

The old man shrugged and repeated, "Sus barbaricus." Then, to explain, he began pointing here and there. "Odoacer and Tufa came leading their columns at a trot along this road, and we local folk gathered to cheer—'Io triumphe!'—as we are bidden to do always on such occasions. It appeared that Odoacer had somewhere won a victory indeed, for there were countless prisoners being hauled along at the horses' heels. Then, suddenly, from yonder, came charging other riders, shouting some barbaric cry, and there was a brief affray. But the attackers were only few in comparison, and quickly laid low. There lies one of them." He pointed at the dead Centurio Brunjo. "When the flurry subsided and those were dead, Tufa gave orders to his men, and all the captives were slain as well. Then he gave orders to us bystanders—'dispose of this lot before they begin to stink!'—and he and the whole army rode on. We have been at this drudgery now for three days, and weary we are. Fortunately the weather has held cool and dry."

The old man waited for me to make some comment, but I was reflecting. Brunjo's brave and self-sacrificing but ineffectual attack would have told Tufa what he wanted to know: that his army had no weightier assault to fear before it reached its haven in Ravenna. He would then have had no further need of the hostages for protection. I heaved a despondent sigh.

795

But for the centurio's foolhardy interference, Freidereikhs and his Rugii would likely have been taken all the way to Ravenna too. They would have been imprisoned, humiliated, possibly ill-treated, but they would still be alive. Akh, well, perhaps not. Tufa might have slain them at the city gates. So I would not lay blame or cast aspersion. If Brunjo had made a lamentable mistake, he had paid for it.

"As you see," the gravedigger resumed, "we are getting little for our labors except the dung to plant under our crops. These prisoners, whoever they are—or were—had already been plundered by the legionaries. Their weapons, armor, everything else of value is gone. Only the blowflies here have a bounty to rejoice about."

It was evident—from the old man's saying, of the prisoners, "whoever they are"—that he did not know that his land of Italia had been invaded by us Ostrogoths and our allies. Probably, considering how many wars this piece of the earth had endured throughout history, the peasant was quite inured to such convulsions and did not much *care* who was fighting whom. At any rate, possibly because I had addressed him in Latin, he had not instinctively taken me, a stranger, to be his enemy. Nor did I consider him to be mine, since it was also evident that he was no ardent admirer of his Dux Tufa.

(I *was* a little surprised to find a simple countryman so well spoken, but I reminded myself that I was now in the Roman heartland; even the rustics here ought rightly to be more articulate than those in outer regions of the empire. Also, I was later to learn that the people hereabout were of Celtic descent. They were paler-skinned and bigger in stature than their Celtic-cousin Veneti we had encountered in Venetia, and, no doubt because these lived closer to Rome, they spoke Latin much more correctly.)

Since the old man was capable of talking, and seemed willing to do so without inhibition, I decided to get from him as much information as I could. I said, "I assume your sus barbaricus Tufa took his army on to Ravenna. Will this road take me there too?"

He cocked his head and asked sardonically, "Are you wanting to take a look at the beast?"

"Perhaps I just wish to thank him, on behalf of the blowflies, for the bounty of their gift."

He chuckled and said, "This Via Aemilia's terminus is the Hadriatic seaport of Ariminum. However"—he waved eastward—"a few miles from here, a very wretched little road forks off to the left and winds its way across the marshes to Ravenna. You would think, in all the years since that city became the capital of the empire, some ruler would have laid a decent Roman road. But none has wanted to make his sanctum easy of access."

"There is no other way in?"

"Yes. Trade your handsome horse for a boat and you can approach Ravenna from the Hadriatic. The only other *road* is the Via Popilia that goes north and south along the coast, but it is no grand highway, either. It is used mostly by mule trains bringing salt from the Alpes to be shipped abroad."

"Very well," I said. "I shall try the marsh road."

"Be warned, though. When Odoacer is in residence, Ravenna is heavily ringed about with guards and sentries. You will at least be challenged. More often, uninvited visitors are shot on sight."

"On behalf of the blowflies," I said lightly, "I must take the risk."

"You need not, if all you wish is to present the flies' compliments to their benefactor. Odoacer often closets himself in Ravenna for months at a time, but Tufa's military duties require him to travel. Also, as I said, he is the legatus of Bononia. You have only to wait at his palace there, and soon or later he will be in residence. Of course, you will not easily get in to see him—not without being rudely interrogated and stripped and searched. Others before you have tried to present certain compliments to the clarissimus Tufa."

Our colloquy was interrupted by rude shouts from the old man's fellow diggers—demanding that he stop shirking and get back to work. He grunted a curse, saluted me with his mattock and said jovially:

"Anyway, stranger, do us a favor and take some of the blowflies with you as you go. Vale, viator."

Then he went to help the others, who were toppling the remains of Freidereikhs and six or seven of his Rugian warriors into a common grave.

✠　✠　✠

Ill paved and rutted and pitted though the marsh road was, I was glad to have it under me. I was advancing along it in the darkness of deep night, and its windings this way and that gave evidence that it was keeping me and Velox safely clear of quaking-sands and other such treacherous spots in the surrounding bogland. I had come about twelve miles since turning off the Aemilian Way, and I knew not how far ahead Ravenna might lie, but I could see no lights of it, and there were no clouds above to show any reflected glow. I was afoot and leading Velox, to move as quietly as possible and, because of the cloudless sky, to make our profile against the stars as inconspicuously low as possible.

I was getting a good appreciation of the stronghold aspects of Ravenna. An army approaching the city by this single twisty road would be slowed to a walk, and the army's striking front could be only four or five horsemen in breadth, meaning no effective front at all. On the road or off it, neither an army nor a lone spying speculator could get close to the city unobserved, day or night, except by creeping on hands and knees. The land was as flat as the road, with no concealing cover higher than swamp grass, reeds and some weedy shrubs. And of course, all that terrain being mud and mire and muck and slime, if an army did attempt to flounder across it, every last man would be as easy a target as a water rat trying the same. I had not yet seen Ravenna from its seaward side, but I was coming to the conclusion that an assailant from the landward had no hope at all, unless he either laid vast fields of pontoons, enough for his whole army to cross at once, or trained the local marsh birds to attack in his stead—the latter option being no more ludicrously impossible than the former.

I knew I could not go much farther this night, as I was going, without soon alerting some sentry. I paused while I considered whether it would be better to tether Velox to a tussock and steal on by myself, or just to stop both of us where we were and wait for dawn to give me a clearer view of our situation. While I was weighing the matter, it was decided for me. At some distance to my front—I could not judge how far—a light was kindled, and so suddenly that at first I took it to be the spectral draco volens common in miasmic swamps like this one. But then the light divided into nine distinct points, and those moved apart into two groups—five on the left, four on the right—and I recognized them as the torches of the Polybian signal system.

To my puzzlement, they did not immediately start a message, but only jiggled up and down. After a moment of perplexity, I somehow thought to turn and look behind me. There, another incalculable distance away, came into existence an identical line of nine lights. I realized that, far to the northwest of these marshlands, some Roman legionaries or speculatores—or, for all I knew, just plain Roman citizens—were preparing to communicate with the troops inside Ravenna. That western line of torches *did* commence a message, and I marveled to think that this news might have come from anywhere in the outside world, passed along by relays of such lights, shortly to be read by Odoacer and Tufa within their sanctum. And by me out here.

But then something happened that did more than puzzle me; it quite dumbfounded me. When the "outside" lights moved—the first torch raised on the left, the third on the right—what was being communicated, unless

Odoacer had recently altered his system, was the third letter of the old-time runic alphabet. And the lights continued to signal the same letter over and over, as if for insistent emphasis, and that third letter of the futhark is the rune called thorn. I was amazed and more than a little dismayed. How could this have happened? Not only had my stealthy progress along the marsh road been noticed; Ravenna was being urgently warned of *who* was approaching.

In another moment, though, I laughed ironically at myself. I had been overpresumptuous of my own importance. The lights stopped repeating the thorn, rested briefly, then signaled the ansus, the dags, the úrus and the ansus again—A, D, U, A—and I comprehended. Such a slow-spelling system must confine itself to the absolute minimum of words, and even must condense those where possible. From this word ADUA an unneeded D had been subtracted. The thorn that I had mistaken for my name signaled only TH, the sound that rune represents, here being used as short-sign for the word "Theodoric." I could gather that the message was telling something about Theodoric and the river Addua. However, the communication consisted of just one more word, or part of one—the runic letters winja, eis, nauths and kaun: V, I, N and C. Then both of the lines of torches did that up-and-down jiggling and abruptly were snuffed out.

I stood in the darkness, which now seemed blacker than before, and pondered. The message sent and received—TH ADUA VINC—was admirably concise and no doubt fully informative to its receivers, but it left me only partly informed. Theodoric had recently been or was right now at the Addua River where Odoacer's other Roman force was stationed; that much was clear enough. And the VINC, in the context, had to stand for "vincere," to conquer. The signalers would know, by prearrangement, the verb's intended voice and mood and tense. But to the uninitiated, meaning me, the truncated VINC could signify that Theodoric was being victorious, or that he was being defeated, or that he was *about* to be one or the other, or that he already *had* been.

Well, I thought, whichever of those eventualities was being reported, the message ought to fetch Tufa out of Ravenna again in rather a hurry. Odoacer might hide there while the rest of his country was or was not being purged of its invaders, but his chief military commander could hardly do that for long. So, I decided, I would be waiting for Tufa when he emerged. And, as the old gravedigger had suggested, Bononia seemed the best place for me to lurk in wait. I turned and began leading Velox back toward the Via Aemilia, frankly relieved that I had *not* had to try some means of sneaking all the way into Ravenna.

As I trudged through the night, still moving cautiously, I had to admit to myself that, in plotting to waylay Tufa, I was actually disobeying orders and exceeding my office. Theodoric had bidden me only to investigate and report on matters here—not to be again his "Parmenio behind enemy lines"—so I ought rightly to be galloping north to find and join him. I could be at the Addua in just two days or so of hard riding, and a marshal's place in battle was at his king's side. I also had to bear in mind that, on another occasion when I sought to bring retribution to a sus barbaricus—the one named Strabo—I had left the job unfinished. Even if I were now to be fully successful in giving Tufa the requital he deserved, Theodoric might not thank me for it. Tufa was guilty of an offense even more heinous than the slaughter of defenseless prisoners. Tufa was a regicide. Custom and tradition would dictate that the slaying of a king be punished by no man of lower rank than a king. Furthermore, Tufa's violation of his given word had been a flagrant insult to Theodoric personally. From any point of view, vengeance properly belonged to Theodoric.

Nevertheless, I would chance my sovereign's displeasure. Freidereikhs had been my friend, my ward, my younger brother. And though Theodoric perhaps was not aware of it, his own princess-daughter had hoped to make Freidereikhs one day her royal husband. So I would not stay my hand. I would avenge the young king and his warriors, needlessly dead. And in the name of all of us who had been bereaved—myself, Theodoric, Thiudagotha, the Rugian nation, the—

My musings were cut short, almost literally, when I walked up against a sharp point and it painfully pricked my belly. Deep in cogitation, I had ignored Velox's whuffle of warning, and then had failed to discern the dark figure crouched against the darkness, until I strode right into the spear leveled at my beltline, and heard a hoarse voice say menacingly:

"I know you, Saio Thorn."

Iésus, I thought, I was right all along: the Romans *have* had me marked from my first arrival in these parts. But no—this man had spoken in the Old Language. I must be again mistaken. And then, to my further confoundment, he demanded:

"Speak the truth, Marshal, or I spill your guts on this spot. Are you Odoacer's man, *niu*?"

"Ne," I said, speaking the truth, whatever the cost. "I am here to *kill* one of Odoacer's men."

The blade did not plunge into my bowels, but neither did it waver. I added, "I am Theodoric's man, and I am here at his behest." After another

800

tense moment of silence, I said also, "Spearman, you know me in the dark. Would I know you in the light?"

He finally moved the spearpoint aside and stood erect, but still he was only a darkness in the dark. He sighed and said, "My name is Tulum. You would not have had reason ever to take note of me. I am a signifer of what was the third turma of what was Brunjo's century of cavalry. It was our century that Theodoric detached at Concordia and sent south on patrol. When we came to Bononia, I was one of the men whom Brunjo posted as lookouts at varying distances outside the city."

"Akh!" I said, enlightened. "So you escaped the shambles."

He sighed again, as if he regretted that, and said, "After some while at my post, during which nothing of interest occurred, I rode into the city to make routine report to my centurio. He was not there, and the townsfolk were talking of the Romans' having scurried through, herding a mass of captive outlanders. When I learned which way Brunjo had gone, and at last caught up to him, at that grainfield east of the city . . . well, you know what I found."

"And there you espied me, too."

"Ja. Of all the outlanders, the only one still alive. Watching the burial and conversing, apparently calmly, with one of the Roman buriers. I will not apologize, Saio Thorn, for my having been provoked to dark suspicions."

"You need not apologize, Signifer Tulum. There have indeed been betrayals aplenty."

"When you went on toward Ravenna, as the Roman columns have done, I thought my suspicions confirmed—that you had long and secretly been in league with the enemy. I followed at a very discreet distance. I was behind you all this night, and moving ever closer, until we had gone so far across the marsh that I expected the city's guards to be surrounding us at any moment. They would welcome you, I supposed, but not me, and I did not wish to be cheated of killing a traitor." He uttered a sort of embarrassed half-laugh. "I can tell you now. When you stopped back there—while those torches briefly burned—had you resumed your course, just one more step toward Ravenna, at that instant I was going to skewer you. But then you turned and came back this way. That made me uncertain. I decided to give you one chance to speak. I am glad now that I did."

"So am I, and right heartily. Thags izvis, Tulum. Come, the dawn will break soon. Let us hasten back to the main road. There is much to relate of the events that have happened since you came south. For one thing, you

801

may be relieved to know that at least one other warrior of your century did not die here. Brunjo sent an optio named Witigis to make report to Theodoric, which is why I am here. I might remark that Witigis was not much pleased to have been spared."

"I can believe that. I know Witigis."

"Now tell me. How many others besides yourself were posted at a distance from Bononia? How many might Brunjo not have had time to collect before he charged the Roman columns?"

"I cannot be sure. I know where three others were stationed before I was assigned my place."

"I hope they are still at their posts, or somewhere to be found. I shall have work for them to do."

We came to where Tulum had left his horse tethered to a loose paving-stone of the road. The night had lightened enough for me to see that the signifer was a man younger than myself, tall and strongly built, wearing cavalry leather armor. What had made him so nearly invisible was that he had obscured his pale Ostrogoth complexion and beard with a smearing of marsh mud. As we proceeded, leading our horses, I recounted to him everything that had happened since Concordia. I concluded by repeating what I had read of the torches' message.

"Everything else, Tulum, you know, except for what I have sworn to myself—here, this very night—that I will make Tufa pay for his treachery and savagery."

"Good. How can I help?"

"I am going into Bononia, and there I shall disappear. You will circle wide around the city. Find as many of those surviving lookouts as you can, and tell them to report to me. Then you go on northward at a good gallop. To Herduic at Verona—or to whichever of our officers you may encounter before—tell everything that has occurred and is occurring here. Be sure the word gets to Theodoric, so that he knows why I have not returned. It may take much time for me to get close enough to Tufa to strike at him. Once you have delivered the news, well . . . you have missed much of our war, Tulum. Go and join the fighting at the Addua or wherever it is now being waged."

"Gladly, Saio Thorn. But how, if you are disappearing inside Bononia, are the men here to report to you?"

"To a surrogate of Saio Thorn, I should have said. I remember seeing a fountain in the central market square. The market is a crowded place, of course, so strangers will be inconspicuous. Have the men doff and hide their armor and weapons. Wearing only street dress, they are to loiter about the fountain—day after day, if necessary—until they are addressed by a certain woman."

"A woman?"

"They are to respect and obey her as if she were wearing my own insignia of marshalcy. Make sure they remember her name. She will introduce herself as Veleda."

✠　　✠　　✠

On arriving in Bononia again, I hired a stall at a stable and left Velox there, along with most of what belongings I had brought from Verona, including even my borrowed sword. I took away with me only a few necessities, among them the two articles of my Veleda attire that I had packed just in case I should find use for them. One was the beaded hipband undergarment that, as Veleda, I always wore to conceal my virile organ and to affect Roman-womanish modesty. The other was the coiled bronze Haustaths breast guard that, as Veleda, I sometimes wore to make my bosom more prominent and pretty.

In shops around the market square I bought—"for my wife"—only rudimentary feminine raiment: gown, kerchief and sandals. Then I slipped into a secluded and unfrequented alley and quickly changed. My masculine clothes and boots I simply left there, for any beggar who might want them. Next I sought out a cheap taberna for visiting traders and rented a room— "while I wait for my husband to arrive and join me," I told the caupo, lest he be reluctant to admit a woman traveling alone. Over the next three or four days, I purchased more apparel, all of the best quality, and some costly cosmetics and a few really good ornaments of Corinthian aes. Then, finely dressed and adorned, I left the lowly taberna and presented myself at Bononia's most elegant hospitium. As I expected, I found the hospes there not at all chary of renting very expensive chambers to such a beautiful and well-spoken and obviously well-to-do lady traveler as myself.

803

I had made Thorn "disappear." It would be up to Veleda to stalk the prey. I had decided on that because I remembered the warning of the old gravedigger. According to him, others before me had made attempts on the person or the life of Bononia's legatus, so now no one was allowed into the man's presence without being scrutinized and searched and avouched in-capable of doing harm to him. It meant that I had to devise a killing weapon that was invisible and undetectable. I already had one in mind, but it was a weapon that could be employed only by a woman, and only at a certain moment—the moment that I well knew from my own experience both as man and woman—the one moment of all moments when *any* man is most vulnerable and helpless. To bring Tufa to that moment, though, I had first to scrape acquaintance with him, and do it in such a way that seemed not at all of my own doing.

So I went again to the market square. At the shop stall of a tool vendor, while I examined various whetstones and finally purchased one of them — "for filing my nails," I explained to the admiring but bemused merchant — I scanned the crowds moving about. In a thriving Roman city like Bononia, there are people of all the world's nationalities to be seen, and of course I did not know the face of every man among Theodoric's thousands of warriors. But almost everybody in the marketplace was busy on some business. I had no trouble in identifying the one man who was unbusily idling about the central fountain and looking very bored. I waited until I could be sure that I was the only person keeping an eye on him. Then I sauntered over and said in an undertone:

"Did the signifer Tulum post you here?"

Instantly he snapped to the military posture of rigid attention and barked, "Ja, Lady Veleda!" Several strollers turned to stare.

I stifled a smile and muttered, "Easy. Be easy. Let us seem old friends casually met. Sit with me here on the fountain curbing." He did so, but still stiffly. I asked, "How many of you did Tulum find?"

"Three, my lady. The signifer has now ridden on northward. We three have waited here for you, as instructed, taking turns at loitering close by this fountain."

"Beckon the others to join us."

The three cavalrymen were named Ewig, Kniva and Hruth. If they found it queer to be submitting themselves to the orders of a woman, they refrained from showing it. In fact, they maintained such martial demeanor and bearing that I had repeatedly to whisper for them to unbend.

"As well as we have been able to ascertain," said Ewig, "we and Tulum are the only survivors of Brunjo's century. Tulum told us that you and the Saio Thorn are here to avenge our fallen fellows by slaying the bestial General Tufa, and we are ready — ne, we are burning — to assist in whatever way you command."

"Let us walk while we talk," I said, because we were attracting notice. Various women passing by, even some ladies of quality, were casting envious glances at me, attended as I was by three such stalwarts.

"Our quarry, the despicable General Tufa," I said as I steered them in the direction of my hospitium, "is at present in Ravenna, some forty miles east. But he must eventually return to his legatus duties here, so it is here that I shall wait for him." They gave me sidelong looks, so I added, "I and our Saio Thorn, I should say. But Thorn must remain out of sight until the time comes to strike. That building yonder—take note of it—is the hospitium where I am quartered, and where you are to report to me. Now, there are various tongues spoken in this city, including our own, but of course Latin is the most common. Are any of you fluent in it?"

Kniva said he could fairly well understand and be understood in Latin. The other two said apologetically that they could not.

"Then, Kniva, you will be my helper here inside Bononia, and you, Hruth and Ewig, will be my speculatores outside. Ewig, I want you to take horse and hasten eastward along the Via Aemilia to where the Ravenna road branches off. Doing your best to be inconspicuous, you are to lurk in that vicinity and watch for Tufa's leaving Ravenna, and then come galloping headlong to tell me. I will hope to hear you report very soon that he is coming this way. But if he seems to be riding toward some other destination, I need to know that too. Go. Ride. Habái ita swe!"

Ewig started to snap his arm up in a salute, but I frowned, so he dropped it, mumbled, "At your command, my lady," and strode off.

I turned to Hruth. "I want you to ride there also and prowl that same area, but you are to watch mainly by night. Ravenna is kept informed of the progress of the war by torch signals. You will intercept those messages for me."

I was quite sure that a simple horse soldier could not read, write or even set down numbers, so I did not try to explain to Hruth the intricacies of the Polybian system. I simply told him how, every time he saw the lights, to make scratch marks on a leaf or a piece of bark to represent the lines of five and four torches, and additional marks to indicate in sequence those lights that got raised to communicate a letter.

"If you can do that," I said, "I can read the marks." Hruth regarded me with some awe, but swore he would most conscientiously comply. I went on, "I want every message recorded thus, and brought to me straightway. It may mean your having to ride back and forth almost every day, between there and here, after your having watched all night. But do it you must. Habái ita swe!"

"And my orders, my lady?" asked Kniva when Hruth had gone.

"I want you to get drunk and stay drunk."

Kniva blinked. "My lady?"

"I want you to go all about Bononia, drinking in every taberna and wineshop and gasts-razns—and buying drinks for the other guests. Here is a purse of silver so you can afford it. In both Latin and our Old Language, you are to proclaim that you are celebrating because you have recently enjoyed a nightlong revel of the most delicious and delirious sexual pleasure you have ever known."

Kniva looked stunned. *"My lady?"*

"You are to boast drunkenly and loudly, in both languages, that you spent that night with the most beautiful, most accomplished, most wanton whore you ever bedded. Say that she is newly arrived in Bononia, that she is hellishly expensive, and that she is fastidious about the partners she accepts, but that she is incomparable in the sexual arts, well worth the cost and the courting."

Kniva looked staggered. *"My lady?"*

"Ja, the lady Veleda, of course. And be sure to mention the hospitium where the lady Veleda is to be found."

Now Kniva looked as if he had been thunderstruck. *"My lady!* You will be besieged and solicited by every man in Bononia!"

"By one in particular, I trust. Look, Kniva." I pointed. "Yonder is the palace and praesidium of the legatus Tufa. See how it is ringed about with armed guards stationed almost shoulder to shoulder. I must somehow get inside there, so I can kill—I mean, so I can somehow admit our Saio Thorn to do the killing. The villain Tufa is notorious as a lecherous libertine. I want him to hear of my talents and prowess, so he will invite me in there."

"My lady!" Kniva protested in a strangled voice. "You would prostitute your body in this cause? You would actually—?"

"Merely spread the word that I do so, for a select few, for a substantial price. I assure you, Kniva, just as people are ever ready to believe the gossip that the most upstanding man has taken to drink, they will as readily believe that the most piously sedate woman has taken to promiscuity. It need only be told of her. Go, Kniva, and tell it everywhere."

806

7

hen I first installed myself in Tufa's city of Bononia, it seemed that I would not have long to lie in wait for him. Only days after I had sent Hruth and Ewig eastward, Hruth came galloping back, delivering to me at my hospitium a small sheaf of tablets of bark.

"Last night . . ." he gasped. "Torches signaled . . . from northwest . . ."

I immediately set to deciphering the message. It began with Hruth's having scratched these marks— | ||| —and I nodded with satisfaction, for that indicated "first torch on the left, third on the right," and *that* indicated "first alphabet group, third letter in the group," and *that* indicated the rune thorn. As I had observed before, the same rune was insistently repeated here: thorn, thorn, thorn, clearly meaning "Theodoric" again. Then came just nine more runes, no two alike, giving me MEDLANPOS. There were any number of ways I could have broken that apart into separate abbreviations of Latin words, hence any number of plausible meanings I might have conjectured. Frowning at what I had set down, I muttered at Hruth:

"This is all of it?"

"Ja, Lady Veleda."

"You are quite sure that you counted correctly?"

"I believe so, my lady. I did my best."

So I puzzled some more over the message and, applying what I knew of Theodoric's recent whereabouts, I perceived that the message should be broken thus: TH MEDLAN POS. "Medlan" does not *look* to be a Latin word, but I divined that it must be the torches' condensation of "Medi-olanum," for that is the name of the biggest city in the vicinity of the Addua River. The third word had to be one of the inflections of the verb "possidere." I grinned exultantly; this was good news. It meant that Theodoric had not been defeated or even stopped at the Addua. He and his army had forged on west of that river to "take possession" of Mediolanum. He already had done that, or was in the process of doing so, or at least was *about* to occupy the city that, after Rome, is the most populous in all Italia.

I said cheerfully, "You have done well, Hruth. I thank you and commend you." I rather surprised him, I think, by giving him a comradely, not very ladylike, clap on his shoulder. "If this news does not yank Tufa out of Ravenna, the man must be already dead. In any case, you hasten back to your watching-post. I trust you will be quick and efficient in bringing to me every further message."

Hruth could not have got far outside Bononia again before he would have passed his fellow trooper galloping in. It was only two hours or so later that Ewig's horse skidded to a halt in the courtyard of the hospitium. Lurching into my chambers, Ewig gasped, "Tufa ... this morning ... emerged from Ravenna ..."

"Good, good," I crooned. "I thought he would. How far behind you is he?"

Ewig shook his head, gulping for breath. "Came not ... this way ... Tufa went south ..."

Again being most unladylike, I snarled, "Skeit!"

When he had got his wind, Ewig told me, "Tufa never passed where I was stationed, my lady. Since I could watch only the marsh road, I have been inquiring of local folk, with gestures and dumb show. They seem not at all reluctant to tell me, as best they can, what they know of Tufa's doings."

"I too have noticed," I murmured, "that his subjects are not overly protective of him."

"If their reports are to be believed, Tufa left Ravenna with only a single turma of horsemen—his own personal palace guard, I gather. He and they rode swiftly south to Ariminum, there to take the Via Flaminia, still going southward."

"The main road to Rome," I said. It was disappointing but understandable. With the second-greatest city of the peninsula in Theodoric's grasp, it made sense for Tufa to hurry to the first-greatest, and see to its defenses. Half to myself, I went on:

"Well, it would be foolish for me to try chasing after him all over the countryside. And his own Bononia is no inconsiderable city. He will hardly abandon it to the enemy. He *must* return here sometime." To Ewig I said:

"If you can catch up to Tufa's company and follow it without being discovered by its outriders, do so. And since you are so clever at enlisting the aid of the Italian peasantry, go on doing that too. Send one of them to let me know when Tufa gets to Rome. You stay on watch there, so you can advise me when he leaves there and where next he is bound."

✠   ✠   ✠

If there is one thing absolutely essential to any murder plot, it is that the murderer be able to get at his victim. And that was *all* I required, because the rest of my plan for killing Tufa was simple in the extreme. But the victim, although he could have had no hint of my presence or intentions, continued to balk me by staying out of my reach. To compress into a few short words what was a frustrating and exasperating time: I was immured in Bononia all winter long.

Now and again, from one of Ewig's conscripted messengers or from some local source, I would hear that Tufa was on the move, but none of his moves during those months brought him to Bononia. After a while in Rome, he reportedly went to the bronze-working town of Capua, then to the iron-working town of Sulmo, from which I deduced that he was urging his Roman weapons-makers to greater effort. I was informed that he was marshaling the various scattered components of southern Roman forces into a cohesive whole. Again I would hear that he was visiting one of the seaports on the western side of the peninsula—Genua or Nicaea—which seemed to indicate that he might be trying to bring into Italia fresh Roman troops from legions stationed in lands abroad.

809

I might have got weary of my wait, and gone north to rejoin Theodoric, where I could have been of some military use. But, early in November, Hruth brought to my hospitium another intercepted torch message, and this one I read as TH MEDLAN HIBERN—Theodoric was settling his army for the winter in his captured city of Mediolanum.

It might be supposed that a Mediterranean land like Italia would not have winters so rigorous as to impede an army's movements and fighting efficiency. However, in Italia's northern provinces, during the months from November to April, the Apenninus mountain range blocks off most of the balmy Mediterranean airs, so that the chill winds coming down from the Alpes are not much mitigated. While it is true that a winter in Mediolanum is mild compared to that in, say, Novae on the Danuvius, still a prudent commander would prefer to keep his army in garrison quarters rather than active in the field. So, since there would be no more warfare waged until spring, I decided to stay where I was.

I must confess that, although I often chafed at my indolence while I resided in Bononia, I was by no means bored. Thanks to the arrangements I had made, I never got bored. I had diversions aplenty.

During my early days here, and for some while afterward, my man Kniva most assiduously followed the instructions I had given him. He went from one drinking place to another, and in every one loudly commended the virtues (if "virtues" is the right word) of the lady Veleda, newly come to the city. In short order, my hospitium was beset by men seeking a taste of those virtues. Of course, in the beginning, most of the men were the roughs and louts that most commonly frequent the wineshops, and those I disdainfully turned away.

Then, as Kniva continued to proclaim my beauty and my accomplishments—and as the rejected early suitors spread the word of my beauty *and* my haughty fastidiousness—I began to be approached by petitioners of better quality. But those too I refused, until eventually I was being visited by the *servants* of men of high rank, sent to solicit my favors on their masters' behalf. When I dismissed those emissaries, I did it not too rudely. I merely told them that I must see and appraise and approve each supplicant in person, whatever his title or entitlements. The servants went away wringing their hands, sure to get a beating when they returned such a supercilious reply to their masters.

It was some while before those notables deigned to come calling, such men being accustomed to summoning such females as myself with no more than a snap of the fingers or a jingle of coins. Then, when they did come to me, they usually came under cover of darkness. But they did come. Before the winter's first snowfall, I was picking and choosing from among the most eminent clarissimi and lustrissimi of Bononia. And my being by now far-famed for my unapproachability made me so irresistibly alluring that, from those I chose, I demanded—and got—a quite incredible remuneration for each smallest favor I dispensed.

What I wanted was to achieve a notoriety that would reach the ears of Tufa and make him, when he did return to his city, urgently desirous of seeing for himself the woman of such resounding acclaim. Therefore, in choosing from the droves of candidates who sought my favors, I maintained strict standards. For example, some of those who called on me, bearing heavy purses generously opened wide, were men young and handsome enough to have been desirable even in pauper rags, but I turned them away. Of the many wealthy and prominent petitioners, I gave consideration only to those whom I could judge to be of Tufa's immediate social circle. Since even those were numerous enough, I could further winnow them down to only the ones I found physically attractive.

There was one other thing I insisted on. As I have said, many of those men made their initial call on me after nightfall, arriving muffled in their cloaks, probably having sidled into the hospitium through its back-alley door. But they did not do that twice; every time we met thereafter, it was in their homes. The local dignitaries might have wished for furtiveness and obscurity in their dealings with me, but I decidedly did not. I wanted Tufa to realize, from the first time he heard of me, that he would have to receive me in his legative palace. So I refused ever to entertain anyone in my hospitium chambers. I made it a condition that, if a man desired to disport himself with me, it would be only and always under his own roof. Some of them made loud protest—most were married, after all—but only a few weak spirits declared themselves unable to comply, and went regretfully away. Others, like the judex Diorio, contrived errands on which to send their families off to distant places. Others openly took me home and dared their wives to object, under threat of violence. One, the medicus Corneto, took me home and brazenly offered his wife a choice: allow our frolicking or join in it with us. Even the venerable Bishop Crescia took me home, in daylight, to his presbytery at Bononia's cathedral of SS. Peter and Paul, to the great scandal (or admiration) of his housekeeper and priests and deacons.

Besides my getting to see the sumptuous interiors of numerous mansions and palaces—and the cathedral's unique relic, the bowl in which Pontius Pilate so famously washed his hands—I found another advantage in visiting those places. A man is always liable to speak more freely in his own accustomed surroundings than in even the most luxurious lupanar or borrowed bedroom, and these men were Tufa's intimates. Thus it was that I heard about Tufa's travels hither and yon, more than I could have learned otherwise, and heard also conjectures about what he was doing here and there throughout Italia.

Since there was no further need for my man Kniva to go on proclaiming Veleda's accomplishments all over the city—because I was now flagrantly flaunting those accomplishments—and since the poor fellow had drunk himself so sodden that he was absolutely reeling from taberna to taberna, I bade him desist and take a rest. Then, when he was sober and steady again, I sent him north to join Theodoric at Mediolanum. I sent also a message, telling everything I had so far heard about Tufa's peregrinations, and what deductions I had made as to the purpose of those travels. I could not know whether the information would be of any value to Theodoric, but it made me feel that I was not spending all my time here in wastrel self-indulgence.

Not until early April did Hruth bring me another intercepted Polybian signal that was anything more than a routine reiteration that TH was still garrisoned in MEDLAN. At least I supposed this message to be something

811

out of the ordinary, because it was the first and only that had not commenced with the repeated "thorn, thorn, thorn." However, that was all I *could* tell about it; the message was incomprehensible to me. In toto, it read thus: VISIGINTCOT. That string of letters I could have broken apart in innumerable ways, making innumerable meanings, but I could trust none of my readings.

I mused aloud, "The first letters . . . could it be that they refer to Visigoths? But that makes no sense whatever. The nearest Visigoths are in far-off Aquitania. Hm, let me think. Vis ignota? Visio ignea? *Skeit!* You must simply keep alert for other signals, Hruth, and fetch them to me instanter."

But the subsequent messages he brought were just as baffling: VISAUG-POS and VISNOVPOS. Could POS again mean "possidere"? If so, *who* was taking possession of *what*? Then Hruth brought me this: VISINTMEDLAN. Well, whatever was happening, it involved Mediolanum, where Theodoric was still encamped. But that was all I could make out.

The next night was one of the three nights a month reserved to the judex Diorio. After I had given him an ample measure of pleasure, I lay back, wearing nothing except my ever present modesty hipband (and my irremovable Venus collar), and said playfully, "I do hope you will recommend me to your friends."

With amused indulgence, he said, "How can I? All my friends tell me you say those selfsame words to *them*. Are you insatiable, woman?"

I tittered girlishly. "There is one I have not met yet. Your friend Tufa."

"You ought shortly to have an opportunity. I hear that the dux is on his way back here from his travels in the south."

In the manner of a vain and silly woman, I cried, "Euax! All that way, just to meet the irresistible Veleda!"

"Do not give yourself airs. The dux has collected a fresh army from the Suburbicaria provinces. He leads it hither on his way to confront your cousinly invaders and their newest allies."

I pouted prettily. "You men are so tedious, so literal-minded. My being of Germanic lineage, dear Diorio, does not make me cousin to the invaders. Or make me the least interested in them. I confine my interest to one man at a time."

"Eheu!" he groaned, feigning dismay. "So now, having drained me dry, your interest fixes on my lord Tufa. Faithless wench!"

"Only a *common* wench would think you drained dry," I said archly. "I wager this *uncommon* wench can plumb deeper wells in you . . . and waken fountains . . ."

When I had done that, and skillfully, I lay back again, waiting until

Diorio finished gasping and composed himself for sleep. Then, pretending drowsiness myself, I murmured, as if it was of no real moment, "What did you mean: newest allies?"

He mumbled, "Visigoths."

"Nonsense. There has not been a Visigoth in Italia since the days of Alaric's depredations."

"*Another* one named Alaric," he muttered. Then he roused himself slightly, to say with mock severity, "And never, my dear, tell a magistrate he is talking nonsense, even when he is. In this case, I am not. I speak of Alaric the Second, current King of the Visigoths away out west in Aquitania."

"He is here? In Italia?"

"Not in person, I think, but I hear that he has sent an army. Alaric apparently expects your cousinly Ostrogoths to be successful in their conquest here. And apparently he wishes to show solidarity with them. So he sent a sizable force from his land, eastward across the Alpes."

In my head, I was dissecting that recent puzzling torch message—VISIGINTCOT—Visigoths, the verb "intrare," the mountain pass called the Alpis Cottia.

"From what I hear," Diorio went on, "they overran our fortress town of Augusta Taurinorum at our northwestern frontier, and then took possession of the next easterly town, Novaria, and at last report they had joined your cousins in Mediolanum. That report—not your notorious allure, dear Veleda—is what occasions Tufa's hasty return from the south. Now, may I beg leave to sleep?"

813

"Sleep?" I said loftily. "When your nation is in such turmoil? You seem to take it very lightly."

He gave a lazy, comfortable chuckle. "My dear young woman, I am the furthest thing from a patriot or a hero. I am a licentiate of the courts of litigation, meaning that I am a champion of the highest bidder, whoever he be. Barbarian invaders are no more repulsive to me than any of the wretches whose causes I have been well paid to plead. In my time I have supported the wrong and the guilty, when the stakes were high enough, as wholeheartedly as the right and the innocent. Now, in wartime, my survival being high stakes indeed, I shall favor the litigant that looks likeliest to win, right or wrong. Unlike Odoacer or Tufa, I need not fret and worry, wondering what will be the name and complexion of Rome's next ruler. My sort will always survive."

"I rejoice to hear it," I said, trying to keep the irony out of my voice. Then I sighed and pouted again. "With all his frets and worries, Dux Tufa may not have time for insignificant little me."

Diorio snorted a laugh. "If I know Tufa—"

"And you do, you do! So *will* you recommend me to him? Promise! Swear you will!"

"I will, I will! No doubt *all* of your friends will recommend you to him. Now, please, allow me just a little refreshment of sleep."

When I returned to my hospitium, I found Hruth again waiting for me, in some excitement and bearing quite a thick bundle of bark. Before he could speak, I said:

"Let me guess. For the first time, the signals came from the south."

He blinked. "How could you have known that, my lady?"

"The message reached here before you did. Other interested parties must be riding relays too. But let me see the tablets, to make sure I heard it right."

"There were several signalings, not just the one," Hruth said as he laid them out in order. "And only the first message came from the south. After that, the torches over in Ravenna made an unusually long signal. Then the same signal, as far as I could determine, was repeated by those customary torches off to the northwest."

"Ja, passing the word farther and farther on," I said, and began to decipher the markings. They confirmed what Diorio had told me. The message from the south gave notice of Tufa's imminent arrival in this region. The message from Ravenna was intended for the northern Roman forces that, like Theodoric's army, had spent the winter there in quarters. Ravenna instructed those troops to stand fast, that General Tufa would soon be on his way with reinforcements.

"Not if I can prevent him," I said to myself, and then to Hruth, "There will be no further need for you to haunt the marshes. From now on, I want you nearby. You are to loiter outside this hospitium. The moment you see Tufa's palace servants or guards escorting me out of here, you are to go to the stable I earlier showed you. Bring from there Thorn's horse, saddled and packed—and have your own horse ready too, and wait out yonder again. Your work and mine—and the marshal Thorn's—will soon be done."

✠   ✠   ✠

Tufa's invitation, when it came, was not a courteous request for my favors; it was a peremptory summons. Two of his Rugian guardsmen came for me, wearing full armor and armament, and the bigger of them said gruffly, "Dux Tufa will have the pleasure of your company, Lady Veleda. Now."

I was given only time enough to don my working clothes. That is to say, I put on my finest raiment, some powder and paint and perfume, a good necklace and fibula—and I grabbed up my little case of cosmetics as we left. Then I was all but frog-marched through the streets. At the palace, one heavy door after another was unbarred before us and barred again behind us. The guards took me to a windowless room deep in the building's interior. It contained nothing but a commodious bed and a Rugian woman of about my own age, well dressed but very plain-faced, and almost as huge as the bed. The guards handed me over, saluted her, then took up stations outside the room's only door, the one we had entered. The woman closed that, to give us privacy, and snapped:

"Give me that box!"

I protested mildly, "It holds nothing but feminine sundries—to make me more comely."

"Slaváith! You would not be here if you were not already comely enough. And no one carries into the presence of the clarissimus Tufa anything that might be injurious to him. Give it here!" She rummaged inside the case and uttered a snort of discovery. "Only feminine sundries, eh? Vái, this is a whetstone!"

"For my fingernails, woman, what else?"

"Even a small stone can be a weapon. And let me see those fingernails." When I showed them, she sniffed as if disappointed, to find them as short and blunt as a man's. "Very well. But the guards will hold the case until time for you to leave. They will also hold that jewelry. A necklace can strangle, a fibula pin can stab. Take them off."

I did. I had protested only for the sake of appearances, and I had brought the case and jewelry only to make sure that Tufa's protectors would have *something* to confiscate. I wanted to afford them the false security of believing that they had adequately disarmed me.

"Now," said the big woman, "take off your clothes."

I had of course expected that, but again I made token protest. "Only at a man's command do I do that."

"Then do so. It is Dux Tufa's command."

"And who are you, woman, to command in his name?"

"I am his wife. Undress!"

I raised my eyebrows and murmured, "Singular employment for a wife." But I complied. I started at the top and, as I doffed each article, Tufa's wife eyed it or felt it for any foreign objects it might conceal. When I was bare to the waist, she curled her fat lip and growled disdainfully:

"You are punily breasted for any real man's taste. No wonder you must resort to augmenting them with disguise. Here, you can put these things back on. Now take off the lower garments."

815

When I was peeled down to the ultimate article, I protested again. "Not even for men do I unloose my modesty band."

She gave a coarse laugh. "Modest, are you? Modest in the classic *Roman* manner? You are nothing but a whore, and you are no more Roman than I am. Do you think I *enjoy* the necessity of searching your whorish clothes and inspecting your even nastier bodily orifices? Give me that hipband and bend over!"

I said spitefully, "I console myself that a whore is morally superior to a procuress. Not to mention a wife who—"

"Slaváith!" she barked, her big face turning red. "I said take that off! And bend over!"

I did both those things in one movement, so that she got no look at my lower front. Then I resignedly endured being twice probed, deeply and roughly, by one of her thick fingers. When she was done, she did not just return my hipband; she slapped it stingingly across my buttocks. As I refastened it and turned around, I said:

"I do not know about procuresses, but we whores are accustomed to being handsomely paid for—"

816

"Slaváith! The guards will have a generous purse waiting with your other possessions."

"But, clarissima," I said sweetly, "I should so much rather receive it from your own tender little hand, and—"

"*Slaváith!* I want never to lay eyes on you again!" And she stormed out of the room.

I sighed with glad relief. The pretend-weapons and my taunting behavior had sufficiently distracted the woman's attention. She had failed to descry the real weapon.

Dressed again, I disposed myself in a fetching attitude upon the bed, and no sooner had I done so than the door banged open and Tufa strode in. We had seen one another on that occasion in Verona, and I readily recognized him, but I had no fear of his seeing me as anyone other than Veleda. He was wearing a fine Roman toga, and he was briskly undoing that as he entered, and he was wearing nothing under it. I already knew him to be a well-built specimen of mature manhood, and now I could see that he was *very* well built indeed, because he approached me with his fascinum ostentatiously preceding him. I smiled, supposing that he was not just eager but urgent for a long and lascivious enjoyment of the talented Veleda. But he stopped short of the bed and rudely demanded:

"Why are you dressed? Why are you not stripped naked? Do you think I have time for foolery? I am a busy man. Let us get on with this."

I bridled, as any woman would, and said coolly, "Excuse me, clarissimus. There seems to be a misunderstanding. I am not here to solicit the favor of being serviced at stud. I thought I was here at your behest."

"Ja, ja," he said impatiently. "But I have many other demands on my time." He tossed his toga onto the bed and stood with arms akimbo, tapping a sandaled foot. "Strip and spread yourself."

"Hold, clarissimus," I said through my teeth. "Reflect that this is costing you a substantial price. Surely you would wish to get your money's worth."

"Vái, wench, you can see that I am *ready* to! But how can I, until you disrobe? Hurry and let me put it in!"

"That is *all* you want?" My womanly resentment was not feigned. "Go and find a knothole somewhere in the wall!"

"Slaváith! Every man of my acquaintance boasts of having had you. So, of course, I must too."

"And *that* is all you want?" I said, in genuinely high dudgeon. "I freely give you leave to say you had me, and you will have wasted none of your precious time, and I promise never to contradict—"

"*Slaváith!*" He shook an immense fist at me and roared, "I said shut your impudent mouth, you ipsitilla wench! Take off those clothes and wires! Open your legs instead of your mouth!"

817

I did not want him to kill me before I could kill him (and I think *any* woman by now would happily have killed him), so I obeyed. But I undressed only slowly, tantalizingly—one piece at a time, beginning with the coiled breast guard he had called "wires"—and saying seductively as I did so:

"Whether you wish it or not, clarissimus, I *like* to give my money's worth. Or even more than that."

"Stop your dawdling or you will get no money at all. I agreed to your exorbitant price only so there would not *be* any delay—of courting, negotiating, haggling, whatever. Duty calls me elsewhere, and I can ill spare even this little while."

I paused, nude to the waist again, and said unbelievingly, "From the most accomplished and loudly lauded ipsitilla ever to honor this city, you want nothing more than *in* and *out* and *away?*"

"Akh, save your auction-mart cajolery. I have already said I would pay your price. And except for your reputation, you are no different from the ugliest kitchen slattern. There is nothing more common than a kunte. Upended, all women are alike."

I said, in utter astonishment, "Why, that is flatly untrue. Women all have the same *things* there, ja, but to a discerning man not any *two* women have nether parts exactly alike. And since every woman has other parts besides the nether, there is an infinite variety of enjoyments to be—"

"*Will* you cease prattling and rip off those last garments?"

Peevishly, I tossed aside everything except my hipband.

"Good. Now splay yourself." He loomed over me, his massive fascinum almost glowing with heat.

I stared up at him, thinking. Granted, his wife might have looked her best with her legs over her head. But what of other women? Had none ever suggested to him that he could do more than *upend* her? I needed some time before I let him do the "in and out and away." I had to keep him occupied and unaware while I readied my killing weapon. So I put up my arms to ward off his flopping full-length upon me—he looked surprised at realizing my strength—and instead drew him down beside me on the bed, saying plaintively:

"Allow me just a bit of time, please, clarissimus, before I splay myself. Your good wife's scrupulous inspection somewhat bruised me down there. However, as I told you, a woman has other useful parts besides the nether. If you will allow a brief recuperation of those, I shall meanwhile show you what I can do with others."

Before he could remonstrate, I commenced doing that. And that must never have been done to him by any woman before, because he exclaimed, scandalized, "That is indecent!" He recoiled only slightly, though, and did not wrench himself loose from me, so I raised my head just long enough to laugh and say, "Ne, this is prelude. Indecency comes later, clarissimus, never fear." Then I bent to my ministrations again, and in a moment he was twitching and whimpering with pleasure. Guilty pleasure, perhaps, but pleasure.

Truth to tell, my paying those intimate attentions to a fascinum already so ripe and palpitant—especially the fascinum of a man like Tufa, accustomed to hasty gratification—risked making it spurt and spend itself untimely soon. But Tufa's amazement at my "indecent" doings apparently had damped his sensitivity to some degree. Also I was very careful not to be *too* stimulating. I simply pretended that the fascinum was my own, signaling its excited feelings to my own consciousness. In such more-than-intimate communion with the organ, I could repeatedly urge it close to the brink of spilling over, and just as repeatedly ease off on my caresses to prevent its doing so. To be further truthful, this activity inevitably wakened excitements in me as well. But I resolutely kept those tamped down, not to chance their interfering with my concentration or their causing my busy hands to fumble at *their* work.

Those hands were working behind Tufa's back—or, rather, behind his legs. I suppose no ordinary woman's hands would have had the strength to do it, but mine were unbending one end of my discarded bronze breast guard from its stiff spiral shape. Without my having to watch what I was doing there, doing it by feel alone, I was able to uncoil and straighten about a forearm's length of the rod—not arrow-straight, but straight enough for my purpose—and it *was* arrow-sharp, because I had months ago whetstoned the metal's blunt end to a point.

When I was satisfied that the weapon was ready, I gave Tufa one final juicy laving of caresses. His fascinum seemed to grow even more in length and girth and rigidity—and the man was involuntarily crying loud cries of "Now! Ja! Liufs Guth! Now!" But I withdrew, just short of *now*, and rolled a little away from him, onto my back, and tugged so that he rolled atop me. Although nearly gone in delirium, he took command and rammed his great fascinum into me. As Tufa began his fervent, rapid pumping, driving deeper and deeper inside me, I clasped my arms about his broad back and my legs about his bouncing hips. I was also doing energetic pumping of my own pelvis and, as if in a real frenzy of passion, I raked the fingernails of my free hand up and down Tufa's back. To be honest again, my passionate involvement was fast *becoming* real, but the sober intent of my nail-clawing was to avert Tufa's noticing when he was touched by the sharp bronze rod waiting in my other hand.

I was waiting only for the proper moment, that moment when any man is totally vulnerable and helpless and unaware, the moment of ultimate sexual spasm and ejaculation, when *nothing else in the universe* matters to a man. For Tufa, that moment must have been the most exultant he had ever known in his life, considering that I had prepared him for it in a way so foreign to him. He clutched me tight, and mashed his bearded lips onto mine, and forced his tongue into my mouth, and I watched his eyes go unfocused. Then he joyously flung his head back and uttered a long, wild, ululating wail, and I felt the first pulsing gush of his ejaculation deep and high inside me, and I stabbed him in the back. I placed the point precisely, just so, to my right of his spine, below the shoulder blade, between two ribs, and I gave the rod a hard yank toward me. Then, hand over hand, as if I were strongly, swiftly climbing the rod, I forced it down through Tufa's body until the point broke through his chest skin and pricked my own.

There was just time for Tufa's eyes to come back into focus, and to glare at me in angry surprise, before they glazed over. But some other things also happened during the brief flicker of his dying. I was already crammed full of his fascinum, but I swear it bulked suddenly bigger inside me, thicker

819

around and vastly longer, as if it were still alive though he was not. And it continued to pulse its gushes of fluid far up in me, even as Tufa's other vital bodily fluid crept stickily over my bare breasts. I remember thinking, in a vague sort of way: well, Tufa has died a happier death than poor Frido did.

And then—I could not help it; I could not hold it back—I convulsed in my own spasm of release. (Surely, I said to myself afterward, it was understandable after so much unavoidable excitation; surely it was impelled by the undeniable fact that I *was* still being rutted on; surely it was *not* impelled by the memory of dear Frido that had come to me unbidden.) As the soft, sweet internal bursting occurred, and copious amounts of my own fluids mingled with those already spilled down there, I cried a long cry of jubilation.

When I had ceased trembling, and recovered my wits and breath and strength, the rest was easy. Tufa's wound had not bled a great deal; it was a very small hole that I had put through him. That closed neatly, and bled no more at all, when I drew out the rod. I slid from under his dead weight, and used his toga to wipe my breasts clean of blood and my lower body clean of the paler juices. Then I dressed again, and rebent the breast guard into its usual spiral—not taking time to do it too tidily—and put that on again too. Then I walked to the door, having to do it carefully because my legs were still quivery, and calmly stepped out between the two waiting guardsmen. I simpered at them in a whorishly shameless way, and flipped a careless hand to indicate Tufa collapsed across the bed back there.

"The clarissimus dux is sated," I said, and giggled. "He sleeps. Now . . ." and I kept my hand out, palm upward.

The guards companionably but a little contemptuously returned my smirk, and one of them dropped a richly jingling leather purse into my waiting hand. The other gave me my cosmetics case and my confiscated ornaments. Unhurriedly, I fastened the necklace about my throat and pinned the fibula to the shoulder of my tunic, then just as unhurriedly closed the bedroom door behind us and said, with another salacious simper:

"Of course, the dux is only sated *for now.* You gallants know where to find me when he wants me again, as he is bound to do. Now, if you will see me out . . . ?"

And they did, unbarring the various doors and gates through which we had come into the palace, and, with further smirks, bidding me "gods dags" at the open street. I strolled away, still outwardly calm and collected, but inwardly quaking for fear that Tufa's wife or one of his chamber servants might dare his wrath to look in on him and see what was taking him so long.

But I got clean away, and Hruth was waiting with the two horses. He glanced at my tousled hair and the smeared fucus and creta of my face, his expression compounded of inquiry, concern and a trace of moralistic disapproval.

I said, "It is done."

"And the marshal?"

"Coming. I will hold his mount. You ride on and Thorn will catch you up."

Thorn did, as soon as I could change clothes and cleanse my face. Hruth's horse was moving at an easy jog trot when Velox cantered up beside him on the Via Aemilia. He heeled his mount to match the faster gait. It was not until we were well clear of Bononia's western outskirts, and I slowed our pace, that Hruth was able to ask:

"The lady Veleda is not going north with us?"

"Ne, she will remain—in covert—in case King Theodoric has need of her services among the enemy again."

"Peculiar services," mused Hruth. "And she seems to feel no self-disgust at what she does in the king's cause. I daresay she is to be commended for her bravery and loyalty, and her wielding so well the only weapon a woman has. Still, it makes a man glad—does it not, Saio Thorn?—that he was born a man, not a mere woman."

821

"Tufa was *mine* to slay," Theodoric said, in a measured voice that conveyed more anger than a bellow could have done. "That obligation and privilege belonged to me, Saio Thorn. You contravened your king's authority and far overstepped your own. Only a king can pretend to be a judex, lictor et exitium all in one."

He and I and a number of his senior officers were met in the Basilica of St. Ambrose, which Theodoric had appropriated for his praitoriaún in Mediolanum. The other men sat stern and silent while our sovereign continued to upbraid me, and I stood with head bowed, enduring the reprimand submissively because I knew I had risked incurring it. Meanwhile, I remembered how curtly Theodoric had expressed his reprehension of a malefactor on other occasions. He had not paused for deliberation or squandered words before he drove his blade into Singidunum's legatus, Camundus, and into Strabo's princeling, Rekitakh. I deemed it a considerable testament to our long friendship that he was chastising me *only* with words.

So I simply stood and let the words wash over me, while I pondered on happier things. Every time I rejoined Theodoric after a lengthy absence, I was struck anew with the realization that he got ever more kinglike in appearance and demeanor as he got older. His beard, as golden-bright as a new-minted solidus, had formerly been heroic of aspect; now it was magisterial. His posture and gestures were dignified; anywhere he sat was a throne. His forehead wore the lines of one who thought deeply, and his cheeks the lines of one who had known sorrow, but the corners of his eyes were crinkled by the lines of ready merriment, and the fine blue eyes themselves could go instantaneously from gleeful to grave to fierce . . .

I recalled how once, long ago, while admiring a younger Theodoric, I had wistfully thought: "Akh, could I but be a *woman!*" Now, admiring the maturer man more ardently still, I wondered why my recent, sudden, startling flights of Veleda imagination should have fixed on the fancy of my embracing young Frido—or *any* other, lesser man than Theodoric. Just days ago, my inmost Veleda mind had substituted an illusory Frido for the real but inconsequential Tufa with whom necessity had coupled me. That made me further wonder: could it be that my imagination, even more fancifully, had all this while been substituting the apparition of Frido for that of Theodoric? Was it possible for a mind to engage in such complexities, independent of its owner's will?

Theodoric now was glowering at me and demanding, "Speak up! Can you justify your preempting of the king's right to condemn Tufa, niu? Have you anything to say in extenuation of your criminal willfulness?"

I might have suggested, and with righteous indignation, that as a holder of both high rank and high office, I ought to be entrusted to make my own decisions when I had to deal with weighty matters in places far from my king's immediate supervision. In fact, that is what I did point out to him, but not indignantly; I made a jest of it.

"The malfeasance was your own fault, my king."

"Eh?" His blue eyes blazed; his bearded jaw dropped; everyone else in the room held his breath.

"You elevated this nonentity Thorn to herizogo. You appointed this upstart Thorn a marshal. Can I be blamed for believing that my sins ought to be equivalent to my status?"

Everyone stared at me. Then Theodoric erupted into hearty laughter and, after him, so did his officers, even the sour old Soas. Well, it was no wonder that I—like all his subjects—admired and adored our king. He was proof that a kingly nature could be warm and engaging as well as majestic and strong.

"Akh," he said, when he was done laughing, "I suppose I ought to be grateful, Thorn, that you did not remain longer at liberty, and single-handedly scour the whole peninsula clean of my opponents. At least you have left Odoacer for me to take care of personally."

"And a few Roman legions here and there," General Pitzias growled warningly.

Theodoric waved a dismissive hand. "Here and there, ja. No unified front. The entire remaining Roman army must be confused and uncertain what to do, with its king in hiding and its chief commander defunct. I expect no formidable resistance. A matter of sweeping up as we go along, no more."

From the ensuing discussion, I learned that Theodoric had inflicted on the Romans at the Addua River a defeat quite as calamitous as the one at

823

the Sontius. And when that army had been dispersed, a few days' hammering at the gates of Mediolanum had sufficed to make its Roman garrison throw open the gates in surrender. Now, the first significant battle of this spring had been fought by the Visigoths who had come from beyond the Alps. Under their General Respa, they had vanquished another Roman force holding the city of Ticinum, and currently were encamped there, awaiting Theodoric's orders.

"Does this mean," I asked warily, "that the Visigoths' King Alaric is going to claim credit for helping in the conquest? That he is going to demand a share of the spoils—a piece of Italia, perhaps—for his own?"

"Ne," said Theodoric. "This contemporary Alaric is not as rapacious as his great-grandfather namesake. He seeks no extension of his own hegemony. Alaric, like many another present-day king, yearns for a return to the time when the Roman Empire comprised the whole of the western world, when its every constituent kingdom could enjoy the security and prosperity of the Pax Romana."

"Remember," Saio Soas said to me, "most of the Germanic rulers supported Odoacer as long as it seemed *he* might bring back the great old days of Rome. Now, clearly, they hope Theodoric can do that. Alaric sent a fighting force to help. But his General Respa brought us embassies, as well, from King Khlodovekh of the Franks and old King Gaiseric of the Vandals and even young King Hermanafrid of the far-north Thuringi. All express their friendship and favor, and offer to contribute any other aid we might require."

General Herduic, grinning broadly, added, "King Clovis even offered to contribute his sister."

"What?" I said. "Who is Clovis?"

"King Khlodovekh. He prefers the Roman version of his name. His sister has at least retained the good Old Language name of Audefleda."

"And what," I inquired, "was Clovis offering his sister to *do?*"

"Why, to be Theodoric's wife and queen."

On hearing that, I confess, I felt a pang of feminine chagrin. It took me quite unexpectedly, because I had never felt any envy or antipathy toward the late Lady Aurora, and never in the time since then had it distressed me to see Theodoric take a woman to share his bed for a while. Well, I thought resignedly, he was bound *someday* to contract a formal marriage. He had so far sired only daughters, and they the offspring of concubinage. He would of course want a son for an heir, and a son of royal blood. However, try though I might, I could not find that thought very consoling.

General Ibba explained further: "Clovis's offer indicates that he fully expects us soon to possess all of Italia—and that his sister, before too long, will be sharing Theodoric's reign over not only Italia but a vast, revivified Roman Empire. Not just Queen Audefleda, *Empress* Audefleda. And if Clovis is so confident of our success, then all the other kings must be too."

"Including this king?" I boldly asked of Theodoric.

He nodded soberly and said, "As of now, we command the entire north of Italia, from the Alpes to the Sontius. I foresee not much difficulty in our sweeping southward over the rest of the peninsula, within another year at most. In effect, ja, it is all over but the shouting of the triumph."

I feigned deep disappointment. "As I feared, you have won the war without me."

"Not quite," grumbled Soas. "A triumph cannot be celebrated without the conferring of the laurel crown. Until Odoacer relinquishes that . . ."

"Come now, Saio Cassandra," I mocked him. "Surely the Emperor Zeno does not require us to deliver Odoacer's smoked head, as we did with Camundus and Babai." I turned again to Theodoric, and urged, "Let Odoacer *have* his little swampy corner of the peninsula. Let him squat there until he rots from the damp. Meanwhile, when all the rest of Italia is yours, and all the rest of the world knows it is yours, Zeno will have no choice but to proclaim you the rightful—"

825

He held up a hand. "Ne, Thorn. Fortune has intervened, and not to our advantage. I have word that Zeno is right now very ill. He may be dying. Anyway, he can proclaim nothing. And no successor can be named until and unless Zeno does die. So if, during this interregnum, I am to be awarded any laurels, I must do it myself. And the world must watch me do it. Now, more than ever, it is necessary that I make ostentatious overthrow of Odoacer."

I sighed. "Then I hate to be the one to tell you this, but we will need something more than our armies to do it. I have observed the terrain around Ravenna. An overland assault is impossible and a landward siege would be futile. The crops of that Flaminia province had just been harvested at the time Odoacer retreated into his stronghold, so he certainly took in with him a bounteous stock of fresh provender."

"And probably," muttered Pitzias, "that is one reason for Tufa's having butchered our men. So they would not be a drain on the city's store of resources."

"If so, it was an unnecessary precaution," I said. "The occupants of Ravenna can live well—and indefinitely—even without having collected those harvests. I remember, when I was Strabo's prisoner in the Black Sea city of Constantiana, how he boasted that all the armies of Europe could not prevent that city's being supplied and fed by seagoing ships. And Ravenna sits beside the Hadriatic Sea. That is why I tell you this. The one and only practical way of assailing Ravenna is to utilize the Roman navy. Have its ships transport our troops and put them ashore there, and—"

"I cannot do that," Theodoric said flatly.

"Proud warrior," I said, "I know you would prefer us to take Ravenna without any outside assistance. So would I. But you must believe me when I say it is beyond our doing. And that Navarchus Lentinus of the Hadriatic Fleet seemed well enough inclined to—"

"Lentinus is *why* I cannot enlist the Roman navy. Vái, Thorn, you were present when I gave that man my word—that I would be his legitimate, lawful, rightful commander before I ever would give him a command. Zeno has not conferred that authority on me, and cannot, and Lentinus knows it. Even if I wished to go back on my given word, there is no way I could make the navarchus obey me. He has only to move his ships out of my reach."

"And such a rebuff," Ibba remarked, unnecessarily, "would demean Theodoric, in the eyes of his soon-to-be subjects, worse than would the most devastating battle defeat."

826

Theodoric went on, "I had already thought of landing seaborne troops, Thorn. And, failing that, of using seaborne catapults to assail Ravenna. And, as a last resort, of employing a naval blockade at least to ward off the ships supplying the city. But ne, I cannot. Lentinus has already very kindly obliged me to the extent of lending his fastest vessels to carry messengers between Aquileia and Constantinople. That is how I learned of Zeno's illness. But more I cannot request of Lentinus, and nothing can I demand."

I shrugged. "I can suggest no other recourse. So lay siege to Ravenna, if you like, when our armies get to Flaminia. It will do no good, except to keep Odoacer in there, when what you really want is to get him out. But at least you will know where he is. Perhaps, by the time we conquerors are settled down and peaceably farming on every other jugerum of Italian ground except that swampy bit of the coast, Odoacer will finally concede that he is beaten and come out voluntarily."

"Habái ita swe," said Theodoric, not in a commanding tone this time, but in a rueful wishing way.

At that, the gathered officers took their leave, and I deliberately lagged to be the last, so I could ask Theodoric, "And what of King Clovis's sister, niu?"

"What?" he said blankly, as if he had quite forgotten her existence.

"What can I say about her? I can hardly contemplate making an empress of Audefleda until I have some claim to an empire."

"Which you will, in time, Guth wiljis. And then? Will you contemplate wedding an alien woman whom you have never even seen?"

"Akh, you know there is nothing uncommon about that, not in the case of royal families arranging marriages of alliance and convenience. However, General Respa *has* met Audefleda. He assures me that she is of passable intelligence, of acceptable graces and of rather more beauty than is usual among princesses."

I said, in the solicitous way in which feminine spitefulness is oftenest expressed, "Such a pity that Frankish women, as is well known, tend to age and wither rather sooner than others. Since, as you remark, it may be some considerable while before you can contemplate—"

"Oh vái!" Theodoric exclaimed, with a robust laugh. "Clovis himself is only a stripling of twenty-three, and Audefleda must be six or seven years younger. I certainly expect to enjoy ample and savory tasting of that plum before it shrivels to a prune."

So I slouched out of the basilica, slightly seething. Even a woman ordinarily as sedate and levelheaded as Veleda cannot help being perturbed when she tries to measure her qualities against those of another woman, and—before she can even begin to tally things like beauty, charm and wit—is confounded to discover that the other woman has the overwhelming, insurmountable, horrendously unjust advantage of being *younger.* And I, Veleda, was—liufs Guth!—something like *twice* the age of the upjumped Audefleda!

I realized that I was gnashing my teeth, so I forcibly reminded myself that I was not yet *old.* The august Christian Church, which purports to be infallible when consulted on every other question that mortals can put to it, has determined *precisely* when a woman is old—old beyond repair, beyond redemption, beyond protest or pretense or appeal for reprieve. The sage Church fathers have decreed that a woman is old at forty, that being the age at which she becomes eligible for the oblivion of the nun's velatio. As little Sister Tilde once explained to me (back when I was so unbelievably, impossibly young), a woman of forty is, by the Church's reckoning, "aged well beyond having any indecent urges of her own . . . so antiquated and dilapidated that she inspires no such urges in any men."

Well, thags Guth, I was still some six years short of toppling over that brink of no return. I might even be one of the few to extend that brink a little further than forty. Although nature had made an appalling error in

827

first giving me human form, nature had since then dealt rather more kindly with me than with most women. I had always been trim and slight of build, and still was. My body had never been thickened and sagged by childbearing, my vigor had never been sapped by the menoths bleeding. And it may have been my lack of certain female glands—or my having them so inextricably mixed with the male—that kept the usual effects of age rather at bay. Granted, my hips had broadened just a *trifle*, my breasts and belly had become just a *little* less springy to the touch. But my skin was still smooth and unblotched, my face not wrinkled or lined, my pores not coarsened. My underchin was still firm, the back of my neck not bunchy, my hair still abundant and bright. My voice had not got strident, my walk not become a waddle. Even compared to an unripe, newly pubescent, barely nubile little minx like the sixteen-year-old Audefleda, I thought, I would hardly be judged decrepit. Still . . .

There is no denying that men who were comely in youth keep their appeal much longer than the comeliest women can hope to do. Veleda would not always be able to take her pick of men of every age and condition, as I had done in Bononia. But her contemporaries Thorn and Theodoric would, for many years yet, go on attracting women of their own age, and women younger and ever younger, not to mention women older. Right now, given their choice of a Veleda nearly ready for the veil, and the budding sprig Audefleda: which would they choose? I was tempted to tear my hair and wail, like that pitiable crone Hildr in the Gutaland cave, "I ask you, is that fair? Is it *fair?*"

Instead, suddenly appalled, I stopped dead in the street where I was walking. In a manner of speaking, Thorn stood back to gaze at Veleda with a mixture of wonder and horror and amusement, and to cry aloud, "Gudisks Himins! Am I being consumed with bitter envy of *myself?*"

At that moment, a patrol of our own warriors marched past in neat formation. They all dutifully saluted my marshal's armor, but gave a very odd look at the marshal wearing it. When they had gone on, I laughed at my lunatic and overlapping vagaries, and now said—not aloud—"Vái, why conjure up so confused a future? It may well be that Fortune or Tykhe or some other goddess of chance has already decided that Thorn and Theodoric and Veleda all will fall in the next battle."

✠　　✠　　✠

But of course we did not, not in the next battle or in any after that. Indeed, the several battles to come were all rather perfunctory affairs, and quickly concluded, costing not too many casualties on either side. That was because the Roman legions, bereft of their chief commander and deserted by their king, were understandably disgruntled and disheartened. None marched out to meet us as we advanced southward along the peninsula, and when we came upon their defensive positions and sent ahead our haughty demand—"tributum aut bellum"—they put up just enough resistance that they could afterward say they had not surrendered without a fight. But surrender they did.

By the August end of the year, we were effectually in command of the entire land of Italia—except for Odoacer's asylum city of Ravenna—though Theodoric had chosen to halt our advance along the east-west line of the Via Aemilia, only about half the distance between Italia's Venetia border and its heart-city of Rome. He elected to stop there for the coming winter, simply to facilitate the travel of his messenger riders, because he was increasingly more occupied with the concerns of administration than of conquest. In the major cities that we had overrun, Theodoric had left detachments of our forces, and now he sent other detachments to police even the smaller towns, and he required quick and easy communication with all of those.

Zeno was still ailing—his life ebbing, said the reports from Constantinople—but no successor emperor or regent had been installed. Since Theodoric still could not be imperially proclaimed the new King of Rome, and since he virtuously refused to arrogate to himself any powers of that office, he lacked the authority to enact and enforce laws for the governance of his conquered land. However, he could and did impose the jus belli, laying down certain rules and regulations for the keeping of order and the conduct of civic affairs. The rules he instituted were by no means harsh; they quite surprised and pleased his "newly conquered subjects"; and they prefigured the beneficent despotism with which Theodoric would govern ever after.

As well as I have been able to determine from my readings in world history, every conqueror who ever lived before Theodoric—Cyrus, Alexander, Caesar, every other—despised the peoples he subdued and made subject. The conqueror always set out to impose on the conquered his own ideas of what was right and wrong, not only in matters of government and law and statecraft but also in every least detail of behavior, beliefs, culture, customs and taste. Theodoric did not. Far from despising these inhabitants of what had been the mighty Western Roman Empire, he honored and admired them for their heritage and, from the very first, made plain that he intended to help them restore and regain that greatness.

For example, it would have been the expectable thing for a conqueror ruthlessly to purge every last subordinate and servitor of his vanquished

829

predecessor, to expunge every last vestige of that predecessor's rulership. Theodoric did not. For the time being, at least, he left in charge of the occupied provinces and cities and towns every Roman legatus or praefectus who had held that office during Odoacer's reign, reasoning that a governor of some longevity and experience would govern better than any newcomer.

However, to assist (and invigilate) each of those governors, Theodoric instituted a kind of tribunal that, for fairness and justice, surely no conquered people ever had known before. At each level of civil administration, Theodoric installed both a Roman judex and an Ostrogoth marshal, coequal in authority. The judex oversaw all matters arising among the Roman populace, and judged according to Roman law. The marshal was responsible for matters pertaining to the occupying outlanders, and judged according to Gothic law. Both magistrates together, somehow managing amiably and equably to correlate their separate bodies of law, arbitrated transactions and adjudicated disputes between Romans and outlanders. Though at first this novel kind of tribunal was intended just to ease friction between the occupied and their occupiers, it proved so eminently serviceable and beneficial to all parties and to the whole nation—even after the influx of many more outlanders—that the system endured and still does to this day.

830

Over time, of course, Theodoric had to weed out numerous Roman legati and praefecti and judices who proved inept or corrupt or stupid, most of those having attained their offices through "amicitia," which is to say favoritism or nepotism or bootlicking or bribery. He replaced the discards with Romans of demonstrable ability, although some of those told him bluntly that, while they would try to serve honestly and efficiently, they were not *joyously* serving under a non-Roman usurper. I think Theodoric best preferred those frankly reluctant holders of office; he could be sure that they were not lickspittles. There was only one kind of office that Theodoric closed to Roman candidates. After the Roman army inevitably came under his command and was merged with our outlander forces, he dismissed the Roman tribunes and would not give to a Roman any other significant military appointment.

"I am trying," he told me once, in those early days of occupation, "to make a reasonable apportionment of responsibilities. Let each man do what he does best, and reward him accordingly. When it comes to cultivating the land and reaping its resources, Romans and outlanders can be equally hardworking and proficient and productive. But the tasks involved in defending the land, maintaining law and order, those are best entrusted to us of Germanic nationality, deservedly notorious as 'battle-loving barbarians.' And since it was the Romans of former times who developed the arts and sciences that have so much enriched mankind, I shall leave today's Romans free of meaner drudgeries—insofar as possible—in hope that they will emulate their forebears, to enhance and enlighten the world anew."

Most of his efforts toward those ends would come later, but, as I say, he made a promising beginning even in those months when martial law was all he had to work with. Though he and his army and his new subjects would continue to regard Mediolanum as Theodoric's "capital city" for some while to come, he did not just go to ground there and rule by fiat, in the remote and uncaring way that most Roman emperors had done. All that winter, he was on the roads, going from one corner of the occupied lands to another, personally seeing to the security and comfort and cheer of "his people," meaning the local folk as well as his troops. And wherever Theodoric might be at a given moment, he was constantly receiving and dispatching messenger riders, so that he was always in touch with every other corner of his domain, and nothing escaped his attention. For one instance, he had put all the land's warehouses and this year's newly stored harvests under martial levy, but not for confiscation. He set his quarter-masters to meting out winter provisions, and doing it with an impartiality that amazed the commonfolk, because they were given as much food as the noble folk. Some of the commoners even got more. At those humble houses where an officer had quartered troops of ours, the family was given extra rations by way of compensation for the inconvenience.

831

I will confidently assert that no other conquered people, before these of Italia, ever had been shown such care and concern by the man who con-quered them. I know for a fact that no other conqueror ever has been given the trust and respect and burgeoning affection with which the people of Italia soon were regarding Theodoric. I do not mean merely the long-downtrodden commonfolk, either. The high-ranking Lentinus, navarchus of the Roman navy's Hadriatic Fleet, rode all the way from his station at Aquileia to call on Theodoric, and to make a friendly proposal that was to prove very helpful to our cause.

While Theodoric had been busy with the deployment of his occupation troops and the imposition of the jus belli and all the other matters of martial administration, General Herduic had been given the mission of laying siege to Odoacer's Ravenna—or, rather, laying it under partial block-ade. As I had warned, the marshlands thereabout gave no firm purchase for the setting up of catapults or the massing of dense ranks of archers. So Herduic could only dispose his infantry in a long thin line about the city's landward outskirts, from the seashore north of it around to the shore to the south. And those men could do nothing but stay there to prevent any supplies being brought into the city along the marsh road, or across the marshes themselves, or down the branch of the river Padus that flows seaward through those marshes, or along the Via Popilia, which goes north and south from Ravenna along the seashore. Except for the occasions when the bored archers dashed up close to the walls to shoot arrows or fire-arrows, just to break the tedium, there was little semblance of a siege. And as I had also warned, even the blockade was as futile—and probably made our enemies inside Ravenna smirk as derisively—as the peevish arrow attacks. Herduic's seaside speculatores reported that, at least once a week, a merchant vessel or a galley-towed string of barges came over the Hadriatic into Ravenna's Classis docks, and there leisurely unloaded a considerable cargo. There was nothing we could do about that, and we could not even be sure where those supply ships came from.

"Not from any of the Hadriatic bases under my command," Lentinus told us officers convened in the Mediolanum praitoriaún. He went on, in his quaint Venetian accent, "I give you my word, Theozoric, those ships are not from Aquileia or Altinum or Ariminum. Just as I will not lend naval vessels to help your conquest, neither will I lend them for Odoacer's last-expedient defenses."

"I know that," said Theodoric, "and I respect your stand of neutrality."

I said, "We are forced to assume that even a failed and discredited ex-ruler must have at least a handful of diehard supporters. We suspect that the supplies are being provided by some Odoacer faction already fled into snug exile, perhaps over the sea in Dalmatia, or even as far away as Sicilia."

"Or," said the bearish old Saio Soas, "Odoacer's supporters may be expatriates wanting, for some reason, to preserve the status quo ante. It is surprising how many people who have long lived outside their native country can be so zealous about meddling into its affairs from a safe distance."

"Well, I am morally barred from meddling," said Lentinus. "However, while my neutrality prevents me from offering you any Roman vessels, Theozoric, nothing forbids my suggesting that you build some of your own."

"The suggestion is kindly taken," said Theodoric with a smile. "But I wager there is not a single man in my ranks who knows anything about shipbuilding."

"Probably not," Lentinus said easily. "But I do."

Theodoric's smile broadened. "You would help us build war craft?"

"Not war craft. That would be a violation of neutrality. And a fleet of those would take years to build, anyway. But all you need, really, are large boxes that can be rowed and steered about the Classis harbor of Ravenna.

Enough of them to float enough armed warriors to discourage any approaching supply ships. Surely you have capable wainwrights and ironsmiths in your ranks. Gather them for me, let me lead them down the Via Aemilia to the shipyards at Ariminum and show them what to do."

"Be it so!" Theodoric exclaimed, right gaily, and sent Generals Pitzias and Ibba scurrying off to collect the workmen.

✠   ✠   ✠

Those preparations for a tighter blockade of Ravenna were not yet completed when spring came. And there came then also one of Lentinus's speedy dolphin vessels from Constantinople, with a Greek messenger on board, bearing the latest news of the Eastern Empire. Zeno had at last succumbed, and his successor in the Purple Palace was a man named Anastasius. He was almost as old as Zeno had been at his death, and he had formerly been only a minor functionary in the imperial treasury, winning no particular distinction in that service. But he had been personally selected for the emperorship by Zeno's widow, the Basílissa Ariadne. Then she exacted payment for what she had done for him; she married Anastasius immediately after his accession.

833

"Take back to the emperor my congratulations—and my condolences," Theodoric told the messenger. "But did he send any word for me? Any acknowledgment of *my* accession?"

"Oukh, nothing, I regret to say." The messenger shrugged. "And if you will permit me the irreverence, I will also say that you had better not expect Anastasius to proffer any worthwhile endowment of his own free will. Like all men who have had the management of much money, he is a tightfisted, cheeseparing old miser. Ouá, do not hope to get *anything* out of Anastasius without having to pry and dig for it."

So Theodoric was still ruling in Italia with no imperial aegis, only by dint of the jus belli and his own growing esteem among the people. And then, shortly after our getting that indifferent news from the far east, we got word of an occurrence in the nearer north that threatened to tarnish what popularity Theodoric had gained.

The report was that another body of foreign troops had come over the Alpes border, this time through the Poenina Pass—and this time Burgund warriors, sent by King Gundobad. However, it was not another cousin-king's welcome gesture of Germanic solidarity. It proved to be Gundobad's taking greedy advantage of Italia's current unsettled conditions. His troops came down from the mountains only as far as the pasture and cropland valleys on the Italia side. This was ground that our Visigoth allies had already won for us on their way hither during the previous spring, and the people there had since been pacific and content with their lot. Theodoric had seen no need to post occupying forces in a region of nothing but farms and tiny farm villages, nor even a judex-and-marshal tribunal anywhere nearer than the Ligurian town of Novaria. So the Burgund troops, unopposed, did some brisk but probably not very profitable sacking and looting in those valleys. And then, worse, they took about a thousand of the local peasants captive, and marched them back across the Alpis Poenina to become slaves in the lands of King Gundobad.

"That son of a fitchet bitch!" Theodoric raged. "Here am I, hoping to band together *all* us outlanders in a new pride and purpose and dignity and respectability. And that tetzte Gundobad decides he will emulate the brute Attila, all on his own, just to run off a herd of slave cattle. May the devil take him napping! May he fry and freeze in hell!"

But there was nothing we could do to repair the damage, short of haring off across the northern Alpes in pursuit of the Burgund raiders. And that was out of the question, because there was all the rest of Italia to be brought under our governance before winter came again. That process took time, but caused us not much exertion, since the cities and towns and legion garrisons were even less inclined to put up a resistance now than they had been a year ago. Several of them, even before we got close enough to send a messenger demanding "tributum aut bellum," had emissaries waiting on the road to meet us and greet us and offer their surrender.

And, as we moved south along the peninsula, we noticed that a good many communities, which *could* have been located on easily defensible high terrain, were instead seated on low ground almost pathetically open to assault or siege. That circumstance baffled us, and at town after town we commented wonderingly on it, until at last we learned the reason for it. The elderly urbis praefectus of one such community—I forget which—said dolefully, as he surrendered it to Theodoric:

"Had my poor town still stood on the high ground yonder, where it once did, instead of down here on the plain, you would not have walked into it uncontested."

"Well?" Theodoric asked. "Why *is* it here? Why would an entire community pick up and move, to its own detriment?"

"Eheu, because thieves stole the aqueduct. Water could no longer be conveyed to the heights, so the town had to move down here by the riverside."

"*Thieves stole the aqueduct?!* Why, man, an aqueduct is as immovable as an amphitheater!"

834

"I meant the pipes of it. The pipes were made of lead. Thieves stole the lead to sell."

Theodoric looked at him in astonishment. "I take it you are not speaking of foreign marauders."

"No, no. Native thieves."

"And you people just *let* them do it? The stealing could hardly have been done overnight. Miles and miles of heavy lead pipe."

"Eheu, we people had been too long peaceable and comfortable. Our town had not enough cohortes vigilum to apprehend the thieves. And Rome seemed uncaring; Rome sent no assistance and took no action. Eheu, our town was not alone in being so helpless. Many others have had their aqueducts similarly ruined over the years, and had to move from secure hilltop to vulnerable low ground."

"So that is why," murmured Theodoric. Then he said, sounding very like my old mentor Wyrd, "By Murtia, the goddess of indolence, but Rome really *had* gone senile and toothless and impotent. It was high time we came."

835

9

t the mountain town of Corfinium, a crossing place of several major Roman roads, we camped for a few days while Theodoric accepted the town's submission to him, acquainted its urbis praefectus with the rules he was to follow under martial law, appointed the usual judex-and-marshal tribunal and detached a mere five contubernia of infantry to be the occupying force. We left town on the Via Salaria, and I happened to be riding and idly conversing with Theodoric at the head of our columns when, just south of Corfinium, we met another, much smaller column approaching: a score of riders escorting a handsome, mule-drawn carruca. When we all stopped, a white-haired, clean-shaven, distinguished-looking man stepped from the carriage and saluted. His red sandals and the broad stripe on his tunic were unmistakable insignia of his rank, and his pronunciation of Theodoric's name was unmistakably Roman:

"Salve, Teodoricus. I am the senator Festus, and I beg a word with you."

"Salve, patricius," Theodoric said politely but not obsequiously. I might have been a trifle awed by the very first Roman senator I had ever seen, but Theodoric was not. After all, he had been a Consul of the Eastern Empire.

"I have come from Rome to seek you out," Festus went on. "But I had expected to meet you nearer there, and now I find you not marching toward Rome at all."

"I am saving Rome for last," Theodoric said carelessly. "Or are you bringing its surrender betimes and unbidden?"

"That is what I would discuss with you. Might we get off the road and sit a while in comfort?"

"This is an army. It does not carry seats and senatorial comforts."

"But I do, of course."

Festus motioned to his men, and while Theodoric summoned forward his other officers and made introductions all around, the senator's escorts speedily erected a very splendid pavilion, laid out cushions in it and even produced skins of Falernian wine and crystal goblets in which to serve it. Festus would have commenced with easy loquacity, but Theodoric remarked crisply that he hoped to reach the next town, Aufidena, by nightfall, so the senator got straight to the point.

"With our former king in obscurity, with a new emperor on the throne in the east, with yourself unquestionably if unofficially our new overlord, the Roman Senate is, like every Roman citizen, in a state of perplexity and uncertainty. I myself should like to see the transfer of title and power done as soon and as smoothly as possible—to make de jure the de facto kingship of Teodoric. Now, I cannot pretend to represent the thinking of all the Senate—"

"The Roman Senate," Theodoric blandly interrupted, "since the days of Diocletian, has not been *required* to do any thinking."

"True. Too true. And over the last century, it has been reduced to little more than a ratifier of the deeds and actions of whatever strongman held preeminence."

"You mean whatever *barbarian* held preeminence. You may use the word without embarrassment, Senator. Ever since Stilikho, the first outlander to wield real influence in the empire, the Roman Senate has had no function except to affirm and assent."

"Come, come," said Festus, seeming unoffended. "A function not entirely superfluous. Regard the very word 'Senate,' derived from 'senex,' and meaning 'an assembly of old men.' From the earliest times, one function of a tribe's old men has been that of giving their blessing to the endeavors of the younger. Just so, Teodoric, you wish your exploits recognized and your claim to kingship made legitimate."

"Only the emperor can make it so. Not the Senate."

"Which is why I am here. As I say, I represent no senatorial majority. I hardly need tell you that the *majority* would rejoice if you and every other barbarus were back lurking deep in the forests of Germania and themselves again the rightful choosers of their rulers. However, I do represent a faction that would very much like to see Italia returned to peace and stability. And we of the Senate are aware, from our own dealings with Anastasius when he was a mere treasury steward, that he is a man inclined to dither and temporize. Therefore, I propose this. If you can provide me transportation and safe-conduct, I will go to Constantinople. I will urge Anastasius to make immediate proclamation that Odoacer is ousted, that you are henceforth Teodoricus Rex Romani Imperii Occidentalis."

"Rex Italiae will suffice," Theodoric said, smiling. "I can hardly decline such a generous offer, Senator, and I welcome your good offices. Go, and with all my wishes for your success. If you keep traveling northward from here, you will come eventually to the Via Flaminia, and that will lead you to Ariminum, where the Navarchus Lentinus of the Hadriatic Fleet is currently engaged in certain projects. My marshal Thorn, here, is acquainted with the roads and with the navarchus. Saio Thorn will accompany you and your men, and will see that Lentinus puts you aboard the first vessel sailing for Constantinople."

837

✠　✠　✠

So Theodoric and the army went on without me, and I turned back the way we had come, guiding Festus's small train. I could not complain of having been given escort duty. It meant no more sleeping outdoors and living on army provender and enduring long days of riding at military pace, because the senator of course traveled as befits a dignitary, and made sure that his servants and I did too. Each day's journey was planned so that it concluded in a city or town having a well-furnished hospitium of well-laden board and well-kept therma.

At Ariminum, Lentinus most obligingly lent Festus a raven craft and crew, and sent him off toward Constantinople straightway. The raven being the smallest of the speedy dromo vessels, the senator could take with him only two of his attendants, so he paid for quartering the rest of them to await his return. That meant a considerable outlay; he could not possibly go out and back by sea in less than four weeks.

I did not have leisure to wander about Ariminum, because Lentinus urged me to go with him to see what he had done in the way of blockading Ravenna. He and our army workmen had only in recent days finished building their makeshift troop carriers and setting them afloat full of warriors. The navarchus seemed very proud and eager to show off the accomplishment, and of course I was eager to see it. So next day we rode north together from Ariminum along the Via Popilia. (It was true, what I had been told: the Popilian Way was not much of a road, its pavement broken and buckled or entirely missing from long stretches.) In late afternoon we came to the place where our landward siege line encircling Ravenna had its termination at the seaside south of the city. Our sentries there were stationed prudently out of bow-shot of Ravenna's defenders, but close enough that the city's harbor works were within our view.

"Actually, Ravenna itself is not visible from here," Lentinus said, as he and I dismounted among the siege troops. "What you see yonder—the docks and piers and sheds and such—that is the working and mercantile end of the city, the seaport suburb called Classis. The patrician part, Ravenna proper, is two or three miles inland. It and Classis are connected by a causeway across the marshes between, and that is lined with shacks and huts where the working people live, the suburb called Caesarea."

It was evident that the port must be a busy place in normal times. The broad, commodious harbor, sheltered from storm waves by two low islands offshore, had room for as many as two hundred and fifty big ships to ride at anchor, and the dockside facilities were ample for doing the loading and unloading and provisioning of all that many at once. But now there were only a few vessels to be seen, all securely moored and battened down and crewless, their sails tight-furled, no skiffs going between them and the shore. In normal times, even from our distance, we would easily have been able to see the crowds of porters and carts and wagons bustling about the wharfs and piers, but now the only discernible movement was that of a few apparent idlers. The waterfront buildings were shuttered, no smithy smokes were rising, the drum-wheel cranes were immobile.

I could see just six things still at work—the six ungainly craft that were paddling sluggishly, one behind another, from one headland of the harbor to the other, on this side of the barrier islands. They yawed and rocked in the water, but they managed to stay in line, a distance apart—in two parallel lines, three vessels going one way, three the other. Except for the warriors' shields hung overlapping along the bulwarks, and the ranks of spearpoints that bristled above, the craft *did* look like nothing more than giant boxes. Each had two banks of oars but no masts, each was slab-sided and square-ended, so that its either end could be prow or stern.

"That way they do not have to turn around as they come and go," Lentinus explained. "It is much easier for the oarsmen to face the other way on their benches than to turn the whole ponderous box around. And, spaced across the harbor as they are, slow though they are, any two of the boxes—one moving forward, one reversing—can converge on any ship that tries to slip between them. Each box carries four contubernia of your spearmen armed also with swords. Enough to swarm aboard and overwhelm any merchant ship's crew."

I asked, "Have the men yet had the pleasure of attacking some enemy craft?"

"So far, no, and I do not expect they will. Since the patrol commenced, one of the immense corn ships and later a galley-towed string of barges came from the sea, between the islands and into the harbor roads. But when they saw the glint of all that waiting steel, they sheered off and went back to sea. I would say we have effectively put an end to the seaborne supplies."

I murmured, "I am glad to hear it."

Lentinus went on, "And I can attest that not so much as a salted flitch has been carried into Ravenna—or out of it, for that matter—along this Via Popilia during the time I have been working with your men here and in Ariminum. If the siege line is equally impermeable all the way around the city, and I believe it is, then the only thing going in and out of Ravenna is the occasional message. Your men have reported seeing the torch lights of the Polybian system, signaling from far across the marshes and being answered from the city walls. Obviously Ozoacer still has some loyal followers reporting from the world outside. But from now on, all that the Ravenna folk have to sustain them is whatever ship's stores they already had squirreled away in there."

Pleased, I said, "Odoacer may still squat in there for a long time, but he cannot do it indefinitely."

"And," said Lentinus, beaming exuberantly, "I am preparing something else—to make Ozoacer's squatting *really* uncomfortable. Let us stop the night here with the troops, Saio Thorn. Then, tomorrow, ride with me around the siege line to where the river flows through it, and I will show you something much more entertaining than floating boxes."

I thought we might have to retrace our ride along the Via Popilia to make our way around Ravenna, but it turned out that our siege soldiers,

839

having little else to do, had paced out and marked a circuitous path of firm ground threading through the bogs and quaking-sands. So the next day we were able to ride almost as quickly and comfortably across country as on the dilapidated highway. The path led us inland, and eventually across the marsh road where I had seen the Polybian signal lights—only we crossed it much closer to Ravenna's walls, here visible in the distance—and at last we came to the river. Our siege line was interrupted by it, but I could see that the line of soldiers resumed on the northern bank. On this side, a score or more of our men, stripped to the waist because of the damp heat, were sweatily at work on the project Lentinus had brought me to see.

"This is the southernmost arm of the Padus River," he said. "Notice how, just to the east of us here, it forks into two branches to flow around Ravenna's walls on its way to the sea. That was not entirely nature's doing; the fossa is man-made, to provide water for the city. The river water, as you can see and smell, is not of the cleanest, coming through these swamps as it does. But it is Ravenna's only supply, because the city's one aqueduct has been derelict for ages. So—the waters flow around the walls, and close against them, and through low arches in them here and there, thence into canals that wind all inside the city. So—I am arranging to have those waters carry into Ravenna some small surprises as well."

I said admiringly, "For a neutral observer, Navarchus, you seem thoroughly to have entered into the spirit of conquest. Those things the men are building, are they *boats*? They look rather small and flimsy to carry soldiers."

"Boats, yes, but they are going in unmanned, so they need not be very sturdy. And they are purposely small, so they can slide easily under the walls' low arches."

"Then why do they each have a mast and sail? Will that not impede their going through arches?"

"They will go in," he said, with a happy grin, "upside down."

"Eh?" I could only stare in puzzlement at him and at the objects under discussion. Lentinus's new-built harbor craft were only giant boxes; these river craft were only shallow, oblong, wooden tubs, not much longer and wider than I was. Now I saw that, on the two or three nearing completion, the workers were fitting the masts to them, and fitting the masts into what *ought* to be the tubs' rounded undersides. And the masts were only crude, stumpy things, supporting very small, square canvas sails.

"The boat rides on the water's surface, like any boat," Lentinus explained, "but with the sail below water. That way the current propels it swiftly along, and the boat does not just drift, at risk of getting caught in the bankside reeds—or of getting caught crosswise in an arch or a narrow canal. Meanwhile, the shallow concavity of the upper side carries the cargo."

"How very clever," I murmured sincerely.

"It is not my own invention. The ancient Greeks, when they were still warlike, called this the khelé, the crab-claw. If an enemy fleet anchored in one of their harbors, they would stealthily send these downstream to infiltrate that fleet and, so to speak, claw at the enemy ships from underneath, in the manner of crabs."

"Claw at the enemy with what?" I asked. "What will be the cargo of these?"

He showed me, for one of the completed khelaí was just then being loaded. "Wet fire, we seafarers call it—another thing the Greeks invented, before they degenerated into a nation of jellyfish. The cargo is a mixture of sulfur, naphtha, pitch and quicklime. As you may or may not know, Saio Thorn, when quicklime is soaked with water, it becomes angry and hot—hot enough to ignite the other ingredients, and that mixture will burn fiercely even underwater. You have already discerned the flimsiness of the khelaí. Well, I have tried to calculate, making them just watertight enough to stay afloat until they are well inside Ravenna. Then they get waterlogged and the quicklime begins to heat and . . . " For a middle-aged man, he grinned like a mischievous boy. ". . . and *euax!* Wet fire!"

841

"Marvelous!" I exclaimed, and still sincerely. But I thought I ought also to speak a word of caution. "I imagine Theodoric would prefer to take Ravenna more or less intact. I doubt that he would applaud your burning the country's capital city to ashes and cinders."

Now he laughed. "Eheu, you and Theozoric need not worry. I am doing this only to bedevil Ozoacer, and to keep his warriors from sleeping soundly at night. Also, I confess, to provide some amusement for myself and some welcome diversion for your poor, bored, sweltering besiegers. After the first few khelaí do their crab-clawing, I doubt that the defenders will let any others get far enough inside the city to cause any real conflagration. But they *will* keep the defenders and the cityfolk awake and nervous and annoyed."

After dark, on Lentinus's instructions, several soldiers swam with one of the khelaí to the middle of the river, and there pointed it downstream and let it go. Then another khelé and another went briskly skimming off into the darkness. When the three were gone, we all lounged about the riverside, eyeing the distant pink sky-glow made by Ravenna's lamps and hearth fires. If any sentries on the city walls noticed the approaching khelaí, they probably took the things to be mere deadfall logs, because the river was thickly scummed with much other floating trash. Anyway, at least one of the crab-claws got through the wall and some way into the city's canals. We watchers saw the sky-glow abruptly and significantly brighten, and we all jumped up with cheers of "Sái!" and "Euax!" and pounded each other on the back. The wet fire went on burning for a long time, and we gleefully imagined the people yonder milling about in consternation and making ineffectual attempts to douse a blaze that mysteriously refused to be put out with water.

When the sky-glow had diminished to normal, I said to Lentinus, "I thank you for the entertainment. Tomorrow I will leave you and your men to your merry pranks. I will ride south again to report to Theodoric what is happening hereabout. And I shall be loud with praise of your ingenuity."

"Please!" he said, smiling and raising a hand in protest. "I beg you to respect my neutrality."

"Very well. I shall praise the *quality* of your neutrality. And, neutral or not, you will be the first to realize it when Ravenna has finally got over-nervous of wet fires, or has eaten its larders to the bare shelves, or simply has got weary of sitting under siege, and can hold out no longer. So I trust you will send a messenger galloping south the minute it does surrender."

✠   ✠   ✠

But Ravenna did not surrender.

It continued to sit stolidly closed and secretive and uncommunicative. Not even a timid emissary emerged to inquire about the possibility of negotiating favorable terms of surrender. Since there was nothing more we could do, except wait for the attrition of long siege to wear down Odoacer's obduracy, Theodoric decided to ignore the situation. He devoted the following months to governing his new domain as if its shuttered capital city and its sequestered ex-king did not even exist.

For example, he began apportioning among his followers the good land that they had won for him. Inasmuch as there were clearly no more major battles in prospect, Theodoric dispersed his troops in small forces all about the country. Then, more or less in emulation of Rome's long-traditional "colonatus" system, he allotted to each soldier of each of those forces a parcel of land in that vicinity (if the man wanted land) on which to build, to farm, to pasture herds, to do what he chose. Of course, many men chose, instead of land, to take an equivalent donative of money, and with it to set up a shop, a smithy, a stable or some other small business in a town or village. Tabernae were very popular enterprises.

✠ ✠ ✠

All those things were going on, and surely Odoacer knew of them from his speculatores' signals. Surely he realized that his onetime dominion was his no longer and never again would be. Surely, too, the living conditions inside Ravenna must be approaching the intolerable. Surely a rational man would by now have been suing for truce. But another winter went by, and no person, no word came out of there. Ravenna still did not surrender.

✠ ✠ ✠

As the veterans of the conquest settled down to be men of property for much of the time, warriors only when summoned by necessity, many of them began—with Theodoric's permission and assistance, and even en-couragement—bringing to Italia their families from back in Moesia. The Danuvius and Savus barges that had earlier served to transport our military supplies now were coming up those rivers laden with women and children and old folks and household goods. From the Savus riverhead in Noricum Mediterraneum, the families came overland, in trains of wagons furnished by the army quartermasters, through Venetia and on to their several desti-nations.

843

Theodoric, early on, sent for his own family, but they naturally traveled hither in rather more comfortable conveyances. His two daughters came in company with two cousins, a young man and woman, all escorted and shepherded by the princesses' aunt, the cousins' mother, who was of course Theodoric's surviving sister, Amalafrida. She, being some years older than Theodoric, might have been averse to leaving her longtime home estate in Moesia, except that she had been recently widowed by the death there of her husband, the herizogo Wulteric. This was the first time I had met the herizogin Amalafrida, and I found her appealingly auntish of aspect—tall, spare, stately, serene. Her daughter, Amalaberga, was fairly handsome, of a meek and retiring nature, likable enough. But the son, Theodahad, was a sullen, heavy-jawed, pimply youth for whom I did not care at all.

The princesses Arevagni and Thiudagotha flung themselves upon me with happy cries and warm embraces. They were both by now full-grown young ladies, very beautiful in their separate ways, and princessly in every degree. I had dreaded Thiudagotha's having to be told of the demise of her intended husband, King Freidereikhs, who had been still the boy Prince Frido when she last saw him. But, as I should have realized, the word of that had been borne back to the Novae palace long before. If Thiudagotha had wept then over her bereavement, she was at least not making a lifelong sorrow of it. On the many occasions that she and I would recollect some mutual memory of Frido, she always regally refrained from tears or mawkishness.

Those members of his family Theodoric housed for a time in a fine Mediolanum mansion that had fallen to him in the spoils, because he had already ordered that a palace be built for himself there, and another in Verona, which would forever be his favorite Italian city. Also, at the beginning of his handing out parcels of Italia's land, he had asked me what *I* would like—another country estate or a residence in some city or town. I had thanked him but declined taking anything, saying that I was more than satisfied with my farm outside Novae and did not wish to be encumbered with *too* many possessions.

✶ ✶ ✶

All those things were going on, and surely Odoacer knew of them from his speculatores' signals. What must have been his state of mind, now that the conqueror's *family* was contentedly installed in what had been his domain? And what, by now, must life have been like inside that sealed city? But still Ravenna did not surrender.

✶ ✶ ✶

844

There are other things I ought to mention in regard to those land allotments. No one would have seen anything remarkable in a conqueror's seizing as his rightful plunder every last jugerum of the conquered land, and everyone would have expected the consequence to be an anguished outcry from the dispossessed landowners. But neither of those things happened here. All that Theodoric appropriated—and then shared with his officers and troops—was the same one-third of Italia's estates that Odoacer had already impounded from the owners some years previous. Even what Theodoric kept for his own—the Mediolanum mansion in which he housed his royal relatives, the land on which he was having the new palaces built— even those he only took from what Odoacer had earlier taken from others. So, to say it simply, the former owners of those lands and properties were no worse off than before. Far from raising any complaint, they were pleasantly surprised and gratified by Theodoric's benevolent restraint, and most were praiseful of it.

Well, *some* people were outraged. Odoacer had made gifts of those selfsame confiscated lands to his accomplices and followers, and those men bitterly resented Theodoric's snatching the gifts away. Some of those held high administrative positions, everywhere from Rome to Ravenna to the outermost provinces, and, for one reason or another, had to be left in those positions. So they still wielded influence and were capable of using it to Theodoric's disadvantage.

The members of the Roman Senate, I hasten to say, were not among the malcontents. True, many senators understandably detested outlanders on principle, but all had the best interests of Rome at heart, and some senators, like Festus, were willing to cooperate with Theodoric from the beginning of his rule. Anyway, none would have dreamed of seeming greedy or petty by sniveling about "dissipation of assets." The Senate was, as it always had been, an assembly of old men from the oldest Roman families, and no patrician family would ever have stooped to such indignity. Anyway, many of those old Roman families could have been deprived of a third of their holdings without feeling much distress, some of them perhaps without even noticing it.

But there were others who, having benefited from Odoacer's reign, had gladly supported it—most notably the Catholic Christian Church and its higher-ranking clerics, whose vast estates Odoacer had conspicuously ex- **845** empted from his land confiscation. When Theodoric commenced the apportioning of land among his soldiers, the churchmen trembled in their liturgical shoes, certain that a "damnable Arian" would naturally, vindictively, gleefully seize upon the Church's lands and their personal estates. Indeed, it was widely rumored that it was nervous apprehension that felled Rome's Patriarch Bishop Felix III with an apoplexy. But Theodoric, like Odoacer, refrained from touching any least piece of Church property. That did not, however, lessen the clerics' execration of him. The same bishops and priests who had lavished hosannahs on their fellow Catholic Odoacer for his having "respected the sanctity" of their holdings now asserted that the Arian Theodoric *dared* not lay a hand on them—that he was a contemptible weakling as well as a despicable enemy. At any rate, and from whatever cause, Papa Felix did drop dead. He was replaced by a fractious old man named Gelasius, and this new Patriarch Bishop brought with him another vexation for Theodoric.

"Bishop Gelasius, or the pontiff, if you prefer," said Senator Festus, "is in extremely bad odor at Constantinople." The senator had just returned from his mission there, and had just been ushered into Theodoric's presence, and those were the first words he spoke. All of us in the room stared at him, mystified.

"What in the name of Pluto do I care about that?" Theodoric demanded. "You went to get the emperor's acknowledgment of my regnancy here. Did you get it?"

"No," Festus said. "I thought I would begin gently, by telling you why Anastasius refuses it."

"*Refuses it?!*"

"Well, withholds it. He maintains that, if you cannot even curb the ill-mannered behavior of a disputatious bishop, you are obviously not yet in full control of your new subjects, and—"

"Senator," Theodoric said icily. "Spare me the oration as well as the gentility. My temper is suddenly on a very short tether."

Festus began to speak quite rapidly. "It seems that Gelasius's first act as Patriarch Bishop of Rome was to denounce his brother prelate, the Patriarch Bishop Akakiós of Constantinople. News of this came while I was there. Papa Gelasius seems to feel that Bishop Akakiós has never been sufficiently severe in suppressing certain contumelious elements in the Eastern Church. The pontiff now demands that Akakiós's name be stricken from the diptych list of Christian fathers deserving the prayers of the faithful. All his cardinal priests at Rome, I am told, are sending letters broadcast, forbidding such prayers all over western Christendom. As you can imagine, this has caused an uproar of indignation in Constantinople. Anastasius says he hesitates to ordain you Teodoricus Rex Romani while his own irate subjects are raging for Rome to be burned to the ground and for everybody even remotely Roman to be banished to Gehenna. That is what he *says.* Of course, it is only a convenient excuse for him to go on postponing your—"

"Skeit!" bellowed Theodoric, smashing down his fist on the arm of his chair, and nearly splintering it. "Does the old fool expect me to intercede between two bickering bishops? I have a whole nation waiting to be governed, and I am denied even the proper authority to govern it. I refuse to believe that a quarrel among ecclesiastics takes precedence."

"As best I could gather," Festus said warily, "the quarrel concerns the Monophysite party in the Eastern Church. Gelasius apparently considers it a divisive element, and considers Akakiós overly tolerant of it. The Monophysites, you see, prefer to believe that the divine and human natures manifested in the person of Jesus—"

"*Iésus Xristus!* Another of those finical quibbles! Fighting over the shadow of an ass, the countryfolk call it. Skeit! Nearly five hundred years of Christianity, now, and still the Christian fathers ignore the real world around them while they pick at theological lint. They pretend to be sages settling

846

weighty questions, when they do not even know how to choose fitting titles for themselves. *Pontiff*, indeed! Is Gelasius ignorant that a pontifex was a *pagan* high priest? And *cardinal* deacons! Are they ignorant that Cardea was the pagan goddess of doorways? By the Styx, if Anastasius wants the Christian Church improved, let him begin by enlightening the stygian ignorance of Christians!"

"Ja, ja," rumbled Saio Soas, when Theodoric had momentarily subsided. "Also, *every* patriarch bishop yearns to be the one and only called Papa, hence to be the only one ranked with the sainted Leo of fifty years ago. And *he* was adoringly called Papa because the Roman Christians credited him with the miracle of having turned back Attila and his Huns from invading Italia. But the truth is that the Huns, being creatures of the cold northern climes, feared fevers and pestilences in these hotter southern lands. *That* is why Attila spared the Italia peninsula. Papa Leo may have been saintly, but he had nothing to do with it."

"Let us get back to the matters of today," said the senator. "Teodoric, if Anastasius will not cede you Rome, let Rome do it. Everyone knows that you are truly the new king, imperial sanction or no. Although Rome is not truly the capital city, I am sure I can persuade the Senate to accord you a triumph there, and—"

"No," Theodoric said gruffly.

"Why not?" Festus asked, in some exasperation. "Rome is yours—the Eternal City—but I am told that you have not yet gone to look at it even from a distance."

"And I will not now," said Theodoric. "I swore to myself that I would not set foot in Rome until I am King of Rome. King I cannot be until I first march into Ravenna, and am accorded the triumph *there*. If Anastasius had given me my due, I would be satisfied to go on waiting for Odoacer to wither on the vine. But now I will wait no longer." He turned to me. "Saio Thorn, you know that region better than any of us here. Go back to Ravenna. Find out how that skulking Odoacer has survived for so long. Then devise a sure way for me to get him out of there. Habái ita swe!"

847

1O

"hat can I say?" Lentinus shrugged. "Perhaps they are subsisting by eating each other in there. I can only tell you that the blockaders report not a single breach of the lines, not once, not by land, not by sea."

"And the men on the river are still nipping at them with the crab-claws?"

848

He nodded, without his former vivacity. "Even after all this time, though, there is no telling whether the eruptions of wet fire have much unnerved the people inside the walls. Outside the wall, I have to say, that little diversion has lost much of its enjoyability. The soldiers building the khelaí are about as weary and bored as the ones manning the floating boxes. So am I, to tell the truth. I can barely remember what it felt like to have a ship's deck beneath my feet."

I left him glooming there at Ariminum's harborside, and went away to ponder the situation. I sat on a marble bench and unseeingly eyed the city's proudest monument, the triumphal arch of Augustus, while I tried to ascertain—by thought alone—how a community the size of Ravenna could possibly have endured for so long without the benefit of provision. There were only three things going unimpeded into that city. One was the Padus River, but our khelaí builders would have intercepted anything attempting that ingress. Then there were the birds of the sea and marshes, but I doubted that Odoacer was, like Elijah, being fed by the birds. Finally, there were the torch signals. They were probably eagerly received by the Ravenna folk so isolated from the rest of the world, but they could not transmit nutriment . . .

Meanwhile, Theodoric was marching determinedly in this direction, leading a substantial attack force and expecting me to tell him, when he got here, how best to employ it. What advice could I proffer? I had no ideas at all, clever or otherwise . . .

Well, I said to myself, there was one aspect of the blockade that I had not yet personally inspected. I had not yet gone to take a look at the *other* end of our siege line, where it terminated at the seashore north of Ravenna.

Neither had Lentinus, it turned out, when I rejoined him. So he insisted, with a resurgence of his former enthusiasm, that we go there by sea. He gave commands, and rounded up a crew of navy men, and they slid a raven down the ways from a shed to the water, and they rowed us away with a will. It was the first time I had been aboard any seagoing vessel since my travels in the Eastern Empire—and the first time for Lentinus, he claimed, in almost as long—so we both thoroughly enjoyed the voyage. From Ariminum, the raven stayed close to the coast until we approached Ravenna, then veered far enough offshore to pass outside the harbor's barrier islands, so we would not risk being mistakenly attacked by our own patrolling troop boxes. We made landfall several miles north of there, where another of the many delta branches of the Padus empties into the Hadriatic, and where a community of butterfly tents lining the Via Popilia marked the siege soldiers' northern command camp.

849

The man in charge of this segment of the line was a Latin-speaking *centurio regionarius* named Gudahals, of oxlike build and oxlike torpidness and evidently oxlike intellect. But then, what better sort of man for the dreary job of supervising a static, tedious, interminable siege? Or that is what I thought until—after he and I and Lentinus had lounged for some while on the pillows in his tent, indulging in congenial conversation, wine and cheese—Gudahals said complacently, for about the eighth time:

"Absolutely *nothing* goes into Ravenna, Saio Thorn," then added, just as complacently, "Except the salt."

Those words hung in the air for a moment, while Lentinus and I regarded them in stunned astonishment. Then he and I said in breathless unison, "What?"

Blithely not noticing our fixed stare, Gudahals said, still with utter complacency, "The mule trains of salt."

The *navarchus* and I were now sitting rigidly upright. I waved a hand for Lentinus to leave this to me, and I said, but only casually, "Tell us about the mule trains, Centurio."

"Why, the ones that come down from the *Regio Salinarum* of the high Alpes, and come hither along the Via Popilia. It was for their convenience that the Popilian Way was built, or so I am told by the drovers. They bring salt from the mines up yonder, as they have been doing for centuries, to be shipped abroad by the merchants of Ravenna."

Gently, as if talking to a child, I said, "Centurio Gudahals, the merchants of Ravenna are no longer doing business."

"Right enough!" he exclaimed, with a comfortable chuckle. "We are seeing to that, are we not? So, since the salt can no longer be shipped out of Ravenna, the mule trains go right on through there, to Ariminum instead."

Because Lentinus had gone so red in the face that he looked ready to imitate Papa Felix's apoplexy, I let him speak. To his credit, he too kept his voice under control. "Meaning that the trains come first through your siege line here, of course."

Gudahals looked puzzled. "But of course, Navarchus. How else would they proceed onward to Ariminum?"

"These trains—how many mules?" I asked. "How much do they carry? Do they come with some frequency?"

"Fairly regularly, Marshal. About twice a week since I have been here. The teamsters say that is normal traffic." He paused to tilt his wineskin above his open mouth and imbibe a long squirt from it. "Twenty to thirty mules in each train. But I could not pretend to estimate the total weight of their load in librae or amphorae. A formidable amount, to be sure."

Lentinus, as if he could not believe what he had heard the first time, said again, "And you and your men have let every one of those trains go through your line here—without argument or impediment."

"But of course," Gudahals also said again. "I would never think of disobeying the orders of my superiors."

"*Orders?!*" Lentinus croaked, his eyes bulging.

Gently, as if talking to a child, Gudahals explained. "When General Herduic posted us here, he instructed me, as commanding centurio, most particularly *not* to do or allow my men to do certain things. Looting, raping, pilfering, any such activities prejudicial to good order. We are outlanders here, the general said; we must gain the respect of the natives, so they will look kindly on Theodoric as their new king. The general also said that we were not to do anything that would disrupt the native peoples' occupations and livelihood—except those people in Ravenna, of course. Well, the mule-train drovers tell me that salt has always been one of the most profitable commodities of Roman commerce."

"Liufs Guth . . ." I breathed, appalled.

"It is true, Marshal! Ever since the Romans first discovered those rich mines of salt in the Alpes, Rome has strictly, jealously kept possession of that salt trade. Naturally, I am most eager to do whatever I can to assist my King Theodoric in winning the affection of his new subjects. I am likewise careful not to do anything that would lower his esteem, such as offending the Roman people by obstructing their commerce in salt."

Lentinus had buried his face in his hands.

"Tell me, Gudahals," I said with a sigh, "when those mule trains come back this way—from Ariminum—do they carry any goods procured in exchange for all that valuable salt?"

"Eheu, Saio Thorn!" he cried cheerfully. "You are trying to catch me out—to make me say that I have been napping." Still cheerfully, he took another swig of his wine. "No, no. Every mule has come back through here *unladen*. What the teamsters are getting for their salt, I do not know— perhaps drafts against payment in the future. But they do not acquire other goods. How could they? If they returned from Ariminum bearing anything of the sort, my counterpart commander at the siege line in the south would halt them and strip them clean. He would not let them proceed on through Ravenna, lest they hand over those goods to Odoacer and his allies there. That would be a breach of the siege, taking provisions to the enemy. However, since every train is unladen when it comes back here, that com-mander is obviously also doing his job at that end. All in accordance with General Herduic's instructions to me."

851

Lentinus and I looked despairingly at one another, and then pityingly at the witless, artless, boastful nauthing who had so ingenuously been so ruinous.

"Just one more thing," I said, almost not caring to hear the reply. "Did it ever occur to you, Centurio, to inspect the mule trains' packs of salt before you let them pass here?"

He spread his hands and smiled. "After the first time, Marshal, the first two or three bales . . . well, salt is salt. And heavy, let me tell you. One feels sorry for the wretched mules, having to stagger so far, so painfully, under such burdens. After the first few mules, one mercifully desists from unload-ing them and inspecting and loading again. That is harder on the poor animals than—"

"Benigne, Centurio. Thags izvis, Gudahals, for the wine and the cheese and the edifying summary of the salt trade." I stood up and reached down his belted sword, emblem of his office, from the tent pole where it hung. "You are relieved of your command and you are under arrest." He was just then taking another squirt from his wineskin, and he choked and splut-tered.

I stepped to the tent opening and bawled for the second-in-command to present himself. He was an optio named Landerit, and he moved smartly when I ordered him to secure Gudahals under guard, to turn out enough armed men to be ready, day and night, to stop and detain the next mule train that came along the Via Popilia from either direction.

"I ought to be arrested and deposed too," Lentinus growled in self-disgust.

"Then so should I," I said. "But how could we have known of this weak link in the chain?" I added, with a rueful attempt at humor, "Anyway, you are a neutral bystander, remember. You and I have no authority to arrest one another."

He spat out an oath. "Shall we fall upon our separate swords, then?"

"Let us try to make the best of Fortune's dice throw here. This is what I propose . . ."

✠   ✠   ✠

Two days later: "Who sent these things?" I demanded of the mule train's chief drover as I kicked a foot at the pile of goods—mostly pickled meats and skins of oil—that Optio Landerit and his guards had found concealed inside the salt bales.

The teamster was gray-faced and quaking, but he answered stoutly enough, "The director of the Saltwaúrtswa Haustaths." I had already half guessed that much, but I would not have known *this* man if he had not added, with wan pride, "My father."

I said, "I should have thought Georgius Honoratus much too old, by now, to be playing such dangerous games."

The son looked startled when I spoke the name, but muttered, "He is still a loyal Roman, and not too old to be brave in the service of our fatherland."

I remembered a remark made by my fellow marshal Soas, about expatriates who meddle in their home country's affairs from a prudent distance. But I did not bother to inquire what reasons old Georgius XIII or XIV might have for wanting to serve the outcast Odoacer. I said only:

"I do not much admire vicarious bravery. Georgius sent you to do his treason for him. And your brother also, I presume. Where is that one?"

"Who are you?" the man said hoarsely, squinting at me. "Do we know you?" When I did not reply, he mumbled, "My brother and I take turn about at leading an occasional train. We need not; there are many other teamsters. But we do it proudly . . . pro patria . . . to participate . . ."

"And to get briefly away from your brave father," I suggested coldly.

"Then I shall look forward to meeting your brother too. And your sister? Does she also participate in your father's vaunted bravery?"

"Who *are* you, man?" Again I replied only with a grim stare, so he said sullenly, "She married, years ago—a rich merchant—and went away from home."

"A pity," I said. "She deserved better than a merchant. But at least she shed her spunkless siblings. I will wager that *you* never married, or your brother. Georgius would not have emancipated his two most abject slaves."

Now it was he who returned no comment, but I made him blink in bewilderment when I snapped, "Take off your clothes." I did not stay to watch that, but told Optio Landerit, "When all the teamsters are undressed, stuff them into the sacks in place of the confiscated provisions. Then top up the sacks again with salt. While that is being done, have Centurio Gudahals brought to my tent."

As it happened, we had caught two mule trains coming through our line almost at the same time—this well-laden one arriving from the north, an unburdened one on its way back from having unloaded in Ravenna. So we had detained, altogether, ten teamsters and forty-odd mules. When Guda-hals arrived at my tent, he was walling his ox eyes back to where the captured smugglers now were uttering cries of horror and pleas for mercy as they were forced into the big canvas sacks. Gudahals no doubt thought I was going to have him salted away in the same manner, so his bovine face brightened when I said:

853

"Centurio, I am giving you an opportunity to redeem yourself." He began to moo in gratitude, but I waved that away. "You will take four horsemen and ride at full tilt northward—the Via Popilia, the Via Claudia Augusta, the Dravus Valley through the Alpes—to Haustaths in the Regio Salinarum, which is where the smugglers come from." I gave him explicit directions for finding the mine, and a description of Georgius Honoratus, as I remembered him. "You are to bring that man back with you, and deliver him to Theodoric or myself, to no lesser officer. Georgius is a very old man by now, so be tender with him. Theodoric will want that man in prime condition when he is crucified upon a patibulum. So I warn you: if you fail to find Georgius, or for any reason fail to abduct him, or if the least harm befalls him on the way back . . ." I waited until Gudahals began to sweat, then said, "Do not come back yourself."

The centurio would have done his best to salute me and run for his horse at the same time, but I had a further instruction. "I do not believe the smuggled goods came all the way from Haustaths. It would have been foolish of the drovers to make their animals carry those burdens from the start of the journey. They came with the pack saddles and sacks, and some amount of salt, but the provisions would have been added somewhere much nearer here. If, on your way, you can find that place, and the person or persons responsible—or perhaps make Georgius tell, if you can do that *without hurting him*—then you will have redeemed yourself amply indeed."

Gudahals and his four men were already pelting out of the camp and off along the Popilian Way when Optio Landerit came to my tent to salute and report:

"When the salt bales ceased their slow squirming, Saio Thorn, they were rather lumpy and contorted. So we poured in more salt to make them as neat and firm and plump as they were before, and we have lashed them across the pack saddles of ten of the fresher mules. On another ten of the fresher mules we have put sacks filled with nothing but salt. So we again have a properly laden twenty-mule train."

"Very good, Optio. The leftover mules you can put with your own herd of draft animals; they will not be needed. Now, we must get our—shall we say—Trojan mules on their way. Obviously, even with this back-door source of supply, Ravenna has been on very skimpy, very stale rations for a very long while. The poor famished people will be anxiously awaiting every new arrival. I hope they like the salt meat they are getting this time."

Landerit murmured, "It will be interesting to see if they are hungry enough to *eat* it."

"However," I said, "Odoacer's sentries around the city are disciplined Roman legionaries. Hungry or not, they will be alert for anything suspicious. The mule train must resemble every previous mule train. That means no more than five drovers. So go and find four good men of ours who are willing to walk unarmed into the enemy's stronghold. Have them start sorting through the teamsters' cast-off clothing and find garments to fit."

"Four men?" The optio grinned in anticipation. "And I will be the fifth Trojan?"

"No, I will be. That is how I planned it with the Navarchus Lentinus before he sailed southward. He will be expecting to meet *me* on the far side of Ravenna—assuming we Trojans get through it. I have something else for you to attend to. There are surely other mule trains on their way here from the north. Confiscate the goods, salt down the teamsters, just as you did with this train. Then send those trains back the way they came, with men of your own as the drovers." I explained to him as I had done to the centurio. "Somewhere along the roads there are other persons who connived in this plot. Gudahals is looking for them; so will your men in disguise."

Landerit looked disappointed, but he nodded. "I understand, Saio Thorn. Any such conspirators are bound to look surprised when they see their supplies returning. They will look even more so if we let them open the bales. By that we shall know them. And . . . we slay them?"

"Of course. I have told Gudahals to bring me the chief conspirator; I do not need the lesser fry. And here, Optio. I will also entrust to you the keeping of my arms and armor while I am gone."

He said, "I know it is none of my concern, Marshal, but I cannot help being curious. How *did* you know so much about the source of the trains, that Haustaths?"

"In my youth I spent part of a summer in that beautiful place. The Place of Echoes." I paused and mused. "I did not suspect, back then, that I would hear an echo of it again in my lifetime."

✠ ✠ ✠

"Blessed are the peacemakers." In a hushed voice Theodoric quoted the apostle Matthew, as he wonderingly regarded me and the other four team-sters and Navarchus Lentinus and the captive prizes that we had waiting for him in Ariminum. "Tell me how you got them."

"It was no great feat," I said modestly. "The Ravenna sentries let our Trojan mule train into the city with no more than stares of scrutiny. At the city's center there was quite a body of soldiers waiting to receive the mules from us. My men kept silent as instructed, and I was able to chatter famil-iarly about Haustaths to the optio to whom I relinquished the train."

"What would you have done," Theodoric asked amusedly, "if the sol-diers had slashed open the Trojan bales then and there?"

"Happily for us, they did not. As might be supposed, they led the mules off to separate quarters of the city, so the provisions could be equitably apportioned and distributed. And by the way, during our brief visit there, I gathered that Ravenna still has a decent store of grains and other dry staples, but the trains were the only source of really *chewable* food and savor-giving oil. Anyway, as soon as the soldiers had the mules, they took no further interest in us drovers. We wandered off without restriction."

Theodoric laughed. "Did you hear the howls that must have gone up when the bales *were* opened?"

"I was expecting to, at any instant. I knew we had to move quickly, before the outraged soldiers came looking for us. Well, we were too few to do any significant damage to the city's defenses, even if we could have gone to ground and labored subversively for weeks. So our best hope was to steal something. Something that would come in useful as a pry bar, so to speak, when we got it outside the city walls. Of course, I should have *liked* to abduct Odoacer, but we had no time to search for him. Besides, I knew he would be heavily guarded, and we were unarmed. Then I espied the Basilica of St. John, and knew it to be Ravenna's Catholic cathedral. Even the conscientious legionaries do not trouble to guard churches. So we entered and, resident in the presbytery there, we found these—our prizes."

Theodoric looked at them appreciatively, appraisingly, lovingly. They looked not so lovingly back.

"By this time," I continued, "there *was* some commotion going on. People running about and shouting. Probably some of them were the soldiers raging in search of us. But part of the confusion was supplied by the good navarchus here." I deferred to Lentinus, and he said:

"As arranged, Theozoric, I had hastened back to my workers at the Padus, carrying fresh supplies of wood and fuel. I made the men work frenziedly at building more and more khelaí—even utilizing the swamp's canes and reeds—and we began sending those in under Ravenna's walls by day as well as night. Thorn tells me that several of them went up in blazes of wet fire, most fortuitously, just as he and his men and their captives emerged from the cathedral. So the crab-claws may have helped, but I believe the escape could have been effected even without them. Remember, a city's guards are concerned with keeping enemies from getting *in*. These were going *out*.".

"And," I said, "we tried to look utterly unconcerned, unhurried, as if we had legitimate business outside the gates. Anyway, it worked. Five travel-worn peasants and two shuffling priests—we got scarcely a glance from the guards as we departed. And the two priests obliged us by not shouting or even whimpering to be rescued. For maintaining silence, a dagger point in the armpit works better than a vow."

"And here you are," said Theodoric, shaking his head in open admiration.

"And here we are," I said. "Allow me to introduce our priestly prizes. The younger and fatter one—at least we have been hospitably feeding him to fatten him up—the one who is trying so hard to look saintly patient and forgiving of his captors, he is Ravenna's Catholic Archbishop John. The other, the wispy, frail and tremulous old man—he really *is* a saint, named a saint in his own time, probably the only saint that you and I, King Theodoric, will ever be privileged to see in *our* time. You have heard of him before. He is Odoacer's lifelong mentor and tutor and confessor and personal chaplain, St. Severinus."

✠　✠　✠

"It is up to Odoacer," said Theodoric. "Give up the city or the saint."

He and we officers and the two newly acquired guests were reclining at refection in the triclinium of Theodoric's borrowed Ariminum palace. We were being lavishly regaled with succulent viands but, while Bishop John was eating with two-fisted vigor, St. Severinus was only indifferently picking at things with his quivery old fingers.

"Teodoric, my son, my son..." the bishop said, with the Roman pronunciation of the name. He swallowed a huge mouthful of meat, and then indicated me. "This person is already damned to be miserable for the rest of his life, and afterward to suffer the torments of Gehenna throughout eternity, because he laid hands on the sainted Severinus. Surely you, Teodoric, will not likewise imperil your hope of heaven by doing harm to a Christian saint."

"A Catholic saint," Theodoric said imperturbably. "I am not a Catholic."

857

"My son, my son, Severinus was sanctified by the sovereign pontiff of *all* Christendom." John piously sketched the sign of the cross on his forehead. "Therefore every Christian must revere and respect a saint who—"

"Balgs-daddja," General Pitzias rudely grunted. "I should expect a saint to be punishing our impieties at this very moment with a divine thunderbolt. But he is not even uttering harsh words."

"Or any words," said Bishop John. "The saint no longer talks."

"Is he injured? Unwell?" asked Theodoric. "I do not want to lose him beforetime. Shall I summon a medicus?"

"No, no," said John. "Since some years now, he has not spoken, nor seemed to hear, nor availed himself of any of his other senses. If he were an ordinary mortal, one would suppose him merely far gone in senile decay. But it is clear, Severinus being a saint, that he is emulating a fellow saint, following Paul's injunction to mind only the things that are above, not the things that are on the earth. You will notice that he even refrains from eating anything except a crumb now and then. To us in Ravenna, since we have *had* to live on crumbs, the saint's serene self-denial has been an inspiration for our imitation."

"If you value and adore him so much, then," said Theodoric, "you will not want anything to happen to him."

"My son, my son," John said yet again, wringing his hands. "Do you really wish me to go back and tell Odoacer that you threaten injury to the sainted Severinus, unless—"

"I do not care *what* you tell him, Bishop. From what I know of Odoacer, he will not risk his skin to save that of even his favorite saint. The man cravenly hid himself among a crowd of his subjects in order to flee unnoticed from Verona. He had several hundred unarmed and helpless captives butchered rather than chance their hindering his flight into Ravenna yonder. Ever since then, he has been subjecting that whole city's populace to deplorable privation, just so he can keep *on* hiding in there. That is why I doubt that any threat to any other person on this earth would make him surrender Ravenna to me. Yet that is what he must do."

"But . . . but . . . if he does not?"

"If he does not, you will learn, Bishop, that I can be as ruthless and brutal as Odoacer. So, if *you* care what becomes of the sainted Severinus, you had better concoct a very persuasive argument, an *irresistible* argument, with which to sway Odoacer. And do it quickly. You will be escorted back to Ravenna tomorrow." He paused to calculate. "Two days to get there, two days back. I will give you until tomorrow week to return here with Odoacer's unconditional surrender. Ita fiat! Be it so!"

858

✠   ✠   ✠

It was I who rode with Bishop John out of Ariminum along the Via Popilia, giving him safe-conduct through our siege lines. And, holding aloft a white signum indutiae, I accompanied him all the way to Ravenna's outer guard lines south of the Classis port. During the two-day ride, I refrained from inquiring how John had decided to put our demands when he faced Odoacer. (And of course I was not going to point out to him that Theodoric never really had said that he *would* harm the fragile and dotard old Severinus.) When I handed over the bishop to the Roman guards, they gave me very sour looks, because by then every last person in and around Ravenna knew of the humiliating Trojan-mule incident.

I returned to our line and waited, not at all sure what to expect next. If any of our soldiers there had proposed a wager on the outcome of this enterprise, I would have been uncertain whether to lay my money on success or failure. Even when a legionary came, riding with a signum indutiae and with Bishop John riding beside him, I still would not have known which way to wager. John *had* returned from the enemy's lair, at any rate, and not carrying his head on his saddle horn. Was that a hopeful sign? His face gave me no hint.

When it was only he and myself riding back along the Popilian Way, I could no longer resist saying, "Well?"

"As Teodoric demanded," he said, not very joyously, "Odoacer capitulates."

"*Euax!*" I exclaimed. "Gratulatio, Bishop John! You have done a good thing, both for your native city and for your native land. But allow me a shrewd and sly conjecture. Odoacer was more than ready to surrender, am I right? His pretending now to do it only for the sake of dear old St. Severinus saves his losing countenance. Even gives him a specious air of noble self-sacrifice. Is that not how it seemed to you?"

"No," he said, rather sulkily. "Teodoric was right. Odoacer would *not* have done it for the sake of Severinus. I had to offer him more than a saint."

"Then you did employ some additional argument? Well, if it served to sway Odoacer, I applaud your powers of invention."

John rode on for several paces without commenting, so I added, "You do not seem very happy about your success."

He still did not comment, so I said, frowning, "Bishop, what *did* you offer Odoacer? His life? Safe exile? A competence? What?"

He blew out a sigh that made his jowls shake. "Co-rulership. Equal kingship with Teodoric. The two of them to reign henceforward side by side, as do the brother-kings of the Burgunds."

I stopped Velox, reached for John's reins and hauled his horse also to a stop, saying in a hiss, *"Are you insane?"*

"Teodoric said—you were there; you heard him—he said that he did not care *what* I proposed."

I stared at the man, aghast. "Theodoric was under the misapprehension that you had good sense. When he learns how wrong he was, he will be exceedingly dismayed. So will you. Eheu. I can see it now."

His heavy underlip quivered, but he said stubbornly, "I have given my word. Odoacer accepted it. So must Teodoric. I am, after all, an archbishop of Holy—"

"You are an imbecile! Theodoric would have done better to send that drooling dotterel Severinus. Who ever heard of the vanquished dictating terms to the victor? Look you. Here stands Theodoric, triumphantly astride this whole land. There lies Odoacer, supine, flattened, crushed—but shaking his fist and crowing—'I am your equal, by order of the Archbishop John!'" Disgustedly, I tossed the reins back. "Come along, then. I can hardly *wait* to see this."

He said again, but shakily now, "I have given my word. The word of a reverend arch—"

"Hold a moment," I said, halting Velox once more. "You must have made some arrangements for the meeting of these two peculiar brotherly kings—the sealing of their comically peculiar partnership. What arrangements?"

"Why, an occasion of great pomp and ceremony, of course. Teodoric marches into Ravenna at the head of his troops. He is accorded the triumph, with all the customary formalities. I myself deck him with the laurel and the toga picta. The defending forces pledge him their oath and their arms. The people lining the streets prostrate themselves in token of submission. After victory prayers at the cathedral, Teodoric proceeds to Odoacer's residence, the palace called the Laurel Grove. There is a banquet laid and waiting. The two men embrace in amity and—"

"That will do," I said, and he sat silent while I pondered on those things. Then I said, "Yes, that will do admirably. Theodoric enters the city; the defenders and the inhabitants submit. That is all he will expect, because that is all you will tell him, Bishop John. Let him believe that when he meets Odoacer it will be only to accept his sword in surrender."

860   John recoiled in horror. "You are suggesting to an archbishop the commission of sin! I would be lying to Teodoric! I would be breaking my pledged word to Odoacer!"

"You would do neither. I suggest only that you trim an edge off the truth. If you were to tell Theodoric the incredible terms you have negotiated, he would certainly have you disemboweled on the spot. But more than that. He is a man of honor. He would refuse to march into the city, even though Odoacer throws it wide open before him. Therefore, Bishop John, you simply omit to mention the equal-king stipulation of the surrender, and you run out of breath before you finish telling of the ceremonial arrangements. After Theodoric's entry and acceptance of the city's submission, he proceeds to the Laurel Grove palace to meet Odoacer. That is all. Stop there. If, at that point, something should occur to blemish your pledged word . . . well, it is hardly your fault, is it?"

"You are still asking of me the sin of omission. And I am an archbishop of Holy—"

"Console yourself with this. A wise abbot once told me that Mother Church allows her ministers occasionally to assist her cause with the aid of pious artifice."

John showed one last flicker of righteous resistance. "You are asking me to assist the cause of *Teodoric*. An Arian. A heretic. How could I persuade even my own conscience that I am thereby helping Mother Church?"

I said pointedly, "You are saving her having to seek a new archbishop for her episcopate of Ravenna. Now come along, and tell Theodoric that he has the unconditional surrender he wanted."

✠   ✠   ✠

And so, because I made sure that my king knew nothing of the "co-rulership" pact that Odoacer had agreed upon, it came to pass that Theodoric commenced his reign with one regrettably unwise deed. I might have foreseen it, because I knew how he had acted on other such occasions, without hesitation or compunction. And later, looking back, I often wished that I had somehow managed to advise against this impulsive action. But at the time I thought nothing except that Theodoric had every reason and right to do what he did.

On a March day in the year 493 by the Christian count, Flavius Theodoricus Rex made his triumphal entry into Ravenna, but what he did on that spring day would cast an autumnal shadow down all the years to follow. When the rites and ovations and prayers were concluded, he and we attendants proceeded on to the Laurel Grove palace, and there met Odoacer for the first time face to face. He was old, bent, bald—and apparently unembarrassed by hypocrisy, because he came to meet us with a welcoming smile, with his arms outstretched for the fraternal embrace. But Theodoric ignored the gesture and reached instead for his sword.

861

On that March day in the 1,246th Year of Rome's Founding, the Western Roman Empire was given rebirth and renewal. It would flourish splendidly in Theodoric's keeping, but it would never quite forgive what he did on that day. Theodoric drew his snake blade. Odoacer backed away in surprise and terror. He gasped, "Huar ist gudja? Ubinam Iohannes? Where is Bishop John?" and his eyes sought here and there about the hall, but the complicitous archbishop had prudently not come with us from the cathedral.

On that March day began a reign the most laudable that any nation in Europe had enjoyed in many centuries. But Theodoric would have his detractors and rivals and enemies, and they would remember—they would see to it that others remembered—what he did on that day. He swung his sword like an ax, two-handed, and cleaved Odoacer from collarbone to beltline. Then, as the sundered corpse crumpled limply to the floor, Theodoric turned to us and said, "Herduic, you were right. You once remarked that Odoacer must have gone boneless with age."

From that long-ago day to this, there would ever be a cloud darkening even the brightest skies of the goodly reign of Theodoric the Great.

THE GOTHIC

KINGDOM

SCOTIA
(IRELAND)

TIN
ISLANDS
(BRITTANIA)

Germanic
Ocean
(North Sea)

SKAND

•Deva
(Chester)

RUGIL
(RÜG

CORNOVIA
(CORNWALL)

TOXANORIA

GERMAN

BELGICA

Rhenus R.

•Isenacum
(Eisenach)

ARMORICA

Durocortorum
(Reims)

Lutetia
(Paris)

GALLIA

Cabillonum
(Châlons-sur-
Marne)

(Rhein/Rhine R.)

Castra
Regina
(Regensburg

Pictavus
(Poitiers)

BURGUND
LANDS

Lugdunum
(Lyons)

Genava
(Geneva)

Mediolanum
(Milan)

Verona

Aqu

AQUITANIA

Arelate
(Arles)

ITAL

Ravenn

Tolosa
(Toulouse)

Massilia
(Marseilles)

Genua (Genoa)

Roma

HISPANIA

Neapolis
(Napl

Mess
(Mess

Panormus
(Palermo)

SICI
(S

Carthage

LIBYA

©A·Karl/J.Kemp, 1992

(ÖTLAND)
TALAND)

matic
an
ic Sea)

Wendic Gulf (Bay of Danzig)
Pomore
(Gdansk)

Bsheshch
(Brest)

Miles
0 ———————————— 400
0 ———————————— 400
Roman Miles

N

S A R M A T I A

• **Lviv** (L'vov)

dobona
(Vienna)

Danuvius R.

Singidunum
(Belgrade)

Noviodunum
(Tulcea)

Novae
(Svishtov)

(*Danube R.*)

Constantiana
(Constanţa)

CHERSONESUS
(CRIMEA)

COLCHIS
(GEORGIA)

LMATIA

Dyrrachium
(Durrës)

Salonika
(Thessaloniki)

Constantinople
(Istanbul)

A S I A
M I N O R

Athens

CYPROS
(CYPRUS)

1

ot even Odoacer's closest friends and associates would have denied that he had deserved his execution. And not even Theodoric's most critical opponents would have denied that a victorious monarch, in dealing with his defeated foes, had every right to play judex, lictor et exitium. Certainly no one anywhere murmured the least complaint when the traitorous Georgius Honoratus was fetched from Haustaths and Theodoric sentenced that old wretch to a punishment rather more severe than mere death. What did cause so many people to look askance at Theodoric, after his slaying of Odoacer, was one particular circumstance: Ravenna's Archbishop John told an outrageous lie.

Although John had been indignantly reluctant to tamper with the truth when I asked him to, he later told a greater lie of his own volition, even though, according to his professed Christian beliefs, that sin put his Christian soul at hazard. What happened was this:

Theodoric had barely got his saddlebags unpacked in Ravenna when a delegation of Church dignitaries arrived from Rome. The Patriarch Bishop Gelasius was not among them—he regarded himself as too exalted to go calling on a king—but the embassy of "cardinal deacons" said he had given them authority to speak for "all of Holy Church." Their speaking was at first obsequious, almost cringing. Indeed, they talked for such a long time in looping circumlocutions that it took Theodoric a while to determine what they were talking *about*. At last he grasped that they and the Church were worried, well-nigh frantic. And what about? Well, he, Theodoric, had overthrown a king who had been a Catholic Christian. He, the new king, was an Arian. The deacons were anxious to know: did he intend (as anyone would expect of a *Catholic* monarch) to impose his own religion as the state religion?

Theodoric laughed. "Why would I? I do not care what beliefs or superstitions my people choose to hold, so long as those do not cause disorderly conduct. Even if I did care, I could not legislate or enforce any change in men's minds."

That put the cardinal deacons at ease—so much so that they shed their servile manner and ventured upon cajolery. If Theodoric did not care what his people believed, then would he have any objection to the Church's doing its best to convert the new Arian and pagan immigrants to the locally prevailing belief, the *true* belief?

Theodoric shrugged tolerantly. "You are free to try. I say again, I have no power over men's minds."

So now the deacons moved from cajolery to importunity. It would greatly aid the Church's campaign of conversion, they said, and would greatly gratify Papa Gelasius if—since Theodoric really did not *care* what the Church did—he would give his *sanction* to what it did. That is, if he would publicly proclaim that he was letting Catholic missionaries and evangelists, with his blessing, move among his Arian and pagan subjects, with the intent of sowing sanctified wheat where only wicked weeds had grown before, and . . .

"Hold," said Theodoric stonily. "I have given you permission. I will not give you privilege. I will no more endorse your proselytizing than I would that of an Old Religion wise-sayer."

At which, the delegation did much forehead-clapping and hand-wringing and dolorous moaning. This might have impressed some observers as sincere affliction, but Theodoric was only annoyed by it. He gruffly bade the clerics begone, and that *did* distress them. Considering how worriedly they had arrived, they should have left relieved, but they departed grumbling that they had been rudely turned away without a fair hearing.

Theodoric clearly did not forget the incident, or minify it. Very soon thereafter, he published a statement that he would stand by throughout his reign. Then and since, many of the world's rulers and divines and philosophers have marveled at the novelty of a monarch's uttering such a sentiment, and just as many others have ruefully shaken their heads at the folly of it:

"Religionem imperare non possumus, quis nemo cogitur ut credat invitus. Galáubeins ni mag weis anabudáima; ni ains hun galáubjáith withra is wilja. We cannot command religion; no one can be forced to believe against his will."

The Church of Rome was, of course, *committed* to making all mankind adopt and embrace and be subject to its creed. So if, until now, its clerics had only mistrusted Theodoric as an unbeliever and an interloper, his "non possumus" pronouncement made them hate and condemn him as a deadly enemy to their mission in this world, their holy calling, their livelihood and their very existence. They could cite the words of Jesus, "He that is not with me is against me." From this time forward, the Catholic Christian Church would ceaselessly, unrelentingly work for Theodoric's downfall, and would implacably oppose his every act of rulership.

That is why, when Ravenna's Archbishop John was stricken with a sudden illness, there were many who whispered that he had been poisoned by his Church superiors, in punishment for the part he had played in securing Theodoric's regnancy. If that was so, John obviously forgave his poisoners, because, on his deathbed, he told a lie intended to discredit his Church's enemy, Theodoric. To the priests giving him the last rites, John repeated what he had once told me: that he had got Odoacer to surrender Ravenna only on condition that the two kings would thereafter reign as co-equals. But then John added the untruth: that *Theodoric had also agreed to that*. And then John died, presumably into hell. But the lie endured and was repeated—the Church saw to that—and the charge was widely believed forever after: that Theodoric had pledged his word to both a holy man and a fellow king, just to get easily inside Ravenna, then had treacherously slain an unarmed, unresisting old man who had trusted his word.

There was no one to refute the accusation except Theodoric and myself. And our word had little weight against that of a high priest about to stand before the Judgment Seat. Not many would believe that John had lied and thereby deliberately invited damnation. But I knew it to be a fact, and I knew that he had done it to *make* the lie that much more believable. For the sake of his Church, John had done a thing that, however reprehensible, was certainly a brave act of self-sacrifice. It earned him a tomb burial with all the Church's honors and reverence, and I—even I—hope that hell dealt leniently with him.

Meanwhile, some of Theodoric's best-intentioned actions were giving the Catholics opportunities to find fault with him—or to impute fault, if they could not find any. When he set his troops in Verona to demolishing the tumbledown old Chapel of St. Stephen there, an outcry of course went up from the churchmen. They were not at all mollified by his patient explanation that the chapel's removal was necessary in order to strengthen the city's defensive wall. Even louder protest went

869

up when Theodoric began *employing Jews* in his service. He recruited a
number of Jewish merchants to handle certain treasury accounts, for
the very good reason that Jews, however cunning they may be at using
numbers to their own business advantage, are certainly scrupulous and
dependable in the counting and adding of numbers, and Theodoric
wanted his accounts to be accurate.

That brought Laurentius, the Catholic Bishop of Mediolanum,
storming all the way from there to Ravenna to thunder, "Christians
could do that work just as well! Why do you give preference to filthy
Jews?"

Theodoric placidly retorted, "Christian workers, Laurentius, are
overly concerned with their right to rest during one day out of every
seven. Jews are more concerned that on the other six days a man ought
to *work*. And you, do not ever dare to shout at me again."

It goes without saying that the Jews in the cities of Italia, like the
city Jews everywhere in the world, had forever been resented and reviled by their Christian neighbors, and for the same reason: not because
they were of alien religion, not because they bore the blame for the
killing of Jesus, but because they generally had made themselves more
prosperous than their immediate Christian neighbors. Now, however,
Italia's Jews began to suffer worse things than revilement. That was
because the Catholics, while they could safely go on preaching and
ranting against the "heretic Arians," obviously could not raise their
hands against an armed occupying force. Against the unarmed, pacific,
defenseless Jews, they could and did.

In Theodoric's own capital city of Ravenna, a crowd was whipped to
riot—apparently by some Christian citizen protesting the rate of interest charged by a Jew who had lent him money—and, during the commotion, the Jews' synagogue was set afire and badly damaged. Since it
was impossible, after the frenzied crowd had been dispersed, to find the
actual arsonists who had set the blaze, Theodoric announced that he
was holding the entire Christian population guilty. He levied a punishing fine on every Catholic *and* Arian Christian, the money to be used
to repair the damaged temple. At that, every last priest of the Church
of Rome—from the Patriarch Bishop Gelasius to hermits in the hinter-
lands—roared out accusation that the heretic Theodoric was *worsening*
his persecution of good Catholics, and *now* on behalf of those sworn
enemies of the faith, the diabolical, irredeemable, unpardonable Jews!

It was at about this time too that the Patriarch Bishop published his
Decretum Gelasianum, with its index of books recommended for the

Christian faithful to read and those books which they were forbidden to read. We advisers to Theodoric suggested that he might want to take action against this infringement on the rights of his subjects.

"Vái," he said dismissively. "How many of the Christian faithful *can* read? And if they are so faithful as to be spineless, I can hardly care if they do get trampled by their priests."

"Gelasius addressed the decree to every Christian, not just Catholics," Soas pointed out. "It is one more attempt to enforce the position that the Bishop of Rome is the overlord of *all* Christendom, and this decree further claims that at no time has he *not* been."

"Let Gelasius pretend what he likes. I cannot pretend to speak for all Christendom and refute him."

"Theodoric," Soas persisted. "It is no secret that, ever since Constantine gave them leave to preach, the bishops of the Church have been preaching one notion in particular. That there is no hope for mankind until it is *Christian bishops* who decide which man is to wear a crown—until every king and emperor is the bishops' anointed *creature*. That might not be an utterly unthinkable notion if it meant a conclave of bishops doing the deciding. But here we have one bishop asserting that he is the mind and the voice of them all."

871

"And you suggest that I enact a law or issue an injunction or publish a decree condemning this? I have already declared that I will not meddle in religion in any way."

"This is a case of religion preparing to encroach on secular affairs and monarchical authority. You are certainly entitled to stop that before it goes any further."

Theodoric sighed. "If I could, I would emulate Lycurgus. He was a ruler of antiquity—a very wise ruler—who made just one law for his land: that no laws should ever be made. Ne, Saio Soas, I believe Gelasius is only maliciously trying to goad me into a response, so he can decry my meddling. Let us ignore him and thereby make him *really* wrathful."

✠ ✠ ✠

I must, in honesty, say that not every high Catholic churchman laid obstacles in Theodoric's way. The Bishop of Ticinum, a man named Epiphanius, came to him with a worthwhile proposal. I might cynically suspect that Epiphanius had in mind only an enhancement of his own standing with the people or with the Church, but it did redound to Theodoric's benefit too. Epiphanius reminded him of the thousand or so Italian peasants who had been carried off by the marauding Burgunds of King Gundobad. The bishop suggested that their rescue and return to their homeland would earn Theodoric much goodwill, and he offered to go himself to do the negotiating for those captives' release. Not only did Theodoric accept the proposal; he gave Epiphanius a cavalry century for an escort and ample gold to pay a ransom. He sent with the bishop, also, something even more precious than gold. He sent his daughter Arevagni, proffering her as bride to King Gundobad's son and crown prince, Sigismund.

"How now, Theodoric?" I protested. "Gundobad took unworthy advantage of you, virtually insulted you, by ordering that foray into Italia while you were embroiled in war. You yourself called him a tetzte son of a fitchet bitch. You owe that man only rebuke, if not violent chastisement. Bad enough that you must pay him a bribe to return the captives. You will also invite him to become affinal father of your royal daughter?"

Theodoric only said patiently, "Arevagni makes no demur. Why should you? The girl must marry somebody, someday, and Sigismund will eventually be king of a stalwart people—a people resident right on Italia's northwest border. Reflect, Saio Thorn. The more prosperous I make this land—as I hope to do—the more tempting a quarry it will be to every covetous outlander. By making other kings my kin, *especially* the sons of fitchet bitches, I lessen the likelihood that they will become my adversaries. Vái, I only wish I had *more* progeny for whom to arrange propitious marriages."

Well, this was Theodoric's domain to hold and defend, and Arevagni was his daughter to do with as he pleased. So I simply accepted the fact that expediency is one of the routine tools of statecraft, and that Theodoric, like every other ruler, had to wield such tools. In this case it worked as warranted. Bishop Epiphanius and his proposal and his sacks of gold were hospitably received in Lugdunum. He was even invited to assist the local Arian bishop in officiating at the wedding of Arevagni and Sigismund. And when in time he returned to Ravenna, he brought, among other things, King Gundobad's avowal of everlasting amity and alliance with Theodoric. Epiphanius brought also every last one of the abducted peasants. And, as he had predicted, that humanitarian rescue made Theodoric even better liked by his Italia subjects—at least by the commonfolk, those who never would pay any heed to the Church's urgings that Theodoric be detested and execrated.

However, if the goddess Fortune was being more or less benign to Theodoric at this time, she seemed not to be smiling much on me. I could almost believe that Bishop John had been right when he threatened that I would be punished for my disrespectful manhandling of the sainted Severinus. I could almost believe that I had been cursed with something like a Christian version of the Old Religion's insandjis, a Sending. What happened was this:

Inasmuch as we never did find out who were the distant Odoacer partisans who had shipped those provisions to Ravenna by sea, I was smugly pleased with myself for having at least effected the capture of the expatriate responsible for the false salt trains. When Centurio Gudahals brought him to us from Haustaths, old Georgius Honoratus was intact, healthy and rightfully terrified. He had been gray of hair and skin and spirit when I first knew him; he was more so now, and I doubt that I would have known him again. He certainly failed to recognize me, so I did not even speak to him, but ordered him held in Ravenna's carcer municipalis for interrogation at my leisure. I congratulated Gudahals, saying that his good work might well have atoned for his earlier lapse.

"I hope so, Saio Thorn," he said earnestly. "We *also* found that traitor's co-conspirators, whom you bade me look for along the way. Caught them in the act, almost—flagrante delicto, anyway. A merchant and his wife."

He told me about it. Gudahals and his riders, after having easily taken old Georgius at the Haustaths mine, were hastening back across country. On this southern side of the Alpes, in a small city called Tridentum, they had been surprised to come upon a salt train just like those they had seen so frequently at their siege line. This train was headed north, as if returning from Ravenna, but its mules were inexplicably still full-laden.

"Then, of course, we recognized the train's drovers as our fellow soldiers in disguise," Gudahals said cheerfully. "And *you* know, Saio Thorn, what the mules were carrying now!"

The soldier-teamsters recounted how they, also sent by Saio Thorn to seek out conspirators, had pulled into Tridentum for the night and there had found cause for suspicion. The merchant and his wife had incriminated themselves, first by too obviously recognizing the mules and then by foolishly querying the drovers: whence came the train and why had it not delivered its freight?

"Naturally, those soldiers took the man and woman in charge," Gudahals said with zest. "They had just done that when I and my riders arrived with our prisoner Georgius."

873

The centurio went on to say that if any further proof of the Tridentum couple's complicity was required, they and Georgius, though taking care not to speak, had exchanged glances of unmistakable significance. So, just for amusement, the gathered soldiers revealed to the prisoners what was now riding inside the salt bales. All three of the culprits had turned as pale as the salt, and the woman had tried to shout something to Georgius, but her husband had cuffed her to silence her words.

"The moment he moved, I cut him down," said Gudahals. "And then the woman too. Both the conspirators executed on the spot, Saio Thorn, as you ordered."

"As I ordered," I repeated, with a sinking heart, because I remembered what Georgius's son had told me. His sister had married a merchant . . . gone away from the Place of Echoes . . .

"Having no further use for the mules and their pickled freight," Gudahals added, "we simply left them there, and all of us soldiers came back here together."

"Those conspirators," I said, "did they have names?"

"The merchant called himself Alypius. He was a man of some property—stores and stables and smithies to accommodate the many trains and teamsters that go back and forth through the Alpes. The prisoner Georgius later mentioned that Alypius's wife was called Livia. I am sure Georgius can tell you much more, Saio Thorn, but we did not ply him with questions on the way hither, because you had ordered that we not trouble him in any manner."

"Yes, yes," I mumbled. "You have indeed followed orders this time, Gudahals, to the veriest syllable. I shall commend you to Theodoric."

I was no longer feeling smugly pleased with myself. As had happened on so many other occasions, I was once again to blame for the death of a onetime friend of mine. I remembered how I had once carved Livia's name and mine in the alpine ice river, and how I had wished the best for the pretty little girl in her later life. Even with the evidence that, in the war just concluded, Livia had been working for the wrong side—and was still, even as a grown woman, obeying the doltish demands of her lackluster father—I was dreadfully sorry for what had happened to her.

I was so downcast and dejected that I did not even visit Georgius in the carcer, either to gloat at the old nauthing or to inquire why he had committed his family to work on behalf of the outcast Odoacer. I did not even attend the hearing at which Theodoric sentenced Georgius to be "turpiter decalvatus, as a mark of perpetual infamy"—and directed that that marking be done "summo gaudio plebis"—and further ordered that Georgius should labor, for as long as life remained to him, alongside the other wretched convicts toiling in "the living hell," the pistrinum of Ravenna's grain mill. ("Turpiter decalvatus" means "foully scalped" and "summo gaudio plebis" meant that Georgius was to be thus mutilated in public, "to the great joy of the masses." But I did not even go to be among those watching masses.)

As Gudahals later reported to me, the warders put onto Georgius's gray head a metal bowl without a bottom, forcing it down as far as his ears and eyebrows, so that his scalp became the bowl's bottom. Then the bowl was filled to the brim with live coals and was held firmly in place by the warders, while Georgius screamed and struggled and contorted, and while all the hair and skin and flesh of the top of his head was burned away to the bone. The crowd, said Gudahals, truly did enjoy the spectacle. A loud cheer had gone up when Georgius's hair went up in flames, but after that there was not much to see except greasy smoke. Then Georgius was dragged off, by now unconscious, to wake up naked and chained to the millstone with the other half-dead slaves of the pistrinum.

Only belatedly did I think of some questions I would like to ask the old man. Perhaps because it was in large measure my fault that his daughter's life had ended so untimely, I had some curiosity to know what kind of man Livia had wed and what their married life had been like. So then I hurried to the grain mill, fearing that old Georgius would not long survive in there. Well, I was right about that, so I did not get to ask him anything. He had died before I got there, and his dishonorable remains had been buried as Odoacer's had been, in tainted ground—which is to say, in the burying ground adjoining the Jews' synagogue.

✠　　✠　　✠

My spirits were not much elevated by the fact that the Frankish Princess Audefleda was now resident in Ravenna. Her brother, King Clovis, had sent her and a considerable escort of guards and servants southward from his capital city of Durocortorum, and her train had come as far as Lugdunum while Epiphanius was there on his ransom mission. So the bishop had brought her with him when he brought the freed captives, and now she was here, and on that account I was feeling half melancholy, half resentful.

Akh, I tried my best not to feel so. I reminded myself that there was at least one thing to be said for the passing of time. I was not *twice* the princess's age any more; I was now only nineteen years older than her twenty-one. And I had to concede that Audefleda was neither a frivolous little dotterel nor an overbearing young virago. She was undeniably handsome of face and figure—wide blue eyes, a cascade of golden curls, ivory skin, proud bosom—and well spoken and of regal bearing. And she did not flaunt her beauty either wheedlingly or demandingly. She was as gracious and pleasant to me as she was to every other member of the court—and, for that matter, even to servants and slaves. Audefleda would, in short, make a perfect queen for Theodoric.

And I did not (I told myself) resent my being neglected by Theodoric when, in addition to all his kingly concerns, he spent so much time in paying court to Audefleda and in making arrangements for a lavish royal wedding. All that bothered me (I told myself) was his behaving like a love-smitten suitor instead of a staid, stern king. For example, I thought he even degraded the dignity of his beard, which was by now of biblical-prophet magnificence, when he so frequently parted it with vapid smiles. And he did not *need* to dance attendance on the princess and cast moon eyes at her. She was, after all, committed to this marriage, even if he had been indifferent or cold or cruel toward her.

On the nowadays seldom occasions that I could gain audience with Theodoric, he would deal summarily with whatever I had come to discuss, so that he could inflict on me some new detail of his nuptial plans, and of those I was already weary. The last time we sat together prior to the wedding day, he said wistfully:

"The ceremony cannot be as elaborate as I should like to make it, simply because there is only the one Arian church in which to hold it. And that one, the Baptistery—did you know, Thorn?—used to be only a Roman bathhouse. It was all that poor Bishop Neon could acquire for Arian worship in a city dominated by the Church of Rome."

"*Only* a bathhouse?" I said, rather waspishly. "There was certainly never anything cramped or cheap about *any* Roman therma. And old Neon did a splendid job of converting this one for religious purposes. The Baptistery is quite big enough and grand enough even for this epochal event."

"Nevertheless, I have promised Neon that I will build a much more sumptuous Arian church, to be his cathedral, and Neon is ecstatic at the prospect. Anyway, the city deserves such an edifice, and will require it, with Arian Christians rapidly outnumbering the Catholics here."

I said, with petulance, "I do not understand why you insist on keeping Ravenna as your capital city. This is a dreary place. Damp, foggy, stinking of swamp. Frogs croaking all night long, *when* one can hear them over the vicious whine of the nasty blood-prickers. The only fresh air to be had is down at the Classis seafront, but one swoons before getting there, in the middle of the causeway, from the stench of the workers' district."

"I have improvements in mind," Theodoric said mildly, but I railed on:

"And the water is worse than the fetid air. What the Padus brings into the canals is brackish, thick with marsh scum—and into that gets mixed the city's rere-dorter offal. It is a ghastly porridge. The Romans here are the only Romans anywhere in the world who drink their wine undiluted, just as it comes from the amphora, because they know better than to mix it with Ravenna water. For ages now, they have been reciting Martial's little verse:

> I had rather, at Ravenna,
> Own a fountain than a vine,
> For I could sell fresh water there
> Much dearer than good wine."

Still mildly, Theodoric said, "This has been the capital city ever since Emperor Honorius made it so."

"All he cared about was its invulnerability as a hiding place. Neither he nor his successors in the ninety years since then ever lifted a finger to make Ravenna more fit for human habitation. They never even repaired the ruined aqueduct, to get decent water. I know *you* do not need a hiding place. You could locate your capital in any of a score of more salubrious—"

"You are right, of course. Thags izvis, Thorn, for thinking of Audefleda."

"What?" That stopped me in mid-stride. "Audefleda?"

"She has already remarked—not complained, mind you—that this humid air loosens the curl of her tresses. But she also says—she is ever cheerful—that such humid air is good for the feminine complexion. Still, it is thoughtful of you, Thorn, to worry that I am being unfair to Audefleda in keeping her here. No need to worry. She is more than willing to share the discomforts of Ravenna while I strive to ameliorate them. I have already discussed with her my plans for draining the marshes, rebuilding the aqueduct, making of this a fair city."

"Discussed the plans with her," I repeated testily. "Your generals and your other marshals and I have heard nothing of such plans."

"You will, you will. In the meantime, while a loving wife is happy to abide with her husband wherever he chooses to be, I hardly expect you to behave like a devoted wife."

That remark may have nettled me more than anything else he could have said. But I only muttered that I would go—and remain—wherever he cared to send me.

"Ne, I know your vagabond nature. I have now appointed enough other marshals that I can put one permanently in every community of any consequence. Soas, for example, will serve as my resident deputy in Mediolanum. But you, Thorn, I will ask to be my roving surrogate, just as you used to be. Go about Italia, go to lands beyond, go wherever you please, and either bring or send word of anything that would be of interest to me. Such a wayfaring commission would be to your taste, would it not?"

Of course it would, and was, but I said a little stiffly, "I ask only to be commanded by my king, not indulged."

878

"Very well. Then I would like you to go first to Rome, since I have not yet decided what deputy I shall settle there, and it will be some while before I shall go there myself. Come back and tell me . . . well . . . tell me *everything* I ought to know about Rome."

I saluted and said, "I go at once."

✠　　✠　　✠

I had said I would go "at once" only so I would have a legitimate excuse for being absent from Ravenna on the wedding day. The herizogo Thorn, staunch marshal and good friend to the king, would otherwise have been expected to stand prominently among the happy day's participants and guests. Having been ordered abroad, Thorn did not attend the nuptial mass. But Veleda did. This is the primordial female way of dealing with an unassuageable itch: since it cannot be relieved by scratching, then scratch it until it hurts and hurts and hurts.

I stood among the many other women of all ages and degrees, on the left side of the Arian Baptistery, and I joined in the responses to the service, but not in the women's muted comments among themselves—mostly concerning the bride and how beautiful she was. Yes, Princess Audefleda was that, and King Theodoric was a model of kingliness, and old Bishop Neon heroically resisted the temptation to make such a noteworthy mass an excruciatingly long one. The duller stretches of it I whiled away by admiring the Baptistery's radiant mosaics. Obviously they had been put in during the building's conversion from the Roman therma, because these were all of Christian subjects, not pagan. For example, the entire ceiling represented the baptism of Jesus, attended by all his apostles as he stood naked in a river clearly labeled the IORDANN. What was so admirable, almost incredible, was that the depiction—done just in chips of colored stone and glass—rendered the water with such limpidity that Jesus's legs and private parts were visible under the water's surface.

Private parts, hovering over a wedding ceremony—*liufs Guth!*—what a thought to be thinking in church! I snatched my vagrant mind to order and scolded it guiltily, angrily, and I wrenched my gaze down from the ceiling mosaic, and I know I must have been blushing bright red, and my eyes as they lowered met those of a tall and comely young man on the opposite side of the chamber, and his eyes were smiling at me.

When we lay together, I recognized him as an optio of one of Ibba's turmae whom I had occasionally encountered as Thorn, but I did not care about that. If I ever had known the young soldier's name, I had forgotten it, and I did not care what his name was. My name he did not even *ask*, but I did not care about that, either. When he tried, rather breathlessly, to compliment me on the avid ardency with which I was embracing him, I bade him hush, for I did not care to hear talk. As I repeatedly convulsed and cried out in rapture and uttered another's name over and over again, and glimpsed the young man's wondering face above mine, I did not care what he was thinking of me. And, after a long while, when he pleaded for a respite, I gave him none, for I wanted to go on and on. And I did, until there was simply no more to go on with. Then the young man tore himself loose from me, as if he had decided that he was in the raptorial grip of a haliuruns hag, and he fled away in shame and terror.

879

2

It was shortly after sunset on a summer day when I and the few escorts I had brought rode into the northern outskirts of Rome on the Via Nomentana. I halted our troop at a wayside taberna that had a sizable yard and stables, to put up for the night. When I entered the taberna's main room, I was surprised to be jovially greeted by a cry from the caupo, "Háils, Saio Thorn!"

880

I stood puzzled as he lumbered toward me with hand outstretched, saying, "I have long been wondering when some more of my comrades would start to arrive!" Now I recognized him, though he had grown very stout. He was the cavalryman Ewig whom I had last seen when I sent him trailing Tufa southward from Bononia. And I was momentarily confused, because at that time Ewig had known me as Veleda. But then I realized that he had, of course, known the marshal Thorn by sight long before then.

As we shook hands in the Roman manner, he prattled on. "I rejoiced when I heard that the evil Tufa was dead, and I knew it was your doing, Saio Thorn, just as the lady Veleda promised. And how fares that gallant lady, by the way?"

I assured him that she was well, and commented that he also seemed to be doing very well, for a common soldier presumably still on speculator duty.

"Ja, the lady Veleda bade me stay in these parts and keep watch. Which I have been doing, right here, all this long time since. But there seemed no harm in my essaying other endeavors. When the caupo of this establishment died, I made haste to woo and wed his widow. And ja, as you see, she and the taberna and I"—he happily patted his paunch—"have prospered handsomely."

So the taberna became, for the time being, the quarters of myself and my little company. And Ewig, nowadays quite fluent in Latin and also well acquainted with the city—or at least with those parts of it accessible to a commoner—became my enthusiastic, informative, loquacious guide to Rome. In his company, I got to see all the notable monuments and landmarks that every visitor to Rome is eager to ogle, and also a good many places that I imagine not many visitors ever know exist—such as the Subura quarter, where all the lupanares are congregated, according to law.

"As you will notice," said Ewig, "every house has its license number prominently displayed, and every ipsitilla is fair-haired. That is also the law: they must either bleach their hair or wear a yellow wig. No one objects to that, neither the women nor their customers. Most Romans being dark-haired, they *like* a change. Some of the whores—if I may express it in cavalry language—even bleach their tails as well as their manes."

I will not trouble to describe the innumerable sights and scenes of Rome that are familiar to people everywhere, even people who have never been there. For example, everybody in the world must know of the Flavian Amphitheater—popularly called the Colosseum because of the towering Colossus of Nero that looms just outside its walls— wherein are held the games, exhibitions, spectacles, contests between wrestlers, between pugiles, between armed men and wild beasts. But I doubt that any casual visitor, merely standing and admiring that immense edifice, would notice one thing that the soldierly and bawdy Ewig pointed out to me:

"Observe, Saio Thorn, the many yellow-haired women lurking about the doorways as the throng comes pouring out. Whores, of course, and they always converge here at the hour the performances end. They do a brisk business, soliciting the men who have been roused to lubricity while watching all the sweat and blood and manly exertion inside."

The single most exciting spectacle I saw (though it did not rouse me to lubricity) was the fighting of a nighttime fire in the city by the special vigiles who perform this function. Other cities have destructive fires, God knows, but a blaze this awesome could only happen in Rome, because only Rome, on its Caelian Hill, has so many residential buildings that are five and six stories high, and it was one of those that was on fire. So the vigiles came swarming, carrying rag-stuffed mattresses soaked in cheap wine, and they held those protective shields in front of them as they dashed inside the building to rescue the occupants. Meanwhile, others were using catapults to fling grappling hooks to the building's high roof and from those grapples depended ropes, enabling

881

persons trapped on upper stories to slither down onto cushioning mattresses laid in the street under them. Meanwhile, too, other vigiles were assaulting the fire itself, using cart-borne machines called Ctesibian siphones. Two men at either side of each cart alternated at ramming down and drawing up stout handles, and that action somehow forced water from a tank through a nozzle which another man was directing at the flames. With the water, pumped as high as the building's roof, and with wine-sodden mattresses and wine-soaked brooms, the vigiles quenched the conflagration of that whole building as thoroughly and almost as quickly as I could put out a campfire by urinating on it.

Ewig several times took me along when he went to market, in a little ass-drawn cart, to procure things he needed for his taberna. However, we almost never went near any of the city's market squares, and I was soon aware that the persons to whom he introduced me were hardly of the highest respectability. We went often to the Street of Janus, where are all the usurers and money-changers and pawnbrokers. And we went often into the district of warehouses called the Pepper Barns, though they store many other commodities besides pepper. Once in a while, we even visited the Via Nova, where are situated Rome's most elegant shops selling the most expensive goods, but all of Ewig's business there seemed to be done at the back doors. We went oftenest to the Emporium docks along the river. When one day Ewig sidled off to a dockside shed, and then slunk back with some leather bags to pile into the cart, I remarked, but not accusingly:

"Caupo, do you provision your taberna entirely by theft?"

"Ne, Saio Thorn, I never steal anything. I merely buy from those who do. These skins of fine Campanian oils and wines I acquired from a seaman on that craft yonder, just in from Neapolis with barrels and barrels full. During the voyage, you see, a seaman slips the hoop of a barrel only a *little*, and with a gimlet bores a hole through a stave, and draws off some of the contents, and slips the hoop back over the hole. And when the freight is delivered, such losses are attributed to 'leakage.' I hope you do not object, Marshal—any more than you object when *drinking* my taberna's wine, or paying the modest prices I am thus enabled to charge for it."

"Ne, ne," I said, laughing, "I have always admired initiative and enterprise."

Every time our wanderings took us near the center of the city, I made sure to go to the Capitoline corner of the Forum to read the *Diurnal* posted at the Temple of Concordia. Ewig seldom bothered to accompany me, because he could not read. Tacked onto the temple wall each noontime by the Forum's accensus (who also bellowed "Meridies!" for the edification of any passersby who did not know what time it was), the *Diurnal* is a written summary of all the previous day's noteworthy occurrences in and around Rome. It lists births and deaths in distinguished families, significant business transactions, accidents and disasters—such as the fire on the Caelian Hill—notices of runaway slaves, announcements of coming games and plays and the like.

And on other occasions I ambled alone in places that held no attraction (or booty) for Ewig, such as the Argiletum, the street of booksellers. And I was interested to find those dealers, ordinarily the most inexcitable of men, in extremely bad humor. I learned that they were nowadays being repeatedly pestered by the Bishop of Rome—or, rather, by his *consultores inquisitionis*, priests who descended on the shops to ransack their shelves and inspect their wares. While those *consultores* had no authority to confiscate any books that were forbidden by Gelasius's Index Vetitae, they did insist on affixing labels to the wares, so that a Christian customer browsing through the scrolls and codices could easily tell which were permissible for him to buy and read and which were "pernicious" on either doctrinal or moral grounds.

I made note of such things as those, and of information I culled from the *Diurnal* that I thought might be useful to Theodoric, and also wrote some observations of my own on the state of Rome, and I periodically sent a rider bearing those writings north to Ravenna. One of my observations, I knew, would be of particular interest to Theodoric.

He and I had seen how the city of Verona had been weakened by the vanity of past emperors, when they erected triumphal monuments in place of stout defensive walls. We had seen how numerous other cities had suffered when indifferent rulers and torpid administrators allowed the destruction of life-sustaining aqueducts. We had seen how the Via Popilia and many other roads had fallen into decay—and bridges too and causeways and canals. Now it was my sad duty to inform Theodoric that Rome itself, the Eternal City, had long been shamefully ill used, and might not for much longer deserve the name Eternal.

During the better part of a millennium and a quarter, Rome had been a-building, spreading, growing ever grander and more beautiful. But at some point in the not too distant past, it had stopped doing so. That would not have mattered much—because a city simply could not *get* much more beautiful—if only that beauty had been maintained and

883

preserved. But the rulers and administrators and inhabitants of Rome seemed to have ceased to care about that. Not only was nothing done to save the city's architectural treasures from the ravages of time and weather; many of those irreplaceable mementos of Rome's heritage were being *let* to fall down, or, worse, to be defaced and demolished piecemeal. Some of the most superb buildings and arches and porticos and arcades were nowadays regarded only as *quarries*. Anyone who wished could use them as a convenient source of materials for the paltriest purposes. Fine marble, limestone, whole columns and friezes, sculptured and polished, were there for the taking and free for the taking.

In some places about the city, such depredations have made it possible for an observer to *look backward* over Rome's twelve and a half centuries of existence. One could literally see how a certain structure, plain and modest at its first upraising, became more lovely and more elegant as Rome's wealth grew and its arts and skills improved. But one looked on that with rue and melancholy.

I shall cite one case, that of the small but enchanting Temple of Eos near the vegetable market square. Had I seen it when Rome was in its prime, this little temple to the dawn must have been an exquisite expression, in purest Parian marble, of high architectural achievement. But now much of the marble has fallen or been pried away, perhaps to put a facing on the villa of some upstart rich man, or the slabs even just leaned together to make a shelter for the market's night watchman. And where the marble used to be, there is revealed an earlier Temple of Eos, of the man-made material called ironstone, probably built at a time when Rome could not yet afford to import costly marble. But chunks of that ironstone have crumbled away or been hacked off, perhaps to fill a hole worn in the paving of some nearby street. And under that is visible an even earlier temple, built of the native gray tufa rock, doubtless erected in the days before Romans learned how to make ironstone. But blocks of the tufa have been carried off too, perhaps to prop up the vegetable vendors' tables in the market. And under what remains of the tufa is what may be the *very* earliest temple, made of humble brown baked-clay bricks, but lovingly made, perhaps away back in the dawn-time when the Rasenar still called this place Ruma and the dawn was called Thesan.

Still, despite its disgraceful self-neglect, Rome had not lost its magnificence. Much of it was simply too well built, and still is, to succumb to any wreckers less strong and crafty and determined than gods. Much of it was simply so splendid, and still is, that I think even the bestial Huns would be ashamed to despoil it. Enough of the sublime public buildings and palaces and fora and gardens and temples remained unsullied that I—although I had previously seen Constantinople—could not help being astonished and gladdened. Not just on this first visit but every time I came to Rome, there was no way I could act the world-weary traveler and pretend to be unimpressed. However often I walked into the vast, high, vaulting interior of a basilica or therma or temple—especially that most awe-inspiring one, the Pantheon—I never failed to feel as small and insignificant as an ant, and at the same time feel a soaring wonder and pride that mere men could have *made* such things.

I would always prefer Rome to Ravenna, even after Theodoric had so thoroughly transfigured that capital city. And while I cannot deny that Constantinople is a sumptuous metropolis, it is, in my view—even now, as that New Rome approaches its two hundredth birthday—still a mere weanling compared to the venerable antiquity of the original and everlasting and only *real* Rome. Of course, I must bear in mind that I first saw Constantinople when I too was young, and never got to Rome until I myself was on the farther slope of the hill of my life.

885

When Ewig had shown me all the parts of the city that he knew best, and had introduced me to all sorts of commonfolk, from thieving seamen to pawnbrokers to lupanar lenae, I decided it was time I saw something of Rome's upper classes. So I inquired as to where Senator Festus might be found, and learned that he owned one of the handsome villas on the Via Flaminia, and I went calling there. The word "villa" correctly means a country estate, and perhaps Festus's mansion had had open country around it when it was first built, but the spread of Rome had long ago put the city walls far beyond the place. It stood in what is still called the Martian Fields, though that expanse of ground between the Flaminian Way and the river consists of fields no longer, but of close-set fine dwellings.

The senator greeted me warmly—as "Torn," of course—and made me welcome and sent his slaves running to fetch sweetmeats and libation. With his own hand, Festus poured Massicus wine for me, and mixed into it Mosylon cinnamon, which is the top-tree grade of that spice. The villa was as richly appointed as a minor palace. There was much statuary, many silk hangings, and the windows were of marble lattice, their multitude of openings filled with slabs of cast glass, blue and green and violet. The room in which we conversed had on its four walls mosaic panels representing the seasons: the flowers of spring, the grain harvest of summer, the grape harvest of autumn, the olive-tree beating of winter. But the villa had its common touches too. Like the meanest hut in the dockside low quarters, the villa had wet mats hung in every doorway, to cool the incoming summer breezes.

Festus kindly offered to help me find a residence of my own, one suitable to the king's marshal and ambassador. And that he did, within just a few days: a town house on the Vicus Jugarius, which had been the street of foreign embassies before all of those removed to Ravenna. The house was no palace or villa, but it was luxurious enough for my taste, and had separate quarters for my domestic slaves, which the senator also helped me buy. (A little later, and without the assistance of either Festus or Ewig, I also acquired a rather more modest house in the Transtiber residential quarter on the other side of the Aurelian Bridge, to be Veleda's residence in Rome.)

Meanwhile, the senator was eager to introduce me to other Romans of his class, and over the next weeks I met many of those. He also took me one day to the Curia to observe a sitting of the Roman Senate, assuring me that I would find this a momentous occasion. I suppose I went, like any wide-eyed provincial, expecting a senate session to be of awesome solemnity and spectacle. Except for one aspect of it, however, I would have found it intolerably dull. The speeches dealt with matters that seemed to me of no import whatever, and even the most fatuous, longest-winded orations were received with cries of "Well spoken!" from all the tiers of benches: "Vere diserte! Nove diserte!"

The one thing that saved this session from boring me utterly was that Senator Festus himself rose to make a proposal: "I ask the concurrence of you senators and of the gods . . ."

Of course, the prefatory verbiage went on and on, like every other speech I heard that day. But it culminated in his proposing a vote of recognition of the rulership of Rome by Flavius "Teodoricus" Rex. His oration was dutifully acclaimed "Nove diserte! Vere diserte!" by all present, including even some senators who then voted *against* the proposal when Festus called for a showing of "the will of you senators and of the gods." The proposal did pass, though, by a comfortable plurimum (of senators, anyway; the gods abstained from voting)—for what little the Senate's blessing was worth. It at least pleased me, because it *displeased* the Patriarch Bishop of Rome, as I discovered when, on another day, Festus arranged for me an audience with that personage.

On my arrival at Gelasius's cathedral, the Basilica of St. John Lateran, I was met by one of the cardinal deacons whom I had earlier seen at

Ravenna. As he escorted me to the bishop's audience chamber, he advised me in all earnestness, "You are expected to address the sovereign pontiff as 'gloriosissimus patricius.'"

"I will not," I said.

That made the deacon gasp and sputter, but I paid him no heed. In my childhood days as exceptor to Dom Clement, I had written many of his letters to other patriarch bishops, and I knew the traditional form of address—Your Authority—so that was the only deference I accorded this one.

"Auctoritas," I said to him, "I bring greetings from *my* sovereign, Flavius Theodoricus Rex. I have the honor to be his deputy in this city, and I offer my services in conveying any communications that you might wish—"

"Convey my greetings in return," he interrupted, and frostily. Then he began gathering up his skirts as if that were to be the end of our colloquy.

Gelasius was a tall, skeletal old man, parchment-pale and ascetic-looking, but his garb was not of corresponding austerity. His vestments were new and voluminous, of rich silks, heavily embroidered, very different from the simple brown robe of peasant cloth worn by every other Christian churchman of my experience, from lowliest monk to the Patriarch Bishop of Constantinople.

When that patriarch came to mind, I recalled the standing quarrel between him and Gelasius, so I said, "My king would be inexpressibly gratified, Auctoritas, if he were to hear that you and the Bishop Akakiós have resolved your differences."

"No doubt he would," Gelasius said through gritted teeth, "That would facilitate his recognition by the emperor. Eheu, what does Teodoric need of that? Has he not already been recognized by the pusillanimous, groveling, sycophantic Senate? I ought to pronounce anathema on every Christian senator in that body. However, if Teodoric wishes to please *me*, all he has to do is join me in denouncing Akakiós for his laxity in the matter of the noxious Monophysites."

"Auctoritas, you know Theodoric refuses to intrude upon matters of religion."

"And so do I refuse to yield on a doctrinal issue to an inferior bishop."

"Inferior?" As tactfully as I could, I remarked that Akakiós had held his patriarchate for nearly ten years before Gelasius was raised to his.

"Eheu! How dare you compare us? His is only Constantinople! Mine

887

is *Rome!* And this"—he indicated the building we were in—"this is the Mother Church of all Christendom!"

I asked mildly, "Is that why you have adopted a more striking style of liturgical costume?"

"Why not?" he snapped, as if I had been scathingly critical. "Those who are unique in the grace of their virtue should also be unique in the richness of their raiment."

I said nothing to that, so he added, "My cardinal deacons and priests too, as they give increasing proofs of their devotion to their Papa, will be rewarded with embellishments of their liturgical dress."

I still said nothing, so he went on, pedantically, "I have long believed that Christianity is too *drab* in comparison with paganism—in costume, in ritual, in ecclesiastical trappings. No wonder paganism seduces the commonfolk, who welcome any gaudery and ostentation that brightens their meager lives. And the finer folk, how can they be expected to accept instruction or admonition from priests clad like wretched peasants? If Christianity is to be more attractive than the pagan and heretic cults, its churches and clerics and ceremonies must outshine theirs in magnificence. It was this basilica's own patron saint, John, who made the suggestion: let the onlookers remark in wonder and admiration, 'You have kept back the *good* wine until now.'"

I still had no comment to make on that, and clearly nothing I could say would soften Gelasius's opposition to his brother bishop and the heretic Theodoric, so I took my leave and did not see him again.

Nor did I mourn when, about a year later, Gelasius died. His replacement was a less rancorous man and, if he and old Akakiós had differing doctrinal beliefs, they somehow conciliated them. I daresay it was only coincidence that this new Patriarch Bishop of Rome took the name Anastasius II, and I doubt that that flattered the emperor of the same name. Nevertheless, very shortly thereafter, Constantinople's Emperor Anastasius *did* proclaim his recognition of King Theodoric and, in token, sent to him the imperial regalia—the diadem, crown, scepter, orb and victoria—all the ornamenta palatii that Odoacer had surrendered to Zeno some thirteen years before.

The now-universal recognition of Theodoric's regnancy did not cause him to put on any airs or affectations. He never took any title other than Flavius Theodoricus Rex. That is to say, he never claimed to be king *of* anything, not of any land or any people. On the coins minted during his reign, on the dedicatory tablets affixed to the many structures built during his reign, never was he styled King of Rome,

King of Italia, King of the Western Empire, not even King of the Ostrogoths. Theodoric was content to express his rulership and his kingliness
in deeds and works and accomplishments.

Churchmen, by contrast, have never been known to abstain from or
give up any entitlement that they have once been granted or can claim
a right to or have invented for themselves. Like Gelasius before him,
Anastasius II continued to insist on the title of sovereign pontiff and
the honorific of Papa and the address of "most glorious patrician"—
and so has every one of the three succeeding Patriarch Bishops of
Rome. Like Gelasius, they all have worn splendiferous raiment, and
their cardinal deacons and priests gradually have assumed costumes
almost equally luxurious. The Church rituals and processions have become ever more bedizened with candles and incense and flowers and
gold-encrusted crosses and staffs and vessels.

Well, even at the time of my interview with Gelasius, I had understood his reasons for wanting his Church to make more flagrant appeal
to both the commonfolk and the finer folk of the city. Before my coming to Rome, I had naturally assumed that the heart-city of the Catholic
Christian Church must be solidly Christian from top to bottom. But I
soon learned that it was Christian only in the *middle*, and I am speaking
literally. The membership of the Church of Rome consisted almost entirely of those persons who make things: smiths, wrights, artisans, crafts-
men—and all those (excluding Jews, of course) who buy and sell things:
merchants, traders, shippers, vendors, brokers, shopkeepers, and their
wives and families. I was unavoidably reminded of the assertion by that
old Gepid hermit, Galindo, that Christianity is a tradesman's religion.

889

The caupo Ewig and numerous other outlanders resident in the city
were Arians, ergo "heretics," and almost all the other lower-class citizens to whom Ewig introduced me, if they professed any faith at all,
were still believers in the teeming Roman pantheon of pagan gods, goddesses and spirits. What surprised me more was that the majority of the
upper-class folk to whom Festus introduced me, including many of his
fellow senators, were also unregenerate pagans. In the ages before Constantine, Rome had recognized—besides its own amorphous pagan
faith—what were called the religiones licitae, meaning the worship of
Isis imported from Egypt, the worship of Astarte imported from Syria,
the worship of Mithras imported from Persia, and the Jews' worship of
Jehovah. Now it became evident to me that those religions, though
frowned upon by the state and violently reprehended by the Christian
clerics, were not by any means dead or moribund or neglected.

Not that anyone really *believed* in any of them. As with the upper-class Romans I had known in Vindobona, these of Rome regarded religion only as one more of the diversions they enjoyed in their ample leisure time. They might profess one faith one day and another the next, just to take advantage of the religions' varying excuses for feasts and convivia. And whichever religion they were observing, the Roman gentry were inclined to like best the indolent or indelicate or even indecent aspects of it. In many dooryards were to be seen statues of the pagan goddess Murtia, and, to emphasize what Murtia was the goddess of—laziness and languor—the families' gardeners would carefully have trained moss to grow over the statues. One of Rome's senators, Symmachus, who was also Rome's highest civil officer, its urbis praefectus, a highly respected patricius and illustris, had in his villa's dooryard a statue of Bacchus. The figure flaunted a massive, uprearing fascinum, and was inscribed "Rumpere, invidia," suggesting that the onlooker should burst and die of envy.

I was among the guests at a convivium in that villa of Praefectus and Senator Symmachus during which we all engaged in a good-natured game of composing palindromes. Done offhand like that, of course, a palindrome could hardly be of the purest Latin, but what struck me was that these wordplays were scarcely of the purest high-mindedness either. The first one, offered by Symmachus's affinal young son Boethius, I thought inelegant for quotation while we all were eating: *Sole medere pede, ede, perede melos.* The next, concocted by another young man, Cassiodorus, had at least the virtue of being the lengthiest composed that night: *Si bene te tua laus taxat, sua laute tenebis.* But the third, *In girum imus nocte et consumimur igni,* was proposed by an illustrious, patrician, newly wed young woman, Rusticiana by name, daughter of Symmachus and wife to Boethius.

Being no stranger to indelicacy myself, and no priggish objector to it, I quite enjoyed the company of these free and easy nobles. And the three men I have mentioned would become high-ranking officers of Theodoric's government, close advisers to him—mainly because of their talents, but partly because I liked them and recommended them to him.

Anicius Manlius Severinus Boethius, as his name indicates, was a scion of one of Rome's first families, the Anicii. He was handsome, wealthy, witty, and his wife, Rusticiana, was a beautiful, spirited woman. Though Boethius was only half my age when we met, I easily recognized in him a prodigy of intelligence and capability. He bore out that promise when he served as Theodoric's chief of all administration, the magister officiorum, and he did many other things besides. In his lifetime he would translate into Latin at least thirty Greek works of science and philosophy, including Ptolemy on astronomy, Nicomachus on arithmetic, Euclid on geometry, Pythagoras on the theory of music and Aristotle on just about everything in creation. Boethius's own library was better filled than any other I ever saw (and the big room was walled with ivory and glass, to make it a fitting container for such treasure). But Boethius was no dust-covered drudge of a scholar; he was also a most inventive artisan. To celebrate one occasion or another, he conceived and built and presented to Theodoric an ornate and intricate clepsydra, an ingenious and complex celestial globe and sundial on which a statue of the king, moved by cunning contrivances, turned always to face the sun.

It may be that Boethius had acquired his literary bent from Praefectus and Senator Symmachus, because that man was also an author, having written a seven-volume history of Rome. Boethius, orphaned in childhood, had been brought up in the house of Symmachus, who, as I have said, later became also his affinal father, and was his lifelong friend and mentor. The good Symmachus had held his office as Rome's urbis praefectum under Odoacer, but, being also of a noble, rich, independent family, he had owed no obligation to that ruler. So Theodoric gladly kept him in that office until, some years afterward, Symmachus was elevated by the Senate to its princeps senatus, or chief member, and so gave his whole time to Senate affairs.

891

The Cassiodorus whom I have mentioned was one of two men of that name, father and son, and both became valued members of Theodoric's court. Cassiodorus Pater was another of Odoacer's appointments in office, and another whom Theodoric retained, for the very good reason that he was the best man for the work. In fact, he held two titles usually entrusted to two different administrators, comes rei privatae and comes sacrarum largitionum, meaning that he was in sole charge of all the government's finances and tax collections and expenditures.

His son Cassiodorus, exactly the same age as Boethius, was engaged to be Theodoric's exceptor and quaestor, writing all his official correspondence and published decrees. Cassiodorus Filius was the author of the lengthiest of those three palindromes I have quoted, and that may give some idea of his style of writing—prolix and flowery. But that was precisely what Theodoric wanted. The "non possumus" proclamation regarding religious beliefs, which Theodoric had set forth in his own blunt words, had been so coldly received by so many persons that Theodoric deemed it politic to couch his later pronouncements in more high-flown language.

And Cassiodorus certainly provided that. I remember when Theodoric received a letter from some troop of soldiers somewhere complaining that they had been paid their January acceptum in underweight solidi. Cassiodorus wrote the reply to them, and it began like this: "The pearl-lustered fingertips of Eos, the young dawn, now tremulously unlock the oriental portals of the golden horizon . . ." and somehow flowed from there into a few reflections on "the sublime nature of Arithmetic, by which both the heavens and earth are ruled . . ." Where it went from there I do not remember, nor do I remember whether the troopers' complaint was ever resolved, but I have long wondered what a bunch of hard-bitten soldiers must have *thought* when they got that florid missive.

Anyway, with such good, wise and capable Romans as those seated about the council tables in Rome and Ravenna (and there were many more than the few men I have mentioned), Theodoric commanded a governing body of more intellect, erudition and ability than had ever been convened in the service of the state since the golden days of Marcus Aurelius.

892

3

ith good Roman administrators and good Gothic men-at-arms attending to the internal concerns of his domain, Theodoric was early able to concentrate his attention on securing the borders of it, by making fraternal alliances with potentially troublesome other kings. In that work he had the assistance of various good women. Already, his daughter Arevagni's wedding to Prince Sigismund had made Theodoric kin to the Burgunds' ruling family, and his own wedding to Audefleda had made him affinal brother to the Franks' King Clovis. Now, in fairly short order, he gave his widowed sister Amalafrida in marriage to King Thrasamund of the Vandals, his younger daughter Thiudagotha to the Visigoths' Alaric II and his niece Amalaberga to King Hermanafrid of the Thuringi.

It was during my first visit to Rome that Theodoric's sister arrived there, on her way to take ship from Ostia to meet her new husband, so I was pleased to welcome her and renew my acquaintance with her and see to her comfort during her brief stay in the city. I quartered Amalafrida and her retinue of servants at my newly acquired ambassadorial residence in the Vicus Jugarius, and I introduced her to my new Roman friends (of the Festus circle, not of the Ewig). I also personally escorted her to games at the Colosseum, plays at the Theatrum Marcelli and other such diversions, because I could see that she was not in very high spirits. Eventually, in her prim, auntish way, she confided to me:

"As the daughter of a king, the sister of a king, the widow of a herizogo, I am naturally accustomed to the demands of statecraft. So I go willingly, of course, to wed King Thrasamund. Indeed"—and she laughed shyly—"a woman of my age, mother of two grown children, ought to rejoice at the chance of marrying *any* new husband, let alone a king. But I am leaving my children behind, while I go far away to a totally foreign continent and a city that is reputed to be nothing but a fortified den of sea pirates. From everything else I have heard of the Vandals, I hardly expect to find the Carthage court very cultivated, or Thrasamund the most loving of husbands."

"Allow me to set you somewhat at ease, Princess," I said. "I myself have never set foot on the continent of Libya, but I have learned some things right here in Rome. The Vandals are a maritime nation, true, and they are ever ready to fight to keep the seas free for their own fleets. But any merchant will tell you that that is only good business. It has certainly made the Vandals rich. And they spend those riches on things more refined than warships and fortifications. Thrasamund has just completed the construction in Carthage of an amphitheater and a vast therma that, I hear, are the grandest in all Libya outside of Egypt."

"And yet," said Amalafrida, "look at what the Vandals did to this very city of Rome, just forty years ago. Why, the rubble is still visible, the evidence of their hacking and tearing at the world's most glorious buildings and monuments."

I shook my head. "The Romans *themselves* have done that, in the years since the Vandals' occupation." I explained to her about the atrocious quarrying of building materials. "When the Vandals were here, they did plunder a good deal of Rome's movable wealth, but they were meticulously careful to cause no damage to the Eternal City itself."

"Can that be true, Thorn? Then why are they known far and wide as wanton destroyers of everything fine and beautiful?"

"Remember, Princess, the Vandals are Arian Christians, like yourself and your royal brother. However, unlike Theodoric, the Vandal kings have never been tolerant of the Catholic Christians. They allow no Catholic bishops anywhere in their lands of Africa. And the Church of Rome has ever been resentful on that account. So, when the Vandals besieged and looted this city, the Romans had their excuse for laying on them a reputation far worse than they deserved. It is the Catholic Christian Church that invented and has perpetuated all those malicious untruths about the Vandals. I confidently expect that, when you get among that people, you will find them no worse than any other Christians."

I do not know whether she did or not, because I personally never visited Carthage, or any other city in Africa, or, for that matter, any place on the whole continent of Libya. But I do know that Amalafrida remained queen to Thrasamund until his death, fifteen years later, which could be taken as testimony that she found her new life not intolerable.

894

I was back in Ravenna again at the time Princess Thiudagotha was preparing to ride west to Aquitania for her marriage to King Alaric of the Visigoths. So I asked Theodoric's permission to ride along with his daughter and her considerable retinue, as far as Genua, just to get my first look at the Ligurian Sea of the Mediterranean. On the way there, Thiudagotha, as she had done in her younger days, confided to me many of her thoughts and feelings, especially her maidenly apprehensions regarding certain aspects of marriage. And I was able, in an avuncular way (or, it might be said, in an auntly way) to give her certain counsels and advices that she could not have got even from her doting father or her attentive female servants (because her father had never been a woman, and her women had never enjoyed my breadth of womanly experience). I heard no thanks afterward from King Alaric, and expected none, but I do hope he properly appreciated the uncommon virtuosity he found his new queen capable of.

By the time I returned from Genua to Ravenna, Theodoric's niece Amalaberga was making ready to ride to the far northern Thuringian lands for *her* marriage to King Hermanafrid. When her train left, I rode partway with that one too, because I had reasons of my own for traveling in that direction—going for a visit to my Novae farm, neglected by its master for so many years. Since Amalaberga and I were only slightly acquainted, not old friends like Thiudagotha and myself, we exchanged no confidences, so she went into wedlock less well prepared than her cousin had done. But I doubted that Hermanafrid would have appreciated any subtle wifely abilities in his new queen. The Thuringi were only a nomadic people, little civilized, and their capital of Isenacum was really only a village, so I imagined that even their king would be of rustic, dull and untutored tastes.

Anyway, as we went north from Ravenna, Amalaberga and I noted with approval the teams of men working on the formerly decrepit Via Popilia—pouring ironstone, laying rock slabs, troweling mortar and tamping marl—making it what a Roman road should be. From that road we travelers could also see the dust clouds rising inland to the west, showing where other work teams were laboring to rebuild the long-derelict aqueduct, in order to bring fresh water once more to Ravenna.

Amalaberga and I parted company at Patavium. Her train kept on northward and I turned westward there, to retrace the course that had brought me and all the other Ostrogoths into Italia. As I proceeded leisurely through Venetia, I saw still other workmen rebuilding the manufactory of army weapons at Concordia that had been in ruins since

895

Attila's time. And, at Aquileia, the Grado harbor was full of teams driving the piles and raising the timbers of new shipyard docks and dry docks for the Roman navy. The whole navy, incidentally, had a new praefectus classiarii, or chief commander, recently promoted by Theodoric from that man's earlier command of just the Hadriatic Fleet. Of course I refer to Lentinus, with whom I happily visited there at Aquileia. His heavier responsibilities had weighted him somewhat with dignity, but when he told me how joyful he was at being "no longer shackled by neutrality," I could perceive that his characteristic enthusiasms were not all outgrown.

✠   ✠   ✠

I was so cordially received by my farm people that I soon felt as if I had never been away. Of course, there were some differences denoting the time that had gone by. One of the slave women whom I had favored in the past, the Alan woman Naranj, wife to my mill steward, no longer had hair as black as moonshade. But their daughter did, and the steward was as proud and honored to lend her to the master as he had once been to lend Naranj. My other favored wench at the farm, the Suevian woman Renata, was rather vexed at that, because she and her husband had only sons, and I politely declined the offer of any of those.

Inasmuch as Theodoric had abdicated his capital of Novae when he took the throne of Rome, this province of Moesia Secunda, lately the mandated Land of the Ostrogoths, had reverted to being again just another province of the Eastern Roman Empire. But that had caused few physical changes in the area. Not every Ostrogoth family had uprooted itself to move west after Theodoric, and many of the men who had fought beside him in Italia had chosen to return here, and Emperor Anastasius was respecting those people's rights to their holdings. Also, there had always been other nationalities resident here besides the Ostrogoths—Greeks, Slovenes, Rumani, various of the Germanic peoples. So there was no noticeable diminution of the population. Some of the farmsteads and workshops and homes (including the town house Veleda had once occupied) had changed owners, but not all, and both the city and the province were flourishing in peace.

This trip back to my farm—and other visits I would make here over the years—I made for a particular purpose. Needless to say, since the farm had been my first real home, I was eager to see it and enjoy it again. But, sentimentality aside, I had a pragmatic aim in view.

I had trusted that I would find my estate still well kept and productive and prosperous, and I did find it so. My free tenants and slaves had not gone lazy or careless for lack of a resident lord. The farm and everyone on it was thriving, and I was pleased to see so many gains, so few losses recorded in the accounts my stewards showed me. It was precisely because I *did* have such capable managers and workers that I had come back here. I had decided to make a business of raising and selling slaves—slaves that were as capable as my own.

I do not mean that I intended to *breed* them, in the way that my farm bred Kehailan horses and earned much profit from the sale of them. (Though I have to remark that my own slave holdings had very much increased in value over the years, simply through their increase in numbers, they having multiplied in the normal human way.) No, what I intended was to found a sort of slave academy—to buy new ones in quantity, young and raw and cheap, and put them to school under my own expert servants, and eventually to sell the finished product at a price much higher than it cost me.

Mind you, I was hardly in need of income. From the Ravenna coffers, Comes Cassiodorus Pater paid me regular stipendia and mercedes commensurate with my office of marshal, and those wages alone would have kept me in ease and comfort. Now, according to my stewards' accounts, I had amassed considerable gold and silver from my Kehailan herd and my farm's other produce. In fact, the stewards had deposited the bulk of that coin with moneylenders in Novae and Prista and Durostorum, with the result that every eight of my invested solidi earned me one additional solidus in interest every year. So I was more than solvent, if nowhere near as rich as, say, Comes Cassiodorus. I was not avaricious to pile up wealth, and I had no loved ones on whom to squander it, and none to bequeath it to when I died. However, in just the first few days of my first visit to Rome, I had discerned there a lack of a certain commodity, and had realized that I could fill that lack by turning slave dealer. So why not try my hand at that? If it earned me an estimable fortune, I would not spurn it.

I hasten to say that Rome suffered no paucity of slave men, women and children; it had multitudes. What it lacked was really *good* slaves. In times past, Roman households might have contained the finest quality of bondsmen—physicians, artists, accountants—but they no longer did. In times past, many Roman slaves had been such able men that they earned the money to buy their freedom, or were so much admired that

897

they were freely manumitted, and then went on to become luminaries of Roman civilization—Phaedrus, Terence, Publilius Syrus—but no slaves did that nowadays.

In most of the rest of the world, as on my Novae farm, bondsmen were regarded as tools and implements, and it made sense to have one's tools sharp, capable, efficient. But in modern Rome and in the other Roman cities of Italia, those tools were being deliberately kept as blunt and clumsy as possible. That is to say, the slave men and women were denied any education or training or encouragement to improve their natural talents. Very few were employed in any positions higher than yard laborer and kitchen trull. The ones of foreign nationality were even discouraged from learning more than enough Latin to understand the commands given them.

There were two reasons for this. Both reasons were as ancient as the institution of slavery itself, but only in these modern times were they being so seriously, solemnly, even *morbidly* regarded by the Romans. Those who owned slaves were naturally accustomed to make sexual use of the attractive females among them. And that naturally provoked in those freemen a dread that their free *women* might take similar liberties in the slave quarters. So they exerted every effort to keep the bondsmen bestial, ignorant, ill favored and unappealing. The other reason was equally inherent in the institution. The slaves in Italia outnumbered the free folk, and the apprehension was that—if the bondsmen were educated above the level of domestic animals—they would soon *realize* their numerical superiority and would unite in uprising against their masters.

It was not long ago that the Roman Senate debated a proposal to make all bondsmen dress in a uniform costume, rather in the same way that all prostitutes are made to wear yellow wigs. That would have averted the possibility of a free woman's mistaking a good-looking, well-spoken slave for a freeman, hence the possibility of her yielding to his embrace. But the proposal was voted down because it conflicted with the other reason for fearing slaves. If they all dressed alike, they could easily see how many they were, and how comparatively few were their masters. There was already one kind of uniformity among the bondsmen that no one had thought to prevent—their widespread adherence to Christianity—and that very much worried the senators and every other Roman.

(I must here qualify an earlier statement of mine. True, Rome's upper and lower classes of freemen—as I have said—are blithely pagan, heretic or totally irreligious. But I erred in saying that Rome is Christian "only in the middle." I neglected to mention the slaves. One does tend to overlook slaves.)

As everyone is aware, Christianity got its first toehold in Rome among just that hapless and despised underclass, and it has been the favored religion of slaves ever since. Nowadays, even those bondsmen imported from abroad—even Nubians and Ethiopes who must have worshipped unimaginably odd gods in their savage Libyan lands—have converted wholeheartedly to Christianity. Slaves, like tradesmen, adopt that faith because they see it as a profitable transaction. For good behavior in this mortal life, they are promised a rich reward in the hereafter, and that is about the only kind of reward the average slave can hope for. But the free Romans, of whatever faith, were forever fretting that the bondsmen's Christianity might somehow prove a unifying force, and someday impel them to revolt in mass.

Well, I knew that to be a baseless apprehension. Christianity teaches that the worse a man's lot here on earth, the better it will be in heaven. So Christianity preaches that slaves should *be* slaves—content, meek, abject, never aspiring above their humble station. "Servants, obey in all things your masters." Clearly, the more Christian the bondsmen, the less chance of their *ever* being unruly. As for the other abiding fear— that free women would make free use of male slaves—I knew that no law, nobody, *nothing* could ensure against that. I was a woman. I could have told the Roman Senate and all of Rome's other freemen that they were flailing at the shadow of an ass. Any woman desiring to disport herself with any man will do so. Let a slave wear an identifying costume, or put on a frightful wig, or be Nubian black and ugly—or even be tightly manacled to a cell wall in Rome's dread Tullianum prison—if a woman wants him, she will have him.

899

✠   ✠   ✠

"So, when I commence peddling my slaves there," I said, "I may find myself accused of perverting the morals of Rome."

Meirus laughed coarsely. "What morals are those?"

He was the same old Mudman. He must be *very* old by now, I thought, but his vast beard was as glossy black as ever, and his vinegar temperament had not at all sweetened with age. If he was changed in the least, it was only in his having got rather stouter yet, and in wearing regal raiment and many rings on his fingers. That was thanks to his increased wealth, he said, and *that* was thanks to his success in the amber trade, and *that* was thanks to his partner Maghib (his *partner* now!) on the Amber Coast.

At the slave mart in Novae I had found only a very few young slaves that met my requirements and were worth buying. It was the same in Prista and Durostorum; the port cities on the lower Danuvius simply do not have sizable slave stocks from which to choose. So I had come all the way downriver to Noviodunum again, because there is a brisk slave trade in the ports around the Black Sea, and of course I had come calling on old Meirus.

"What you must do," he went on, as he poured more wine for us both, "you must make your slaves so *very* competent at their occupations that, if one is sometime caught in bed with his master's wife, the master will discharge the *wife*."

"I hope to make them so. The boys and girls that I have already bought, I put immediately to apprentice under my own flawless servants—my cellarer, my house steward, my notary and so on—put each child to whichever calling seemed best suited to what I could perceive of its aptitudes. But I would like to have every tutor working with several at once. And in the river cities I found not many to select from."

"You have come now to the right place. Noviodunum gets all sizes, shapes, ages and colors. Males, females, eunuchs, charismatics. Persians, Khazars, Mysians, Cherkesses, everything else you ever heard of, and some you probably never did. Have you any particular preferences? The Cherkess people are the handsomest, I think."

"I care only that they be young—none older than adolescent—bright, sturdy, untrained and therefore *cheap*. I am not dealing in concubines or toys or love-boys. All I want is good raw material that my academy can mill and refine and forge and polish."

"Understood. We will cast about the marts tomorrow, and I imagine you will net a whole bargeful to take back upriver. Allow me to be your nose here in Noviodunum from now on, as Maghib is mine in Pomore. I will continue supplying your farm, and with only the best stock. Speaking of races and colors, there lately came to the market here two or three young women of the far-eastern people called Seres. Exquisite, tiny, fine-boned and *yellow* of skin—all over. I marvel that such fragile beauties came safely all the way from there to here. And cheap, those were not. Only one is still here. She was bought by Apostolides, leno of the best lupanar in Noviodunum. After our nahtamats, I shall introduce you there. You must try the young lady. *That* will not come cheap, either, but worth the cost, I am assured."

As we dined, on oysters, asparagus and hare jugged with tart plums, accompanied by a Cephalene wine, I asked Meirus how Theodoric's rule in the formerly Western Empire was being regarded here in the Eastern.

"Vái, the same way it is being regarded, I should suppose, by every ruler and noble and commoner and slave from here to the Tin Islands. It is universally said that his reign bids fair to be Rome's most contented and peaceful and prosperous since the time of 'the five good emperors.' That is to say, the period from Nerva the Kindly to Marcus the Golden, and that was four centuries ago."

I said, "I am pleased to hear that so many approve of him."

"Well, they approve of his ability at governing, not necessarily of *him*. No one forgets the treacherous way in which he slew Odoacer. The general opinion is that every one of Theodoric's close advisers must be walking on tiptoe, not to chance a sudden sword stroke."

"Balgs-daddja," I growled. "I am one of the closest. I do not walk on tiptoe."

"And there are others who are openly envious of his skill at kingship. Our Emperor Anastasius, for one, does not like Theodoric. Of course, the crabbed Anastasius has never liked anything much. But it naturally chafes him to see a ruler of a lesser title outshining him in statecraft."

901

"Do you think Anastasius will cause trouble?"

"Not any time soon. He has more pressing things to worry about—a renewal of the eternal contention with the Persians on his eastern borders. Ne, Theodoric's problems will not come from abroad, but from right under his nose. When I said he is admired from here to the Tin Islands, that is because the Catholic Christian Church holds no sway here or in the Tin Islands. In Italia and the other provinces where it does wield influence, it will do its best to belittle and beleaguer Theodoric."

"I know. It is despicable. Why cannot the Church clerics treat him with the same innocuous indifference he accords them?"

"You have just said why. *Because* he pays them no mind at all. They would be genuinely happy if he persecuted them, oppressed them, banished them. To them, his indifference is a much more hateful attack than forthright molestation would be. He begrudges them the pleasure and honor of martyrdom. He makes them suffer *not* suffering for the sake of their Mother Church."

"You are probably right."

"What is worse, he has set the churchmen back in one area where they thought they were advancing."

"Eh? He has done nothing to any churchmen."

"Again, by ignoring them. Look here. When Anastasius took the imperial crown and the purple robe and all the other regalia of the Eastern Empire, he was given them from the hands of the Patriarch Bishop of Constantinople. And Anastasius was lying prone at the bishop's feet, in the demeaning position of proskynésis. But what did Theodoric do? He took his throne by conquest, by popular acclaim, by vote of the Roman Senate. Unlike Anastasius, he did not once pause to ask the blessing of God or of any church whatever. He was not crowned by a bishop of his own Arian creed, much less by the so-called Papa. That sets back all the bishops in Christendom, and it must gall the very soul of the one at Rome."

Later, at the lupanar, the girl of the Seres proved such a delicious experience that I was half tempted to leave an order with the local slave dealers to procure one for me. She was exotic of color and features, and as soft, smooth, sleek as the silk that also comes hither from her homeland. She spoke no human language, only twittered like a bird, but she made up for that deficiency with her venereal talent. She was a veritable gymnast and contortionist—and *tight*, as of course I had expected on first seeing her budlike little mouth. As I was leaving the house, I asked its leno, Apostolides, whether the girl was also shrewish of temper, as a small-mouthed western woman would be.

"Not in the least, Saio Thorn. I am told that *all* Seres are narrowly pursed of mouth, above and below. This one, I am given to understand, has a larger mouth than most, so it follows that she is of sweet and amiable humor. Perhaps her even more puckered sisters may be mean-tempered in the western womanly way. Who can say? But ah! just imagine how tight *they* must be in their nether apertures."

Anyway, I refrained from ordering the procurement of one for myself. I decided my money would be better spent on less frivolous indulgences. So, when I left Noviodunum again, my barge was heavy-laden with boys and girls of more familiar aspect, mostly Khazars, a few Greeks and Cherkesses. On the long, slow haul upriver, I had time to begin their education—teaching them some rudiments of the Latin tongue—before I delivered them into the care and tutelage of my Novae academicians.

✠ ✠ ✠

When I returned to Ravenna, along the now level and smooth Via Popilia, that city was already a much more gracious place. Its workers' suburb of Caesarea, formerly squalid and noisome, had been cleaned up considerably. The aqueduct was bringing drinkable water to the spouts and fountains that had for so long been dry, and, as if that new flow had irrigated a new growth of stone and brick and tile in the city, some impressive new buildings were under construction. Most notable of those were Theodoric's palace and the Arian cathedral he had promised Bishop Neon, though that worthy man had been dead for some time.

The high central portion of Theodoric's palace was, in imitation of the Golden Gate of the city in which he had passed his childhood, fronted with three soaring arches. In the triangular tympanum between the arches' tops and the slanting roof was carved a figure of the king on horseback. From either flank of the central building extended a slightly less high loggia of two stories, the lower having three arches, the upper having five. And in those ten upper arches would stand statues representing Victories. Sculptors imported from Greece were already at work on those, and others were just beginning the more colossal group of figures that was to stand atop the roof. It would consist of Theodoric on his horse, holding shield and spear, attended by female figures representing Rome and Ravenna, the whole assemblage to be gold-leafed. When complete, the sculpture was to be so huge and high that the gleam of its gilding would guide mariners coming from the Hadriatic into the Classis harbor.

903

The cathedral Church of St. Apollinaris, named for a distinguished early bishop of Arian Christianity, was the biggest Arian church anywhere in the world; to my knowledge, it still is. It also contains a tasteful feature that I have seen in no other church. Down either side wall of its vast, twenty-four-columned chamber stretch panels of rich mosaic, of brilliant figures on a dark blue background. Along the right wall, on the side where the men of a congregation stand to worship, the mosaic figures are of Christ, the apostles and other saints, all the usual biblical males. But the panel along the left wall, where the women stand, shows all female figures: the Virgin, the Magdalen and other biblical women. I have never known any other Christian church to make such a nice gesture of recognition of its female parishioners.

Also underway, all about Ravenna, was the staggeringly ambitious and laborious work intended to make the city really livable. That was the draining of the miasmic, stinking, vermin-ridden marshes. Thousands of men and hundreds of oxen were plowing the flat, wet land into ridges and furrows—the water to run off the former into the latter, thence into deeper ditches and still deeper trenches, thence into permanent canals of stone and ironstone that would convey the effluent out to the seashore. That was no work of just a few years. It is still going on, and may have to go on for decades more. But even when I first saw the dredgers at work, Ravenna's many street canals were carrying water almost as clear and odorless as that coming from the spouts and fountains.

It was young Boethius, magister officiorum, who was guiding me about the city and showing me all these things. One of his duties as Master of the Offices was the finding and collecting of special workers like architects and artificers and sculptors, sometimes having to fetch them from distant places.

"And this," he said proudly, indicating another grand edifice under construction, "will be Theodoric's mausoleum. May Fortune grant that it will be many years before he shall have use for it."

The solid and tranquil-looking building was all of marble blocks. Its two-story exterior was ten-sided, but the lofty interior was round and would be capped with a dome.

904

"Not the usual kind of dome, however," said Boethius. "A single massive piece of marble, to be smoothly rounded off by the sculptors. Yonder it lies. That enormous monolith came from the quarries of Istria—a formidable undertaking, to bring it here—and, if it could be weighed, would weigh more than six hundred libramenta."

"Theodoric should sleep comfortably under it," I said. "He will certainly have plenty of room in there to stretch and thrash in his sleep."

"Eheu, he did not plan to sleep alone," said Boethius, a little sadly. "He planned for this to be the resting place of all his descendants as well. However, his Queen Audefleda has just been delivered of their first child. You had heard? Yes, another daughter. Unless the queen soon produces some sons for Theodoric, he will have only matrilineal and collateral descendants lying beside him in that tomb."

That did not yet seem to be worrying Theodoric. He was in fine spirits when I dined with him and recounted to him my latest travels and doings.

"And you are now headed back to Rome again, Thorn? Then you can deliver a mandatum for me. Did you know? I made my own first visit there while you were away."

Boethius had told me about that. Theodoric had been welcomed with an imperial triumph, a splendid procession, and had been extravagantly entertained during his stay—chariot races at the circus, men-versus-beasts fights at the Colosseum, plays at the Marcellian Theater, feasts and convivia in all the finest homes. He had been invited to address the Senate, and his oration had brought all the senators up standing and cheering.

"Mainly, though," he said, "I got to see with my own eyes the piece-meal ruination of the city that you have so much deplored. I ordered that every possible measure be taken to stop that desecration of artistic and architectural treasures. And, to that end, I am going to pay to Rome an annual grant of two hundred librae of gold, strictly to be spent on the restoration and preservation of buildings, monuments, walls and such."

"I applaud you," I said. "But can the treasury afford such benefi-cence?"

"Well, the frugal Comes Cassiodorus grumbled a bit. But he has lev-ied a new duty on imported wines. That will provide the money."

"Then I applaud him too. You mentioned a mandatum. Something to do with this matter?"

"Ja, I must correct an oversight of my own. When I spoke to the Senate, and announced this grant, I specified *only* buildings and monu-ments and such. I neglected to mention the city's *statues*. As you know, they are likewise being nibbled away. So I wish to make clear that they are also to be repaired and preserved with this money. The quaestor and exceptor Cassiodorus Filius is preparing the mandatum. Get it from him, Thorn, and please see that it is read in the Senate, posted in the *Diurnal* and cried in the streets."

So I sought out the younger Cassiodorus, who smiled and said, "You may wish to read this before I seal it," and slid a stack of papyri across his table to me.

"Which one is the mandatum I am to carry?" I asked, riffling through the sheets.

"What?" He looked surprised. "Why, all of those are the mandatum."

"This entire sheaf? This is Theodoric's order to stop the destruction of things in Rome?"

"Yes, of course." He looked perplexed. "Is that not what you came for?"

"Cassiodorus, good Cassiodorus," I said. "A mandatum is only to make the order official. All I really have to do is go to Rome and utter two words. 'Stop this.' Two words."

"Well?" He looked slightly hurt. "That is what *this* says. Read it."

"Read it? I can barely lift it." I was exaggerating, of course, but not much. The top papyrus, addressed "to the Senate and People of Rome," began:

"The noble and praiseworthy art of statuary is said to have been first practiced in Italia by the Etruscans. Posterity has embraced it, and given to the city of Rome an artificial population almost equal to its natural one. I refer to the abundance of statues of gods and heroes and distinguished Romans of the past, and to the mighty herd of horses of stone and metal adorning our streets and squares and fora. If there were any reverence in human nature, it, and not the cohortes vigilum, ought to be a sufficient guardian of the statuary treasures of Rome. But what shall we say of the costly marbles, the expensive bronzes, precious both in material and workmanship, which too many a hand yearns, if it has opportunity, to pluck from their settings? . . . As well as to Rome's forest of walls, it is desirable that the necessary repairs be made to its population of statues. And meanwhile, all upstanding citizens must be on guard that this artificial population is no further molested and mutilated and carried off in pieces. Oh, honest citizens, we ask you, who, when entrusted with such a charge, can be negligent? Who can be venal? You must watch for such pilfering scoundrels as we have described. Then, when the villain is taken, rightly will the grieving public punish him who has marred the beauty of the ancients with amputation of limbs, by inflicting on him that which he had made our monuments to suffer . . ."

I stopped, shuffled the pages together, cleared my throat and said, "You were right, Cassiodorus, it *does* say 'stop this.' Only much more . . . much more . . ."

"Much more unmistakably," he offered. "Much more fully."

"Fully. That was the word I wanted."

"If you will read on, Saio Thorn, you will like it even better. Where I have King Theodoric expatiate on the need for—"

"No, no, Cassiodorus," I said, shoving the pages back to him. "I think I will save the rest. I do not wish to spoil the pleasure of getting its impact. Fully. When its ringing sounds are given forth in the hall of the Curia."

"Declaimed in the Senate!" he said joyfully as he rolled the papyri into a tube shape, dripped melted lead to hold them scrolled, and stamped that with Theodoric's seal. "In the Senate!"

"Yes," I said. "And I would wager everything I own that it will be received there with cries of 'Vere diserte! Nove diserte!'"

906

4

uring most of the years of Theodoric's reign, I was chiefly occupied in doing what I had been doing practically all my life—traveling, observing, learning, experiencing. Every other one of the king's marshals was glad to be given a settled, secure position, but I was much more glad to be the king's wandering emissary, his far-reaching arm and far-seeing eye. Theodoric might sometimes require me to spend some while in attendance at his court, or I might choose to stay for a while in one of my residences in Rome or Novae, but I was oftenest to be found somewhere else within Theodoric's realm, or beyond it, or on my way to or fro.

907

Sometimes at the express command of Theodoric, sometimes of my own accord, I went everywhere from the luxurious Baiae seaside resort of the Roman nobility to the remotest outlands of alien tribes. Sometimes I went in the boar-ornamented armor and other insignia of my marshalcy, sometimes in the elegant raiment that a herizogo or dux is entitled to flaunt, but most often I went in the anonymous dress of a simple country wayfarer. Sometimes I took along a troop of soldiers, sometimes just a few serving men so that I would have messengers available to carry dispatches, but most often I went alone and brought back my reports in person.

I might return to say, "Theodoric, in yonder place your subjects are commendably obeying your laws and orders."

Or: "In another place, Theodoric, your subjects require governors more strict than those now in office."

Or: "In a certain land beyond your borders I detected smoldering envy of your rich realm, and those people may attempt a plundering incursion."

Or: "In another land beyond your borders, the envy is so wistful that those people might welcome your annexing them to your domain."

Or I might report on the progress of one or another of Theodoric's many projects intended to better the life of his subjects. Under his direction, the old Roman roads and aqueducts and bridges and cloacae were put in good repair, and new ones constructed where needed. As was being done with the marshes of Ravenna, he set additional swarms of men and oxen to work at draining the Pomptine Marshes around Rome, and similar swampy areas around Spoletium and the pretty promontory of Anxur.

But, akh, I need not cite every one of the innumerable achievements and benefices of Theodoric's reign. They can all be found in the official history of these years. Cassiodorus Filius, in addition to his routine writings, has long been working on that. The exceptor and quaestor has personal experience of everything that has occurred since Theodoric took the throne, and for the time before that, he has relied much on my own manuscript account of the Goths' past. (I only wish that the writing of the official history had been entrusted to Boethius—it would have proved far more readable—but Cassiodorus's *Historia Gothorum* assuredly will be nothing if not *voluminous*.)

908   Under the rule and care of Theodoric, the once Roman Empire of the West *has* attained to its finest flowering since that long-ago era of "the five good emperors." Well before the king's beard began to turn from gold to silver, he was being called Theodoric the Great, not just by sycophants and flatterers but also by many of his fellow monarchs. Even those not allied with him, or not especially fond of him, have frequently deferred to his sage advice and counsels. As for Theodoric's subjects . . . well, the more hidebound Romans never ceased resenting his being an outlander, and the purblind Catholic Christians never ceased despising his being an Arian, and many other people never ceased regarding him with dubiety for the manner of his slaying Odoacer. But not one of those people can deny today that he is living better, and in a better land, thanks to Theodoric.

As I have said, Theodoric did not, in the manner of earlier conquerors, try to impose his own or his people's standards of morality, custom, culture or religion upon his new subjects. Instead, he did what he could to make the Roman citizens more conscious of their own heritage, and more respectful of it, as when he put an end to the detrition of antique monuments, and encouraged their restoration.

He tampered with Rome's venerable body of laws only to the extent of making some of those laws more lenient, some more strict. For example, under the Roman code, whatever the punishment of a convicted criminal, it almost always included the confiscation of his property, wealth and personal belongings—and not just *his*; every remotest relative of his could be similarly stripped of every last possession. Theodoric made that law more merciful, exempting from confiscation all the convict's relatives beyond the third degree of kinship.

On the other hand, the crime of bribery was only mildly punished—by banishment of the perpetrator—*when* bribery was punished at all. It was so rife among officeholders that none of them ever denounced another. Indeed it was so accepted as a fact of life that the civil servants had formulated a system setting certain perquisites for every level of administration. Say a citizen went to a tabularius to get a license to set up a stall in the market. That clerk, besides taking the citizen's money for the license fee, would also consult his schedule of bribes to see what sum he could extort for this particular request. However, when Theodoric decreed that the penalty for bribery would henceforth be death, the incidence of such extortions quickly diminished.

Death was already the punishment fixed, by Roman law, for any person found guilty of making false accusation against another. And it would seem that there could be no punishment more draconian than death, but Theodoric felt that this crime deserved one. He considered false accusation so despicably craven an act that he ordered such perjurers to be burned alive.

909

And Theodoric found in the Roman lands one kind of fraudulence that was unknown in the outlands. Here, both the man who produced a commodity and the man who needed that commodity were long accustomed to being cheated by the intermediary man—the tradesman who bought from the one and sold to the other. That was because every tradesman was so adept at paying for his supplies of merchandise with filed, chipped or cased coins, and equally adept at giving short measure to the customers who bought from him. So Theodoric had the clever Boethius devise new, inflexible standards of coinage and of weights and measures. The moneyers of the mint produced the new coins, and Boethius set overseers in the markets to enforce the new standards.

In undertaking to eradicate Rome's rampant corruption and favoritism in high circles and the "amicitia" that was only a polite word for complicity in dishonesty, Theodoric spared not even one of his own close relations. His nephew Theodahad was accused of having engaged in questionable practices in acquiring for himself a sizable estate in Liguria. I was not surprised, for this was the son of Amalafrida whom I had found unattractive even in his youth. It was never proved that there really was any fraud involved in the land transaction, so Theodahad was not punished, but the mere suspicion of impropriety was enough to make Theodoric command him to return the land to its original owners.

Theodoric's determination to provide justice impartially for all his subjects led him to decree another modification of Roman law, though he knew well that it would earn him increased invective from his detractors. It might have seemed a minor alteration, a matter of just a few words—stipulating that the courts must treat with fairness even "those who err from the faith"—but that was enough to excite wrath among both the hidebound Romans and the Church of Rome. "Those who err from the faith" would have included even Theodoric himself, since he was not a Catholic Christian, and every other Arian, heretic and pagan as well. But most particularly, that phrase extended justice even to *Jews*. Not within the memory of the oldest Roman had a Jew been allowed to bring suit in court against anybody but another Jew. And the Church of Rome was infinitely more scandalized, horrified, outraged. "A detestable Jew will now be able to testify against an upright Christian!" roared every one of its priests from every one of its ambos. *"And be believed!"*

However, one of Theodoric's innovations was admired and approved even by those who might be cursing him on other accounts. He and his stern administrator of finances, Comes Cassiodorus Pater, put a new and tight rein on the government's tax collectors. In the past, those exactores had not been paid by the state for their labors. Their emolument was whatever they could gouge out of a taxpayer *above* what he was legitimately assessed. True, that system had ensured Rome's collection of every last nummus it was owed, but it also had made the tax collectors wealthy and the taxpayers murderously mutinous. Now the exactores were paid a fixed stipendium and were scrupulously supervised to prevent their abusing their office. It may have made them less rigorous in their collecting, and probably cost Theodoric's treasury some revenue, but his people were much happier. Anyway, Cassiodorus Pater so ably managed the realm's finances that there seemed usually to be a comfortable surplus in the treasury, enabling Theodoric sometimes to lessen taxes or rescind them entirely in districts that suffered a poor harvest or some other kind of calamity.

He was always more mindful of the welfare of the commonfolk than of the nobility and the merchant classes, and he angered many of the latter when he set fixed prices on staple foodstuffs and other necessities of life. But the tradesmen were few, compared to the many of the plebecula who benefited from that decree. A family could buy a whole modius of wheat, enough for a week of meals, for just three denarii, and a whole congius of fairly palatable wine for a single sesterce. Only occasionally did Theodoric's concern for the lower classes make him err in judgment. Probably his least wise move was his forbidding grain merchants to export that product out of Italia in search of better profits abroad. Theodoric's advisers Boethius and Cassiodorus Pater hastened to explain to him that such a sanction would redound to the ruin of all the grain farmers in Campania, and he immediately revoked the decree. From then on, he was careful always to consult Comes Cassiodorus and Magister Boethius on matters of good intention that could have adverse effects, and they kept him from making too many such mistakes.

In Theodoric's address to the Roman Senate, he had said that "reverently to preserve the old is even more commendable than to erect the new," but he did both.

It was not long before, all over Italia and in outlying provinces too, there stood newly erected edifices and lovingly refurbished old ones bearing dedicatory tiles gratefully affixed by the local folk: REG DN THEOD FELIX ROMAE. But whenever some foreign dignitary, newcome to these lands, complimented the king on his having made so many contributions to the felicity of the Roman Empire, Theodoric would relate an ironic little tale:

911

"There was in ancient times a talented sculptor. He was commanded to raise a monument to the ruling king, and he sculptured a most impressive one. But on the base of it he chiseled a lavish encomium to *himself.* Over that he plastered a layer of ironstone, in which he chiseled the expected encomium to the king. During the course of years, the ironstone flaked away, exposing the original inscription. So the king's name was forgotten, and the name of the long-dead sculptor meant nothing to anybody."

I suspect that Theodoric was thinking, and perhaps not too cheerfully, of the subsequence of his own reign.

After the birth of the latest daughter, Amalaswintha, there were no more children. One might have thought that the king, despairing of *ever* siring a son, had ceased to bed his queen. I knew that was not so, for he and Audefleda were ever tender and loving to one another, and I saw them as often in private as in public. Nevertheless, for whatever reason, the queen never gave birth again. The daughter meanwhile, in one respect, excelled her heritage. The product of two handsome races and of exceptionally handsome parents, Amalaswintha grew up to be more beautiful even than might have been expected. Unfortunately, she being an only child, the *last* child, she was too much catered to and spoiled by her father, mother, nurses, servants and everyone else at court. Inevitably, she grew to be a haughty, demanding, petulant, self-centered young lady, unlikable in spite of her physical charms.

I remember how once, when she was no more than ten years of age, in my presence she gave a vicious tongue-lashing to a palace maid who had committed some trifling error of service. Since Amalaswintha's parents were not in the room, and since I was more than old enough to be her parent myself, I presumed to chide her:

"Girl, your royal father would never speak that way to his meanest slave. Certainly not when someone else was present to hear."

She drew herself up to her tallest and, though she had only a snub nose, managed to look down it at me, and said coldly, "My father may sometimes forget that he is a king, and neglect to demand the respect due him as a king, but I will never forget that I am a king's daughter."

When Amalaswintha's pettiness of nature became apparent even to Theodoric and Audefleda, they were of course grieved and troubled, but by then there was nothing to be done in the way of remolding her. And I think Theodoric might be forgiven, to some degree, for his part in the overcoddling that had made the princess such a virago. His other two daughters were wives of foreign kings, so this one would be his successor, Amalaswintha Regina or even Amalaswintha Imperatrix. She and her eventual consort—and *he* would have to be most painstakingly chosen—would provide whatever royal lineage was to descend from Theodoric the Great.

✠　　✠　　✠

In some of Theodoric's farther-flung ventures aimed at developing the produce and trade of his domain, I was his principal agent. I led a troop of legionaries and military fabri south into Campania to reopen a long-abandoned gold mine there and to recruit native workers for it, then led another troop around the Hadriatic into Dalmatia to do the same at three disused iron mines in that province. At each location, I appointed a faber to oversee the workings and left a turma of soldiers to keep order, and I stayed long enough to satisfy myself that the mine *would* produce before I moved on.

Although Rome in its great days had been the center of a network of trade routes spraddled all over Europe, practically the only such channel of trade still in continuous use by the time Theodoric came to rule was the salt trail between Ravenna and the Regio Salinarum. Naturally wishing to revive the once bustling traffic of commerce, Theodoric directed me to start laying out the routes again, and those projects occupied me for several years.

The reopening of an east-west corridor was not too difficult, because all of it lay within the more or less civilized nations and provinces, from Aquitania to the Black Sea. Some of the old Roman roads required repair, but in general they were passable, kept safe for travel by frequent guard posts, sufficiently provided with lodging, eating and resting places for the merchants and their trains. The Danuvius River, providing a water route for those who preferred it, was likewise well guarded by the Pannonian and Moesian fleets of the Roman navy, and was likewise dotted with villages and other stopping places along its banks. Meirus the Mudman was pleased when I appointed him Theodoric's praefectus in charge of supervising the eastern end of those trails. His own city of Noviodunum was the Black Sea terminus of the river travel, and he scuttled back and forth, as necessary, to the other port cities—Constantiana, Kallatis, Odessus, Anchialus—that were the termini of the overland roads. Not at all to my surprise, Meirus did an irreproachable job of maintaining that end of the line, while never neglecting his own several businesses and his supplying of slaves for my Novae academy.

The reopening of Rome's north-south trade corridor was much more arduous and took much more time, because the lands north of the Danuvius never *had* been Roman or much civilized by Rome or much inclined to friendship with Rome. But I did get that laid out, with the result that Italia had an access to the Sarmatic Ocean more secure and reliable than the empire had ever had before. To forge the trail itself, I followed pretty much the same route that had brought me and Prince Frido south from the Amber Coast, only seeking paths and roads that would accommodate carts and wagons and spans of draft animals.

On my first journey, I took along a sizable force of cavalry—not legionaries but Ostrogothic and other Germanic warriors. If we had resembled a Roman invasion, we would have encountered much more opposition than we did. But I was able to convince the petty kings and tribal chiefs along the way that we were their kinsmen, representatives of their *great* kinsman Theodoric (or Dieterikh af Bern, as many of them now called him), whose only intent was to make a peaceable highway through their lands, as much to their benefit as to his. Only three or four of those rustic rulers made any objection, and only one or two

913

threatened active resistance, in which cases we simply made a circuitous way around their little patches of territory. At intervals, I dropped off detachments of my troops, instructing them to set up guard posts and enlist native warriors to help man them. On a second journey along the same route—a much, much slower journey—I took with me not only another troop of cavalry but also a considerable population of town and country men and their families, all of whom desired to seek their fortunes in far and uncrowded places. Those I dropped off—one or two or three families at a time—to start the building of roadside tabernae and stables, each establishment perhaps to be the nucleus of a future community of some size.

Before the first of those journeys northward brought me again to Pomore on the Wendic Gulf, I had already heard from other travelers that the Rugii were no longer ruled by Queen Giso. She had been dead almost as long as had her royal husband, and had been succeeded by a young man named Eraric, a nephew of the late Feva-called-Feletheus. This new King Eraric, having got word of my approach, was waiting to welcome me with open arms, because he was as eager as Theodoric to

have an overland, all-year trade route between their two countries. As I already knew, the Viswa River, the Rugians' main avenue to the interior of Europe, was useless during the long northern winter and, in the best of weather, enabled only a tediously slow voyage for travelers going south against its strong current.

So Eraric gladly dispatched numbers of his Rugian soldiers and Kashube and Wilzi peasants from his end of the trail to supplement those I had posted. The soldiers would occupy the guard posts, the Slovene peasants would clear and grade the path to make it more easily travelable, and would build lodging places along it. The Slovenes being good only for hard labor, they would return to Pomore when their work was done, and higher-grade Rugian peasant families would be sent out to manage those establishments.

As soon as Eraric and I had completed our arrangements, I hurried off to find my old companion Maghib, and found him living in a very grand stone house. The Armenian was nowadays almost as fat as his partner Meirus, of equally elegant dress, even oilier of complexion, and as loquacious as he had always been.

"Ja, Saio Thorn, Queen Giso is long gone from among us. When the word came that both her husband and her son had fallen in battle, she flew into a frenzy that ended with the rupture of a blood vessel in her head. Perhaps she severed it by gnashing her extraordinary teeth. Giso was not mourning her menfolk, you understand, she was enraged to realize that her dreams of greater queenship had been dashed. Well, it happened none too soon for me, I can tell you. That tiresome woman had been intolerably tiring my—er, my nose, as you will recall. Later I married a maiden of nearer my own humble station in life, and side by side we have been improving our station ever since." He broke off to introduce me to the wife, a broad-faced, broad-beamed woman of the local Wilzi Slovenes. "As you can see, Hujek and I have richly prospered from the flourishing amber trade."

"It should flourish even more with the new and quicker route of transport southward," I said. "Many years ago, Maghib, I promised that Theodoric would reward you for your gallant surrender of your nose to that Giso creature. I would now like to offer you the post of the king's praefectus here at this end of the new route. It pays only a modest stipendium, but of course you will know ways to profit from the office. Charge the merchants for the affixing of your official seal, or—"

"Ne, ne," he said virtuously. "This is such a high honor for a mere maggot of an Armenian that I would not sully it for any amount of money. Tell the king that I gratefully accept that post, and that his praefectus here will never graft so much as a nummus onto the prices of the wares that he and his people receive from Pomore."

So, eventually, both the north-south and the east-west trade routes were as heavily and profitably traveled as they had been in the empire's palmiest days. And various lesser trails and sea lanes brought to those main routes the products of nations distant from Europe, those lands on the farther shores of the Germanic Ocean and the Sarmatic Ocean and the Black Sea—merchandise from Britannia, Scotia, Skandza, Colchis, the Chersonesus, even silk and other rare treasures from the land of the Seres. Meanwhile, the new ships built at Theodoric's instigation were doing a brisk trade all around the Mediterranean: with the Vandals in Africa, the Suevians in Hispania, the Roman colonies in Egypt, Palestine, Syria, Arabia Petraea.

Of course, as always throughout history, the prosperous and beneficent foreign trade was sometimes interrupted by wars or uprisings. Several of those occurred in countries too far away for Theodoric or Emperor Anastasius or any of their allies to do anything about them. But some flared up close enough to Theodoric's domain so that he sent armies to quell them. Neither he nor I rode with those troops, and even their commanders were not the men who had led when he and I were active warriors. Old Saio Soas, the generals Ibba and Pitzias and Her-

915

duic had all died or retired from service by this time. The generals now were Thulwin and Odoin, whom I had not met at all, and Witigis and Tulum, whom I had briefly known when they held the ranks only of optio and signifer at the time of the siege of Verona.

One of the insurgents they went to fight, however, was an old familiar. It was the Gepid tribe that had vainly tried to impede our advance toward Italia those many years ago. Their ambush of us at Vadum on the river Savus had cost them many men and their king, Thrausila, and cost us our Rugian ally King Feletheus. Now it seemed the Gepids were again brashly testing our mettle, and not far away from the first place they had tried it. Under their new king, Thrasaric, son of the dead Thrausila, they besieged, overwhelmed and occupied Sirmium, that pig-producing city in Pannonia where our army had wintered on the way west from Novae.

Remembering how Sirmium smelled, I personally might have been inclined to let the Gepids keep it, but of course that was out of the question. For one thing, the Gepids there could put a permanent squeeze on the river traffic. But more important, the city of Sirmium marked the easternmost extent of Theodoric's lands. Notwithstanding the official amity existing between him and Anastasius, that province of Pannonia *still* was the place where east and west never had quite settled the border between them, and where neither would tolerate any encroachment by anybody.

Thus, when our army swept through Pannonia, Anastasius angrily declared that it trespassed on the soil of the Eastern Empire. That may have been true, because our troops very easily flushed the Gepids out of Sirmium, and then chased them some distance eastward before turning around to march home to Italia. Anyway, the incursion gave Anastasius an excuse to declare war on Theodoric to punish his "presumption and insubordination." Actually, the emperor was only making a gesture to assert his supremacy, because the war never amounted to more than harassment. Since he could not spare any of his land forces from their perpetual entanglement with the Persian Empire, he sent only some war galleys to attack Italia. And all they did was sail to several of our southern seaports and drop anchor in the harbor mouths, with a view to cutting off our trade with other Mediterranean countries. But the warships did not squat there for long.

The Roman navy's commander, Lentinus, boyishly gleeful at having the opportunity again, ordered the building of some more of the khelé boats, and sent them out by night on the ebb tide. When three or four of the blockading galleys, in three or four separate harbors, had thus been mysteriously burned to the waterline, the rest of them upped anchor and scuttled back to their bases in the Propontís. That war was never officially declared over, and never officially declared won or lost by either side. But, for many years afterward, Theodoric and the eastern emperor—Anastasius, then Justin—stayed on the best of terms, and worked to their peoples' and their own mutual advantage.

The next war took place in the west, and it was of more consequence. Theodoric's having made himself related by marriage to so many neighboring monarchs had secured lasting concord between them and him, but those marital connections had not made all of them friendly toward *each other*. So, after some time, a friction and a dispute developed between one of Theodoric's affinal brothers and one of his affinal sons.

King Clovis of the Franks and King Alaric of the Visigoths both laid claim to certain lands along the river Liger, which was the boundary separating their respective domains of Gallia and Aquitania. For some years, it caused only border affrays between their peoples settled thereabout—skirmishes that were repeatedly conciliated by truces and treaties that never lasted for long. But finally the two kings began mobilizing and arming in earnest for a full-scale war over those lands. Theodoric did his best to play the neutral peacemaker between his kingly kinfolk, sending numerous embassies to arbitrate with Alaric at Tolosa and with Clovis at his new capital city of Lutetia. But nothing could pacify the two fretful kings, and when it became clear that war was inevitable, Theodoric chose to ally himself with Alaric. It must have cost him a pang, siding against the brother and the people of his own queen, Audefleda. But of course the Balting Alaric and his Visigoths had more than just a marital bond with us Ostrogoths.

917

As things turned out, though, our warriors had to do very little fighting at all in Aquitania. Before they could join the Visigoth forces, King Alaric had fallen in battle near a town called Pictavus, and it appeared that the Visigoths had lost the war. But as soon as our army made its first assault upon the Frankish lines, King Clovis downed weapons and sued for peace. In exchange for keeping what ground he had already won—those disputed lands along the Liger—he would pledge a new and lasting alliance with the Visigoths' new king, Amalaric. When our generals Tulum and Odoin accepted the terms and the pledge, Clovis and his Franks withdrew, and so did the Visigoth forces, and our own came back to Italia practically unbloodied.

Now, what was most consequential in this was the fact that the Visigoths' new king, the dead Alaric's son Amalaric, was still an infant in arms. Since he was too young to reign, his mother, Queen Thiudagotha, would be regent in his stead. And further—the boy being Theodoric's grandson and his mother being Theodoric's daughter—the practical result was that *Theodoric* now ruled the Visigoths. They and we Ostrogoths, for the first time in centuries, were subjects of a single king. Now Theodoric reigned over all the lands bordering the Mediterranean from Pannonia and Dalmatia through Italia and Aquitania to Hispania. His domain need no longer be referred to as the once Roman Empire of the West. From this time on, it was more accurately—and proudly—the Gothic Kingdom.

5

918

et me illustrate how tranquil and contented was the kingdom during the halcyon days of Theodoric's reign.

I was in residence at the king's Mediolanum palace on one of the days regularly appointed for his hearing in person the pleas and grievances of any of his subjects who felt they had not properly been dealt with by lesser authorities or inferior magistrates. I accompanied Theodoric and his several attending counselors to the audience chamber, and we were all greatly surprised to find not one single citizen waiting to be heard. The counselors and I did some temperate jesting at the king, suggesting that he ruled a people so sunk in hebetude that they were no longer even litigious.

As Boethius put it: "Plebecula inerte, inerudite, inexcita."

"No, no, no," said Theodoric, with good-humored toleration. "A quiet people constitutes a monarch's highest praise."

I asked, "Why do you suppose the citizens seem more content under your rule than they did under their previous lords, who were not—as they deem us—uncouth aliens and base heretics?"

He pondered the question before replying. "Perhaps it is because I try to keep in mind one thing that all people should, but seldom do. It is that every person—king, commoner, slave—man, woman, eunuch, child—every dog and cat too, for all I know—is the center of the universe. That fact ought to be self-evident to each of us. But we—being *each* the center of the universe—we do not often pause to realize that *so is everyone else.*"

Cassiodorus Filius looked slightly incredulous. "How can a slave or a dog be master of the universe?" he asked, as if *he* might be, but no one else.

"I did not say master of anything. A man may defer to a god, or to several gods, to an overlord, to family elders, to any number of acknowledged superiors. And I was not speaking of self-love or self-importance. A man may love, say, his children more than himself. And he may never feel important at all. Very few people ever do have any legitimate reason for feeling important."

Now Cassiodorus looked slightly offended, as if taking that for personal criticism. Theodoric went on:

"Nevertheless, to any man's sight and hearing and understanding, every other thing in the universe revolves about him. How could it seem otherwise? From inside his head, he regards everything else as *outside*, existing only insofar as it affects himself. Thus his own interest must be paramount. What he believes is, to him, the only necessary truth. What he does not know is not worth knowing. What things he does not love or hate are, to him, matters of no concern whatever. His own needs and wants and complaints deserve the most immediate attention. His own rheumatism is of more moment than another's dying of the carrion worm. His own impending death means the veritable end of the world."

Theodoric paused and looked at each of us in turn. "Can any of you, worthy men, conceive of even the grass growing when you can no longer feel it springy underfoot? When you can no longer smell its sweet aroma after rain? When you can no longer loose your faithful horse to graze upon it? When the grass has no other reason for growing but to mantle your grave—and you not able even to look and admire that?"

None of us said anything. There seemed a sudden touch of chill in the empty, echoing audience chamber.

"So," Theodoric concluded, "when any person requires my attention—senator, swineherd, prostitute—I try to remind myself: the grass grows, the world exists, only because this person lives. His or her con-

919

cerns are the most pressing ever brought before me. And then, in addressing those concerns, I try to bear in mind that the disposition I make of them will inexorably affect *other* centers of the universe." He smiled at our faces of concentrated attention. "Perhaps I make it sound either fatuously simplistic or confoundingly tangled. But I believe my attempt at perspective enables me to judge and pronounce and rule more providently." He gave a small deprecating shrug. "Anyway, the people seem satisfied."

And still none of the rest of us said anything. We stood in silent admiration of a king who could regard his people, great and small, from such a compassionate point of view. It may have been, also, that we all were remembering persons, named or nameless, whom we—indifferent to that perspective—in the past had wronged or slighted or even loved too lightly.

✠ ✠ ✠

I, like senators and swineherds and prostitutes and almost every other human center of the universe here in Theodoric's domains, have lived my centripetal life very comfortably, through all the years of his reign. My trade in slaves proved profitable, and required not much of my personal attention—which, of course, I could not have given it, what with all my traveling and my frequent necessary attendance at court. My own farm workers at Novae produced the first two or three crops of well-enough-trained, educated, mannerly slaves, and they were so superior to the common kind found in the Roman cities that they sold for good-enough prices. But then Meirus sent to Novae, in one of his consignments from Noviodunum, a young Greek—not a youth, but a grown eunuch—and a letter suggesting that I take special note of this particular slave.

"He is Artemidorus," said the letter, "formerly slavemaster to the minor court of a certain Prince Balash of Persia. You will find him *really* knowledgeable in the arts and practices of manufacturing the finest grade of servants."

I asked Artemidorus a number of questions about his methods of teaching, concluding with this one: "How do you determine when a student has finished the schooling—when he or she is fully trained and ready to be sold into service?"

The eunuch's classic Greek nose sniffed rather haughtily and he said, "A student is *never* finished with my schooling. All my charges, of course, learn to read and write in one language or another. Then, when they go forth into the world, they remain in communication with me, to benefit from my continued instruction. They may seek advice on small matters or large—on new fashions for their lady's hair-setting or on concerns of great confidentiality. They never cease their learning and I never cease their refining."

I thought the answer eminently satisfactory, and so put him in full authority, and thereafter the Novae farm truly did become an academy. Many of Artemidorus's early products I took into my own household, there at the farm and at both Thorn's and Veleda's residences in Rome. Even when each of my houses had more of a complement of servants than most rich Roman villas owned, Artemidorus kept sending on such elegant young men and women, boys and girls, that I was honestly loath to part with them. But I did sell them, and I asked staggering prices, and I got them.

There was only one person to whom I refused ever to sell one of my slaves. That was Crown Princess Amalaswintha, grown now and married and living in a palace of her own, newly built by Theodoric for her and her consort. On my first visit there, when Amalaswintha bade me come and admire its sumptuousness, I saw her again go into a rage at one of her own servants, a young maid who had misheard a command. The house steward was angrily bidden to drag the girl away and "wash out her ears." Curious to see how that would be done, I tagged surreptitiously along. The washing consisted of boiling water being poured into each of the maid's ears, leaving her both totally deaf and lamentably scarred. Thereafter, whenever the crown princess came to wheedle from "Uncle Thorn" a well-trained tonstrix or cosmeta, I always found that I was out of stock.

I could afford to be selective of my customers because I soon had so many of them, mostly the Romans who had for so long lacked *any* decent servants. I might have expected that I would have to preach to change the Romans' way of thinking about slaves in general, but I found that unnecessary. I did not have to persuade them to cease fearing that male slaves would despoil their free women or would unite in uprising. All I had to do was let some of the leading Romans see my own slaves in service at the Saio Thorn's mansion on the Vicus Jugarius.

Whenever I was in residence there, I kept the place alive and lively with feasts and convivia, and invited all the best people. They had only to be attended by my servants—skilled coqui preparing superb meals that were served by punctilious bearers; fastidious chambermaids and cosmetae and ornatrices of talent and dedication; gardeners working

921

wonders in my little plot of dooryard; stewards who could address foreign visitors in their own tongues and exceptores who could write their correspondence for them; even chore boys and scullions and other menials doing their lowly work with earnest devotion in hope of rising higher—and my guests would plead to own the like of them.

I never even had to mention the extreme unlikelihood that my male slaves would overstep their station, either in a free woman's chamber or in a militant bid for freedom. That was obvious from the servants' demeanor. Artemidorus, naturally believing that Greeks are superior to every other human, imbued his students with a similar notion: that they, being of eastern races, were superior to all the western. So the graduates of his academy would have deemed it *beneath* them to seek intimacy with a Roman (or a Goth). And they were given a genuine respect for their calling that inhibited any tendency to rebellion. Artemidorus taught them that "a man must work hard to be a good slave; there is nothing hard in being born a free man, and nothing particularly praiseworthy about it." Artemidorus, himself a Platonist, also inclined his students to look askance at every religion. Anyway, they all being intelligent and eventually well educated, none of them ever succumbed to the blandishments of Rome's Christian clerics or Christian neighbor slaves.

Indeed, so very sapient and alert were all the graduates of Artemidorus's academy that it required some effort for me to find the *duller* among them, to be servants in my Veleda house in the Transtiber. I wanted eyes and minds not sharp enough to discern anything amiss if perhaps I should sometime absentmindedly do something unfeminine in the presence of an attendant. Also I took only boys to serve me there, because even dull and very young females would have been likelier to notice any lapse of feminine behavior or mannerisms. And of course I made sure to take only boys who had never laid eyes on their owner Thorn, and made sure never to let them mingle with the slaves of Thorn's house across the river. I kept the households as separate as I kept my identities—and as I kept Thorn's and Veleda's circles of close friends, and our invitation lists, and the markets and shops in which we traded, and the arenas and theaters we attended, and even the public fora and gardens in which we strolled at evening.

The slaves at all three of my residences, besides being so numerous that none was overworked, lived very well and in luxurious surroundings—as I did too, of course—because the slave trade brought me money far exceeding my marshal's stipendium and mercedes, and I spent it freely on the things that money can buy.

In each of my houses I had couches stuffed with real down, and furniture made of Taenarian marble and Capuan bronze and citrus wood from Libya, and in the two town houses mosaic walls done by the same artists who had decorated the Apollinaris cathedral. In Thorn's house I and my guests dined from a table service of pure silver, every vessel having for its handle a sculptured swan. In Veleda's house every bedchamber contained an Etruscan speculum, a real looking *glass* that, when one looked into it, reflected also a floral design that was etched on the *back* of the glass. In both town houses my drinking ware was also of glass—this from Egypt, and as expensive as gemstones, because it was what is called the "singing glass." In use upon the table or just sitting on the shelf, every goblet and bowl and tumbler would *ring* in harmony with the conversing voices in the room.

At my Novae house I hung a musical instrument that I had found in a remote Bajo-Varia village, of a sort that I never saw in any other house anywhere. The peasant who sold it to me had no idea who had made the thing, or how many aeons ago, but it was clearly of ancient origin. It consisted of stones of graduated sizes, every one laboriously hollowed out to make a sort of upside-down cup. They were of weights ranging from perhaps four unciae to four librae, and each was hung on a separate rope (though I rehung them on silver chains), and when tapped or struck they gave out different sounds, every sound as pure and melodious as human song. One of my Novae domestics proved to have musical talent and learned to play that contrivance with little mallets as artfully and tunefully as if it had been a cithara.

At any of my tables, my guests and I ate viands redolent of the ripest garon sauce and Mosylon-flavored oil, and drank seven-year-aged Peparethus wine, and dipped freely from saucers of sacchari imported from Farther India or pale honey brought from the Plains of Enna. While we dined, we heard soft music played by a pretty slave on— depending on which mood I wished to convey—the amorous beech flute or the nostalgic bone flute or the lively elder flute. In the thermae of my houses, the guests found every nicety of appointment, right down to Magaleion unguent for the skin and rose-and-cinnamon pastilli for the breath. All the fine trappings notwithstanding, I flattered myself that, when I held a convivium in any of my houses, the real worth was to be found in the conversation, not the setting.

923

But sometimes, when I was alone, I would remember that I had not always been much concerned with correctness and uniqueness. I might be sitting and gloating over some ornament I owned, something that was one of a kind, turning it over to observe the maker's mark—"Kheirosophos" or whoever the proud artisan might have been—and I would suddenly laugh at myself, recalling how I had gone often into battle wielding a borrowed, battered weapon, or even one snatched from a dead man's hand, without the least regard for the appearance or value or provenience of it.

Well, those were days long gone. As I grew older, my age more and more insisted on its right to be indulged and treated with solicitude— by me as well as by my peers and my juniors and my servitors. In time, my journeys became less frequent and shorter of extent, and I made longer stays at one of my residences or at one of Theodoric's palaces. Still, I have never yet become infirm. I have never got too stiff of sinew or too soft of bone to straddle a horse and ride. This very day, I could mount my stallion—he is Velox V, almost indistinguishable from his great-great-grandsire—and ride to any far place that I might care to go. I just cannot, at the moment of this writing, think of any place that urgently and irresistibly calls me to come there.

But I have not been preoccupied during all these years with my own negligible doings and feelings. There did occur many happenings of more general interest, even of genuine historical interest. I was at least vicariously involved in one of them, since it was my written compilation of the Amal family lineage that Theodoric, his queen, his quaestor and other counselors consulted and pored over when they were seeking a suitable Gothic husband for Crown Princess Amalaswintha. The one they decided on was named Eutharic, and he was of the right age, and he was the son of a Herizogo Veteric, who had settled in the Visigoth lands of Hispania, and he was of better than just acceptable blood. He was a descendant of the same branch of the Amal line that had produced both Queen Giso and Theodoric Strabo, so the uniting of him with Amalaswintha would finally knit together those long-divided and frequently dissentient branches of the family. I am glad to record that young Eutharic was nothing like Giso or Strabo. He was of presentable appearance, pleasing manner and alert intelligence.

The royal wedding was celebrated by the Arian Bishop of Ravenna in the Apollinaris cathedral (reportedly making the Catholic Patriarch Bishop of Rome seethe with outrage and chagrin at being able neither to officiate at the ceremony nor to prevent it). The occasion was one of grand pomp and magnificence, and it inspired Cassiodorus to write a poem. It combined a hymeneal to the beautiful bride, an epithalamium to the loving couple and a panegyric to Theodoric on his wisdom in uniting the pair. And the poem was what one would expect from Cassiodorus. When it was copied out for *Diurnal* publication in Rome, it ran to so many pages that the papyri quite covered the front of the Concordia temple. Guests came to the celebration from every corner of the Gothic Kingdom and beyond (and stayed for weeks afterward, enjoying Roman-Ostrogothic hospitality). Emperor Anastasius sent congratulatory envoys and rich gifts from Constantinople. The bride's royal relations and her father's allies sent—from Carthage, from Tolosa, from Lugdunum, Genava, Lutetia, Pomore, Isenacum, from every capital city—congratulatory envoys and rich gifts and cordial wishes that the young couple live happily ever after.

But they did not, for Eutharic took sick and died shortly after he and his bride moved into their new-built Ravenna palace. I had not been alone in wondering how happily any man could have lived with the overbearing Amalaswintha for *any* length of time, and some averred that he died just to get away from her. However, he and the marriage did endure long enough to produce a child, and Theodoric was overjoyed that this latest addition to the family line was a *male* child. So were we of his court and counsel, but our joy was severely diminished by Eutharic's untimely death. That must have much tempered Theodoric's pride in his grandson too, though he manfully refrained from ever dwelling on it. What troubled everybody was that the king, like myself, was past sixty years of age when the new Prince Athalaric was born. If Theodoric should die before the boy reached his majority, as was almost certain, then Amalaswintha would rule as regent, and everyone in the realm dreaded that prospect.

925

Not only the Gothic Kingdom had reason for apprehension of the future; so did the Eastern Roman Empire, because, about this same time, Emperor Anastasius also died. The man had had a lifelong fear of thunderstorms; he had gone to hide from one of those, in a closet of the Purple Palace, and his stewards next morning found him dead in there. The general opinion was that he had succumbed to stark terror, but he was, after all, eighty-seven years old, and a man must die of *something*.

Anastasius may not have been one of the outstanding emperors of all time, but his successor at Constantinople was very near being a cipher, a blank, a nothing. He was named Justin, and he had been a common foot soldier who, through battlefield valor, had risen through the ranks to become commander of Anastasius's imperial palace guard. So his accession to the purple was owing to his having been, as the saying goes, "raised on the shields" of his admiring fellow officers. The attribute of bravery and the honor of acclamation are fine things, but Justin had numerous balancing deficiencies—most notable among them his total inability to read and write. Merely to sign his name to an imperial pronouncement, he had to brush an inked stylus over a cutout thin metal stencil of his monogram. And he was thus signing into law commands and edicts and statutes that, for all he could read of them, might as well have been bawdy taberna songs.

What most worried Justin's subjects (and brother monarchs) was not his appalling incapacity for his high office—many a nation has enjoyed its best years under a featureless cipher of a ruler—but the fact that he brought with him to the Purple Palace his much more capable, strong-minded and ambitious nephew Justinian. This young noble was officially the emperor's quaestor and exceptor, what Cassiodorus was to Theodoric, and assuredly Justin *needed* a literate and educated assistant. But where Cassiodorus merely performed, so to speak, as Theodoric's amplifying trumpeter, it soon became obvious that Justinian composed the notes for his uncle's trumpet, and not everybody liked the music that now began to be played. Since Justinian was the real ruler, and at the fairly tender age of thirty-five, and since Uncle Justin was already sixty-six, the Eastern Empire and its neighbor nations faced the unappealing likelihood of having to deal with an Emperor Justinian—today de facto, tomorrow de jure—for a long time to come.

Bad enough, people muttered, that old Justin relied on his upstart nephew; what was really horrific, people agreed, was that Justinian in turn relied on a person absolutely unspeakable. This was a young woman who, under ordinary circumstances, would have been snubbed in the street even by folk of the working class. Theodora was her name; her father had been a bear-keeper at the Hippodrome, and she herself had since childhood been a stage mima. Her origin and her trade would have sufficed for obloquy, but Theodora had managed to achieve infamy. As she traveled and performed everywhere from Constantinople to Cyprus to Alexandria and back, she became notorious for pleasing her male admirers in private as well as in public. And those private performances were so much to her taste that, according to rumor, she once *complained* because "a woman has not enough orifices to admit more than a mere three lovers at one time."

Somewhere during her travels, she met the patrician Justinian, and he was smitten with her. Now Theodora, at the ripe age of nineteen, had "retired" and become "respectable"—meaning that she was concubine to Justinian alone. And even those who most virulently detested her had to concede that she was bright and shrewd and calculating— in short, that her hand was discernible in many of the decrees and edicts that Justinian published to the empire as the proclamations of Emperor Justin.

Theodora wanted to marry Justinian; she saw empressdom in it. He wanted to marry her; as a devout Orthodox Christian, he was anxious to make their union legitimate. But one of the Roman Empire's oldest laws forbade noblemen to marry "mulieres scenicae, libertinae, tabernariae"—women of the stage, the streets or the drinking houses. The lovers wanted to have that law amended, so that a tainted woman, by making a "glorious repentance," would be legally washed clean, reviresced, even revirginated, enabled to marry whomever she might. To have the new law look anything but farcical, the repentance would have to be made to look passably believable, and who else could validate a repentance as "glorious" except the Church? Small wonder that Justinian and Theodora did everything possible to conciliate the Christian clergy.

Their labors early bore fruit. One of the loudest-praised achievements of Justin's reign was the "diplomatic exploit" of healing the schism that had for so many years divided the Church of Rome and the Church of Constantinople. Indubitably, to the faithful of those sister churches, that was a commendable action. However, having so overtly allied himself with those two sects of Christianity, Justin had tacitly declared himself *against* every other religion existing in the empire— including the Christian "heresy" of Arianism. In other words, the Emperor of the East was now an avowed religious enemy of his co-ruler in the West. That lent some weight and impetus to the Roman Church's vilification of Theodoric.

For many years, the churchmen's ill-humored sniping only occasionally annoyed Theodoric, and more frequently amused him, but their implacable resistance to his reign did have some troublesome aspects. It kept Romans and outlanders from ever having the complete and amicable integration that the king had envisioned for his diverse peoples. It made Romans distrustful and unappreciative of his best efforts in that direction, and at the same time caused his fellow Goths to grumble that he was *too* propitiatory of the ungrateful natives. Theodoric was

927

not a worrying kind of man, but he did have to stay on the alert for enemies both without and within his realm. Had any Christian foreign ruler aspired to invade the Gothic Kingdom, or had any disaffected Christian inhabitant aspired to insurgency, either aggressor might have been emboldened by the knowledge that the Church of Rome could incite its faithful to side with "the Christian liberator" and take up arms against the incumbent "heretic." It was partly for that reason that Theodoric early dismissed all the higher-ranking Romans from his standing army, and later decreed that no persons not in military service would be allowed to own weapons of any sort.

Not since the quick defeat of the Gepids at Sirmium and the running off of Anastasius's war galleys from the southern seaports had Theodoric's domain been harried from abroad. But there came, not long ago, a menace from an unexpected direction. I heard the first murmur of it when a train of new slaves from my academy arrived in Rome, accompanied by the slavemaster Artemidorus. I was surprised that the Greek had brought the slaves in person, because he almost never left the Novae farm. He was no longer young and no longer boasted a classic Greek profile, having become, as eunuchs do, very corpulent and therefore unsuited to hard travel. But his presence was explained when he immediately took me aside to say:

928

"Saio Thorn, I bring this word directly to your ear. It could be entrusted to no messenger. Within the ranks of King Theodoric's most trusted men, there is treachery stirring."

6

hen Artemidorus had explained, I said rather frostily, "I became a slave dealer to provide a valuable service for people of the better classes, *not* to put an ear inside their households."

Just as frostily, the Greek said, "I also, Saio Thorn. My students are cautioned most severely against eavesdropping and tattling. Even the females manage to learn reticence and decent behavior. But this case seems to involve more than idle gossip."

"Indeed, yes. It involves the reputation of the Ostrogoth Odoin, who boasts the status of herizogo, as I do, and whose rank of general is equivalent to mine of marshal. Against such a man, you would believe the word of a slave?"

"Of *my* slave," Artemidorus said, really icily now. "A product of my school. And young Hakat is of the Cherkess, a people renowned for their ingrained honesty."

"I remember the lad. I sold him to Odoin to be his exceptor. For all his titles and honors, the general cannot read or write. But his residence is right here in Rome. If this is a matter of such moment, why did the slave Hakat not come to me? Why send a slow message to you, away off there in Novae?"

"The Cherkesses have one racial peculiarity—an exaggerated reverence for the superiority of their immediate elders. Even a younger brother, if his elder enters a room, will jump to his feet, respectfully at attention, and never speak until his brother has spoken. To my Cherkess students, it seems, I stand in loco frateri as a surrogate elder. They bring their concerns to me."

"Very well. Then I shall provide young Hakat with an elder *sister*, to help ascertain the truths of this matter. Get word to him that, at his earliest opportunity, he is to go across the Tiber and seek out the house of a lady named Veleda . . ."

General Odoin and I had never been close acquaintances, but we had been frequently in company at Theodoric's court. So, since I intended now to insinuate myself as a speculator inside his residence, I wished to be someone he would not recognize. When Hakat presented himself at my Transtiber house, I said:

"Your master cannot possibly know or care how many slaves he owns. You have only to put me among them for some little while. And the slaves themselves will not question the authority of their master's exceptor to do that. Tell them I am your widowed and impoverished elder sister, seeking to work for mere sustenance."

"Excuse me, Caia Veleda," and the young man coughed discreetly. He was of the comeliness for which all the Cherkesses are noted, male as well as female, and he was trying now to exhibit the good manners Artemidorus taught all his charges. "The thing is . . . there are *not* many slaves — anywhere — of my lady's obvious gentility and, er, distinguished age."

930   That stung me enough that I snapped, "Hakat, I am not yet ready to be propped useless in a hearth corner. And I can simulate slave humility with sufficient abjection to deceive even your sharp and knowing eyes."

"I meant no disrespect," he said hastily. "And of course my lady is more than handsome enough to pass as my Cherkess sister. Only command me, Caia Veleda. In what capacity would you prefer to serve?"

"Vái, introduce me to the household kitchen, the pantry, the scullery, I do not care. I wish only to be in a position to observe your master's visitors and take heed of his converse with them."

And so, some fifty years after my kitchen youthtime, and very much to my wry amusement, I found myself again doing duty as a lowly scullion. While, this time, I was doing it to worthwhile purpose, and while it did soon accomplish the ends I sought, I must report that playing the spy turned out to be rather easier than playing the servant slave. What I remembered of menial tasks from my St. Damian days did not greatly avail me here, because a noble Roman household is much more efficiently and formally managed than any Christian abbey. I was constantly being rebuked, scolded and berated by my fellow slaves. I was not even accorded the small dignity of being chastised by name.

"Imbecile old woman, that is no way to carry a salver! Hold it underneath, not with your thumbs in the gravy!"

"Filthy old sloven! You may have scrubbed your own hovel so carelessly, but in this kitchen you clean also between the floor stones! Use your old gray tongue, if necessary!"

"Shambling old slattern! When you cross the threshold into the triclinium, you cease that shuffling and pick up your feet. In the master's presence, you walk noiselessly, no matter how weary you may be!"

The other slaves pretended that they chided me only because they took pride in their communal giving of good service, so they were distressed to have it marred by my many clumsinesses and derelictions. But it became evident to me that they took pleasure in having me to heap scorn on, and took self-importance from doing so. Among slaves, obviously, there is as much of a pecking order as there is in any poultry yard, and rather less of mutual respect. Slaves have none but each other to look down on, and that they do, that they do. Artemidorus might assert that a good slave is innately superior to any man freeborn, but I now perceived the one really demeaning aspect of being a slave. It is not in *being* a slave, but in having to live one's life in consort with none but *other* slaves. As the lowliest in this household, I had to bear the contumely of every other one of us slaves. Even Hakat, in his ostensibly higher status as exceptor, felt constrained to carp at me occasionally:

931

"Old woman! You call these pinfeathers good enough for me to cut pens from? Go back to the yard and pluck some proper quills!"

Our master, Odoin, probably never appreciated his servants' meticulous service and probably never would have noticed any small lapses in it. He was a burly, bearded, rough-hewn military man, more accustomed to life in the field than in a refined Roman residence. Anyway, as I soon learned, he had weightier things on his mind than a concern for housekeeping. Nevertheless, he too was younger than myself and, on the one occasion when he took the trouble of correcting me, addressed me by what had become my new name:

"Old woman! Vái, can you not clear the tables without clattering things? My guests and I cannot hear ourselves speak!"

True, that night I was being inattentive to my duty, because my attention was all on the identity of those triclinium guests and the import of the words spoken. In the course of a fortnight or so, I was able to lurk on the fringes of several such gatherings and, after each, I recorded what I had seen and heard. Of course, to preserve my imposture, I could not let the other slaves see me *writing*, so, late each night, Hakat would join me while I took my meager nahtamats of manchet crusts and table scraps, and he would set down what I repeated to him.

There finally came a night when I said, "We have ample evidence to convict and condemn the man. You did well, younger brother, in confiding your suspicions to Artemidorus."

And on the next day, without leave, we departed from Odoin's house and went to Veleda's. I set Hakat to making a fair copy of the papyri we had compiled, while I took a very long bath to rid myself of kitchen grime and grease. When the copy was done, I gave it to a messenger and sent him off at a gallop, and bade Hakat, "Remain here, younger brother, until I return. You would not be safe today outside these doors."

I went again to my Thorn house, donned my boar-ornamented marshal costume, gave orders to various of my guardsmen, then proceeded once more to Odoin's residence. At his door, I made polite request—to a steward who had yesterday been reviling me as "old woman," but was now unrecognizing and obsequious—for private audience with the general. When Odoin and I sat at ease, over an amphora of Falernian, I produced my papyri and said without preamble:

"These documents accuse you of fomenting treason against our King Theodoric, and of plotting his overthrow."

Odoin looked surprised, but tried for cool indifference. "Say you so? I will summon my exceptor Hakat to read them to me."

"He is not here. It was your exceptor who wrote these pages, and that is why he is not here. I have Hakat in my keeping, to give witness, if necessary, that these words he recorded are words that were uttered by you and your fellow conspirators."

The general's face darkened and his beard bristled, and he growled, "By Allfather Wotan, it was *you*, Thorn, who sold me that overpretty and overeducated little foreigner. If we are to speak of plotting and conspiracy and betrayal . . ."

I ignored that and said, "Your reader being absent, allow me to do the reading to you."

As I did so, Odoin's color ebbed from livid to ashen. Some of the things he and his guests had discussed I had been aware of even before Artemidorus came calling on me. For instance, it was public knowledge that Odoin believed he had been cheated in some kind of land transaction, at which he took the matter to court, and was ruled against, and appealed the judgment upward through higher courts, each time unsuccessfully, and finally was ruled against by Theodoric himself. Well, that was very similar to what had once happened with Theodoric's own nephew Theodahad. But where the sullen Theodahad had only retired to sulk over his frustration, Odoin—it was now clear—had determined to requite the "injustice" done to him.

"You recruited everyone else you could find who bore a grievance or a grudge," I said. "These documents attest your meeting with them here under your own roof. The names are those of other malcontent Goths like yourself, and of dissident Roman citizens, and of numerous Catholic Christians inimical to Theodoric—including two cardinal deacons of the Patriarch Bishop's own retinue."

Odoin made a movement that splashed some wine out of his goblet, as if he would like either to dash that in my face or to snatch the papyri from my hands, so I said:

"A copy of these pages is already on its way to Ravenna. At this moment, also, every one of your conspirators is being taken into custody."

"And I?" he asked hoarsely.

"Let me conclude by reading these words of your own. 'In his old age, Theodoric has become as spineless and boneless as the deposed Odoacer. It is time Theodoric was supplanted by a better man.' Tell me, Odoin, would that better man have been you? And what do you suppose will be Theodoric's emotion when he reads those words?"

Odoin made no reply to that, but said, "You did not come here, Thorn, alone and unarmed, to take *me* into custody."

I gave him a level look. "You were a valiant warrior, a capable general and, until now, a faithful follower of the king. Because of what you were, I came to afford you the opportunity of anticipating and avoiding your public disgrace."

Cassiodorus's *Historia Gothorum* records that Herizogo Odoin, together with his numerous accomplices, was three days later beheaded in the Forum Romanorum. And so he was. But only Artemidorus, Hakat and I—and my two trusted guardsmen who supported the traitor's trudge to the block—know that Odoin had already been three days dead. In the manner of a noble Roman, in my presence, that day I confronted him, he had unsheathed his sword, pressed its point to his breast and its pommel to the mosaic floor, and leaned his weight against it until it pierced him and let him fall.

✠ ✠ ✠

For me personally, there were two consequences of those events. One was a conversation between myself and Artemidorus before his departure from Rome.

933

"Saio Thorn," he said, "our venerable slave supplier, old Meirus the Mudman, has achieved an age to rival his ancestor Methushelach, and he desires to retire from commerce. I would ask your permission to consult with him regarding our appointment of a new factor in Noviodunum."

"I give you that leave and more," I said. "I have amassed more than fortune enough to last me the rest of my life, even if I should outlive Meirus and Methushelach both, and I have lately become disenchanted with the slave trade. I would not myself wish to be a slave, therefore I no longer wish to be responsible for the creation of slaves. Here, Artemidorus—I have already prepared and signed it—I give you title to my Novae estate." He reeled in astonishment and was momentarily stricken most un-Greekly mute. "Take good care of the place, Artemidorus, and its people and its livestock. They all were very good to me."

The other thing affecting me personally had happened earlier, on the day I left Odoin dead on his mosaic floor, when I went from his house to Veleda's and changed into my most fetching feminine garb, and sought out the handsome young Hakat.

934

✠   ✠   ✠

For some years now, just as travel and trade and far horizons have gradually lost their appeal for me, so have certain other things in my life, once urgent and irresistible, become less so. Akh, I know that I shall never be entirely glutted and finished with sexual enjoyments, but, over the course of time, I found that I required fewer of those and less frequently. That is not to be attributed to any dearth of available partners. Even today, even as Veleda, and certainly as Thorn, I could take my pick of the opposite sex, if I wanted a partner *of my own age*. But what man or woman past the prime of youth and beauty *wants* to bed a woman or man who is equally worn and weathered?

Long ago, at the Mouths of the Danuvius, I had observed that the aged husband and wife Fillein and Baúhts looked almost exactly alike. Now, eyeing the men and women growing old about me, I saw that *so did they*. Except for their dress, they showed almost no sexual distinctness. Some men were bald, some women were hairy about the face, some of each were scrawny, some obese, some were more wrinkled than others, but they all had the identical bland, medium, tepid look of neuterdom. I have been not at all tempted to investigate beneath the clothes of any of them, but I think I do not have to. It is obvious that *every* once normal man and woman, if he or she lives long enough, turns at last into something very like a eunuch. I suppose I will too. But evidently because I never have been normal, I am blessedly taking longer to get there.

It has not been difficult for me, as Thorn, to avail myself of partners younger and ever younger than myself. That is not difficult for even the oldest and most repulsive of men; there are plenty of lupanares and street-corner noctilucae. But I was in the fortunate position of not having to resort to those. Everywhere I went, there were attractive young women (young men and boys as well) eager to oblige a man of status in exchange for a small official favor, or a letter of reference, or just to earn his continuing good regard—or, often, simply to be able to boast of having been so honored.

But even my most harmonious encounters—whether as Thorn or as Veleda—began to make me aware of one unbridgeable rift between me and my young lovers. Those youths so desirable as sexual partners proved rather less appealing in the aftermath of our frolics. As Thorn, I would be unutterably bored by a young woman lying beside me and chattering of the latest Rome fashion in hairstyles or house pets. As Veleda, I would lie yawning while the young man beside me prattled of his wagers on the Greens or the Blues contending in the Circus games. By the same token, if Thorn chanced to mention the siege of Verona, or if Veleda spoke of the squint-eyed Strabo, the bedmates would regard me with amused amazement, as if I were senilely discoursing on ancient history. More and more often, just to preclude our parting in absolute contempt of each other, I would get rid of those young persons as early as possible the next morning.

I must make mention of another thing, and I can put it most succinctly in kitchen terms. There are only so many ways of cooking pork and beans. The most expert and ingenious coquus, in the best-equipped kitchen, can devise only so many ways and no more. After my lifetime of experiencing every sexual combination possible to men and women, including the extraordinary variations introduced by my brother-sister mannamavi Thor, there cannot now be for me any thrill of discovery or surprise, only familiarity and sameness. There is no such thing as a *bad* sexual coupling, but even the good and the better and the best, after innumerable repetitions, tend to lose their onetime savor.

Also, in these latter years, conquests came not so easily to Veleda as to Thorn. While I did indeed, as I had hoped, keep my youthful female features and firm figure for many more years than most women do— until I was fifty, or near it—I imagine even Venus herself, after some

935

centuries, must have begun to show signs of wear and tear. The graying hair that made Herizogo Thorn look (as others said) "dignified and wise," the facial lines that made him look "experienced and wise," the eye folds that made him look "pensive and wise"—oh vái!—ask any woman seeing those things in her speculum what they mean to *her*.

However, I made good use of those years of grace that *were* allotted to me. As had happened with that young optio in the Ravenna Baptistery, I often would lock glances with a personable young stranger among a convivium crowd, or across my own dining table, or in a public garden, and with pleasant consequences. But in time the room's lamps or the table's candles had to be fewer, the garden had to be deeper in dusk, as I came to know what all women come to know: that the dark is kinder than the light. And inevitably there came the time . . .

It came the day I said to that beauteous young Cherkess slave Hakat, "For your services to King Theodoric, in helping to expose the traitor Odoin, you are granted manumission. You are a free man henceforth. Furthermore, for your help in her imposture in Odoin's household, your elder sister Veleda would like to grant you a reward of another sort."

During the hours thereafter, Hakat several times said very Cherkessly respectful things like "A younger brother can deny nothing to an elder sister . . ." and "An elder sister's every entreaty is her younger brother's command . . ." and I tried hard not to realize that he was every time averting his face or clenching his eyes closed or stifling a sigh of resignation.

But I did realize those things. That is why Hakat was the last man ever to couple with Veleda. That is why I closed the house in the Transtiber, and gave away all but the most precious of my Veleda garments and trappings, and sold or liberated all the slaves that had attended Veleda.

And Veleda's virtual retirement from the world seemed further to diminish Thorn's enterprisingness in that particular field of endeavor. Although, as Thorn, I still can heartily enjoy a coupling—and do, whenever one offers, and hope I shall on my very deathbed—I no longer go avidly seeking such enjoyments. To the act itself I am less and less impelled; young lovers I find ultimately unsatisfactory, and old ones pathetically impossible. Nevertheless, the men and women of my own age, albeit unthinkable as amative partners, do at least have other interests and ideas and memories in common with myself. That is why I gradually have come to accept the sedate pleasures of convivial company around a bounteous table in place of the more frivolous pleasures of the bedchamber.

Having said that, however, I must ironically reflect that it was a sexual adventure — of a sort — that tempested the serene weather I had supposed would last to the end of my days.

7

hat had its beginning only in rumors, and the first was brought to me by that onetime soldier and longtime taberna caupo Ewig. Ever since my earliest arrival in Rome, he has been my personal speculator among the city's commonfolk, keeping me apprised of their doings and opinions and attitudes — contentment, complaint, murmurs of unrest, whatever — so that I might in turn help Theodoric keep in touch with his subject masses. One day, reporting to me, Ewig chanced to mention that a Caia Melania, a widow newly come to Rome, had purchased a fine old house on the Esquiline Hill and had hired a goodly number of artisans to renovate it. Gratifying, I thought, a new resident providing employment for the local folk, but nothing particularly noteworthy in the tidings.

937

When, over succeeding weeks, I heard other friends of other classes speak of Caia Melania — generally with approving or even awed comment on the money she was spending — I still took little note. I remembered having heard of a woman by that name in Vindobona, long ago, and idly wondered if it might possibly be the same person. But then, Melania is no uncommon feminine name.

It really first engaged my attention when I heard it bruited about the triclinium during a feast at the villa of Rome's princeps senatus, old Senator Symmachus. There were many notable personages around the tables that evening — various other senators and their wives; Theodoric's magister officiorum, Boethius, and his wife; Rome's current urbis praefectus, Liberius; perhaps another score of the city's leading citizens—and all of them seemed better informed about the widow Melania than I was. At any rate, there was considerable comment on the woman's extravagant spending, and gossipy speculation as to what sort of establishment her new house was turning into.

Then, when the ladies of the company had withdrawn from the triclinium, to allow us men to talk freely, Senator Symmachus told us what *he* knew of the mystery woman. And, old and respectable though he was, Symmachus obviously took a wicked delight in making the revelation. (Well, old and respectable though he was, he still had standing in his dooryard that little statue of Bacchus with the massively erect fascinum, which some of his guests preferred to walk past with averted eyes.)

"This woman Melania," he said with relish, "is a wealthy widow come from somewhere in the provinces. But she is more than just a middle-aged woman indulging herself at the expense of her late, rich husband. She comes to us with a mission, a vocation, perhaps a divine inspiration. What she is building there on the Esquiline she intends to be the most elegant—and most expensive—house of assignation ever seen since the legendary days of Babylon."

"Eheu, the mystery woman is only a lena?" said Praefectus Liberius. "Has she applied for a license, then?"

"I did not call her house a lupanar," said Symmachus, chuckling. "The word is inadequate. And so would be the word 'lena' to describe the widow Melania. I have met her, a most gracious and distinguished lady, and she did me the honor of showing me about the establishment. To require a tabularius to issue a license for such a place would be like insisting that King Theodoric's palaces be licensed."

"Still, a commercial enterprise . . ." grumbled Liberius, ever concerned with fees and taxes.

Symmachus ignored him. "The house, for all its richness, is small, a jewel box. Only one, ahem, client will be admitted each night. And *no* client will be admitted until he has sat down in an antechamber face to face with Caia Melania herself. She will closely interrogate him—not only asking his name and rank and status and character and his capacity to pay her exorbitant prices—but also his tastes and preferences and most intimate inclinations. Even his previous experience of women— respectable women and not so."

"Impudent prurience, I should call that," said Boethius. "What decent man would discuss his wife, or even his concubines, with a pandering bawd? What is the point of her interrogation?"

938

Symmachus winked and laid a finger alongside his nose. "Not until Melania shall have appraised the applicant and thoroughly taken his measure—not until then will she give some secret signal to a hidden servant. There are doors all about that antechamber. One of them will open. In the doorway will be standing the one woman in all the world of whom that man shall have dreamt, for whom he shall have yearned, all his life long. That is what Caia Melania promises, and I am inclined to believe her. Eheu, my friends, what I would give to be a stripling of sixty again! Or even a youth of seventy. I should be the first in that antechamber."

Another senator laughed and said, "Go anyway, you imperishable old satyr. Take along your evil little Bacchus and let him perform in your stead."

There was more laughter, and more of that kind of banter, and much more speculation—as to where Melania might be procuring her "dream women"—but I paid little heed. I had seen lupanares in my time. Jewel-box pretensions this one might have, but it would be just another house full of whores, and the Caia Vidua Melania just another mercenary old lena.

939

Then Symmachus changed the subject of conversation, saying more soberly, "I am troubled by a recent occurrence, and I should like to know if I am alone in finding it worrisome. Yesterday came a messenger bearing a missive from the king. Theodoric's compliments, and would I please lend my support in the Senate to the proposed statute setting stricter limits to the moneylenders' rates of interest."

"That troubles you?" said Liberius. "It is a worthwhile measure, from what I hear."

"Of course it is," said Symmachus. "What bothers me is that Theodoric sent me the identical message more than a month ago, and I lent my support to the statute by making a lengthy speech, and the proposal will easily pass when it comes to the vote. I had already so advised the king. Boethius, you know that. So why is Theodoric repeating himself?"

There was a short silence. Then someone said charitably, "Well, older men can be forgetful . . ."

Symmachus snorted. "I am older than Theodoric. I am not yet forgetting to redrape my toga modestly when I emerge from a latrina. I am certainly not forgetting the whereabouts of major legislation."

"Well . . ." someone else said, also charitably, "a king does have more things to keep in mind than even we senators do."

"True," said Boethius, ever the loyal supporter of his king. "And one matter weighing heavily on Theodoric's mind these days is the lingering illness of his queen. He is much distracted. I notice it. Cassiodorus notices it. We do what we can to prevent his manifesting too many lapses of attention, but sometimes he sends out messages without consulting us. We trust that he will be himself again as soon as Audefleda is well."

"If Theodoric, even at his age, is being deprived of conjugal intercourse," said a medicus, "he could be suffering a congestion of his animal spirits. It is well known that the normal ducts are constipated by prolonged sexual abstinence. That could account for all manner of derangements."

"Then," spoke up a brash young nobleman, "let us invite the king to come south to Rome. Until his Audefleda is again fit for service, he can frequent the lady Melania's new lupanar. *That* ought to unclog his ducts."

Some of the other younger men laughed uproariously at that, but the elder guests angrily rebuked the impertinence, and the name of Melania was not mentioned again that night.

But, over the following months, I kept hearing that name, from one after another of my male friends and associates. These were men of substance, men mostly about my own age and of rank at least equal to my own, men usually of dignified reticence. Now they spoke in voices of wonder, without being prompted, of the fantastic women they had enjoyed at the house on the Esquiline Hill.

"A gray-eyed Cherkess girl, of contortions simply unbelievable . . ."

"An Ethiope, black as midnight, but like the sun coming up for me . . ."

"An Armenian, each breast exactly as big as her head . . ."

"A pale Polan, just eight years old. The Polanie females are only good as children, you understand, because they grow grossly fat at puberty . . ."

"A Sarmatian, fierce, wild, insatiable. I think she must have been an Amazon . . ."

"However, the real prize of Melania's collection, so I hear, she has not yet found the proper man for. Or perhaps the man rich and profligate enough to pay for it. A female creature of genuine rarity, I am told. Every man in Rome is avid to know what it is, and prays he will be the fortunate claimant of it."

"A beautiful virgin, Saio Thorn, a girl of the people called Seres," said my speculator Ewig, who knew everything furtive that went on in

940

Rome. "Brought hither under close wraps and kept hidden ever since. A girl who is pale *yellow* all over, if you can credit such a thing."

"I can," I murmured. "Pale *peach*-colored is more accurate."

Ewig gave me a look. "If you know things like that, Saio Thorn, perhaps you are the man the virgin is being reserved for."

Well, as the long-ago St. Damian monks were the first to remark, curiosity has always been my chief besetting vice.

"Ewig," I said, "you are acquainted with the artisans who worked on that house. I believe it is no immense edifice. Find out what you can about the plan and arrangement of it, and let me know."

So, on a summer evening, I presented myself at the house on the Esquiline Hill, and an only fairly pretty maid ushered me into the antechamber. It was circular and spacious, and in the old warrior's way I scanned it with a single glance. There was a pink marble table in the center of the room, with pink marble benches on either side of it, no other furnishings. Caia Melania was half sitting, half reclining on the bench facing me and the door through which I had entered. In the curved wall behind her were five other doors, all closed. At one end of the marble table stood a shallow crystal bowl full of just-picked peaches, every one perfect and unblemished, flecked with dewdrops, and atop them lay a tiny red-gold knife. At the other end of the table stood a much bigger, deeper crystal bowl of water in which lazily swam some small fish, also peach-colored, undulating filmy, veil-like fins and tails.

Apparently pink, or peach, was Melania's favorite color, this day anyway, because her samite stola was of the same hue. As reported, she was no young woman, but a matron only eight or ten years younger than myself. For her age, though, she was strikingly handsome—well shaped but slender—and I could see the winsome girl she would once have been. Now, through her golden hair, time's tremulous old finger had scribbled a few locks of silver, and down her ivory-translucent cheeks had scrawled a line here and there. But her blue eyes were large and lustrous, her lips still pink and unwithered; she needed no cosmetic plastering or coloring, and wore none.

She made a curt gesture and I took the bench across from her, sitting rectitudinously upright. Without a greeting, without a smile, without ceremony, she began her interrogation. As I had been warned, there were many questions, but—though her voice was pleasant enough— she asked them only in a somewhat perfunctory manner, making me suspect that she must already have done a very thorough investigation of each applicant before he ever walked through her street door. When she got to the questions about my tastes and proclivities, but still seemed little interested, I interrupted the inquisition to remark lightly:

"I take it, Caia Melania, that you have already judged me unqualified for the one famously invaluable gem in your jewel box."

She raised an eyebrow, sat back a little and regarded me coolly. "Why do you think that?"

"Well, I have answered your every question with utmost honesty. Clearly I do not pretend to be a patricius or anything of the sort. And you must have surmised by now that neither am I one of Rome's leading lechers."

"So you believe you do not deserve the best in this house?"

"It is your house. You decide. Do I?"

"Take a look and see."

She had somehow given her secret signal, for one of the doors behind her swung silently open, and the girl of the Seres stood there. As I had discovered years before, the females of that race grow no concealing escutcheon tuft, and this one's gown of transparent goose-summer fabric concealed nothing either. Every pretty feature was unabashedly presented for my admiration, and she had clearly practiced at posing her peach-flesh body in a fetching attitude.

I said, "That is the rarity? The prize of your collection? For me? I had hardly dared hope. Really, I am overwhelmed." And I gave the lie to that by yawning elaborately.

The girl in the doorway looked hurt, and Melania said tartly, "You do not *sound* exactly overwhelmed."

I cocked my head and said judiciously, "I think . . . when you were her age, Caia Melania, you must have been much more beautiful."

She blinked and almost flinched, but snapped, "I am not for hire. The Seres girl is. Are you telling me that you could *resist* her?"

"Yes. I have tried to abide by one of the sayings of the poet Martial." Pedantically I quoted, " 'To have lived so as to look back with pleasure on one's life is to have lived twice.' So, you see, much earlier in my life I made sure to enjoy a girl of the Seres. Now I have my memories, my second life, so to speak. I suggest that you save this girl for someone less jaded, someone more callow—"

Melania said through her teeth, "She is reserved for one man alone."

"And I am that man? Why me?"

Now she looked slightly disconcerted. "I mean . . . a virgin is a once-only thing. Should you decline this opportunity, and some other man qualify . . ."

I nodded. "He would have the once-only. You are right. Eheu, but risks do abound in this world."

Melania glanced at the Seres girl, who was now glumly pouting, then gave me another long regard. She evidently decided that my air of world-weariness was only my attempt to disguise a foolishly puerile nervousness. So she made a visible effort to contain her own impatience and, to put me more at ease, said, "Perhaps I have seemed to hurry you, Saio Thorn." She gestured and the door closed on the girl. "Let us simply sit and talk leisurely for a bit. Here, share one of these plump peaches with me."

She took up the miniature gold knife, but politely waited for me to pick out a peach from the bowl and hand it to her. With scrupulous care, she sliced the dewy fruit in half, flicked aside the pit and pushed my half across the table toward me. Pointedly, I did not touch it until she took a bite of her half, which she did with seemingly unfeigned enjoyment. She smiled and munched and said moistly, "Delicious. It is one of those peaches that you almost drink rather than eat."

At which, I picked up my half. But I held it over the crystal fishbowl and gave it one powerful squeeze that wrung all its juice and pulp into the water. Almost on the instant, the several fish began flirting about in agitation, and one rolled over and came to the water's surface belly-up. I looked from it to Melania, who had gone very white and wide-eyed. She started shakily to stand, but I shook my head and rapped on the table, a signal of my own. All five of the doors behind her opened, and in each stood one of the soldiers I had brought, a bare sword in his hand. They waited for my signal to advance, but I only sat and waited too, until the woman spoke.

"I thought I had planned so perfectly," she said, with just a hint of tremor in her voice. "I thought I had prepared so painstakingly. You could not possibly have known who I was. I have been exceedingly careful never to be seen in public in Rome. Yet you knew even before you got here to the house. How?"

"I knew fairly well what to expect, not whom," I said. "I myself once laid a very similar trap for a man. I did not have such alluringly exotic bait—and, for that matter, not such patience as you have shown—but the general design was familiar. Also, I have had some experience of administering poisons. The girl is a venefica, is she not?"

The woman nodded dejectedly.

"And just in case I spurned her"—I picked up the little fruit knife—"one side of the blade was coated with poison, but only the one side,

943

is that right?" She nodded again. "How would I have died? In convulsions, so you could watch and laugh? Or paralyzed numb and dumb, so you could tell me *why* I was dying? Or—?"

"No," she interrupted. "Instantly, painlessly, mercifully. Just like that." She indicated the bowl, where all the fish were now floating upside down.

"And if I had embraced the venefica?"

"The same. The swiftest, surest, kindest poison known. It is extracted from the spines of the sea hedgehog. I would not have made you suffer. I was bent on revenge, yes, for those you slew. But needless torment . . . I would not do that."

I sighed. "It has been so many years since I slew *anybody*. Why did you wait so long?"

"I was not waiting. I was very busy, very dedicated during all the years. It was easy enough for me to find out who had done the actual killing, but I was not interested in the mere instruments. I wanted the one who had given the orders. It took a long time to find that out. Then, when I learned it was you, I had to set about devising a plan. And for that, I had to have you accessible."

I laughed a small laugh. "I encountered that problem too, the time I set a similar trap for an enemy."

"For years, you kept journeying hither and yon, and I had always to keep track of you. At last, when you did seem to settle down somewhat, here in Rome, I determined that Rome would be the place for my trap. So . . . more time had to pass. I wanted a bait that was certain to draw you, that you absolutely could not refuse." She smiled ruefully. "I failed to reckon with your vast experience. By the way, what kind of female bait did you use in *your* man trap?"

"Only myself. I had none other to use."

She looked a trifle puzzled at that, but went on. "So, fourteen years ago, I made arrangements to buy a baby girl of the rarest possible sort. Sending emissaries halfway across the world—you can imagine what a long and complicated and frustrating process that was. And then, rearing her on the poison, inuring her to it, saturating her with it. The spines of that sea fish exude their venom in only minute amounts, so I was practically having to manage a fishing fleet at the same time I was doing everything else." She shrugged. "All for nothing."

I said, "You exempted the actual killers from your revenge. But you must have known that I gave the orders only in the service of Theodoric. Why did you not exempt me too, and go after him?"

"I would have done, if I had thought I could lure him out from behind all his defenses." She added thoughtfully, "That would yet have been possible if I had succeeded with you. It might still be."

I turned to the optio of my swordsmen. "You heard. A threat against the king."

"I heard, Saio Thorn." He took a step forward. "Do we slay her?"

I motioned for him to hold his arm, and at the same moment the woman said, "I would prefer that, Thorn, to the Tullianum."

I deferred comment on that, asking, "And the name? Melania?"

"A small disguise. I took the name of the woman your soldiers slew in mistake for me. She was my husband's sister."

I nodded, recalling the circumstances as they had been reported to me. Then I asked, "And the name I knew you by—did you ever go back to the river of ice, to see if our two names had moved downhill from where I carved them?"

"No. I waited a long time, hoping you would return someday. When finally I married Alypius, I moved south with him, and I never since then went back to visit Haustaths. Alypius and I built up a very respectable business in Tridentum."

945

"So I heard. And I remember your saying once that you intended to make your own way in the world."

"I did. I worked hard. I was not just a Caia Alypia, a barnacle riding the hull of my husband's prosperous galley. I worked as much and as productively as he did. Indeed, it was because I was off in a distant mountain orchard, negotiating to purchase the olive crop, that I was not at home on the day your soldiers came. I returned to find Alypius and Melania dead, and the neighbors told me also that my father was a captive, probably taken to die as well. That was bad enough, but then they showed me my brother in the salt sack. Shriveled and desiccated and gray, like a flitch of bacon. There never was a worse day in my life, except . . ." She faltered.

I said, "Alypius sacrificed his sister to save you that day. You and he had no children?"

With a flash of her old childhood spirit, Livia demanded, "Would they have died too?" I said nothing, so she went on. "No, there were no children. Had there been, I might have wavered in my determination on revenge. But when I heard that my father and my other brother also were dead, that strengthened my resolve. I know, Thorn, that you always considered them worthless. Perhaps I did too, but they were all I had. Now I should like to join them. Can we get this over with?"

"You said the day you returned to Tridentum was the worst of your life, except . . . What was worse, Livia?"

She hesitated, then whispered, "The day I learned who was the slayer I was hunting. That it was you." She stood up and faced me, unafraid. "May I die now?"

"I think not. You were kind enough to wish me an easy death. In return, I can at least emulate Alypius, and preserve your life. But you will appreciate that I cannot grant liberty to such a dedicated and determined opponent. I might tolerate your being a hazard to myself, but to the king, no."

I turned again to the optio. "Collect everyone in the house, tenants and servants alike, all but the girl of the Seres. Leave her here. Take all the rest to the Praefectus Liberius. Have him apportion them out to the regular licensed lupanares. He ought to enjoy that chore. This house is closed. Put a guard on it, day and night, from this time forward."

The optio saluted, and he and the others disappeared.

To Livia I said, "You will be under house arrest for the remainder of your life. The Seres girl will be your only servant. The guards will fetch and carry for you—supplies, messages, whatever. But you will never again go out of doors, and no one else will ever be allowed in."

"Thorn, I told you I would prefer death to prison."

"This is hardly the Tullianum. I assume you have never seen the inside of that. I have."

"Please, Thorn. Just give me back the little paring knife, for only a moment. For the sake of what we once—"

"Livia, we are far, very far, from what we once were. Look at us. We are old now. Even I, for all my wandering ways, even I probably would not find house arrest impossible to endure, what time I have left."

She slumped a little. "I suppose you are right."

"And if you ever do find it unendurable, Livia—either imprisonment or old age—well, you do not need the knife. You have only to kiss your servant girl."

She laughed without humor. "I do not kiss women."

I thought about that for a moment, then said, "You never even once kissed *me*."

And I took her in my arms and put my lips on hers. For a long minute, she only accepted the kiss, then she sweetly returned it. But in a moment more, I felt her shudder slightly and she drew back from me. Her eyes were searching my face, but her own face showed nothing like anger or offense or dislike. It wore an expression of perplexity that changed slowly to a sort of wonderment, and I went away and left her standing like that.

8

Time was when I regarded with amusement the Roman pagans' superabundance of gods and goddesses. In the Old Religion of us Germanic peoples there is only one goddess of flowers, Nerthus, and she is credited with responsibility, as well, for almost everything else that flourishes on Mother Earth. By contrast, the pagan Romans believe in not just a single flower deity, but four or five. According to them, a goddess named Proserpina is in charge of a plant when it first sprouts, then Velutia takes charge as its foliage unfolds, then Nodinus when the plant is in bud, and finally Flora when the plant is in full bloom. If it is a food-bearing plant, then still another, Ceres, is responsible for its fruiting. I used to be amused by that: so many goddesses caring for every green growing thing. But I have come to think, now, that there is yet one lacking. There is no goddess in attendance during the time of fading blossom and yellowing leaf and the dying fall of what was once beautiful and pleasing and enriching to the world.

947

Theodoric, all through his autumn years, had remained as vigorous and alert as ever I had known him, but I saw the winter of his life begin when Queen Audefleda sickened and died. That bereavement clearly affected him much more deeply than had the loss of his Aurora—probably because he and Audefleda had shared the experience of growing old together. I have observed that that often makes more of a bond between a man and a woman than even love does, though love there certainly had been between those two. Anyway, in the five years since the queen's death, I have watched Theodoric age much more rapidly. His hair and beard, once radiant gold, later gleaming silver, now can only be called ash-white. Though he is still erect of posture and carriage, he is thin and his hands sometimes tremble and he is too restless ever to sit still for long. His blue eyes, that once could change so easily from merry to fierce and back again, have not been leached of their color, as are those of many old men, but now his eyes are a blue without light or depth, like blue slate. His voice is still firm and resonant, not at all thin or quavery, but he can sometimes be as rambling of speech as Cassiodorus is of pen.

On that occasion when Symmachus made worried remark about the king's having twice sent him the identical message, the senator was only voicing what all of us of Theodoric's court had begun to notice—and tried hard not to. It first came to my notice one day when I was at the Ravenna palace, conversing with the king, and Princess Amalaswintha unexpectedly came calling, bringing along her son, Prince Athalaric. I forget what Theodoric and I were discussing, but he kept right on talking to me, flicking at his daughter and grandson only a blue-slate glance as blank and uninterested as if they had been servants coming in to dust the room. Only when the escorting steward announced them, enunciating their names very loudly and carefully, did Theodoric blink, shake his head and finally give them a rather bleak smile of acknowledgment.

948

Tactfully, I made my excuses and departed, so I do not know what had brought Amalaswintha visiting that day. But it was common gossip among the palace servants that she never did communicate with her father except to make some greedy demand or petulant complaint— just as she never called on "Uncle Thorn" except to try to get from me a costly slave at a "niecely" price. Not wifehood, motherhood or widowhood had changed the princess from the Xantippe she had always been.

And she had made little Athalaric no more likable than she was. The spoiled princess had grown up to be a spoiler, and turned the poor prince into as odious a brat as a five-year-old child could be. He was seldom out from behind his mother's skirts, and even in that soft sanctuary he did nothing but whine and whimper. So, on the occasion of Theodoric's seeming not to recognize his own offspring, I assumed that he had been deliberately feigning forgetfulness, and that the paternal smile he finally gave them was only forced by my having been present.

But evidently that had been no pretense. Not long afterward there came a night when I was among the many guests at a feast the king gave for some visiting Frankish nobles. During the meal, Theodoric regaled the company with stories from our wartimes past, including the time our army broke open the supposedly impregnable treasury building at Siscia.

"With nothing more than *oats*, would you believe it?" he said gleefully. "Oat-filled tin wedges that we dubbed our trumpets of Jaíriko. That was the ingenious idea of the young marshal here . . ." He indicated me, then stammered, "The young marshal . . . er . . ."

"Thorn," I murmured, in some embarrassment.

"Ja, young Saio Thorn here," and he went on with the story—while the guests eyed me, obviously wondering why he called me *young*—and he told how those tin trumpets had worked, and how successfully.

The company laughed and buzzed in appreciation when the tale was done, but one of the Franks said, "Curious. I have visited Siscia since those days. The treasury building seems unimpaired. And not one of the citizens made mention of any such occurrence. I should think an event so memorable—"

"The Siscians probably prefer *not* to remember," Boethius interrupted, laughing, and deftly turned the talk to something else.

No one of Theodoric's court would have dreamt of correcting him in public, of course. But I felt I was a close enough friend to tell him later, in private:

"It was at *Singidunum* that we employed the trumpets of Jaíriko. At Siscia, we undermined the treasury and threatened to topple it, and that was how we got in."

Theodoric looked momentarily flustered. "Was it?" Then he looked indignant. "What of it? Have you some complaint? I gave you credit for the ingenuity, did I not?" Then he clapped me on the shoulder and chuckled dismissively. "Well, well. A good story need not be overburdened with accuracy. It is still a good story, eh, Soas?"

✠　✠　✠

"The marshal Soas died a decade ago," I said, downcast. "Theodoric and I have been friends for nearly fifty years, but nowadays he is frequently forgetting or miscalling my name."

"Which one of your names?" Livia asked, a little mockingly.

"Thorn, of course. He has never known me as Veleda. Not many ever have, besides you."

"Why not tell him?" She grinned as impishly as she used to do when she was a child. "Forgetful he may be. But if Theodoric knew both your names, he might be better able to remember you by one of them."

I grinned too, but ruefully. "No, that secret I have kept from him

949

through all these years. It will go to the grave with whichever of us goes there first. Anyway, I have not even *been* Veleda for a long time now. Except with you."

That was true. My having closed the house in the Transtiber, I supposed, was one of the reasons—having no place now in which to be my female self—that I began visiting the house of Livia from time to time. She never refused me admittance, and even seemed glad to see me, and I do not think that was just because I was almost the *only* person she ever saw.

Except for my own visits, I allowed no relaxation of the terms of Livia's imprisonment. She was never let to leave the house and no one else from the outside world was ever let in. Her only human contact was with myself and her guards and her sole remaining servant. She and that slave had no language in common, except for basic commands and responses, and the Seres girl seemed indisposed to affability, anyway. She served Livia efficiently enough, but went about her duties in glum silence, and I gathered that she had been made permanently morose when I denied her the one function she had been bred for.

It had not been difficult for me to reveal to Livia the fact of my dual nature. I knew, when I kissed her that one time, that she sensed something of the truth about me—if, indeed, she had not divined it years ago, when she was a little girl. The revelation did not shock, scandalize, horrify or amuse her. She took it calmly, which would hardly have been the case if she and I had been younger. Happily for both of us, we were past the age when every woman and every man regards one another with speculation, as a possible lover—when even a woman as sensible as Livia would receive such a disclosure with amazement, perhaps with disappointment, possibly with some perverse interest in "experimenting," but certainly not with equanimity.

When I told her, "I am a mannamavi, an androgynus, a creature of both sexes in one," Livia made no exclamation, asked no questions, only waited with composure to be told whatever else I might care to tell her. Not once since then has she ever hinted that she might be curious to see the physical evidence of my abnormity. Not once has she ever pried to know what the life and loves of a mannamavi must have been like. Over time, though, I have freely told her much about myself—my selves—because nowadays, whenever I am in Rome, I go more and more often to see her.

We are comfortable together—all three of us, I might say. Of course, I go always dressed as Thorn, but, once indoors, I can talk easily to

Livia either as man to woman or as woman to woman. And I do talk of many things that I cannot or care not to discuss with other people. After all, I made Livia's acquaintance long before that of any other person in my life at present. I met her even before I met Theodoric. And, here lately, it is of Theodoric that I oftenest come to talk to her.

"I spoke only partly in jest," she said now. "Why *not* tell the king the truth about yourself?"

"Liufs Guth!" I said. "Tell him I have been deluding him for nearly half a century? If he did not drop dead of an apoplexy, Theodoric would assuredly see that I got dead of something worse."

"I doubt it," said Livia. She delicately refrained from pointing out the obvious: that no one was likely to care *what* sex an old relic like myself used to be. "Try it. Tell him."

"To what end? We of the court are already concerned that the king's mind and memory seem to be clouding. It might be calamitous to startle him with—"

"You said yourself that his lapses began during the queen's illness and worsened with her departure. You said yourself that the only woman near him now is his daughter, and that she is only an affliction to him. Theodoric might be much improved by the companionship of a new woman. One of his own age. One who knows him well. One who turns out, however surprisingly, to have been his friend all his life long. Veleda might be just what he needs."

"As you are for me?" I said, smiling, but shaking my head. "I thank you for the suggestion, Livia, but . . . *eheu!* Before I could bring myself to break my long silence, Theodoric would have to be in dire need indeed."

"And then," she said, "it may be too late."

✠　✠　✠

Not even the Christian priests and Roman augurs and Gothic wise-sayers, all of whom pretend to know the wiles of every kind of demon, have ever been able to fend off those that can prey on a man's mind as it ages and lets down its defenses. If there *is* such a thing as a demon of forgetfulness, and if that one first crept upon Theodoric while he was disarmed by his grief for Audefleda, then other demons were waiting their chances to find chinks in his armor. And they found them, because each year since that time has brought some event that, like a siege ram, has further battered at Theodoric's defenses.

His queen died in the year 520 by the Christian count. In the year

951

521 came word from Lugdunum that his eldest daughter, Arevagni, was dead. Theodoric should have found that bereavement not too unbearable, because it was reported that she died easily, in her sleep, and Arevagni's life had been a good one. For the five years before her death she had gloried in being Queen of the Burgunds, her husband, Sigismund, having succeeded to his father's crown in the year 516. Also, Arevagni had attained to motherhood; she was survived by a young son, Segeric, another grandson to Theodoric and heir apparent to the regnancy of the Burgunds.

However, less than a year later, in 522, came further news from Lugdunum, really appalling news. The widowed King Sigismund had remarried, and his new wife, of course intending to bear children of her own and wanting them to have no impediment to their royal inheritance, had persuaded Sigismund to slay his own firstborn, that young Crown Prince Segeric. I suppose it will never be known whether King Sigismund, to have done such a horrendous thing, was overweening of his own almightiness, or was the most weakling husband in the history of henpeckery, or was out-and-out insane. If he was cognizant of Theodoric's tendency to forgetfulness, and counted on that to make Theodoric overlook this atrocious filicide—or if he thought that *any* Goth would let such an insult go unavenged—then Sigismund was much mistaken.

Theodoric convened all of us, his advisers, in his throne room, and we perceived him to be, in his fulminating rage, again the man we all remembered. His eyes had lost their slaty dullness and blazed blue, like the Gemini fires. His beard no longer hung limp and lank, but bristled like a patch of stinging nettles. When Magister Boethius counseled that the king postpone any retaliatory action "until you are more composed, my lord," Theodoric roared at him, "That is a tradesman's suggestion, if not a traitor's!" and Boethius prudently sidled out of his sight. When Exceptor Cassiodorus recommended scolding the Burgunds with a stern missive, Theodoric bellowed, "*Words?* Words be damned to Gehenna! Get me General Thulwin!" He would have gone charging off himself, I think, except that he knew he could not ride at a flat-out gallop over that distance, and he wanted his army there *now.* So, led by Thulwin, a hastily assembled but formidable and angry army thundered westward.

However, Fortune, in her whimsical but implacable way, had already avenged the filicide. Before Thulwin could arrive at Lugdunum, the Burgunds had got embroiled in a war with the Franks, and in an early battle Sigismund was slain. Since he had eliminated his own lineal successor, Sigismund's crown went to a cousin named Godemar. And that man, impelled so abruptly into both the responsibilities of kingship and the throes of a war with the Franks, was disinclined to cross swords as well with the Gothic army that came pounding up to the walls of Lugdunum. King Godemar abjectly offered to recompense King Theodoric for the loss of his grandson by ceding to him the entire southern half of the Burgund lands, and General Thulwin readily accepted that concession. Thus, with no cost in Gothic lives lost—except that of the hapless little Prince Segeric—the Gothic Kingdom made a great gain in territory, its western borders now extending to the river Isara on that side of the Alpes.

So Theodoric's pride and puissance had been upheld, and his domain unexpectedly enlarged besides, but none of that assuaged his grief at having been deprived of two generations of his own family. When the pinnacle of his rage subsided, it let him down into a gully of despondency, and subsequent events only deepened that. The next bad news came from Carthage, and involved not only another insult to one of Theodoric's family but also a threat to the stability of his reign.

The news was that Thrasamund, King of the Vandals and husband to Theodoric's sister Amalafrida, was dead and had been succeeded by a cousin, Hilderic. As I have mentioned, the Vandals always were predominantly of the Arian Christian faith, and their kings had been not even *tolerant* of Catholic Christianity, but always antagonistic to it. However, this Hilderic was an anomaly among Vandals, a devout, even rabid Catholic Christian, and now he was king. Thrasamund, on his deathbed, had exacted a solemn promise from this cousin that he would preserve Arianism as the state religion, but Hilderic broke that promise as soon as Thrasamund expired.

The first thing he did was to imprison Thrasamund's widow, Theodoric's sister, in a remote palace, because she was an Arian, was much respected by the people and so might be able to hinder his plans. Second, Hilderic took possession of every Arian church in his African lands, expelled their bishops and priests and solicited "good, godly, heretic-hating" replacements from both the Church of Rome and the Church of Constantinople. Third, because Theodoric's Gothic Kingdom was Arian, therefore detestable, Hilderic forbade any further Vandal trade with that former ally, and he began fawning on Emperor Justin, seeking closer ties with the Empire of the East.

Theodoric was again infuriated, but this time he had no way of venting his fury. He could not just utter a command and send an army

953

galloping across the Mediterranean waters. All he could do was order the immediate start of construction of a naval fleet adequate to attack Carthage and bring Hilderic to his knees.

"A thousand ships!" the king barked at the navarchus of the Roman navy. "I want a thousand ships, half of them armed with seagoing weapons, the other half to carry armored troops and horses. And I want those ships in a hurry."

"You shall have them," said Lentinus, unruffled. "And in a hurry. But for an undertaking of this magnitude, Theodoric, I must advise you that a *hurry* means perhaps three years."

Even a king, with all the suasions and incentives and threats and goads and penalties at his disposal, cannot do much about the intransigency of time. Theodoric could only wait for the ships to be built. So, frustrated by his impotence, depressed by his frustration, made vulnerable by his depression, he was even more frequently fretted by that demon of forgetfulness, and now also by the demons of suspicion and distrust and anxiety.

He might give a trifling order—do this or do that—to some palace servant, and have the servant say meekly, "But I attended to that yesterday, King Theodoric."

"What? How dare you do something like that until I tell you to?"

"But you did tell me to, my lord. Yesterday."

"I never did! Impudent nauthing, first you presume to anticipate my wishes, then you lie about it. Steward, take this wretch away and give him fitting punishment."

Since the steward, like everyone else, was growing accustomed to such episodes, the servant's only "punishment" would consist of his being kept out of the king's sight until the king forgot the incident.

I should remark, though, that not all of Theodoric's suspicions of persecution and conspiracy were entirely baseless delusions. In a very real sense, he *was* now ringed about by persons—by whole nations of people—inimical to his Arian religion, hence to himself, his reign and the existence of his Gothic Kingdom. In the east, Emperor Justin, Justinian and Theodora were in such cozy affinity with the Church of Constantinople that the Eastern Empire was, in effect, an Orthodox Christian theocracy. In the northwest, the formerly pagan King Clovis of the Franks had, some while previous, become a Catholic Christian. (Indeed, he had made a mass spectacle of his baptism, requiring some four thousand of his Lutetia citizens to get baptized in the same cere-

954

mony.) Now, in the south, King Hilderic had decreed Catholic Christianity the state religion of Vandal Africa. So Theodoric's domain was literally surrounded by anti-Arians. Granted, none of those was yet being overtly bellicose, and only Carthage had broken off trading. But the Church of Rome, of course, had its agents busy in all those places, urging every *genuine* Christian to pray and tithe and strive for the overthrow of the heretic Theodoric, and then for the conversion or utter extirpation of all his heretic subjects.

Yes, our king had real vexations to be anxious about, and they were of a nature that would have absorbed the full attention of even a Caesar or an Alexander, and Theodoric certainly should have bent his whole concern on them. But those weevil demons infesting his mind were more and more frequently making him ignore the problems abroad to swat imaginary pests closer at hand.

Unlike the palace servants, we of Theodoric's court and counsel could not easily hide, and did not so easily escape chastisement. Boethius, Cassiodorus Pater and Filius, myself and other marshals, nobles and officials of every degree were continually being accused by Theodoric of having misheard his orders, misread his decrees or misinterpreted his intentions. Partly out of our prudent self-concern, but mostly out of our fondness and pity for the king, we did our best to pretend that his lapses did not happen, and quietly tried to repair whatever damage they caused. But sometimes the episodes were unconcealable, and even Theodoric had to be aware of them. I think, to his other woes, that added the terror that he *might* be losing his mind. And I think he was trying to deny that more to himself than to us when, even in his lucid intervals, he sought to blame others for his own derelictions.

I was present once when, some minor endeavor of his having gone awry—no one's fault but his—Theodoric castigated Boethius for it, as fiercely as ever Amalaswintha had railed at one of her slaves. Boethius bore it manfully, without protest or rebuttal or even a hurt look, then took himself wearily from the room. Again presuming on our long friendship, I told Theodoric, "That was unjust, uncalled for and unlike you."

He snarled, "Ineptitude deserves rebuke!"

I dared to retort, "*You* appointed that man your magister officiorum, more than twenty years ago. Are you now saying that *you* were inept?"

"Vái! If he is not guilty of ineptitude, then perhaps he is of perfidy. Boethius may have held his office for so long that he now entertains

955

insidious ambitions. You remember, Thorn—you were present—how he urged cowardly caution when I wanted to smite the murderer Sigismund."

"Come, come, Theodoric. There is an old saying—that the right hand is the smiter, because it is the stronger. Therefore the gentler, slower left hand is for dispensing justice and mercy and tolerance. You appointed Boethius to be your left hand. To temper your impulsiveness. To save you from acting rashly . . ."

"Nevertheless," he grumbled, "ever since that time I have wondered. Could Boethius possibly be now in the secret employ of foreign powers?"

"Akh!" I said. "Old friend, what has become of your belief in a perspective of sympathy? Of your wanting to view other men with insight and understanding? Of your respecting each man's being the center of his own universe?"

"I still try to look at men so," he said, but darkly. "And I see some men greedy to expand their universes—to gulp and engulf and engorge others. I intend to take care that no one encroaches on mine."

956

✠ ✠ ✠

"Theodoric was always impetuous of action," I said to Livia, "as witness the way he struck down Camundus and Rekitakh and Odoacer—sometimes with unhappy consequences. But now his whole character is changing. He is almost never cheerful any more, but wary and misgiving. It troubles me enough when he merely mopes in despondency, but in one of his seizures of vehemence, who can say what folly he may commit?"

Livia thought about that, while her maid set on the table between us a tray of sweetmeats. Then she said:

"You and Theodoric's other friends and counselors must emulate the ancient Macedonians."

"Eh? How is that?" I said as I bit into a small cake.

"The Macedonian king Philip was a drunkard, alternately demented by wine and deranged by its withdrawal. His much abused courtiers and subjects, it is said, had only one resort—appeal from Philip drunk to Philip sober."

I smiled at her, appreciative and admiring. Livia had been bright and clever even as a child. Evidently, during the years that had put gray in her hair and lines in her face, she had also got an education.

"And wisdom too," I murmured. Then I frowned at the sweet I was eating. "I thought, Livia, you long ago abandoned your intended vengeance on me. For a honey cake, this tastes uncommonly bitter."

She laughed. "No, I am not trying again to poison you. Quite the contrary. The cakes are made with Corsican honey, and that is tart, because the island is all yews and hemlocks. But it is well known that the Corsicans live to a great age, so their honey is highly recommended by the medici as an aid to prolonging one's life." She added, with mischievous good humor, "You see? Since you keep me prisoner here, and you alone come to visit me, I am trying to keep you alive forever."

"Forever?" I put the cake down, unfinished, and said, more to myself than to her, "Forever? I have already lived long. I have seen much and done many things—not all of them pleasant. To live forever? To have always as much in prospect as is past? No . . . that is rather daunting to contemplate. I think not."

Livia was watching me with the warm concern of a wife or sister, so I went on. "In truth, that is what is so sad about Theodoric. He has simply lived too long. Everything good he has done, all his greatness, is in danger of being overshadowed and blotted out by some foolish act that his age, not his will, may impel him to commit."

Still looking wifely-sisterly, Livia said, "I told you. What he needs is the care of some good woman."

I shook my head. "Not this woman."

"Why not? Who better?"

"I swore my auths to Theodoric as Thorn. If, as Thorn, I should sometime be compelled to do something contrary to that auths, I would be dishonored and damned in all men's regard, including my own. However, as Veleda, I never swore any such auths . . ."

In some alarm, Livia said, "I almost fear to ask. What do you have in mind?"

"You are a literate woman. Do you know the real meaning of the word 'devotion'?"

"I think so. Nowadays it means an emotion, an ardent attachment. But originally it referred to an *act*, did it not?"

"Yes. The word derives from votum, a vow, a consecration. On the battlefield, a Roman commander would pray to Mars or Mithras, promising to court death for himself in the combat if that god of war would grant victory and survival to his army, his nation, his emperor."

"Giving up one life that others might live and prevail," said Livia in a hushed voice. "Oh, my dear, my dear . . . are you planning an act of devotion?"

957

9

In the year 523 there appeared in the sky, visible all over the world, even in daylight, for the space of more than two weeks, that kind of star that some call a smoking star, and others a long-haired star, and others a star bearing a torch. In consequence, every Christian and Jewish priest, every pagan augur and wise-sayer cried, "Woe!"—that God and the other gods were warning us of dire calamities to come.

Well, numerous untoward things did happen during that year, but I could see no touch of God or the gods in them; they were all the doings of mortal men and women. To illustrate, Justinian and his concubine, Theodora, finally, with the connivance of the Church, managed to promulgate the "glorious repentance" law that enabled the two of them to marry. Then, no longer having to concentrate his energies on tidying his personal affairs, Justinian turned to what he saw as his major mission in life: tidying all the rest of the world to fit the precepts of the established Christian Church. The edicts were still, of course, ostensibly issued by Emperor Justin, but the words were Justinian's. For example, when he decreed that henceforth no pagan or unbeliever or heretic would be allowed to hold any office in the Eastern Empire, either military or civil, he added, "All men will now perceive that, from those who do not properly worship the true God, not only the blessings of the afterlife but also this world's material goods are withheld."

That mandate did not—or not yet—extend westward beyond the province of Pannonia, but Theodoric understandably regarded it as ominous. By the terms of his long-ago agreement with Zeno, he was still, at least nominally, the eastern emperor's "deputy and vicar." If and when Justin should ever issue such an obnoxious decree aimed at the inhabitants of Theodoric's domain, then Theodoric would have to yield to it or declare himself in open rebellion against his acknowledged overlord. And Theodoric and his Arian subjects were not alone in seeing trouble in the offing. The more sensible Catholic Christians in the Gothic Kingdom and the senators at Rome were also disturbed. After all, the senators considered themselves the caretakers of what remained of the Western Roman Empire, and the Western and the Eastern had for two hundred years been vying to outdo the other in authority and influence.

So had the Church of Rome been vying with the Church of Constantinople. It might be supposed that all devout Catholic Christians should have been delighted by an imperial edict that—anywhere in the world—worked evil to Jews and pagans and heretics. But remember, every patriarch bishop in Christendom had long been striving for recognition as *the* patriarch, the primus inter pares, the sovereign pontiff, the Papa. Almost simultaneous with Justin's publication of his decree, Rome's Patriarch Bishop Hormisdas died and was replaced by a man named John. As can be imagined, John was mightily disgruntled to find himself assuming a bishopric that had, in effect, just now been eclipsed by the one in Constantinople. The complaisant Emperor Justin had given a considerable escalation to the power and prestige of *his* patriarch bishop, Ibas. John had no hope of getting any such help from Theodoric. So, naturally, John and his clerics and his loyal laymen had one more grudge to hold against Theodoric. But they were only the *most* hostile of Theodoric's adversaries. If there was one thing that united in brotherhood all Christians everywhere who adhered to the Anastasian creed—the Orthodox in the Eastern Empire, the Catholic in Africa and Gallia and the Gothic Kingdom—it was their determination to put an end to Theodoric and his fellow Arians and the Arians' abominable tolerance of pagans and Jews and heretics and everything else unChristian.

959

Still, the clouds around the horizons of our Gothic Kingdom were not yet so dark as those looming right overhead. We who were closest to Theodoric had, for some time now, been fearful that one of his spells of irrationality might mar or disastrously undo the achievements of his entire reign. But even if Theodoric had been still at the zenith of his mental and physical prowess, there was no denying the fact of his age. In no very long time, he was going to die. Even if, mercifully, that happened before his increasing senility might harm the kingdom, *who* was to succeed him? Who was capable of carrying on the noble work he had done? Was there anyone, anywhere, in prospect fit to don the fallen mantle of a king rightly called "the Great"?

The heir apparent, of course, was Theodoric's grandson in Ravenna, Athalaric. But in this year of which I am speaking the crown prince was only seven years old. If he succeeded to the throne any time soon, the kingdom would have to be ruled for some years by his regent-mother, and—as I believe I have indicated—Amalaswintha was about as lovingly regarded in the Gothic Kingdom as Theodora was in the Eastern Empire. Even supposing that the kingdom should survive her regency until Athalaric came to his majority, what kind of king would *he* make? I can offer one adumbration:

I and Theodoric's three senior generals were in an antechamber of his palace, waiting to have audience with him. We were amusing ourselves meanwhile by trying to outdo each other's war stories, when a door opened and young Prince Athalaric came shuffling in. Evidently he and his mother were also visiting the palace, probably on one of her errands of petulance. Anyway, the prince was blubbering and sobbing, one of his hands rubbing his red eyes and running nose while the other hand rubbed his backside.

General Tulum said gruffly, "Here, here, lad. What ails you?"

"Amma," whimpered the boy, between sniffs and gasps. "Amma spanked me with her sandal."

Tulum looked scandalized, but not sympathetically so.

General Witigis growled, "I hope, Athalaric, you had done something really heroically wicked to deserve it."

"All I did"—snuffle, slobber—"was get a reprimand . . . from my Greek tutor . . . for misspelling the word 'andreía" . . . and Amma overheard . . ."

Still blubbering and rubbing himself, the prince drifted on out of the room. There was a moment of silence while the warrior generals looked at each other in blank astonishment. Then Thulwin said unbelievingly:

"By the great leather balls of Allfather Wotan! Have I just seen an Amaling Ostrogoth—a *male* Ostrogoth—puling and mewling in *tears?*"

"After a whipping by a *woman!*" said General Tulum, equally appalled. "After *letting* a woman whip him!"

"Ne, ne, *spanked* he got," said Witigis wonderingly. "With a woman's sandal. By the Styx, when my brute of a father used to belt *me*, I was happy enough if he did not use the *buckle* end."

"At that boy's age," said Thulwin, "I was breaking my first horse to the saddle, and breaking the nose of my drillmaster in cudgel practice."

"Ja," grunted Tulum. "Men-children should shed blood, not tears."

Witigis said, with distaste, *"This* man-child is being *tutored.* In Greek. And being reprimanded. By a *Greek."*

Thulwin asked, "What kind of word is 'andreía,' anyway?"

I said, "It means manliness."

"Liufs Guth! And he does not even know how to *spell* it!"

Theodoric did have another grandson still living: Amalaric, the son of the Visigoths' late King Alaric and Theodoric's daughter Thiudago-tha. That prince, now sixteen years old, could have been considered an acceptable alternate to the milksop brat Athalaric. However, he was not even being seriously expected to succeed his own father as King of the Visigoths—and, sad to relate, this was again the fault of Theodoric's overprotection and overindulgence of his offspring. Ever since King Alaric's death in battle, his queen, Thiudagotha, had been regent of that kingdom, and she had gratefully relegated the regnancy to her father, and Theodoric had all these years done the actual ruling, by means of the deputies he appointed there in Aquitania and Hispania. In other words, that Crown Prince Amalaric in Tolosa had grown up devoid of kingly responsibilities, devoid of kingly experience and apparently devoid of the least ambition to *be* king of anything. All in all, as a putative ruler of the entire Gothic Kingdom, he had to be judged about as inadequate as his cousin in Ravenna.

There was yet one other candidate: Theodahad, the son of Theodoric's sister Amalafrida by her first husband, who had been an Ostrogoth herizogo. In truth, Theodahad could have made a very plausible claim to precedence as Theodoric's successor, on the ground of close Amaling blood-kinship. Also, he had the requisite maturity for kingship, being now a man of middle age. However, in addition to lacking training and experience, Theodahad lacked the *moral* qualities for any post higher than that of a money-gouging tradesman. This was the Theodahad whom I had disliked when he was a pimply, surly youth, the Theodahad whom his uncle the king had publicly discredited in the matter of one of his land-grabbing transactions, the Theodahad who since then had done many other questionable dealings to his own aggrandizement, and thereby earned the contempt of many other people.

There was only one person in high circles who seemed to think Theodahad *might* have a slight chance of Fortune's favor—and that was, unlikely though it would seem, Theodoric's own daughter, unquestionably his direct heir, Princess Amalaswintha. She could not have helped knowing of her own unpopularity at court—indeed, throughout

961

the kingdom—and, even as a doting mother, she must have been aware that her son, Athalaric, was no better loved. So she sought out and made friends with the cousin Theodahad that she, like every other respectable person, had long shunned. Amalaswintha's reasoning was clear. She and her son and her cousin were Theodoric's closest relatives and likeliest claimants to his crown. If all three of them clung together, they could repel any more distant pretenders, the Gothic Kingdom would *have* to accept one of them as Theodoric's successor, and whichever one succeeded would share the spoils with the other two.

So, in that year of the daytime star, anno domini 523, ab urbe condita 1276, fifth year of the reign of Emperor Justin, thirtieth year of the reign of King Theodoric the Great, the situation was this:

We, Theodoric's closest friends and counselors, were rather desperately casting about for someone fit to succeed the monarch we loved, to be ruler of the kingdom he and we had fought to win, then had worked to make great. The ideal replacement, a worthy Ostrogoth of Amal lineage, was simply nonexistent. The military men among us proposed an appealing alternative, General Tulum. He had no familial claim, but he *was* an Ostrogoth, and we all agreed that he possessed the attributes of a king. We were all disappointed when he gruffly refused the honor, on the ground that he and his every forebear had loyally served the Amaling kings, and he would not presume to break the long-standing traditions of succession.

Meanwhile, the Eastern Empire—that is to say, the trinity of Justin, Justinian and Theodora—was not exactly menacing the Gothic Kingdom, but was certainly making gestures of asserting its power and authority in the world. The intent appeared to be not to provoke Theodoric to belligerence, but to give his subjects unmistakable notice that, once his domain was bereft of his strong presence, it could be easily annexed by Constantinople. No doubt the rulers of other nations roundabout our borders entertained similar ideas. And they may not even have worried about having to fight each other over the carcass of the Gothic Kingdom. Considering that so many of our neighbors now shared the bond of Catholic or Orthodox Christianity, they may already have been peaceably agreeing on which of them were to get which scraps. As long as Theodoric lived, and did not visibly succumb to total senility, those surrounding neighbors had not the courage to be raptors, but they were avidly waiting to be scavengers.

Meanwhile, too, the Church of Rome, after thirty years of trying but failing to make any significant trouble for Theodoric, had not lessened by one iota in its loathing of him. Almost every Catholic Christian in the kingdom, from Rome's Patriarch Bishop John down to cave-dwelling hermits, would have rejoiced to see *any* non-Arian usurp the throne. I say "almost" because there were, of course, men and women high and low who, even though their vows bound them to uphold the Church's views and forbade them to reason for themselves, yet were sensible enough to realize what disaster the land would suffer from an overthrow of the Gothic Kingdom.

The senators at Rome realized that too. Although most of them were Catholic Christians, therefore required to abhor Arians—and although almost all of them were Italia-born Romans, who would naturally have preferred to be ruled again by a Roman—they were pragmatic men. They recognized that Rome and Italia and everything else that had once been the Western Roman Empire had enjoyed, under Theodoric, a reprieve from the brink of oblivion, and then an enduring security, peace and prosperity unequaled in more than four centuries. Also, they realized the threat posed by the surrounding Franks and Vandals—even by lesser peoples, once subdued or allied or negligible, like the Gepids and Rugii and Langobardi—should the Gothic Kingdom find itself ruled by a lesser man than Theodoric. The senators took the attitude of "better the barbarians we know than those we do not." Like us of Theodoric's court, they debated and argued the merits of this and that candidate for the kingship—and did not count it a demerit if the candidate was of Gothic nationality and Arian faith. But, like us, the senators found no one suitable.

However, while those senators were justifiably wary of every outland nation, they were most apprehensive of a nation that was not barbarian at all—their old rival and contender for supremacy, the Eastern Roman Empire. And the Senate's mood of apprehension caused the most lamentable of all the events that occurred in that year of the daytime star.

One senator, named Cyprianus, accused another, named Albinus, of having engaged in treasonous correspondence with Constantinople. This could have been mere windy calumniating; there was nothing novel in any senator's ascribing to another the most disgusting depravities; it has always been an accepted manner of playing for political advantage. Or, for all I know, Senator Albinus really *had* been secretly conspiring with alien enemies of the state. That hardly matters now.

What caused such grievous consequences was that the accused Albinus was a close friend of Magister Officiorum Boethius. Perhaps, if

963

Boethius had stayed aloof from the commotion, nothing much would have come of it. But he was a good man, not one to stand aside while a friend was defamed, and treason is, after all, a capital offense. So when the Senate convened a formal court to try Albinus on that charge, Boethius came to stand before the judges and plead for the defense, concluding with these words:

"If Albinus be guilty, then so am I."

✠　　✠　　✠

"I was made to study rhetoric in my youth," I said to Livia, mournfully shaking my head. "That peroration by Boethius came straight from the classic texts. Any schoolboy would have shrugged it off for what it was. An elenctic argument on the topic of reasonable probability. But the Senate court . . ."

"Surely they are reasonable men." She made it more of a question than a statement.

I sighed. "One can reason from the facts presented or one can reason from the testimony offered. I do not know the facts, and I did not attend the trial. There were letters produced in evidence. They may or may not have been genuine. I cannot say. Anyway, it was apparently on the basis of the facts that the judges found Albinus guilty. Then, since Boethius had said *so am I,* they took him at his word."

"That is preposterous! The king's master of the offices—a traitor?"

"He freely offered that testimony. Rhetorical, yes, but there it is." I sighed again. "Let me be charitable and give the judges their due. They are well aware of Theodoric's altered nature—his inclination nowadays to doubt and suspect all around him. They could hardly help being infected by the same suspicion. And if the evidence convinced them of Albinus's guilt . . ."

"But Boethius! Why, Rome honored him as its Consul Ordinarius when he was just thirty! One of the youngest ever—"

"And now, in his forties, by his own admission, guilty of treason to Rome."

"Inconceivable. Ridiculous."

"The court concurred in his admission. That was the verdict."

"And the sentence?"

"For high treason, Livia, there is only one sentence."

She gasped, "Death . . ."

"The sentence must be ratified by the full Senate, then confirmed by the king. I devoutly hope and trust that it will be overturned. Boethius's affinal father, old Symmachus, still is princeps senatus. He will assuredly influence the Senate vote. Meanwhile, at Ravenna, Cassiodorus Filius has been appointed to Boethius's vacant office. Those two were friends, so Cassiodorus will be pleading his case to Theodoric. And if anyone has a wealth of words for persuasion, it is Cassiodorus."

"You must go and plead as well."

"I was traveling north in any case," I said gloomily. "I am the king's marshal, so I have a duty to perform. I am escorting poor Boethius, under heavy guard, to the Calventianus prison at Ticinum. At least he does not have to rot in the Tullianum here. I was able to arrange for him a more comfortable imprisonment while he awaits his deliverance."

Livia smiled an equivocal smile and murmured, "You have always been kind to your captives."

✠   ✠   ✠

It was during the twelve months that Boethius languished in the Calventianus prison, while every rational man outside it entreated for his release, that he wrote a book entitled *The Consolation of Philosophy*—and that book, I believe, is what determined the outcome of all the appeals for mercy. I well remember one of the passages in it:

"Mortal, it was you yourself who cast your lot not with Security but with Fortune. Never rejoice overmuch when she leads you to great victories; never repine when she leads you into sad adversity."

While the legal processes in Rome did their ponderously slow progression, Theodoric in Ravenna listened attentively to me and Cassiodorus and Symmachus and Boethius's brave wife, Rusticiana, and many other persons who argued on the prisoner's behalf. But to none of us did Theodoric give any sign of his own feelings in the matter. Surely, I thought, he realized what a gross travesty of justice had occurred. Surely he took into account all the years of Boethius's irreproachable service to himself and the kingdom. Surely he knew that Boethius was innocent, blameless, unfairly imprisoned, cruelly kept in anxiety by the sentence hanging over him like the sword of Damocles, probably even more cruelly tormented by his inability to ease the anguish of his wife and children. Still, Theodoric was the king, and he had to show at least the semblance of abiding by the laws of his realm. So, to me and every other appellant, he said only:

"I cannot anticipate the Senate of Rome. I must await its vote to ratify the sentence or not, before I can address the question of clemency."

965

I visited Boethius occasionally, and I saw his hair turn gray during that year. But he endured, evidently sustained by his unquenchably active mind. As I have mentioned, he had written many books during his life, on a variety of subjects, but they had been appreciated mainly by persons concerned with those specific subjects—arithmeticians, astronomers, musicians and so on. His *De Consolatione Philosophiae* had much more universal appeal, because it dealt with despair and the overcoming of despair, and there are few persons in the world who have never known despair. There are few who could not echo Boethius's sigh of resignation:

"Remember, mortal, if Fortune ever should stand still, she is no longer Fortune."

When the book was completed, the governor of the prison was uncertain whether it should be allowed to see the light of day. So I personally *commanded* him to make sure it was delivered, safe and intact, to Boethius's wife. The gallant Rusticiana then made it available to every person who could read and who cared to have a copy made of it. The copies multiplied, proliferated. The book was much discussed and praised and quoted. Eventually, inevitably, it came to the attention of the Church.

Now, mind you, Boethius could have made that book his own plea for pardon, but he did not. Only briefly did it deplore the grim situation in which its author found himself. Not once did it lay blame for that on any person or persons. It personified Philosophy as a sort of goddess who visited the author in his prison cell and, whenever his spirits sank to melancholy, prescribed one or another source of consolation. Those included natural theology, Platonist and Stoic concepts, simple meditation and, over and over again, the saving grace of God.

But nowhere did Philosophy, nowhere did Boethius, nowhere did the book suggest that solace could be found in any Christian belief. So the Church decried the book, called it "pernicious" and, under the Decretum Gelasianum, forbade its reading by the faithful. It could hardly have been coincidental, then, that the Senate finally voted, by a plurimum almost exactly reflecting its Catholic Christian majority of membership, to ratify Boethius's death sentence and remand it to the king for final review.

I daresay that Boethius's book will survive the Church's ban and live for a long, long time to come. Boethius did not.

✠   ✠   ✠

"Your strong right hand, Theodoric," I said bitterly, "has chopped off your left. How could you allow such a thing?"

"The Senate court found him guilty. The full Senate confirmed that verdict."

I sneered, "By a majority of old-womanish old men, overfearful of the Eastern Empire, jealous of their authority *and* bullied by the Church. You know Boethius was guilty of nothing."

Theodoric said, enunciating carefully, as if to convince himself more than me, "If Boethius could be suspected of treason and accused of treason and charged with treason, then he was clearly *capable* of treason, and it follows—"

"By the Styx!" I interrupted recklessly. "Now you are reasoning like a Christian churchman. Only in an ecclesiastical court is defamation accepted as evidence, and accusation as conviction."

"Have a care, Saio Thorn," he growled. "You remember that I was given cause to wonder about Boethius's loyalty and motives as long ago as the Sigismund affair."

Undeterred, I went on angrily, "I hear Boethius was killed with a cord tightened around his skull. They say his eyeballs crept out upon his cheeks long before he died. To have done that work with such needless cruelty, the prison executioner must be a Christian too, I assume."

"Be still. You know I am indifferent in regard to all religions, and I assuredly have no love for Athanasian Christians. Especially now. This document just arrived from Constantinople. Read it. You will see that the senators may not have been *overfearful* of the Eastern Empire."

It was written in both Greek and Latin, and signed both with Emperor Justin's crudely stenciled monogram and with the recognizably more literate signature of Patriarch Bishop Ibas. As was customary, the text was prolix with fulsome greetings and regards and good wishes, but the content could be summed up in a single sentence. It decreed that all Arian Christian churches throughout the empire were immediately to be confiscated, then consecrated anew for Catholic Christian worship.

I said, marveling, "This is as much unwarranted presumption as it is a flagrant personal insult to you. Justin and his influencers must realize that you will not obey—that they are inviting a war. Will you oblige them?"

"Not just yet. I have another war I wish to fight first, to expunge an even *more* personal insult—the Vandals' treatment of my royal sister.

967

Lentinus's fleets of warships are very nearly ready, in every southern port of Italia, to be boarded by our armies and sail against Carthage."

I asked, "Is it wise, at this time, to commit such a mass of our forces to such a distant—?"

"I have already committed *myself*," he said impatiently. "A king cannot renege on his decisions."

I sighed and was silent. Theodoric would never have maintained such inflexible haughtiness in former days.

"As for this," he said, contemptuously flicking the document, "for the time being, I shall simply fight priest with priest. I have sent a troop to Rome to fetch hither *our* patriarch bishop, either escorted in dignity or dragged by his tonsure fringe of hair, whichever he chooses. I shall dispatch him from here to Constantinople, by fast dromo, to demand the rescission of this decree."

"What? Send the haughty Bishop of Rome to abase himself before the Bishop of Constantinople? Send the man who styles himself sovereign pontiff to plead on behalf of *heretics*? Why, if John has even a splinter of manly backbone and the least adherence to his professed beliefs, he will suffer martyrdom rather than do that."

Theodoric said again, and grimly, "Whichever he chooses. I imagine Papa John will remember, since he colluded in it, how gruesomely Boethius died. Any number of eyeballs—John's and his patriarch successors'—can be extruded, if necessary, until I get a sovereign pontiff who will do what I want done."

✠ ✠ ✠

"It required no eyeballs, and only the one pontiff," I told Livia. "Papa John may not have gone joyously or even willingly, but he went. Theodoric may sometimes act irrationally, but he was lucid enough to realize that patriarch bishops, like lesser men, prefer living in this world rather than risking the next one. And not only did John go to Constantinople; he did what the king sent him to do. May I have some more wine?"

I was tired, dusty and parched, having just then arrived back in Rome. While the servant girl poured, Livia said:

"The patriarch bishop actually asked *not* to have the Arian churches here given to the Catholics? Why, they would have been *his*. He was declining a veritable windfall."

"That is what Theodoric demanded of him. So that is what John asked. And that is what he got. He brought back to Ravenna another document signed by Justin and Ibas. It amends the earlier decree. The confiscation will be done only within the bounds of the Eastern Empire. By the emperor's kind dispensation, all the Arian properties in the Gothic Kingdom will be exempted."

"It is almost unbelievable—that Bishop John would agree to go on such an embassy—still less that he would succeed. But you do not seem very happy about it."

"Neither is John. Almost immediately upon his return to Ravenna, Theodoric had him seized and imprisoned."

"What? *Why?* Since he did exactly as the king asked . . ."

"Livia, you just now called it unbelievable. The king finds it so too. He is enduring another of his spells of dark suspicion. The document of exemption is genuine enough; the Arian churches are safe enough. But Theodoric suspects that Papa John must have traded something to get that parchment. Perhaps a promise that the Church of Rome and all its faithful will aid the Eastern Empire if and when a war breaks out. John, of course, swears on the Bible that he did nothing seditious. Theodoric thinks that putting him for a while in Boethius's old cell in Ticinum might jog his recollection."

"And what do you think?"

969

"Iésus." I shrugged. "I thought the king was out of his senses when he sent the bishop on that mission. I think he is out of his senses now, but I could be wrong again. Anyway, I should be the last to trust the word of any churchman. Or of Justin, Justinian and Theodora. An ignorant, feeble simulacrum of an emperor. A reformed whore. And Justinian, who will be the next emperor, never eats meat or drinks wine. Would *you* trust such a man?"

"But still . . . for Theodoric to imprison the Patriarch Bishop of Rome! John may be less high and mighty than he thinks he is, but countless thousands regard him as their sanctified Papa. Those countless thousands of Theodoric's subjects will be furious when they hear what he has done."

"I know . . . I know . . ." I sighed. "That is why I am back in Rome. I came to seek advice from wiser heads than mine. I stopped here only to rest a bit after the long ride—and to rest my aching head on your soft shoulder, so to speak." I stood up and brushed at my dusty tunic. "I shall go now and find old Senator Symmachus. He, if anyone, will be able to suggest some way to placate—"

Livia shook her head. "You will not find Symmachus."

"Oh vái. Not in Rome?"

"Not on earth. A few days ago, his steward came upon his dead body.

In his front garden, near that ugly little Bacchus statue of his. The guard here at my door told me about it."

I groaned in dismay. Livia added, "The guards also have no one else to talk to, so sometimes we talk, they and I."

I said, though I disbelieved it even as I said it, "I presume Symmachus died of old age."

"No. Of many stab wounds." She paused, then said, "On Theodoric's orders, the gossip has it."

Which was what I had feared, but I tried to dispute it—as if convincing Livia could change anything. "Theodoric and that noble old man had the highest regard for one another."

"They did. Until Theodoric let Boethius be slain." She did not have to remind me that Symmachus had raised and taught and loved Boethius like a real son. "All these months now, the old man had been making bitter lament. Rumor says he *could* have raised an insurrection."

"So Theodoric simply removed him," I muttered. "Eheu! True or not, it is calamitous. I worried that Theodoric had outraged only the Catholic Christians here and everywhere else in the world. This will have alienated the Senate, the first families, the plebecula. Even his own most loyal Goths will feel their heads insecure on their necks." I went wearily to the door. "I must go and hear what the commonfolk are saying. I will be back, Livia. I shall probably have need of your soft shoulder again."

✠ ✠ ✠

"Talk?!" exclaimed Ewig. "Of course there is talk, Saio Thorn, and of little else. The universal opinion is that King Theodoric has gone incurably insane. Surely you must have realized that every least manifestation of his madness would be instantly reported throughout the land. The peasants, especially, have means of communication far swifter than courier horses and dromo boats. Why, I could tell you this minute anything that happened in the Ravenna palace yesterday."

I asked apprehensively, "Did anything happen?"

"The king was served a fine broiled Padus fish for his nahtamats last evening, and—"

"Liufs Guth! The gossips report even his *diet*? What earthly interest—?"

"Wait, wait. The king recoiled from the platter in wild-eyed horror. He saw there not a cooked fish's head, but the face of a dead man. The face of his old friend and counselor, Symmachus, glaring at him with reproach and accusation. Theodoric fled screaming from the dining room, they say."

"They say. Are the sayers believed?"

"I regret to tell you, they are." Ewig sniffled sadly. "Saio Thorn, our beloved king and comrade is no longer being called 'the Great.' Not Theodoric Magnus but Madidus, the raving drunk."

"Surely not on the basis of *fish stories.*"

"Surely not. Evidence abounds. This very noontime came galloping a messenger from the king, and a new royal decree has been published. Have you been yet to the Forum, Saio Thorn?"

"Not yet. I knew you would have more dependable information than any senator or—"

"You remember how you and I used to go together to the Concordia temple, so you could peruse the *Diurnal.* Well, I still cannot read, but the new decree is posted there. People are crowding in from all over the city to read it, and getting angrier as they do so. I expect I will soon hear what bad news it—"

"We cannot wait." I seized his sleeve. "Come!"

971

Ewig, being somewhat younger than myself and a great deal fatter, served as a battering ram to make a way for me through the throng about the temple. Those people were muttering and growling—not at our rude elbowing, but in amazement or consternation or perplexity at what they read of the *Diurnal.* The announcement to the public comprised many sheets of papyrus, of course, having been composed by the wordy Cassiodorus, but I was able from experience to scan through the dross and pick out the significant phrases. I nudged Ewig and he turned to shove a way for us to get out of the crowd again.

When we stood, somewhat disheveled, in a clear space on the Forum pavement, I said firmly, "This cannot go on, Ewig. Our king and comrade must be saved from himself. Theodoric must be now and always known as 'the Great.'"

"Only command me, Saio Thorn."

"There is nothing to be done here. I must go back to Ravenna, to Theodoric's side. And I shall not be returning to Rome, but there may later be some few things . . ."

"Only command me, Saio Thorn. Send a message and I will comply. If you can somehow preserve our king's good name, you will have the gratitude of every man who ever loved him."

✠   ✠   ✠

To Livia too I said, "This cannot go on. Theodoric must be saved from himself. The *Diurnal* announces that Patriarch Bishop John has died in that Ticinum prison. Whether the wretch died naturally or in the manner of Boethius, I cannot know. But I *can* deduce that he died without confessing anything to ease the king's mad suspicions, because his death has clearly enraged Theodoric. The king has committed the worst folly yet. He has issued a decree exactly as abominable as the one Justin tried to impose. There it is on the Concordia temple for all to read. Every *Catholic* Christian church in the kingdom is to be confiscated, made into an Arian church, and all Catholic worship is henceforth forbidden."

I downed my goblet of wine in one gulp. Livia said nothing, but her gaze was somber.

"Theodoric might as well have posted a suicide note of farewell," I went on, through gritted teeth. "If this does not provoke a nationwide uprising against his rule, or a kingdom-shattering civil war, Arian against Catholic, Theodoric is most certainly baring his throat for it to be slashed from behind."

"From behind?"

"From abroad. Right now, Lentinus's fleets are waiting the king's word to sail off to attack the Vandals. That war is justified—Theodoric's sister is still a captive of King Hilderic—and that war might be winnable under ordinary circumstances. But we will be committing all our forces there on the southern side of the Mediterranean. Meanwhile, in the east are Justin's Orthodox Christians, in the north are Clovis's Catholic Christians, all of them inimical and soon to be irate when they learn of this latest lunacy. The moment we assail the Vandals, their fellow Catholics, what would *you* expect those other nations to do?"

Livia beckoned for more wine to be brought, and said, "I know your name Veleda means an unveiler, a far-seer. So you foresee either devastating foreign war or civil war. Do you suppose you are the only one who does?"

"Of course not. But since the demise of Symmachus and Boethius, who is there to talk sense to Theodoric? His chief remaining counselors are his comes of finances and his master of the offices, Cassiodorus Pater and Filius. The elder knows only numbers and solidi and librae. He will be happy enough keeping count of the arrows expended in any war. The younger Cassiodorus knows nothing but words. A war would give him ample opportunity to blather to his heart's content. Theodoric's only other intimates are his generals. They would go cheerfully off to any war in any cause. Who else is there but me?"

"So. You will go to Ravenna. You will hope to find the king lucid. You will tell him—forcefully—what you have just been telling me. You will try to persuade him to recall the decree before it is imposed, and to withhold the fleet before it sails. And if you succeed in convincing him—what then?"

"Iésus, Livia. *That* much is likely too much to hope for. Even if he is lucid enough to recognize me and call me by my name and listen to me, he may fly into a fury and send *me* off to prison. What do you mean: what then?"

"Supposing the Gothic Kingdom survives this period of crisis, is not Theodoric likely to cause another? And if the kingdom survives them all, and outlasts Theodoric himself, what happens when he is gone? That cannot be long now. You have told me there is no one fit to succeed him."

"Yes." Then I was silent for a long time, brooding into my wine. Finally I said, "Well, perhaps one of those successors will astound the world by turning out to be worthy, after all. Or perhaps some totally new and better claimant will step forward when the time comes. Or perhaps the Gothic Kingdom *is* doomed. If not today, tomorrow. If not by Theodoric, by his heirs. You are right, my dear. If that is what Fortune ordains, I cannot save the kingdom from ruin. But I can save Theodoric's having to see it. Livia, how would you like to be free?"

She blinked once, in surprise, but then gave me a long and level look, reminding me how luminous and beautiful her blue eyes still were, though her facial beauty had faded. Sounding half amused, half wary, she asked:

"Free to do what?"

"To go away with me. Tomorrow. I have here in Rome an honest Ostrogoth friend who will arrange the sale of my house and slaves and possessions, or will send along anything I may care to keep. He could do the same for you. Would you wish to come?"

"To where? Ravenna?"

"Ravenna first. Then, if I am not summarily slain during my audience with Theodoric, I thought we might go on to Haustaths, where we first met. It should be lovely now in high summer. And I am curious to see if the names I carved in the ice river have moved from where we last saw them."

973

Livia laughed, but kindly. "We are rather old and rickety now, my dear, to go cavorting about an eisflodus on the heights of the Roof-stone."

"Perhaps the names will have come downhill to meet us. Truly, Livia, I have long yearned to visit again the Place of Echoes. The more I think about it, the more fondly I remember it, and the more I believe that I might stay there the rest of my days. I think, also, that I should like to have your soft shoulder beside me always. And you? What would you say to that?"

"Who is asking? Thorn or Veleda?"

"Saio Thorn, with full marshal's escort, will accompany you and your maidservant as far as Ravenna. Then, when I have done what I hope to do there, Thorn will disappear. It will be Veleda, with no escorting troop, who accompanies you the rest of the way to the Place of Echoes. Thereafter . . . you and I . . . well . . ." I held out my arms to her. "We are old and we are friends. We shall be old friends."

974

10

he next-to-last thing that Theodoric ever said to me was, in melancholy tones, "Think back, old Thorn. Whenever we set out to destroy, we succeeded beyond measure. Whenever we sought to build and preserve and glorify, we failed utterly."

"Not utterly, Theodoric, not yet," I said. "And even if failure should be inevitable, it is no small thing to have attempted nobly."

I could have wept for him, he looked so pitiably ravaged and frail and unhappy and near to despair. But at least he knew me; he was in command of his senses; so I went on:

"Let us talk of brighter topics. A lady friend of mine has suggested that these latter years of yours, Theodoric, might have been better, more joyful, even more full of achievement, if you had not been deprived of Audefleda's loving companionship—with no other good woman to take her place. The Bible itself, you know, in its earliest pages, recommends a woman as a help meet for a man. It may well be that—with a soft, fair, feminine hand gently holding yours—you *would* now be standing straighter and stronger. Most certainly, you would have warmth and comfort against the storms and strangers without."

Theodoric's silent regard of me had gone from surprised to dubious to reflective in expression. I cleared my throat and went on:

"This friend of whom I speak is an old woman named Veleda. The name will tell you that she is an Ostrogoth, therefore trustworthy, and I can personally attest that she is, like her ancient namesake—the legendary prophetess, the unveiler of secrets—a very wise old woman indeed."

Now the king looked slightly alarmed, so I hastened to say:

"Ne, ne, Veleda does not propose *herself* as your help and companion. Ni allis. She is as aged and decrepit as I am. When Veleda put forth the idea, she too quoted the Bible—where it tells of another king, David, when he was advanced in years. His servants said: Let us seek for our lord the king a young virgin, and let her stand before the king, and cherish him, and sleep in his bosom, and warm our lord the king. So they sought and they found and they brought her, and the maiden was exceeding beautiful."

Now Theodoric was looking as near amused as I had seen him in many a year, so I went on even more hurriedly:

"It happens that my friend Veleda owns a young female slave. A genuine rarity, a girl of the Seres people. A virgin, surpassingly beautiful and unique in many other respects. I presume on our lifelong comradeship, Theodoric, to ask your permission to send old Veleda to you, so that she can offer you this exquisite maiden. She can fetch the girl this very night. You have only to order Magister Cassiodorus—I know how he guards your privacy—to see that they are admitted without hindrance. I entreat you, dear friend, not to refuse. It is a heartfelt favor I would do you. I believe you will thank me and Veleda for it. I assure you it cannot hurt."

Theodoric nodded tolerantly, actually smiling just a little, and said—with unfeigned love for me, with gratitude for my love for him—the last thing he ever said to me, "Very well, old Thorn. Send me Veleda, the unveiler."

975

✠　✠　✠

I could not be doing this as Thorn—and not because, as Thorn, I swore my auths to uphold and defend the king's greatness. I believe I *am* defending the king's greatness. No, I will do it as Veleda because, when I give him the girl, it will be a vicarious giving of what I, as Veleda, so many times in all these years *wished* could be given.

Tonight I will take the venefica to the palace, and in Theodoric's chamber I will unveil her of the transparent gown. I know he will accept the offering, if only to indulge the well-meant whim of his old friend Thorn. I will take also these many, many pages of parchment and vellum and papyrus, and deliver them to Cassiodorus, and ask him to store them wherever the kingdom's other archives are kept, for future readers who might wish to learn of the time of Theodoric the Great. I and Livia may have some few pages of life yet to live, but this story that began so long ago is done.

976

11

TRANSLATOR'S NOTE:
THE FOLLOWING IS IN ANOTHER HAND.

The newly co-regnant Emperor Justinian, most Christian of nobles at Constantinople, when he commanded the closing of the Platonist schools of philosophy at Athens, wisely observed of those pagan pedagogues, "If they speak what is false, they are pernicious. If they speak what is truth, they are unnecessary. Silence them."

The mass of manuscript composed by Saio Thorn contains many truths. But all of those—facts and details and battle accounts and other verifiable events—I have already incorporated into my own *Historia Gothorum*, where they will be much more easily accessible to scholars than they are in the marshal's ponderous and diffuse volumes.

As a narrative of truth, then, Thorn's work is unnecessary.

If the remainder, which is to say the bulk, of his chronicle is not outright and incredible invention, it is so scandalously impious, blasphemous, scurrilous and obscene as to offend and disgust any reader who is not a professional historian like myself, well practiced in dispassionate objectivity. As a historian, I resolutely decline to judge the worth of any written work according to its moral propriety. However, as a Christian, I must regard this book with horror and revulsion. As a normal male human being, even, I must regard it as a compilation of vile perversities. Therefore, since everything worthwhile in it is readily available elsewhere, I must denounce this work as both unnecessary *and* pernicious.

Nevertheless, the disposition of this work was entrusted to me, and I have no way of returning it to its author. The marshal Thorn has not been seen or heard of since sometime before King Theodoric was found dead in bed, and it is widely supposed that Thorn, in his grief at the king's decease, must have cast himself into the Padus or the sea. So, nolens volens, I am encumbered with his manuscript and cannot, in conscience, destroy it.

While I refuse to deposit this work in the royal archives or in any   977
scriptorium accessible to the public, I can put it where it will never by remotest chance assault the eyes of the unwary. Tomorrow, the late King Theodoric will be ceremoniously laid to rest in his mausoleum, together with certain of his regalia, favorite possessions, artifacts and mementos of his reign. This manuscript I will put there too, so it will be entombed and invisible and silent forever.

(*ecce signum*) Flavius Magnus Aurelius Cassiodorus Senator Filius
MAGISTER OFFICIORUM
QUAESTOR
EXCEPTOR

TRANSLATOR'S FINAL NOTE

 heodoric died on the next-to-last day of the 1,279th Year of the Founding of Rome—that is, the 30th of August, A.D. 526—and with him died the very last afterglow of what had been the Western Roman Empire. Bereft of able leadership, his Gothic Kingdom was, within thirty years, fragmented into petty warring states. And bereft of that kingdom's civilizing influence, all of Europe was doomed to centuries of wretchedness, despair, superstition, brute ignorance and lethargy—the era known as the Dark Ages.

Theodoric's marble mausoleum still stands in Ravenna. But during the Dark Ages that city was more than once despoiled by invasion, siege, sack, uprising, famine, plague and destitution. At some time—no one now knows when—Theodoric's tomb was broken open and desecrated by grave-robbers. His embalmed body, clad in golden helmet and armor, was removed, stripped of its valuables and never seen again. The robbers also took his snake-blade sword, his shield, his regalia of office, everything else that had been laid away with him. Except for his marshal Thorn's manuscript, recently rediscovered, none of those lost treasures has ever come to light again.

The other books mentioned by Thorn as being the repositories of Gothic history, traditions, deeds and accomplishments—the *Biuhtjos jah Anabusteis af Gutam*, the *Saggwasteis af Gut-Thiudam*, Ablabius's *De Origine Actibusque Getarum*, even Cassiodorus's *Historia Gothorum*—all were condemned, banned, destroyed by later rulers and Christian bishops. Those books, like the Gothic Kingdom, its Arian Christianity and the Goths themselves, are long gone from the world.

G.J.

ACKNOWLEDGMENTS

This book could not have been completed without the help of these friends, advisers and counselors:

Herman Begega, Pompton Lakes, New Jersey
Chavdar Borislavov, Sofia, Bulgaria
The late L. R. Boyd, Jr., Teague, Texas
Robert Claytor, Staunton, Virginia
David L. Copeland, M.D., Lexington, Virginia
John J. Delany, Jr., Lexington, Virginia
Donald Dryfoos, Donan Books, New York, N.Y.
Glenn and Janet Garvey, East Pepperell, Mass.
The late Joseph Garvey, M.D., Montréal, Québec
Hugo and Lorraine Gerstl, Carmel, California
John Haverkamp, Waynesboro, Virginia
Jesse Glen Jennings, The Woodlands, Texas
The late Michael Glen Jennings, West Milford, New Jersey
George and Grethe Johnson, Lexington, Virginia
Gloria Martin, Buena Vista, Virginia
Norma McMillen, Branson, Missouri
Karla Mehedintzi, Constanţa, Romania
Aylâ Meryem Midhat, Tunçeli, Turkey
Sam Moran, Glasgow, Virginia
Isidora Nenadovic, Belgrade, Yugoslavia
David Parker, Washington and Lee University
Diana Perkinson, Boones Mill, Virginia
Cathryn B. Perotti, Novato, California
Robert M. Pickral, M.D., Lexington, Virginia
Taylor Sanders, Washington and Lee University
Joyce Osborne Servis, Caldwell, New Jersey
Nedelia Shapkareva, Varna, Bulgaria
Sanger and Patricia Stabler, Avilla, Indiana
Lawrence Sutker, M.D., Staunton, Virginia
Sven Swedborg, Göteborg, Sweden

979

Ali Kemal Vefik, Istanbul, Turkey
Hunter Wilson, San Miguel de Allende, Gto., México
Eugene and Ina Winick, Hastings-on-Hudson, New York
Mary Winston, R.N., N.P., Natural Bridge, Virginia

. . . and Ivan Stoianov Ivanov of Sofia, Bulgaria, who, from the Iron Gate to the Valley of Roses to the Black Sea, was my guide, interpreter and frequently my rescuer.

G.J.